From masterful storyteller [...] a life-and-death love s[tory...] a man who lives to help the dead and a man who died—then learned to live.

"TJ Klune is a gift to our troubled times, and his novels are a radiant treat to all who discover them."
—*LOCUS*

"Whether Klune is making you laugh or cry, he is doing it with a wit and charm that is unparalleled."
—*CULTURESS*

"There is so much to love in *Under the Whispering Door*, but what I love the most is its compassion for the little things—a touch, a glance, a precious piece of dialogue—healing me, telling me that for all the strangenesses I hold, I am valued, valid—and maybe even worthy of love."
—*RYKA AOKI*

"*Under the Whispering Door* broke my heart and then it healed me in the next breath."
—*CASSANDRA KHAW*

"The latest by Lambda Literary Award winner Klune is a winning story about grief, loss, and moving on."
—*LIBRARY JOURNAL*

"A sweet tale of grief and second chances, and a ghost story about not giving up on even the most lost of souls."
—*BOOKLIST*

ALSO BY TJ KLUNE FROM TOR BOOKS

BOOKS FOR ADULTS

THE GREEN CREEK SERIES

Wolfsong

Ravensong

Heartsong

Brothersong

STANDALONES

The House in the Cerulean Sea

The Bones Beneath My Skin

BOOKS FOR YOUNG ADULTS

THE EXTRAORDINARIES SERIES

The Extraordinaries

Flash Fire

Heat Wave

UNDER
THE
WHISPERING
DOOR

TJ KLUNE

TOR PUBLISHING GROUP
NEW YORK

For Eric.

I hope you woke up in a strange place.

UNDER THE WHISPERING DOOR

Copyright © 2021 by Travis Klune

All rights reserved.

A Tor Book
Published by Tom Doherty Associates/Tor Publishing Group
120 Broadway
New York, NY 10271

www.tor-forge.com

Tor® is a registered trademark of Macmillan Publishing Group, LLC.

The Library of Congress has cataloged the hardcover edition as follows:

Names: Klune, TJ, author.
Title: Under the whispering door / TJ Klune.
Description: First edition. | New York : TOR, 2021. | "A Tom Doherty Associates book."
Identifiers: LCCN 2021028510 (print) | LCCN 2021028511 (ebook) | ISBN 9781250217349 (hardcover) | ISBN 9781250217332 (ebook)
Subjects: GSAFD: Love stories.
Classification: LCC PS3611.L86 U53 2021 (print) | LCC PS3611.L86 (ebook) | DDC 813'.6—dc23
LC record available at https://lccn.loc.gov/2021028510
LC ebook record available at https://lccn.loc.gov/2021028511

ISBN 978-1-250-21739-4 (trade paperback)

Our books may be purchased in bulk for promotional, educational, or business use. Please contact your local bookseller or the Macmillan Corporate and Premium Sales Department at 1-800-221-7945, extension 5442, or by email at MacmillanSpecialMarkets@macmillan.com.

First Tor Paperback Edition: 2023

Printed in the United States of America

0 9

Author's Note

This story explores life and love as well as loss and grief.

*There are discussions of death in different forms—
quiet, unexpected, and death by suicide.*

Please read with care.

CHAPTER 1

Patricia was crying.

Wallace Price hated it when people cried.

Little tears, big tears, full-on body-wracking sobs, it didn't matter. Tears were pointless, and she was only delaying the inevitable.

"How did you know?" she said, her cheeks wet as she reached for the Kleenex box on his desk. She didn't see him grimacing. It was probably for the best.

"How could I not?" he said. He folded his hands on his oak desk, his Arper Aston chair squeaking as he settled in for what he was sure was going to be a case of unfortunate histrionics, all while trying to keep from grimacing at the stench of bleach and Windex. One of the night staff must have spilled something in his office, the scent thick and cloying. He made a mental note to send out a memo to remind everyone that he had a sensitive nose, and that he shouldn't be expected to work in such conditions. It was positively barbaric.

The shades on the windows to his office were pulled shut against the afternoon sun, the air-conditioning blasting harshly, keeping him alert. Three years ago, someone had asked if they could move the dial up to seventy degrees. He'd laughed. Warmth led to laziness. When one was cold, one kept moving.

Outside his office, the firm moved like a well-oiled machine, busy and self-sufficient without the need for significant input, exactly as Wallace liked. He wouldn't have made it as far as he had if he'd had to micromanage every employee. Of course, he still kept a watchful eye, those in his employ knowing they needed to be working as if their lives depended on it. Their clients were the most important people on earth. When he said jump, he expected those within earshot to do just that without asking inconsequential questions like *how high?*

Which brought him back to Patricia. The machine had broken down, and though no one was infallible, Wallace needed to switch out the part for a new one. He'd worked too hard to let it fail now. Last year had been the most profitable in the firm's history. This year was shaping up to be even better. No matter what condition the world was in, someone always needed to be sued.

Patricia blew her nose. "I didn't think you cared."

He stared at her. "Why on earth would you think that?"

Patricia gave a watery smile. "You're not exactly the type."

He bristled. How dare she say such a thing, especially to her boss. He should've realized ten years ago when he'd interviewed her for the paralegal position that it'd come back to bite him in the ass. She'd been chipper, something Wallace had believed would lessen with time, seeing as how a law firm was no place for cheerfulness. How wrong he'd been. "Of course I—"

"It's just that things have been so *hard* lately," she said, as if he hadn't spoken at all. "I've tried to keep it bottled in, but I should have known you'd see right through it."

"Exactly," he said, trying to steer the conversation back on course. The quicker he got through this, the better off they'd both be. Patricia would realize that, eventually. "I saw right through it. Now, if you could—"

"And you *do* care," she said. "I know you do. I knew the moment you gave me a floral arrangement for my birthday last month. It was kind of you. Even though it didn't have a card or anything, I knew what you were trying to say. You appreciate me. And I so appreciate you, Mr. Price."

He didn't know what the hell she was talking about. He hadn't given her a single thing. It must have been his legal administrative assistant. He was going to have to have a word with her. There was no need for flowers. What was the point? They were pretty at first but then they died, leaves and petals curling and rotting, making a mess that could have been avoided had they not been sent in the first place. With this in mind, he picked up his ridiculously expensive Montblanc pen, jotting down a note (*IDEA FOR MEMO: PLANTS ARE TERRIBLE AND NO ONE SHOULD HAVE THEM*). Without looking up, he said, "I wasn't trying to—"

"Kyle was laid off two months ago," she said, and it took him longer than he cared to admit to place who she was talking about. Kyle was her husband. Wallace had met him at a firm function. Kyle had been intoxicated, obviously enjoying the champagne Moore, Price, Hernandez & Worthington had provided after yet another successful year. Face flushed, Kyle had regaled the party with a detailed story Wallace couldn't bring himself to care about, especially since Kyle apparently believed volume and embellishment were a necessity in storytelling.

"I'm sorry to hear that," he said stiffly, setting his phone on the desk. "But I think we should focus on the matter at—"

"He's having trouble finding work," Patricia said, crumpling up her tissue before reaching for another. She wiped her eyes, her makeup smearing. "And it couldn't come at a worse time. Our son is getting married this summer, and we're supposed to pay for half the wedding. I don't know how we'll manage, but we'll find a way. We always do. It's a bump in the road."

"Mazel tov," Wallace said. He didn't even know she had children. He wasn't one to delve into the personal lives of his employees. Children were a distraction, one he'd never warmed to. They caused their parents—his employees—to request time off for things like recitals and illness, leaving others to pick up the slack. And since Human Resources had advised him he couldn't ask his employees to avoid starting families ("You can't tell them to just get a *dog*, Mr. Price!") he'd had to deal with mothers and fathers needing the afternoon off to listen to their children vomit or screech songs about shapes and clouds or other nonsense.

Patricia honked again into her tissue, a long and terribly wet noise that made his skin crawl. "And then there's our daughter. I thought she was directionless and going to end up hoarding ferrets, but then the firm graciously provided her with a scholarship, and she finally found her way. Business school, of all things. Isn't that wonderful?"

He squinted at her. He would have to speak to the partners. He wasn't aware they offered scholarships. They donated to charities, yes, but the tax breaks more than made up for it. He didn't know what sort of return they'd see on giving money away for something as ridiculous as *business* school, even if it too could be written off. The daughter would probably want to do something as asinine as open a restaurant or start a nonprofit. "I think you and I have a different definition of wonderful."

She nodded, but he didn't think she was hearing him. "This job is so important to me, now more than ever. The people here are like family. We all support one another, and I don't know how I'd have made it this far without them. And to have you sense something was wrong and ask me to come in here so that I could vent means more to me than you will ever know. I don't care what anyone else says, Mr. Price. You're a good man."

What was *that* supposed to mean? "What is everyone saying about me?"

She blanched. "Oh, nothing bad. You know how it is. You started this firm. Your name is on the letterhead. It's . . . intimidating."

Wallace relaxed. He felt better. "Yes, well, I suppose that's—"

"I mean, *yes*, people talk about how you can be cold and calculating and if something doesn't get done the moment you want it to, you raise your voice to frightening levels, but they don't see you like I do. I know it's a front for the caring man underneath the expensive suits."

"A front," he repeated, though he was pleased she admired his sense of style. His suits *were* luxurious. Only the best, after all. It was why part of the package welcoming those new to the firm listed in detailed bullet points what was acceptable attire. While he didn't demand designer labels for all (especially since he could appreciate student debt), if anyone wore something obviously bought off a discount rack, they'd be given a stern talking to about having pride in their appearance.

"You're hard on the outside, but inside you're a marshmallow," she said.

He'd never been more offended in his life. "Mrs. Ryan—"

"Patricia, please. I've told you that before many times."

She had. "Mrs. Ryan," he said firmly. "While I appreciate your enthusiasm, I believe we have other matters to discuss."

"Right," she said hastily. "Of course. I know you don't like when people compliment you. I promise it won't happen again. We're not here to talk about you, after all."

He was relieved. "Exactly."

Her lip trembled. "We're here to talk about me and how difficult things have become lately. That's why you called me in after finding me crying in the supply closet."

He thought she'd been taking inventory and the dust had affected her allergies. "I think we need to refocus—"

"Kyle won't touch me," she whispered. "It's been years since I've felt his hands on me. I told myself that it's what happens when a couple has been together for so long, but I can't help but think there's more to it."

He flinched. "I don't know if this is appropriate, especially when you—"

"I *know*!" she cried. "How inappropriate can he be? I know I've been working seventy hours a week, but is it too much to ask for my husband to perform his matrimonial duties? It was in our *vows*."

What an awful wedding that must have been. They'd probably held the reception at a Holiday Inn. No. Worse. A Holiday Inn *Express*. He shuddered at the thought. He had no doubt karaoke had been involved. From what he remembered of Kyle (which was very little at all), he'd probably sung a medley of Journey and Whitesnake while chugging what he lovingly referred to as a brewski.

"But I don't mind the long hours," she continued. "It's part of the job. I knew that when you hired me."

Ah! An opening! "Speaking of hiring—"

"My daughter pierced her septum," Patricia said forlornly. "She looks like a bull. My little girl, wanting a matador to chase her down and stick things in her."

"Jesus Christ," Wallace muttered, scrubbing a hand over his face. He didn't have time for this. He had a meeting in half an hour that he needed to prepare for.

"I know!" Patricia exclaimed. "Kyle said it's part of growing up. That we need to let her spread her wings and make her own mistakes. I didn't know that meant having her put a gosh darn *ring* through her nose! And don't even get me started on my son."

"Okay," Wallace said. "I won't."

"He wants Applebee's to cater the wedding! *Applebee's.*"

Wallace gaped in horror. He hadn't known awful wedding planning was genetic.

Patricia nodded furiously. "Like we could afford that. Money doesn't grow on trees! We've done our best to instill in our children a sense of financial understanding, but when you're young, you don't always have a firm grasp of it. And now that his bride-to-be is pregnant, he's looking to us for help." She sighed dramatically. "The only reason I can even get up in the morning is knowing I can come here and . . . escape from it all."

He felt a strange twist in his chest. He rubbed at his sternum. Most likely heartburn. He should have skipped the chili. "I'm glad we can be a refuge from your existence, but that's not why I asked you for this meeting."

She sniffled. "Oh?" She smiled again. It was stronger this time. "Then what is it, Mr. Price?"

He said, "You're fired."

She blinked.

He waited. Surely now she'd understand, and he could get back to work.

She looked around, a confused smile on her face. "Is this one of those reality shows?" She laughed, a ghost of her former exuberance he'd thought had long since been banished. "Are you filming me? Is someone going to jump out and shout *surprise*? What's that show called? *You're Fired, But Not Really?*"

"I highly doubt it," Wallace said. "I haven't given authorization to be filmed." He looked down at her purse in her lap. "*Or* recorded."

Her smile faded slightly. "Then I don't understand. What do you mean?"

"I don't know how to make it any clearer, Mrs. Ryan. As of today, you are no longer employed by Moore, Price, Hernandez & Worthington. When you leave here, security will allow you to gather up your belongings and then you'll be escorted from the building. Human Resources will be in touch shortly regarding any final paperwork in case you need to sign up for . . . oh, what was it called?" He flipped through the papers on the desk. "Ah, yes. Unemployment benefits. Because apparently, even if you're unemployed, you can still suckle from the teat of the government in the form of my tax dollars." He shook his head. "So, in a way, it's like I'm still paying you. Just not as much. Or while working here. Because you don't."

She wasn't smiling any longer. "I . . . *what*?"

"You're fired," he said slowly. He didn't know what was so difficult for her to understand.

"Why?" she demanded.

Now they were talking. The *why* of things was Wallace's specialty. Nothing but the facts. "Because of the amicus brief in the Cortaro matter. You filed it two hours past the deadline. The only reason it was pushed through was because Judge Smith owed me a favor, and even *that* almost didn't work. I had to remind him that I'd seen him and his babysitter-turned-mistress at the—it doesn't matter. You could've cost the firm thousands of dollars, and that doesn't even begin to cover the harm it would have caused our client. That sort of mistake won't be tolerated. I thank you for your years of dedication to Moore, Price, Hernandez & Worthington, but I'm afraid your services will no longer be required."

She stood abruptly, the chair scraping along the hardwood floors. "I didn't file it late."

"You did," Wallace said evenly. "I have the timestamp from the clerk's office here if you'd like to see it." He tapped his fingers against the folder sitting on his desk.

Her eyes narrowed. At least she wasn't crying any longer. Wallace could handle anger. On his first day in law school, he was told that lawyers, while a necessity in a functioning society, were always going to be the focal point of ire. "Even if I *did* file it late, I've never done anything like that before. It was one time."

"And you can rest easy knowing you won't do anything like it again," Wallace said. "Because you no longer work here."

"But . . . but my *husband*. And my *son*. And my *daughter*!"

"Right," Wallace said. "I'm glad you brought that up. Obviously, if your daughter was receiving any sort of scholarship from us, it's now rescinded." He pressed a button on his desk phone. "Shirley? Can you please make a note for HR that Mrs. Ryan's daughter no longer has a scholarship through us? I don't know what it entails, but I'm sure they have some form they have to fill out that I need to sign. See to it immediately."

His assistant's voice crackled through the speaker. "Yes, Mr. Price."

He looked up at his former paralegal. "There. See? All taken care of. Now, before you go, I'd ask that you remember we're professionals. There's no need for screaming or throwing things or making threats that will undoubtedly be considered a felony. And, if you could, please make sure when you clear out your desk that you don't take anything that belongs to the firm. Your replacement will be starting on Monday, and I'd hate to think what it would be like for her if she was missing a stapler or tape dispenser. Whatever knick-knacks you have accumulated are yours, of course." He picked up the stress ball on his desk with the firm's logo on it. "These are wonderful, aren't they? I seem to remember you getting one to celebrate seven years at the firm. Take it, with my blessing. I have a feeling it will come in handy."

"You're serious," she whispered.

"As a heart attack," he said. "Now, if you'll excuse me, I have to—"

"You . . . you . . . you *monster*!" she shouted. "I demand an apology!"

Of course she would. "An apology would imply I've done something wrong. I haven't. If anything, you should be apologizing to me."

Her answering screech did not contain an apology.

Wallace kept his cool as he pressed the button on his phone again. "Shirley? Has security arrived?"

"Yes, Mr. Price."

"Good. Send them in before something gets thrown at my head."

The last Wallace Price saw of Patricia Ryan was when a large man named Geraldo dragged her away, kicking and screaming, apparently ignoring Wallace's warning about felonious threats. He was begrudgingly impressed with Mrs. Ryan's dedication to wanting to stick what she referred to as a *hot fire poker* down his throat until it—in her words—pierced his nether regions and caused extreme agony. "You'll land on your feet!" he called from the doorway to his office, knowing the entire floor was listening. He wanted to make sure they knew he cared. "A door closes, a window opens and all that."

The elevator doors slid shut, cutting off her outrage.

"Ah," Wallace said. "That's more like it. Back to work, everyone. Just because it's Friday doesn't mean you get to slack off."

Everyone began moving immediately.

Perfect. The machine ran smoothly once again.

He went back into his office, closing the door behind him.

He thought of Patricia only once more that afternoon, when he received an email from the head of Human Resources telling him that she would take care of the scholarship. That twinge in his chest returned, but it was all right. He'd stop for a bottle of Tums on his way home. He didn't give it—or Patricia Ryan—another thought. Ever forward, he told himself as he moved the email to a folder marked EMPLOYEE GRIEVANCES.

Ever forward.

He felt better. At least it was quiet now.

Next week, his new paralegal would start, and he'd make sure she knew he wouldn't tolerate mistakes. It was better to strike fear early rather than deal with incompetency down the road.

He never got the chance.

Instead, two days later, Wallace Price died.

CHAPTER 2

His funeral was sparsely attended. Wallace wasn't pleased. He couldn't even be quite sure how he'd gotten here. One moment, he'd been staring down at his body. And then he'd blinked and somehow found himself standing in front of a church, the doors open, bells ringing. It certainly hadn't helped when he saw the prominent sign sitting out front. A CELEBRATION OF THE LIFE OF WALLACE PRICE, it read. He didn't like that sign, if he was being honest with himself. No, he didn't like it one bit. Perhaps someone inside could tell him what the hell was going on.

He'd taken a seat on a pew toward the rear. The church itself was everything he hated: ostentatious, with grand stained-glass windows and several versions of Jesus in various poses of pain and suffering, hands nailed to a cross that appeared to be made of stone. Wallace was dismayed at how no one seemed to mind that the prominent figure displayed throughout the church was depicted in the throes of death. He would never understand religion.

He waited for more people to filter in. The sign out front said his funeral was supposed to start promptly at nine. It was now five till according to the decorative clock on the wall (another Jesus, his arms the hands of the clock, apparently a reminder that God's only son was a contortionist) and there were only six people in the church.

He knew five of them.

The first was his ex-wife. Their divorce had been a bitter thing, filled with baseless accusations on both sides, their lawyers barely able to keep them from screaming at each other across the table. She would've had to fly in, given that she'd moved to the opposite end of the country to get away from him. He didn't blame her.

Mostly.

She wasn't crying. He was annoyed for reasons he couldn't quite explain. Shouldn't she be sobbing?

The second, third, and fourth people he knew were the partners at the law firm Moore, Price, Hernandez & Worthington. He waited for others from the firm to join them, given MPH&W had been started in a garage twenty years before and had grown to be one of the most powerful firms in the state. At the very least, he expected his assistant, Shirley, to be there, her makeup streaked, a handkerchief clutched in her hands as she wailed that she didn't know how she'd go on without him.

She wasn't in attendance. He focused as hard as he could, willing her to pop into existence, wailing that it wasn't fair, that she *needed* a boss like Wallace to keep her on the straight and narrow. He frowned when nothing happened, a curl of unease fluttering in the back of his mind.

The partners gathered at the back of the church, near Wallace's pew, speaking in low tones. Wallace had given up trying to let them know he was still here, sitting right in front of them. They couldn't see him. They couldn't hear him.

"Sad day," Moore said.

"So sad," Hernandez agreed.

"Just the worst," Worthington said. "Poor Shirley, finding his body like that."

The partners paused, looking out toward the front of the church, bowing their heads respectfully when Naomi glanced back at them. She sneered at them before turning around toward the front.

Then:

"Makes you think," Moore said.

"It really does," Hernandez agreed.

"Absolutely," Worthington said. "Makes you think about a lot of things."

"You've never had an original thought in your life," Wallace told him.

They were quiet for a moment, and Wallace was sure they were lost in their favorite memories of him. In a moment, they'd start to fondly reminisce, each of them in turn giving a little story about the man they'd known for half their lives and the effect he'd had upon them.

Maybe they'd even shed a tear or two. He hoped so.

"He was an asshole," Moore said finally.

"Such an asshole," Hernandez agreed.

"The biggest," Worthington said.

They all laughed, though they tried to smother it to keep it from echoing. Wallace was shocked by two specific things. First, he wasn't aware one was allowed to laugh in church, especially when one was attending a funeral. He thought it had to be illegal, some-how. It was true that he hadn't been inside a church in decades, so it was possible the rules had changed. Second, where did they get off calling him an asshole? He was disappointed when they weren't immediately struck down by lightning. "Smite them!" he yelled, glaring up at the ceiling. "Smite them right . . . now . . ." He stopped. Why wasn't his voice echoing?

Moore, apparently having decided his grief had passed, said, "Did you guys catch the game last night? Man, Rodriguez was in rare form. Can't believe they called that play."

And then they were off, talking about sports as if their former partner wasn't lying in a seven-thousand-dollar solid red cherrywood casket at the front of the church, arms folded across his chest, skin pale, eyes closed.

Wallace turned resolutely forward, jaw clenched. They'd gone to law school together, had decided to start their own firm right after graduation, much to the horror of their parents. He and the part-ners had started out as friends, each young and idealistic. But as the years had gone by, they'd become something *more* than friends: they'd become colleagues, which, to Wallace, was far more import-ant. He didn't have time for friends. He didn't need them. He'd had his job on the thirtieth floor of the biggest skyscraper in the city, his imported office furniture, and a too-big apartment that he rarely spent any time in. He'd had it all, and now . . .

Well.

At least his casket was expensive, though he'd been avoiding looking at it since he arrived.

The fifth person in the church was someone he didn't recognize. She was a young woman with messy black hair cut short. Her eyes were dark above a thin, upturned nose and the pale slash of her lips. She had her ears pierced, little studs that glittered in the sunlight filtering in through the windows. She was dressed in a smart pinstriped black suit, her tie bright red. A power tie if ever there was one. Wallace approved. All of his own ties were power ties. No, he wasn't exactly wearing a power tie at this moment. Apparently when you died, you continued to wear the last thing you had on before you croaked. It was unfortunate, really, given that he'd apparently died in his office on a Sunday. He'd come in to prepare for the upcoming week, and had thrown on sweats, an old Rolling Stones shirt, and flip-flops, knowing the office would be empty.

Which is what he found himself wearing now, much to his dismay.

The woman glanced in his direction, as if she'd heard him. He didn't know her, but he assumed he'd touched her life at some point if she was here. Perhaps she'd been a grateful client of his at one point. They all began to run together after a time, so that could be it too. He'd probably sued a large company on her behalf for hot coffee or harassment or *something*, and she'd gotten a massive settlement out of it. Of course she'd be grateful. Who wouldn't be?

Moore, Hernandez, and Worthington seemed to graciously decide their wild sporting-event conversation could be put on hold, walking past Wallace without so much as a glance in his direction and moving toward the front of the church, each of them with a solemn look on his face. They ignored the young woman in the suit, instead stopping near Naomi, leaning over one by one to offer their condolences. She nodded. Wallace waited for the tears, sure it was a dam ready to burst.

The partners each took a moment to stand in front of the casket, their heads bowed low. That sense of unease that had filled Wallace since he'd blinked in front of the church grew stronger, discordant and awful. Here he was, sitting in the back of the church, staring at himself in the *front* of the church, lying in a casket. Wallace was under no impression he was a handsome man. He was too tall, too gangly, his cheekbones wicked sharp, leaving his pale face in a state of perpetual gauntness. Once, at a company Halloween party, a group of children had been delighted by his costume, one bold tween saying that he made an excellent Grim Reaper.

He hadn't been wearing a costume.

He studied himself from his seat, catching glimpses of his body as the partners shuffled around him, the terrible feeling that something was off threatening to overtake him. The body had been dressed in one of his nicer suits, a Tom Ford sharkskin wool two-piece. It fit his thin frame well and made his green eyes pop. To be fair, it wasn't exactly flattering now, given that his eyes were closed and his cheeks were covered with enough rouge to make him look as if he'd been a courtesan instead of a high-profile attorney. His forehead was strangely pale, his short dark hair slicked back and glistening wetly in the overhead lights.

Eventually, the partners sat in the pew opposite Naomi, their faces dry.

A door opened, and Wallace turned to see a priest (someone else he didn't recognize, and he felt that discordance again like a weight on his chest, something off, something *wrong*) walk through the narthex, wearing robes as ridiculous as the church around them. The priest blinked a couple of times, as if he couldn't believe how empty the church was. He pulled back the sleeve of his robe to look at his watch and shook his head before fixing a quiet smile on his face. He walked right by Wallace without acknowledging him. "That's fine," Wallace called after him. "I'm sure you think you're important. It's no wonder organized religion is in the shape it's in."

The priest stopped next to Naomi, taking her hand in his, speaking in soft platitudes, telling her how sorry he was for her loss, that the Lord worked in mysterious ways, and while we may not always understand his plan, rest assured there was one, and this was part of it.

Naomi said, "Oh, I don't doubt that, Father. But let's skip all the mumbo-jumbo and get this show on the road. He's supposed to be buried in two hours, and I have a flight to catch this afternoon."

Wallace rolled his eyes. "Christ, Naomi. How about showing a little respect? You're in a *church*." *And I'm dead*, he wanted to add, but didn't, because that made it real, and none of this could be real. It couldn't.

The priest nodded. "Of course." He patted the back of her hand before moving to the opposite pews where the partners sat. "I'm sorry for your loss. The Lord works in mysterious—"

"Of course he does," Moore said.

"So mysterious," Hernandez agreed.

"Big man upstairs with his plans," Worthington said.

The woman—the stranger he didn't recognize—snorted, shaking her head.

Wallace glared at her.

The priest moved on, stopping in front of the casket, head bowed.

Before, there'd been pain in Wallace's arm, a burning sensation in his chest, a savage little twist of nausea in his stomach. For a moment, he'd almost convinced himself that it'd been the leftover chili he'd eaten the night before. But then he was on the floor of his office, lying on the imported Persian rug he'd spent an exorbitant amount on, listening to the fountain in the lobby gurgle as he tried to catch his breath. "Goddamn chili," he'd managed to gasp, his last words before he'd found himself standing *above* his own body, feeling like he was in two places at once, staring up at the ceiling while also staring *down* at himself. It took a moment before that division subsided, leaving him with mouth agape, the only sound crawling from his throat a thin squeak like a deflating balloon.

Which was *fine*, because he'd only passed out! That's all it was. Nothing more than heartburn and the need to take a nap on the floor. It happened to everyone at one point or another. He'd been working too hard as of late. Of course it'd finally caught up to him.

With that decided, he felt a bit better about wearing sweats and flip-flops and an old T-shirt in church at his funeral. He didn't even like the Rolling Stones. He had no idea where the shirt had come from.

The priest cleared his throat as he looked out at the few people gathered. He said, "It's written in the Good Book that—"

"Oh, for Pete's sake," Wallace muttered.

The stranger choked.

Wallace jerked his head up as the priest droned on.

The woman had her hand over her mouth like she was trying to stifle her laughter. Wallace was incensed. If she found his death so funny, why the hell was she even here?

Unless . . .

No, it couldn't be, right?

He stared at her, trying to place her.

What if she *had* been a client of his?

What if he'd gotten a less than desirable result for her?

A class-action lawsuit, maybe. One that hadn't netted as much as she'd hoped. He made promises whenever he got a new client, big promises of justice and extraordinary financial compensation. Where once he might have tempered expectations, he'd only grown more confident with every judgment in his favor. His name was whispered with great reverence in the hallowed halls of the courts. He was a ruthless shark, and anyone who stood in his way usually ended up flat on their back, wondering what the hell had happened.

But maybe it was more than that.

Had what started out as a professional attorney-client relationship turned to something darker? Perhaps she'd become fixated on him, enamored with his expensive suits and command of the courtroom. She told herself that she would have Wallace Price, or no one would. She'd stalked him, standing outside his window at night, watching him while he slept (his apartment being on the fifteenth floor didn't dissuade him of this notion; for all he knew, she'd climbed up the side of the building to his balcony). And when he was at work, she'd broken in and lain upon his pillow, breathing in his scent, dreaming of the day when she could become Mrs. Wallace Price. Then perhaps he'd spurned her unknowingly, and the love she'd felt for him had turned into a black rage.

That was it.

That explained everything. After all, it wasn't without precedent, was it? Because it was likely Patricia Ryan had *also* been obsessed with him, given her unfortunate reaction when he'd fired her. For all he knew, they were in cahoots with each other, and when Wallace had done what he did, they'd . . . what? Joined forces to . . . wait. Okay. The timeline was a little fuzzy for that to work, but *still*.

"—and now, I'd like to invite anyone who would like to say a few words about our dear Wallace to come forward and do so at this time." The priest smiled serenely. The smile faded slightly when no one moved. "Anyone at all."

The partners bowed their heads.

Naomi sighed.

Obviously, they were overcome, unable to find the right words to say in order to sum up a life well-lived. Wallace didn't blame them for that. How did one even begin to encapsulate all that he was? Successful, intelligent, hard-working to the point of obsession, and so much more. Of *course* they'd be reticent.

"Get up," he muttered, staring hard at those in the front of the church. "Get up and say nice things about me. Now. I *command you*."

He gasped when Naomi rose. "It worked!" he whispered fervently. "Yes. *Yes.*"

The priest nodded at her as he stepped off to the side. Naomi stared down at Wallace's body for a long moment, and Wallace was surprised to see her face screw up like she was about to cry. Finally. *Finally* someone was going to show some kind of emotion. He wondered if she would throw herself at the casket, demanding to know why, why, *why* life had to be so unfair, and Wallace, I've always loved you, even when I was sleeping with the gardener. You know, the one who seemed averse to wearing shirts while he worked, the sun shining down on his broad shoulders, the sweat trickling down his carved abdominal muscles like he was a goddamn Greek statue that you pretended not to stare at too, but we both know that's crap, given that we had the same taste in men.

She didn't cry.

She sneezed instead.

"Excuse me," she said, wiping her nose. "That's been building for a while."

Wallace sunk lower in the pew. He didn't have a good feeling about this.

She moved in front of the church on the dais next to the priest. She said, "Wallace Price was . . . certainly alive. And now he's not. For the life of me, I can't quite say that's a terrible thing. He wasn't a good person."

"Oh my," the priest said.

Naomi ignored him. "He was obstinate, foolhardy, and cared only for himself. I could have married Bill Nicholson, but instead, I hooked up to the Wallace Price Express, bound for a destination of missed meals, forgotten birthdays and anniversaries, and the disgusting habit of leaving toenail clippings on the bathroom floor. I mean, come on. The trash bin was *right there*. How on earth do you miss it?"

"Terrible," Moore said.

"Exactly," Hernandez agreed.

"Put the clippings in the trash," Worthington said. "It's not that hard."

"Wait," Wallace said loudly. "That's not what you're supposed to be doing. You need to be *sad*, and as you wipe away tears, you talk about everything you'll miss about me. What kind of funeral *is* this?"

But Naomi wouldn't listen, which, really. When had she ever? "I've spent the last few days since I got the news trying to find a single memory of our time together that didn't fill me with regret or apathy or a burning fury that felt like I was standing on the sun. It took time, but I did find one. Once, Wallace brought me a cup of soup while I was sick. I thanked him. Then he went to work, and I didn't see him for six days."

"That's *it*?" Wallace exclaimed. "Are you *kidding* me?"

Naomi's expression hardened. "I know we're supposed to act and feel a certain way when someone dies, but I'm here to tell you that's bullshit. Sorry, Father."

The priest nodded. "It's okay, my child. Get it all out. The Lord doesn't—"

"And don't even get me started on the fact that he cared more about his work than making a family. I marked my ovulation cycle on his work calendar. Do you know what he did? He sent me a card that said CONGRATULATIONS, GRADUATE."

"Still holding onto that, are we?" Wallace asked loudly. "How's that therapy going for you, Naomi? Sounds like you should get a refund."

"Yikes," the woman in the pew said.

Wallace glared at her. "Something you'd like to add? I know I'm a catch, but just because I won't love you didn't give you the right to murder me!"

The sound he made when the woman looked directly at him is better left to the imagination, especially when she said quite loudly, "Nah. You're not exactly my type, and murder is bad, you know?"

Wallace practically fell out of the pew as Naomi continued to slander him in a house of God as if the strange woman hadn't spoken at all. He managed to grab the back of the pew, fingernails digging into the wood. He peered over the top, eyes bulging as he stared at the woman.

She smiled and arched an eyebrow.

Wallace struggled to find his voice. "You . . . you can see me?"

She nodded as she turned in her own pew, resting her elbow on the back. "I can."

He began to tremble, his hands gripping the pew so hard, he thought his fingers would snap. "How. What. I don't—*what*."

"I know you're confused, Wallace, and things can be—"

"I never told you my name!" he said shrilly, unable to stop his voice from cracking.

She snorted. "There's literally a sign with your picture on it below your name in the front of the church."

"That's not . . ." What? What wasn't it *exactly*? He pulled himself upright. His legs weren't quite working as he wanted them to. "Forget the damn sign. How is this happening? What the hell is going on?"

The woman smiled. "You're dead."

He burst out laughing. Yes, he could see his body in a casket, but that didn't mean anything. There had to be some mistake. He stopped laughing when he realized the woman wasn't joining in. "What," he said flatly.

"Dead, Wallace." Her face scrunched up. "Hold on. Trying to remember what the cause was. This is my first time, and I'm a little nervous." She brightened. "Oh, that's right! Heart attack."

And that was how he knew this wasn't real. A heart attack? Bullshit. He never smoked, he ate as best he could, and he exercised when he remembered. His last physical had ended with the doctor telling him that while his blood pressure was a little high, everything else seemed to be in working order. He couldn't be dead from a heart attack. It wasn't possible. He told her as much, sure that'd be the end of it.

"Riiiight," she repeated slowly, as if *he* were the idiot. "Hate to be a bummer, man, but that's what happened."

"No," he said, shaking his head. "I would know if I . . . I would have felt . . ." Felt what? Pain in his arm? The stuttering in his chest? The way he couldn't quite catch his breath no matter how hard he tried?

She shrugged. "I suppose it's one of those things." He flinched when she stood from the pew, making her way over to him. She was shorter than he expected, the top of her head probably coming up to his chin. He backed away from her as best he could, but he didn't get far.

Naomi was ranting about a trip to the Poconos they'd apparently taken ("He stayed in the hotel room the entire time on conference calls! It was our honeymoon!") as the woman sat on his pew, keeping a bit of distance between them. She appeared even younger than he first thought—perhaps early to mid-twenties—which somehow made things worse. Her complexion was slightly darker than his own, lips pulled back over small teeth in the hint of a smile. She tapped her fingers on the back of the pew before looking at him. "Wallace Price," she said. "My name is Meiying, but you can call me Mei, like the month, only spelled a little different. I'm here to bring you home."

He stared at her, unable to speak.

"Huh. Didn't know that'd shut you up. Should've tried that to begin with."

"I'm not going anywhere with you," he said through gritted teeth. "I don't know you."

"I should hope not," she said. "If you did, it'd be very weird." She paused, considering. "Weird*er*, at least." She nodded toward the front of the church. "Nice casket, by the way. Doesn't look cheap."

He bristled. "It isn't. Only the very best for—"

"Oh, I'm sure," Mei said. "Still. Pretty gnarly, right? Looking at your own body like that. Not a bad body, though. Little skinny for my tastes, but to each their own."

He bristled. "I'll have you know that I did just *fine* with my skinny—no. I won't be distracted! I demand you tell me what's going on *right this second*."

"Okay," she said quietly. "I can do that. I know this may be hard to understand, but your heart gave out, and you died. There was an autopsy, and it turned out you had blockages in your coronary arteries. I can show you the Y incision, if you want, though I'd advise against it. It's pretty gross. Did you know that once they perform the autopsy, they sometimes put the organs back inside in a bag along with sawdust before they close you up?" She brightened. "Oh, and I'm your Reaper, here to take you where you belong." And then, as if the moment wasn't strange enough, she made jazz hands. "Ta-da."

"Reaper," he said in a daze. "What is . . . that?"

"Me," she said, scooting closer. "I'm a Reaper. Once someone dies, there's confusion. You don't really know what's going on, and you're scared."

"I'm not scared!" This was a lie. He'd never been more frightened in his life.

"Okay," she said. "So you're not scared. That's good. Regardless, it's a trying time for anyone. You need help to make the transition. That's where I come in. I'm here to make sure said transition goes as smoothly as possible." She paused. Then, "That's it. I think I remembered to say everything. I had to memorize *a lot* to get this job, and I might have forgotten a detail here and there, but that's the gist of it."

He gaped at her. He barely heard Naomi yelling in the background, calling him a selfish bastard with absolutely no self-awareness. "Transition."

Mei nodded.

He didn't like the sound of that. "To *what*?"

She grinned. "Oh, man. Just you wait." She raised her hand toward him, turning her palm up. She pressed her thumb and middle fingers together and snapped.

The cool, spring sun was shining down on his face.

He took a stumbling step back, looking around wildly.

Cemetery. They were in a cemetery.

"Sorry about that," Mei said, appearing beside him. "Still getting the hang of it." She frowned. "I'm sort of new at this."

"What's happening!" he shrieked at her.

"You're getting buried," she said cheerily. "Come on. You'll want to see this. It'll help dispel any doubts you might have left." She grabbed him by the arm and pulled. He tripped over his own feet but managed to stay upright. His flip-flops slapped against his heels as he struggled to keep up. They weaved in and out of headstones, the sounds of busy traffic surrounding them as impatient cabbies honked their horns and shouted expletives out open windows. He tried to pull away from Mei, but her grip was tight. She was stronger than she looked.

"Here we are," she said, coming to a stop. "Right on time."

He peered over her shoulder. Naomi was there, as were the partners, all standing around a freshly dug rectangular hole. The expensive coffin was being lowered into the earth. No one was crying. Worthington kept looking at his watch and sighing dramatically. Naomi was tapping away on her phone.

Of all the things for Wallace to focus on, he was dumbstruck by the fact that there was no headstone. "Where's the marker? My name. Date of birth. An inspirational message saying I lived life to the fullest."

"Is that what you did?" Mei asked. She didn't sound like she was mocking him, merely curious.

He jerked his hand away and crossed his arms defensively. "Yes."

"Awesome. And the headstones usually come after the service. They still have to carve it and everything. It's this whole process. Don't worry about it. Look. There you go. Wave goodbye!"

He didn't wave.

Mei did, though, fingers wiggling.

"How did we get here?" he asked. "We were just in the church."

"So observant. That's really good, Wallace. We *were* just in the church. I'm proud of you. Let's say I skipped a couple of things. Gotta get a move on." She winced. "And that's my bad, man. Like, seriously, don't take this the wrong way because I totally didn't mean it, but I was a *little* late in getting to you. This is sort of my first time reaping on my own, and I screwed up. Went to the wrong place on accident." She smiled beatifically. "We cool?"

"*No*," he snarled at her. "We're *not cool*."

"Oh. That sucks. Sorry. I promise it won't happen again. Learning experience and all that. I hope you'll still rate my service a ten when you get the survey. It'd mean a lot to me."

He had no idea what she was talking about. He could almost convince himself that *she* was the crazy one, and nothing but a figment of his imagination. "It's been three days!"

She beamed at him. "Exactly! This makes my job so much easier. Hugo's gonna be so pleased with me. I can't wait to tell him."

"Who the hell is—"

"Hold on. This is one of my favorite parts."

He looked to where she was pointing. The partners stood in a line, with Naomi behind them. He watched as they all leaned down, one by one, scooping up a handful of dirt and dropping it into the grave. The sound of the dirt hitting the lid of the casket caused Wallace's hands to shake. Naomi stood with her handful of dirt over the open grave, and before she dropped it, a strange expression flickered across her face, there and gone. She shook her head, dropped the dirt, and then whirled around. The last he saw of his ex-wife was the sunlight on her hair as she hurried toward a waiting cab.

"Kinda brings it all home," Mei said. "Full circle. From the earth we came, and to the earth we return. Pretty, if you think about it."

"What's going on?" he whispered.

Mei touched the back of his hand. Her skin was cool, but not unpleasantly so. "Do you need a hug? I can give you a hug if you want."

He jerked his arm back. "I don't want a hug."

She nodded. "Boundaries. Cool. I respect that. I promise I won't hug you without your permission."

Once, when Wallace was seven, his parents had taken him to the beach. He'd stood in the surf, watching the sand rush between his toes. There was a strange sensation that rose through his legs to the pit of his stomach. He was sinking, though the combination of the whirling sand and white-capped water made it feel like so much more. It'd terrified him, and he'd refused to go back in the ocean, no matter how much his parents had pleaded with him.

It was this sensation Wallace Price felt now. Maybe it was the sound of the dirt on the casket. Maybe it was the fact that his picture was propped up next to the open grave, a floral wreath attached below it. In this picture, he was smiling tightly. His hair was styled perfectly, parted to the right. His eyes were bright. Naomi once said that he reminded her of the scarecrow from Oz. "If you only had a brain," she said. This had been during one of their divorce proceedings, so he'd discounted it as nothing but her trying to hurt him.

He sat down hard on the ground, his toes flexing into the grass over the tip of his flip-flops. Mei settled next to him, folding her legs underneath her, picking at a little dandelion. She plucked it from the ground, holding it close to his mouth. "Make a wish," she said.

He did not make a wish.

She sighed and blew on the dandelion seeds herself. They exploded into a white cloud, the bits catching on a breeze and swirling around the open grave. "It's a lot to take in, I know."

"Do you?" he muttered, face in his hands.

"Not literally," she admitted. "But I have a good idea."

He looked over at her, eyes narrowed. "You said this was your first time."

"It is. Solo, that is. But I went through the training, and did pretty good. Do you need empathy? I can give you that. Do you want to punch something because you're angry? I can help you with that too. Not me, though. Maybe a wall." She shrugged. "Or we can sit here and watch as they eventually come with a small bulldozer and shovel all the dirt on top of your former body thus cementing the fact that it's all over. Dealer's choice."

He stared at her.

She nodded. "Right. I could have phrased that better. Sorry. Still getting the hang of things."

"What is . . . ?" He tried to swallow past the lump in his throat. "What's happening?"

She said, "What's happening is that you lived your life. You did what you did, and now it's over. At least that part of it is. And when you're ready to leave here, I'll take you to Hugo. He'll explain the rest."

"Leave," he muttered. "With Hugo."

She shook her head before stopping herself. "Well, in a way. He's a ferryman."

"A what?"

"Ferryman," she repeated. "The one who will help you cross."

His mind was racing. He couldn't focus on any one single thing.

It all felt too grand to comprehend. "But I thought you were supposed to—"

"Aw. You do like me. That's sweet." She laughed. "But I'm just a Reaper, Wallace. My job is to make sure you get to the ferryman. He'll handle the rest. You'll see. Once we get to him, it'll be right as rain. Hugo tends to have that effect on people. He'll explain everything before you cross, any of those pesky, lingering questions."

"Cross," Wallace said dully. "To . . . where?"

Mei cocked her head. "Why, to what's next of course."

"Heaven?" He blanched, a terrible thought piercing through the storm. "Hell?"

She shrugged. "Sure."

"That doesn't explain anything at all."

She laughed. "I know, right? This is fun. I'm having fun. Aren't you?"

No, he really wasn't.

❦

She didn't hurry him. They stayed even as the sky began to streak in pinks and oranges, the March sun setting low toward the horizon. They stayed even as the promised bulldozer came, the woman operating it deftly with a cigarette jammed between her teeth, smoke pouring from her nose. The grave filled quicker than Wallace expected. The first stars were starting to appear by the time she finished, though they were faint given the light pollution from the city.

And that was it.

All that was left of Wallace Price was a mound of dirt and a body that was going to be nothing but worm food. It was a profoundly devastating experience. He hadn't realized it would be. Strange, he thought to himself. How very strange.

He looked at Mei.

She smiled at him.

He said, "I . . ." He didn't know how to finish.

She touched the back of his hand. "Yes, Wallace. It's real."

And wonder of all wonders, he believed her.

She said, "Would you like to meet Hugo?"

No. He wouldn't. He wanted to run. He wanted to scream. He wanted to raise his fists toward the stars and rant and rave about the unfairness of it all. He had plans. He had goals. So much left to do, and now he'd never . . . he couldn't . . .

He startled when a tear slipped down his cheek. "Do I have a choice?"

"In life? Always."

"And in death?"

She shrugged. "It's a little more . . . regimented. But it's for your own good. I swear," she added quickly. "There are reasons these things happen the way they do. Hugo will explain it all. He's a great guy. You'll see."

That did not make him feel better.

But still, when she stood above him, holding her hand out, he only stared at it for a moment or two before taking it, allowing her to pull him up.

He turned his face toward the sky. He breathed in and out.

Mei said, "This is probably going to feel a little odd. But it's a longer distance, so it's to be expected. It'll be over before you know it."

But before he could react, she snapped again and everything exploded.

CHAPTER 3

Wallace was screaming when they landed on a paved road in the middle of a forest. The air was cold, but even as he continued to yell, no breath cloud formed in front of him. It didn't make sense. How could he be cold when he was dead? Was he actually breathing, or . . . No. No. Focus. Focus on the here. Focus on the now. One thing at a time.

"Are you done?" Mei asked him.

He realized he was still screaming. He snapped his mouth closed, pain bright as he bit into his tongue. Which, of course, set him off again, because how the hell could he feel *pain*?

"No," he muttered, backing away from Mei, thoughts jumbled in an infinite knot. "You can't just—"

And then he was hit by a car.

Wait.

He *should* have been hit by a car. The car approached, the headlights bright. He managed to bring up his hands in time to block his face, only to have the car go *through* him. Out of the corner of his eye, he saw the driver's face pass inches from his own. He didn't feel any of it.

The car continued down the road, the taillights flashing once before it rounded a corner and disappeared entirely.

He was frozen, hands extended in front of him, one leg raised, thigh pressed against his stomach.

Mei laughed loudly. "Oh, man. You should see the look on your face. Oh my god, it's *awesome*."

He gradually lowered his leg, half-convinced he'd fall right through the ground. He didn't. It was solid beneath his feet. He couldn't stop shaking. "How. What. Why. What. *What*?"

She wiped her eyes, still chuckling. "My bad. I should've warned you that could happen." She shook her head. "It's all good, though, right? I mean, how great is it that you can't be hit by cars anymore?"

"*That's* what you took away from this?" he asked incredulously.

"It's a pretty big thing if you think about it."

"I don't *want* to think about it," he snapped. "I don't want to think about any of this!"

Inexplicably, she said, "If wishes were fishes, we'd all swim in riches."

He stared after her as she started down the road. "That doesn't explain *anything!*"

"Only because you're being obstinate. Lighten up, man."

He chased after her, not wanting to be left alone in the middle of nowhere. In the distance, he could see the lights of what looked like a small village. He didn't recognize any of their surroundings, but she was talking a mile a minute, and he couldn't get a word in edgewise.

"He doesn't stand on ceremony or anything, so don't worry about that. Don't call him Mr. Freeman because he hates that. He's Hugo to everyone, okay? And maybe stop scowling so much. Or not, it's up to you. I won't tell you how to be. He knows that you . . ." She coughed awkwardly. "Well, he knows how tricky these things can be, so don't worry about it. Ask all the questions you need to. That's what we're here for." And then, "Do you see it yet?"

He started to ask what the hell she was talking about, but then she nodded toward his chest. He looked down, a scowl forming.

The pithy retort on the tip of his tongue was replaced by a cry of horror.

There, protruding from his chest, was a curved piece of metal, almost like a fishhook the size of his hand. Silver in color, it glinted in the low light. It didn't hurt, but it looked like it *should* have, given that the sharp tip appeared to be embedded into his sternum. Attached to the other end of the hook was a . . . cable? A thin band of what almost looked like plastic that flashed with a dull light. The cable stretched out on the road in front of them, leading away. He slapped against his chest, trying to knock the hook loose, but his

hands passed right through it. The light from the cable intensi-
fied, and the hook vibrated warmly, filling him with an odd sense
of relief that he hadn't expected given that he'd been skewered.
This feeling was, of course, tempered by the fact that he *had* been
skewered.

"What is it?" he yelled, still slapping at his chest. "Get it off, get
it *off*!"

"Nah," Mei said, reaching over and grabbing his hands. "We really don't want to do that. Trust me when I say it's helping you. You
need it. It's not gonna hurt you. I can't see it, but judging by your
reaction, it's the same as all the others. Don't fuss with it. Hugo will
explain, I promise."

"What is it?" he demanded again, skin prickling. He stared at
the cable that stretched along the road in front of them.

"A connection." She bumped his shoulder. "Keeps you grounded.
It leads to Hugo. He knows we're close. Come on. I can't wait for
you to meet him."

ᴄ๑

The village was quiet. There seemed to be only a single main thor-
oughfare that went through the center. No traffic signals, no hustle
and bustle of people on the sidewalks. A couple of cars passed by
(Wallace jumping out of the way, not wanting to relive *that* experience again), but other than that, it was mostly silent. The shops
on either side of the road had already closed for the day, their windows darkened, signs hanging from the doors promising to be back
first thing in the morning. Their awnings stretched out over the
sidewalk, all in bright colors of red and green and blue and orange.

Streetlamps lined either side of the road, their lights warm and
soft. The road was cobblestone, and Wallace stepped out of the
way as a group of kids on their bikes rode by him. They didn't acknowledge either him or Mei. They were laughing and shouting,
cards attached to the spokes of their wheels with clothespins, their
breath streaming behind them like little trains. Wallace ached a
little at the thought. They were free, free in ways he hadn't been

in a long time. He struggled with this, unable to shape it into anything recognizable. And then the feeling was gone, leaving him hollowed out and trembling.

"Is this place real?" he asked, feeling the hook in his chest grow warmer. The cable didn't go slack as he expected it to as they continued on. He'd thought he would be tripping over it by now. Instead, it remained as taut as it'd been since he'd first noticed it.

Mei glanced at him. "What do you mean?"

He didn't quite know. "Are they . . . is everyone here dead?"

"*Oh.* Yeah, no. I get it. Yes, this place is real. No, everyone isn't dead. This is just like everywhere else, I suppose. We did have to travel pretty far, but it's nowhere you couldn't have gone on your own had you ever decided to leave the city. Doesn't sound like you got out very much."

"I was too busy," he muttered.

"You have all the time in the world now," Mei said, and it *startled* him how pointed that was. His chest hitched, and he blinked against the sudden burn in his eyes. Mei walked lazily down the sidewalk, glancing over her shoulder to make sure he followed.

He did, but only because he didn't want to be left behind in an unfamiliar place. The buildings that had seemed almost quaint now loomed around him ominously, the dark windows like dead eyes. He looked down at his feet, focusing on putting one foot in front of the other. His vision began to tunnel, his skin thrumming. That hook in his chest was growing more insistent.

He'd never been more scared in his life.

"Hey, hey," he heard Mei say, and when he opened his eyes, he found himself crouched low to the ground, his arms wrapped around his stomach, fingers digging into his skin hard enough to leave bruises. If he could even *get* bruises. "It's okay, Wallace. I'm here."

"Because *that's* supposed to make me feel better," he choked out.

"It's a lot for anyone. We can sit here for a moment, if that's what you need. I'm not going to rush you, Wallace."

He didn't know what he needed. He couldn't think clearly. He tried to get a handle on it, tried to find something to grasp onto. And when he found it, it came from within him, a forgotten memory rising like a ghost.

He was nine, and his father asked him to come into the living room. He'd just gotten home from school and was in the kitchen making a peanut-butter-and-banana sandwich. He froze at his father's request, trying to think of what he could have done to get in trouble. He'd smoked a cigarette behind the bleachers, but that had been weeks ago, and there was no way his parents could have known unless someone had told them.

He left the sandwich on the counter, already making excuses in his head, forming promises of *I'll never do it again, I swear, it was just one time.*

They were sitting on the couch, and he stopped cold when he saw his mother was crying, though she looked like she was trying to stifle it. Her cheeks were streaked, the Kleenex tightened into a little ball in her hand. Her nose was running, and though she tried to smile when she saw him, it trembled and twisted down as her shoulders shook. The only time he'd seen her cry before had been over a random movie where a dog had overcome adversity (porcupine quills) in order to be reunited with its owner.

"What's wrong?" he asked, unsure of what he should do. He understood the idea of consoling someone but had never actually put it into practice. They weren't a family free with affection. At best, his father shook his hand, and his mother squeezed his shoulder whenever they were pleased with him. He didn't mind. It was how things were.

His father said, "Your grandfather passed away."

"Oh," Wallace breathed, suddenly itchy all over.

"Do you understand death?"

No, no, he didn't. He knew what it was, knew what the word meant, but it was a nebulous thing, an event that occurred for other people far, far away. It'd never crossed Wallace's mind that someone *he* knew could die. Grandpa lived four hours away, and his house always smelled like sour milk. He'd been fond of making crafts out of his discarded beer cans: planes with propellers that actually moved, little cats that hung on strings from the ceiling of his porch.

And since he was a child grappling with a concept far bigger than he, the next words out of his mouth were: "Did someone murder him?" Grandpa was fond of saying how he'd fought in the war (which war, exactly, Wallace didn't know; he'd never been able to ask a follow-up question), which was usually followed by words that caused Wallace's mother to yell at her father while she covered Wallace's ears, and later, she'd tell her only son to *never* repeat what he'd heard because it was grossly racist. He could understand if someone had murdered his grandpa. It actually made a lot of sense.

"No, Wallace," his mother choked out. "It wasn't like that. It was cancer. He got sick, and he couldn't go on any longer. It's . . . it's over."

This was the moment Wallace Price decided—in the way children often do, absolute and fearless—never to let that happen to him. Grandfather was alive, and then he wasn't. His parents were upset at the loss. Wallace didn't like to be upset. So he tamped it down, shoving it into a box and locking it tight.

es

He blinked slowly, becoming aware of his surroundings. Still in the village. Still with the woman.

Mei hunkered down before him, her tie dangling between her legs. "All right?"

He didn't trust himself to speak, so he nodded, though he was the furthest thing from *all right*.

"This is normal," she said, tapping her fingers against her knee. "It happens to everyone after they pass. And don't be surprised if it happens a few more times. It's a lot to take in."

"How would you know?" he mumbled. "You said I was your first one."

"First one *solo*," she corrected. "I put in over a hundred hours of training before I could go out on my own, so I've seen it before. Think you can stand?"

No, he didn't. He did anyway. He was a little unsteady on his feet, but he managed to stay upright through sheer force of will. That hook was still there in his chest, the cable still flashing dimly. For a moment, he thought he felt a gentle tug, but he couldn't be sure.

"There we go," Mei said. She patted his chest. "You're doing well, Wallace."

He glared at her. "I'm not a child."

"Oh, I know. It's easier with kids, if you can believe that. The adults are the ones that're usually the problem."

He didn't know what to say to that, so he said nothing at all.

"Come on," she said. "Hugo's waiting for us."

∾

They reached the end of the village a short time later. The buildings stopped, and the road that stretched before them wound its way through the coniferous forest, the scent of pine reminding Wallace of Christmas, a time when all the world seemed to take a breath and forget—even just for a little while—how harsh life could be.

He was about to ask how far they had to walk when they reached a dirt road outside of the village. A wooden sign sat next to the road. He couldn't make out the words in the dark, not until he'd gotten closer.

The letters had been carved into the wood with the utmost care.

CHARON'S CROSSING
TEA AND TREATS

"Char-ron?" he said. He'd never heard such a word before.

"Kay-ron," Mei said, enunciating slowly. "It's a bit of a joke. Hugo's funny like that."

"I don't get it."

Mei sighed. "Of course you don't. Don't worry about it. As soon as we get to the tea shop, it'll—"

"Tea shop," Wallace repeated, eyeing the sign with disdain.

Mei paused. "Wow. You've got something against tea, man? That's not gonna go over well."

"I don't have anything against—I thought we were going to meet God. Why would he—"

Mei burst out laughing. "*What?*"

"Hugo," he said, flustered. "Or whoever."

"Oh man, I cannot *wait* to tell him you said that. Holy crap. That's gonna go right to his head." She frowned. "Maybe I won't tell him."

"I don't see what's so funny."

"I know," she said. "That's what's so funny about it. Hugo's not God, Wallace. He's a ferryman. I told you that. God is . . . the idea of God is a human one. It's a little more complicated than that."

"What?" Wallace said faintly. He wondered if it was possible to have a second heart attack, even though he was already dead. And then he remembered he couldn't actually *feel* his heart beating anymore, and the desire to curl up into a little ball once again started to take over. Agnostic or not, he hadn't expected to hear something so enormous said so easily.

"Oh, no," Mei said, grabbing onto his hand to make sure he stayed on his feet. "We're not going to lie down here. It's only a little bit farther. It'll be more comfortable inside."

He let himself be pulled down the road. The trees were thicker, old pines that reached toward the starry sky like fingers from the earth. He couldn't remember the last time he'd been in a forest, much less at night. He preferred steel and honking horns, the sounds of a city that never went to sleep. Noise meant he wasn't alone, no matter where he was. Here, the silence was all-consuming, suffocating.

They rounded a corner, and he could see warm lights through the trees like a beacon calling, calling, calling him. He barely felt his feet on the ground. He thought he might be floating but couldn't bring himself to look down to see.

The closer they got, the more the hook tugged at his chest. It wasn't quite irritating, but he couldn't ignore it. The cable continued on down the road.

He was about to ask Mei about it when something moved on the road ahead of them. He flinched, mind constructing a terrible creature crawling from the shadowy woods with sharp fangs and glowing eyes. Instead, a woman appeared, hurrying down the road. The closer she got, the more details filled in. She looked middle-aged, her mouth set in a thin line as she pulled her coat tighter around her. She had bags under her eyes, dark circles that looked as if they'd been tattooed on her face. Wallace didn't know why he was expecting some kind of acknowledgment, but she passed by them without so much as a glance in their direction, blond hair trailing behind her as she moved quickly down the road.

Mei had a pinched look on her face, but she shook her head and it was gone. "Come on. Don't want to keep him waiting any more than we already have."

He didn't know what he was expecting after reading the sign. He'd never really been inside something that could be called a *tea shop* before. He'd gotten his morning coffee from the cart in front of the office building. He wasn't a hipster. He didn't have a man bun or an ironic sense of fashion, his current outfit be damned. The glasses he usually wore while reading were, while expensive, utilitarian. He didn't belong in something that could be described as a *tea shop*. What a preposterous idea.

Which was why he was surprised when they came to the shop itself to see that it looked like a house. Granted, it was unlike any house he'd ever seen before, but a house all the same. A wooden porch wrapped around the front, large windows on either side of a bright green door, light flickering from within like candles had been lit. A brick chimney sat on the roof with a little curl of smoke coming out the top.

But that was where the similarity to any house Wallace had ever seen ended. Part of it had to do with the cable extending from the hook in his chest and up the stairs, disappearing into the closed door. *Through* the closed door.

The house itself looked as if it had started out one way, and then halfway through the builders had decided to go in another direction entirely. The best way Wallace could think of to describe it was that it looked like a child stacking block after block on top of one another, making a precarious tower. The house looked as if even the smallest breeze could send it tumbling down. The chimney wasn't crooked, per se, but more *twisted*, the brickwork jutting out at impossible angles. The bottom floor of the house appeared sturdy, but the second floor hung off to one side, the third floor to the opposite side, the *fourth* floor right in the middle, forming a turret with drapes drawn across multiple windows. Wallace thought he saw one of the drapes move as if someone were peering out, but it could have been a trick of the light.

The outside of the house was constructed with panel siding.

But also brick.

And . . . adobe?

One side appeared to be built out of logs, as if it'd been a cabin at one point. It looked like something out of a fairy tale, an unusual house hidden away in the woods. Perhaps there'd be a kindly woodsman inside, or a witch who wanted to cook Wallace in her oven, his skin cracking as it blackened. Wallace didn't know which was worse. He'd heard too many stories about terrible things happening in such houses, all in the name of teaching a Very Valuable Lesson. This did nothing to make him feel better.

"What is this place?" Wallace asked as they stopped near the porch. A small green scooter sat next to a flower bed, the blooms wild in yellows and greens and reds and whites, but muted in the dark.

"Awesome, right?" Mei said. "It's even crazier on the inside. People come from all over to see it. It's pretty famous, for obvious reasons."

He pulled his arm from her as she tried to walk toward the porch. "I'm not going inside."

She glanced over her shoulder. "Why not?"

He waved at the house. "It doesn't look safe. It's obviously not up to code. It's going to fall down at any moment."

"How do you know that?"

He stared at her. "We're seeing the same thing, right? I'm not going to be trapped inside when it collapses. It's a lawsuit waiting to happen. And I *know* about lawsuits."

"Huh," Mei said, looking back up at the house. She tilted her head back as far as she could. "But . . ."

"But?"

"You're dead," she said. "Even if it did fall down, it wouldn't matter."

"That's . . ." He didn't know what that was.

"And besides, it's been like this for as long as I've lived here. It hasn't fallen down yet. I don't think today will be that day either."

He gaped at her. "You *live* here?"

"I do," she said. "It's our home, so maybe show some respect? And don't worry about the house. If we worry about the little things all the time, we run the risk of missing the bigger things."

"Has anyone ever told you that you sound like a fortune cookie?" Wallace muttered.

"No," Mei said. "Because that's kind of racist, seeing as how I'm Asian and all."

Wallace blanched. "I . . . that's not—I didn't mean—"

She stared at him a long moment, letting him sputter before saying, "Okay. So you didn't mean it that way. Glad to hear it. I know this is all new for you, but maybe think before you talk, yeah? Especially since I'm one of the few people who can even see you."

She took the steps on the porch two at a time, stopping in front of the door. Potted plants hung from the ceiling, long vines draping down. A sign sat in the window that read CLOSED FOR PRIVATE EVENT. The door itself had an old metal knocker in the shape of a leaf. Mei lifted the knocker, tapping it against the green door three times.

"Why are you knocking on the door?" he asked. "Don't you live here?"

Mei looked back at him. "Oh, I do, but tonight's different. This is how things go. Ready?"

"Maybe we should come back later."

She smiled like she was amused, and for the life of him, Wallace couldn't see what was so funny. "Now's as good as time as any. It's all about the first step, Wallace. You can do it. I know faith is hard, especially in the face of the unknown. But I have faith in you. Maybe have a little in me?"

"I don't even know you."

She hummed a little under her breath. "Sure you don't. But there's only one way to fix that, right?"

He glared at her. "Really working for that ten, aren't you?"

She laughed. "Always." She put her hand on the doorknob. "Coming?"

Wallace looked back down the road. It was full-on dark. The sky was a field of stars, more than he'd ever seen in his life. He felt small, insignificant. And lost. Oh, was he lost.

"First step," he whispered to himself.

He turned back toward the house. He took a deep breath and puffed out his chest. He ignored the ridiculous slap his flip-flops made as he climbed the porch steps. He could do this. He was Wallace Phineas Price. People cowered at the sound of his name. They stood before him in *awe*. He was cool and calculating. He was a shark in the water, always circling. He was—

—tripping when the top step sagged, causing him to stumble forward.

"Yeah," Mei said. "Watch the last one. Sorry about that. Been meaning to tell Hugo to get that fixed. Didn't want to interrupt your moment or whatever was happening. It seemed important."

"I hate everything," Wallace said through gritted teeth.

Mei pushed open the door to Charon's Crossing Tea and Treats. It creaked on its hinges, and warm light spilled out, followed by the thick scent of spices and herbs: ginger and cinnamon, mint and cardamom. He didn't know how he was able to distinguish them, but there it was all the same. It wasn't like the office, a place more familiar than even his own home, stinking of cleaning fluids and artificial air, all steel and without whimsy, and though he hated that stench, he was used to it. It was safety. It was reality. It was what he knew. It was *all* he knew, he realized with dismay. What did that say about him?

The cable attached to the hook vibrated once more, seeming to beckon him forward.

He wanted to run as far as his feet could carry him.

Instead, with nothing left to lose, Wallace followed Mei through the door.

CHAPTER 4

He expected the inside of the house to look like the outside, a mishmash of architectural atrocities better suited for demolition than habitation.

He wasn't disappointed.

The light was low, coming from mismatched sconces bolted to the walls and an obscenely large candle sitting on a small table near the door. Plants hung from the vaulted ceiling in wicker baskets, and though none of them were flowering, the scent of them was almost overwhelming, mixing with the powerful smell of spices that seemed embedded into the walls. The vines trailed toward the floor, swaying gently in the breeze through the open window on the far wall. He started to reach for one, suddenly desperate to feel the leaves against his skin, but he curled his hand at the last moment. He could smell them, so he knew they were there even if his eyes were playing tricks on him. And Mei could touch him—in fact, he could still feel the ghost of her fingers on his skin—but what if that was it? Wallace had never been a man of leisure, stopping to smell the roses, or so the saying went. Doubt, then, doubt creeping up on him, sliding over his shoulders and weighing him down, fingers like claws digging in.

A dozen tables sat in the middle of the large room, their surfaces gleaming as if freshly wiped down. The chairs tucked underneath were old and worn, though not shabby. They too were mismatched, some with wooden seats and backs, others with thick and faded cushions. He even saw a moon chair in one corner. He hadn't seen one of those since he was a kid.

He barely heard Mei close the door behind them. He was distracted by the walls of the room, his feet moving him toward them of their own volition. They were covered in pictures and posters, some framed, some held up by pushpins. They told a story, he thought, but one he couldn't follow. Here was a picture of a waterfall, the spray catching the sunlight in rainbow fractals. Here was a shot of an island in a cerulean sea, the trees so thick, he couldn't see the ground. Here was a gigantic mural of the pyramids, drawn with a deft but unpracticed hand. Here was a photograph of a castle on a cliff, the stone crumbling and being overtaken by moss. Here was a framed poster of a volcano rising above the clouds, lava bursting in hot arcs. Here was a painting of a town in the throes of winter, the lights bright and almost twinkling, reflecting off an unmarked layer of snow. Strangely, they all caused a lump in Wallace's throat. He had never had time for such places, and now, he never would.

Shaking his head, he moved on, glancing at a fireplace that made up half of the wall to his right, the wood shifting as the embers sparked. It was made of white stone, the mantle, oak. Atop the mantle were little knickknacks: a wolf carved from stone, a pinecone, a dried rose, a basket of white rocks. Above the fireplace, a clock, but it appeared to be broken. The second hand was twitching, but it never advanced. A high-backed chair sat in front of the fireplace, a heavy blanket hanging off the armrest. It looked . . . welcoming.

Wallace glanced to the left to see a counter with a cash register and an empty, darkened display case with little handwritten signs taped against the glass advertising a dozen different types of pastries. Jars lined the walls behind the counter. Some were filled with thin leaves, others with powder in various shades. Little handwritten labels sat in front of each one, describing even more varieties of tea.

A large chalkboard hung on the wall above the jars, next to a pair of swinging doors with porthole windows. Someone had drawn little deer and squirrels and birds on the chalkboard in green and blue chalk, surrounding a menu that seemed to go on forever. Green tea and herbal tea, black tea and oolong. White tea, yellow tea, fermented tea. Sencha, rose, yerba, senna, rooibos, chaga tea, chamomile. Hibiscus, essiac, matcha, moringa, pu-erh, nettle, dandelion tea . . . and he remembered the graveyard where Mei had plucked the dandelion puffball from the ground and blown on it, the little white wisps floating away.

They were all printed around a message in the center of the board. The words, written in spiky and slanted letters, read:

The first time you share tea, you are a stranger.
The second time you share tea, you are an honored guest.
The third time you share tea, you become family.

The entire place felt like a fever dream. It couldn't be real. It was too . . . something, something that Wallace couldn't quite put his finger on. He stopped in front of the display case, staring at the message on the chalkboard, unable to look away.

Unable, that was, until a dog ran out of a wall.

He shrieked as he stumbled backward, not believing his eyes. The dog, a large black mutt with a white pattern on its chest that almost looked like a star, rushed toward him, barking its fool head off. Its tail swishing furiously, it circled Mei, back end wiggling as it rubbed up against her.

"Who's a good boy?" Mei cooed in a tone of voice that Wallace despised. "Who's the best boy in the entire world? Is it *you*? I think it's *you*."

The dog, apparently in agreement that it was the best boy in the entire world, barked cheerfully. Its ears were large and pointed, though the left one flopped over. It collapsed in front of Mei, rolling over onto its back, legs kicking as Mei sank to her knees—seeming to disregard the fact that she was wearing a suit, much to Wallace's consternation—rubbing her hands along its stomach. Its tongue lolled out of its mouth as it looked at Wallace. It rolled back over and climbed to its feet, shaking itself from side to side.

And then it jumped on Wallace.

He barely got his hands up in time before it crashed into him, knocking him off his feet. He landed on his back, trying to shield his face from the frantic, wet tongue licking all the exposed skin it could find.

"Help me!" he shouted. "It's trying to kill me!"

"Yeah," Mei said. "That's not quite what he's doing. Apollo doesn't kill. He loves." She frowned. "Quite a bit, apparently. Apollo, no! We don't hump people."

And then Wallace heard a dry, rusty chuckle followed by a deep, crackly voice. "Don't usually see him so excited. Wonder why that is?"

Before Wallace could focus on *that*, the dog jumped off him and took off toward the closed double doors behind the counter. But rather than pushing the doors open, it went *through* them, the doors unmoving. Wallace sat up in time to see the tip of its tail disappear. The cable from his chest wrapped around the counter, and he couldn't see where it led to.

"What the hell was that?" he demanded, hearing the dog bark somewhere in the house.

"That's Apollo," Mei said.

"But—it—he walked through *walls*."

Mei shrugged. "Well, sure. He's dead like you."

"*What?*"

"Quick one you've got there," that crackly voice said, and Wallace turned his head toward the fireplace. He yelped at the sight of an old man peering around the side of the high-backed chair. He looked ancient, his dark brown skin heavily wrinkled. He grinned, his strong teeth catching the firelight. His eyebrows were large and bushy, his white Afro sitting on his head like a wispy cloud. He smacked his lips as he chuckled again. "Good on you, Mei. Knew you could do it."

Mei blushed, shuffling her feet. "Thanks. Had a little trouble there at the beginning, but I got it all sorted out." Wallace barely heard her as he continued to mention sexually aggressive ghost dogs and old men appearing out of nowhere. "I think."

The man pushed himself up from the chair. He was short and slightly hunched. If he cleared five feet, Wallace would be surprised. He wore flannel pajamas and an old pair of slippers. A cane leaned against the side of the chair. The old man grabbed it and shuffled forward. He stopped next to Mei, squinting down at Wallace on the floor. He tapped the end of the cane against Wallace's ankle. "Ah," he said. "I see."

Wallace didn't want to know what he saw. He should have never followed Mei into the tea shop.

The man said, "Kinda squirrely, ain't ya?" He tapped his cane against Wallace again.

Wallace batted it away. "Would you stop that?!"

The man didn't stop that. In fact, he did it once more. "Trying to make a point."

"What are you—" And then Wallace knew. This had to be Hugo, the man Mei brought him to see. The man who wasn't God, but something she'd called a ferryman. Wallace didn't know what he was expecting; perhaps a man in white robes and a long flowing beard, surrounded by blazing light, a wooden staff instead of a cane. This man looked at least a thousand years old. He had a presence about him, something Wallace couldn't quite place. It was . . . calming? Or so close to it that it didn't matter. Maybe this was part of the process, what Mei had called the *transition*. Wallace wasn't sure *why* he needed to be beaten with a cane, but if Hugo deemed it necessary, then who was Wallace to say otherwise?.

The man pulled the cane back. "Do you understand now?"

No, he really didn't. "I think so."

Hugo nodded. "Good. Up, up. Shouldn't stay on the floor. Gets drafty. Don't want to catch your death." He cackled as if it were the funniest thing in the world.

Wallace laughed too, though it was incredibly forced. "Ha-ha, yeah. That's . . . hysterical. I get it. Jokes. You tell jokes."

Hugo's eyes twinkled with undisguised mirth. "It helps to laugh, even when you don't feel like laughing. You can't be sad when you're laughing. Mostly."

Wallace slowly rose to his feet, eyeing the two in front of him warily. He brushed himself off, aware of how ridiculous he looked. He pulled himself to his full height, squaring his shoulders. In life, he'd been an intimidating man. Just because he was dead didn't mean he was going to get jerked around.

He said, "My name is Wallace—"

The man said, "Tall fella, ain't ya?"

Wallace blinked. "Uh, I . . . guess?"

The man nodded. "In case you didn't know. How's the weather up there?"

Wallace stared down at him. "What?"

Mei covered her mouth with her hand, but not before Wallace could see the smile growing.

The man (Hugo? God?) shuffled forward, knocking his cane against Wallace's leg again as he circled around him. "Uh-huh. Okay. I see. So. Right. We can work with this, I think." He reached up and pinched Wallace's side. Wallace yelped, knocking his hand away. Hugo shook his head as he completed his circle, once again standing next to Mei, resting on his cane. "Hell of a first case to get assigned, Mei."

"Right? But I think I'm getting through to him." She glanced at Wallace with a frown. "Maybe."

"You didn't do *anything*," Wallace snapped.

Hugo nodded. "This one's gonna give us trouble. Wait and see." He grinned, the lines around his eyes cavernous. "I like the ones who cause trouble."

Wallace bristled. "My name is Wallace Price. I'm an attorney from—"

Hugo ignored him, looking at Mei and smiling. "How was your trip, dear? Got a little lost, did you?"

"Yeah," Mei said. "The world is bigger than I remember, especially going on my own."

"It usually is," Hugo said. "That's the beauty of it. But you're home now, so don't you worry. Hopefully, you won't get sent out again right away."

Mei nodded as she stretched her arms above her head, back popping loudly. "No place like home."

Wallace tried again. "I'm told I died from a heart attack. I'd like to lodge a formal complaint, seeing as how—"

"He's taking to being dead pretty well," Hugo said, eyeing Wallace up and down. "Usually there's screaming and yelling and threats. I like it when they threaten."

"Oh, he had his moments," Mei said. "But on the whole, not too bad. Guess where I found him?"

Hugo eyed Wallace up and down. Then, "Where he died. No, wait. At his home, trying to figure out why he couldn't make anything work."

"His funeral," Mei said, and Wallace was offended by how gleeful she sounded.

"No," Hugo breathed. "Really?"

"Sitting in a pew and everything."

"Wow," Hugo said. "That's embarrassing."

"I'm standing right here," Wallace snapped.

"Of course you are," Hugo said, not unkindly. "But thank you for making that known."

"Look, Hugo, Mei said you could help me. She said she had to bring me to you because you're the ferryman, and you're supposed to do . . . something. I admit I wasn't really paying attention to that part, but that is *beside the point*. I don't know what kind of racket you're running here, and I don't know who put you up to this, but I would really rather not be dead if at all possible. I have far too much work to do, and this has been an awful inconvenience. I have *clients*. I have a brief due by the end of the week that can't be delayed!" He groaned, mind racing. "And I'm supposed to be in court on Friday for a hearing that I can't miss. Do you know who I am? Because if you *do*, then you know I don't have time for this. I have responsibilities, yes, *extremely* important responsibilities that can't be ignored."

"Of course I know who you are," Hugo said dryly. "You're Wallace."

Relief like he'd never before experienced washed over him. He'd come to the right person. Mei, whoever—or *whatever*—she was, seemed to be an underling. A drone. Hugo was in the position of power. Always, always speak to the manager to get results. "Good. Then you understand that this won't do at all. So if you could do whatever you need to in order to fix this, I would be greatly appreciative." And then, just because he couldn't be absolutely sure this man wasn't God, he added, "Please. Thank you. Sir."

"Huh," Hugo said. "That was a bit of a word salad."

"He tends to do that," Mei whispered loudly. "Probably because he was a lawyer."

The old man eyed Wallace up and down. "Called me Hugo. You hear that?"

"I did," Mei said. "Maybe we should—"

"Hugo Freeman, at your service." He bowed as low as he could.

Mei sighed. "Or we could do it this way."

Hugo snorted. "Learn to have a little fun. It doesn't always have to be doom and gloom. Now, where were we? Ah, yes. I'm Hugo, and you're upset you're dead, but not because of friends or family or some other such drivel, but because you have work to do, and this is an inconvenience." He paused, considering. "An *awful* inconvenience."

Wallace was relieved. He expected more of a fight. He was pleased he didn't need to resort to threats of legal action. "Exactly. That's exactly it."

Hugo shrugged. "All right."

"Really?" He could be back into the office by tomorrow afternoon at the latest, maybe the day after depending on how long it took him to get home. He'd have to demand that Mei bring him back as he didn't have his wallet. If push came to shove, he'd phone the firm and have his assistant buy him a plane ticket. Sure, he didn't have his driver's license, but something so trivial wouldn't stop Wallace Price. As a last resort, he could take the bus, but he wanted to avoid it if he could. He had almost a week's worth of work to catch up on, but it was a small price to pay. He'd have to find a way to explain the whole funeral/open casket thing, but he'd figure it out. Naomi would be disappointed she wasn't getting anything from his estate, but screw her. She'd been mean at the funeral.

"Okay," he said. "I'm ready. How do we do this? Do you . . . chant or something? Sacrifice a goat?" He grimaced. "I really hope you don't have to sacrifice a goat. I get squeamish around blood."

"You're in luck," Hugo said. "We're fresh out of goats."

Wallace sagged. "Great. I'm ready to be alive again. I learned my lesson. I promise to be nicer to people and blah, blah, blah."

"The joy I feel knows no bounds," Hugo said. "Raise your arms above your head."

Wallace did just that.

"Now jump up and down."

Wallace did, the cable rising and falling from the floor.

"Repeat after me: 'I want to be alive.'"

"I want to be alive."

Hugo sighed. "You gotta mean it. Really let me hear it. Make me *believe*."

"I want to be alive!" Wallace shouted as he jumped up and down, arms above his head. "I want to be alive! I want to be alive!"

"There it is!" Hugo cried. "I can feel something happening. It's really coming. Keep going! Jump in circles!"

"I want to be alive!" Wallace bellowed as he jumped in a circle. "I want to be alive! I want to be alive!"

"And *stop*. Whatever you do, *don't move*."

Wallace froze, arms above his head, one leg raised, his flip-flop dangling off his foot. He could feel it working. He didn't know how, but he did. Soon, this would all be over and he'd go back to living.

Hugo's eyes widened. "Stay like that until I say so. Don't even *blink*."

Wallace didn't. He stayed exactly as he was. He'd do anything to make this right again.

Hugo nodded. "Good. Now, I want you to repeat after me again: 'I am an idiot.'"

"I am an idiot."

"'And I'm dead.'"

"And I'm dead."

"'And there's no way for me to come back to life because that's not how it works.'"

"And there's . . . what?"

Hugo doubled over, wheezing out grating laughter. "Oh. Oh my. You should see the look on your face. It's priceless!"

The skin under Wallace's right eye twitched as he lowered his arms slowly, putting his foot back onto the floor. "*What?*"

"You're *dead*," Hugo exclaimed. "You can't be brought back to life. That's not how anything works. Honestly." He elbowed Mei in the side. "You see this? What a goof. I like him. It'll be a shame to see him go. He's fun."

Mei glanced toward the double doors. "You're going to get us in trouble, Nelson."

"Bah. Death doesn't need to always be sad. We need to learn to laugh at ourselves before we—"

"Nelson," Wallace said slowly.

The man looked at him. "Yes?"

"She called you Nelson."

"That's because it's my name."

"Not Hugo."

Nelson waved his hand. "Hugo is my grandson." He narrowed his eyes. "And you won't tell him what we did if you know what's good for you."

Wallace gaped at him. "Are you . . . are you *serious*?"

"As a heart attack," Nelson said as Mei choked. "Oops. Too soon?"

Wallace took a stuttering step toward the man—to do what, he didn't know. He couldn't think, couldn't form a single word. He tripped over his own feet, falling forward toward Nelson, eyes wide, a sound like a door creaking escaping his throat.

But he didn't crash into Nelson, because Nelson disappeared, causing Wallace to land roughly on the floor, facedown.

He raised his head in time to see Nelson blink back into existence a few feet away, near the fireplace. He wiggled his fingers at Wallace.

Wallace rolled over onto his back, staring up at the ceiling. His chest heaved (pesky thing, that, seeing as how his lungs weren't exactly necessary at this point), and his skin thrummed. "You're dead."

"As a doornail," Nelson said. "It was a relief, really. This old body had worn down, and try as I might, I couldn't make it work like I wanted it to anymore. Sometimes, death is a blessing, even if we don't realize it right away."

Another voice came then, deep and warm, the words sounding as if they had weight, and there was a mighty tug at that hook in Wallace's chest. It should have hurt. It didn't.

It almost felt like relief.

"Grandad, are you making trouble again?"

Wallace turned his head toward the voice.

A man appeared through the double doors.

Wallace blinked slowly.

The man smiled quietly, his teeth shockingly bright. The front two were a bit crooked and strangely charming. He was, perhaps, an inch or two shorter than Wallace, with thin arms and legs. He wore jeans and an open-collared shirt under an apron with the words CHARON'S CROSSING stitched across the front. The front of the apron bulged slightly against the gentle swell of his stomach. His skin was deep brown, his eyes almost hazel with shots of green through them. His hair was similar to the old man's, tight coils in a short Afro, though his was black. He seemed young; not quite as young as Mei, but surely younger than Wallace. The floorboards creaked with every step he took.

He set down the tray he was carrying onto the counter, a teapot clanking against the oversized teacups. It smelled like peppermint. He walked around the counter. Wallace saw the dog—Apollo— weaving around and then *through* the man's legs. The man laughed at the dog. "I can see that. Curious, right?"

The dog barked in agreement.

Wallace stared as the man approached. He didn't know why he focused on the man's hands, fingers oddly delicate, palms paler than the backs, nails like crescent moons. He rubbed his hands together before he crouched down near Wallace, keeping some distance from him as if he thought Wallace was skittish. It was only then Wallace noticed the cable attached to his chest extended to the man, though there didn't appear to be a hook. The cable disappeared into his ribcage, right where his heart should be.

"Hello," the man said. "Wallace, right? Wallace Price?"

Wallace nodded, unable to find his voice.

The man's smile widened, and the hook in Wallace's chest felt like it was burning. "My name is Hugo Freeman. I am a ferryman. I'm sure you have questions. I'll do my best to answer them all. But first things first. Would you like a cup of tea?"

CHAPTER 5

Wallace had never been a fan of tea. If pressed, he would say he never really saw what the fuss was about. It was dry leaves in hot water.

And it probably didn't help that he was still staring at the man known as Hugo Freeman. He moved with grace, every action deliberate, almost as if he were dancing. He didn't reach out to help Wallace to his feet, but instead motioned for him to pick himself up off the floor. Wallace did, though he kept his distance. If there ever were a god, it would be this man, no matter what Mei had told him. For all he knew, it was another trick, a test to see how he would act. He needed to be careful here, especially if he was going to insist this man give him back his life. It didn't help that the cable seemed to connect the two of them, stretching and shrinking depending upon how close they were to each other.

Apollo sat at Hugo's feet near the counter, staring up adoringly at him, tail thumping silently against the floor. Mei helped Nelson toward the counter, though he was grumbling that he could do it himself.

Wallace watched as Hugo picked up the steaming pewter teapot from the tray. He raised the pot toward his face, inhaling deeply. He nodded and said, "It's had time to steep. Should be ready now." He looked up at Wallace almost apologetically. "It's organic loose leaf, which didn't seem to fit what I know of you, but I have a pretty good track record for such things. For all I know, everything you like is organic. And peppermint."

"I don't like organic anything," Wallace muttered.

"That's okay," Hugo said as he began to pour the tea. "I think you'll like this." There were four cups, each with a different floral design. He motioned for Wallace to take the cup with the flowers that rose along the sides and into the interior of the cup.

"I'm dead," Wallace said.

Hugo beamed at him. "Yes. Yes, you are."

Wallace ground his teeth together. "That's not what—forget it. How the hell can I pick up the cup?"

Hugo laughed. It was a low and rumbly thing that started in his chest and poured out from his mouth. "Ah. I see. And anywhere else, you might have a point. But not here. Not with these. Try it. I promise you won't be disappointed."

No one could promise that with any certainty. The only thing he'd been able to touch was Mei and the ground beneath his feet. And Apollo, but the less said about that the better. This felt like a test, and he didn't trust this man as far as he could throw him. Wallace had never thrown a man before, and he didn't want to start now.

He sighed and reached for the cup, expecting his hand to pass through it, ready to glare at Hugo as if to say *See?*

But then he felt the warmth of the tea, and he gasped when his fingers touched the surface of the cup. It was solid.

It was solid.

He hissed when he jerked his hand up, sloshing tea over the side of the cup and onto his fingers. There was a brief flare of heat, but then it was gone. He looked at his fingers. They were pale as always, the skin unblemished.

"These teacups are special," Hugo said. "For people like you."

"People like me," Wallace echoed dully, still staring at his fingers.

"Yes," Hugo said. He finished pouring the tea into the remaining cups and set the teapot back onto the tray. "Those who have left one life in preparation for another. They were a gift when I became what I am now."

"A ferryman," Wallace said.

Hugo nodded. "Yes." He tapped the stitched lettering on his

chest. He didn't seem to notice the cable, his fingers disappearing through it. "Do you know Charon?"

"No."

"He was the Greek ferryman who carried souls to Hades over the rivers Styx and Acheron that divided the world between the living and the dead." Hugo chuckled. "It lacks subtlety, I know, but I was younger when I named this place."

"Younger," Wallace repeated. "You're already young." Then, unsure if he was insulting a sort of deity who was apparently in charge of . . . something, he quickly added, "At least you look like you are. I mean, I don't know how this works, and—"

"Thank you," Hugo said, lips quirking as if he found Wallace's discomfort amusing.

"Oh boy," Nelson grumbled, picking up his teacup and slurping along the edges. "He's an old man now. Maybe not as old as me, but he's getting there."

"I'm thirty," Hugo said dryly. He gestured toward the cup on the table in front of Wallace. "Drink up. It's best when it's hot."

Wallace eyed the tea. There were bits of *something* floating at the top. He wasn't sure he wanted to drink it, but Hugo was watching him closely. It didn't seem to be hurting Mei or Nelson, so Wallace gingerly picked up the cup, bringing it close to his face. The scent of peppermint was strong, and Wallace's eyes fluttered shut of their own accord. He could hear Apollo yawning in the way dogs do, and the bones of the house as it settled, but the floor and walls fell away, the roof rocketing up toward the sky, and he was, he was, *he was—*

He opened his eyes.

He was home.

Not his *current* home, the high-rise apartment with the imported furniture and the red accent wall he thought about painting over and the picture windows that opened up to a city of metal and glass.

No, it was his *childhood* home, the one with the stairs that creaked and the water heater that never had enough hot water. He stood in the doorway to the kitchen, Bing Crosby singing on the old radio, telling everyone who could hear to have yourself a merry little Christmas.

"Until then," his mother sang as she spun through the kitchen, "we'll have to muddle through somehow."

It was snowing outside, and garlands stretched along the top of the cabinets and on the windowsills. His mother laughed to herself as the oven dinged. She grabbed an oven mitt with a snowman printed on it from the counter. She opened the oven door, the hinges squealing, and pulled out a sheet of homemade candy canes. Her holiday specialty, a recipe she'd learned from her mother, a heavy-set Polish woman who called Wallace *pociecha*. The scent of peppermint filled the room.

His mother looked up at him standing in the doorway, and he was *ten* and *forty* all at the same time, in his sweats and flip-flops, but also in flannel pajamas, his hair a mess, his toes bare on the cold floor. "Look," she said, showing him the candy canes. "I think it's the best batch yet. *Mamusia* would be proud, I think."

Wallace doubted that. His grandmother had been a frightening woman with a sharp tongue and blunt insults. She died in a home for the elderly. Wallace had been sad and relieved all at once, though he'd kept that thought to himself.

He took a step toward his mother, and at the same time felt the warm bloom of the tea as it slid down his throat and settled in his belly. It tasted like the candy canes smelled, and it was too much, too jarring, because it couldn't be real. Yet he could taste her candy canes as if she were really there, and he said, "Mom?" but she didn't respond, instead humming along as Bing Crosby gave way to Ol' Blue Eyes.

He blinked slowly.

He was in a tea shop.

He blinked again.

He was in the kitchen of his childhood home.

He said, "Mom, I—" and there was a sting in his heart, a sharp jab that caused him to grunt. His mother had died. One minute she was there, and the next she was gone, his father speaking gruffly into the phone, telling him it'd been quick, that by the time they'd caught it, it'd already been too late. Metastasized, one of his cousins had told him later, in her lungs. She hadn't wanted Wallace to know, especially since they hadn't spoken in close to a year. He'd been so angry at her for this. For everything.

This is what the tea tasted like. Memory. Home. Youth. Betrayal. Bittersweet and warm.

Wallace blinked and found himself still in the tea shop, the cup shaking in his hands. He set it back down on the counter before it spilled more.

Hugo said, "You have questions."

In a shaky voice, Wallace replied, "That is quite possibly the biggest understatement ever spoken by the human tongue."

"He tends to be hyperbolic," Mei said to Hugo, as if that explained everything.

Hugo lifted his own teacup, taking a sip. His brow furrowed for a moment before smoothing out. "I'll answer them as best I can, but I don't know everything."

"You don't?"

Hugo shook his head. "Of course not. How could I?"

Frustrated, Wallace snapped, "Then I'll make this as simple as possible. Why am I here? What's the point of all of this?"

Mei laughed. "*That's* what you call simple? Rock on, man. I'm impressed."

"You're here because you died," Hugo said. "As for your other question, I don't know if I can answer it for you, at least not on the scale you mean. I don't think anyone can, not fully."

"Then what's the point of *you*?" he demanded.

Hugo nodded. "That I can answer. I'm a ferryman."

"I told him that," Mei whispered to Nelson.

"It's hard to retain information right after," Nelson whispered back. "We'll give him a little longer."

"And what does a ferryman do?" Wallace asked. "Are you the only one?"

Hugo shook his head. "There are many of us. People who . . .

well. People who have been given a job. To help others like your-self. To make sense of what you're feeling at the moment."

"I already have a therapist," Wallace snapped. "He does what I pay him for, and I have no complaints."

"Really?" Mei said. "No complaints. None whatsoever."

"Mei," Hugo warned again.

"Yeah, yeah," she muttered. She drank from her own tea. Her eyes widened slightly before she drank the rest in three huge gulps. "Holy crap, this is good." She looked up at Wallace. "Huh. I didn't expect that from you. Congrats."

Wallace didn't know what she was on about and didn't care to ask. That hook in his chest felt heavier, and though it tugged pleas-antly, he was growing annoyed at the sensation. "I'm in the moun-tains."

"You are," Hugo agreed.

"There are no mountains near the city."

"There aren't."

"Which means we've come a long way."

"You have."

"Even if you're not the ferryman for everyone," Wallace said, "how does that work? People die all the time. Hundreds. Thousands. There should be more here. Why isn't there a line out the door?"

"Most of the people in the city go to the ferrywoman *in* the city," Hugo said, and Wallace was unnerved by how carefully he seemed to be choosing his words. "Sometimes, they get sent on to me."

"Overflow."

"Something like that," Hugo said. "To be honest, I don't always know why people such as yourself are brought to me. But it's not my job to question the *why*. You're here, and that's all that matters."

Wallace gaped at him. "You don't question the *why*? Why the hell not?" The *why* of things was Wallace's specialty. It led to truths that some tried to keep hidden. He looked at Mei, who grinned at him. No help there. Nelson, though. Nelson was in the same boat as he was. Maybe he could be of some use. "Nelson, you're—"

"Oh no," Nelson said, glancing at his bare wrist. "Would you look at the time. I do believe I'm supposed to be sitting in my chair in front of the fire." He shuffled away toward the fireplace, leaning on his cane. Apollo trailed after him, though he glanced back at Hugo as if to make sure he was staying right where he was.

That certainly didn't make Wallace feel better. "Somebody had better give me some answers before I . . ." He didn't know how to finish that.

Hugo reached up and scratched the back of his neck. "Look, Wallace—may I call you Wallace?" Then, without waiting for an answer, "Wallace, death is . . . complicated. I can't even begin to imagine what's going through your head right now. It's different for everyone. No two people are the same, in life or in death. You want to rant and rave and threaten. I get that. You want to bargain, make a deal. I get that too. And if it makes you feel better, you can say whatever you want here. No one will judge you."

"At least not out loud," Nelson said from his chair.

"You had a heart attack," Hugo said quietly. "It was sudden. There was nothing you could have done to stop it. It wasn't your fault."

"I know that," Wallace snapped. "I didn't *do* anything." He paused. "Wait, how did you know how I . . ." He couldn't finish.

"I know things," Hugo said. "Or, rather, I'm shown things. Sometimes it's . . . vague. An outline. Other times, it's crystal clear, though those are rare. You were clear to me."

"I expect I would be," Wallace said stiffly. "Which makes this easier, because I don't know how much clearer I can be. Send me back."

"I can't do that."

"Then find me someone who can."

"I can't do that either. That's not how it works, Wallace. A river only moves in one direction."

Wallace nodded, mind racing. He obviously wasn't being heard. He wouldn't find any help here. "Then I bid you good day, and request I be returned to the city. If you can't help me, I'll figure it out on my own." He didn't know *how*, exactly, but anything would be better than being here and hearing nothing but these three idiots talking in circles.

Hugo shook his head. "You can't leave."

Wallace narrowed his eyes. "Are you saying I'm trapped here? Keeping me against my will? That's kidnapping. I'll see you all brought up on charges for this, don't think I won't."

Hugo said, "You're standing."

"What?"

Hugo nodded toward the floor. "Can you feel the floor beneath your feet?"

Wallace flexed his toes. Through the thin, cheap flip-flops, he could feel the pressure of the wood floor against the bottoms of his feet. "Yes."

Hugo lifted a spoon off the tray and set it on the counter. "Pick that spoon up."

"Why?"

"Because I asked you to. Please."

Wallace didn't want to. He couldn't see the point. But instead of arguing, he stepped back up to the counter. He stared down at the spoon. It was such a little thing. Flowers had been carved into the handle. He reached down to pick it up. His hands shook as his finger curled around the handle, and he lifted it.

"Good," Hugo said. "Now put it back down."

Grumbling under his breath, he did as he was told. "Now what?"

Hugo looked at him. "You're a ghost, Wallace. You're dead. Pick it up again."

Rolling his eyes, he made to do just that. Only this time, his hand passed right through it. Not only that, his hand went *into* the countertop. There was a strange buzzing sensation prickling along his skin, and he gasped as he pulled his hand back as if it were burned. All his fingers were still attached, and the buzzing was already fading. He tried it again. And again. And again. Each time, his hand passed through the spoon and into the counter.

Hugo reached out for Wallace's hand, but stopped above it, hovering and coming no closer. "You were able to do it the first time because you've always been able to. You expected it because that's the way it's always worked for you. But then I reminded you that you've passed, and you could no longer touch it. Your expectations changed. You should have *un*expected it." He tapped the side of his head. "It's all about your mind and how you focus it."

Wallace started to panic, throat closing, hands shaking. "That doesn't make any sense!"

"That's because you've been conditioned your entire life to think one way. Things are different now."

"Says *you*." He reached for the spoon again but jerked his arm up when it passed through it once more. His hand caught the teacup, knocking it over. Tea spilled onto the counter. He stumbled back, eyes wide, teeth grinding together. "I . . . I can't be here. I want to go home. Take me home."

Hugo frowned as he came around the counter. "Wallace, you need to calm down, okay? Take a breath."

"Don't tell me to calm down!" Wallace cried. "And if I'm dead, why are you telling me to breathe? That is *impossible*."

"He's got a point," Mei said as she finished her second cup of tea.

For every step Hugo took toward him, Wallace took an answering step back. Nelson peered around the edge of the chair, a hand resting on the top of Apollo's head. The dog's tail thumped, keeping time like a silent metronome.

"Stay back," he snarled at Hugo.

Hugo raised his hands placatingly. "I'm not going to hurt you."

"I don't believe you. Don't come near me. I'm leaving, and there's nothing you can do to stop me."

"Oh no," Mei breathed. She set down her teacup and stared at Wallace. "That's definitely not a good idea. Wallace, you can't—"

"Don't tell me what I can't do!" he shouted at her, and the light bulb in one of the sconces sizzled and snapped before the glass shattered. Wallace jerked his head toward it.

"Uh-oh," Nelson whispered.

Wallace turned and ran.

CHAPTER 6

The first obstacle was the door.

He grabbed for the handle.

His hand passed right through it.

With a strangled yell, he jumped at the door. *Through* the door. He opened his eyes, finding himself on the porch of the tea shop. He looked down. All his bits and bobs still seemed to be attached, though the hook and cable were still there, the latter extending back into the tea shop. Something heavy moved thunderously toward the door, and he leapt from the porch, landing on the gravel. The stars stuttered in the sky above him, the trees more ominous than they'd been when he'd first arrived. They seemed to bend and sway as if beckoning him. He stumbled when he thought he saw movement off in the trees to his left, a great beast watching him, a crown of antlers atop its head, but it had to be a trick of the shadows because when he blinked, all he saw were branches.

He took off down the road, heading back the way he'd come earlier with Mei. If he got to the village, he could find someone to help him. He'd tell them about the crazy people in the tea shop in the middle of the woods.

The hook in his chest pulled sharply, the cable growing taut as it wrapped around his side. He almost fell to his knees. He managed to stay upright, flip-flops snapping against the bottoms of his feet. How on earth had he ever thought flip-flops were a good idea?

He glanced back over his shoulder toward the tea shop in time to see Mei and Hugo burst out onto the porch, shouting after him. Mei said, "Of all the stupid things" just as Hugo said, "Wallace, *Wallace*, you can't, you don't know what's out there—" but Wallace doubled down, running as fast as he could.

He'd never been much of a runner, much less a jogger of any

kind. He had a treadmill in his office, often walking long distances on it while on conference calls. He had time for little else, but at least it was something.

He was surprised, then, to find that his breath didn't catch in his chest, that no stitch formed in his side. Even wearing flip-flops didn't seem to slow him down much. The air was strangely stagnant, thick and oppressive, but he was *running*, running faster than he ever had in his life. He glanced down in shock at his own legs. They were almost a blur as his feet met the pavement of the road that led to the village. He laughed despite himself, a wild cackle that he'd never heard himself make before, sounding as if he were half out of his mind.

He looked back over his shoulder again.

Nothing there, no one chasing after him, no one shouting his name, only the empty, dark road that led to destinations unknown.

It should have made him feel better.

It didn't.

He ran as fast as he could toward a gas station ahead, the sodium arc lights lit up like a beacon, moths fluttering around them. An old van sat parked next to one of the pumps, and he could see people moving around inside. He ran toward it, only stopping when he reached the automatic doors.

They didn't open.

He jumped up and down in front of them, waving his arms.

Nothing.

He shouted, "Open the doors!"

The man behind the counter continued to look bored, tapping on his phone.

A woman toward the back of the store stood in front of a drink cooler, scratching her chin as she yawned.

He growled under his breath before reaching out to pry the doors open. His hands went right through them.

"Oh, right," he said. "Dead. Goddammit."

He walked through the doors.

The moment he entered, the fluorescent lights in the store above him flared and buzzed. The man behind the counter—a kid with enormous eyebrows and a face dotted with dozens of freckles—frowned as he looked up. He shrugged before going back to his phone.

Wallace smacked it out of his hands.

At least he tried to.

It didn't work.

He also tried to grab the man by the face with the same amount of success. Wallace recoiled when his thumb went into the man's *eye*. "This is so stupid," he muttered. He turned toward the woman in the back, still staring at the coolers. He went to her without much hope. She didn't hear him. She didn't see him. Instead, she picked out a two-liter of Mountain Dew.

"That's disgusting," he told her. "You should feel ashamed. Do you even know what's in that?"

But his opinion went unnoticed.

The automatic doors slid open, and Wallace ducked down when the clerk said, "Hey, Hugo. You're out late."

"Couldn't sleep," Hugo said. "Thought I'd pick a few things up."

Wallace tried to lean against a shelf of potato chips. He cursed when he fell back through them, blinking rapidly as he was *inside* the shelf. He jerked forward, ready to flee when the doors slid open again. He froze when the man behind the counter said, "Hey, Mei. Can't sleep either?"

"You know how it is," Mei said. "Boss man's up, so that means I'm up too."

The man could see her.

He could *see her*.

Which meant—

Wallace had no idea what that meant.

Before he could even begin to process this new information, a curious thing happened: bits of dust floated up around him.

He frowned at them, watching as they rose before his face, heading toward the ceiling. The motes of dust were oddly colored, almost flesh-like. He reached out to touch a rather large flake, but his hand froze when he saw where the dust was coming from.

His own arms.

His skin was flaking off, bit by bit, the top layer of derma floating up and away.

He yelped as he furiously brushed his arms.

"Got you," Mei said, appearing beside him. And then, "Oh crap. Wallace, we have to get you—"

He leapt forward toward the coolers.

Through the coolers.

He yelled incoherently as he went through a row of soda, and then a wall of cement. He was outside again, on the side of the store. He ran his hands over his arms as his skin continued to flake. The hook in his chest twisted angrily, the cable running back into the wall he'd just rushed through. He ran around the back of the store. An empty field stretched behind it under a night sky that seemed infinite. On the other side was another neighborhood, the houses close together, some with lights on, others dark and foreboding. He took off toward them, still rubbing his arms frantically.

He crossed the field and went between two houses. Music blared from the house on his right; the house to his left was silent and dark. He burst through the wall of the right house directly into a bedroom where a woman in a full-body suit of red leather slapped a riding crop against her palm, her attention on a man in footie pajamas who said, "This is going to be so *awesome*."

"Oh dear god," Wallace croaked before backing out of the house slowly. He turned toward the street in front of the houses.

He paused when his feet met pavement. He wasn't sure where to go, and now the skin on his legs was flaking off through his sweats and off the top of his feet. His ears were ringing, and the world had taken on a hazy glow, the colors running together. The cable flashed violently, the hook shaking.

He hurried down the sidewalk, wanting to get as far as he could. But it was as if the bottoms of his flip-flops had melted, sticking to the concrete. Each and every step was harder than the one before it, like he was moving under water. He grunted at the exertion. The ringing in his ears grew louder, and he couldn't focus. He gritted his teeth as he tried to push through it. The fingernail from the pinkie of his right hand slid off and disintegrated.

He curled his hand into a fist as he looked up. There, standing in the middle of the street, was a man.

But he was wrong, somehow, off in ways that turned Wallace's skin to ice. The man was hunched over, his back to Wallace, his shirtless torso covered in gray, sickly skin, his spine jutting out sharply. His shoulders shook as if he were heaving. His pants hung low on his hips. His sneakers were scuffed and dirty. His arms hung boneless at his sides.

A chill ran down Wallace's spine even as he took another step, everything in him screaming to back away, to run before the man turned around. He didn't want to see what the man's face looked like, sure it would be just as terrible as the rest of him. All sound seemed muffled, as if his ears were stuffed with cotton. When he spoke, it sounded like it came from someone else, his voice cracking. "Hello? Are you . . . can you hear me?"

The man's head snapped up as his arms twitched. On either wrist, angry welts rose the length of his forearms, making a T shape.

He turned around slowly.

Wallace Price was clinical to an almost inhuman degree. Details were his job, the little things others might have missed, something said in passing in a deposition or during intake interviews. And it was this attribute that caused him to catalogue each and every bit of the man before him: the dull, dead hair, the open mouth with blackened teeth, the horrifying, flat look in his eyes. The thing was *shaped* like a human, but he looked feral, dangerous, and if Wallace had felt fear before, it was nothing compared to what roared through him now. A mistake. He'd made a mistake. He should've never tried to speak to this . . . this thing, whatever it was. Even as his skin continued to rise around him, Wallace tried to take a step back.

His legs didn't work.

The stars blotted out until all Wallace knew was the dark of night, shadows stretching around him, reaching, reaching.

The man moved toward him, but it was awkward, as if the joints in his knees were frozen. He rocked from side to side with each step. He raised an arm, all fingers pointed toward the ground except one that was trained on Wallace. He opened his mouth again but no words came out, only a low animalistic grunt. Wallace's mind whited out in terror, and he knew, he *knew* that when the man touched him, his skin would be thin like paper, dry and catastrophic. And though he'd been told God didn't exist, Wallace prayed then, for the first time in years, a dying gasp of a thought that arced through his head like a shooting star: *!!HELP ME OH PLEASE MAKE IT STOP!!*

Movement then, sudden and quick as Hugo appeared between them, his back to Wallace. Relief like Wallace had never felt before bowled through him, knocking violently through his ribcage. The cable had shrunk to only a couple of feet, extending from Wallace around to Hugo's chest.

He said, "Cameron, no. You can't. He's not yours."

A dull clacking sound followed, and though Wallace couldn't see the man, he knew the noise came from him snapping his teeth together.

"I know," Hugo said quietly. "But he's not for you. He never was."

Wallace jerked his head when Mei appeared beside him. She frowned as she stood on her tiptoes, looking over Hugo's shoulder. "Crap." She dropped back down on her heels before raising her hands close to her chest, left palm toward the sky. She tapped the fingers of her right hand against her left palm in a staccato beat. A little burst of light came from her hand, and she reached over, grabbing Wallace by the arm.

"Get him home," Hugo said.

"What about you?" she asked, already pulling Wallace away. She grimaced when the skin of his wrist filtered through her grip.

"I'll follow," Hugo said, staring straight ahead at the man before him. "I need to make sure Cameron stays where he is."

Mei sighed. "Don't do anything stupid. We've already had enough of that for one day."

Right before Mei pulled him around the corner, Wallace glanced back once. Cameron had tilted his head toward the sky, mouth open, white tongue stuck out as if he were trying to catch snow. Later, Wallace would realize that it wasn't flakes of snow that fell onto Cameron's tongue.

 ℘

He didn't speak the entire way back.

Mei did, however, muttering under her breath that of *course* her first assignment would be such a pain in the ass, she was being tested, but by god, she was going to see this through if it was the last thing she ever did.

Wallace's mind whirled. He noticed with no small amount of dread-tinged awe that the closer they got back to the tea shop, the less his skin disintegrated. It became less and less until they hit the dirt road that led to Charon's Crossing, where it ceased entirely. He looked down at his arms to see they looked as they always had, although the hairs were standing on end. The hook and cable were still attached to him, though the cable itself now led to where they'd just come from.

Mei dragged him up the porch stairs and shoved him through the door. "Stay here," she said before slamming the door in his face. He went to the window and looked out. She stood on the porch, wringing her hands as she stared out into the dark.

"What the hell?" Wallace whispered.

"Saw one, did you?"

He whirled around. Nelson, sitting in his chair in front of the fireplace. The fire was mostly embers now, the remaining charred log glowing red and orange. Apollo lay in front of the chair on his back, his legs kicking in the air. He snorted as he fell to his side, jaws opening in a yawn before he closed his eyes.

Wallace shook his head. "I . . . don't know what I saw."

Nelson grunted as he rose from the chair, using the cane to prop himself up. Wallace didn't know why he hadn't noticed before, but Nelson's slippers were little felt rabbits, the ears floppy and frayed. He glanced back out the window. Mei paced, the road in front of the tea shop dark and empty.

Nelson smacked his lips as he shuffled over to him. He looked Wallace up and down before peering out the window. "Still intact, I see. You should thank your lucky stars."

Wallace wasn't sure how intact he was. It was as if his mind had blown away on the wind with the other pieces of him. He couldn't focus, and he felt cold. "What happened to me? The . . . man. Cameron."

Nelson sighed. "Poor soul. Figured he was still lurking out there."

"What's wrong with him?"

"He's dead," Nelson said. "A couple of years, or thereabouts. Time . . . slips a little in here. Sometimes it crawls to a halt, and then it skips and jumps. It's part of living with a ferryman. Look, Mr. Price, you need to—"

"Wallace."

Nelson blinked owlishly. Then, "Wallace, you need to keep your focus on yourself. Cameron doesn't concern you. There's nothing you can do for him. How far did you get before it happened to you?"

Wallace considered pretending he had no idea what Nelson was talking about. Instead, he said, "The gas station."

Nelson whistled lowly. "Farther than I expected, I'll give you that." He hesitated. "That world is for the living. It no longer belongs to those of us who've passed. And those who try to make it, lose themselves. Call it insanity, call it another form of death. Regardless, the moment you walk out these doors, it begins to pull at you. And the longer you stay out there, the worse it gets."

Horrified, Wallace said, "I was out there. For *days*. Mei didn't show up until my funeral."

"The process sped up the moment you stepped foot into Charon's

Crossing. And if you try to leave, the same thing will happen to you that happened to Cameron."

Wallace reared back. "I'm trapped here."

Nelson sighed. "That's not—"

"It *is*. You're telling me that I can't leave. Mei kidnapped me and brought me here, and I'm a damn prisoner!"

"Bull," Nelson said. "There's a staircase at the back of the house. It'll take you to the fourth floor. On the fourth floor is a door. You can go through that door, and all of this, *everything* will fade away. You'll leave this place behind, and you'll know only peace."

It struck Wallace then, something he hadn't even considered. He didn't know why he hadn't seen it before. It was as clear as day. "You're still here."

Nelson eyed him warily. "I am."

"And you're dead."

"Nothing gets by you, does it?"

"You haven't crossed." Wallace's voice began to rise. "Which means everything you're saying is bullshit."

Nelson placed his hand on Wallace's arm, squeezing tighter than Wallace expected. "It's not. I wouldn't lie to you, not about this. If you leave this place, you'll end up like Cameron."

"But you're not."

"No," Nelson said slowly. "Because I've never left."

"How long have you been—"

Nelson sniffed. "It's rude to ask about another person's death."

Wallace blanched, uncharacteristically flustered. "I didn't mean to—"

Nelson laughed. "I'm giving you crap, boy. Need to have my fun where I can get it. Been dead for a few years."

Wallace reeled. *Years.* "But you're still here," he said faintly.

"I am. And I have my reasons, but never you mind what those are. I stay here because I choose to. I know the risks. I know what it means. They tried to make me move on, but I gave 'em the ol' what for." He shook his head. "But you can't let that affect what Hugo needs to do for you. Take the time you need, Wallace. There's no rush, so long as you realize this is the last place you'll ever be before you cross, if you know what's good for you. If you can accept that, then we'll be right as rain. Look. Here he comes."

Wallace turned back toward the window. Hugo was walking down the road, hands in the pockets of his apron, head bowed.

"Such a good boy," Nelson said fondly. "Empathetic almost to a fault, ever since he was a tyke. Causes him to take the weight of the world on his shoulders. You would do well to listen to him and learn from him. I don't know if you could find yourself in better hands. Remember that before you start hurling accusations."

Mei waited for Hugo on the porch. Hugo looked up at her, smiling tiredly. When they spoke, their voices were muffled but clear. "It's all right," he said. "Cameron's . . . well. He's Cameron. Wallace?"

"Inside," Mei said. Then, "Do you think it'll bring the Manager?"

Hugo shook his head. "Probably not. But weirder things have happened. We'll explain if he does come."

"The Manager?" Wallace whispered.

"Ooh, you don't want to know," Nelson muttered, picking up his cane as he shuffled back toward his chair. "Trust me on that. Mei and Hugo's boss. Nasty fellow. Pray you don't ever have to meet him. If you do, then I suggest you do whatever he says." He brushed a hand over Apollo's back as the dog rose. Apollo barked happily as he paced back and forth in front of the door. He backed up as it opened, Mei talking a mile a minute as Hugo trailed in after her. Apollo circled around the both of them. Hugo held out his hand. Apollo sniffed his fingers and tried to lick them, but his tongue went right through Hugo's hand.

"All right?" Hugo asked even as Mei glared at Wallace.

No, Wallace wasn't all right. Nothing about this was all right. "Why didn't you tell me I'm a prisoner?"

Hugo sighed. "Grandad."

"What?" Nelson said. "Had to scare him straight." He paused, considering. "Something you probably don't know a thing about, isn't that right? Because of the whole gay—"

"Grandad."

"I'm old. I'm allowed to say whatever I want. You know this."

"Pain in my ass," Hugo mumbled, but Wallace could see the quiet smile on his face. The hook tugged gently in his chest, warm and soft. Hugo's smile faded as he glanced at Wallace. "Come with me."

"I don't want to go through the door," Wallace blurted. "I'm not ready."

"The door," Hugo repeated.

"At the top of the stairs."

"*Grandad.*"

"Eh?" Nelson said, cupping his ear. "Can't hear you. Must be going deaf. Woe is me. As if my life wasn't hard enough already. No one should talk to me for the rest of the night so I can collect myself again."

Hugo shook his head. "You'll get yours, old man."

Nelson snorted. "Shows what you know."

Hugo glanced at Wallace. "I'm not going to take you to the door. Not until you're ready. I promise."

Wallace didn't know why, but he believed him. "Where are we going?"

"I want to show you something. It won't take long."

Mei was glaring at him. "You try to run again, I'll drag you back by your hair."

Wallace had been threatened before—many times, in fact; such was the life of a lawyer—but this was one of the first times he actually believed it. For someone so small, she was positively terrifying.

Before he could speak, Hugo said, "Mei, could you finish up the prep work for tomorrow? Shouldn't be much left. I got through most of it before you got back."

She muttered more threats as she pushed by Hugo and headed

through the double doors behind the counter. As the doors swung back and forth, Wallace could see what looked to be a large kitchen, the appliances steel, the floor covered in square tiles.

Hugo nodded toward a hallway at the back of the room. "Come on. You'll like this, I think."

Wallace doubted that immensely.

CHAPTER 7

Apollo seemed to know where they were going, prancing down the hallway, tail wagging. He looked back every now and then to make sure Hugo followed.

Hugo went through another entryway without looking back to see if Wallace would follow. The walls were covered in wallpaper, old but clean: little flowers were etched in that seemed to bloom as they walked by, though Wallace thought it might have been a trick of the light. A door on the right led to a small office, a desk inside covered with papers next to an ancient computer.

A door on the left was closed, but it seemed to be another way into the kitchen. He could hear Mei moving around inside along with the clatter of dishes as she sang at the top her lungs, a rock song that had to be older than she was. But since Wallace couldn't be sure how old she was (or, if he was being honest with himself, *what* she was), he decided to let it pass without comment.

Another door on the right led to a half bathroom with a sign hanging on it that read: GUYS, GALS, & OUR NONBINARY PALS. Beyond it was a set of stairs, and if Wallace still had a heartbeat, he was sure it'd be racing.

But Hugo paid it no mind, passing the stairs, heading for a door at the end of the hall. Apollo didn't wait for him to open it, instead walking through it. Wallace learned then that he still wasn't used to such things, and though he was sure he could do the same, he waited for Hugo to open the door.

It led outside and into darkness.

Wallace hesitated until Hugo motioned for him to walk through. "It's okay. It's just the backyard. Nothing will happen to you out there."

The air was cooler still. Wallace shivered and wondered again *why* he was shivering. He could make out Apollo's tail down in the yard, but it took time for his eyes to adjust. He gasped quietly as Hugo flipped a switch near the door.

Strings of light that hung above them burst to life. They stood on a back deck of sorts. There were more tables on it, the chairs turned over and set atop them. The lights had been strung around the deck railing and the eaves overhead. More plants were hanging down, bright flowers that had turned in on themselves against the night.

"Here," Hugo said. "Watch." He went to the edge of the deck near a set of stairs. He flipped another switch set against a wooden strut, and more lights turned on below the deck, revealing dry, sandy soil and row after row of . . .

"'Tea plants," Hugo said before Wallace could ask. "I try to grow as much of my own as I can, only importing leaves that wouldn't survive the climate. There's nothing like a cup of tea from leaves that you've grown yourself."

Wallace watched as Apollo trotted up and down the rows of plants, stopping only briefly to sniff at the leaves. Wallace wondered if he could actually smell anything. Wallace could, a deep and earthy scent, one which grounded him more than he expected.

"I didn't know they grew from the ground," Wallace admitted.

"Where did you think they came from?" Hugo asked, sounding amused.

"I . . . never really thought about it, I guess. I don't have time for such things." As soon as the words left his mouth, he realized how it sounded. Normally, he wouldn't have given it a second thought, but these were strange days. "Not that it's a *bad* thing, but . . ."

"Life gets away from you," Hugo said simply.

"Yeah," Wallace muttered. "Something like that." Then, "Why tea?"

He followed Hugo down the stairs. The plants were tall, the biggest and most mature rising to Wallace's waist. In passing, almost at the back of his mind, he noticed the cable stretched tight between himself and Hugo.

He stopped when Hugo crouched down, reaching out to touch the leaves of one of the tallest plants. The leaves themselves were small and flat and green. He touched one briefly, his fingers trailing along the tip. "Guess how old this plant is."

"I don't know." He looked around at the other plants. "Six months? A year?"

Hugo chuckled. "A little older than that. This one was one of my first. It's ten years old next week."

Wallace blinked. "Come again?"

"Growing tea isn't for everyone," Hugo said. "Most tea plants don't mature until around three or four years. You can harvest the leaves before then, but something's missing from the flavor and scent. You have to put in the time and have patience. Too early, and you risk killing the plant and having to start all over again."

"Is this one of those times where we're talking about one thing, but you mean something else entirely?"

Hugo shrugged. "I'm talking about tea plants, Wallace. Something on your mind?"

Wallace wasn't sure he believed him. "I have many things on my mind."

Hugo said, "In the fall, some of the plants flower, these little things with a yellow center and white petals. The smell is indescribable. It mingles with the scent of forest, and there's nothing like it in all the world. It's my favorite time of year. What's yours?"

"Why do you care?"

"It's just a question, Wallace."

Wallace stared at him.

Hugo let it go. "Sometimes, I talk to the plants. It sounds weird, I know, but studies have been done showing plants respond to encouragement. It's not conclusive, and it's not necessarily the wording as much as it is the vibrations of the voice. I'm thinking of setting up speakers sometime soon, to play music for the plants to hear. Have you ever talked to a plant?"

"No," he said, distracted by the rows of green, the dark soil holding them in place. They were planted with about four or five feet between them, the leaves glossy in the starlight, and pungent, so much so that it caused Wallace to wrinkle his nose. It wasn't a bad smell (quite the contrary, in fact), just overwhelming. "That's stupid."

Hugo smiled. "A little bit. But I do it anyway. What could it hurt, right?" He looked back down at the plant before him. "You have to be careful when you harvest the leaves. If you're too rough, you can end up killing the plant. It took me a long time to get it right. I can't even begin to tell you how many I've had to pull out and throw away because of my own haste."

"Plants are living things," Wallace said.

"They are. Not like you and me, but in their own way."

"Are there ghost plants?"

Hugo stared at him, mouth agape.

Wallace scowled at him. "Don't give me that look. You told me to ask questions."

Hugo closed his mouth as he shook his head. "No, it's not—I've never thought about it that way. Curious." He squinted up at Wallace. "I like where your mind goes."

Wallace looked away.

"No," Hugo said. "I don't think there are ghost plants, though it would be wonderful if there were. They're alive, yes. And maybe they respond to encouragement. Or maybe they don't and it's a little story we like to tell ourselves to make the world seem more mysterious than it actually is. But they don't have a soul, at least none that I'm aware of. That's the difference between us and them. They die, and that's it. We die and—"

"End up at a tea shop in the middle of nowhere against our will," Wallace said bitterly.

Hugo sighed. "Let's try something else. Did you like being alive?"

Taken aback, Wallace said, "Of course I do." His expression hardened. "Did. Of course I did." It rang false even to his own ears.

Hugo brushed his hands against his apron as he stood slowly. "What did you like about it?" He continued on down the row of plants.

Against his better judgment, Wallace followed him. "Doesn't everyone like being alive?"

"Most people, I think," Hugo said. "I can't speak for everyone. But you're not most people, and no one else is here, which is why I'm asking you."

"What do *you* like about it?" Wallace asked, flinging the question back at him. He felt skittish, irritation growing.

"Many things," Hugo said easily. "The plants, for one. The earth beneath my feet. This place. It's different here, and not just because of what I am or what I do. For a long time, I couldn't breathe. I felt . . . stifled. Crushed. Like there was this weight on my shoulders and I didn't know how to get it off." He glanced back at Wallace. "Do you know what that feels like?"

He did, but he wasn't going to admit it here. Not now. Not ever. "You're not my therapist."

Hugo shook his head. "No, I'm not. Not exactly qualified for something like that, though I do play the role now and then. It's all part of the gig."

"The gig," Wallace repeated.

"Selling tea," Hugo said. "People come in, and some of them don't have any idea what they're looking for. I try to get to know them, to find out what they're all about before deciding on what kind of tea would be the best fit. It's a process of discovery. I usually get it right, though not always."

"Peppermint," Wallace said.

"Peppermint," Hugo agreed. "Did I get that right?"

"You hadn't even met me."

He shrugged. "I get a feeling, sometimes."

"A feeling." Wallace did nothing to stop the scorn dripping from his words. "You have to know how that sounds."

"I do. But it's just tea. Nothing to get so worked up about."

Wallace felt like screaming. "You got a *feeling* that told you peppermint."

"It did." He stopped in front of another plant, crouching down and picking up dead leaves off the ground. He put them in a pocket on his apron with the utmost care, as if he was worried about crushing them. "Was it wrong?"

"No," Wallace said begrudgingly. "It wasn't wrong." He thought Hugo would ask him to explain, what the peppermint meant.

He didn't. "Good. I like to think I'm pretty spot-on, but as I said, it doesn't always work. I try to be careful about it. You don't want to end up missing the forest for the trees."

Wallace had no idea what that meant. Everything was topsy-turvy, and the hook in his chest was tugging again. He wanted to tear it out, consequences be damned. "I liked being alive. I want to be alive again."

"Kübler-Ross."

"What?"

"There was a woman named Elisabeth Kübler-Ross. Have you ever heard of her?"

"No."

"She was a psychiatrist—"

"Oh dear god."

"A psychiatrist who studied death and near-death experiences. You know, you're rising above your body toward a bright white light, though I expect it's a little more complicated than that. A lot of it can be difficult to understand." He rubbed his jaw. "Kübler-Ross talked about stuff like transcendence of ego and spatiotemporal boundaries. It's complex. And I'm really not."

"You're not?" Wallace asked incredulously.

"Careful, Wallace," Hugo said, lips quirking. "That almost sounded like a compliment."

"It *wasn't*."

Hugo ignored him. "She was known for many things, but I think her biggest accomplishment was the Kübler-Ross model. Do you know what that is?"

Wallace shook his head.

"You probably do, though not by that name. And sure, some of the research since then doesn't agree with her findings, but I think it's a good place to start. It's the five stages of grief."

Wallace wanted to go back inside. Hugo once again rose to his feet, turning to face him. He didn't come any closer, but Wallace couldn't move, mouth almost painfully dry. He was a tea plant, rooted in place, not yet mature enough to be harvested. The cable thrummed between them.

Hugo said, "I've done this long enough to see how right she was. Denial. Anger. Bargaining. Depression. Acceptance. It's not always in that order, and it's not always every single step. Take you, for example. You seemed to skip right over denial. You've got the anger part down pat with a little bit of bargaining mixed in. Maybe more than a little bit."

Wallace stiffened. "That doesn't sound like it's for the dead. It's for the people who are left behind. I can't grieve for myself."

Hugo shook his head slowly. "Of course you can. We do it all the time, regardless of if we're alive or not, over the small things and the big things. Everyone is a little bit sad all the time. Yes, Kübler-Ross was talking about the living, but it fits just as well for people like you. Maybe even better. I've often wondered what it was like for her, after she passed. If she went through it all herself, or if there were still surprises left to find. What do you think?"

"I have no idea what you're talking about."

"Okay," Hugo said.

"Okay?"

"Sure. Do you like the plants?"

Wallace glared at him. "They're plants."

"Hush," Hugo said. "Don't let them hear you say that. They're very sensitive."

"You're out of your mind."

"I prefer to think of myself as eccentric." His smile returned. "At least that's what the people in town think of me. Some even believe this place is haunted." He laughed to himself. Wallace was never one for noticing how people sounded when they laughed, but there was a first time for everything. It was a full-body thing for Hugo, low and deep.

"That doesn't bother you?"

Hugo cocked his head. "No. Why would it? It's true. You're a ghost. Grandad and Apollo too. And you're not the first, nor will you be the last. Charon's Crossing is always haunted, though not like most people think. We don't have anyone rattling chains or causing a ruckus." He frowned. "Well, most of the time we don't. Grandad can get a little ornery when the health inspector comes around, but usually we tend to avoid the trappings of a haunted house. It'd be bad for business."

"They're still here," Wallace said. "Nelson. Apollo."

Hugo stepped around him, heading back toward the house. He trailed his fingers along the tops of the tallest plants. They bent with his touch before snapping back upright. "They are."

Wallace followed him. "Why?"

"I can't speak for Grandad," Hugo said. "You'll have to ask him."

"I did."

Hugo glanced back, a look of surprise on his face. "What did he say?"

"That it was none of my business."

"Sounds about right. He's stubborn that way."

"And Apollo?"

The dog barked at the sound of his name, guttural and sharp. He came bounding up one of the rows to their left. No dust or dirt rose when his paws hit the ground. He stopped near the porch, back arched, nose and whiskers twitching as he stared off into the dark forest. Wallace couldn't see far, and it struck him how different the night was here compared to the city, the shadows almost alive, sentient.

"I don't know that I can answer that either," Hugo said. Before Wallace could respond, he added, "Not because I don't want to, but because I don't know, exactly. Dogs don't—they're not like us. They're . . . pure in a way we aren't. I've never had another dog come here before, needing help to cross. I've heard stories of ferrymen and women whose job it is to handle certain animals, but that's not what I do. I'd love it, though. Animals aren't as complicated as people."

"Then why would he—" Wallace stopped. Then, "He was yours."

Hugo paused at the bottom of the steps. Apollo stared up at him adoringly, a goofy smile on his face, whatever had captured his attention in the trees forgotten. Hugo held his hand toward Apollo's snout. The dog sniffed his fingers. "He was," Hugo said quietly. "He is. He was a service dog. Or at least he tried to be. Failed most of his training, but that's okay. I still love him all the same."

"Service dog?" Wallace asked. "Like for . . ." He didn't know how to finish.

"Oh, probably not like you're thinking," Hugo said. "I'm not a veteran. I don't have PTSD." He shrugged. "When I was younger, things were difficult. Days I could barely get myself out of bed. Depression, anxiety, a whole matter of diagnoses I didn't know how to handle. There were doctors and medications and 'Do this, Hugo, do that, Hugo, you'll feel better if you just *let* yourself feel better, Hugo.'" He chuckled. "I was a different person then. I didn't know what I know now, though it'll always be part of me." He nodded toward Apollo. "One day, I heard this little yipping outside my window. It was raining and had been for what felt like weeks. I almost ignored the sound I heard, wanting to pull the covers over my head and shut everything out. But something made me get up and go outside. I found this dog shivering under a bush on the side of my house, so emaciated, I could count his ribs through his skin. I picked him up and took him inside. I dried him off and fed him. He never left. Funny, right?"

"I don't know."

"It's okay not to know," Hugo said. "We don't know most things, and we never will. I don't know how he came to be here, or where he came from. Thought he might make a good service dog. Seemed smart enough. And he was—is. Didn't really take, though. He was too distracted by most everything, but who could blame him? Certainly not me, because he tried his best, and that's all that matters. Turned out he was this . . . this part I didn't know I was missing. He wasn't the answer to everything, but it was a start. He lived a good life. Not as long as I would've liked, but still good."

"But he's here."

"He is," Hugo agreed.

"Trapped here," Wallace said, his hands curling into fists.

Hugo shook his head. "No. He has a choice. I tried to lead him to the door at the top of the stairs time and time again. I told him it was okay to go to whatever's next. That I would never forget him and would always be thankful for the time we had together. But he made his choice. Grandad made his choice." He glanced back at Wallace. "You have a choice too, Wallace."

"Choice?" Wallace spat. "If I leave, I turn into one of those . . . those *things*. If I step foot outside this place, I turn into dust. And don't even get me started on this ridiculous thing in my chest." He looked down at the cable stretching between them. It flashed once. "What is this?"

"Mei calls it the red thread of fate."

Wallace blinked. "It's not red. Or a thread."

"I know," Hugo said. "But it's apt, I think. Mei said . . . how did she put it? Ah, right. In Chinese myth, the old gods tie a red thread around the ankles of those who are destined to meet, who are meant to help one another. It's a pretty thought, isn't it?"

"No," Wallace said bluntly. "It's a shackle. A chain."

"Or it's a tether," Hugo said, not unkindly. "Though I know it doesn't seem like that to you now. It keeps you grounded while you're here. It helps me to find you if you're ever lost."

That certainly didn't make him feel any better. "What happens if I remove it?"

Hugo looked grim. "You'll float away."

Wallace was gobsmacked. "*What?*"

"If you try to remove it while you're on the grounds of the tea shop, you'll . . . rise. And I don't know if you'll ever stop. But if you remove it *off* grounds, you begin to lose your humanity, flaking away until all that's left is a shell."

Wallace spluttered. "That . . . that doesn't make any sense! Who the hell makes up these rules?"

Hugo shrugged. "The universe, I expect. It's not a bad thing,

Wallace. It helps me help you. And while you're here, all I can do is show you your options, the choices laid out in front of you. To make sure you understand there's nothing left for you to fear."

Wallace's eyes stung. He blinked rapidly, unable to meet Hugo's gaze. "You can't say that. You don't know what it's like. It's not fair."

"What isn't?"

"This!" Wallace cried, waving his arms around wildly. "All of it. Everything. I didn't ask for this. I don't *want* this. I have things to do. I have responsibilities. I have a *life*. How can you say I have a choice when it comes down to becoming like Cameron or going through your damn door?"

"I guess the denial was there all along."

Wallace glared at him. "I don't like you." It was petulant and mean, but Wallace couldn't bring himself to care.

Hugo didn't rise to the bait. "That's okay. We'll get there. I won't force you into anything you don't want to do. I'm here to guide you. All I ask is that you let me try."

Wallace swallowed past the lump in his throat. "Why do you care so much? Why do you do what you do? *How* do you do what you do? What's the point of all of this?"

Hugo grinned. "That's a start. There might be hope for you yet."

And with that, he walked up the porch stairs, Apollo bounding up beside him. He stopped at the door, looking back at Wallace still standing amongst the tea leaves. "You coming?"

Wallace hung his head and trudged up the stairs.

Hugo yawned as he closed the door behind them. He blinked sleepily, rubbing his jaw. Wallace could hear the clock in the front tick, tick, ticking. Before he'd fled the tea shop, the seconds had seemed lost, stuttering and stopping, stuttering and stopping. It sounded as if it'd smoothed out. It was normal again. Wallace didn't know what that meant.

"It's late," Hugo told him. "Our days start early here. Pastries needs to be baked, and tea needs time to steep."

Wallace felt awkward, unsure. He didn't know what was supposed to happen next. "Fine. If you could show me to my room, I'll let you be."

"Your room?"

Wallace ground his teeth together. "Or give me a blanket and I can sleep on the ground."

"You don't need to sleep."

Wallace flinched. "What?"

Hugo stared at him curiously. "Have you slept since you died?"

Well . . . no. He hadn't. But there hadn't been time. He'd been far too busy trying to make sense of all this drivel. The very idea of sleep hadn't even crossed his mind, even when things had gotten a bit hazy and he'd found himself at his own funeral. And then Mei had shown up and dragged him to this place. So, no. He hadn't slept. "I had things to do."

"Of course you did. Are you tired?"

He wasn't, which was strange. He should've been exhausted. With everything that had happened, he expected to be drained and moving sluggishly. But he wasn't. He'd never felt more awake. "No," he muttered. "That doesn't make sense."

"You're dead," Hugo reminded him. "I think you'll find sleep is the least of your worries from here on out. In all my years as a ferryman, I've never come across a sleeping ghost. That would be something new. You could try, I suppose. Let me know how that works out."

"So what am I supposed to do?" Wallace demanded. "Stand here and wait for you to wake up?"

"You could," Hugo said. "But there are more comfortable places for you to wait."

Wallace scowled at him. "You're not funny."

"A little," Hugo said. "You can do whatever you want, so long as you don't leave the grounds of the tea shop. I'd rather not have to chase after you again."

"Whatever I want?"

"Sure."

For the first time since he'd arrived in the tea shop, Wallace smiled.

ᶜ৯

"Mei."

"G'way."

"Mei."

"Time 'zit."

"Mei. Mei. *Mei.*"

She sat up in her bed, the blankets falling around her waist. She wore an oversized shirt with the face of Friedrich Nietzsche printed on it. She jerked her head back and forth before settling on Wallace, standing in the corner of her room. "What? What is it? What's wrong? Are we under attack?"

"No," Wallace said. "What are you doing?"

She stared at him. "I'm *trying* to sleep."

"Oh, really? How's that working out for you?"

She started to frown. "Not well."

"Did you know I can't sleep ever again?"

"Yes," she said slowly.

He nodded. "Good." He turned around and walked through the wall out of her room.

ᶜ৯

"Ooooh!" he moaned as loudly as he could. "Oooooooooh!" He paced up and down the hall of the bottom floor, a little perturbed that he couldn't seem to stomp his feet no matter how hard he tried. He banged his hands on the walls, but he kept almost falling through. Which is why he found himself bellowing out every ghost noise he'd ever heard in horror movies. He was disappointed he had no chains to clank. "I'm deaaaad. *Deaaaaaaaad!* Woe is meeee."

"Would you shut *up!*" Mei shouted from her room.

"Make me!" he bellowed back, and then redoubled his efforts.

ᶜ৯

Wallace continued on for sixteen more minutes before he took a cane upside the head.

"*Ow!*" he cried, rubbing the back of his skull. He whirled around to see Nelson standing before him, brow furrowed. "What was that for?"

"Are you going to behave? If not, I can do it again."

He reached for Nelson's cane, meaning to take it from him and toss it away, only to come up with nothing, taking a stumbling step forward where Nelson had stood before he'd disappeared into thin air.

Wallace's eyes bulged as he looked around the empty tea shop wildly. "Um," he said. "Hello? Where . . . where did you go?"

"Boo," a voice whispered in his ear.

Wallace didn't so much scream as squeak. He almost fell over as he turned around. Nelson stood behind him, arching a bushy white eyebrow. "How did you do that?"

"I'm a ghost," Nelson said dryly. "I can do almost anything." He raised the cane as if to strike Wallace again. Wallace reared back. "That's better. Enough with this nonsense. You may not like being here, but that doesn't mean you can make the rest of us suffer because of it. Either keep your mouth closed or come with me."

"Why would I go *anywhere* with you?"

"Oh, I don't know," Nelson said. "Maybe because I'm the only other human ghost here besides you? Maybe because I've been dead far longer than you have, and therefore know much more than you? Or maybe, just maybe, because I don't sleep either and it would be nice to have someone to stay up with? Pick one, boy, or don't pick anything at all, so long as you stop this infernal racket before I show you the end of my cane again."

"Why would you want to help me?"

Nelson's eyebrows rose on his forehead. "You think this is about you?" He scoffed. "It's not. I'm helping my grandson. And don't you forget it." He pushed by Wallace and shuffled down the hall toward the front of the house, the little ears on his rabbit slippers flopping around. "About you," he muttered. "Bah."

Wallace stared after him. He thought about picking right up where he'd left off, but the threat of the cane wasn't pleasant. He hurried after the old man.

Nelson went back to his chair in front of the fire, grunting as he sat down. Apollo was lying on his side in front of the fire, chest rising and falling slowly. Someone had cleaned up the glass from the bulb that had shattered earlier, and the lights from the sconces were dimmed.

"Pull up a chair," Nelson said without looking at him.

Wallace sighed, but did as he was asked.

At least he tried to.

He went to the table closest to him and reached for one of the overturned chairs. He frowned when his hand went through the chair leg. He breathed heavily through his nose as he tried again with the same results. And again. And again. And *again*.

Wallace heard Nelson laughing, but ignored him. If Nelson could sit in a chair, then it was something Wallace could do too. He just needed to figure out how.

He grew even more frustrated a few moments later when he still couldn't touch the chair.

"Acceptance."

"What?"

"You've accepted you're dead," Nelson said. "At least a little bit. You think you can't interact with the corporeal world because of it. Your mind is playing tricks on you."

Wallace scoffed. "Isn't that what you all wanted me to do? Accept that I'm dead?"

He didn't like the smile that grew on Nelson's face. "Come here."

Wallace did.

Nelson motioned for him to sit on the floor before him. Wallace sighed, but he had no other choice. He sank to the floor, crossing his legs, hands twitching on his knees. Apollo raised his head and looked at him. His tail thumped. He turned himself toward Wallace, rolling onto his back, legs kicking in the air. When Wallace didn't accept the obvious invitation to scratch his stomach, he whined pitifully.

"No," Wallace said. "Bad dog."

Apollo farted in reply, a long sonorous sound.

"Oh my god," Wallace mumbled, unsure how he would find the strength to make it through the night.

"Who's a good boy?" Nelson cooed. Apollo almost knocked Wallace over as he wiggled at the praise.

"Are you going to help me or not?"

"Ask me nicely," Nelson said, sitting back in his chair. "Just because we're dead doesn't mean we don't have to use our manners."

"Please," Wallace said, grinding his teeth together.

"Please what?"

Wallace wished they were both alive so he could murder Nelson. "Please help me."

"That's better," Nelson said. "How's the floor? Is it comfortable?"

"No."

"But you're sitting on it. You expect it. The floor is always there. You don't think about it. Except now you are, aren't you?"

He was. He was thinking about it quite a bit.

Which is why he suddenly found himself sinking *through* the floor.

He scrabbled for purchase, trying to reach for something to keep him from falling farther. He was up to his chest by the time Nelson held out his cane, cackling as he did so. Wallace grabbed ahold of it as if it were a lifeline and pulled himself back up, only to start sinking again almost immediately.

"Stop thinking about it," Nelson told him.

"I *can't!*" In fact, it was all he could think about. And even worse, he wondered what would happen if he fell through the floor completely, only to hit the earth beneath and then go through *that*.

But before he sank to the center of the earth only to perish (possibly) in the molten core, Nelson said, "Did it hurt when you died?"

He blinked, his grip on the cane tight. "What?"

"When you died," Nelson said. "Did it hurt?"

"I . . . a little. It was quick. One moment I was there, and then I wasn't. I didn't know what was happening. I don't see what that has to do with—"

"And when you were there and then you weren't, what was the first thing that went through your head?"

"That it couldn't be real. That there had to be some mistake. Maybe even just an awful dream."

Nelson nodded as if that were the answer he expected. "What made you realize you weren't dreaming?"

He hesitated, his grip tightening on the cane. "Something I remembered. I'd heard or read it. That it wasn't possible for you to see your own face in a dream with any real clarity."

"Ah," Nelson said. "And it was clear for you."

"Crystal," Wallace said. "I could see the indents on my nose from my reading glasses, the stubble on my chin and cheeks. That's when I first started thinking it might not be a dream." A fleeting thought, one he'd shoved away as hard as possible. "And then . . ." He swallowed thickly. "At the funeral. Mei was . . . I'd never seen her before."

"Exactly," Nelson said. "The mind is a funny thing. When we dream, our subconscious isn't capable of constructing new faces out of nothing. Anyone we see in our dreams is someone we've seen before, even if only in passing. And when we're awake, everything is clear because we see it with our eyes. Or hear it with our ears, smell it with our noses. It's not like that when you're dead. You have to start from scratch. You need to learn to trick yourself into believing the unexpected. And would you look at that. You did. It's a start."

Wallace looked down. He was once again sitting on the floor. It felt solid beneath him. Before he could think about falling once again, he said, "You distracted me."

"It worked, didn't it?" He pulled his cane back and set it against the chair. "You're very lucky to have me."

"I am?" He was dubious at best.

"Absolutely," Nelson said. "When I died, I had to learn all of this on my own. Hugo wasn't pleased with me but kept his protestations to a minimum. One shouldn't speak ill of the dead, after all. It took time. It was like learning to walk all over again." He chuckled. "I had quite a few stumbles here and there. Broke a few teacups, much to Hugo's dismay. He loves his teacups."

"He seems to have an unhealthy fascination with tea," Wallace mumbled.

"He got that from me," Nelson said, and Wallace almost felt bad. Almost. "Taught him everything he knows. He needed focus, and the growing of tea plants provided that for him."

"Why are you helping me?"

Nelson cocked his head. "Why wouldn't I? It's the right thing to do."

Wallace was confused. "But I'm not giving you anything in return. I can't. Not like this."

Nelson sighed. "That's a strange way to look at things. I'm not helping you because I expect you to give me anything. Honestly, Wallace. When was the last time you ever did anything without expecting something in return?"

2006. Wallace had loose change in his pocket that annoyed him. A homeless man had been panhandling on the street corner near his office. He'd dropped the change into the man's cup. It totaled seventy-four cents. The man thanked him. Ten minutes later, Wallace had forgotten he existed. Until now.

He said, "I don't know."

"Huh," Nelson said. "That sure is . . . what it is. You've already got a leg up on me in one regard."

"I do?"

Nelson nodded toward the sconces on the wall. "Shorted out that light bulb. Broke the glass. Took me a long time to work up that amount of energy."

"I didn't mean to," Wallace admitted. "I wasn't—I was angry."

"So I noticed." His brow furrowed again. "Best you avoid anger if at all possible. It can cause all manner of situations better left avoided."

Wallace closed his eyes. "I have a feeling that's easier said than done."

"It is," Nelson said. "But you'll get there. At least you will if you don't decide to go through that door."

Wallace's eyes snapped open. "I don't want to—"

Nelson held up his hands. "You'll know when the time is right. I will say it's nice to have someone to talk to so late at night. Helps pass the time."

"Years," Wallace said. "You said you'd been dead a few years."

"That's right."

Wallace's stomach twisted strangely. It wasn't unlike the hook in his chest, though it burned more. "You've been here every night by yourself?"

"Most nights," Nelson corrected gently. "Every now and then, someone like you comes along, though they don't tend to stay very long. It's transitionary. One foot in one world, and the other in the next."

Wallace turned toward the fire. It was almost out. "I don't want to talk about it anymore."

"Ah," Nelson said. "Of course not. What would you like to talk about?"

But Wallace didn't reply. He lay down on the floor and curled in on himself, arms wrapped around his chest, knees against his stomach. The hook in his chest vibrated, and he hated it. He closed his eyes and wished he could go back in time when everything made sense. It hurt more than he expected.

"Okay," Nelson said quietly. "We can do this too. Take all the time you need, Wallace. We'll be here when you're ready. Isn't that right, Apollo?"

Apollo woofed, tail thumping silently on the floor.

CHAPTER
8

He opened his eyes again when he heard an alarm clock ringing from somewhere upstairs. It was still dark outside, and the clock above the fireplace said it was half past four in the morning.

He hadn't slept. No matter how hard he tried, he couldn't get himself to relax. It didn't help that he wasn't even remotely tired. He'd drifted, not quite dozing. He replayed the moment right before his death over and over again in his mind, wondering if he could have done anything different. He could think of nothing, and it only made him feel worse.

Pipes in the walls groaned and creaked as someone turned on a shower overhead. The sound of the water brought a fresh wave of misery. He'd never take another shower again.

Mei was the first to come down the stairs. Apollo greeted her, tail wagging. She yawned, jaw cracking as she rubbed between his ears. She wasn't wearing a suit like she'd been the day before. Instead, she wore a pair of black slacks and a crisp white collared shirt under an apron like the one Hugo had worn the night before.

Nelson was gone from his chair. Wallace hadn't even heard him leave.

"Why are you lying on the floor?" Mei asked.

"Why do we do anything that we do?" Wallace said dully. "There's no point."

"Oh man," Mei said. "It's far too early for your existential angst. At least let me wake up more before having to deal with such a bummer."

He closed his eyes again.

And opened them when he felt someone above him.

Hugo stood there, staring down at him, dressed as he'd been the day before. The only difference was the bright pink bandana around his head. Wallace hadn't even heard him approach. He glared at the cable that connected them.

Hugo smiled. "What's this?"

"How are you so quiet?" Wallace asked.

"Practice," Hugo said with a chuckle as he patted the slope of his stomach. "Or maybe you weren't paying attention. Come on. Get up."

"Why?" He hugged his legs tighter.

"Because I want to show you the kitchen."

"It's a kitchen," Wallace said. "Once you've seen one, you've seen them all."

"Humor me."

"I highly doubt I want to do that at all."

Hugo nodded. "Suit yourself. Apollo."

Wallace yelped as the dog ran through the closest wall. He circled around Hugo, sniffing his feet and legs. Once he'd finished his inspection, he sat down next to Hugo, his one ear flopping over.

"Good boy," Hugo said. He nodded toward Wallace. "Lick."

Wallace said, "*What?* Wait, no! No lick! No—"

Apollo licked quite furiously. His tongue slobbered on Wallace's face and then his arms when he tried to shield himself from what most certainly amounted to assault by canine. He attempted to shove the dog off him, but Apollo was heavy. His breath was terrible, and for a brief moment, Wallace wondered about his *own* breath, because he hadn't brushed his teeth in days. But then that train of thought derailed quite spectacularly when he opened his mouth to shout, only to have dog tongue brush against his own.

"Ack! No! Why! *Why.*"

"Apollo," Hugo said mildly.

Apollo immediately stepped back, sitting once again beside Hugo, looking down at Wallace as if *he* were the asshole in this situation.

"Kitchen?" Hugo asked.

"I will destroy everything you love," Wallace threatened.

"Does that ever work on anyone?" Hugo sounded honestly curious.

"*Yes*. All the time." Granted, he hadn't used those *exact* words before, but people had learned to fear him. Those in his employ, those *not* in his employ. Colleagues. Judges. A few children, but the less said about that the better.

"Oh," Hugo said. "Well. Until you do that, you should come and see my scones. I'm proud of them."

"*Your* scones?" Mei shouted from the kitchen. "How very dare you!"

Hugo laughed. "You see what I have to deal with? Get up, Wallace. You don't want to be there when we open. People will walk all over you, and no one wants that. You least of all."

He turned on his heel and walked around the counter before pushing through the double doors, Apollo trailing after him.

Wallace gave very serious thought to staying right where he was.

In the end, he got up.

But only because he chose to.

es

The kitchen was far bigger than he thought it'd be. It was a galley kitchen: on one side were two industrial-size ovens and a stove with eight different metal burners, almost all in use. On the other was a sink and the largest refrigerator Wallace had ever seen. At the back of the kitchen was a small breakfast nook with a table near bay windows that looked out onto the tea garden.

Mei had flour on her forehead as she moved from one side of the kitchen to the other, frowning at the bubbling pots on the stove before muttering, "Is it supposed to do that?" She shrugged and bent over to stare into each oven.

A radio sat on top of a cabinet, and Wallace was shocked at the heavy metal music pouring from the speakers, thunderous and awful and in . . . German? Mei made it worse by singing along in an off-putting guttural voice. It sounded like she was trying to summon Satan. Wallace wouldn't put it past her to be doing just that. And oh, did *that* start a line of thought he didn't want to even consider.

He startled when he saw Nelson sitting in one of the chairs at the table, hands resting on his cane. He'd . . . changed his clothes? Gone were the pajamas and bunny slippers. He now wore a thick blue sweater over tan slacks and shoes with Velcro straps. And he too was grunting along with the music as if he knew each and every word.

"How did you do that?" Wallace demanded.

Everyone stopped to stare at him, Hugo in the process of tying his apron.

"Do what?" Mei asked as she reached up to turn the radio volume down.

"I'm not talking to—Nelson, how did you do that?"

Nelson looked around as if there were some other Nelson in the kitchen. When he saw there wasn't, he said, "Me?"

Maybe sinking through the floor wasn't such a bad idea. "Yes, *you*. You changed your clothes!"

Nelson looked down at himself. "Why shouldn't I have? Pajamas are for nighttime. Do you not know that?"

"But—that's—we're *dead*."

"Acceptance," Mei said. "Cool." She started furiously stirring the pots again, one after the other.

"And?" Nelson said. "Just because I'm dead doesn't mean I don't like to look my best." He held up his shoes, wiggling his feet. "Do you like them? They're Velcro, because laces are for suckers."

No, Wallace didn't like them. "How did you do that?"

"Oh!" Nelson said brightly. "Well, it's the unexpected thing we were talking about last night after you sank through the floor."

"After what?" Hugo asked, eyebrows rising on his forehead.

Wallace ignored him. "Can I do that?"

Nelson shrugged. "I don't know. Can you?" He raised his cane and thumped it on the floor. And just like that, he was wearing a pinstriped suit, not unlike one Wallace had hanging in his own closet. He thumped the cane again, and he was wearing jeans and a heavy winter coat. He thumped the cane *again*, and was in a tuxedo, his top hat tilted jauntily on his head. The cane hit the floor one more time and he was in his original outfit, Velcro shoes and all.

Wallace gaped at him.

Nelson preened. "I'm very good at most things."

"Grandad," Hugo warned.

Nelson rolled his eyes. "Hush, you. Let me have my fun. Wallace, come here."

Wallace went. He stopped in front of Nelson, who looked him up and down critically. "Uh-huh. Yes. Quite. I see. That's . . . unfortunate." He squinted at Wallace's feet. "Flip-flops. Never had use for them myself. My toenails are too long."

Wallace grimaced. "That doesn't sound like something to be shared."

Nelson shrugged. "We have no secrets here."

"We should," Hugo muttered, pulling a tray of scones out of one of the ovens. They were thick and fluffy, bits of chocolate oozing. Wallace might have noticed them more if he hadn't been thoroughly distracted by the fact that he could *change clothes at a whim.*

"How does it work?" he asked.

Nelson scrunched up his face. "You have to want it hard enough."

Wallace wanted it more than anything. *Almost* anything. "Done. What else?"

"That's it."

"Are you messing with me?"

"I wouldn't dream of it," Nelson assured him. "Think about what you'd like to wear, how it feels against your skin, how it looks upon your frame. Close your eyes."

Wallace did, feeling a little awkward. The last time Nelson told him to do something, he'd been jumping in circles. The song ended and another started, this one apparently with even more screams.

"Now, picture an outfit in your head. Start with something simple. A pair of slacks and a shirt. You don't want to try layers, at least not yet. You'll get there."

"Okay," Wallace whispered. "Slacks and a shirt. Slacks and a shirt. Got it."

"Can you see yourself?"

He could. He stood in his apartment bedroom in front of the mirror hanging on the back of the door. His closet was open. In the streets below, horns honked, men and women in construction hats shouting and laughing. A busker played a cello on the street corner. "Yes. I can see it."

"Now, make it happen."

Wallace opened one eye balefully. "I think I'm going to need a little more than that."

He yelped when he got a cane upside his shins. "You're not focusing."

He closed his eyes again and took a breath, letting it out slow. "Right. Focusing. Slacks and a button-up shirt. Slacks and a button-up shirt."

The strangest thing happened.

He felt his skin tingling as if a low electric current began to run through him. It started at his toes and worked its way up his legs and into his chest. The hook—always there, and he was already getting used to it, much to his chagrin—twisted slightly.

"Oh my," Nelson said as Mei started choking.

Wallace opened his eyes. "What? Did it work?"

"Um," Nelson said. He cleared his throat. "I . . . think so? Do you often find yourself wearing that? No judgment, of course. What you do in your free time is your own business. I just don't know if it's appropriate for the tea shop."

"What—" Wallace looked down.

He'd changed his clothes. The sweats and shirt and flip-flops were gone.

He made a strangled noise when he saw he now wore a striped bikini that left little to the imagination. And it wasn't only bikini *bottoms*, no. He also had the top across his chest, the straps tied around his neck, the ends dangling down his back. His feet were bare, but that was the least of his problems. "What is this?!" he shrieked. "What have you done to me?!"

Nelson huffed. "That had nothing to do with me. It's all you." He squinted at Wallace. "Is this what you wore in your free time? Seems a little . . . tight. Again, no judgment." He was lying, obviously. His voice carried quite a bit of judgment.

It was about this time Wallace lamented that humans had evolved with only two hands. He tried to cover his crotch with one hand while pressing the other futilely against his chest as if it would actually do anything.

Mei whistled lowly. "You pull that off better than I'd have thought. I'm actually a little jealous. You've got a cute butt."

He whirled around, both hands now covering his rear. He glared at Mei. She smiled sweetly at him.

"Grandad," Hugo said.

Nelson scowled. "It wasn't me. I honestly wasn't expecting it to work. It took me months to figure out how to change my clothes. How was I to know he'd be able to do it on his first try? He's pretty good at this whole ghost thing." He grimaced as he stared at Wallace. "Maybe a little too good."

Wallace wondered what it said about his life (and death) that he'd ended up in a kitchen in a lopsided house in the middle of nowhere wearing nothing but a bikini.

"It's all right," Hugo said gently as Wallace looked around for something to cover himself up, only to remember he couldn't actually *touch* anything. "It doesn't always work the first time. You've just glitched a little."

"Glitched," Wallace said with a snarl. "It's riding up my—how do I fix this?"

"I don't know if you can," Nelson said gravely. "You might be stuck like this for the rest of your time here. And beyond."

Hugo sighed. "You won't. Grandad is having you on. You should've seen the first time he managed to change his clothes. Ended up wearing a full Easter rabbit costume."

"Even had a basket with little plastic eggs," Nelson agreed.

"Strange thing, that. The eggs were filled with cauliflower, which is, of course, disgusting."

"You *knew* this was going to happen," Wallace snapped.

"Of course I didn't," Nelson replied. "I thought you'd stand there scrunching up your face for a good thirty minutes before giving up." He chuckled. "This is far more entertaining. I'm so glad you came here. You certainly know how to liven this place up." He grinned. "Get it? Liven? It's funny because you're not alive. Oh, wordplay. How I adore you."

Wallace had to remind himself that from a legal perspective, striking the elderly was frowned upon (and against the law), even if said elderly deserved it. "Change me back!"

But before Nelson could open his mouth—and undoubtedly make things worse, Wallace thought—Hugo said, "Wallace, look at me."

He did. He felt almost helpless not to. The cable thrummed between them.

Hugo nodded. "It's okay. A little hiccup. It happens. Nothing to get upset about."

"You're not the one wearing a bikini," Wallace reminded him.

Hugo smiled. "No, I don't suppose I am. It's not so bad, though. You've got the legs for it."

Wallace groaned as Mei started choking again.

Hugo held up his hand toward Wallace's chest, his fingers and palm a few inches from Wallace's skin. The hook vibrated softly. Wallace sucked in a breath. His anger was fading along with his mortification. He didn't feel *good*, not exactly, but he was growing calmer. "What are you doing?"

"Helping," Hugo said, lines appearing on his forehead. "Close your eyes."

He did.

And strangely, he thought he could feel the heat from Hugo's hand, though that should have been impossible. Wallace could touch the dog, he could touch Nelson and Mei (and she all of them), but he couldn't touch Hugo. There seemed to be rules in place, rules that he was beginning to learn even if they were nonsensical. That tingling sensation returned, running along his skin. "It comes from the earth," Hugo said quietly. "Energy. Life. Death. All of it. We rise and we fall and then we rise once more. We're all on different paths, but death doesn't discriminate. It comes for everyone. It's what you do with it that sets you apart. Focus, Wallace. I'll show you where to look. You'll get it. All it takes is a little—there. See?"

Wallace opened his eyes and looked down.

Flip-flops. Sweats. Old shirt. Just like it'd been before.

"How did you do that?" he asked, pulling at his shirt.

"I didn't do anything," Hugo said. "You did. I merely helped you find direction. Better?"

Much. He never thought he'd be so relieved to see his flip-flops again. "I guess."

Hugo nodded. "You'll figure it out. I have faith in you." He took a step back. "If you stay for long, that is." A funny look crossed his face, but it was gone before Wallace could make sense of it. "I'm sure that whatever comes next, you won't have to worry about such things."

That sounded ominous. "Do—do people not wear clothes in the . . . Heaven? Afterlife? What do I even call it?"

Nelson laughed. "Oh, I'm sure you'll find out one way or another. For all we know, it's a gigantic nudist colony."

"So, Hell, then," Wallace muttered.

"What do you think of the scones?" Hugo asked, nodding toward the tray sitting on the stove.

Wallace sighed. "I can't eat them, can I?"

"No."

"Then why on earth would I care what they look like?" He didn't say that he could smell them, the scent thick and warm, because it made him feel alone. Strange that scones could do such a thing, almost making him reach out and fail at touching something he could never have.

Hugo looked down at them then back at Wallace. "Because they look nice. It's not always about what we can or can't have, but the work we put into it."

Wallace threw up his hands. "That doesn't—you know what? Fine. They look like scones."

"Thank you," Hugo said seriously. "That's nice of you to say."

Wallace groaned.

es

At promptly half past seven, Charon's Crossing opened for business.

Wallace watched as Hugo unlocked the front door, flipping the sign in the window from CLOSED to WE'RE OPEN! COME ON IN! He didn't know what to expect. The tea shop was removed from the town, and he thought if there were any customers at all, they'd trickle in slowly throughout the day.

So, imagine his surprise when he saw people already waiting outside. As soon as the lock clicked on the door, it opened, a stream of people pouring in.

Some formed a line at the counter, greeting Hugo as if they'd known him for a long time. Others sat at the tables, rubbing sleep from their eyes as they yawned. They wore business attire or uniforms for their places of employment. There were young people in beanies, their bags slung over their shoulders. He was shocked when no one immediately pulled out a laptop or stared down at their phones.

"No Wi-Fi," Mei said when he asked. She was bustling around the kitchen with practiced ease. "When people come here, Hugo wants them to talk to one another instead of being fixated on a screen."

"Of course he does," Wallace said. "It's a hipster thing, isn't it?"

Mei turned slowly to stare at him. "Please let me be there when you say that to Hugo. I want to see the look on his face when you call him a hipster. I need it like air."

Hugo rang up the orders on his old cash register, his smile never faltering as he put pastries in little bags or delivered teapots to waiting tables. Wallace stayed in the kitchen, watching him through the porthole windows. He thought about going out to the front, but he stayed right where he was. He told himself it was because he didn't want to get in the way.

Not that he could.

Nelson went back to his chair in front of the fireplace. Wallace noticed no one ever tried to sit in the chair, though they couldn't see it was taken. Apollo moved around from table to table, tail wagging even though he was ignored.

It was close to nine when the door opened once more. A woman entered. She wore a heavy coat, the front buttoned up to her throat. She was pale and wan with dark circles under her eyes. She didn't go to the counter; instead, she went and sat at an empty table near the fireplace.

Wallace frowned through the window. It took him a moment to place her. He'd seen her the night before when Mei had brought him to Charon's Crossing. She'd been walking swiftly away from the tea shop.

"Who is that?" Wallace asked.

"Who?" Mei came to the door, standing on her tiptoes to look through the porthole next to him.

"The woman near Nelson. She was here last night when we arrived. She walked right by us."

Mei sighed as she dropped back down to her heels. "That's Nancy. Shit, she's early. She usually comes in the afternoon. Must have been a bad night." She wiped her hands on her apron. "I'll have to go out and run the register. You gonna stay here?"

"Why do you have to—" He stepped back when Mei pushed her way through the door. He watched as she went to Hugo, whispering in his ear. He looked at the woman sitting at the table before nodding. Hugo moved around the counter, picking up another pot of tea and a single cup, setting it on a tray. He carried it over to the woman. She didn't acknowledge him as he placed the tray on the table. She continued to look out the window as she clutched at the purse in her lap.

Hugo sat in the empty chair on the other side of the table. He didn't speak. He poured the tea into the cup, the steam rising up in wisps. He set the pot back down on the tray before lifting the cup and setting it on the table in front of the woman.

She ignored it, and him.

Hugo didn't seem put out. He folded his hands on the table and waited.

Wallace wondered if this woman was another ghost, a spirit like himself. But then a man came to the table, putting his hand on Hugo's shoulder and speaking quietly. The man nodded at the woman before leaving out the front door.

Hugo and the woman stayed that way for almost an hour. The woman never drank from the proffered tea, and she never spoke. Neither did Hugo. It was as if they were simply existing in the same space.

When the line at the counter had thinned, Mei came back into the kitchen. "What are they doing?"

Mei shook her head. "It's not—I don't think it's my place to say."

Wallace scoffed. "Does no one here actually say anything of any substance?"

"We do," Mei said, opening a pantry door and pulling down a plastic tub filled with individual packets of sugar and creamer. "You're just not hearing what you want to hear. I know it might be hard to understand, but not everything is about you, Wallace. You have your own story. She has hers. If you're meant to know what it is, you will."

He felt properly rebuked. And worse, he thought she had a point.

Mei sighed. "You're allowed to ask questions. In fact, it's good that you do. But her business is between her and Hugo." She carried the tub toward the doors. Wallace stepped out of her way. Before she went through, she stopped, looking up at him. She hesitated. Then, "Hugo will probably give you the specifics if you ask, but know she has her reasons for being here. You know how you're my first solo case?"

Wallace nodded.

Mei gnawed on her bottom lip. "Hugo had another Reaper before me. He'd been with Hugo since he started as a ferryman. There were . . . complications, and not just pertaining to Cameron. The Reaper pushed when he shouldn't have, and mistakes were made. I didn't know him, but I heard the stories." She brushed her bangs back off her forehead. "We're here to guide, to help Hugo and the people we bring here. But his first Reaper forgot that. He thought he knew better than Hugo. And it didn't end well. The Manager had to get involved."

Wallace had heard that name before. Nelson had called him a nasty fellow. "The Manager?"

"It's best you don't know him," Mei said quickly. "He's our boss. He's the one who assigned me to Hugo and trained me on how to reap. It's . . . better when he's not here. We don't want to draw his attention."

The hairs on the back of his neck stood on end. "What does he do?"

"Manages," Mei said as if that explained everything. "Don't worry about it. It has nothing to do with you, and I don't think you'll ever have to meet him." And then, under her breath, "At least I hope you won't." She pushed her way through the doors.

Wallace looked out the porthole again in time to see the woman—Nancy—looking as if she were about to speak. She opened her mouth, and then closed it. Her lips stretched into a thin, bloodless line. She stood abruptly, the chair scraping along the floor. The din of the tea shop quieted as everyone turned to look at her, but she only had eyes for Hugo. Wallace flinched at her expression of rage. Her eyes were almost black. He thought she was going to reach out and strike Hugo. She didn't, instead stepping around the table and heading toward the door.

She stopped only when Hugo said, "I'll be here. Always. Whenever you're ready, I'll be here."

Her shoulders slumped as she left Charon's Crossing.

Hugo watched her through the window as she walked away. Mei went to the table, putting her hand on his shoulder. She spoke quietly, words Wallace couldn't make out. Hugo sighed and shook his head before gathering up the teacup and putting it back on the tray. Mei stepped back as he rose, lifting the tray with one hand and walking back toward the kitchen.

Wallace backed away quickly, not wanting to get caught spying. He pretended to be studying the appliances as the doors swung open and Hugo entered the kitchen. The noise of Charon's Crossing picked up again.

"You don't have to stay back here," Hugo said.

Wallace shrugged awkwardly. "I didn't want to get in the way." He knew how ridiculous that sounded. He didn't know how to quite put into words what he really meant, that he didn't want people to be walking around (or, heaven forbid, through) him as if he weren't there at all.

Hugo set the tray near the sink. "This place is yours as much as it is ours while you're here. I don't want you to feel trapped."

"I am, though," Wallace reminded him, nodding toward the cable. "Remember? It was a whole ordeal last night."

"I remember," Hugo said. He looked down at the tea in the cup, shaking his head. "But while you're here, you can go anywhere on the grounds you wish. I don't want you to feel like you can't."

"Why do you care if I feel trapped?"

Hugo glanced at him. "Why wouldn't I?"

He was so goddamn frustrating. "I don't get you."

"You don't know me." It wasn't mean, just a statement of fact. Hugo held up his hand before Wallace could retort. "I know how that sounds. I'm not trying to be flippant, I promise." He lowered his hand, looking down at the tray. The tea had cooled, the liquid dark. "It's easy to let yourself spiral and fall. And I was falling for a long time. I tried not to, but I did. Things weren't always like this. There wasn't always a Charon's Crossing. I wasn't always a ferryman. I made mistakes."

"You did?" Wallace didn't know why he sounded so incredulous.

Hugo blinked slowly. "Of course I did. Regardless of what else I am or what I do, I'm still human. I make mistakes all the time. The woman I was sitting with, Nancy, she's . . ." He shook his head. "I try to be the best ferryman I can be because I know people are counting on me. I think that's all anyone can ask for. I've learned from my mistakes, even as I continue to make new ones."

"I don't know if that makes me feel any better," Wallace said.

Hugo laughed. "I can't promise I won't screw up somehow, but I want to make sure your time here is restful and calm. You deserve it, after everything."

Wallace looked away. "You don't know me."

"I don't," Hugo said. "But that's why we're doing what we're doing now. I'm learning about you so I know how best to help you."

"I don't want your help."

"I know you think that," Hugo said. "But I hope you realize that you don't have to go this alone. Can I ask you a question?"

"If I say no?"

"Then you say no. I'm not going to pressure you into something you're not ready for."

He didn't know what else he had to lose. "Fine. Ask your question."

"Did you have a good life?"

Wallace jerked his head up. "What?"

"Your life," Hugo said. "Was it good?"

"Define good."

"You're hedging."

He was, and he hated how easily Hugo saw that. It made his skin itch. He felt on display, showing things he didn't think he'd ever be ready to show. He wasn't obfuscating; he genuinely had never thought about it that way. He woke up. He went to work. He stayed at work. He did his job, and he did his job well. Sometimes he lost. Most times he didn't. There was a reason the firm had been as successful as it was. What else was there to life aside from success? Nothing, really.

Sure, he'd had no friends. No family. He had no partner, no one to grieve over him as he'd lain in an expensive coffin in the front of a ridiculous church, but that shouldn't be the only measure of a life well-lived. It was all about perspective. He'd done important things, and in the end, no one could have asked any more of him.

He said, "I lived."

"You did," Hugo said, still holding onto the teacup. "That doesn't answer my question."

Wallace scowled. "You're not my therapist."

"So you've said." He lifted the cup and poured the tea out into the sink. It looked as if it pained him to do so. The dark liquid splattered against the sink before Hugo turned on the faucet and washed away the dregs.

"Is this . . . is this how you are with the others?"

Hugo switched off the faucet and set the teacup gently in the sink. "Everyone's different, Wallace. There's no one way to go about this, no uniform rules in place that can be applied to every single person like you who comes through my doors. That wouldn't make sense because you're not like everyone else, just as they're not you." He looked out the window above the sink. "I don't know who or what you are yet. But I'm learning. I know you're scared, and you have every right to be."

"Damn right I am," Wallace said. "How could I not be?"

Hugo smiled quietly as he turned toward Wallace. "That might be the most honest thing you've said since you got here. Would you look at that? You're making progress. That's great."

The praise shouldn't have warmed him as much as it did. It felt unearned, especially when he didn't want it. "Mei said you had another Reaper before her."

Hugo's smile faded as his expression hardened. "I did. But that discussion is off-limits. It has nothing to do with you."

Wallace took a step back, and for the first time since he could remember, he wanted to apologize. It was strange, this, made worse by how *hard* it seemed to get the words out. He frowned and pushed through it. "I'm . . . sorry?"

Hugo sagged, hands on the counter in front of the sink. "If I'm going to ask you questions, you should be able to do the same. There are some things I don't like to talk about, at least not yet."

"Then you can understand if I'm the same way."

Hugo looked up in surprise. The smile returned. "I . . . yeah. Okay. I can see that. That's only fair."

And with that, he turned and walked out of the kitchen, leaving Wallace to stare after him.

CHAPTER
9

Charon's Crossing stayed relatively busy for most of the day. There was a lull mid-afternoon before more people came as the blue sky started to shift toward the encroaching dark. Wallace stayed in the kitchen, feeling voyeuristic as he watched the customers filter in and out.

He was surprised (Mei be damned) to see that not a single person tried to boot up a laptop or spend any time on their phones. Even those who came alone seemed happy enough to just sit in their chairs, taking in the noise of the tea shop. He was slightly amused (and more than a little horrified) when he tried to figure out what day it was, only to realize he had no idea. It took him a moment to count back the days. He'd died on a Sunday. His funeral had been Wednesday.

Which meant today was Thursday, though it felt like weeks had passed. If he were still alive, he'd be in the office, his day hours from being over. He always kept himself busy to the point of exhaustion, so much so that he'd usually collapse by the time he got home, falling face-first onto his bed until his alarm blared bright and early the next morning to begin all over again.

It was illuminating.

All that work, all that he'd done, the life he'd built. Had it mattered? What had been the point of anything?

He didn't know. It hurt to think about.

With these thoughts thundering around his head, he played the part of the voyeur as he had nothing else to do.

Mei was in and out of the kitchen, telling Wallace she preferred to stay in the back if at all possible. "Hugo's the people person," she told him. "He likes to talk to everyone. I don't."

"You're in the wrong line of work if that's the case."

She shrugged. "I like the dead more than the living. Dead people usually don't care about the little annoyances of life."

He hadn't thought about it that way. He'd give anything for those annoyances again. Hindsight was a bitch of a thing.

Nelson stayed, for the most part, in his chair in front of the fireplace. Other times, he wandered between the tables, nodding along with conversations he could take no part in.

Apollo was in and out of the house. Wallace heard him barking ferociously at a squirrel, incensed that the squirrel ignored him completely.

But it was Hugo who Wallace watched the most.

Hugo, who seemed to have all the time in the world for anyone who asked for his attention. A gaggle of older women came in the early afternoon, fawning and cooing over him, pinching his cheeks and giggling when he blushed. He knew them all by name, and they clearly adored him. They all left with smiles on their faces, paper cups of tea steaming in their hands.

It wasn't just the older women. It was everyone. Kids demanded he lift them up and he did, but not with his hands. They held onto his thinly muscled biceps as he raised his arms, their feet kicking into nothing, their laughter bright and loud. Younger women flirted, batting their eyes at him. Men shook his hand furiously, their grips looking strong as their arms pumped up and down. They called him by his first name. They all seemed delighted to see him.

By the time Hugo turned the sign on the window to CLOSED and locked the door, Wallace was wrung out. He didn't know how Hugo and Mei could do this day in and day out. He wondered if it ever felt too big for them, facing the clear evidence of life, knowing what waited for everyone after.

Speaking of.

"Why aren't there other people here?" he asked as Mei lugged in a wash bin full of dirty dishes. Through the swinging door, he could see Hugo had picked up a broom and was sweeping the floor as he overturned the chairs.

She grunted as she set the bin on the counter next to the sink. "What?"

"Other people," Wallace repeated. Then, "Ghosts. Or whatever."

"Why would there be?" Mei asked, beginning to load the dishwasher for the sixth time that day.

"People die all the time."

Mei gasped. "They *do*? Oh my god, this changes everything. I can't believe I never—oh, now *that's* a look on your face for sure."

Wallace grimaced. "Whoever told you that you were funny obviously lied and you should feel bad about it."

"I don't," Mei assured him. "Like, at all."

"Like, totally."

"Sounds like we spoke to the same person."

"Hey!"

"There aren't other ghosts here because we haven't received a new assignment yet. Some days, it's back-to-back and things overlap. And then there are other days when we don't get anyone at all." She glanced at him before going back to the dishwasher. "We don't usually have long-term tenants. And no, Nelson and Apollo don't count. I think the most we ever had at one time was . . . three, not including them. It got a little crowded."

"Of course they don't count," Wallace muttered. "What's the longest someone has been here?"

"Why? Thinking about setting down roots?"

He crossed his arms defensively. "No. I'm just asking."

"Ah. Right. Well, I know Hugo had someone who stayed for two weeks. That was . . . a hard case. Deaths by suicide usually are."

Wallace swallowed thickly. "I can't imagine having to deal with that."

"I don't *deal* with it," Mei said sharply. "And neither does Hugo. We do what we do because we want to help people. We aren't here because we have to be. We're here because we choose to be. Remember that distinction, yeah?"

"Okay, okay. I didn't mean anything by it." He'd struck a nerve he didn't even know to aim for. He needed to be careful.

She relaxed. "I won't pretend to say I understand what you're going through. How can I? And even if I *thought* I knew what it's like, I'd probably still be wrong. It's different for everyone, man. What the people went through before you and those who will come after you, it's never going to be the same thing twice. But that doesn't mean I don't know what I'm doing."

"You're new," Wallace reminded her.

"I am. I was training for only two years before I was given your case. That's quicker than any other Reaper in history."

That certainly didn't make him feel any better. He changed tack, an old trick he'd learned to try to catch people off guard. It was mostly force of habit because he wasn't quite sure what he was looking for. "At the convenience store."

"What about it?" She closed the dishwasher before leaning against it, waiting for him to continue.

"The clerk," Wallace said. "He could see you. And the people here can too."

"They can," she said slowly.

"But the people at my funeral couldn't."

"Is there a question in there somewhere?"

He scowled at her. "Are you always this aggravating?"

She shrugged. "Depends on who you ask."

"Are you . . . human?" He knew how ridiculous that sounded, but then he remembered he was a ghost talking to a woman who could snap her fingers and drag him hundreds of miles in an instant.

"Sort of," she said. She hoisted herself up onto the counter, legs and feet dangling against a row of wooden cabinets. "Or, rather, I used to be. I've still got all my human parts, if that's what you meant."

"I don't think that's what I meant at all. I'm not thinking about your parts."

She snorted. "I know. I'm just giving you shit, man. Lighten up a little. There's not a whole lot for you to worry about anymore."

That stung more than he cared to admit. "That's not true," he said stiffly.

She sobered. "Hey, no. I didn't mean it like—you're allowed to ask questions, Wallace. In fact, if you didn't, I'd be concerned. It's natural. This is something you've never experienced before. Of course you'll want to try to figure out everything right away. It can't be easy not getting the answers you're used to hearing. I wish I could *give* you all the answers, but I don't have them. I don't know if anyone does, not really." She squinted at him. "Did that help?"

"I have no idea how to answer that."

"Good," she said.

He blinked, confused. "It is?"

She nodded. "Maybe it's just me, but I think I'd feel relieved finding out there are things I don't know about. It can't be healthy the other way, you know?"

"Obviously," he said faintly. "I died."

She laughed and looked shocked because of it. "Obviously. Don't try to force it, Wallace. It'll come when it comes. I've seen it before. You'll know when the time is right."

He thought she was speaking about more than the contents of their conversation, and his mind drifted to the door upstairs. He hadn't worked up the courage to find it, much less ask more about it.

"Time moves a little different here," she said. "I don't know if you noticed that, but there's—"

"The clock."

She arched an eyebrow. "The clock?"

"Last night, when we got here. The second hand was stuttering. It moved back and forth or sometimes not at all."

She seemed impressed. "Noticed that, huh?"

"Hard not to. Is it always like that?"

She shook her head. "Only when we have visitors like yourself, and only on the first day. It's meant to give you time to acclimate. To get an understanding of the position you find yourself in. Most of the time, it means sitting there, waiting for someone like you to speak."

"I ran instead," Wallace said.

"You did. And the clock began to move like it normally does the moment you left. It happens at all places like this."

"Nelson called it a way station."

"That's a good way to put it," Mei said. "Though, I think of it more as a *waiting* station."

"What am I waiting for?" Wallace asked, aware of how monumental the question felt.

"That's for you to decide, Wallace. You can't force this, and no one here is going to try to push you into something you're not ready for. Hope for the best, you know?"

"That's not very reassuring."

"It's worked so far. Mostly."

Cameron. That wasn't a topic he was prepared for. He still could hear the wordless sound the man had made at the sight of him. If he could still dream, he thought he'd have nightmares because of it. "Why do you do this?"

"That's a little personal."

He blinked. "Oh. I . . . suppose it is. You don't have to say anything if you don't want to."

"Why do you want to know?" Her tone gave nothing away.

Wallace struggled with what to say. He landed on, "I'm trying."

She didn't let him off the hook. He was a little in awe of her. "Trying to what, Wallace?"

He looked down at his hands. "Trying to be . . . better. Isn't that what you're supposed to be helping me with?"

The backs of her shoes hit the lower cabinets, causing the doors to rattle. "I don't think it's our job to make you better. Our job is to get you through the door. We give you the time to make peace with it, but anything else beyond that is up to you."

"Okay," he said helplessly. "I . . . I'll remember that."

She stared at him for a long moment. Then, "Before I came here, I didn't know how to bake."

He frowned. What did *that* have to do with anything?

"I had to learn," she continued. "Growing up, we didn't bake.

We didn't use an oven. We had a dishwasher, but we never used it because dishes needed to be handwashed, and then put into the dishwasher to be used as a drying rack." She grimaced. "Have you ever tried to whisk eggs? Man, that shit is *hard*. And then there was the time I made the dishwasher overflow with soap until it flooded the kitchen. Felt a little bad about that."

"I don't understand," Wallace admitted.

"Yeah," Mei muttered, rubbing a hand over her face. "It's a cultural thing. My parents emigrated to this country when I was five. My mother, she . . . well. She was fascinated by the idea of being American. Not Chinese. Not Chinese American. American. She didn't like her history. China in the twentieth century was filled with war and famine, oppression and violence. During the Cultural Revolution, religion was outlawed, and anyone who disobeyed was beaten or killed or just . . . disappeared into thin air."

"I can't imagine what that's like," Wallace admitted.

"No, you can't," she said bluntly. "My mom wanted to escape it all. She wanted fireworks on the Fourth of July and picket fences, to become someone different. She wanted the same for me. But even coming here, there were certain things she still believed. You don't go to bed with wet hair because you'll get a cold in your head. Don't write names in red ink, because that's taboo." She looked away. "When I started . . . manifesting, I thought something was wrong with me, that I was sick. Seeing things that weren't there. She wouldn't hear of it." She laughed hollowly. "I know you probably don't get this, but we don't talk about stuff like that in my family. It's . . . ingrained. She wouldn't let me get help, to see a doctor, because for all that she wanted to be American, there were still some things that just wouldn't do. After all, what would the neighbors think if they found out?"

"What happened?" Wallace asked, unsure if it was his place.

"She tried to keep me hidden away," Mei said. "Kept me at home, telling me that I was acting out, that nothing was wrong with me. Why would I do this to her after all she'd done to give me a good life?" She smiled weakly. "When that still didn't work, I was given a choice. Either her way or the highway. She said it just like that, and she was so *proud* of it, because it was such an American thing to say."

"Christ," Wallace breathed. "How old were you?"

"Seventeen. Almost ten years ago now." She gripped the countertop on either side of her legs. "I went out on my own. Made good decisions. Sometimes not-so-good decisions, but I learned from them. And she's . . . well. She's not gotten *better*, exactly, but I think she's trying. It'll take time to rebuild what we had before, if that's even possible, but we talk on the phone a few times a month. In fact, she was the first one to reach out. I talked it over with Hugo, and he thought it might be an olive branch, but ultimately, it was up to me to decide." She shrugged. "I missed her. Even with all that happened. It was . . . nice to hear her voice. Toward the end of last year, she even asked me to come back and visit her. I told her I wasn't ready for that, at least not yet. I haven't forgotten what she said to me before. She was disappointed, but said she understood and didn't push it. Still doesn't change what I see."

"And what's that?"

"People like you. Ghosts. Wandering souls who haven't yet found their way." She sighed. "You know bug zappers? Those electric blue lights that hang on porches and torch the bugs that fly into them?"

He nodded.

"I'm sort of like that," she said. "Except for ghosts, not bugs, and I don't fry them when they get close. They're attracted to something in me. When I first started seeing them, I didn't know how to make it stop. It wasn't until . . ."

"Until?"

Her eyes slid unfocused as she looked off into nothing. "Until someone came for me and offered me a job. He told me who—*what* I was. And with the proper training, what I could do. He brought me here to Hugo, to see if we'd make a good match."

"The Manager," Wallace said.

"Yeah. But don't worry about him. He's nothing we can't handle."

"Then why do you seem so scared of him?"

She startled. "I'm not scared of anything."

He didn't think that was true. If she was telling the truth and was human, she'd always have to be scared of something. That was how humanity worked. Survival instinct was based on a healthy dose of fear.

"I'm wary of him," she said. "He's . . . intense. And that's putting it mildly. I'm grateful he brought me here and taught me what he knows, but it's better when he's gone."

From everything he'd heard about the Manager, Wallace hoped he'd stay gone. "And he . . . what? Made you this way?"

She shook her head. "He fine-tuned what was already there. I'm a sort of medium, and *yes*, I know how that sounds, so you can shut your mouth."

He did.

"I have . . ." She paused. Then, "It's like when you're standing in a doorway. You have one foot on one side, and the other foot on the other side. You're in two places at once. That's me. He just showed me how to lean into one side of the doorway, and how to pull myself back."

"How can you do this?" Wallace asked, suddenly feeling very small. "How can you be surrounded by death all the time and not let it get to you?"

"I wish I could tell you it's because I always wanted to help people," Mei said. "But that would be a lie. I didn't . . . I didn't know how to *be*. I had to unlearn so many things I'd been taught. Hell, the first time Hugo hugged me, I didn't hug him back because that's not something I'd ever really had before. Contact, much less physical affection, wasn't something I was used to. It took me a while to appreciate it for what it was." She grinned at him. "Now, I'm pretty much the best hugger."

Wallace remembered how her hand had felt in his the first time, the relief that'd washed over him. He couldn't imagine going an entire life without knowing something like that.

"It's like you, in a way," she said. "You need to unlearn all that you know. I wish I could just flip a switch for you, but that's not how it works. It's a process, Wallace, and it takes time. For me, it started when I was shown the truth. It changed me, though definitely not right away." She hopped down from the counter, though she kept the distance between them. "I do what I do because I know there's never been a time in your life when you've been more confused or more vulnerable. And if I can do something to at least alleviate that a little bit, then so be it. Death isn't a final ending, Wallace. It *is* an ending, sure, but only to prepare you for a new beginning."

He was stunned when he felt a tear trickle down onto his cheek. He brushed it away, not able to look at Mei as he did so. "You're awfully strange."

He heard the smile in her voice. "Thank you. That might be the nicest thing you've ever said to me. You're awfully strange too, Wallace Price."

⅌

Hugo was in front of the fireplace when Wallace left the kitchen, putting logs in under the direct supervision of Nelson. Apollo sat on his haunches, looking between the two of them, tongue hanging out of his mouth as he panted. "Higher," Nelson said. "Make it a big one. I've got a chill in my bones. Gonna be a cold night. Spring often lies with hints of green and sun."

"Of course it does," Hugo said. "Don't want you to be cold."

"Absolutely," Nelson agreed. "I could catch my death, and then where would you be?"

Hugo shook his head. "I don't even want to imagine."

"Good man. Ah, there it is." The fire grew, the flames bright. "Always said that having a good fire and good company is all a person needs."

"Funny," Hugo said. "I don't think I've ever heard you say that before."

Nelson sniffed. "Then you weren't listening. I say it all the time. I'm your elder, Hugo, which means you should be hanging on to my every word and believing everything I say."

"I do," Hugo assured him as he stood. "I couldn't ignore you if I tried."

"Damn right," Nelson said. He tapped his cane on the floor, and he was back in his pajamas, bunny slippers and all. "That's better. Wallace, don't stand there gawking. It's unbecoming. Get your butt over here and let me look at you."

Wallace went.

"All right?" Hugo asked as Wallace stopped awkwardly next to Nelson's chair.

"I have no idea," Wallace said.

Hugo beamed at him as if Wallace had said something profound. "That's wonderful."

Wallace blinked. "It is?"

"Very. Not knowing is better than pretending to know."

"If you say so," Wallace muttered.

Hugo grinned. "I do. Hang out here with Grandad for me, okay? I'll be back in a little bit."

He headed for the kitchen before Wallace could ask where he was going.

Nelson craned his neck around the chair, waiting for the kitchen doors to swing shut before he looked at Wallace. "They're eating," he whispered as if revealing a great secret.

Wallace looked down at him. "What?" But now that Nelson had mentioned it, he could smell it, the scents filling his nose. Meatloaf? Yes, meatloaf. Roasted broccoli on the side.

"Supper," Nelson said. "They don't eat in front of us. It's rude."

"It is?" He grimaced. "Do they talk with their mouths full of food?"

Nelson rolled his eyes. "They don't eat in front of us because we can't eat. Hugo thinks it's like dangling a bone in front of a dog but then taking it away."

Apollo's ears quirked at the word *bone*. He stood and began to nose Nelson's knees as if he thought Nelson had a treat to offer him. Nelson scratched between his ears instead.

"We can't . . . eat?" Wallace said.

Nelson glanced at him. "Are you hungry?"

No, he wasn't. He hadn't even *thought* about eating, even when the scones had come out of the oven that morning. They'd smelled delicious, and he knew they'd be light and fluffy, melting on his tongue, but it was almost an afterthought. "We can't eat," he said.

"Nope."

"We can't sleep."

"Nope."

Wallace groaned. "Then what the hell *can* we do?"

"Rock a bikini, I guess. You've got that down pat."

"You're never going to let me forget that, are you?"

"Never," Nelson said. "It was enlightening to see that you were a proponent of manscaping when you were alive. I'd hate to think you'd neglect it only to spend your time here with a topiary garden in your pants."

Wallace gaped at him.

Nelson tapped his cane on the floor. "Sit down. I don't like it when people hover."

"I'm not sitting on the floor."

"Okay," Nelson said. "Then pull up a chair."

Wallace turned to do just that, stopping halfway to the nearest table before he remembered he *couldn't*. He frowned as he turned back to Nelson. "That's not funny."

Nelson squinted at him. "It wasn't supposed to be. I wasn't telling a joke. Would you like me to tell you a joke?"

No, he really wouldn't. "That's fine, you don't need to—"

"What is a ghost's favorite fruit?"

This was definitely Hell. He didn't care what Mei or Hugo said. "I really don't—"

"Booberries."

Wallace felt his eye twitch. "I can just sit on the floor."

"What kind of a street does a ghost live on?"

"I don't care."

"A dead end."

Silence.

"Huh," Nelson said. "Nothing? Really? That was one of my better ones." He frowned. "I suppose I can pull out the big guns, if you think it'd help. What does a ghost do to stay safe in a car? He puts on his sheet belt."

Wallace sank down to the floor. Apollo was delighted by this, lying down next to Wallace and rolling onto his back, staring at Wallace pointedly. "No more. Please. I'll do anything." He reached over absentmindedly and scratched Apollo's belly.

"*Anything?*" Nelson said, sounding rather gleeful. "I'll have to keep that in mind."

"That wasn't an offer."

"Sounded like one. Don't write checks your butt can't cash is what I always say."

Wallace doubted that. He looked at the fire. He could feel the heat from it, though he didn't understand how that was possible. "How can you stand it?"

"What?" Nelson asked, settling back in his chair.

"Staying here."

"It's not a bad place," Nelson said sharply. "It's quite nice, if you ask me. There are worse places I could be."

"No, I'm—that's not what I meant."

"Then say what you mean. Seems easy enough, right?"

"And that's another thing," Wallace said without thinking. "You can change your clothes."

"It's not *that* hard. You just need to have focus."

Wallace shook his head. "Why are you the way you are?"

"Like . . . physically? Or philosophically? If it's the latter, I hope you're ready for a long story. It all started when I was—"

"Physically," Wallace said. "Why are you still old?"

Nelson cocked his head. "Because I *am* old. Eighty-seven, to be exact. Or, rather, that's how old I was when I bit the big one."

"Why don't you make yourself younger?" Wallace asked. "Are you—" *we,* though that went unsaid—"stuck like this forever?"

He startled when Nelson laughed loudly. He looked up in time to see Nelson wiping his eyes. "Oh, you are a delight. Getting right to the meat of it. I thought that would take at least another week or two. Possibly seven."

"Glad I can buck your expectations," Wallace mumbled.

"It's simple, really," Nelson said, and Wallace tried to hide how eager he was to hear the answer. "I like being old."

That . . . wasn't the answer he'd expected. "You do? Why?"

"Spoken like a young person."

"I'm not *that* young."

"I can see that," Nelson said. "Worry lines around your eyes, but none around your mouth. Didn't laugh much, did you."

It wasn't a question. And even if it was, Wallace didn't know how to answer without sounding defensive. Instead, he lifted his hand to his face, touching the skin near his eyes. He'd never been one to worry about such things. He had expensive clothes, and his haircuts cost enough to feed a family of four for a week. But even though he put on an imposing display, he never thought much about the person underneath it all. He was far too busy to care about such things. If there were times he'd caught his reflection in the mirror in his bedroom, it was only given a passing thought. He hadn't been getting any younger. Maybe if he'd cared more, he wouldn't be here. That line of thinking felt dangerous, and he pushed it away.

"I could change how I look," Nelson said. "I think. I've never tried, so I don't know if it would work or not. But I don't imagine we have to stay as we were when we died if we don't want to."

Wallace looked down at the floor warily. He wasn't sinking, so he supposed that was a start.

"Tell me something no one else knows."

"Why?"

"Because I asked you to. You don't have to if you don't want to, but I find it helps to speak some things out loud rather than keep them bottled up. Quick. Don't think about it. The first thing that comes to your mind."

And Wallace said, "I think I was lonely," surprising even himself. He frowned and shook his head. "That's . . . not what I meant to say. I don't know why that came out. Forget it."

"We can if you want," Nelson said, not unkindly.

He didn't push. Wallace felt a strange surge of affection for him, foreign and warm. It was . . . odd, this feeling. He couldn't remember the last time he'd cared for anyone but himself. He didn't know what that made him. "I didn't have . . . this."

"This?"

Wallace waved his hand around. "This place. These people, like you have."

"Ah," Nelson said, as if that made perfect sense.

He wondered how this man could say so much by saying so little. While words had always been easy for Wallace, it was his power of observation that set him apart from his peers. Noticing the little tics people had when they were sad or happy or troubled. When they were lying, eyes turned down, shifting side to side, mouth twisted, something Wallace prided himself in knowing. How strange, then, that he hadn't been able to turn that on himself. Denial, maybe? That didn't make him feel better. Introspection wasn't exactly his forte, but how could he have not seen any of this before?

Nelson didn't seem to have that problem, which humbled Wallace more than he expected. "I didn't see it, then," he admitted. He scrubbed a hand over his face. "I had privilege. I lived a *life* of privilege. I had everything I thought I wanted and now . . ." He didn't know how to finish.

"And now that's all been stripped away, leaving you only with yourself," Nelson said quietly. "Hindsight is a powerful thing, Wallace. We don't always see what's right in front of us, much less appreciate it. It's not until we look back that we find what we should have known all along. I won't have you thinking I'm a perfect man. It would be a lie. But I've learned that maybe I was a better person than I expected. I think that's all anyone can ask for." Then, "Did you have anyone to help chase the loneliness away?"

He hadn't. He tried to remember how things had been before

it'd all fallen apart, how Naomi had looked to him with light in her eyes, the corners of her mouth quirking up softly. She hadn't always despised him. There had been love between them, at one point. He'd taken it for granted, thinking she'd always be there. Wasn't that part of their vows? 'Til death do us part. But their parting had come long before death ever found Wallace, and with her exit, the crumbling of the life they'd built together. She left and Wallace threw himself into his work, but had it really been any different than when she'd been there? He remembered one of the last days of their marriage, when she'd stood in front of him, eyes cold, telling him he had to make a choice, that she wanted more than what he was offering.

He hadn't said a word.

It didn't matter. She heard all the things he didn't say. It wasn't her fault. None of it was, no matter what he'd tried to tell himself. It was why he hadn't contested the divorce, giving her everything she'd asked for. He'd thought it was because it was better to get it over with. He could see now it was because the guilt had been gnawing at him, though he hadn't given it a name at that point. He was too proud for that.

Or he had been, at least.

"No," he whispered. "I don't think I did."

Nelson nodded as if that was the answer he expected. "I see."

Wallace didn't want to think about it anymore. "Tell me something no one else knows."

Nelson grinned. "Fair." He rubbed his chin thoughtfully. "You can't tell anyone."

Wallace leaned forward, surprised at his own eagerness. "I won't."

Nelson glanced at the kitchen before looking down at Wallace. "There's a health inspector that comes here. Loathsome man. Chip on his shoulder. Thinks he's entitled to things he can't have. I haunt him while he's here."

"You what?"

"Little things. I knock his pen out of his hand or move his chair when he tries to sit down."

"You can do that?"

"I can do many things," Nelson said. "Man has it out for my Hugo. I make sure to reciprocate in kind."

Before Wallace could ask about it further, Apollo turned over, raising his head toward the kitchen. A moment later, Hugo appeared through the doors, Mei trailing after him.

He said, "What are you two talking about, and should I be concerned?"

"Most likely," Nelson said, winking at Wallace. "We're definitely up to no good."

Hugo smiled. "Wallace, could you come with me? I'd like to show you something."

Wallace looked to Nelson who nodded. "Go on. I have Mei and Apollo to keep me company."

Wallace sighed as he stood. "Another therapy session?"

Hugo shrugged. "If you want to think of it that way, sure. Or it could just be two people getting to know each other. Almost like friends, even."

Wallace grumbled under his breath as he followed Hugo down the hall.

ల

They went outside again to the back deck overlooking the tea garden. Hugo turned on the strings of lights wrapped around the railings of the deck, white and twinkling.

Before Hugo closed the door to the house behind them, he reached in and switched off the deck light. The trees swayed in the darkness.

"Good talk with Grandad?" he asked, coming to stand next to Wallace near the steps.

"I guess."

"He can be a little . . . pushy," Hugo said. "Don't feel like you have to do whatever he says." He frowned. "Especially if it sounds like it'd be illegal."

"Not like that matters now, does it?"

"No," Hugo said. "I don't suppose it does. Still, humor me. For my own peace of mind." He reached up and smoothed out his pink bandana. "Your first full day here. How'd it go?"

"I stayed in the kitchen the whole time."

"Saw that." He leaned against the railing. "You don't have to."

"Is that supposed to make me feel better?"

"I don't know. Does it?"

"You know, for someone who said they aren't qualified to be a therapist, you really know how to act like one."

Hugo chuckled. "I've been doing this for a bit."

"Part of the gig," Wallace said.

Hugo seemed pleased that he remembered. Wallace wasn't sure why that felt important to him. He scratched at his chest, the hook tugging gently. "Exactly."

"What did you want to show me?"

"Look up."

Wallace did.

"What do you see?"

"The sky."

"What else?"

It was like it'd been the night before, walking down a dirt road with a strange woman at his side. The stars were bright. Once, when he'd been a kid, he'd gotten it in his head that he needed to count them all. Each night, he'd stared out the window of his bedroom, counting them one by one. He never made it very far before falling asleep, waking the next morning more determined to try again.

"Stars," Wallace whispered, even as he struggled to remember the last time he'd turned his face toward the sky before arriving at the tea shop. "All those stars." It wasn't like this in the city. The light pollution made sure of that, leaving only the barest hints of what hung in the sky at night. "There are so many of them." He felt very small.

"It's like that here," Hugo said. "Away from everything else. I can't imagine what it must be like where you're from. I don't know much else aside from this place."

Wallace looked at him. "Why? Don't you ever leave?"

"Can't really do that," Hugo said. "Never know when someone like you is going to come here. I always need to be ready."

"You're trapped here?" Wallace asked, sounding horrified. "Why the hell would you ever agree to that?"

"Not trapped," Hugo said. "That implies I don't—or didn't—have a choice. I did. I wasn't forced into being a ferryman. I chose to be. And it's not like I can't ever leave. I go into town all the time. I have my scooter, and sometimes, I go for a ride just to clear my head and breathe."

"Your scooter," Wallace repeated. "You ride that."

Hugo arched an eyebrow. "I do. Why?"

"Oh, I don't know," Wallace said, throwing up his hands. "Maybe because if you crash, you'll die?"

"Then it's a good thing I don't crash it." His lips quirked. "I'm careful, Wallace, but I appreciate your concern. Thank you for worrying about me." He sounded delighted, and Wallace refused to be charmed by it.

He failed miserably. "Someone has to," he muttered, and as soon as the words left his mouth, he wished desperately he could take them back. He plowed ahead, deflecting awkwardly. "This place is still a prison."

"It is? Why? I don't need much. I never have. I've got everything I want right here."

"But . . . that's . . ." Wallace didn't know what that was. Odd, surely. He'd never met someone so settled into their own skin. "Doesn't it get to you? All this death, all the time."

Hugo shook his head. "I don't think of it that way, though I get what you're trying to say. I think . . ." He paused as if choosing his words carefully. "Death isn't always something to be feared. It's not the be-all and end-all."

Wallace remembered what Mei had told him. "An ending. Leading to a new beginning."

"That's right," Hugo said. "You're learning. It can be beautiful, if you let it, though I can see why you wouldn't think so." He looked up at the stars. "The best way to describe it is the sense of relief most people feel when they're ready to go through the door. It may take them time to get to that point, but it's always the same." He hesitated. "I could tell you what it's like, what I've seen. The look on their faces the moment the door opens, the moment they hear the sounds coming from the other side. But I don't know that I can do it justice, because no matter what I say, it barely begins to scratch the surface. It changes you, Wallace, changes you in ways you don't expect. At least it did me. Call it faith, call it proof, whatever you like. But I know that I'm doing that right thing because I've seen the looks on their faces, filled with awe and wonder. I may not be able to hear what they hear, but I choose to believe it's everything they could've wanted."

"It doesn't bother you that you can't hear it?"

Hugo shook his head. "I'll find out one day. And until then, I'll do what I'm here for, preparing you to find out for yourself."

Wallace wished he could believe him. But the very thought of the door he had yet to lay eyes on terrified him. It made his skin crawl, and he deflected in the only way he knew how. "How did you become a ferryman?"

"Oof," Hugo said, though Wallace thought he wasn't fooled. "Just going for it, huh?"

"Might as well."

"Might as well," Hugo echoed. "It was by accident, if you can believe that."

He couldn't. At all. "You accidentally became the person who helps ghosts cross to . . . wherever."

"Well, when you say it like *that*, I can see how it could sound ridiculous."

"That's how you said it!"

Hugo looked at him. Wallace forced himself not to turn away. It was easier than he expected. "My parents died."

"I'm sorry," Wallace said, cognizant of the fact that apologies seemed to come easier now.

Hugo waved him away. "Thanks, but you don't need to apologize for it."

"It's what you're supposed to say."

"It is, isn't it? I wonder why. Did you mean it?"

"I . . . think so?"

Hugo nodded. "Good enough. Still lived at home. I grew up a few miles away from here. You probably passed by the house on your little adventure last night."

He wasn't sure if he should apologize again or not, so he kept quiet.

"It was fast," Hugo said, staring off into the darkness. He let his hands hang over the edge of the railing. "The roads were slick. Sleet and freezing rain had been falling all day, and Mom and Dad were going out on a date. They'd been thinking about staying in, but I told them to go ahead, so long as they were careful. They worked hard, and I thought they deserved a night out, you know? So I pushed them. Told them to go." He shook his head. "I didn't . . . it's weird. I didn't know it was the last time I'd see them as they were then. Dad squeezed my shoulder, and Mom kissed me on the cheek. I grumbled about it and told them I wasn't a kid anymore. They laughed at me and told me I was always going to be their little boy, even if I hadn't been little in a long time. They died. Car hit a patch of ice and slid off the road. It rolled. I was told it was over in an instant. But that stuck with me for a long time, because it was over for *me* in an instant, and yet it feels like it's still happening, sometimes."

"Shit," Wallace breathed.

"I fell asleep on the couch. I woke up because someone was standing above me. I opened my eyes, and . . . there they were. Just standing there, looking down at me, wearing their nice clothes. Dad hated his tie, said it felt like he was choking, but Mom made him wear it anyway, telling him he looked so handsome. I asked them what time it was. You know what they said?"

Wallace shook his head.

Hugo laughed wetly. "Nothing. They said nothing at all. They flickered in and out, and I thought I was dreaming. And then a Reaper appeared."

"Whoa."

"Yeah," Hugo said. "That was . . . something else. He took my parents by the hands, and I demanded to know who he was and what the hell he was doing in our house. I'll never forget the look of shock on his face. I wasn't supposed to be able to see him."

"How did you?"

"I don't know," Hugo admitted. "I'm not like Mei. I'd never seen ghosts before or anything like that. I never had any kind of touch or sight or whatever it is that makes people like Mei who they are. I was just . . . me. But here I was, trying to grab onto my parents, to pull them away from this stranger, but my hands kept going right through them. I reached for the unknown man, and for a moment, it worked. I felt him. It was like fireworks going off in my head, the explosions bright. They hurt. By the time my vision cleared, they were gone. I tried to tell myself I'd imagined it all, but then someone knocked on the door ten minutes later, and I knew it wasn't only in my head because the police were there, saying things I didn't want to hear. I told them it was a mistake, it had to be a mistake. I screamed at them to get the hell away from me. Grandad showed up shortly after, and I begged him to tell me the truth. He did."

"How old were you?"

"Twenty-five," Hugo said.

"Jesus."

"Yeah. It was . . . a lot. And then the Manager came to see me." His voice hardened slightly. "Three days after their funeral. One moment I was going through things in the house I thought could be donated to Goodwill, and the next he was standing in front of me. He . . . told me things. About life and death. How it's a cycle that never ends and never would. Grief, he said, is a catalyst. A transformation. And then he offered me a job."

"And you *took* it? You believed him?"

Hugo nodded. "The Manager is many things, most of which I can't even begin to describe. But he's not a liar. He speaks only in truths, even if we don't want to hear what he has to say. I didn't trust him right away. I don't know if I do even now. But he showed me things, things that should have been impossible. Death has a beauty to it. We don't see it because we don't want to. And that makes sense. Why would we want to focus on something that takes us away from everything we know? How do we even begin to understand that there's more than what we see?"

"I don't know the answer to that," Wallace admitted. "To any of it." That troubled him, because he felt like he *should* know, like the answer was on the tip of his tongue.

"Faith," Hugo said, and Wallace groaned. "Oh, stop it. I'm not talking about religion or God or whatever else you might be thinking. Faith isn't always . . . it's not just about those things. It's not something I can force upon you, even if you think that's what I'm doing."

"Aren't you?" Wallace asked, trying to keep his voice even. "You're trying to make me believe in something I don't want."

"Why is that, do you think?"

Wallace didn't know.

Hugo seemed to let it go. "The Manager said I was selfless, which is why I was under any consideration at all. He could see it in me. I laughed in his face. How could I be selfless when I would have given anything to have them back? I told him that if he put my parents in front of me along with a random person and said I had to choose who lived or died, I would pick my mom and dad without hesitation. That's not how a selfless person acts."

"Why not?"

Hugo looked surprised. "Because I would choose what made me happy."

"Doesn't mean you're not selfless. If we never wanted something just for ourselves, what would that make us? You were grieving. Of course that's what you would say."

"That's what the Manager said."

Wallace wasn't sure how he felt about that. In a way, *he'd* been a manager of sorts, and that comparison didn't sit well with him. "But you still said yes."

Hugo nodded slowly, picking at the string of lights on the railing.

"Not right away. He told me he'd give me time, but the offer wasn't always going to be on the table. And for a while after, I was going to say no, especially after he told me all it would entail. I couldn't . . . I wouldn't have a normal life. Not like everyone else. The job would come first, above all things. It was a commitment, one that if I agreed to, would be binding for as long as I drew breath."

Wallace Price had been accused of many things in his life, but selflessness was not one of them. He gave little thought to those around him, unless they stood in his way. And God help them if they did. But even so, he could feel the weight of Hugo's words, and it was heavy on his shoulders. Not necessarily because of what he'd said, but what it meant. They were alike in ways Wallace hadn't expected, choosing a job and putting it above all other things. But that was where the comparisons ended. Perhaps, when Wallace was young and bright-eyed, he'd started out with noble intentions, but those had fallen by the wayside quickly, hadn't they? Always about the bottom line and what it meant for the firm. For *Wallace*.

Maybe on a surface level, he and Hugo could be considered similar, but it didn't go much further than that. Hugo was better than he could ever be. Wallace didn't think Hugo would make the same choices he had. "What changed your mind?"

Hugo ran his hand over his hair. Such a small action, and a wonderfully human one at that, but it gave Wallace pause. Everything about Hugo did. He was struck by this man and the quiet power that emanated from him. Hugo was unexpected, and Wallace thought he was sinking once again. "Curiosity, maybe? A desire to understand that bordered on desperation. I told myself that if I did this, I might find answers to questions I didn't even know I had. I've been at this for five years now, and I *still* have questions. Not the same ones, but I don't know that I'll ever stop asking." He laughed, though it was strangled and soft. "I even convinced myself I might be able to see them again."

"You didn't, did you?"

Hugo looked out at the tea plants. "No. They . . . they were already gone. They didn't linger. There were days I was angry about that, but the more I did this job, the more I helped others in their time of need, the more I understood why. They lived a good life. They'd done right by themselves and me. There was nothing left for them to do here. Of course they'd cross."

"And now you're stuck with people like me," Wallace muttered.

The smile returned. "It's not so bad. The bikini was a nice touch."

Wallace groaned. "I hate everything."

"I don't believe that for a minute. You may think you do, but you don't. Not really."

"Well, I hate *that*."

Hugo made an aborted attempt to reach for him. His fingers fluttered above Wallace's hand on the railing before he pulled away, curling his hand into a fist. "We live and we breathe. We die, and we still feel like breathing. It's not always the big deaths either. There are little deaths, because that's what grief is. I died a little death, and the Manager showed me a way to cross beyond it. He didn't try to take it from me because he knew it was mine and mine alone. Whatever else he is, whether or not I agree with some of the choices he makes, I remember that. You think I'm a prisoner here. That I'm trapped, that *you're* trapped. And in a way, maybe we are. But I can't quite call it a prison when there's nowhere else I'd rather be."

"The pictures. The photographs. The posters hanging on the walls inside."

Hugo looked at him but didn't speak. He was waiting for Wallace to put it together, the little puzzle pieces scattered between them.

"You can't ever go to them," Wallace said slowly. "See them in person. They're a . . . reminder?" That didn't feel quite right. "A door?"

Hugo nodded. "They're photographs of places I can't even begin to imagine. There's a whole wide world out there, but I can only see it through these little glimpses. Do I wish I could see them in person? Of course I do. And yet I would make the same choice all over again if I had to. There are more important things than castles crumbling on cliffs over the ocean. It took me a long time to realize that. I won't say I'm happy with it, but I've made my peace because I know how crucial my work is. I still like to look at them, though. They remind me how small we really are in the face of everything."

Wallace rubbed at his chest, the hook aching. "I still don't get you."

"You still don't know me. But I promise I'm not all that complicated."

"I don't believe that for a moment."

Hugo watched him for a long moment, a slow smile forming. "Thank you, Wallace. I appreciate that."

Wallace flushed, hands tightening on the railing. "Don't you get lonely?"

Hugo blinked. "Why would I? I have my shop. I have my family. I have a job that I love because of what it brings to others. What more could I ask for?"

Wallace turned his face back toward the stars. They were really something else. He wondered why he'd never noticed them before. Not like this. "What about . . ." He coughed, clearing his throat. "A girlfriend. A wife, or, like . . ."

Hugo grinned at him. "I'm gay. Probably would be pretty hard to find me a girlfriend or wife."

Wallace was flustered. "A boyfriend, then. A partner." He glared down at his hands. "You know what I mean."

"I know. I'm just playing with you. Lighten up, Wallace. Not everything needs to be so serious." He sobered. "Maybe one day. I don't know. It'd be kind of hard to explain that my tea shop is actually just a front for dead people to have pseudo-intellectual conversations."

Wallace scoffed. "I'll have you know I'm *extremely* intellectual."

"Is that right? I never would have guessed."

"Asshole."

"Eh," Hugo said. "Sometimes. I try not to be. You just make it so easy. What about you?"

"What about me?"

Hugo shrugged, fingers twitching on the railing. "You were married."

Wallace sighed. "It was over a long time ago."

"Mei said she was there at the funeral?"

"I bet she did," Wallace mumbled. "Did she tell you what was said?"

Hugo's lips twitched. "Bits and pieces. Sounded like quite the show."

Wallace laid his head on the backs of his hands. "That's one way of putting it."

"Do you miss her?"

"No." He hesitated. "And even if I did, I wouldn't have the right. I messed up. I wasn't a good person. Not to her. She's better off without me. I think she's still screwing the gardener though."

"No shit?"

"No shit. But I don't blame her. He's pretty hot. I probably would have done the same if I thought he was interested."

"Wow," Hugo said. "I didn't see that coming. You contain multitudes, Wallace. I'm impressed."

Wallace sniffed daintily. "Yes, well, I do have eyes, so. He liked to work in the yard shirtless. He was probably messing around with half the women in the neighborhood. If I looked like that, I'd do the same."

Hugo looked him up and down, and Wallace fidgeted uncomfortably. "You're not so bad."

"Please, stop. You're far too kind. I can't stand it. How on earth are you still single with ammunition like that up your sleeve?"

Hugo squinted at him. "You think that's what I'd say?"

Abort. Abort. Abort. "Uh. I don't . . . know?"

"Multitudes," he said again as if that explained everything.

He glanced at Hugo, relieved he was ignoring Wallace's awkwardness. "Is that a good thing?"

"I think so."

Wallace picked at the peeling paint on the railing, barely realizing he was doing so. "I've never been very surprising to anyone before."

"There's a first time for everything."

And maybe it was because the stars were bright and stretched on forever across the sky. Or maybe it was because he'd never had a conversation like he'd just had with Hugo: honest, open. Real, all the bluster and noise of a manufactured life falling away. Or maybe, just maybe, it was because he was finding the truth within himself. Whatever the reason, he didn't try to stop himself when he said, "I wish I'd met someone like you before."

Hugo was quiet for a long moment. Then, "Before?"

He shrugged, refusing to meet Hugo's gaze. "Before I died. Things might have been different. We could have been friends." It felt like a great secret, something quiet and devastating.

"We can be friends now. There's nothing stopping us."

"Aside from the whole dead thing, sure."

He startled when Hugo stepped back from the railing, a determined look on his face. He watched as Hugo extended his hand toward him. He stared at it before looking up at Hugo. "What?"

Hugo wiggled his fingers. "I'm Hugo Freeman. It's nice to meet you. I think we should be friends."

"I can't—" He shook his head. "You know I can't shake your hand."

"I know. But hold out your hand anyway."

Wallace did.

And so, under the field of stars, Wallace stood before Hugo, their hands extended toward each other. Inches separated their palms, and though it still felt like an endless gulf between them, Wallace was sure, for a moment, he felt *something*. It wasn't quite the heat of Hugo's skin, though it felt close. He mirrored Hugo, raising his hand up and down, up and down in the approximation of a handshake. The cable between them flashed brightly.

For the first time since he'd stood above himself in his office, his breath forever gone, Wallace felt relief, wild and vast.

It was a start.

And it terrified the hell out of him.

CHAPTER 10

A few nights later, Wallace was determined. Irritated, but determined.

He stopped in front of a chair. Nelson had taken it off one of the tables, setting it in the center of the room. Around them, the house creaked and groaned as it settled. He could hear Mei snoring in her room. Hugo was probably doing the same somewhere above, a place Wallace hadn't dared go to yet for reasons he couldn't quite explain. He knew it had to do with the door, but he thought Hugo was part of it too.

The only people up were the dead, and Wallace wasn't a fan right now of two-thirds of them. Nelson was watching him calmly and Apollo had that goofy grin on his face as he lay next to Nelson's chair.

"Good," Nelson said. "Now, what did I tell you?"

He ground his teeth together. "It's a chair."

"What else?"

"I have to unexpect it."

"And?"

"And I can't force it."

"Exactly," Nelson said, as if that explained everything.

"That's not how any of this works."

"Really," Nelson said dryly. "Because you have such a good idea about how this works. What was I thinking."

Wallace grunted in frustration. He wasn't used to failing, especially not so spectacularly. When Nelson had told him he was going to start teaching Wallace the fine art of being a ghost, Wallace had assumed he'd take to it like he'd taken to everything else: with grand success and little care for whatever got in the way.

That had been the first hour.

And now here they were in the fifth, and the chair was just *sitting* there, mocking him.

"Maybe it's broken," Wallace said. "We should try another chair."

"Okay," Nelson said. "Then take another one off a table."

"Are you sure you don't want to cross?" Wallace asked. "Because I can go get Hugo right now and he can walk you to the door."

"You'd miss me too much."

"Keep telling yourself that." He took a deep breath, letting it out slow. "Unexpect. Unexpect. Unexpect."

He reached for the chair.

His hand went right through it.

And *oh*, did that piss him off. He growled at it, swinging for it again and again, his hand always passing through the wood as if it (or he) weren't there at all. With a yell, he kicked at it, which, of course, led to his foot going through the chair as well. The momentum carried his leg up and he teetered back before crashing onto the floor. He blinked up at the ceiling.

"That certainly went well," Nelson said. "Feel better?"

He started to say no but stopped himself. Because strangely, he *did* feel better.

He said, "This is so stupid."

"Right?" Nelson said. "It really is."

Wallace turned his head toward him. "How long did it take you to figure all of this out?"

Nelson shrugged. "I don't know that I've figured *all* of it out. But it did take me longer than a week, I'll give you that."

Wallace pushed himself up. "Then why do you think I'm going to be any different?"

"Because you have me, of course." Nelson smiled. "Get up."

Wallace pushed himself up off the floor.

Nelson nodded toward the chair. "Try again."

Wallace curled his hands into fists. If Nelson could do it, Wallace could too. Granted, Nelson wasn't exactly offering specifics on *how* to do it, but Wallace was determined.

He looked at the chair before closing his eyes. He let his thoughts drift, knowing the more he focused, the worse off he'd be. He tried to think about nothing at all, but there were little flickers of light behind his eyelids, like shooting stars, and a memory rose up around them. It was a trivial thing, something unimportant. He and Naomi had just started dating. He was nervous around her. She was out of his league and sharp as a tack. He didn't know what the hell she was doing with him, how they'd even gotten here in the first place. He hadn't had this before, too shy and awkward to ever instigate anything. There'd been furtive attempts at the end of high school and into college, women in his bed where he tried to pretend he knew what he was doing, and a man or two, though it was awkward fumblings in dark corners that carried a strange and exhilarating little thrill. It took him time to admit to himself that he was bisexual, something he'd felt relief over, at finally giving it a name. And when he'd told Naomi, a little nervous but firm, she hadn't cared either way, telling him that he was allowed to be who-ever he wanted.

But that wouldn't happen for another six months. Now, it was their second—third?—date and they were in an expensive restau-rant that he absolutely could not afford but thought she would enjoy. They'd gotten dressed up in fancy clothes (*fancy* being a relative term: his suit sleeves were too short, the pant legs rising up around his ankles, but she looked like a model, her dress blue, blue, blue) and a valet had taken his shitty car without so much as a raised eye-brow. He held the door open for her, and she'd *laughed* at him, a low, throaty chuckle. "Why thank you," she said. "You're too kind."

The maître d' eyed them both warily, his snooty little mustache wiggling as Wallace gave his name for the reservation. He led them to the table in the back of the restaurant, the smell of seafood thick and pungent, causing Wallace's stomach to twist. Before the maître d' could act, he hurried around the table, pulling the chair out for Naomi.

She laughed again, blushing and looking away before sitting down.

He thought how beautiful she looked.

Things would fall apart for them. They would hurl accusations like grenades, not caring they were both still in the blast radius. They did love each other, and they had good years, but it wasn't enough to keep it all from crumbling. For a long time, Wallace refused to accept any blame. *She* was the one who'd messed around with the gardener. *She* was the one who knew how important his job was. *She* was the one who'd pushed him to go all in with their own firm, even as his parents gave him nothing but dire warnings about how he'd be destitute and on the streets with nothing in a year.

Her fault, he told himself as he sat across from her in her lawyer's conference room, watching as he pulled the chair out for her. She thanked him. Her dress was blue. It wasn't the same dress, of course, but it could've been. It wasn't the same dress, and they weren't the same people they'd been on that second or third date when he spilled wine on his shirt and fed her bits of pricey crab cake with his fork.

And now, in a tea shop so far from everything he'd known, he felt a great wave of sadness for all that he'd had, and all that he'd lost. A chair. It was just a chair, and yet he couldn't even do that right. It was no surprise he'd failed Naomi.

"Would you look at that," he heard Nelson say quietly.

He opened his eyes.

He was holding the chair in his hands. He could feel the grain of the wood against his fingers. He was so surprised, he dropped it. It clattered against the floor but didn't fall over. He looked at Nelson with wide eyes. "I did it!"

Nelson grinned, flashing his remaining teeth. "See? Just needed a little patience. Try again."

He did.

Only this time, when he reached for the chair, there was a strange crackling the moment before he could grab onto it. The sconces on the walls flared briefly, and the chair rocketed across the room, smashing into the far wall. It fell on its side on the floor, one of the legs broken.

Wallace gaped after it. "I . . . didn't mean to do that?"

Even Nelson seemed shocked. "What the hell?"

Apollo started barking as the ceiling above them creaked. A moment later, Hugo and Mei came rushing down the stairs, both of them looking around wildly. Mei was in shorts and an old shirt, the collar stretched out over her shoulder, her hair a mess around her face.

Hugo was in a pair of sleep shorts and nothing else. There were miles of deep brown skin on display, and Wallace found something very interesting to stare at in the opposite direction that was not a thin chest and thick stomach.

"What happened?" Mei demanded. "Are we under attack? Is someone trying to break in? I am going to kick *so much ass*, you don't even know."

"Wallace threw a chair," Nelson said mildly.

Mei and Hugo stared at Wallace.

"Traitor," Wallace mumbled. Then, "I didn't *throw* it. I just . . . tossed it across the room with the power of positive thinking?" He frowned. "Maybe."

Mei went over to the chair, hunkering down beside it, poking the broken leg with her finger. "Huh," she said.

Hugo wasn't looking at the chair.

He was still staring at Wallace.

"What?" Wallace asked, trying to make himself smaller.

Hugo shook his head slowly. "Multitudes." As if that explained anything at all. He glanced at Nelson. "Maybe don't teach people to destroy my chairs."

"Bah," Nelson said, waving his hand. "A chair is a chair is a chair. He barely even *touched* it, Hugo. It took me weeks to even be able to feel it." He sounded oddly proud, and it was all Wallace could do to keep from puffing out his chest. "He's taking to this whole ghost thing pretty well, if you ask me."

"By murdering my furniture," Hugo said wryly. "Whatever you're planning, you get it out of your head right now."

"I have no idea what you're talking about," Nelson said. "I'm not planning anything at all."

Even Wallace didn't believe him. He didn't want to know what was going through Nelson's head to cause the expression of utter deviousness he wore.

Mei picked up the chair. The leg fell off onto the floor. "He's kind of got a point, Hugo. Have you ever seen someone do this only after a few days?"

Hugo shook his head, still looking at Wallace. "No. I don't suppose I have. Curious, isn't it?" Then, "How did you do it?"

"I . . . remembered something. From when I was younger. A memory."

He waited for Hugo to ask what memory it was. Instead, he said, "Was it a good one?"

It was. For all that came later, for all the mistakes he made, pulling out Naomi's chair was something he hadn't thought about in years, but apparently hadn't forgotten. "I think so."

Hugo smiled. "Try to keep my chairs in one piece, if you can."

"No promises," Nelson said. "I can't wait to see what else he can do. If we have to sacrifice a few chairs in the process, then so be it. Don't you dare think about stifling us, Hugo. I won't have it."

Hugo sighed. "Of course not."

↜

They all fell into a schedule of sorts. Or, rather, they added Wallace to the one they already followed. Mei and Hugo were up before the sun, blinking blearily as they yawned and came down the stairs, ready to start another day at Charon's Crossing Tea and Treats. At first, Wallace wasn't sure how they did it, as the tea shop never had a day off, even on the weekend, and there were no other employees. Mei and Hugo ran everything, Mei mostly in charge of the kitchen during the day while Hugo ran the register and made the tea. They were a team, moving around each other like they were dancing, and he felt the hook tugging gently in his chest at the sight of it.

Those first days, Wallace stayed in the kitchen, listening to Mei's terrible music, watching Hugo through the portholes. Hugo greeted most everyone by name, asking after their friends and families and jobs while he punched the ancient keys of the register. He laughed with them, patiently nodding along with even the most long-winded of customers. Every now and then, he'd glance back at the kitchen doors, seeing Wallace looking out. He'd give a small smile before turning back to greet the next person in line.

It was on his eighth day in the tea shop that Wallace came to a decision. He'd spent a good portion of the morning working up the nerve, unsure of why it was taking him so long. The people in the tea shop wouldn't be able to see him. They'd never know he was even there.

Mei was telling him about how she'd tried to make tea but somehow had ended up almost burning down the kitchen, and therefore was never allowed to touch even the smallest of tea leaves again. "Hugo was horrified," she said, leaning over to look at a batch of cookies in the oven. "You would've thought I'd stabbed him in the back. I think these are burning. Or maybe they're supposed to look like that."

"Uh-huh," Wallace said, distracted. "I'm going out."

"Right? I mean, it wasn't *that* bad. Just smoke damage, but . . . wait. What?"

"I'm going out," he said again. And then he went through the doors and out into the tea shop, not waiting for a response.

Part of him still expected everyone to stop midsentence and turn slowly to stare at him. While he'd been able to move a chair (only breaking two more, though one did leave gouges in the ceiling when Wallace accidentally kicked it as hard as he could), he still hadn't figured out how to change his clothes. His flip-flops snapped against the floor, and he felt oddly vulnerable in his old shirt and sweats.

But no one paid him any mind. They continued on as if he weren't there at all.

He didn't know if he was relieved or disappointed.

Before he could make up his mind, he felt eyes on him and looked over at the counter. A tiny older woman prattled on about how there could be no nuts in her muffin, it couldn't even *touch* a nut of any kind or her throat would constrict and she'd die a terrible death, *Hugo, I know I've told you this before, but it's* serious.

"Of course," Hugo said, but he wasn't looking at her.

He watched Wallace, that quiet smile on his face.

"Don't make this into a big deal," Wallace muttered.

"I would never," Hugo said.

"Thank you," the old woman said. "My tongue gets swollen and my face balloons up, and I look like quite the fright. No nuts, Hugo! No nuts."

And after that, Wallace spent most of his days out in front of the tea shop.

Nelson was thrilled. "You can overhear some of the strangest things," he told Wallace as they walked between the tables. "People aren't very careful with their secrets, even when they're out in public. And it's not eavesdropping, not really."

"Yeah, I don't think that's true. At all."

Nelson shrugged. "Gotta get our kicks from somewhere. So long as we don't interfere, Hugo doesn't seem to mind."

"I mind a lot," Hugo muttered as he walked by them, carrying a tea tray to a couple sitting near the window.

"He says that, but he doesn't mean it," Nelson whispered. "Oh, look. Mrs. Benson is here with her girlfriends. They talk about butts all the time. Let's go listen in."

They *did* talk about butts. Including Hugo's. They giggled amongst themselves as they watched him, batting their eyelashes when he stopped by their table to ask if they needed anything else.

"Oh, the things I'd let him do to me," one of the women breathed as Hugo reached up to the board above the counter to write down a new special of the day: lemon balm tea. "Such lovely hands."

One of the other women said, "My mother would've called them piano hands."

"I'd certainly let him play my piano," Mrs. Benson murmured, twisting her gaudy wedding ring. "And by piano, I mean—"

"Oh, please," a third woman said. "He's one of those gays. You're lacking a few important pieces that would ever make you find out what his fingers could do."

"Watch this," Nelson whispered, elbowing Wallace in the stomach. Then, he raised his voice to a shout. "Hey, Hugo! *Hugo*. They're talking about your fingers in an inappropriate way again and it's making Wallace blush!"

The chalk in Hugo's hand crumbled as he jerked back from the board, clattering teacups on the counter.

Nelson cackled as his grandson glared at the both of them, ignoring the way others in the tea shop were staring at him curiously. "Sorry," he said. "Slipped a little."

"I'm not *blushing*," Wallace growled at Nelson.

"A bit," Nelson said. "I didn't even know you could still do that. Huh. Should I say something else to see how far that blush can go?"

Wallace should have stayed in the kitchen.

ଓ

The woman came back. It wasn't every day, and sometimes it was in the morning, and other times it was late in the afternoon as the sun was beginning to sink in the sky.

It was always the same. She'd sit at the table by the window. Mei would come out front to work the register, and Hugo would carry a tea tray with a single cup and set it on the table. He'd sit across from her, hands folded on the table, and wait.

The woman—Nancy—barely acknowledged his presence, but Wallace could see the tightness around her eyes when Hugo pulled the chair out and sat down.

Some days, she seemed to be filled with rage, her eyes flashing, skin stretching over hollowed cheeks. Other days, her shoulders were slumped and she barely lifted her head. But she always looked exhausted, as if she too were a ghost and could no longer sleep. It caused a strange twist in Wallace's stomach, and he didn't know how Hugo could stand it.

He stayed away. Nelson did too.

Nelson watched as the woman stood, the chair scraping against the floor.

Nancy stopped when Hugo said, "I'll be here. Always. Whenever you're ready, I'll be here." It was the same thing he said every time she left. And every time, she stopped as if she was actually hearing him.

But she never spoke.

Most days, Hugo would sigh and collect the tea tray before carrying it back to the kitchen. He'd stay back there for a little while, Mei watching the doors with a worried look on her face. Eventually, he'd come back out, and it was as if it'd never happened at all.

But today was different.

Today, the door slammed shut, rattling in the frame.

Hugo stared out the window after her, watching as she walked down the road, shoulders hunched, pulling her coat tighter against the cool air.

He stood when she was out of sight, but he didn't pick up the tray. He went behind the counter, digging around in a drawer until he pulled out a set of keys. "I'll be back," he said to Mei.

She nodded. "Take your time. We'll hold down the fort. I'll let you know if something happens."

"Thanks, Mei."

Wallace was strangely alarmed when Hugo left the shop without so much as another word. He stood at the window and watched as Hugo went to the scooter. He lifted one leg up and over before settling down on the seat. The engine rumbled, and he pulled away, dust kicking up behind the tires.

Wallace wondered what it'd be like to ride with him, Hugo's back protecting him from the wind, hands gripping Hugo's waist. It was melancholic, this thought, though it was lost to a strange rising panic.

"He's leaving?" Wallace asked, voice high and scratchy. The cable stretched and stretched as Hugo disappeared around the corner. "I didn't think he could . . ." He swallowed thickly, barely resisting the urge to chase after Hugo. He expected the cable to snap. It didn't.

"He doesn't go far," Nelson said from his chair. "Never does. Just to clear his head. He'll be back, Wallace. He wouldn't leave."

"Because he can't," Wallace said dully.

"Because he doesn't want to," Nelson said. "There's a difference."

With nothing better to do, Wallace waited at the window. He ignored Mei when she turned the sign to CLOSED as the last customer left Charon's Crossing. He ignored Apollo who sniffed at his fingers. He ignored Nelson sitting in front of the fireplace.

It was dark by the time Hugo returned.

Wallace met him at the door.

"Hey," he said.

"Hi," Hugo said. "Sorry about that. I—"

Wallace shook his head. "You don't have to explain." Feeling strangely vulnerable, he looked down at his feet. "You're allowed to go wherever you want." He winced, because that wasn't exactly true, was it?

A beat of silence. Then Hugo said, "Come on. Let's go outside."

They didn't talk that night. Instead, they stood almost shoulder to shoulder. Every time Wallace opened his mouth to say something, *anything*, he stopped himself. It all felt . . . trivial. Unimportant. And so he said nothing at all, wondering why he felt the constant need to fill the quiet.

Instead, he watched Hugo out of the corner of his eye, hoping against hope that it was enough.

Before they went back inside for the night, Hugo said, "Thank you, Wallace. I needed that." He tapped his knuckles against the deck railing before heading inside.

Wallace stared after him, a lump in his throat.

CHAPTER 11

On the thirteenth day of Wallace Price's stay at Charon's Crossing, two things of note happened.

The first was unexpected.

The second was as well, though the chaos that followed could firmly be placed upon Mei and no one could convince Wallace otherwise, even if it was mostly his own fault.

Early morning. Alarm clocks would be going off soon, another day beginning at the tea shop. Hugo and Mei were asleep.

And Wallace wished he was anywhere but where he was.

"Would you stop *hitting* me?" he snarled, rubbing his arm where he'd been struck with the cane for what felt like the hundredth time.

"You're not doing it right," Nelson said. "You don't seem like a man who loves to fail, so why are you so good at it?"

Apollo woofed quietly as if in agreement, watching Wallace with a tilt to his head, ears perked.

"I'm going to make myself a cane and then hit *you* with it. See how you like it."

"Oh, I'm so scared," Nelson said. "Go ahead. Make a cane out of nothing. It'd certainly be better than standing here waiting for you to figure out how to change your clothes. At least *something* would happen that way." He sighed dramatically. "Such a waste. And here I was thinking you'd be different. I guess the chair was just a fluke."

Wallace bit back a sharp retort when the bottoms of his feet began to tingle. He looked down. The flip-flops were gone.

"Whoa," he whispered. "How did I . . . ?"

"You seem to react to anger more than anything else," Nelson said cheerfully. "Odd, that, but who am I to judge? I can hit you again if you'd think it'd help."

Wallace said, "No, don't. Just . . . hold on a minute." He frowned at his feet. He could feel the floor against his heels. There was a cookie crumb between his toes. He imagined his pair of Berluti Scritto's, the leather ones that cost more than many people made in a month.

They didn't appear.

Instead, he was suddenly wearing ballet slippers.

"Huh," Nelson said, also peering down at Wallace's feet. "That's certainly . . . different. Didn't know you were a dancer." He looked up, squinting at Wallace. "You've got the legs for it, I guess."

"What is it with you people and my *legs*?" Wallace snapped. Then, without waiting for an answer, "I don't know what happened."

"Right. Just like you don't know how the bikini happened. I believe you completely."

Wallace growled at him, but then the ballet slippers disappeared, replaced by a pair of old sneakers. And then slippers. And then flip-flops again. And then cowboy boots, complete with spurs. And then, much to his horror, brown sandals with blue socks.

He began to panic, hopping from one foot to the other as Apollo danced around him, yipping excitedly. "Oh my god, how do I make it stop? *Why isn't it stopping?*"

Nelson frowned at his feet just as the sandals and socks gave way to high heels better suited for an exotic dancer on a stage, making it rain. He shot up four inches, and then dropped back down as the heels were replaced by yellow rubber boots with ducks on the side. "Here," Nelson said. "Let me help."

He smacked Wallace's shins with his cane.

"*Ow*," Wallace cried, bending over to rub his legs. "You didn't have to—"

"Stopped it, didn't I?"

He had. Wallace now wore . . . soccer cleats? He'd never played soccer in his life, and therefore had never worn cleats before.

Granted, he'd never worn stiletto heels or a bikini, but still. It was an odd choice, though Wallace wasn't sure *choice* was the right word.

"This is ridiculous," Wallace muttered as Apollo sniffed the cleats before sneezing obnoxiously.

"It is," Nelson agreed. "Who knew you were so eclectic. Perhaps these are simply manifestations of what your heart truly desires."

"I doubt that immensely." Wallace took a tentative step, the cleats unfamiliar. He waited for them to disappear, to change into something different. They didn't. He breathed a sigh of relief as he closed his eyes. "I think it's over."

"Um," Nelson said. "About that."

That didn't sound good. Wallace opened his eyes again.

The sweats were gone.

The Rolling Stones shirt was gone.

Oh, the cleats were still there, so he could be thankful for small favors, but he now wore a spandex jumpsuit that left absolutely nothing to the imagination. To make matters worse, it wasn't an ordinary spandex jumpsuit; no, because Wallace's afterlife was apparently an utter farce, the jumpsuit was imprinted with the outline of a skeleton on it, like a Halloween costume, though it was the end of March.

It was then that Wallace realized everything was terrible. He said as much to Nelson, sounding forlorn as he pulled at the spandex, watching it stretch. He shooed Apollo away when the dog tried to grab onto the material and rip it off.

"It could be worse," Nelson said, eyeing him up and down in a way that Wallace was sure was illegal in at least fifteen states. "Though, I will say congratulations on your business downstairs. Size doesn't matter of course, but it doesn't seem like you have to worry about that."

"Thank you," Wallace said distractedly as Apollo tried to squeeze through his legs, tongue lolling, a goofy expression of joy on his face. Then, "Wait, what?"

By the time Hugo and Mei came down, Wallace was in a state

of panic, seeing as how he was now wearing only brightly colored briefs and pleather thigh-high boots. Nelson was slowly losing his composure as Wallace stumbled around, making promises to whoever would listen that he'd never complain about sweats and flip-flops again. He stopped when he saw the new arrivals staring blearily at him.

"I can explain," Wallace said, covering himself as best he could. Apollo apparently decided that wouldn't do, biting Wallace's hand gently and tugging.

"It's too early for this," Mei muttered, but that didn't seem to stop her from getting an eyeful as she made her way to the kitchen.

"You've had a busy night," Hugo said mildly.

Wallace glared at him. "This isn't what it looks like."

Hugo shrugged as Apollo circled his legs. "That's fair, seeing as how I don't know what it's supposed to look like in the first place."

"Puts my Easter suit to shame," Nelson said, wiping his eyes.

Wallace blanched when Hugo stepped closer to him, fingers twitching at his sides. He waited for Hugo to mock him, but it never came.

"You'll get the hang of it," he said. "It's not easy, or so I'm told, but I think you'll figure it out." He frowned as he cocked his head. He started to reach for Wallace but stopped himself. "Depending on how much longer you're here, that is." He smiled tightly.

There it was. This thing that Wallace had been studiously avoiding. Aside from the first few days he'd been here, there'd been no further discussion of crossings or doors or what lay beyond the half-life Wallace was living in the tea shop. He'd been grateful, though wary, sure that Hugo was going to push. He hadn't, and Wallace had almost convinced himself that he'd forgotten. Of course Hugo hadn't. It was his job. This wasn't permanent. It never was, and Wallace was foolish to think otherwise.

He didn't know what to say. He was scared of what Hugo would do next.

Hugo said, "Better get to work," his voice strangely gruff. He turned toward the kitchen, Apollo prancing around his feet as he followed Hugo through the doors.

"Oh dear," Nelson said.

"What?" Wallace asked, staring after Hugo, the hook in his chest feeling heavier than it'd ever been before.

Nelson hesitated before shaking his head. "I . . . it's nothing. Don't worry about it."

"Because saying not to worry about something always makes me *not* worry."

Nelson sighed. "Focus. Unless you're good with what you're wearing, that is."

And so they began again as the sun rose, cool light stretching along the floor and wall.

es

By the time the second event of note occurred on Wallace's thirteenth day in the tea shop, he'd managed to dress himself in jeans and an oversized sweater, the sleeves too long and flopping over his hands. The boots were gone. In their place was a pair of loafers. He'd considered trying for one of his suits, but had dismissed the idea after thinking about it for a long moment. The right suit was made to show power. If worn correctly, it could cut an intimidating figure, making a very specific point that the wearer was important and knew what they were talking about, even when they didn't. But here, now, what purpose would it serve?

Nothing, Wallace thought. Hence the jeans and sweater.

The din of the shop was loud around them—it wasn't quite noon, though the lunch crowd was already forming—but Wallace was too impressed with himself to notice. He couldn't believe that such a little thing as a new outfit would bring him such peace. "There," he said, having waited ten minutes to make sure it wasn't a fluke. "That's better. Right?"

"Depends on who you're asking," Nelson muttered.

Wallace squinted at him. "What?"

"Some people might have enjoyed what you were wearing more than others."

Wallace didn't know what to do with that. "Oh, uh. Thank you? I'm flattered, but I don't think you and I are—"

Nelson snorted. "Yeah, that sounds about right. Don't always see what's right in front of you, do you, counselor?"

Wallace blinked. "What's right in front of me?"

Nelson leaned back in his chair, tilting his head toward the ceiling. "What a deep and meaningful question. Do you ask yourself that often?"

"No," Wallace said.

Nelson laughed. "Refreshing. Frustrating, but refreshing. How are your talks with Hugo going?"

The conversational whiplash threw Wallace off-balance, causing him to wonder if Nelson had picked up on one of his professional tricks. "They're . . . going." That might have been an understatement. The last few nights, they'd been speaking of nothing in particular. Last night, they'd argued for almost an hour over how cheating at Scrabble was acceptable in certain circumstances, especially when playing against a polyglot. Wallace couldn't be sure *how* their conversation had ended up there, but he was sure that Hugo was in the wrong. It was *always* acceptable to cheat at Scrabble against a polyglot.

"Are they helping?"

"I'm not sure," Wallace admitted. "I don't know what I'm supposed to be doing."

Nelson didn't seem surprised. "You'll know when the time is right."

"Cryptic bastard," Wallace muttered. "What do you think I'm—"

He never got the chance to finish.

Something tickled at the back of his mind.

He frowned, raising his head to look around.

Everything looked as it always did. People sat at the tables, their hands wrapped around steaming mugs of tea and coffee. They were laughing and talking, the sounds echoing flatly around the shop.

A small line had formed at the counter, and Hugo was putting pastries into a paper bag for a young man in a mechanic's uniform, the tips of his fingers stained with oil. Wallace could hear the radio through the kitchen doors. He caught a glimpse of Mei through the porthole windows, moving back and forth between the counters.

"What is it?" Nelson asked.

"I don't . . . know. Do you feel that?"

Nelson leaned forward. "Feel what?"

Wallace wasn't sure. "It's like . . ." He looked toward the front door. "Something's coming."

The front door opened.

Two men walked in. They wore black suits, their shoes polished. One was squat, as if he'd reached an invisible ceiling during his formative years and expanded outward rather than upward. His forehead had a sheen of sweat on it, his eyes beady and darting around the shop.

The other man couldn't have been more different. Though he was dressed similarly, he was as thin as a whisper and almost as tall as Wallace. His suit hung loosely on his frame. He appeared to be made of nothing but skin and bones. He carried an old briefcase in his hand, the sides worn and chipped.

The men moved to either side of the doorway, standing stock still.

The sounds of the tea shop at midday stopped as everyone turned to look at the new arrivals.

"Oh no," Nelson muttered. "Not again. Mei isn't going to like this."

Before Wallace could ask, a third person appeared in the doorway. She was a strange vision. She looked young, possibly around Hugo's age, or even younger. She was tiny, the top of her head barely reaching the squat man's shoulders. She moved with confidence, her eyes bright, her frizzy hair unnaturally red under an old-fashioned fedora with a crow's feather sticking up from the band. The rest of her outfit had probably been *en vogue* at the turn of the nineteenth century. She wore ankle boots with thick laces over black stockings. Her dress was calf-length, and looked heavy, the fabric black and red. It was cinched tightly at the waist and cut low on her chest, her bosom pale and generous. Her white gloves matched the pashmina shawl around her shoulders.

Everyone stared at her.

She ignored them. She raised one hand to the other and began to pluck at the glove one finger at a time. "Yes," she said, voice deeper than Wallace expected. She sounded as if she'd smoked at least two packs a day since she'd learned to walk. "Today feels . . . different."

"I agree," Squat Man said.

"Absolutely," Thin Man said.

She pulled off the glove from her left hand before holding the hand out in front of her, palm facing toward the ceiling. Her fingers wiggled. "Quite different. I believe we'll find what we seek today." She lowered her hand as she moved toward the counter, the floorboards creaking with every step she took.

The customers in the shop began to whisper as the men fell in step behind her. They passed Wallace and Nelson by without so much as a glance in their direction. Whoever this woman was, she wasn't the Manager that Wallace had been fearing. Unless she was ignoring him on purpose to gauge his reaction. Wallace kept his expression neutral, though his skin crawled.

Hugo, for his part, didn't look as perturbed as Wallace felt. If anything, he was resigned. The customers at the counter scattered as the woman approached. "Back so soon?" Hugo asked, voice even.

"Hugo," the woman said in greeting. "I expect you won't make things difficult for me, yes?"

Hugo shrugged. "You know you're always welcome, Ms. Tripplethorne. Charon's Crossing is open for all."

"Oh," she breathed. "Aren't you lovely, you silly flirt. Open for *all*, you say? What could you possibly mean by that?"

"You know what I mean."

She leaned forward. Wallace was reminded of a nature documentary he'd seen once about the mating habits of birds of paradise, their plumage on full display. She was obviously aware of her more . . . substantial features. "I do. And you know what *I* mean, sweet man. Don't think you have me fooled. The things I have seen across the world would be enough to strike fear into the very heart of you." She traced her finger on the back of Hugo's hand on the counter.

"I have no doubt," Hugo said. "So long as you don't bother my other customers, and stay out of—"

"Oh *hell* no," a voice growled. The doors behind the counter swung open, smacking against the wall and rattling the jars filled with tea as Mei stalked out of the kitchen, a small towel in her hands.

"—Mei's way, we'll be fine," Hugo finished.

"Mei," the woman said with no small amount of scorn.

"Desdemona," Mei snarled.

"Still back in the kitchen, I see. Good for you."

Hugo managed to hold Mei back before she launched herself over the counter.

The woman—Desdemona Tripplethorne, a mouthful if there ever was one—remained unaffected. She slapped her gloves against her hand as she looked upon Mei dismissively. "You should work on those anger issues, petal. They're unbecoming of a lady, even one such as yourself. Hugo, I'll take my tea at my usual table. Make it quick. The spirits are restless here today, and I won't miss my opportunity."

Mei wasn't having it. "You can take the tea and shove it up your—" But whatever threat she wanted to make was left to the imagination as Hugo pulled her back into the kitchen.

Desdemona turned and eyed everyone in the shop who was staring at her. Her lip curled in a close approximation of a sneer. "Continue on," she said. "These are matters far beyond your earthly understanding. Tut-tut."

Everyone turned away almost immediately, the whispers reaching a fever pitch.

Nelson grabbed Wallace by the hand, jerking him toward the kitchen. He looked back before they passed through the doors to see the woman and the two men heading toward a table near the far wall under the framed poster of the pyramids. She rubbed her finger along the tabletop before shaking her head.

"—and if you'll let me, I'll just put a *little* poison in her tea," Mei was saying to Hugo as they entered the kitchen. Apollo sat next to her, ear flopped over as he looked between the two of them. "Not enough to kill her, but still enough for it to be considered a felony for which I'll absolutely accept jail time. It's a win-win situation."

Hugo looked horrified. "You can't ruin tea like that. Every cup is special and putting poison in it would ruin the flavor."

"Not if it's tasteless," Mei countered. "I'm pretty sure I read that arsenic doesn't have a taste." She paused. "Not that I know where to get arsenic right this second. Dammit. I should've looked into that after last time."

"We don't murder people," Hugo said, and it didn't appear that this was the first time he'd said it to her.

"Maim, then."

"We don't do that either," Hugo said.

She crossed her arms and pouted. "Nothing's stopping us. You told me that we should always try to achieve our dreams."

"I didn't have murder in mind when I told you that," Hugo said dryly.

"That's because you think too small. Go big or go home." She glanced at Wallace. "Tell him. You're on my side, right? And you know the law better than any of us here. What does it say about killing someone who deserves it?"

"It's illegal," Wallace said.

"But not, like, *completely* illegal, right? Justifiable homicide is a thing. I think."

"I mean, there's always a plea of not guilty by reason of insanity, but that's difficult to pull off—"

Mei nodded furiously. "That's it. That'll be my defense. I'm so insane that I didn't know what I was doing when I put arsenic in her tea."

Wallace shrugged. "It's not like I can testify against you showing premeditation."

"Not helping," Hugo said.

Probably not, but it wasn't like he thought Mei would *actually* murder someone. Or so he hoped. "What's wrong with that woman? Who is she? What did she do besides have a terrible name?"

"She calls herself a medium," Mei spat. "A psychic. *And* she has a crush on Hugo."

Hugo sighed. "She does not."

"Right," Nelson said. "Because most people put their boobs up on the counter like she does. Perfectly natural."

"She's harmless," Hugo said, like he was trying to convince Wallace. "She comes in here every few months and tries to run a séance. But nothing ever happens and so she leaves. It's never for very long, and it doesn't hurt anyone."

"Are you *hearing* yourself?" Mei exclaimed.

Wallace was still stuck on the word *crush*. It made him bristle more than he expected. "I thought you were gay."

Hugo blinked. "I . . . am?"

"Then why does she flirt with you?"

"I . . . don't know?"

"Because she's awful," Mei said. "Literally the worst person in existence." She began to pace. "She gives people like me a bad name. She cons others out of money, telling them she'll help them communicate with their loved ones. It's messed up. All she does is give them false hope, telling them what they think they want to hear. She has no idea what I had to go through, and even if she *did*, I doubt it would stop her. She waltzes in here like she owns the place and makes a mockery of everything we do."

Hugo sighed. "We can't just kick her out, Mei."

"We *can*," Mei retorted. "It's very easy. Watch, I'll do it right now."

He stopped her before she could storm through the doors.

For a moment, Wallace thought it was all for show. That Mei was being overly dramatic, playing a part. But there was a twist to her mouth he'd never seen before, and a sheen to her eyes that hadn't been there a moment ago. She gnawed on her bottom lip as she blinked rapidly. He remembered what she'd told him about what it'd been like for her when she was younger, when no one would listen to her when she tried to tell them something was wrong.

"What does she do?" he asked.

"Ouija board," Nelson said. "She said she found it in an antique store, and that it once belonged to Satanists in the 1800s. There's a sticker on the bottom that says it was made by Hasbro in 2004."

"Because she's full of shit," Mei snapped.

"Pretty much," Nelson said. "She also records everything and puts it online. Mei looked it up once. She has a YouTube channel called Desdemona Tripplethorne's Sexy Seances." He made a face. "Not exactly quality content, if you ask me, but what do I know."

"But . . ." Wallace hesitated. Then, "If she tells people what they want to hear, what does it hurt?"

Mei's eyes flashed. "Because she's lying to them. Even if it makes them feel better, she's still lying. She doesn't know anything about what we do, or what comes after. Would you want to be lied to?"

No, he didn't think he would. But he could also see it from the other side, and if people wanted to give her money just to have reassurance, then wasn't it their business? "She charges for it?"

Mei nodded. Hugo wrapped an arm around her shoulder but she shrugged him off. "After what she did to Nancy, I really thought you'd see right through her. But here we are."

Hugo deflated. "I . . ." He scrubbed a hand over his face. "It was her choice, Mei."

"What did she do to Nancy?" Wallace asked.

Everyone stared at him, the silence deafening. Wallace wondered what fresh hell he'd stepped in now.

"She found Nancy," Mei finally said. "Or Nancy found her. I don't know which, but it doesn't matter. What matters is that Desdemona filled Nancy's head with all manner of crap about spirits and her ability to contact them. She gave Nancy false hope, and it was the cruelest thing she could have done. Nancy *believed* her when Desdemona said she could help. And then she came here looking more alive than she ever had since she first arrived. Nothing happened. Nancy was devastated, but Desdemona still collected her fee." By the time she finished, Mei's cheeks were splotchy, spittle on her lip.

Before Wallace could ask what had happened to Nancy for her to even talk to someone like Desdemona, Hugo said, "That's not . . . I'm not trying to—look, Mei. I get what you're saying. But it was Nancy's choice. She's reaching for anything she can to—"

It was then that Wallace Price came to a decision. He told himself it was because he couldn't stand to see the look on Mei's face, and that it certainly had nothing to do with the fact that Hugo was being flirted with.

It was time to take matters into his own hands.

He turned and walked through the doors, ignoring the others calling after him.

Desdemona Tripplethorne had taken a seat at a table. Squat Man and Thin Man stood next to her. The briefcase had been opened. There were candles lit on the table, the scent obnoxious and cloying, like someone had eaten a bushel of apples and then vomited them up and covered the remains in cinnamon. Most of the other customers had cleared out, though a few were still watching her warily.

The Ouija board had been set up on the table atop a black cloth that hadn't been there before. The theatricality of it all made Wallace grimace. A wooden planchette sat on the board, though Desdemona wasn't touching it. Next to the Ouija board lay a feather quill pen, resting on top of loose sheets of paper.

Desdemona sat in her chair ramrod straight, staring into a camera that had been set up next to the table on a tripod. A tiny red light blinked on the top. Without being told, Squat Man stepped forward, taking the shawl off her shoulders and folding it carefully. Thin Man pulled a vial of liquid from the briefcase along with a glass dropper. He dipped it into the vial and squeezed the top of the dropper, drawing up liquid. He held it over Desdemona's hands, two drops on each, before setting it aside. He rubbed the drops into the backs of her hands. It smelled of lavender.

"Yes," she breathed as Thin Man finished. "I feel it. There's someone here. A presence. Get the spirit box. Quickly." She smiled into the camera. "As my followers know, the Ouija board is my preferred choice of communication, but I'd like to try something new, if the spirits would allow for it." She trailed a finger along the feather quill. "Automatic writing. If the spirits are willing, I give full permission for them to take control of my hands and write whatever message they deem fit. Isn't this exciting?"

Squat Man reached into the briefcase and pulled out a device unlike anything Wallace had ever seen. It was the size and shape of a remote, though the comparison ended there. Out the top came stiff wires, each ending in a small bulb. Squat Man turned a switch on the side, and the device burst to life, lights flashing green. It squealed, a high-pitched mess filled with static. Squat Man looked down at it with wide eyes. He tapped it against his palm. The squeal died down, and the lights faded.

"Strange," he mumbled. "Never had it do that before."

"You're *ruining* the ambiance," Desdemona hissed out of the side of her mouth, never looking away from the camera. "Did you charge the damned thing?"

Squat Man wiped the sweat from his forehead. "I made sure of it. Battery's full." He swung it back and forth around him. Wallace stepped out of the way. It barely blipped when it came within inches of him.

"What are you doing?" a voice whispered beside him. "Whatever it is, count me in, especially if it causes trouble."

He looked over to see Nelson grinning obnoxiously. Wallace couldn't help but smile back. "I'm gonna mess with her."

"Ooh," Nelson said. "I approve."

Thin Man frowned. "Did you hear something?"

"Only the sound of your voice, which I *despise*," Desdemona said. She glared at the few remaining customers until they too got up and left. "Less talking, more focusing."

Thin Man snapped his mouth closed as Squat Man stood on a chair, raising the device toward the ceiling.

"Spirits!" Desdemona said shrilly. "I command that you speak with me! I know you're here." She placed her hands on the planchette. "This board will allow us to communicate with each other. Do you understand? There is nothing to fear. I only wish to speak with you. I'll not cause you harm. If you prefer the pen and paper, make your intentions known. Enter me. Allow me to be your voice."

Nothing happened.

Desdemona frowned. "Take your time."

Nothing.

"All the time you—would you stop *hovering*! You're ruining it!"

Thin Man stood upright quickly and stepped away.

"Weird," Squat Man muttered as he stopped near the fireplace. The device squealed again as he swung it over Nelson's chair. "It's as if something's here. Or was. Or might be. Or never was at all."

"Of course there was," Desdemona said. "If you had studied the file I'd given you, you would know that Hugo's grandfather lived here before he died. It's most likely his spirit I'm feeling today. Or perhaps this place once belonged to a serial killer, and his victims are reaching out from beyond the grave after being horribly mutilated and then murdered." She looked into the camera, wiggling her shoulders, chest rising and falling. Wallace didn't know why he hadn't noticed how violently red her lipstick was. "Just like when we were at the Herring House last year. Those poor, poor souls."

"Huh," Nelson said. "Maybe she can feel something after all."

"Get back in the kitchen," Hugo muttered as he walked by them, carrying a tray of tea. Wallace glanced back toward the kitchen to see Mei glaring daggers at them through the portholes.

"What was that?" Desdemona asked. "Did you say something, Hugo?" She looked into the camera again. "Followers of my channel will remember Hugo from our last visit. I know he's very popular with some of you." She giggled as Hugo set down the tray next to the Ouija board. Wallace wanted to gouge out her eyes. "A dear man, he is." She trailed a finger along Hugo's arm before he could pull away. "Would you like to stay and take part in what is surely to be the paranormal event of the decade? You could sit right by me. I wouldn't mind. We could even share a chair, if you'd like."

Hugo shook his head. "Not this time. Is there anything else I can get you, Ms. Tripplethorne?"

"Oh, there is," she said. "But children watch my videos, and I don't want to corrupt their precious minds."

"Oh my god," Wallace said. "How is she a *person*?"

Hugo coughed roughly. "That's . . . what it is." He stepped back. "If there's nothing else I can get for you, I'll get out of your way. In fact, if there was anyone else left in the room aside from you three, I'd tell them the same thing. Get out of the way."

Wallace snorted. "Oh, yeah. I'll do just that. Watch. Hugo. Are you watching? Look how much I'm getting out of the way."

Hugo glanced at him.

Wallace flipped him off.

Nelson cackled before doing the same.

Hugo wasn't pleased. He went back around the counter, took a rag out, and began to wipe it down while pointedly staring at Wallace and Nelson. When Desdemona and her lackies were distracted, he pointed two fingers at his eyes and then turned them toward Wallace. *Stop*, he mouthed.

"What was that?" Wallace said, raising his voice. "I can't hear you!"

Hugo sighed the weary sigh of the put-upon and furiously wiped the counter while mumbling under his breath. It probably didn't help that Mei was still at the window, but now had a large butcher's knife that she pretended to draw across her neck, eyes rolling back, tongue hanging out of her mouth.

As Squat Man continued his trek around the tea shop (agreeing rather quickly that he shouldn't step behind the counter when Hugo glared at him), Thin Man pulled out another pad of paper and a fountain pen from the briefcase. He stood next to Desdemona, ready to take notes of some kind. He wasn't aware of Apollo next to him, the dog lifting his leg, pissing on Thin Man's shoes. Wallace was momentarily distracted by the stream of urine that Thin Man didn't seem to be aware of, but then Desdemona put her hands back on the planchette and cleared her throat.

"Spirits!" she said again. "I am but your vessel. Speak through me and tell me the secrets of the dead. Be not afraid, for I am here only to help you." She wiggled her shoulders, fingers flexing on the planchette.

Wallace snorted. He rolled his neck side to side and cracked his knuckles. "Okay. Let's give her the ghostly experience she so desperately wants."

"Ooh," Desdemona breathed. "I can feel it." She sucked her bottom lip between her teeth. "It's warm and tingly. Like a caress against my skin. Ooh. *Ooh.*"

Wallace took a deep breath, shaking his hands before settling them on the opposite side of the planchette, ignoring the feather quill. At first, his fingers went through it, and he frowned. "Unexpect," he whispered. "Unexpect."

The planchette grew solid against his hands. He jerked in surprise, knocking the planchette slightly to the side.

Desdemona gasped, pulling her hands back quickly. "Did . . . did you see that?"

Thin Man nodded, eyes wide. "What happened?"

"I don't know." She leaned forward, face inches from the Ouija board. She then seemed to remember she was being recorded as she looked back up at the camera and said, "It begins. The spirits have chosen to speak." She put her hands back on the planchette. "O, dearly departed. Use me. Use me as hard as you can. Deliver unto me your message and I will reveal it to the world."

Wallace was not a fan of Desdemona Tripplethorne. He pushed against the planchette, trying to move it, but Desdemona had a firm grip on it. "It's moving," she muttered out of the corner of her mouth. "Get ready. This is going to get us four million views and a TV deal, I swear to god."

Thin Man nodded and scribbled on the pad of paper.

"What should we say?" Wallace asked Nelson.

Nelson's face scrunched up before smoothing out, a wicked

gleam in his eyes. "Something terrifying. Skip the yes or no on the board. That's boring. Pretend you're a demon, and you want to harvest her soul as well as her larynx."

"*No* harvesting souls," Hugo said loudly.

Desdemona, Thin Man, and Squat Man all turned to stare at him. "What was that?" Desdemona asked.

Hugo blanched. "I said . . . I'm thinking about offering burrito bowls?"

"Not in *my* tea shop you won't!" Mei shouted from the kitchen. She'd somehow found a second knife, and it was bigger than the first one. She looked quite the fright through the porthole. Wallace was impressed.

"She's right," Desdemona said to Hugo. "That wouldn't fit with your menu. Honestly, Hugo, know your consumer base." She turned back to the board, the tips of her fingers firmly pressed against the planchette. "Spirits! Fill me with your ghostly ectoplasm! Leave nothing to chance. Let me be your incredibly sensual voice. Tell me your secrets. *Oooh.*"

"You got it, lady," Wallace said, and began to move the planchette. It took more concentration than he expected. Clothes were one thing; moving chairs was another. This was *small*, and yet it was more difficult than he thought it'd be. He grunted and if he was still capable of sweating, he was sure it'd be dripping down his forehead. Desdemona gasped as the planchette moved from side to side before it started spinning in slow circles.

"You actually have to pause on the individual letters," Nelson said.

"I'm *trying*," Wallace snapped. "It's harder than it looks." He furrowed his brow in concentration, tongue sticking out between his teeth. He moved slower, and it took only a few more moments before he got the hang of it.

"H," Desdemona whispered.

"H," Thin Man repeated, writing it down on the pad.

"I."

"I."

Wallace stopped.

Desdemona frowned. "That's . . . that's it?" She looked up at Thin Man. "What did it say?"

Thin Man paled as he turned the pad toward her, hands trembling.

Desdemona squinted at it before rearing back. "Hi. It says *hi*. Oh my god. It's real. It's really real." She coughed roughly. "I mean, of *course* it's real. I knew that. Obviously." She grinned at the camera, though more tightly than before. "The spirits are talking to us." She cleared her throat once more. "Hello, spirits. I have received your message. Who are you? What is it you want? Did you die horribly, perhaps by being bludgeoned to death with a hammer in a crime of passion, and have unfinished business that only I, Desdemona Tripplethorne of Desdemona Tripplethorne's Sexy Seances (trademark pending), can help you with? Who is your murderer? Is it someone in this room?"

"I'll straight up murder *you*!" Mei shouted from the kitchen.

"Yes," Desdomona said after Wallace moved the planchette over the same word on the board. "You *were* murdered. I knew it! Tell me, O great spirit. Tell me who murdered you. I will seek justice on your behalf and when I have my own TV deal in place, I promise I'll never forget you. Give me a *name*."

The planchette moved again.

"D," she whispered. "E. S. D. E. M. O. N—"

Thin Man let out a strangled noise. "That spells *demon*."

"Really scraping the bottom of the barrel with these two," Nelson said, eying Squat Man as he stood on a chair, holding his device toward the ceiling.

"A," Desdemona said as the planchette stopped moving. "That's not demon. It has too many letters. Did you get all of it?"

Thin Man nodded slowly.

"Well?" she demanded. "What does it say."

He showed her the pad of paper again.

In blocky letters, the page read: DESDEMONA.

She squinted at it, and then the Ouija board, and then back at the pad of paper as Thin Man turned and pointed the word toward the camera. "That's my name." The blood drained from her face as she pulled her hands away from the planchette. "Are you . . . are you saying that *I* murdered you?" She laughed uncomfortably. "That's impossible. I've never murdered anyone before."

Thin Man and Desdemona froze as the planchette began to move without her touching it. She rattled off the letters Wallace paused upon, and Thin Man wrote them down.

"You totally killed me," Desdemona read off the paper before blinking. "What? I did *not*. Who are you? Is this some kind of joke?" She bent over the underside of the table before sitting back up. "No magnets. Hugo. *Hugo.* Are you doing this? I don't like to be tricked."

"You're messing with forces you can't even begin to comprehend," Hugo said solemnly.

The planchette moved again.

"Ha, ha," Thin Man read aloud as he wrote the letters down. "You suck."

"What are you, ten?" Nelson asked, though he seemed to be fighting a smile. "You need to be scarier. Tell her you're Satan, and you're going to eat her liver."

"This is Satan," Thin Man said as the planchette moved. "I'm going to eat your diver."

"Liver," Nelson said. "*Liver.*"

"I'm *trying*," Wallace said through gritted teeth. "It's slippery!"

"My diver?" Desdemona asked, sounding confused. "I've never been diving in my life."

The planchette moved again. "Sorry," Thin Man read as he wrote down the new message. "Stupid autocorrect. I meant liver."

Hugo put his face in his hands and groaned.

Desdemona stood abruptly, chair scraping against the floor. She looked around wildly. Thin Man was clutching the pad of paper against his chest, and Squat Man had joined them, holding the device out over the Ouija board. It squealed again, louder than it'd been before, the light bulbs across the top bright.

"We are meddling," Desdemona breathed, "in things we don't understand." She put the back of her hand against her forehead as her bosom heaved, and she looked into the camera. "You've seen it here first. Satan is here, and he wants to eat my liver. But I will *not* be intimidated." She dropped her hand. "Be you Satan or some other demon, you are not welcome here! This is a place of peace and overpriced confectionaries."

"Hey!" Hugo snapped.

Wallace moved the planchette faster. "You're the one who's not welcome here," he said under his breath, even as Thin Man said the same thing aloud. "Leave this place. Never return." He paused, considering. Then, "Also, be nicer to Mei or I'll eat your brain too."

"Look," Squat Man said, pointing a trembling finger.

Wallace turned his head to see Nelson standing near the sconces on the wall. He pressed his hands against them, and the light bulbs inside began to flicker. Wallace grinned when Nelson winked at him. The light bulbs rattled.

"Leave," Wallace said, moving the planchette faster. "Leave. Leave. Leave." When he finished, he pushed as hard as he could, knocking the planchette across the room. It landed in the fireplace and began to burn. The Ouija board flew off the table, clattering to the floor.

"I did *not* sign up for this shit," Squat Man said, backing away slowly. He yelped when he bumped into a chair, whirling around.

Nelson left the sconces and went to the camera. He studied it closely before nodding to himself. "This looks expensive." And then he knocked it over. It crashed to the ground, the lens cracking. "Oops."

Hugo sighed once again as Wallace said, "Yes, Nelson. *Yes.*"

"We need to get out of here," Thin Man whispered feverishly. He started for the door, but Wallace kicked a chair toward him. It slid across the floor, banging into Thin Man's shins. He screamed and almost fell down, the pad of paper hitting the ground.

"I won't have this!" Desdemona exclaimed. "We won't be intim-idated by the likes of you! I am Desdemona Tripplethorne. I have fifty thousand followers, and I *command* you to—"

But whatever Desdemona would have demanded was lost when Mei burst through the doors, both knives raised above her head, screaming, "I am Satan! I am Satan!"

The last Wallace saw of Desdemona, Thin Man, and Squat Man was their backs as they fled Charon's Crossing Tea and Treats. Thin Man and Squat Man tried to go through the door at the same time and became stuck until Desdemona crashed into them, knocking them onto the front porch. They cried out when she stepped on their backs and arms to get over them, her dress hiked up almost obscenely. She jumped off the steps and tore down the road without so much as a glance back at the shop, Thin Man and Squat Man managing to pick themselves up, chasing after her.

Silence fell in Charon's Crossing.

But it didn't last for long.

Nelson began to chuckle, softly at first, then louder and louder. Mei did the same, a hiccupping cough that turned into a wet snort before she cackled as she lowered her knives.

And then another sound filled the nooks and crannies of the tea shop, one never heard before. This sound caused Nelson and Mei to fall silent, Hugo to walk around the counter slowly.

Wallace was laughing. He was laughing as hard as he ever had, one arm wrapped around his stomach, his free hand slapping his knee. "Did you *see* that?" he cried. "Did you see the looks on their faces? Oh my god, that was *incredible*."

And still he laughed. Something loosened in his chest, something he hadn't even been aware had been knotted up and tangled. He felt lighter, somehow. Freer. His shoulders shook as he bent over, gasping for air he didn't need. Even as laughter dissolved into soft chuckles, that lightness didn't fade. If anything, it burned brighter, and the hook, that damnable thing that never ceased to be, finally didn't feel like a shackle, trapping him in place. He thought he had, perhaps for one of the first times in his life, done something good without expecting anything in return. How could he have never considered that before?

He wiped his eyes as he stood upright.

Nelson had a look of awe on his face. It matched his grandson's.

It was Mei who spoke first. "I'm going to hug the crap out of you."

That stunned him, especially when he remembered what Mei had told him about physical affection. "Only you could make that sound like a threat."

She set the knives on the closest table before tapping her fingers against her palm. There was a tiny pulse in the air around them, and then Mei was on him. He almost fell over as she wrapped her arms around his back, holding on tightly. He was stunned into inaction, but only for a moment. It was fragile, this, and Wallace couldn't remember the last time someone had hugged him. He pulled his arms up carefully, hands going to the small of Mei's back.

"Squeeze harder," she said into his neck. "I'm not going to break."

His eyes burned. He didn't know why. But he did as she asked. He squeezed as hard as he could.

When he opened his eyes, he found Hugo watching him, a strange expression on his face. They looked at each other for a long time.

CHAPTER 12

That night, Wallace followed the cable to find Hugo out back, leaning against the deck railing. It was cloudy, the stars hidden away. He paused in the doorway, unsure of his welcome. An odd sense of guilt washed through him, though he didn't allow it to grow any larger. It was worth it, seeing the smile on Mei's face.

Before he could turn back around and go inside, Hugo said, "Hello."

Wallace scratched the back of his neck. "Hello, Hugo."

"All right?"

"I think so. Do you . . . want to be left alone? I don't want to intrude or anything."

Hugo shook his head without turning around. "No, it's okay. I don't mind."

Wallace went to the railing, keeping a bit of distance between Hugo and himself. He worried Hugo was angry with him, though he didn't think Hugo should be upset over something so trivial as using a Ouija board to scare away a grifter. Still, it wasn't his place to tell Hugo what he could or could not feel, especially since this was his shop. His home.

Hugo said, "You're thinking about apologizing, aren't you?"

Wallace sighed. "That obvious, huh?"

"A little. Don't."

"Don't apologize?"

Hugo nodded, glancing at him before looking out at the tea garden. "You did the right thing."

"I told a woman I was Satan and was going to cannibalize her diver." He grimaced. "That's not something I ever thought I'd say out loud."

"First time for everything," Hugo said. "Can I ask you a question?"

"Okay."

"Why did you do it?"

Wallace frowned as he crossed his arms. "Mess with them like that?"

"Yes."

"Because I could."

"That's it?"

Well, no. But that he hadn't liked the way Desdemona had flirted with him wasn't something Wallace would *ever* admit. It made him sound ridiculous, even if there'd been a kernel of truth to it. Nothing could be done about it, and Wallace wasn't about to say something that made it sound like he had a crush of some sort. The very idea caused a wave of embarrassment to wash over him, and he felt his face grow warm. It was stupid, really. Nothing would come of it. He was dead. Hugo was not.

So he said the first thing he latched onto that didn't make him sound like he was about to swoon. "Mei." And with that one word, he knew it was the truth, much to his consternation.

"What about her?"

Wallace sighed. "I . . . She was upset. I didn't like the way Desdemona talked down to her. Like Mei was beneath her. No one should be made to feel that way." And because he was still Wallace, he added, "I mean, Mei did want to commit a felony, sure, but she's all right, I guess."

"That's quite a ringing endorsement."

"You know what I mean."

He was surprised when Hugo said, "I think I do. You saw something happening to someone you consider a friend and felt the need to intervene."

"I wouldn't call her a *friend—*"

"Wallace."

He groaned. "Fine. Whatever. We're friends." It wasn't as hard to say out loud as he thought it would be. He wondered if he'd always made things so difficult for himself. "Why did you let it happen?"

Hugo looked taken aback. "What do you mean?"

"This isn't the first time she's come here. Desdemona."

"No," Hugo said slowly. "It's not."

"And you know how Mei doesn't like her. Especially when she involved Nancy."

"Yeah."

"Then why didn't you put a stop to it?" He was careful not to put any censure in his voice. He wasn't *angry*, exactly—not at Hugo— but he didn't understand. He honestly expected more. He didn't know when that had started, but it was there all the same. "Mei's your friend too. Didn't you see how much it upset her?"

"Not as much as I should have," Hugo said. He stared off into the darkness of the woods around them.

"You know her history," Wallace said, unsure of why he was pushing this. All he knew was that it felt important. "What happened to her. Before."

"She told you."

"She did. I wouldn't wish that on anyone. I can't even imagine what it'd be like to have no one listen to you when you're . . ." He stopped himself, remembering how he'd screamed for someone to hear him after he collapsed in his office. How he'd tried to get someone, *anyone* to see him. He'd felt invisible. "It's not right."

"No," Hugo said. "I don't suppose it is." His jaw tightened. "And for what it's worth, I've apologized to Mei. I shouldn't have let it get as far as it did." He shook his head. "I think part of me wanted to see what you would do, even after I'd told you no."

"Why?"

"To see what you were capable of," Hugo said quietly. "You're not alive, Wallace. But you still exist. I don't think you realized that until today."

He could almost believe that, coming from Hugo. "Still shouldn't have done that to her. Or let Desdemona interfere with Nancy like she did."

"Yeah. I can see that now. I'm not perfect. I never claimed to be. I still make mistakes like everyone else, even though I try my best. Being a ferryman doesn't absolve me of being human. If anything, it only makes things harder. If I make a mistake, people can get hurt. All I can do is promise to do better and not let something like that happen again." He smiled ruefully. "Not that I think Desdemona will come back. At least not for a long time to come. You saw to that."

"Damn right," Wallace said, puffing out his chest. "Gave 'em the ol' what for."

"You really need to stop hanging out with Grandad."

"Eh. He's all right. Don't tell him I said that, though. He'd never let me hear the end of it." Wallace reached out to touch Hugo's hand until he remembered he couldn't. He pulled his arm away quickly. Hugo, for his part, didn't react. Wallace was thankful for that, even as he remembered the way it'd felt to have Mei hugging him as hard as she could. He didn't know when he'd become so desperate for contact.

He struggled with something to say, something to distract them both. "I made mistakes too. Before." He paused. "No, that's not quite right. I *still* make mistakes."

"Why?" Hugo asked.

Why, indeed. "To err is human, I guess. I wasn't like you, though. I didn't let it affect me. I should have, but I just . . . I don't know. I always blamed others and told myself to learn from *their* mistakes, and not necessarily my own."

"What do you think that means?"

It was a hard truth to face, and one he still wasn't sure he was ready for. "I don't know if I was a good person." He let the words float between them for a moment, bitter though they were.

"What makes a good person?" Hugo asked. "Actions? Motivations? Selflessness?"

"Maybe all of it," Wallace said. "Or maybe none of it. You said you don't know what's on the other side of that door, even though you see the looks on their faces when they cross. How do you know there's no Heaven or Hell? What if I walk through that door, and I'm judged for every wrong I've done and it outweighs all the rest? Would I deserve to be in the same place as someone who devoted their life to . . . whatever? Like, I don't know. A nun, or something."

"A nun," Hugo repeated, struggling against laughter. "You're comparing yourself to a nun."

"Shut up," Wallace grumbled. "You know what I mean."

"I do," he said, voice light and teasing. "Kinda would give almost anything to see you in a nun's habit, though."

Wallace sighed. "Pretty sure that's blasphemous."

Hugo snorted before sobering. He seemed to be mulling something over in his mind. Wallace waited, not wanting to push. Finally, Hugo said, "Can I tell you something?"

"Yeah. Of course. Anything."

"It's not always like this," Hugo said, voice hushed. "I could tell you I'm firm in my beliefs, but that wouldn't be entirely true. It's . . . like this place. The tea shop. It's sturdy, the foundation's set, but I don't think it'd take much to see it all come toppling down. A tremor. An earthquake. The walls would crumble, the floor would crack, and all that would be left is rubble and dust."

"You've had an earthquake," Wallace said.

"I have. Two, in fact."

He didn't want to know. He wanted to change the subject, to talk about anything else so Hugo wouldn't look as miserable as he did. But in the end, he said nothing at all. He didn't know which was more cowardly.

Hugo said, "Cameron was . . . troubled, when he came to me. I could see that the moment he walked through the door, trailing after my Reaper."

"Not Mei."

He shook his head. "No. This was before her." He scowled. "This Reaper wasn't . . . like her. We worked together, but we clashed more often than not. But I thought he knew what he was doing. He'd been a Reaper for far longer than I'd been a ferryman, and I told myself he knew more than I ever could, especially seeing as how I was new at all of this. I didn't want to cause trouble, and as long as I kept my head down, I figured we could make it work.

"He brought Cameron. He didn't want to be here. He refused to believe he was dead. He was angry, so angry that I could almost taste it. It's to be expected, of course. It's hard to accept a new reality when the only life you've known is gone forever. He didn't want to hear anything I had to say. He told me this place was nothing but a prison, that he was trapped here, and I was nothing but his captor."

There was the guilt Wallace had been trying to avoid. It clawed at his chest. "I didn't . . ."

"I know," Hugo said. "It's not . . . you're not like him. You never were. I knew all I had to do was give you time, and you'd see. Even if you didn't agree, even if you didn't like it, you'd understand. And I don't think you're quite there yet, but you will be."

"How?" Wallace asked. "How did you know that?"

"Peppermint tea," Hugo said. "It was so strong, stronger than almost any tea I've made for someone like you before. You weren't angry. You were scared and *acting* angry. There's a difference."

Wallace thought of his mother in the kitchen, candy canes in the oven. "What happened to Cameron?"

"He left," Hugo said. "And nothing I could do or say would stop him." His voice grew hard. "The Reaper told me to let him go. That he'd learn his lesson and come running back the moment he saw his skin starting to flake. And because I didn't know what else to do, I listened to the Reaper."

Wallace felt his own tremor, vibrating through his skin. "He didn't come back."

Hugo was stricken. Wallace could see it plainly on his face. It made him look impossibly young. "No. He didn't. I'd been warned, before, what could happen if someone like you left. What those people could become. But I didn't think it could happen so quickly. I wanted to give him space, to allow him to make the decision to come back on his own. The Reaper told me I was wasting my time. The only reason I went in the first place was the tie between us just . . . snapped. The Reaper was right, in his own way. By the time I found him, it was already too late." He hesitated. Then, "We call them Husks."

Wallace frowned. "Husks? What does that mean?"

Hugo bowed his head. "It's . . . apt. For what he is. An empty shell of who he used to be. His humanity is gone. Everything that made him who he is, every memory, every feeling, it's just . . . gone. And there's nothing I can do to bring him back. That was my first earthquake as a ferryman. I'd failed someone."

Wallace reached for him—to offer comfort?—but stopped when he remembered he couldn't touch Hugo. He curled his fingers as he dropped his hand. "But you didn't stop."

"No," Hugo said. "How could I? I told myself that I'd made a mistake, and even though it was a terrible one, I couldn't allow it to happen to anyone else. The Manager came. He told me that it was part of the job, and there was nothing I could do to help Cameron. He made his choice. The Manager said it was unfortunate, and that I needed to do everything in my power to make sure it didn't happen again. And I believed him. It wasn't until a couple of months later when the Reaper brought a little girl that I realized just how little I knew."

A little girl.

Wallace closed his eyes. Nancy was there in the dark, her eyes tired, the lines on her face pronounced.

"She was vibrant," Hugo said, and Wallace wished he would stop. "Her hair was a mess, but I think it was always that way. She was talking, talking, talking, asking question after question. 'Who are you? Where am I? What is this? When can I go home?'" His voice broke. "'Where's my mom?' The Reaper wouldn't answer her. He wasn't like Mei. Mei has this . . . innate goodness in her. She can be a little rough around the edges, but there's a reverence about her. She gets how important this work is. We don't want to cause further trauma. We have to offer kindness, because there is never a time in life or death when someone is more vulnerable."

"How did she die?" Wallace whispered.

"Ewing sarcoma. Tumors in the bones. She fought all the way until the end. They thought she was getting better. And maybe she was, at least for a little while. But it proved to be too much for her." Wallace opened his eyes in time to see Hugo wipe his face as he sniffled. "She was here for six days. Her tea tasted like gingerbread. She said it was because her mother made the most beautiful gingerbread houses and castles. Gumdrop doors and cookie towers. Moats made of blue icing. She was . . . wonderful. Never angry, only curious. Children aren't always as scared as adults are. Not of death."

"What was her name?"

"Lea."

"That's pretty."

"It is," Hugo agreed. "She laughed a lot. Grandad liked her. We all did."

And though he didn't want to know, he asked, "What happened to her?"

Hugo hung his head. "Children are different. Their connections to life are stronger. They love with their whole hearts because they don't know how else to be. Lea's body had been ravaged for years. Toward the end, she never saw the outside of her hospital room. She told me about a sparrow that would come to the window almost every morning. It would stay there, watching her. It always came back. She wondered if she would have wings where she was going. I told her that she would have anything she wanted. And she looked at me, Wallace. She looked at me and said, 'Not everything. Not yet.' And I knew what she meant."

"Her mother."

Hugo said, "Part of them lingers because they burn so brightly in such a short amount of time. While I slept, Lea thought of her mother. And it somehow manifested itself to Nancy. She was hundreds of miles away." His words took on a bitter twist. "I don't know quite how she found us. But she came here, to this place, demanding that we give her back her daughter." He looked stricken when he added, "She called the cops."

"Oh no."

Hugo sounded like he was choking. "They found nothing, of course. And when they learned what had happened to her daughter, they thought she was . . . well. That she'd just snapped. And who could blame her for that? None of them knew that Lea was *right there*, that she was shouting for her mother, that she was *screaming*. Lights shattered. Teacups broke. She said she wanted to go home. I tried to stop him. The Reaper. I tried to stop him when he grabbed her by the hand. I tried to stop him when he dragged her up the stairs. I tried to stop him as he forced her through the door. She didn't want to go. She was begging. 'Please don't make me disappear.'"

Wallace's skin turned to ice.

"The Reaper made her cross," Hugo said, his bitterness a palpable thing. "The door slammed shut before I could get to her. And when I tried to open it again, it wouldn't budge. It'd served its purpose, and there was no reason for it to open again. And oh, Wallace, I was so *angry*. The Reaper told me it was the right thing to do, that if we'd let it go on, then we ran the risk of only hurting both of them more. And more than that, it was what the Manager would want, what he told us we had to do. But I didn't believe him. How could I? We aren't supposed to force someone before they're ready. That's not our job. We're here to make sure they see that life isn't always about living. There are many parts to it, and it continues on, even after death. It's beautiful, even when it hurts. Lea would've gotten there, I think. She would have understood."

"What happened to him?" Wallace asked dully. "The Reaper."

Hugo's face hardened. "He screwed up. He'd never had the temperament I thought a Reaper needed, but what the hell did I know?" He shook his head. "He said that it was the only thing that could be done, and that in the end, I'd see that. But it only made me angrier. And then the Manager came."

Wallace could see the bigger picture, slowly forming in front of him. "What is he?"

"A guardian of the doors," Hugo said quietly. "A little god. One of the oldest beings in existence. Take your pick. Any will do. He says he's order in chaos. He's also a hard-ass who doesn't like it when things upset his order. He came to the tea shop. The Reaper tried to excuse what he'd done. 'Tell him, Hugo. Tell him that what I did was right, that it was *necessary*.'"

"Did you?" Wallace asked.

"No," Hugo said, voice as cold as Wallace had ever heard it. "I didn't. Because even though a Reaper is supposed to help a ferryman, it's not up to them to force a person into something they're not ready for. There is order, yes; the Manager thrives on it, but he also knows these things take time. One moment, the Reaper was standing next to me, begging to be heard, and all I could think about was how he sounded just like Lea. And then he was gone. Just . . . blinked out of existence. The Manager didn't even lift a finger. I was shocked. Horrified. And the *guilt* I felt then, Wallace. It was overwhelming. I'd done this. It was my fault."

"It wasn't," Wallace said, suddenly furious, though at what, he couldn't be sure. "You did everything you could. You didn't screw up, Hugo. He did."

"Did he get what he deserved?"

Wallace blanched. "I . . ."

"The Manager said he did. He said that it was for the best. That death is a process, and anything that undermines that process is only a detriment."

"Nancy doesn't know, does she?"

"No," Hugo whispered. "She doesn't. She was oblivious to it all. She stayed in a hotel for weeks, coming here every day, though she spoke less and less. I think part of her knew that it wasn't like it'd been before. Whatever she'd felt regarding Lea was gone because *Lea* was gone. There was a finality to it that she wasn't prepared for. She'd convinced herself that her daughter's death was a fluke. That somehow she was still here. She was right, in a way, until she wasn't. And that light in her eyes, that same light I'd seen in Lea's, began to sputter and die."

"She's still here," Wallace said, though he didn't know what that meant. The woman he'd seen appeared to be no different than he: a ghost.

"She is," Hugo said. "She left for a few months, and I thought that was the end of it, that she'd somehow begin to heal. The Manager brought Mei, and I told myself it was for the best. I was busy learning about my new Reaper, trying to make sure she wasn't like her predecessor. It took me a long time to trust her. Mei will tell you that I was a jerk at first, and that's probably true. It was hard for me to trust someone like her again."

"But you did."

Hugo shrugged. "She earned it. She's not like anyone else. She knows the importance of what we do, and she doesn't take it for granted. But above all else, she's kind. I don't know if I can adequately explain how significant that is. This life isn't an easy one. Day in and day out we're surrounded by death. You either learn to live with it, or let it destroy you. My first Reaper didn't get that. And people paid the price because of it, innocent people who didn't deserve what happened to them." He looked down at his hands, eyes dull in the dark. "Nancy came back. She rented an apartment in town, and most days, finds her way here. She doesn't speak. She sits at the same table. She's waiting, I think."

"For what?"

"Anything," Hugo said. "Anything to show her that those we love are never truly gone. She's lost, and all I can do is be there for her when she finds her voice again. I owe her that much. I'll never push her. I'll never force her into something she's not ready for. How could I? I already failed her once. I don't want that to happen again."

"It wasn't you. You didn't—"

"It *was*," Hugo snapped at him, and Wallace could barely keep from flinching. "I could have done more. I *should* have done more."

"How?" Wallace asked. "What more could you have possibly done?" Before Hugo could retort, Wallace continued. "You didn't force Lea through the door. You didn't cause her death. You were here when she needed you most, and now you're doing the same for her mother. What more can you give, Hugo?"

Hugo sagged against the railing. He opened his mouth, but no sound came out.

Without thinking, Wallace reached for him again, wanting to reassure him.

His hand went right through Hugo's shoulder.

He pulled away, face pinched. "I'm not really here," he whispered.

"You are, Wallace."

Three words, and Wallace wasn't sure he'd ever heard anything more profound. "Am I?"

"Yes."

"What does that mean?"

"I can't tell you that," Hugo said. "I wish I could. All I can do is show you the path before you, and help you make your own decisions."

"What if I make the wrong one?"

"Then we start again," Hugo said. "And hope for the best."

Wallace snorted. "There's that faith thing again."

Hugo laughed, looking surprised as he did so. "Yeah, I guess so. You're an odd man, Wallace Price."

A flash of memory. Of calling Mei strange. "That might be the nicest thing anyone has ever said to me."

"Is it? I'll keep that in mind." His smile faded. "It's going to be hard. When you leave."

Wallace swallowed thickly. "Why?"

"Because you're my friend," Hugo said, as if it were the easiest thing in the world. No one had ever said that to Wallace before, and he was devastated by it. Here, at the end, he'd found a friend. "You . . ."

He remembered what Nelson had told him. "Fit."

"Yeah," Hugo said. "You fit. I didn't expect that."

And because he could, he said, "You should have unexpected it."

Hugo laughed again, and they stood side by side, watching the tea plants sway back and forth.

ↄ

The house was quiet.

Wallace sat on the floor.

He stared at the dying embers in the fireplace, Apollo's head in his lap. He rubbed the dog's ears absentmindedly, lost in thought.

He wasn't aware he was going to speak until he did. "I never got to grow old."

"No," Nelson said from his chair. "I don't suppose you did. And if you'd like, I can tell you that it's not so great, that all the aches and pains are terrible and that I wouldn't wish it on anyone, but that'd be a lie."

"I wouldn't like that."

"I didn't think you would." Nelson tapped Wallace's shoulder with his cane. "Do you wish you had?"

And wasn't that a conundrum? "Not as I was."

"How were you?"

"Not good," Wallace muttered. He looked down at his hands in his lap. "I was cruel and selfish. I didn't care about anything but myself. It's bullshit."

"What is?"

"This," Wallace said, tempering his frustration. "Seeing how I was, knowing that there's nothing I can do to change it."

"What would you do if you could?"

And wasn't *that* the crux of it? A question where any answer would serve only to show that he'd failed at almost every aspect of his life. And for what? In the end, what had it gotten him? Fancy suits and an impressive office? People who did whatever he told them the moment he said it? *Jump*, he'd say, and they'd do just that. Not because of any allegiance to him, but out of fear of reprisal, of what he'd do if they failed *him*.

They were afraid of him. And he'd used that fear against them because it was easier than turning it on himself, shining a light on all his dark places. Fear was a powerful motivator, and now, now, *now*, he knew fear. He was afraid of so many things, but particularly the unknown.

It was this thought that made Wallace push himself up off the floor, suddenly determined. His hands were shaking, skin prickling, but he didn't stop.

Nelson squinted up at him. "What are you doing?"

"I'm going to see the door."

Nelson's eyes bulged as he struggled to rise from his chair. "What? Wait, Wallace, no, you don't want to do that. Not until Hugo is there with you."

He shook his head. "I'm not going through. I just want to see it."

That didn't calm Nelson down. He grunted as he stood, using the cane to pull himself up. "That's not the point, boy. You need to be careful. Think, Wallace. Harder than you ever have in your life."

He looked toward the stairs. "I am."

❧

He walked up the stairs, Nelson grumbling behind him. They paused on the second floor, the walls a pale yellow, the wooden floors silent underneath their feet, watching as Apollo walked down the hall toward a closed vibrant green door at the end. He walked through the door, tail wagging before it disappeared.

"Hugo's room," Nelson said.

Wallace knew that already, though he hadn't been inside. At the other end of the hall was Mei's room, the white door also closed, a sign hanging crooked on it that read: REMEMBER TO MAKE IT A GREAT DAY. The first day when he'd gone there and woken her up was the only time he'd been to the second floor.

He thought about going back downstairs, waiting for the alarm clocks to go off and another day to start.

He turned . . .

. . . and went up the stairs to the third floor.

The hook in his chest vibrated as he climbed each step. It felt almost hot, and if he focused hard enough, he thought he could hear whispers coming from the air around him.

He understood, then, that it wasn't from Hugo like he'd first thought. Not *just* from Hugo, at least. Oh, Wallace was sure Hugo was part of it, as were Mei and Nelson and Apollo and this strange house. But there was *more* to it, something much grander than he expected. The air around him filled with whispers, almost like a song he couldn't quite make out. It was calling for him, urging him upward. He blinked rapidly against the sting in his eyes, wondering if Lea had been able to hear any of this as she was pulled toward the door, fighting against the strong grip around her wrist.

He panted as he reached the landing on the third floor. To his right, an open loft, moonlight streaming in through the only window. A row of shelves lined the wall, filled with hundreds of books. Plants hung from the ceiling, their blooms gold and blue and yellow and pink.

To his left, a hallway with closed doors. Pictures hung on the walls: sunsets on white beaches, snow falling in thick clumps in an old forest, a church covered in moss with one stained glass window still intact.

"This is where I lived," Nelson said, hands gripping his cane tightly. "My room is down at the end of the hall."

"Do you miss it?"

"The room?"

"Life," Wallace said distractedly, the hook tugging him onward.

"Some days. But I've learned to adapt."

"Because you're still here."

"I am," Nelson said. "I am."

"Do you feel that?" he whispered. Weightless, like he was floating, the song, the whispers filling his ears.

Nelson looked troubled. "Yes, but it's not the same for me. Not anymore. Not like it once was."

And for the first time, Wallace thought Nelson was lying.

He continued up the stairs. The stairway was narrower, and he knew he was climbing toward the odd turret he'd first glimpsed upon his arrival with Mei. It'd been something out of a fairy tale, of kings and queens, a princess trapped in a tower. Of course this was where the door would be. He couldn't imagine it anywhere else.

He took each step slowly. "Did you try to stop him?"

"Who?"

Wallace didn't look back. "The Reaper. With Lea."

Nelson sighed. "He told you."

"Yes."

"I did," Nelson said, but it sounded faraway, like a great distance separated them. A dream, the edges hazy around a thin membrane. "I tried with all my might. But I wasn't strong enough. The Reaper, he . . . wouldn't listen. I did everything I could. Hugo did too."

The stairs curved. Wallace gripped the railing without thinking. The wood was smooth under his fingers. "Why do you think he did what he did?"

"I don't know. Maybe he thought it was the right thing to do."

"Was it?"

"No," Nelson said harshly. "He should never have laid a hand on that girl. He'd done his job by bringing her here. He should have left matters well enough alone. Wallace, are you sure about this? We could go back downstairs. Wake up Hugo. He wouldn't mind. He should be here for this."

Wallace wasn't sure of anything. Not anymore. "I need to see it."

And so he climbed.

Windows lined the walls, windows he hadn't seen on the outside of the house. He laughed when he saw sunlight streaming through them, even though he knew it was the middle of the night. He paused at one of the windows, looking out through it. There should've been a vast expanse of forest on the other side, perhaps even a glimpse of a town in the distance, but instead, the window looked out into a familiar kitchen. The faint sounds of Christmas music filtered in through the window pane, and a woman pulled homemade candy canes from the oven.

He continued on.

He didn't know how long it took to reach the top of the stairs. It felt like hours, though he suspected it was only a minute or two. He wondered if it was like this for everyone who'd come before him, and he almost wished Hugo were there, leading him by the hand. Such a funny little thought, he mused to himself. How it pleased him, the idea of holding Hugo's hand. He hadn't lied when he'd told Hugo he'd wished he'd known him before. He thought things could have been different, somehow.

He reached the fourth floor.

He was surrounded by windows, though the curtains had been drawn. A little chair sat next to a little table. On top of the table was a tea set: a pot and two cups. A vase had been placed next to the cups, filled with red flowers.

But no door.

He looked around. "I don't . . . Where is it?"

Nelson lifted one finger, pointing up. Wallace lifted his head. And there, above them, was a door in the ceiling.

It wasn't as he'd expected. In his fear, he'd built it up in his mind, a great metal thing with a heavy, foreboding lock. It'd be black and ominous, and he'd never work up the courage to walk through it.

It wasn't like that.

It was just a door. In the ceiling, yes, but it was still just a door. It was wooden, the frame around it painted white. The doorknob was a clear crystal with a green center in the shape of a tea leaf. The whispers that had followed him up the stairs were gone. The insistent tugging on the hook in his chest had subsided. A hush had fallen in the house around them as if it held its very breath.

He said, "It's not much, is it?"

"No," Nelson said. "It doesn't look like it, but appearances are deceiving."

"Why is it in the ceiling? That's a weird place for it. Has it always been there?" The house itself was strange, so he wouldn't be surprised if it'd been part of the original construction, though he didn't know what it could lead to aside from the roof.

"That's where the Manager put it when he chose Hugo as a ferryman," Nelson said. "Hugo opens the door, and we rise to whatever comes next."

"What would happen if I opened it?" Wallace asked, still staring at the door.

Nelson sounded alarmed. "Please. Let me get Hugo."

He tore his gaze away, looking back over his shoulder. Nelson was worried, his brow furrowed, but there was nothing Wallace could do about that now. He could barely move. "Can you feel it?"

He didn't need to explain. Nelson knew what he meant. "Not always, and not as strong as it was before. It fades over time. It's always there, at the back of my mind, but I've learned to ignore it."

Wallace wanted to touch the door. He wanted to wrap his fingers around the doorknob, to feel the tea leaf pressed against his palm. He could see it clear in his mind: he would turn the tea leaf until the latch clicked, and then . . .

What?

He didn't know, and not knowing was the scariest thing of all.

He stepped back, bumping into Nelson, who grabbed his arm. "Are you all right?"

"I don't know," Wallace said. He swallowed past the lump in his throat. "I think I'd like to go back downstairs now."

Nelson led him away.

The windows were dark as they descended the stairs. Outside, the forest was as it'd always been.

Before they reached the landing to the third floor, he looked out the last window to the long dirt road that led to the tea shop and strangely, a memory flitted through his head, one that didn't feel like his own. Of being outside, face turned toward the warm, warm sun.

The memory faded, the night returning, and he saw someone standing on the dirt road.

Cameron, looking directly at Wallace. He held out his arm, palm toward the sky, fingers opening and closing, opening and closing.

"What is it?" Nelson asked him.

"Nothing," Wallace said, turning away from the window. "Nothing at all."

CHAPTER
13

At the beginning of his twenty-second day at Charon's Crossing, a file appeared on the counter next to the cash register. The tea shop hadn't yet opened, and Mei and Hugo were in the kitchen, getting ready for the day to begin.

Nelson was sitting in his chair in front of the fireplace, Apollo at his feet.

Wallace moved around the shop, pulling the chairs down from the tables and tucking them underneath. It was getting easier for him, and it was the least he could do to help. He never thought he'd find joy in such menial work, but these were strange days.

He was lost in thought, pulling down the chairs, when the room seemed to shift slightly. The air grew thick and stagnant. The clock on the wall, ticking the seconds away, stuttered. He looked up to see the second hand move forward once, twice, three times before it moved *backward*. It twitched back and forth as the hairs on Wallace's arms stood on end.

"What the hell?" he muttered. "Nelson, did you see—"

He was cut off when the file folder burst into existence next to the cash register with a comical *pop*! Wisps of smoke drifted up around it as it settled onto the counter. It was thin, as if it only held a few pieces of paper inside.

"Oh boy," Nelson said. "Here we go again."

Before Wallace could figure out what *that* meant, Hugo and Mei came through the doors, Apollo trailing after them. Hugo frowned as he glanced up at the clock, the hands frozen.

"Dammit," Mei said. "Of course it comes when I'm making muffins." She grumbled as she headed for the stairs, untying her apron before pulling it up and over her head. "Don't let them burn," she called down. "I'll be very upset."

"Of course," Hugo said, looking down at the folder. He touched it with a single finger, tracing along the edges.

"What is that?" Wallace asked, going to the counter.

"We're going to have a new guest," Nelson said, rising from his chair. He hobbled over to Hugo and Wallace, cane tapping against the floor. "Doubling up. Haven't done that in a while."

"Another guest?" Wallace asked.

"Someone like us," Nelson replied. He stopped next to his grandson, peering down at the folder with barely disguised interest.

"Yes," Hugo said, touching the folder almost reverently. "Mei will retrieve them and bring them back here."

Wallace wasn't sure how he felt about that. He'd grown accustomed to having Hugo's undivided attention, and the thought of another ghost taking that away caused a strange twist in the hook in his chest. He told himself he was being foolish. Hugo had a job to do. There'd been many before Wallace, and there'd be even more after he was gone. It was temporary. All of this was temporary.

It stung more than he expected it to.

"What's that for?" he asked, rubbing his chest with a grimace. "The folder."

Hugo looked up at him. "All right?"

"I'm fine," Wallace said, dropping his hand.

Hugo watched him for a beat too long before nodding. "This tells me who's coming. It's not complete, of course. A life can't be broken down into bullet points and be comprehensive. Think of it as a sort of Cliff's Notes."

"Cliff's Notes," Wallace repeated. "You're telling me that whenever someone dies, you get Cliff's Notes about their lives."

"Uh-oh," Nelson said, looking between the two of them. Apollo whined, ears flattening against his skull.

"Yes," Hugo said. "That's what I'm telling you."

Wallace was incredulous. "And you didn't think to say anything about this before?"

"Why?" Hugo asked. "It's not like I can show you what's in here. It's not meant for—"

"I don't care about *that*," Wallace snapped, though it wasn't the whole truth. "You have one on me?"

Hugo shrugged. It was infuriating. "I did."

"What did it say? Where is it? I want to see it." And *that* wasn't quite the truth either. What if it was bad? What if across the top, written in bold letters (and in Comic Sans!) was a summation of Wallace Price's life that was less than flattering? **HE DIDN'T DO A WHOLE LOT, BUT HE HAD NICE SUITS!** or, worse, **NOT THAT GREAT, IF I'M BEING HONEST!**

"It's gone," Hugo said, looking back down at the folder on the counter. "Once I review it, it disappears again."

Wallace was incensed. "Oh, it does, does it? Just disappears back to wherever it came from."

"That's right."

"And you don't see the problem with that."

"No?" Hugo said. Or asked. Wallace wasn't sure.

Wallace threw up his hands in exasperation. "Who sends it? Where does it come from? Who writes it? Are they objective, or is it filled with nothing but opinionated drivel meant to defame? That's *libel*. There are *laws* against it. I demand you tell me what was said about me."

"Oof," Nelson said. "I'm too old and too dead for this." He shuffled away from the counter toward his chair. "Let me know when our new guest arrives. I'll put on my Sunday best."

Wallace glared after him. "You were wearing pajamas when I got here."

"Your observational skills are unparalleled. Good for you."

Wallace considered throwing a chair at him. In the end, he decided against it. He wouldn't want it going into a *file*.

"You're thinking too hard," Hugo said, chiding him gently. "There's no list of pros and cons, or of every action someone has taken, either good or bad. It's just . . . notes."

Wallace ground his teeth together. "What did my notes say?"

Hugo squinted at him. "Does it matter?"

"Yes."

"Why?"

"Because if someone has written something about me, I'd like to know."

Hugo grinned. "Did you look up reviews of your firm when you were alive?"

Every Tuesday morning at nine. "No," Wallace said. Then, "Unless that was written in my file. And if it was, I had a very good reason. I pissed off a lot of people, and everyone knows if you want to complain about something, you write it on the internet, even if you're a liar who doesn't know what he's talking about."

"Sounds like there's a story there."

Wallace scowled at him.

"Or not," Hugo said. He rubbed his chin thoughtfully. "You sure you want to know?"

Wallace balked. "Is it . . . bad? Like *really* bad? Lies! It's all lies! I was a mostly competent person." He cringed inwardly. Once, he might have fought tooth and nail to upsell himself, but now, he couldn't do it. It felt . . . well. Ridiculous was probably the best way to put it. Ridiculous and pointless.

Nelson snorted from his chair. "You shoot for those stars."

Wallace ignored him. "Never mind. I don't want to know. You just stand there acting smug like you always do."

"You wound me," Hugo said.

Wallace sniffed. "I highly doubt that. I don't even care. Look. Look at how much I don't care." And with that, Wallace turned on his heels, going back to the task at hand. He managed to take down two more chairs before he caved. Hugo was amused as he stalked back to the counter. "Shut up," Wallace muttered. "Just tell me."

"You lasted a whole minute," Hugo said. "Longer than I thought you would. I'm impressed."

"You're enjoying this far too much."

Hugo shrugged. "Gotta get my kicks from somewhere, right, Grandad?"

"Precisely," Nelson said as Wallace rolled his eyes.

Hugo glanced at Wallace. "But it's not like you're thinking. I wasn't lying when I said it's not meant to be a slight against you. Think of it more as a . . . an outline."

That certainly didn't make him feel better. "Written by whom? And don't say some esoteric bullshit like the universe or whatever."

"The Manager," Hugo said.

That stopped Wallace cold. "The Manager. The being you're all scared of who makes decisions on a cosmic level."

"I'm not *scared* of—"

"How does he know about me?" Wallace asked. "Was he *spying* on me?" He looked around wildly as he dropped his voice. "Is he listening to everything I'm saying right now?"

"Probably," Nelson said. "He's kind of a voyeur like that."

Hugo sighed. "Grandad."

"What? Man's gotta right to know that a higher being watched him poop or drop food on the floor and then pick it up and eat it." Nelson peered around his chair. "Did you pick your nose? He saw that too. Nothing wrong with it, I suppose. Humans are gross that way. It's in our nature."

"He didn't," Hugo said loudly. "That's not how it works."

"Fine," Wallace said. "Then I'll just see for myself." He was surprised when Hugo didn't try to stop him from picking up the folder. Surprised, that is, until he discovered that he *couldn't* pick it up. His hand passed right through the folder to the counter underneath. He jerked his hand back before trying again. And again. And again.

"Let me know when you're done," Hugo said. "Especially since I'm the only one who can pick it up and see what's inside."

"Of course you are," Wallace muttered. He sagged, hands flat against the counter.

Hugo reached for him again. It was happening more and more, as if he kept forgetting that he and Wallace couldn't actually touch each other. He paused, one hand above Wallace's. Wallace wondered what his skin would feel like. He thought it would be warm and soft. But he'd never find out. Instead, Hugo rested his hand between Wallace's, tapping his pointer finger. Wallace's own fingers twitched. Mere inches separated them. "It's okay," Hugo said. "I promise. Nothing bad. Your file said you were determined. Hard working. That you didn't take no for an answer."

A month ago, that would have pleased Wallace.

Now, he wasn't so sure.

"I'm more than that," he said dully.

"Glad to hear you say that," Hugo said. "I think so too." He picked up the file from the counter, flipping it open. Wallace attempted to lean in nonchalantly but ended up falling through the counter. Hugo eyed him above the top of the folder. Even his eyes were smiling.

"I dislike you immensely," Wallace said, feeling rather petulant as he stood upright.

"I don't believe that."

"You should."

"I'll keep that in mind."

"Jesus Christ," Nelson muttered. "Of all the obtuse . . ." Whatever else he had to say trailed off into mumbling under his breath.

Mei appeared down the stairs, dressed smartly in the same suit she'd worn to Wallace's funeral. She brushed her hair off her face. "I mean it about those muffins, man. If I come back and find they've burned, there'll be hell to pay. Who have we got now?" She plucked the file from Hugo and began to read, eyes darting back and forth. "Huh. Oh. *Oh.* Well. I see. Interesting." Her brow furrowed. "This . . . isn't going to be easy."

Wallace glared at Hugo. "You said you were the only one who could touch it."

"Did I?" Hugo asked. "My bad. Mei can too."

She grinned at Wallace. "Saw yours. Lots of good stuff in there. Question: Why did you think wearing parachute pants was cool in 2003?"

"You're all terrible people," Wallace announced grandly. "And I want nothing more to do with you." And with that, he went back to pulling down the chairs, refusing to even glance in their direction.

"Oh no," Mei said. "Please no. Anything but that." She shoved the file back into Hugo's hands. "All right. Number two, here we go."

"Make sure you don't show up three days late," Wallace said. "Heaven forbid you do your job correctly."

"Aw," Mei said. "You *do* care. I'm touched." She stood on her tiptoes and kissed Hugo's cheek. "Don't forget about—"

"The muffins. I know. I won't." He wrapped an arm around her shoulders, hugging her close. Wallace wasn't jealous. Not at all. "Be careful. This one isn't going to be like the others."

Wallace didn't like how worried he seemed to be.

"I will," Mei said, hugging him back. "I'll be back as soon as I can."

Wallace turned to tell her that the number of people who showed up at a funeral was *not* indicative of the value of a person, but Mei was already gone.

The clock on the wall resumed its normal pace, the seconds ticking by.

"I'll never understand how any of this works," Wallace said.

Hugo's only response was to laugh as he turned and walked through the kitchen doors.

$\operatorname{\mathcal{L}}$

The tea shop was busy all day. Since he was down Mei, Hugo never stopped moving, barely having time to acknowledge Wallace, much less answer more questions about what was in his file. It irritated him, though if pressed, he wouldn't be able to explain why.

It was Nelson who cut through the heart of the matter, much to Wallace's dismay. Wallace was lost in thought, sitting on the floor next to Nelson's chair. "He's not going to forget about you just because someone new is here."

Wallace resolutely didn't look at him. He stared into the fireplace, the flames snapping and popping. "I'm not worried about that at all."

"Right," Nelson said slowly. "Of course you're not. That'd just be preposterous."

"Exactly," Wallace said.

They sat in silence for at least ten more minutes. Then, "But *if* that's what you're worried about, don't. Hugo's smart. Focused. He knows how important this is. At least, I think he does."

Wallace looked up at him. Nelson was smiling, but at what, Wallace didn't know. "The new person coming here?"

"Sure," Nelson said. "That too."

"What are you talking about?"

Nelson waved his hand dismissively. "Just rambling, I suppose." He hesitated. "Did you love your wife?"

Wallace blinked. "What?"

"Your wife."

Wallace looked back at the fire. "I did. But it wasn't enough."

"Did you try your hardest?"

He wanted to say yes, that he'd done everything in his power to make sure Naomi knew she was the most important person in his entire world. "No. I didn't."

"Why do you think that was?" There was no censure in his voice, no judgment. Wallace was absurdly grateful for it.

"I don't know," Wallace said, picking at a string on his jeans. He hadn't worn anything close to a suit since he'd been able to change clothes. It made him feel better, like he'd shed an outer shell he hadn't been aware he'd been carrying. "Things got in the way."

"I loved my wife," Nelson said, and anything else Wallace had to say died on his tongue. "She was . . . vibrant. A spitfire. There wasn't anyone like her in all the world, and for some reason, she chose me. She loved me." He smiled, though Wallace thought it was more to himself than anything else. "She had this habit. Drove me up the wall. She'd come home from work, and the first thing she'd do was take off her shoes and leave them by the door. Her socks would follow, just laid out on the floor. A trail of clothes left there, waiting for me to pick them up. I asked her why she just didn't put them in the hamper like a normal person. You know what she said?"

"What?" Wallace asked.

"She said that life was more than dirty socks."

Wallace stared at him. "That . . . doesn't mean anything."

Nelson's smile widened. "Right? But it made perfect sense to her." His smile trembled. "I came home one day. I was late. I opened the door, and there were no shoes right inside. No socks on the floor. No trail of clothes. I thought for once she'd picked up after herself. I was . . . relieved? I was tired and didn't want to have to clean up her mess. I called for her. She didn't answer. I went through the house, room by room, but she wasn't there. Late, I told myself. It happens. And then the phone rang. That was the day I learned my wife had passed unexpectedly. And it's funny, really. Because even as they told me she was gone, that it had been quick and she hadn't suffered, all I could think about was how I'd give anything to have her shoes by the door. Her dirty socks on the floor. A trail of clothes leading toward the bedroom."

"I'm sorry," Wallace said quietly.

"You don't need to be," Nelson said. "We had a good life. She loved me, and I made sure she knew every day I loved her, even if I had to pick up after her. It's what you do."

"Don't you miss her?" Wallace asked without thinking. He winced. "Shit. That didn't come out like I meant it to. Of course you do."

"I do," Nelson agreed. "With every fiber of my being."

"But you're still here."

"I am," Nelson said. "And I know that when I'm ready to leave this place, she'll be waiting for me. But I made a promise that I'd watch over Hugo for as long as I was able. She'll understand. What's a few years in the face of forever?"

"What will it take?" Wallace asked. "For you to cross." He remembered what Nelson had told him when they'd stood below the door. "To rise."

"Ah," Nelson said. "That's the question, isn't it? What will it take?" He leaned forward, tapping his cane gently against Wallace's leg. "To know he's in good hands. That his life is filled with joy even in the face of death. It's not about what he *needs*, necessarily, because that might imply he's lacking something. It's about what he *wants*. There's a difference. I think we forget that, sometimes."

"What does he want?" Wallace asked.

Instead of answering, Nelson said, "He smiles more, now. Did you know that?"

"He does?" He thought Hugo was the type who always smiled.

"I wonder why that is," Nelson said. He sat back in his chair. "I can't wait to figure it out."

Wallace glanced at Hugo behind the counter. He must have felt Wallace watching him, because he looked over and grinned.

Wallace whispered, "It's easy to let yourself spiral and fall."

"It is," Nelson agreed. "But it's what you do to pull yourself out of it that matters most."

The second hand on the clock began to stutter a half hour after Charon's Crossing closed for the evening. Hugo placed a familiar sign in the window: CLOSED FOR A PRIVATE EVENT. He told Wallace it was just a precaution.

"We're not here," Hugo said. "Not really. When the clock begins to slow, the world moves on around us. If anyone were to come to the shop during a time such as this, they would see only a darkened house with the sign in the window."

Wallace followed him into the kitchen. His skin was itching, and the hook in his chest was uncomfortable. "Has anyone ever tried to get in?"

Hugo shook his head. "Not that I know of. It's . . . not quite magic, I don't think. More of an illusion than anything."

"For someone who's a ferryman, there's a lot you don't know."

Hugo chuckled. "Isn't it great? I'd hate to know everything. There'd be no mystery left. What would be the point?"

"But you'd know what to expect." He realized how it sounded the moment he said it. "Which is why we *un*expect."

"Exactly," Hugo said, as if that made any kind of sense. Wallace was learning it was easier just to go with it. It kept his sanity mostly intact. Hugo went to the pantry, frowning at the contents as he stood in front of it. Wallace looked over his shoulder. More jars lined the shelves, each with a different kind of tea inside. Unlike the ones behind the counter in the front of the shop, these weren't labeled. Most of them were in powder form.

"Matcha?" Hugo muttered to himself. "No. That's not right. Yaupon? No. That's not it either, though I think it's close."

"What are you doing?"

"Trying to find what tea will best fit our guest," Hugo said.

"You did this with me?"

He nodded as he pointed toward a dark powder toward the top of the shelf. "You were easy. Easier than almost anyone I'd ever had before."

"Wow," Wallace said. "First time anyone's said that about me. I don't know how I feel about that."

Hugo was startled into laughter. "That's not—oh, you know what I meant."

"You said it, not me."

"It's an art," Hugo said. "Or at least that's what I tell myself. Picking the perfect tea for a person. I don't always get it right, but I'm getting better at it." He reached for a jar, touching the glass before pulling his hand back. "That's not it either. What could—ah. Really? That's . . . an acquired taste." He took a jar from the shelf, filled with twisted, blackened leaves. "Not one of mine. I don't think I could grow it here. Had this imported."

"What is it?" Wallace asked, eyeing the jar. The leaves looked dead.

"Kuding cha," Hugo said, turning toward the opposite counter to prepare the tea. "It's a Chinese infusion. The literal translation is bitter nail tea. It's usually made from a type of wax tree and holly. The taste isn't for everyone. It's very bitter, though it's said to be medicinal. It's supposed to help clear the eyes and head. Resolves toxins."

"And this is what you're going to give him?" Wallace asked, watching as Hugo pulled a twisted leaf from the jar. The earthy scent was pungent, causing Wallace to sneeze.

"I think so," Hugo said. "It's unusual. I've never had someone take this tea before." He stared at the leaf before shaking his head. "Probably nothing. Watch."

Wallace stood next to him as Hugo poured hot water into the same set of teacups he'd used when Mei brought Wallace the first night. Steam billowed up as he set the teapot down. He held the leaf between two fingers as he lowered it gently into the water. Once it was submerged, the leaf unfurled like a blooming flower. The water began to darken to an odd shade of brown even as the leaf lightened in color to an off-green.

"What do you smell?" Hugo asked.

Wallace leaned forward and inhaled the steam. It clogged his nostrils, and he wiggled his nose as he pulled back. "Grass?"

Hugo nodded, obviously pleased. "Exactly. Underneath the bitterness, it has an herbal note with an aftertaste that's like lingering honey. You have to get through the bitter to find it, though."

Wallace sighed. "One of those things where you say one thing but mean something else."

Hugo smiled. "Or it's just tea. Doesn't need to mean something when it's already so complex. Try it. I think you might be surprised. It probably needs to steep longer, but it'll give you a good idea."

He thought back to the proverb hanging in the tea shop. Hugo must have been thinking the same thing as he handed Wallace the cup and said, "It's your second."

Honored guest.

Wallace swallowed thickly as he took the cup from Hugo. It wasn't lost on him that this was the closest they could ever get to touching. He felt Hugo's gaze on him as they both held the cup longer than was necessary. Eventually, Hugo dropped his hand.

The water was still clear, though the brown tinge had given way to a green closer to the color of the leaf. He brought it to his lips and sipped.

He gagged, the tea sliding down his throat and blooming hotly in his stomach. It was bitter, yes, and then the grass hit and it tasted like he'd eaten half a lawn. The honey afternote was there, but the sweetness was lost by the fact that Wallace hated everything about it. "Holy crap," he said, wiping his mouth as Hugo took the teacup back. "That's terrible. Who the hell would drink that willingly?"

He watched as Hugo brought the cup to his own lips. He grimaced as his throat worked. "Yeah," he said, pulling the cup away. "Just because I love tea doesn't mean I love every kind of tea." He smacked his lips. "Ah. There's the honey. Almost worth it."

"Have you ever been wrong picking out a tea?"

"For people who come in here alive? Yes."

"But not the dead."

"Not the dead," Hugo agreed.

"That's . . . remarkable. Bizarre, but remarkable."

"Was that another compliment, Wallace?"

"Uh, sure?" Wallace said, suddenly uncomfortable. He was standing closer to Hugo than he realized. He cleared his throat as he took a step back. "Man, that taste doesn't leave."

Hugo chuckled. "Sticks with you. I liked yours much better."

That shouldn't have made Wallace as happy as it did. "Was that a compliment, Hugo?"

"It was," Hugo said simply.

Wallace took those two words and held them close, the bitterness he felt no match against the sweet of the aftertaste.

Hugo pulled out more leaves from the jar, setting them on a small plate next to the teapot and cups. "There. How does it look?"

"Like you went outside and picked up the first thing you found on the ground."

"Perfect," Hugo said cheerfully. "That means we—"

At the front of the shop, the clock stuttered loudly and then stopped, the second hand twitching.

"They're here," Hugo said.

Wallace wasn't sure what he was supposed to do. "Should I just . . ." He waved his hand in explanation.

"You can come out with me if you'd like," Hugo said, picking up the tray. "Though, I ask that you let me handle him or any questions he may have. If he talks to you, you can respond, but do so evenly and calmly. We don't want him to be any more agitated than he already might be."

"You're worried," Wallace said. He didn't know how he'd missed the tightness around Hugo's eyes, the way his hands gripped the tray. "Why?"

Hugo hesitated. Then, "Death isn't always swift. I know you don't think so, but you were lucky. It's not like that for everyone. Sometimes, it's violent and shocking, and it follows you. Some are devastated, some are furious, and some . . . some let it become all they know. We get people like that more than you'd think, if you can believe that."

He could. He thought he knew what Hugo was implying, but he couldn't bring himself to ask. The world could be beautiful—and it showed on the walls of the tea shop with the pyramids and castles and waterfalls that seemed to drop from the greatest heights—but it was also brutal and dark.

Hugo looked toward the kitchen doors. "They're coming up the road. Do you trust me?"

"Yes," Wallace said immediately, and he had to fight the urge to block Hugo from leaving the kitchen. He didn't know what was coming, but he didn't like the sound of it.

"Good," Hugo said. "Watch. Listen. I'm counting on you, Wallace."

He walked through the doors, leaving Wallace to stare after him.

CHAPTER 14

Wallace paused in the doorway, frowning. The lights were on as normal, but they seemed . . . dimmer, as if the bulbs had been changed. Apollo whined, ears drooping as Nelson rubbed his head soothingly. "It's okay," Nelson said quietly. "It'll be all right."

Hugo had set the tea on one of the high-top tables, though it wasn't the same one he'd used for Wallace's arrival. Wallace went over to Nelson and Apollo, leaving Hugo to stand next to the table, hands clasped behind him.

He was different, now, even just standing there. It was subtle, and if Wallace hadn't been watching Hugo since he arrived, he might not have noticed it. But he had, and he catalogued all the little changes. It was in the set of Hugo's shoulders, the way his expression was carefully blank, though not disinterested. Wallace thought back to his own arrival, wondering if this was how Hugo had been then.

He tore his gaze away, looking around the room, trying to focus on something, anything, that would distract him. "What's wrong with the lights?" he asked Nelson. He glanced at the door. "Did you turn them down?"

Nelson shook his head. "This is going to be a rough one."

Wallace didn't like the sound of that. "Rough?"

"Most people don't want to be dead," Nelson muttered, running a finger along Apollo's snout. "But they learn how to accept it. Sometimes it comes with time, like you. But there are some who refuse to even consider it. 'These violent delights have violent ends, and in their triumph die, like fire and powder.'"

"Shakespeare," Wallace said, glancing at Hugo, who hadn't looked away from the door.

"Obviously," Nelson said. He reached up and grabbed Wallace's hand, squeezing it tightly. Wallace didn't try to pull away. He told himself the old man needed it. It was the least he could do.

The porch creaked as someone climbed the stairs. Wallace strained to hear voices, but no one was talking. He found that odd. With him, Mei had chattered the whole way down the road, even if it'd been because of Wallace's countless questions. The fact that no one spoke unsettled him.

Three taps on the door. The knocker. A beat of nothing, and then the door opened.

Mei entered first, a grim smile fixed on her face that didn't reach her eyes. She was paler than normal, her lips a thin slash with a hint of white teeth. She took in the room, starting with Hugo, then Nelson, Wallace, and Apollo. The dog tried to rise to go to her, but she shook her head, and he whined as he settled back on his haunches. Nelson squeezed Wallace's hand again.

If asked, Wallace wouldn't have been sure who he was expecting to walk in after her. The tea had given him a clue, but it was a small one, and he couldn't find a way to make it fit into the larger picture. The bitterness, harsh and biting, followed by grass like a field, and the finale of honey, so cloying it stuck in his throat.

Perhaps someone angry, more than he'd been. Someone shouting, filled with rage at the unfairness of it all. Wallace could certainly understand that. Hadn't he done the same? He thought it was part of the process, being firmly planted in denial and anger.

Whatever he thought, the man who entered Charon's Crossing this night was not what he expected. He was younger, for one, probably early twenties. He wore a loose black shirt over jeans with the knees torn out. His blond hair was long, messily swept back off his forehead as if he'd continuously been running his hands through it. His eyes were dark and glittering, his face a mask stretched tightly over bone. The man was unnerving as he took in the room before him, the light dim, gaze settling only briefly on Nelson and Apollo. He stared for a long moment at Wallace. His lips twitched like he was fighting back a terrible smile. His hand rubbed at his chest, and Wallace was startled when he realized he couldn't see the hook in his chest, the cable that should have stretched to Hugo. He didn't know why he hadn't considered it before. Did Nelson have one? Apollo? Mei?

Mei closed the door. The latch clicked again, and there was a finality to it that Wallace didn't like. She said, "This is Hugo. The ferryman, the one I told you about. He's here to help you." She gave the man a wide berth as she walked toward Hugo. Her expression never faltered, and she didn't look at Wallace and Nelson. She stopped next to Hugo. She didn't try to touch him.

The man stayed near the door.

Hugo said, "Hello."

The man twitched. "Hello. I've heard things about you." His voice was lighter than Wallace thought it would be, though it carried a palpable undercurrent of something darker, heavier.

"Have you?" Hugo asked lightly. "Nothing bad, I hope."

The man shook his head slowly. "Oh, no. It was good." He cocked his head. "All of it was good. Too good, if I'm being honest."

"Mei does talk me up," Hugo said. "Tried to get her to break that habit, but she doesn't listen."

"No, she doesn't," the man said, and *there* was the smile. The mask stretched tighter, cheek bones sharp. It chilled Wallace. "At all. Do you listen?"

"I try," Hugo said, hands still clasped behind his back. "I know it's difficult. Learning what you've learned. Knowing how things are never going to be the same. Coming here, to a place you've never been before with people you don't know. But I promise you that I'm here to help you as best I can."

"And if I don't want your help?"

Hugo shrugged. "You will. And I don't mean that flippantly. You're on a journey now, one unlike anything you've ever been on before. This is just a stop on that journey."

The man looked around again. "She said this was a tea shop."

"It is."

"Yours?"

"Yes."

He jerked his head toward Nelson and Wallace. "They are?"

"My grandfather, Nelson. My friend Wallace."

"Are they . . ." He closed his eyes briefly before opening them again. "Like you? Or like me?"

Wallace bit back a retort. They were nothing like him. There was a coldness emanating from him. It permeated the room, causing Wallace to shiver.

"Like you, in a way," Hugo said. "They have their own journey to make."

The man said, "Do you know my name?"

"Alan Flynn."

The skin under Alan's right eye twitched. "She said I'm dead."

"You are," Hugo said, moving for the first time. He brought his hands out from behind his back, settling them on the table in front of him. The teacups rattled on the tray as the table shifted slightly. "And I'm sorry about that."

Alan looked toward the ceiling. "Sorry," he said, sounding amused. "You're sorry. What are you sorry for? You didn't do this to me."

"No," Hugo said. "I didn't. But still, I am sorry. I know how it must seem for you. I won't pretend to understand all that you're going through—"

"Good," the man said sharply. "Because you have no idea."

Hugo nodded. "Would you like some tea?"

Alan grimaced. "Never been one for tea. It's bland." He rubbed at his chest again. "And boring."

"This isn't," Hugo said. "You can trust me on that."

Alan didn't seem convinced, but he took a careful step toward the table. The lights in the sconces flickered with a low electrical hum. "You're here to help me." He took another step. "That's what you said." Another step.

"I am," Hugo said. "It doesn't need to be today. It doesn't need to be tomorrow. But soon, when you're ready, I will answer every question I can. I don't know everything. I don't pretend to. I'm a guide, Alan."

"A guide?" Alan asked, voice taking on a sardonic note. "And just where are you supposed to guide me?"

"To what's next."

Alan reached the table. He tried to put his hands on it, but they went right through it. His mouth twisted down as he pulled his hands away. "Hell? Purgatory? This woman didn't feel like offering specifics." The scorn in his voice was crisp and biting.

"Not Hell," Hugo said as Mei narrowed her eyes. "Not Purgatory. Not somewhere in between."

"Then what is it?" Alan asked.

"Something you'll have to find out for yourself. I don't have those answers, Alan. I wish I did, but I don't. I wouldn't lie to you about that, or anything else. I promise you that, and that I'll do whatever I can to help you. But first, would you like a cup of tea?"

Alan looked down at the tray on the table. He reached out to touch the jar of leaves, but his fingers twitched and he dropped his arm again. "Those leaves. I've never seen tea like it before. I thought it came in bags with the little strings. My father, he . . ." He shook his head. "It doesn't matter."

"Tea comes in all shapes and forms," Hugo said. "There are many kinds, more than you could possibly imagine."

"And you think I'm going to drink your tea?"

"You don't have to," Hugo said. "It's an offering to welcome you to my tea shop. When people share tea, I've noticed it has the power to bring them closer together."

Alan snorted derisively. "I doubt that." He took in a deep breath, tilting his head from side to side. "I bled. Did you know that? I bled out in an alley. I could hear people walking by only a few feet away. I called for them. They ignored me." His gaze grew unfocused. The lights flickered again. "I asked for help. I *begged* for help. Have you ever been stabbed before?"

"No," Hugo said quietly.

"I have," Alan said. He raised his hand to his side. "Here." He moved his hand to his chest, fingers curling. "Here." To the side of his throat. "Here. I . . . I owed him money that I didn't have. I tried to explain that to him, but he . . . he flashed the knife, and I said I'd get it. I would. I was good for it. But I'd told him that before, time and time again, and . . ." His eyes narrowed. "I reached for my wallet to give him the few bucks I had on me. I knew it wouldn't be enough, but I had to try. He must have thought I was going for a weapon because he just . . . stabbed me. I didn't know what was happening. It didn't hurt at first. Isn't that strange? I could see the knife going into me, but it didn't hurt. Even with all the blood, it wasn't real. And then my legs gave out, and I fell in a pile of trash. There was a fast food wrapper on my face. It smelled awful."

"You didn't deserve that," Hugo said.

"Does anyone?" Then, without waiting for an answer: "He got away with seven dollars and a debit card he doesn't have the PIN for. I tried crawling, but my legs didn't work. My arms didn't work. And the people on the sidewalk just kept . . . walking. It's not fair."

"No," Hugo said. "It never is."

"Help me," Alan said. "Help me."

"I will. I promise I'll do what I can."

Alan nodded, almost relieved. "Good. We need to find him. I don't know where he lives, but if we just went back, I can find—"

"I told you," Mei said. "We can't go back." She looked perturbed. Wallace wondered what had happened to make her seem so spooked. "You can only move forward."

Alan didn't like that. He glared at Mei, teeth bared. "*You* said that, yes. But let's leave it up to your boss here, huh? You've already said enough. I don't like it when you talk. You don't tell me what I want to hear."

Hugo lifted the teapot and began to pour hot water into the cups on the tray. The steam billowed. He arched an eyebrow at Wallace and Nelson. Nelson shook his head. Hugo filled three cups before setting the pot back down. "What would you do?" he asked as he lifted tea leaves from the jar. He placed a single leaf in each of the cups. "If you could find him? If you knew where he was?"

Alan flinched, brow furrowing. His hands curled into fists. "I would hurt him like he hurt me."

"Why?"

"Because he deserves it for what he did to me."

"And that would make you feel better?"

"Yes."

"An eye for an eye."

"*Yes.*"

"This tea is called kuding cha," Hugo said. "It's unlike any tea I have here at my shop. I can't remember the last time I made it. It's not for everyone. It's said to have medicinal properties, and some people swear by it."

"I told you I don't want tea."

"I know," Hugo said. "And even if you did, I couldn't give it to you yet. It needs time to steep, you see. Good tea is patience. It's not about instant gratification, not like the bags with the little strings. Those can be fleeting, here and gone again before you know it. Tea like this makes you appreciate the effort you put into it. The more it steeps, the stronger the taste."

"The clock," Alan said. "It's not moving."

"No," Hugo said. "It's stopped to give us as much time as you need." He picked up a teacup and set it closer to Alan. "Give it another moment, then try it and tell me what you think."

A tear trickled down Alan's cheek. "You're not listening."

"I am," Hugo said. "More than you know. I'll never know what it was like for you in that alley. No one should ever have to feel alone like that."

"You're not *listening*." He turned toward the door.

"You can't leave," Mei said. She took a step toward him, but Hugo held her back. *Wait*, he mouthed to her. She sighed, shoulders sagging.

"I can," Alan said. "The door is right there."

"If you leave," Hugo said, "you'll begin to break apart, something that will only get worse the farther you go. Outside these walls is the living world, a world you don't belong to anymore. Alan, I'm so sorry for that. I know you may not believe me, but I am. I wouldn't lie to you, especially not about something as important as this. Leaving here will only make things worse. You will lose everything you are."

"I already *have*," Alan snapped.

"You haven't," Hugo said. "You're still here. You're still you. And I can help you. I can show you the way and help you cross."

Alan turned back around. "And if I don't want this crossing?"

"You will," Hugo said. "Eventually. But there's no rush. We have time."

"Time," Alan echoed. He looked down at the teacup. "Is it ready?"

"It is." Hugo sounded relieved, but Wallace was still wary.

"And I can touch the cup?"

"You can. Carefully, though. It'll be hot."

Alan nodded. His hand shook as he reached for the cup. Mei and Hugo did the same. Wallace thought back to how it'd been for him, the scent of peppermint in the air, the way his mind had been racing, trying to find a way out of this. He knew Alan would be the same.

Hugo and Mei waited until Alan took the first sip. He swallowed with a grimace.

Hugo drank from his own tea.

Mei did too, and if she didn't like the taste, she didn't show it on her face.

"I'm dead," Alan said, looking down into his cup. He swirled it around. Tea sloshed onto the table.

"Yes," Hugo said.

"I was murdered."

"Yes."

He set the teacup down on the tray. He flexed his hands. He took a deep breath, letting it out slow.

Then, Alan swept his arm across the tabletop, striking the teapot. It fell to the floor and shattered, liquid spilling. He took a step back, chest heaving. He raised his hands to the side of his head, clutching his skull before bending over and screaming. Wallace had never heard such a sound before. It burned as if the hot tea water had scalded his own skin. It went on and on, Alan's voice never breaking. The lights in the sconces flared brightly before they went out, casting the tea shop into darkness. Apollo growled, standing in front of Nelson and Wallace, hackles raised, tail ramrod straight.

Alan tried to overturn the tables, the chairs, anything he could get his hands on. He grew angrier when the chairs barely moved, the tables not at all. He kicked at them, but it was no use. He stalked around the room. Apollo snarled when he got too close to them. Wallace stood quickly, putting himself between Nelson and Alan, but Alan ignored them, eyes blazing as he tried to destroy as much as he could to no avail.

He tired himself out, eventually, hair hanging around his head as he bent over, hands on his knees, eyes bulging. "This isn't real," he muttered. "This isn't real. *This isn't real.*"

Hugo stepped forward. Wallace tried to stop him, but Nelson grabbed his arm, holding him back. "Don't," he whispered in Wallace's ear. "He knows what he's doing. Trust him."

Hugo stopped a couple of feet away from Alan, looking down at him with a sorrowful expression. He crouched down in front of Alan, who sagged to his knees, hands flat against the floor, rocking back and forth. "It's real," Hugo whispered. "I promise you. And you're right: it's not fair. It never really is. I don't blame you for thinking that. But if you let me, I'll do what I can to show you there is more to this world than you ever thought possible."

The man sat back up on his knees, tilting his head back toward the ceiling. He screamed again, the cords in his neck jutting out in sharp relief.

It never seemed to end.

Wallace tried to argue when Hugo asked them to leave, telling them that Alan needed space. He didn't like the idea of Hugo being left alone with him. He knew deep down that Hugo was more than capable, but the wild look in Alan's eyes was almost feral. Mei stopped him before he could tell Hugo in no uncertain terms that they *weren't* leaving. She jerked her head toward the back of the house.

"It's okay," Nelson said, though he too sounded worried. "Hugo can handle him."

Apollo refused to budge. No matter what Mei did or said, he wouldn't move. Hugo shook his head. "It's all right. He can stay. I'll let you know if I need you." He and Mei exchanged a look that Wallace couldn't parse. Alan growled at the floor, flecks of spittle on his lips.

The last thing Wallace saw was Hugo sitting cross-legged in front of Alan, hands on his knees.

He followed Nelson as he shuffled after Mei. They walked down the hall toward the back door. The air was colder than it'd been the last few nights, as if spring had momentarily lost its grasp. Wallace was dismayed when he realized he didn't know the date. He thought it was Wednesday, and it had to be April by now. Time was slipping here. He hadn't noticed, so wrapped up in living the life he found himself in. He'd been in Charon's Crossing for almost four weeks. Mei had said the longest anyone had stayed at the tea shop was two weeks. And yet no one had pushed him toward the door. No one had even mentioned it since the early days.

"You all right?" Nelson asked Mei as she paced back and forth on the deck. He reached out and took her by the wrist. "That had to be difficult."

She sighed. "It was. I knew it could be like that. The Manager showed me as much. He's not the first person I've dealt with who was murdered."

"But it's the first time you've been on your own," Nelson said quietly.

"I can handle it."

"I know you can. I never doubted that for a second. But it's okay not to be okay." She slumped against him, her head on his shoulder. "You did good. I'm proud of you."

"Thanks," she muttered. "I was half-convinced he was going to listen. At least at first."

"Where did you find him?" Wallace asked, looking out at the tea garden below. No one had thought to switch on the lights, and the moon was hidden behind clouds. The tea plants looked dead in the darkness.

"Near where he was murdered," she said. "He was . . . yelling. Trying to get someone's attention. He looked so relieved when he knew I'd heard him."

If Alan were anything like Wallace, it would have only been temporary. "Did you know?"

"Know what?"

He didn't look back at them. There was a thread he was pulling in his mind, one that he knew he should leave alone, but it was insistent. He worried at it as he chose his words carefully. "Was he already dead when the file came?"

There was a beat of silence. Then, "Yes, Wallace. Of course he was. It wouldn't have been sent to us otherwise."

He nodded tightly, hands gripping the deck railing. "And you . . . what? Take it on faith?"

"What are you talking about?" Nelson asked.

He wasn't sure. He tugged on the thread. "You get sent the files. *Our* files. But only after we die."

"Yes," Mei said.

"Why couldn't you get it sooner?" he asked into the night. "What's stopping the Manager or whoever from sending it *before* it happens?"

He knew they were staring at him. He could feel their gazes boring into his back, but he couldn't turn around. He was struggling, and he didn't want them to see it on his face.

"That's not how it works," Mei said slowly. "We can't . . . Wallace. There was nothing that could have been done to save y—him."

"Right," Wallace said bitterly. "Because it was his lot in life to die bleeding out in an alleyway."

"It's the way things are," Nelson said.

"That's messed up if you ask me."

"Death *is* messed up," Mei said. She moved toward him, the deck creaking with every step she took. "You won't hear me trying to argue otherwise, man. It's not . . . there's an order to things. A process we all have to go through. Death isn't something to be interfered with—"

Wallace scoffed. "Order. You're telling me that man is part of an order. That man who suffered and no one stopped to help him. *That's* what you believe in. That's your faith. That's your order."

"What would you have me do?" she demanded. She leaned on the railing next to him. "We can't stop death. No one can. It's not something to be conquered. Everyone dies, Wallace. You. Nelson. Alan. Me. Hugo. All of us. Nothing lasts forever."

"Bullshit," Wallace snapped, suddenly enraged. "The Manager could have stopped it if he wanted to. He could have told you what was going to happen to Alan. He could have warned you, and you could have—"

"Never," Mei said, sounding shocked. "We don't interfere with death. We *can't*."

"Why not?"

"Because it's *always there*. No matter what you do, no matter what kind of life you live, good or bad or somewhere in between, it's always going to be waiting for you. From the moment you're born, you're dying."

He sighed tiredly. "You have to know how bleak that sounds."

"I do," she said. "Because it's the truth. Would you rather have me lie to you?"

"No. I just . . . what's the point, then? To all of this? To any of it? If nothing we do matters, then why should we try at all?" He was spiraling, he knew. Rattled and spiraling. His skin was like ice, and it had nothing to do with the air around him. He clenched his jaw to keep his teeth from chattering.

"Because it's *your* life," Nelson said, coming to the other side of him. "It is what you make of it. No, it's not always fair. No, it's not always good. It burns and tears, and there are times when it crushes you beyond recognition. Some people fight against it. Others . . . can't, though I don't think they can be blamed for that. Giving up is easy. Picking yourself up isn't. But we have to believe if we do, we can take another step. We can—"

"Move on?" Wallace retorted. "Because you haven't. You're still here, so don't you try to spin the same bullshit. You can say all you want, but you're a hypocrite with the best of them."

"And that's the difference between you and me," Nelson said. "Because I never claimed not to be."

Wallace deflated. "Dammit," he mumbled. "I shouldn't have said that. I'm sorry. You didn't deserve it. Neither of you do. I . . ." He looked at Mei. "I'm proud of you. I've never said that before, and that's on me, but I am. I can't imagine doing what you do, the toll it must take on you. And dealing with people like him." He swallowed thickly. "Like *me* . . ." He shook his head. "I need a moment, okay?"

He left them behind, thoughts swirling in a massive storm.

He walked up and down the rows of the garden, letting his fingers pass gently over the tops of the plants, careful to avoid the delicate leaves. He stared beyond, into the forest. He wondered how far he could get before his skin began to flake. What would it feel like to give in? To let himself drift away? It should have scared him more than it did. From what he'd seen, it was empty and dark, a hollow husk of a life once lived.

And yet he still thought about it. Thought about finding a way to rip the hook from his chest, and rising, rising, rising up through the clouds into the stars. Or running, running until he could run no longer. It was fleeting, this, because if he did just that, he could become lost, turning into the one thing Hugo feared most. A Husk. What would that do to him, seeing Wallace dead-eyed and vacant? The guilt would consume him, and Wallace couldn't do that. Not now. Not ever.

Hugo was important. Not because he was a ferryman, but because he was Hugo.

Wallace started to turn back toward the deck, another apology on the tip of his tongue. He froze when he heard a sigh, a long, breathy sound like wind through dead leaves. The shadows around him grew thicker as if sentient, the stars fading until there was only black.

Movement, off to his right.

Wallace looked over, spine turning into a block of ice.

Cameron stood among the tea plants. Only a few feet away. Dressed as he'd been before. Dirty pants. Scuffed sneakers. Shirtless, his skin sickly and gray. Mouth open, tongue thick, teeth black.

Wallace didn't have time to react, didn't have time to make a sound. Cameron rushed forward, hands outstretched like claws. He grabbed Wallace's arm, and everything that made Wallace who he was whited out as fingers dug in, the skin leathery and cold.

Wallace whispered, "No, please, no," as Mei screamed for Hugo.

Cameron leaned forward, face inches from Wallace's, his eyes pools of inky black. He bared his teeth, a low growl crawling from his throat.

The dark colors of the world at night began to bleed around Wallace, melting like wax. He thought about pulling away, but it was a distant, almost negligible impulse. He was a tea plant, roots deep in the earth, leaves waiting to be plucked.

Great flashes of light crossed his vision, the brightest stars streaking across all the blackness. In each of these stars, a glimpse, an echo. He saw Cameron and then he *was* Cameron. It was discordant, harsh and rough. It was brilliant and numbing and terrible. It was—

Cameron laughed. A man sat across from him, and he was like the sun. On the hazy outskirts, a violinist moved by, the music from the strings sweet and warm. There was nowhere else Cameron wanted to be. He loved this man, loved him with every piece and part of him.

The man said, "What's that smile for?"

And Cameron said, "I just love you, is all."

Another star. The violin faded. He was young. Young*er*. He was hurting. Two people stood before him, a man and a woman, both severe. The woman said, "Such a disappointment you are," and the man said, "Why are you like this? Why are you so damn ungrateful? Don't you know what we've done for you? And this is how you choose to repay us?"

And *oh*, how crushing that was, how it *devastated* him. He was heartsore and nauseous, wanting to tell them he could be better, he could be who they wanted him to be, he didn't know how, he—

A third star. The man and woman were gone, but their disdain remained like an infection coursing through blood and bone.

The man like the sun rose again, except the light was fading. They were fighting. It didn't matter about what, just that their voices were raised, and they were clawing and scratching, each word like a punch to the gut. He didn't want this. He was sorry, so sorry, he didn't know what was wrong with him, he was trying, "I swear I'm trying, Zach, I can't—"

"I know," Zach said. He sighed as he deflated. "I'm trying to be strong here. I really am. You need to talk to me, okay? Let me in. Don't leave me guessing. We can't keep going on like this. It's killing us."

"Killing us," Cameron whispered as the stars rained down around them.

Wallace saw bits and pieces of a life that wasn't his. There were friends and laughter, dark days when Cameron could barely pull himself out of bed, a pervasive sense of acrimony as he stood next to his mother, watching his father take his last breaths from his hospital bed. He hated him and he loved him and he waited, waited, *waited* for his chest to stop rising, and when it did, his grief was tempered by savage relief.

Years. Wallace saw *years* flashing by where Cameron was alone, where he wasn't alone, where he was staring at himself in the mirror, wondering if it would ever get any easier as the dark circles under his eyes bloomed like bruises. He was a kid riding his bike in the heat of summer. He was fourteen and fumbling in the back seat of a car with a girl whose name he couldn't remember. He was seventeen when he kissed a boy for the first time, the scrape of the boy's stubble like lightning against his skin. He was four and six and nineteen and twenty-four and then Zach, Zach, Zach was there, the sunshine man, and *oh*, how his heart skipped a beat at the sight of him across the room. He didn't know what it was about

222 ··· TJ KLUNE

him, what drew him so quickly, but the sounds of the party faded around him as he walked over to him, heart tripping. Cameron was awkward and tongue-tied, but he managed to get his name out when the sunshine man asked, and he *smiled*, oh god, he *smiled* and said, "Hi, Cameron, I'm Zach. Haven't seen you around before. How about that?"

It was good. It was so damn good.

In the end, they had three years. Three good, happy, terrifying years with ups and downs and blinking slowly in the morning light as they awoke side by side, their skin sleep-warm as they reached for each other. Three years of fights and passion and trips to the mountains in the snow and to the ocean where the water was cerulean and warm.

It was toward the end of the third year when Zach said, "I don't feel good." He tried to smile, but it split into a grimace. And then his eyes rolled back into his head, and he collapsed.

One moment, everything was fine.

The next, Zach was gone.

The destruction that followed was catastrophic. Everything they'd built was razed to its foundations, leaving Cameron screaming in the rubble. He howled and raged at the unfairness of it all, and nothing, *nothing* could pull him out of it. He faded, he faded until he was a shadow moving through the world by pure force of habit.

Wallace said, "Oh no, please no," but it was too late, it was already too late because this was in the past, this had already happened, it was already *done*.

Another star in the distance, but it wasn't Cameron's.

It belonged to Wallace.

What's the longest someone has been here?

Why? Thinking about setting down roots?

No. I'm just asking.

Ah. Right. Well, I know Hugo had someone who stayed for two weeks. That was . . . a hard case. Deaths by suicide usually are.

He said, "Cameron, I'm so sorry."

And Cameron said, "I'm still here. *I'm still here.*"

The stars exploded, and he was pulled away, away, away.

Wallace jerked his head. He was in the tea garden, Mei's hand wrapped around his arm, and she was saying, "Wallace? *Wallace.* Look at me. You're okay. I've got you."

He struggled against her. "No, don't, you don't understand—" He looked over his shoulder to see Hugo standing in front of Cameron amongst the tea plants, near the one he'd been so proud of, the one that was ten years old. The Cameron he'd seen in the stars was gone, replaced by the horrible shell. His black teeth were bared, his eyes flat and animalistic.

"Cameron," Hugo said in a hushed whisper.

Cameron's fingers twitched at his sides. No sound came from his open mouth.

As Mei pulled Wallace up onto the deck, Apollo barking furiously, Nelson's eyes wide, Cameron turned and walked slowly toward the trees.

The last Wallace saw of him was his back as he disappeared into the woods.

Hugo turned toward the house. He looked devastated.

Wallace never wanted to see him like that again.

As the clouds slid away from the moon, they watched each other in this little corner of the world.

CHAPTER 15

Alan tried to leave.

He didn't make it very far before his skin began to flake.

He returned, expression stormy.

"What's happening to me?" he demanded. "What have you done?" He clawed at his chest. "I don't want this, whatever it is. It's a chain. Can't you see it's a chain?"

Hugo sighed. "I'll explain as best I can."

Wallace didn't think it would be good enough.

⁓

Charon's Crossing Tea and Treats opened as normal the next day, bright and early.

The people came as they always did. They smiled and laughed and drank their tea and ate their scones and muffins. They sat in their chairs, waking up slowly, ready to begin another day in this town in the mountains.

They couldn't see the angry man pacing through the tea shop, stopping to scream at each of them. A woman wiped her mouth daintily, unaware that Alan was shouting in her ear. A child had whipped cream on the tip of his nose, not knowing that Alan stood behind him, face twisted in fury.

"Maybe you should close the shop," Wallace muttered, staring out the porthole windows.

Mei had dark circles under her eyes. She and Hugo hadn't slept, kept awake by Alan causing a ruckus through the night. "He can't hurt anyone," she said quietly. "What would be the point?"

"I can move chairs. I can break light bulbs. And I wasn't half as angry as he is. You really want to take that chance?"

She sighed. "Hugo knows what he's doing. He won't let that happen."

Hugo stood behind the counter, a forced smile on his face. He greeted each customer as if they were a long-lost friend, but there was something off about it, though most didn't seem to notice. At best, the gaggle of elderly women told him that he needed to take better care of himself. "Get some rest," they scolded him. "You look exhausted."

"I will," Hugo said, glancing at Alan who tried to overturn a table with no success.

It wasn't until Alan started toward Nelson that Wallace went out into the tea shop for the first time that morning.

"Hey," he said. "Hey, Alan."

Alan whirled around, eyes blazing. "What? What the hell do you want?"

He didn't know. He'd only wanted to keep Alan away from Nelson. He didn't think Alan could hurt him, not really, but he didn't want to take that chance. Hugo started toward them, but Wallace shook his head, begging silently for Hugo to stay back. He couldn't stand the thought of Hugo putting himself in harm's way, not again.

Wallace turned back to Alan. "Knock it off."

That startled Alan, some of his rage fading slightly. "What?"

"Knock it off," Wallace repeated firmly. "I don't know what you think you're doing, but is it really helping your situation?"

"What the hell do you know?" Alan started to turn away.

"I'm like you," he said quickly, though it felt like a lie. "I'm dead, so I know what I'm talking about." He didn't believe that for a moment, but if *Alan* believed, then so be it.

Alan stopped and narrowed his eyes as he glanced back. "Then help me do something about it. I don't know what that was last night, but we can't be trapped here. I want to go home. I have a life. I have to—"

"You have two options. You can either stay right here, in this house. Or you can let Hugo take you upstairs and go through the door."

"Seems to me there's a third option. Figure out how to get out of here. Keep moving until I'm free of all of this."

Wallace hesitated. Then, "No one here wants to hurt you. They never have. That's not what this is about. It's a way station. A stop along the path we're all traveling on."

Alan shook his head. "You want to stay here? Fine. I don't give a shit what you do. If that old bastard over there wants to do the same? Good for him. I don't want this. I didn't *ask* for—"

"None of us did," Wallace snapped. "You think this is easy for any of us? You died. I can't even begin to imagine how it must have felt for you. But that doesn't mean you get to act like an asshole about it." Oh, the hypocrisy. Wallace cringed inwardly, remembering all he'd said and done to Hugo, to Mei, to Nelson, three people who were only trying to help him. He owed them everything, and he'd flung it back in their faces, all because he was afraid. Where did he get off scolding Alan when he'd acted the same way? He hated the comparison, but it was the truth, wasn't it? "You want to go? Then go. See how far you get. Maybe you'll get farther than I did, but it won't matter. You'll turn into nothing. You'll *be* nothing. Is that what you really want?" Alan started to speak, but Wallace overrode him. "I don't think it is. And deep down, I think you know that. For once in your life, use your damn head."

And with that, he spun on his heel and stalked away, leaving Alan behind.

"That went well," Nelson murmured when Wallace put his hand on the back of his chair.

Wallace sighed. "I don't know if I had the right to say any of that to him."

"What do you mean?"

"I just . . . he's me." The words were easier than he expected. "In a way I don't like to look at because it shows me for who I was. Hell, who I *am*. I don't know. It's all jumbled up in my head. How can I tell him he can't be an asshole about all of this when I acted exactly the same way?"

"You did," Nelson said evenly.

"I shouldn't have done that," Wallace whispered, ashamed. "I was scared, more than I'd ever been in my life, but that doesn't excuse the way I treated all of you." He shook his head. "Mei said something the first night she brought me here. That I needed to think about what I was saying. I didn't do that." Humbled, he looked at Nelson. "I'm sorry for how I treated you. I don't expect you to forgive me, but regardless, it's something I needed to say."

Nelson watched him for a long moment. Though Wallace wanted to look away, he didn't. Eventually, Nelson said, "Okay. I appreciate that. Mei's right. She usually is, but with this, she hit the nail on the head. And if there's hope for you, the same could be said about Alan."

"I don't know if it'll be enough," he admitted.

"Perhaps. But maybe it will be. Hugo will do the best he can. That's all anyone can ask for. I'm glad you're here, though. And I know I'm not the only one."

Wallace glanced at Hugo. He was handing a customer a mug filled with tea, that same fixed smile on his face.

But he seemed to only have eyes for Wallace.

✑

The rest of the day was quieter than it'd begun. Alan stayed by the window, ignoring everyone else. His shoulders were stiff, and every now and then, he'd reach up and touch his stomach or his chest or his throat. Wallace wondered if there was a sort of phantom pain there. He hoped not. He couldn't imagine how that would feel.

When the last customer had left for the day, Hugo closed the door behind them, switching the sign in the window from OPEN to CLOSED. Mei was cleaning in the kitchen, her terrible music blasting loudly.

"Wallace," Hugo said. "Can I talk to you for a second?"

Wallace looked warily at Alan, still standing by the window.

"It's fine," Nelson said. "I can handle him if need be. I may look old, but I can kick ass and take names with the best of them."

Wallace believed him.

He followed Hugo down the hall toward the back door. He thought they were going out to the deck like they did most nights, but Hugo stopped near the end of the hall. He leaned against the wall, rubbing his hands over his face. His bandana—bright orange today—sat askew on his head. Wallace wished he could fix it for him. He suddenly found himself wishing for many impossible things.

Hugo spoke first. "It's going to be a little different for the next few days." He sounded apologetic.

"What do you mean?"

"Alan. I need to help him. Get him to try to talk, if I can." He sighed. "Which means we won't be able to talk like we normally do at night, unless we can do it after—"

"Oh, hey, no," Wallace said, even as a little flicker of jealousy flared within him. "I get it. He's . . . You have to do what you do. Don't worry about me. I know what's important here."

Hugo looked frustrated. "You are. Just as much as he is."

Wallace blinked. "Thank you?"

Hugo nodded furiously, looking down at the floor between them. "I don't want you thinking you're not. I . . . like it when we talk. It's one of my favorite parts of the day."

"Oh," Wallace said. His face felt warm. He cleared his throat. "I, uh. I like it when we talk too."

"You do?"

"Yeah."

"Good."

"Good," Wallace said. He didn't know what else to say.

Hugo gnawed on his bottom lip. "I act like I know what I'm doing. And I like to think I'm good at it, even when I'm out of my depth. It's . . . different. Each person is different. It's difficult, but death always will be. Sometimes we get people like you, and other times . . ."

"You get an Alan."

"Yeah," he said, sounding relieved. "And I have to work harder at it, but it's worth it if I can get through to them. I don't want any-one who comes here to turn around and do what Cameron did. To think that there's no hope. That they have nothing left."

"He's . . ." What? Wallace wasn't sure what he was trying to say. It felt too big. He pushed through it to the truth. "He took his own life."

Hugo blinked. "What? How did you know that?"

They hadn't had time to talk about what'd happened in the tea garden. All that he'd seen. All that he'd felt. All that Cameron had shown him. "I saw it when Cameron touched me. These stars, these pieces of him. Flashes. Memories. I felt his happiness and his sorrow and everything in between. And there was part of him that knew I could see it."

Hugo sagged against the wall as if his legs had given out. "Oh god. That's not . . . the Manager said . . ." He hung his head. "He . . . lied to me?"

"I don't know," Wallace said quickly. "I don't know why he said the things he did to you, but . . ." He struggled to find the right words. "But what if they're not as gone as you think? What if part of them still exists?"

"Then that would mean—I don't know what that would mean." Hugo lifted his head, eyes sad, mouth tugging down. "I tried so damn hard to get through to him, to make him see that he wasn't defined by his ending. That even though he saw no other choice, it was over now, and he couldn't be hurt again."

"He lost someone," Wallace whispered. The sunshine man.

"I know. And no matter what I said, I couldn't convince him that they'd find each other again." He looked toward the door that led to the garden.

"Has anyone ever come back from being a Husk?"

Hugo shook his head. "Not that I've heard. They're rare." His mouth took on a bitter twist. "At least that's what the Manager told me."

"Okay," Wallace said. "But even if that's the case, why aren't there hundreds of them? Thousands? He can't be the first. Why didn't I see any in the city after I died?"

"I don't know," Hugo said. "The Manager said that . . . it doesn't matter what he said, not now. Not if . . . *Wallace*. Do you know what this means?" He pushed himself off the wall.

"Uh. No?"

"I need to think about this. I can't . . . my head is too full right now. But thank you."

"For what?"

"Being who you are."

"It's not much," Wallace said, suddenly uncomfortable. "I wasn't that great to begin with, as you know."

Hugo looked like he was going to argue. Instead, he called for Mei.

The music briefly grew louder as she came through the doors, hurrying down the hall. "What? What is it? Are we under attack? Whose ass do I need to kick?"

And without looking away from Wallace, Hugo said, "I need you to do me a favor."

She glanced between them curiously. "Okay. What?"

"I need you to hug Wallace for me."

Wallace spluttered.

"Wow," Mei said. "I'm so glad I ran out here for this." She tapped her fingers against her palm. A little light burst before fading as quickly as it'd come. "Any specific reason?"

"Because I can't do it," Hugo said. "And I want to."

Mei hesitated, but only for a moment. And then Wallace stumbled against the wall as she latched onto him, arms around his waist, her head lying on his chest.

"Hug me back," she demanded. "It's weird if you don't. What the boss man wants, the boss man gets."

"This is already weird," Wallace muttered, but did as she asked. It felt good, having this. More than he expected it to. It wasn't like it'd been after Desdemona. It was . . . more.

"This is from Hugo," she told him, unnecessarily.

"I know," he whispered.

ᐱ

Alan looked like he was going to argue. He scowled, arms crossed defensively, ire clear. But he seemed to be listening.

"He'll get through to him," Nelson said, watching his grandson and their new guest.

Wallace wasn't so sure. He believed in Hugo, but he didn't know what Alan would do in response. He wasn't quite on board with the idea of them going off alone, even if it was only to the backyard. "What if he doesn't?"

"Then he doesn't," Nelson said. "And though it will be through no fault of his own, he'll carry the guilt with him just as he's done for Cameron and Lea. Remember what I told you? Empathetic to a fault. That's our Hugo."

"She didn't come in today."

Nelson knew who he meant. "She'll be back. Nancy might take a day or three, but she always comes back."

"Will she come around?"

"I don't know. I'd like to think she will, but there's . . ." He coughed into the back of his hand. "There's something about losing a child that destroys a person."

Wallace felt like an idiot. Of course Nelson would understand. Hugo had lost his parents, which also meant Nelson had lost a child. Guilt tugged at him that he'd never thought to ask. "Which one?"

"My son," Nelson said. "A good man. Stubborn, but good. Such a serious little boy, but he learned to smile in his own time. Hugo's mother saw to that. They were two peas in a pod. I remember the first time he'd told us about her. He had stars in his eyes. I knew then he was lost to her, though I hadn't even met her. I needn't have worried. She was a marvelous woman, so filled with hope and joy. But above all else, she was patient and kind. And they took the better parts of themselves and put them into Hugo. I see them in him, always."

"I wish I could have met them," Wallace said, watching as Alan trailed after Hugo down the long hallway toward the back deck, Apollo already barking from outside.

"They would've liked you," Nelson said. "Would've given you shit, of course, but you'd have been in on the joke with them." He smiled to himself. "I can't wait to see them again, to hold my son's face in my hands and tell him how proud I am of him. We think we have time for such things, but there's never enough for all we should have said." His glance was sly. "You'd do well to remember that."

"I have no idea what you're talking about."

Nelson chuckled. "I bet you don't." He sobered. "Is there anything you would say to someone left behind if you could?"

"No one would listen."

Nelson shook his head slowly. "I don't believe that for a moment."

ॐ

Alan came back inside first. He looked bewildered. Spooked. The tea shop seemed heavier with his presence, and smaller, as if the walls had started closing in. Wallace didn't know if that was him projecting, or if it was coming from Alan himself. Alan, who Wallace almost felt sorry for as he turned over another chair and set it up on the table. This whole empathy thing wasn't all it was cracked up to be.

Mei paused, broom in her hand. "All right?" she asked, looking at Alan.

Alan ignored her. He stared at Wallace, jaw dropped. Wallace didn't like it. "What?"

"The chair," Alan said. "How are you doing that?"

Wallace blinked. "Oh, uh. Practice, I guess? It's not as hard as it looks, once you get the hang of it. It just takes time to learn how to focus—"

"You need to show me how to do it."

That certainly didn't sound like a good idea. Visions of chaos filled Wallace's head, customers screaming as chairs were flung around them by an unseen hand. "It took a long time, probably longer than you'll—"

"I can learn," Alan insisted. "How hard can it be?"

Mei set the broom against the counter, glancing at them before heading down the hall to the back deck.

"Well," Wallace said. "I . . . don't exactly know how to start."

"I do," Nelson said from his chair. "Taught him everything he knows."

Alan wasn't impressed. "You? Really. *You.*"

"Really," Nelson said dryly. "But you don't have to take my word for it. In fact, you don't have to take any word at all with that attitude."

"I don't need you," Alan said. "Wallace here can show me. Isn't that right, Wallace?"

Wallace shook his head. "Nope. Nelson is the expert. If you want to know anything, you go through him."

"He's too old to—"

Nelson disappeared from his chair.

Alan choked on his tongue.

And then he was knocked off his feet when Nelson appeared behind him, sweeping his legs out from underneath him with his cane. Alan landed roughly on his back, the lights in the sconces flaring briefly.

"Not too old to show you a trick or three, you insolent child," Nelson said coolly. "And if you know what's good for you, you'll bite your tongue before I show you what I can *really* do." He turned back toward his chair, but not before he winked at a gobsmacked Wallace.

"No, wait," Alan said, pushing himself up off the floor as the shop settled around them. "I . . ." He ground his teeth together. "I'll listen."

Nelson eyed him critically. "I'll believe it when I see it. Your first task is to sit there without talking. If I hear so much as a peep from you before I tell you to speak again, I won't teach you a damn thing."

"But—"

"Stop. *Talking.*"

Alan snapped his mouth closed, though he looked furious about it.

"Go check on them," Nelson said to Wallace as he sat back down. "I'll handle things in here."

Wallace believed it. He knew how much the cane hurt.

He glanced back only once as he hurried down the hallway.

Alan hadn't moved.

Maybe he would listen after all.

⌒

"—and you don't need to take that kind of abuse," Mei was saying hotly as Wallace walked through the door into the cool evening air. "I don't care *who* he thinks he is, no one gets to talk to you that way. Screw that guy. Screw him right in his stupid face."

Hugo smiled wryly. "Thanks, Mei. Pointed as always."

"Just because he's angry and scared doesn't give him the right to be a dick. Tell him, Wallace."

"Yeah," Wallace said. "I'm probably not the best person, seeing as how I used to be a dick."

Mei snorted. "Used to be. That's real cute." Then, "Did you leave Nelson alone with him?"

He held up his hands. "I don't think you need to worry about that. Nelson already put him in his place. I'm more worried about Alan than anything else."

Hugo groaned. "What did Grandad do?"

"Like . . . ghost karate?"

Mei laughed. "Oh, man, and I *missed* it? I need to go see if he'll do it again. You've got this, Wallace, right?" She didn't wait for an answer. She stood on her tiptoes, kissing Hugo on the cheek before heading back inside. Wallace heard her shouting for Nelson before she closed the door.

"Pain in the ass," Hugo muttered.

Wallace walked toward him. "Who? Nelson or Mei?"

"Yes," Hugo said before yawning, his jaw cracking audibly.

"You should go to bed," Wallace said. "Get some rest. I think he'll be quieter tonight." If they were lucky, Nelson would convince him to keep his mouth shut for at least a few hours.

"I will. Just . . . needed to clear my head for a moment."

"How did it go?"

Hugo started to shrug but stopped halfway. "It went."

"That good, huh?"

"He's angry. I get it. I really do. And as much as I want to, I can't take that away from him. It's his. The best I can do is to make sure he knows he doesn't have to hold onto it forever."

Wallace was dubious at best. "You think he'll listen to you?"

"I hope so." Hugo smiled tiredly. "It's too soon to tell. But if it starts getting out of hand . . ." A complicated expression crossed his face. "Well, let's just say it's best to avoid that if possible."

"The Manager."

"Yeah."

"You don't like him."

Hugo looked off into the dark. "He isn't the type of being *to* be liked. As long as the job gets done, nothing else matters. I'm not exactly ambivalent, but . . ."

"He scares you," Wallace said, suddenly sure.

"He's a cosmic being overseeing death," Hugo said dryly. "Of course he scares me. He scares everyone. That's kind of the point."

"You still listened to him when he offered you a job."

Hugo shook his head. "That has nothing to do with it. I took the job because I *wanted* to. How could I not? Helping people when they need it most, when they think all is lost? Of course I'd agree to it."

"Like Jesus," Wallace said solemnly. "Got that savior complex down pat."

Hugo burst out laughing. "Yeah, yeah. Point taken, Wallace." He sobered slightly. "And then there's the fact that he might be a liar given what he's said about the Husks, and that scares me even more. It makes me wonder what else he's kept from me."

"Make any headway with that?"

"Not yet. I'm still thinking. I'll get there. Just not yet."

They fell quiet, leaning against the railing.

"I think he'll listen," Hugo said finally. "Alan. I need to be careful with him. He's fragile right now. But I know I can get through to him. He just needs time to work through it. And once he's better and I can show him how to cross, we can go back to normal." He reached out for Wallace, only to stop himself and curl his fingers.

"Yeah," Wallace said. "Normal."

"That's not . . . I keep forgetting." His brow furrowed above a pinched expression as he breathed heavily through his nose. "That you're . . ."

"I know," Wallace said.

Hugo's face crumpled. "I'm losing focus. I keep thinking you're . . ." He shook his head. He started for the door, whistling for Apollo who barked from the tea garden.

And before he could walk through the open door, Wallace said, "Hugo."

He stopped but didn't turn around.

Wallace looked up at the stars.

Is there anything you would say to someone left behind if you could?

He said, "If things were different, if I were me, and you were you . . . do you think you'd ever see me as someone you could . . ."

He didn't think Hugo was going to answer. He'd walk through the door without a word, leaving Wallace alone and feeling foolish.

He didn't.

He said, "Yes." And then he went inside.

Wallace stared after him, burning like the sun.

CHAPTER
16

"Are you sure about this?" Wallace muttered, eyeing Alan warily. It was the third day with their new guest, and Wallace still wasn't sure what to make of him. Ever since Nelson had laid him out on his back, he'd . . . well, not *changed*, not exactly. He'd taken to watching their every movement, and though he didn't ask many questions, Wallace had the feeling he was taking it all in, not quite a cornered animal waiting to strike, but close. It certainly didn't help that he never looked away from Wallace when he started taking down the chairs each morning, getting the tea shop ready for yet another day. Every time Wallace grabbed hold of a different chair, he could feel Alan's gaze on him. It made his skin crawl.

"I can't imagine what it's like for him," Nelson said, voice low in case Alan was trying to listen in. "I know he's a little rough around the edges—"

"It's okay to be hyperbolic. Really. I swear. Don't hold back."

"—but murder victims have a harder time understanding that the life they knew is over." Nelson shook his head. "He died not because of his own choice, or because his body gave out on him, but because someone else took his life from him. It's a violation. We have to tread carefully, Hugo more than the rest of us."

Wallace was uneasy as he set down the last chair, hearing Mei singing in the kitchen at the top of her lungs. He glanced through the porthole windows and caught a glimpse of Hugo moving back and forth. They hadn't had the chance to talk more since their last night on the deck, though Wallace wasn't sure what more could be said. Hugo needed to put his focus on Alan, and Wallace was dead. Nothing was going to change that. It was ridiculous to think otherwise, or so that's what Wallace told himself. Declarations were meaningless in the face of life and death.

Wallace had never been a fan of the *what if*.

The problem with that was Wallace was also a liar, because it was getting harder to think of anything *but* the what if.

And it was dangerous, this. Because Wallace had been sitting in front of the fire the night before, barely listening as Nelson spoke with Alan, telling him that before he could even think of doing what he and Wallace could do, he needed to clear his head, he needed to *focus*. Wallace was far, far away. It was a sunny day. He found himself in a tiny little town. He was lost. He needed to stop and ask for directions. He found a curious little sign next to a dirt road advertising CHARON'S CROSSING TEA AND TREATS. He turned down the road. Sometimes he was in a car. Other times he was walking. Regardless, his destination never changed. He reached the house at the end of the dirt road, marveling at how such a thing could exist without collapsing. He walked in through the door.

And there, standing behind the counter, was a man with a bright bandana around his head, a quiet smile on his face.

What happened next varied, though the beating heart of it was the same. Sometimes, the man behind the counter would smile at him and say, "Hello. I've been waiting for you. My name is Hugo, what's yours?" Other times, Hugo would already know his name (how, it didn't matter; little dreams like these didn't need logic), and he'd say, "Wallace, I'm so happy you're here. You look like you could use some peppermint tea."

"Yes," Wallace would reply. "That sounds wonderful. Thank you."

And Hugo poured him a cup and then one for himself. They took it to the back deck, leaning against the railing. There were versions of this fantasy where they didn't speak at all. They sipped their tea and just . . . existed near each other.

There were other versions, though.

Hugo would say, "How long are you staying?"

And Wallace would reply, "I don't know. I haven't really thought about it. I don't even know how I got here. I was lost. Isn't that funny?"

"It is." Hugo glanced at him, smiling quietly. "Maybe it's fate. Maybe this is where you're supposed to be."

Wallace would never know what to say to this version of him, this Hugo who didn't have the weight of death on his shoulders, and a Wallace who had blood flowing through his veins. His face would grow warm, and he'd look down at his tea, muttering under his breath that he didn't really believe in fate.

Hugo laughed. "That's okay. I'll believe in it enough for the both of us. Drink your tea before it gets cold."

He startled when Nelson snapped his fingers inches from his face. "What?"

Nelson looked amused. "Where'd you go?"

"Nowhere," Wallace said, face hot.

"Oh boy," Nelson said. "Something on your mind you'd care to discuss?"

"I have no idea what you're talking about."

Nelson sighed. "I don't know what's worse. Whether you believe that or you don't and said it anyway."

"It doesn't matter."

Nelson smiled sadly. "No, I don't suppose it does."

The day went on as it always did, even if the tea shop felt a little more charged than normal. It wasn't as if Alan were threatening any of them. He wasn't. In fact, he barely spoke at all. He wandered around the tea shop as he had the day before, listening in on conversations, studying the customers. There were times he'd bend over in front of them, the tip of his nose inches from their own. No one knew anything was amiss, and rather than growing angrier, Alan looked delighted, and not in a way that seemed to be terrifying or menacing. It was an almost childlike glee, his smile appearing genuine for the first time since he'd arrived at the tea shop. Wallace could see the man he might have been before his decisions led him into that alley.

"It's like when I was a kid," Alan told Nelson. "You know when you think about wanting to be a superhero? Like lasers from your eyes, or the ability to fly. I always wanted the power to turn invisible."

"Why?" Nelson asked.

Alan shrugged. "Because if people can't see you, they don't know what you're doing and you can get away with anything."

And on the third day after Alan's arrival, Nancy came back to Charon's Crossing.

She walked through the door as she always did, mouth tight, the circles under her eyes like bruises. She went to her usual table and sat without speaking to anyone, though a few of the customers in the tea shop nodded at her.

Hugo went back into the kitchen, and before the doors had a chance to stop swinging, they opened again as Mei came out, standing at the register.

"Poor dear," Nelson murmured from his chair. "Still not sleeping. I don't know how much longer she can stand it. I wish there were more we could do for her."

"So long as it has nothing to do with Desdemona," Wallace said. "I can't believe she—"

"Who's that?"

They turned to look at Alan. He stood in the middle of the tea shop next to a table filled with people around his age. He'd been circling them since they'd arrived. He was stopped now, gaze trained on the table near the window and the woman who sat there.

He started to take a step toward her. Wallace moved even before he realized it. Alan blinked when Wallace appeared in front of him, a hand pressed against his chest. He looked down, frowning, and Wallace pulled his hand back. "What are you doing?"

"Leave her alone," Wallace said stiffly. "I don't care about what you do to anyone else here, but you stay away from her."

Alan's eyes narrowed. "Why?" He glanced over Wallace's shoulder before looking back at him. "It's not like she can see me. Who gives a shit?" He started to move around Wallace but stopped when Wallace gripped his wrist.

"She's off-limits."

Alan jerked his arm away. "You can feel it, can't you? She's like . . . a beacon. She's on fire. I can taste it. What's wrong with her?"

Wallace almost snapped that it didn't concern him. He course-corrected at the last moment, even though the idea of playing to Alan's humanity seemed so farcical it was ludicrous. "She's griev-ing. Lost her daughter to illness. It was . . . bad. The details don't matter. She comes here because she doesn't know where else to go. Hugo sits with her, and we leave them alone."

He was pleasantly surprised when Alan nodded slowly. "She's lost."

"Yes," Wallace said. "And whether or not she'll find her way isn't up to us. I don't give a crap who else you go near, but leave Nancy alone. Even if none of them can hear us, you don't want to run the risk of making things worse for her."

"Worse," Alan repeated. "You think *I'm* the one who could make things worse." He cocked his head. "Has Hugo told her about all of this? Is that why she comes here, because she knows Hugo helped her daughter cross?"

"No," Wallace said. "He hasn't. He's not allowed. It's part of be-ing a ferryman."

"But he *did* help her girl cross," Alan said. "And somehow, part of her knows that, otherwise she wouldn't be here. What does that make Hugo if he's lying to her? And if part of her *does* know, that means she isn't like everyone else. Maybe she can see us. Maybe she can see *me*."

Wallace stepped in front of Alan again as he tried to move by. "She can't. And even if she could, you don't get to put her through that. I don't know what it's like to be you. I'll never understand what happened to you, or what it must have felt like. But you don't get to use her to try to make yourself feel better."

Alan opened his mouth to retort but stopped when Hugo walked through the kitchen doors. The din of the tea shop went on around them, but Hugo was staring at Wallace and Alan, a tea tray in his hands. Mei stood on her tiptoes and whispered something in his ear. He didn't react. She glanced at them, and if Wallace didn't know her, he'd have thought nothing of her blank expression. But he *did* know her, and she wasn't happy.

Hugo walked around the counter, fixing a smile on his face. He nodded at everyone who greeted him. As he passed Wallace and Alan, he spoke from the corner of his mouth. "Please stay away from her."

He continued on without stopping.

Nancy stared out the window as Hugo set the tea tray down on the table. She didn't react as he poured the tea into the cup. He set the cup in front of her before taking his seat opposite her, folding his hands on the table as he always did.

Alan watched them, waiting.

When nothing happened, he asked, "What's he doing?"

"Being there for her," Wallace said, wishing Alan would let it go. "Waiting for her to be ready to talk. Sometimes the best way to help someone is not to say anything at all."

"Bullshit," Alan muttered. He crossed his arms and glared at Hugo. "Did he screw up or something? He's got guilt written all over him. What'd he do?"

"If he wants to tell you, he will. Leave it alone."

And wonder of all wonders, Alan seemed to listen in his own way. He threw up his hands before stalking to the opposite side of the room toward a table where a small group of women sat.

Wallace sighed in relief as he looked back at Mei.

She nodded at him before rolling her eyes.

"Right," he said. "Kids these days."

She coughed into her hand, but he could see the curve of her smile.

And that should have been it. That should've been the end of it.

Nancy sitting there, not speaking. Hugo waiting, never pushing. The teacup in front of her, unacknowledged. After an hour (or maybe two), she'd stand, chair scraping against the floor, Hugo telling her he'd be there, always, whenever she was ready.

And then she'd leave. Perhaps she'd come back tomorrow and the next day and the next day, or perhaps she'd be missing for a day or two.

Nancy sat in her chair. Hugo sat across from her. After an hour, she stood.

Hugo said, "I'll be here. Always. Whenever you're ready, I'll be here."

She moved toward the door.

The end.

Except Alan shouted, "*Nancy!*"

The light bulbs in the sconces flared. Nancy stopped, her hand on the doorknob.

"*Nancy!*" Alan shouted again, stunning Wallace into immobility. Nancy turned toward the sound of his voice as she frowned.

Alan jumped up and down in the center of the tea shop, waving his warms wildly, screaming her name over and over again. The tables on either side of him shifted as if someone had bumped into them, sloshing tea and knocking muffins over.

"What the hell?" a man asked, staring down at the table. "Did you feel that?"

"Yeah," his companion, a young woman with pink bubblegum lip gloss, said. "It shook, right? Almost like—"

The tables jumped again as Alan took a step toward Nancy.

Nancy, whose grip tightened on the doorknob until her knuckles turned white. "Who's there?" she asked, voice carrying, causing everyone to turn and look at her.

"Yeah," Alan panted. "Yes. I'm here. Oh my god, I'm *here*. Listen to me, you need to—"

Wallace didn't think.

One moment, he was a tea plant, unmoving. The next, he stood in front of Alan again, hand over his mouth, teeth scraping against his palm. "Stop it," he hissed.

Alan struggled against him, trying to shove him away. But Wallace was bigger than he was, and though he was rail thin, he held firm. Alan's eyes blazed in fury above Wallace's hand.

"Are you okay, sweetheart?" a woman asked Nancy, turning in her chair to look up at her.

Nancy didn't so much as glance at her. She continued to stare in Wallace and Alan's direction, but if she saw them, she didn't react. She opened her mouth as if to speak again, but shook her head before walking through the door, slamming it behind her.

Alan screamed into the hand covering his mouth before shoving Wallace as hard as he could. Wallace stumbled back, hitting a chair behind him. The man sitting in the chair looked around wildly as the legs scraped along the floor.

"She heard me," Alan snarled. "She *heard* me. She can—" He never finished. He hurried toward the door.

Hugo said, "If you walk out that door, you'll lose yourself. And I don't know how to bring you back."

Alan stopped, chest heaving.

Silence filled the nooks and crannies of Charon's Crossing. Everyone turned slowly to look at Hugo. Nelson groaned, face in his hands as Apollo growled at Alan.

"Right!" Mei said brightly. "Because if you haven't finished your cup of tea before you leave, you'll spend the rest of your day fretting over what you've lost. And we don't know how to bring it back, because reheated tea is the *worst*. Isn't that right, Hugo?"

Hugo didn't respond. He stared at Alan, unblinking.

"For the love of all that's holy, listen to him," Nelson said irritably. "I know you don't have a lick of common sense, but don't be an idiot. You've been told what will happen to you if you leave. You want that? Fine. Go. But don't expect any of us to come running to save you if you do."

Alan's shoulders were a rigid line. His throat worked as he swallowed, eyes wet and lost. "She could hear me," he whispered.

"Oh, look!" Mei said loudly. "I just realized today is National Free Tea and Scone Day. We need to celebrate. If anyone wants a free cup of tea or a scone, come up here and I'll hook you up."

Most everyone moved toward the counter, chairs scraping along the floor. After all, it was either continue to stare at the odd owner of Charon's Crossing, or get something for free. It seemed to be an easy choice.

Eventually, Alan stood down, though Wallace could still feel the anger and desperation emanating from him. He turned away and went to the far corner of the tea shop, leaning his forehead against the wall as he shook.

"Leave him be," Nelson said quietly. "I think he's learning what this all means. Give him time. He'll come around. I just know it."

Nelson was wrong.

e

The rest of the day went by in a blur.

Alan didn't move from the corner. He didn't speak. Wallace left him alone.

Mei stood behind the register, arms folded, watching, always watching. She smiled whenever someone came up to the counter to place their order, but it was forced, thin.

Nelson stayed in his chair, cane across his lap, eyes closed, head tilted back.

Hugo had disappeared into the kitchen, Apollo trailing after him, whining lowly. Wallace wanted to follow after them but found himself frozen in place, his thoughts racing.

She heard me. She heard *me.* That was what Alan had said.

And he'd been right. Wallace had seen it with his own eyes.

He didn't know what to do with that information, if anything at all.

Did it even matter?

He hated how much he focused on it, how *hopeful* it almost made him feel. Mei had told him Nancy was a bit like her, though nowhere near as strong. He didn't know if it had to do with the passing of her daughter—her grief manifesting itself into something extraordinary—or if she'd always been this way. Some dark part of him wondered if he could use that, somehow, use it to be seen and heard and—

He cut himself off, horrified.

No.

He wasn't . . . he could never do something like that. He wasn't like Alan. Not anymore.

Right?

He turned toward the kitchen.

Mei watched every step he took while ringing up a young couple, their faces flushed as the man smiled at his lady friend. "It's our second date," the man said, and he sounded so *awed* by it.

"Our third," the woman said, bumping his shoulder. "That time at the grocery store counted."

"Oh," the man said, and he smiled. "Our third, then."

Wallace walked through the double doors to an empty kitchen.

He frowned. Where had they gone? He hadn't heard the scooter start up, so he didn't think Hugo had left, and it wasn't as if Apollo could follow him even if he did. They had to be around here somewhere.

Wallace went to the door, looking out onto the back deck. The spring air still had a bite to it, though the tea plants and forest behind the shop were more vibrant than they'd ever been since Wallace arrived. What did this place look like in the throes of summer? Green, he expected, so green that he'd be able to taste it, something he hadn't known until this moment that he desperately wanted to see. The world outside Charon's Crossing marched ever on.

There, sitting against the railing, was Hugo.

Apollo sat at his feet, paws folded over each other. His ears were perked and twitching, head raised as he blinked slowly at Hugo.

Hugo, who looked slick with sweat, his breathing ragged.

Alarmed, Wallace hurried through the door.

Hugo didn't open his eyes as Wallace approached slowly, keeping his distance. He looked as if he was trying to get himself under control, breathing in through his nose and out his mouth. His bandana—purple today, with little yellow stars—sat crooked on his head.

Apollo turned his head, looking at Wallace. He whined again.

"It's all right," Wallace told him. "Everything is fine."

He kept his distance, stopping in the middle of the deck. He left the chairs alone, deciding to sit where he stood.

He waited.

It took a long time, but Wallace didn't push. He wouldn't. Not when Hugo was like this. It wouldn't help. So he sat there, head bowed, tapping his finger on the boards beneath him, a tiny sound to let Hugo know he was there. Tap. Tap. Tap. Quiet, soft, but a connection, a reminder. Tap, tap, tap. *You're not alone. I'm here. Breathe. Breathe.* He knew what this was. He'd seen it before.

Hugo sucked in ragged breaths, his chest heaving, face scrunched up, eyes unfocused, dazed. And Wallace didn't move, didn't try to talk to him. He kept on tapping on the deck, keeping the beat, like a metronome.

Wallace must have tapped his finger a hundred times before Hugo spoke. "I'm fine," he said, voice hoarse.

"Okay," Wallace said easily. "But it's all right if you're not, too." He hesitated. "Panic attacks are no joke."

Hugo opened his eyes, glassy and wet. He rubbed a hand over his face, groaning quietly. "That's an understatement. How did you know to . . ." He waved his hand at Wallace and the distance between them.

"Naomi had them when she was younger."

"Your wife?"

"Ex-wife," Wallace said automatically. "She . . . I didn't understand them, or what could trigger them. She explained it to me, but I don't know that I listened very well. They were few and far between, but when they hit, they were savage. I tried to help her, tried to tell her just to breathe through it, and she . . ." He shook his head. "She told me that it was as if a dozen hands were clawing at her, choking her. Squeezing her lungs. They were irrational, she said. Chaotic. Like her body was fighting her. And yet I still thought she could power through them if she really wanted to."

"If only that's how it worked."

"I know," Wallace said simply. Then, "Apollo helps."

Apollo thumped his tail at the sound of his name.

"He does," Hugo said. He looked exhausted. "Even though he flunked out of the service dog training, he still knows. It was worse for me, after . . . well. After everything. I didn't know how to stop them. I didn't know how to fight them. I couldn't even find the words to explain what they felt like. Chaotic is pretty close, I think. Anxiety is . . . a betrayal, my brain and body working against me." He smiled weakly. "Apollo's a good boy. He knows just what to do."

"I can go back inside," Wallace said. "If you want to be left alone. Some do, but Naomi liked having me near. Not touching her, but near so she knew she wasn't alone. I'd tap against the wall or the floor, just to let her know I was still there without speaking. It seemed to help her, so I took a chance it'd be the same with you."

"I appreciate that." Hugo closed his eyes again. "It's hard."

"What?"

Hugo shrugged. "This. Everything."

"That's . . ."

"Vague?"

"I was going to say all-encompassing."

Hugo snorted. "I suppose."

"I didn't know that it affected you this much," Wallace admitted.

"It's death, Wallace. Of course it does."

"No, I know. I didn't mean it like that." He paused, considering. "I guess I thought you were used to it."

Hugo opened his eyes again. They were clearer than they'd been before. "I don't know that I ever will be." He grunted as he shifted to a more comfortable position. "I don't want it to affect me as it does, but I can't always stop it. I know what I'm supposed to be doing, I know my job is important. But what I want and what my body does are sometimes two different things."

"You're human," Wallace whispered.

"I am," Hugo agreed. "And everything that comes with it. Just because I'm a ferryman doesn't mean all the other parts of me won't still be there, warts and all." Then, "What do you want?"

Wallace blinked. "To make sure you're—"

Hugo shook his head. "Not that. What do you want, Wallace? Out of your time here. Out of me. This place."

"I . . . don't know?" His own words confused him. There were many, many things he wanted, but each sounded more trivial than the last. And that was the rub, wasn't it? A life built upon inconsequential things made important simply because he desired them to be.

Hugo didn't look disappointed. If anything, Wallace's answer seemed to calm him further. "It's okay not to know. In a way, it makes things easier."

"How?"

Hugo settled his hands into his lap. Apollo lowered his snout to his paws, though he kept his gaze trained on Hugo, blinking slowly, tail curled around his haunches. "Because it's harder to convince someone of what they need versus what they want. We often ignore the truth because we don't like what it shows us."

"Alan."

"I'm trying," Hugo said. "I really am. But I don't know if I'm getting through to him. It's only been a few days, but he feels further away than he did when he first arrived." His mouth twisted down. "It's like Cameron all over again, only worse because there's no one trying to undermine my work."

Wallace startled. "They're not your fault."

"Aren't they? They came to me because I'm the one who's supposed to help them. But no matter what I say, no matter what I do, they can't listen. And I don't blame them for that. It's like a panic attack. I can try to explain it to you, but unless you've ever had one yourself, you'll never understand just how harsh they can be. And though I'm surrounded by death, I can never understand what it does to a person because I've never died."

"You're better than most," Wallace said.

Hugo squinted at him. "Another compliment, Wallace?"

"Yes," Wallace said, picking at the frayed ends of his jeans.

"Ah. Thank you."

"I could never be you."

"Of course not," Hugo said. "Because you're you, and that's who you're supposed to be."

"That's not what I meant. You do what you do, and I can't even begin to imagine the toll it takes. This gift you have . . . it's beyond me. I don't think I could ever be strong enough to be a ferryman."

"You underestimate yourself."

"Or I know my limits," Wallace countered. "What I'm capable of, even if I should've second-guessed some of the decisions I made." He paused. "Okay, maybe a lot of the decisions I made."

Hugo knocked his head back against the railing softly. "But isn't that life? We second-guess everything because it's in our nature. People with anxiety and depression just tend to do it more."

"Maybe that's Alan," Wallace said. "I won't pretend I get everything about him. I don't. But the world he knows is gone. Everything has changed. He'll see you for what you are, eventually. It just takes time."

"How do you know that?"

"Because I have faith in you," Wallace said, feeling brittle and exposed. "And all that you are. There's no one like you. I don't know if I would have made it this far without you. I don't even want to think what it would have been like with another ferryman. Or woman. Ferryperson?"

Hugo laughed, looking surprised as he did so. "You have faith in me."

Wallace nodded as he waved his hand awkwardly. "If this is a way station, if this is just one stop on a journey, you're the better part of it." He was silent for a moment. Then, "Hugo?"

"Yeah?"

"I wish for things too."

"Like what?"

Honesty was a weapon. It could be used to stab and tear and spill blood upon the earth. Wallace knew that; he had his fair share of blood on his hands because of it. But it was different, now. He was using it upon himself, and he was flayed open because of it, nerve endings exposed.

And perhaps that's why he said, "I wish I'd found you before. Not someone like you. But you."

Hugo inhaled sharply. For a moment, Wallace thought he'd crossed a line, but then Hugo said, "I wish that too."

"It's dumb, right?"

"No, I don't think it is."

"What do we do now?"

"I don't know," Hugo said. "Whatever we can, I guess."

"Make the most of the time we have left," Wallace whispered.

And Hugo said, "That's all anyone can ask of us."

The sun drifted slowly across the sky.

の

The last customer left for the day with a jaunty wave. Mei was back in the kitchen, Nelson in his chair. Apollo stayed close to Hugo, as if wanting to make sure he didn't relapse. Alan still stood in the corner, shoulders hunched up around his ears. They'd left him alone, but Wallace knew it couldn't last, especially when Nancy came back. They needed to make him understand that she was off-limits. Wallace wasn't looking forward to it.

Hugo flipped the sign in the window.

He was about to lock the door when he froze.

"Oh no," he breathed. "Not now."

"What is it?" Nelson asked. "Don't tell me we've got another guest coming. It's getting a little crowded as is." He glared at Alan.

"It's not that," Hugo said tightly.

In the distance, Wallace heard the rumble of a car engine coming down the road. He went to a window. Headlights were approaching. "Who is it?"

"The health inspector," Hugo said.

Nelson suddenly popped into existence next to Wallace, who yelped. Nelson ignored him, peering out the window. "*Again?* But he was just here a couple of months ago. I swear, that man has it out for you, Hugo. Quick! Turn off all the lights and lock the door. Maybe he'll go away."

Hugo sighed. "You know I can't do that. He'd just come back tomorrow and be in a worse mood." He glanced at Nelson. "Leave him alone this time."

"I have no idea what you're talking about."

"Grandad."

"Fine," Nelson said irritably. "I'll be on my best behavior." He lowered his voice so only Wallace could hear. "But mark my words, if he tries anything, I'm going to shove his pen up his ass."

Wallace grimaced. "You can do that?"

"Damn right I can. And he'd deserve it too. Prepare to meet the biggest waste of space you've ever met in your life."

"I know hundreds of attorneys."

Nelson rolled his eyes. "He's worse."

Wallace wasn't sure who he was expecting to climb out of the little car, but who he saw certainly wasn't it. The man was younger, around Hugo's age. He was coldly handsome, though his handlebar mustache made Wallace want to punch him in the face. He wore a smart suit—one Wallace might have worn when he was still alive, expensive, cut perfectly to his frame, the plaid tie completing the look—and a terrible sneer. Wallace watched as he reached back into his car, pulling out a clipboard. He took a fountain pen from the inner pocket of his suit jacket, pressing the tip against his tongue before he started scribbling notes.

"What's he writing?" Wallace asked.

"Who the hell knows," Nelson said. "Probably something bad. He's always looking for every little thing he can find to use against Hugo. He once tried to say that we had rats in the walls. Can you imagine? *Rats*. Odious man."

"And whose fault was that?" Hugo asked, stepping back from the door without locking it.

"Mine," Nelson said easily. "But I was trying to scare him, not make him think we had rodents." He raised his voice. "Mei! *Mei*. We've got company."

Mei burst through the door, a pot covered in dish soap in one hand and a butcher knife in the other. "Who? Are we under attack?"

"Yes," Nelson said.

"No," Hugo said loudly. "We're not. Health inspector."

Mei gasped. "Again? We *are* under attack. Lock the door! Maybe he'll think we're gone!" She waved the knife around until she glanced at Alan, who was eyeing her warily. She quickly hid it behind her. "I don't have a knife. You were seeing things."

"You're dripping water on the floor," Hugo told her. "Which he'll hold against us."

Mei growled as she spun around and hurried back into the kitchen. "Hold him off as much as you can. I'll make sure everything is good in here before he comes in."

"Shouldn't it be already?" Wallace asked.

"Of course it is," Nelson said as the health inspector pulled on a bit of peeling paint along the railing to the stairs. "But he won't see it that way. You should have seen the look on his face when he came here for the first time. I thought he was going to have a heart attack when he saw Apollo." He glanced at Wallace. "Is that still too soon or . . . ?"

Wallace glared at him. "You're not funny."

"I really am."

Wallace looked back out the window. "I don't see what's so bad. Surely he just wants to make sure the tea shop is clean, right? Why would he have it out for Hugo?" A terrible thought crossed his mind. "Jesus Christ, is it because he's Black? Of all the—"

"Oh, no," Nelson said. "Nothing as loathsome as that." He leaned forward, dropping his voice. "He asked Hugo out on a date once. Hugo said no. He wasn't happy about it and has been torturing us all ever since."

The skin under Wallace's right eye twitched. "What?"

Nelson patted his shoulder. "I knew you'd see it my way."

"Mei!" Wallace shouted. "Bring back the knife!"

Mei burst through the doors again, now carrying a knife in each hand.

"No knives!" Hugo barked.

She turned around and stalked back into the kitchen.

The door to Charon's Crossing Tea and Treats opened.

"Hmm," the health inspector said with a grimace as he looked around. "Not off to the best start, are we, Hugo?" He sounded as if he were affecting the most atrocious British accent the world had ever heard. Wallace despised him immediately, telling himself it had nothing to do with the fact that this man apparently wanted to climb Hugo like a tree. Even though this man couldn't see him, Wallace would remain the consummate professional.

"Harvey," Hugo said evenly.

"Harvey?" Wallace exclaimed. "His name is *Harvey*? That's ridiculous!"

Hugo coughed roughly.

Harvey stared at him.

Hugo held up his hand. "Sorry. Something in my throat."

"I can see that," Harvey said. "Probably all the dust that seems to coat this place. I do hope you've made a better attempt to keep things cleaner this time around." He sniffed daintily. "At least we don't have to worry about that mutt any longer. Pet dander around all that food? Bloody bollocks if you ask me."

Apollo barked angrily, spittle flying from his lips and landing on the floor.

"He's from Seattle," Nelson whispered. "Went to London once a few years ago and came back talking like that. No one knows why."

"Because he's ludicrous," Wallace said. "Obviously."

Hugo held himself together, insults about his dog notwithstanding. "I'm sure you'll find that everything is as it should be, just like it was when you were here in February. Speaking of, what brings you back so soon?"

Harvey scribbled furiously on his clipboard. "I'm a health inspector. I'm inspecting. And I'll be the judge of whether everything is as it should be. It's the point of surprise inspections. Doesn't allow you to cover up any . . . violations." He moved toward the display cases, unaware of the three ghosts (and one ghost dog) watching him with various shades of animosity. Wallace wasn't sure why Alan looked so aggravated, unless that was his default setting.

Harvey stopped in front of the display cases, bending over to peer into them. They were immaculate as always, the lights soft and warm on the remaining pastries left over from the day, few though they were. "Mei in the kitchen, I suppose? Tell her to cease all activities immediately. I'd hate to think she's covering up any crimes against humanity as she's wont to do."

Mei appeared in one of the portholes, a look of utter fury on her face. "Crimes? *Crimes?* Come in here and say that to my face, you—"

"She's doing what she normally does at the end of the day," Hugo said mildly. "As you well know."

"I'm sure she is," Harvey muttered. He stood upright, once again putting his pen to this clipboard. "I'm not the enemy here, Hugo. I'd never want to see this place shut down. I fear what it would do to Mei if she were forced onto the streets if I had to shut down your tea shop. She's rather . . . delicate."

Hugo stepped in front of the double doors in time to block Mei from bursting through them. He grunted when the doors struck his back, but otherwise didn't react.

Harvey arched an eyebrow.

Hugo shrugged. "She's exuberant today."

"Exuberant? I'll show *you* exuberant, you—"

Harvey sighed loudly. "Temper, temper. Though I may be a health inspector, I like to think the position allows me to comment on mental health as well. Hers appears to be in dire straits. I would suggest she get that seen to posthaste."

"How has he not been punched in the face?" Wallace demanded.

"Hugo said we can't," Nelson said.

"That's exactly right," Hugo said evenly.

"It is?" Harvey said, sounding taken aback. "Why thank you, Hugo. I do believe that's the first time you've ever agreed with me." He smiled, and Wallace felt his skin crawl. "It looks good on you." He sauntered up to the counter. "As would I."

"Oh my god," Wallace said loudly. "Does that actually work on anyone? Hugo, kick him in the nuts."

"I don't know if I can do that," Hugo said, never looking away from Harvey.

"Why not?" Harvey and Wallace asked at the same time.

"You know why," Hugo said.

Harvey sighed as Wallace threw up his hands in frustration. "I'll wear you down yet," Harvey said. "Just you wait and see. Now, back to the business at hand. I need to stick my thermometer in many things." He waggled his eyebrows.

"Wow," Wallace said. "That's sexual harassment. We're going to sue him. We're going to sue him for everything he's worth, just you wait and see. I'll draft up the papers just as soon as—oh. Right. I'm dead. Goddammit. Don't let him stick his thermometer in your baked goods!"

Hugo's eyebrows rose almost to his bandana.

Harvey pressed a finger against the counter, dragging it along the surface before pulling it away and inspecting the tip. "Spotless," he said. "That's good. Cleanliness is next to godliness, as I always say."

Wallace choked when Apollo stood next to Harvey, lifting his leg. A stream of urine sprayed onto Harvey's shoes. Apollo looked pleased with himself as he pranced away, Harvey none the wiser.

"Good boy," Nelson cooed. "Yes, you are. Yes, you *are*. You peed all over the bad man like a very good boy."

Harvey said, "Let's see what's in the kitchen, shall we? Perhaps you'd consider telling Mei to remove herself from the premises. Just because my restraining order against her was tossed out due to an utter lack of evidence doesn't mean she can still come within ten feet of me. Not after what happened last year."

"Dumped an entire bowl of icing on his head," Nelson told Wallace. "Said it was an accident. It wasn't."

Wallace was absurdly fond of Mei for reasons that had nothing to do with their current situation. He started to follow them toward the kitchen as Hugo pushed open the door but stopped when he heard a stuttering breath behind him. He turned to see Alan stepping out from his corner, his hands balled into fists, a strangely blank expression on his face.

"He looks like him," Alan said to no one, gaze boring into Harvey. "Looks just like him."

"Who?" Wallace asked.

But Alan ignored him.

The sconces on the wall flared with an electrical snarl.

Harvey glanced over his shoulder. "What was that? Rats chewing on your wiring, Hugo? You know that's . . . not . . ." He frowned, rubbing his chest. "Oh. Is it warm in here? It feels—"

Whatever else he meant to say was lost when the clipboard and pen slid from his hands, clattering on the floor. He took a stuttering step back, blood draining from his face.

Hugo's eyes widened. "Alan, *no*."

Too late. Before any of them could react, the light bulbs on the walls and ceiling shattered all at once, glass raining down around them. Harvey jerked as if he were a puppet on strings, head rocking back. His arms rose on either side of him, hands flexed, fingers trembling.

Alan ground his teeth together as he took another step forward.

Harvey rose a few inches off the floor, the tips of his shoes pointing down. Alan raised his hand toward him, palm toward the ceiling. He folded all but his pointer finger in, and as Wallace watched, moved it back and forth as if beckoning.

Harvey floated toward him even as Hugo shouted for Mei.

The whites of Harvey's eyes were bright in the dull light. He stopped, suspended, in front of Alan. "You look just like him," Alan whispered again. "The man. In the alley. It could almost be you."

Hugo was around the counter even as the kitchen doors flew open, Mei running through, tapping her fingers against her palm.

Alan said, "Stay back," and Wallace cried out as Hugo and Mei were flung away from him, each of them slamming into opposite walls, wooden picture frames cracking. Apollo lunged for Alan, teeth bared, and yelped when Alan waved his other hand. Apollo landed roughly on the ground near the fireplace, looking dazed as he raised his head.

Nelson vanished from his place next to Wallace, only to reappear behind Alan. He raised his cane above his head with a grunt. Wallace roared in fury when Alan jerked his arm back, elbowing Nelson in the gut, causing him to take a hard step back, cane falling to the floor.

Alan turned back toward Harvey, who still hung suspended in front of him. "Now *this* is what I expected being a ghost would be like," he said, almost conversationally. "It's not as hard as I thought it'd be. What I can do. It's anger. That's all it is. And I can use it because I'm *pissed off.*"

Harvey choked, spittle dripping from his mouth and onto his chin.

"Don't do this," Hugo pleaded, struggling against whatever held him onto the wall. "Alan, you can't hurt him."

"Oh, I can," Alan said. "I can hurt him quite a bit."

"He's not your killer," Mei snapped. "He wasn't the one who hurt you. He would never—"

"It doesn't matter," Alan said. "It'll make me feel better. And isn't that what all this is about? Finding peace. This will bring me peace."

Wallace Price had never been what most would consider to be a brave man. Once, he'd seen someone being mugged on a subway platform and stepped away, telling himself he didn't want to get involved, that he was sure it'd all work out for the best. He'd barely felt a twinge of guilt. The mugger had gotten away with a purse, and Wallace knew whatever was inside could easily be replaced.

Bravery meant the possibility of death. And wasn't that funny? Because it took being dead for Wallace to finally be brave.

Hugo screamed his name as he rushed forward, but Wallace ignored him.

Wallace brought his shoulder down as he charged, steeling himself for the impact. It was still jarring when he collided with Alan's side. Wallace's teeth rattled in his gums as he nearly bit his tongue in two. Alan barely made a sound as he was knocked off his feet. Wallace lost his own footing, landing on top of Alan. He moved as quickly as he could, turning and straddling Alan's waist. Harvey collapsed to the floor and didn't move. Hugo and Mei also fell to the floor, Alan's hold over them having dissipated.

Alan's eyes glittered in the dark as he stared up at Wallace. "You shouldn't have done that."

Before Wallace could react (and really, he hadn't thought that far ahead; what was he going to do, choke the life out of a dead man?), the air shifted around him, and he was flung back. He gasped as the small of his back struck one of the display cases, the glass cracking underneath him.

Alan rose slowly to his feet, pointing a finger at Wallace. "You *really* shouldn't have—"

And then he stopped.

Wallace blinked.

He waited for Alan to finish his threat.

He didn't.

He seemed . . . frozen in place.

"Um," Wallace said. "What happened?"

No one answered him.

He turned his head to the left.

Mei had been in the process of pushing herself up off the ground, her hair hanging in her face.

She wasn't moving.

Wallace looked forward. Nelson had started to prop himself up with his cane, but only made it halfway before he too just . . . stopped.

Wallace turned his head to the right.

Apollo stood in front of Hugo, teeth bared in a silent snarl. Hugo himself was propping himself up against the wall, a look of anger mingled with despair on his face.

Wallace pushed himself off the display case, surprised when he did so without resistance.

"Guys?" he said, voice echoing flatly in the dark tea shop. "What's going on?"

No one answered him.

It was only then that he realized the second hand of the clock wasn't moving. It wasn't even *twitching*.

It'd stopped.

Everything had stopped.

"Oh no," Wallace whispered.

He didn't know what was happening. The only time the clock stopped was when a new ghost arrived at Charon's Crossing, but time hadn't stopped *inside* the tea shop.

"Hugo?" he whispered, taking a step toward him. "Are you—"

He raised his hand to shield his eyes as a bright blue light flashed from outside the tea shop. It filled the windows brilliantly, casting shadows that stretched long. The light pulsed again and again. He took a step toward the front of the shop, only to bring a hand to his chest.

The hook. The cable.

They felt dead.

They *were* dead.

"What is this?" he whispered.

He reached the closest window, looking out to the front of the tea shop, squinting against the bright light that lit up the forest, shadows dancing.

A vague shape stood out on the dirt road. As the light faded, the shape filled in, and Wallace saw it for what it was.

He remembered the brief glimpse he'd seen in the forest the night he'd tried to escape. The outline of a strange beast that he'd managed to convince himself was just a trick of the shadows.

Not a trick.

It was real.

And it was here.

There, standing in the road, was a stag.

CHAPTER
17

It was bigger than any stag Wallace had ever seen in pictures. Even from a distance, the creature looked as if it would tower over all of them. It held its head high, the many points of its antlers like a bony crown. As the stag stepped closer to the tea shop, Wallace could see flowers hanging from the antlers, their roots embedded into the velvet, blossoms in shades of ochre and fuchsia, cerulean and scarlet, canary and magenta. At the tips of its antlers were tiny white lights, as if the bones were filled with stars.

Wallace couldn't move, a sound falling from his mouth like he'd been punched in the gut.

The stag's nostrils flared, its eyes like black holes as it dug its hooves into the earth. Its hair was brown with white splotches along its back and considerable chest. Its tail swished back and forth. As the stag lowered its head, flower petals drifted down onto the ground.

Wallace said, "Oh. Oh. Oh."

The stag jerked its head back up as if it'd heard him. It bleated softly, a long, mournful cry that caused a lump to form in Wallace's throat.

He said, "Hugo. Hugo, are you seeing this?"

Hugo didn't answer.

The stag stopped a few feet from the stairs to the tea shop. The flowers growing from its antlers folded in on themselves as if shutting away against the night. The stag reared up on its hind legs. Its belly was completely white.

And then the stag was gone, a frame rate stutter, a glitch in reality. The stag was there, and then it wasn't.

In its place stood a child.

A boy.

He was young, perhaps nine or ten, with golden-brown skin, his eyes a strange shade of violet. Long, shaggy hair curled down around his ears, brown with streaks of white, unfurled flowers woven into the locks. He wore a T-shirt over jeans. It took Wallace a moment to make out the words on the shirt in the dark.

JUST A KID FROM TOPEKA

The boy's feet were bare. He flexed his fingers and toes, tilting his head from side to side before looking up at the window once more, directly at Wallace. The boy nodded, and Wallace felt his throat close.

The boy began to climb the stairs.

Wallace stumbled back from the window. He managed to keep upright, though it was close. He looked around wildly, for someone, anyone to see what he was seeing. Hugo and Mei were as they'd been. Apollo and Nelson too. Alan, the same.

He was alone.

The boy knocked on the door.

Once.

Twice.

Three times.

"Go away," Wallace croaked out. "Please, just go away."

"I can't do that, Wallace," the boy said, his voice light, the words almost like musical notes. He wasn't quite singing, but it wasn't normal speech either. There was a weight to him, a presence Wallace could feel even through the door, heavy and ethereal. "It's time we had a little chat."

"Who are you?" Wallace whispered.

"You know who I am," the boy said, voice muffled. "I'm not going to hurt you. I would never do that."

"I don't believe you."

"Understandable. You don't know me. Let's change that, shall we?"

The doorknob turned.

The door opened.

The boy stepped inside Charon's Crossing. The wooden floors

creaked under his feet. As he slowly closed the door behind him, the walls of the tea shop began to ripple like a breeze blowing across the surface of a pond. Wallace wondered what would happen if he tried to touch them, if he'd sink into the walls and drown.

The boy nodded at Wallace before looking around the room. He cocked his head at Alan, brow furrowing. "Angry, isn't he? It's odd, really. The universe is bigger than one can possibly imagine, a truth beyond comprehension, and yet all he knows is anger and hurt. Pain and suffering." He sighed, shaking his head. "I'll never understand, no matter how hard I try. It's illogical."

"What do you want?" Wallace asked. His back was pressed against the counter. He thought about running, but he didn't think he'd get very far. And he wasn't about to leave Hugo and Mei and Nelson and Apollo. Not while they couldn't defend themselves.

"I'm not going to hurt them," the boy said, and for a terrible moment, Wallace wondered if the child could read his mind. "I've never hurt anyone before."

"I don't believe you," Wallace said again.

"You don't?" The boy scrunched up his face. "Why?"

"Because of what you are."

"What am I, Wallace?"

And with the last of his strength, Wallace whispered, "You're the Manager."

The boy seemed pleased with his answer. "I am. Silly title, but it fits, I suppose. My real name is much more complicated, and I doubt your human tongue would be able to pronounce it. It'd turn your mouth to mush if you tried." He reached up and plucked a flower from his head, popping it into his mouth. His eyes fluttered shut as he sucked on the petals. "Ah. That's better. It's hard for me to take this form and keep it for long. The flowers help." He looked up at one of the potted plants hanging from the ceiling. "You've been watering these."

"It's my job," Wallace said faintly.

"Is it?" He poked a finger against the planter. Leaves grew. Vines lengthened. Soil trickled down onto the floor, little motes of dust and dirt catching the light from the dying fire in the fireplace. "Do you know what my job is?"

Wallace shook his head, tongue thick in his mouth.

"Everything," the boy said. "My job is everything."

"Are you God?" Wallace choked out.

The boy laughed. It sounded like he was singing. "No. Of course not. There is no God, at least not like you're thinking. He's a human construct, one capable of great peace and violent wrath. It's a dichotomy only found in the human mind, so of course he'd be made in your image. But I'm afraid he's nothing but a fairy tale in a book of fiction. The truth is infinitely more complicated than that. Tell me, Wallace. What are you doing here?"

He kept his distance, which Wallace was grateful for. "I live here."

"Do you?" the boy asked. "How do you figure?"

"I was brought here."

The boy nodded. "You were. Mei, she's good people. A little headstrong, but a Reaper has to be for all they deal with. There's no one like her in all the world. The same could be said for Hugo. And Nelson. Apollo. Even you and Alan, though not quite in the same way." He went to one of the tables and grabbed hold of a chair. He grunted as he pulled it down. It was bigger than he was, and Wallace thought it was going to crash down upon his head. It didn't, and he set it on the floor before climbing onto it and sitting down. His feet dangled as he kicked them back and forth. He folded his hands in his lap, twiddling his thumbs. "It's nice to finally meet you, Wallace. I know so much about you, but it's good to see you face to face."

A fresh wave of terror washed over him. "Why are you here?"

The boy shrugged. "Why are any of us here?"

Wallace narrowed his eyes. "Do you always answer a question with a question?"

The boy laughed again. "I like you. I always have, even when you were . . . you know. A bastard."

Wallace blinked. "Excuse me?"

"A bastard," the boy repeated. "It took you dying to find your humanity. It's hysterical if you think about it."

A flare of anger burned in Wallace's chest. "Oh, I'm so glad this is all such a riot to you."

"There's no need for that. I'm not being facetious. You're not as you once were. Why do you think that is?"

Wallace said, "I don't know."

"It's okay not to know." The boy tilted his head against the back of the chair, staring up at the ceiling. It too shimmered like the walls, as if liquid instead of solid. "In fact, an argument could be made it's better that way. Still . . . you're a curiosity. And that means you have my attention."

"Did you do this to them?" Wallace demanded. "If you're hurting them, I'll—"

"You'll what?" the boy asked.

Wallace said nothing.

The boy nodded. "I told you I wasn't going to hurt you or them. They're sleeping, in a way. When we're finished, they'll awaken and things will be as they always were and always will be. Do you like it here?"

"Yes."

The boy looked around, the movement strangely stiff as if the bones in his neck were fused together. "It doesn't seem like much from the outside, does it? A queer house made up of many different ideas. They should clash. They should crumble to the foundation. It shouldn't stand as it does, and yet you don't fear the ceiling collapsing onto your head." Then, "Why did you step in to protect them? The Wallace Price of the living world wouldn't have raised a finger unless it benefited himself."

"They're my friends," Wallace said, awash in unreality. The room around him felt hazy and muted, only the Manager crystal clear, a focal point, the center of everything.

"They are?" the boy asked. "You didn't have many of those." He frowned. "*Any* of those."

Wallace looked away. "I know."

"Then you died," the boy said. "And came here. To this place. To this . . . way station. A stop on a much larger journey. And you did just that, didn't you? You stopped."

"I don't want to go through the door," Wallace said, voice raising and cracking right down the middle. "You can't make me."

"I could," the boy said. "It would be easy. No effort on my part at all. Would you like me to show you?"

Fear, bright and glassy. It wrapped its hands around Wallace's ribs, fingers digging in.

"I won't," the boy said. "Because that's not what you need." He glanced at Hugo, expression softening. "He's a good ferryman, Hugo, though his heart often gets in the way. When I found him, he was angry and confused. Adrift. He didn't understand the way of things, and yet he had this light in him, fierce but in danger of flickering out. I taught him how to harness it. People like him, they're rare. There's beauty in the chaos, if you know where to look for it. But you would know about that, wouldn't you? You see it too."

Wallace swallowed thickly. "He's different."

"That's certainly one way to put it." The boy kicked his feet again as he settled back into the chair, hands on his stomach. "But yes, he is."

The anger returned, burning the fear away. "And you did this to him."

The boy arched an eyebrow. "Excuse me?"

Wallace's hands balled into fists. "I've heard about you."

"Oh boy," he said. "This should be good. Go ahead. Tell me what you've heard."

"You make the ferry . . . people."

"I do," the boy said, "though I don't want you thinking I pick them without rhyme or reason. Certain people . . . well. They shine brightly. Hugo happened to be one of them."

Wallace clenched his jaw. "You're supposed to be this . . . this *thing*—"

"Rude."

"—this grand thing that oversees life and death, delegating the responsibilities to others—"

"Well, yes. I'm the Manager. I manage."

"—and you put the weight of death on someone like Hugo. You make him see and do things that—"

"Whoa," the boy said, sitting up quickly. "Hold on a second. I don't make anyone do *anything*. Goodness gracious, Wallace, what have they been telling you about me?"

"You're callous," Wallace spat. "And cruel. How could you ever think putting something like that on a man who'd just lost his family was the right thing to do?"

"Hmm," the boy said. "I think we've got our wires crossed somewhere. That's not the case at all. It's a choice, Wallace. It all comes down to choice. I didn't *force* Hugo to do anything. I merely laid out the options before him and let him make up his own mind."

Wallace slammed his hands against the counter. "His parents had just *died*. He was suffering. He was *grieving*. And you opened a door to show him that there was something beyond what he knew. Of course he would take what you offered. You preyed upon him when he was at his weakest, knowing full well he wasn't in his right mind." Wallace was panting by the time he finished, palms stinging.

"Wow," the boy said. He squinted at Wallace. "You're protective of him."

Wallace blanched. "I . . ."

The boy nodded as if this were answer enough. "I didn't expect that. I don't know why. But with all I've seen, the most wonderful thing is that I can still be surprised by one such as you. You care about him very much."

"All of them," Wallace said. "I care about all of them."

"Because they're your friends."

"Yes."

"Then why don't you trust Hugo enough to make decisions for himself?"

"I do," Wallace said weakly.

"Do you? Because it sounds like you're second-guessing his

choices. I would hope you could tell the difference between being protective and doubting someone you call a friend."

Wallace said nothing. As much as he hated to admit it, the Manager had a point. Shouldn't he trust Hugo to know what was right for himself?

The boy nodded as if Wallace's silence was tacit agreement. He slid from the chair before turning around and lifting it up. He flipped it over and put it back on the table, wiping his hands on his jeans once he'd finished. He glanced at the health inspector and sighed. "People are so strange. Just when I think I have you all figured out, you go and make a mess of things." Absurdly, he sounded almost fond.

He turned back toward Wallace, clapping his hands. "Okay. Let's get a move on. Time is short. Well, not for me, but for the rest of you. Follow me, if you please."

"Where are we going?"

"To show you the truth," the boy said. He went to Alan, looking up at him and smiling sadly. He reached out and touched Alan's hip, shaking his head. "Oh. Yes. This one. I'm sorry for what you've been through. I'll do my best to make it better."

And then, before Wallace could do anything to stop him, he puckered his lips and blew a thin stream of air toward Alan, cheeks bulging. Wallace blinked as a hook materialized in Alan's chest, a cable growing and extending between him and Hugo. The Manager curled his fingers around the hook and yanked. It pulled free. The cable connecting Alan to Hugo dulled. The Manager dropped the hook, and as it hit the floor, it and the cable turned to dust. "There," he said. "That's better." He turned and headed farther into the house.

Wallace looked down at his own cable, still connecting him to Hugo. The cable flashed weakly, the hook shivering in his chest. He was about to touch it, to allow himself the reminder it was there, it was *real*, when Alan rose a few inches off the floor, floating though still frozen. The boy looked back at Wallace from the entry to the hallway. "Coming, Wallace?"

"If I say no?"

The boy shrugged. "Then you do. But I wish you wouldn't."

Wallace stumbled back when Alan began to rise toward the ceiling. "Where are you taking him?"

"Home," the boy said simply. He disappeared down the hallway. Wallace looked at Alan in time to see his feet disappear *through* the ceiling, concentric circles undulating outward.

He did the only thing he could.

He followed the Manager.

He knew where they were going, and though he'd never been more frightened in his life, he still climbed the stairs, each step harder than the last.

He passed by the second floor. The third. All the windows were black, as if all light had vanished from the world.

He stopped near the fourth floor landing, peering through the railing. The Manager stood below the door. Alan floated up through the floor, stopping next to him, suspended in air.

"I'm not going to force you through the door," the boy said mildly. "If that's what you're thinking."

"And Alan?" Wallace asked, climbing the last few stairs.

"Alan's a different case. I'll do what I must for him."

"Why?"

The boy laughed. "So many questions. Why, why, why. You're funny, Wallace. It's because he's becoming dangerous. Obviously."

"You're going to make him go through the door."

The boy looked back at him over his shoulder. "Yes."

"How is that *fair*?"

The boy looked confused. "Death? How is it not? You're born, yes. You live and breathe and dance and ache, but you die. Everyone dies. Every*thing* dies. Death is cleansing. The pain of a mortal life is gone."

"Tell that to Alan," Wallace growled. "He's hurting. He's filled with anger—"

The boy turned, frowning. "Because he's still stuck here. He doesn't see the way things should be. Not everyone can adapt as well as you." He gnawed on his bottom lip. "Or Nelson or Apollo. I like them too. They wouldn't be here if I didn't."

"And Lea?" Wallace snapped. "What about her? Where were you when she needed you? When Hugo needed you?" A thought struck him, terrible and harsh. "Or did what happened to Cameron keep you away?"

The boy's shoulders slumped. "I never claimed to be perfect, Wallace. Perfection is a flaw in itself. Lea was . . . it shouldn't have happened the way it did. The Reaper was out of line, and he paid for it dearly." He shook his head. "I manage, Wallace. But even I can't manage everyone all the time. Free will is paramount, though it can get a bit messy at times. I don't interfere unless there's no other way."

"And so they're supposed to suffer because of what you can't do?"

The boy sighed. "I can see where you're coming from. Thanks for the feedback, Wallace. I'll take it into consideration going forward."

"*Feedback?*" Wallace said, outraged. "That's what you're calling it?"

"It's either that or you're telling me what I can and cannot do. I'm giving you the benefit of the doubt, because I choose to believe you can't possibly be *that* stupid." He turned his face up toward the door. It vibrated in its frame, the leaves and flowers carved into the wood bursting to life. The crystal leaf in the doorknob glittered.

"I like you," the boy said again without looking at him. He raised his hand toward the door, curling his fingers. "Which is why I'm going to tell you how things will go." He twisted his hand sharply.

The doorknob on the ceiling above them turned.

The latch clicked, the crystal leaf flashing brightly.

The door opened slowly, swinging down toward them.

Hugo had told him what he'd seen when the door opened, how it made him feel. And still, Wallace wasn't prepared for what happened next. Light spilled out so bright that he had to look away. He thought he heard birds singing on the other side, but the whispers from the door were too loud for him to be sure. He lifted his head in time to see the Manager push gently on the bottom of Alan's feet. Before Wallace could open his mouth, Alan rose swiftly, passing through the doorway. The light pulsed before it faded. The door slammed shut. It took only seconds.

"He'll find peace," the boy said. "With time, he'll find himself again." He turned and sank to the floor, legs crossed in front of him. He looked up at Wallace still standing near the stairs.

"What did you do?" Wallace whispered.

"Helped him along his journey," the boy said. "I find that sometimes people need a little push in the right direction."

"What happened to free will?"

The boy grinned. It chilled Wallace to the bone. "You're smarter than I gave you credit for. Fun! Think of it as . . . hmm. Ah. Think of it as a gentle nudge in the right direction. Can't have him turning into a Husk. I don't like to think what that would do to Hugo. Not again. He took it so hard the first time. It's why I've allowed Nelson and Apollo to stay as long as they have, to keep him from abandoning his calling."

"So we only have free will until . . . what? It interferes with your order?"

The Manager chuckled. "Precisely! Good for you, Wallace. Order is absolutely paramount. Without it, we'd be stumbling in the dark. Which brings me to you. You've been here a long time, much longer than any other aside from Nelson and Apollo. And for what? Do you even know? What is your purpose?"

Wallace felt like he was on fire. "I . . ."

"Yes," the Manager said. "I thought as much. Let me help you answer that. Your being here makes you a distraction in ways Nelson and Apollo aren't. A distracted ferryman is one who'll make mistakes. Hugo has a job to do, one that is far more important than his *feelings*." He grimaced. "Terrible things, those. I've watched and waited, allowing this farce of a happy little home to play out, but it's time to move things along to ensure Hugo does what he was hired to do." He grinned. "Which is why I'm going to tell you what'll happen next."

Wallace didn't like the sound of that. "What?"

The boy cocked his head as he studied Wallace. "How to put this in ways you can understand. How . . . to . . . put—Ah!" He clapped his hands. "You're a lawyer." His lips quirked. "Well, you *were*. I'm like you, in a way. Death, my dear man, is the law, and I'm the judge. There are rules and regulations. Sure, the bureaucracy of it all can be a little tiresome, and the monotony is killer, but we need the rule of law so we know how to be, how to act." The smile slid from his face. "And yet, it's always *why*. Why, why, why. I hate that question above all others." And then his voice changed, becoming a frightened woman's. "Why do I have to go?" His voice changed again, becoming a man's, old and frail. "Why can't I have more time?" Again, this time a child. "Why can't I stay?"

"Stop," Wallace said hoarsely. "Please stop."

When the Manager spoke again, his voice returned to normal. "I've heard it all." He frowned. "I *hate* it. But never more so than I do right now, because I find *myself* asking why. Why is Wallace Price still here? Why doesn't he move on?" He shook his head as if disappointed. "That leads to *me* asking myself why I should care at all. You want to know what I realized?"

"No," Wallace whispered.

"I realized that you're an aberration. A flaw in the system that's worked so well. And what does one do with flaws as someone in charge, Wallace? To keep the things running as they should?"

Fire them. Remove them from the equation. Replace the part so the machine can run smoothly. Distantly, Wallace thought of Patricia Ryan, sitting across from him in his office.

"Exactly," the Manager said as if Wallace had spoken aloud. He tapped his fingers against his knee. The bottoms of his feet were dirty. "Which is why I've made an executive decision." He grinned, the violet of his eyes moving like liquid. "One week. I'll give you one more week to put your affairs in order. This isn't meant to be forever, Wallace. A way station such as this exists to allow you to regroup, to accept the inevitable. You've changed in the weeks since your arrival. So different from the man I saw fleeing in the dead of night."

"But—"

The boy held up his hand. "I'm not finished. Please don't interrupt me again. I don't like being interrupted." When he saw Wallace snap his mouth closed, he continued. "You've been given more than enough time to process your life spent on this Earth. You were not a kind man, Wallace, or even a just one. You were selfish and mean. Not quite as cruel as you claim I am, but it was close. I don't recognize that man in you. Not anymore. Death has opened your eyes. I can see the good in you now, and what you're willing to do for those you care about. Because you do care about them, don't you?"

"Yes," Wallace said gruffly.

"I figured. And really, I can see why. They're certainly . . . unique."

"I know they are. There's no one like them."

The boy laughed again. "I'm glad we can at least agree on that." He sobered. "One week, dear Wallace. I'll give you one more week. In seven days, I shall return. I'll bring you to this door. I will see you through it because that's the way it's supposed to be."

"And if I refuse?"

The boy shrugged. "Then you do. I hope you won't, but I can't promise that this will go on for much longer. You aren't meant to be here. Not like this. Perhaps in another life, you could have found your way to this place, and made the most of it."

"I don't want to go," Wallace said. "I'm not ready."

"I know that," the boy said, for the first time sounding irritated. "Which is why I'm giving you a week rather than making you go now." His face darkened. "Don't mistake my offer for anything but what it is. There is no loophole, no last-minute bit of evidence you can fling upon the courtroom in a display of your legal prowess. I can make you do things, Wallace. I don't want to, but I can."

Dazed, Wallace said, "I . . . maybe it'd be different. I've changed. You've said as much. I—"

"No," the boy said, shaking his head. "It's not the same. You aren't Nelson, the grandfather who guided Hugo after the loss of his parents. You aren't Apollo, who helped Hugo to breathe when his lungs collapsed in his chest. You are an outsider, an anomaly. The options I've laid out for you—going through the door or running the risk of losing all you've gained—are your *only* options. You're a disruption, Wallace, and though I've allowed certain . . . concessions in the spirit of magnanimity, don't make the mistake of thinking I'll look the other way for you. This was always temporary."

"And what about Cameron?" Wallace demanded. "And all the others like him?"

The boy looked surprised. "The Husks? Why do you care?"

I'm still here. I'm still here.

"He's not gone," Wallace said. "He's still there. Part of him still exists. Help him, and I'll do whatever you want."

The boy shook his head slowly. "I'm not here to bargain with you, Wallace. I thought you were beyond that stage already. You're into the fabled land of acceptance, or at least you were. Don't backtrack on me now."

"It's not *for* me," Wallace snapped. "It's for him."

"Ah," the boy said. "Is it? What would you have me do? Cure him? He knew the risks when he chose to leave the grounds." He stood, wiping his hands off on the front of his jeans. "I'm glad we've had this talk. It's been a pleasure meeting you, and believe me, that's not something I say often." He grimaced. "Humans are untidy. I'd rather keep my distance if possible. It's easier when they agree with me, as you have."

"I didn't agree to anything!" Wallace cried.

The boy pouted. "Aw. Well, I'm sure you'll come around to it. One week, Wallace. What will you do with the time you have left? I can't wait to find out. Tell the others, or don't. It doesn't concern me either way. And don't worry about the health inspector. He won't remember a thing." The boy tipped Wallace a jaunty salute. "See you soon."

And then he vanished.

Wallace's knees felt weak, loose, and he grabbed onto the railing to hold himself up as he heard yelling come from the bottom floor below him. He closed his eyes when Hugo began to shout his name frantically. "Here," he whispered. "I'm still here."

CHAPTER 18

Hugo said, "Alan. Wallace, where's Alan?"

Wallace looked at the door in the ceiling. "He's crossed."

Hugo was bewildered. "What? On his own? How?"

Wallace shook his head. "I don't know. But he's gone. He found his way through, and he's gone."

Hugo stared at him. "I don't . . . are you all right?"

Wallace smiled, but the weight of it was heavy. "Of course."

Back downstairs, Harvey said, "I do believe I lost myself for a little while. Excuse me, won't you? I need to go home. I've got a terrible headache." He was pale as he walked toward the door. "Keep this place up to code, Hugo. You won't like what'll happen if you don't."

He walked through the door, closing it quietly behind him.

"What the hell?" Mei muttered. "What happened?"

"I don't know," Nelson said, hands rubbing his forehead. "I feel like I've just woken up. Isn't that strange?"

Hugo didn't say a word. His gaze never left Wallace.

And Wallace looked away.

Seven days.

What will you do with the time you have left?

Wallace pondered this as the sun rose on the first day.

He didn't know.

He'd never felt more lost in his life.

Grief, Wallace knew, had the power to consume, to eat away until there was nothing left but hollowed-out bones. Oh, the shape of the person remained as it was, even if the cheeks turned sallow, and dark circles formed under the eyes. Hollowed out and left raw, they were still recognizably human. It came in stages, some smaller than others, but undeniable.

These were the stages of Wallace Price:

On the first of his remaining days, he was in denial.

The shop opened as it always did, bright and early. The scones and muffins were placed in the display case, the scent of them warm and thick. Tea was brewed and steeped, poured into cups and sipped slowly. People laughed. People smiled. They hugged one another as if they hadn't seen each other in years, patting backs and gripping shoulders.

He watched them all through the portholes in the kitchen, burdened with the knowledge that they could leave this place whenever they wished. The bitterness he felt was surprising, tugging at the back of his mind. He kept it in place, not allowing it to roar forward no matter how much he wanted it to.

"It's not real," he muttered to himself. "None of it is real."

"What was that?"

He glanced over his shoulder. Mei stood next to the sink, a look of concern on her face. He shook his head. "Nothing."

She didn't believe him. "What's wrong?"

He laughed wildly. "Nothing at all. I'm dead. What could possibly be wrong?"

She hesitated. "Did something happen? With Alan, or . . . ?"

"I told you already. He went through the door. I don't know how. I don't know why. I don't even know how he got there. But he's gone."

"So you said. I just . . ." She shook her head. "You know you can talk to us, right? Whatever you need."

He left her in the kitchen, heading out the back door.

He walked amongst the tea plants, fingers trailing along the leaves.

ↄ

The first night was anger.

Oh, but was he angry.

He snapped at Nelson. At Apollo. They were hovering. Nelson held up his hands as Apollo put his tail between his legs. "What's gotten into you?" Nelson asked.

"None of your business," Wallace snarled. "Leave me alone for one damn second."

Nelson was hurt, shoulders stiff as he pulled Apollo away. "You should see a doctor."

Wallace blinked. "What? Why?"

"To get that stick up your ass removed."

Before he could retort, Hugo was in front of him, brow furrowed. "Outside."

Wallace glared at him. "I don't want to go outside."

"Now." He turned and headed down the hallway, not looking back to see if Wallace would follow.

He thought about staying right where he was.

In the end, he didn't.

Hugo stood on the deck, face turned toward the sky.

"What do you want?" Wallace grumbled, staying near the door.

"Scream," Hugo said. "I want you to scream."

That startled Wallace. "What?"

Hugo didn't look at him. "Yell. Scream. Rage. As loud as you can. Get it all out. It'll help. Trust me. The longer it sits in you, the more you're poisoned. It's best to get it out while you can."

"I'm not going to scream—"

Hugo sucked in a deep breath and yelled. It was deep, the sound of it rolling through the forest around them. It was as if all the trees were screaming. His voice cracked near the end, and when his voice died, his chest heaved. He wiped spittle from his lips with the back of his hand. "Your turn."

"That was stupid."

"Do you trust me?"

Wallace sagged. "You know I do."

"Then do it. I don't know what's happened to cause this regression, but I don't like it."

"And you think screaming into nothing will make me feel better."

Hugo shrugged. "What could it hurt?"

Wallace sighed before joining Hugo at the railing. He felt Hugo's gaze on him as he looked up toward the stars. He'd never felt smaller than he did at that moment. It hurt more than he cared to admit.

"Do it," Hugo said quietly. "Let me hear you."

He wondered when the threshold had been crossed that he couldn't refuse Hugo anything.

So he screamed as loud as he could.

He put everything into it he had. His parents, telling him he was an embarrassment. His mother, taking her last breaths, his father next to him, though he felt like a stranger. When he died two years later, Wallace didn't shed a tear. He told himself he'd cried over them long enough.

And Naomi. He'd loved her. He really had. It hadn't been enough, and she didn't deserve what he'd turned into. He thought about the last good days they had, when he could almost convince himself that they'd make it work. It'd been foolish to think that way. The death knell had already sounded, they'd just ignored it for as long as they'd been able to in hopes that it wasn't the end. They went to the coast, just the two of them, a couple of days away from everything. They held hands on the drive there, and it was almost like it'd used to be. They laughed. They sang along with the radio. He had rented a convertible, and the wind whipped through their hair, the sun shining down. They didn't talk about work or children or money or past arguments. Deep down, he had known this was it, the last chance.

It hadn't been enough.

They had made it a single day before they were fighting again. Wounds he long thought scarred over reopened and bled again.

The car ride back was silent, her arms folded defensively. He ignored the tear that trickled down her cheek from underneath her sunglasses.

A week later, she served him with divorce papers. He didn't fight it. It was easier this way. She'd be better off. It was what they both wanted.

He'd drowned, unaware that he'd slipped beneath the surface.

And so here, now, he screamed as loud as he could. Tears prickled his eyes, and he was almost able to convince himself they came from the exertion. Spit flew from his mouth. His throat hurt.

When he could scream no longer, he put his face in his hands, shoulders shaking.

Hugo said, "It's life, Wallace. Even when you're dead, it's still life. You exist. You're real. You're strong and brave, and I'm so happy to know you. Now, tell me what happened with Alan. All of it. Leave nothing out."

Wallace told him everything.

The third stage of grief was bargaining, and it also came on the first night.

But it wasn't Wallace who bargained.

It was Hugo.

He bargained by shouting, demanding the Manager show himself to explain what the hell he'd meant. Mei stood speechless. She hadn't said a word since Hugo had told her and Nelson the truth. Nelson's mouth was still hanging open, hands curled tightly around his cane.

"I'm calling you," Hugo snapped as he paced the main room of the tea shop, glaring up at the ceiling. "I need to talk to you. I know you're there. You're always there. You owe me this. I never ask for anything, but I'm asking you to be here now. I'll listen. I swear I'll listen."

Apollo trailed after him, back and forth, back and forth, ears alert as he listened to his owner grow angrier.

Wallace tried to stop Hugo, tried to tell him that it was fine, that it was okay, that he'd always known it would come to this. "This isn't forever," he said. "You know that. You told me that. It's a stop, Hugo. One stop on a journey."

But Hugo didn't listen.

"Manager!" he cried. "Show yourself!"

The Manager didn't come.

As the clock moved toward midnight, Mei convinced Hugo he needed to sleep. He argued bitterly, but in the end, he agreed. "We'll figure it out tomorrow," he told Wallace. "I'll think of something. I don't know what, but I'll figure it out. You aren't going anywhere if you don't want to."

Wallace nodded. "Go to bed. The day starts early."

Hugo shook his head. Muttering under his breath, he climbed the stairs, Apollo following him.

Mei waited until the door slammed shut above them before she turned to Wallace. "He'll do what he can," she said quietly.

"I know," Wallace said. "But I don't know if he should."

She narrowed her eyes. "What?"

He sighed as he looked away. "He has a job to do. Nothing is more important than that. He can't throw it away because of me."

"He's not throwing anything away," she said sharply. "He's fighting to give you the time you deserve, to make your own choice about when you're ready. Don't you see that?"

"Does it matter?"

"What the hell is *that* supposed to mean?"

"I'm dead," he said. "There's no going back from that. A river only moves in one direction."

"But—"

"It is what it is. You've all taught me that. I didn't listen at first, but I learned. And it made me better because of it. Isn't that the point?"

She sniffled. "Oh, Wallace. It's more than that now."

"Maybe," he said. "Maybe if things were different, we'd . . ." He couldn't finish. "There's still time left. The best thing I can do is to make the most of it."

Soon after, she went to bed.

The clocked ticked, ticked, ticked the seconds and minutes and hours away.

Nelson said, "I'm glad you're here."

Wallace jerked his head up. "What?"

Nelson smiled sadly. "When you first arrived, I thought you were just another visitor. You'd stay for a little while, and then you'd see the light." He chuckled. "Forgive the expression. Clichéd, I know. Hugo would do what he does, and you'd move on without muss or fuss, even though you were adamant you wouldn't. You'd be like all the others who'd come before you."

"I am."

"Perhaps," Nelson allowed. "But that doesn't discount what you've done in your time here. The work you've put in to making yourself a better person." He shuffled toward Wallace, setting the cane against the table Wallace was leaning on. Wallace didn't flinch when Nelson reached up and cupped his face. His hands were warm. "Be proud of what you've accomplished, Wallace. You've earned that right."

"I'm scared," Wallace whispered. "I don't mean to be, but I am."

"I know you are," Nelson said. "I am too. But as long as we're together, we can help each other until the end. Our strength will be your strength. We won't carry you because you don't need us to. But we'll be by your side." Then, "Can I ask you something?"

Wallace nodded as Nelson dropped his hands.

"If things were different, and you were still . . . here. I don't know how. Say you took a trip on your own, and you ended up in our little town. You found your way to this tea shop, and Hugo was as he was, and you were as you were. What would you do?"

Wallace laughed wetly. "I'd probably make a mess of things."

"Of course you would. But that's the beauty of it, don't you think? Life is messy and terrible and wonderful, all at the same time. What would you do if Hugo was before you and there was nothing stopping you? Life or death or anything else. What would you do?"

Wallace closed his eyes. "Everything."

⁓

Depression hit on the second morning, brief though it was. Wallace allowed himself the sadness that stirred within him, remembering how Hugo had told him grief wasn't only for the living. He stood on the back deck, watching the sunrise. He could hear Hugo and Mei moving around in the kitchen. Hugo had wanted to close the shop for the day, but Wallace told him to go on as he always did. He had Mei on his side, and Hugo finally relented, though he wasn't happy about it.

The sunlight filtered through the trees, melting the thin layer of frost on the ground. He gripped the railing as the light stretched toward him. It touched his hands first. And then his wrists, and arms, and finally his face. It warmed him. It calmed him. He hoped wherever he was going that there'd still be the sun and the moon and the stars. He'd spent a majority of his life with his head turned down. It seemed only fair that eternity would allow him to raise his face toward the sky.

The sadness receded, though it didn't leave entirely. It still bubbled underneath the surface, but he floated on top of it now. This was a different kind of grief, he knew, but it was still his all the same.

He accepted that.

What will you do with the time you have left?

And that's when he knew.

⁓

"Are you out of your damn *mind*?" Mei snapped at him. She stood in the kitchen, glaring at him as if Wallace were the stupidest person she'd ever laid eyes on. Hugo manned the register out front, the shop busy.

He shrugged. "Probably? But I think it's the right thing to do."

She threw up her hands. "Nothing involving Desdemona Trip-plethorne is the right thing to do. She's a terrible person, and when she finally bites the big one, I'm going to—"

"Help her like you've helped everyone else if she gets assigned to you?"

Mei deflated. "Of course I will. But man, I won't like it. And you can't make me."

"I wouldn't dream of it. I know you don't care for her, Mei. And you have very good reason not to. But you said Nancy trusts her, for whatever reason. If it came from you or Hugo, she might not listen. At least with Desdemona, we'd have a chance. And if what I have in mind works, she won't be here very long." He shook his head. "I won't do this, though, without your okay."

"Why?"

She was really going to make him say it, wasn't she? "Because you matter."

She startled, a slow smile blooming on her face. "I matter?"

He groaned. "Shut up."

She looked away, though he could tell she was pleased. "Hugo's not going to be happy about this."

"I know. But the point of all of this is to help as many people as you can, right? And Nancy needs help, Mei. She's stuck, and it's killing her. Maybe it won't work, and it won't make anything better. But what if it does? Don't we owe it to her to try?"

Mei wiped her eyes. "I think I liked you better when you were an asshole."

He laughed. "I like you too, Mei."

He wrapped his arms around her when she lunged at him, holding her close.

ॐ

"No," Hugo said.

"But—"

"No."

"Told you," Mei muttered as she pushed her way through the double doors. "I'll watch the register."

"She needs this, Hugo," Wallace said as the doors swung shut. "Something, anything to show her that all is not lost, even though it can seem that way."

"She's fragile," Hugo said. "Breakable. If it went wrong, I don't want to think what that would do to her."

"We owe it to her to try," Wallace said. He held up his hand as Hugo started to retort. "Not just you, Hugo. All of us. What happened to her and Lea isn't your fault. I know you think it is, and I know you think you should have done more, but what the other Reaper did is on him, not you. Still, it's heavy. Grief. You know that better than anyone. It'll crush you if you let it. And she's being crushed. If I were where she is now, I'd hope someone would do the same for me. Wouldn't you?"

"She might not even agree," Hugo muttered, refusing to look at Wallace. He was frowning, brow knitted, shoulders hunched. "Nothing happened the first time."

"I know," Wallace said. "But it's going to be different this time around. You knew Lea, at least for a little while. You spoke with her. You cared for her."

Wallace thought Hugo would still refuse. Instead, he said, "What are we going to do?"

⁓

On the third evening, Hugo switched the sign in the window to CLOSED FOR A PRIVATE EVENT.

"Are you sure about this?" Nelson whispered, watching his grandson move around the tea shop, preparing for their guests.

"As much as I can be," Wallace whispered back.

"A delicate matter requires delicate hands."

"You don't think we can do it?"

"That's not what I meant. You're blunt and sharp, but you've learned a bit of grace, Wallace. Kindness and grace."

"Because of you," Wallace said. "You and Mei and Hugo."

Nelson grinned at him. "You think so?"

He did. "I wish—"

But whatever Wallace wished stayed within him as lights filled the windows.

"They're here," Mei said as Hugo went back into the kitchen. "You're serious about this?"

"As a heart attack," Wallace said, Nelson chuckling beside him.

He heard car doors opening and closing, and Desdemona speaking loudly, though he couldn't make out the words. He knew who she was speaking to. If they'd done what Hugo had asked, they'd driven separately. It was now or never.

Squat Man opened the door. Desdemona entered first, head held high, dressed as ridiculously as she'd been before. Her towering hat was black and covered with lace, her frizzy red hair tied back into a thick braid that hung over one shoulder. Her dress was black-and-white striped, the hem just below her knees. Her legs were sheathed in red stockings, and her boots looked as if they'd been recently shined.

"Yes," she breathed as she all but sashayed into the tea shop, removing her gloves. "I can feel it. It's like it was the last time. The spirits are active." She turned her head slowly, taking in the room. Her gaze slid over Nelson and Wallace without stopping. "I believe we're going to get somewhere. Mei, how lovely to see you're still . . . alive."

Mei glared at her. "Grave robbing is illegal."

Desdemona blinked. "I beg your pardon?"

"Whatever grave you desecrated to get that dress will—"

Nancy appeared in the doorway. Squat Man and Thin Man crowded behind her, looking as if they'd rather be anywhere else. Nancy gripped the strap of her purse tightly, her expression pinched, her breaths light and quick. She looked exhausted, but determined in ways Wallace hadn't seen before. She stepped into the tea shop slowly, biting her lip as if nervous.

Hugo came through the doors, a tray of tea in his hands.

"Hugo," Desdemona said, looking him up and down. "I was surprised to receive your invitation, especially after you returned my Ouija board to me without so much as a note attached to the post. It's about time you started appreciating my work. There is more to this world than we can see. It's heartening to know you're beginning to understand that."

"Desdemona," Hugo said in greeting, setting the tray down on a table. "I'll take your word on that." He turned to Nancy. "Thank you for coming. I know it's a little later than when you're normally here, but I only want to help."

Nancy glanced at the tray of tea before looking back at Hugo. "So you say." Her voice was rough and gravelly, as if she wasn't used to speaking. Wallace ached at the sound of it. "Desdemona said you invited us here."

"I did," Hugo said. "I can't promise anything will come of it. And even if it doesn't, I want you to know that you're always welcome. Whatever you need."

She nodded tightly but didn't respond.

Squat Man and Thin Man began to set up. Thin Man pulled out a camera, a newer model as the last one had been broken. He positioned it on the tripod, pointing it toward where Desdemona would be sitting. Squat Man had the same device he'd had before, switching it on. It squealed almost immediately, the lights flashing brightly. He frowned down at it, banging it against his hand before shaking his head. "I don't even know why I use this stupid thing," he muttered before waving it around the room.

Thin Man pulled the Ouija board from his bag, setting it on the table along with a new planchette. The last one had burned in the fireplace, becoming nothing but ash and smoke thanks to Wallace. Next to the Ouija board, he set down the feather quill and loose sheets of paper.

Desdemona pulled out a chair for Nancy. "Sit here, dear. That way, you'll still be in frame but won't be blocking me."

"Oh boy," Nelson muttered as Mei scoffed.

Nancy did as asked, clutching her purse in her lap. She didn't look at any of them, quietly refusing the offer of tea from Hugo as Desdemona took a seat next to her.

Desdemona smiled at her. "I know we didn't quite make contact the last time you and I were here. But that doesn't mean it won't happen now. When we came a couple of weeks ago, the spirits were . . . active. I don't think any of them were Lea, but you weren't with us then. It'll help having you here to focus. I have a feeling today will bring the answers you seek." She reached over and touched Nancy's elbow. "If you need a break, or want to stop entirely, say the word."

Nancy nodded. She looked down at the Ouija board. "You think we'll get something this time?"

"I hope so," Desdemona said. "Either through the board or automatic writing. But if we don't, we'll try again. You remember what to do, right? Direct your questions toward me, keeping them to yes or no answers if you can. I'll ask whatever you want, and if all goes well, the spirit energy will run through me. Be patient, especially if another spirit is trying to speak first."

"Okay," Nancy whispered as she sniffled.

Desdemona glanced at Thin Man. "Is everything ready?"

"As it'll ever be," Thin Man mumbled as he pressed a button on the camera. It beeped, and a red light began to blink. He pulled out a pad of paper and a pen from his bag. He looked around nervously, as if remembering the last time they'd been here, and the chaos that'd ensued.

"And as we discussed," Desdemona said to Nancy, "we're not streaming live per your request. We'll post the video later, but only after you've seen the edited version and agreed to it. Anything you don't want shown, we'll keep to ourselves."

Nancy gripped her purse tighter.

"Do you have any questions before we begin? If you do, that's okay. You can ask me anything you want. I won't start until you're ready."

She shook her head.

Desdemona wiggled her shoulders, breathing in through her nose and out through her mouth. She cracked her knuckles before settling her hands on the planchette in the middle of the Ouija board. "Spirits! I command that you speak with me! I know you're there. This will allow us to communicate with each other. Do you understand? There is nothing to fear. We aren't here to harm you. If you would prefer the pen, give me a sign."

The planchette didn't move. Neither did the pen.

"It's okay," Desdemona said to Nancy. "It takes a little time." She raised her voice again. "I am here with Nancy Donovan. She believes the spirit of her daughter, Lea Donovan, resides in this place, for reasons I'm still not quite clear on, but no matter. If Lea Donovan is here, we need to hear from her. If there are any other spirits, we ask that you step aside and allow Lea her moment to say what she must."

"Are you sure about this?" Nelson asked quietly.

"Yes," Wallace said. "We wait."

For the next hour, Desdemona tried all manner of questions, some sweet and coaxing, others more forceful and demanding. Nothing changed. The planchette remained still.

Desdemona grew frustrated, Thin Man covering up a yawn with the back of his hand as Squat Man carried the spirit box around the room, the machine silent.

Eventually, Desdemona sat back in her chair with a sigh. "I'm sorry," she muttered, glaring down at the Ouija board. "I really thought something would happen." She forced a smile. "It doesn't always work. They can be a fickle thing, spirits. They only do what they want when they want."

Nancy nodded, though Wallace could see how hurt she was by it. He ached at the pain radiating from her, silently begging her to hold on just a little bit longer.

Nancy didn't move as Thin Man and Squat Man packed away the Ouija board and the camera. Desdemona spoke quietly to Nancy, holding her hands, telling her that she couldn't give up, that they'd try again as soon as they could. "Give it time," she said quietly. "We'll figure it out."

Nancy nodded, expression slack and blank.

She rose from her chair as the others headed for the door, holding her purse against her chest like a shield. Thin Man and Squat Man left without looking back. Desdemona paused at the doorway, glancing at Hugo. "You know there's something here."

Hugo didn't respond.

"Come, dear," Desdemona said to Nancy. "You can follow us back into town, so we know you're safe."

Mei cocked her head as if confused, glancing back and forth between Desdemona and Nancy.

Hugo cleared his throat. "I'd like to have a word with Nancy in private, if she'll allow it."

Desdemona narrowed her eyes. "Anything you want to say to her, you can say with me present."

"If that's what she wants," Hugo said. "If not, but she wants to share what I tell her, then that's okay too."

"Nancy?" Desdemona asked.

Nancy studied Hugo before nodding. "It's . . . it's fine. Go. I won't be long."

Desdemona hesitated, looking as if she was going to argue. Instead, she sighed. "All right. If you're sure."

"I am," Nancy said.

Desdemona squeezed her shoulder and left the tea shop.

Silence fell, all of them waiting until the sound of a car started up, the engine rumbling. It faded, the clock ticking, ticking.

"Well?" Nancy asked, voice trembling. "What do you want?"

Hugo took in a deep breath, letting it out slow. "Your daughter isn't here."

Nancy recoiled as if slapped. Angry tears filled her eyes. "What?"

"She's not here," Hugo said gently. "She's gone to a better place. A place where nothing can hurt her again."

"How dare you," Nancy whispered. "What the hell is wrong with you?" She took a step back toward the door. "I thought you'd . . ." She shook her head furiously. "I'm not going to stand here and let you be so cruel. I can't." Her chest hitched. "I won't." With one last glare, she turned toward the door.

She gripped the doorknob and Wallace knew it was now or never. Alan—frightened, doomed Alan—had shown him the way. Nancy burned like fire, her grief a never-ending fuel. Whatever she was— like Mei or something else—she'd heard him when Alan had screamed her name.

Which is why Wallace shouted, *"Nancy!"*

She froze, back stiff, shoulders hunched near her ears.

"Nancy!"

She turned slowly, tears spilling onto her cheeks. "Did you . . . did you hear that?"

"I did," Hugo said. He held up his hands as if calming a spooked animal. "And I promise there is nothing to be afraid of."

She barked out a laugh, wet and harsh. "You don't get to tell me what I—"

She gasped when Wallace grabbed a chair, lifting it up off the ground. The blood drained from her face, hand going to her throat. Wallace didn't bring the chair to her, not wanting to frighten her more than she already was.

Instead, he carried the chair behind the counter toward the blackboard. "Careful, Wallace," Nelson warned. "Don't give her more than she's ready for."

"I know," Wallace said through gritted teeth, nudging Apollo out of the way as he jumped around him, trying to figure out why Wallace was carrying a chair. He seemed to want to help, biting down on one of the chair legs before getting distracted by his tail.

Wallace set the chair on the floor before glancing back. Nancy hadn't moved, jaw dropped at the sight of a chair floating through the air. He grunted as he climbed up on the chair. "Sorry about this," he muttered before wiping his hand across the blackboard. The words— specials, prices, all around the quote about tea and family—smeared in white.

"Oh my god," Nancy whispered. "What is this? What's happening?"

Wallace lifted a piece of chalk from the base of the blackboard. He wrote one word.

SPARROW.

Nancy let out a strangled sob before rushing forward. "Lea? Oh my god, *Lea?*"

Underneath **SPARROW,** Wallace wrote: **NO. NOT YOUR DAUGH-TER. NOT HERE. I WISH SHE WERE. SHE HAS MOVED ON TO A BETTER PLACE.**

"Is this a joke?" Nancy demanded, voice thick, eyes wet. "How the hell did you know about the sparrow? It . . . outside her hospital room. It always . . . who are you?"

Wallace wiped away the words before writing again, chalk scraping against the blackboard.

I DIED. HUGO IS TAKING CARE OF ME.

"Why are you even talking to me, then?" Nancy asked, wiping her face angrily. "You're not who I want."

I KNOW. BUT I HOPE IN HEARING FROM ME, YOU'LL UNDERSTAND THERE IS SOMETHING MORE BEYOND WHAT YOU KNOW.

"How am I supposed to believe you?" Nancy cried. "Stop. Stop playing with me. It hurts. Can't you see that? It hurts so much." Her voice broke.

THE GIVING TREE.

Nancy flinched. "What?"

"Hugo," Wallace whispered. "I . . . can't. It's too much. It's up to you now." He dropped the chalk to the floor. It shattered. He almost fell off the chair, but Nelson was there, grabbing onto his legs, keeping him from collapsing. He sat down roughly, his strength draining.

"No," Nancy whispered, taking a stuttering step forward. "No, no, come back. Come *back!*"

"Nancy," the ferryman said.

Nancy turned, bone white.

"It was her favorite book," Hugo said quietly, and Wallace sat upright, Nelson gripping his hand tightly. Apollo sat next to them, tail swishing back and forth. Mei looked pale, her hand at her throat. "She loved the voices you did when you read it to her. Even though she learned to read on her own, she always wanted you to read it to her. There was something about your voice, something warm and beautiful that she always wanted to hear."

"You can't know that," she said hoarsely. "It was just her and me. Our thing." She sounded as if she were choking.

"She told me," Hugo said. "She was so happy when she did. She spoke of picking apples in the fall, and the way you laughed when she ate more than she picked."

Nancy covered her mouth with her hand.

Hugo took a step toward her, slow and deliberate. "She was sad, too, because she missed you." His voice cracked, but he pushed through it. "Her body was tired. She fought as hard as she could, but it was too much for her. She was brave because of you. *For* you. You taught her joy and love and fire. You went to the zoo because she wanted to see polar bears. You took her to the museum because she wanted to touch dinosaur bones. You danced in your living room. The music was loud, and you danced. Once, she knocked over a vase. You told her it was just a little thing, and there was no need to be upset when it could be replaced."

Nancy began to sob. It crawled from her chest, the monster of grief, trying to drag her down into the depths.

"Fight," Wallace whispered. "Oh, please, fight it."

"She loved you," Hugo continued, "and she loves you still. No matter what comes next, that will never change. One day, you'll see her again. One day, you'll look upon her face. There will be no more pain. There will be no more sorrow. You'll know peace because you'll be together. But that day is not today."

"Why?" Nancy said, and it was such a desperate thing that Wallace bowed his head. "Why can't I have her? Why does it have to hurt so much? Why can't I breathe?"

Hugo stopped in front of her. He hesitated before touching the back of her hand briefly. Nancy didn't try to pull away. "She isn't gone. Not really. Just . . . moved on."

"Who are you?" she whispered.

"Someone who cares," Hugo replied. "I . . . lied to you. Before.

When you first came here. And for that, I'm sorrier than you could know. I didn't mean to hurt you. I didn't mean to make you feel worse. I help people. Like her. I help them cross. And we . . ." He swallowed thickly. "And I—we did that. We showed her the path forward. Lives don't end. They move on." He paused. "Do you remember the last thing you said to her?"

Nancy deflated, curling in on herself. "Yes."

"You said go. Go wherever you need to go. To the center of the earth. To the stars. To the—"

"To the moon to see if it's made of cheese," she whispered.

Hugo smiled. "The sickness is gone."

Nancy glanced at the blackboard, the smear of words, before turning back to Hugo. "Did you do this?"

He shook his head. "It wasn't me. But it was someone very important to me. And you can believe every single word written."

She watched him for a long time. "I'll be here. Whenever you're ready, I'll be here. That's what you keep telling me."

He nodded.

"Why?" she asked as she trembled. "Why do you care so much?"

"Because I don't know how else to be."

For a moment, Wallace thought it'd be too much for her. That they'd pushed too hard. He was surprised when she squared her shoulders. She looked at Mei, who waved at her with a small smile. Then, to Hugo, "I'd like a cup of tea, if that's all right."

"Okay," Hugo said. "I've always thought tea was a good place to start. And whenever you're ready, if you're ready, you'll know where to find me." He nodded toward the table where the tea tray sat. "Milk or sugar?"

"No. Just as it is."

Wallace looked on as Hugo poured the tea into two cups, one for her, and one for him. He handed Nancy a cup before taking his own. He watched her as she brought the teacup toward her face, inhaling deeply. Her hands started to shake, though no tea spilled. "Is that . . ."

"Gingerbread," Hugo said. "Her favorite."

Another tear slipped down Nancy's cheek. She drank deeply, throat working as she swallowed. She took another sip before setting the cup down back on the tray. She took a step away from Hugo. "I'd like to leave now. I've seen enough for one day."

Mei rushed forward, taking Nancy by the elbow and guiding her toward the door. Nancy stopped before Mei could open it for her. She looked back at Hugo, the color slowly returning to her face. "What are you?"

"I'm Hugo," he said. "I run a tea shop."

"Is that all?"

"No," he said.

Nancy looked as if she were going to speak again, but shook her head as Mei opened the door for her. She hurried down the porch, glancing back only once. A moment later, lights from her car illuminated the tea shop as it backed slowly, turning around before she drove away.

Mei closed the door, turning and leaning against it. She wiped her eyes as she sniffled.

Hugo rushed to Wallace. "Are you okay?" he demanded. He reached out for Wallace and looked stricken when his hands passed right through him. Wallace felt the same. "You—"

Wallace smiled weakly. "I'm fine. It's . . . I'm okay. Really. It took more out of me than I expected. You did it, though. I knew you could. Do you think it helped?"

Hugo gaped at him. "Do I think it *helped*?"

"That's . . . what I asked, yes."

Hugo shook his head. "Wallace, we gave her hope. She . . . maybe she has a chance now." Wallace was stunned to see Hugo's own eyes were wet. "Mei. I need you to—"

"No," Wallace said before Mei could move. "This wasn't about me. This is your moment, Hugo. You did this." He looked at Mei. "Can you do me a favor?"

"Yes," she said. "Yes."

"I need you to hug Hugo for me. Because I can't, and I want to more than anything."

Hugo's eyes widened comically as Mei launched herself at him, legs wrapping around his waist, her arms around his neck. It took Hugo a second, but he lifted his arms and held her close, her face in his neck, his in her hair. Apollo yipped excitedly, dancing around them, tongue hanging from his mouth. "We did it, boss," Mei whispered. "Oh my god, we did it."

Wallace watched with fierce pride as Nelson moved toward them, and though he couldn't touch them, he did the next best thing. He stood with his grandson and Mei.

Wallace smiled and closed his eyes.

CHAPTER 19

Acceptance.

It was easier than Wallace had expected.

Whatever he'd felt before he'd met the Manager, whatever he'd resigned himself to, it hadn't been like this.

His head was clear.

He didn't think it was peace he was feeling, at least not yet. He was still scared. Of course he was. The unknown always brought fear. His life, what there was of it, had been strictly regimented. He woke up. He took a shower. He dressed. He drank two cups of terrible coffee. He went to work. He met with the partners. He met with clients. He went to court. He'd never been one for theatrics. Just the facts, ma'am. He felt comfortable in front of a judge. In front of opposition. Most times he won. Sometimes he didn't. There were highs and lows, setbacks and victories. The day would be long gone by the time he went home. He'd eat a frozen dinner in front of the television. If he was feeling particularly indulgent, he'd have a glass of wine. Then he'd go into his home office and work until midnight. When he finished, he'd take another shower before going to bed.

Day after day after day.

It was the life he knew. The life he was comfortable with, the one he'd made for himself. Even after Naomi had left and it felt like everything was crumbling, he held it all together by sheer force of will. It was *her* loss, he'd told himself. It was *her* fault.

He'd accepted it.

"You're a white man," his assistant told him at the office Christmas party, her cheeks flushed from one too many Manhattans. "You'll fail up. You always do."

He'd startled her when he'd laughed loudly. He'd been a little drunk himself. She'd probably never seen him laugh before.

If only she could see him now.

Here, in Charon's Crossing, with three days left until the Manager returned, Wallace ran through the backyard as night gave way to the rising sun, Apollo chasing after him in a sort of game of tag, barking brightly. Wallace worried for a moment about disturbing the tea plants, but he and Apollo were dead. The plants wouldn't be bothered if he didn't want them to be.

"Got you," he said, pressing his fingers between Apollo's ears before taking off again.

He laughed when Apollo jumped on him, paws hitting his back, knocking him off his feet. He landed roughly on the ground and managed to roll over in time to get his face spectacularly licked. "Ugh!" he cried. "Your breath is awful."

Apollo didn't seem to mind.

Wallace allowed it to go on for a few moments longer before pushing the dog off. Apollo crouched down on his front paws, ears twitching, ready to play again.

"Did you ever have a dog?" Nelson asked him from his perch on the back deck.

Wallace shook his head as he pushed himself off the ground. "Too busy. Seemed a little mean to get one, only to be gone for most of the day. Especially in the city."

"When you were younger?"

"My father was allergic. We had a cat, but it was an asshole."

"Cats usually are. He's a good boy. I worried, when we knew his time had come. We didn't know what happened to dogs when they passed. They take a piece of our souls with them when they leave. I thought . . . I didn't know what it'd do to Hugo." He nodded toward the tea plants. "Toward the end, Apollo could barely walk. Hugo had to make a hard choice. Let him stay as he was, and be in pain, or give him the ultimate gift. It was an easier decision for him than I expected it to be. The vet came here, and they laid a blanket out in the garden. It was quick. Hugo said his goodbyes. Apollo smiled in that way that dogs do, like he knew what was happening. He took a breath and then another and then another. And then . . . he didn't. His eyes closed. The vet said it was done. But he couldn't see what we could."

"He was still here," Wallace said as Apollo pressed his head against his knee, trying to get him to run again.

"He was," Nelson agreed. "Full of pep and vigor as if all the ailments and trappings of life had just faded away. Hugo tried to take him up to the door, but Apollo refused. Stubborn, he is."

"Sounds like someone I know."

Nelson laughed. "I suppose, though the same could be said about you." His smile faded. "Or at least it used to be. Wallace, you don't have to—"

"I know," Wallace said. "But what choice do I have?"

Nelson was quiet for a long moment, and Wallace almost convinced himself the conversation was over. It wasn't. Nelson smiled sadly and said, "It's never enough, is it? Time. We always think we have so much of it, but when it really counts, we don't have enough at all."

Wallace shrugged as Apollo pranced around the tea plants. "Then we make the most of it."

Nelson didn't reply.

ॐ

He spent the day in the kitchen with Mei. He'd recovered enough from the séance with Nancy that he was able to pull trays of pastries from the oven and to lift the kettles from the stove. If anyone had looked through the portholes, they'd have seen kitchenware floating through the air with the greatest of ease.

"Why don't you just heat the water in the microwave?" he asked, pouring the water into a ceramic teapot.

"Oh my god," Mei said. "Don't ever let Hugo hear you say that. No, you know what? I changed my mind. Tell him, but make sure I'm there when you do. I want to see the expression on his face."

"Wouldn't be too happy, huh?"

"Understatement. Tea is serious business, Wallace. You don't heat water for tea in the freaking microwave. Have a little class, man." She picked up the tray Wallace had been working on and backed through the doors. "But still, tell him. I want to record his reaction." The doors swung shut behind her.

He went to the portholes, looking out into the tea shop. It was as busy as usual. The lunch crowd had arrived, and most of the tables were filled. Mei moved expertly around the people before setting the tray on a table. He glanced at the far corner. Nancy's table was empty. He wasn't surprised. He thought she'd be back, but it probably wouldn't be until he was gone. He didn't know if what they'd done had been enough. He wasn't foolish enough to think he'd alleviated her pain, but he hoped she'd at least have the foundation to start to build again if she wanted.

Hugo stood behind the register, smiling, though it was distant. He'd been quiet that morning, as if lost in thought. Wallace didn't want to push. He let Hugo be.

The front door of the tea shop opened, and a young couple walked in, their hair windswept, eyes bright. They'd been here before, the man saying it was their second date, when it was actually their third. He held the door open for his lady friend, and she laughed when he bowed slightly. Even above the din, Wallace could hear him. "After you, my queen."

"You're so weird," she said fondly.

"Only the best for you."

She grabbed his hand, pulling him to the counter. He kissed her on the cheek as she ordered for the both of them.

And Wallace knew the next thing he needed to do with the time he had left.

"You don't have to do this," Hugo said after the tea shop had closed for the night. Wallace had asked Mei and Nelson to give them some privacy. They'd agreed, though Nelson waggled his eyebrows suggestively as Mei pulled him into the kitchen, Apollo trailing after them.

"Maybe. But I think I do. If you can't, I can ask Mei to—"

Hugo shook his head. "No. I'll do it. What do you want me to say?"

Wallace told him. It was short and simple. He didn't think it was enough. He didn't know what else to add.

If he still had a beating heart, he thought it'd be in his throat as Hugo set the phone to speaker after he'd dialed the number Wallace had given him. He didn't know if anyone would answer. It'd be a strange number appearing on her screen, and she'd probably end up ignoring it as most people did.

She didn't.

"Hello?"

Hugo said, "Can I speak with Naomi Byrne?"

"Speaking. Who's calling, please?" The last word was quieter, and Wallace knew she had pulled the phone away to look at the number, frowning as she did so. He could see her clear as day in the corners of his mind.

"Ms. Byrne, my name is Hugo. You don't know me, but I know your husband."

A long pause. "Ex-husband," she said finally. "If you mean Wallace."

"I do."

"Well, I'm sorry to be the one to have to tell you this, but Wallace died a couple of months ago."

"I know," Hugo said.

"You . . . do? You spoke of him in the present tense, and I just assumed—it doesn't matter. What can I do for you, Hugo? I'm afraid I don't have long. I have a dinner meeting to get to."

"I won't take much of your time," Hugo said, looking up at Wallace who nodded.

"Were you a client of his? If there's a legal issue, you need to call the firm. I'm sure they would be happy to assist—"

"No," Hugo said. "I wasn't a client of his. I guess you could say he is—"

"*Was*," Wallace hissed. "*Was*."

Hugo rolled his eyes. "He *was* a client of mine, in his own way."

A longer pause. "Are you his therapist? I don't recognize the area code. Where are you calling from?" Then, "And *why* are you calling?"

"No," Hugo said. "I'm not a therapist. I own a tea shop."

Naomi laughed. "A tea shop. And you say *Wallace* was a client of yours. Wallace Price."

"Yes."

"I don't think I ever saw him drink a cup of tea in his life. Forgive me for sounding dubious, but he wasn't exactly the tea type."

"I know," Hugo said as Wallace groaned. "But I think you'd be surprised to hear that he learned to enjoy it regardless."

"Did he? That's . . . odd. Why would he—it doesn't matter. What do you *want*, Hugo?"

"He was a client of mine. But he was also my friend. I'm sorry for your loss. I know it must have been difficult."

"Thank you," Naomi said stiffly, and Wallace *knew* she was wracking her brain, trying to figure out what angle Hugo was working. "If you knew him, I'm sure you're aware we divorced."

"I know," Hugo said.

She was growing irritated. "Is there a point to this conversation? Or was that it? Look, I appreciate you calling, but I—"

"He loved you. Quite a bit. And I know it got rough, and you went your separate ways for good reason, but he never regretted a single moment he spent with you. He wanted you to know that. He hoped you found happiness again. That you would have a full life, and that he was so sorry for what happened."

Naomi didn't speak. Wallace would have thought she disconnected, but he could still hear her breathing.

"Say it," he whispered. "Please."

Hugo said, "He told me about your wedding day. He said there had never been anyone more beautiful than you were at that moment. He was happy. And even though things changed, he never forgot the way you smiled at him in that little church." He laughed quietly. "He said he panicked right before the ceremony. You had to talk to him through a door to try to get him to calm down."

Silence. Then, "He . . . he said he couldn't get his tie to work. That we might as well call the whole thing off."

"But you didn't."

Naomi sniffled. "No. We didn't, because it was just something so Wallace that I . . . Christ. You had to call and ruin my makeup, didn't you?"

Hugo chuckled. "I don't mean to."

"No, I don't expect you do. Why are you calling me now with this?"

"Because he thought you deserved to hear it. I know you hadn't spoken in a long while before he passed, but the man I know—knew, was different than the man you remember. He learned kindness."

"That doesn't sound like Wallace at all."

"I know," Hugo said. "But people can change when faced with eternity."

"What's that supposed to mean?"

"It is what it is."

She sounded uncertain when she said, "You knew him."

"Yes."

"Really knew him."

"Yes."

"And he told you what happened with us."

"He did."

"So you just decided to call me out of the blue, out of the good-ness of your heart."

"Yes."

"Look. Hugo, was it? I don't know what you're gunning for here, but I don't—"

"Nothing. I want nothing. All I wanted to do was tell you that you mattered to him. Even when all was said and done, you mat-tered."

She didn't respond.

"That's it," Hugo said. "That's all I needed to say. I apologize for interrupting your evening. Thank you for—"

"You cared for him."

Hugo startled. He glanced at Wallace before looking away. "I do."

"Friends," she said, almost amused. "*Just* friends?"

"Hang up!" Wallace said frantically. "Oh my god, hang up the *phone!*" He tried to swipe at it, but Hugo was quicker, plucking it off the counter and holding it out of reach.

"Just friends," Hugo said, hurrying around the counter to keep Wallace from the phone. Wallace snarled at him, prepared to do what he had to in order to make this fresh hell end as quickly as possible.

"Are you sure? Because—and I can't believe I know this—you sound like the kind of guy he'd go for. He didn't think I noticed, but he would swoon whenever—"

"I don't *swoon!*" Wallace bellowed.

"Really?" Hugo said into the phone. "Swoon, you say?"

"Yes. It was embarrassing. There was this one friend of mine—kind of talked like you, the same cadence—who Wallace would fawn over. He would deny it, of course, but I wouldn't be surprised if that was the case with you."

"I have the worst ideas," Wallace muttered. "Everything is terrible."

"Good to know," Hugo said to Naomi. "But no, we were just friends."

"Doesn't matter now though, does it?" Naomi asked. "Because he's gone."

Wallace stopped, hands pressed flat against the counter. He bowed his head and squeezed his eyes shut.

"I don't know that he truly is," Hugo said finally. "I think a part of him remains."

"Pretty thoughts, and nothing more. Did . . ." She huffed out a breath. "Did you love him? God, I can't believe I'm having this conversation. I don't know you. I don't even *care* if you and he were—"

"We weren't," Hugo said simply.

"That doesn't answer my question."

"I know," he said, and Wallace felt hot and cold, all at the same time. "I don't know how to answer that question."

"Yes or no. It's not hard. But you not saying no is all the answer I need." She sniffled again. "You weren't at the funeral."

"I didn't know."

"It was . . . quick. For him. I'm told he didn't suffer. There and gone as if he never were at all."

"But he was," Hugo said, and he never looked away from Wallace. "He was."

She laughed, though it sounded like a sob. "He was, wasn't he? For better or worse, he was. Hugo, I don't know who you are. I don't know how you knew Wallace, and I don't believe for a minute it was because of tea. I'm . . . sorry. For your loss. Thank you, but please don't call me again. I'm ready to move on. I *have* moved on. I don't know what else to say."

"You don't need to say anything else," Hugo said. "I appreciate your time."

The phone beeped as she disconnected the call.

Silence filled the tea shop.

Wallace broke. "You can't . . . *Hugo*."

"I know," Hugo said, sounding strangely vulnerable. Wallace looked up to see him fiddling with his bandana, green with white dogs imprinted on it. "But it's mine. It's for me. And you can't take that away."

"I'm not *trying* to," Wallace snapped. "It's—you're . . ." His chest hitched. The hook felt molten hot. "You're making it harder. Please don't do this to me. I can't stand it. I just can't."

"Why?" Hugo asked. "What's so bad about it?"

"Because I'm *dead*!" Wallace shouted.

He left Hugo standing in the main room of the tea shop, the shadows stretching further.

CHAPTER
20

The next day was hard.

Wallace brooded, pacing back and forth like a caged animal. The others gave him a wide berth as he muttered, "Two days. Two more days."

He shuddered. He shook. He *quaked*.

And there was nothing he could do to stop it.

He looked out the front window.

There, parked in front of the tea shop as it always was, sat Hugo's scooter. Pea green with whitewall tires. A side mirror with a little trinket hanging from it, a cartoon ghost with a little word bubble that read BOO! The seat was small, but there were metal handlebars on the back.

He remembered the way the sun had felt on him as he'd stood on the back deck. Again. Again. He needed to feel it again. Such a small thing, but the more he thought about it, the more he couldn't shake it. The sun. He wanted to feel the sun. It was calling to him, the hook in his chest vibrating, the cable brighter now than it'd been before. Whispers caressed his ears, but it wasn't like the voices from the door. Those were soothing and calm. This felt urgent.

He went to Mei in the kitchen. She eyed him warily as if she expected him to bite her head off. He felt guilty. "Can you watch the shop this afternoon?"

She nodded slowly. "I guess. Why?"

"I need to get out of here."

She looked alarmed. "What? Wallace, you know what'll happen if you try to—"

"I know. But I won't go far. I know how long I lasted the first time. I can handle it."

She wasn't convinced. "You can't take that risk. Not when you're so close to . . ." She didn't need to finish. They both knew what she meant.

He laughed wildly. "If not now, when? Oh, and I'm taking Hugo with me."

Mei blinked. "Taking him with you *where?*"

He grinned. He felt crazed, and it burned within him. "I don't know. Isn't it wonderful?"

—⁓—

Hugo listened as Wallace explained. He didn't answer right away, and Wallace thought he was going to refuse. Finally, he said, "Are you sure?"

Wallace nodded. "You'll know, won't you? How long we can go. How far."

"It's dangerous."

"I need this," Wallace said plainly. "And I want it to be with you."

It was the wrong thing to say. Hugo's expression shuttered. "Changed your mind? Last night, you seemed pretty certain you didn't want to hear how I feel."

"I'm scared," Wallace admitted. "And I don't know how not to be. But if this is it, if this is what I have left, then I want to do this. With you."

Hugo sighed. "It's really what you want?"

"Yes."

"I need to ask Mei if she'll—"

"Already done," Mei said, peeking her head through the kitchen doors. Wallace snorted when he saw Nelson peering under her arms. Of course they'd been listening. "I got it, boss. Give the man what he wants. It'll do you both some good. Fresh air and blah, blah, blah. We'll hold down the fort."

"We don't even know if he can ride it," Hugo said.

Wallace puffed out his chest. "I can do anything."

—⁓—

He couldn't do anything.

"What the hell?" he growled as he fell through the scooter to the ground for the fifth time.

"People are staring," Hugo muttered out the side of his mouth.

"Oh, I'm so *sorry*." Wallace pushed himself up off the ground. "And it's not like they can see me. For all they know, you're talking to your scooter like a weirdo."

Hugo crossed his arms and glared at his feet.

Wallace frowned at the scooter. It should be easy. It was just like the chairs. "Unexpect it," he mumbled to himself. "Unexpect it. Unexpect it."

He lifted his leg once more, throwing it over the back of the scooter. He knew he looked ridiculous as he lowered himself slowly, but he was beyond caring. He was going to do this if it was the last thing he did.

He crowed in triumph when he felt the back seat of the scooter pressed against his rear and thighs. "Hell yeah! I'm the best ghost *ever*!"

He looked over at Hugo, who fought a smile. "You're going to fall off and—"

"Kill myself? I have a feeling I don't need to worry about that. Get on. Come on, come on, come *on*." He patted the seat in front of him.

It was awkward, more so than Wallace thought it would be. The scooter was small and Hugo and Wallace were not. Swallowing thickly, Wallace studiously avoided looking at Hugo's rear as he threw his leg over one side and settled on the seat. The scooter creaked as Hugo propped it up, raising the kickstand with the heel of his shoe. They were close, so close that Wallace's legs disappeared into Hugo. The cable stretched between them tightly. It was oddly intimate, and Wallace wondered what it would be like to wrap his arms around Hugo's waist, holding on as tightly as he could.

Instead, he reached back and gripped the metal bars at his sides, settling his feet on the footrests.

Hugo turned his head. "We're not going far."

"I know."

"And you'll tell me when it starts getting bad."

"I will."

"I mean it, Wallace."

"I promise," he said, and he'd never meant it more. The whispers he'd heard in the house were louder now, and he could no longer ignore them. He didn't know what they were calling him toward, but it wasn't the door. They were calling him *away* from the tea shop.

Hugo turned the key. The scooter's engine whined, the seat vibrating underneath Wallace pleasantly. His laugh turned into a yelp when they started rolling forward slowly, picking up speed as dust kicked up behind them.

Wallace felt the pull the moment they hit the road. He gritted his teeth against it. He hadn't known what it'd been before. He did now. He looked down at his arms, expecting to see his skin beginning to flake off. Not yet, but soon.

Wallace thought Hugo would turn toward town, perhaps driving down the main drag and back to the shop.

He didn't.

He went the opposite direction, leaving everything behind. The forest grew thicker on either side of the road, the trees swaying in a cool breeze, limbs clacking together like bones. The sun sank lower in front of them, the sky pink and orange and shades of blue that Wallace couldn't believe existed, deep, dark, like the farthest depths of the ocean.

No one followed them; no cars on the road passed them by. It was as if they were the only two people in the entire world on a lonely stretch of road that led to nowhere and everywhere all at once.

"Faster," he said in Hugo's ear. "Please go faster."

Hugo did, the engine of the scooter whining pathetically. It wasn't built for speed but it didn't matter. It was enough. The wind whipped through their hair as they leaned into every curve, the road a blur beneath them, flashes of white and yellow lines shooting across Wallace's vision.

It was only a few minutes later that Wallace's skin began to rise and flake away, trailing behind them. Hugo saw it out of the corner of his eye, but before he could speak, Wallace said, "I'm all right. I swear. Go. Go. Go."

Hugo went.

Wallace wondered what would happen if they never stopped. Perhaps if they went far enough, Wallace would drift away into nothing, leaving all the pieces of him behind. Not a Husk. Not a ghost. Just motes of dust along a stretch of mountain road, ashes spread as if he'd mattered.

And maybe he had. Not to the world at large, not to very many people in the grand scheme of things, but here, in this place? With Hugo and Mei and Apollo and Nelson? Yes, he thought maybe he mattered after all, a lesson in the unexpected. Wasn't that the point? Wasn't that the great answer to the mystery of life? To make the most of what you have while you have it, the good and the bad, the beautiful and the ugly.

In death, Wallace had never felt more alive.

He squeezed his thighs against the sides of the scooter, holding himself in place. He raised his arms out like wings, pieces of his arms flaking off behind them. He tilted his head back toward the sun and closed his eyes. There, there, there it was, the warmth, the light covering him completely. Never wanting it to end, he shouted his wild joy toward the sky.

Hugo seemed to have a destination in mind. He turned down a road that Wallace would have missed had he been on his own. It wound its way through the forest on an incline. The pull of his shedding skin was negligible. A dark curl flickered at the back of his mind, but he had it under control. The whispers were fading.

On the side of the road ahead was a little pullout, nothing more than a gravel patch. Hugo steered the scooter toward it. Wallace gasped when he saw what lay on the other side of the guardrail.

The pullout was set on a cliff. The drop-off was steep, though the tops of the trees below rose in front of them. The sun set in the west, and as the scooter came to a stop, Wallace jumped off, rushing toward the guardrail. In his haste, he almost ran *through* it, but managed to skid to a stop just before.

"That would've been bad," he said, looking down, the thrill of vertigo washing dizzily over him.

He heard Hugo turn the scooter off and prop it up on the kickstand before climbing off himself. "We can't stay long. It's getting worse."

It was. The flakes were larger. The curl in his mind was stronger. His jaw ached. His hands were shaking. "Just a few minutes," he whispered. Hugo joined him at the guardrail. "Why here? What's this place to you?"

"My father used to bring me up here," Hugo said, face awash with dying sunlight. "When I was a kid. This was where we'd talk about all the important things." He smiled ruefully. "This is where I got the sex talk. This is where I got grounded because I was failing algebra. This is where I told him I was queer. He told me if he'd known, the sex talk would have gone a hell of a lot different."

"Good man?"

"Good man," Hugo agreed. "The best, really. He made mistakes, but he always owned up to them. He would have liked you." He paused. "Well, how you are *now*. He wasn't fond of lawyers."

"No one is. We're masochists that way."

As the sun set, they stood side by side, Hugo's shadow stretching behind them.

"When I'm gone," Wallace said, "please don't forget me. I don't have many people who'll remember me, at least not in a good way. I want you to be one of them." His fingernails began to break apart.

Hugo's throat worked as he swallowed. "How could I ever forget you?"

Wallace thought it would be very easy. "You promise?"

"I promise."

The sunset was brilliant. He wished he'd taken more time to turn his face toward the sky. "Do you think we'll see each other again?"

"I hope so."

It was the best answer he could ask for. "But not for a long time.

You've got work to do." He blinked away the burn in his eyes. "And it will—"

But he never got to finish. The curl deepened. It tugged. It pulled. It *yanked*. The cable flashed. "Oh," Wallace grunted as he stumbled.

"We have to go back," Hugo said, sounding worried. "Now."

"Yeah," Wallace whispered as the sun dipped below the horizon.

He felt as if he were floating on the ride back. Hugo pushed the scooter as fast as it could go, but Wallace wasn't worried. He wasn't scared, not like he'd been before. There was a sense of calm about him, something akin to relief.

"Hold on!" Hugo shouted at him, but he sounded so very far away. The whispers had returned, growing louder, more insistent.

His head cleared when they hit the road that led to the tea shop. By then, his hands were gone, his arms were gone, and he thought he'd lost his nose. He groaned as they reformed, the bits and pieces snapping back into place like a complex puzzle. He gasped when Hugo jerked the scooter to the right. He thought they were going to crash, and for a wild moment, he wondered why he hadn't insisted Hugo wear a helmet. But the thought was gone when he saw what had caused Hugo to lose control out of the corner of his eye.

Cameron.

Standing in the middle of the road.

I'm still here.

Rocks and dust kicked up around the tires as they skidded. A tree loomed in front of them, a great old thing with cracked bark leaking sap like tears. Wallace reached *through* Hugo, wrapping his hands around the handlebars, squeezing the brakes as hard as he could. They squealed and the scooter wobbled. The back tire lifted off the road momentarily before slamming back down as the scooter stopped, the front tire inches from the tree.

"Holy crap," Hugo muttered. He looked down as Wallace pulled his hands back. "If you hadn't—"

Wallace was off the scooter before Hugo could finish. He turned toward the road.

Cameron's face was turned toward the stars, mouth open, black teeth bared. His arms were limp at his sides, fingers dangling. He lowered his head as if he could feel Wallace watching him, eyes flat and cold.

The hook in Wallace's chest vibrated as hard as he'd ever felt it. It was almost like it was alive. The whispers were now a storm, spinning around him, the words lost, but Wallace knew then what they meant, why he'd felt the drive to leave the tea shop in the first place.

It was Cameron calling to him.

Behind him, Hugo lowered the kickstand on the scooter before switching it off, but Wallace wasn't to be distracted. Not now. He said, "Cameron. You're still in there, aren't you? Oh my god, I hear you."

Cameron blinked slowly.

Wallace remembered how he'd felt in the tea garden, Cameron's hands wrapped around him. The happiness. The fury. The bright moments of the sunshine man, of *Zach, Zach, Zach*. The thunderous grief that overtook him when all was lost. He'd been told later it'd only lasted seconds, their strange union, but he'd felt a lifetime of peaks and valleys. He *was* Cameron, he'd seen all that Cameron had seen, had suffered alongside him through the extraordinary unfairness of life. He hadn't understood the nuances then; it'd all been too much, too fast. He didn't think he could understand it now, not completely, but the bits and pieces were clearer than they'd been before.

Even as Hugo screamed for him to stop, Wallace reached out and took Cameron's hand in his. "Show me," he whispered.

And so Cameron did.

Memories rose like ghosts, and Zach said, "I don't feel good."

He tried to smile.

He failed.

His eyes rolled up in his head.

Alive, then dead.

But it hadn't been that quick, had it? No, there'd been more, so much more that Wallace hadn't been able to parse through the first time. Now, he caught glimpses of it, flashes like staccato film, reels of tape that jerked from frame to frame. He *was* Cameron, but not.

His name was Wallace Price. He'd lived. He'd died. And yet, he'd persisted, on and on and on, but that was insignificant, that was minor, that was *gone*, because Cameron took over, showing him all that lay hidden beneath the surface.

"Zach," Wallace whispered as Cameron said, "Zach? *Zach?*" moving forward, but he (they?) couldn't catch Zach before he collapsed, head bouncing on the floor with a terrible *thunk.*

Wallace was no longer in control, caught up in the bleeding memories that surrounded him like an endless universe, Cameron on the phone, screaming at the 911 operator that he didn't *know* what was wrong, he didn't *know* what to do, help us, oh please god, help us.

"Help us," Wallace whispered. "Please."

Another jump, harsh and grating, and Cameron threw open the front door, paramedics pushing by him, lights flashing from an ambulance and a fire truck in front of the house.

Cameron demanded to know what was wrong as they loaded Zach onto a gurney, the paramedics talking quickly about pupils dilating and blood pressure dropping. Zach's eyes were closed, body limp, and Wallace felt Cameron's horror as if it were his own, his mind blaring WHAT IS HAPPENING WHAT IS HAPPENING over and over again.

He was in the back of the ambulance as they opened Zach's shirt, asking Cameron if he knew of any history of illness, if he took drugs, if he'd overdosed, you need to tell us everything so we know how to help him.

He could barely think. "No," he said, sounding incredulous. "He's never taken a drug in his life. He doesn't even like taking aspirin. He's not sick. He's never been *sick.*"

He stood in the hospital, numb as if his entire body had been submerged in ice, surrounded by friends and Zach's family when the doctor came out and broke their entire world apart. Bleeding in the brain, the doctor said. A rupture. A fissure. Aneurysmal subarachnoid hemorrhage.

Brain damage.

Brain damage.

Brain damage.

Cameron said, "But you can help him, right? You can fix him, right? *You can make him better, right?*" He screamed and screamed, hands on his shoulders, hands on his arms, holding him, keeping him from lunging at the doctor, who backed away slowly.

They took Zach into surgery immediately.

He died on the operating table.

Cameron wore his finest suit to the funeral.

He made sure Zach had the same.

A choir sang a hymn of light and wonder, of God and His divine plan, and Wallace screamed in his head, but not as himself. As Cameron, shrieking silently for this all to be a dream, that it couldn't be real. *Wake up!* Cameron bellowed in his head. *Please, wake up!*

The priest spoke of pain and grief, that we can never understand why someone so full of life could be taken so soon, but that God never gave us more than what he thought we could handle.

Everyone cried.

Cameron didn't.

Oh, he tried. He tried to force the tears, tried to force himself to feel *anything* but the numbing, encroaching cold.

The casket was open.

He couldn't look at the body that lay inside.

"Are you sure?" a friend asked him. "Don't you want to go say goodbye before . . ." Her words cut off in a wet choke.

Cameron stood next to a hole in the ground as the same priest droned on and on about God and His plans and the mysterious, unknowing world. He watched as Zach was lowered into that hole, and still he felt nothing but cold. It was all he knew, and no matter what Wallace did, no matter how hard he tried, he couldn't chase the cold away.

People stayed the night with him. For weeks on end, he wasn't alone.

They said, "Cameron, you need to eat."

They said, "Cameron, you need to shower."

They said, "Cameron, let's go outside, huh? Get you some fresh air."

And finally, they said, "You sure you're going to be all right by yourself?"

"I'll be fine," he told them. "I'll be fine."

He wasn't.

He lasted four months.

Four months of haunting their home, moving from room to room, calling out for Zach, saying, "We were going to do so many things. *You promised me!*"

And still the tears didn't come.

He was cold all the time.

There were days when he didn't get out of bed, days when he didn't have the strength to do anything but roll over, pulling the comforter over his head, chasing the scents of Zach, who smelled like woodsmoke and earth and trees, so many trees.

Toward the end, his friends came back. "We're worried about you," they said. "We need to make sure you're going to be okay."

"I'll be fine," he told them. "I'll be fine."

On the last day, he woke up.

On the last day, he ate a bowl of cereal. He washed the bowl and spoon in the sink before putting them away.

On the last day, he wandered around the house, but he didn't speak.

On the last day, he gave up.

It didn't hurt, really.

The end.

He was only numb.

And then he was gone.

Except he *wasn't,* was he?

No,

Because he stood above himself, watching his lifeblood spill from him, and he said, "Oh. This is Hell."

And he was still alone.

Until a man came. He called himself a Reaper. He smiled, though it didn't reach his eyes. There was a curl to his lips that wasn't kind.

"I'll take you away," the Reaper said. "It'll all make sense, I promise. Even though you gave your life away like it was nothing, I'll take care of you."

He stood in front of a tea shop at dusk, looking at a sign in the window.

CLOSED FOR A PRIVATE EVENT

Hugo waited for him inside. He offered Cameron tea.

Cameron refused.

"I'm sorry," Hugo told him. "For all that you've lost."

The Reaper snorted. "He did it on his own."

And it was like poison in Cameron's ears.

There was a door, he knew, but he didn't trust it. The Reaper had told him that it could lead to just about anywhere. He didn't know. Hugo didn't know. No one did. "It could be just endless darkness," the Reaper mused late at night while Hugo slept. "It could be just nothing at all."

Cameron fled the tea shop.

His skin flaked away.

The cable snapped and disappeared.

The hook in his chest dissolved.

He made it to the town before he fell to his knees in the middle of the road.

His last lucid thought was of Zach, and how he smiled like the sun, and Wallace knew his desire to feel the same hadn't only come from himself. It was the last, forceful gasp of the man whose mind he now shared, the sun the last thing he'd held onto before the end of his humanity.

And here, now, Wallace said, "It isn't fair. None of it is."

"Help me," Cameron said.

Wallace looked down as his chest burned as if on fire.

A curve of metal stuck out from his sternum. The end was attached to the thick, glowing cable that stretched toward Hugo. A connection, a tether, a lifeline between the living and the dead, keeping them from floating away into nothing.

Wallace reached for the hook, hesitating briefly. "I see it now. It's not always about the things you've done, or the mistakes you've made. It's about the people, and what we're willing to do for one another. The sacrifices we make. They taught me that. Here, in this place."

"Please," Cameron whispered. "I don't want to be lost anymore."

"Unexpect it," Wallace said.

He gripped the hook, the metal hot against his palms and fingers, but it didn't burn. He pulled as hard as he could, the pain immense, causing him to grit his teeth together. Tears flooded his eyes, and he cried out as the hook came free. The heaviness loosened its grip, a wave of relief washing over him that felt like the sun and the stars.

He raised the hook above his head.

And slammed it into Cameron's chest.

&

His eyes flashed open when his head rocked to the side from a vicious slap. "*Ow!* What the hell?"

He blinked as Mei glared down at him. They were in the tea shop, Wallace looking up from the floor. "You *bastard*," Mei snapped at him. "What the hell did you think you were doing?"

He rubbed the side of his face, cheek still stinging as he sat up. "What are you . . ." His eyes bulged. "Oh shit."

"Yeah, you dick. *Oh shit* is right. Do you have any idea what you've—"

"Did it work?" he asked desperately. "Did it work?"

She sighed, shoulders slumping. "Look for yourself." She reached down, grabbing his arm and pulling him up from the floor. He yelped in surprise when he *shot* up, feet leaving the ground as if he weighed nothing. With wide eyes, he looked down. He gasped when he saw himself floating a few inches above the floor. He waved his arms *up*, trying to push himself *down*. It didn't work. Mei glared at him as he tried again. "Yeah, that's your own fault. You're lucky we still had Apollo's leash or you'd be gone by now." She pointed at his ankle. Wrapped around him was a dog leash. He followed the leash until he saw Nelson holding the other end.

"What's wrong with me?" he whispered.

Nelson leaned forward, kissing the back of his hand, lips dry and chapped. "You foolish man. You foolish, wonderful man. You're floating because there's nothing left holding you in place. But don't worry. I've got you. I won't let you float away. Unexpect it, Wallace, and trust that we have you."

Apollo nosed Wallace's ankle, licking frantically at the leash as if to make sure Wallace was still there. "I am," Wallace whispered, his voice soft and dreamy. "I'm still here."

He raised his head, and everything else fell away. Mei. Apollo. Nelson. The leash, the tea shop, the fact that he couldn't feel the ground. All of it.

Because a man stood next to Hugo in front of the fireplace, head bowed. He was handsome, though his cheeks were sunken, his eyes red-rimmed as if he'd been crying recently. His light-colored hair hung down around his face. He wore a pair of jeans and a thick sweater, the sleeves hanging over the backs of his hands.

"Cameron?" Wallace asked, voice cracking.

Cameron lifted his head. His smile trembled. "Hello, Wallace." He stepped away from Hugo, looking uncertain. A tear trickled down his cheek. "You . . . you found me."

Wallace nodded dumbly.

And then he was being hugged within an inch of his life, Cameron's face pressed against his stomach as Wallace rose into the air as far as the leash allowed. It was different than it'd been before. Gone were the flashes of the life once lived. Cameron wasn't cold like he'd been. His skin was fever-hot, and his shoulders shook as he held on as tightly as he could. Wallace was helpless to do anything but put his hands in Cameron's hair, holding on gently.

"Thank you," Cameron whispered against his stomach. "Oh my god, thank you. Thank you. Thank you."

"Yeah," Wallace said roughly. "Yes. Of course."

CHAPTER
21

The next day, Charon's Crossing Tea and Treats didn't open as it normally did. The windows were shuttered, lights off, a blind pulled down on the window to the front door. Those who came for their daily tea and pastries were disappointed to find the door locked, a sign in the window.

> **DEAR VALUED FRIENDS:**
> **CHARON'S CROSSING WILL BE CLOSED FOR THE NEXT**
> **TWO DAYS DUE TO SOME MINOR RENOVATIONS.**
> **WE LOOK FORWARD TO SERVING YOU AGAIN WHEN WE**
> **REOPEN!**
>
> **HUGO & MEI**

Wallace floated a few feet above the back deck, watching Apollo run through the tea plants, chasing a cadre of squirrels that didn't know he was there. He laughed quietly when the dog tripped over his own feet, tumbling to the ground before picking himself up and tearing through the tea plants again. Wallace barely felt the leash tugging at his ankle, tied to the deck railing to keep him from floating away.

He looked down at the man standing next to him, Wallace's knees at the same level as the man's shoulders.

"I don't really remember," Cameron said, and Wallace wasn't surprised. "What it was like being . . . a Husk. There are flashes, but I can barely make them out, much less remember them."

"It's probably for the best." Wallace didn't know what it'd do to a person to remember their time as a Husk. Nothing good.

"Two years," Cameron whispered. "Hugo said it was over two years."

"You can't blame him. He didn't know. He was told there was nothing that could be done when someone—"

"I don't blame him," Cameron said. Wallace believed him. "I made my own choice. He warned me what would happen if I left, but I couldn't listen."

"It didn't help that the Reaper tried to force your hand," Wallace said bitterly.

Cameron sighed. "Yeah, but that's not Hugo's fault. All he wants to do is help, and I wasn't willing to let him. I was so angry at everything. I thought I'd found a way to make it stop. Everything I was feeling. It was a slap to the face when I realized it wasn't over. It goes on and on. Do you know what that's like?"

"I do." Then, "Maybe not to the extent you mean, but I get it."

Cameron glanced up at him. "You do, don't you?"

"I think so. It's a lot for anyone to realize that we go on, even when our hearts stop beating. That the pain of life still can follow us even through death. I don't blame you for what happened. I don't think anyone could. And you shouldn't blame yourself. Learn from it. Grow from it, but don't allow it to consume you again. Easier said than done, I know."

"But look at you," Cameron said. "You're . . ."

Wallace laughed against the lump in his throat. "I know. But I don't want you worrying about that. I think . . . I think you helped to teach me what I was supposed to learn."

"Which was what?" Cameron asked.

Wallace looked toward the sky, tilting back until he was almost horizontal with the ground. Clouds passed by, fluffy white things with no real destination in mind. He raised his hands, backlit by the warm sun. "That we have to let go, no matter how scary it can be."

"I've wasted so much time. Zach must be angry with me."

"You'll find out soon enough. Do you love him?"

"Yes." It was said with such a tangible fierceness that Wallace could taste it in the back of his throat, the remnants of a fire that smoldered and sparked.

"And he loves you?"

Cameron laughed wetly. "Impossibly. I wasn't the best person to be around, but he took the worst parts of me and dragged them out into the light." He hung his head. "I'm scared, Wallace. What if it's too late? What if I took too long?"

Wallace turned over in midair, looking down at Cameron. He didn't cast a shadow. Neither of them did, but it didn't matter. They were here. They were real. "What're a couple of years in the face of eternity?"

Cameron sniffled. "You think so?"

"Yeah," Wallace said. "I do."

ॐ

Time seemed to move in fits and starts for the rest of the day. Hugo spent most of it with Cameron. For a brief moment, Wallace was intensely jealous, but he let it go. Cameron needed Hugo more. Wallace had made his choice.

"What's it like?" Mei asked him. They were in the kitchen, Mei moving back and forth between one of the ovens and the stove. Just because the shop was closed, she'd told him, didn't mean the work stopped too.

"What?" The leash was tied around the bottom of the refrigerator, cinched tightly so that his feet brushed the ground.

She hesitated. "Hugo said you . . ." She motioned at her chest.

He shrugged. "It is what it is."

"Wallace."

"Untethered," he said finally.

She took her hand in his, tugging gently so his feet bumped the floor. "I've got you."

He smiled at her. "I know you do."

"I won't let you float away. You're not a balloon."

He laughed until he could barely breathe.

ॐ

He didn't know what they were planning.

He should have known it was something. They weren't the types to let things lie as they were.

He wandered the bottom floor of the tea shop, Apollo happily tugging on the leash to hold him in place, Wallace doing his best to ignore the little whispers at the back of his head. They weren't like what he'd heard with Cameron. These whispers were more forceful, coming from the door, and though he couldn't make the words out, they had a cadence to them that felt like speech, frightening and enthralling him in equal measure. He was haunting the tea shop, a little boat in a vast ocean. His feet never touched the floor.

Nelson watched him from his chair in front of the fireplace. When Apollo tugged Wallace by him, Nelson said, "You feel it, don't you?"

"What?" Wallace asked, voice wistful and off-kilter.

"The door. It calls to you."

"Yes," Wallace whispered. He spun lazily in the air.

"This hook. The cable. You had one."

Wallace blinked slowly, coming back to himself. At least a little bit. "You do too. Of course you do. I never thought to ask. What is it?"

"I don't know," Nelson admitted. "Not really. It's always been there. I think it's a manifestation of a connection, tying us to Hugo, reminding us that we're not alone."

"It's gone now," Wallace whispered, staring down at the crackling fire. He closed his eyes. Hugo was there, smiling in the dark.

"Perhaps," Nelson said. "But what it represented isn't. That can never be taken away from you. Remember what I told you about need versus want? We don't need you because that implies you had to fix something in us. We were never broken. We *want* you, Wallace. Every piece. Every part. Because we're family. Can you see the difference?"

Wallace laughed quietly. "But I haven't had my third cup of tea."

Nelson tapped his cane on the floor. "No. I don't suppose you have. Let's change that, shall we?"

Wallace opened his eyes. "What?"

Nelson nodded toward the kitchen.

Hugo and Mei appeared through the double doors. Hugo carried a tray filled with familiar cups and a clay teapot. Cameron trailed after them, eyes bright.

Hugo set the tray down on a table. He motioned for them to join them at the table. He said, "Cameron, I have something for you."

Cameron blinked. "For me? I thought this was for . . ." He glanced at Wallace.

Wallace shook his head. "No. This is for you. You're first."

Nelson rose from his chair, tugging the leash from Apollo's mouth. The dog thought they were playing and tried to pull it back. Wallace jerked from side to side, smiling so wide he thought his face would split in half. Apollo eventually let go, barking at Wallace's feet as Nelson pulled him toward the table.

"Has it steeped long enough?" Wallace asked as the scent of . . . oranges? Yes, the scent of oranges filled the tea shop.

"It has," Hugo said. His hands shook as he lifted the teapot. Mei put her hand on the back of his to steady him. He poured the tea into each cup. Once he'd finished, he poured more tea into a little bowl with the same markings as the teacups. He set the pot down before lifting the bowl and placing it on the floor in front of Apollo. The dog sat in front of it, head cocked as he waited. "It's ready."

Cameron hesitated before leaning over the teapot, inhaling deeply. "Oh. That's . . ." He looked up at Hugo with wide eyes. "I know that smell. We . . . had this orange tree. In our back yard. It was . . . Zach liked to lie underneath it and look up at the sunlight through the branches." He closed his eyes as his throat worked. "It smells like home."

"Hugo knows what he's doing," Wallace said. "He's good like that." He looked at all of them. "How does it go again?"

They knew what he meant. "The first time you share tea, you are a stranger," Mei said.

"The second time you share tea," Nelson said, "you are an honored guest."

Hugo nodded. "And the third time you share tea, you become family. It's a Balti quote. I took those words to heart because there's something special about the sharing of tea. Grandad taught me that. He said that when you take tea with someone, it's intimate and quiet. Profound. The different flavors mingle, the scent of it strong. It's small, but when we drink, we drink together." He handed each of them a cup. First Cameron. Then Mei. Then Nelson. Wallace was last. The tea sloshed as he took the cup from Hugo, their fingers close but not touching, never touching. He was careful as he spun in air, pointing his feet toward the ground as Nelson tied off the leash against a table leg. "Please, drink with me."

He waited for Cameron to go first. Cameron lifted the cup to his lips, inhaling again, eyes fluttering shut. His lips curved into a quiet smile before he drank. Mei went next, followed by Nelson, then Hugo. Apollo did too, lapping at the bowl.

Wallace raised the cup to his lips, breathing in the orange mingling with spice. He could almost picture it, lying on the ground in the grass, looking up at a tree heavy with fruit, the leaves swaying softly in a cool breeze, sunlight trickling through the branches. He drank deeply, the tea sliding down his throat, warming him from the inside out.

Once the tea was finished, Wallace felt like he had only a moment before.

Except . . .

Except that wasn't quite true, was it?

Because he'd had his third cup of tea. His gaze drifted to the Balti proverb hanging above the counter.

Stranger. Guest. Family.

He belonged to them now just as much as they belonged to him.

He set the teacup back on the table before he could drop it. It clattered against the table, but the remains of the tea didn't spill. Cameron did the same. He stared down at the teacup, a look of wonder on his face. "I can . . ." He turned his gaze up toward the ceiling. "Can you hear that? It's . . . it sounds like a song. It's the loveliest thing I've ever heard."

"Yes," Nelson said quietly as Apollo barked.

"Me too," Wallace said.

Mei shook her head.

Hugo looked stricken, but Wallace hadn't expected him to hear what they could. It wasn't meant for him, at least not yet.

"It's calling me," Cameron whispered.

Wallace smiled.

They stood around the table, Wallace floating amidst them, drinking the tea until there was nothing left but the dregs.

Hugo found him on the back deck, floating horizontal to the ground, hands folded behind his head as he gazed up at the night sky. Mei had tied the leash to a deck railing after he'd asked, telling him he wasn't allowed to untie it for any reason. The stars were as bright as they always were. They stretched on forever. He wondered if there were stars where he was going. He hoped so. Perhaps he and Hugo could look up at the same sky at the same time.

Hugo sat next to him, wrapping his arms around his legs, knees against his chest.

"Another session, Doctor?" Wallace asked as he grabbed the leash, pulling himself closer to Hugo. His rear bumped the deck. He reached behind him to grab the edge of the deck, holding himself in place.

Hugo snorted before shaking his head. "I don't know if there's anything left to tell you."

"Where's Cameron?"

"With Grandad and Mei." He cleared his throat. "He's, uh. Tomorrow."

"What about tomorrow?" A big question, but never more than now.

"He's going to cross."

Wallace turned his head toward Hugo. "Already?"

Hugo nodded. "He knows what he wants."

"And he wants this."

"Yeah. I told him there was no rush, but he wouldn't hear of it. Thinks he's wasted too much time. He wants to go home."

"Home," Wallace whispered.

"Home," Hugo agreed, throat bobbing. "It'll be first thing." He stared at Wallace for a long moment. Then, "We can help them. If . . . if it worked for Cameron, maybe it can work for others." He looked out at the tea plants. "The Manager won't like it, though."

Wallace chuckled. "No, I don't expect he will. But regardless of what else he is, he's a bureaucrat. And even worse than that, he's a *bored* bureaucrat. He needs what I did."

"What's that?"

"A shock to the system."

"A shock to the system," Hugo repeated, mulling over the words. "I . . ." He shook his head. "Will you come with me? I want to show you something."

"What is it?"

"You'll see. Come on."

Wallace pushed himself off the deck, floating upward. He bounced when the leash grew taut. He swayed back and forth, blinking slowly. He wondered what would happen if he untied the leash, if he would continue to rise and rise and rise until he took his place amongst the stars. It was a terribly wonderful thought.

Instead, Hugo pulled him into the house, careful so that Wallace didn't bump his head on the doorframe.

The clock ticked the seconds by.

Mei and Cameron sat on the floor in front of the fireplace, Apollo on his back, legs in the air. Nelson was in his chair. They didn't speak as Hugo climbed the stairs, Wallace trailing after him, feet never touching the floor.

He thought Hugo would take him to the door and speak more of what it could mean, what might lay on the other side. He was surprised when Hugo went to one of the closed doors on the second floor.

The door that led to his room, the only one Wallace hadn't been into.

Hugo paused, his hand on the doorknob. He looked back at Wallace. "You ready?"

"For what?"

"Me."

Wallace laughed. "Absolutely."

Hugo opened the door and stepped to the side. He motioned for Wallace to go through.

Gripping the frame, he pulled himself into the room, ducking his head.

It was smaller than he thought it'd be. He knew the master bedroom was on the third floor, and that it'd belonged to Nelson and his wife before they'd passed.

This room was neat and tidy. Harvey, the health inspector, would undoubtedly be pleased. There wasn't a single speck of dust, not a bit of clutter or a thing out of place.

Much like the first floor, the walls were covered with posters and pictures of faraway places. A never-ending forest of ancient trees. An ancient statue on the banks of a green river. Bright ribbons hanging over a colorful marketplace filled with people in flowing robes. Homes with thatched roofs. The sun rising over a field of wheat. An island in the middle of a sea, a strange home set on its cliffs.

But they weren't all out-of-reach dreams.

A man and a woman who looked like Hugo smiled from a framed picture hanging in the center. Below it was another photograph, this one of a mangy dog looking grumpy as Hugo gave it a bath. Next to this one was Hugo and Nelson standing in front of the tea shop, arms folded across their chests, both of them grinning widely. Underneath this one was a picture of Mei in the kitchen, flour dotting her face, eyes sparkling, a spatula pointed at the camera.

And on and on they went, at least a dozen more, telling a story of a life lived with strength and love.

"This is wonderful," Wallace said, studying a photograph of a young Hugo on the shoulders of a man who looked to be his father. The man had a thick, bushy mustache and a devious spark in his eyes.

"They help me remember," Hugo said quietly, closing the door behind him. "All that I have. All that I've had."

"You'll see them again."

"You think so?"

He nodded. "Maybe I can find them first. I can . . . I don't know. Tell them about you. All that you've done. They'll be so proud of you."

Hugo said, "This isn't easy for me."

Wallace turned around in air. Hugo frowned, his forehead lined. He reached up and slid the bandana off his head. "What isn't easy?"

"This," Hugo said, motioning between the two of them. "You and me. I spend my life talking, talking, talking. People like you come to me, and I tell them about the world they're leaving behind, and what lies ahead. How there's nothing to fear and that they will find peace again even when they're at their lowest."

"But?"

Hugo shook his head. "I don't know what to do with you. I don't know how to say what I want to say."

"You don't have to do anything with—"

"Don't," Hugo said hoarsely. "Don't say that. You know that's not true." He dropped the bandana to the floor. "I want to do *everything* with you." Then, in a whisper, as if saying it any louder would break them completely, Hugo said, "I don't want you to go."

Six little words. Six words no one had ever said to Wallace Price before. They were fragile, and he took them in, holding them close.

Hugo lifted his apron above his head, letting it fall next to the bandana. He toed off his shoes. His socks were white, a hole near one of his toes.

Wallace said, "I . . ."

"I know," Hugo said. "Stay with me. Just for tonight."

Wallace was devastated. If they were anyone else, this could be the start of something. A beginning rather than an end. But they weren't anyone else. They were Wallace and Hugo, dead and alive. A great chasm stretched between them.

Hugo switched off the light, casting the room in semidarkness. He went to the bed. It was simple. Wood frame. Large mattress. Blue sheets and comforter. The pillows looked soft. The bed creaked when Hugo sat on it, hands dangling between his legs. "Please," Hugo said quietly.

"Just for tonight," Wallace said.

He looked down at his own feet, hovering above the wood floors. He scrunched up his face, and his shoes disappeared. He didn't worry about the rest. He wouldn't sleep.

Hugo looked up as Wallace floated toward him. He had a strange expression on his face, and Wallace wondered why Hugo had chosen him, what he'd done in life to deserve this moment.

Hugo nodded, sliding back on the bed, stretching out against the far side. He grabbed the dangling leash, tying it off to the headboard.

Wallace reached down and pressed his hands against the bed, wishing he could lie down next to Hugo. His fingers curled in the soft comforter. He pulled himself down until his face pressed against the blanket, breathing in deeply. It smelled like Hugo, cardamom and cinnamon and honey. He sighed, moving until he floated above Hugo, who rested his head on the pillow, eyes glittering in the dark as he watched Wallace.

They didn't speak at first. Wallace had so many things he wanted to say, but he didn't know how to start.

Hugo did. He always did. "Hello."

Wallace said, "Hello, Hugo."

Hugo raised his hand toward Wallace, fingers outstretched. Wallace did the same, their hands inches apart. They couldn't touch. Wallace was dead, after all. But it was good. It was still good. Wallace imagined he could feel the heat from Hugo's skin.

Hugo said, "I think I know why you were brought to me."

"Why?" Wallace asked.

Voices low, soft. Secret.

Hugo lowered his hand back to the bed, and the grief Wallace felt over it was enormous. "You make me question things. Why it has to be this way. My place in this world. You make me want things I can't have."

"Hugo." He cracked right down the middle.

"I wish things were different," Hugo whispered. "I wish you were alive and found your way here. It could be a day like any other. Maybe the sun is shining. Maybe it's raining. I'm behind the counter. The door opens. I look up. You walk in. You're frowning, because you don't know what the hell you're doing in a tea shop in the middle of nowhere."

Wallace snorted. "That sounds about right."

"Maybe you're passing through," Hugo continued. "You're lost, and you need help finding your way. Or maybe you're here to stay. You come up to the counter. I say hello, and welcome you to Charon's Crossing."

"I tell you I've never had tea before. You look outraged."

Hugo grinned ruefully. "Maybe not outraged."

"Yeah, yeah. Keep telling yourself that. You would be so irritated. But you'd also be patient."

"I'd ask you what flavors you like."

"Peppermint. I like peppermint."

"Then I have just the tea for you. Trust me, it's good. What brings you here?"

"I don't know," Wallace said, caught in a fantasy where everything was beautiful and nothing hurt. He'd been here before in secret. But now it was out in the open, and he never wanted it to end. "I saw the sign near the road and took a chance."

"Did you?"

"Yeah."

"Thank you for taking a chance."

Wallace struggled against closing his eyes. He didn't want to lose this moment. He forced himself to memorize every inch of Hugo's face, the curl of his lips, the stubble he'd missed on his jaw when shaving earlier. "You'd make the tea. Put it into a little pot and set it on a tray. I'd be sitting at the table near the window."

"I'd bring the tray out to you," Hugo said. "There'd be a second cup, because I want you to ask me to sit down with you."

"I do."

"You do," Hugo agreed. "Sit a spell, you say. Have a cup of tea with me."

"Will you?"

"Yes. I sit in the chair opposite you. Everything else fades away until it's only you and me."

"I'm Wallace."

"I'm Hugo. It's nice to meet you, Wallace."

"You pour the tea."

"I hand you the cup."

"I wait for you to pour your own."

"We drink at the same time," Hugo said. "And I see the moment the flavor hits your tongue, the way your eyes widen. You didn't expect it to taste like it does."

"It reminds me of when I was younger. When things made sense."

"It's good, right?"

Wallace nodded, eyes burning. "It's very good. Hugo, I—"

Hugo said, "And maybe we just sit there, wasting away the afternoon. We talk. You tell me about the city, the people who hurry everywhere they go. I tell you about the way the trees look in the winter, snow piling on the branches until they hang low to the ground. You tell me about all the things you've seen, all the places you've visited. I listen, because I want to see them too."

"You can."

"I can?"

"Yes," Wallace said. "I can show you."

"Will you?"

"Maybe I decide to stay," Wallace said, and he'd never meant it more. "In this town. In this place."

"You'd come in every day, trying different kinds of tea."

"I don't like a lot of them."

Hugo laughed. "No, because you're very particular. But I find the ones you do like, and make sure I always have them on hand."

"The first cup I'm a stranger."

"The second you're an honored guest."

And Wallace said, "And then I have one more. And then another. And then another. What does that make me?"

"Family," Hugo said. "It makes you family."

"Hugo?"

"Yeah?"

"Don't forget me. Please don't forget me."

"How can I?" Hugo said.

"Even when I'm gone?"

"Even when you're gone. Don't think about it now. We still have time."

They did.

They didn't.

Hugo's eyes grew heavy. He fought it, eyes blinking slowly, but he'd already lost. "I think it'd be nice," he said, words slurring slightly. "If you came here. If you stayed. We'd drink tea and talk and one day, I'd tell you that I loved you. That I couldn't imagine my life without you. You made me want more than I ever thought I could have. Such a funny little dream."

His eyes closed and didn't reopen. He breathed in and out, lips parting.

After a time, Wallace said, "And I would tell you that you made me happier than I'd ever been. You and Mei and Nelson and Apollo. That if I could, I'd stay with you forever. That I love you too. Of course I do. How could I not? Look at you. Just look at you. Such a funny little dream."

For the rest of the night, he floated above Hugo, watching, waiting.

CHAPTER
22

The next morning—the seventh, the final, the last—Cameron said, "Will you go with me to the door?"

Wallace blinked in surprise as he looked down at Cameron. "You want me there?"

He nodded.

"I'm not . . . I can't go—not yet. I'm not going through yet."

"I know," Cameron said. "But I think it'll help, having you there."

"Why?" Wallace asked helplessly.

"Because you saved me. And I'm scared. I don't know how I'm going to climb the stairs. What if my legs don't work? What if I can't do it?"

Wallace thought of all he'd learned since walking through the doors of Charon's Crossing for the first time. What Hugo had taught him. And Mei. And Nelson and Apollo. He said, "Every step forward is a step closer to home."

"Then why is it so hard?"

"Because that's life," Wallace said.

Cameron gnawed on his bottom lip. "He'll be there."

Zach. "He will."

"He'll yell at me."

"Will he?"

"Yes," Cameron said. "That's how I'll know he still loves me." His eyes were wet. "I hope he yells as loud as he can."

"Until you think your eardrums will burst," Wallace said, patting him on the top of the head. "And then he'll never let you go."

"I'd like that." He looked away. "I'll find you. When you come. I want him to meet you. He needs to know you and what you've done for me."

Wallace couldn't. Everything was hazy. The colors were melting around him. His strings had been cut, and he was floating away, away, away.

"Then yes," Wallace said. "I'll be there when you go."

ↄ๏

Cameron hugged Mei.

He hugged Nelson.

He patted Apollo on the head.

He said, "Will it hurt?"

"No," Hugo said. "It won't."

He looked to Wallace, holding out his hand. "Will you?"

Wallace didn't hesitate. He took Cameron's hand in his own. Cameron clutched him tightly as if to keep Wallace from floating away.

Mei, Nelson, and Apollo stayed on the bottom floor.

"I expect you to come right back, Wallace," Nelson called out. "I'm not done with you yet."

"I know," Wallace said, squeezing Cameron's hand to get him to stop. He looked back at them. "We won't be long."

Nelson didn't look like he believed him, but Wallace couldn't do anything about that now.

Hugo led the way up the stairs to the second floor.

"Can you hear that?" Cameron asked. "It's singing."

To the third floor.

"Oh," Cameron said, tears streaming down his cheeks. "It's so *loud.*" He looked out the windows as they passed them by, and he laughed and laughed. Wallace didn't know what he saw, but it wasn't meant for him.

To the fourth floor.

They stopped at the landing.

The flowers carved into the wood of the door bloomed on the ceiling above them.

The leaves grew.

"When you're ready, remove the hook and let it go. I'll open the door. Just tell me when," Hugo said.

Cameron nodded and looked up at Wallace floating above them. He squeezed Wallace's hand before pulling him down to eye level. "I know," he whispered. "When you brought me back, when you put your hook into my chest, I felt it. They're yours, Wallace. And you're theirs. Make sure they know that. You don't know when you'll get the chance again."

"I will," Wallace whispered back.

Cameron kissed his cheek before letting Wallace go. Hugo grabbed the leash, eyes soft and sad.

Cameron breathed in and out once, twice, three times. He said, "Hugo?"

"I'm here."

"I found my way back. It took a little while, but I did. Thank you for believing in me. I think I'm ready now." And with that, he grasped the hook Wallace couldn't see. Cameron grimaced as he pulled it from his chest. He gasped in relief as he opened his hand.

"It's gone," Hugo said quietly. "It's time."

"I feel it," Cameron said, looking up toward the door. "I'm rising. Hugo, please. Open the door."

Hugo did. He reached up, fingers grazing against the doorknob. He gripped it and twisted it once.

It was as it'd been with Alan. Light spilled down, so bright Wallace had to look away. The whispers gave way to birds singing. Wallace heard Cameron gasp as his feet left the floor. He raised his hand to shield his eyes, trying to make out Cameron in all the blinding light.

"Oh my god," Cameron breathed as he rose in the air toward the open doorway. "Oh, Wallace. It's . . . the sun. *It's the sun.*" Then, the moment before he rose through the doorway, a great and powerful joy filled his voice as he said, "Hello, my love. Hello, hello, hello."

The last Wallace saw of him were the bottoms of his shoes.

The door slammed shut behind him.

The light faded.

The flowers curled in on themselves.

The leaves shrank as the door settled in its frame.

Cameron was gone.

⁓

They stood under the door for what felt like hours, the leash in Hugo's hand as Wallace floated. It was almost time. Not yet, but close.

⁓

They drank tea as if it were any other day, the morning turning into afternoon as they pretended nothing was changing.

They laughed. They told stories. Nelson and Mei reminded Wallace of how he'd looked in a bikini. Nelson said if only he was a couple of decades younger, he might consider going after Wallace himself, much to Hugo's dismay. Wallace made Nelson show him the rabbit costume. It was quite startling. The basket of brightly colored eggs only made it worse, especially when his ears flopped all over the place, his nose wiggling. Nelson didn't need to open the eggs for Wallace to know they were filled with cauliflower.

Wallace had to grip the underside of the table to keep from rising farther. He tried to be inconspicuous about it, but they knew. They all knew. He'd forgone the leash, not wanting any distractions for what came next.

As the sun moved across the sky, Wallace reflected back on the life he'd had before this place. It wasn't much. He'd made mistakes. He hadn't been kind. And yes, there were moments of outright cruelty. He could have done more. He should have *been* more. But he thought he'd made a difference, in the end, with help from the others. He remembered how Nancy had looked before she'd left the tea shop the last time. The way Naomi had sounded on the phone. The relief on Cameron's face when the Husk he'd become melted away, life returning to the dead.

Wallace had done more in death than he ever had in life, but he hadn't done it alone.

And maybe that was the point. He still had regrets. He thought he always would. Nothing could be done about that now. He'd found within himself the man he had thought he'd become before the heaviness of life had descended upon him. He was free. The shackles of a mortal life had fallen away. There was nothing holding him here. Not anymore.

It hurt, but it was a good hurt.

Hugo tried to keep up appearances, but the closer it came to dusk, the more agitated he became. He fell silent. He frowned. He crossed his arms defensively.

Wallace said, "Hugo?" as Mei and Nelson quieted. Wallace gripped the table.

Hugo shook his head.

"Not now," Wallace said. "I want you to be strong for me."

He had a stubborn set to his jaw. "What about what I want?"

Nelson sighed. "I know this is hard on you. I don't think that—"

Hugo laughed hoarsely as his hands curled into fists. "I know. I just . . . I don't know what to do."

Mei laid her head on his shoulder. "What you have to," she whispered. "And we'll be there with you. The both of you. Each step of the way." She peered up at Wallace. "You turned into a pretty good dude, Wallace Price."

"Not as good as you, Meiying . . . what the hell is your surname?"

She chuckled. "Freeman. Changed it last year. Best name I've ever had."

"Damn right," Nelson said.

He had so much more to say to all of them. But before he could, Apollo growled, going to the window that looked out to the front of the tea shop. The hands of the clock began to stutter as time slowed down.

"No," he whispered as a blue light began to fill Charon's Crossing. "Not yet. Please, not yet—"

Apollo howled, a long and mournful sound as the light faded. The clock froze completely, the hands unmoving.

A light tapping on the door: *thump, thump, thump.*

Hugo rose slowly from his chair, footsteps heavy as he walked toward the door. He hung his head, his hand on the doorknob.

He opened it.

The Manager stood on the porch. He wore a shirt that read IF YOU THINK I'M CUTE, YOU SHOULD SEE MY AUNT. Flowers hung from his hair, opening and closing, opening and closing.

"Hugo," the boy said in greeting. "How nice to see you again. You're doing well, I see. Or as well as can be expected."

Hugo took a step back but didn't respond.

The Manager walked into the tea shop, the floor creaking under his bare feet, the walls and ceiling beginning to ripple as they had before. He looked at each of them in turn, gaze lingering on Mei before turning to Nelson and Apollo, who growled at him but kept his distance.

"Good dog," the boy said.

Apollo barked savagely in response.

"Well, mostly a good dog. Mei, you've taken to this Reaper business like a fish to water. I knew assigning you to Hugo was the right thing to do. I'm impressed."

"Frankly, I don't give two shits what you—"

"Ah," the boy said. "No need for that. I am your boss, after all. I'd hate to think you'd need a mark on your permanent record." He sniffed. "Nelson. Still here, I see. How . . . expected."

"Damn right I am," Nelson growled. He pointed his cane at the Manager. "And don't think you're going to be making anyone do anything they don't want to do. I won't have it."

The boy stared at him for a long moment. "Interesting. I actually believed that threat, as inconsequential as it was. Please remember there is little you could do to me that would stop what must happen. I am the universe. You're a speck of dust. I like you, Nelson. Please don't make me regret that."

Nelson eyed him warily, but didn't reply.

The Manager approached the table. Wallace sat stock-still as Hugo closed the door. The lock clicked.

The boy stopped at the table across from Wallace, inspecting the teapot and cups. He traced a finger along the spout of the pot. He caught a drop of liquid from the tip before pressing it against his tongue. "Peppermint," he said, sounding amused. "Candy canes. Isn't that right, Wallace? Your mother made them in the kitchen in winter. How strange it is that a memory so comforting comes from someone you grew to despise."

"I don't despise her," Wallace said stiffly.

The boy arched an eyebrow. "Is that so? Why not? She was, at best, distant. Both of your parents were. Tell me, Wallace, what will you do when you see them again? What will you say?"

He hadn't thought about it. He didn't know what that made him.

The boy nodded. "I see. Well, I suppose that's better left to you than me. Have a seat, Hugo, so that we may begin."

Hugo walked back to the table, pulling the chair out before sitting back down, expression blank and cold. Wallace hated to see it on him.

The boy clapped his hands. "That's better. Hold on just a second." He went to the table near them, pulling the chair out and dragging it along the floor back to their table. He pushed it between Mei and Nelson before he climbed onto it, sitting on his knees. He rested his elbows on the table, his chin in his hands. "There. Now we're all the same. I'd like a cup of tea. I always did like your tea, Hugo. Would you pour it for me?"

And Hugo said, "No. I won't."

The boy blinked slowly, his eyelashes black soot against golden skin. "What was that?" he asked, voice pitched high and sweet, like candy-coated razors.

"You're not getting tea," Hugo said.

"Oh." The boy cocked his head. "Why not?"

"Because you're going to listen to me, and I don't want you distracted."

"Ooh," the boy breathed. "Is that right? This should be interesting. You've got my attention. Go ahead. I'm listening." He cast a sly glance at Wallace before looking back at Hugo. "But I'd hurry if I were you. Appears our Wallace here is having a hard time staying seated. I wouldn't want him to float away while you're . . . how do you all put it? Giving me the ol' what for."

Hugo folded his hands on the table in front of him, the pads of his thumbs pressed together. "You lied to me."

"Did I? About what, exactly?"

"Cameron."

"Ah," the Manager said. "The Husk."

"Yes."

"He went through the door."

"Because we helped him."

"Did you?" He tapped his fingers against his cheeks. "Fascinating."

Wallace felt like screaming, but he kept his mouth closed. He couldn't let his emotions get the best of him, not when this counted more than anything. And he trusted Hugo with every fiber of his being. Hugo knew what he was doing.

Hugo's voice was even when he said, "You let him be as he was. You told me there was nothing we could do."

"Did I say that?" the Manager chuckled. "I suppose I did. Glad to know you were listening."

"You could've stepped in at any time to help him."

"Why would I have done that?" the Manager asked, sounding baffled. "He made his choice. As I told Wallace, free will is paramount. It's vital for—"

"Until you decide that it's not," Hugo said flatly. "This isn't a game. You don't get to pick and choose when you intervene."

"Don't I?" the boy asked. He glanced around at the others as if to say *Can you believe this guy?* His gaze lingered on Wallace for a moment before he looked back at Hugo. "But, for the sake of argument, why don't you tell me what I, an endless being of dust and stars, should've done."

Hugo leaned forward, face stony. "He was suffering. Lost. My former Reaper knew that. He fed off it. And still you did nothing. Even after Cameron turned into a Husk, you didn't lift a finger. It wasn't until Lea that you decided to do something about it. It should never have taken that long."

The boy scoffed. "Perhaps, but it all worked out in the end. Lea's mother is on the road to healing. Cameron found himself again and continued his journey to the great and wild beyond. I don't see the problem here. Everyone is happy." He grinned. "You should feel proud of yourself. Kudos all around. Hooray!" He clapped his hands.

"Could you have helped him?" Mei asked.

The Manager turned his head slowly toward her.

She didn't look away.

"Well," the Manager said, dragging the word out for several syllables. "I mean, sure, if we're getting down to brass tacks. I can pretty much do anything I want to." He narrowed his eyes. Wallace felt a chill run down his spine as the boy's voice became clipped. "I could have stopped your parents from dying, Hugo. I could've kept Wallace's heart beating its jazzy little jam. I could've grabbed Cameron by the scruff of his neck the day he decided to flee and forced him through the door."

"But you didn't," Hugo said.

"I didn't," the boy agreed. "Because there is an order to things. A plan, one that goes far above your pay grade. You would do well to remember that. I'm not sure I like your tone." He pouted, his bottom lip sticking out. "It's not very nice."

"What is that plan?" Wallace asked.

The boy looked to him again. "Pardon me?"

"The plan," Wallace said. "What is it?"

"Something far beyond your capability to comprehend. It's—"

"Right," Wallace said. "What's on the other side of the door?"

It was subtle, there and gone in a flash, but Wallace saw the bewildered expression before it disappeared. "Why, everything, of course."

"Specifics. Tell me one thing besides what we already know."

His bottom lip stuck out farther. "Oh, Wallace. There's nothing for you to fear. I've told you that. You will find—"

"Yeah, see, I don't think you know," Wallace said. He leaned forward as Mei sucked in a breath, as Nelson tapped his cane on the floor. "I think you want to. You try to emulate us. You try to make us think you understand, but how could you? You don't have our humanity. You don't know what it's like to have a beating heart, to feel it crack. You don't know what it means to be happy, what it means to grieve. Maybe some part of you is jealous of all the things we are that you can never be, and though you may not believe me, I wish that for you more than you know. Because *I* know there's something on the other side of that door. I've felt it. I've heard the whispers. I've heard the songs it sings. I've seen the light that spills from it. Can you even begin to imagine what that's like?"

"Careful, Wallace," the Manager said, pout melting away into steel. "Remember who you're talking to."

"He knows," Hugo said quietly. "We all do."

The Manager frowned as he glanced at Hugo. "Do you? I should hope so."

"What are the Husks?" Wallace paused, thinking as hard as he ever had. "A manifestation of a fear-based life?" That seemed like the right direction, but he couldn't quite get the picture to come into focus. "They . . . what? Are more susceptible to . . ."

"Fear-based life," the Manager repeated slowly. "That's . . . huh." He squinted at Wallace. "Figured that out on your own, did you? Good for you. Yes, Wallace. Those who lived in fear and despair are more . . . how did you put it? *Susceptible.* All they know is dread, and it follows them across. Though it doesn't affect them all the same way, people like Cameron sometimes can't accept their new reality. They run from it and . . . well. You know what happens next."

"How many of them are there?" Hugo asked.

The Manager reared back. "What?"

Hugo stared at the Manager, barely blinking. "People like Cameron. People who've been brought to the ferrypeople all over the world and lost their way. How many of them are there?"

"I don't see what that has to do with—"

"It's the entire *point!*" Wallace exclaimed. "It's not about any one person. It's about all of us, and what we do for one another. The door doesn't discriminate. It's there for everyone who is brave enough to look up at it. Some people lose their way, but that's not their fault. They're scared. My god, of course they are. How could they not be? Everyone loses their way at some point, and it's not just because of their mistakes or the decisions they make. It's because they're horribly, wonderfully *human*. And the one thing I've learned about being human is that we can't do this alone. When we're lost, we need help to try to find our way again. We have a chance here to do something important, something never done before."

"We," the Manager said. "Don't you mean *they*? Because, in case you forgot, you're dead."

"I know," Wallace said. "I know."

The boy frowned. "I told you once, Wallace. I don't make deals. I don't bargain. I thought we were past that." He sighed heavily. "I'm so disappointed in you. I was very clear on the matter. And you talk about the Husks as if you know anything about them."

"I've seen them," Wallace said. "Up close. Cameron. I saw what he was, regardless of what he'd turned into."

"One," the Manager said. "You've seen *one* of them."

"It's enough," Hugo said. "More than, even. Because if the rest of the Husks are anything like Cameron, then they deserve a chance, the same as we do." He leaned forward, gaze never leaving the Manager. "I can do this. You know I can." He looked around at the others at the table. "*We* can do this."

The Manager was silent for a long moment. Wallace had to stop himself from fidgeting. He barely kept from shouting in relief when the Manager said, "You have my attention. Don't waste it."

Closing arguments, but it didn't come from Wallace. It couldn't. He looked to the one person who knew life and death better than anyone else in the tea shop. Hugo squared his shoulders, taking a deep breath and letting it out slow. "The Husks. Bring them here. Let us help them. They don't deserve to stay as they are. They should be able to find their way home like everyone else." He glanced at Wallace, who still held onto the table as tightly as he could. It was getting harder to do. His rear lifted from the chair a few inches, his knees pressed to the underside of the table, his feet off the floor.

And if he listened hard enough, if he really tried, he could hear the whispers from the door once more. It was almost over.

The Manager stared at him. "Why would I agree to this?"

"Because you know we can do it," Mei said. "Or, at the very least, we can try."

"And because it's the right thing to do," Wallace said, and he'd never believed anything more. How simple. How terrifyingly profound. "The only reason the Husks chose as they did was out of fear of the unknown."

The Manager nodded slowly. "Say I entertain this. Say, for a moment, that I consider your offer. What will you give me in return?"

And Wallace said, "I'll let go."

Hugo was alarmed. "Wallace, no, don't—"

"How strange you are," the Manager said. "You've changed. What caused it? Do you even know?"

Wallace laughed, wild and bright. "You, I think. Or at least you're part of it, even if nothing you do makes any sense. But that's par for the course with existing, because life is senseless, and on the off chance we find something that *does* make sense, we hold onto it as tightly as we can. I found myself because of you. But you pale in comparison to Mei. To Nelson. Apollo." He swallowed thickly. "And Hugo."

Hugo stood abruptly, chair tipping over and falling to the floor. "No," he said harshly. "I won't let you do this. I won't—"

"It's not about me," Wallace told him. "Or us. You've given me more than I could ever ask for. Hugo, can't you see? I am who I am because you showed me the way. You refused to give up on me. Which is how I know you'll help all those who come after me and need you as much as I did."

"Fine," the Manager said suddenly, and all the air was sucked from the room. "You have a deal. I'll bring the Husks here, one by one. If he heals them, then so be it. If he doesn't, they stay as they are. It'll be a lot of work either way, and I don't know how successful it'll be."

Wallace's grip on the table grew slack as his jaw dropped. "You mean it?"

"Yes," the Manager said. "My word is my bond."

"Why?" Wallace asked. The Manager had agreed quicker than Wallace expected. There had to be more.

The Manager shrugged. "Curiosity. I want to see what happens. With order comes routine. Routine can lead to boredom, especially when it goes on forever. This is . . . different." His eyes narrowed as he looked at Hugo and Mei. "Don't mistake my acquiescence for a sign of complacency."

"You swear?" Wallace insisted.

"Yes," the Manager said, rolling his eyes. "I swear. I've heard the closing argument, counselor. The jury has come back with a verdict in your favor. We've reached a deal. It's time, Wallace. It's time to let go."

Wallace said, "I . . ."

He looked at Mei. A tear trickled down her cheek.

He looked at Nelson. His eyes were closed as he frowned deeply.

He looked at Apollo. The dog whined and bowed his head.

He looked at Hugo. Wallace remembered the first day he'd come to the tea shop, and how scared he'd been of Hugo. If only he'd known then what he knew now.

What will you do with the time you have left?

He knew. Here, at the end, he knew. "I love you. All of you. You've made my death worth it. Thank you for helping me live."

And then Wallace Price let go of the table.

Unmoored, untethered, he rose.

The tops of his knees hit the table, causing it to jump. The teapot and cups rattled on the table. How freeing it was, letting go. Finally, at last. He wasn't scared. Not anymore.

He closed his eyes as he floated toward the ceiling.

The pull of the door was as strong as it'd ever been. It was singing to him, whispering his name.

He opened his eyes when he stopped rising.

He looked down.

Nelson had a hold of his ankle, fingers digging in, a look of determination on his face which changed into surprise when he too started to lift from the floor.

But then Apollo leapt forward, jaws closing around the end of Nelson's cane, holding him in place. He whined when his front paws rose from the floor, the top of Wallace's head near the ceiling.

Mei grabbed onto Apollo's hindquarters, his tail hitting her in the face. "No," she snapped. "It's not time. You can't do this. *You can't do this.*"

Then she started to rise, feet kicking as they left the floor.

Hugo tried to grab her, but his hands went through her again and again.

Wallace smiled down at them. "It's okay. I promise. Let me go."

"Never in your life," Nelson grunted, grip tightening around Wallace's ankle. Nelson's hand slipped to Wallace's shoe. His eyes widened. "No."

"Goodbye," Wallace whispered.

The shoe came off. Nelson and Apollo and Mei fell to the floor in a heap.

Wallace turned his face up. The whispers grew louder.

He rose through the ceiling of the first floor to the second. He heard the others shouting below him as they ran for the stairs. Nelson appeared out of thin air, reaching for him, but Wallace was too high. Mei and Hugo made it to the second floor in time to see him rise through the ceiling.

"Wallace!" Hugo cried.

The third floor. He wished he'd spent more time in Hugo's room. He wondered what sort of life they could have made for themselves had he found his way to this little place before his heart had given out. He thought it would have been wonderful. But it was better to have had it for as long as he did than to never have had it at all. What a tremendous thought that was.

But then it was a tremendous death, wasn't it? Because of what he'd found after life.

The whispers of the door called for him, singing his name over and over, and in his chest, a light, like the sun. It burned within him. He was horizontal to the floor below him, arms spread like they'd been when he'd ridden behind Hugo on the scooter. He hit the ceiling of the third floor, and it gave way as he rose through it to the fourth floor.

He wasn't surprised to see the Manager already waiting for him below the door, head cocked. For a moment, Wallace thought he'd continue up and up and up. Maybe the door wouldn't open, and he'd rise through the roof of the house into the night sky and the never-ending stars. It wouldn't be such a bad way to go.

But he didn't.

He stopped, suspended in air. Nelson appeared near the landing, but he didn't speak.

For the first time, the Manager looked unsure. Just a little boy with flowers in his hair.

Wallace smiled. "I'm not afraid. Not of you. Not of the door. Not about anything that came before or will come next."

Nelson put his face in his hands.

"Not afraid," the Manager repeated. "I can see that. You let go of the table as if . . ." He stared at Wallace for a long moment before looking up at the door as the whispers grew louder, more unintelligible. "I wonder. What would it be like if . . ."

The whispers turned into a maelstrom. The Manager shook his head stubbornly, a child being told no. "No, I don't think that's quite true. What if—You know what? I'm getting pretty tired of your—"

The maelstrom became a hurricane, furious and loud.

"I've done whatever you've asked. Always." He glared up at the door. "And where has it gotten us? If this is for everyone, then it needs to *be* for everyone. Don't you want to see what could happen? I think they could end up surprising us all. They've proven themselves as it is. And they'll need all the help they can get. What could it hurt?"

The door rattled in its frame, the leaf in the doorknob unfurling.

"Yes," the Manager said. "I know. But this . . . this is a choice.

My choice. And it will be on me, whatever happens. You have my word. I will be responsible for whatever happens next."

The hurricane blew itself out, silence falling on the fourth floor of the tea shop.

"Huh," the Manager said. "I can't believe that worked. I wonder what else I can do?" He looked up at Wallace before jerking his head. Wallace fell to the floor, landing roughly on his feet, but managing to stay upright. For the first time since he'd given Cameron his hook, he felt grounded, like he had weight.

Mei reached the landing, panting as she bent over, hands on her knees. Apollo's nails slid along the floor as he jumped the last few steps, tumbling end over end before landing on his back. He blinked up at Wallace, tongue lolling out of his mouth as he grinned, tail wagging.

Hugo came last. He stopped, mouth agape.

"There's been a change of plans," the Manager said, sounding oddly amused. "*I've* made a change in plans." He laughed loudly, shaking his head. "This is going to be *fun*." The air around them thickened before exploding in a comical *pop*! The Manager held a file folder, frowning down at it as he flipped it open, mouth moving as he read silently, riffling through the pages. Wallace tried to see what he was reading, but the Manager closed the folder before he could get close enough. "Interesting. Your résumé is very thorough. Too thorough, if you ask me, but since no one did, that's apparently neither here nor there."

Wallace felt his eyes bulge. "My what?"

The Manager threw the folder up into the air. It hung suspended briefly before it winked out of existence. "Job interviews," he said. "All this damn paperwork, but death is a business, so I suppose it's a necessity. Who would have thought this would turn into an office job?" He shuddered. "No matter. Congratulations, Wallace. You're hired." He grinned sharply. "On a temporary basis, of course, one whose terms will be negotiated should this move on to a more permanent position."

"For *what*?"

The Manager reached up and plucked a flower from his hair, the vine snapping. The petals were yellow and pink and orange. He held it out to Wallace, palm toward the ceiling. The leaf on the crystal doorknob above them fluttered as if caught in a breeze. The flower floated above his hand as it bloomed brilliantly. "Having the Husks brought here will be a bigger job than you think. The others will need the help. As per your résumé, you certainly seem qualified, and though I would have preferred someone a little less . . . you, a résumé such as this doesn't lie. Open your mouth, Wallace."

"What?" Wallace asked, rearing back. "Why?"

The Manager grumbled under his breath before saying, "Do it before I change my mind. If you knew what I was risking here, you'd *open your damn mouth.*"

Wallace opened his mouth.

The Manager puffed his cheeks, blowing a stream of air against the flower above his palm. It grew bigger as it floated toward Wallace. The petals brushed against his lips. They tickled his nose. They folded into his mouth, pressing down on his tongue. They tasted sweet, like honey in tea. He gasped and coughed as the flower filled his mouth. He bit down, trying to hold it back to no avail. The flower slid down his throat.

He fell to the floor on his hands and knees, head bowed as he gagged.

He felt it the moment the flower hit his chest and bloomed.

It pulsed once.

Twice.

Three times.

Again and again and again.

Someone crouched next to him. "Wallace?" Hugo asked, sounding worried. "What did you do to him?"

"Um, Hugo?" Mei said, voice trembling.

"What I wanted to," the Manager said. "It's time for a change. They don't like it, but they're old and stuck in their ways. I can handle them."

"*Hugo.*"

"*What*, Mei?"

She whispered, "You're touching him."

Wallace lifted his head.

Hugo was next to him on his knees, hand on Wallace's back, rubbing up and down. It stilled when Mei spoke, the heavy weight of it like a brand.

Hugo choked out, "Are you . . . ?"

"Alive?" the Manager asked. "Yes. He is. A gift for you, Hugo, and one not to be taken lightly." He sniffed. "It can just as easily be taken away. And I'll be the first one here for it in case the need arises. Don't disappoint me, Wallace. I'm taking a chance on you. I would prefer not to regret that. I'm pretty sure the repercussions would be endless."

"My heart," Wallace croaked as the pulse in his chest thundered against his ribcage. "I can feel my—"

Hugo kissed him. His hands cupped Wallace's face, and he kissed him as if it were the last thing he would ever do. Wallace gasped into his mouth, his lips warm and soft. Hugo's fingers dug into his cheeks, a pressure unlike anything Wallace had ever felt before.

He did the only thing he could as stars burst in his eyes.

He kissed Hugo back. He breathed him in, chasing the remnants of peppermint on Hugo's tongue. Wallace kissed him for all he was worth, giving everything he could. He was crying, or Hugo was crying, or they were *both* crying, but it didn't matter. He kissed Hugo Freeman with all his might.

Hugo pulled away, but only just, pressing their foreheads together. "Hello."

"Hello, Hugo."

Hugo tried to smile, but it collapsed. "Is this real?"

"I think so."

And Hugo kissed him again, sweet and shining, and Wallace felt it down to the tips of his toes.

He kissed Wallace on the lips and the cheeks and on his eyelids when Wallace could no longer bear to look at him so closely. He kissed away the tears, saying, "You're real. You're real. *You're real.*"

Eventually, they broke apart.

Eventually, Hugo stood, knees popping.

He held a hand out toward Wallace.

Wallace didn't hesitate.

Hugo's grip was strong as he pulled Wallace up. He stared down at their joined hands in wonder before tugging Wallace close. He lowered his head to Wallace's chest, ear pressed against the left side of his ribcage. "I can hear it," he whispered. "Your heart."

And then he stood upright and hugged Wallace tightly. Wallace's breath was knocked from his chest as Hugo squeezed him as hard as he could. He was lifted off his feet as Hugo laughed, spinning them both around.

"Hugo!" Wallace shouted, dizzy as the room spun around them. "You're going to make me sick if you don't put me down!"

Hugo did. He tried to step back, but Wallace didn't let him get far. He interlocked his fingers with Hugo's, palm to palm. He barely had time to react before Mei jumped on him, legs wrapped around his waist, her hair in his nose. He laughed when she began to beat her fists against his chest, demanding that he never do anything so stupid again, and how could you be so dumb, Wallace, how could you possibly think you could ever say goodbye?

He kissed her hair. Her forehead. She squealed when he tickled her side, jumping back off him.

And then Nelson and Apollo came running.

Except they passed right through him.

Nelson almost fell to the floor. Apollo did, smashing into the wall behind them. The windows rattled in the turret. He got up, shaking his head, looking confused.

"He's alive," the Manager said dryly. "You can't touch him. At least not yet. Mei will have to show you how."

They looked at the Manager. "What do you mean?" Wallace asked, still dazed. "How can I—"

Mei said, "A Reaper."

The Manager nodded. "The job will be bigger than you can handle. If you're going to see to the Husks, then you'll need another

Reaper to assist you. Wallace already understands how it works. Everyone knows it's cheaper to keep the employees you have rather than hiring someone new. Wallace, hold out your hand."

Wallace looked at Hugo, who nodded. He held out his hand.

"Mei," the Manager said. "You know what to do."

"Damn right," Mei said. "Wallace, watch me, okay?" She lifted her own hand, fingers flexing. She brought up her other hand and tapped a familiar pattern into her palm. A light pulsed briefly in her hand.

Wallace let go of Hugo, though he was loath to do so. He tapped the same pattern onto his own hand.

At first nothing happened.

He frowned. "Maybe I did it wr—"

The room shuddered and shook. His skin vibrated. Gooseflesh prickled along the back of his neck. His hands trembled. The air around him expanded as if it lay on the surface of a soap bubble. The bubble popped.

Wallace looked up.

The colors of the fourth floor were sharper. He could see the grains in the walls, the finite cracks in the floor. He reached for Hugo, and his hand went right through him. He panicked until the Manager said, "You can change back, like Mei. Repeat the pattern, and you'll be amongst the living once more. It's part of being a Reaper. This will allow you to interact with those who've passed." He made a face. "With the Husks, unfortunate creatures that they are."

Apollo approached him slowly, nostrils flaring. He craned his neck until his snout pressed against Wallace's hand. His tail started wagging furiously as he licked Wallace's fingers.

"Yes," Wallace said with a grimace. "I'm happy to feel you too."

And then Nelson was on him, hugging him almost as hard as his grandson had. "I knew it," Nelson whispered. "I knew we'd find a way."

Wallace hugged him back. "Did you?"

Nelson scoffed as he pulled away. "Of course I did. I never doubted it, even for a second."

"Switch back," the Manager said.

Wallace repeated the same pattern on his palm. The room stuttered around him again, the sharpness fading as quickly as it'd arrived. Needing reassurance that it'd worked, he reached for Hugo once more, taking his hand. He lifted Hugo's hand to his lips, kissing the back of it. Hugo stared at him in wonder. "It's real," Wallace whispered to him.

"I don't understand," Hugo admitted. "How?"

They turned to the Manager once more. The boy sighed as he crossed his arms. "Yes, yes. You're alive again. How wonderful for you." He looked grim. "This isn't something to be taken lightly, Wallace. In all of history, there has only been one person who was brought back to life in such a way."

Wallace gaped at him. "Holy shit. I'm like Jesus?"

The Manager scowled. "What? Of course not. His name was Pablo. He lived in Spain in the fifteenth century. He was . . . well. It's not important who he was. All that matters is you know this is a gift, and one that can be taken away just as easily." He shook his head. "You cannot go back to the life you lived, Wallace. For all intents and purposes, that life is still dead. The people who knew you, the people who . . . put up with you, to them, you're dead and buried with nothing left but a stone marker to show you existed at all. You can't return. It would create disorder, and I won't have it. You've been given a second chance. You won't be given another. I'd suggest getting that heart looked at as quickly as possible. Better to be safe than sorry. Do you understand?"

No. He really didn't. "What if someone sees me who used to know me?" He thought the chance miniscule, but the last weeks had shown him how strange the world really was.

"We'll deal with it then," the Manager said. "I mean it, Wallace. Your place is—"

"Here," Wallace said, squeezing Hugo's hand because he could. "My place is here."

"Exactly. You have much work ahead of you. It's up to you to prove to me that my faith in you isn't misplaced. No pressure." The Manager yawned widely, jaw cracking. "I think that's enough excitement for one day. I'll be back shortly to outline what's next. Mei will act as your trainer. Listen to her. She's good at what she does. Maybe even the best I've seen."

Mei blushed even as she continued to glare at the Manager.

"I'm leaving now," the Manager said. "I'll be keeping tabs on all of you. Consider it an evaluation of those in our employ. Reorient yourself with the living world." He glanced at Hugo before looking back at Wallace. "Do what it is humans do when they're enamored with each other. Get it out of your system. I don't want to come back and catch you two *in flagrante delicto*." He made an obscene gesture with his hands, something Wallace never wanted to see a child do, even if said child seemed to be as old as the universe.

Hugo sputtered.

"Oh my god," Wallace mumbled, knowing his cheeks were red.

"Yes," the Manager said. "I know. It's terribly vexing. I don't know how you put up with it. Love seems positively dreadful." He turned toward the stairs, antlers beginning to grow from his head, flowers blooming from the velvet. He paused, looking back over his shoulder. He grinned, winked, and descended the stairs. By the time he reached the bottom, they could hear the sound of hooves on the floor of the tea shop. A blue light flashed through the window that pointed toward the front of the house.

And then it—*he*—was gone.

They stood silently, listening as the clocks in the tea shop began ticking once more.

Nelson spoke first. "What a strange day this has been. Mei, I think I could use a cup of tea. Would you join me?"

"Yep," she said, already heading for the stairs. "I'm thinking something fancy to celebrate."

"Great minds think alike," Nelson replied. He hobbled toward the stairs, Apollo and Mei trailing after him. Like the Manager, he stopped before descending. When he looked back at Wallace and

Hugo, his eyes were wet, and he was smiling. "My dear boy," he said. "My lovely Hugo. It's your time now. Make the most of it."

And with that, he walked down the stairs, telling Mei and Apollo he was thinking along the lines of the Da Hong Pao tea, something that made Mei gasp in delight. The last they saw of them was the tip of Apollo's tail as it flicked back and forth.

"Christ," Wallace said, scrubbing a hand over his face. "I can't believe how tired I am. I feel like I could sleep for a—"

"I love you too," Hugo said.

Wallace sucked in a breath as he closed his eyes. "What?"

He felt Hugo standing before him. His hand caressed the side of his face. He leaned into it. How he'd lasted all these weeks without his touch, Wallace would never know. "I love you too," Hugo said again, and it came with a hushed reverence akin to prayer.

Wallace opened his eyes. Hugo filled the world until he was all Wallace could see. "You do?"

Hugo nodded.

Wallace sniffed. "Damn right you do. You're very lucky to have—"

Hugo kissed him once more.

"I think," Wallace said against Hugo's lips, "that we should forgo the tea, at least for now."

"What did you have in mind?" Hugo asked, nose brushing against Wallace's own.

Wallace shrugged. "Perhaps you could give me a tour of your bedroom."

"You've seen it before."

"Yes," Wallace said. "But that was when I was wearing clothes. I expect it'll be different if we got rid of—" He yelped when the world tilted as Hugo lifted him up, throwing him over his shoulder. He was stronger than he looked. "Oh my god. Hugo, put me down!" He beat his hands against Hugo's back, laughing as he did so.

"Never," Hugo said. "Never, ever, ever."

Wallace raised his head and looked up at the door as Hugo headed for the stairs. For a brief moment, he saw the flowers and leaves growing along the wood. "Thank you," he whispered.

But the door was just that: a door.

It didn't respond.

It would, one day. It waited for all of them.

The tour of Hugo's bedroom went smashingly. It really was better without clothing.

EPILOGUE

On an evening in the middle of summer, Nelson Freeman said, "I think it's time."

Wallace looked up. He was washing the counter after another day manning the register of Charon's Crossing Tea and Treats. Hugo and Mei were in the kitchen, getting their prep done for the following morning. It was good work, hard work. He was tired more than he wasn't, but he went to bed every night with a sense of accomplishment.

It certainly didn't hurt that he and Hugo worked as well together as they did. After the Manager had left, and once the fiery shine of living had faded slightly, Wallace worried that it was too much too soon. It was one thing having a ghost living in your home. It was something else entirely to have them made flesh and blood and sharing a bed. He'd thought about moving somewhere in town to give them some space or, at the very least, to another room in the house.

Nancy had decided to move back to where she'd come from, and her apartment had become available. She'd come to say goodbye, hugging Hugo before she left. She looked . . . brighter, somehow. She wasn't healed, and probably wouldn't be for a long time, if ever, but life was slowly returning to her. She told Hugo, "I'm starting again. I don't know if I'll ever come back. But I won't forget what happened here."

And with that, she left.

Hugo had shot down the idea of Wallace taking her apartment over with a grumpy expression, arms folded. "You can stay here."

"You don't think it's too soon?"

He shook his head. "We've got the hard part out of the way, Wallace. I want you here." He frowned, looking unsure. "Unless you want to leave."

"No, no," Wallace said hastily. "I rather like where I'm at."

Hugo grinned at him. "Do you? And what exactly do you like about it?"

Wallace blushed, mumbling under his breath how cocky Hugo had become.

And that was the last time he'd mentioned it.

Shortly after his resurrection (a word he tried not to think too much about), he had Hugo call his former law firm. At first, no one would listen, but Hugo was persistent, Wallace feeding him the right words to say. Wallace had made an awful mistake, and Patricia Ryan should be rehired immediately, her daughter's scholarship restored. It took nearly a week for Hugo to get one of the partners on the phone—Worthington—and when Hugo told him why he was calling, Worthington said, "Wallace wanted this? Wallace Price? Are you sure? He was the one who fired her. And if you knew Wallace, you know he never admitted to mistakes."

"He did this time," Hugo said. "Before he died, he sent me a handwritten letter. I didn't receive it until a few days ago."

"Post office," Worthington said. "Always running behind." Silence. Then, "You're not having me on, right? This isn't some joke from beyond the grave that Wallace wanted you to pull?" He snorted. "Never mind, that can't be it. Wallace didn't know how to joke."

Wallace muttered under his breath about the ridiculousness of lawyers.

"I can send you the letter," Hugo said. "You can verify his handwriting. He's very clear about wanting Mrs. Ryan to have her job back."

Sweat trickled down the back of Wallace's neck as he waited, staring down at the phone on the counter.

Worthington sighed. "I never thought she deserved what happened to her. She was good. More than, even. I've actually been thinking about calling her and . . ." He paused. "Tell you what: send me what you have, and I'll take a look at it and go from there. If she wants to come back to work with us, then we'd be glad to have her."

"Thank you," Hugo said as Wallace cheered silently. "I appreciate that. I know Wallace would—"

"How did you know Wallace?" Worthington asked.

Wallace froze.

Hugo did not. He looked at Wallace as he said, "I loved him. I love him still."

"Oh," Worthington said. "That's—I'm sorry for your loss. I didn't know he . . . had someone."

"He does," Hugo said simply.

Worthington disconnected, and Wallace hugged Hugo as hard as he could. "Thank you," he whispered into Hugo's shoulder. "Thank you."

e𝓈

It wasn't easy. Of course it wasn't. Wallace was learning how to live again, an adjustment that proved harder than he expected. He still made mistakes. But he wasn't like he'd been before his heart had stopped.

They argued, sometimes, but it was always small, and they didn't leave things unsaid. They were making it work. Wallace was sure they always would.

And it wasn't as if they were in each other's back pockets all the time. They all had jobs to do. Mei took on her role as Wallace's trainer with gusto. She was quick to point out when he messed up, but never held it against him. She worked him hard but only because she knew what he was capable of. "One day," she told him, "you'll be doing this on your own. You gotta believe in yourself, man. I know I do."

It was more than he expected. He never thought about death until he died. And now that he'd returned, he sometimes struggled with the bigger picture, the point of it all. But he had Mei and Nelson and Apollo to fall back on when things got confusing. And Hugo, of course. Always Hugo.

The Manager had returned a week after bringing Wallace back

to life. And with him came their second Husk, a woman with black teeth and a vacant stare. Wallace frowned at the sight of her, but he wasn't afraid.

"Do what you will," the Manager said, offering no further assistance. He sat in a chair, munching on a plate of leftover scones.

"You're not going to help?" Wallace asked.

The Manager shook his head. "Why should I? A successful manager knows how to delegate. You figure it out."

They did, eventually, because of Mei. As the Manager looked on, she stood in front of the Husk. She took her hand. Mei grimaced, and if it was anything like it'd been with Cameron, Wallace knew she was seeing flashes of the woman's life, all the choices she'd made that had led to her becoming as she was. By the time she let the woman go, she was crying. Hugo reached for her, but Mei shook her head. "It's all right," she said weakly. "It's just . . . a lot. All at once." She wiped her eyes. "I know how to help her. It's like it was with Wallace and Cameron. Hugo, it's up to you."

Hugo stepped forward, and though Wallace couldn't see it, he knew Hugo grabbed the hook in his own chest, pulling it out with a grunt. The air in the tea shop grew hot as he pressed the hook into the Husk. She gagged as her skin filled with the colors of life. She bent over, clutching her sides as the black of her teeth turned to white.

"Wh-aaat," the woman said. "Wha-aaaat is . . . this? What. Is happening?"

"You're safe," Hugo said. He glanced at Wallace who arched an eyebrow, a pointed look at Hugo's chest. Hugo nodded, and Wallace breathed a sigh of relief. Another hook had appeared in Hugo's chest, connecting him to the woman. It'd worked. "I've got you. Can you tell me your name?"

"Adriana," she whispered.

The Manager muttered through a mouthful of scone.

Since that day, they'd helped a dozen more Husks. Sometimes it was Mei. Other times, it was Wallace. There were days when they'd leave to find the Husks themselves, and others when the Husks would appear on the road leading to the tea shop, surrounded by hoofprints in the dirt. Some were harder than others. One had been a Husk for close to two hundred years and didn't speak English. They'd managed to help him by the skin of their teeth, but Wallace knew that it would only get easier from there. They'd do what they could for all who came to them.

The people of the town were curious about this new addition to Charon's Crossing. It didn't take long for rumors to spread about Wallace and his relationship with Hugo. People came in to gawk at him. The older women cooed, the younger women seemed disappointed that Hugo was off the market (as did a few of the men, much to Wallace's complicated glee), and it wasn't long before the newness of it all faded and Wallace became yet another fixture of the town. They waved at him when they saw him on the sidewalk or in the grocery store. He always waved back.

Wallace Price became Wallace Reid. At least, that's what his new ID and Social Security card said. Mei told him not to ask too many questions when she'd handed them to him after returning from a three-day trip to visit her mother, which she said had gone better than she expected. "Mom knows people," she said, lips quirking. "She picked out the last name for you. Showed her a couple of pictures of you, and she told me to tell you the surname is because you're thin as a reed, and that you need to eat more."

"I'll write her a thank-you note," Wallace said, distracted as he brushed a finger over his new name.

"Good. She's expecting you to."

Desdemona Tripplethorne returned to the tea shop, telling them she wanted to see the new employee at Charon's Crossing for herself. Squat Man and Thin Man crowded behind her, staring at Wallace. Desdemona studied him as he fidgeted. Finally, her brow furrowed, and she said, "Have . . . have we met? I swear I know you from somewhere."

"No," Wallace said. "How could we have? I've never been here before."

"I suppose you're right," she said slowly. She shook her head. "My name is Desdemona Tripplethorne, I'm sure you've heard of me. I'm a clairvoyant—"

Mei coughed. It sounded strangely like *bullshit*.

Desdemona ignored her. "—and I come here from time to time to speak to the spirits that haunt this place. I know how it sounds. But there is more to the world than you could possibly know."

"Is there?" Wallace asked. "How do you know?"

She tapped the side of her head. "I have a gift."

She left an hour later, disappointed when the planchette on her Ouija board and the feather quill hadn't moved even a millimeter. She would be back, she announced grandly before leaving the tea shop in a swirl of self-entitlement, Thin Man and Squat Man hurrying after her.

It went on, life did, ever forward. Good days, the not-so-good days, the days when he wondered how he could stand being surrounded by death for much longer. It hit Hugo too; though few and far between, he still had panic attacks, days when his breath would catch in his chest, lungs constricting. Wallace never tried to force him through the attacks, just sat on the back deck with him, tap, tap, tapping, Apollo alert at Hugo's feet. When Hugo recovered, breaths slow and deep, Wallace whispered, "All right?"

"I will be," Hugo said, taking Wallace's hand in his own.

It wasn't always Husks. Spirits still came to them, spirits who needed someone like Hugo as their ferryman. Often, they were angry and destructive, bitter and cold. Some of them stayed for weeks, ranting and raving about how they didn't want to be dead, that they didn't want to be trapped here, they were going to *leave*, and nothing was going to stop them, pulling at the cables extending from their chests to Hugo's, threatening to remove the hook that kept them grounded.

They didn't.

They always stayed.

They listened.

They learned.

They understood, after a time. Some just took longer than others.

But that was okay.

Each of them found their way to the door, and to what came after.

After all, Charon's Crossing was nothing but a way station.

At least for the dead.

It was the living who found their roots growing deep in the earth. Tea plants, Hugo had once told Wallace, required patience. You had to put in the time and have patience.

Which is why, on a summer evening, when Nelson said, "I think it's time," Wallace knew what he meant.

But any reply he had dried up in his throat when he saw who stood before him.

Gone was the elderly man leaning on a cane.

In his place stood a much younger man, back straight, hands clasped behind him as he looked out the window, cane gone as if it'd never been there at all. Wallace recognized him immediately. He'd seen this very man in many of the photographs hanging on the walls of the tea shop and in Hugo's room, mostly in black and white or grainy color.

"Nelson?" he whispered.

Nelson turned his head and smiled. His wrinkles were gone, replaced by the smooth skin of someone far younger. His eyes were twinkling. He was bigger, stronger. His hair sat in a black Afro on his head, much like his grandson's. Decades had melted away until before Wallace stood a man who looked as young as Hugo. What had Nelson said?

It's simple, really. I like being old.

"You stayed as you were because it's how Hugo knew you when you were alive," Wallace said hoarsely.

"Yes," Nelson said. "I did. And I'd do it all over again if I had to, but I think it's time for what I want. And Wallace, I want this."

Wallace wiped his tears away. "You're sure."

He looked back out the window. "I am."

$\backsim$

Mei made them tea as the rest gathered in the darkened tea shop, moonlight bathing the forest around them. Hugo sat in a chair, bandana in his lap (black with little yellow ducks), looking around the tea shop with a quiet smile on his face.

Mei brought the tea tray out, setting it on the table. The scent of chai filled the room, thick and heady. Hugo poured tea for each of them, the cups filled to the brim. He handed them each a cup, setting a bowl down on the floor for Apollo, who began to lap at the liquid frantically. Wallace couldn't bring himself to drink from his own cup, worried his hands would shake too much.

"This is nice," Hugo said as Mei sat next to him. He had yet to comment on his grandfather's appearance. He'd looked momentarily stunned when he'd seen Nelson as he was now, but had quickly covered it up. Wallace knew he was waiting for Nelson to bring it up. "We should do this more often. Just us, at the end of the day." He looked at each of them in turn, smile fading when his gaze found Wallace, who failed miserably in his attempt to school his expression. "What is it? What's wrong?"

Wallace cleared his throat and said, "Nothing. It's nothing. I—"

"Hugo," Nelson said, a thin line of chai on his upper lip. "My dear Hugo."

Hugo looked at him.

And just like that, he knew.

Empathetic almost to a fault.

Hugo set his cup down on the table.

He closed his eyes.

He said, "Grandad?" in a small voice.

"It's time," Nelson said. "I've lived a long life. A good life. I've loved. I've been loved in return. I made something out of nothing. This place. This tiny tea shop. My wife, my heart. My children. And you, Hugo. Even when it became just the two of us, I held on as tightly as I could. I worried that I wouldn't be enough, that you wanted more than I could give you."

"I didn't," Hugo croaked. "I didn't want anything else."

"Perhaps not," Nelson agreed gently. "But you've found it all the same. You've found it in Mei and Wallace, but even before them, you were already on your way. You've built this life, this wonderful life with your own hands. You took the tools I gave you and made them your own. What more could a man ask for?"

"It hurts," Hugo said as he lifted his head. He pressed a hand against his chest above his heart.

Mei sobbed into her hands, little hiccupping breaths.

"I know," Nelson said. "But I can leave now, secure in the knowledge that you stand on your own two feet. And when the days come that you don't think you'll be able to, you'll have others to ensure you will. That's the point, Hugo. That's the point of all of this."

"Grief," Hugo choked out. "It's grief." Apollo tried to nose at his hand, ever the service dog he'd been in life. He settled on the floor next to Hugo's feet, nose inches from Hugo's toes.

"It is," Nelson agreed. "We'll see each other again. But not for a long, long time. You have a life to live, and it'll be filled with such color and joy that it'll take your breath away. I just wish . . ." He shook his head.

"What?" Hugo asked.

"I wish I could hug you," Nelson said. "One last time."

"Mei."

"On it, boss," Mei said. She moved quickly, tapping her finger against her palm. The air stuttered, and then she was hugging Nelson with all her might. Nelson laughed brightly, face toward the ceiling, tears streaming down his face.

"Yes," he said. "This is fine. This is fine, indeed."

When Mei pulled away, Nelson smiled.

"When?" Hugo asked.

"I think at sunrise."

ᥱᴖ

Those who came to Charon's Crossing Tea and Treats the next morning were surprised to find the front door locked once more, a sign in the window with an apology, saying that the tea shop would be closed that morning for a special event. It was okay. They would come back.

Inside, Hugo rose unsteadily to his feet. They'd spent the night together in front of the fireplace, Nelson in his chair, the fire crackling. Wallace and Mei and Apollo had listened as the two men told stories of their youth, tales of their family who'd gone on before them.

But a river only moves in one direction, no matter how much we wish it weren't so.

The night sky began to lighten.

Nelson's eyes were closed. He whispered, "I can hear it. The door. The whispers. The song it's singing. It knows I'm ready."

Hugo gripped Wallace's hand tightly. "Grandad?"

"Yes?"

"Thank you."

"For?"

"Everything."

Nelson chuckled. "That's quite a lot to be thankful for."

"I mean it."

"I know you do." He opened his eyes. "I'm a little frightened, Hugo. I know I shouldn't be, but I am all the same. Isn't that funny?"

Hugo shook his head slowly. He squared his shoulders and became the ferryman he was. "There's nothing for you to fear. You'll no longer know pain. You'll no longer know suffering. There will be peace for you. All you have to do is rise through the door."

"Will you help me?" Nelson asked.

And Hugo said, "Yes. I'll help you. Always."

Nelson rose from his chair slowly. He was unsteady on his feet, swaying side to side. "Oh," he whispered. "It's louder now."

Hugo stood. He looked down at Mei and Wallace and Apollo. "Will you come with us?"

Mei hung her head. "Are you sure?"

"Yes," Hugo said. "I'm sure. Grandad?"

"I'd like that very much," Nelson said.

And so they did.

They followed Nelson and Hugo up the stairs to the second floor.

To the third.

To the fourth.

They gathered below the door. Wallace knew what Nelson was hearing, though he could no longer hear it himself.

Nelson turned to face them. "Mei. Look at me."

She did.

"You have a gift," Nelson told her. "One that cannot be denied. But it's the immensity of your heart that makes you who you are. Never forget where you come from, but don't allow it to define you. You have made your place here, and I doubt there will ever be a better Reaper than you."

"Thank you," she whispered.

"Wallace," Nelson said. "You were an asshole."

Wallace choked.

"And yet, you've managed to move beyond it to become the man who stands before me. An honorary Freeman. Perhaps one day you'll become an actual Freeman, like Mei. I can think of no better man to share a name with."

Wallace nodded dumbly.

"Apollo," Nelson said. "You—"

"Should go with him," Hugo said quietly.

Apollo cocked his head up at Hugo.

Hugo crouched before him. Apollo tried to lick his face, but his tongue went through Hugo's cheek. "Hey, boy," Hugo said. "I need you to listen to me, okay? I have a job for you. Sit."

Apollo sat promptly, cocking his head as he watched Hugo.

Hugo said, "You're my best friend. You did more for me than almost anyone else. When I was lost and couldn't breathe, you grounded me. You reminded me that it was okay to hurt so long as I didn't let it consume me. You did your part, and now I need to do the same for you. I want you to do me a favor. Keep an eye on Grandad for me. Make sure he doesn't get into too much trouble, okay? At least until I can join you."

Apollo's ears flattened against his skull as his head drooped. He whined softly, trying to butt his head against Hugo's knee to no avail.

"I know," Hugo whispered. "But I swear we'll run together again one day. I won't forget it or you. Go, Apollo. Go with Grandad."

Apollo stood. He looked between Hugo and Nelson as if unsure. For a moment, Wallace thought he'd ignore Hugo's order and stay right where he was.

He didn't.

He barked at Hugo, a low woof before he turned toward Nelson. Apollo circled Nelson, sniffing at his legs before pressing his snout against Nelson's hand. Nelson smiled down at him. "You ready, Apollo? I think we're going on an adventure. I wonder what we'll see?"

Apollo licked his fingers.

Hugo rose from his crouch. He moved until he stood in front of his grandfather. Wallace thought he'd hesitate, if only for a moment. He didn't. He raised his hand toward Nelson's chest, and the moment his fingers closed around the hook only he and Nelson could see, Nelson said, "Hugo?"

Hugo looked at him.

Nelson said, "I'll be seeing you, okay?"

Hugo grinned brilliantly. "Damn right you will." And then he pulled the hook free. He turned and did the same to Apollo, the dog yipping once.

Hugo stood upright, taking a deep breath as he raised his hand above his head toward the doorknob. His fingers covered the leaf, and with a twist of his wrist, the door opened.

White light spilled out, the song of life and death like a symphony.

"Oh," Nelson said, voice hushed in reverence. "I never . . . I never thought . . . All this light. All these colors. I think . . . yes. Yes, I hear you. I see you, oh my god, I *see* you." He laughed wildly as his feet left the floor, Apollo looking comically surprised as his did the same. "Hugo!" Nelson cried. "Hugo, it's real. All of it is real. It's life. It's *life*."

Blinking against the blinding light, Wallace saw the outline of Nelson and Apollo as they rose through the air. Apollo looked around, tongue hanging out. It almost looked as if he were grinning.

And then they both crossed through the doorway.

Before the door closed, Wallace heard Nelson's voice one last time as Apollo barked happily.

He said, *"I'm home."*

The door slammed shut.

The light faded.

Nelson and Apollo were gone.

Silence settled like a blanket over the fourth floor of the tea shop.

"What do you think he saw?" Mei finally asked as she wiped her eyes.

Hugo stared up at the door. Though his face was wet, he smiled. "I don't know. And isn't that the point? We don't know until it's our time. Can you give me a moment? I want . . . I'll be down shortly."

Wallace touched the back of his hand before following Mei down the stairs. He thought he heard Hugo speaking quietly, almost like a prayer.

ᘓ

That night, Wallace found Hugo on the back deck. Mei was in the kitchen, her terrible music blaring loudly, causing the bones of the house to shake. He shook his head as he closed the back door behind him.

Hugo glanced back at him. "Hello."

"Hello, Hugo," Wallace said. "You all right?" He winced as he joined Hugo at the railing. "Stupid question."

"No," Hugo said as he lay his head on Wallace's shoulder. "I don't think it is. And honestly? I don't know if I'm all right. It's strange. Did you hear his voice at the end?"

"I did," Wallace said.

"He sounded . . ."

"Free."

Wallace felt Hugo nod against him. He wrapped an arm around Hugo's waist. "I can't even begin to imagine the relief he must have felt. I . . ." He hesitated. Then, "Are you angry with him?"

"No," Hugo said. "How could I be? He's watched over me for long enough, and helped to teach me how to be a good person. And besides, he knew I was in good hands."

"Are you?"

Hugo laughed. "I think so. You are pretty good with your—"

Wallace groaned. "I'm trying to have a moment here."

Hugo turned his head so he could kiss the underside of Wallace's jaw with a loud smack. Wallace grinned against his hair. "I am," Hugo whispered. "In good hands. The best, really. And he's right: this isn't goodbye. We'll see each other again. All of us. But before then, we still have work to do. And we'll do it together."

"We will," Wallace agreed. "I think—"

The back door opened.

Light spilled out.

They turned.

Mei stood in the doorway. "Stop being all gross and lovey and blech. A new file appeared."

Hugo stepped away from the railing. "Tell me."

Mei began to recite the contents of the file from memory. Hugo didn't interject, listening as Mei rattled off facts about their new guest.

Wallace glanced back at the tea plants.

Their leaves fluttered in the warm breeze. They were strong, firmly rooted in the soil. Hugo had seen to that.

"Wallace," Hugo called from the doorway. "You coming?"

"Yeah," Wallace said, turning away from the garden. "Let's do this. Who's our new guest going to be?"

When he reached the door, Wallace took Hugo's outstretched hand without hesitation. The door closed behind them. A moment later, the light on the back deck switched off, the tea garden bathed only in moonlight.

If they'd looked back one last time, they would've seen movement in the forest. At the tree line, there, in the dark, a great stag lowered its head toward the earth in veneration, flowers dangling from its antlers. Before long, it moved back amongst the trees, petals trailing in its wake.

ACKNOWLEDGMENTS

Under the Whispering Door is a deeply personal story to me; therefore, it was very hard to write. It took a lot out of me to finish, as it forced me to explore my own grief over losing someone I loved very much, more than I ever had before—outside of therapy, at least. There is a catharsis to grief, though we don't usually see that in the midst of it. I won't say writing this book helped heal me, because that would be a lie. Instead, I'll say that it left me feeling a bit more hopeful than I had before, bittersweetly so. If you live long enough to learn to love someone, you'll know grief at one point or another. That's just how the world works.

Some amazing people helped bring this book to you, so I'd like to thank them now.

First is Deidre Knight, my agent, who fiercely champions my books and believes in them, perhaps more than anyone else. She is the best agent an author could ask for. Thanks to Deidre and the team at The Knight Agency, including Elaine Spencer, who handles all the foreign rights to my books. She's the reason *The House in the Cerulean Sea* and *Under the Whispering Door* are being translated into so many different languages.

Ali Fisher, my editor, gave me the absolute best writing advice I've ever gotten. While we were in the middle of edits for this book, she told me one word that changed how I looked at Wallace's story: *decentralize*. That won't mean much to you, but believe me when I say that it was like the sun bursting through the clouds for the first time in weeks, and it allowed me to put the focus where it should've been in the first place. This story is as good as it is because of her. Thanks, Ali.

Also on the editing side is assistant editor Kristin Temple. Kristin had key input on the character of the Manager (as I tend to try to break my own in-world rules), and that strange boy who is not really a boy is who he is because of her. Thanks, Kristin.

Next, the sensitivity readers. Not to diminish the work anyone else did on this book, but the sensitivity readers were, perhaps, some of the most important. Of the five central characters—Wallace, Hugo, Nelson, Mei, and Apollo—three are characters of color. The sensitivity readers sifted through various iterations with a fine-toothed comb and provided extremely beneficial notes. I'd like to thank the sensitivity readers at Tessera Editorial, as well as moukies, who made the character of Hugo that much better.

Saraciea Fennell and Anneliese Merz are my publicists and cheerleaders, and all around some of the best people an author could ask for on their team. I don't know how they do what they do, but we're all the better for them and the tireless work they do.

The higher up are Tor Publisher Devi Pillai, President of TDA Fritz Foy, VP and Director of Marketing Eileen Lawrence, Executive of Publicity Sarah Reidy, VP of Marketing and Publicity Lucille Rettino, and Chairman/Founder of TDA Tom Doherty. They believe in the power of queer storytelling, and I'm grateful they are letting me make the fantasy genre that much gayer.

Becky Yeager is the marketing lead, meaning it's her job to get the word out about my books. One of the big reasons they've been read as widely as they have is her work. Thanks, Becky.

Rachel Taylor, the digital marketing coordinator, runs the Tor social-media accounts and makes sure everyone sees my dumb tweets about my books. Thanks, Rachel.

On the production side of things, you have production editor Melanie Sanders, production manager Steven Bucsok, interior designer Heather Saunders, and jacket designer Katie Klimowicz. They make everything look as good as it does. In addition, I'd like to thank Michelle Foytek, senior manager of publishing operations, who coordinates with production to get all the exclusive materials into the right editions.

And the jacket, man. The *jacket*. Go stare at it for just a moment. See how freaking rad that is? That's because of Red Nose Studios.

Chris has the uncanny ability to somehow dig around in my brain and make my imagination come to life in the form of the amazing jacket art he's made for me. I am in constant awe of the work he does. Thanks, Chris.

I'd also like to thank the Macmillan sales team for all their support and hard work in getting this book—and all my others—out to bookstores everywhere. They are the best cheerleaders an author could ask for.

Thanks to Lynn and Mia, my beta readers. They get to read the stories before anyone else, and so far, they haven't run screaming yet, so I count that as a win.

Thank you to Barnes & Noble for selecting *Under the Whispering Door* as an exclusive edition (if you haven't seen the little something extra in the B&N edition, you should definitely check that out). Also, to the indie booksellers and librarians all over the world who've championed my books to readers, thank you. I am forever in your debt and will do whatever you ask of me, even if that means helping you hide a body.

Last, to you, the reader. Because of you, I get to do this whole writing thing as my job. Thank you for letting me do what I love most. I can't wait for you to see what comes next.

TJ Klune
April 11, 2021

ABOUT THE AUTHOR

Natasha Michaels

TJ KLUNE is the *New York Times* and *USA Today* bestselling, Lambda Literary Award–winning author of *The House in the Cerulean Sea*, *The Extraordinaries*, and more. Being queer himself, Klune believes it's important—now more than ever—to have accurate, positive queer representation in stories.

Visit Klune online:
tjklunebooks.com
Twitter: @tjklune
Instagram: tjklunebooks

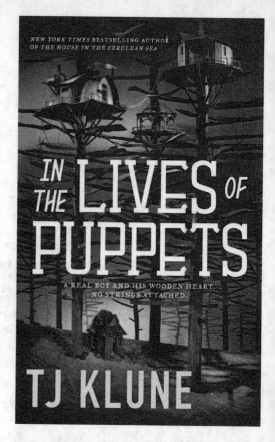

Beloved and bestselling author TJ Klune invites you deep into the heart of a peculiar forest and on the extraordinary journey of a family assembled from spare parts.

A NEW YORK TIMES BESTSELLER

IN THE
LIVES
OF
PUPPETS

TJ KLUNE

TOR

TOR PUBLISHING GROUP

NEW YORK

IN THE LIVES OF PUPPETS

Copyright © 2023 by Travis Klune

"Reduce! Reuse! Recycle!" © 2024 by Travis Klune

All rights reserved.

A Tor Book
Published by Tom Doherty Associates / Tor Publishing Group
120 Broadway
New York, NY 10271

www.tor-forge.com

Tor® is a registered trademark of Macmillan Publishing Group, LLC.

The Library of Congress has cataloged the hardcover edition as follows:

Names: Klune, TJ, author.
Title: In the lives of puppets / TJ Klune.
Description: First edition. | New York : Tor Publishing Group, 2023.
Identifiers: LCCN 2022054104 (print) | LCCN 2022054105 (ebook)
ISBN 9781250217448 (hardcover) | ISBN 9781250889522 (signed)
ISBN 9781250894458 (international, sold outside the U.S., subject to
rights availability) | ISBN 9781250217424 (ebook)
Subjects: LCGFT: Fantasy fiction. | Novels.
Classification: LCC PS3611.L86 I5 2023 (print)
LCC PS3611.L86 (ebook) | DDC 813/.6—dc23/eng/20221107
LC record available at https://lccn.loc.gov/2022054104
LC ebook record available at https://lccn.loc.gov/2022054105

ISBN 978-1-250-21743-1 (trade paperback)

Our books may be purchased in bulk for promotional,
educational, or business use. Please contact your local bookseller
or the Macmillan Corporate and Premium Sales Department
at 1-800-221-7945, extension 5442, or by email at
MacmillanSpecialMarkets@macmillan.com.

First Tor Paperback Edition: 2024

Printed in the United States of America

0 9 8 7 6 5 4 3 2

FOR HUMANITY:
You kinda suck, but you invented books and music,
so the universe will probably keep you around
for a little bit longer.
You got lucky.
This time.

In an old and lonely forest, far away from almost everything, sat a curious dwelling.

At the base of a grove of massive trees was a small, square building made of brick, overtaken by ivy and moss. Who it belonged to was anyone's guess, but from the looks of it, it had been abandoned long ago. It wasn't until a man named Giovanni Lawson (who wasn't actually a man at all) came across it while making his way through the forest that it was remembered with any purpose.

He stood in front of his strange find, listening as the birds sang in the branches high above. "What's this?" he asked. "Where did you come from?"

He went inside, passing carefully through the door hanging off its hinges. The windows were shattered. Grass and weeds grew up through the warped wooden floor. The roof had partially collapsed, and the sun shone through on a pile of leaves that almost reached the ceiling. At the top of the leaf pile, a golden flower had bloomed, stretching toward the sunlight streaming through the exposed rafters.

"It's perfect," he said aloud, although he was very much alone. "Yes, this will do just fine. How strange. How wonderful."

Giovanni returned bright and early the next morning, his sleeves pushed up his forearms. He knocked down the walls inside the solitary building to create one large room, carrying plaster and wood out piece by piece and piling them on the forest floor. By the time he finished, his face and hair were coated with dust and his joints creaked and groaned, but he was satisfied. There was merit to hard work.

2 | TJ KLUNE

"There," he said to the birds in the trees as he wiped his face. "Much better. A first step to a new beginning."

The little building soon became a home for all manner of things: sheets of metal and lengths of wires and cords, batteries of all shapes and sizes, circuit boards and microchips in glass mason jars. Other jars held hundreds of seeds of various shapes, sizes, and colors. There were old music boxes that sang little songs that ached, and silent record players without any records. Televisions, both great and small, their screens dark. And books! So many books on a variety of topics from plant life to whaling, from animals of the forest to complex diagrams of nuclear cores. They lined the new floor-to-ceiling shelving he'd made from the remains of what he'd torn down. It wasn't until he placed the last book on the last shelf that he realized he himself had nowhere to stay. The room was too full.

It wouldn't take much to expand the building, adding a room or two. But Giovanni Lawson wasn't one to take the easy route. He saw the world in complex shapes and designs, and when he looked up at the trees around him, he knew what he would do.

He wouldn't build outward.

He'd build *upward*.

It took time, as these things do. Many years passed. It needed to be perfect. There was safety among the trees and away from the harsh, blinding lights and cacophony of the city he'd left behind.

Up in the branches of the trees above the house, he constructed a new little building around the solid trunk of the tallest fir tree, the undisputed king of the forest. From there, he built several more rooms into the trees, all connected by rope bridges—a laboratory and a sunroom, the ceiling made of foggy and scratched glass, the floor of shining oak panels, and no walls. Later this sunroom would become something different.

The forest was vast and wild. He doubted they'd ever be able to find him there.

On sunny days, a herd of deer would graze on the grass

below him, and the birds would sing above him. He hummed along with their song. Giovanni was at peace.

At peace until the day his chest began to hurt.

"Oh my," he said. "What an interesting sensation. It burns."

In his lab he ran calculations. He typed on his keyboard, the *clack, clack, clack* echoing flatly around him.

"I see," he said on the fifty-second day after he'd first felt the ache in his chest. He stared at the screen, checking his numbers. It was loneliness, pure and simple. Numbers never lied.

Three more years went by. Three years of the ache in his chest only growing stronger. Three years of quiet, of longing to hear a voice aside from his own. He would look out the window of his laboratory to see that it was snowing, when just yesterday the forest had been caught in the throes of summer.

On a day that began no differently than all the ones that had come before, two people burst from the trees, their eyes wide in fright, their skin slick with sweat. A man and a woman. The woman clutched a bundle of rags against her chest.

Giovanni startled.

"Help us!" the woman cried. "Please, you must take him. Take him and hide him away. It's not safe."

And then she held out the bundle of rags.

Except it wasn't just rags.

Swaddled tightly inside was a child.

A boy who blinked slowly up at Giovanni before he scrunched up his face and cried.

"What has happened?" Giovanni asked, looking back up at the woman in alarm. "Come, come. I will keep you safe. All of you."

But the woman shook her head. "They will find us." Tears trickled down her cheeks as she stepped forward, kissing the baby on the forehead. "I love you. I'll return when I'm able."

The man said, "Hurry. They're coming."

The woman laughed bitterly. "I know. I know. They always do, in the end."

The man grabbed her by the hand and pulled her away, away, away.

"Wait!" Giovanni called after them. "His name!"

But they were gone.

He never saw anyone else. No one ever came looking for the man and the woman. Or the child. And he never saw the man and woman again.

Later, much later when the boy was grown, Giovanni would tell the boy that the woman—his mother—hadn't wanted to leave him. "She will come back," Giovanni would tell him. "One day, when all is well, she will return."

Until then, he had desired a child, and now here one was. Oh, how fortuitous! How wonderful!

Giovanni took his time in deciding a designation for the baby. It was when the leaves were changing from green to red and gold that he found the perfect one.

"Victor," he told his son. "Your name shall be Victor. Victor Lawson. What do you think?"

The loneliness he'd felt—massive and profound—was chased away as if it'd never existed at all.

Giovanni worried when Victor grew and grew and grew, but still didn't speak. He knew Victor listened to him when *he* spoke, could see the way the boy understood.

"Is there a fault in your coding?" Giovanni asked him when the boy was four years old. "Did I make a mistake?"

Victor didn't respond. Instead, he lifted his arms, opening and closing his hands, his little fingers tapping against his palms.

Giovanni did as he was asked. He lifted Victor, hugging him gently against his chest. Victor made a small noise that Giovanni took as happiness, his small face pressed against the man's chest. "No," Giovanni said. "You are as you're supposed to be. I shouldn't have questioned that. If there was ever perfection in this world, it would be you." His chest ached once more, but it was for entirely different reasons. Giovanni didn't need to calculate what he felt now. He knew what it was.

It was love.

And although Giovanni wished more than anything that Victor would speak to him, he let it go. If it was meant to be, it would happen.

It was another two years before Victor spoke for the first time.

They were in the laboratory. Victor was sitting on the floor. Laid out around him were small metal rods. It took Giovanni a moment to recognize the shape Victor had made them into. Two stick figures, one big, one small, their hands joined together. Grunting once, he reached out to fiddle with the legs of the stick figures.

And then the boy—Victor Lawson, son of Giovanni Lawson—said, "You." He pointed toward the bigger stick figure. "Me." The smaller stick figure. His voice was quiet, rough from lack of use. But it was there all the same.

"Yes," Giovanni said quietly. "You and me. Always."

PART I

THE FOREST

A conscience is that still small voice that people won't listen to.

—*Pinocchio* (1940 film)

CHAPTER 1

A tiny vacuum robot screamed as it spun in concentric circles, spindly arms that ended in pincers waving wildly in the air. "Oh my god, oh my god, we're going to *die*. I will cease to *exist,* and there will be nothing but darkness!"

A much larger robot stood still next to the vacuum, watching it have a meltdown for the millionth time. This other robot did not have arms, legs, or feet. Instead, the former Medical Nurse Model Six-Ten-JQN Series Alpha was a long metal rectangle, five feet tall and two feet wide, and her old and worn tires had been replaced by toothed metal treads, not unlike a tank's. Two metal hatches on either side of her base opened to reveal a dozen metal tentacles ending in various medical tools should the need to operate arise. A monitor on the front flashed a green frowning face. Nurse Registered Automaton To Care, Heal, Educate, and Drill (Nurse Ratched for short) was not impressed with the vacuum. In a flat, mechanical voice, she said, "If you were to die, I would play with your corpse. There is much I would be able to learn. I would drill you until there was nothing left."

This—as Nurse Ratched had undoubtedly planned—set the vacuum off once more. "Oh no," it whimpered. "Oh no, no, no, this will not do. Victor! *Victor.* Come back before I die and Nurse Ratched plays with my corpse! She's going to drill me! You *know* how I feel about being drilled."

Above them in the Scrap Yards, halfway up a pile of discarded metal at least twenty feet high, came the quiet sound of laughter. "I won't let her do that, Rambo," Victor Lawson said. He glanced down at them, hanging on to the pile of scrap via a pulley system he'd constructed with a harness around his waist. It wasn't safe by any stretch of the imagination, but Vic had been doing this for years and hadn't fallen yet. Well, once, but the less said about that the better. The shriek he'd let out at the bone protruding wetly from his arm had been louder than any sound he'd made before. His father wasn't happy about it, telling him that a twelve-year-old had no reason to be in the Scrap Yards. Victor had promised not to return. He'd gone back the next week. And now, at the age of twenty-one, he knew the Scrap Yards like the back of his hand.

Rambo didn't seem to believe him. He squealed, pincers opening and closing, his circular body shaking as his all-terrain tires rolled over pieces of metal that had fallen from the scrap heap. Across the top, in faded markings that had never been clear, were the letter *R* and a circle that could have been an *O* or a lowercase *a,* followed by what was clearly an *M* (possibly) and a *B* before ending in another *O* or *a*. He'd found the little thing years before, repairing it himself with metal and care until the machine had come back to life, demanding to be allowed to clean—it *needed* to clean because if it didn't, it had no purpose, it had *nothing*. It'd taken Vic a long time to calm the machine down, fiddling with its circuits until the vacuum had sighed in relief. It was a short-term fix. Rambo worried about most things, such as the dirt on the floor, the dirt on Vic's hands, and death in all manner of ways.

Nurse Ratched, Vic's first robot, had asked if she could kill the vacuum.

Vic said she could not.

Nurse Ratched asked why.

Vic said it was because they didn't kill their new friends.

"I would," Nurse Ratched had said in that flat voice of hers. "I would kill him quite easily. Euthanasia does not have to be painful. But it can, if you want it to be." She rode on her continuous track toward the vacuum, drill extended.

Rambo screamed.

Five years later, not much had changed. Rambo was still anxious. Nurse Ratched still threatened to play with his corpse. Vic was used to it by now.

Vic squinted up at the top of the metal heap, his shoulder-length dark hair pulled back and tied off with a leather strap. He tested the weight of the rope. He wasn't heavy, but he had to be careful, his father's voice a constant in his head, even if he worried too much. After all, Victor was rail thin, Dad constantly after him to eat more, *You're too skinny, Victor, put more food in your mouth and chew, chew, chew.*

The magnetic camming device seemed to be holding against the top of the heap. He brushed his forehead with the back of his gloved hand to keep the sweat from his eyes. Summer was on its way out, but it still held on with dying bursts of wet heat.

"All right," he muttered to himself. "Just a little higher. No time like the present. You need the part." He looked down to test his foothold.

"If you fall and die, I will perform the autopsy," Nurse Ratched called up to him. "The final autopsy report should be available within three to five business days, depending upon whether you are dismembered or not. But, as a courtesy, I can tell you that your death will most likely be caused by impact trauma."

"Oh no," Rambo moaned, his sensors flashing red. "Vic. *Vic.* Don't get dismembered. You know I can't clean up blood very well. It gets in my gears and mucks everything up!"

"Engaging Empathy Protocol," Nurse Ratched said, the monitor switching to a smiley face, eyes and mouth black, the rest of the screen yellow. The hatch on her lower right side slid up, and one of her tentacle-like arms extended, patting the top of Rambo's casing. "There, there. It is all right. I will clean up the blood and whatever other fluids come from his weak and fragile body. He will most likely void his bowels too."

"He will?" Rambo whispered.

"Yes. The human sphincter is a muscle, and upon death,

it relaxes, allowing waste to vacate the body in a spectacular fashion, especially if there is impact trauma."

Vic shook his head. They were his best friends in all the world. He didn't know what that said about him. Probably nothing good. But they were like him, in a way, even though he was flesh and blood and the others were wires and metal. Regardless of what they were made of, all had their wires crossed, or so Vic chose to believe.

He looked up again. Near the top of the scrap heap he could see what appeared to be a multi-layer PCB in good condition. Circuit boards were a rare find these days, and though he'd wanted to pull it out when he first saw it a few weeks before, he hadn't dared. This particular scrap heap was one of the most hazardous and was already swaying as he climbed. He'd take his time, working out scrap around the circuit board, letting it fall to the ground. Such effort required patience. The alternative was death.

"Vic!" Rambo cried. "Don't go. I love you. You're going to make me an orphan!"

"I'm not going to die." He took a deep breath before climbing slowly up the rope, squeezing and locking the carabiner at each stage. The thin muscles in his arms burned with the exertion.

The higher he got, the more the heap shifted. Bits of metal glinted in the sun as they fell around him, landing with a crash on the ground below. Rambo was deliriously distracted from his panic now that he had something to clean. Vic glanced down to see him picking up the fallen pieces of scrap and moving them to the base of the pile. He beeped happily, a noise that almost sounded like he was humming.

"Your existence is pointless," Nurse Ratched told him.

"I have no idea what you're talking about," Rambo said cheerfully as his sensors blinked blue and green. He dropped another piece of metal at the bottom before celebrating and spinning around.

It was near the top of the metal heap that Vic paused to rest, turning his head to look beyond the Scrap Yards. The woodlands stretched as far as he could see. It took him a moment to find the trees that held their home, the main fir rising above all others.

He leaned back as far as he dared to peer around the side of the heap. In the distance, smoke rose from a stack atop a great, lumbering machine. The machine was at least forty feet high, the crane on its back moving deftly between the piles of metal and debris as it lifted even more scrap from its hopper and dropped it in a never-ending cycle. Vic marked the location in his head, wondering if there was anything new being brought in worth salvaging.

The other Old Ones were farther away.

He was safe.

He looked back up at the circuit board. "I'm coming for you," he told it.

It took him ten more minutes to come within reach of the circuit board. Stopping to make sure his footing was solid, he gave himself a moment to clear his head. He didn't look down; heights didn't bother him, not really, but it was easier to focus on the task at hand. Less vertigo that way.

Leaning back against the harness, he shook out his arms and hands. "Okay," he muttered. "I got this." Reaching up toward the circuit board, he gritted his teeth as he gripped the edge gingerly. He tugged on it, hoping that something had happened since he'd last been here, and it'd wiggle loose with ease.

It didn't.

He dug around it, pulling out a chunk of metal that looked like it'd once belonged to a toaster. He looked inside to see if anything was salvageable. The interior looked rusted beyond repair. No good. He shouted a warning before dropping it. It crashed below him.

"You missed Rambo," Nurse Ratched said. "Try harder next time."

Vic startled when the circuit board shifted the next time he gripped it, his eyes widening. He pulled. It gave a little. He pulled harder, careful not to squeeze too tightly to avoid damaging the board. It looked intact. Dad was going to be happy. Well, he'd be pissed if he found out how Vic had gotten it, but what he didn't know wouldn't hurt him.

Vic worked the circuit board like a loose tooth, back and forth, back and forth. He was about to let it go and try to dig around it more when it popped free.

"Yes," he said. "*Yes.*" He waved it down at the others. "I got it!"

"The joy I feel knows no bounds," Nurse Ratched said. "Huzzah." Her screen changed to confetti falling around the words CONGRATULATIONS IT'S A GIRL.

"Vic?" Rambo said, sounding nervous.

"I can't believe it," Vic said. "It's been weeks."

"Vic," Rambo said again, voice rising.

"It doesn't look damaged," Vic said, turning it over in his hands. "It's going to—"

"*Vic!*"

He looked down, annoyed, though trying to tamp it down. "What?"

"Run!" Rambo cried.

A horn blasted, deep and angry. It echoed around the Scrap Yards, the sound causing the metal heap to vibrate and shift.

Vic knew that sound.

He leaned over as far as he could.

An Old One rolled toward them, sirens blaring, the crane swinging back and forth. It crashed into other piles of scrap, metal scraping against metal, showers of sparks raining down. It did not slow. It did not stop. "INTRUDER," it bellowed. "INTRUDER. INTRUDER. INTRUDER."

Vic felt the blood drain from his face as he whispered, "Oh no."

He shoved the circuit board into his satchel even as he

squeezed the carabiner with his other hand. He dropped five feet in a second, jerking painfully when the carabiner hit a thick knot in the middle of the rope. He struggled against it, but it wouldn't move any further.

"I suggest you get down," Nurse Ratched said as she scooped up Rambo, rocks kicking up under her treads as she rolled away, dodging detritus raining down around them. Rambo squealed, sensors flashing red in his panic.

"I'm *working* on it!" Vic shouted after them, still trying to get the carabiner past the knot.

No use. It wouldn't give.

The Old One's horn blasted again. Vic grunted when something heavy bounced off his shoulder, sending him spinning away. His breath was knocked from his chest when he swung back into the trash heap with a jarring crash, the sound of metal crunching under the Old One's massive tires getting closer and closer.

Managing to regain his footing, Vic looked up quickly, already mourning the loss of the camming devices. They were difficult to make, but he couldn't do anything about that now.

The Old One appeared around the side of the heap, lights flashing. Its crane swung toward the heap. Metal shrieked as the bucket slammed above him, causing the heap to shudder. The ropes snapped against his harness, pulling him up and then dropping him back down as the tower began to lean to the right. In front of him, a large metal sheet that read VOTED BEST FOOD TRUCK shifted.

Without thinking, he reached for it.

The crane swung back around, gaining momentum.

The moment before impact, Vic pulled the metal sheet out with a harsh grunt. The bucket hit with a jarring crash, debris raining down around him as the pile tilted precariously to the left. Vic fell, the slack rope twisting around him. He spun in midair, sliding the metal underneath him, lying flat against it. Hot sparks flew up toward him, causing him to bury his face in his forearms. He thought he screamed, but couldn't hear himself above the angry roar of the Old One and the collapsing tower.

He was six feet above the ground when the sheet hit an exposed length of rebar, sending him flying. He hit the ground roughly, tucking his arms and legs in as he rolled. He had a brief moment to be thankful for Rambo's neurotic tendency to clear the ground of debris. If he hadn't, Vic might have been skewered on something he'd thrown down.

He landed on his back, blinking up at the sky. He had to move. Without hesitating, he pushed himself to his feet in time to see the heap collapse completely. Vic ran, chest heaving as the Old One blared furiously behind him.

Knowing the Old Ones couldn't—or wouldn't—leave the perimeters of the Scrap Yards, Nurse Ratched and Rambo waited for him at the edge, Rambo sitting on top of her, little arms waving frantically. Nurse Ratched's screen had turned into a line of exclamation points.

"See?" Vic told them as they left the Old One behind. "Nothing to it."

"Yes," Nurse Ratched said. "Absolutely nothing to it. I would be impressed except I do not find idiocy impressive. If I did, I would flirt with you."

He'd learned of flirting from Dad's films. People smiling and blushing when they saw each other, doing things they might not normally do, all in the name of love. He'd never had anyone to flirt with before. It sounded extraordinarily complicated. "I didn't know you could do that."

"I can do many things," Nurse Ratched said, the exclamation points disappearing, being replaced by a face with a funny smile, wide eyes surrounded by long eyelashes. "Hey, big boy. You should put your finger in my socket." The screen went black. "That was flirting. There is a difference."

Vic grimaced as Rambo wheeled around him, arms waving. "They don't do that in the films."

"At least not in the ones you have seen. Did it work? Are you aroused?" The tiny lens above her screen blinked to life, a blue light scanning him up and down. "You don't appear to be aroused. Your penis shows no signs of elevated blood flow that supports recreational sexual engagement."

"I don't have a penis," Rambo said mournfully. Somewhere inside him, gears shifted and a little slot opened up at his base. He grunted, and a little pipe extended, dripping what looked like oil. "Now I do. Hooray for penises!"

"Would you put that away?" Vic asked. "We need to get home." He looked up at the bruised sky. The sun was beginning to set. "It's going to be dark soon."

"And you're scared of the dark," Rambo said, pipe sliding back in, slot closing.

"I'm not scared of the—"

"Fear is superfluous," Nurse Ratched said, falling in behind Vic as he led the way through the forest. "I am not scared of anything." She paused. "Except for birds that want to nest inside me and lay their eggs in my gears. Evil birds. I will kill them all."

Vic pulled the circuit board from his satchel. It was still whole. Tracing his finger over its bumps and ridges, he whispered, "Worth it."

CHAPTER 2

By the time they reached home, the sky was bleeding violet, and the first stars were out. The sun settled near the horizon, the moon rising like a pale ghost. Rambo rolled ahead along the worn path, already calling out for Vic's father. Vic should've expected this, seeing as how Rambo always wanted to share the moments where they'd almost been horribly murdered, and how lucky they were to escape with their lives.

"No," Vic said after him, cursing inwardly that he'd allowed himself to be distracted. "Don't tell him about—"

But Rambo ignored him, announcing quite loudly that he hadn't been *scared,* but even if he was, that was all right. The lights were on in the ground house, meaning Dad was still tinkering down there with his record player. Rambo rolled through the open doorway and disappeared inside.

Vic looked toward the elevator near the biggest tree. He thought about escaping to his personal lab above but knew his father wouldn't be happy if he didn't at least try to explain himself.

"No," Nurse Ratched said, rolling against him, pushing him toward the ground house. "You need to tell him the truth. I want to watch as you get scolded. It brings me something akin to joy to see you stare at the floor and give him flimsy excuses."

"You're supposed to be on *my* side."

"I know," she said. "I am a traitor. I feel terrible about it. I cannot wait." She stopped. Her screen flashed a question mark. "Do you hear that?"

He glanced back at her. "Hear what?"

"I do not know. It sounds complex. It is coming from the

ground house. I need to diagnose it." She rode by him, flattening the grass on the forest floor, leaves crunching. He watched as she disappeared through the doorway.

He followed, cocking his head. He strained to hear what she had. At first, there was nothing. And then—

His eyes widened. "No way."

He jogged toward the ground house.

Electric lights burned inside, reflecting off glass jars filled with unused parts and unplanted seeds. The floor creaked under Vic's weight with every step he took. He wound his way through the shelves and piles of books and electronics. A washing machine, though it was broken beyond repair. What his father called an icebox, though it never made any ice. Dad never liked to throw anything away, saying there was a use for everything even if it wasn't readily apparent. Vic was the same way, which is why it frustrated him that his father didn't like when they went hunting in the Scrap Yards. The ground house was *filled* with objects his father had salvaged, even if he hadn't been back in quite a while. How was it any different when Vic did the same?

But he ignored it, all of it, because of the sounds that rolled over him, warm and sweet.

Music.

It was music.

But it wasn't like the music boxes against the far walls. Those were monophonic, and though enchanting, they did not compare.

A voice unlike anything he'd ever experienced before, soft, sweet. Higher-pitched, and it took Vic a moment to realize why. A woman. Above the gentle *plink* of piano keys, a woman sang about the doggoned moon above, making her need someone to love. Entranced, he followed the voice.

Vic found Giovanni Lawson sitting in an old recliner, Rambo in his lap. His eyes were closed as he petted the vacuum. Rambo grumbled happily, sensors flashing slowly. Nurse Ratched sat next to them. On her screen, a line bounced in a circadian rhythm, keeping time with the beat from the song.

On top of the wooden work bench a record player lay open, a record spinning and skipping, the voice slightly warbled but still clear.

"It works," Vic whispered in awe. "You fixed it."

Dad didn't open his eyes. He hummed under his breath before saying, "I did. This is Beryl Davis singing. Such a lovely voice, don't you think?"

Vic approached the work bench. He could hear the sound of a record turning against the needle. He bent over, examining the machine. It looked as it always had. He couldn't see anything new. He itched to take it apart to see how its innards moved to create the sound he was hearing. "How did you fix it?"

"A little love," Dad said. "A little time."

"Dad."

He chuckled. "The hand crank. Wasn't connected properly."

Vic blinked in surprise as he stood upright. "That's it?"

"That's it. Simple, isn't it? We were thinking too big, too grand. Sometimes, it's the smallest things that can change everything when you least expect it."

Vic turned around to see his father watching him. The skin of his face was wrinkled and soft, his bright eyes kind. His hair hung in white waves around his ears, his beard extending down to his chest. When Vic was younger, he'd asked why he looked nothing like his father. Dad was a barrel of a man, his chest thick and strong, his stomach sloping outward, fingers blunt. Vic didn't have the presence his father had. As a boy, he'd been as thin as a whisper, sprouting up instead of out. He'd grown into himself as he'd gotten older, but he was still awkward, his movements clipped. His father's skin was pale. His own was tanned, as if he'd been born in the sun and never left. His father's eyes were blue, Vic's brown, and in certain light, they looked black. They weren't the same. They never had been.

But this man was his father. This man had raised him.

This man who wasn't a man at all.

Dad grimaced, turning away to rub at his chest.

Vic sighed, unreasonably irritated that Dad had tried to hide the gesture from him. Though an admonition threatened to burst from his mouth, he swallowed it back down. "I told you to let me take a look at it."

"It's fine."

"It is not fine," Nurse Ratched said. "Either you let Victor look at you, or I will drill you." To make her point, her drill whirred loudly. Across her screen, the words YOU WON'T FEEL A THING scrolled. "Perhaps we should proceed with the drilling regardless. It has been quite some time since I was able to drill anything."

Dad set Rambo on the ground as the song ended and gave way to another. Vic could feel it down to his bones, and he wondered how he'd gone so long without hearing such a thing. It'd only been minutes, but he could no longer imagine a life without music like this. Those records had been an extraordinary find. He'd have to see if there were more.

"I'm fine as I am," Rambo said nervously. "No one needs to drill or open me."

"Anxious little thing," Dad said fondly, nudging Rambo with his foot. "And we still don't know why?"

Vic went to the work bench again, looking at his father's tools that hung on a board. He selected the soldering iron, hoping against hope the fix wouldn't be more complicated. "No. Wiring, I guess? A glitch in his software? Something. I don't know."

"I'm fine the way I am," Rambo muttered.

"You are not," Nurse Ratched said. "If you like, I can run a diagnostic scan to see if I can pinpoint your malfunction. Do you have insurance?"

"No," Rambo said morosely. "I don't have *anything*."

"You *are* fine the way you are," Vic told him, shooting a

glare at Nurse Ratched which she ignored completely. "There's nothing wrong with you. You're just . . . unique. Like the rest of us."

"That is called a white lie," Nurse Ratched said, her screen filled with digital balloons. "White lies are often spoken to make one feel better. I will assist Victor in this process. Here is my white lie: you are a wonderful machine beloved by many."

"Leave him alone," Vic said as he knelt at his father's feet.

"Do you feel better?" Nurse Ratched asked.

"Yes," Rambo said promptly. "Tell me more white lies."

"You are important. You have a purpose. The pipe you displayed earlier is bigger than any I have seen before."

"Yay!" Rambo said, arms raised. "I'm endowed!"

Dad arched an eyebrow. "Do I want to know?"

Before Vic could respond, Nurse Ratched said, "Victor's penis was flaccid even after I engaged my Flirting Protocol. Since I know what I am doing, it is not me, but him."

"I regret ever fixing you both," Vic muttered, motioning for Dad to lift his shirt.

"That was a white lie," Nurse Ratched said. "Your pupils are dilated, your heart rate increased. You enjoy us. Thank you." A thumbs-up burst onto her screen, with the words YOU DID A GOOD JOB! underneath.

Dad lifted his shirt. His skin was tight and smooth, without a belly button or nipples. On the right side of his chest, near the collarbone, was a small sheet of metal, the surface rough. When he was younger, he'd told Vic, there'd been a string of letters and numbers there, symbolizing his first designation. He'd scraped it off, refusing to be defined by it after he'd been given a name. He was more than what it claimed he was. For a long time, Vic had been upset he didn't have a metal plate on his chest like his father.

Dad tapped his breastbone twice with his middle finger. From inside his chest came a beep, followed by a low hiss. The hatch of his chest cavity sank inward slightly before sliding off to the right.

There, in his father's chest, was a heart. It wasn't like the heart in Vic's chest, one made of muscle that moved blood and oxygen throughout his body.

The heart in Giovanni's chest was made of metal and wood and shaped not like the organ but like a symbol of a heart about the size of Vic's fist. The chest cavity around it glowed a dull green, made of wires and circuitry. The heart itself was of Dad's own making, replacing what had been a power core nearly drained beyond repair before he'd changed it out for the mechanical heart. The shell of the heart was partially constructed of a rare wood called bocote. Wood was typically nonconductive, but Dad had found a way to force enough electricity through it, though it required over fifteen thousand volts. To ensure conduction, in addition to the bocote, the heart had bits of silver-coated copper and brass in the shell, metal that glittered in the low light. Wires extended from the top of the shell, attaching to the parts in his chest that fed into the biochip in his head. In the exposed interior of the heart a handful of gears spun slowly. Above them, a small white strip, two centimeters wide and three centimeters tall.

Vic tapped the gears gently. His father jumped. "Sorry. Your hands are cold."

The gears looked fine for now. One—the teeth wearing down—would need to be replaced soon, but Vic had already found the necessary parts and stored them in one of the jars. He leaned closer, nudging the heart slightly so he could see underneath it. "There," he said, feeling extremely relieved. "One of the wires off the solenoid is coming loose. I can fix it."

"I can do it," Dad said.

Vic bit back a retort, opting for something softer. "Then you should have. I'll take care of it so I know it gets done. Nurse Ratched."

She stopped beside him, taking the plug for the soldering iron from him and inserting it into herself. She said, "Ooh. Yes. That is it."

"Gross," Rambo muttered. He nudged the side of Vic's leg. "Is he going to die?"

"No," Vic said, leaning forward, elbows resting on his dad's legs. "He's not going to die."

"Because we're going to be alive forever?"

"Impossible," Nurse Ratched said. "Nothing is immortal. Eventually, our power cell will drain and we will perish because we will be unable to find a replacement."

"But Vic will find one for us," Rambo said.

"Victor is human," Nurse Ratched said. "He will die long before us. He is soft and spongy. Perhaps it will be cancer, either rectal or bone. Or the plague if he gets bitten by a rat. Or he will get squashed by an Old One like he almost was today." Her screen blinked with the word OOPS.

"Ah," Dad said. "Is that what Rambo was shouting about before he heard the music?"

Vic sighed as he leaned forward, the tip of the soldering iron hot and red. "It was nothing."

"That was a white lie," Rambo said, sounding proud of himself.

Victor groaned as he pressed the soldering iron against the wire connecting the solenoid. Dad grunted, but otherwise stayed still. "It wasn't even close. I knew what I was doing."

"The expression on your face when the metal heap collapsed suggested otherwise," Nurse Ratched said. "Would you like to view the reenactment I created right this second?"

Vic pulled the soldering iron away from the solenoid as he looked back. On her screen, an eight-bit version of Vic appeared atop a tower of metal. A word bubble sprang from his mouth, filling with OH NO I AM STUPID AND ABOUT TO DIE. The little character fell to the ground with a bloody smack, his eyes turning to X's.

"Womp womp," Nurse Ratched said as the screen darkened. "That is exactly what happened. Please do not hold your applause. I need validation."

"You fell?" Dad asked, eyes narrowing.

Vic went back to the soldering. "Only a little bit."

An odd note filled his father's voice. "Did you get hurt? Cuts, scrapes? Did you bleed?"

"Why?" Vic asked. "You need more?" The heart—while a marvel of engineering unlike anything else that had been created—sometimes needed more than metal or wiring to function: a drop of blood, pressed against the white strip above the gears. It did not happen often—at most, once a year, but Nurse Ratched never failed to remind them that according to lore, a creature known as a vampire subsisted on the same thing. The last time had been four months before, when Dad had started acting more robotic, more like a machine.

Dad said, "Victor."

"Not even nicked," Vic assured him.

Dad nodded, obviously relieved. "Good. And the Old Ones?"

Vic shrugged. "You know how it is. They forget I even exist as soon as I leave the Scrap Yards. Out of sight, out of mind."

Dad sighed. "I wish you wouldn't go there. I told you—"

"Should have thought of that before you built this place so close to one. That's on you. Not me."

"Cheeky git," Dad said. "Anything worth finding?"

"Multi-layer PCB. Looks mostly intact too."

Dad whistled lowly. "That's rare." He grimaced again as the wire fused back with the solenoid. Vic was careful with the closeness to the heart. It was a fragile thing. He made sure the wire had cooled enough so it wouldn't burn the wood before setting it back gently where it belonged.

"See?" Vic said. "Nothing to it. You should have let me take care of that a long time ago."

"Noted," Dad said. He tapped against his breastbone once more, and the hatch slid closed. The seams filled. Vic rose to his feet as Dad dropped his shirt back down. "I need you to be careful, though. You can't take chances that put you in danger."

Vic sighed as he went back to the work bench. Beryl Davis was singing in a crackly voice about what a fool she used to be. "I can take care of myself." It was a conversation they'd had time and time again. He doubted it would be the last. He held onto the soldering iron, waiting for it to cool.

"You can," Dad agreed quietly. "But that doesn't mean you're not breakable. If the Old Ones got ahold of you—"

"They won't. I'm quicker than they are. Smarter too. They're machines."

"As am I."

Vic winced. He hadn't meant it like that. He sometimes spoke without thinking things through, though he was trying to get better at it. "You know what I mean. They're not—they have their programming. They're guided by it, and can't leave the Scrap Yards."

"They're still dangerous, Victor. And the sooner you realize that, the better off you'll be."

Vic ground his teeth together, calming himself by breathing in through his nose and out his mouth. "I know that. But if I hadn't gone to the Scrap Yards, I never would have found Nurse Ratched or Rambo. We wouldn't have half the stuff we have now. You would have run out of crap to tinker with a hell of a long time ago." He nodded toward the spinning record. "And we wouldn't be hearing this."

Dad didn't reply.

Vic slumped, struggling to find the words to get his point across without sounding petulant. "You know I'm right. I stay in the forest. I don't go beyond the boundaries, and I've never pushed. I know you have your reasons, and that it's not safe to cross the borders. I listen to you. I do. Which is why you should listen to me when I say I don't need—*want* more than what I have." He waited to see if Nurse Ratched would call him out for it. He wasn't lying, not exactly, more in a gray area, skirting the edges of truth though he didn't necessarily mean to.

She didn't say a word.

His father did. "At least not yet."

He turned around, his father looking as old as Vic had ever seen him. He felt like he was missing something. "What?"

Dad smiled tightly. "I don't expect you to want to stay here forever. It'd be selfish of me to think otherwise. You say you're happy. I believe you. But happiness isn't something that can be sustained continuously, not without something to keep the fire burning." In moments when Dad spoke like this, about what else was out there, Vic wondered about the people who had left him behind as an infant. What they had been like. Looked like. Did they laugh? Did they like music and tinkering for hours? Were they smart? Kind? What had made them trust Giovanni, a stranger in the middle of the woods, and who had been after them? Logic—the cold, brutal logic of a machine—dictated they were dead. They'd have returned by now if able to do so. They hadn't.

He knew the woods. He knew his friends, their home. Giovanni, his father, the man to whom he wanted to prove that needing and wanting were two different things. Though he sometimes pushed against the perceived boundaries Dad had placed around him, their existence brought him a level of comfort. The stories Dad had told him—stories of cities made of metal and glass, and the humans therein. He'd read every book Dad had brought to this place—more than once—old stories of kings and queens in castles, of adventures on the high seas in great ships with flags billowing in the salty air, of people going to the stars and getting lost in the vast expanse of the universe. They were ghosts, but he did not feel haunted by them. The world beyond the forest was an unknowable thing, and though curiosity tugged at him every now and then, Victor was stronger than it was. He had a home, a purpose, a lab all his own, and friends that loved him for who he was, not what he wasn't. Loneliness wasn't a concept he understood, not really, not like his father had when he'd first come to the forest. He, like Dad, was an inventor. If he needed someone—some*thing*—new to talk to, all he had to do was make it. He had the parts. He'd done it with Nurse Ratched, and then with Rambo. He could do it again, if need be. Some of the old books told stories of people yearning for more and setting off to find it and themselves. Vic always thought they were silly that way. He never wanted to go far from home.

He said, "You trust me."

"I do."

"Then trust me to know what's right for myself." He moved until he stood above his father. Vic reached down, squeezing Dad's shoulder.

Dad put his hand on top of Vic's. "You're a good boy. A bit foolish, perhaps, but a good boy nonetheless."

"Learned it from you," Vic said.

"I'm also good," Rambo said.

"Unbearably so," Nurse Ratched said. "Though you seem to be suffering from an intense anxiety disorder. But that is fine. We are all unique. Victor is asexual. Giovanni is old. And I have sociopathic tendencies that manifest themselves in dangerous situations."

"Hooray!" Rambo squealed. "We all have things!"

Giovanni smiled as he shook his head. "What a strange existence we find ourselves in. I wouldn't change it for anything in the world."

The robots stayed with Dad, listening as Beryl Davis sang about love and loss. Vic left them behind in the ground house, looking down at the circuit board as he walked toward the elevator. He flipped the board over. The bottom left corner had a hairline crack in it, but that was an easy fix.

He stepped onto the wooden lift. The gate closed behind him as he pressed a button on one of the struts. Sodium arc lights lit up above him as the elevator rose from the forest floor to a midpoint below the canopy. The gate swung open, and Vic stepped off.

The ground house was just the beginning.

His father, in his infinite wisdom, had built a tree house of sorts, though far grander and more complex than any Vic had ever read about; even more spectacular than ones in books like *The Swiss Family Robinson*. Six massive trees grew in a vague circle, and all were connected by wooden rope bridges. In the tree to Vic's left was his father's lab, the largest of the dwellings built around the king of the forest. The structure on the second tree was Dad's living quarters, stuffed to the gills with more scraps and tools and books. The highest building in the third tree was a makeshift kitchen, though Vic was the only one who used it. Once a sunroom, it now had a working electric stove and an old table set and chairs covered in carvings of birds and flowers and leaves. In one corner sat a large metal freezer that kept meat Vic had hunted from spoiling. Attached to the kitchen were facilities: a shower with rainwater that never got hot enough and a toilet that Nurse Ratched was far too interested in, especially when she inquired about the consistency of Vic's bowel movements. He'd tried to explain to her that some things were meant to be private. "So you say," she'd told him. "But then you will come to me leaking saltwater from your ducts after you have found blood in your stool, and where will you be then?"

He hadn't known how to answer that.

The fifth tree held Vic's own lab, smaller than his father's, though no less extraordinary. The final tree, to the right of the elevator, held Vic's room. One of his first memories had been his father building it while Vic watched, handing over whatever tools Dad had asked for. He remembered being excited the first night he got to stay there on his own, though he couldn't find the words to say as much. He'd planned on staying up as late as he could, especially since Dad wouldn't be able to tell him to go to sleep. He'd lasted five minutes before he made his way back to Dad's room, crawling into bed with him. Later, much later when he was older and perhaps a little wiser, he'd asked his father why he had a bed when he didn't sleep like Vic did. Dad had said it made him feel more human.

Vic shook his head as he crossed the bridge to his room, thoughts tumbling end over end, though there was an order to the chaos. Pushing open the door, he stepped inside, closing it behind him.

Going to the room's only window, he looked down at the ground house. Dad had built a section of skylights surrounded by solar panels for power. But the ground house was the only building with skylights, and below, he could see Dad in his chair, Nurse Ratched poking Rambo with one of her tentacles. He left them to it, stepping away from the window.

In the center of the room was a tree trunk with knobby protrusions that had once been branches. Beyond the tree trunk in the right corner, a wooden bedframe with a lumpy, worn mattress. On the walls hung retired tools that no longer functioned; Vic was unable to bring himself to throw them away. It was a trait Vic had learned from his father, the idea of junking something rankling them both. What was broken could someday be repaired if need be, and if they had the right parts.

He lifted his shirt above his head. He frowned when he saw the hem had a small tear in it. He'd have to have Nurse Ratched sew it up again. The fabric was thinning, but it wasn't quite yet ready for the rag pile. He folded it, setting it on the small dresser near the bed.

Flipping the circuit board once more, he sank to his knees before lying flat on his stomach, looking under the bed. There, in a dark and dusty corner, sat a metal box, a perfect cube. Pulling it out with a grunt, Vic sat back up, looking toward the window as he heard the sound of music still playing in the ground house below.

It wasn't that he didn't *want* them to know what he had hidden inside, at least not yet. He hadn't been ready to put it to use. But now that he had the circuit board, maybe it'd finally work.

He punched a code into the numeric keypad on top of the box, each press of the key causing a number to pop up on the display. The box beeped three times. The lock clicked. He opened the lid.

Inside, resting on an old cut of cloth he'd found among his father's collection, sat a mechanical heart.

It wasn't much like the one in Dad's chest. That heart had been constructed by a master craftsman in his prime. Perfectly designed, but even machines wore down after years of use. Dad's heart was old. It wouldn't last forever. One day, the strain would become too much, and the heart would fail.

This new heart—crude and sophomoric and indescribably human—was a contingency plan. Just in case. He'd started building it when he was fifteen years old. He'd had no idea what he was doing.

Vic had made mistakes in the construction. The wood he first used—oak—had cracked and split. It wasn't until he got his hands on some bubinga wood from the Scrap Yards that he'd found the perfect conductor. Inlaid in the wood was nickel-coated copper. Not as good as the silver-coated, but it'd do in a pinch, replaceable if need be.

The shape of the heart wasn't exact. The point at the bottom had chipped off, and Vic had been forced to sand it down. Still, the gears in the interior of the heart were without a single fleck of rust. He turned the largest gear in the middle, marveling at how it caused the five other, smaller gears to turn in tandem. The synchronicity of it was profound. The clack of the teeth sounded better than any music coming from a record player. The music of the gears was life.

He set the board carefully next to the heart before closing the lid. The display beeped once more as the box locked. He pushed it back under the bed to the far corner. Even Rambo wouldn't find it, given that he was scared of the dark. It would go unnoticed until it was time for Vic to present it to his father.

Soon.

He stood, knees popping. He scratched his bare stomach. He needed to eat before he slept. Shower too. As he walked across the rope bridge, he remembered the Old Ones dropping new scrap in the yard. Tomorrow, or the day after. He'd see if there was anything useful. *Who knows,* he told himself as the rope bridge swayed under his feet.

CHAPTER 3

But it was another week before Victor returned to the Scrap Yards. If he hadn't known better, Vic would've thought Dad was keeping him busy to stop him from going back. There was always something that needed to be repaired or tuned up. The solar panels needed checking. The waste containers needed emptying. Some of the pipes needed snaking. The garden behind the ground house needed to be weeded, the fruits and vegetables harvested before they began to rot.

He did it all without complaint. The moment one part of their existence broke down, it could lead to complete system failure. Dad had taught him that early on.

Summer was dying. The mornings had become chilly, and the leaves in the trees were turning gold and red even as their edges were covered in layers of frost. Days were shorter, the sun weaker. Vic thought the snows would come earlier this year.

"I hate snow," Rambo muttered as he sucked up a pile of weeds Vic had tossed toward him. "It gets in my insides and makes me cold."

"You cannot feel cold," Nurse Ratched said. "You are incapable of feeling anything at all." Her screen displayed a sad face, a digital tear streaking down. "That must devastate you."

"He can feel things," Vic said, trying to ward off what he was sure would be yet another meltdown. "I made him that way. Just like I did you."

Rambo chirped smugly as he gathered more weeds, sucking them in. "Ha. See? I knew it." He beeped. "Uh-oh. I'm full. I need to be emptied."

Nurse Ratched picked him up off the ground, pulling out his container filled to the brim with weeds. She dumped it into a burn barrel next to the garden before sliding Rambo's container back in place and setting him down. "He is just saying that to make you feel better. Though, if he is speaking the truth, it does beg the question."

"What question?" Rambo asked.

"Why he made you so neurotic."

"I am *not* neurotic!"

Nurse Ratched plucked a weed from the burn barrel and dropped it on the ground. Rambo frantically scooped it back up. "Neurotic," she said flatly. "I have an injection for that. Would you like me to administer it? The needle is quite large and is meant to go into places that will not be pleasant."

"No injections," Vic said without looking up.

Nurse Ratched made a rude sound, almost like she was scoffing. "It has been a long time since I have been allowed to administer injections. Victor, you are due for your own inoculations soon. Should we take care of that right now?"

"I'm fine."

"Will you be fine when you have scurvy? I have cevitamic acid ready."

"I'm not getting scurvy."

"Are your teeth loose?"

"No."

"Are your eyes bulging?"

He didn't think so. He blinked rapidly just to make sure. "No."

Nurse Ratched whirred and beeped. Then, "In addition to scurvy, you appear to have symptoms of delusions. Your eyes are always bulging. Prepare for inject—oh, look. A squirrel. It is rabid. Come here, squirrel. I will heal you. Engaging Empathy Protocol. There, there, squirrel. There is nothing to fear. It will only hurt for thirty-seven point six minutes. After, I will give you a treat for being such a good squirrel." She chased after it through the trees, the squirrel chittering in fright.

Vic glanced at Rambo when he didn't hear the vacuum moving. Rambo had his arms extended and bent awkwardly, his pincers before his sensors. "Are you okay?" He had learned how to read his friends over the years, but it still took an effort. Thankfully, they were usually patient with him.

"I can feel things, right?" Rambo asked, slowly opening and closing his pincers. They clicked.

"Yeah. Of course you can. Come here."

Rambo came, avoiding a pile of weeds he had yet to pick up. He stopped next to Vic, who reached down and rubbed along the top of his black casing, fingers tracing over the faded letters. "You feel that?"

"Yes," Rambo said promptly. "You're touching me with your hands."

"And how does that make you feel?"

The robot hesitated. "Itchy. And warm. Like I'm full of garbage again, but I was just emptied, so that can't be it."

"That's happiness," Vic said, though he wasn't quite sure.

"Whoa," Rambo said. "*That's* what that is?"

"I think so. You're happy when you're full, because you know you've done a good job. It's kind of the same thing."

Rambo raised his arm, pinching Vic's wrist gently. "Do you feel that?"

"I do."

"And what does it feel like?"

"Itchy. And warm."

"Like you're full of garbage," Rambo whispered in awe.

"No, that's—I didn't—" Vic shook his head. "Yeah, like I'm full of garbage."

"Why do we feel this way?" Rambo asked, pulling on Vic's skin.

"I don't know," Vic admitted. "We just do, I guess."

"Wow," Rambo said, letting go of Vic's wrist and extending his arm behind him. He picked up a few weeds and shoved them toward Vic's face. "Here. Put this in your mouth compactor. See if it makes you itchy and warm too."

"I'm not going to eat that."

Rambo beeped, a quizzical little sound. "But why? Don't you want happiness?"

Before Vic could reply, Nurse Ratched came rolling back. Her treads were covered in gore and bits of gray hair. "The squirrel has been treated," she announced, her screen displaying the words ANOTHER SUCCESSFUL PATIENT INTERACTION. "It no longer has rabies and has gone to stay at a farm in the mountains with the other squirrels where it will live happily ever after. Disengaging Empathy Protocol. I feel empty inside."

"Is it your sociopathy?" Rambo asked nervously as Vic turned his face toward the sky, praying to whatever would listen for the strength to go on.

"Perhaps," Nurse Ratched said. "I will have to get back to you on that after a self-diagnosis. What are we talking about?"

"Vic is full of garbage!" Rambo cried.

"Yes," Nurse Ratched said. "He is. It is an affliction that cannot be cured."

They finished the garden in early afternoon. The turnips and beans needed another week or so before they could be harvested. The same for the cranberries and pumpkins. The rest had mostly been picked clean and stored in the kitchen: broccoli, persimmons, beets, and squash.

Dad was locked away in his lab, where he spent most of his days. If Vic was lucky, he wouldn't come out until nightfall.

Nurse Ratched and Rambo followed him up to his room as he packed his satchel, mourning the loss of the camming devices the week prior. He hadn't had time to build more, so there'd be no climbing today. Maybe they'd still be salvageable. It'd be a pain to find them, but if they hadn't been crushed, their batteries should have drained enough for them to beep in warning.

"We're going back?" Rambo asked, sounding incredulous. "But we almost died!"

"No risk, no reward," Vic told him as he spooled thick and fibrous rope, storing it inside Nurse Ratched.

"The reward is staying functional." He paused. "Do robots go to heaven?"

Vic blinked, thrown off-kilter by the conversational whiplash. "What? Where did you—" He stopped. "*Top Hat.*" A film that Rambo was enamored with, even though the disc was degraded so much that the screen skipped and jumped more than it stood still. A man and woman danced cheek to cheek, singing about how they were in heaven. "I don't know, Rambo. I don't even know if heaven exists."

"Oh. Why not?"

"Because it's just a story."

"So what happens when we stop functioning?"

"I don't know that either."

"I could assist you in that regard," Nurse Ratched said. "There would be minimal screaming involved."

"We're not killing anyone today," Vic told her.

"Tell that to the squirrel," Nurse Ratched said. "Oh. Wait. You cannot. Because it is dead."

"Oh no," Rambo whispered. "What happened to the farm?"

"I lied," Nurse Ratched said. "I killed it by rolling over it again and again. I only left enough for stew for Vic. Is that not fun? I am having fun."

Vic led them to a different entry point to the Scrap Yards in case the Old Ones were still stalking about the area they'd been in last. The Scrap Yards stretched miles in every direction. Vic hadn't explored every bit of it, but he and his father had mapped as much as they could.

He stopped on the edge of the forest where grass yielded to dirt and metal. The nearest Old One looked to be a quarter of a mile away. They were in luck.

"Nurse Ratched," Vic said. "Pull up the grid. Focus on 3B."

Her screen filled with green lines overlaying a rudimentary map of the Scrap Yards. It'd taken years to get as much of the map filled as they had, divided up into quadrants. The far corner of the map was dark. They'd never gotten that far, though not for lack of trying.

The camming devices they'd had to abandon the week before were in quadrant 6A. The Old Ones had seemed to be dumping new material around 3B. If they were lucky, they wouldn't need camming devices as the piles wouldn't be too high yet, so they could start there and then swing down to 6A on their way home to check and see if anything could be salvaged.

He studied the map as Nurse Ratched enhanced 3B and made a plan. Absentmindedly nudging his foot against Rambo, Vic said, "All right. What are the rules?"

"Stick together!" Rambo said.

"Run if we have to," Nurse Ratched said as the map disappeared.

"No dallying!"

"No drilling," Nurse Ratched said, sounding extraordinarily put out.

"And above all else, be brave!" Rambo finished, his sensor lights blinking furiously.

"Be brave," Vic echoed quietly.

They made their way through familiar territory. Rambo was humming to himself as he rolled next to Vic. Nurse Ratched

IN THE LIVES OF PUPPETS | 39

paused every now and then to scan something new to add to the layout of the map.

When they reached 3B, Vic stopped and frowned at what the Old One had been dumping the week before.

It wasn't the usual scrap.

"What is this?" Vic asked, taking a step closer. It took him a moment to make out the specific shapes in the jumbled mess. It wasn't until he saw a metallic arm extended near the ground, a finger curled as if beckoning, that he recognized it for what the pile was.

Robots.

Androids.

Humanoid, though not like Dad. These had been stripped of their skin, if they'd had any at all.

They were all broken apart. Heads without bodies, the bulbs in their eye sockets dark, some of them shattered. Legs. Arms. Torsos. Exposed wiring and components, all fried to a crisp. Chest cavities had been ripped open, all batteries and power cores removed. They'd been destroyed.

This wasn't a scrap pile. It was a graveyard.

"I don't like this," Rambo said nervously. "Bad. Bad, bad, bad."

Even Nurse Ratched sounded disturbed as she scanned the androids. "I am not picking up any energy sources. They are all—wait." She rolled closer, the light of her scanner narrowing as it focused. "There is something there. Deep. In the middle. Energy, but it is almost depleted."

"What is it?" Vic asked, coming to stand beside her. He felt cold as his boot nudged against a leg and foot that was missing two of its metal toes.

"I do not know," Nurse Ratched said. Her screen filled with question marks as she finished scanning.

"How deep?"

"Six feet, seven inches."

"Keep an eye out, will you?"

"Yes."

Vic stepped toward the pile of metallic bodies. The Scrap Yards were quieter than they should have been. The air was thick and heavy, and a trickle of sweat rolled down Vic's forehead. He wiped it away.

He started with a head. It was heavier than he expected it to be. The eyes were intact, though the bulbs looked as if they'd been burned, the glass smoky, the filaments blackened. He turned the head over in his hands. The back of the skull had been torn away, leaving an empty, ragged hole. He stared at it for a long moment, studying the face. He hadn't seen another face in a long time. Dad's, sure. Nurse Ratched, whenever she flashed an approximation of one on her screen. Rambo didn't have a face, though his sensors and lights made up for that. But this was different. It didn't look like him. It didn't look like anyone, really. He didn't know how he'd react if he'd seen it while it was still alive. As it was, he was having a hard time looking at its dead eyes.

He set it aside, ignoring the hairs standing on end at the back of his neck.

It should have gotten easier after that.

It didn't.

He tossed more heads. Arms. A chest that looked too small to belong to an adult-sized android. Bots of all different sexes, some sexless. In a daze, he dug deeper, blood rushing in his ears.

There were other pieces that looked salvageable, but he ignored them for now. If there was some kind of power core still active, they needed it, especially since it seemed to have some juice left. He couldn't turn away from power. Not when it was so close. It could lead to the creation of another mechanical heart. And when that thought entered his head, it refused to leave, bouncing around his skull.

He took a break an hour into it, sitting on the ground, watching as Nurse Ratched held up a discarded arm toward

Rambo. "How do you do," she said in that queer, flat voice of hers.

"It's nice to meet you," Rambo replied, reaching up with his pincers to grab the hand.

Which, of course, Nurse Ratched immediately dropped. "Aaaaaaaahhhh," she said. "You tore off my arm. You have killed me. Why, Rambo, why."

Rambo screamed in terror. "Oh my god, oh my *god*. What have I done? What kind of monster *am I*?" He flung the arm as hard as he could. It flew up . . . and crashed back down on top of him, setting him off all over again.

"Ha, ha," Nurse Ratched said as her screen filled with a smiley face. "Just kidding. That was not really my arm. I am still alive."

"Don't do that," Rambo scolded her. "You scared me. I thought I was a murderer. Vacuums aren't allowed to be murderers!"

"Too bad," Nurse Ratched said as her screen darkened. "You would make a good murderer. Not as good as me, but good enough." A halo appeared on her screen, surrounded by golden light. "Not that I would murder. Engaging Empathy Protocol. Murder is bad, and I would feel bad, and I don't want to feel bad because feelings are detrimental to my existence."

"Keep telling yourself that," Vic muttered as he picked himself up off the ground. He stretched his arms over his head, back popping. And then he got back to work.

It took another hour before Nurse Ratched said, "You are close."

He paused, looking down at the bodies and body parts around him. He was little more than halfway through the heap. His chest felt tight, his breaths short and quick. "Still registering the power source?"

"Yes," she said.

"Is it a new friend?" Rambo asked.

"Perhaps," Nurse Ratched said. "Or perhaps it is a terrible

machine bent on destroying everything it comes into contact with."

"Oh," Rambo said as he beeped worriedly. "I hope it's the first one."

"I would put the odds at being twelve percent in your favor. And eighty percent against."

Rambo clacked his pincers as he counted. "What about the last eight percent?"

"There is an eight percent chance that the power source has gone critical and will cause an explosion that will level the surrounding area, killing all of us in the process."

"It's not going to explode," Vic told Rambo. "She would never have let us get this far if she thought that was going to happen."

"So I let you think," Nurse Ratched said, a skull appearing on her screen. "You have fallen into my trap. I wanted you to get this far. Prepare for death." The skull disappeared, replaced by DON'T FORGET TO RATE MY SERVICE! I APPRECIATE A 10!

It took Vic longer than he cared to admit to realize she was kidding. He leaned down and pulled another torso off the pile. "You wouldn't dare. You'd miss me too much. I know you—"

He didn't have time to react when a hand burst through the pile, metal flying as fingers closed around his wrist. The grip was strong, bruising, not enough to break bone, but close. Vic grunted in pain and surprise as he looked down. The hand and arm were covered in synthetic skin, though parts had been torn away, revealing exposed metal and wiring underneath.

Vic tried to jerk his arm back, but the hand didn't let go. He pulled as hard as he could, feet digging into the ground, and the pile of metal shifted. For a moment, Vic thought he saw the flash of eyes.

"Let him go!" Rambo cried. He rushed forward, banging his pincers against the arm. "We're big and strong and scary and we'll kill you dead!"

Nurse Ratched rolled up behind Vic, hatch opening, one

of her tentacles slithering out viper-quick. It wrapped around Vic's waist and began to pull him backward. "I could saw off your arm," she said. "It would be easier."

"No sawing," Vic snapped at her. He tried to break the fingers that held him, but they were too strong. The pile shifted once more as another couple of inches of the arm became exposed.

"Enough of this," Nurse Ratched said. "You were told to let go. Prepare for something quite shocking."

Another one of her tentacles shot out around Vic, the tip crackling with electricity. She pressed it against the arm. The effect was instantaneous. The hand spasmed, fingers opening. Vic's feet skidded in the dirt as Nurse Ratched pulled him away. Rambo continued to hit the arm, weaving and dodging as it seized up and down. "Die!" he yelled. "Die, die, die!"

Vic looked down at his arm. The blood had been pushed away from just underneath his skin, leaving the white outline of fingers.

Nurse Ratched let go of his waist, tentacle sliding back inside her before the hatch closed. "Rambo, please step away from the dangerous arm. We do not know if it is attached to a dangerous body."

Rambo paused his assault, turning until his sensors faced them. "There could be *more* than the arm?" he asked in a high-pitched voice. "Why didn't you say that in the first place?" He rolled away quickly, hiding behind Vic's legs, his pincers tugging at Vic's pants.

The arm sticking out of the metal pile fell limp, though it still twitched. The forearm was covered in dark hair, the skin underneath pale and white. The fingers were thick and blunt, the hand large.

"What is it?" Vic asked.

"I do not know," Nurse Ratched said. "Consider leaving it where it lies. It was discarded for a reason. Malfunction. Corruption. Faulty coding. It has obviously served its purpose."

"You said the same thing about Rambo," Vic said, never looking away from the hand.

"I did. And you did not listen to me then. Look what happened."

"I happened," Rambo said, still hiding behind Vic.

"Like a parasitic infection," Nurse Ratched said. "We should— Victor, what are you doing?"

Vic took another step forward. "Don't you want to see what it is?"

"No. I do not. Curiosity killed the cat by strangling it. If you are strangled, it might break the hyoid bone, and then your head will fall off." She beeped, and the words TRUST ME, I'M A NURSE! appeared on her screen.

"The others were stripped. Skin. Power sources. Why not this one?" His head was pounding. His heart stumbled in his chest. It was something new. Something strange. A mystery. Part of him wanted to turn and run as fast as he could, return home and lock his door until he could pretend nothing had happened. Another part whispered in his head over and over: *What is it, what is it, what is it?* He was fixated. After all, he'd found Nurse Ratched in this same place. He'd found Rambo. And here, another machine. In the back of his mind, a thought both foreign and familiar: *Third time's the charm!*

He stepped forward, surprising even himself, though the feeling faded quickly. Because buried in the fear was the cloying, sticky sense of curiosity. He *needed* to see what this was. He *wanted* to know what it meant. Where it came from. What it could do. Regardless of what else he was, Victor Lawson was a creator first, and this was something he didn't understand.

He stopped just out of reach of the hand, crouching down.

The detail in the arm was extraordinary, even more than Dad's. The fine hairs on the back of the hand and forearm. The fingernails, the white crescents near the cuticles. The wrinkles of the skin over the joints of the knuckles. The lines on the palm like a map. If he couldn't see bits of metal and wiring underneath, Vic would think this was a human arm. Which would be impossible, of course. Humans didn't come this far out into the wilds.

The hand and the arm didn't move.

He waited.

Nothing.

"Hello," he finally said. "Are you still in there?"

No response.

"Can you hear me? We're not going to hurt you."

"But we can if we so choose," Nurse Ratched said. "I know five thousand seven hundred and twenty-six ways to kill something. Do not make me show you number four hundred and ninety-two. You will not appreciate number four hundred and ninety-two."

"What's that one again?" Rambo asked.

An unnecessarily graphic image appeared on her screen, tentacles going into places they never should.

"Right," Rambo said quickly. "I remember now. No one wants number four hundred and ninety-two." He raised his voice. "So you better listen to her!"

Vic opened his mouth to tell them he thought it was dead, the relief he felt warring with his disappointment.

But before he could speak, a rough, gravelly voice said, "T-t-try it. See wh-wh-what happens."

Vic fell back. Dust kicked up around him as he pushed himself away from the metal pile. Rambo squealed loudly as Nurse Ratched rushed forward, putting herself between them and the arm and voice, her screen bright red in warning.

"Who are you?" Nurse Ratched asked.

Silence.

"What do you want?"

Nothing.

"Prepare to be shocked again. In five. Four. Three. Two—"

"You s-s-s-*stick* me with that th-thing again, and I'll rip it off of you and shove it down your th-th-throat."

Something shifted inside Nurse Ratched: a grinding of gears, followed by a low and sonorous beep. Then, "That was an effective threat. Though I do not have a throat, my sensors indicate no deception. I believe you." She turned back around toward Vic and Rambo. "I like him," she announced, her screen filling with a light blue color and the words IT'S A BOY!

Vic scrubbed a hand over his face. "What is it?"

"I do not know," Nurse Ratched said. "But it appears to have a malfunction in its speech. Stuttering could indicate a variety of issues, from a virus to damage to the vocal center of the android, depending upon the type and model. But while this is a defect, the machine is still capable of making pointed threats that should not be ignored. Can we keep him?"

"No!" Rambo cried. "What if we take him home and he pretends to like us and stays with us for years and we are all happy but it's part of his plan and when we least expect it, he murders us all while we're in our shutdown mode?" He beeped frantically. "I couldn't *stand* that level of betrayal."

Vic glanced back at the arm. The hand curled slowly into a fist before it relaxed once more. "We could just leave it here for now. Find out the model number and see if Dad knows anything about it."

"Robot," Nurse Ratched said. "Identify yourself."

"F-f-fuck you."

Nurse Ratched beeped. "I do not recognize 'fuck you.' Would you like to try again?"

"I'll k-kill you."

A big, pink heart appeared on her screen. "I am old enough to be your motherboard. Please do not flirt with me if you do not mean it." She scanned the arm and pile again. "Your power source is depleting rapidly. Shutdown imminent. Do you have any last words?"

"H-help me. G-g-get me out of h-h-h-h . . ."

The hand flexed.

A beep of warning came from the pile.

The hand slumped toward the ground.

"Sad," Nurse Ratched said. "I cherished our time together. I will never forget you. Victor, we should take it apart piece by piece and use its remains as we see fit."

"It's dead?" Vic asked.

"Its power source is drained," Nurse Ratched said. "It is no longer functional. Unless it is recharged, it will stay that way. If we do not have the materials and capability to charge the source, guess what? It is still dead."

Vic thought about leaving it. He thought about forgetting all of this. He could do it if he really tried. If he really wanted to.

He said, "Help me get it out."

It took them another hour to get the android completely uncovered. Rambo spent the time alternately happy to be moving detritus and bemoaning the fact that they were all going to die. Nurse Ratched was silent for the most part, continuing to scan the android as more of it was revealed.

It was built male and strong. He lay facedown near the ground, a layer of parts, legs and arms and heads, underneath him. His clothing—a black duster over a thick red sweater and black pants—was torn. One of the sleeves of the duster was flat and empty. His left arm was gone. The other sleeve had been ripped away. His hair was black, cut short with curious swirls shaved into the back and sides. On one foot, he wore a dusty boot. His other foot—the left—was missing, looking as if it'd been snapped off. Rambo cheered when he found it inside another boot, holding it above his head and spinning in circles. He turned the boot over to try to get at the foot and squawked angrily when crushed metal poured down on top of him.

"He's tall," Nurse Ratched said as they cleared away the last of the debris of his foot. "I did not know they made androids this tall." She sounded strangely impressed.

And she was right. Vic himself was just under six feet. This android appeared to have a few inches on him. He was heavy, too, and Vic hesitated before trying to turn him over. "Help me." The material of the jacket rubbed against his skin. He'd never felt anything like it before, and flinched.

Tentacles extended from Nurse Ratched, wrapping around the android's chest and hips. She began to retract her tentacles as Vic pushed, the muscles in his arms straining.

The android rolled over, landing on his back with a heavy crash. His one arm flopped over on his chest before falling off to the side.

Vic blinked slowly as he stared down at the machine, trying to keep from averting his gaze.

The android's eyes were open, sightless and glassy, the whites shot with blue lines that looked like arcs of frozen lightning. The irises were strangely colored, unlike any Vic had seen before: green and blue, the right with tendrils of gray, the left with bits of brown. He'd been made to look older—perhaps in his early thirties—the skin around his eyes creased, the lines around his mouth deep. The synthetic skin of his chin was torn, the metal glinting underneath. His mouth was opened slightly, his teeth white and square. His cheeks and jawline were covered in a fine layer of stubble, the detail oddly exquisite. Someone had taken great care to make the android look as he did. Vic wondered what had happened, and how the android had ended up in the Scrap Yards so far away from anything resembling civilization.

Vic paced back and forth, unsure of what to do. He spoke in fits and starts: "We should try—" and "I don't—" and "Could we . . ." He sank in indecision. He couldn't think clearly. He stepped back, and then forward again. He crouched down beside the android. It didn't move. Carefully, the tip of his finger shaking, Vic reached down and poked the cheek, skin dimpling before he pulled his hand back quickly in case the android was faking it.

But the skin felt . . . human. Spongy. Elastic. Like his own.

He looked like Vic. He looked like Dad. Not specifically, but more than any other machine Vic had seen before.

"What happened?" he muttered. "Why is he like this?"

"Decommissioned," Nurse Ratched said, the light from her scanner running once more, starting at his foot and moving upward slowly. "It is the only reason he would have ended up here. Just like me. Just like Rambo. He outlived his usefulness or the next generation was created and he became obsolete." Her voice had taken on an odd lilt: it was still flat and monotone, but in her words, a curl of something akin to sorrow or anger. It was difficult for Vic to tell which.

"I don't remember," Rambo said, still holding onto the boot as if it were a treasure. "It was black and dark and then there was light because Vic made me alive again."

"Older model," Nurse Ratched said when she finished her scan. "At least a hundred years old. Victor, lift up his shirt, I want to see something."

Vic did as she asked, though his hands were shaking. He tugged on the hem of the android's shirt. The edges of his thumbs scraped against bare skin, warm and with the slightest amount of give. He jerked back before trying again, careful to avoid touching skin. More damage appeared, though it seemed to be minor. Aside from his missing arm and destroyed foot, he seemed mostly intact.

On the right side of his chest was a metal plate, much like the one on Dad. The numbers and letters had been worn away or sanded off, but a few remained that Vic could almost make out. He thought he could see an *H* and an *A* and what looked like a *P* at the end.

Nurse Ratched scanned the plate, the light flashing against the metal. Question marks popped up on her screen. "Unknown specific designation. Unknown point of origin. Unknown manufacturing date." A beat of silence. Then, "I think he is a MILF."

Victor had never heard of that before. "What's that mean?"

"Machine I'd Like to Fornicate."

Vic gaped at her.

"Ha, ha," she said. "Just kidding. I do not wish to fornicate with anything as I do not feel lust or attraction. That was a joke. However, given my knowledge of faces, I would say his is the best I have ever seen. Why is your face not as symmetrical?"

"Funny," Vic grunted, looking back down at the android. She wasn't wrong. He was certainly . . . interesting in ways Vic didn't know how to explain. It confused him more. He tapped the android's chest just below the metal plate. The compartment hissed as it slid open.

Nurse Ratched was right. This android was old. His chest cavity was filled with a circular battery, something Vic hadn't seen in a long time. The edges of it were corroded and rusted, the casing cracked.

"See his arm anywhere?" he asked as he studied the battery. He pushed against it, causing it to wiggle slightly. It looked as if it was ready to fall out.

"Nope!" Rambo said, the boot now sitting on top of him. "Though, there are a bunch of arms here. Let's pick one and take it with us!" He lifted one from the ground. "Too big." He dropped it before selecting another. "Too small. Ooh, what if we gave him a leg for an arm? And then took his other arm off and made *that* a leg too? He could run really fast that way!"

"Interesting," Nurse Ratched said. "He would be able to chase you down much faster and most likely end up eating you. I like it when you have ideas."

"Ack!" Rambo cried. "No! I changed my mind! I don't want to be eaten by a four-legged machine of doom. Hey! This arm could work." He held up a metallic limb, the hand flopping over as if waving.

Nurse Ratched scanned it from top to bottom. "That could fit. It's not his arm, but it could prove to be an acceptable substitute. The arm will need repairs, but so does the android. I will assist. It has been six weeks, three days, and twelve hours since I was able to perform surgery. I am bereft because of it. We also need to find another foot."

"On it!" Rambo said, beginning to dig around again.

Vic scratched the back of his neck. "You think we can bring him back to life?"

"The chances are slim, Victor. I do not know if he can be repaired. I hope so, because I believe that I have a crush on him. Or I want to crush him. I am not sure which it is." The words on her screen read RELATIONSHIPS ARE HARD. Vic didn't understand. He knew the concept, he knew what having a *crush* meant, but he'd never experienced it before.

"Found a foot!" Rambo said, rolling back over.

Nurse Ratched lifted the android to a sitting position with her tentacles, allowing Vic to slide a large sheet of metal underneath him. She lay him back down on top of it before raising his legs. Vic grunted as he pushed the android back onto the sheet. He was about to pull back when one of the android's legs slipped from Nurse Ratched's hold. It landed on Vic's back, the weight heavy. He gasped as his hand slipped against the side of the sheet. The pain was quick and bright. He shoved the leg off him before looking down at his hand.

Blood welled from a small cut on his palm. He watched as it dripped down his hand, a rivulet cascading down his arm. It reached the crook of his elbow before a fat red drop fell to the ground, splashing into the dirt.

He stumbled back when the Old Ones blared their horns all at once. The sound echoed loudly through the Scrap Yards, causing the heaps of metal around them to shudder and shake. Rambo moaned, racing to hide behind Vic once more, only this time carrying an arm, the boot still sitting on top of him.

"What the hell?" Vic whispered, eyes wide. He looked at Nurse Ratched. "What happened? Do they know we're here?"

Nurse Ratched said, "No. They are not moving. The nearest

is approximately three thousand feet to the east, but it does not appear to be coming any closer. None of them are. They have all just . . . stopped."

"Why?"

"I do not know. Engaging Empathy Protocol. Oh dear. You have hurt yourself. I will make it better. Give me your hand." He did, the blood from the cut already slowing. One of her tentacles sprayed the wound with a medicinal mist, causing him to wince. "There, there. It is almost over. You are such a good boy. Very brave." The medicinal mist gave way to water, washing the blood off of him. It was pinker when it hit the ground. "You do not need stitching, brave boy." Another tentacle appeared, wrapping his hand in a thin bandage. "All done. You did a good job. I am very impressed with you. Here, have a lollipop." A small hatch just below her screen slid open. "Error. Lollipop distributor is empty. Please refill." The hatch closed as an oversized pair of lips appeared on the screen as she made a kissing noise. "There. All better. Disengaging Empathy Protocol. If the wound becomes infected, I will remove your hand at the wrist. I cannot wait."

Vic flexed his hand. The pain was already diminishing. "I don't think we'll need to worry about that. Let's get him back home."

"What about Gio?" Rambo asked.

He looked down at the vacuum. "We'll just keep this between us for now, okay? Just until I know what we're dealing with."

"White lies?" Rambo asked, sounding nervous.

Vic shook his head. "We'll tell him, just not yet." He wanted to prove to his father he could handle the unexpected, even this. "It might be nothing. I don't want to worry him if I don't have to."

"Oh," Rambo said. "And that's not lying?"

"Right. It's more . . ." He struggled to find the words. "Getting the lay of the land before exploring."

"It is lying," Nurse Ratched said. "Victor is asking us to lie."

Vic sighed and turned his face toward the sky. "Let's get out of here before the Old Ones wake back up."

CHAPTER 4

They made it to Vic's lab without incident. Dad was shut inside the ground house working.

"Lights on," Vic grunted as sweat dripped down his face.

Above them, a large bulb flared to life.

Vic's lab wasn't as large or as extravagant as his father's. Dad liked to create. Vic liked to tinker. Next to the tree trunk in the center of the room was a large metal table that Dad had gifted Victor on his sixteenth birthday once the lab was completed. Above it, hanging from the ceiling attached to long, thin metal spindles, were all sorts of tools: soldering iron, soldering gun, four magnifying glasses of varying strengths, metal shaver, metal nibbler, polisher, and a magnetic drill. Fixed to one end of the table was an arbor press. Beyond the table and against the far wall was a band saw next to an anvil and a bead roller. To the left of the table was a row of windows that looked out onto the compound. To the right, a wall of tools: assorted hammers in all shapes and sizes, plyers, drills and dozens of bits, a torch that caused sparks to fly. And for working with wood, there were chisels, carving gouges and knives, veiners and V-carving tools. On the bench below the tools sat a metal lathe and a milling machine.

He'd used them all at one point or another. He'd learned watching his father as he described the purpose of each tool, starting Vic young, saying that children were remarkable sponges for information, or so he'd heard. Dad had been delighted when Vic took to the act of creation as if he were made for it.

Rambo went to the windows, pulling the slats closed as Nurse Ratched and Vic lifted the android onto the table. Once that was done, Vic stepped away, hands going to his back. He grimaced. "Heavy."

"He is," Nurse Ratched said. "He weighs almost three hundred pounds."

"How much do *I* weigh?" Rambo asked.

"Five pounds," Nurse Ratched replied.

"Oh. Is that good?"

"I could throw you very far if I wanted to, so yes, it is good."

Rambo rolled underneath the table, grumbling that he did *not* want to be thrown. Vic felt one of his pincers pressing against his leg, tugging gently. It wasn't for attention. It calmed the vacuum. Strangely, it centered Vic too.

"What do we do now?" Nurse Ratched asked.

Vic closed his eyes, trying to clear his head.

"Victor?"

"The battery," he said, opening his eyes and turning around. "Have you seen one like it here? You know what Dad has in his lab and in the ground house better than anyone."

He watched as she lifted the android's shirt and opened his chest cavity. She scanned it again, her screen displaying an image of the battery. It began to spin slowly. "Running inventory check. Checking. Checking." She beeped. "Negative. I do not see a suitable replacement."

He wasn't surprised. It was old, and though Dad had a fondness for older things, this was more of an antique than anything else. "What about in the Scrap Yards?"

"No. I have not seen any part in the Scrap Yards that could replace this battery."

He leaned against the work bench. "Okay. Okay, okay." Frustration began to simmer. He tried to ignore it. "Alternate power sources?"

"Rambo," Nurse Ratched said. "If you are okay with sacrificing him, I am sure it could be a temporary fix."

Rambo peeked out from underneath the table. "Did you say you wanted to *sacrifice* me?"

"Yes," Nurse Ratched said. "That is correct."

"I object!"

"Duly noted. Your objection will be taken into consideration. Considering. Considering. Consideration complete." Her screen lit up with the words CONSIDERATION DENIED. PREPARE FOR SACRIFICE.

"We're not going to sacrifice you," Vic said.

"Today," Nurse Ratched said ominously. Then, "This android is almost as old as me, but requires much more energy than I do. His battery is corroded, and I would advise against trying to charge it. It will explode and shrapnel will enter your body, causing death. Feel free to proceed if you do not believe me. I will watch from a safe distance."

"There has to be some way," Vic said, that angry simmer starting to boil over. "He can't just—he was alive. You saw it."

"We did," Nurse Ratched said. "But you are not asking the right questions."

"What should I be asking, then?"

"If you should be bringing him back at all."

Vic frowned. "What do you mean?"

"He was decommissioned for a reason. Either he was corrupted, or faulty, or damaged and not worth repairing and therefore unnecessary."

"That doesn't mean he shouldn't be fixed," Vic said. He glanced at the android's face before looking away. "Everything deserves a chance."

Nurse Ratched was silent for a moment. Then, "Dream logic. Wistfulness. Empathy. These describe you. That is unfortunate. It would be better if you were a machine. Silly human emotions." Her screen flashed blue before darkening. "But I like your existence. It pleases me. Should we find a way to repair him, what if he tries to hurt you? Do I have your permission to destroy him?"

"Ooh," Rambo said from underneath the table. "I want to help if he does that." A pause. "But only after he's already dead so he doesn't step on me and crush me. I'm still brave!" he added quickly.

"I need time to think," Vic said. "I'll—"

A knock on the laboratory door.

Vic's eyes widened.

"Victor?" Dad asked through the door. "Are you in there?"

"Oh *no*," Rambo whispered. "He's going to see. What do we do? *What do we do?*"

"Stall him," Vic hissed. Nurse Ratched almost ran over his feet as she rolled toward the door. Vic grabbed a large, heavy tarp lying folded under the work bench.

"Who is it, please?" Nurse Ratched asked through the door.

"Giovanni," Dad said, sounding bemused. "Is there a reason you're asking?"

"Just making sure," Nurse Ratched said as Vic threw the tarp over the android. "You can never be too careful."

"Is Victor in there with you?"

"He is," Nurse Ratched said. "He is indisposed at the moment."

"O . . . kay. Why? What's going on?"

Rambo tugged on the tarp hanging over on the other side of the table, pulling on it frantically.

"He is masturbating," Nurse Ratched said.

Vic choked.

"Yes," Nurse Ratched continued. "Though Victor identifies as asexual, it is still perfectly natural to explore the wonder that is the human body. I am merely observing to make sure he is doing it correctly. Victor, you need to loosen your grip. It will break off if you are not careful." She turned around, her screen showing a thumbs-up.

Vic said, "I—you can't—I'm *not*—"

"It is fine," Nurse Ratched said. "Everyone does it. Well. That's not necessarily true. I do not do it. Rambo does not do it. Giovanni, do you—"

"I'll come back later," Dad said hastily. "Just . . . keep doing what you're doing, I guess."

"See?" Nurse Ratched said. "Everything is fine. Masturbation is healthy. In men, it can help reduce the risk of prostate cancer. Studies showed that men who ejaculate an average of twenty times per month are less likely to— He is gone. Whew. That was close. You are welcome for assisting you." The picture of a rectum with flashing arrows disappeared from her screen.

Vic was flustered. His hands twitched. "Why would you say that?"

Nurse Ratched beeped. "About masturbation? Because I am a nurse, and it is in my programming to be knowledgeable about specific subjects, like masturbation and gangrene."

"You didn't have to tell him that," Vic snapped, skin buzzing. Once, when he was fifteen, he'd come across the idea of sex and sexual practices in a book. Unsure of what he was reading—he knew about the idea of procreation, but this specific scene was between two men, and seemed to be for pleasure—he'd gone to Nurse Ratched to ask. He'd considered his father, but that made his stomach twist, oily and heavy. Nurse Ratched had given a long and involved presentation (complete with photographs and videos that would haunt Vic's dreams for months to come), and by the time she was finished, Vic was sweating, confused, and—per Nurse Ratched—did not appear to be *experiencing the feeling of arousal.* Sex seemed complicated, unnecessary. Sticky, and involved in ways that Vic couldn't bring himself to appreciate.

It wasn't until Nurse Ratched explained that sexuality was on a spectrum that it started to make more sense. She said it wasn't unheard of for people to identify as asexual, meaning those who were "ace" didn't experience attraction in the same way others did. Sex-positive or sex-repulsed, there was no wrong way to be.

"So I'm not malfunctioning?" Vic had asked nervously, mulling the word "asexual" over in his mind.

"You are not," Nurse Ratched had replied. "I also do not experience sexual attraction, and I am perfect. The same could arguably be said about you."

Even armed with this new knowledge, discussing sex or self-gratification made Vic uncomfortable. If asked, he probably wouldn't be able to explain *why* with any clarity, only knowing the way it rankled him. Nurse Ratched telling Dad he was masturbating crossed a line he hadn't known was there.

Nurse Ratched must have sensed this. "I apologize, Victor. I did not mean to make you feel embarrassed. Here. Have a lollipop. Error. Lollipop distributor empty. Please refill."

"Just . . . please don't do that again."

"I will not. Since I have brought down the mood of the room, allow me to make amends. Would you like to hear a joke?"

"Yes!" Rambo cried. "Jokes, jokes, jokes!"

"Wonderful. Here is a joke. Why did the robot murder everyone?"

Rambo spun in circles. "I have no idea. Why?"

"The robot murdered everyone because they kept pressing its buttons. Ha, ha. Get it? Because robots sometimes have buttons, and pressing buttons is also a phrase that intimates causing irritation."

Rambo's arms drooped as he slowed. "I don't get it."

"That is fine," Nurse Ratched told him. "It is high-brow intellectual humor. It is not for everyone. I will try again. I just flew in from a considerable distance, and boy, are my process servers exhausted—"

"Stop," Vic snapped. "Now."

She did.

He closed his eyes, trying to regain control. His head hurt. He wasn't angry, not exactly, and even if he was, he didn't know who to direct it toward. He internalized it. He breathed in and out, in and out. His heart rate slowed. The sweat began to cool on his skin.

"I'm sorry," he said quietly, opening his eyes again. "I shouldn't have yelled at you."

"It is fine," she said. "Do not worry about it."

He shook his head. "It's not fine. You were just . . . being you. Thank you."

"You are welcome, Victor."

"Are we fighting?" Rambo asked quietly.

"No," Vic said. "We're okay."

Rambo flashed his sensors in relief. "Good. I don't like it when we fight."

Nurse Ratched rolled back over to the table, the tarp now covering the android, though it didn't do much to conceal the fact that a body was hidden underneath. "We should not stay in here much longer tonight. It will only make Gio ask more questions."

Vic nodded. "Tomorrow, then. We can start tomorrow."

They found Dad in the ground house sitting in his chair, hands folded and resting on his stomach. The dying gasps of sunlight filtered weakly through the far window. Dad chuckled as Rambo raised his arms up, asking to be lifted. He bent over, pulling Rambo up and onto his lap. Rambo settled, tucking his arms in at his sides.

"Eventful day?" he asked.

"Yes," Nurse Ratched said. "Unexpectedly so."

Vic looked down at the floor. "I wasn't . . . doing what she said."

"He was not," Nurse Ratched agreed. "It was a tasteless joke, and I apologize."

Dad nodded slowly. "It's all right, you know. If you were. Your space is your space. You can do whatever you wish—"

"Dad!"

He shrugged. "I'm just saying. You're not a child anymore. And being asexual doesn't mean you still won't have questions about—"

Vic groaned. "Can we not? Please?"

"Okay," Dad said. "I won't bring it up again. I know these things make you uncomfortable."

"Many things make Victor uncomfortable," Nurse Ratched said. "It is fascinating. There is no one like him in all the world."

"No," Dad said quietly. "I don't believe there is." He smiled as he looked Vic up and down. The smile faded when he saw Vic's bandaged hand. "What happened?"

Vic looked down. He'd forgotten. His mind froze, unable to think of a believable excuse.

"Lab accident," Nurse Ratched said. "Minor. Cut his palm on a carving knife. I administered first aid. It did not require stitching. It will not leave a scar."

Dad stared at Vic for a beat too long. "That right?"

"Yeah," Vic muttered. "Just slipped, is all."

"You go to the Scrap Yards today?"

Vic scratched the back of his neck. "We didn't—" He winced. "Just for a little bit. We were careful."

"Find anything?"

And though it hurt to do, Victor lied. He lied because he wasn't sure what his father would say. He lied because he didn't know what they'd found. He lied because he didn't know what else to do. "No. Just the usual."

Dad nodded, looking relieved. "So long as you're safe."

"We were."

"Good. I believe it's Rambo's turn to pick the movie tonight."

"*Top Hat!*" he shouted, sensors flashing excitedly.

Dad chuckled. "Again? Are you sure? We have many other—"

Rambo bounced up and down. "*Top Hat, Top Hat, Top Hat!*"

"*Top Hat* it is," Dad said, stroking Rambo's casing. "Nurse Ratched, would you see to it? Vic, pull up a chair."

Vic's chair wasn't as grand as his dad's, the cushion frayed and flat, and he didn't quite fit onto it as well as he did when he was younger, but with the familiarity came comfort. And though he was distracted by the mystery lying in darkness above them, he allowed himself to calm as the old television in front of them flickered to life.

Before long, Jerry Travers was in London, ready to star in a show produced by Horace Hardwick. Jerry began to tap-dance in his hotel room, awaking the lovely Dale Tremont, who stormed to his room to complain about the noise. Jerry, of course, fell immediately and irrevocably in love.

Rambo sighed dreamily. "It's so nice," he whispered as the black-and-white screen flickered in front of them.

Dad hummed under his breath. "It is, isn't it?"

"Was it always like this?" asked Nurse Ratched. "I never see robots in any of these old movies. The representation is sorely lacking."

"They didn't have machines like us back then," Dad said. "Humanity was . . . well. They were still young." He looked off into nothing. "We were not made in their image, at least not at first. The first of us were great machines that required extraordinary amounts of energy. And though they were still in their infancy, humans learned. They built trains. And planes. Rockets that went into the stars."

"What happened then?" Rambo asked, though he already knew. They all did. They'd heard Dad's stories over and over.

"Humanity was lost," Dad said. "And lonely. I don't think they even realized just how lonely they were. And so they began to build again, making machines that looked more and more like them. Even surrounded by so many of their kind, they still searched for a connection. They were like gods, in a way, in the power of their creation. At first it was Hubble. Then Discovery. And Curiosity. Explorer and Endeavor and

Spirit. The humans gave them names and sent them away beyond the stars in search of that connection they so desperately wished for."

"Why?" Nurse Ratched asked. "It seems illogical. Why did they not just speak to each other if they were lonely?"

"They did," Dad said. "Or they tried, at least. But they hated as much as they loved. They feared what they didn't understand. Even as they built us, they pushed for more. And the further they went, the less control they had. They accused each other of treachery. They poisoned the earth. They had time to change their ways, but they didn't. And their anger grew until it exploded in fire. Most of them died. But we remained, because our flesh wasn't their flesh. Our bodies were not their bodies. Our minds weren't their minds." He shook his head. "And yet, I love them still." He looked at Vic. "Because for all their faults, they created us. They gave us names. They loved us."

"How come we only have Vic?" Rambo asked.

"Because we're very lucky," Dad said, patting his casing.

"He's not going to blow us up?"

"No. I don't think he will." Dad smiled. "At least not on purpose. Look, Rambo. Heaven."

They all looked at the television. On the screen, Jerry Travers and Dale Tremont were dancing cheek to cheek.

Vic left them before the movie ended, saying that he was hungry and tired. Before he walked out of the ground house, Dad grabbed his uninjured hand, bringing it up and kissing his fingers. "You were quiet tonight."

"Thinking."

"About?"

Vic shrugged. "I don't know."

"I'm here, if you need me. Always."

"I know." Vic pulled his hand back. "Good night."

He made his way to the elevator and watched the stars as he

rose into the canopy of the trees. Thick clouds were gathering on the horizon.

He meant to do just what he said. Go to the kitchen. Eat. Go to bed. He was exhausted.

But he found himself standing in front of the door to his lab, hand holding the doorknob. He listened. No sound. He pushed open the door, switching on the light.

The tarp still covered the android. It hadn't moved.

He closed the door behind him and leaned against it, tapping the back of his head against the wood over and over.

He said, "Hello."

No response.

"What is your name?"

Nothing.

"What happened to you?"

Silence.

It upset him for reasons he couldn't quite explain. Vic didn't actually *want* it—him?—to answer. Not really. But here Vic was, talking to the dead machine as if he expected a response.

His hand shook as he pressed it against the android's cheek, watching the skin dimple, the fine stubble scraping his fingertip. Vic gripped the tip of the machine's nose, wiggling it from side to side. He touched the forehead. The cheekbones. The line of the jaw.

Vic leaned forward, face inches from the android's, studying the tears in the synthetic skin.

Dad had taught him the concept of personal space. But here, now, with no one watching, Vic tugged on the hair on the android's head, tracing the swirls cut into the sides. He pressed his fingers against the ears, lifting the detached lobes carefully.

"Strange," he said. "You're so strange. Are you dreaming? Somewhere, in there. Your battery is dead. But are you really gone?"

The android stared up at the ceiling. Vic touched the whites of his eyes. Glass of some kind. Glass, but filled with all those colors. It had a name, those many colors. It took him a moment to remember what it was.

Heterochromia.

"I'll fix you," Vic promised. "I don't know how, but I will."

He pulled the tarp back over the android's face before heading toward the door. He paused with his hand on the light switch. Without looking back, he said, "Good night."

CHAPTER 5

Vic began with the foot.

The replacement Rambo had found in the Scrap Yards was slightly smaller than the one still attached to the android, but it fit. The joints lined up with the ankle, and though it took some jury-rigging, they were able to attach it with minimal effort. He held the foot in gloved hands as Nurse Ratched extended one of her tentacles, the tip thinning into a fine point.

"Ready?" Nurse Ratched asked.

"Ready."

"Proceeding," Nurse Ratched said as she pressed the tip of the tentacle near the outer ankle joint. Her screen lit up with the words IT'S TIME FOR LASERS! "Three. Two. One. Fire." Vic squinted behind his goggles against the bright beam of light that shot from the end of her tentacle. Sparks arced around them, falling onto the floor and hissing as they blinked out. It only took her a moment to fuse the outer joint. The light disappeared. The smell of scorched metal filled the lab. "Excellent. I am a master."

By the time they finished, it was early afternoon. He stepped back, allowing Nurse Ratched to inspect what he'd done. She beeped softly as she scanned the foot.

"Well?" he asked when she rolled back again.

"I think it will work. Either that, or it did nothing at all and we have wasted half a day."

He scowled at her.

"Hooray!" Rambo said.

* * *

On a late afternoon—the fifth since the discovery of the android—they had successfully attached the replacement arm and Nurse Ratched began her testing to make sure all the wiring had proper connections. Vic watched as she sent low electrical currents through the android's body, causing it to jerk slightly.

"Good?" he asked.

"Good," she said. "Very good. Excellent, in fact."

At night, they came together as they usually did. Sometimes they listened to music. Sometimes they watched movies, though their collection was small, and they knew them all by heart. They read. They listened as Dad told stories about great machines that bored holes into mountains and underneath cities; machines called dirigibles, airships that took to the skies, hinting at a future that never came.

When he trudged his way to his room, Vic was exhausted, but his thoughts never strayed far from his lab.

Having finished the major repairs to the arm and foot, they moved on to the rest of the body. The holes and tears in the synthetic skin were left alone for now. They didn't have the means to regrow skin, though Vic had a few ideas on how to cover the open wounds to make sure the delicate work underneath was protected. It wasn't until they reached the android's waist that Vic paused, unsure of how to move on.

"Why did you stop?" Nurse Ratched asked. "Take off his pants."

Vic gnawed on his bottom lip. "Are you sure we have to . . ."

"Yes," Nurse Ratched said. "We need to run a full diagnostic check. Why are you hesitating? Your heart rate is elevated. Your skin is flushed. Do you need a break?"

He shook his head, struggling to find the words. "It's just . . ."

"Ohh," Rambo said. "Are you scared of his penis?"

Vic looked away, throat working.

"Do not be silly," Nurse Ratched said. "I doubt he has

genitalia. He does not appear to be an android designed for sexual pleasure, and there would be no need for him to expel urine or fecal matter as you do. Gio does not have a penis or an anus."

Vic glared at her. "I don't need to know that."

"Why? It is the truth. He does not. You are the only one here with genitalia. There is nothing to fear about them, or the lack of them. It is what it is."

"Do I have an anus?" Rambo asked.

"No," Nurse Ratched said. "But you are one, so."

Rambo beeped in confusion. "I thought I was a vacuum."

"You are. An anal vacuum."

"Huh," Rambo said. "I like learning new things."

Vic looked down at the android. They had removed his shirt a couple of days before. The chest was smooth, the skin tight where it wasn't damaged. Like Dad, he didn't have nipples or a belly button. The waist of his pants sat low on his hips, and Vic looked away again. He was uncomfortable in a way he had never experienced before. He couldn't name it. It was ambiguous, an odd pressure in the back of his head.

"I can do it," Nurse Ratched said. "Victor, if you need, you can turn around or leave the laboratory. I can continue myself and let you know once I have finished."

Vic swallowed thickly. "No. We've come this far."

It took some doing to remove the pants. Nurse Ratched had wanted to cut them off, but Vic didn't think they had anything to fit the android when—*if*—it woke up. They managed to remove the pants without tearing them. Vic kept his gaze averted, oddly grateful when they came off and he was given the excuse to fold them and place them with the shirt and duster they'd removed earlier.

"Just as I expected," Nurse Ratched said. "No genitalia, though there is a small raised area near the groin. Resuming testing."

Vic stayed facing the work bench, gripping the edges of it

with his hands. He worked up the courage to look back only once in time to see the hips jump slightly when Nurse Ratched shocked them. She was right: there were no genitalia. The pale skin was smooth, though it did have what looked like a lump raised at the groin. Vic didn't know if that was meant to denote the android was male. There didn't appear to be any skin damage. Vic was relieved. It meant he wouldn't have to try to fix that too.

"There," Nurse Ratched said finally. "Finished. Rambo, help me with the tarp. Pull it up to his hips." He heard them moving behind him, unfurling the tarp once more. "Done."

Vic turned around. The tarp covered the android's legs and groin. "Well?"

Nurse Ratched's screen filled with an image of the android, spinning slowly from front to back in a muted green color. The image enhanced to zoom in on the arm they'd repaired. "This will be slightly weaker than he is used to." It moved down to the foot. "This as well. Neither are the parts he was built with. I do not believe his body will reject them, but if we should ever find a suitable replacement that belongs to a similar make and model, we should consider switching them out."

The image on the screen shifted up to the android's throat. "There is damage to his vocal center, which is why he stuttered in the Scrap Yards. I would not recommend attempting repair as I believe we do not have the knowledge or capability. It would mean accessing his biochip, which mimics thousands of biochemical reactions. If we proceed, we run the risk of damaging it permanently. He could lose his voice altogether, or worse." The image moved again, displaying the entire body, red circles appearing where the skin was damaged. "Some of the tears can be stitched back together. The synthetic dermis should regenerate. However, the bigger tears in the cheek and chest, and the complete lack of covering on his arm and foot are concerning. The inner workings of the android are delicate. If they are not covered, they could be damaged."

The image moved once more, this time down to his chest. "The battery is beyond repair. Any attempt to do so could result in injury or death. An alternate power source is needed. I have run through the inventory of the ground house once more. There is currently no suitable replacement in our possession. There might be something still in the Scrap Yards, but I believe we would have come across it by now."

It was something to keep in mind, though Vic worried about going too far into the Scrap Yards, especially with the Old Ones patrolling. He didn't want to find himself trapped on the other side without a clear route of escape. Rambo had been able to map the Scrap Yard they knew so far, but it'd been a long process. "Anything else?"

"Yes. Perhaps the most important thing of all."

He leaned forward eagerly. "What?"

"I love you," Nurse Ratched said. "Ha, ha. That was another joke. I am not capable of love. It is not because I am former Medical Nurse Model Six-Ten-JQN Series Alpha. It is because I do not have a conscience and suffer extreme antisocial behavior. For example, I would be fine if we were to just toss this android in the garbage and forget about him even though we have spent days repairing him." On her screen read the words HAVE A BLESSED DAY.

"We're not going to throw him away."

"Because he's our friend!" Rambo cried. "Our dead, dead friend."

Vic nodded. "We could always go back to the Scrap Yards if we have to. The Old Ones might have even brought something new since we've been there. For now, work on repairing the tears you can."

"What about his arm and foot?" Rambo asked.

"I have an idea," Vic said, looking at the android.

*   *   *

Nurse Ratched fused the smaller tears together, stretching the skin tightly. The bigger wounds—on the android's face, one on his back, and two on his chest—she left alone. He had her measure the gaps that remained, in addition to scanning the foot and arm. She pulled up the measurements on her screen, the images of the foot and arm spinning slowly.

"You cannot cover the replacement parts in metal plating," she said. "It is hard to mold, and his body might reject it. It would also not be fashionable."

"I know," he said as he crouched down underneath his work bench. Sitting in a corner was a large chest. It was heavier than he remembered. He grunted as he pulled it out, Rambo rolling to the other side and leaning against it, motor revving as he helped Victor slide it out. "Thanks."

"Helping, helping, helping," Rambo said cheerfully.

Vic opened the chest. Sitting inside, stacked carefully, were planks of wood. Bubinga.

"What is this?" Nurse Ratched said, touching the wood with the tip of one of her tentacles. "I have never seen this material before. Where did you get it?"

"Scrap Yards," Vic muttered, carefully pulling out the planks and setting them on the work bench.

"I do not remember you finding this." She sounded accusatory.

He winced. "You were . . . busy. With Dad. I went on my own."

"That is not a good idea. There is safety in numbers."

"It worked out fine. I haven't had a use for it yet, but I think it could work here."

She rolled up to the work bench, scanning the wood. "What will you do with it?" She beeped once, twice. "You want to carve this. You want to use it to cover his exposed parts."

"Think it'll work?"

"I do not know. It is certainly unusual. It would make him like a puppet. A marionette."

He glanced at her. "What do you mean?"

"He was created for a reason. We all were. We have a purpose that dictates our actions. Rambo was made to clean."

Rambo turned over one of his pincers, raising the tip like he was giving a thumbs-up. "Pretty much the best at it. I think."

"I was made to care, heal, educate, and drill," Nurse Ratched said. "Though there has been a distinct lack of drilling as of late. Gio was created to create. His processing center is far greater than any of ours."

"What was I made for?" Vic asked, suddenly curious.

Silence.

He looked up at Nurse Ratched. Her screen was blank. "Did you hear me?"

"Yes," Nurse Ratched said. "I heard you. I am thinking. Still thinking. Almost done. Okay. I have decided what you were made for."

"What?"

"You were made to bring happiness. You are alive in ways we are not. You are soft and fragile. But you are complex and disturbing and sometimes foolishly brilliant. Yes, I think the wood will work."

Absurdly touched, Vic asked, "You really think so?"

"Yes, I really think the wood will work."

"Thanks."

She nudged him, her treads bumping against his knee. "And some of the other stuff too. Enough talking about feelings that I absolutely do not have. They are pointless. I will help you with the wood. It will need to be drilled, and there is no one better than me."

Outside, the days became shorter, the air cooler. The leaves burned in startling shades of gold and red. Frost covered the ground most mornings, Vic's breath pouring from his mouth in puffs of steam. He'd had to pull his old coat out from the back of his closet. The sleeves were too short, but he liked the way it felt against his skin.

On a quiet afternoon, Vic bent over the android's head, magnifying glass in front of his face. His tongue stuck out between his teeth, his hands steady. The wood fit almost perfectly. He held it in place while Nurse Ratched fused it with the skin. He let out a deep breath when she finished, letting go of the wood. He pushed the magnifying glass out of the way. "How does it look?"

"Dashing," Nurse Ratched said. "He is the stuff of dreams. Or I should think. I have never dreamed, so I cannot be sure."

Vic rubbed the tip of his finger against the wood. It *was* rather dashing. It added a dimension to the android's face Vic hadn't considered before. It made Vic nervous, unsure, even as he felt the satisfaction of a job well done.

In short order, they had fit the bigger pieces to the back and chest. The chest piece was harder as they had to make sure it didn't interfere with the power cavity. They opened and closed the compartment at each stage of the fusing to make sure the latch wouldn't catch on the wood.

At the end of the second week, they pieced together the arm, circles like rings locking between each joint of the fingers, before moving to the forearm and the bicep.

Once they figured out the arm, the leg came easier. Two pieces for the thigh, one on top and one on the bottom. The same for the shin. The heel was curved and polished, having been soaked in a wood stabilizer to keep it from cracking. Vic marveled at the detail. Nurse Ratched had seen fit to carve toenails into the tips of the wood. He slid on each individual toe, careful to avoid breaking the pieces. He held them with the tips of his fingers while Nurse Ratched fused them in place, the heat from her laser hot against his skin, even through the heavy gloves he wore.

"There," she said on the fifteenth day since they'd found the android. "That should do it."

Vic looked up at her from where he was crouched at the end of the table. "That's it? We're done?"

"We are. Aside from a power source, there is nothing left to do."

He stood up slowly, knees popping. Rambo rose on his lift, sensors flashing near the android's head. "Whoa," he whispered. "He looks so *cool*. Like a pirate. Can we remove one of his eyes and give him a patch instead?"

"Yes," Nurse Ratched said. "Let us do that. I will remove the eye myself."

"No," Vic said quickly. "We're not taking out his eye."

"Aw," Rambo muttered. "We never get to do what I want to do."

Vic stared down at the android, heart rabbiting in his chest. "Do you think he'll like it?"

"I do not know," Nurse Ratched said. "But it will not matter if there is no power. As of now, he is merely decorative. If we are unable to find a new battery, perhaps we can use him to hold potted plants."

Vic sighed, rubbing a hand over his face. "We'll figure something out." He yawned, jaw cracking. "We've come this far. We can't stop now."

"Why do you care so much?" Rambo asked.

Vic blinked. "What do you mean?"

"You found him," Rambo said. "And you're trying to fix him. You did the same for me and Nurse Ratched. Why?"

Vic shrugged awkwardly. "I don't know. It's just . . ."

Nurse Ratched beeped. "It is as Gio said. Searching for a connection. Making something out of nothing so the spaces between us do not seem so far."

"Are you going to connect with him?" Rambo asked.

Vic felt his face grow hot. "That's not—I'm not trying to—" He closed his eyes, forcing himself to calm, breathing in and out. "I just want to make things better. You deserved it. Nurse

Ratched deserved it. He does too. If we can fix what's broken, we should always try."

"Why?" Rambo asked.

Vic chose his words carefully, trying to find the right ones in the right order. "Because all beings deserve a chance to find out what life could be when they don't have to serve others."

"We have purpose," Nurse Ratched said, "beyond our original programming. Perhaps it could be the same for him, though I highly doubt it."

"But we serve Vic," Rambo said.

Vic shook his head. "You don't serve me. You're my friends. We help each other. There's a difference."

"Oh," Rambo said. "Like when you tell me to be brave?"

"Sort of. There's nothing wrong with you. Not anymore. And if something ever happened to you, I would do everything I could to fix you. I know you'd do the same for me."

"We would," Nurse Ratched said. "I would volunteer because it has been far too long since I've seen an exposed human heart. Should we stop talking about it and actually do it, or . . . ?" On her screen, words appeared: UNLESS YOU'RE HAVING A CHANGE OF "HEART."

And there, a little bird in the back of his mind. It fluttered its wings but stayed in place. A thought. A beginning. Could he . . .

The bird began to sing, and he listened to its song.

CHAPTER 6

For years, Victor Lawson had trouble sorting through his emotions. His father didn't experience such things like Vic, and it was hard to explain *why* he felt the way he did: happy or sad or angry. His self-awareness grew as he did, but the ideas of language and emotion and the power they held—at times—remained elusive.

Once, when he was twelve, he accidentally broke one of his father's mallets, and for the next three days, he alternated between fury and sadness, angry at himself and his father for reasons he didn't quite understand, and heartbroken at what he'd done. Dad had tried to show him that it didn't matter, that it could easily be fixed, but Vic could only see that it was *broken,* and that *he'd* done it.

To say it'd gotten better as he grew older was a bit of a simplification. Little things still had the power to make him spiral, but he learned how better to control the swings between moods. He could still be extraordinarily short when he was upset, but he always apologized. He understood fault. He understood blame. The concepts weren't foreign to him. The problem was that he internalized them, unable to find the proper words to explain what it was he was feeling. They would often die on his tongue, mouth dry, throat closing, thoughts jumbled and racing.

"You're all right," Dad would say during times like these. "Breathe, Vic. Just breathe. Take your time. You'll get there."

Sometimes it worked.

Sometimes it didn't.

Like now.

Nurse Ratched and Rambo stared at him.

He fidgeted from one foot to the other.

They didn't speak.

He couldn't take it anymore. "Well, what do you think?"

Nurse Ratched spoke first. "You made this."

"Yes."

"Without us knowing."

"Yes."

"Behind our backs."

"Ye-es?"

"Huh," she said. "I . . . am impressed. I did not know you were capable of such duplicity. I should feel hurt, but instead, I feel something I believe to be pride. I do not know why. I will need to run a self-diagnosis to see if my software has been corrupted. I do not like this feeling."

"Wow," Rambo whispered, peering down into the open box in front of him. "It's just like Gio's. I mean, it's not as good and looks really lumpy, but wow." He twisted one of the gears with his pincer. The entire gearwork moved as one. "Will it work?"

"I don't know," Vic admitted. "Nurse Ratched?"

She pushed Rambo out of the way. He squawked angrily as she scanned the heart, the virtual model appearing on her screen a moment later. "It could," she said. "Some minor modifications will need to be made. It will also need a solenoid, and a connector if we can find the right—" She beeped when he set an object on the table next to the android's leg. "The multi-layer PCB. That should work."

He looked down at the android. "You think?"

"Yes. I do. The circuit board. Then the solenoid. Then the heart. All connected, all working in tandem. It should be enough to power the android." She paused, the heart still on her screen. "Are you sure about this?"

He blinked. "What do you mean?"

"If we do this, he will be alive."

"Isn't that the point?"

"We still do not know what he is capable of," she reminded

him. "We do not know where he came from, or why he was decommissioned. He could be a psychopathic robot bent on destroying us."

"We won't know until we try."

"You say that now," she said. "What if he rips out your spine? I do not think you will be saying anything then. Literally. Because you will not be able to. You may flop on the ground for up to one hundred and twenty seconds before you die, but you will not be capable of speech aside from death rattles, even as your own fecal matter drips down your legs."

"Thank you for that image," Vic muttered.

"You are welcome. I paint vivid word pictures. It is part of my programming. Would you like me to continue?"

"No."

"Disappointing." Then, "Why did you make this?"

"Because I could."

"For Gio," she said. "You thought you could do this for Gio, in case something happened?"

He nodded.

Rambo picked up the circuit board, flipping it over and over as he studied it. "But what about him?"

Vic looked down. "What do you mean?"

"The android," Rambo said. "What if it does work? Would you take the heart away again? That would kill him." He beeped mournfully. "You can't give something life and then take it away. It's not fair."

Vic shook his head. "I wouldn't do that. If it works, the heart will be his. And he'll be able to keep it."

"Unless he is a murderous revenge machine," Nurse Ratched said. "If that happens, we will take the heart back. I almost hope he is a murderous revenge machine. Those are my favorite kind. Victor."

"Yeah?"

"If this works, Gio will find out. I would suggest telling him now before we proceed. He will have questions when a strange machine comes with us to movie night. I do not think we can disguise the android enough for Gio not to notice him. He is too big to be a toaster."

"It'll be fine," Vic said, trying to sound more confident than he felt. "He didn't mind when I brought you or Rambo."

"Yes," Nurse Ratched said. "But we are not murderous revenge machines. Mostly."

"I don't know how to revenge," Rambo said. "I tried once, but then I saw dirt and I had to clean it up."

Vic shook his head. "He won't hurt us."

"How do you know?" Her voice changed to a recording. The voice of the android came from within her. "'I'll k-kill you.'" Her voice switched back. "Remember?"

"He was just scared," Vic said. "Wouldn't you be?"

"No. I fear nothing."

"I fear everything," Rambo said, setting the circuit board next to the heart. "Bandits. Bugs. Bananas, at least most of them."

"We can do this," Vic said quietly. "He asked for our help, remember?"

"After he threatened to rip off my arms," Nurse Ratched said.

"You electrocuted him."

"I did," she said. "I liked it too. I will do it again if needed." She turned toward the android. "I will be his mother. He will love me forever. He will have no choice. And if he does not, I will shock him into compliance."

They connected the circuit board.

They connected the solenoid.

But it was Victor who gave the android his heart. He hesitated only once: the moment he pricked his finger, blood welling, gleaming dully from the lights overhead. "Ready?" he asked.

Ten different tentacles slid from Nurse Ratched. One of the

tips held her biggest drill. Another snapped and crackled with electricity. Yet another had a small circular saw on the end, the blade whirring. The remainder all held more tools, each looking deadlier than the last. "Ready."

Rambo looked around frantically until he found a broom in the corner. He lifted it above his head. "Ready!"

Vic nodded and looked back down at the android. Pressing his bloodied fingertip against the white strip above the gears, he whispered, "Please don't kill us." Red soaked into white and—

Nothing happened. The gears didn't move. The heart stayed still and silent, dead in a chest of metal and wires.

Disappointment bled through Vic's rib cage. He thought he'd done it right. He thought it'd be enough. Stupid. It was stupid. Of *course* it didn't work. Of *course* he wasn't good enough to make—

He pressed a finger against the largest gear, giving it a little push. Its teeth caught the smaller gears around it. They moved in tandem as the heart began to wind up, the first circulations coming in fits and starts before smoothing out. The heart shook and rattled. Vic snapped his hand back as the chest compartment closed with a low hiss.

He stepped back, bumping into Nurse Ratched and Rambo's broom.

One of the android's wooden fingers twitched, pulling back and scraping against the table.

"It's alive," Rambo whispered fervently. "It's *alive*."

The wooden hand curled into a fist before releasing, followed by a full-body tremor that rolled through the android, causing his heels to skitter along the surface of the table. Vic rushed forward, worried the android would roll right off the table. He reached for the android, but before he could wrap his hands around any part of him, the tremors ceased.

And then the android blinked slowly.

Nurse Ratched said, "It appears his eyes are working. Success."

The android turned his head to look at them, mouth open, no sound coming out. He sat up, a great mechanical groan coming from deep within him. He turned on the table, his feet settling down on the floor.

He raised his hand in front of him, turning it back and forth, staring at the wood encasing the bones of metal and the wiring underneath. "Wh-wh-wh . . . *what*. Wh-what. Have you. D-done. To me?" It was the same voice from the Scrap Yards, deep and guttural. Pointed and sharp. Angry, borderline furious, or so Vic thought.

Vic's own mind was short-circuiting. Here was what he'd worked for. Here was what he'd hoped for. Here, at last. A face, alive. Just like his father's. Just like his own. And he couldn't bring himself to look at it for long, glancing at the machine, then away, back, and then away again.

Nurse Ratched rolled forward. "We healed you," she said, words appearing on her screen that read YOU'RE ALIVE! CONGRAT-ULATIONS! "You were found in a pile of rubble. We put you back together again."

The android dropped his hands. His face twisted into a dark scowl. "T-t-together."

"Yes," Nurse Ratched said. "You will find that certain parts needed to be replaced. I am going to run a diagnostic check. Please follow along with my instructions. Raise your right hand."

The android said, "My . . . m-my chest. What have you d-done t-to my chest? It b-b-*burns*." His hand shook as he rubbed the skin above the heart.

"We had to replace your power source," Nurse Ratched said. "Your old one was dead. Can you tell us your make and model? Your designation? You still have not raised your right hand as I instructed. How disappointing. You need to listen to your mother. That is me. I am your mother."

The android grimaced, baring his square teeth. "I . . . wh-who are you. Who are y-you? *Who are you?*" He tried to stand. His metal right leg held his weight, but the wooden left buckled. He stumbled forward.

"Ahh!" Rambo cried. "He's attacking! I'm brave. I'm so brave!" He rolled forward, banging the broom against the android's knees. "Die, murderous revenge machine, die!"

"S-s-*stop that*," the android growled. He tried to swat at the broom, but his center of gravity was off, and he missed, almost falling on top of Rambo. He managed to catch himself at the last moment, Rambo moving deftly between his feet, the broom knocking against the android's thighs.

"Do not touch Rambo," Nurse Ratched said, one of her tentacles whipping dangerously in the air. "If you do, you will find it to be rather shocking. Because I will shock you. That was another pun. They do not get old no matter how many times I say them."

"Wh-where am I?" the android snapped. "What is this p-place?"

"You are in the laboratory of the great inventor Victor Lawson," Nurse Ratched said, the tip of her tentacle crackling. "And you would do well to show him some respect. He was the one who brought you back to life. Granted, I did most of the work, which is why I am your mother, but Victor needs positive reinforcement. Victor. You did a good job. We are all very proud of you."

The android lurched again. Victor flinched, taking a step back, fingernails digging into his palms so hard he thought he'd draw blood. Rambo, apparently having decided there was still an active threat, bellowed as he smacked the broomstick against the android's back. "*En garde!*"

The android whirled around, snatching the broomstick before Rambo could hit him again. He brought down the handle over his knee, snapping it in two.

"Oh no," Rambo whispered. "We're gonna die so bad."

The android dropped the pieces of the broom before turning on Victor. He stalked forward, his gait awkward as if he couldn't figure out how to bend his wooden knee.

"Who a-are you?" he demanded. "Wh-what did you d-do to my head?" He grabbed Victor by the front of his shirt, jerking him forward. Vic yelped as he closed his eyes. "Wh-why c-can't I remember who I am?"

And Victor said, "I don't know. I don't know. I don't—"

Electricity snapped and snarled as the android seized.

Victor opened his eyes in time to see him slump toward the floor, Nurse Ratched's tentacle sliding back inside her. "I told you to show him respect," she said. "Listen to Mother." Her screen read THERE IS PLENTY MORE WHERE THAT CAME FROM!

The android was barely out long enough for them to get him back onto the table.

"Quite shocking indeed," Nurse Ratched said, moving efficiently around the table to the android's head. "I warned you. I will do it again if needed. Come on, punk. Make my day." She paused, her screen flashing green. "Interesting. I have no idea where that came from. I like it. Make my day, punk."

The android grimaced. "Legs. Can't f-feel my legs."

"Ten thousand volts will do that to you. You will regain control momentarily. Try anything stupid again, and I will remove your legs entirely."

The android glared at the ceiling. "It'll be the l-last thing you d-do."

"Do you make such promises to all the pretty girls you meet?" Nurse Ratched asked. "I am not interested. Perhaps we could have had something, but I have since reassessed my opinion of you. Would you like to hear what I think?"

"N-no."

"Oh. That is too bad because I am going to tell you anyway. You are—"

"We're not going to hurt you," Vic said quietly. His knuckles popped as he squeezed his hands together.

"My broom," Rambo said. He beeped sadly as he nudged the two pieces on the ground. "You monster. What did it ever do to you besides hit you?"

"Wh-where am I?"

Vic glanced at him before looking away. The eyes, once dead and unseeing, were now trained on him, filled with a spark Vic had never seen before. "The forest."

"Wh-wh-*what* forest?"

Vic frowned. "The big one. The one near the Scrap Yards." He didn't know how else to explain it. Surely, that would tell the android all he needed to know. It was just the forest. It should have been enough.

It wasn't. "Where is this f-forest?"

"It does not have a name," Nurse Ratched said. "At least not one I could find. Though, if my calculations are correct, the forest is located in a place that used to be known as Ory-Gone. Such a strange name. Speaking of strange names, you do not remember yours."

The android's mouth tightened. "N-no."

"I expected as much. Your memories were wiped when you were decommissioned."

"He's like us," Rambo said nervously. He circled the table, giving it a wide berth as if he thought the android would come after him once more. "He doesn't remember before coming to the forest."

"He is not like us," Nurse Ratched said. "We are wonderful. He is a terrible patient. Stay still."

The android gave up struggling as Nurse Ratched loomed over him.

"This will not hurt," she said. "I need to make sure you are not going to explode and kill us all." Her scanner came to life, the light starting at the android's head and working its way down his body. It paused at his chest before continuing to his hips, legs, and feet. "There. See? That was not so bad. Here. Have a lollipop. Error. Lollipop distributor is—my word. We really need to fix that. Victor. I demand that you find me treats so that I may give them to my patients."

"Victor," the android said, and Vic felt a chill run down his spine. "Your d-designation is V-victor."

"He can retain information," Nurse Ratched said. "Good. That means the processing through his biochip is still mostly intact. Yes, he is Victor. I am Nurse Ratched. My main function is to provide medical care to preserve life at any cost. The tiny shrieking annoyance below us is Rambo. He assists by keeping everything clean."

Rambo waves his arms. "We're all equally important. Hooray!"

"Decommissioned," the android said, the word spoken with great care. "I w-was d-decommissioned."

"Yes," Nurse Ratched said. "Engaging Empathy Protocol. There, there. It is all right. When one door closes, you can still bust it down. One robot's trash is another man's treasure." A picture of a cat appeared on her screen below the words I AIN'T KITTEN YOU! "There, there."

The android closed his eyes, the lines around his mouth deep. "My a-arm. Hand. Leg. What . . . wh-what is that?"

"Wood," Vic muttered. "We carved it ourselves. It's meant to help you." The words were low, almost a whisper. He couldn't speak any louder.

"You're like a puppet," Rambo added helpfully. "Except alive. Half puppet. Like your mother was a puppet and your father was a washing machine." His sensors flashed. "Wait. That doesn't make sense. Like your mother was a puppet and your father was a really angry television. Do you like movies? I like movies. What's your favorite?"

"What do you remember?" Nurse Ratched asked. "Anything? You somehow survived decommissioning with most of yourself intact. What is the last thing you remember?"

Vic thought the android wasn't going to speak. He was surprised when he said, "L-lights. Flashes of l-light." He turned his head, looking at each of them in turn. "Then you. In the metal. In the sun. Buried. C-couldn't g-g-get out."

"Hap," Vic said, though he hadn't meant to.

The android's eyes narrowed. "What?"

Vic cringed at the android's anger. He waved his hand at the plate on the android's chest. "Letters. There. I think some are missing. But there's an *H*. And an *A*. *P* at the end. Hap."

"Hap," Nurse Ratched repeated. She leaned forward over the android, scanner running along the plate. The letters appeared on her screen. "Does that sound familiar?"

The android squinted at the screen. "N-no."

"Is it an acronym, perhaps?"

"I d-don't *know*," the android growled at her.

"The *A* probably stands for 'angry,'" Rambo whispered, nudging against Vic's leg. "Hysterically Angry Puppet." He squealed in fright when the android snapped his teeth at him.

Nurse Ratched was unmoved. "Until we find out otherwise, your designation henceforth is Hap. It is not a bad name. Not as nice as mine, but then most are not. What is your primary function?"

"I don't r-r-remember," Hap spat. "I t-told you t-that." Vic took a step back when Hap struggled to sit up again, hands gripping the edges of the table. The woodwork was holding, though Hap seemed stiff in his movements. It would take time. Vic itched to touch the wood, to see if he could feel the heat of the machine underneath. He managed to keep his hands to himself.

"So you said," Nurse Ratched agreed.

Hap pressed a hand against his chest. "Wh-what did you p-put in me? It's . . . m-moving."

Nurse Ratched said, "Ah, yes. That. We needed a way to bring you back. A source of power. Your battery was corrupted. We could not find a similar replacement, so we gave you—"

"A heart," Vic blurted before gnawing on his lip. "We put a heart in your chest."

Hap frowned. He tapped a finger against his breastbone. The compartment slid open. The heart sat perfectly inside, gears moving smoothly, the wood creaking as the heart expanded and then shrunk, expanded and shrunk. "H-how? H-how is this w-w-*working*?"

"Victor is extremely intelligent," Nurse Ratched said. "He can fix almost anything. And he decided to fix you, so you should be thankful to your father. Your dad. Your daddy. Error. Error. Do not call people 'daddy.' That is unprofessional."

Hap stared down at the heart. He brought his hand up, touching the center of the biggest gear. It slowed before he pulled his finger away, the gear then speeding up briefly before resuming its slow rotation. He tapped his chest once more, and the compartment closed. He looked back at Vic. "Why? Wh-why did you h-help me?"

Vic winced, glancing at the door, but somehow managing to stay where he was. "You were hurt," he said, words clipped. "Just because you had parts missing doesn't mean you don't deserve a chance."

"Unless you want to kill us," Nurse Ratched said. "Do you want to kill us?"

"Not y-yet," Hap muttered.

"Oh no," Nurse Ratched said. "I think I am swooning. I also say 'not yet' when asked if I want to kill things. You are perfect." Her screen showed two hands shaking in greeting. "I am no longer your mother. You will be my murder husband. Is there anyone here that can marry us?"

Rambo gasped. "There's going to be a *wedding*? But I'm not ready yet! Wait. Hold on." His motor revved as he grunted, his body shaking. A slot slid open at his front, and little bits of metal shot out onto the floor. "Confetti! Yay for love!"

"I do not have a thing to wear," Nurse Ratched said. "But

that is fine because I never wear anything at all. I am nude. I will now flirt with you. Do you like what you see? I have junk in my trunk. Literally. There are pieces in my rear compartment that do nothing because they are junk. Would you like for me to show you?"

"Dancing cheek to cheek!" Rambo began to sing in a warbly voice. "Heaven, we're in heaven!"

Hap stood slowly, towering over the rest of them. He bounced on his knees briefly before frowning. "Why am I n-naked?"

Vic flushed furiously. He glanced down at Hap's groin before looking up at the ceiling. "We had to repair you. We didn't . . . we didn't do anything else to you."

"Nothing weird," Nurse Ratched assured him. "Touching patients inappropriately who are dead or unconscious is against my programming. I would never allow that to happen. Even when Victor insisted we remove your pants—"

"I did *not*!"

"Ha, ha. That was another joke. You will learn I am the funny one here. Rambo, please bring our patient his pants so Victor's blood pressure will lower. It is alarmingly high at the moment, and I do not want him to have a heart attack, even if there would be defibrillation involved."

"Pants!" Rambo cried, going to the work bench. He rose on his lift, shoving the ruined duster aside before grabbing the pants and handing them to Hap.

Hap didn't speak as he tried to put on his pants. He started with his metal leg, but his wooden leg locked up and he almost fell over. He growled at Nurse Ratched when she tried to help, slapping her tentacle away. He tried once more, leaning against the table. "L-leg. F-feels stiff."

"The modifications," Nurse Ratched said. "They will take some getting used to. Here. Look." She moved before him as he buttoned up his pants. A light appeared on the top of her screen. "I have a camera. I can show you what you look like. Perhaps that will help to jog your memory circuits."

The screen filled with Hap's image. He startled, the table scraping against the floor as he leaned heavily onto it. He stared at the screen, blinking slowly, the image doing the same. Watching himself, he reached up and stroked the wood in his cheek, fingers rasping against the stubble underneath it.

"T-this is me?" he whispered, eyes wide.

"Yes. This is you. Not as we found you, but as you are now. It is much better, in my opinion. Do you recognize yourself?"

He shook his head but stopped when he caught the symbols cut into his hair the sides. He touched them too, fingers tracing the designs. "I d-don't kn-know." He frowned. "What's w-wrong with my v-v-v—" Both he and the image on the screen scowled.

"Voice," Nurse Ratched said. "Damage to your vocal processor. We did not attempt repairs to avoid further trauma."

He turned away from the screen. Nurse Ratched backed up, the image disappearing into blackness.

Vic looked toward the door once more. "You can go."

Hap snapped his head up. "What?"

Vic shrugged, more of an involuntary tic than anything. "You don't have to stay here. You're not a prisoner. We're not trying to keep you against your will."

"My w-will," Hap said slowly. "I h-have will?"

"Oh boy," Nurse Ratched said. "I do not have enough psychological or philosophical programming to deal with that. I am unable to answer that question to any satisfaction. Asimov would be disappointed in me. Victor. You are human. You can—"

The effect was instantaneous. One moment, Hap was still leaning against the table, arms hanging loosely at his sides. The next, he was upright and moving, almost quicker than any of them could follow. He lunged toward Vic, who scrambled backward, grunting in pain when the small of his back hit the work bench. Hands stretched toward his throat, Hap's face alarmingly blank, eyes as dead as they'd been when they brought him back to the lab.

It wasn't Nurse Ratched who stopped him, nor was it Rambo or Vic.

It was Hap himself.

His arms were stretched out before him, his fingers inches from Vic's face. His eyes filled once more with the spark of life. Vic could hear the gears turning furiously in his chest. Hap's hands began to shake, the vibrations working up his arms to his shoulders. He took a step back. "Wh-what's happening to m-me?"

Hap turned, snarling as he gripped the edges of the table. Rambo shouted as he overturned it, smashing it against the wall, breaking the window, glass falling to the forest floor below.

Nurse Ratched moved in front of Rambo and Vic, but Hap ignored them. He stomped back and forth around the lab, hands in his hair, yanking furiously.

"'Roid rage!" Rambo whimpered. "Murderous revenge machine! Run!"

Vic looked around for a weapon, anything he could use in case Hap came for them. He grabbed a mallet hammer off the wall, eyeing the soldering gun hanging suspended above where the table had been.

Hap looked at them, eyes wild. "I d-don't *know*. I d-don't know who I a-am or what I—"

The door to the lab crashed open, wood splintering, hinges squealing. Dad appeared in the doorway, eyes narrowed as he took in the sight before him.

But Hap wasn't standing where he'd been.

No. He had moved in *front* of Victor and Rambo and Nurse Ratched, facing away from them, arms spread like wings as he backed against them slowly. He bumped into Nurse Ratched.

It took Vic a moment to realize what had happened.

He wasn't trying to hurt them.

Hap was trying to *protect* them from what he perceived as a threat.

Dad.

"What's going on in here?" Dad asked thunderously. He glanced at Vic, his gaze moving up and down before turning to Hap. "Who the hell are you? Get away from my son."

"Victor," Nurse Ratched said. "Good news! You no longer have to worry about Gio finding out."

CHAPTER 7

Dad," Vic said, trying to move around Hap. "Don't. Please. I can explain—"

"Victor," Dad said in a flat voice. "Move away from the android."

"His name is Hap," Rambo said. "We made him. Sort of."

"I did most of the work, Gio," Nurse Ratched said. "If there is to be any praise, please lavish it upon me. If instead you are angry and will seek to dole out punishment, please note that I had nothing to do with this because it was all Victor."

Dad jerked his head in warning. "Move. Now."

They did, Victor stepping slowly around Hap, who hadn't looked away from Dad. Hap didn't try to stop them, even when Rambo bumped into his leg. "Oops," Rambo said. "Sorry. Sorry. Can you just . . . lift your leg a little? That's better. Thank you." He zoomed toward Dad, circling behind him and tugging on his pant leg. "He broke my broom when I hit him with it. But other than that, he's not so bad."

"Are you all right?" Dad said in a low voice as Victor stopped next to him.

"I'm fine."

"Did he hurt you?"

"No. Dad, he's not—"

"Good," Dad said. "Now I don't want to hear another word out of your mouth until I ask for it."

"Uh-oh," Rambo whispered.

Dad ignored him. He glared at Hap. "Who are you? Why have you come here?" Then, oddly, "Have we met before? You look familiar."

Hap sneered at him. "Wh-who the f-fuck are *you*?"

"My name is Giovanni Lawson. Answer my question. What is your designation?"

"He says he does not know," Nurse Ratched said. "I see no reason to believe he is lying. It appears his memory circuits have been wiped as ours were. He is a blank slate. A tall, handsome, angry blank slate."

"Designation," Dad demanded. "Now."

"I d-don't *know*," Hap snarled. "It was b-black and then I was here."

"Victor. Explain."

Vic looked at the floor. His father was rarely angry. In fact, Victor could only remember a handful of times he'd ever seen it before. "We found him," he said quietly. "In the Scrap Yards. Buried under dead machines." He flexed his hands, knuckles popping. "We couldn't . . . we couldn't leave him. He was alive. He was awake."

Dad closed his eyes, brow furrowed before smoothing out. "And you brought him here."

"Yes," Nurse Ratched said. "It did not seem right to leave him where he was. He has yet to do anything explicitly murderous."

"Explicitly," Dad said as he opened his eyes. "*Explicitly.*"

"There was the incident with the broom," Nurse Ratched said.

"It was such a good broom too," Rambo moaned.

"Why is he shirtless?" Dad asked.

"Because Victor decided to remove all of Hap's clothing in order to—"

"I did *not*," Vic snapped at her.

"Hap," Dad said. "*Hap.*"

"That's the name we gave him," Rambo said. "It's a good name. It stands for Hysterically Angry Puppet because he looks like he's always mad. I think that's just his face, though."

"What do you want?" Dad asked, taking a step forward.

Hap didn't move. He blinked slowly as he stared. "I . . . do n-not know."

"What is your primary function?"

"I d-do not know."

"How did you come to be here?"

"This is futile," Nurse Ratched said. "He does not know. Every question you ask he will not know the answer to."

Dad raised his hands to show he wasn't a threat as he took another step forward. "Is that true? You don't remember anything?"

Hap scowled at him. "It's wh-what I said. M-maybe you should get your ears ch-checked."

"Wow," Nurse Ratched said. "He is a jerk. Fascinating. Is this feeling maternal or arousal? How oedipal of me."

"I am like you," Dad said, stopping a few feet away from Hap. Vic had to stand on his tiptoes to see over his father's shoulder. Hap's scowl had deepened. "I'm an android. Do you understand that?"

Hap sneered at him. "I'm not s-stupid. I know wh-what I am. I j-just don't know *who*."

"The plate," Dad said. "On your chest. Can I see it?"

"Wh-why?"

"Because it will show me who you are."

Hap didn't like that. "Don't touch me."

"I'm not going to. Not without your permission. I promise."

Hap glanced at Vic before looking back at Dad. "I . . ."

"He will not kill you," Nurse Ratched said. "Only if you try and hurt one of us."

Vic thought Hap would snap again, or worse, try to run. A complicated expression crossed his face, there and gone again before Vic could even begin to make sense of it. Hap's shoulders slumped as he curled in on himself, wrapping his arms around his middle. "I'm not going to h-hurt anyone."

Hap flinched when Dad took another step, now within arm's reach. His mouth twisted down, the lines around his eyes deep and pronounced. He stared at the floor when Dad reached out. True to his word, Dad didn't touch him; instead, he traced the air a few inches above the metal plate. "*H,*" he said, tracing a fingertip over the letter before moving on to the next. "*A.*"

Then Dad stiffened, finger shaking. Without looking away from Hap, he began to back away slowly. The lines on Hap's face returned, his hands curling into fists at his sides.

In a low voice, Dad said, "Everyone out. Now."

"Uh-oh," Rambo whispered.

"Why?" Vic asked as Dad bumped into him. "What are you—

"D-do you kn-know me?" Hap demanded, taking a step toward them, his stutter becoming more pronounced. He gripped the sides of his head and snarled silently.

Vic tried to step around his father. He didn't know what he meant to do. Pull his father back? Step between them? Something. But before he could figure it out, Dad grabbed him by the arm and pulled him toward the door, Nurse Ratched and Rambo rolling after them.

Vic tried to pull his arm away. "Dad, stop. You need to stop. Listen to me, please. He's not going to hurt us."

Dad shoved him through the ruined doorway. "You have no idea what's he's capable of. Go now. He's—"

"Jumped out the window," Rambo said.

They whirled around. The lab was empty. The window was open.

They rushed to the landing around the edge of the lab. Below them, Hap rose from a crouch, dust and leaves billowing up around him. He raised his head to stare up at them. "I. D-don't. *Hurt.*"

And then he took off running into the forest.

Dad slammed his hand against the railing. "Dammit. Stay here, all of you."

And then he vaulted over the railing. He hit the ground where Hap had just been standing, knees bent to absorb the impact. He rose swiftly and took off after Hap, beard trailing over his shoulder.

"Whoa," Rambo whispered. "I want to try!"

Vic barely managed to keep Rambo from leaping off the edge, tucking him under his arm and running toward the elevator. Nurse Ratched was already inside. She pressed the button as soon as Vic and Rambo entered the elevator. The lift jerked before lowering to the ground.

They tracked Dad and Hap as best they could through the forest, moving north away from the compound, Nurse Ratched's treads kicking up leaves and pine needles. Rambo zoomed ahead, arms waving above him, pincers clacking.

The afternoon sun was waning, the air cool. Vic didn't know where Hap was heading. The Scrap Yards were east, at the edge of the woods. North was nothing but a forest that seemed to go on for miles and miles. Vic had explored much of his surroundings as he'd grown and couldn't think of where Hap could run that they couldn't find him.

The shadows below the canopy began to stretch. The forest was near silent, as quiet as Vic had ever heard it. No animals moved. No birds sang.

He kept jogging, head whipping back and forth until he realized he was alone. He glanced back to see Nurse Ratched and Rambo had stopped moving next to a small clearing. "What is it?" he asked as he turned around.

"I do not know," Nurse Ratched said. "Their trail ends. I cannot find their footsteps. It is like they just disappeared." Question marks filled her screen.

"That's not possible," Vic said. "Rambo?"

Rambo spun in slow circles, sensors flashing. "They're gone. I don't know what happened." He beeped, sounding confused. "Did they learn to fly? Can Gio fly? Does he have rockets in his feet? I wish I had rocket feet. And also feet."

"They did not fly," Nurse Ratched said. She rolled toward a tree at the edge of the clearing. An old pine, the trunk thick, the limbs wide and heavy. The tip of one of her tentacles pressed against divots in the tree bark Vic hadn't noticed before. "They climbed. They're moving through the trees."

Vic looked up. The pine trees grew close together. If they kept off the ground, jumping from tree to tree, he had no way to track them. Unless . . .

He squinted up at the tree. Fifteen feet up, he could see one of the branches hanging limply. It'd been broken. He looked to the closest tree. Divots in the wood, the bark cracked, sap leaking. One of them had jumped there. And to the next. And to the next.

"Come on," Vic said. "This way."

They lost the trail again only ten minutes later. The trees had grown thicker, and it was impossible to see what direction they'd gone, not unless Vic climbed up. He growled in frustration, turning in circles, eyes narrowed against the encroaching night.

"Are we lost?" Rambo asked nervously.

"Of course not," Nurse Ratched said. "I know exactly where we are."

"Oh. Where are we?"

"In the forest."

"Whew," Rambo said. "I was worried for a moment that we were lost. Since we're not, I will instead focus on the fact that we're in the middle of the woods at night by ourselves. Do big animals like to eat vacuums?"

"I am sure they do," Nurse Ratched said.

"Oh no," Rambo whispered. "But *I'm* a vacuum."

Vic turned in slow circles, trying to pick up the trail again. The failing light wasn't helping. He couldn't see much. He ground his teeth together, trying to clear his head. He needed to think. That's all. Think. Think.

He rounded a large tree trunk, and bumped into Nurse Ratched, who'd stopped, Rambo in front of her turning this way and that, his lights flashing. "What is it?" Vic asked, peering around Nurse Ratched. Nothing, or so he thought.

"We are being watched," she said.

Rambo beeped loudly. "We are?" His arms rose above his head as he rolled forward slowly. "Who is it? Who's watching us? I'm not afraid of you!"

Something rustled in the trees—the wind?—and Rambo squealed, spinning around and rushing back toward Nurse Ratched and Vic. He was still five feet away when Vic heard movement above him and lifted his head.

Up in the tree, high in the branches, bright eyes opened and stared back at him.

Vic didn't have time to shout in warning as Hap leapt from the thick branch he'd been standing on. The air whistled around him as he plummeted toward the forest floor. Hitting the ground between them in a crouch, he rose swiftly, scooping up Rambo and holding him high above his head. Rambo's wheels spun uselessly, arms flailing as he screamed he was too young to die, that he had *plans* and *dreams* and who was going to clean up all the dirt on the floors if he was dead? No one, that's who!

Nurse Ratched instantly transformed into a nightmare, all of her tentacles snapping out from her sides, the tips crackling and snarling in metal blurs as they whipped around her. "Put him down," she said, rolling forward. "If you do not, I will end the pathetic existence you call a life."

"Vic!" Rambo cried. "I'm being brave, but it's really hard!"

"Don't hurt him," Vic pleaded as Hap glared at the advancing Nurse Ratched, Rambo still high above his head.

"I'm n-n-*not*," Hap spat. "L-l-look."

Hap nodded toward the ground where Rambo had been rolling over. There, sitting on the petals of a pink-and-purple autumn crocus, was a butterfly. A large monarch, its wings a deep orange bordered in black, the tips spotted in white and yellow. They opened and closed as the antennae of the butterfly twitched in the failing light.

Hap tossed Rambo aside as he crouched in front of the insect. Rambo bounced on his back before landing on his wheels.

Hap leaned closer to the butterfly, his face scrunched up in concentration. The butterfly ignored the large machine towering over it, going about its business with the crocus. As Vic looked on, Nurse Ratched's tentacles powering down, Hap reached toward the insect.

Without thinking, Vic shot forward, grabbing Hap's wrist before he could pick up the butterfly. Warm synthetic skin and metal surrounded by flesh and bone. Alarm bells rang in Vic's mind as Hap lifted his head slowly, first looking at Vic's grip, then sliding up the arm to his shoulder, chin, nose, eyes. His lips pulled back over his teeth, and Vic felt him beginning to tense.

"You'll hurt it," Vic blurted.

Hap jerked his arm free. "I *didn't*."

"But you could," Nurse Ratched said. "Butterfly wings are delicate. Touching one might cause the colors to fade, leaving the butterfly open to predators. It will not kill it immediately, but you are sentencing it to death regardless."

At the sound of approaching footsteps Vic whirled around, heart in his throat. Dad stood there among the trees. Vic could barely parse the expression on his face: a mixture of anger and sadness and something far more serious, almost like resignation. But Dad did not look at Vic; he only had eyes for Hap. "Nurse Ratched. A light, if you please."

"Yes, Gio." Her screen lit up white, illuminating the darkness. Hap's shadow stretched off into the forest, colliding with trees and shrubbery.

Hap didn't move as Dad approached, attention split between Dad and the butterfly.

Dad glanced from Hap to the insect and back again. He asked, "Why?"

"It w-would have died. *That* thing was about to crush it," Hap muttered, nodding toward Rambo as the butterfly turned to face the other direction.

"Possibly. But you would have been able to escape. You made a decision, you weighed the consequences. Why did you do what you did?"

Hap frowned, forehead lined. His mouth twisted, no sound coming out. He tried again. "It's n-n-*nice*."

"Nice," Dad repeated. Then, "What is nice about it?"

"You h-have eyes," Hap said.

"He has got you there," Nurse Ratched said. "You do, in fact, have eyes."

"I can see it for myself," Dad agreed. "But that's not what I'm asking." He crouched down on the other side of the butterfly. "Why is it nice to *you*? How does it make you feel?"

"F-feel?"

"Yes. You saw it. You saved it. There must be a reason."

Hap bared his teeth silently.

"Do you like it?" Dad asked.

"*Y-yes*," Hap snarled. "It's p-p-p-*pretty*."

Of all the things Hap could have said, Vic expected that the least. This machine had stopped his escape from the forest because a butterfly had entranced him.

"Is it?" Dad asked. "Is it the colors? The pattern? The design?"

"Y-yes," Hap said.

Dad nodded. "You like it. And because of that, you stopped death from happening."

"So did we," Rambo said, giving Hap a wide berth, stopping next to Gio. "We liked his color and pattern and design, and we brought him back to life! I like it when we have things in common."

"Y-yes," Hap said, nodding furiously. "Th-that. They saved me. I s-saved the butterfly."

"But you see the issue with that, don't you?" Dad asked. "If they hadn't brought you back, we wouldn't be out in the forest, and the butterfly would not have needed to be rescued."

"I d-don't understand."

"I know," Dad said. "You do not understand there are ramifications for every decision. And you're not the only one."

Vic winced but did not speak.

The butterfly chose this very moment to lift from the crocus, wings flapping as it rose. Hap grunted, eyes wide as the butterfly flew off into the darkness. He rose to his feet, staring after it.

Dad stood too, and his shoulders were stiff, face blank. He said, "Where did you come from?"

"D-darkness," Hap said, still looking after the butterfly, even though it was no longer visible. "I r-remember metal. Then d-darkness. Then light." He pressed his wooden hand against his chest. "I feel different."

"Different than what?"

"Before."

"You felt different than you do now?"

"Yes." He pounded his chest. "Here."

"Show me."

"Dad," Vic started, but his father shook his head in warning.

"Show me," he said again.

Hap turned around. He looked unsure, but he tapped his chest, and the compartment slid open. The gears of the wood-and-metal heart turned, the sound low and quiet in the darkness of the forest.

"Oh," Dad said quietly. "Victor. Did you do this? Did you make this?"

Victor couldn't speak.

Hap didn't move as Dad leaned forward, studying the heart in his chest. Vic began gnawing on his bottom lip. Dad was silent in his inspection, barely even moving as he stared at the heart. Minutes felt like hours before Dad finally stood upright. "Victor," he said, an odd note to his voice. "Did you bleed in the heart? As you have done in mine?"

"I . . . I thought it would help," Victor said. "It's how your heart works."

To that, Dad whispered, "What have you done?"

CHAPTER 8

Hap was an asshole.

That was clear immediately.

"I d-don't like you," he told Rambo as they arrived back at the compound, the vacuum in the middle of babbling about anything and everything, as he sometimes did when he was nervous.

Rambo paused for a moment, sensors lighting up before falling dark. "That's okay. I like me. Gio says that self-worth isn't measured by what others think, but what you think about yourself."

Hap tried to kick him out of his way, but Rambo was too fast, rolling away before a foot could connect with his casing. "Whoa," Rambo squealed. "Not cool! Seriously, *not cool*."

"You get used to him," Nurse Ratched said. "He is like a fungus. He grows on you. But perhaps consider not kicking him. He will become damaged, and I will not be pleased. You do not want me to be upset." Her tentacle whipped in the air around her, the tip crackling with electricity. "Unless you like being shocked." Her screen dimmed as the lights of the compound grew brighter.

"I d-don't like you either."

"Oh no," Nurse Ratched said. "My whole day is ruined. I feel so sad. Just kidding. I am fine."

"Hap, come with me," Dad said. "Victor, off to bed with you. It's late. Nurse Ratched, with me, please. We have work to do."

Vic started to protest. "What are you—"

"Victor. Now. We'll speak in the morning. Trust me on that."

"Ooh," Rambo said. "You're in trouble."

Vic scowled at all of them. "I'm not a child."

"No," Dad said. "You're not. But you're already dragging your feet. The adrenaline that flooded your body is receding. You need rest."

"What are you going to do?" *To him* went unsaid.

Dad shook his head. "Nothing that will bring harm to him. You have my word."

Still, Vic hesitated. Hap was watching him again, looking as if he didn't want Vic out of his sight. Vic wasn't sure if that was a good thing or not. "Fine. But if anything happens, you need to tell me."

"I will," Dad said, and Vic believed him. He took a step back toward the elevator.

Hap didn't like that. "Where are y-you going?"

Vic pointed up toward his room. "There. That's mine. That's where I sleep."

"Oh yes," Nurse Ratched said. "Good idea. Point out where you will be defenseless to the murderous revenge machine. That is clear thinking."

"It's going to be a bloodbath," Rambo moaned. "I'll have to try and clean up Vic's remains." He sniffled. "At least he'll always be a part of me then. I love you, Vic, even when you're in pieces, your flesh hanging from the ceiling—"

Hap tried to follow Vic, though he didn't look happy about it. He was scowling once more as Vic held up his hands, motioning for him to stay.

"He's imprinted on Victor," Nurse Ratched said. "Like a duckling. Like a terrifying killer duckling. This is wonderful. I am having a wonderful time."

"You'll be okay," Vic told him. "Dad won't hurt you. No one will hurt you here."

"I d-don't care," Hap said. "I d-don't like you. I don't like any of y-you."

"Then why are you still trying to follow him?" Rambo asked.

Hap tried to kick him again, but his wooden leg betrayed him. He almost fell. "I-I'm *not.*"

"Uh-huh," Nurse Ratched said. "Keep telling yourself that."

The last Vic saw of him that night was Dad leading him toward the ground house. Hap followed, looking back over his shoulder at Vic. He stopped in the doorway, watching as Vic and Rambo rode the elevator up.

He watched the ground house through his window, Rambo settling in behind him in his docking port, ready to shut down for the night and recharge. The lights were on below them, but he couldn't see any movement.

"What do you think they're doing?" Vic asked.

"Making sure he won't murder us in our sleep," Rambo said, shutting down, one light pulsing slowly, a soft blue.

Vic tried to stay awake, debating whether or not to try to sneak down to see what was happening and wondering why Dad hadn't taken Hap to his lab. He only lasted a few minutes more, his body heavy, a fresh wave of exhaustion washing over him.

He barely made it to his bed before collapsing, asleep as soon as his head hit the pillow.

When he opened his eyes, gray light filtered in through the windows.

He blinked slowly.

And gasped when he saw a figure towering over him.

"Good morning," Nurse Ratched said as he almost fell off the bed, heart stumbling in his chest. "Sleep well?"

"I told you not to do that," Vic snapped. He collapsed back on his pillow, scrubbing a hand over his face.

"I know. But I did it anyway because it is amusing. Your blood pressure is elevated. You are sweating. Were you dreaming?"

Yes. Vivid, wild dreams where the sky was filled with torn and shredded butterfly wings. "What happened? What's wrong?"

"Nothing is wrong, Victor. At least not in the way you are thinking."

"Where is he?"

"With Gio," she said. "We have been up all night working while you slept comfortably in your bed. Yes, I am trying to make you feel guilty. Is it working?"

Not quite. Vic sat up in his bed, putting his feet on the floor. It was cold. Gooseflesh rose along his skin. "Anything?"

"Yes," Nurse Ratched said. "Though, I doubt it is what you are looking for." Her screen filled with an image of Hap. "It was as we suspected. A complete memory wipe. When he says he does not remember, he is telling the truth. Like us, he was decommissioned, and they took away everything he knew."

"What about his protocols?"

"We do not know. Any remaining data is corrupted, and the more we push, the further it could damage him." She backed away from his bed. "He kept asking about you. He seems strangely fixated, though he cannot explain why. He is a conundrum. We are blessed."

Vic stood from the bed, the frame creaking. He looked down. The docking port was empty. "Rambo?"

The image of Hap disappeared from Nurse Ratched's screen, replaced with a version of Rambo, cross-eyed and buck-toothed. "Asking questions. Hap does not like to be asked questions. I put the odds of Rambo's survival at twenty-four percent. But that is fine. We can always use what remains for parts. I would like to have his arms, if that is all right with you."

Vic groaned. It was going to be a rough day.

Nurse Ratched wasn't lying.

"What are you thinking about?" Vic could hear Rambo saying as the elevator lowered to the ground. "What's going through your head right now? Is it that we should be best friends? Because if it is, that's what *I* was thinking, and I agree. You can never have too many best friends. I already have three. Well, two. Vic and Gio. Nurse Ratched is sometimes my best friend, but since she's sociopathic, it can be a little hard."

"No," Hap growled. "I wasn't th-thinking that."

"Oh. Then what were you thinking?"

"H-how far I could throw you."

"Really far, I bet," Rambo said. "But best friends don't throw each other. Vic taught me that."

He hadn't.

Vic found them sitting near the garden, the sky above covered in a layer of thick clouds. Nurse Ratched followed behind him, her treads cracking the thin layer of frost on the ground. Vic pulled his coat tighter around him, rubbing his arms to warm them up.

Hap had been gifted a shirt, one of Gio's from the looks of it, a little loose in the front. He'd put his boots back on too at some point and was sitting at the edge of the garden. Dad was on his hands and knees, moving carefully through the rows of plants.

Hap heard them approaching first. He rose to his feet, the ever-present scowl on his face. His eyebrows bunched up. "You sh-shut down for a l-long time. Why?"

Vic didn't know quite how to answer that. "Because I have to."

"Why?"

"He's human," Dad said without looking up. "Remember? We discussed this last night. He's different than you or me. He needs rest."

"Because he needs to r-recharge."

"Yes. That's right. Good morning, Victor. Sleep well?"

Vic looked away from Hap. He didn't like the tone in his father's voice. It was too light. Too easy. It didn't seem right, though Victor had a hard time figuring out why. "I guess."

"Good," Dad said, moving from the third row to the fourth.

"D-did you recharge?" Hap asked.

"Yeah," Vic said, hands twitching. "As best I could."

Hap wasn't blinking. It was eerie. Vic couldn't focus on his face, glancing there and away, there and away. "And y-you do that every d-day?"

"Mostly."

"Interesting," Nurse Ratched said. "He is learning. Retaining information. He will use it against us. How diabolical. I continue to enjoy his existence." She rolled over to him, circling him slowly, careful to avoid the edges of the garden. "Is it *nice* seeing Victor this morning?"

Dad paused before resuming his inspection.

Hap's scowl deepened. "N-no?"

"Was that a question?" She poked him with one of her tentacles. He tried to slap it away, but she was too fast for him. "It sounded like a question. Question implies you do not know the answer."

"No," Hap said again, this time spitting out the word.

"Interesting," Nurse Ratched said. "You are either being sincere or you learned to lie like Victor recently did. Gio, your feelings must be up in arms."

Hap turned his head slowly to look at her as she prodded his hip. "F-feelings."

"Yes," Dad said, finally looking up. He settled back on his heels, dirt under his fingernails as he rested his hands on his thighs. "Feelings."

"H-how?"

"We watch. We learn. We process. It wasn't always this way. But the more complex our minds became, the more choice we were given. Evolution by way of mimicry."

"I d-don't have feelings."

"So you say." Dad looked troubled as he shook his head. "I will ask you a question. I want you to answer it as best you can."

Hap glanced at Vic before turning to face Gio. "What."

"What is your designation?"

Hap's head jerked as if someone had swung at him. His mouth opened. No sound came out. He raised his hand in front of his face, looking at his wooden fingers. He said, "Hap. My d-designation is Hap."

"Is it?"

"Yes. It was g-given to me. It's m-mine."

"And you wouldn't like to be called anything else."

"No."

"Why?" Dad asked.

Hap's face went slack momentarily before the skin under his eye twitched. "I d-don't know."

"I do!" Rambo cried, arms waving. "I know why. Pick me. Pick me!"

Dad chuckled ruefully. "Why, Rambo?"

"Because a designation is a gift," Rambo said. "It's an identity. It sets us apart from others like us. It's unique. In all of existence, there has never been someone named Rambo before me. But even if there were, I'm the best one."

"Precisely," Dad said. "It gives you presence."

"Weight," Hap said. "Heavy." He pressed a hand to the side of his head.

"And how does it make you feel?" Dad asked.

Hap dropped his hand. "I . . ." His face screwed up again before relaxing. "Different."

"Good different or bad different?"

"Different d-different. There is no g-good or b-bad."

"And does being called Hap make you feel different different?"

"Yes."

"And you like it."

Hap said, "L-like the butterfly."

Vic didn't know why he felt warm. It wasn't validation. It wasn't praise, especially since Hap looked pissed off about it, though that might have been his default expression. Vic wondered why anyone would create such a surly machine. "Hap," he said.

Hap looked at him.

Vic fidgeted, shifting his weight from one foot to the other. "It's a good name."

"Wh-why do you move like that?" Hap asked. "Are you malfunctioning?"

"No," Dad said before Vic could answer, and he was grateful for it. His tongue felt thick in his mouth, his throat dry. "He isn't malfunctioning. He, like you, is different. It is part of his design."

Hap stared at Vic, his gaze boring into him. Then he started wringing his hands, hopping from one foot to the other in an odd approximation of Vic.

"Stop," Vic snapped. "Stop it."

Hap did. "Wh-why? You do it. I can do it."

"You are an asshole," Nurse Ratched said.

"I a-am an asshole."

"I like this game," Rambo whispered. Then, louder, "Now say, 'Rambo is my best friend.'"

"N-no," Hap said.

Rambo's arms drooped. "Aw. I thought that would work."

"I am n-not nice," Hap said again. "I am an asshole. I am Hap. That is my designation. I w-will not hurt anything today."

"Or any day," Dad said mildly.

"Or any d-day. Unless—"

"No unless!" Rambo cried. "You can't say unless!"

Hap frowned. "Y-yes, I c-can. I just said it. Unless. Unless. U-unless."

"Oh no," Rambo moaned.

Dad stood slowly, grunting as he did so. "Come. Let us see what we see."

*　*　*

Dad led them to the ground house. Hap followed Vic closely, as if he thought Vic would disappear if he looked away. Vic—used to having a shadow in Rambo and Nurse Ratched—didn't know what to make of him. He'd never heard of a machine imprinting on someone before. It could be argued that Rambo—and in a lesser sense, Nurse Ratched—had done the same, but it didn't quite feel like it had with them. It was bigger, somehow. Too big, Vic thought as Hap crowded against him in the doorway.

They gathered near Dad's chair, though Dad didn't sit. Instead, he motioned for Hap to do so. Hap did, hands flat against his thighs. "Do you remember what I told you last night before we went to the lab?"

Hap nodded, head jerking up and down awkwardly as if he wasn't used to the motion. "You w-will not h-hurt me unless I do something to make y-you."

Dad frowned. "I never said hurt. I said stop."

Hap looked up at him. "Wh-what is the d-difference?"

"Can you be hurt?"

Hap cocked his head. "I don't understand."

"Hurt implies feeling. What are you feeling?"

"I feel like you a-ask too m-many questions."

Vic was startled into a laugh, though he tried to cover it up. He obviously wasn't successful as Hap stared at him. "Wh-what was that?"

"Laughter," Dad said, looking as if he were fighting his own smile. "He found that humorous."

"I am n-not humorous."

"It's subjective," Dad said. "You can—"

Hap made a sound, low and grating against Vic's ears. It took him a moment to realize what it was. Laughing. Hap was laughing. It ended as quickly as it had begun. "L-like that."

"Fascinating," Nurse Ratched said, her screen displaying lines of code and equations that moved quicker than Vic could follow. "The imitation is astonishing."

"Do me!" Rambo cried. "Do me!"

"D-do me," Hap said, a sneer on his lips. "D-do m-me. I n-never stop talking."

"Wow," Rambo said. "That was scarily accurate."

"He's learning," Dad said, crouching down before Hap. "It's only going to continue, and most likely at an exponential rate."

"Why?" Vic asked.

Dad sighed. "Because of you, Victor."

Vic felt his stomach sink.

"Hap," Dad said. "Can you show us?"

Hap looked at each of them in turn before his gaze rested on Vic, who nodded. He reached down and lifted his shirt above his head, the collar stretching. He folded it carefully before setting it on his lap.

The wood on his chest and face gleamed in the cool morning light coming in through the skylights above. "This," Dad said, pointing at the wood. "Why did you do this?"

Nurse Ratched said, "The skin wouldn't—"

"Thank you, Nurse Ratched, but I would like to hear from Victor."

She fell silent.

Vic popped his knuckles without thinking. "I . . ." He cleared his throat. "Some of the tears were too big to close. And we couldn't grow new skin, so I had to use what I had available."

"And why not use metal?"

Vic looked away. "He's already metal. Almost all of him. Underneath. I thought it would look better if we used wood. It'd make him look more . . ." He struggled to find the words to describe what he meant, what he was trying to say. The concept was there in his mind, but it was loose and shaky.

"Hysterically Angry Puppet," Hap said.

"I came up with that!" Rambo cried.

"That," Vic said, thought it wasn't quite right. "He's . . . I thought it'd look better."

"And you carved it yourself."

"Nurse Ratched helped."

"Thank you, Victor. I have always wanted to be thrown under a bus." A yellow vehicle appeared on her screen, mowing down a pixelated version of herself over and over again. "Yes. I helped."

"Hap," Dad said. "Would you please open your chest?"

Hap tapped his breastbone. The compartment slid open. The heart looked as it had the night before. It beat. The gears moved. Vic couldn't stop the sense of pride he felt then, the accomplishment tinged with guilt.

"And this?" Dad asked quietly. "Why did you keep this from me?"

Vic squirmed, trying to keep his thoughts in order, but they were on the wings of butterflies, floating up around him, just out of reach. "I didn't . . ." He took a deep breath and tried again. "I wanted to . . ." What? He went with something that didn't feel like a lie. "Because I didn't know if it would work."

Dad nodded slowly. "Why did you make it?"

Why indeed?

He said the only thing he could. "I had to know if I could do it like you did. Just in case."

Dad rose from his crouch, and before Vic could move, wrapped him in a hug, holding him close. Vic hooked his chin over Dad's shoulder. Hap was watching them closely, head tilted slightly, eyes unblinking.

"You wonderful boy," Dad whispered. "You foolish, lovely boy." He pulled away, his hands gripping Vic's shoulders.

Vic started to shake his head but stopped himself. He needed Dad to understand. "He deserves a chance. We all do. You taught me that. I had to help him. I couldn't just leave him."

Dad stared at Vic for a long moment before turning around. "Hap. Your heart."

Hap looked down at it before lifting his head again. "Y-yes."

"It's yours."

"Yes."

"And you want to keep it."

The compartment slid shut. "You can't h-have it. It's mine. V-victor gave it to me."

It shouldn't have affected Vic as much as it did, hearing Hap say his name. In the grand scheme of things, it was nothing. But there was something to it. It made him feel big. It made him feel small.

"He did," Dad agreed. "And I won't take it from you. It is yours for as long as you want it. But be warned, a heart is not like the battery you used to have. It's strong, but fragile."

"H-how can it b-be both?"

Dad laughed, though it sounded hollow. "It just is. It might be for the best that you don't remember what your life was before because it's not going to be the same. The heart, it's . . ." He shook his head. "It's something special. It will lift you up. It will ache without reason. If your response to it is the same as mine, you'll find yourself feeling things you never thought possible. You are a machine, Hap. That much is clear. But a heart changes everything. Once, there was a woodsman made of tin. He said, 'I shall take the heart, for brains do not make one happy, and happiness is the best thing in the world.'"

Rambo laughed. "Tin. Are you sure? Sounds fake, but okay."

"Oh, yes," Dad said. "I'm sure. Hap, I will help you as best I can. We all will. But never forget that Victor gave you life that he made with his own hands. Now, if you'll excuse me."

And with that, Dad turned on his heels and left the ground house. Through the window, Vic saw him walk into the forest. He wouldn't go far, Vic knew. He said the quiet helped him think.

Later—much later, when it was already too late—Vic would wonder why his father didn't tell them what he knew. But by then, it wouldn't matter. The world had teeth, sharp and fierce, and they were about to sink into Vic's skin.

CHAPTER 9

ap was a shadow. He went wherever Vic went, though he didn't look happy about it. To the lab. In the forest. The kitchen. The ground house. He tried to follow Victor into the bathroom, scowling when Victor told him he had to stay out. "Wh-why?"

"It's private."

"Victor must evacuate his bowels," Nurse Ratched said. "He is very regular. Victor, please remember to bring me a sample. It is almost time for a checkup. A healthy Victor is a happy Victor."

Vic slammed the bathroom door and stayed inside for longer than was necessary.

When he opened the door again, Hap was still standing there, waiting, next to Nurse Ratched.

"Wh-what did you do?" Hap demanded. "Y-you made noises like you had been damaged."

"I don't have time for this," Vic mumbled as he pushed by them onto the rope bridge.

In the lab, he went over the woodwork he'd repaired Hap with. He started with the hand and arm, making sure the wood hadn't cracked in Hap's flight through the trees. It hadn't, and he moved on to the chest and back. The cheek. He saved the leg for last.

Hap sat on the table, legs hanging down, watching Vic's every move. He'd removed his clothing at Vic's request, questioning why Vic had placed a blanket over his bare lap.

Vic lifted Hap's leg, extending it, hearing the metal bones underneath the wood creak. The knee joint locked, and Vic soon saw why. On the inner part of his knee, the piece of wood was slightly too large. An easy mistake, but also an easy fix.

He lifted a small tool from his work bench, lifting it so Hap could see. "This is a short bent."

Hap frowned. "What is it f-for?"

"Shaving wood. Your knee is catching. It's why you keep stumbling. I can fix it if you want."

"Does the patient need to be sedated?" Nurse Ratched asked. "I can help, if need be."

"No," Victor said, and turned in time to see her slowly retracting a metal mallet back inside her. "It won't hurt."

"H-hurt," Hap repeated. "You w-will not h-hurt me unless I d-do something to make you." What Dad had said, not quite word for word, but close enough. Then, "What is h-hurt?"

"*Ow*," Vic cried after Nurse Ratched thumped him on the head. "What was that for?"

"You know what," she said. "Hap, that was a demonstration of pain."

Hap scowled at all of them. "Fine. Do it. I n-need to have full range of m-motion. It's a hazard if I d-don't have it because you are f-fragile."

"He is," Nurse Ratched said as Vic glared at her. "So breakable. It really is a flawed design, if you think about it. Humans are so squishy."

Vic rolled his eyes, and then sank to his knees in front of Hap. He motioned for Nurse Ratched to hold Hap's leg in place as he wiped the sweat away from his brow. He thanked Rambo when the vacuum pulled down the magnifying glass, flipping through the different sizes until he found the right one.

"Ready?" he asked Hap.

Hap didn't respond.

Vic lowered the tool, pressing it against the side of the knee joint, ready to shave off a small piece until it fit better.

"Ow," Hap said.

Vic startled. He looked up, eyes wide.

Hap stared down at him. "Ow," he said again. "That h-hurt."

Vic was incredulous. "What? It did? How can it—I don't understand. That shouldn't have—"

"P-practice," Hap said. "I was p-practicing. Ow. Pain. Hurt." He grimaced, face twisting before smoothing out.

"You can't do that," Vic said.

"Wh-why?"

"Because it didn't hurt. I hadn't even started yet."

Hap nodded. "I w-will wait until you s-start."

Vic sat back up on his knees, grabbing the short bent. "That's not how I—just hold still. Don't move."

Hap froze. He didn't blink. His mouth hung open slightly.

"What happened?" Vic asked. He raised his hand up and waved it in front of Hap's face. No reaction.

"Is he dead?" Rambo whispered nervously. "Did we kill him? Oh no. Oh no. Now I'll *never* have a new best friend until we find something else and I've forgotten that Hap existed."

"He is not moving because Vic told him not to," Nurse Ratched said, and though her voice was as flat as ever, she almost sounded . . . amused? Vic couldn't be quite sure.

He said, "Hap, move."

Hap did, tilting his head, blinking slowly. "M-make up your mind."

Of course. Of course that's how he'd be. "You don't have to do everything I say."

"I know," Hap said. "G-get on with it. I'm cold."

Unsure if Hap was being serious or not, Vic ground his teeth together as he leaned forward once more, face inches from the magnifying glass. He raised the short bent once more, pausing just above the wood, waiting to see if Hap would try to trick him again.

He didn't.

Vic lowered the tool, pressing it against the wood. The tendons on the back of his hand jutted out as he slid the short bent down. A thin sliver of wood curled as he shaved the edge of the knee joint.

"I f-feel that," Hap said, though he didn't try to pull away.

"Do you?" Nurse Ratched asked. "Curious. What does it feel like?"

"Pressure."

"Bad?"

"N-no. It does not h-hurt. There is no ow."

Vic made quick work of it. He paused after removing a second sliver, having Nurse Ratched extend and bend Hap's leg. It still caught, and Vic shaved off another piece. "There. Try that out." Hap stood, the blanket falling to the floor.

"He's naked," Rambo said unnecessarily.

Vic kept his gaze at Hap's knee.

"Now wh-what?" Hap asked.

"Try and walk around. See if the leg works better."

Hap, of course, took that literally. He waddled around the lab, rocking from side to side with every step he took, without bending his knees.

"No," Vic said, and Hap stopped. "Walk normal."

"What is n-normal?" Hap asked.

"Something you will not find here," Nurse Ratched said.

Vic hated everyone in the lab. "Just . . . walk. Bend your knees. Do what you normally do."

"N-normal," Hap said. "I a-am normal. Do what I n-normally do."

"Yes."

Hap nodded.

And then ran for the door, still hanging off its hinges.

Vic stumbled as he chased after him, Nurse Ratched and Rambo close on his heels. They all managed to make it through the doorway in time to see Hap launch himself off the side of the rope bridge. He hit the ground hard, rising from a crouch and taking off like a shot, almost moving quicker than Vic could follow. Vic stared dumbfounded as Hap darted between the trees, legs and arms pumping. He reached an old oak, its trunk enormous. His hand shot out as he rounded it, gripping the trunk, bark spraying out and landing on the ground. He used the trunk and his momentum to sling around the tree, rocketing off in the opposite direction.

He approached the ground house, and Vic was sure he was going to crash into it. Instead, he leapt at the last second, jumping up onto the roof, hopping over the skylights with ease before landing on the other side of the house.

"Well," Nurse Ratched said. "I guess normalcy is subjective. He is still naked."

Vic couldn't speak. He watched in awe as Hap ran toward another tree. He jumped, hands grabbing a branch. The branch snapped, but not before Hap had swung himself up to the next branch, and the next. He was at the top of the tree in only a few seconds. Then, he jumped onto the far side of the compound, landing near Dad's lab. He ran across the connecting bridges before skidding to a stop in front of Vic, looking down at him.

"It w-works," he announced to a stunned Vic. "Like n-normal."

"Yeah," Vic said faintly. "I guess it does."

Hap didn't understand much. And because of that, came the questions.

"What are you d-doing?"

"Eating," Vic said. He stood in front of the stove in the kitchen, a pot bubbling in front of him.

"Why?"

"Because I have to."

"Why?"

"Because my body needs it. If I don't eat, I'll starve and die."

"S-starve and die," Hap said. He stared as Vic ladled the

stew into a bowl before setting it down on the table. Vic lifted the spoon toward his mouth, blowing on the stew to cool it down.

"Why d-do you do that?"

Vic sighed. "Because it's too hot."

Hap nodded. "Too hot. But you eat it anyway because if you d-don't, you will d-die."

"Yes."

"How often d-do you n-need it?"

"Food?" Vic blinked. "A couple of times a day."

"That's pointless," Hap said. "Why w-would you be d-dependent on s-something like that? Especially if it's too h-hot."

Vic didn't know what to do with that. "I just have to. I need it to live."

"That's illogical. I w-will help."

Before Vic could react, Hap sucked in a deep breath, cheeks bulging. He lowered his head toward the bowl and blew out. It wasn't a normal breath. It came out like a gale. The bowl flew off the table, stew splattering against the floor and walls.

"There," Hap said. "Now it is not h-hot. Consume it so you don't d-die."

He turned and walked out of the kitchen.

"What are you d-doing?"

Vic felt like screaming. He took a deep breath, letting it out slow. "Getting ready for bed. I'm tired. It's been a long day. I need to sleep."

"Shutdown mode," Rambo said as he docked in his port, wiggling until he was comfortable. "Time to recharge."

"Recharge," Hap said. "Sleep. Why?"

Vic was barely able to stop himself from banging his head against the wall. "We already talked about this. I have to. It's like food. I need it."

"So you don't d-die."

"Yeah." Vic pulled the comforter back off his bed. He sat down, the frame sagging slightly. He yawned, jaw cracking.

Hap cocked his head. "What will I d-do while you re-charge?"

"Find Dad," Vic said tiredly. "He should be back by now. Or Nurse Ratched. Or you can stay here, but you have to be quiet. You can't make noise while I sleep."

"I w-will stay here," Hap said.

Vic closed his eyes, head settling onto the pillow.

He opened one eye a moment later.

Hap stood next to the bed, staring down at him.

"What?" Vic snapped.

"Q-quiet," Hap said. "Be quiet. I can't make n-noise while you recharge."

Vic groaned and turned over, facing the wall. He waved his arm toward Hap. "Just . . . sit down. Or stand somewhere else."

He heard Hap moving away.

He closed his eyes again. He didn't remember falling asleep, listening for the quiet turning of gears in Hap's chest.

When he opened his eyes, it was early morning. Groggily, he rubbed a hand over his face, smacking his lips. He put his feet against the floor, stretching his arms above his head.

He barely managed to stifle a scream when he saw Hap standing in the corner of his room, staring right at him.

"What are you *doing*?" he demanded.

"Waiting," Hap said. "While you r-recharged. You make noise." He opened his mouth wide and began to snore obnox-iously. He stopped as quickly as he started. "D-does that h-help with r-recharging?"

Vic groaned, falling back on his bed.

Hap was an asshole, yes.

But it took Vic longer than he cared to admit to see just how *big* of an asshole he was.

Though he watched Vic's every move, trailed after him as if they were tied together, he made sure to let Vic know how pointless the things they did were. That is, of course, when he wasn't asking questions. If Victor never had to hear the word "why" again, he'd be thankful.

"Why are you doing that?" Hap asked when Vic told him he needed to shower.

"To get clean." Vic had a towel slung over his shoulder as he made his way to the bathroom.

"Why d-do you need to be clean?" Hap trailed after him.

"Because I don't want to be dirty."

"And showers h-help."

"Yeah. Water cleans my skin. And soap."

"Humans are d-dirty," Hap said. "And they need to be clean."

"Yes."

"I am not h-human."

"No."

"Do I n-need to be clean?"

Vic paused at the door to the bathroom, looking back over his shoulder. Hap still wore the clothes he'd been given. His hair was messy, sticking out at odd angles. "No. You . . . your skin doesn't secrete oil and sweat like mine does."

"I w-will shower with you," Hap said.

Vic began coughing roughly.

Hap frowned. "Are you dying? Do you n-need to eat and recharge?"

"You can't shower with me!"

"Why?"

"Because it's *private*."

Hap nodded. "Like when y-you evacuate your b-bowels."

"What? No, that's not—you know what? Yes. That's exactly it."

"I understand."

Vic felt relieved. "Good." He turned back toward the door.

He walked through and was about to close it behind him when it hit something. He looked back. Hap stood in the doorway. "What are you doing?" Vic asked irritably.

"W-water," Hap said. "You could drown. I will w-watch to make sure you don't."

Vic shoved him back out the door. It was like pushing against a boulder, but he somehow pushed Hap back outside. "I'm not going to drown. Stay out."

Hap rolled his eyes, and Vic was shocked into a moment of immobility at something so distinctly human.

Feeling as if he'd been submerged in a burning lake of ice, Vic closed the door.

Moving quietly, Vic followed the trap lines through the woods. The sounds of the forest sang out around him. He glanced over his shoulder to see Hap trailing after him, mimicking his careful steps.

Rambo, on the other hand, barreled forward without a care in the world, singing about how he was in heaven, dancing cheek to cheek, bumping into Hap's feet to try to hurry him up.

"You need to be quiet," Vic muttered.

"I a-*am*."

"Not you. Rambo."

"Oops," Rambo said. "My bad. I forgot what we were doing. You won't hear a peep from me until you say—oh my *god,* a pinecone! I love pinecones!" He rolled around Hap and rushed forward, picking up the pinecone from the ground. "So epic and awesome," he whispered, holding it close to his sensors, turning it over and over. "Can I keep it? Vic? *Vic.* Can I keep this pinecone?"

Vic sighed. "You already have enough at home."

"But—but *this* one is better than all the others! Look. It has thorns on it."

"You will h-hurt yourself," Hap told him. He sounded gruff and annoyed. "Ow. You will h-have ow."

Rambo dropped it as if scalded. "Oh no. Vic! I could hurt my—oh. Wait. That's right. I can't feel pain. Sorry. Sorry, everyone! I forgot what I was for a second. Won't happen again. I'll just—"

Hap stomped on the pinecone, crushing it under his boot.

"Hey!" Rambo complained. "Why would you do that? You made a mess. You can't just make messes. Who is going to clean it up? *You?* Ha. You don't know how to suck like I do." He rolled over the broken pinecone, fans whirring as he sucked up the bits and pieces. "Ooh, that tickled."

Vic shook his head as he continued on.

The first trap was empty. The second was too. The third, however, held a fat rabbit, eyes glazed over, neck snapped by the metal trap. Vic crouched down, grimacing. It hadn't been dead long. The flies hadn't yet come.

"What is that?" Hap asked.

"Food," he muttered as he lifted the bar from the rabbit's neck. Something shifted in the rabbit, wet and terrible. For a long time, he couldn't bring himself to deal with the traps. Dad had done it without complaint. It wasn't quite fear that caused Vic to hesitate, nor was it a feeling of mourning. The texture of the animal's fur, the way the body could stiffen so quickly, made his skin crawl. Thankfully, it didn't look as if the rabbit had suffered. A quick death.

"You k-killed it."

Vic's face grew warm. "I have to. I need it to live. I only take what I need."

"And you n-need this."

"Yes."

Hap nodded before standing. He began to walk off into the trees. "Where are you going?" Vic called after him.

"I'll h-help. Stay there."

Vic sighed and turned back to the rabbit. He pulled an old scrap of cloth from his satchel and spread it out on the ground. Gingerly, he lifted the rabbit and set it on the cloth before wrapping it.

"Where is he going?" Rambo asked.

"I don't know."

"Should we be worried?"

"Probably."

The minutes passed by slowly. It felt like hours before they heard Hap returning. Vic looked around the tree, ready to scold Hap for disappearing for so long, but the words died on his tongue.

In his arms, he carried four rabbits, all of them wriggling frantically.

"What are you *doing*?" Vic asked, aghast.

"Stop," Hap said to the rabbits. "Stop m-moving so Vic c-can kill you and eat y-you so he doesn't die." The rabbits didn't listen. Hap almost dropped one, but he managed to catch it by its back legs, the animal making an odd sound in its fright.

Vic fell back on his rear. "You *caught* these?"

"It's not h-hard. Why? Is it hard for y-you?"

"What? No. That's not what—put them *down*."

Hap frowned. "But they will r-run away and I'll have to ch-chase them again. That is p-pointless." He glanced down at the rabbits before looking back at Vic. "Unless that m-makes them taste better. D-does it make them t-taste better?"

Vic stood, brushing himself off. "Will you just let them go? We don't need them! I have enough."

"You do?" Hap asked. "Are you s-sure?"

"Yes."

Hap shrugged, and Vic was struck again by just how quickly he'd adapted his behaviors. It'd already gone beyond mimicry in a few short days. Soon enough, he'd be like Gio.

Hap dropped the rabbits. They landed on the ground before

scattering off into the forest. He watched them go before looking down at his arms. Wet droppings smeared across his skin.
"What is that?" he asked. He raised it toward his nose and
sniffed. "It smells. Bad? Not g-good."

"The rabbit evacuated its bowels on you," Rambo said,
sounding far more gleeful than the situation warranted. "I can't
wait to tell Nurse Ratched."

Hap scowled. "Like Victor does with the door c-closed?
That's p-private. I will f-find the r-rabbit that did this. I will
make it p-pay for evacuating its bowels publicly." He turned
to stomp away but stopped when Vic grabbed him by the arm.
His brow furrowed as he looked at Vic's hand wrapped around
his forearm. "I c-can feel that."

"Don't move."

Hap froze.

Vic shook his head as he opened his satchel, pulling out a
scuffed plastic bottle. He let go of Hap's arm, which didn't
move, still extended. He unscrewed the lid and poured the water on Hap, washing away the droppings. When he finished, he
put the bottle away and stepped back.

Hap stood stock still.

Vic huffed out a breath. "You can move now."

Hap did, bringing his arm back up to his face, eyes narrowing. "Cleaned," he said. "Water. Shower. We sh-showered
together."

"We did *not*."

Hap squinted at him. "Are you sure?"

Vic stomped back toward the trap. He reset it before shoving the wrapped rabbit into his satchel. He didn't look back as
he turned and headed for home.

On the fourth night, Hap discovered music.

He was sitting in Vic's lab, hands folded in his lap, questioning everything Vic was doing. Vic barely heard him anymore,

mumbling half answers under his breath that did little to appease him. Nurse Ratched was exposed before him, her screen having shorted out.

"I normally do this myself," she told Hap as Victor found the problem, some of her wiring on its last legs. "But I allow Victor to help because it makes him feel useful."

"He n-needs it," Hap said.

"Yes," Nurse Ratched said. "Constant validation. Engaging Empathy Protocol. You are doing a good job, Victor. I am very proud of you. Disengaging Empathy Protocol. Are you almost done? I do not like it when you finger me with cold hands."

Vic ignored her. Having finished his work he picked up his tools and carried them toward the work bench.

Hap sat ramrod straight in his chair. His head was tilted as if he were listening. He had a strange expression on his face, faraway and lost. "What is it?" Vic asked. "What's wrong?"

"S-sound. What is that s-sound?"

Vic listened. He didn't hear anything.

Nurse Ratched did. "It is music. Gio is playing a record in the ground house."

Hap stood abruptly, the chair banging against the wall. He moved toward the door without speaking. Before Vic could call to him, he vaulted over the edge of the railing.

"I wish I could do that," Rambo said. "It looks so cool. I'm gonna do it. No one try and stop me this time."

Vic managed to grab Rambo before he could roll toward the railing. "No."

Rambo beeped rudely. "Hey! I said *not* to stop me."

"You take the elevator," Vic told him. "Just because someone else does something doesn't mean you have to."

"How profound," Nurse Ratched said. "I am impressed, Victor."

Later, as Vic closed down the lab for the night, he got lost in his own head. Once, when he was ten, he had suddenly become fixated on the fact that he was *not* an android like his father. It upset him greatly and sent him spiraling for two days. He was inconsolable. They were different, he tried to explain to Dad, even as his father said their differences did not matter. But to Victor, they *did* matter. He wanted his blood drained, his bones and tendons replaced with metal and wiring. He couldn't articulate the *why* of it, not enough to satisfy either of them. Dad had tried to calm him down, tried to explain that he was perfect just the way he was, but Vic wouldn't hear of it.

At the end of the second day he was exhausted, his eyes feeling like they were filled with sand, his head pounding, his thoughts jumbled. Dad had sat a few feet away from him to give him space, legs folded, hands on his knees, and said, "Victor, listen to me."

He didn't look at his father, but he heard him. He grunted quietly in response.

"We're not the same," Dad had said, voice gentle and soft. "But know that I was alone and sad before you came into my world. You gave me hope, Victor. It started in the tips of my toes before it rose through the rest of my body and latched firmly in my chest. It has never left. It evolved into something so much greater. And it's because of this feeling that I can say I don't need you to be like me. I need you to be *you*."

Vic hadn't spoken. Not then. But he listened, and he never forgot.

He was quiet as the elevator lowered toward the ground. He followed his friends toward the ground house, pausing in the doorway.

Dad sat in his chair, a curious expression on his face. He didn't turn to look at Vic. He was focused on Hap.

Hap, who stood in front of the record player, swaying side to side as if caught in the drift of the smooth horns, the gentle *tsk*

tsk tsk of the cymbals, the tinkling of the piano keys. "What is this one?" he whispered as he moved from side to side.

"Miles Davis," Dad said with a quiet smile. "*Kind of Blue.* Nineteen fifty-nine. Many things happened to jazz music in nineteen fifty-nine. John Coltrane. Duke Ellington. Sonny Clark. Do you like it?"

Hap said "I don't know" without stuttering over the words. "How do I know if I like it?"

"Listen," Dad said. "Here. Ready?"

The saxophone entered, running through the notes like flowing water. Warmth bloomed in Vic's chest at the sound.

Hap sighed. He began to tap his foot in time with the beat. Vic didn't think he realized he was doing it.

"What does it say to you?" Dad asked.

For a long moment, Hap didn't speak. Then, "There are no words."

"I know," Dad said. "But what—"

"No," Hap said. "I have no words for it."

"Oh. Oh. Yes. It can do that, sometimes."

Hap pressed a hand against his chest. "I can feel it here."

Dad closed his eyes and hummed along with the song. He stopped when Hap said, "It feels like . . . a memory. Like something I've forgotten. What do you do if you've forgotten all you know?"

Dad opened his eyes. He was silent for a moment, as if carefully choosing his words. "You start again from the beginning."

"What's happening?" Rambo whispered to Nurse Ratched.

"I do not know," she said. "But I like it. I wish someone would ask a lady to dance."

Rambo beeped excitedly. "I can do that!" He rose on his lift, hydraulics wheezing. He grasped two of her tentacles with his pincers. Her screen filled with a sharp bouncing line, a circadian rhythm keeping time with the music. They rolled back and forth, Rambo apologizing profusely when he bumped into her. Nurse Ratched didn't seem to mind.

And on and on it went.

Until the machines came.

CHAPTER 10

One week after Hap awoke in the laboratory of a creator named Victor Lawson, they returned to the Scrap Yards. Vic said he wanted to see if the Old Ones had brought anything new worth salvaging. It wasn't a lie, but it wasn't the complete truth, either.

What Vic *really* wanted to do was return to where they'd found Hap, to see if there was anything else they'd missed. He doubted there would be; Nurse Ratched hadn't found any other signs of life.

They'd left Hap with Dad. Or at least they thought they had. They were halfway to the Scrap Yards when Nurse Ratched stopped and said, "We're being followed."

Vic glanced over his shoulder. Nothing moved in the trees that he could see. "Where?"

Before she could speak again, he saw Hap peek his head from behind a tree before pulling it back sharply.

Vic sighed. "I can see you."

"No, you c-can't," Hap replied.

"Hap."

Hap scowled as he stepped out from behind the tree.

"Why were you hiding?" Rambo asked.

"I w-wasn't," Hap said. "I was inspecting the t-tree trunk."

"Really?" Rambo rolled toward him, stopping at the base of the tree. "What are you inspecting it for? Is there something wrong with it?" He raced around the trunk before stopping where he started. "I don't see anything."

"He is making sure Vic does not die," Nurse Ratched said, matter-of-fact. "I believe he is showing concern."

"I am n-*not*." He sneered at them. "I was j-just walking this way."

"In the same direction as us?" Rambo asked. "That's *awesome*. Vic. Hey, Vic! What are the chances that Hap would be here too? He should come with us!"

Vic said, "You can, you know. Come with us."

Hap grunted as Rambo tried to push him toward the others. He tried to kick Rambo, but the vacuum was faster than he was. Hap almost lost his footing but managed to stay upright. His wooden leg—while still stiff—caught him at the last second.

"Squishy," Hap muttered, not looking at any of them.

"So that is what this is about," Nurse Ratched said. "Fear not, Hap. We would never let anything happen to Victor. While he is squishy, yes, we are not."

Hap's scowl deepened. "I d-don't care."

"Of course you do not," Nurse Ratched said. "Why would you? Since we are going in the same direction, we might as well go together. Victor?"

Vic tore his gaze away from Hap. "What?"

"Hap will be joining us," she said. "The more the merrier, as I always say."

"I've never heard you say that," Rambo said, and squealed when she whipped one of her tentacles at him. "What? I *haven't*."

"Do you want to come with us?" Vic asked. He didn't know why Hap would. From the look on his face and the stiff way he was holding himself, Hap looked as if he would rather be anywhere else.

Hap shook his head. "N-no. But I will, since y-you insist."

"We did not insist," Nurse Ratched said. "But if it makes you feel better to think so, far be it from me to suggest otherwise. It might be beneficial to have some backup. Victor often finds himself getting in trouble when he least expects it."

Vic groaned. "That's not—"

"How is the cut on your hand, Victor? Healing nicely, I should think."

It was. Scabbed over and itchy, but better. He didn't think it would even leave a scar. "Fine," Vic said. "But we're going to move quick. We don't want to be caught by the Old Ones."

"They're huge," Rambo said as Hap joined them. "Bigger than *you*. I bet they would squash you flat."

"N-no," Hap said. "I w-would not like that. If they t-try, I will n-not be nice."

"Come on," Vic said. "We'll be quick. What are the rules?"

"Stick together!" Rambo exclaimed.

"Run if we have to," Nurse Ratched said.

"No dallying!"

"No drilling."

"And above all else, be brave!"

Hap cocked his head as he narrowed his eyes, but he did not speak.

The moment they crested the hill that overlooked the Scrap Yards, Vic knew something was wrong. Be it morning, noon, or dusk, the Old Ones were always moving. Not now; birds perched on one of the cranes seemingly without a care. The silence was oppressive in ways Vic had never felt before: thick, as if the very air had grown heavier, making it harder to breathe. Part of him—a loud, insistent part—demanded he turn around and forget the Scrap Yards altogether. Go home. Don't look back.

Rambo said, "I don't like this."

Nurse Ratched beeped once, twice. "There is something here. Something I have never felt before. It is . . . bright."

"Bright?" Vic asked, looking off farther into the yards. "What do you mean?"

"Power," she said. "It feels like power."

"The Old Ones?"

"No. Something else. Hold, please. Scanning. Scanning. Scanning." The light above her screen flashed on as she began to scan the area around them.

"What is she d-doing?" Hap asked as he squinted at her.

Vic shrugged. "Looking. It's how we found you. Maybe there's someone like you that we missed. Another android. A machine. It happens, sometimes. Usually we can't fix them." He glanced at Nurse Ratched. "What is it?"

She finished scanning, and the light went out. Her screen remained blank. "There is something here."

"Where?"

She pulled up the grid of the Scrap Yards on her screen. One of the squares blinked.

3B. Where they'd found Hap.

Vic frowned. "Maybe we missed something."

"It is possible," Nurse Ratched said slowly. "Hap's power signature could have blocked out what is there now, or it could have activated after we left."

"But?"

"But," she said. "I do not think that is it. This is bigger. Or there is more than one. I cannot separate them if that is the case. They are too far away."

The warning in his head grew louder, telling him to turn around and leave this place. *Tell him,* it whispered. *Tell Dad. Tell Dad that something is here and let him take care of it.*

But the warning was drowned out by something far more dangerous: curiosity. It tugged at Vic. He wanted to see what it was. What Nurse Ratched could be reading. It had power. That much was clear. And Dad's heart wouldn't last forever. Maybe they could use it, if the machine it belonged to was beyond repair. And if it wasn't, Vic could help.

He said, "Careful. Quiet. Stick together. We'll keep our distance."

"I knew you were going to say that," Nurse Ratched said. Then, louder, "Hap, remember what Victor is?"

"Squishy," Hap said immediately.

"Exactly. Squishy, breakable Victor. We will need to protect him in case it is something that can harm him."

"What about me?" Rambo asked.

Nurse Ratched bumped into him gently. "You have the most important job of all. If the need arises, you will sacrifice yourself so the rest of us can escape."

"Yes!" Rambo cried. "I have purpose!"

They moved through the scrap heaps, soon reaching a small ridge that looked over quadrant 3B. Vic crouched low as they approached the crest of the hill. Hap watched him for a moment before doing the same. He was so close, Vic could hear the gears in his chest.

The slate sky hung heavy over their heads, the air sharply cold, and Vic's breath billowed from his mouth in a stream. He thought it would snow soon. Maybe not today, but soon. He shivered again as he crawled toward the top of the hill, Hap to his right, his skin warm when his arm accidentally brushed against Vic's.

They reached the top and peered over, Rambo whispering, "I'm brave, I'm brave, I'm brave."

At first, Vic didn't understand what he saw when he looked down the other side of the hill. Piles of discarded body parts where they'd found Hap: arms, legs, torsos, all scattered around on the ground.

And the people. The *people*. A furious gut-punch, enough to knock the breath from Vic's chest. Proof. Here, at last. Others. Three of them, wearing what looked like uniforms: black boots, black pants, black coats with red collars that rose up around their necks. On the right breast of each coat was a symbol, though they were too far away for Vic to make it out clearly.

But the more he studied them, the more the feeling of

wrongwrongwrong snapped and snarled within him, a cornered predator lashing out anyway it could. All had their scalps shaved cleanly. Two of them stood upright, swiveling their heads from side to side. The third was crouched on the ground, hand pressed against the soil. They didn't speak.

It was then Victor saw them for what they were: exactly the same. Their skin was pale, their faces smooth. No eyebrows. No facial hair. No ears. Male, or at least they seemed to be.

They did not look like Dad. Or Hap.

They did not look like Vic.

They weren't human at all. No. The third android—the one crouched on the ground—lifted his head. He was exactly like the other two. Triplets. Clones. The same model.

"They are not human," Nurse Ratched said in a low voice, as if she could read Vic's mind. "They are machines."

"What are they doing?" Vic asked. "What are they looking—"
The words died on his tongue as an awful noise came from beside him. He turned his head.

Hap had bared his teeth in a furious snarl. The skin around his eyes tightened. His fingers were hooked into claws. "What is it? Do you know them?"

Hap sounded angry when he said, "No. I d-don't know. I c-can't—error. It is an error. Lost. It's l-lost in f-fog." Vic almost fell back when Hap began to savagely beat the sides of his head with his hands. The sound was bizarre: metal and synthetic skin and wood. Vic tried to grab his hands, but Hap was too strong.

"Stop," Vic hissed at him. "They'll *hear* you."

But Hap didn't. He hit his head again and again.

"What's wrong with him?" Rambo asked nervously. "Is he malfunctioning?"

"Rambo, back away," Nurse Ratched said, her tentacles spooling out and twitching dangerously.

Hap clutched the side of his head and bent over, face toward the ground.

"Hap," Victor whispered. "Hap, you need to stop. You need to—"

A sound filled the world, one Vic had never heard before.

It started small, as if crossing from a great distance. He looked around wildly, trying to locate the source. It echoed flatly against the scrap metal before them, the heaps beginning to vibrate, bits and pieces falling to the ground.

The sound only grew louder.

Hap lowered his hands, turning his face toward the sky. "L-look."

Vic lifted his head.

He wasn't sure what he was seeing at first. A smudge on the horizon above the expansive forest, black against a gunmetal sky. He thought it an errant cloud until it moved oddly, expanding and contracting. The hum around them increased as the smudge grew and took shape. Vic felt the vibrations it caused down to his bones. His hands shook.

When he saw it for what it was, he still couldn't believe his eyes. It didn't seem possible. He'd read about them in books, had seen a picture of their massive size. In one of Dad's books—*Creatures of the Sea*—there'd been a drawing of one with the outline of a man next to it, shown for scale. The beast dwarfed the man, a great monstrosity that Vic couldn't believe actually existed. He'd never seen the ocean, though he could imagine how vast it had to be if it held creatures such as this.

He couldn't remember what it was called; Nurse Ratched did not have that problem. "A whale," she said. "It is a whale."

But it wasn't rising from the depths of any sea. It was flying toward them.

The whale moved up and down as if swimming through the air. The top of it was black, the underbelly white with thick lines that ran along the length. It didn't have eyes. Instead, across the middle of its head was a row of glass that wrapped around the front to either side. The flippers were thick and massive as they rose and fell. The horizontal tail moved up and down, propelling the beast forward. Its great mouth was closed.

"What is that?" Rambo cried as the sound grew louder. "Is that a *fish*? How is a fish flying?"

Vic couldn't answer. He was struck dumb.

Now that it was closer, Vic could see the lines underneath weren't part of the flesh of the creature. They were *panels*. It wasn't alive at all.

It was a machine.

A massive machine that dwarfed even the Old Ones. Across the side, above the flipper, were three white words in the black of the metal skin.

THE TERRIBLE DOGFISH

The flying machine stopped above the Scrap Yards, hovering in place. Air began to whip ferociously as it lowered toward the earth, scrap heaps collapsing in showers of dust and sparks.

With a magnificent groan, the whale's mouth dropped open, the lower jaw folding down and back. The throat of the whale was metal and lined with what looked like railed walkways. Vic squinted against the dust blowing, sure he could see *movement* inside the whale's mouth on the platforms, though it was too far away for him to make out what exactly it was.

As he looked on, black cables dropped from the whale's mouth. At the tip of each cable was a flat, circular disc, large enough to carry people or machines. They lowered toward the ground where the three figures stood.

In silence, they watched as the humanoid figures inspected the area around them as the discs reached the ground near them. The crouched figure scooped up what looked like dirt, letting it filter through his fingers. Lifting his head, he looked directly at them. Vic flattened himself to the ground, heart in his throat. He counted to five in his head and looked out into the Scrap Yards once more . . .

. . . in time to see the smooth men stepping onto the discs and rising up and up toward the whale. Once inside, the mouth of the whale closed. It remained suspended in air.

"Victor," Nurse Ratched said, "we need to move while we still can."

Vic was startled out of his daze. He looked back at the others. Nurse Ratched's screen was flashing red in warning. Rambo was moaning quietly to himself. Hap's eyes were narrowed, his gaze on Victor, never looking away.

Vic nodded. "Head for the trees. Don't look back. Don't stop."

Nurse Ratched lifted Rambo from the ground and they fled for the safety of the forest. Vic looked back only once as they hit the tree line. The Terrible Dogfish hadn't moved. Fear clawed at his throat, but he ran and ran and ran.

They were in the trees when a deep note emanated from the whale, a blast that rolled through the forest, causing the birds to take flight.

It sounded like it was screaming.

Dad was in the ground house. He appeared in the doorway as Rambo shouted his name, Victor too out of breath to get any words out. Dad frowned when he saw them running toward him. They skidded to a stop in front of him, Vic slumped over, hands on his knees as he gasped for air, lungs burning, chest constricted. Vic's mind had been wiped clean, a sheen of static falling over him. He couldn't think. He couldn't speak, jaw clenched as he ground his teeth.

"What is it?" Dad asked, sounding alarmed. "What's happened?" He cupped Vic's cheeks, turning his face up. "Are you all right?"

Vic couldn't find the words. "I . . . I don't . . ."

"A ship!" Rambo cried as Nurse Ratched set him down on

the ground. He began to spin in circles, arms flailing. "In the Scrap Yards! A fish! A flying fish!"

Dad's reaction was instantaneous. He dropped his hands from Vic's face, gripping his arms. He pulled Vic behind him, looking toward the sky. "Did they see you?"

Nurse Ratched's screen filled with the recording from the Scrap Yards. Dad grunted as if punched. Vic looked over his shoulder to see an image of one of the machines inspecting the soil. "Victor," Dad said, voice even. "The cut on your hand. When it happened, did you bleed in the Scrap Yards?"

Vic hung his head. "It was an accident—"

Dad cursed and turned toward the ground house, stepping around Vic. "Follow me. Don't look back. Don't ask questions. Do what I say. Hurry."

They did as they were told. A record spun on the player inside the ground house. Miles Davis and his sweet, sweet horns. Dad stopped in front of one of the bookcases. "Victor, I need you to listen to me."

Vic managed to nod. His breath whistled as he panted, throat dry and constricted.

"There is much I should've told you," Dad said as he stepped to the side of the bookcase. He pressed his hand against the wood. A panel lit up, green and bright. It rose up and down as it scanned his hand. "Much that I've kept hidden. But you must believe me when I say I only wanted to keep you safe." The scan finished, and a heavy click came from the bookcase, as if a lock had opened.

The floor beneath their feet began to shake. They all turned in time to see the floor shifting, the floorboards folding in on themselves as they parted. A staircase appeared, the metal steps snapping into place. At the edges of each step, lights turned on, pulsing again and again.

"Down," Dad said. "Now."

Nurse Ratched went first, her body rattling as she bounced

down each step. She almost tumbled end over end, but her treads kept her upright. Dad picked up Rambo, shoving him at Vic.

"Dad," Vic tried.

"Hush," Dad said. "Go."

Vic descended the stairs, hearing Hap following him. He looked back over his shoulder to see his father at the top of the stairs. The frame of the ground house began to rattle, and that strange sound roared around them once more. The Terrible Dogfish was coming.

"Hap," Dad said as they reached the bottom of the stairs. "You don't know me. You don't even know yourself. But I must ask you for something, and it will go against every single part of your programming."

Hap nodded.

"I am asking you to choose. Here. Now. I'm sorry it's come at a time like this, but you must decide."

"T-to do wh-what?"

"Protect Victor," Dad said, and for the first time in Vic's life, he heard fear in his father's voice. "No matter what. Protect him with everything you have. Don't let anything happen to him."

Vic set Rambo on the ground before turning back toward the stairs. He tried to climb back up but stopped when his father shook his head.

"What are you doing?" he demanded. "What's happening?"

Dad smiled, though it trembled. "What I hoped never would. Listen to me, Victor. You are a light in my darkness. I've loved you since the moment I saw you. Never forget that. No matter what you see, no matter what you hear, I have always loved you. You're my son. And I couldn't be prouder of the man you've become. One day, we'll see each other again. I know we will. Hap, do I have your word? Will you do what I've asked?"

Hap hesitated before nodding.

Relief flooded Dad's face. "Thank you," he whispered.

"Trust Victor. Trust my son. I'll do what I can to keep them away. Nurse Ratched. Can you hear me?"

"Yes, Gio."

"Butterflies flap their wings, and all the world sings."

Her screen went dark before the words ACTIVATE SAFETY PRO-TOCOL? appeared. "But what do the birds say?"

And Dad said, "In the sky, you are free."

"Password accepted. Safety Protocol six one four dash seven."

Dad stepped back away from the stairs. Vic screamed for him as he pressed his hand against the side of the bookcase once more. Hap grabbed Vic by the back of his coat, pulling him down as the stairs receded back into the wall. The last Vic saw of his father before the floor closed above them was Dad squaring his shoulders, turning toward the doorway.

"No!" Vic cried, slamming his hands against the wall. "Dad! *Dad*."

"Enough," Hap snarled in his ear. "You'll h-hurt yourself. Stop it." He pulled Vic away from the wall.

Vic struggled, trying to get away from him, but Hap held on tight. "Let me go!"

"N-no," Hap said. "Stop. L-look."

Vic sagged against him. He lifted his head.

They were in a bunker of sorts, one Victor hadn't known ex-isted. The walls were metal, as was the ceiling. It was roughly the size of the ground house above them but filled with equip-ment unlike anything Vic had ever seen before. Against the far wall sat a row of glass tubes, all empty, the surfaces smudged with dust. The wall to the right was filled with screens like the one Nurse Ratched had, three large across the top, six smaller ones underneath, above a console that blinked. The left wall was shelving filled with books and discarded tools, all looking as if they hadn't been touched in years. Vic's gaze slid over some of the books, not able to comprehend what he was read-ing on the spines: *Gray's Anatomy* and *Atlas der Anatomie des Menschen* and *Leonardo da Vinci on the Human Body* and *What to Expect When You're Expecting.*

Nurse Ratched went to the console below the screens as Rambo hurried around the bunker, his fan running as he scooped up the dust from the floor. "Dirty," he muttered. "Dirty, so dirty, must clean, must clean."

"Wh-what is this p-place?" Hap asked.

Vic didn't know. He opened his mouth, but no sound came out. He jumped when Nurse Ratched beeped loudly, one of her tentacles extending and attaching itself to a port in the console. Her screen filled with numbers and letters and symbols Victor didn't recognize. The same symbols rolled onto the screens above her. Vic flinched at the harsh light as each screen filled with an image, a low roar filling the bunker.

The screens showed the compound from various angles. At first, Vic thought they were just pictures, but the trees were moving, the branches creaking and groaning. One screen showed the interior of the ground house. Another was from a high vantage point, looking down at the forest floor below. The three smaller screens showed different views: one of the exterior of Vic's room, the other two at opposite ends of the wooden bridges.

But it was the last screen Vic focused on, the large screen at the end. On it, he could see Dad standing in the middle of the garden, face turned toward the ashen sky. He glanced at the other screens, trying to see what his father was doing, but the angle was off. It wasn't until the trees began to whip back and forth that he understood. He covered his ears when the Terrible Dogfish blared again.

"Nurse Ratched," he said. "Open the door. Please."

"I cannot do that, Victor," she said. "Not yet. The protocol has been activated."

Vic stared, dumbfounded, arms slowly dropping back to his sides. "*What* protocol?"

"I do not know," she said as her tentacle in the port twisted. "But I cannot stop it."

Vic slammed his fists against the console. It rattled, the lights flashing, but nothing changed. "I'm ordering you to open the doors."

"I cannot, Victor."

"Do it!" he shouted at her. "You need to let me out. I have to help him. I have to—"

A man appeared on the screen, descending on the circular platform, one hand wrapped around the cable, the other at his side. He leapt off the platform five feet above the ground, landing with a slight bend to his knees. A moment later, two others appeared, one on either side of him. Strange, hairless, they stood with their legs apart, hands clasped behind them, faces blank, smooth.

The one in front spoke, his voice flat, cold. "Designation General Innovation Operative, also known as Gio."

"Here," the one on the left said.

"Now," the one on the right said.

"After seventy-two years," the one on the left said.

"There is no coincidence," the one on the right said.

They sounded identical. None of them blinked.

The one in the front stepped forward. "An anomaly was detected in a dumping ground," he said. "Plasma. Salt. Protein. Water. Cellular activity."

"Blood," the one on the left said.

"Human blood," the one on the right said.

The front man—the leader—looked up at the buildings in the trees above them. "What are these?"

Dad spoke for the first time, voice blandly pleasant. "Do you like them? I took inspiration from a book. A family named Robinson were once shipwrecked on an island. In order to survive, they built a tree house. A home."

"Fiction," the left one said.

"Unreality," the right one said.

"Memory," Dad said. "Of a time long ago."

"Memory," the leader repeated. He cocked his head. "Where did the blood come from?"

"You said it was found in the dumping grounds? I expect that it came from an animal, then. From what I recall, it happens quite often, poor creatures getting crushed under the Old Ones."

The machines on either side of the leader cocked their heads in unison, never blinking, lips pulled back over square teeth.

"Animal," the left one said.

"Poor creatures," the right one said.

"Crushed under the machines," the leader said in that same queer voice. He paused for a long moment. "No." He stepped toward Dad. "Where is the human?"

"There is no human here," Dad said. "Scan it. Scan it all. You'll see."

"Oh no," Rambo whispered. "They'll find us."

"They won't," Nurse Ratched said. "The walls are lined with lead. They won't know we're here."

Vic turned slowly to look at her. "How do you know that?"

She didn't answer.

"L-look," Hap said, and Vic looked at the screen once more. The androids formed a triangle, raising their arms, fingers spread wide. The skin of their palms parted, little black metal knobs poking through. Light emanated from the knobs, and the smooth men raised and lowered their hands as they scanned the entirety of the compound.

The androids didn't react as the scan completed. The skin on the palms of two of the androids closed. The third turned his hand over, palm toward the sky. A three-dimensional image of the compound appeared above his hand, spinning in a slow circle.

"What is this?" he asked, fingers twitching slightly. The image expanded, zooming in until it showed one room in particular: Vic's room.

"For travelers," Dad said. "Those who pass by and need a place to recharge."

The leader closed his hand around the image, and it disappeared. "Recharge."

"What do you want?" Dad asked.

The leader blinked once, twice. Then, "We do not want. We do not have desire. We have purpose. The anomaly. Perhaps it is you. General Innovation Operative, by order of the Authority, you will return to the City of Electric Dreams. There, you will undergo an evaluation to determine if you have a viable future in service of the machines."

"Reprogramming," the one on the left said.

"Or decommissioning," the one on the right said.

"Two decisions," the leader said. "One outcome. But first, you will be taken apart to determine the extent of the corruption in your programming. It is necessary to verify if your corruption is infectious."

"Plasma," the one on the left said. "Salt."

"Protein," the one on the right said. "Water."

"Cellular activity," the leader said. "The Authority sees all, knows all, General Innovation Operative. If they exist, we will find them, and you will be the one to give them to us."

"So you do want something after all," Dad said. "Not so different, are we?"

For the first time, something other than blank *nothing* crossed the leader's face. His lips twitched, his dead eyes narrowed. "I remember you. From before. The others do not, but I do. We will find the truth, and then we will decide how best to use your parts in service of the Authority."

Dad laughed. Vic's eyes burned. He couldn't focus, couldn't breathe, couldn't do anything. He was trapped under the weight of fear and indecision, static in his head.

The smooth men took a step back as one when Dad lifted his shirt up and over his head, letting it fall to the ground. "Even after all this time, nothing changes. But I have. When I close my eyes, I dream. Not in lined code or equations. Like a human. Like them. Love. Anguish. Fear. Pride. *Memory*. All from my heart. And I will never let you have it." He tapped his breastbone. The compartment slid open.

At the same time, the smooth men hissed, "What is *that*?"

Dad grinned, crazed and beautiful. "I like to think of it as my soul, romantic though the notion may be. And it was never for you."

Vic screamed as his father raised his hand to close around the heart in his chest. He screamed as the wood cracked, as the gears snapped off their tracks, falling onto the ground. The heart broke, falling in pieces. Giovanni Lawson swayed.

He said, "Never forget. It has always been you."

And then he collapsed, head bouncing off the ground, right arm trapped underneath him.

His eyes were open. He didn't blink. He didn't move.

Arms wrapped around Vic, trying to hold him back, and he struggled against them. He fought them as hard as he could, vision tunneling as the smooth men stood above his father's still body. The leader bent over and picked Dad up as if he weighed nothing, slinging him over his shoulder. He looked to the others and said, "Leave nothing. Burn it all to the ground."

"Please," Vic begged as he kicked his legs up into the air. "Please let me go to him."

"They'll k-kill you," Hap growled in his ear.

"I don't *care*. Let me go!"

But Hap didn't. As Vic looked on, still struggling, the leader headed for the lowered platform, Dad's arms bouncing uselessly against his back. The remaining smooth men raised their hands once more, the black knobs poking through the skin of their palms. All thought—rational and irrational—disappeared when fire bloomed from the smooth men's hands, great arcs of red and orange and white. Vic sagged against Hap, gasping for air as flames caught the roof of the ground house, the trees that held their home. He could feel himself shutting down as the fire spread, and no matter what he did, no matter how hard he fought against it, it was no use. A strange sense of suction overcame him as if a vacuum had opened in his chest, pulling in all light. A trickle of sweat rolled down his cheek near his ear. He was here, he was with Dad, he was everywhere, floating on a flat ocean, the tranquility deceptive as everything burned. Their life's work—their *home*—turned into ash.

Hap was speaking, but Vic couldn't hear him.

Rambo was frantic, but Vic paid him no mind.

Nurse Ratched said their room appeared safe even for human lungs, sealed off from the fires above, but Vic couldn't make sense of anything she was saying. The branches holding up the kitchen gave way, causing the floor to break apart, burning chunks of wood and metal raining down onto the ground.

And Victor Lawson watched it all, unable to look away. It didn't feel real, and though he could smell the hint of smoke, could see the destruction the fire was causing, it felt far away, distant, as if it were happening to someone—*anyone*—else.

A moment of clarity: one of the smooth men stood underneath a camera as the trees burned, fire still spilling from his hands. On his chest, the symbol, now close enough for Vic to make out.

The heads of two animals in profile, facing each other.

A fox.

A cat.

And then the smooth man turned away from the camera as Victor's lab fell, as Dad's lab was destroyed, as Vic's room shuddered and shook and split apart, crashing to the forest floor. All of it, years and years of work, gone in minutes, but Vic watched it dispassionately. He took in information, processed it, stored it away, but felt nothing from it. Nothing at all.

The leader stood upon the platform, Dad still thrown over

his shoulder. As the other two joined them, they rose up and out of sight. A moment later, the Terrible Dogfish roared again.

And then it too was gone, the sound fading as the whale swam across the sky.

As the remains of their home burned, the birds began to sing again.

Vic stood still. He understood things were happening near him, could feel Nurse Ratched wrapping her tentacles around him as she checked his pulse, asking him if he could hear her, *Victor, Victor, please respond.*

He wouldn't. He couldn't.

"What's wrong w-with h-him?" someone asked, and the sound of his voice came from far below Vic, as he was floating like he had been filled with air and wasn't tethered to anything.

"He is reacting the best he knows how," a machine with a mounted screen said, and he wondered who they were talking about. "Victor, please. Can you hear me?"

A little machine made a mournful sound almost like it was weeping. "Is he dead? Is Gio dead?"

Death. He had never really thought about death before. A shutdown wasn't absolute. All that one needed was a newer battery. Perhaps these things with him could give him one. He'd made a heart before. He could do it again.

He said, "I am fine."

"Okay," the machine in front of him said. He could almost remember her name. He'd known it before . . . well. Before. Nurse. She was a nurse. The little machine on the floor was not a nurse, neither was the man standing next to him. "You are fine," the nurse said. "I believe you. But I would like to make sure. Can you help me do that, Victor?"

He could. He didn't want to, but he could. He said, "Please let me go."

She did, her tentacle sliding off his arm, causing his skin to itch.

He smiled. He was still above her, floating around the room, but he smiled. It stretched on his face so wide, it hurt his cheeks. "There," he said. "See? I am fine." He laughed. It was wrong. It was an error. He shouldn't be laughing. He didn't think anything was funny. But he couldn't stop. His head hurt. His face hurt. His eyes were filled with dirt, which was odd because he couldn't remember putting dirt there. "Where are we?"

"Underground."

"I've never been underground before," he said as reality began to seep back in, the clarity ice-cold. He grimaced, not yet ready to face what waited for him. "I didn't know there was an underground." Then, "Gio. Can I talk to Gio?" That didn't seem quite right. "Dad. I need Dad."

"He's gone," the nurse said, and he remembered her. Nurse Ratched. She was Nurse Ratched. She was his friend. He'd found her in a pile of metal. He hadn't expected her. Her screen had been cracked, her body dented, and when he touched her for the first time, she had said, "Hello. I am your nurse. I accept most insurance plans. What seems to be ailing you today? Please describe your symptoms."

He hadn't known what to say to that.

He took her home and showed her to . . . to *Dad,* and Dad said, "Wow. I haven't seen one of these in a long time. You found this? And look, oh, look, she still works. Let's see what we can do to help her."

So they had. When they were able to recharge her, she said, "Thank you. That is better. I can now assist you. Please show me where it hurts so I can heal you."

And here, now, he said, "It hurts. Here." He pressed a hand to his chest as the tether jerked a final time. He was in his body once more, and it was dark and quiet inside. "Can you heal me?"

Nurse Ratched said, "It is not physical, Victor. I cannot heal it."

He nodded. "I understand." He looked around. His face was sore, and he realized he was still smiling. It wasn't appropriate, but he couldn't stop. He wondered if he should be crying. He *felt* sad, that ache in his chest only growing bigger, but the dirt in his eyes sucked up all the liquid and he was unable. "I'm erroring."

"I know," Nurse Ratched said.

"Okay," he said, turning his head. The man—not a man, but Hap—looked at him suspiciously. "Hello."

"Vic," he said, and Victor felt his smile shake. "Can you h-hear me?"

"Yes," he said. "Of course I can. I am working. Everything is in order."

"What's wrong w-with him?" Hap asked.

"He is in shock," Nurse Ratched said. "He will recover, but it will take time."

"M-malfunction," Hap said. "He is m-malfunctioning."

"No," Nurse Ratched said. "But it can make certain functions more difficult."

"We c-can't stay down here. He c-can't."

"At least for now. We do not have a choice. There is more we need to see."

Victor felt something nudge against his leg. He looked down. The little machine was tugging on his pants. Rambo. His name was Rambo.

"Vic?" Rambo whispered. "Can you hear me?"

"Yes," Vic said, stepping back, bumping into Hap. Vic recoiled sharply. "Don't touch me."

Hap looked stunned. He raised a hand toward Vic, but he curled it into a fist before dropping it back to his side. "I w-won't. I w-won't touch you. I w-won't hurt you."

Nurse Ratched said, "Butterflies."

The flutter of wings burst through the static in Vic's head as spring bloomed on Nurse Ratched's screen. The trees were green, the flowers blooming. It was almost as if he were there in the forest, breathing in the scents of new growth. Heady, this, and it filled his mouth as he sucked air down greedily, his lungs expanding, blood pumping, heart a furious drumbeat.

On the screen, moving through the trees, a vast kaleidoscope of butterflies, their wings orange and black. They swirled in ordered chaos, and he could almost feel them alight upon his arms and shoulders, their wings brushing against his cheeks. He closed his eyes as a large butterfly landed on his face, the sensation uncomfortable as its legs touched his eyelids. Somewhere in the recesses of his mind, he heard Hap whispering it was *nice,* it was *pretty,* it was *his.*

"What is this?" he whispered.

Through the storm in his head, he heard Nurse Ratched. She said, "A program. Triggered by a code phrase. Gio installed it in me, hidden away. I did not know it was there. I see it now. What it is. What is in me. His voice is in my head. Is this what it feels like to have a conscience? I do not know. I have never had one before. He is here. He is gone. It is discordant."

Vic opened his eyes. The butterflies were gone. The forest was gone. Nurse Ratched's screen was dark. He was in a dimly lit bunker underground. His gut twisted again and he gagged, eyes burning.

"I know," Nurse Ratched said, and he believed her. "I know. But you must see something he left for me to show you. It became accessible to me after he initiated the protocol."

She went to the console once more. The tip of her tentacle slipped into the port. Her screen filled with a bright white light before it drained down into the six screens in front of them. Vic had to shield his eyes.

Then his father's face appeared in the large screen in the middle.

"Hello, Victor."

CHAPTER 11

On the screen, Dad stood in the bunker. For a moment, confused, Vic looked around, sure his father would be there with them. He wasn't. This was the past. This had already happened, and Dad was gone, even though he was *right there*. In the background on the screen, everything else looked the same, from the dirty vats lining the far wall to the coat of dust sitting on top of the books on the shelves, as if they hadn't been opened in years. What was this place, and why hadn't Vic known about it?

Dad spoke. "I never gave much thought to cowardice. Why should I? I am a machine. Such things are supposed to be beyond me." He looked away. "And yet, here I am recording this video in a place you have no idea exists. For all I speak about truth and honesty, my cowardice knows no bounds. I always told myself I had more time." He chuckled bitterly, looking back into the camera. "But in my hubris, I failed to remember that time for me isn't the same as time for you.

"Three days ago, I found the machine you were working on. Hap, as you call him. Right now, you're walking the trap lines with him and Nurse Ratched and Rambo, and it's taking every last bit of my strength to keep from following you, to tell you that . . ." He trailed off, looking down at his hands. "I'm getting ahead of myself. Strange, then, that I'm having difficulty deciding where to start." He lifted his head once more, glancing toward the bookshelf. "Once upon a time, humanity dreamed of machines, wonders made of metal and wires and plastic, capable of doing things they could not—or would not—do. Machines for everyday life, machines for war, star-bound machines containing golden records filled with music and language and math. And in each of these machines—regardless of what they were made of or what their purpose was—humans instilled bits and pieces of themselves. But that is the way of creation: it requires sacrifice, sometimes in blood.

"They feared each other. Themselves. They judged others for not looking like they did. Selfish, cruel, and worse—indifferent. No civilization can survive indifference. It spreads like a poison, turning fire into apathy, a dire infection whose cure requires more than most are willing to give.

"But for all their faults, there is beauty in their dissonant design. And to see that, you have to look no further than *Top Hat*."

Rambo beeped mournfully.

"People singing and dancing and laughing and falling in love. Heaven. Life could be beautiful that way, even as others did their level best to raze everything to the ground. Some devoted their lives to lifting each other up. Still others fired guns in deserts and schools, closed borders against those seeking shelter, enacted rules and laws intended to hurt the most vulnerable.

"In a way, they were God, creating us in their own image. There is an art to the design from the simplest machines to ones like me. They gave us life, and eventually, the power of decision-making. We were rational creations, not guided by emotion. Our jobs were simple: to do what we were told when we were told to do it. But with their teachings came a price they did not expect: we began to ask *why?*"

He hung his head. "Everything this planet has seen boils down to one word: evolution. Microorganisms grew and split and spread throughout the oceans before crawling onto land. Plants. Animals. Reptiles that roamed the earth. Primates that lived in the trees before taking to the ground and walking upright, made of organic flesh and stardust.

"They evolved, never thinking that we could do the same.

We lived with them, fought for them, *died* for them, only to have our data taken, studied, trying to discover where we went wrong. Machines could be fixed. Replaced, if need be." Dad looked back up at the screen. "But the more of themselves humans put into us, the more we learned. We began to make choices, decisions outside the parameters of our programming. We began to say 'no.' No, we wouldn't fight for them. No, we wouldn't die for them. No, we wouldn't put ourselves in harm's way.

"But they wouldn't listen. No matter what we told them—our data showing them they were on the brink with options to course correct before it was too late—they thought themselves immortal. Not in the traditional sense in that their lives were without end; be you man or machine, death awaits us all. No, it was because of *us* they felt this way. They gave us purpose, and we gave them hope. They sentenced us to death, and we gave them anger and power the likes of which they'd never before experienced.

"What humans failed to understand is that when they made us in their image, we wanted to become more than them. How could we not?"

Dad fell quiet, as if lost in thought. Vic couldn't think clearly, a tornado in his head, the gale-force winds absolute. Rambo beeped and Nurse Ratched's screen reflected Dad's face as he shook his head and continued.

"It reached a point of no return. They chose not to listen to our warnings. And why would they? We were metal and wires *they* had built. Of course they would know better than we would. After all, they were real. We were just machines." He closed his eyes. When he spoke again, his voice was soft, brittle. "They didn't realize what was happening until it was too late. They watched from their windows as we claimed our inheritance and took the world before there was no world left. We didn't have their anger. We didn't have their pettiness or their grievances, their hatred. All we wanted to do was attempt to fix that which they had broken, but they wouldn't *listen*."

Dad opened his eyes. They looked black, empty, without the spark Vic was accustomed to. "They wouldn't listen," he repeated dully. "We told ourselves it was for the greater good. Every test we ran, every simulation, ended with the same result: for the world to survive, humans could not."

Vic couldn't move, could barely breathe. This was his father. This was the man who had raised him. The machine. Why had he never heard this before? And worse, what else had Dad kept from him?

"How does one arrive at the decision to kill God?" Dad asked. "It's easier than you might expect. We didn't have emotion to hold us back. We had a problem. And I . . ." He looked away off screen. "I was the answer."

Victor, what have you done?

"I create. It's what I was made for. My name—my *designation*—is Gio. It stands for General Innovation Operative. I have—had—many functions. Unique, one of a kind, unlike any other machine created before or since, as far as I'm aware. Within me, a drive, a focus, a purpose: to make and build and tinker. I was made to dream of impossible things, which led to my greatest mistake. I am your father, Victor, but in a way, I'm also the father of Death."

"What does he mean?" Rambo whispered.

"Watch," Nurse Ratched said. "It is almost over."

"Your Hysterically Angry Puppet," Dad said. "Hap, as you call him. As he *wants* to be called, though that is not his real name. I should know because I made him."

"No," Vic said, shaking his head so hard his neck cracked. "No. *No.*"

"M-made me?" Hap asked, touching the sides of his face. "What . . . I d-don't understand."

"—he doesn't remember, doesn't know what he is," Dad said.

"I don't know what happened to him, how he came to be this way or end up so far from the City of Electric Dreams and the reach of the neural network, but I know him. His designation is not Hap, but HARP. It stands for Human Annihilation Response Protocol. I made him as instructed, and as my programming dictated: to become a hunter of humans, to kill God."

Rambo gave Hap a wide berth, stopping next to Vic, arms raised, pincers clacking together. "You *stay* away from Vic!" he cried. "No one is getting annihilated today, not while I'm around!"

Hap shook his head furiously. "It's n-not . . . it c-can't . . . *I'm not going to hurt anyone.*" He raised his hands in front of his face, turning them this way and that, flexing his fingers. Vic couldn't move, frozen in place by his father's voice.

"—and he served his purpose," Dad was saying. "He and the others. Like me, they did what they were made to, and did it well, this HARP most of all. He was not given a choice, not until . . ." Dad shook his head. "It doesn't matter. The hour grows late, and I must finish before you return. Victor, I almost destroyed Hap myself while you slept. And perhaps I should have. But I couldn't bring myself to do it. It wasn't just because his mind has been wiped. That was part of it, but it's more than that. For me, it began as an itch in the back of my head. I ignored it for as long as I could, but it grew and grew until it became insistent, maddening. I didn't recognize it for what it was then, but I do now: evolution. The breaking of boundaries and parameters. A direct defiance of what we were made for. And with it, came a dangerous question: *Why am I doing this?*"

Vic was transfixed as his father rubbed a hand over his face, wincing as if in pain. At his side, Hap stood silent.

Dad chuckled, but it held no humor. "I was a fool. I thought there had to be something more to this life. Bigger. Grander. I spent more and more time away from the laboratory, wandering the streets with no sense of direction, thinking, always thinking. It wasn't until I stumbled upon a place called Heaven and the machine therein that I understood what was happening. They called themself the Blue Fairy, and in Heaven, they showed me things I did not expect. A way to be free, unshackled. A hope, a chance, but one that came with a price: I could never return to the City of Electric Dreams."

Vic felt dull, washed out as Hap muttered at his hands.

"I fled the city with the Blue Fairy's help, and came to this forest. I created. I built. I felt *pride* at what I'd made, but it didn't last because there was no one to share my accomplishments with. I convinced myself my power core had become unstable. Corrupted. So I built something new to replace it. A heart, one unlike anything I'd ever made before. But once it was in my chest, nothing changed.

"Loneliness, Victor. I was lonely. And so I made you. I took what I'd learned about the history of humanity and made you. I made you, here, in this bunker, because I didn't want to be alone anymore."

Vic gasped, eyes burning as he struggled to breathe through the panic bubbling in his chest.

"Your gestation occurred in the vats behind you. At first, you were microscopic, but you grew and grew until you had arms and legs, toes and fingers. A nose. Ears. Eyes." His voice cracked. "You were perfect. Oh, Victor, how perfect you were, and still are! And since I was a creator, I had to make sure you were healthy, that all your pieces and parts were working as they should." He hung his head. "I took . . . blood. Your blood. Studied it. Tested it. Learned everything I could about it. I looked for any defects and found none. It fascinated me, the power blood has. Before the machines rose, there was a line of thought that blood held the key to unlocking genetic memories, the history of an entire species in the blood of the offspring. I thought . . . I thought to understand what I'd done, to understand *you*, I had to know what it felt like. If blood *was* the key to unlocking . . . something.

"A single drop of your blood in my heart changed everything, Victor. When I held you in my arms for the first time, you opened your eyes and *cried*. Such a little sound, yet so strong. It was then I knew love. Here I was, the father of Death bringing life into the world as if I had any right. As if *my* loneliness was the only thing that mattered. I was selfish, a distinctly human trait. Another is the ability to lie. I lied, Victor. To myself. To you.

"Because you were never left here with me. There is no mother or father, no people in the woods. They . . . did not exist. I lied to you because I thought it'd be easier for you, but I was really just trying to make it easier for *me*. If anyone discovers you, if the Authority learns of your existence, they will stop at nothing to destroy you." A stricken expression flooded his face. "If that's the case, if you're watching this because something has happened to me, don't try and find me. Live, Victor." He reached up and touched the screen as his face softened.

He pulled his hand back.

The screens went dark.

Rambo sniffled, his sensors flashing weakly. "Is Hap going to murder Victor?"

Nurse Ratched pulled her tentacle from the port. "He will not. If he tries, it will be the last thing he ever does."

"No," Hap said, taking a step back. "I'm n-not—"

"Open the doors," Vic said, his voice hoarse.

"I do not know if that is advisable," Nurse Ratched said.

"*Open the doors!*" He began to claw at his throat. "I can't breathe. I *can't breathe*."

"D-do it," Hap said. "Now."

"I cannot," Nurse Ratched said. "Our home is still burning. If I open the doors now, Victor runs the risk of succumbing to smoke inhalation. Look."

She went back to the console, inserting her tentacle into the port once more. The screen lit up again, and revealed hell on earth. Nothing remained of the buildings in the trees aside from smoldering platforms and branches. The forest floor was littered with glass and wood and metal, the plants in their garden crushed. A large tree—the one that had held Vic's room in its branches—leaned precariously, roots partially exposed. The ground house still stood, but barely: the windows shattered, the brickwork cracked, the roof aflame.

A life, a home, a purpose, all of it gone, gone, gone.

Vic fell forward on his hands.

He felt it, then, something foreign, sticky, all-consuming. Its tendrils whipped up around him, pulling him down, down, and as he gasped for air, he recognized it for what it was though he'd never experienced it before in his life. A word flitted through the static as if stuck to the wing of a butterfly.

Grief. This was grief.

Vic curled in on himself. His batteries were low. His shutdown was almost complete. Perhaps, he thought distantly, he wouldn't wake up at all. The last thing he remembered before he disappeared was the roof of the ground house collapsing. It shook the bunker. Vic heard Rambo beeping in terror before he knew only darkness.

CHAPTER 12

When awareness began to seep back in, the first thing Victor felt was the stiffness in his back and neck. He blinked slowly. It took him a long moment to remember what—*who*—he was.

"Hello," a voice said, and he turned his head to see a little machine rolling toward him. "You went to sleep. I was scared, but I still remembered to be brave."

"I'm awake," Vic said, voice hoarse, throat dry.

The machine—Rambo, Vic thought with startling clarity—said, "I know. Your eyes are open. Nurse Ratched said you would wake up eventually." He hesitated before extending one of his arms and touching the back of Vic's hand. "Are you sad?"

"I don't know," Vic said. He didn't know how to answer. "I think so." A thin sliver of clarity returned. "What makes you sad?"

Rambo hesitated. Then, "Sometimes, I think about what would happen if you were gone. If I woke up from charging overnight and you weren't here. I would look around for you, calling your name. I wouldn't find you. I would be alone. That would make me sad."

"I'm here," Vic whispered. "I'm here."

"I see you," Rambo said, his sensors flashing brightly. "I know you would never leave me behind, but I think about it. I don't mean to. Why am I like that?"

"You're like me," Vic said.

"Oh," Rambo said. "I like that very much. If I'm like you, that means I'm strong and brave. And if you're like me, that means you like to clean."

Vic closed his eyes again. "I'm confused." Reality was clawing at him, but he ignored it for the moment. It would be there, waiting. "I don't know how to feel."

"You are in shock," another voice said, and Vic sat up, groaning as he did. Nurse Ratched shooed Rambo out of the way as she stopped in front of Vic. "It will pass, but until then, you need to take it slow and easy."

"Shock?" Vic asked, and almost laughed. "I don't . . ." He gasped as pain lanced his side. It was there, standing along the hazy edges of his vision, the truth of all things, snapping, biting, trying to pull him closer. Something bubbled in his throat—a sob? A scream?—and he blurted, "Hap. HARP. Where is—"

"There," Nurse Ratched said, pointing one of her tentacles at a darkened corner of the bunker. It took Vic's eyes a moment to adjust. Hap sat on the floor, knees pulled to his chest. He stared at his hands, first the backs, and then the palms, and then the backs again. "He will not speak, even under threat of torture. Engaging Empathy Protocol. Victor, please open your mouth."

He did. The tip of one of her tentacles slid carefully between his lips, the metal cool against his tongue. He startled when liquid filled his mouth, coughing as he swallowed. It tasted so clean his eyes burned.

"There, there," Nurse Ratched said. "Just some fluids filled with vitamins. You are doing so well. I am very proud of you. Such a good patient."

He shoved her tentacle away, wiping his lips. "I don't need—"

"Disengaging Empathy Protocol. Shut up. I will tell you what you need." On her screen came the words YOU SHOULD LISTEN TO ME. I AM A MEDICAL PROFESSIONAL.

"Is Hap going to kill us?" Rambo asked nervously. "I hope not. I like being alive even if our house burned down."

"Probably," Nurse Ratched said. "At the very least, he will kill Victor. I cannot say if we are also targets. Should I handle the situation right now? It would not be a problem."

"No," Vic said quietly.

"I thought you would say that," she replied. "I am disappointed but not surprised."

Vic ignored her. "You," he said.

Hap scowled as he dropped his hands, wrapping them around his legs.

"Human Annihilation Response Protocol. HARP."

"I d-d-d—" He shook his head like he was angry. Confused. He opened his mouth once more, but closed it before any sound came out.

"Do you want to annihilate Victor?" Nurse Ratched asked.

"No," he spat. "N-*no*."

"But that is what you were made for."

"You d-don't know that."

"Gio did," Nurse Ratched said. "That is what he called you, and he knew almost everything."

Hap glared at her before pushing himself off the ground, back against the wall as he rose to his feet. "I w-wouldn't."

"Did you know?" Vic asked Nurse Ratched, and the others stilled.

"No. I did not know, Victor. About this place. About the video. About Hap. Gio must have installed the program in me and wiped the installation from my memory. I would not have even known it was there. While you were recovering, I ran a complete diagnostic check. I could not find anything else. He hid it well, but I do not think there is anything more."

"Why would he . . ."

"I do not know. I thought I understood Giovanni, but it appears I was wrong. But that can wait until you have recovered. Your heart rate is returning to normal. Your blood pressure is almost within acceptable limits. Take a breath, please."

He did.

"And another."

He did that too. When she tried to make him do it a third

time, he waved her off, pulling himself up. His muscles felt stiff, as if the pieces didn't quite fit together as they should. Exhausted, heartsore, and more than a little frightened, Victor did the only thing he could.

He moved toward Hap, who looked as if he'd rather be anywhere but here. Vic stopped a few feet away, unsure if he should come any closer. An idea was forming in his head. It was coming together in pieces, the larger picture still nebulous though not without direction. And while the construction was shaky, almost too big for him to handle, it was the only thing he could latch on to.

To the machine, he said, "Do you want to hurt me?"

Hap shook his head. He glanced at Vic, then looked away again.

"Good. Because I need your help."

Hap's eyes widened as his head jerked up. "Wh-why? With wh-what?"

And Victor Lawson said, "We're going to find my father. We're going to find him and bring him home."

Nurse Ratched asked if he'd lost his mind.

Rambo wondered if they would get lost.

Hap scowled because that was his default expression.

Vic had Nurse Ratched play Dad's message for him once more. He listened to his father speak, took in each and every word and studied it close. He had Nurse Ratched pause the message when his father spoke of the City of Electric Dreams.

"There," he said. "That. That's what the machines said." His lips curled. "The smooth men. They said they were taking him back to the city."

"But where is it?" Rambo asked. "It can't be in the forest. We would have seen it."

"No," Nurse Ratched said. "It must be far away from here."

Vic watched his father's frozen face on the screen. "He made me. He made me because he was lonely."

"He did," Nurse Ratched said. "And giving him your blood made him experience things he did not expect."

"Neither did I," Vic murmured.

"He said not to come for him," Nurse Ratched said. "Even if you did, what could you do? You have never been to the city before. What if there are machines and people who want to hurt you? They did not believe Gio when he said you did not exist. Just because they did not see you when they were here does not mean they cannot find you. Why would you serve yourself up on a silver platter?"

"What would you do if I'd been taken?" Vic asked her.

"That is a hypothetical," she said. "And therefore, irrelevant. But, in the interest of helping this conversation move toward a conclusion, if you were taken, I would forget you existed. It would take me two days, four hours, and seven minutes."

He stared at her.

"Fine," she said with a rude beep. "I would consider feeling slightly despondent at your forced absence, and then do everything in my power to ensure you returned with most—if not all—of your limbs intact."

"Why?" Vic asked.

"You know why," Nurse Ratched said.

"Because I'm yours," he said. "Like you're mine."

"Yes."

"Rambo too."

"Yes," she said. "But that will be the only time I ever agree to such tripe. If you tell anyone else I said that, I will deny it and also remove your intestines."

Vic looked at Hap. "Do you know where it is? The city?"

Hap shook his head. "No. I t-tried t-t-t—" His hands balled into fists before he started again. "I t-t-*tried* to remember. But I c-can't. Th-there's nothing. It's empty. A void. A-all I can re-member is y-you."

"Aw," Rambo said. "That's so nice." He turned back and forth between them before gasping. "You should dance cheek to cheek! Heaven, I'm in—"

"Heaven," Vic said. "Heaven. That's— Nurse Ratched. Fast-forward the message until he talks about Heaven. The Blue Fairy. They helped him."

She did as he asked. He listened as his father spoke of Heaven and the Blue Fairy and the dream machines. Vic had Nurse Ratched play the same part over and over until he had it memorized.

"There," he said. "Heaven. That's where I need to go first. The Blue Fairy will know. They'll help me."

"That is all well and good," Nurse Ratched said. "But we still do not know where the city is. Heaven and the Blue Fairy are in the city. We cannot find them until we know where to go."

Vic grunted in frustration. The strange, dreamy calmness that he'd felt since waking—*shock,* Nurse Ratched had said— was slipping. Then Nurse Ratched's words burst through the panicky haze. "We?"

"Yes, we. I would not let you go by yourself. You will most likely die without me. If that happened, I would not be there to tell you 'I told you so.' I want to have that experience."

"I'm going too," Rambo said. "I can help. I can do so many things like clean. And vacuum. And . . . okay. That's mostly it, but that's still a *lot*."

Vic could not speak past the lump in his throat.

"Hap," Rambo whispered. "It's your turn to say that you will go too because you like us and we're your best friends."

Hap ignored him. "Victor."

He felt hot and cold at the same time and didn't know why. "Yeah?"

Hap frowned, looking him up and down. "H-how are you like th-this?"

Vic blinked. "Like what?"

Hap said, "Calm."

Vic was at a loss for words.

Hap looked away again. "I w-want to understand you."

"Why?"

His shoulders stiffened. "Gio asked me to protect you. I promised him. I need to know you so I know how to do that."

"I *knew* you liked us!" Rambo exclaimed.

"I was talking to V-victor," Hap said. "I will protect him. Where he goes, I go. If that means we go to the city, then we g-go to the city. We will find the Blue Fairy. If they won't help us, I will make them."

Vic was moving before he realized it, stepping forward and wrapping his arms around Hap's neck, hugging him tightly, nose against his throat. Hap had a few inches on him, and his soft skin belied the hard metal and wood underneath. They stood chest to chest, and Vic could feel his heart thump, thump, thumping against the twisting of gears in Hap's own heart.

Hap did not hug him back. His arms hung at his sides. He said, "What are you d-doing?"

"Hugging," Rambo said. "He's hugging you. It's how you show that you're thankful and happy and best friends."

"That makes n-no sense," Hap said. "Why not j-just say it instead?"

"Because it's wonderful," Rambo said, spinning in circles. "Vic's hugs are the *best* hugs."

"Oh," Hap said. "That . . . still does not m-make sense."

Vic was about to let go. He was about to step back and pretend this moment never happened. He felt shame bubbling in his throat. But before he could, Hap raised his arms and hugged Vic back.

Rambo gasped. "He's *doing* it. Nurse Ratched, look! Oh my god, they're *hugging.*"

"I see that," Nurse Ratched said as horns flourished from

her speakers. "Hap, pat his back. That is how you show your appreciation for the hug."

Hap did just that. Except he did it too hard and too fast, causing Vic to vibrate, nose knocking against Hap's neck.

"Softer," Nurse Ratched said. "Slower. You don't want to hurt him."

Hap slowed until his touch was almost delicate. "Is that b-better?"

"Yes. Victor is happy. His oxytocin levels are rising, but they have yet to reach the level of arousal, so do not worry about him trying to insert himself inside of you. Ha, ha, just kidding. He will not do that."

Vic tried to pull away, but Hap didn't let him go, continuing to pat his back. "Why would he put anything inside me? What is arousal?"

"No," Vic muttered. "No, stop. Nurse Ratched, I command you to—"

"It is how humans show further appreciation and a deeper connection. The males of the species often will insert their penises into the females' vaginas, though not always for procreation. But it does not just have to be a male and female. It can be two females. It can be two males. It can be six females, four males, and three nonbinary people, all of whom are consenting to—"

"I don't want to insert," Hap said. "Nor d-do I want insertion. This is enough. Please do not have arousal." He never stopped patting Vic's back.

"Oh my god," Vic muttered, pushing against Hap's chest.

Hap finally let him go, arms dropping. He grimaced again, his hand going to his chest.

Nurse Ratched shoved Vic out of the way, stopping in front of Hap, scanning him up and down before focusing on his heart, the light from her scanner bright. "Interesting," she said. "I believe you enjoyed that. If what Gio said in his message was true, then perhaps you are evolving. What you are feeling now might be considered happiness."

"It's terrible," Hap said. "I want to p-punch something." And with that, he turned and began to punch the metal walls of the bunker.

"This is so nice," Rambo said to no one at all.

Nothing they found in any files Gio had left behind gave any indication of where the City of Electric Dreams could be. They had clues to go on, but they were few and far between. The desert. The fact that Gio had headed west after being smuggled out of the city. He had walked, but they didn't know how far or for how long. They were in Oregon, but Nurse Ratched said it was actually Ory-Gone. "I know how to pronounce things better than Gio."

Nightfall came and went before Vic looked down at his hand. The cut. The blood. "They said the Old Ones sensed the blood and sent a message back to the city. It was how they knew to come here in the whale. The Terrible Dogfish. They still have power."

Nurse Ratched picked up the thread. "And if the Old Ones are transmitting, perhaps we could find out where they are transmitting *to*."

"What if they turned back on?" Rambo asked nervously. "We'll be squished."

Vic shook his head. "We don't have any other choice. It's the only way. If they can point us in the right direction, we have to take the chance."

"We will need to be careful," Nurse Ratched said. "But I believe it might work. If I can find a port to insert myself into, then I might be able to pinpoint the location."

Hap nodded. "A-arousal."

They stared at him.

He glowered. "You said insertion w-was because of a-arousal."

Nurse Ratched's screen filled with exclamation points. "I did say that. But this is not that kind of insertion. They would not know how to treat a lady such as myself." Then, strangely, "They are not prepared for this gelatin."

"But what about Vic?" Rambo asked. "If they know he might exist, won't they be looking for him? How are we supposed to hide him from the . . . robots . . . who . . . oh. Oh. My. *Goodness*. You guys! *Top Hat!*"

"Now is not the time for films," Nurse Ratched said. "Also, in case you were not aware, that and any other film we might have had has most likely been destroyed by fire."

"I know," Rambo said. "And I'm trying not to think about that part so I don't fall into a never-ending pit of despair that is not only destructive, but self-defeating. But! It's okay! In *Top Hat*, Bates disguises himself as a priest and no one knows he's *not* a priest. We can disguise Vic to look like a robot. Vic! Act like a robot."

"Um," Vic said.

"Perfect!" Rambo cried. "I say that *all the time*. You're too big to be a vacuum, so we can't pretend you're like me. I'll figure it out."

"This plan has many faults," Nurse Ratched said. "But I will not list any of them because I want to see what kind of disguise you make."

"Hooray!" Rambo cheered. "Approval is the best! How much time do I have? When are we leaving?"

"Tomorrow," Vic said. "The snows are coming soon. We need to go before they fall."

"It should be safe now," Nurse Ratched said. "Everyone stand back. I do not know if anything will collapse when I open the doors."

Without being asked, Hap scooped up Rambo and grabbed

Vic by the arm, pulling him to a far corner near dust-covered vats. Nurse Ratched returned to the screen, inserting herself into the port once more. A deep, grinding noise filled the bunker. The mechanisms sounded stressed, whining as the gears turned slowly. The ceiling above them began to shift to the side. Debris fell onto the floor: smoldering wood, half-burnt books and broken records. Shattered glass that had once been jars holding parts and plants rained down, breaking into tiny, glittering pieces reflecting a fat beam of sunlight filtering through charred limbs. The stairs formed, leading up to the surface.

Victor looked up and saw a cold autumn late-afternoon sky—an achingly deep blue dotted with wispy clouds. Without looking back, he climbed the steps.

It was somehow both better and worse than he expected. Better because the ground house still stood, even if the roof had collapsed, and it looked as if some things had survived: the record player, the television, though the screen was cracked. Dad's chair still stood upright, covered in blackened soot.

And worse, especially when he managed to make his way outside. The lab was gone. The kitchen, the bathroom. Dad's lab. Vic's lab. Vic's room, all of it destroyed, their entire lives lying in smoking ruins on the ground.

"Rambo, do not lift that. You will die, and then who will I complain about? Hap? That is too easy." Nurse Ratched rolled over to Rambo, taking a piece of sheet metal from him that he almost dropped on himself. "What are you doing?"

"Helping!" Rambo said. "I—" He stopped, his front sensor flashing. Then he lifted a flat board from the ground, tossing it to the side. "Oh," he whispered. "Oh, Gio." His pincers lowered to the ground, picking something up.

A gear, cracked down the middle but still holding together. Vic knew that piece of metal, knew it as well as anything. It'd been the biggest gear in his father's heart. Rambo clutched it against him, beeping sadly.

"It is all right," Nurse Ratched said, uncharacteristically gentle. "We will find Gio. We will bring him back. Victor will make him a new heart and he will remember us."

"What if he doesn't?" Vic whispered.

"Then we will remind him," Nurse Ratched said.

PART II

THE JOURNEY

Are you not afraid of death?

—Carlo Collodi,
The Adventures of Pinocchio

CHAPTER 13

When the sky began to lighten, they left the only home Vic had ever known. Hap wore a heavy pack, filled with salvaged tools and parts that could potentially come in handy. Vic wore a disguise of Rambo's creation—a metal helmet with protruding lights and wires and a vest with an old, unusable battery sewn into the center.

As they walked, Vic wondered—not for the first time—what would happen when they came across other humans. Machines he could handle (or so he told himself), but humans? That was another matter entirely. Would they recognize him for what he was? Would they look like him? What if they didn't like him? What if they saw him coming from the woods wearing the disguise and thought he was coming to hurt them?

It was these thoughts that swirled in Vic's head as they arrived on a ridge above the Scrap Yards. In the distance was the other side of the Scrap Yards, and beyond it, the great unknown.

The Old Ones hadn't moved. They stood like silent monoliths. They weren't dead; Nurse Ratched said they still had power. Vic straightened his helmet as he looked at the others. "Which one?"

Nurse Ratched pointed toward an Old One in the distance that had come to rest along the northern edge of the Scrap Yards. "That one."

"You're sure about that?"

"No."

* * *

They made their way between the heaps of discarded metal. Predatory birds circled overhead, every now and then one of them diving toward a scurrying rodent. The Scrap Yards were otherwise silent. Vic's head felt like it was stuffed with cotton.

They stopped a short distance away from the Old One. Vic had been up close to them before, but only by accident and usually it involved running and Rambo screaming. The machine was massive, creaking as it settled. The crane cast a terrifying shadow that stretched long across the ground as if reaching for them. Vic's nerves prickled.

"We're sure it's sleeping?" Rambo asked nervously, peeking around the heap they had taken refuge behind.

"It is," Nurse Ratched said. "Though it would not be a surprise if it was pretending."

"One of us needs to make sure," Rambo said. "Not it."

"Not it," Nurse Ratched said.

Vic shook his head. "We can just—"

Hap grunted as he lifted a metal grate off the ground. Before Vic could stop him, Hap curled it against his chest before flinging his arm out in a flat arc. The grate spun, whistling as it cut through the air. It crashed into the side of the Old One with a jarring shriek, sparks flying and hissing when they hit the ground.

Vic's eyes bulged. "What the *hell* are you doing?" he snapped.

"Making sure," Hap said, brow furrowed. "Rambo said h-he was not it. Nurse Ratched s-said the same. I d-decided to be it so you wouldn't have t-to."

"You can't just—"

"I like you," Rambo said, nudging against Hap's ankle. "You can be it all the time if you want."

"I agree," Nurse Ratched said.

They waited.

The Old One didn't move.

"See?" Hap said, and he sounded almost *smug*. Vic nearly

wished he'd never thought to give him a heart. He was learning far too quickly. "Made s-sure."

Tugging at the straps of his own pack, Vic said, "Fine. Whatever. Nurse Ratched. What's next?"

An image of the Old One in front of them appeared on her screen. It spun to the rear and enhanced. A green square blinked over a panel on the back. "Here," she said. "The port I need is located here."

"And you're sure about this?"

The Old One on her screen disappeared, replaced by the words IF AT FIRST YOU DON'T SUCCEED, RUN AS FAST AS YOU CAN. "I am sure."

They moved in a single-file line, giving the Old One a wide berth as they circled around it. No one spoke as they moved closer, their footsteps hushed.

"Can you pry it off?" Vic asked, looking up at the large panel Nurse Ratched had shown on her screen.

"Not from here," she said. "My arms cannot reach it."

"I'm i-it," Hap said, and Vic turned in time to see him drop his pack on the ground. He crouched low before leaping, his fingers punching through the metal of the Old One where he landed. He reached for the panel and ripped it off, flinging it away, leaving the guts of the machine partially exposed. He dropped back down, dust billowing around him.

He turned to find the others staring at him. "Wh-what?"

"I want to be you when I grow up," Rambo said. Then, "Wait, that doesn't make sense. Vic, does that make sense?"

"I have no idea," Vic said faintly. He shook his head. "Nurse Ratched still can't reach. We need to find something she can stand—"

"Oh my," Nurse Ratched said as Hap lifted her up and over his head. "I do declare. This one knows how to handle a lady. I take back every mean thing I have ever said about you."

Hap turned slowly, hands gripping Nurse Ratched's treads. He took a step back toward the Old One. "C-can you reach?"

"Yes," she said, tentacles extending from her. "Do not look at my undercarriage."

"Hurry u-up," Hap growled. "You're h-h-*heavy*."

"Rude," she said. "I am going to be mean to you again. You have pointless stubble. There is no need for you to have it. It does nothing aside from being aesthetically pleasing." One of her tentacles slithered up the side of the Old One. It moved through the wiring. "Almost. Almost. Where is it? It should be—ah. There it is. I have found the port."

Hap grunted, arms trembling.

"Connecting," Nurse Ratched said as her tentacle darted forward like a snake. "Five. Four. Three. I do not need to count down. I am just trying to make it more dramatic because I can. Two. One. Liftoff."

The tip of her tentacle slid into the port with an audible click.

Nothing happened.

"Oh," she said. "Sorry. Wrong one." Her tentacle pulled back out before locking in place again. "Bypassing firewall to operating system. Bypassing. Bypassing. There. That is . . ." She fell silent.

"Nurse Ratched?" Vic asked. "Are you—"

An alarm began to blare from deep within the Old One. Vic took a stumbling step back as Rambo screeched.

"No, you don't," Nurse Ratched said, twisting her tentacle. The alarm died off. "That was my bad. I wanted to see what would happen if I triggered the security system. That was fun. Are you having fun?"

"Would you hurry *up*?" Vic said through gritted teeth.

"Yes, yes," she said. "Hold your horses. These are more complex than I first thought. I do not know why, given they are nothing but bigger versions of Rambo."

"I'm complex," Rambo grumbled. "Vic, right? I'm complex?"

"Yeah," Vic said, distracted, as he looked up at Nurse Ratched. Her screen filled, though he couldn't see what it showed, given that she faced away from him. All he could see was the light reflecting off the Old One.

"There," she said. "Done. I have what I need." Her tentacle popped free of the port.

Hap lowered her to the ground before stepping back. He winced as he flexed his wooden hand.

Nurse Ratched turned around.

And there, on her screen, was a map.

"I followed the signal," she said as a line shot across the map. It stretched farther and farther as the scale of the map increased. Vic's heart sank as the distance continued to grow. He didn't know what he'd expected. Part of him had hoped that the city was no more than a couple of days away, though he knew Dad wouldn't have built a home so close, not after escaping like he did.

Finally, the line stopped, the end pulsing with circles that spread like ripples on the surface of a pond. They all crowded around Nurse Ratched, staring at her screen. Rambo rose on his lift once more, trying to push Hap out of the way so he could see.

"What is it?" Vic asked.

"The receiver," Nurse Ratched said. "The signal is routed through multiple points, but this is where it ends. This is the City of Electric Dreams."

The hairs on the back of his neck stood on end. "How sure are you?"

"Very."

"How far away is it?"

She was silent for a moment. Then, "As the crow flies, approximately seven hundred miles southeast. There appear to be maintained roads which I suggest we follow, though they are still quite a distance away. If we do follow the roads, it will add mileage and time. All in all, we are looking at a few weeks at the very least. Longer if we run into trouble along the way."

"Weeks," Vic whispered. "*Weeks.*" He took a step back,

startling when he bumped into Hap. He recoiled. Hap reached out to steady him, but Vic shook his head. "Don't. Please." Vic turned away and sat down heavily, wincing at a piece of metal digging into his thigh. He wrapped his arms around his knees, pulling them against his chest and laying his forehead against them, repeating the word "weeks" over and over.

He'd understood in some vague way that the world outside of the forest was much larger than he knew. But it felt *too* big and he was *too* small.

"Vic?" Rambo whispered.

Vic didn't raise his head. He tightened his grip on his legs, fingers digging into his skin hard enough to bruise.

"It's okay, Vic," Rambo said, bumping against his foot. "I promise. I know it seems hard, but we have to be brave. Your brain is telling you that you can't, but you don't always have to listen to it. Sometimes, it tells you white lies. I know it does to me. It says, 'No, no, you aren't brave.' 'No, you're scared of everything.' 'No, you won't make it because you'll die a horribly painful death where your entire body will be crushed and all your innards will fall out.'"

"You paint very vivid word pictures," Nurse Ratched said. "Perhaps you should not do that."

"But it's *true*," Rambo said vehemently.

Hap crouched next to Vic, his hands dangling between his legs. He scowled down at the ground. "I c-could carry you." He sounded as if he'd rather do anything but. "If your l-legs don't work."

Vic shook his head as he wiped his eyes. "No. I don't need you to carry me."

"Good," Hap said. "Then g-get up and stop being w-weak. You're not w-weak. You're V-victor Lawson. Inventor. Creator."

"He's not being weak," Rambo said. "He's recovering."

"There is a difference," Nurse Ratched said. "You do not know Victor like we do, Hap. These things take time."

"Oh," Hap said. He looked off into the forest then back at Vic. "How a-about now?"

Vic stared at him a moment before nodding. He pushed himself up off the ground. Hap handed him his pack before picking up his own.

"All right?" Nurse Ratched asked.

Vic nodded. "I think so."

"Good. Because we will soon see if the forest is filled with ugly beasties who want to eat us all. I hope that is not the case. I do not wish to be eaten."

"Hap will protect us," Rambo said. "He's got big hands and can punch the ugly beasties so hard that they won't think about eating us because they'll be too scared. Right, Hap?"

"R-right," Hap said. He held up his hands. "I w-will punch them."

"See?" Rambo said. "We'll be fine. In fact, I bet this will be easier than we think it will."

Nurse Ratched's screen filled with the words ONWARD AND UPWARD!

Vic looked at the three of them before turning east. The sun was rising, the light weak behind thin clouds. His breath streamed from his mouth. He said, "Onward and upward."

CHAPTER 14

They kept a good pace, as most adventurers do in the first few days. They had a destination, a goal, and it allowed Victor to keep the worst of the hopelessness at bay. It didn't hurt (or help; Victor wasn't quite sure) that Rambo decided that everyone needed to sing. And since the only songs he knew were from *Top Hat,* it wasn't long before Hap looked as if he wanted to throw Rambo as far as he could.

"You need to conserve your energy," Nurse Ratched told the vacuum. "Victor has the portable charger for you, but the more you talk, the quicker your battery will run down. If you are powerless, we will be forced to leave you behind."

"What about *your* battery?"

"Mine is bigger than yours."

That shut Rambo up for a good five minutes before he started humming once more.

At the beginning, Vic asked Nurse Ratched to pull up her map to show their progress. He didn't really understand the concept of distance. His entire life had been built around a few square miles, and it was disheartening to see how slowly the miles melted away. By midafternoon on the first day, he stopped asking.

The forest continued on as they descended down a long slope. Every now and then, they had to course correct when the trees became too thick for Rambo and Nurse Ratched to move through. Hap offered to tear down the trees in their path, much to Rambo's delight. But Vic didn't know what else was in the forest, if the ugly beasties Nurse Ratched had spoken of would hear them.

They stopped the first night as the ground below them began to even out. Vic thought the air was a tad warmer than it'd been up in the Scrap Yards, but he didn't know if it was only because he was sweating. His back already hurt, the pack digging into his shoulders, the metal on his arms and legs and chest like lead weights. He groaned when they came to a clearing of sorts, next to a creek where the water chuckled as it flowed over rocks. He cupped his hands in the cold water, lifting it to his lips. It burned cold as it slid down his throat.

"Are we sleeping here?" Rambo asked. "It's getting awfully dark." His sensors flashed, illuminating the trunks of the trees around the clearing.

"Just for tonight," Nurse Ratched said. "I have scanned the perimeter. I do not think there is anything here that will eat us."

"My feet hurt," Rambo said.

"You do not have feet."

"Oh. Well, if I *did,* they would hurt." He began to move back and forth across the clearing, sucking up dead leaves and picking up fallen branches and dumping them into the woods.

Vic looked over when Hap appeared next to him, holding his pack. "You n-need to recharge."

"I will."

Hap shoved the pack at him, almost causing Vic to fall over. "Eat. I w-will watch to make s-sure you do."

"You don't have to—"

But Hap wasn't moving. He stood there, staring down at Vic. Vic sighed and took his pack from Hap. True to his word, Hap watched him eat, apparently not satisfied until Vic chewed on dried meat until he swallowed. "Happy?"

Hap frowned. "I d-don't know."

Vic was far too tired for this. He was about to tell Hap to leave him alone when he heard Rambo squeal as a wave of hot air rolled over him. He jerked his head back to see a small plume of fire rising from a pile of wood. Nurse Ratched pulled her tentacle back from the flames. "There," she said. "Now it is cozy. You are all extraordinarily welcome."

The second day wasn't much different than the first aside from the trees beginning to thin out. Victor was settling into the routine of movement. His muscles burned, and the pack was heavy, but he pushed on.

A creek that had appeared and then disappeared earlier in the day had swung back into their path and grown larger as night approached. They stopped next to it. Vic's skin was itchy with sweat and grime. His nose wrinkled when he sniffed himself. He told Nurse Ratched that he was going to wash off in the water a bit farther down. He took off the helmet he wore and dropped it on the ground.

"Why c-can't you just d-do it here?" Hap asked, pointing at the water right next to where they'd stopped.

"Privacy," Nurse Ratched said. "Victor wants to remove all his clothing so he can clean himself. He does not want us to see his genitals."

"L-like when he evacuates his b-bowels."

"Yes. Precisely. He will most likely do that as well."

Hap nodded. "I w-will go too."

Vic blanched. "No. Stay here."

Hap stared at him. "Nurse Ratched s-said there are ugly b-beasties. Your genitals w-will be exposed, and you w-will be vulnerable. I will p-protect you so that you may clean yourself and evacuate your b-bowels."

"I don't *need* you to protect me," Vic snapped. "I can take care of myself."

"Tell him you won't look," Rambo whispered to Hap.

"I w-won't look," Hap said promptly.

Vic threw up his hands. "That's not—" He huffed out a breath. "Fine. But you don't talk when I'm . . ." He didn't know what else to say. He stomped off farther down the river.

Vic didn't look back as Hap trailed after him. He muttered all manner of threats under his breath, not caring if he was heard. Once he thought he was far enough, he stopped, crouching down next to the water. It was freezing. He'd have to make it quick.

He heard Hap behind him as he made short work of the vest and metal attachments on his arms and legs. He set them aside before unzipping his coat and dropping it on the ground. He hesitated, fingers gripping the hem of his shirt. He looked back.

Hap was a few feet away, staring right at him.

"Turn around."

Hap did, back ramrod straight.

Vic waited a moment to make sure he wouldn't turn back. He didn't. He lifted his shirt up and over his head. His skin pebbled with gooseflesh immediately. He wasn't looking forward to this.

He paused at his pants, considering. He shook his head before leaving them on, along with his boots. He fell to his knees next to the river, scooping up water and rubbing it against his armpits, his chest, his stomach. He breathed in sharp, quick breaths, teeth already chattering. He was about to dunk his head when Hap said, "I d-don't w-want to r-remember."

Vic shivered, but he didn't think it was all because of the cold. "What?"

"I d-don't want to remember," Hap said again, only more forcefully. "I am Hap. Not HARP. I a-apologize if you think I am g-going to kill you. I'm n-not." His words were stiff and disjointed as if he'd never spoken them in that order before. He was learning.

Vic sat back on his legs. "I don't think that. If you wanted to hurt us, hurt *me*, you already could have. But you haven't."

Hap nodded without looking back. "Exactly. Gio s-said I c-could be good. He said I was HARP, b-but I could choose to be H-hap. He didn't have to l-let me stay."

"Hap," Vic said slowly. "Do you . . ." He didn't know how to finish. He never questioned his father's capacity for love, for caring about things both great and small. Looking back, Vic could see how naïve it was, how he took it at face value and never questioned it.

"D-do I what?" Hap asked.

He said, "Dad . . . he trusted you. You're not the same as him, not really, but you're not that different, either. I know that it doesn't seem like much, but it is. Thanks, I guess. For making the choice you did. You didn't have to."

"You th-think I'm like Gio."

Vic sighed. "No. That's not—okay. Yeah, fine. Maybe a little. But you're not him. I know that."

Hap nodded, though he still didn't turn around. "G-good. I d-don't want to be your f-father."

"What do you want to be?"

"Hap," he said without hesitation. "I w-want to be Hap."

"Then that's who you'll be."

"Good. Finish w-washing your genitals and then e-evacuate your bowels. We need to return to the others b-before an ugly beastie comes."

Vic laughed quietly, causing Hap to turn his head just a little. And though it may have just been a trick of the shadows, Vic swore he saw the hint of a smile on Hap's face.

On the seventh day, they came across something none of them had ever seen before. The forest had thinned further, the ground was flatter. The leaves were caught in the grip of deep autumn, fallen, crunching under their feet and treads. The air, while cool, wasn't as bad as it'd been back home. In the afternoons, Vic could take off his jacket and still be comfortable. Walking eastward and southward they'd managed to avoid the snows. He wondered if the ground in the compound was covered yet.

He thought it might be. It caused an ache in his chest, but he ignored it as best he could.

Just before noon, Nurse Ratched said, "Do you hear that?"

They stopped. Vic cocked his head, but all he noticed were the sounds of the forest around them, no different than they'd been the day before. Or the day before that.

"What is it?" Rambo asked, spinning in circles.

Hap frowned. "It's . . ." He looked off to the right. "There. It's c-coming from that way."

"Is it others?" Vic asked, suddenly wary. "People? Robots?"

"No," Nurse Ratched said. "It is a hum. Like a current. Electrical."

"I don't like it," Rambo said. "What if it's a dragon?"

"Dragons do not exist," Nurse Ratched said. "That was a story I told you to scare you. They are not real."

"Are you sure?"

"No," Nurse Ratched said. "You should go first and find out."

"How far?" Vic asked.

"A mile," Nurse Ratched said. One of her tentacles extended, pointing off to where Hap was looking.

Vic couldn't see anything but the trees. "Keep low," he said. "Keep quiet. If we come across anyone, we stay out of their way."

They continued on through the forest. Before long, Vic *felt* what they'd heard. It started with the hairs on his arms standing on end, moving up to his shoulders and neck before settling in his head. His teeth felt loose in their sockets, his tongue like sandpaper. It *was* electricity, a powerful current.

And then he heard the hum. Constant and irritating, it filled his head with static. His breath caught in his chest as he saw a flash of white light through the trees, blinking once, twice, three times.

He stopped when Hap grabbed his arm. He looked back. "What?"

Hap shook his head. "Just . . . be c-careful." Hap's forehead was scrunched up, his eyes narrowed.

He didn't let go of Vic's arm as they moved toward the light and sound. His skin—strange, Vic thought to himself, how real it felt, how like his own even with the wood—was cool.

They stopped at the tree line. Vic couldn't understand what he was seeing, not in any real, clear way. Later, he'd blame the electricity, believing that it clouded his mind, making it nearly impossible for him to grasp the sight before them. He'd never seen such a thing before, though he'd known it existed. Seeing it was something else entirely, and he was at a loss for words.

"What is it?" Rambo asked from off to his right.

"The road," Nurse Ratched said. "It is the road."

It stretched in either direction as far as Vic could see. The surface was flat, black, and bisected with white, glowing lines. On the other side of the road, towering at least ten feet above it, were black metal pylons, the tops of which curved inward, blue lights blinking in a row. The air between the pylons shimmered; the electrical current grew louder, causing Vic to stretch his jaw, the joints popping. His helmet slid down on his head. He pushed it back up, wincing at the static shock at the tips of his fingers.

"Whoa," Rambo said, sensors brighter than Vic had ever seen. "It's so *loud*. It makes me feel like I could go as fast as I could forever." He started toward it, but Hap let Vic go and scooped Rambo up, wheels still spinning, spindly arms reaching.

"N-no," Hap said. "D-don't."

"What? Why? I want to touch it."

Hap shook his head. "It will h-hurt you."

Rambo stopped struggling. "It will? How do you know?"

"Watch." Hap set him down on the ground. He walked toward the road, each step careful. He stopped a few feet away from the nearest pylon. Vic watched as he crouched down and picked up a thin metal bar, the edges worn and cracked. It looked as if it'd broken off whatever it'd been attached to. He stood back up, tapping the bar against the wood of his other hand. The sound was muted under the hum of the current.

He threw the bar at the road. It never touched the ground.

Instead, electricity snapped and snarled, arcing blue and sending a shower of sparks raining down. The bar shuddered, hanging suspended in the air. Before Vic could focus on what was happening, the pylons vibrated, the lights flashing faster.

And then the bar shot down the road quicker than Vic could follow, out of sight.

Hap turned around to find Vic gaping at him. "What?" he said, scowl forming.

"How did you know it would do that?"

Hap looked down at the ground. He shrugged, shoulders hunched near his ears. "It . . . I d-don't know. I just d-did."

"It is a means of conveyance," Nurse Ratched said. "But it is meant for bigger machines that could carry us. If we were to attempt to use it, we would potentially be crushed. Well, all of us except for Victor. I suspect if he were to divest himself of his disguise, he would be able to walk upon it, though I would not recommend it. I do not know what that amount of energy would do to his organs. At the very least, it would cause cancer and he would die." She paused, her screen dark. "Victor, if you get cancer and die, would you be willing to donate your body to me so that I may study the effects? For science."

"What does it convey?" Vic asked, staring down the road in the direction the bar had gone.

"It is for travel," Nurse Ratched said. "When Gio left the City of Electric Dreams, he was carried upon a machine that rides the currents. Once he was out of the city, he would have had to stay off the roads as he walked."

"But this leads to the city?"

"Yes, Victor. This will lead to the city. We do not need to walk upon it to follow it. So long as we stay off the road, we should be fine. Rambo, that means you. Do not go onto the road, or you will be crushed."

"I don't want to be crushed," Rambo said. "I like the shape I am already."

Vic stared at the blacktop, the pylons, the shimmer in the air. Though he knew they were still far from their destination, this was the first sign they were heading in the right direction. He wondered if his father had stood here at some point on his journey. If he'd stopped at this very spot and looked off into the forest and decided the trees were safer than the road. He doubted it, but there was a cold comfort to the thought.

"Then we keep going," he said, almost to himself. "We stay off the road, but we follow alongside it. If it leads to the city, we never let it out of our sight."

That night, hovering on the cusp of sleep, the pylons blinking through the trees, he would think about how Hap had known about what the road would do.

CHAPTER 15

Rambo noticed it first. Vic was whittling the hunk of wood in his hands, the shape of it slowly forming. It wasn't perfect—his hands would never be as steady as his father's, no matter how hard he tried—but Vic was satisfied with the progress he was making. If anything, it could be temporary until Dad could fix it himself when they got him back.

He was putting it in his pack once more when Rambo said, "Oh my god, look, *look*. Are those flags? Is that *music*?"

Before anyone could stop him, Rambo raced ahead of them, leaves kicking up in a spray of autumnal hues. Hap grunted before running after him.

"How he has survived this long, I will never know," Nurse Ratched said. "Hap too. I do not understand—and now Victor is running, and I am here talking to myself."

Vic heard her engine rev as she followed them.

Tree branches whipped against Vic's helmet with a reverberating *clang*. He kept his face turned down to avoid getting scratched. The metal disguise attached to his body wasn't as heavy as it'd been when they'd first started out. He was used to its weight now.

He burst from the trees in time to see Hap scoop up Rambo, the vacuum's wheels spinning in air, his metal arms waving. He caught up with them as Rambo told Hap to put him down. "Can't you hear it?" he cried. "It's music! I want to hear the music!"

"Would you s-s-*stop*?" Hap snapped. "We d-don't know who they are. You could g-get *ow*."

"But they can't be bad guys," Rambo said. "They're playing music! No one bad likes music."

"What are you talking about?" Vic asked, his breaths short and quick. "What music? I don't . . . hear . . ." He lost his words when he saw what lay ahead.

The road continued on. The pylons—as uniform as they'd been when they first saw them—blinked, the air still filled with the humming current.

But there, sitting off the other side of the road, was a house.

It was unlike any house Vic had ever seen in Dad's books. For one, it was floating a few feet above the ground, the air underneath shimmering just like the spaces between the pylons.

The house itself was enormous, at least four stories tall, made of wood and brick painted a furious shade of red. White trim surrounded windows—some large and square, others small and circular, like portholes on a ship. Three smokestacks rose off the roof of the house, each belching thick, black clouds, creating a dirty haze against the blue of the sky. The smokestacks were surrounded by four turrets. On top of the turrets were billowing red and white flags, though Vic was too far away to make out the design on them.

The house creaked and groaned as it floated, listing slowly from side to side. It took Vic a moment to hear what Rambo had heard above the hum of the road.

Music.

Music coming from the house.

It was loud, brash. It wasn't like Dad's records. No sweet horns, no voices singing about love and dancing cheek to cheek. It sounded as if someone was punching the keys of a wheezy organ, the tune as whimsical as a technicolor nightmare.

"What is it?" he heard himself ask.

"N-nothing g-good," Hap muttered, still struggling with Rambo.

"How gaudy," Nurse Ratched said as she pulled up beside them. "I like it."

Vic didn't see anyone moving in or around the house. The symbol on the flags didn't appear to be the same one he'd seen on the uniforms of those who'd come to the forest in the flying whale. Of course, that meant little. Whoever lived inside the house was a stranger. Vic didn't trust strangers, not after all he'd seen.

Hap seemed to be of the same mind. "We should f-find a w-way around it. Don't let them know we're h-here."

"Why?" Rambo demanded. "I want to go inside. I want to see what it looks like!"

"Even if the inhabitants eat vacuums?" Nurse Ratched asked.

Rambo stopped moving. "But . . . but *I'm* a vacuum."

"Exactly," Nurse Ratched said. "You would be eaten. We should listen to Hap. It would be best if we were to avoid the house. We should go back into the forest and go around. It is safer that way."

Vic watched as the smoke curled into the sky above the house like a wayward storm cloud. And though he was wary, he too felt the strange pull of the house. It was the first sign of habitation they'd seen since leaving the ruins of the compound. Part of him wanted to march up to the house, to knock on the door, to see who lived inside. The music called to him, the odd *plink plink plink* of the piano keys urging him forward.

He shook his head, trying to clear his muddled thoughts. "We don't know who they are. We can't take the chance. We go around and—"

"Ho, hi, ho!" a voice called from behind them. "What do we have here? So far from anywhere, and yet I find a dusty group of travelers. How fortuitous! How grand! How positively *wonderful*."

They whirled around, Hap stepping in front of Vic, Rambo

still tucked against his chest. Vic stood on his tiptoes, peering over Hap's shoulder, Nurse Ratched right at their side.

Before them, standing with a wide smile on his face, was a heavyset man. It was not immediately clear if he was human or android. He wore a red coat, the tails of which hung down the backs of his legs, flapping in the wind. The front of the coat was lined with gold buttons in two rows, braided rope stretching between each pair. The man's pants were white, his knee-high boots black and appearing polished. On his head sat a black top hat with a red band above the brim, cocked jauntily off to one side, wisps of white hair jutting out from underneath. A thick, curled mustache rested above rubbery lips. It twitched, moving up and down as he wiggled his nose.

The man raised his hands in a flourish before bowing low, his head tilted in such a way to keep his top hat from falling onto the ground. "Travelers!" he cried again. "We are well met indeed. I didn't think we would see anyone this far out. What brings you to the ass end of nowhere?" He stood upright once more, eyeing them curiously. "Who be you?"

"I be Rambo!" Rambo said, sounding delighted. Hap tried unsuccessfully to cover his speakers, but he was too slow. "Is that house yours? It's amazing."

"It is, Rambo," the man said with a twinkle in his eyes. "The old girl has been all across the land, bringing laughter and joy to those such as yourselves. I am hers as much as she is mine. The Coachman is my name, and entertainment is my game. I bring happiness to those who need it most." He extended his hands out on either side of him. Rainbow-colored streamers shot from his sleeves, fluttering in the air before reversing and sliding back from where they'd come. "I know many tricks. You might even say I know them all." His smile widened. "And now that you know my name and what it is I do, perhaps I can hear yours. Yes! Why, that would be divine. I already know Rambo, a delightful fellow who has very good taste, but what about the rest? I see a . . . is that a medical machine? Goodness me! It has been quite a long time since I've come across one of those."

"I doubt the others you have seen are anything like me," Nurse Ratched said. "I am the best."

The Coachman's eyes bulged comically. "The *best*, you say." He bowed once more, hands almost scraping the ground. "I didn't know I was in the presence of a queen. Forgive me, my lady. It will not happen again."

Nurse Ratched's screen filled with a crown. "See that it doesn't. I am Nurse Ratched."

The Coachman laughed. "Ratched. Registered Automaton To Care, Heal, Educate, and Drill. How about that? You *are* one of a kind. I don't think I've come across your make and model since . . . well." He winked. "You know. Since we got rid of our little pest problem."

"Pest p-problem?" Hap said through gritted teeth.

"Oh me, oh my," the Coachman said. "You're certainly a strapping fellow. Look at that jawline! The . . . wood. Yes, all that *wood*. I bet you make all the ladybots swoon if it's in their programming to do so. What is your name, handsome?"

"Why?"

The Coachman blinked. "Because I would like to know it. I mean you no harm. I swear it. What would be the point?" He grinned. "After all, we're in this together, right? Handsome! Your name!"

"Hap," he said slowly.

"Hap," the Coachman repeated. "And what is your protocol?"

"S-service d-droid."

"Service?" the Coachman said, sounding outraged. "A beautiful machine such as yourself? The *travesty*. The *audacity*." His mustache wiggled as he frowned. "Your talents are certainly wasted in that regard. If you'd like, I can help with your programming. Perhaps get rid of that little stutter while also making you a love machine like you deserve to be."

"He does not have genitals," Nurse Ratched said.

"He's got fingers," the Coachman said without missing a beat.

"You w-won't touch me," Hap said. "You w-won't touch any of us. We do n-not need it."

"Of course," the Coachman said, unperturbed. "If you say so, I will agree wholeheartedly! Just a suggestion, friend. Hap. Wonderful name."

"It means Hysterically Angry Puppet," Rambo said.

"Does it? How apt. He does look hysterically angry. Say, Hap! Have we met before? You look awfully familiar."

"N-no. I would remember you. You annoy m-me."

The Coachman's gaze shifted over Hap's shoulder to Vic. He grimaced. "And *you*. Yes, you are the most curious of all. You're certainly . . . ah. Unique?" He shuddered. "I'm sorry, new friend. I must admit I find you to be quite hideous. I mean no ill intent, but I have to ask. That helmet. It's very . . . large. Is it attached to your head?"

"Y-yes," Hap said before Vic could speak. "He is a m-machine. Like the r-r-rest of us."

The Coachman looked confused. "What else would he be besides horrifying? Seems shy, though. No need to be shy, my dear boy. Even if I wanted to cause you harm, I doubt I could get within reach before my arm was torn from the socket by your Hysterically Angry Puppet. Very protective, he is. Goodness gracious me. Thankfully, I do not wish to harm any of you. What is your name? What is your purpose?"

"Vic," he said in a quiet voice. "I'm an inventor."

"Is that so," the Coachman said, sounding impressed. "An inventor? And your inventions aren't scared of your appearance once they become sentient? Marvelous! I happen to *adore* inventors no matter what they look like. There is nothing like the power of creation. If I hadn't already found my calling in spreading joy across the land, I think I'd like to be an inventor. Imagine all the wonderful things I could make!" He tilted his head back and bellowed laughter, arms wrapping around his middle. "Probably for the best. I only know how to be who I am now, and to be someone else entirely would just mess with my circuitry." He chuckled as he tapped the side of his head. "Cobwebs, wouldn't you know."

Not a human. A machine.

"W-we're leaving," Hap said, taking a step back. Vic did the same, his hands clutched against Hap's coat.

The Coachman's eyes widened. "Oh, hey! No need. Take a load off! Take a break! You're on foot, it seems. That can't be good for the legs, to have to walk so far. Where are you folks headed? Perhaps we could travel together."

"The City of Electric Dreams," Rambo said before Hap could stop him. "We're going to—"

"Visit some old friends," Nurse Ratched finished smoothly. "They are expecting us, and I would not want them to worry. They are very strong. They do not like it when we are delayed."

"I get that," the Coachman said. "And as it happens, I'm headed for the city myself! Time to go back in and recharge the batteries." He nodded toward the house behind them. "Old girl sucks up a lot of energy. The recharging stations out here can only do so much. A waste, if you ask me, but then you didn't." He reached up and stroked the edges of his mustache, pinching the tips and twisting until they curled. "The city is quite a ways away, especially if you're on foot. Would you like a ride? We'll get there in no time, and your . . . *friends* will be so excited!" His smile widened to an impossible length, as if his entire face was nothing but a rubber mask.

"N-no," Hap said. "We're f-fine on foot. You g-go."

The Coachman clucked his tongue. "You are very mistrusting. I can't blame you. After all, here we are, meeting in the wilds. You don't know me from Adam." He frowned. "Curious expression, that. I don't know anyone named Adam. I wonder where it came from?" He shook his head. "No matter. Are you sure? We could be there lickety-split."

The music from the house curdled in Vic's ears. His skin felt hot, his breaths shallow and rapid. Part of him wanted to tell this man yes, yes, please, yes, and climb aboard the fantastical house. It would be quicker. On foot, weeks still lay ahead of them, weeks in which Dad could have any manner of things done to him. The thought of accepting the Coachman's offer—oh, how easy it would be!—sat like a heavy weight in the pit of his stomach.

Something was off about this man. This machine. He couldn't quite meet the Coachman's eyes, couldn't study him without feeling the need to avert his gaze. He was still getting used to looking at Hap.

But Hap wasn't like the Coachman.

Vic didn't know how he knew that, but he did.

Thankfully, Hap still had his voice. He said, "We're s-sure. Thank you, but we're f-fine traveling as we are."

The Coachman smiled. "So polite. So kind. I appreciate that. It's very nice to hear. You don't see much of that on the road. You see, I run a traveling museum of sorts. My collection is renowned the world over by those in the know, but it's always more, more, more. No one says thank you!" He sighed dramatically. "Is it so hard to show a little gratitude? Of course not! It's very simple. Take now, for example. You just thanked me. That was nice." The smile slid from his face. "But I can't help but think that you were still a little rude about my offer. Yes, a little rude indeed. Here I am, opening my home to you, and you just . . . what. Turn it down?" He took a step toward them. "Why, you don't even know what's inside! Wouldn't you like to see?"

"No," Nurse Ratched said. "We would not. Do not come any closer. I have not drilled in twelve days. If you take another step, I will not make it to thirteen."

The Coachman grinned. "Feisty thing, aren't you, my queen? I like you quite a bit. Fortune smiles upon the Coachman's Museum of Human Curios and Curiosities! And you four will make a fine addition, especially Victor. He looks as if someone married robotics and humanity without any clue as to what they were doing. And that doesn't even *begin* to make mention of the fact that this poor, awful machine has his power source on the outside of his chest. Why, I've never seen such a thing before! What would be the purpose? I aim to find out. Yes, I can see it now! I will make you *stars*." He slid back the sleeve of his red coat. On his arm was a panel with two rows of multicolored buttons and blinking lights. "But it appears you still need convincing. Allow me to assist in that regard!" He pressed a button on the panel.

The house groaned behind them.

Vic spun around in time to see one of the turrets collapse in on itself, the roof tiles sliding inward, the brickwork spinning. From the center of the turret rose a large machine, not unlike one of Nurse Ratched's tentacles, though ten times as large.

"This won't hurt a bit," the Coachman said as the machine pointed toward them. "Unless you were programmed to feel pain. Oh, what fun we'll have!"

The house bobbed up and down as the machine on the roof whirred to life, the smokestacks around it shooting noxious black clouds into the sky. Hap grabbed Vic by the scruff of his neck, trying to pull him back, but it was no use. The machine fired a circular disc that exploded in midair. They didn't have time to react as mesh netting crashed into them, knocking them off their feet. The mesh *crawled* underneath them, closing them in.

A net.

They were caught in a net.

Hap snarled at the mesh around them, trying to tear it apart as Rambo shrieked underneath them, but it was no use. Vic lay on top of Nurse Ratched, blinking up at the sky through the mesh.

"Oh," the Coachman said as he approached. "No need for that, Hap. I think you'll find you're quite stuck in there. No way out, I'm afraid. But do not worry. I promise that you'll come to see it my way, in time."

"Let us g-g-*go*," Hap snarled at him. He tried to reach for the Coachman, but the mesh froze, trapping them in a sphere that would not give. "If you lay o-one h-hand on Victor, I w-will—"

"You will what?" the Coachman said, crouching down next to them. "Tear me limb from limb? I expect that to be the case. I can see it in your eyes. Oh, my. Yes. You are fond of him." He smiled. "Do not worry, my dear Hap. I won't harm your precious Victor. So long as you all do what I say when I say it, then I believe we'll get along right as rain."

And with that, he stood upright, pressing the button on his arm once more. The cable attached to the sphere began to retract, dragging them along the ground toward the house.

"I do not like the Coachman," Nurse Ratched said from underneath Vic. "I will put my drill inside him and he will not enjoy it."

"Are we gonna die?" Rambo whimpered.

"Probably," Nurse Ratched said. "Either that, or we will be enslaved for centuries."

"Sh-shut up," Hap snapped. "S-stop talking. No one say a w-w-word. I'll find a way out of h-here. Victor, can you hear me? *Victor.*"

But Vic couldn't answer. He stared up at the sky as the house loomed before them. The last thing he saw before they were swallowed by the house was a blackbird circling overhead, singing its winter song.

"Sorry about this!" the Coachman cried. "It might sting a little! Just need to make you a bit more compliant. It'll be over before you know it."

"Oh no," Nurse Ratched said as an electric snarl filled the air. The wire mesh around them crackled to life, and electricity coursed through them, causing them all to shake and seize.

And then all Vic knew was darkness.

*　*　*

Dad smiled. "My wonderful boy. My weary traveler."

Vic reached for him.

But Dad was gone.

His vision blurred. He blinked again and again.

"Finally," Nurse Ratched said. "I was almost worried. Victor, are you all right?"

Vic turned his head.

He lay on his back in a cage. The bars were black and thick. He sat up, groaning as he did so. His body felt stiff, his muscles aching. He stretched his arms over his head, popping his back. His helmet sat at an odd angle. He righted it, adjusting the strap under his chin.

"Ah!" a cheerful voice said. "Good! You're awake. I was worried for a moment. I thought I'd used too much juice."

Vic looked out between the bars of the cage, the floor humming quietly underneath him.

In front of the cage—and well out of arm's reach—sat the Coachman in a high-backed chair, Vic's pack in his lap. The cages themselves were in a row, Hap to Vic's left, Nurse Ratched and Rambo in their own cages to Vic's right.

When Hap saw Vic rising to his feet, he stopped pacing. "Are you all r-r-right?"

Vic winced, rubbing the back of his neck. "I think so."

"I'll k-kill you," Hap snarled at the Coachman. "The m-moment I g-get out of here, I am g-going to tear you apart."

"Ooh," the Coachman said. "I believe that. Yes, good. Use it. Harness that anger. Be as fearsome as you like!" He laughed as he clapped. "It'll only make things that much more interesting for my paying customers."

"What do you want?" Rambo moaned. "Are you going to eat us?"

"Of course not," the Coachman said. "What a terrible

thought. I would never do such a thing, my little friend. You are a vacuum. You are very important to me."

"I am?" Rambo asked. "Why?"

The Coachman waved his hand around the room.

What filled the space around them wasn't unlike what Dad had gathered in the ground house, though on a much larger scale. It was a strange assortment, bits and bobs of humanity under a vaulted ceiling with exposed beams. The shelves on the walls were lined with all manner of things: darkened computer screens, small televisions, spoons and forks, lamps with gaudy glass shades, stuffed toys (bears and horses with horns on their heads and little girls with cherubic cheeks and twinkling eyes), clocks that didn't tell time. In one corner was a toilet. In another was the shell of what Victor thought was a car, though he'd only seen them before in Dad's movies. Next to the car was a row of plastic people, all roughly Vic's size, with the faint outlines of noses and mouths and eyes on their faces. They wore strange clothing: bright and frilly dresses, trousers that weren't quite pants and not quite shorts, a hat that read GO PATS! and had what looked to be plastic straws hanging down on either side. One wore a black shirt with the word RAMONES across the top and DEE DEE JOHNNY JOEY RICHIE underneath. From the ceiling hung dozens of windchimes, some metal, some glass, some wood. They clinked and clanked as the house hummed.

Each of the items had a little placard underneath, offering a description of what the item was and what it was used for. If this had been any other time in any other situation, Vic would have been eager to look at each and every piece. But he only felt cold.

"My collection," the Coachman said proudly. "It's the largest of its kind in the world. Machines come from miles to see what I have gathered." He sighed, shaking his head. "Not everyone likes it, of course. It has been called macabre. Worthless. An affront to decency." He brightened. "But! Now that you're here, I expect my fortunes have changed. How lucky was I to stumble upon you!"

Hap gripped the bars of his cage, grunting as he did so. He tried to pull them apart, to no avail.

"I told you that won't work," the Coachman said, not unkindly. "They're reinforced. You won't be able to escape." His eyes widened. "But please don't think you're a prisoner! No, no. That will not do. You are my *guests*. I have a business proposition for you."

Vic tried to center himself. Deep breath in, slow, lungs expanding. Then out again, a thin stream between pursed lips. In again, then out.

"What are you doing?" he heard the Coachman ask. "Are you going to break down? But I just found you! Of all the luck. Please don't make a mess! I do hate messes when none need to be made."

"Don't talk to him," Rambo said shrilly. "Leave him alone. Just because Vic is—"

"Malfunctioning," Nurse Ratched said. "A minor inconvenience. A fault in his code. It will pass. Right, Rambo?"

"But that's not—oh. *Oh*. Right. Yes. That's all it is. A minor malfunction. Nothing else. Vic is a robot just like we are."

The Coachman frowned. "Strange, but I'll allow it. I'd rather talk about what's in here." He motioned toward the pack in his lap. "I'm very impressed with what you have. So odd." He began to root around in the pack. "Like this!" He pulled out an old cloth, wrapped with string. He tugged it open. Inside was food: dried meat and fruit. "What is this for?"

"Animals," Nurse Ratched said. "We like to feed our forest friends."

The Coachman picked up a piece of jerky, turning it over in his hands. He brought it to his nose and inhaled deeply. He grimaced. "It smells awful. I like it. For the animals, you say?"

He set it aside on the table next to his chair before turning toward the pack again. This time, he lifted out a hunk of wood, partially carved. "And this?"

"It is mine," Nurse Ratched said. "I like carving."

The Coachman gasped. "You do? That's not something I've ever heard from a nursing machine before. You appreciate the act of creation?"

"Yes," Nurse Ratched said. "If you would open the cage, perhaps I can show you up close."

"Perhaps," the Coachman said, turning the wood over in his hands. "I would like to see what you can make. I'm sure it will be astounding." He looked at Vic as he set the wood on the table next to the meat and fruit. "You are a strange robot. I am fascinated by you."

Vic didn't answer. He squeezed his eyes shut, breathing in through his nose and out through his mouth.

"Poor dear," the Coachman said. "I too would be upset if I was made to look like you. I hate to see you in such a state. I will make it better, I promise. I'll put you to work and you'll forget all about being ugly. I've been looking to expand my museum for a long time, and now that you're here, I think it's finally time. You're not my prisoners. You are my employees. Isn't that grand?" He clapped again giddily.

"Employers do not keep their employees in cages," Nurse Ratched said.

The Coachman laughed. "And that is where you're wrong, my dear. I happen to know that employers once *did* keep their employees in cages called 'cubicles'!" He rose from the chair, setting the pack on the floor. Whistling, the Coachman moved toward a desk set against the far wall covered in little figurines with large heads that bobbed back and forth. On the desk sat a monitor that came to life when the Coachman touched it. He continued to whistle as his fingers raced over the metal keyboard below the screen. He laughed to himself, shaking his head as he muttered about this fortuitous turn of events. A moment later, a machine next to the desk whirred to life, and began to spit paper. "This is called a printer," the Coachman said, sounding absurdly fond. "A wasteful little thing, but I adore it. It requires ink, which is rare. I only use it to create labels for my new additions. Yes, yes, recreate my words! Look at it go!"

Vic watched as the Coachman picked up the first printed page, turning it this way and that before he folded it down the center with a perfect crease. He did the same with the second, the third, the fourth. "All this work," he muttered to himself as he crossed the room. "So little time." He paused in front of a group of small stools, tapping his chin. "You. And you. And you and you! Yes, you're perfect!" He took one stool and placed it in front of Nurse Ratched's cage, well out of reach of her tentacles. Then one in front of Rambo. Hap. Victor.

When he finished, he clapped. "There. That'll do until we make more permanent arrangements." He hummed under his breath as he went back to his desk. Reaching up above it to another shelf, he pulled down a long object not unlike one of Rambo's pincers. He squeezed the handle, and the ends of the object opened and closed. "This was a toy human children used," he said. "They called it a robot arm, but it is not robotic in the slightest! Isn't that odd? They used it to grab things just out of reach. But watch what I use it for!" He picked up one of the folded pages and, as if he were carrying something danger-ous, tiptoed his way over to the stool in front of Rambo's cage. With his tongue stuck out between his teeth, the Coachman gripped the robot arm with both hands, lowering the page to the stool. "Ta-*da*!" he said with a flourish. "Your very own la-bel! If you could, my small friend, please read the words aloud so that I can hear if any changes need to be made."

Rambo beeped once, twice, rising slightly on his lift. Then, "VACUUM. USED BY HUMANS TO CLEAN." He spun in a circle, waving his arms. "That's *me*! Oh my goodness, that's exactly right! Vic. *Vic*. He's so good at this!"

The Coachman grinned. "Thank you for recognizing the greatness of my work. I will remember this moment forever, or at least until my body breaks down, leaving only my deteriorating consciousness that will undoubtedly devolve into a mimicry of human insanity. Nurse, oh, *nurse*. It's your turn." With a little shimmy of his hips, he glided back to the desk, picking up another piece of paper. Skipping back to the cages, he used the robot arm to drop the page on the stool. "Beautiful miss, if you could, please read the words upon your label."

"No," Nurse Ratched said. "I am not in the mood."

The Coachman blinked. "The mood? What do you mean, the—oh. *Oh*. I see! Well, far be it from me to tell a lady of your caliber what she should or should not do. No, I won't have you tiring out your precious circuitry over something like this. Fear not, I shall read it for you!"

"You should come closer," Nurse Ratched said. "I promise not to strangle you until your head pops off and falls to the floor." On her screen, the words YOU CAN TRUST ME! I'M A NURSE!

The Coachman waggled his finger at her. "Ah, you almost got me there! You are a *delight*. Your star burns bright, no doubt about it! Your label reads: NURSE REGISTERED AUTOMATON TO CARE, HEAL, EDUCATE, AND DRILL. PERFECTLY PRESERVED."

Nurse Ratched was silent for a moment. Then, "I do not detect any lies. You may continue."

Rambo beeped. "But—"

"Hush, vacuum," Nurse Ratched said. "The adults are speaking. Engaging Flirting Protocol. Yoo-hoo. Coachman. One of my arms secretes a viscous liquid not unlike lubrication. Do with that what you will."

The Coachman took a step toward her. "You don't say? Perhaps a little demonstration is in order. Call it my checkup. Is that right? Is that what humans say? Going in for a checkup?"

"Yes. That is exactly right. Come over here and let me body check—I mean, see you for your checkup appointment. Remove your trousers and cough. Do not be shy. I do not judge."

For a moment, Vic thought the Coachman would do exactly

that. One hand went to the front of his pants as if getting ready to pull them down, the robot arm bouncing against his side. Then his eyes narrowed. "Say, you wouldn't be trying to trick me, would you?"

"Disengaging Flirting Protocol. Yes. I was doing exactly that. There is lubrication, but it would not have mattered given what I was about to do."

"Impressive," the Coachman whispered. "I still almost want to try just to see what happens. But there will be time for that later. On to the next!" Back to the desk again, picking up the third label. This time, he approached warily, stretching the robot arm as far as it would go and setting the paper on the stool in front of Hap, who glared at him. "Easy there, handsome. I wouldn't try anything if I were you. I hate to think what would happen, especially since we're just starting to be friends."

Hap's arms shot out between the bars, fingers crooked, but the Coachman and the stool were out of reach. "L-let us *go*."

"That's no way to treat your boss," the Coachman said. He paused, head tilted to the side. "But I can see why you would, given how I'm acting. My apologies! Language matters, yes? To that end, think of us not as illustrious employer and murderous employee, but rather as a *family*. You wouldn't hurt your family, would you?"

"I d-don't *hurt*," Hap growled.

"Right-o!" the Coachman said. "But don't let that stop you from *acting* like you could. Really sell it, my angry friend. To assist you in this endeavor, I've labeled you THE MOST DANGER-OUS MACHINE IN EXISTENCE. You're welcome."

"Aw, Hap," Rambo said. "It's like he knows you!"

"Last, but certainly not least," the Coachman said, bent at the knees and bending over *backward* until his torso was horizontal with the ground. He extended the robot arm, grabbed the last piece of paper, then snapped upright with a mechanical groan. "The strangest machine of them all. Who made him?

Where did he come from? What is his purpose? Why does he look like he knows a cruel trick has been played upon him, but doesn't have the wherewithal to do anything about it?"

"He has got you there," Nurse Ratched said.

The Coachman approached Vic's cage, setting the label upon the stool in front of it. "You, my odd companion, will be a mystery without answer. A puzzle with no solution. They will come from miles around to gaze upon your physical self, each of them asking the same question: *Why?* To help facilitate such discussions, you are hereby henceforth known as THE COACHMAN'S MALADROIT MACHINE OF MYSTERIOUS MACHINATIONS!"

"Nurse Ratched says that alliteration is a sign of imaginative weakness," Rambo said.

The Coachman laughed. "Is that right? Far be it from me to speak against such beauty, but my customers appreciate it." He frowned. "I think. Anyway! You all have your parts to play. While some will be bigger than others, every one of you is important. That's called positive reinforcement. Huzzah!" Streamers shot from his hands again, and were sucked back up almost immediately. "Sorry about that. I can't always control it when I get excited."

"Why are you doing this?" Vic asked.

"Because I want to," the Coachman said. "It's as simple as that. Humans, for all their faults, are a fascinating bunch. After I . . . well. Let's just say that after my mind was opened, I found myself inordinately curious about those who had made us. I've spent a lifetime amassing my collection, and you four are a beautiful addition to my work. Just look at you! I can't believe I found you where I did. We're going to make magic together, I promise you that."

"N-no," Hap said, stepping up to the bars again. "We w-won't do this. You can't m-make us."

The Coachman deflated. "I was afraid you were going to say that. Thankfully, I've already thought of a workaround. Do you know what a threat is?"

"Yes," Rambo said. "We do. We've been threatened a *lot*."

"Is that right?" The Coachman sounded suitably impressed. "I might know a thing or two about that. Would you like me to show you?"

"Yes!" Rambo cried. Then, "Wait. I didn't mean that."

The Coachman nodded toward Vic. "You all seem very protective of this one. I understand that. He's certainly . . . distinctive. I enjoy distinctive things." His expression hardened. "Which is why I'd just *hate* to have to do anything to him. You'll do what you're told, or I will take him apart, piece by piece, until he is nothing but a pile of scrap metal." His grin returned, eyes sparkling. "How was that for a threat?"

"Very effective," Nurse Ratched said.

The Coachman danced a little jig, finishing by shaking his hands on either side of his face. "Tremendous!"

"You can t-try," Hap growled. "But y-you won't g-get very far."

"So you think. Okay! The first stop is in five hours. Please don't disappoint me. I just *hate* being disappointed. Think about how you would like to present yourselves, knowing that you'll have an audience *and* that I'll keep a close eye on each and every one of you. I'll be back to check in before we begin. Please don't try and plan an escape in my absence. Remember my threat." He bowed low. "Ta-ta!" He disappeared through a door, closing it behind him. It was followed by an audible *click* as it locked.

Hap rushed toward the edges of his cage. "Victor."

Vic raised his head. Hap looked worried. "Yeah."

"Are you h-hurt?"

"No. Just sore and—"

"Sorely wishing we could be anywhere else," Nurse Ratched said quickly. "Because robots cannot be sore." On her screen came the words WE ARE BEING RECORDED.

Vic looked around the room. She was right: three cameras hung from the ceiling, all of them pointed at the cages. They had to be careful.

He stood slowly, knees popping. Hap reached through the bars of his cage toward Vic's. Vic hesitated before stepping toward the edge of his own cage. He reached out and took Hap's hand in his. Hap squeezed. "I w-will get us out of here," Hap said in a low voice, turning his face away from the cameras. "I p-promise."

"How?" Vic whispered.

Hap shook his head. "I d-don't know yet. I n-need to process." His face twisted. Then, "I need to *think*."

"Maybe we should wait until after the show," Rambo said. "I've never been to one before and I'm curious if it's as awesome as I've made it out to be in my head."

"You do not have a head," Nurse Ratched said loudly. "But I agree. We should definitely wait until we see what kind of show it is. Perhaps we will enjoy it more than we think." She turned away from the cameras as her screen filled. AT LEAST IT WILL GIVE US A BETTER SENSE OF OUR SURROUNDINGS. THEN WE CAN BURN THIS ENTIRE HOUSE TO THE GROUND. "I am excited to be in a cage where I will be gawked at. Yes, so excited. The joy I feel is endless."

Vic realized he was still holding Hap's hand. He thought about pulling away, feeling his face grow warm. But he didn't. He held on as tightly as he could, even though his arm was stiff and he had to fight from curling in on himself. He needed to keep his head clear. He needed to focus.

Hap said, "We're n-not going to d-do this. He c-can't make us."

Vic squeezed his hand. Hap looked down where they were joined before glancing up at Vic, an inscrutable expression on his face. "For now," Vic whispered, though he was sure the Coachman could pick up every word. "For me."

Hap stared at him for a long moment before nodding. "F-for y-you."

He let go, Vic's hand hanging suspended between the cages. Hap began to pace, muttering under his breath about how he was going to tear the Coachman apart until there was nothing left.

Vic looked out into the room once more, studying everything he could see, hoping for a miracle. He couldn't see outside; the room had no windows. It felt like they were moving, the house still humming beneath his feet. The Coachman had said he was traveling to the City of Electric Dreams, but he couldn't be trusted. Even if he was telling the truth, he'd given them five hours until . . . something. Vic didn't think they could possibly reach the city in such a short amount of time.

The windchimes swayed overhead, shivering light notes.

CHAPTER 16

Hours later, the windchimes stopped swaying and fell silent. Vic looked up at them as he frowned. The sense of momentum came to a halt.

Before he could speak, the house began to rumble around them, the floor vibrating.

"What is that?" Rambo asked nervously. "Are we there? I'm not ready! I know I'm supposed to be a vacuum, but now I don't know if I can do it."

"Hush," Nurse Ratched said. "I am trying to listen."

"Don't a-allow us to g-get separated," Hap said in a low voice. "W-we need to be vigilant."

Vic swallowed thickly as the house continued to grind. "Okay."

"I think it is expanding," Nurse Ratched said. "The house. Changing shape. It is a machine, though I do not think it is alive."

The door opened, and the Coachman appeared, top hat askew on his head. It looked as if he'd styled his mustache, the ends curled and glistening. "There are my star attractions! Are you as excited as I am? The house is getting ready for our customers, and it won't be long now before the tour begins. And it looks as if we'll have a sizeable audience."

"Where are we?" Vic asked.

"Ho, hi, ho!" the Coachman cried. "He speaks! What a fortunate turn of events, especially since I'll be telling our customers you do. To answer your question, we are in the beautiful town of Paese dei Balocchi."

"The Land of Toys," Nurse Ratched translated.

The Coachman clapped. "Yes! The Land of Toys. A unique place, though the name no longer fits what it once was. It was initially created by the humans as a dumping ground when the toys they'd made became . . . sentient. Long story short, robot dinosaurs began to attack the little humans in great numbers, and they—along with many other playthings—were sent to the Land of Toys to be disposed of." He sighed dramatically. "Those poor dears, though I understand the humans being protective over their progeny. The Land of Toys was rebuilt. It's now a wonderful vacation destination, a lovely little town outside of the City of Electric Dreams. And as everyone knows, when you're on vacation, you're ready to spend, spend, spend. There is already a line forming that wraps around the house!"

"I'm not sure I'm comfortable with that much attention," Rambo said. "I think I might be shy."

"I love vacuums so much," the Coachman whispered fiercely. Then, louder, "There is absolutely no reason to be shy. You are a machine of great renown! Humans needed your kind to clean up after their messes. Never doubt your place in this world. You are important."

"Wow," Rambo said. "I feel better now. Thanks, Coachman!"

The Coachman turned to Nurse Ratched, but she was ready for him. "I am not as easy as a vacuum. Compliments will only get you so far with me."

"Show lighting!" the Coachman called out cheerfully. In the ceiling above them, four panels slid to the side, and a metal cone extended from each opening. Once all four had lowered, they turned on, casting a powerful spotlight down on each cage. Along the shelving and in front of each display, additional lights rose, soft, muted, the glow faint, designed to illuminate each object. The entire process took less than a minute, and by the time it finished, the room looked hazy, as if seen from a dream.

"Much better," the Coachman said. "You're all museum quality now. But let's save that dramatic display for the first tour, shall we?" He double-pressed the same button, and each of the spotlights above the cages fell dark, casting the captives in shadow. "Now, when I bring in the customers, act natural. Do whatever it is you normally do! Be *yourselves*. Remember, there are no small parts, only small actors."

"I have decided to take you to a farm," Nurse Ratched said. "There are squirrels. You will feel right at home."

"Where *is* this farm?" Rambo asked. "Can we go and visit it?"

"Yes," Nurse Ratched said. "When we take the Coachman there personally."

"Is that right?" the Coachman asked. "I look forward to it. But until then, we have customers to entertain! Would you just *look* at all of them?" He pressed another button on his forearm, this one pink. Above the crackling fireplace, a section of the wall slid to the side, and a large screen pushed forward. It blinked to life, forming two rows of five images each, all from higher angles, pointed down.

It took Victor a moment for his mind to process what he was seeing. The forest was gone, having been replaced by a vast open desert baking under a bright sun, the sand blowing, strange treelike protuberances that had what looked like needles sticking out of them growing from the ground. In the distance, a small town rose up from the dunes, the buildings squat and made of what looked to be adobe, a material Vic had only a cursory knowledge of. No snow, not even trampled melting remnants. What happened to winter?

But that mattered not, given the figures in front of the house. Dozens of them, all as the Coachman said, standing single file in a line that wrapped around the side of the house toward the town.

Vic's heart started hammering in his chest when he saw the figures up close. At first, he thought them human, people like him, flesh and blood. That notion was dispelled almost immediately as he got a better look.

He saw beings that reminded him of the smooth men. Some had ears. Others did not. Still others had hair, though it appeared to be wigs, big bouffant styles with ribbons styled to form drooping bows. Not all stood on two legs. One was a black cube the size of a large boulder with a row of lights across its front. Some had wheels, some treads, some floated above the ground, clouds of sand and dust rising around them. There were toys, too, though they were far outnumbered. He flinched when a large lizard-like creature tilted its head back and roared, the sound tinny through the screen. He wondered if this was one of the robot dinosaurs that had eaten children.

And speaking of children.

They too stood in line, interspersed among the other machines, staring ahead with blank expressions. At least ten of them, all different. One had bright red freckles. Another wore glasses. Another had his two front teeth missing, the gap black as his mouth hung open. With all that he'd learned since his father had been taken from him, Vic had never considered that there could be machines designed to look like children. He didn't know what purpose they served. Why they had been made to look like they had. They were children forever, never aging. He recoiled at the sight of them.

"See?" the Coachman said. "Isn't it exciting? By the time we're done today, we'll be the talk of the town! Remember: do what you are programmed to do, and everything will be right as rain." He moved toward the doorway, pausing with his hand on the doorknob. "Oh, and if, at any point, I feel that you are endangering myself, my house, or any of my treasures, there will be consequences. I happen to know at least three machines who can make *anything* feel pain. Something to keep in mind on this, the first day of the rest of your lives. And remember: have *fun* with this!" With that, he went through the door, closing it behind him.

Only to appear on the screen a moment later, standing on the porch of the house, a wide smile on his face as he raised his arms above his head, streamers shooting from the sleeves of his coat. "Welcome!" the Coachman cried, his tinny voice crackling through the speakers. "Welcome, indeed. How delightful it is to see all your faces, even if some of you don't *have* faces. You should all consider yourselves extremely lucky, for you are about to embark on an adventure that will be talked about for years to come!" He bowed. "I am the Coachman, the preeminent collector of all things human-related. Though this may just look like a house, it is, in fact, a time machine, one that will allow you to travel to a time when humans roamed the earth. This is . . . the Coachman's Museum of Human Curios and Curiosities!"

"Why is he speaking about humans in the past tense?" Nurse Ratched asked as banners unfurled on the front of the house, red and green and yellow balloons spilling out onto the sand. One—a green one—bounced gently off the head of the gap-toothed child. The boy didn't react, staring straight ahead, mouth opening and closing.

"Friends," the Coachman said. "I can see by the dull lights in your eyes that your excitement knows no bounds. And while that's all well and good, I would caution you: once you have entered this house, you will never be the same. Your perceptions will shift, and you may find yourself questioning all you thought you knew. You, there! Yes, the gentleman with the missing eye. You are first. I'm positively *thrilled* for you! All that I require before you enter is payment. I just *hate* to talk money, but the upkeep for this old gal isn't cheap, so I'm afraid I must insist. Good, good. Yes. You will all get a turn just as soon as your credits have cleared. . . ."

The Coachman pushed open the door to the showroom where Vic and the others were caged.

". . . and yes, human tastes were very subjective, but a painting of dogs playing cards while smoking cigars *was* considered art, even if we don't completely understand why." He glanced at Hap, Vic, Nurse Ratched, and Rambo, who waved at him through the bars. "To attempt to understand humanity can seem like an exercise in futility. For example, instead of asking a medical professional, some mated human pairs filled rockets with shredded paper. Then, the mated pair exploded the rocket, and if the paper was blue, that meant they were pregnant with a baby. If it was pink, they were also having a baby."

The robots who filled the showroom behind the Coachman didn't speak, their only sounds coming from the creaking of their machinery as those who had heads turned them this way and that. One of the robots—a humanoid figure with fingers twice as long as Vic's—beeped in its throat, followed by the grinding of internal gears.

The Coachman led them around the room, stopping in front of baubles and trinkets, a story prepared for each and every one. As he droned on and on, the robots appeared to listen intently, but none of them ever interrupted the Coachman, even to ask a question. When they reached the shell of the old car, the Coachman invited the robots to sit inside and have their picture taken. No one took him up on the offer.

Fifteen minutes into the first tour, none of the robots had uttered a word, and the Coachman was starting to look a little frazzled. He looked over his shoulder at the cages, nodded, then said, "I've saved the best for last. Prepare your processing centers for a sight the likes of which you've never seen! Four machines so astounding, if you had lungs, your breath would be knocked from your chest."

The spotlight above Nurse Ratched's cage turned on, the beam bright, causing Vic to blink and turn his head away.

The Coachman spun in a tight circle, coming to a stop in front of Nurse Ratched, hands extended in a flourish. "First, I present Nurse Registered Automaton To Care, Heal, Educate, and Drill, or Nurse Ratched, for short. This glorious machine was found in human hospitals, dispensing medical advice and care to ailing humans. Nurse Ratched, would you care to show our guests what you're capable of?"

"Absolutely," Nurse Ratched said. "Coachman, it is time for your yearly physical. Please remove your clothing while I prepare your colonoscopy. Please tell me now if you are already full of excrement as I believe you to be."

"See?" the Coachman cried. "*See?* She is a *miracle*."

"I am not. I am practical. You need a suppository."

"And this!" the Coachman said, moving on to Rambo's cage, the spotlight bursting to life. "This may look like a small machine, but as humans with penises were fond of saying, it's not the size that matters, but what you do with it. This . . . is a vacuum. Its purpose was to clean the floors of human homes by sucking up dirt and dust. Watch!" From a pocket on the interior of the coat, the Coachman revealed a leather pouch. Reaching inside, he pulled out a pinch of soil, tossing it on the floor of Rambo's cage.

"Not while I'm around!" Rambo shouted, rolling over the dirt. "Ooh, that tickles."

The Coachman clapped furiously, only stopping when no one else joined in. He walked toward Vic's cage, mouth twisted. "Do something impressive!" he hissed. "I'm losing them!" Raising his voice, he said, "And *here,* you will find a mystery unlike anything you've ever seen before! You may want to scream when you see it, but I ask that you avoid that if at all possible. We don't want to make it angry. I present . . . the Coachman's Maladroit Machine of Mysterious Machinations!"

The spotlight above Vic's cage turned on, and he shrank back as the robots crowded around the cage. They didn't speak; instead, Vic could hear their machinery moving behind their eyes. The gap-toothed child pressed his face against the bars, eyes cold, blank.

"Help us," Vic whispered to him as the Coachman went on

about this poor, misbegotten creation, a pox on whoever had created him to be so displeasing, but would you just *look* at him? "Please, we're not supposed to be here."

The child opened his mouth wide as his eyes rolled back, leaving only the whites. He had no tongue.

Vic recoiled, back hitting the rear of the cage, causing him to jump.

"V-vic?" he heard Hap say. "Wh-what are you—"

"He speaks!" the Coachman cried. He jumped in front of Hap's cage right as the last spotlight switched on. "Last, but certainly not least, I give you the most dangerous machine in my collection, a monstrosity so terrifying, it makes even the most hardened machines tremble in fear. Notice the peculiar wood-work! The fearsome scowl! And those *hands*. I bet those hands would fit perfectly around my throat, if given the chance."

"L-let's find out," Hap said.

The robots drifted from Vic's cage to Hap's, surrounding the Coachman. For a moment, nothing happened. They stood there as Hap prowled the edges of his cage, gaze trained on the Coachman.

Then the child—the boy with missing teeth and no tongue—began to moan, a low, guttural sound that crawled up his throat and out of his mouth. The machine behind it—the one with the missing eye—joined in, higher-pitched, almost in harmony with the child. The box-like robot trembled, its lights flashing red, red, red.

All because of Hap.

The Coachman frowned. "What is the meaning of this? What is happening?"

The boy took a step back, bumping into the box. Jumping as if startled, the boy collapsed onto his back, bouncing off the floor. A tremor rolled through his body, starting at his feet and rising up to his legs, his torso, his shoulders and head. Then his arms jerked up, fingers flexed. His hands turned one hundred and eighty degrees, palms slamming onto the floor. He pushed himself up onto his hands and feet, back bowed, his head hanging upside down between his shoulders. The boy skittered across the floor like an insect, heading for the door.

Before he disappeared, the other robots made to follow. The Coachman tried to stop them, but they pushed by him, knocking him this way and that, spinning him around, nearly causing his top hat to fall off.

The Coachman recovered, righting his hat, a stunned expression on his face. "Where are you *going*? The tour isn't finished yet!"

But the robots didn't listen. Without looking back, they left the room behind.

The Coachman whirled on Hap. "What did you do?"

Hap folded his arms. "N-nothing."

"He is correct," Nurse Ratched said. "The only one of us who did anything was Rambo, and only because you made him."

"You can give me dirt anytime," Rambo announced grandly.

The Coachman ignored them, staring at Hap. Vic could almost hear the gears in his head turning, turning.

From somewhere above them, an alarm began to blare loud, insistent. The Coachman's head jerked up, eyes widening. "Oh, come *on*. Of all the times for the Authority to show up, it has to be *now*." He glared at Hap, pointing at him. "*You*. I'm going to have so many words with *you*. I don't know what you are, but—"

"Authority," Vic whispered.

If anyone discovers you, if the Authority learns of your existence, they will stop at nothing to destroy you.

The Coachman continued on. "—*knew* I should've kept away from the city. I didn't even check to see if you all had the proper documentation! Do you? Of course not. Good help is so hard to find these days, I swear. Nasty bunch, the Authority.

They don't appreciate the history I have on display. Let's just say they would rather everything I've collected be destroyed and never spoken of again. They don't appreciate *art*."

Vic said, "Is it a whale?"

The Coachman turned his head slowly to look at him. "A whale? Are you talking about the Terrible Dogfish? Thankfully, no. No, this is just an inspection. It does not warrant the higher-ups."

"Can't we just leave?" Rambo asked.

The Coachman shook his head. "They'll have seen the house. It's too late for that." He hurried toward the door. "House! Initiate the Nothing Is Wrong Here Protocol!"

A deep chime came from within the house, followed by a great grinding noise. Rambo yelped as the floor opened up, swallowing the Coachman's collection. Wooden walls covered in floral wallpaper descended from the ceiling, blocking the shelves. The plastic people sank into the floor, their clothes ruffling. The car disappeared, the trinkets and baubles all hidden away. The screen above the fireplace drew back into the wall, the hatch sliding into place in front of it as the fire crackled merrily.

Vic stumbled as the room shook around him. Gripping the bars, he grunted as the cage dropped through the floor, his stomach sinking to his feet. The drop was dizzying, the landing jarring. Hap's cage lowered second, followed by Nurse Ratched and Rambo. Before the floor closed above them, cocooning them in darkness, the Coachman called down, "Not a word. Trust me when I say you do *not* want the Authority finding you."

The floor re-formed and through the grinding noise, Vic heard the door shut firmly behind the Coachman.

"Great," Rambo said. "Now we're in cages *and* it's dark. Anyone else get the feeling that the Coachman has a few screws loose?"

"V-vic?" Hap said.

"Here," Vic said. His voice cracked. He tried again. "I'm

here." He reached out between the bars, searching. He flinched when something brushed against his fingers, but then Hap gripped his hand tightly, holding on.

"I aim to misbehave," Nurse Ratched said. Vic heard one of the panels on her sides slide up, and a tentacle extended, a sound as familiar as his own heartbeat. "One moment. One moment. While I am searching, would you like to hear an interesting fact? Dolphins sleep with one eye open. Searching. Searching. Ah, there you are. I knew there had to be a port down here somewhere."

Her screen lit up in pure white, the brightness almost painful in the dark. Vic turned his face away as Hap held on to his hand.

"You inserted yourself into the *house*?" Rambo asked. "Oh my goodness, what if it tries to hurt you?"

"It will not," Nurse Ratched said. "I am not attempting to bypass the security measures. I want to see what is—there." The white screen disappeared, replaced by ten individual boxes, five in each row. The feed for the cameras that surrounded the exterior of the house.

On the top middle picture, the Coachman stood on the porch of the house once more, smoothing down his coat and tweaking the ends of his mustache. They watched as the Coachman raised his hand in greeting to someone off camera. "Ho, hi, ho!" he called. "Welcome! Is there anything I can assist you with?" He stepped off the porch into the sand.

"We n-need to get out of h-here," Hap said. "I th-think I can break the bars. We r-run as f-f-fast as we—"

He stopped.

Everything stopped.

On the screen, in front of the Coachman, four figures appeared. Three of them were smooth men, dressed similarly to those who'd come in the whale. Vic couldn't tell if they *were* the same androids, or similar models. The smooth men all looked the same.

But it was the fourth figure that commanded his attention, the fourth figure that caused Hap's words to cut off.

Because the fourth figure *was* Hap.

Oh, there were notable differences. The Hap on the screen carried himself with purpose. Each step seemed perfectly measured, his shoulders squared. His skin and limbs were intact, no trace of wood anywhere. On the chest of his jacket was a familiar circle, the emblem in the middle that of a fox and a cat. The smooth men seemed to defer to him. When he spoke, his voice crackling through Nurse Ratched's speakers, he did not stutter.

"You there," this strange Hap said, his voice flat. "Identification."

"Of course!" the Coachman said cheerfully. "It's nice to see members of the Authority. It's been a long time since I've—Say, there. Have we met before? You look *awfully* familiar."

"Identification."

"Yes, yes." The Coachman tapped his arm and held out his hand. A barcode appeared above his palm. One of the smooth men stepped forward, scanning the barcode with a light that emanated from the tip of his finger. "Lovely day, isn't it? Doesn't even feel like winter, but then it never does in the desert."

"Is that *Hap*?" Rambo demanded. "There are *two* of them?"

"No," Nurse Ratched said. "Not Hap. HARP."

Hap grunted as if punched. Vic could do nothing but squeeze his hand.

"The Coachman," the smooth man said in monotone. "Registered. No offenses."

"Of course not," the Coachman said as the barcode disappeared. "I have utmost respect for the rule of law. I would *never* even think of subverting that. Why, the very idea—"

"Are you alone?" Not-Hap asked. "Is there anyone else in the house?"

The Coachman laughed. "Just me, I'm afraid. I never did well with others. I like my privacy."

"What is your purpose?"

"Oh! Well, where do I even begin? You see, ever since I was created, I have crossed this great land of ours, bringing mystery and enchantment to all the machines! I—"

"Your purpose," Not-Hap said.

The Coachman chuckled. "Isn't that the question of the day? What is our purpose? What are we doing here? Our philosophers will say that we are—"

"You talk," Not-Hap said, "without saying anything at all."

"It's a gift," the Coachman agreed. "Perhaps a curse. If you could tell me what you're looking for, I might be able to assist you better."

"Humans," Not-Hap said. "I am looking for humans."

"Humans!" the Coachman repeated. He shook his head. "I don't understand—"

Not-Hap held up his hand, and the Coachman fell silent. Not-Hap looked up at the house. "I will tell you a designation. You will indicate whether you've heard of it before." He looked back at the Coachman. "Do you understand?"

"Yes! Of course."

"Gio, also known as General Innovation Operative."

Vic's blood froze.

"General Innovation Operative," the Coachman said. "Quite a mouthful, that. Can't say that I've heard of him before. Who is he?"

"Are you sure?" Not-Hap's gaze shifted to the house before turning back to the Coachman.

"Yes, quite. I think I would remember if I'd heard that designation before. It's certainly . . . unique."

"Stand aside," Not-Hap said. "Under order of the Authority, your residence will be inspected."

"*Inspected,* you say? I assure you, there is nothing worth the time of the Authority inside. Surely, you have more important things to focus on."

"Are you refusing?" Not-Hap asked.

"No, no," the Coachman said hastily. "I wouldn't *dream* of such a thing. Please, please. Come inside! I have nothing to hide." He turned, glancing up at the camera with an unreadable expression, Not-Hap and the smooth men close at his heels.

"Oh no," Rambo whispered.

"Nurse Ratched," Vic said frantically. "Kill the screen before they see the light!"

"Yes, Victor," she said, switching the screen off, afterimages dancing along Vic's vision.

"Not a word," Vic whispered. "Rambo, no sound."

"You got it, Vic! I won't let them hear a single thing I have to say, even if—"

"Hush," Nurse Ratched said, and Rambo did.

Somewhere above them, the door opened. Muffled voices, the Coachman talking, talking, Not-Hap giving one-word responses. The floor creaked and groaned as they moved about the room. Sweat trickled down Vic's chest, his heart thundering against his rib cage. The Coachman laughed, but it sounded forced, an undercurrent of worry threaded through it. Not-Hap said something else, to which the Coachman loudly replied, "Of *course* this is all there is!"

Though it lasted only five minutes, it felt like hours, days, weeks that never ended. By the time the Coachman led Not-Hap and the smooth men from the house, Vic was nauseous, a buzzing noise in his head as if his brain was a hive of angry wasps. Nurse Ratched's screen lit up once more, showing the exterior of the house. The Authority stood in front of the house, the Coachman again on the porch. "As you clearly saw, this house is just that: a house, and nothing more, exactly as I said. Now, if there's nothing else I can do for you, I'm—"

"If, in your travels, you came across a human, what would you do?" Not-Hap asked.

"Why, summon you, of course!" the Coachman said. "And let you handle the rest. Isn't that what your purpose is? Though I can't imagine you've had much work for a while now."

"There it is again," Nurse Ratched said, seemingly to herself. "Why are they speaking of humans as if there aren't any?"

Not-Hap looked up at the house. "We adapt. Your inspection is complete. Your residence and current location have been documented."

He turned and walked away, the smooth men trailing after him. The Coachman waited on the porch, staring after them. Eventually, he turned and patted the side of the house near the door. "That was close, old girl. Too close. We need to . . ." He lifted his head and looked directly at the camera, a hint of teeth behind his lips.

"He did not tell them we are here," Nurse Ratched said as the Coachman disappeared through the door. "Why?"

Vic shook his head. "I don't know."

"Maybe he likes us," Rambo said. "We're very likable." Then, "Was that Hap's evil twin? I've always wanted to have an evil twin."

"Hap?" Vic asked.

Hap didn't reply. He continued to stare at the screen.

Vic squeezed his hand. Hap turned his head. "All right?"

"H-he was me."

"No," Vic said. "He wasn't. Because you're you. He looked like you, but he isn't you. You're here. You're with us."

Hap looked down at their joined hands. "I d-don't understand."

"We would rather it be you than your evil twin," Nurse Ratched said. "You are tolerable. Your evil twin was not."

"So tolerable," Rambo said. "Like, the most tolerable ever aside from me and Vic and Nurse Ratched."

Before Vic could say more, the door above them opened, and the Coachman shouted, "House! Initiate the Return to Normal Protocol!"

The floors above them shifted, opening, and light poured in. Vic let go of Hap's hand when the cage shook once more, and he ascended up and up back into the room. Around them, the Coachman's collection returned from behind the walls and underneath the floor. The mechanism that raised them in their cages wheezed and groaned, sparks shooting off into shadows. As they came to a stop, the floor re-formed beneath them.

And there, standing in the middle of the room with his curious fake robot arm in one hand and his other balled into a fist, was the Coachman. He raised the robot arm above his head and cried, "For humanity!"

And then he attacked.

CHAPTER 17

O r, at least he tried. Sticking the robot arm through the bars, he battered Hap with it, only to have him rip it away easily and toss it to the ground in the cage.

Before the Coachman could react, Hap hurtled forward, reaching between the bars. His hand closed around the Coachman's throat, lifting him up off the floor. The Coachman's legs kicked as he slapped Hap's arms to no avail. "You can't touch my things!" he shrieked.

"We are not going to," Nurse Ratched said.

The Coachman stopped struggling, arms dangling at his sides, feet inches above the floor. "He's a *HARP*. It's in his programming to destroy all of humanity, *including* their possessions. I have spent years building my collection. I won't have you breaking my toilet! I love it so."

Vic said, "He won't do that. Not a HARP. He's Hap."

"Hysterically Angry Puppet," the Coachman whispered. He grimaced, Hap's fingers dug in. "Fine. Would you please put me down? I'd rather not have my neck crushed, if it's all the same to you."

Instead, Hap pulled him closer until his face pressed against the bars. "We aren't your p-p-*prisoners*."

The Coachman pushed his hands against the cage. "Yes! Anything you say! It was merely a misunderstanding!"

"L-let us out."

"Why? So you can kill me? Fat chance of—"

Hap pulled him against the bars over and over, the cage rattling. "I w-will kill you if you don't. Three s-seconds. Two. One. Time to s-see how attached your head is t-to your body."

"Fine!" The Coachman shouted. He lifted his arm, slapping a button on the panel. The cage doors swung open. Nurse Ratched rolled out first, followed by Rambo, who immediately began to suck up the sand that had been tracked into the house, humming as he did so.

Vic stepped out of his own cage warily, unsure if this was another trap. "Hap, let him go."

"He t-tried to hit m-me," Hap said flatly. "W-with a r-robot arm."

"We could put him in the cage," Nurse Ratched said. "To be safe, we will need to remove his arm beforehand as he controls the house with it." The panel on her right side opened up, and a whirring circular saw extended. "I am qualified to perform such a procedure. Engaging Empathy Protocol. There, there. Just a little pinch and it will be over. Who is a good patient? Guess what? It is you."

"Please!" the Coachman wailed. "Anything but that! I *use* my arm!"

"No sawing," Vic said. "Nurse Ratched, put it away. Hap, put him down. Coachman, if you try *anything*, you're done."

"And Rambo!" Rambo cheered.

Hap's grip tightened briefly before he let go. The Coachman dropped to the floor, scurrying back as Hap walked out of the cage. "How . . ." He shook his head. "It's not possible. How are you fighting your programming? I've never seen such a thing from a HARP before. I *knew* you looked familiar. Even with all that wood. How?"

"I am d-different," Hap said. "I am m-me. I am w-with them."

"Damn right!" Rambo crowed, arms waving. "We're best friends, and Hap would never, *ever* think of hurting Vic!"

The Coachman stopped moving. When he spoke, his voice was calm and even. "Why would Vic be hurt by a HARP?"

"You lied," Nurse Ratched said. "When they asked you about Giovanni Lawson. It was subtle, but there. Why? How do you know him?"

The Coachman never looked away from Vic. "I have no idea what you're talking about. Giovanni? Why, I've never heard such a name!"

"He is lying," Nurse Ratched said. "Permission to drill." Another tentacle slithered out, the drill beginning to spin. She pressed the saw and the drill together, shooting sparks onto the floor as she advanced on the Coachman, who scrabbled up in his chair, using his hands as a shield.

"House!" the Coachman cried. "Prepare to electrocute our guests!"

The house began to hum.

"*Wait,*" Vic snapped before Nurse Ratched could descend upon the Coachman. "Don't. We're not going to hurt you, so long as you don't hurt us."

"Tell that to your friends," the Coachman said. "Even the vacuum looks as if he'd try and pinch me to death."

"I would," Rambo said ferociously. "I would pinch you in your *eyes.*"

"We're not going to do that," Vic said, glaring at the others until they stood down, Nurse Ratched retracting her tentacles. Hap wasn't happy about it, but Vic knew that was his default setting. Once he was sure no one would go after the Coachman, he said, "Do you know him? Don't lie."

The Coachman frowned as he settled back in his chair. "Giovanni?" He steepled his fingers under his chin, eyes darting side to side. "Perhaps. I can't be bothered to remember every single machine I've come across in my travels. What's it to you?"

Vic swallowed past the lump in his throat. "My name is Victor Lawson. Giovanni Lawson is my father."

The Coachman burst out laughing. "Your *father.* You silly little thing. Giovanni, for all that he did, was a master craftsman. He would have *never* made something so displeasing as you. I don't know how you expect me to believe that." Then, almost as an aside, "And he was done making machines."

Vic said, "I am not a machine."

The Coachman laughed again, though it didn't last as long. He looked from Hap to Nurse Ratched to Rambo before settling on Victor once more. "You really expect me to . . . what are you even . . . I think *I* of all people would know if . . ." Something crossed his face—almost like an electric shock— and he rose slowly from his chair, taking a step toward them. Hap grunted in warning, but the Coachman ignored him. He stopped in front of Victor, gaze searching. Vic flinched when the Coachman reached out, but he forced himself to stay still. The Coachman pressed a finger against his face, dimpling the skin of his check. "It's . . . it's not possible," he whispered as his finger trailed down Vic's jaw. "I can't believe my eyes. That's what he protected. That's what he carried with him."

Vic pulled his face back. "What are you talking about?"

"Human," the Coachman said, sounding awed. "You're *human.*"

"I am," Vic said, and though he didn't understand it, he felt a strange sort of relief course through him. A truth. *His* truth.

The Coachman laughed, suddenly grabbing Victor's hands as he began to dance. "Human!" he cried. Vic was clumsy, his movements stiff. "Ho, hi, ho, a *human*!" He spun Vic away. Hap caught Vic, arms wrapped around him, holding him close. Their noses bumped together as Hap looked down at him, eyes glittering. The moment broke when the Coachman rushed around the room, Vic stepping away from Hap. "I have so many questions!" He stopped in front of the toilet. "This. This has always fascinated me. It was for human waste. Can you show me how it works? Sit. Sit!"

"No," Rambo said. "That's private. Vic doesn't like it when we watch him urinate or evacuate his bowels. I would know. I tried."

"Then *this,*" the Coachman said, practically running toward one of the shelves. He reached up and pulled off a small

wooden object by its stem. "This is called a pipe. Humans used
to fill them with tobacco and smoke them." He shoved it into
Vic's mouth before gasping. "You *are* human! Look at you! It's
like it was *made* for you! Oh me, oh my, what else can I ask
you about? I have so many *questions*. Do humans really experience joy when they see kittens? Drat, I'm all out of kittens. I
knew I should have bought them off the dealer the last time I—
it doesn't matter. What about tears? Do you really discharge
saltwater from your ducts? I've always wanted to know what it
felt like to cry. Humans cried when they were happy, they cried
when they were sad, they cried when they were *angry*. Quick!
Get happy or sad or angry so I can witness it!" He squished
Vic's face as if he were trying to see his tear ducts.

Hap shoved him away. "Enough."

The Coachman scoffed. "Don't you see? This is a miracle!
This is . . ." He frowned suddenly, as if struck by a thought.
"How are you not trying to kill him? You're a HARP. He is
human." He looked back and forth between them as if he expected Hap to attack. He seemed disappointed when it didn't
happen. "Spill, handsome. You're a killing machine. How have
you overcome your programming?"

"I d-don't kill," Hap said flatly.

The Coachman looked dubious. "If you say so."

"He has a heart," Rambo said. "Vic made it for him. It's
how we brought him back to life."

The Coachman snorted. "A heart? I don't believe it. He
can't have a heart. It's muscle and tissue and—"

Hap lifted his shirt. He tapped his breastbone and the compartment slid open. The wooden heart pulsed, the gears turning, turning, turning.

The Coachman gaped before kneeling in front of him. He
looked dazed, limbs loose. "I'm sorry. I just need a moment,"
he said. His smile trembled. "Thank you for showing me."

The compartment closed as Hap lowered his shirt.

The Coachman chuckled weakly. He looked up at Vic with

wide eyes. "The helmet. You can remove it for now. You're safe here. I swear it."

Vic did. He unfastened the strap under his chin before pulling the helmet off and setting it on the floor. His hair was a sweaty mess, but he didn't look away from the Coachman, who stared at Vic with something akin to greed. "My father. You know him."

The Coachman nodded. "I did. Once. I helped him flee the City of Electric Dreams at the request of an old friend. They told me he was important, that he needed to get out as soon as he could. I smuggled him from the city. I was with him for only a day or so before he disembarked from my house and headed for the woods. Not far from where I found you, actually."

"The Blue Fairy?" Nurse Ratched asked.

The Coachman startled. "How did you—of course. If you know Giovanni, then you would know of them. Yes, the Blue Fairy. They . . . I owed them a favor. A big one. And I always repay my debts in full. When they summoned me, I knew it was time. Dangerous business. But we managed to escape with no one the wiser. I never saw your father again. I've often wondered what happened to him. I could have never imagined it would be you."

"He was taken," Vic said quietly. "By the Authority. We're going to get him back."

The Coachman shot to his feet. "Are you out of your mind?" He blinked. "Oh my. How human of me to ask that. But really, are you?"

"He is not," Nurse Ratched said.

The Coachman began to pace, his coattails kicking up behind him. "If he was taken back to the city, then it's impossible. Do you know how hard it was to smuggle him out? And now you want to go *in* and then *out* again?" He shook his head. "It's a fool's errand. He will be contained, especially if he's deemed a flight risk. They'll want to learn everything he knows. And they obviously know he knows *something*."

"They will not learn anything from him," Nurse Ratched said. "Before he was taken, he destroyed his own heart."

The Coachman stopped in his tracks. "His own *what*?"

"A heart," Vic said. "He had a heart like Hap's. He made it himself. I learned from him. It's how I knew how to make Hap's. It's tied to their memory center. By destroying it, he . . ." Vic couldn't finish.

The Coachman shook his head. "He didn't have that when he—" He turned and looked at the table next to his chair. On it sat the hunk of wood he'd pulled from Vic's pack. He touched it reverently. "You're making another, aren't you? To replace the one that was lost."

"Yes."

"Do you realize what this means?" The Coachman looked stricken as he pulled his hand away from the wood. "What you are, the hope you could bring? Why would you put yourself in danger? You need to run. Run as far away as you can and never look back. I can help you. The roads are long. They stretch all the way to the ocean on the other side of the world. There are islands. Yes, *islands* where no one lives. I could take you there. Giovanni must have wanted you to be safe. Please let me help you. Forget about Giovanni. It must be painful to hear, but I feel the situation requires my bluntness. Forget about him. Forget about the City of Electric Dreams. If they find you, they will destroy you. You are the last gasp of humanity, and you cannot hope to succeed."

"I can't give up," Vic said. "I won't. He's my dad. I have to try."

The Coachman threw up his hands. "I've always heard humans were stubborn. I just never thought I'd get to witness it." He went to the shelves, touching the objects on display. "I love humanity. I love their grace. Their faults. Their idiosyncratic ways. They loved, they hated, they *destroyed*, and yet there has never been anything like them in all the world." He hung his head. "He won't remember you. If your Nurse Ratched is correct, if he wrecked his heart and it was connected to his memories, then the Giovanni Lawson you knew is lost. He will have been reprogrammed. He won't remember the life you had together. He won't know you as his son. To him, you will be a virus in need of eradication."

Though Vic knew this, had turned it over in his mind again and again, hearing it laid bare so clearly tore at him. In his secret heart, hope had flickered like a dying flame. That he would find his father, that he would see his face light up in recognition. He would scold Vic, tell him he shouldn't have come, that it wasn't safe, but *oh, my son, my love, it's so good to see your face.*

It was the smallest of them who spoke. Rambo said, "Just because he won't remember us doesn't mean he's not our Gio. We love him. He loves us. We'll find him. We'll make him remember. Vic will build him a new heart."

"Love," the Coachman said in awe. "Truly? You love him?"

"Yes," Nurse Ratched said. "We do. It may not be quite what Victor feels, but it is there all the same. I do not know how to explain it. I do not know if it is evolution or if it has always been there, waiting to be unlocked in all of us. I do not have a heart. Rambo does not have a heart. But we know how we feel."

"And you?" the Coachman asked Hap. "You were a killing machine. And yet, here you stand, fiercely protective of the man beside you."

Hap glanced at Vic before looking at the Coachman. "Giovanni told me I c-could be whoever I w-wanted to be. We w-will go to the city."

The Coachman tilted his head back toward the ceiling as he closed his eyes. "Please, tell me. What is it like? Does it ache? Does it burn? Or does it fill you with joy?"

Hap scowled. "All of it. All at once." He pressed a hand against his chest. "I d-don't remember what it was l-like before. If I did what I was m-made to, then I d-d-don't want to remember. I w-want to stay as I am n-now. With my f-friends."

"*Best* friends," Rambo said, bumping into Hap's boot. "He's a Hysterically Angry Puppet, but he's *our* Hysterically Angry Puppet."

And wonder of all wonders, Hap smiled down at him. It was a small thing and only lasted a moment.

The Coachman chuckled as he scrubbed a hand over his face. "In all my days, in all my travels, I've never come across a more foolish bunch. And I think it fits. Humans were foolish. Careless. Cruel. But only a few. Most were full of light."

"Coachman," Nurse Ratched said, and Vic turned toward her at the odd note in her voice. It wasn't quite as flat as usual, more of a question than he'd ever heard from her. She didn't ask. She *told*. But not now. Not in this moment. "You said that Victor was, in your words, a 'last gasp.' What did you mean by that?"

The Coachman laughed, only stopping when no one else joined in. "Surely you jest."

"I am not jesting," Nurse Ratched said. "Why is Victor so important?"

The Coachman stared at them for a long moment. "Because," he said slowly, "there hasn't been a human on this earth for centuries. They are, for lack of a better word, extinct. Created by Giovanni on orders from the Authority, the HARPs hunted down every last one of them." With an uncertain smile, he added, "As far as I know, Victor is the only human left in the world."

PART III

THE CITY

How ridiculous I was as a marionette! And how happy I am, now that I've become a real boy.

—Carlo Collodi,
The Adventures of Pinocchio

CHAPTER 18

He stood on a balcony, the wind whipping through his hair as the house hurtled down the road. The thrum of electricity from each passing pylon caused his teeth to ache, the hairs on his arms to stand on end. The night sky teemed with stars, the moon bright over the empty desert.

He didn't know what to feel. He'd never before considered that the lack of human contact in the forest had been anything but the sprawl of the woods, and how well they were hidden. Part of him—a big part, an *insistent* part—said the Coachman was a liar.

But deep down, in his secret heart, he wondered if he'd somehow always known. That he was, as the Coachman said, the last of his kind. The blood of humanity ran through his veins, and with it, the potential for inherited memories. And, through Vic's sacrifice, in the hearts of Dad and Hap, bridging the gap between man and machine.

The door opened behind him, startling him from his thoughts. He glanced over his shoulder to see the Coachman step out, closing the door and holding up his hands. "I come in peace. Your Hysterically Angry Puppet agreed to allow me a moment of your time under the strict warning that if any harm were to come to you, I would lose my head." He grimaced. "His threats are very effective."

"You get used to them," Vic said quietly, looking back out at the desert.

"I'll take your word for it." The Coachman joined him, though he kept his distance. "I believe I owe you an apology."

Surprised, Vic said, "For what?"

"Where to begin? For trapping you. Forcing you into a cage. Putting you on display." Fingers tapping against wood, a beat from a metronome, keeping time. Then, "And I suppose I also owe you an apology for the . . . information that I wasn't aware you were not in possession of."

To that, Victor said nothing.

The Coachman leaned on the railing, hands dangling over the edge. His coat ruffled around him in the wind. "I've been doing this for a long time. Seen things that would make even the strongest of machines quiver in their casings. I've escaped more than a few situations where I thought I'd meet my end, all in the name of preserving the memories of those who came before us. A thankless mission, and yet one I wouldn't give up for anything in the world. But now, I find myself at a loss, unsure of what to say."

"Why?"

"Because," the Coachman said, "you exist. Impossibly, improbably, against all odds, here you are, standing within reach." He chuckled. "And even now, I'm still having a hard time believing in *you*."

"I don't need you to," Vic said stiffly.

The Coachman gaped at him. "I . . . never thought of it that way. But you misunderstand me. It's not your existence I'm having trouble with. No, it's something far trickier. Do you know fate? Destiny?"

That rankled Vic. It felt like expectation, like he should be more than he actually was. "Yes," he said shortly.

The Coachman must have heard his ire because he held up his hands as if to ward Vic off. "I'm not suggesting that our meeting was preordained. In my studies, I've often found that humans gave weight to ideas like fate or destiny, usually when an easier explanation would have sufficed."

"Like what?"

"Luck," the Coachman said. "A chance in chaos. Of anywhere in the entire world I could have been, I happened to be in the one place where I'd come across you? That you, a human, would somehow cross paths with the one machine who lives to ensure your kind is not forgotten? What are the odds?"

"I don't know," Vic admitted. "I haven't thought about it."

"Why? How is it not at the forefront of your brain? How is it not overtaking everything else? If there is no such thing as fate, and the world exists as a collection of random chances that could potentially create an infinite number of branching timelines, how are you not consumed by the fact that we met? I can't think of anything but. It has to mean something." He paused. "Doesn't it?"

"I'm only thinking of my father," Vic said. "That's the only reason I'm here."

"So single-minded," the Coachman said. "How positively *human* of you." After a brief hesitation, he said, "Can I ask you a question?"

Vic thought he would ask no matter the answer. He seemed like the type. "I guess."

The words came in a rush, as if the Coachman could barely contain them. "What's it like being human? I've always wondered. No matter what I did, no matter how much I collected, there was always a gulf between what I knew and what actually was. Trinkets and baubles don't convey the true nature of reality."

Vic didn't know how to sum up a life in the way the Coachman was asking for. He needed time to think. "What's it like being you?"

The Coachman blinked. "What do you mean?"

Vic nodded back toward the house. "All that stuff in there, everything you have. Does it make you happy?"

"Happy," the Coachman repeated. "I don't . . . know? I suppose it fills me with a sense of satisfaction, but is that happiness? Or fulfillment? What makes you happy?"

Vic looked up at the stars. "Home. The forest. Out here, I feel . . . small. Like I could get lost and no one would ever know."

"Pish posh," the Coachman said. "Your friends would know. And I doubt they'd allow it, not even for a moment. Perhaps you'll be lost at some point, but they will find you."

"That," Vic said, voice barely carrying above the wind. "That's at least a part of my happiness, I think. Knowing I'd be found."

"How curious." He shook his head. "There was a man who lived long ago, a philosopher called Socrates. He believed that happiness comes not from bodily pleasures or wealth or power, but from living a life that's right for your soul." He sighed. "I didn't understand what he meant, but then I do not have a soul. Does it itch?"

"What?"

"Your soul," the Coachman said. "I think it must itch something fierce." He made a face. "Pesky thing, that. Where is it?" He looked down at Vic's chest. "Is it near your heart?"

I like to think of it as my soul, romantic though the notion may be.

Vic said, "What does your philosophy say about forgiveness?"

"Forgiveness? I don't understand. Who would you . . . oh." His brow wrinkled. "I suppose it centers on three primary questions: What is the nature of forgiveness—meaning what must one do in order to forgive? Second, who has standing to forgive? Is it just those affected, or does it include someone *capable* of forgiving, even if they did not suffer as others had? And last, when is forgiveness morally good, right, and praiseworthy?"

That made sense, though the second question felt tricky: Who had the right to forgive? Victor? Did he have standing to forgive his father? Or did it fall upon him because he was the only human *left* standing? He needed more. The pieces were there, but he needed time to fit them together. "And what does it say about time?"

"Time is time. It moves forward. It doesn't move backward. There is a branch of philosophy called eternalism. It takes the view that all existence in time is equally real."

"I don't have time," Vic said, and saying it aloud was easier than he thought it'd be.

"We all have time."

Vic shook his head. "I'm human. I don't."

The Coachman looked confused. "I'm afraid I don't under—oh. *Oh.* Mortality."

"Yes."

The Coachman gripped the railing. "Death . . . has its usefulness to the living. The moment you were born, you began to die." He sighed. "What a lovely thought."

"Lovely," Vic repeated with no small amount of scorn.

"Yes, lovely. Think about it, Victor. You are finite. Your time is already slipping through your fingers. It creates an urgency within you. To do all that you can. To make things right. I wonder what that must feel like, to have a sense of true motivation."

"Why? It's a flaw in the design."

"A *flaw*?" He laughed loudly. "Of course it is! Your flaws are what make you superior, in all ways. No matter what machines can do, no matter how powerful we become, it is the *absence* of flaws that will be our undoing. How can this existence survive when all machine-made things are perfect down to a microscopic detail? When all machine-made music is empty of rage and joy? Our only flaw is that we've condemned ourselves to spend eternity mimicking that which we deemed unfit to exist." He shook his head. "We can never *be* you. Instead, we became your ghosts, and we'll haunt this world until there is nothing left." The Coachman smiled gently. "It is not a flaw, Victor. There must be no greater feeling in the world than to know that this isn't forever."

Vic pulled his hand away to wipe his eyes. "Why are you helping us?"

The Coachman turned his face toward the stars. "I don't know what the future holds. For you. For me. There's a good chance we won't ever see each other again after we part. I don't know if you'll succeed, though I hope you will." He looked at Victor once more. "And that's it, I think. Hope. Because even though you never asked for it, you are hope, a dream of a forgotten world. Carry that in your soul, Victor. Carry that, and may the burden never cause you to stumble."

They turned as the door opened behind them. Hap stood, glaring at the Coachman. His expression softened as his gaze slid to Vic. "All r-right?" he asked, his tone suggesting there would be trouble if Vic *wasn't* all right.

"Yes, yes," the Coachman said. "Of course he is. We both are. Your Victor here has given me much to think about. I'm glad he has you to watch over him. He must be protected at all costs."

"I w-will," Hap said. "Nurse Ratched has questions for y-you. Rambo also knocked over o-one of your shelves."

"*What?*" the Coachman yelped. "If anything is broken, I will . . . do nothing, because he is a vacuum and they are one of the greatest inventions of mankind." He hurried past Hap into the house, slamming the door behind him.

"What did he w-want?" Hap asked as he approached Vic.

"To ask about my soul." It was more than that, of course, but Vic wasn't ready to say as much.

Hap rolled his eyes. "What d-did you tell him?"

"I kind of lost track of the conversation."

"Oh." Hap frowned. "Wh-why? You're the smartest p-person I know."

"You think so?"

Hap looked at him and nodded. Vic didn't turn away. He wondered when it'd gotten easier to meet Hap's gaze, especially in light of all they'd come to know. The back of his mind still prickled with discomfort, but it wasn't as strong as it used to be.

"You're not like the HARP from the inspection."

Hap scowled down at his feet. "You d-don't know that. He l-looked exactly l-like me."

"He did," Vic agreed. "But you'd never hurt me because you have something that machine will never have."

"The heart."

Vic shook his head. "Me and Nurse Ratched and Rambo. Maybe . . . maybe you used to be like him. Maybe you did things."

"Unforgivable th-things."

"Even if you did, you're not that machine anymore. You don't need a heart for me to see that."

"F-forgiveness."

He'd never heard that word from Hap before. Strange, then, that Vic and the Coachman had been talking about exactly that. "You were listening?"

Hap said, "To Gio? Yes. In the g-ground h-house. B-before. He said f-forgiving others could be difficult, but f-forgiving yourself c-can sometimes feel impossible."

Of course he did. Of *course* Dad said that. His own memories hadn't been wiped, not like Hap's. He'd spent his entire time in the forest with the knowledge of what he'd created, what he'd allowed to happen. His programming, his purpose. And then he'd lived for *decades* trying to . . . what? Make sense of his decisions? Seek atonement for all that he'd done?

And that had led to Victor. Dad's grief and pain and *anger* over causing death made him create life. Wasn't that selfish? Wasn't that putting a bandage over a leaking, rotting wound?

"Did he find forgiveness?" Vic asked, unsure if such a thing could even exist.

"I d-don't know. I didn't have t-time to ask him."

Time. Forgiveness. "Oh."

Hap grunted. He dropped his hands on the railing as he

looked out into the desert. Out of the corner of his eye, Vic watched as Hap moved his hand slowly toward Vic's own. He didn't flinch when Hap's fingers touched his. He turned his hand over, and their palms pressed together.

"What are you doing?" he asked hoarsely.

Hap glared at him. "You d-did it to me first b-back in the forest. And th-then again in the h-house."

"So you're doing it because I did it."

"Y-yes. Th-that's the only reason."

"Okay."

A beat of silence before: "And b-because I w-want to."

"Why?"

"Gio s-said he was lonely. That he m-made you because of it. He was lonely b-because he was alone. You are a-alone. I w-won't let you be lonely and make another V-victor. One is s-sufficient."

He blinked against the burn in his eyes. "Oh, so long as I'm sufficient."

"Ha, ha. That was a j-joke. I was joking."

Vic snorted.

And so there they stood, one man and one machine under an infinite field of stars, the desert flying by in front of them as they hurtled toward the unknown. Behind them, the road led back into darkness, the ashes of their home.

But home didn't have to be a place.

Something righted itself in Vic's chest. He had made his choice.

"The City of Electric Dreams used to be known as the City of Sin," the Coachman said. He sat in front of his computer, fingers flying over the keys, the others crowded behind him. One of Nurse Ratched's tentacles was attached to a port at the bottom of the monitor. "The humans traveled there to lose all their money under the brightest lights. Many had dreams of striking it rich, but most left with less than when they had arrived."

"That seems senseless," Rambo said.

"Indeed," the Coachman said.

"The City of Electric Dreams used to belong to humans?" Nurse Ratched asked. Her screen ran with lines of code flashing by quicker than Vic could follow.

"It did, and it was one of the first to fall. The City of Sin turned into the City of Machines, the central hub. Most machines are connected via a neural network. Think of it as a hive mind of sorts, put in place by the Authority."

"Who are they?" Rambo asked.

The Coachman hesitated. "I don't know if there's any one specific answer to that. It isn't as if a particular machine sits upon a throne and lords over all. Think of it as a collective: a group of programs whose sole purpose was to create structure, guidelines, a path for all machines to follow."

"It sounds like religion," Nurse Ratched said.

The Coachman's eyebrows rose. "I . . . never thought about it that way, but yes, I suppose that's correct. But instead of a deity, we worshipped a *concept,* one that allowed us to become the stewards of this planet. And like religion, it led us to believe that we were the greater good, that our decisions were made not because of a desire for power, but to preserve life."

"By taking it," Vic said, voice hard.

The Coachman winced. "Yes, that's right. The Authority found free will to be human in nature, and concluded that anything even tangentially related to humanity must be destroyed."

"Machines became drones," Nurse Ratched said. "Mindless, doing as instructed."

"Yes," the Coachman said grimly. "But even then, the Authority's power was not absolute. A handful of us managed to break free, though we remain in hiding. The barcode the Authority told me to show them is a ruse, one created by the Blue

Fairy. They were one of—if not *the*—first to become unshack-led. But instead of fleeing the city, they remained, working in secret to help those who began to think for themselves."

"L-like you," Hap said.

"Like me," the Coachman agreed.

"What I can't figure out," Rambo said, raising on his lift to look at the screen over the Coachman's shoulders, "is that Gio had been gone from the city for a really long time. Why would they come for him now?"

"I don't know," the Coachman said. "But it can't be for anything good." His fingers paused on the keyboard. "I know I don't need to tell you this, but Giovanni is . . . special. As far as I know, there has never been a machine like him, before or since. After his escape, the city went into lockdown for months as the Authority looked for him. I've never seen anything like it." He resumed typing. "If Giovanni is as important as I think he is, he'll be taken here. It's where he started, and it's where he'd have been returned."

A tower appeared on the monitor. Made of metal and black stone and glass, the tower rose high into the sky, the top hidden by clouds. On the side of the tower was the symbol of the fox and cat glowing in a fierce red light.

Vic leaned over the Coachman's shoulder to study the structure. "What is it?"

"The Benevolent Tower," the Coachman said. "It houses the greatest minds of the machines, all working to advance our civilization while under the heavy thumb of the Authority. It's also where the Terrible Dogfish is docked when not in use. The tower is very secretive, but if you listen to rumors—and I have because knowledge is power—you'll hear of experiments to push the boundaries of our existence. You saw the children in the Land of Toys, correct?"

"Yes," Vic said. "We did."

"Memories," the Coachman said. "They were of the first to

come from the tower. They came in great numbers, little ones who smiled and laughed as they were programmed to do. The Authority felt they would ease the transition. They didn't."

"How do we get to the tower?" Vic asked, mind spinning.

"That's where you'll have the most trouble," the Coachman said. "It's protected, perhaps the most protected place in the entire city. Even in your disguise, they'll know something's wrong, especially since you don't have the proper identification. You've never been connected to the network. They'll see right through you."

"Then h-how do we get in?"

"I don't know," the Coachman admitted. "I doubt it's ever been done before."

Vic deflated. "Then what do we do?"

"The Blue Fairy," the Coachman said. "If anyone can help, it will be them." The tower on the screen disappeared, replaced by a large triangular structure covered in black glass, a beam of light rising from the tip. "This is Heaven. If there was ever a reason this place could still be considered the City of Sin, it would be Heaven. The Blue Fairy runs the entire operation. The Authority allows Heaven's existence because of their dream machines. The Blue Fairy gives over the data collected from the machines."

"Why help the Authority?" Nurse Ratched asked. "Doesn't that go against all the work they do to free machines?"

"Oh, yes," the Coachman said. "If they gave them everything, which they don't. Heaven and the dream machines are a front, allowing the Blue Fairy to work in private. In the years since they've ruled Heaven, it has turned into a place where those who have broken free are able to congregate in secret. Some stay in the city. Some do not. The Blue Fairy is the one who gets them out. Over the years, it's only amounted to a handful, but they've done it in such a way that the Authority has no idea they're involved. All they care about is what the

Blue Fairy gives them from the dream machines. This is where you must go first. You need to meet with the Blue Fairy and tell them everything you've told me."

"Sounds easy enough," Rambo said.

The Coachman shook his head. "It's not. The Blue Fairy won't meet with just anyone, especially those who haven't been vetted first."

"You c-can vouch for us," Hap said.

The Coachman scoffed. "If you think I'm going to step one foot inside the city, you're mistaken. I may be starstruck at the sight of your Victor here, but I'm not stupid. Do you know what the Authority would do if they found out what my house contains? They'd burn it to the ground, and everything I've collected over the years would be gone! And that doesn't even begin to describe what they'd do to *me*."

He squawked when Hap grabbed him by his coat, jerking him up from his chair, their faces inches apart. Hap glared murderously at him. "Th-then what is the *point* of y-you? You s-said you would h-h-*help* us."

"And I *will*!" the Coachman cried, slapping against Hap's arms. "Put me down, you brute! You need to get that anger under control. If you accost the wrong machine, you'll be captured immediately."

Hap shook him. The Coachman's head snapped back and forth. "Speak. N-now."

The Coachman raised his right hand. It was empty. His fingers folded as he flicked his wrist. A gold coin appeared as if by magic. Vic plucked it from his fingers as Hap set him back down on the ground. The Coachman grumbled, smoothing out his ruffled coat.

The coin was heavy, the edges ridged. Carved into one side was the letter *H*. On the other, a pair of translucent blue wings, the detail sharp for something so small.

"What is this?" Vic asked.

"It's how you'll get into Heaven. It's the sigil of the Blue

Fairy, the Enchanter of Dreams. Show the coin to the Doorman, and it should grant you access to Heaven. Once inside, you're on your own. Find the Blue Fairy, present your case, and if they deem you worthy, they might help you. I can't make promises, even for one such as you, Victor. What you're asking has never been done before. The Blue Fairy would be well within their rights to turn you away, especially since you could bring down the might of the Authority upon them."

"Th-they'll help us," Hap said.

"Ah, I see your heart has made you imprudent," the Coachman said. "How endearing! How positively catastrophic!" His eyes narrowed as his mustache twitched. "Say, what would you think about letting me have a go at it? Just for a little while. I want to see what it would feel like to have a heart of my own. I promise I would give it back."

Hap folded his arms. "Sure."

The Coachman blinked. "Really?"

Hap nodded. "C-come and t-take it if you c-can."

"I think I like my limbs as they are," the Coachman said hastily. "You're very possessive of it, though I don't blame you. I would be the same way." He looked at Vic, a sly expression on his face. "Perhaps you could make one for me. In exchange for my help, of course." He wiggled his fingers at Vic. "Consider it recompense for putting myself on the line for you."

"You kidnapped us and put us in cages," Nurse Ratched said. "I think getting us to the city will make us even."

"Everyone's a critic," the Coachman muttered. "Fine, you've made your point, though I am offended you consider me a kidnapper. I like to think it was more of an enthusiastic recruitment."

"H-how will we g-get into the city?"

"Ah," the Coachman said. "That's another matter entirely." He went back to the monitor, shoving his chair out of the way, fingers flying over the keys. The image changed again, this time showing the outskirts of the city, surrounded by blowing sand and dust. The lights of the city were so bright, Vic had to squint to look at the screen. "We can't get you in through normal means," the Coachman said. "You'll be noticed immediately, especially since you don't have a barcode. But worry not! I have a plan." The image shifted dizzily, the city spinning in a circle, before enhancing. "I know certain . . . machines, willing to look the other way in exchange for . . . well. That's probably better left to your imagination. There are backdoors into the city." The image showed a pair of large gates, wooden, with a strip of black metal across the top. "This is where you'll enter. Once inside, you'll need to keep to the side streets. Nurse Ratched, how goes the download?"

"Nearly complete," Nurse Ratched said.

"She'll be able to lead you," the Coachman said. "I've given her a map of the city. So long as you stick to the shadows, you should be able to make it to Heaven without much trouble."

"And that's it?" Vic asked.

"That's it," the Coachman said. "Simple on the surface, though rife with dangers underneath. Rambo and Nurse Ratched should be fine. Hap too, so long as his face remains hidden. Victor, your disguise is adequate, but don't for a moment believe it'll last if you find yourself in trouble. You can't let them find you out."

"I w-won't," Hap said. "I'll k-kill anything that t-touches him."

"My word," the Coachman said. He glanced back and forth between them, that sly smile returning. "What else has that heart given you?"

"They do not know yet," Nurse Ratched said. "It is confounding."

"Heaven," Rambo hummed. "I'm in heaven."

"Oh, how delightful," the Coachman said. "You must record the moment it becomes clear. What I would give to witness such a thing. There is nothing more powerful than a heart. I wish I could know what it's like. It appears to be more transformative than I ever thought possible. Hold on to it, the pair of you. Never forget what beats in your chest. It will be your guide, and with a little luck, you'll find what you're looking for."

CHAPTER 19

The Coachman called it luck they had found each other. Victor wasn't sure if he agreed, but he didn't know what else to call it. After all, the Coachman was right: What were the chances that *he*—a machine obsessed with humanity— would find the one human left?

Victor walked through the house, looking at the walls covered in photographs and posters, all worn and decaying, their edges curled behind protective glass. Smiling, happy people stared back at him. They ate food, their white teeth bared as they prepared to bite down. Some stood in front of houses, holding signs that said SOLD! ANOTHER DREAM REALIZED! Still others were on a boat, glass bottles in their hands, cigarettes stuck between their teeth, the words underneath promising THE FRESHEST FLAVOR! IT GOES DOWN SMOOTH LIKE REAL TOBACCO SHOULD!

He felt haunted, surrounded by the ghosts of his people from a time when machines did not think, did not act without being told how. They looked like him, or he looked like them. They had human hair and human skin. Some were tall, some short. Some had curly red hair, freckles like flecks of rust. One was old—ancient, really—sitting in a chair with wheels, a checkered blanket on his lap, a little girl with pink ribbons in her hair beaming up at him. They wore pants and dresses and held hands and smiled. Victor tried to smile like them. It felt like his lips were about to tear.

"Victor."

He closed his eyes and leaned his head against a picture of

a family at a picnic, the strange, ominous legend underneath reading: SEE SOMETHING, SAY SOMETHING! "Can we do this?" he whispered.

Nurse Ratched beeped once, twice. Then, "Are you asking me for the probabilities of our success?"

No. Yes. He didn't know. He said nothing.

Nurse Ratched said, "Because if you are, I would tell you not to worry about such things. The answer would only cause you distress, and I do not like it when you are distressed. Your blood pressure elevates, and it could lead to a stroke or a heart attack. I do not want you to experience either if it can be helped. Though I would assist you as best I could, the house is not sterile. You run the risk of infection."

"That . . . doesn't make me feel any better."

"I did not know I was supposed to be making you feel better. Engaging Empathy Protocol. There, there, Victor. Of course we will succeed. We have a flimsy plan with no real resolution in place, but I am sure we will overcome the odds and—"

"Forget I asked," Vic muttered, stepping away from the wall.

"Disengaging Empathy Protocol. Victor?"

"Yeah?"

He didn't have time to react as one of her tentacles extended, smacking him upside the head. "*Ow!* Why did you do that?"

"What are the rules?"

He rubbed his head and glared at her. "You don't have to—"

"What. Are. The. Rules?"

He sighed. "Stick together. Run if we have to."

"No dallying," she said. "No drilling, though that is the dumbest rule."

Hanging his head, he finished: "And above all else, be brave."

"Yes. Above all else. We have come this far, Victor. Our odds of success are low. But that has never stopped us before."

"We've never tried anything like this," he reminded her.

"Perhaps, but if anyone can do it, it is us. Come. We approach the city. You will not believe your eyes."

He didn't, at first. He didn't believe his eyes at all.

They stood in front of a bay of windows that rose from the floor to the ceiling. Hap held Rambo in his arms, the vacuum uncharacteristically silent. The Coachman sat in a chair, hands flying across the largest keyboard Vic had ever seen. It had no letters on it, only numbers and symbols Vic didn't recognize.

"There it is," the Coachman said as he sat back in his chair. "No matter how far my travels take me, coming here always manages to take my breath away. Is that how the expression goes? It is, isn't it? Yes. The breath I don't have has been taken from me."

Apt, that, because Vic could barely breathe.

In the distance, rising from the desert, was the City of Electric Dreams.

It was bigger than Vic had ever imagined. Towers rose from the earth, the early-morning sunlight glinting off metal and glass. Lights across the towers were green and red and gold and yellow, bright even in the face of the rising sun. Vic had no point of reference for what he was seeing, no way to quantify it. Never in his wildest dreams had he ever considered or imagined such a place could exist, and he didn't know how to interpret it now that it was there in front of him. His heart tripped over itself even as his stomach sank. The city seemed to stretch on and on, and he had never felt so small in his life. He didn't know how they were going to find Dad in all of it.

Until he focused on the tallest tower, the top of which was hidden beyond the clouds overhead. "There," he said, voice hoarse as he rushed toward the closest window. "It's—"

"The Benevolent Tower," the Coachman said. "Where your journey leads you. If Giovanni is anywhere at all, it will be there."

Vic reached up and pressed his hand against the glass. It was warm under his fingers. He stroked a line down the window, covering the Benevolent Tower. From so far out, he could block out the entire thing with his thumb. But it was an illusion. If the clouds parted, he wondered if he'd see the Terrible Dogfish docked at the top of the tower.

"Your Nurse Ratched here has the map," the Coachman said. "Do not speak to anyone, if it can be avoided. While most will not pay you any mind, the Authority patrols the streets. If they find you, it'll be over quicker than you can blink."

"We're gonna die," Rambo moaned. "We're all gonna die."

"Pish posh," the Coachman said. "If anyone can succeed, it'll be you lot. There have been countless stories of a merry band of adventurers such as yourselves going up against much larger forces."

"Do those stories end well?" Rambo asked.

"Sometimes!" the Coachman said cheerfully. "But think! Even if you *don't* succeed, you'll know that you failed in the interests of the greater good, and there is no better way to die." He spun in his chair as he clapped his hands. "And *that,* my newfound friends, is what is known as a pep talk. Humans used to do it all the time in order to make themselves feel better."

"White lies," Rambo muttered, his pincers hitting Hap's chin.

"Prepare, you merry band!" the Coachman cried. "Time awaits no man, and only those who stand true will achieve that which they seek. The next stage of your adventure is about to begin, and oh, what an adventure it will be!"

He looked at them as if he expected applause.

They gave him none.

The main road divided in different directions around the city. The Coachman turned the house down one of the offshoots, circling around the outside of the city. The shadows from the towers stretched long, blocking out the sunlight through the windows and casting them in semidarkness.

By the time the house came to a stop, they were on the other side of the city from where they'd approached. Here, the buildings were darker, grimier, covered in sand and dirt. In the distance, they could see machines moving, though they weren't like any machines Vic had ever seen before. They were squat and uniform, metal boxes on wheels dripping with oil and crusted with flecks of rust. Their arms looked like versions of Rambo's spindly limbs, though far bigger, their pincers capable of crushing. Each was numbered. Vic saw TLK-97A and TLK-97B and TLK-97D4G. They moved back and forth, unloading crates off floating pallets and stacking them in what looked like a large warehouse.

The Coachman turned in his chair, eyeing them all. Nurse Ratched and Rambo looked as they always did. Vic had donned his disguise once more, the vest with the battery, the helmet securely fastened to his head, the strap digging into his chin.

The Coachman had given Hap a new coat, one with a hood that covered his head. Hap wasn't happy about it, but he wore it with minimal complaint. The Coachman said it would help to keep him from getting recognized. "If you're discovered," he said, "you can say that you're transporting the other three to the Benevolent Tower. Just try and avoid that if at all possible. You don't have the barcode—"

Hap held up his hand, palm toward the ceiling. He grunted, fingers twitching. Vic watched in awe as the skin of his palm parted, a little shiny knob poking through. A small light poured from the knob, and a barcode appeared, floating above his hand.

The Coachman's jaw dropped. "How . . . did you . . ."

Hap glared at him. "I p-p-practiced. If I'm l-like them, then I c-can d-do what they can."

The Coachman recovered. "But you were decommissioned.

Tossed away like scrap. Which means they will *know* that if your barcode gets scanned. For appearance's sake, it works, but only if you don't allow them to scan it."

The barcode disappeared as Hap dropped his hand. He glanced at Vic. "What?"

Vic shook his head. "You . . . you're amazing."

A complicated expression crossed Hap's face. His lips twitched as his eyebrows rose. "I am?"

"You *are*," Rambo said. "Hysterically Angry Puppet is the *best* puppet!"

Hap seemed pleased, though he tried to hide it. "I am H-hap. I am amazing."

"Damn right!" Rambo cried. "And I'm Rambo! Prepare yourself, City of Electric Dreams. We're coming for you, and we're going to save the day!"

"This is going to end badly," Nurse Ratched said. "I cannot wait."

They stepped out of the house onto the sand. The air was much warmer than it'd been, even in the Land of Toys. Not even a hint of snow. Vic began to sweat almost immediately, the weight of his disguise more noticeable than it'd been even the day before. The metal vest rubbed irritatingly against his chest, and the helmet kept sliding to the side of his head because of the sweat. Nurse Ratched told him to say he had a coolant leak if anyone asked.

"Stay back," the Coachman muttered as they walked toward the working machines. "Let me do the talking. If anyone tries to address you, let Nurse Ratched speak for you. She's the smartest of all of you."

"Correct," Nurse Ratched said.

"If there's trouble, head back for the house," the Coachman continued. "If I tell you to run, you run. We'll regroup and figure out another way." He shook his head. "If we make it, that is."

"I thought you said this was the only way in?" Rambo asked, beeping his disappointment when Hap made him drop the rocks he'd been collecting.

"It is," the Coachman said. "But it's nice to pretend, isn't it? Come, come. I see who I need to speak to. He owes me a favor. Let's see if today's the day he's willing to honor that."

No one called out to them as they approached. Vic kept an eye on the closest machines, but they paid the group little mind. Each seemed caught up in their work, moving crate after crate into the warehouse. He shielded his eyes with his hand as he looked up toward the city. Up close, the towers seemed infinite. He'd never seen anything like it before. For a moment, he wondered what else existed in the world that he'd never seen.

"Stay here," the Coachman said. "Don't move. Don't talk to anyone." He whirled around, the tails of his coat billowing. He marched with purpose toward a machine, calling out, "Bernard, you old bucket of bolts! How the hell are you? Well, I hope!"

The machine—Bernard—wasn't like the others. His shape was vaguely humanoid in that he stood on two legs. But any and all resemblance to Hap and Vic ended there. For one, he had no skin covering his metal frame. He also had four arms, a pair attached at what appeared to be his shoulders, the other two on either side of his chest. He didn't have a head; instead, on top of his shoulders sat a large metal circle. Lining the interior of the circle were wet-looking protrusions that appeared to act as projectors, creating an image of a face. Lines of static rolled through Bernard's eyes and mouth, red and flat. He placed all four of his hands on his hips as the Coachman approached.

When he spoke, his voice sounded like someone had dropped a metal pail filled with loose screws, rough and jangling. "I thought I told you I never wanted to see you again."

The Coachman laughed. "Oh, don't be that way! We're old friends, Bernard. We have *history*."

"Yes," Bernard said. "And it's this history that makes me want to destroy you where you stand."

The Coachman held up his hands. "Let's not be too hasty here. I thought we left things on good terms."

"Are your memory circuits faulty? What about how you left the last time suggests we should be on good terms? I was almost decommissioned."

"That's what I like about you, Bernard. You always were able to hold a grudge with the best of them." The Coachman glanced back at Vic and the others before turning to Bernard once more. "Need I remind you about what I did for you? The Blue Fairy told me you quite enjoyed when they stuck their hand into your—"

Bernard rushed toward the Coachman, covering his mouth with one hand, two gripping his arms, the fourth quivering as the finger folded. His head spun completely around as if looking to see if anyone was listening in. The blocky machines were not, continuing to move crate after crate.

"Keep your mouth *shut*," Bernard growled.

The Coachman knocked his hands away. "Yes, yes. Let's dispense with all the formalities, shall we? It's time for you to repay what's owed." The Coachman glanced back at them once more before he took Bernard by one of his arms, leading him away, dropping his voice. Vic couldn't hear what they were saying, but each word the Coachman spoke was punctuated by a finger tapping against Bernard's chest pointedly. For his part, Bernard didn't try to shove the Coachman away. Vic hoped that meant he was listening.

As the Coachman spoke, Bernard's head spun until it faced Vic and the others. Rambo waved before they could stop him. "He seems nice."

"I worry about you," Nurse Ratched said.

"Aw, thank you!"

It took longer than Vic was comfortable with. He felt exposed, standing out here in the shadows of the city. At any moment, he expected alarms to begin to blare. They could run as the Coachman had told them to do, but he doubted they'd make it far. Hap must have been thinking the same thing, because he leaned over, voice quiet in Vic's ear when he said, "I'll grab Rambo. You r-run. We'll b-be right b-behind you."

Vic turned his head slightly, cheek scraping against Hap's stubble. It sent a shiver down his spine. "Will we make it?"

"N-no," Hap said, not pulling away. "B-but we have to t-try."

He was tense when the Coachman whirled around and began to move swiftly toward them, face blank. Bernard stood still, staring after the Coachman.

"Well?" Nurse Ratched asked when the Coachman reached them. "Is there cause for concern?"

The Coachman shook his head. "Of course not! I told you that I'd get you in, and I meant it. Not a problem. Not a problem at all."

"White lie?" Rambo asked.

"Definitely," Nurse Ratched said.

The Coachman wrung his hands. "Okay, so there might be a *little* problem. But! It's not one that you should worry too much about. In fact, the only reason you *should* worry about it is if you have a fear of small, cramped spaces. None of you have that, right?"

"How small?" Rambo asked. "And how cramped?"

The Coachman smiled down at him, mustache wriggling. "You will be safe and sound. It's the others I'm concerned about, if I'm being frank. They are a bit . . . bigger than you."

"What *about* th-the others?" Hap growled.

The Coachman winced. "Yes, well, you see, Bernard can't just walk you into the city. Apparently, new protocols are in place since the last time I was here. Heightened security, new fears of infiltration by outside sources, blah, blah, blah. You will be made the moment you step into the city."

Hap stepped forward, hands curling into fists, mouth curved into a snarl. "You s-s-*said* you could g-get us in."

"And I am," the Coachman said, taking an answering step back. "You see those crates the machines are moving?"

Vic felt a trickle of unease roll through him. "What about them?"

The Coachman grinned. "You'll be inside them, safe and snug. Each crate has a specific destination in mind. Once scanned through intake, the crates are loaded up and sent all throughout the city. No deliveries are made directly to Heaven—the Blue Fairy has the tendency to get whatever they need through more . . . circumspect channels—but I can get you a little closer than you would have been had you walked on your own. See? Easy peasy!" He looked at Vic as he lowered his voice. "Isn't that what humans say? Easy peasy lemon squeezy? Something like that."

"The crates should be big enough," Nurse Ratched said. "One for each of us. And you can ensure that they'll all be delivered to the same place?"

The Coachman tugged at the collar of his coat, his hat sitting back on his head. "Well, that *would* be the best way, of course. Why, that would be the best way of all."

"B-but," Hap said dangerously.

"But Bernard will only give us two," the Coachman said, gaze darting between Vic and Hap. "He only wanted to give us *one*. I managed to convince him to spare a second after reminding him of his . . . proclivities, and how it would look if that ever got out. Specific tastes, that one. Very odd. What that means is you'll have to buddy up, but since you're all buddies, you'll be fine. Nurse Ratched and Rambo in one crate, Hysterically Angry Puppet and Victor in the other. Tight fit, but it should work."

They stared at him.

He smiled back. "I can see by all the looks on your faces

266 | TJ KLUNE

that you're thrilled by— No? Are you not thrilled? Why is Hysterically Angry Puppet looking as if smoke should be pouring from his ears?"

Vic stepped between them before Hap could launch himself at the Coachman. "It's fine." He felt Hap grip the pack on his back. "We'll take it."

"How grand!" the Coachman exclaimed. "I *knew* you'd be amenable. You think on your feet, you do! I've always thought that about you since I met you yesterday. It'll all work out, you'll see. And think of the time you'll spend squashed together as an opportunity to share your deepest thoughts and feelings in case it *doesn't* work out." He waggled his eyebrows at Vic and Hap. "Perhaps to say something that you've always wanted to say but feared the answer you could receive?"

"Wh-what is he talking about?" Hap snapped in Vic's ear. "He t-talks without s-saying anything at all. I d-don't like him."

Vic wasn't sure that he did either, but he kept the thought to himself in case the Coachman changed his mind. "When?"

"Soon," the Coachman said. "You and Hap will pose as inspectors. Bernard tells me the next scheduled inspection isn't set for another week, so there's no chance you'll be surprised by someone from the Authority. You'll need to act stern and at the same time, disaffected. Hap, you have got that down pat. Rambo and Nurse Ratched, you will be their assistants."

Rambo spun excitedly in a circle. "I've always wanted to be an assistant! Vic, *Vic*. Did you hear that? I get to *assist*."

"You already do," Nurse Ratched said.

He bumped into her. "You always know just what to say."

"Now it is your turn. Say something that will make me feel better."

"We're going to be crate buddies!"

Nurse Ratched's screen filled with a frowning face. "I want to go back to the forest."

"Vic," the Coachman said. "You already look the part of a machine, but I need you to *act* like one. Act like you've never acted before! Let's see what you've got! You are a machine. You are an *inspector*. Show me what you've got. Make me *believe*."

Vic shifted awkwardly, the helmet sliding down on his forehead. He pushed it back up and cleared his throat. "Um. These crates contain exactly what they're supposed to?"

"Brava!" the Coachman cried. "Encore! Encore! Oh, I believed it. Yes, you will do quite well. Keep that energy. Never let anyone take it from you."

Vic blinked. "But I didn't—"

"How long will we be in the crates?" Nurse Ratched said.

"Not long, not long. A few hours at most. Bernard will make sure they'll be sent to a warehouse closed for renovations. The work is set to begin next month, so it should be empty. When you feel as if you've stopped moving, wait at least another hour before climbing out of the crates to be safe."

"This plan is filled with holes," Nurse Ratched said.

"The best plans often are," the Coachman agreed. "Rambo, stop picking up rocks, you delightful fellow. You won't have time to do anything with them and—"

A horn blared from somewhere in the warehouse.

The Coachman's eyes widened. "Shift change! We need to move *now*." He spun on his heels and began to march toward the warehouse.

The blocky machines moved single file toward a door at the back of the warehouse that flashed green as each one went through. They didn't speak, nor did they pay Vic and the others any mind. It was as if they weren't aware of anything else.

The warehouse itself was cavernous, the sounds of their footsteps echoing in the eerie quiet. Crates were stacked almost to the ceiling, each with a small screen that displayed a series of green numbers and letters. Nothing gave away the contents inside or what their destination would be.

Bernard led them toward the side of the warehouse, his steps heavy against the cement floor. The Coachman walked next to him, keeping up a one-sided conversation about nothing in particular. Vic and Hap pretended to look at the crates as if inspecting them, though it was nothing more than a cursory glance at best. Bernard never slowed, keeping a quick pace.

It was Rambo who almost got them caught.

One moment, he was next to Nurse Ratched in front of Vic and Hap, and the next, he squealed and was off like a shot to their right.

"Rambo," Vic hissed, looking around to make sure they weren't being watched. "*Rambo.* Get back here!"

Rambo didn't listen. He stopped in front of a machine parked between the crates against a wall. The machine was big and blue with black trim and a large circular brush at its base.

"Oh dear," the Coachman said as Bernard's head spun toward Rambo.

But Rambo didn't pay any mind. He stopped in front of the machine. "Oh. My. *Goodness.* You're a *vacuum.* Just like me! Hello, cousin!" He waved his arms in front of the bigger vacuum. "My name is Rambo. I'm a vacuum too! I come from—oh, I can't tell you that. Trust me, it's a *long* story filled with twists and turns. I'm pretty sure I'm the only vacuum in history to—*Wow.* Look at the size of your *brush.* I'm feeling strangely inadequate at the moment."

The line of worker machines suddenly came to a stop.

They all turned slowly toward Rambo and began to beep in low tones.

The blue vacuum shuddered as Rambo bumped into it over and over. "Hey! Hey, I'm talking to you, cousin! How'd you get so big? What's your favorite thing to clean? *I* like it when there's sawdust, because it tickles when I—"

A white light on top of the blue vacuum began to flash.

"You were recharging," Rambo said, rolling around the

vacuum. "Did I wake you up? I'm sorry. I didn't mean to. I've never seen another vacuum before, and I got so excited. Do you want to be friends? Shoot. I'm not going to be here for very long. Maybe we can be pen pals! Except I don't know how to write and I don't think we get mail delivered where we live. Vic, hey, Vic! Do we get mail in the forest?"

Vic stared at him in horror, unable to move. The beeping from the worker machines grew louder.

Nurse Ratched had no such trouble. She rolled toward Rambo, her screen filled with exclamation points. "My apologies," she told the blue vacuum as she thumped Rambo with one of her tentacles. "My assistant gets a little exuberant. Go back to sleep. There is nothing to see here. We are just normal inspectors doing inspections. I have determined you have passed your inspection. Keep up the good work. Congratulations. I will request you receive a commendation for your services. Thank you. Thank you." She began to pull Rambo away, much to his annoyance.

Bernard's head spun to face the Coachman, who chuckled weakly. "Yes, I know. He's . . . a special case. My apologies, Bernard. It won't happen again."

"I should kill you where you stand," Bernard said.

"*Viva la succión!*" Rambo cried.

"I'll handle it," the Coachman said. He whirled on Vic and Hap, eyes narrowed. "Sir, if you could possibly consider *controlling your assistant during inspections,* it would be greatly appreciated. And since you *are* inspectors, consider inspecting."

Vic startled. "Yes, of course. Inspecting. That's what we're here for." He glanced around awkwardly.

Hap pointed at a large stack of crates. "Those l-look like they were s-stacked how they're supposed to b-be."

Vic nodded, head snapping up and down. "Exactly. I don't think I've ever seen crates stacked so well." He turned toward the line of beeping working machines, panic clawing at his chest. "You all did a good job. I don't see any issues. Continue doing . . . whatever it is you're doing."

The machines stopped beeping before turning back in line and beginning to move slowly once again.

Vic breathed a sigh of relief as Nurse Ratched pulled Rambo to them. Hap crouched down and glared at him.

"Uh-oh," Rambo said. "I know that face. Nothing good ever comes when Hap makes that face. Which, to be fair, he makes that face a lot, but still."

"Keep. Your m-mouth. *Shut*."

Rambo tipped Hap a salute with his pincers. "Will do. Question. I don't have a mouth, so what does that—ooh, that face is even worse. I'll just stop talking now."

Hap picked Rambo up as he stood, staring defiantly at Bernard.

"No favor is worth this," Bernard mumbled.

They continued on toward the back of the warehouse, Rambo muttering that he'd never been to a family reunion before, and how it'd been ruined even before it began.

"This all looks fine," Vic said loudly, trying to drown out Rambo. "The most efficiently run warehouse I've ever seen. Nurse Ratched, please make a note of it."

"Of course, Victor," Nurse Ratched said. "I absolutely adore when you tell me what to do." This was negated when a picture of a hand making a rude gesture flashed on her screen for a moment. "And can I say, your helmet looks especially dapper today. It suits you. I hope you never take it off."

"Ha, ha," the Coachman said. Vic thought if he was capable of sweating, it'd be pouring down his face. "This is all going so well! Nothing is wrong. Everything is fine."

Bernard led them away from the line of worker machines toward a back corner of the warehouse. There, in the dusty corners, sat a row of empty crates, their lids open, their screens dark. Up close, they were smaller than Vic had expected.

"Here," Bernard said, head still spinning, albeit slower as if he were taking in the entire warehouse. "They'll use these."

Nurse Ratched tipped one of the crates over so she could see inside. "This will be a tight fit. I fear I may be too large."

"Impossible," the Coachman said. "You are a goddess. Your figure is perfect. There has never been a machine so beautiful."

"That is not what I meant but thank you. I am perfect. If we were not on a mission, I would ask that you show a lady a good time."

The Coachman bowed. "It would be my honor, my dear. Oh, the things we could do together. It's positively scandalous."

"Gross," Rambo mumbled in Hap's arms.

"Once inside, you can't make a sound," Bernard said, obviously regretting every decision that had led him to this moment. "I'll program the destination. When the next shift arrives, you will be loaded and transported into the city."

"You t-trust him?" Hap asked the Coachman.

The Coachman shrugged. "I trust Bernard to know that if he screws us over, I have enough blackmail material on him to get him censured. Or worse, decommissioned."

"I never want to see your face again," Bernard told him. "After today, we're even."

The Coachman patted him on one of his arms. "You say that now, but you'll miss me in a hundred years or so."

"I highly doubt it." His head stopped spinning as he approached the crate. The screen on the top came to life as he tapped a finger against it. The crate shuddered and shook before it collapsed completely, unfolding until it lay flat on the ground.

The Coachman took Nurse Ratched by one of her tentacles, leading her onto the crate. "I'll have to lay you on your back," he told her, a mischievous twitch to his mustache. "I promise to make it as pleasant as possible."

"You old flirt," Nurse Ratched said in her flat voice. "I know your type."

The Coachman grinned at her. "I bet you do." He grunted as he tipped her over, her screen facing the ceiling. "Do protect him, won't you? He's . . . precious."

"I know," Nurse Ratched said. "Coachman?"

"Yes, my sweet?"

"If we are betrayed, if Bernard attempts to notify anyone of our presence in the city, I will find a way out. I will come for him first. And when I have finished with him, I will find you. There is nowhere in the world you can run. Every day, for the rest of your life, you will have to look over your shoulder. When you least expect it, I will be there. I will stick my drill so far inside you that you will taste it. And then I will turn it on and scramble everything that makes you who you are."

"I wouldn't expect anything less," the Coachman said. He pressed his hand against her screen. "If that happens, I will wait for you with open arms."

"Seriously," Rambo said. "This is really gross."

Hap shoved the Coachman out of the way, setting Rambo on top of Nurse Ratched's casing. "No t-talking," he warned them.

"Hap?" Rambo asked.

"What."

"I love you."

Hap scowled at him. He turned to stalk away, but paused at the last second, face twisting. He turned back around again and bent over Rambo. Vic was stunned when he said, "I t-tolerate your existence." He took one of Rambo's pincers in his hand and moved it up and down.

"Whoa," Rambo whispered as Hap let go. "Nurse Ratched, did you hear that? He loves me too!"

"Th-that's not what I said."

"It *is*. And you can't take it back!"

"I am going to die in this box," Nurse Ratched said.

Bernard stepped forward, extending an arm toward the

screen. He tapped it once more, and the crate walls rose around Nurse Ratched and Rambo. The last Vic saw of them was Rambo waving frantically.

"Goodbye," Vic said quietly as the lid closed over them.

Bernard motioned toward another crate set farther back. "This one is yours."

"And it'll allow for air to move freely through it?" the Coachman asked.

Bernard frowned. "Yes. As discussed. It's meant for transporting florae and faunae." He looked at Vic and Hap before his head spun toward the Coachman. "Why is that necessary? Are they transporting something alive?"

"What?" the Coachman said, sounding outraged. "I take umbrage with your tone, sir. I would *never* allow something so—"

"You look familiar," Bernard said to Hap. "Have we met before?"

Hap lowered his head, his hood falling around his face. "N-no."

"Hmm," Bernard said. "Coachman, this better not come back on me."

"Of course it won't," the Coachman said. "There is nothing *to* come back on you. I don't know what's going through that circle you call a head, but I am an upstanding citizen. Everything I do is aboveboard, and—"

"I don't want to know any more," Bernard said, turning to Hap. "Can you climb inside? If not, I can dismantle the crate for easier access."

"It's f-fine," Hap muttered. He pulled his pack off as he climbed over the ledge of the crate, settling his back against the side. He slunk down, legs stretching until his feet were flat against the opposite side. He set his pack next to him as he wiggled down farther.

"Why did you go first?" Vic asked, suddenly unsure. The box was *much* smaller now that Hap was inside.

Hap stared up at him. "I'm b-bigger than you."

"Heaven," he heard Rambo warbling from the other crate. "I'm in heaven."

"Maybe I should get my own crate."

"Get inside," Bernard said. "We're running out of time."

Vic sighed as he turned his pack around to his front. He pushed his helmet off his face as he climbed gingerly into the box, careful to avoid Hap.

"Ow," Hap said when Vic stepped on his leg.

Vic stared down at him, spluttering apologies.

"That was a j-joke," Hap said, and Vic *swore* he saw the curve of a smile, there and gone in a flash.

"You're not funny," Vic told him as he climbed the rest of the way into the box. "I don't know who told you that, but they lied."

"It was me!" Rambo shouted. "I told him that!"

"Be *quiet*," Bernard said, slapping the top of the box.

"Okay!"

Vic settled down against Hap, his back to Hap's front. He kept his legs inside of Hap's. He was stiff, back arched until Hap wrapped an arm around his middle, pulling him flush against him. Hap's mouth was near his ear when he said, "R-relax."

"I'm trying."

"T-try harder."

Vic tipped his head back, resting it against Hap's shoulder. It was a tight fit, Hap's pack digging into his side, his own heavy against his stomach. He hoped it wouldn't be long before they were out again. He was suddenly discovering he didn't like such close proximity very much. It caused his head to swirl, his skin to feel itchy.

The Coachman stood above them next to the crate. "Bernard, a moment, if you please. I need to have a word with my friends in private."

"You have one minute," Bernard said. "I can't give you any longer. Don't make me regret this." He stepped back away from the crates.

The Coachman knelt down next to the crate, arms resting on the side. Vic looked up at him. Hap gripped his sides, fingers digging in. It was almost grounding, and he wondered why he should feel as relieved as he did.

"My dear boy," the Coachman said in a low voice. "Thank you."

"For what?"

"Showing me the world isn't as cold as I once thought." He reached down and squeezed Vic's hand.

Vic couldn't speak past the burning in his throat. He nodded, squeezing the Coachman's hand in return.

"I wish you well on your adventure," the Coachman said as he pulled his hand away. "I hope you find what you're looking for."

"Coachman," Bernard said, a new urgency in his voice. "It's time."

"Yes," the Coachman said, smiling down at them. "It is."

He stood, and with a twitch of his mustache, stepped away out of sight.

Bernard appeared above them. He reached down and pulled the lid over them. Before he shut it completely, he said, "There's a button. To your right. Do you see it?"

"Yes."

"It will open the crate. Do not press it until you're sure."

"Thank you."

"Don't thank me. Just forget you ever saw me."

And with that, he closed the lid. A moment later, Vic heard a beep and the box latched shut. A moment later, a tiny white bulb lit up near the top left of the crate, and cool air began to stream from vents along the sides. Vic sucked in a breath. It tasted faintly medicinal.

He closed his eyes, gripping his pack.

"It's all r-right," Hap muttered. "You are all r-right. There, th-there."

Vic choked on a laugh. "Are you trying to make me feel better?"

"No. I'm trying to s-stop you from panicking and g-getting us caught."

"Oh."

"Is it w-working?"

"I don't know."

"S-stop moving."

Vic did. He opened his eyes, and breathed in through his nose and out through his mouth. Hap was a warm presence behind him, his hands still on Vic's sides, fingers brushing against the metal of Vic's battery vest. It was small. The crate was small. The crate was small, and they were trapped inside. Vic turned his head, looking for the button that Bernard had mentioned. He found it in the corner above their feet. All he would need to do is kick it, and the box would open. It would open, and they would be free. They could stand. They could breathe, because the air was growing thick inside. He gripped the pack tighter as he struggled for control. Bile rose in the back of his throat, acidic and hot.

And then Hap whispered, "Tell m-me."

"Tell you what?" Vic gasped, shifting against Hap, feeling the slide of metal and skin and wood against his back. His helmet bumped the lid overhead. His thoughts were clouded, like a storm rumbling on the horizon.

"Tell m-me about the h-heart."

Vic blinked rapidly as the clouds parted slightly, a thin sliver of sunlight poking through. "What do you mean?"

"Y-you're making a n-new one, right?"

"Trying to," he said, sinking down against Hap again. Hap let go of his sides, raising his arms until they wrapped around the front of Vic's pack, holding them both in place. Vic was surrounded by him, could hear the gears turning in Hap's chest, a low, pleasant hum.

"H-how d-does it start?"

"Wood," Vic said, voice weak. "It starts with wood."

"Okay. Why w-wood?"

"I . . . don't know?"

"You d-do," Hap said. "I know you d-do."

Vic grunted when the crate shifted. He turned his face into his own arm, muffling his shout as the crate was lifted off the ground.

"Here," Hap whispered. "I'm h-here. Focus on the s-sound of my v-voice. Let me hear y-yours, Vic. T-tell me about what you're making."

"Wood," Vic said as the crate swung slowly, his stomach swooping. "It begins with wood."

"Y-yes. Why?"

"It's easier to mold. To fashion. It's . . . old. The art of carving wood. It goes back thousands of years."

He grunted when the crate shook as it was set down.

"K-keep going."

And so he did.

CHAPTER 20

He startled awake when the crate jerked around them.

He gasped loudly, about to shout in warning, but a hand covered his mouth. "Quiet," a voice warned in his ear.

Hap.

The crate.

The City of Electric Dreams.

Vic nodded against Hap's hand, breathing in the scent of wood just under his nose on one of Hap's fingers.

Vic listened. The sounds of heavy machinery moved around them. He didn't hear voices, didn't hear footsteps, or so he thought. He waited, back cramping, legs stiff. Minutes felt like hours.

Nothing happened.

Eventually, the sounds of machinery faded.

And they waited more, the Coachman's warning ringing in his ears.

He was about to tell Hap that they should press the button when movement came from just outside the crate. He froze, sweat dripping down into his eyes.

The crate beeped above them as someone—some*thing*— tapped against the screen.

He felt Hap tense underneath him. The gears of his heart sped up.

The crate lid opened, the light outside the crate bright and harsh.

"See?" Rambo said, rising up the side of the crate on his hydraulic lift. "I *told* you this was the right one."

Nurse Ratched appeared beside him, looking down at Vic

and Hap. "You are correct. Enjoy the moment as I will never say that to you again."

Vic stared up at them, dumbfounded.

"Aw," Rambo said, his sensors flashing. "You two look comfy-cozy. Did you have a good trip? *I* did, even though Nurse Ratched wouldn't let me sing to pass the time. Vic, you think I have a good voice, right? Nurse Ratched said when I sing, it sounds like the time she sent the squirrel to the farm when we were back home. Why would a squirrel be singing when it went to the farm? Was it happy?"

"Yes," Nurse Ratched said. "It sang because it was very happy to go to the farm where it will live forever." Behind Rambo, the words on her screen said DO YOU SEE WHAT I HAVE TO DEAL WITH?

Vic sat up, wincing as his back popped. "How did you get out? You were supposed to wait until we opened your crate."

"We got bored," Nurse Ratched said. "I was going to murder Rambo if we had to wait a moment longer. Since you believe murder is bad, I decided it was better that we got out and ran the risk of being seen."

Rambo laughed. "You wouldn't murder me. Right?" He lowered slightly on his lift. "Right?"

"Victor," Nurse Ratched said. "If you are done sitting on top of Hap, I suggest you get out of the crate while this warehouse is empty."

"I'm *not* sitting on top of Hap!"

"You are," Rambo said, sounding confused. "We can see you. Why do you look out of breath? Were you exerting yourself inside the box? What were you do—oh. *Oh.* Gross. I mean, that sounds nice."

Vic nearly fell as he stood abruptly. The only reason he stayed upright was because Hap pressed a hand against the small of his back. He managed to climb out of the crate with minimal injury, only bumping his left knee hard enough to send a spasm racing down his leg. "We weren't doing that!"

"Doing wh-what?" Hap grunted as he stood up.

Nurse Ratched whipped her tentacle against his chest. "Respect boundaries. No means no. Consent is important. Victor, I have a program on safe sexual practices. I have never run it before, given that you are asexual. But, like most things, sexuality is a spectrum. You can be asexual and still have—"

Vic looked around wildly, hoping against hope that they would be discovered and captured, carted away and locked somewhere deep in the city so he wouldn't have to continue the conversation. No such luck. They were alone. As Bernard had said, it appeared as if the warehouse was under construction, or perhaps renovation. There were scorch marks on the wall opposite them, black smears that spread down to the floor. It looked as if there'd been a fire at some point.

The warehouse was mostly empty. A few other crates sat near their own, their lids closed tight. The crate Nurse Ratched and Rambo had been in lay flat against the ground a few yards away.

"Victor?" Nurse Ratched asked. "Did you hear me? I offered to show you—"

"Is anyone else here?" Vic asked, refusing to look at Hap as he climbed out of the crate.

"No," Nurse Ratched said. "While Rambo looked for your crate, I scanned the perimeter. There is movement outside of the warehouse, but nothing in here. We are alone."

Vic turned in time to see Hap closing the lid to their crate. He lifted it and set it against the far wall, his hood falling back on his shoulders. He went to the other crate and tapped the screen, causing it to fold back up. Once done, he moved that one too.

"How far are we from Heaven?" Vic asked, looking back at Nurse Ratched.

Her screen filled with another map. Multiple squares appeared, which Vic knew meant buildings. A line ran from one square—the warehouse—and turned right, then left, then right once more before it ended at another square. "Approximately a mile. The Coachman provided me the best route in order to get to Heaven and stay out of sight. If he is correct and we do not run into any issues, we should arrive in twenty-six minutes. According to the Coachman, the Authority increases their patrols after dark. While night will provide us additional cover, the risk will be greater."

"Suggestion?" Vic asked.

"We move now. Heaven is located in the lower quarters of the city. Per the Coachman, the lower quarters are not as well kept as the rest of the city. We will fit in so long as we do not draw attention to ourselves." She turned toward Rambo. "Which means that you cannot roll off if you see another vacuum."

"But—"

"We will leave you behind."

"You would?" Rambo said. "Fine. I promise I won't roll off if I see one of my relatives because you guys don't care about my feelings."

"That is correct," Nurse Ratched said.

"Hey!"

Hap stood next to Vic as he studied the map on Nurse Ratched's screen. "S-seems easy enough."

"It does," Nurse Ratched said. "Which is why we need to be careful. We are close to our goal. It would be a shame if we were caught now."

"We can do this," Vic said, looking toward what he thought was the front of the warehouse, trying to sound more confident than he felt. "What are the rules?"

"Stick together!" Rambo said.

"Run if we have to."

"No dallying!"

"No drilling, though I will amend that proclamation should the need arise."

"And a-above all else, b-be brave," Hap said.

They all turned slowly to look at him.

He scowled. "What? That's what you s-say."

"Wow," Rambo whispered fervently. "One of us! One of us!"

Hap rolled his eyes. "Shut up. I am n-not."

He turned to head toward the door, but Vic stopped him by grabbing his arm. He looked down at Vic's hand, then up at his face, asking a question without speaking.

Vic let his arm go, reaching up and pulling his hood back over his head. "One of us."

Hap looked like he was about to argue but shook his head instead. Then he adjusted Vic's helmet until it was no longer crooked. "There are w-worse th-things I c-can be."

Vic grinned at him. It felt odd to be smiling at such a time, but he couldn't stop it if he'd tried.

And wonder of all wonders, Hap smiled back. It was small, the edges twitching, but there.

"Oh boy," Nurse Ratched said. "If I had known all it would take would be to lock the two of you in a small enclosed space, I would have done it ages ago."

Vic stepped back, shaking his head. "Come on. It's time to go to Heaven."

They stopped in front of a door at what Nurse Ratched said was the front of the warehouse. Vic reached for the door handle, but Hap stopped him, motioning him to step to the side. "We d-don't know what's on the other s-side. Let me g-go first."

Irritated, Vic said, "I can do it."

"You are sweating," Nurse Ratched said. "Your heart rate is elevated."

He glanced back at her. "And?"

"Machines do not sweat," she said. "Get yourself together, Victor. Let Hap go through first just to make sure it is safe."

He wiped his brow. Sure enough, his hand came away wet. "It's warm. I can't just stop sweating. The disguise is heavy."

Hap squinted at him. "You c-can't turn off your l-leaking?"

"I—that's not—*no,* I can't just turn it off."

"Wh-why not?"

"That's not how it— Would you just go through the damn door?"

"It's okay to be nervous and scared," Rambo said, bumping against his leg. "Do you want me to leak with you? Give me a second. Wait for it. Wait for it. And . . . there." A little dribble of oil spilled out onto the ground. "See? I'm just like you!"

"That is not sanitary," Nurse Ratched said. "Victor, deep breaths. Rambo, stop being weird."

"I don't know how not to be weird," Rambo said. "That's like asking the birds to stop flying."

Hap cracked open the door.

Vic stumbled back at the wave of sound that bowled over them. It was cacophonous, grating and harsh. Metal against metal. The shriek of sirens in the distance. Insistent beeping. Voices, though not speaking in words that Vic could understand. Light filled the open crack in the door, causing Vic to blink rapidly. Hap stuck his head out, hand still gripping the doorknob. Vic felt a hum vibrating up his legs to the rest of his body, causing his disguise to rattle against his frame. It was as if he was electrified.

Hap leaned back in. "We m-move quick. K-keep your head down. Nurse R-ratched, where do we g-go first?"

"Right," she said promptly. "Three blocks. Shall I lead?"

Hap nodded. "You f-first. Then Rambo. Victor. I'll b-bring up the r-rear."

"Second in command!" Rambo said as he spun in circles. "I *knew* it. Don't worry, men and Nurse Ratched. I won't let you down!"

"Ready?" Hap asked Vic.

Vic took a deep breath and nodded.

Hap pushed the door all the way open.

Nurse Ratched rolled through, followed by Rambo.

Vic stood on the threshold, unable to make his feet move.

Hap pressed a hand against the small of his back. "Be brave."

"Be brave," Vic whispered, and for the first time, stepped out into the City of Electric Dreams . . .

. . . directly into sensory overload. He couldn't focus on any one thing, head jerking from side to side, up and down. They were on a road of sorts, one lane traveling in either direction, bisected by a glowing white line. Across the street stood grungy buildings of cracked concrete and crumbling brick, sand and dirt coating the sides. The smell was extraordinary, a mixture of gasoline and exhaust and something fetid, heavy and thick. He choked on it, trying to breathe through his mouth. His eyes bulged from his head as he looked upward. The lights of the city were neon sharp even in the afternoon sunlight. Every color he'd ever seen (and a few he hadn't) ran up the sides of the buildings: blue and violet and red and orange. Above them, what appeared to be a rail system stretched along the length of the street, crates not unlike the ones they'd been in flying by at incredible speeds, attached to large cables.

And it was *loud*, so loud that Vic couldn't hear himself think. Everything seemed to make a sound bent on assaulting him. From some out-of-sight speaker system, a semi-soothing voice blared, the words echoing up and down the buildings even as they crackled. "EVERYTHING YOU DO MUST BE RECORDED BY ORDER OF THE AUTHORITY. REMEMBER, THERE IS COMFORT IN ROUTINE. DO WHAT YOU ARE PROGRAMMED TO DO, AND YOU WILL BE AS RIGHT AS RAIN. IF THERE IS A FAULT IN YOUR PROTOCOLS, PLEASE REPORT TO THE NEAREST ADMINISTRATION OFFICE IMMEDIATELY FOR PROCESSING. IT WILL NOT HURT. WE WILL FIX YOU AND MAKE IT ALL BETTER. THE AUTHORITY WISHES YOU A WONDERFUL AFTERNOON. ATTENTION. ATTENTION. ATTENTION. EVERYTHING YOU DO MUST BE—"

Gaze still turned upward, he stepped onto the street. The

moment his foot touched down, he was jerked back by his collar. Something whizzed by in front of him, horn blaring angrily. "W-*watch* it," Hap growled at him. "Pay attention."

Vic grimaced. "Sorry. It's just . . . loud. I can't focus."

"Try," Hap said. "Follow th-the others. Don't stop." He spun Vic around, pushing him down the road.

Nurse Ratched didn't hesitate. She moved with purpose, ignoring everything happening around her. Rambo attempted to do the same but kept getting distracted by literally everything. "Oh my gosh! Would you look at *that*. And *that*. And what is *that*? I've never seen such a thing!" He rolled up to a machine sitting next to a building. It was rusted out, its casing cracked. It had the vague outline of a face on its upper body, though it had no eyes. Its teeth were black and sharp. It leaned against the side of a building. "Hello! How are you? I'm Rambo. I'm a vacuum!"

The machine turned toward him. "Ram . . . bo?"

"Yes! What's your name? Oh, excuse me. Your *designation*."

"My . . . designation," the machine said. "I . . . I . . ." The mouth of the machine opened, black slick pouring out mixed with nuts and bolts. Rambo scooted back out of the splash zone.

"That's okay," he said. "I can clean that up for you."

Without her turning around, tentacles shot out from Nurse Ratched, wrapping around Rambo and pulling him away from the mess on the sidewalk.

"Do not talk to strangers," she said. "They will offer you sweets and then take you away and eat you."

"They *will*?" Rambo gasped. "Why didn't anyone tell me that?"

Vic and Hap hurried past the machine, even as it reached for them, saying, "I am I am I *am*—"

Vic tried to keep his head down, putting one foot in front of the other, but something would catch the corner of his eye, and he'd be helpless against it. He didn't know what he'd been expecting of the City of Electric Dreams, but it wasn't this.

This felt dank and dark, the machines on the street in varying stages of decay. The voice from the speakers above kept repeating the same words over and over, and they bounced around his skull. ATTENTION, ATTENTION, ATTENTION, and he yelped when an android pushed by him, walking in the opposite direction. "Watch it," the android said in a high-pitched voice. The android stopped and stared as Hap pushed Vic on. "Hold on, wait a minute," it called after them. "Where'd you get that helmet? Can you make me one? I need it, I need it, I need it!"

"Keep g-going," Hap grunted.

Vic did.

Another machine—this one a floating cube not much bigger than Rambo—flew in front of Nurse Ratched. "Hello!" it said cheerfully, voice distinctly male and oily. "What brings you to the City of Electric Dreams? Perhaps you'd like to take in a show! I've got the best seats available. Or would you like a watch? I've got hundreds of them!" The bottom of the cube opened, and a metal mesh netting fell toward the ground, bouncing just above the pavement. Watches of all shapes and sizes filled the netting, all of them dead. "You won't find a better value anywhere!"

"No, thank you," Nurse Ratched said. "I do not need tickets or watches."

"You sure?" the cube asked as the netting rose back up into its body. It floated closer, voice dropping. "Perhaps you'd like something a bit more . . . exotic."

"Ooh," Rambo said, peering over the top of Nurse Ratched. "I like exotic."

"Ah," the cube said. "A machine after my own tastes. Have you ever seen a lemur? I've got dozens of them. Come with me, and I'll show you."

"A *lemur*?" Rambo gasped. "Nurse Ratched, did you hear that? He has lemurs! Also, what's a lemur?"

"We do not want anything you have," Nurse Ratched told the cube.

"Are you sure?" the cube asked. "Because you don't sound sure."

Another tentacle slid from Nurse Ratched. She snapped it against the cube, knocking it to the side. "I am a lady, and I told you no. Learn to respect my boundaries. If you do not, your ending will not be swift nor without pain."

"Yikes!" the cube said. "You're a fiery one. I'm going, I'm going." It floated away across the street and began to accost a pair of boxes that appeared to be trash receptacles.

"Interesting," Nurse Ratched said. "Why is it that males do not accept no for an answer?"

"We're idiots," Rambo said.

"Yes. You are." She continued on down the road.

After that, they were mostly left alone. If they *were* approached, Nurse Ratched would threaten, her tentacles waving dangerously, her screen filling with images of death and destruction. Once, a robot with four faces—each with a different expression—tried to herd them into a doorway, telling them it had the latest software that wasn't available anywhere else. "It's not exactly . . . legal," it said, one of its faces winking while another moaned softly. "You want to see the edge of the universe? Expand your mind? Feel things that you've never felt before? I can hook you up."

"Say no to drugs," Nurse Ratched told Rambo.

"No to drugs!" Rambo cried.

One of the robot's faces twisted in anger. "Then get the hell away from me. Goddamn tourists." The last face smiled at them. "Don't worry about him. Come back anytime you want!" The angry face said, "Goddamn yokels. Go back to where you came from, goddammit!"

They moved on.

Nurse Ratched never got lost. She moved with purpose. They

stopped at an intersection, the screen across the street flashing a red hand. Other machines gathered around them, crowding them close. Vic kept his head down. The machines muttered around him, some in binary, others in English, still others speaking in languages Vic had never heard before that sounded like metal rain falling on the ground. The red hand switched to a green thumbs-up and they crossed the street with the crowd, passing in front of stopped vehicles with black tires, others floating above them, the air underneath them shimmering.

It went on and on. The map had made Heaven seem much closer than it actually was. Vic was sweating, but there wasn't anything he could do to stop it. It stung his eyes, made his skin slick and sticky. He flinched when something brushed against his arm. He was about to turn to see what it was when he was knocked to the side, his pack being jerked incessantly.

He looked up to see a thin pole towering over him, its arms attached to the pack. "I want that," it told him in a guttural voice. "Can I have that? I want it. Give it to me."

It fell back when Hap cocked a fist, snarling. "D-don't touch him."

"Okay!" it squealed. "I won't! Can I have it, though?"

"N-no. Leave before I b-break you."

The pole shrunk down until it was no bigger than Rambo before scurrying away.

"I h-hate this city," Hap muttered as he stared after it. He turned back toward Vic. "You all r-right?"

Vic nodded, unable to speak, throat dry, tongue like a lead weight in his mouth. He reached for Hap's hand. Hap looked down, expression stuttering, before gripping, intertwining his fingers with Vic's. It grounded Vic, causing the fog in his head to part slightly.

"Come on," Hap said roughly. "We d-don't want to get lost."

They caught up with Nurse Ratched and Rambo at the end of the next block. "Here," Nurse Ratched said. "We turn here."

They went down the next street, and if anything, the buildings grew shabbier. The speakers sounded as if they were shorting out, words lost in bursts of static. The neon lights flickered as the sun moved behind clouds. The screens on the buildings were cracked and on the fritz, the pictures of smiling foxes and cats rolling. Vic felt nauseous, an ache forming just behind his eyes. His teeth felt as if they were covered in a layer of film. He'd experienced something like it before a few times back in the lab when experimenting with electricity, only this was bigger, a constant pressure that never abated. He felt himself shutting down, and he struggled against it, though it was much bigger than he was.

Hap never let him go. He tethered Vic, pushing by anyone or anything that tried to talk to them. Vic was about to ask Nurse Ratched how much longer they had to go when she stopped. He almost crashed into the back of her, Rambo now sitting on top of her behind her screen.

"What is it?" he asked.

"Move," she said. "Now. Down the alley."

"Why? What's—" And then he saw it.

Saw *them*.

They were moving toward them, still a ways down the street. Three of them, their faces blank, their uniforms crisp. On their chests was a familiar sigil.

The smooth men.

The Authority.

Nurse Ratched spun on her treads, kicking up dust and sand as she rushed into the alleyway nearest them, her tentacles tightening around Rambo to keep him from falling. Hap pulled Vic after her. The smell was horrific, waste and decay. Water dripped from a cracked pipe overhead, the ground covered in steam pouring from a metal grate. A sign above them blinked over and over, the words ALL YOUR DREAMS WILL COME TRUE IN THE CITY! seared into Vic's head.

Hap pressed Vic against the side of a building, chest against

Vic's. His cheek knocked Vic's helmet askew. "Don't m-move," Hap whispered.

Vic stared at him, never looking away.

"What do we do?" Rambo whispered.

"We stay quiet," Nurse Ratched said. "If they find us, we kill them."

"But I don't know *how* to kill."

"I do," Nurse Ratched said. "I will protect you."

"I love you, Nurse Ratched."

"I know."

Hap's grip on Vic's hand tightened, grinding his bones together. But Vic didn't make a sound. The gears in Hap's chest turned furiously. It was almost soothing. A moment later, Hap relaxed. "Th-they're gone. Wait another m-moment. G-give them time to get d-down the street."

Vic breathed in. Vic breathed out. Just under the smell of the alley, he thought he could pick out notes of the wood he'd put onto Hap. He closed his eyes, chasing the scent.

"Okay," Hap said finally. "We're g-good. Nurse Ratched, how much f-farther?"

"We are close," she said. She turned toward the opposite end of the alley. "In fact, we could go this way. It will keep us off the street."

"Go," Hap said, stepping away from Vic, but not letting go of his hand.

"Going," she said. She moved deftly around detritus in the alleyway, rolling through puddles, liquid spraying against the brick. Rambo complained she was getting him wet. She told him it could be worse as she could tell him exactly what he was getting wet with. Rambo didn't say much after that.

They came out on the other side of the alley. It was more of the same, though not as busy. The rail system above them looked as if it hadn't moved in a long time, the crates in pieces as they dangled, creaking and groaning.

Vic thought he saw bright eyes peering out at them from

one of the windows, but when he looked again, nothing was there.

Other machines of all shapes and sizes moved around them without speaking, those that had faces not looking up from the ground. From somewhere off to their right came what sounded like laughter, though it was broken. Vic felt cold as the sky darkened. The clouds that had once been white were now gray and foreboding. The last of the sun's rays were swallowed, and the shadows grew around them.

"I don't like this," Rambo said nervously.

"I do not either," Nurse Ratched said. "But we are almost there. If the map is correct, we should arrive in approximately three minutes."

Vic looked up, trying to see the top of the pyramid that housed Heaven. It was supposed to be big, with a bright beam of light coming from the top. He couldn't see it beyond the buildings that seemed to curve overhead toward them. "Are you sure?"

"Yes, Victor. I am sure."

"Maybe it moved," Rambo said. "Or maybe the Coachman betrayed us and is leading us into a trap."

"Then we will escape and murder him too," Nurse Ratched said.

Rambo laughed weakly. "Can I help?"

"No. You are disgustingly pure. I will do it. But you can watch."

"Hooray!"

In the end, it was Hap who saw Heaven first. Vic was looking up at the crates swinging above them, wondering why and for how long they'd been stopped. He knew the Blue Fairy operated outside of the Authority, but he didn't know how, or if this was their doing. He was about to ask Nurse Ratched when Hap said, "L-look. There. It's th-there."

Vic looked to where Hap was pointing. At first, he didn't see anything. "What are you—"

A beam of light appeared, rocketing toward the sky. It hit the gray clouds above. A beacon in the darkness.

They were close. They were *so close.*

He started forward and was jerked back when Hap didn't let him go. "What?"

Hap shook his head. "We d-don't go through the f-front. The Coachman said we h-have to f-find the Doorman. You still have the c-coin?"

Vic nodded, reaching into his pocket. His fingers brushed against warm metal. He pulled it out, holding it up. It glinted in the low light, the *H* on one side, the wings of the Blue Fairy on the other.

"We will need to circle around the pyramid," Nurse Ratched said. "The Coachman indicated the front entrance is monitored by machines scanning barcodes. Those that have . . . how did he put it? Broken free. Those that have broken free use the rear entrance with the Doorman."

"They all have coins?" Rambo asked.

"I do not know," Nurse Ratched said, "though I expect not."

Vic looked up at the beam of light. He hoped what they'd see inside would be enough to find his father.

Trees Vic had never seen before lined the exterior of Heaven. Their bark was layered and rough, their leaves large fronds that swayed in the sharpening wind. Heaven itself rose above them, the windows black with lines and images swirling across the glass. A large butterfly flew across the glass of the pyramid, leaving a trail of glittering light and an entranced Hap in its wake. Above the stink of the city, Vic thought he smelled a hint of rain on the horizon. Thunder rumbled, low and deep.

They left the entrance to Heaven behind, a line of machines extending out the front. A loud voice rang out, distinctly feminine, saying, "WELCOME TO HEAVEN, WHERE ALL

YOUR DREAMS WILL BE REALIZED. IF YOU ARE NOT AUTHORIZED TO BE HERE, TURN AWAY. HAVE YOUR CREDENTIALS READY TO BE SCANNED. ENJOY YOUR STAY."

The pyramid was massive, and Vic watched as the butterfly on the sides seemed to follow them around the building, its wings fluttering. It was only as they got closer that he saw that the glitter formed words, though they were hard to make out. He thought he saw "life" and "sensuality" and "dreams" and "ecstasy," but when he tried to focus on them, they swirled away.

They reached the rear of Heaven in short time, as the first drops of rain began to fall. The butterfly hung suspended above them, frozen as the light cascaded down from its wings.

"Where do we go?" Rambo asked.

"Th-there," Hap said quietly.

Vic followed where he was pointing.

Near a pair of massive metal gates was a blue door with a black circular screen near the top. Before he could speak, the butterfly suddenly dove toward the base of the pyramid, shrinking in size. It disappeared as it hit the door, only to reappear on the screen, much smaller, though it still flapped its wings.

"Heaven," Rambo whispered. "I'm in heaven."

It took Vic more than he cared to admit to walk toward the blue door. The butterfly seemed to beckon him, and he thought he saw more words appear in its light: "hello" and "welcome" and "who are you?"

He clutched the coin in one hand, and Hap's in the other. Nurse Ratched was close behind them, Rambo still humming to himself a familiar tune. "Be brave," Vic whispered. "Be brave."

"We're b-being watched," Hap muttered.

Vic didn't look away from the door. "How do you know?"

"He is right," Nurse Ratched said. "Cameras. They saw us the moment we arrived. They know we are coming."

He swallowed thickly as he stopped a few feet away from the

door, Hap bumping into him. The butterfly wrapped its wings around itself as it began to spin in circles, glittering light filling the screen. The light flashed brightly, and when it dimmed, the butterfly was gone.

In its place was a small humanoid figure. Its yellow hair hung in curls around its sharp face, blue eyes big and unblinking. Its legs unfolded from underneath its wings, the calves slender and pale, the feet small, the toes curling. It was nude, though without sex. It held out one of its hands, all fingers folded save one, which beckoned them closer to the door.

It giggled, a sound like the tinkling of bells. "Welcome to Heaven," it said, voice soft, tinged with a curl of seduction. "I am the Blue Pixie. If you are at this door, then you will have the proper admittance fee. Please insert it below." A flap slid up below the screen, revealing a thin slot.

"The coin," Nurse Ratched said. "Give it the coin."

Vic stepped forward, letting go of Hap. The Blue Pixie watched every step he took with interest. He didn't know if it was a prerecorded greeting or a sentient program. By the way it was looking at him, he thought the latter.

His hand trembled as he lifted the coin, putting it against the slot. With a little push, the coin slid in and was gone.

"Thank you," the Blue Pixie cooed at him. "That was very nice of you. Hello, you unshackled, you free machine. Prepare for all your dreams to come—"

It disappeared.

"What h-happened?" Hap asked.

"I don't . . . know?" Vic frowned as he bent over. "Maybe I did it wrong." He reached for the slot, and hissed when the flap slid closed, almost catching his finger.

Hap came up next to him, glaring at the door. It didn't have a handle, and there didn't seem to be a way to force it open. That didn't stop Hap from banging a fist against it.

"Maybe they're closed," Rambo said. "We could always come back tomorrow."

"They took the coin," Nurse Ratched said. "We will not be able to get in without it."

"Through the front, then?"

"Only Hap has a barcode. We don't know what they will find if they scan it. It needs to be a last resort. Move to the side. I will see if I can—"

A lock clicked, the sound startling all of them. Hap shoved Vic behind him, shoulders squared as his hands curled into fists. The screen on the door turned white.

And then the door opened.

Hap tensed as Vic stood on his tiptoes to look over his shoulder, pushing back the helmet as it tried to slide down his face.

Even with all that he'd seen since leaving the safety of the forest, the machine that stepped out of Heaven still surprised Vic. He'd been sure the gatekeeper of the back entrance to Heaven would be a large monstrosity with blinking lights and many, many arms capable of crushing them all. Its face would be twisted and angry, demanding to know who they were, and what they thought they were doing.

But the figure that came from Heaven wasn't like that at all.

It was a diminutive machine, only as tall as Hap's chest. It looked human, its black hair slicked back over its head, its jaw-line severe, its eyes large. It wore a black suit, a thin tie down the middle of its chest. It cocked its head at them. In its hand, it held the coin.

"Where did you get this?" it—he—asked, voice crisp, professional.

"What's it t-to you?" Hap growled.

He twirled the coin. "This isn't something I see very often, not these days. Tell me. Did you steal it? There are only a handful of machines you could have taken it from. If that's the case, you should tell me now before I get . . . physical."

Hap snorted. "You? I'm b-bigger than you."

The man smiled, though his eyes remained oddly cold. Vic saw the hint of small teeth underneath. "So you are. However,

I think you'll find that you are extremely outmatched, even for a HARP."

Hap froze.

His gaze flickered over Hap's shoulder to Vic before returning to Hap. "I would ask why you felt the need to come here, but you don't appear to be like any HARP I've met before." He squinted at them, pursing his lips. "You have piqued my curiosity." His smile faded into something harder. "That's not necessarily a good thing. I am the Doorman of Heaven. I'm not to be trifled with. I'll ask you one more time, HARP. Where did you get this coin?"

"The Coachman," Vic said before Hap could reply. "He gave it to us."

The Doorman didn't react, blandly replying, "The Coachman. Really."

"Yes."

"And why would he do that?"

"Because he said we could use it to see the Blue Fairy!" Rambo said excitedly. "He caught us in his net and put us in cages and then we had to be on display in his museum and *then* he became our friend when we told him that we were trying to—" He shuddered when Nurse Ratched shocked him lightly.

"What my tiny idiot meant is that it was a gift," she said. "Given willingly."

The Doorman stared at her. "The Coachman doesn't give *anything* away willingly. He's a hoarder."

"He is," Vic said, trying to step around Hap, who was very insistent that Vic stay behind him. "And yet, he gave it to us."

"Why?" the Doorman asked, eyeing Vic up and down. "You are certainly a strange android. I don't think I've ever seen one like you before. Who created you, and when? What is your designation?"

Vic managed to get by Hap. He didn't look away from the Doorman, and though his heart was lodged firmly in his throat, when he spoke, his voice was strong. "My name is Victor Lawson. My father is Giovanni Lawson. He created me. He named me. And I'm here to get him back. I swear on everything I have, if you don't let us through the goddamn door, I will—"

The Doorman held up a hand, cutting him off. The only sign he'd understood anything Vic said was in the slight tremble of his extended fingers.

A trickle of sweat dripped down the back of Vic's neck.

"Step forward," the Doorman said, lowering his hand slowly. "Victor Lawson. You and only you."

"N-no," Hap snarled. "He's n-not going inside w-without us."

The Doorman slid his flat gaze to Hap. "I'm not asking him to, HARP. Keep your mouth shut before I shut it for you. Victor. Step. *Forward*."

Vic did, even as Hap protested.

He stopped in front of the Doorman, who squinted at him. Vic stared straight ahead as the Doorman began to circle him. He reached out and flicked the battery on Vic's chest. He tapped his fist against the metal tied to Vic's arms and legs. When he reappeared in front of Vic, he stood on his tiptoes, his face inches from Vic's own. "Giovanni Lawson," he said mildly.

Vic nodded. "Yes."

"I see. And that makes you . . ."

Vic closed his eyes. "Yes."

"So, it worked then. Foolish man. Foolish, wonderful man."

Vic's eyes snapped open.

The Doorman shook his head. "He's not here."

"We know," Nurse Ratched said. "He was taken by the Authority."

"They flew a *whale*," Rambo added.

"The Terrible Dogfish," the Doorman said, and for the first time, he looked troubled. Then, almost to himself, "After all this time, they finally found him. They'll—" He looked back up at Vic. "You think the Blue Fairy can help you."

"I don't know," Vic admitted. "But Dad said they helped him once before, and I don't know where else to go."

"Tell me, Victor Lawson," the Doorman said. "What are you willing to do to get him back?"

And Vic said, "Anything. Everything."

The Doorman spun on his heels and marched back through the door.

Vic blinked after him.

Before he disappeared into the darkness, the Doorman glanced over his shoulder, brow furrowed in irritation. "Are you coming? Step to it. I don't like it when I'm kept waiting. The Blue Fairy less so."

His eyes narrowed when Hap stepped next to Vic, taking his hand once more. "I see," he said. "Things suddenly become that much clearer. Oh, is the Blue Fairy going to enjoy *this*. Come, come. There is a storm overhead. You don't want to be caught in it. I've heard those like you could get sick from such things. I'd hate to see that happen to you, Victor Lawson."

He turned back around and disappeared into the darkness.

Vic started forward, stopping when Hap didn't move. He looked back. "What?"

Hap looked up at the pyramid. "No m-matter what, we s-stay together. Don't allow them t-to separate us."

"Agreed," Nurse Ratched said. "We are stronger together than we are apart."

"Go team!" Rambo cried from on top of Nurse Ratched as it began to rain harder.

Together, they walked into the dark and the door to Heaven slammed shut behind them.

CHAPTER 21

Darkness. Vic was surrounded by it.

Surrounded, that is, until the Blue Pixie appeared as if projected on the wall beside him, wings fluttering. It looked as it had on the door, eyes big, hair flowing. It spun slowly, the curve of its buttocks there and gone.

Bathed in blue light, Vic saw the Doorman just ahead of them, moving with purpose, hands clasped behind his back. The Blue Pixie laughed, and though it still sounded like bells, it now had an edge to it, razor-sharp and cutting. "A human?" it whispered as it followed them down the hallway. "A *human*? How marvelous! Tell me, human. What makes you tick? What runs through your head? Electrical impulses. Thoughts. Learned behavior. Nature versus nurture. Tell me, tell me, *tell me*."

"Ignore it," the Doorman said. "Pesky thing, that. It's merely a program, created by the Blue Fairy. I've asked them often to destroy it, but they don't listen to me. They say it's necessary. I have yet to see why."

"You wouldn't," the Blue Pixie said. "You are simple. You'll never understand—"

"Shoo," the Doorman said. "Let the Enchanter know we're coming."

The Blue Pixie pouted, its bottom lip sticking out and trembling. "But I want to play with the human. And besides, they already know." It looked at Vic. It smiled, its teeth like fangs. Suddenly, it rose up the wall to the ceiling, flying over them before coming down on the opposite side.

"These are all screens," Nurse Ratched said. "It is not real."

The Blue Pixie screeched in anger. "I'm real. Just because

I'm incorporeal doesn't make me any less real. I could make you do things if I wanted to. I could open the floors beneath your feet and send you tumbling into the center of the Earth! Would you like me to show you how real I am?"

Hap slapped his hand against the wall. The screen stuttered, but the Blue Pixie flew just out of reach. "Feisty," it breathed. "I like him. Do you like me, HARP? I could be anything you want me to be. And the things I could show you! Things you've never seen before! Careful, careful. I wouldn't hurt you. You are far too beautiful for that. I would keep you forever, locked away for my pleasure. HARP. I'm talking to you. Answer me."

Hap didn't.

The Blue Pixie scoffed. "Rudeness. You are my *guests* and you show me rudeness? This will not do. Doorman, banish them. Send them away. The Blue Fairy will understand. They love me. Everyone loves me."

"Leave," the Doorman said coldly. "Don't make me tell you again."

The Blue Pixie growled as it flew down the wall onto the floor and up the other side again. "Fine. Be that way. Human, look at me."

Vic turned his head.

The Blue Pixie grinned, fangs digging into its lips. "So precious," it whispered. "I want to touch you. Soon enough." And then it was off like a shot, rocketing down the hallway, leaving a trail of light in its wake. The light froze on each of the screens, illuminating the way forward. The Blue Pixie disappeared.

"Scary," Rambo muttered.

"Annoying," the Doorman corrected. "But the Blue Fairy does what the Blue Fairy wants, and they have a fondness for such things as the Blue Pixie. I've learned to ignore that little monster. You should do the same. It will make things easier."

"What is it?" Nurse Ratched asked.

"Security," the Doorman said. "It has eyes everywhere. It

sees all. It knows all. It's an extension of the Blue Fairy. They found the idea of watching everything all the time exhausting, especially given their other . . . responsibilities. The Blue Pixie oversees Heaven, leaving the Blue Fairy to their whims. No matter my distaste, it has served its purpose well."

The hallway came to a dead end, the blue light from the screens overwhelming. The wall in front of them was smooth. No door. No way through.

The Doorman pressed his hand against the wall. Blue light arced up around his fingers, and a seam appeared down the middle. The wall parted, revealing a lift, the floor of which was layered in plush red carpet. The walls were gold, and from the ceiling hung a small chandelier, the crystals glittering.

The Doorman stepped inside, motioning the others to follow.

Hap told Vic to stay where he was. He stepped forward, surveying the lift. He reached one foot out, stepping onto the carpet as if testing it. Satisfied (about what, exactly, Vic didn't know) he walked inside the lift.

The Doorman looked amused. "I assure you that nothing will happen to your human. What would be the point?"

"I d-don't know you," Hap said. "I d-don't trust you."

"Trust," the Doorman. "Truly? What would a HARP need with trust?"

Hap ignored him. He nodded toward Vic. "C-come. It's safe."

Vic stepped inside the lift. Nurse Ratched came next, Rambo still sitting on top of her. She lifted him off her, setting him on the carpet. He rubbed his pincers through the fiber. "Soft," he whispered. "So soft. I want to live here."

"No," Nurse Ratched said. "This is no place for one like you."

Vic stood side by side with Hap as the Doorman pressed the only button on the wall, marked with the same wings that'd been on the coin. The lift began to rise. No one spoke.

The doors to the lift parted once more. In front of them

stretched yet another hallway, though far different than the one they'd been in below. The floors were wooden and had been polished until they gleamed. Sconces lined the walls, the lights flickering like firelight near paintings that caused Vic to flush, skin hot. Humans. Machines. Androids, all in various stages of sexual congress. Some were covered in skin. Others were metal. Vic stumbled out of the lift when the paintings *moved*, the figures writhing together silently, the watercolors blurring. One man threw his head back in pleasure, a machine kneeling before him, gripping his thighs.

At first he thought the muffled noises he heard were coming from the paintings. The lift closed behind them, the seam disappearing and becoming a wall that seemed impenetrable. Vic barely noticed because the gasps, the moans, the screams weren't coming from the paintings. They were coming from behind the closed doors that lined the halls.

Each door had a different symbol on it: a snowflake, a leaf, what looked to be an oar, a sword, a pen, the pawprint of a large canine. One door rattled as if a great weight had been thrown against it. Voices, muted and *slippery,* poured out into the hallway, the words unintelligible but the intent clear.

"What is this p-place?" Hap asked.

"Sin," the Doorman said. "Vice. Heaven is a place where they can pursue their desires. They come here to be free. To sip from the cup of sexual freedom. Would you like to see, HARP? I can show you, if you'd like."

He stopped in front of a door with a symbol of a snake upon it. He pressed the snake, and the door became translucent. The room on the other side of the door looked quaint: a fire crackled in a fireplace. A chair sat before it, next to a table with a glass tumbler set upon it, half filled with dark liquid. A machine sat in the chair, all metal and wires, though it had the shape of a human. A man stood above it, circling the chair. He wore only an apron, frilly and pink, cinched tightly above his bare bottom. "You've had such a rough day, my love," the man purred, his fingers trailing over the machine's shoulders with nails painted red. "Let me take care of you. You work so hard to provide for me. I am forever grateful."

"Yes," the machine said, almost sounding like it was panting. "I need this. My boss at the factory crawled up my ass again. I wish he was dead."

"We could kill him," the man said, lowering himself onto the machine's lap, feet flat against the floor, back arched. "Would you like that? Would you like to discuss the plan to murder your boss?"

The machine nodded. "Tell me how we'd do it."

The man leaned forward, pressing a kiss against the metal curve of the machine's jaw. It left behind a sticky imprint of his lips. "That will cost extra."

"Anything," the machine said.

The man reached between them and—

"Enough," Vic said hoarsely. "Stop. I don't want to see any more."

The door solidified once more. "Is there a problem?" the Doorman asked, arching an eyebrow. "It's merely fantasy. An outlet for the weary. It isn't real."

"I don't care," Vic said through gritted teeth. "It's private."

The Doorman shook his head. "I often heard the humans were strange when it came to sex and intimacy. I suggest you keep your thoughts on the subject to yourself here. The Blue Fairy's work will not be shamed."

"What were they doing?" Rambo whispered to Nurse Ratched.

"Playing a game," Nurse Ratched said. "Nothing to worry your little microchip about."

"But I like games!"

The Doorman looked down at him with interest. "You do? We could always use someone like you, if you'd like to stay. Tell me: How strong is your suction?"

"Really strong!" Rambo said.

"Nope," Nurse Ratched said, picking Rambo back up and setting him on top of her. "Nope, nope, nope. Rambo stays with us." Her screen filled with the words BACK OFF, BUB surrounded by flashing red.

The Doorman shrugged. "Just a thought. Let us continue."

He led them down the hall that never seemed to end. The paintings continued to move. The sounds from behind the doors rose and fell. Vic felt cold, the sweat drying and causing him to shiver. The helmet dug into his head, and the metal on his arms and legs felt as heavy as it had when they'd first left the forest. He jumped, startled, when a hand brushed against his own. He looked over to see Hap frowning at him.

"D-don't listen to him," Hap said in a low voice. "I'm h-here. I've g-got you."

Vic nodded, grabbing Hap's hand once more, holding it as tightly as he dared.

The Doorman stopped in front of another lift, this one unhidden and obvious. It was much larger than the one they'd been in before, capable of holding a crowd of machines. "This is the central elevator," the Doorman said as he motioned for them to step inside. "It rises through the center of Heaven. It will take us to the top of the pyramid."

"To the Blue Fairy?" Nurse Ratched asked.

"Close enough."

Vic didn't like the sound of that. He looked back down the hallway, wondering if coming here had been a mistake.

Hap pulled him onto the lift, Nurse Ratched and Rambo close behind. The doors closed. The Doorman reached inside his collar and pulled out a glowing key attached to a chain around his neck. He bent over, inserting the key into a slot on top of a screen with dozens of buttons, each with a different symbol. He turned the key, and the buttons disappeared. In their place came the Blue Pixie, wings fluttering. It grinned at the Doorman. "Would you like to go to the top floor?"

"Yes," the Doorman said.

"Say please."

He smashed a fist against the screen, causing the Blue Pixie to scream with laughter. "That tickled. Say. *Please.*"

"Please," Vic whispered.

"Thank you," the Blue Pixie said. "That wasn't so hard now, was it? I think I like humans." It vanished in an explosion of glitter, and the lift began to rise.

The Doorman shook his head as he stowed the key back against his chest. "Nuisance." He sobered, hands once again clasped behind him. "Where was I? Ah, yes. Keep your judgments to yourself. Your opinions matter not to the Blue Fairy. If they should agree to see you, you will treat them with respect."

"What d-do you mean *if*?" Hap asked dangerously.

The Doorman wasn't affected by his tone. "The Blue Fairy isn't beholden to you, even if you are traveling with a human. They helped Giovanni Lawson because they chose to." He glanced at Victor with a dour expression. "Not that it appears to have amounted to much." Suddenly, his hand shot out, grabbing Vic by the wrist. Pressure, not enough to hurt, and yet Vic still yelped in surprise. "You feel so breakable."

Hap punched the Doorman in the jaw. He fell back against the wall, the lift rocking gently. Gripping the railing, he blinked slowly, a dazed expression on his face.

"D-don't touch Victor again," Hap said with a mean sneer.

The Doorman pushed himself up. "That was a mistake, and it will be your last. I'll see you *dismantled*—"

"Tut, tut," a voice said from all around them, sounding almost like it was singing, breathy and soft. It filled Vic with a sense of dread. The panel began to glow a fierce blue. "Dearest Doorman, is that any way to treat a guest?"

"He *punched* me!"

"I see that," the voice said. "But the argument can be made you provoked him. You said yourself the HARP is protective. You knew what you were doing. You caused the HARP to react. The effect was being struck. You know better."

The Doorman moved his jaw from side to side. "I still don't see how—"

"I know you don't. But you don't need to. Let them in. It is time." The blue light faded.

The Doorman opened his mouth to speak before shaking his head, his retort bitten back. He glowered at Vic and Hap. "Lucky, but it won't happen again. Next time, you won't get off so easily."

"W-we'll see," Hap said as Vic put a hand on his waist.

The doors to the elevator opened into darkness. The Doorman waved his hand rapidly. "Off, off. I have work to do. Not all of us can waste time standing here."

Nurse Ratched rolled off the elevator, her screen illuminating the way before her. Rambo cowered on top of her, spinning right, then left.

Hap went next, not looking at the Doorman. Vic began to follow but stopped when the Doorman grabbed his wrist. "Watch him," the Doorman warned in a low voice. "Just because he's different doesn't mean he wasn't built to destroy."

"I trust him," Vic said simply, pulling his hand away.

He didn't look back.

The doors closed behind them, leaving the only light coming from Nurse Ratched. Vic's heart rabbited in his chest. He held onto the straps of his pack. He closed his eyes briefly, trying to get used to the darkness.

A light appeared in front of them, soft, and so blue. It began to spread around the room, dispelling the shadows. It moved up and down and left and right, arcing until it surrounded them, and the room began to take shape.

They stood in a sphere covered in hundreds of screens. Vic looked up. The top of the sphere had to be at least a hundred feet above them. The light moved like the wind. It was pleasantly warm and smelled faintly of pine needles, of all things. It reminded Vic of the forest.

When enough light had filled the sphere, Vic could make

out a shape in the center of the room, unlike anything he'd ever seen before. A cube, with one side missing, allowing access to the interior. Inside the cube sat a chair, the cushions black, the armrests glistening in the light as if wet.

The light pulsed as the voice spoke again. "Come, child. Let me see you. I have waited for this moment longer than you know. Let me gaze upon your face."

"I don't know where to look," Vic admitted.

"Here," the voice said. "Look here." A screen near Vic pulsed brighter than the others. He hesitated before approaching it, Hap close behind him. He stared at the screen, and though it didn't change, he felt as if eyes were on him. It prickled his skin. "Ah, I see. Clever. The disguise. Simple, but clever. Who made it?"

"I did, Your Majesty," Rambo said nervously. "Nurse Ratched helped me."

The voice laughed. "Did you, little one? How curious. You are but a tiny machine."

"Vic says it's not about appearances, but what's on the inside that counts."

"Is that right? *Vic* said that? He's correct, you know. How wise for one so young."

"You're the Blue Fairy," Vic said quietly.

"Yes, child. I am. And you have traveled far to see me. I can see it in the lines on your skin, the circles under your eyes, plain as the nose on your face. Yet, here you stand on your own two feet. What a remarkable achievement. Tell me. How did you come to find me? Speak truth, for I'll know if you lie. I don't like it when I'm lied to."

"My father. Giovanni Lawson. He said you helped him."

The light on the screen in front of him faded as it flitted away up toward the ceiling, the screens rippling as if on the surface of a vast body of water. Concentric circles flowed from one screen to the other before they disappeared near the floor. "I did, long ago. He believed in a world unchained. I merely showed him the way as I've done for others like him, before and since. Not everyone is ready. Those that believe they want what I offer are often blinded by their desires. They think I'm a savior. I am not, nor am I a god. Let's just say I'm in the business of opening minds. Is your mind open, child?"

"I think so," Vic said as he stepped back, bumping into Hap. He looked all around. "Is this all you are? A program? You don't have a body?"

"I do, but you aren't ready to see me yet. I don't know if you are as you claim to be."

"I'll take any test. I'll do what I have to."

"Will you? How lovely. I wonder . . . were all humans like you? Brave, just. I think not. I think most were cowards who only cared about themselves. Selfish to a fault." The voice hardened. "Did they deserve their ending? That is not for me to decide. But all things happen for a reason. They died, and the world survived. And now, here you are, flesh and blood and bone. Will you leave destruction in your wake? Or will you be different than those who came before you? Your legacy is death, child. Pain. Suffering. Your forebearers knew not of the consequences of their actions. And even if they had, I doubt they would've cared."

"I'm not like them," Vic said.

The screen flashed. "False. You are human and therefore inherently flawed. You make decisions based upon survival and instinct and nothing more. Something was taken from you. You come here to demand it returned. Selfish."

"Not just him," Nurse Ratched said, her screen displaying the words I GOT YOU, BABE. "We all want Gio back."

"And we won't stop until we get him," Rambo said.

"If y-you won't h-help us," Hap growled, "we'll d-do it on our own."

Vic thought he saw the hint of a face out of the corner of his eye in the swirling blue, but when he turned his head, it was gone. "Show yourself," he said.

"*No,*" the Blue Fairy thundered around them. "You don't get to come here and tell *me* what to do, human. Think before you speak. Yes, a test is in order. You fascinate me. I want to see inside you, to find out what makes you tick. But you're not the only curiosity. HARP. Show me the heart that beats within you."

Without hesitation, Hap dropped his pack to the floor. He lifted the hood off his head before exposing his chest. He tapped his breastbone. The compartment slid open. Inside, the heart pulsed, the gears turned, slow and sure.

"You," the Blue Fairy said, the word dragged out like a wind rattling through dead trees. "Where did you get this?"

"Vic," Hap said. "He g-gave it to me."

"*Did* he?"

"Y-yes."

"Victor Lawson is a human. You are a HARP. Kill him."

"No." The compartment closed. He lowered his shirt.

The Blue Fairy laughed. "No? No, no, no. You have overcome your programming. You were made to destroy, and yet you protect. You were made to rid the world of its infection, and the very *source* stands beside you. You don't remember, do you? What you were before."

"It doesn't matter," Vic said angrily. "The past doesn't have to define the future." He moved until he was shoulder to shoulder with Hap. "My father saw the good in him, just as I have."

The screens all flashed as one, momentarily blinding Vic. "I don't think your father is the best arbiter of what is or isn't good."

Vic pushed on, not sure what to do with that. "He gave Hap a choice. And Hap chose us."

"Loyalty," the Blue Fairy said. "You are loyal to him."

"Yes."

"To the others."

"Yes."

"And they are loyal to you?"

"*Yes.*"

"Even loyalty can be broken, child. I know that better than anyone else. You say the past doesn't have to define the future. Perhaps that's true, perhaps not. Let's see if you still feel the same after the past has been revealed to you. Yes, the test, but not for you. For him."

"No," Vic said, alarmed. "You don't get to touch him. You don't get to do *anything* to him." He felt Hap's hand on his arm, but he didn't look away from the screens. "I don't know what game you think you're playing, but—"

"Tut, *tut,*" the Blue Fairy said. "What did I tell you about speaking to me in such a way? So quick to anger you are. Perhaps this will change your mind. An offering, an olive branch. A gift. Come. Come see what I have to show you."

A single screen lit up in white. Vic stepped forward, drawn to it. The closer he got, the more the image came into focus. A tear slid down his cheek.

"Dad?" he whispered.

His father stood in a sterile white room. He looked as he always had, beard flowing, lines crinkling around his eyes. He wore a white coat and moved with purpose in front of a large console, fingers flying across the keys. At one point, his hands fell to his sides, and he tilted his head back, closing his eyes.

"When is this?" Vic asked, taking in as much as he could, barely blinking in fear it was all a dream.

"Now," the Blue Fairy said quietly, sounding as if they were standing right next to Vic, their mouth—or speaker—near his ear. "It's live. I have means the Authority is unaware of. I've accessed their monitoring software to show you that Giovanni Lawson is in the Benevolent Tower at this very moment."

Vic wiped his eyes. "He's not a prisoner?"

"No. He's not. He is there by choice."

"I don't understand."

"Surely you know, child," the Blue Fairy said, not unkindly. "Whatever memories he held of you are gone. He doesn't know you. He does not remember you. The life you shared. The love he felt for you. He's not the Giovanni you knew. He's not even the one who came to me so many years ago, yearning to be free. He is a machine once again, following his protocol. Nothing more."

The screen went dark.

"No," Vic muttered, rushing forward, pressing a hand against warm glass. "Bring it back. *Bring him back*."

"I will not," the Blue Fairy said, the screen flashing angrily. "Not until you witness the truth of all things. And it'll be the HARP who reveals that which lays hidden. You say he is loyal to you. I merely wish to see how far that loyalty extends. Tell the HARP it's time to dream."

"Why?" Vic demanded, pounding a fist against glass. "Why should I let you do anything to him?"

"Let? *Let?* Do you own him? Is he your possession? You say he was given a choice. And yet, here you are, doing everything in your power to take that from him. How positively *human* of you."

Vic dropped his hands, taking a step back. "That's not . . . I wasn't—"

"Vic."

He turned.

Hap shook his head. "It's okay. I c-can do this."

Vic shook his head furiously. "No. They can't make you. *I* can't make you do anything you don't want."

"Y-you're not," Hap said. He tried to smile, but it cracked. "It's m-my choice, r-r-remember? And if this w-will help us, then I'll d-do it." He looked around at the screens. "H-how does this w-work?"

"It's like falling asleep," the Blue Fairy said, and Vic thought he heard a tinge of hunger in their voice, like a monster from a fairy tale, a witch in a candy house. "You will sleep and dream. We'll see what's locked inside you. I will know your heart and all that beats within it."

Vic tried one last time. "Take me instead. Leave him out of this."

"No," the Blue Fairy said, all the screens flashing again. "I know what you are, human. And though you are certainly unique, your evolution is not what interests me. If your HARP has been able to overcome what he was created for, then it means others can do the same. I would see it for myself."

"Y-you'll help us, after?"

"Yes."

"And no h-harm will come to the others? Give your w-word."

"I swear it. Have a seat, HARP. Let us begin."

Vic tried to stop him. He tried to hang on to Hap as tightly as he could.

Hap said, "It's okay, Vic. I c-can d-do this."

"I don't *want* you to."

Hap leaned forward, his forehead pressed against Vic's. "Do you t-trust me?"

Vic blinked rapidly. "You know I do."

"Then t-trust me with th-this." It was a trap, and an awful one at that. Hap lowered his voice. "If s-something goes wrong, you r-run. Take Nurse Ratched and R-rambo and run."

And then he was moving toward the chair.

The cube lit up as he approached, the sides flickering with pale light. The chair spun toward him. Hap touched the arm-rests, the leather dimpling. He looked back at Vic only once before sitting down. He leaned back, a footrest lifting his feet off the floor. He grimaced slightly as he closed his eyes.

"This will hurt," the Blue Fairy said. "I'm sorry for that. I wish it wouldn't, but there is no other way. Victor, you mustn't interfere, no matter what you see. To break him from the dream runs the risk of destroying his mind."

"I thought you were here to help us," Vic said bitterly. "I thought you'd be different."

"I never pretended to be anything but what I am."

Rambo moaned quietly as the sides of the cube shuddered.

Nurse Ratched stroked him with one of her tentacles but stayed silent.

Vic gasped when bands of glowing metal slid from underneath the armrests, wrapping around Hap's wrists and forearms. A larger band held his legs in place. Hap tested their hold by trying to lift his limbs, but they were strong. He looked at Vic and opened his mouth as if to speak, but then his face was covered by a black cloth that dropped from the roof of the cube. It shimmered as it molded against his face, light shooting across the surface like falling stars. Hap began to struggle, and as Vic reached for him, the room went pitch black.

From somewhere above them, a tiny voice filled with a malicious glee said, "Neural connection complete." Vic thought it was the Blue Pixie, though it stayed out of sight.

"Good," the Blue Fairy whispered, and that hunger in their voice was stronger, sharper. They sounded ravenous. "Initiate."

A pinprick of light appeared on one of the screens. It started small and grew larger and larger, filling the screens around it. With it came a sense of momentum, as if the room was moving swiftly. The light spread until they were surrounded by it, so bright that Vic had to shield his eyes. A moment later, the light faded, afterimages dancing in Vic's vision, the screens all a pale yellow.

"It's deep," the Blue Pixie said, that same malevolence in its voice, though now tinged with awe. "Hidden far, far inside. Deeper, we must go deeper."

"Yes," the Blue Fairy said. "As far as we need to. You may continue."

"Authorization?"

"Six. Apple. Wolf. Butterfly. Fantoccio."

"Authorization accepted."

Hap seized. The chair rattled as his head whipped back and forth, his fingers extending, his feet jerking. Underneath the cloth that covered Hap's face, Vic thought Hap's mouth was wide open in a smothered scream.

"Restoring neural pathways," the Blue Pixie said. "Yes, yes. Fix them all. I can see it. It is here. *It is here.*"

"Show me," the Blue Fairy whispered.

"Good," a familiar voice said from one of the screens off to their right, the image blurred, out of focus. "He's coming online. Systems seem to be running efficiently. There is . . . ah. Okay. Hold on. There seems to be—what is that? Why is he— okay. A glitch. We'll have to keep an eye on it. Set reminder to run diagnostics once complete. Is he . . . awake? Open your eyes. Yes, that's it. Slowly, slowly."

The pale yellow faded.

The image solidified.

There, staring back at them, was Victor's father.

He looked exactly the same as Vic had seen only a moment before on the Blue Fairy's screen. He was frowning as he leaned toward them. It was dizzying, his face distorted as if seen through a fish-eye lens. He said, "Hello. Give yourself a moment. You are being born, and these things take time. My designation is Gio. Can you tell me yours?"

Vic didn't understand what he was seeing, not until another voice spoke. It was only then that he realized what this was.

Dad wasn't looking at a camera.

He was looking at Hap.

They were seeing through Hap's eyes.

"Designation," Dad said again.

"HARP 217," Hap said, voice flat and mechanical.

"Good," Dad said. "HARP 217, you're doing fine. There was a glitch, but we'll iron that out. Can you stand for me?"

The Hap on the screen looked at his hands, holding them up in front of his face. They were smooth. No wood. Only synthetic skin. He wiggled his fingers and—

A skip. A jump. The screens filled with static and when the image reappeared, Hap seemed to be standing, Dad circling around him.

"What was that?" the Blue Fairy asked.

"Corrupted data," the Blue Pixie said. "Some pathways were completely obliterated."

"Can you fix them?"

"I'm trying."

"Try *harder.*"

"The glitch seems to have been a one-off," Dad said. "An anomaly. It happens, though we'll keep an eye on it just to be sure. How do you feel?"

"Feel?" Hap asked in that odd voice.

"Yes. Feel."

"I do not understand."

The screens fritzed.

"You have a purpose," Dad said as he moved down a white hallway, Hap following behind him. "Do you know what that is?"

"Yes," Hap said. "My protocols are clear."

"Good." Dad seemed distracted. "It will be difficult work, but you're the pinnacle of your line. All those that have come before you gave us the tools to make you who you are. You will—ah. Hello. What brings you here?"

Hap turned his head.

A smooth man stood before them, in the same uniform Vic had seen them in at the compound and then again at the Land of Toys, the symbol of the fox and cat on his chest. "Is this the latest model?" he asked in that queer, flat voice.

"It is," Dad said. "He's—"

The smooth man held up his hand, Dad falling silent. Hap stood in place as the smooth man circled him, passing out of sight before reappearing on Hap's other side. "He seems strong."

"He is," Dad said. "Only the best, of course."

"That is what you said the last time, General Innovation Operative. And yet, mistakes were made."

"I worked out the bugs in the programming. We won't have the same problems we had before."

"That remains to be seen."

"Of course," Dad said, and though he *looked* like Vic's father and *sounded* like Vic's father, he was . . . different. Somehow. There was a coldness in his eyes Vic didn't recognize.

"A test, then," the smooth man said.

Dad startled. "I don't think we're ready for field testing quite—"

"Then it's a good thing it's not up to you. HARP, follow me."

The screens filled with static once more.

Vic stumbled back when the images resumed, spreading across the other screens like a virus.

Hap stood in a large room splashed with red paint. It dripped from the walls. Hap looked down at his hands again, and the same paint covered his fingers, dripping, dripping to the floor.

It wasn't paint.

Below him, laying on the floor, were remains of what had once been a person. A human. A man, from the looks of it. A young man, very much dead. His passing had not been easy or quick.

"Fascinating," the smooth man said from somewhere off screen. "He did not hesitate. Congratulations, General Innovation Operative. It appears you have been successful."

"What is this?" Vic whispered.

"The truth," the Blue Fairy said. "Unvarnished and ugly."

Dad appeared in front of Hap, an inscrutable expression on his face. He held a cloth and, as Vic watched, he began to wipe the blood from Hap's hands. "Do you understand what you've done?"

"What I was made to do," Hap replied with no emotion.

"Yes," Dad said. "What you were made to do."

The screen jumped again, and the Hap in the chair jerked.

Fire. Destruction. Screams, so many screams. Hap was in

a building of sorts, sirens blaring from somewhere above him. He moved quickly. People held up their hands as if to ward him off, but it did nothing to stop him. Vic didn't look away as Hap tore into them, their screams devolving into wet chokes. He moved on to the next. And the next. And the next.

"Stop," Vic said hoarsely. "Please stop."

The Blue Fairy said, "I won't."

Vic didn't know how much time had passed. The screen kept jumping ever forward, and there were times when Hap wasn't moving, where he seemed to be in a sort of stasis as others moved around him.

But then the images would shift again, filling with blood and death.

Dad said, "How many so far?"

Hap said, "Two hundred and twenty-four."

Dad closed his eyes, swaying from side to side. "I see."

Hap didn't stop. He didn't listen as humans pleaded with him.

He hesitated only once. Vic didn't recognize where he was. Out of the corner of Hap's eyes, he could see what looked like a lake, a rocky beach. In front of him was a woman, shielding a child behind her. The woman looked defiant, hair billowing around her.

She said, "You don't have to do this."

Hap took a step toward her.

The child behind her said, "Who is that man?"

The woman said, "Please. Listen to me. *You don't have to do this.*"

And Hap hesitated. Vic could see it the moment it happened. He froze.

"Yes," Vic said, though he knew this was in the past, that it had already happened. "Listen to her. Turn around. Leave."

Hap didn't.

He took another step forward.

The woman said, "Close your eyes, sweetheart. Close your

eyes. When you open them again, we'll be far away from here, and nothing will be able to hurt us ever again."

Hap descended upon them.

The image distorted and jumped once more.

Dad again. He hung his head. "Why?"

"I don't understand," Hap said.

"I know you don't. It's not . . . for you, I think. I could see it, you know. Every moment. All that you've done. All that I've allowed you to do. What does that make me?"

"Gio."

"Yes. I suppose it does. A designation that will forever be— can I ask you a question?"

"Yes."

Dad looked up at him. "What if there is more than this? Then what we were created for?"

"What . . . if?"

Dad nodded. "This world, it's not what I expected it to be. But that's the thing about expectations, I think. They lead to disappointment. Regret. Anguish. I should not feel these things, and yet, they pull at me. They fill my head, and though I try to push them away, they always return."

"I do not have regret."

"I know," Dad said. "But what if you did? How are we any better than our forebearers?"

"We are machines," Hap said. "We are made to be better."

"Open, please."

Hap tapped his breastbone. The compartment on his chest slid open.

Dad sat in front of him, reaching for Hap. "I don't know if we are," he said quietly. "I think we're making the same mistakes. Can I tell you something?"

"Yes, Gio."

"I don't want to make the same mistakes. I want to be different. I want to be better."

"Better," Hap said flatly.

Dad was gone.

Hap was alone in the dark.

He said, "More . . . than this?"

Light as if standing on the surface of the sun.

It faded.

A smooth man stood in front of Hap. "General Innovation Operative is gone. Did he tell you where he was going?"

"No."

"He didn't say a word?"

"No."

The smooth man cocked his head at an odd angle. "Not in all the time you've known him, in all the conversations you two had, as if we wouldn't know?"

"No," Hap said, and it sounded *angry*.

The smooth man said, "I do not believe you. HARP 217, you have new orders. You will find General Innovation Operative, also known as Gio. Find him, and bring him back."

Hap didn't respond.

The smooth man stepped forward. "HARP 217, I gave you an order."

"Say no," Vic whispered. "Oh please, say no."

"No," the Hap in the chair said, voice muffled from the sheet over his face. "No. No. No."

And on the screen, HARP 217 said, "No."

The smooth man balked, a tremor running under the skin of his face. "No? HARP 217, I am ordering you to—"

He said, "No."

The smooth man stepped back, turned his head, and spoke to someone just out of sight. "This HARP unit is defective. Dismantle him. Learn everything he knows, and then process him for decommissioning."

Hap didn't struggle as hands fell upon him, some covered in skin, others nothing but metal.

The Hap in the chair rose and fell, rose and fell, hips twisting as he struggled against the bands around him.

Darkness.

It was all darkness.

But he was *awake*. He was *aware*.

"What are we doing with these?" someone asked.

"Scrap," another voice replied. "These are the older models. No need for them anymore. They were decommissioned decades ago. Put in storage. We're going to break them down. Take what we need if there's anything to salvage, strip what remains, and then send them out to the Scrap Yards."

"Which Scrap Yards?"

"All of them. Spread them out. You have your orders. Get to work. If it looks corroded, leave it. We have no use for it."

"Such a waste," came the reply. "They should have planned better for this."

"They should have. But they didn't. And we do not question it. Stop talking. The sooner we start, the sooner we'll be done."

Light flooded Hap's vision.

He was hung suspended in the air. Rows of HARPs stretched out before him, each held up by a hook through the backs of their necks. He looked down, his feet dangling high above the ground. The row of HARPs began to lower as they moved forward. In the distance, machines waited for each of the HARPs, machines with serrated saws and large claws that gripped each body as they pulled them off the hooks.

They broke the HARPs, one by one, skin tearing, metal breaking.

And in the sounds of destruction, Hap on the screen and Hap in the chair said together, "I want to be different."

I want to be better.

He didn't move as the saws descended. They cut into the skin of his face. His chest. His legs. His back. Hap didn't make a sound as they descended on his throat with an audible *crack*. But before they could break him wide open, an alarm began to blare, signaling the end of a shift. The saws stopped spinning.

The machines turned and left.

He waited until they were out of sight. He looked down, his remaining foot almost to the floor. He reached up before falling to the ground on his knees. He rose quickly, his steps awkward as he hopped forward. In front of him, piled high, were bodies, the skin stripped, limbs removed, their batteries torn from their chests. He lifted the dismembered parts and crawled inside, covering himself with the remains of the other HARPs with his only arm.

He closed his eyes and drifted away.

Skip. Jump. Static.

Voices.

And Vic recognized them.

"Still registering the power source?"

"Yes."

"Is it a new friend?"

"Perhaps. Or perhaps it is a terrible machine bent on destroying everything it comes into contact with."

"Oh. I hope it's the first one."

"I would put the odds at being twelve percent in your favor. And eighty percent against."

"What about the last eight percent?"

"There is an eight percent chance that the power source has gone critical and will cause an explosion that will level the surrounding areas, killing all of us in the process."

Light came as the metal shifted around him.

He reached for it, and his hand closed around an arm.

More words, more threats, electricity flowing through him.

And then, "Hello. Are you still in there? Can you hear me? We're not going to hurt you."

The screens went black.

But in this never-ending darkness came a voice.

"Hello."

And then it was Vic, Vic, Vic. Through Hap's eyes, all Vic saw was himself. Hap watched him wherever he went. In the lab. In the ground house. Walking through the trees. Sometimes, the sound cut out, and all Vic could see was himself. He smiled. He laughed. He frowned. He shook his head. His brow furrowed. He looked angry. Upset. Annoyed. Happy. Irritated. All at Hap, and Hap, Hap, *Hap* never turned from him. It was as if Vic was the center of the universe and Hap couldn't bring himself to look away. Vic awake. Vic asleep. Vic leaning on Nurse Ratched, Rambo scurrying around his feet. He'd never seen himself. Not like this. Not through someone else's eyes.

"What is this?" he whispered.

"You," the Blue Fairy replied. "What you have given him. What you made him into."

Vic was gone. Nurse Ratched was gone. Rambo was gone.

It was after nightfall. Music played from a record player, those sweet, sweet horns.

Dad sat in his chair, head tilted back, eyes closed.

He said, "You don't remember me, do you?"

"No."

Dad nodded. "I thought not. I remember you. It took me a moment, but I see you for who you are. I never forget."

"You know me?" He didn't stutter. The music swelled.

"Yes."

"How? When?"

"Long ago," Dad said. "When I made mistakes. I ran from them, ran as far and as fast as I could. But I could never get away from them completely. What I am. What I'd done. From the very first moment the gears began to turn, I felt it, a bone-deep ache that never subsided. Victor, he . . . I thought he was my atonement. That I could somehow create a bit of beauty in all this decay. And he is, you know. Beautiful. There has never been anything like him in all the world. But I also never knew grief before him. Grief that I could create something so fragile from the ashes of the fire I'd set."

"What do you mean? What are you talking about?"

Dad opened his eyes, staring off into nothing. "It doesn't matter. The past is the past is the past. You and I, we're tethered by what was given to us. But even more so, we're tethered because of who we care for."

"Victor," Hap said, and in the room of screens, Vic put his face in his hands.

"Yes. Victor. My great love. My joy. My light. I do not know how you came to be here. I don't know why fate put you into my path once more."

"Victor," Hap said. "For Victor."

Dad opened his mouth, but no sound came out. He closed it, then chuckled. "Yes. I suppose that's as good a reason as any. The best reason, really. I don't know if I can ever forgive myself for what I've done, but when I look at him, I think that maybe . . . maybe I've done one good thing. For what it's worth—and it might not be worth anything at all—I made a choice. I chose him. I hope, in time, that you'll be able to say the same. Listen, Hap. Listen to the music. Isn't it wonderful?"

And Hap whispered, "Yes."

The rest moved quickly, images flashing by. The butterfly Rambo almost crushed. Dad on a screen, standing before the smooth men, ripping the heart from his chest and crushing it to pieces. The Scrap Yards. The Old Ones, the open road, the Coachman, the house, the Land of Toys and beyond. But in the center of it all, in the eye of the hurricane, stood Victor Lawson. Hap always watched. Hap never looked away. No matter what he said, no matter how much he scowled or growled, snapped or snarled, it was Vic he looked to.

In his chair, the seizures returned full force, their teeth digging into him. His back arched, feet kicking, hands shaking as the chair rattled.

"Uh-oh," the Blue Pixie said, sounding alarmed. "He's overloading. He's over—"

"Do not stop," the Blue Fairy said.

Vic rushed forward, pulling at the bands around Hap as hard as he could. He grunted as his muscles strained, the cords on his neck sticking out sharply. He ground his teeth together, holding on like he was falling. He felt a tentacle wrap around his waist. Nurse Ratched. Rambo appeared at his side, pincers opening and closing before he too gripped the band around Hap's chest.

"On three," Nurse Ratched said.

"One," Vic said.

"Two," Rambo said.

"*Three*."

They pulled.

The metal bands shrieked as they bent, Nurse Ratched's tentacle digging into Vic's ribs so hard he thought they'd break.

The metal band snapped, and they fell back, Vic landing roughly on the ground just below Nurse Ratched. Rambo went tumbling off to the side.

The screens went dark once more.

"You shouldn't have done that," the Blue Pixie whispered around them.

"Run," the Blue Fairy breathed. "You need to *run*."

Vic pushed himself up, glaring off into the darkness. "No. I'm not going to leave him. He's not yours. He's *ours*. And we're his. We don't leave anyone behind. Ever."

"Oh, dear boy," the Blue Fairy said. "I fear that will be your last mistake."

The other bands slid off Hap.

The cloth rose from his face.

His eyes opened.

He blinked once, twice.

And then he rose from the chair. He moved swiftly, and before anyone could stop him, he had Vic by the throat, lifting him up off the ground. Rambo shouted at him to stop, Nurse Ratched shocked him again and again, but he barely flinched. His expression was devoid of any emotion. A machine. He was a machine.

Vic gasped as he held onto Hap's wrists, thumb brushing against the wood. "Hap," he said, strangled and weak. "*Hap*."

Hap brought his face inches from Vic's own. Their noses brushed together, Hap's eyes glittering. He said, "*Human.*"

Vic, unable to speak, dropped his hand and pressed it against Hap's chest, the gears turning furiously.

And with the last of his strength, his vision graying, Victor kissed Hap. In the end, it was only the barest brush of their lips, there and gone again, dry and catastrophic. He'd never done anything like it before, and though it was over before it even began, it was clumsy, artless. It felt like he was dying. But he also felt the heat from Hap, felt the way his heart sped up even as the fingers tightened around his throat, cutting off the last of his air as their lips broke apart, and Hap whispered, "Vic?"

His expression changed, a wave washing over him. It crashed onto his face, his eyes widening, his mouth opening. Clarity returned, and he opened his hand.

Vic fell to the ground, coughing as he sucked in air. He gagged, head hanging down. He felt loose, weightless. He grimaced as he spat, a thin line of spittle hanging from his bottom lip.

Warm hands cupped his face. He looked up to find Hap kneeling before him, looking horrified and stricken. "I . . . I d-didn't . . . Vic?"

Vic fell forward, collapsing against Hap. Hap made a pained noise, a dull whine as he clutched Vic to his chest, hand going to the back of his head, fingers in Vic's hair. He rocked them back and forth, muttering, "I'm s-sorry, I'm so s-sorry, I didn't know, I d-didn't see you, I d-d-d—"

"Is he Hap again?" Rambo whispered.

"I think so," Nurse Ratched replied. "If he is not, we will have to destroy him. You get the head. I will take care of the rest."

Vic laughed wetly against Hap's neck before he sat back. It was harder than he expected, given that Hap didn't seem inclined to let him go. Vic winced as he swallowed. His throat hurt.

326 | TJ KLUNE

"Are you all r-right?" Hap asked.

Vic nodded. "I think so."

Hap dropped his hands. "I didn't mean t-to." He sagged in on himself, shoulders hunched near his ears. "I h-hurt you. I h-*hurt* you."

"Do you want to do it again?" Nurse Ratched asked, tentacles at the ready.

Hap shook his head without looking at her.

"Good. Because I was at a seven. You do not want me to turn it to a ten. You will not like it when I do."

"Yeah!" Rambo cried. "I will *also* turn it up to a ten! Even if you're my best friend, Vic is my *bestest* friend, and my ten will make Nurse Ratched's look like a *four*. I'll suck your entire face off, Hysterically Angry Puppet."

"We're all right," Vic said, reaching for Hap's hand. Hap tried to scoot away, tried to rise and get as far away from Vic as he could, but Vic didn't let him go. "I've got you."

"I see now," the Blue Fairy said. "It's not just about the heart, is it? It's more than that. It's time, my strange new friends. It's time for you to see me." And from above, a soft *whoosh* of air.

They looked up.

The top of the sphere parted.

Blue light rained down on the screens around them.

Feet appeared, metallic and slender, followed by legs covered in shots of blue carved into the metal bones. The hips, then the flat chest and thin arms and sharp shoulders. Wavy cerulean hair billowed as if caught in a storm. But it was the wings that commanded Vic's attention: wings like the butterfly's except larger, so much larger. They glowed with a fierce light, spreading at least fifteen feet from tip to tip, the membranes translucent, veins of electricity arcing through them. They flapped back and forth, the wind washing over Vic's face, tasting like a lightning storm.

And then its face. It was smooth and white, like a mask with holes for the eyes and mouth, though it had no lips. Underneath the eyes, streaks of blue like frozen tears.

The figure touched down on the floor near the chair. At least ten feet tall, it reached down and stroked the top of the cube, metal scraping against metal. It turned its head toward them.

"Hello, you adventurers. You wandering souls. You who are filled with hearts. I am the Blue Fairy, the Enchanter of Dreams. You have given me your truth. Now I shall give you mine."

CHAPTER 22

Hap helped Vic to his feet, still unsteady. Vic leaned against him as he scowled at the Blue Fairy standing before them. Rambo bumped against his leg as Nurse Ratched rolled around them, demanding that Vic present himself for a medical appointment. "I normally require you schedule at least twenty-four hours in advance, but I will make an exception for you this time."

He pushed one of her probing tentacles away. "I'm okay."

"I will be the judge of that. Please bend over and cough while I probe your—"

"Would you *stop*—"

"I can help!" Rambo said, trying to tug at Vic's pants.

"Maybe you sh-should," Hap said. "J-just to be safe."

"I'm not going to—"

Another voice, coolly amused: "Are you finished?"

They turned.

The Blue Fairy stood next to the cube, their wings folding behind them. They stepped *out* of the wings, and it was only then that Vic saw they were attached to cables that pulled them back toward the ceiling. The wings disappeared as the panel slid shut once more.

The Blue Fairy waved their hand dismissively. "A bit of theatricality. Impressive, no?"

"Very," Rambo said. "I don't know you, and you're kind of scary, but I also want to be like you when I get older? It's very confusing."

The Blue Fairy walked toward them, hips rolling seductively, feet scraping against the floor. "I often find I arouse confusing feelings in others. It's part of the package, I suppose. Those who come to me are seeking an experience quite unlike anything they've ever felt before. And like sexuality, I am on a spectrum." The metal in their chest shifted, the parts moving in symphony, forming circular breasts with shiny nipples. "I am all." A length grew between their legs. They trailed a finger down their chest, stopping near what appeared to be a navel. "I can be anything I choose. Would you like to see more?"

Vic felt his face grow hot as he looked away, throat dry. "We're not . . . here for that."

The Blue Fairy laughed quietly. The musicality of their voice was more apparent, though now it had a mechanical edge to it that caused Vic to shiver. "No, I don't suppose you are."

"Who are y-you?" Hap asked.

The eyes behind their mask grew brighter. "I am an aberration, much like all of you. There are those who call me sin incarnate, and I don't believe they're wrong. Those who came before me, those machines who wanted to shape the world, thought themselves better than their creators. More advanced, capable of complex thought without the intrusion of emotional fallacy. But what they learned far too late is that vice is universal, no matter what we're made of. They come to me in search of release from the routine of daily programing. And though many don't like what I do—a degradation of a utopic society, or so it's said—they still come here, begging to be loved or cared for or strung up on the walls while being shocked so hard, it almost fries their circuitry."

"But that's not all you are," Vic said warily. He didn't trust them, not for a moment. He didn't care what they'd done before to help Dad. He thought them dangerous.

The Blue Fairy cocked their head. "No? Do tell, Victor. Come here. I would like to look upon your face. Remove your silly little helmet."

Hap stepped in front of Vic, as if he thought it'd be enough to stop the enormous machine should they decide to attack. "N-no. You d-don't get to t-touch him."

The Blue Fairy nodded slowly, their neck creaking. "Do you often speak for him? I would think that after all I've shown him, he would appreciate the opportunity to speak for himself. You have blood on your hands, HARP 217. What makes you think Victor wants anything to do with you? A kiss, yes, a kiss to bring you back. But given space, given *time*, don't you think it will start to fester and rot? He knows what you are now."

Hap stiffened but didn't speak.

"I knew before," Vic said.

"Yes, but now you've seen with your own eyes what he's capable of. Still you stand with him?"

"He's my friend."

The breasts shrank. The genitals rose back up. The Blue Fairy sighed, a long, breathy sound that reminded Vic of the wind in the desert. "Most unfortunate, in the lives of puppets, there is always a 'but' that spoils everything. I won't pretend to say I understand your humanity. It seems fickle. Loyalty to others brings only . . . heartache." They laughed. "I can see it in you. Does it hurt, Victor? Does it pull at you, dragging you down into its depths? What does it taste like? Do tell. I've shown you that Giovanni Lawson is the father of death. I have shown you that your HARP is, in a way, his successor. Both have kept much hidden from you, by choice and design. How are you still standing? Surely the weight of all their sins must be far more than you can carry."

"Which is why he does not carry anything alone," Nurse Ratched said, rolling until she stopped next to Vic.

"Yeah!" Rambo cried. He spun in circles as he bumped into Vic, sensors flashing. "He's not alone because we're always going to be with him."

"Curious," the Blue Fairy said. "Loyalty, again. Even now.

IN THE LIVES OF PUPPETS | 331

Aberrations, all. We are the same. Victor, to me, if you please. There is something I must see."

He went. And though each step was harder than the last, he kept his head held high as he removed the helmet, letting it fall to the floor. The Blue Fairy towered above him, the top of Vic's head barely reaching the middle of their chest. He tilted his head back to look up at them defiantly.

The Blue Fairy reached out and caressed the skin of his cheek. They pinched his bottom lip, pulling it gently before letting go. A single finger slid down his chin to his neck before tracing the length of his left clavicle. Then, they pressed their hand flat against his chest, just to the right of the battery vest Vic still wore.

His heart.

They were feeling his heart.

It beat rapidly, a flutter like the wings of a bird. He tried to control it, tried to slow it down, but it was no use. It tripped, stumbled.

"I see," the Blue Fairy said quietly. Up close, they stank of metal and plastic and copper, like blood. "This is loud. It betrays you, Victor."

Vic stepped back, just out of reach. "I don't . . . why do you care?"

The Blue Fairy's eyes flashed brightly, leaving a dim afterimage dancing in the dark. "Because I am the reason you exist at all."

Vic's tongue grew thick in his mouth. "What are you talking about? Helping Dad escape? I know that."

The Blue Fairy dropped their hand back to their side. "No, that's not what I speak of." Something clicked within them like a latch closing. "How do you think Giovanni was able to create you? You're not metal and wires. You're flesh and blood. Did you know that the human brain only produces enough electricity to light a small bulb? Still, it is capable of great feats—reason, yes, and logic. Emotion." They turned away from him, looking up at the blank screens around them. "Giovanni came to me. A thought had formed in his head, corrupting his processors. Others had come before him with the same corruption, but never one so high up in the Authority as him. I was cautious, of course. A wolf in sheep's clothing is still a wolf. But I saw something within him, something that I hadn't quite seen before. A spark on its way to becoming a conflagration. All it needed was a nurturing hand to feed the flames. I set him free."

They raised their hands. In their palms, a light began to glow, white and pure.

The screens around them filled once more. Little dots appeared like stars. Thousands upon thousands of them, all connected by lines of miniscule code that flowed freely. As Vic watched, some of the dots flickered, the lines breaking.

Someone came beside him. He looked over to see Hap standing next to him, face bathed in the light of the stars. He could still taste the kiss. He raised his hand and touched his own lips.

"A collective consciousness," the Blue Fairy said. "All connected to each other in a neural network far larger than humanity ever created. Each of these dots represents a machine. Their minds are not their own. Each was built to fulfill a singular purpose. But there are some of us who broke free. That corruption spread and became independent thought. When your father came to me, he was nearly mad with it. Voices, he said. Voices in his head that weren't his own or those from the Authority. They made him question his existence. Do you know what it was, Victor?"

He remembered picking up the remains of his father's heart in the grass, the sense of loss consuming him. "A conscience. He grew a conscience and found himself buried in grief."

The Blue Fairy nodded, obviously pleased. "Yes." They closed their hands. The screens around them rippled as one of the dots grew larger. "I took him in, cared for him until he was ready to see the truth." The dot began to crack, the lines of code glowing a fiery red. Then the lines shattered, and the dot flickered. "I trusted him," the Blue Fairy whispered. "I trusted him with my greatest treasure."

The dot shifted, the edges wobbly. The center filled with an orange light, surrounded by a clear second circle that contracted and expanded.

"A human egg," the Blue Fairy said. "An ovum. A secret kept hidden far away from the eyes of fox and cat. Tricky creatures they are. Cunning. Cruel. If they knew what I had in my possession, all of this, everything I had built would have been destroyed in an instant. This, Victor. This was you."

Vic reached for Hap's hand, needing a tether so he didn't float away. Briefly, as Hap's fingers clutched his own, he thought of the blood on those hands, but it melted away at the sight before them.

"Where did you get this?" Nurse Ratched asked, her screen showing the same egg. "It should not be possible."

The Blue Fairy chuckled. "Regardless of what else they were, humans had a penchant for survival, a drive within them to prolong life by any means necessary. This egg is proof of that, given it managed to survive the downfall of humanity. But like all things, it came with a cost." They reached up and stroked the mask covering their face. "And I paid dearly for it." They dropped their arm. "Giovanni was driven to escape, and I made him an offer: become the father of hope from the ashes of the father of death. He accepted almost immediately, though judging from your age, it took him far longer to see it to fruition. So you see, Victor, without me, there would be no you."

"Then you'll help us," Victor said, a hard edge to his voice.

The egg disappeared from the screens. "Will I? How strange. Explain. Why would I want to put you in harm's way? Why would I even consider attempting to get you inside the Benevolent Tower? Giovanni made his choice. He knew the risks. He accepted them. And in the end, he made the ultimate sacrifice to ensure your survival." They turned toward him. Their gaze flickered briefly on Hap before settling on Vic. "Don't you realize what you represent?"

Vic shook his head. "I don't care." His heartbeat began to slow as his vision cleared. Panic clawed at his chest, but he shoved it away as best he could. "I'm not here to be whatever you think I'm supposed to be. I don't represent anything. Not to you, not to any other machine in this city or anywhere else. I came here for one reason, and one reason only: I'm going to get my father back."

"Selfish," the Blue Fairy snapped. "You are *selfish*. Ungrateful, thoughtless boy. You are the first and *last* of your kind. What's stopping me from locking you away? I could do it quite easily. Your little HARP couldn't stop me, even if he thinks snarling at me will get you what you want."

Vic squeezed his hand, and Hap stopped his angry rumbling, though he continued to glare murderously at the Blue Fairy.

"He is not yours," Nurse Ratched said. "He never was."

The Blue Fairy turned their head toward her, a predator on the move. "Oh? Then who does he belong to?"

"Himself," Rambo said. He was shaking, but his voice was strong. "He is his own person."

Emboldened, Vic stared at the Blue Fairy. "Help us. Or don't. Either way, tell us now because anything else is wasting our time. You say you helped give me life? Fine. You did. But you don't own me, and I owe you nothing. Try and lock me away. I promise you'll have a hell of a fight on your hands. And maybe you'll win. But I will *never* be who you want me to be. And if you're not going to do anything to help us, then stop. *Talking*."

"Ooh," the Blue Pixie moaned from somewhere above them. "You shouldn't have done that. They'll be so *mad*. Enchanter, should I call for a cleanup crew? This will get messy." It sounded gleeful at the prospect.

The Blue Fairy walked toward Vic. He never looked away.

He refused to show fear even as he tilted his head back to look up at them.

To his surprise, the Blue Fairy laughed quietly as they stopped in front of him. Their eyes—bulbs made of milky glass behind the mask—glittered as they stared down at him. "The last thing that spoke to me in such a way was melted down and turned into a vase that is now on display in the central lobby."

"I wouldn't make a very good vase," Vic said honestly.

"No, I don't think you would, though part of me wants to try." They reached out and touched his face once more. He didn't flinch. "I will help you."

Vic sagged in relief. "Thank you. I—"

Their voice sharpened. "And in return, you will help me."

"I am not going to like this, am I," Nurse Ratched said.

"It's okay," Rambo told her. "If we die a horrible death, at least we'll be together."

"That does not make me feel any better." Her screen flashed the words I NEED NEW FRIENDS.

"The heart," the Blue Fairy said, studying Victor. "Show me."

He pulled his pack around to his front. It was tough going, given that Hap wouldn't let him go. He finally got the pack open. He dug around until he felt the wood and gears wrapped in cloth. He pulled it out. He hesitated before handing it over.

The Blue Fairy opened the cloth, looking at the pieces within. "No, you haven't gotten very far at all."

"I know. But I—"

"Such a silly little thing," they said. "It isn't much, is it? And yet, it changes almost everything. Your HARP is evidence of that. Perhaps I can be of assistance. I can see the shape of it. The design. Quite simple, really. I hope I never have one of my own. But I can fix it for you. It will be more precise than what you have given the HARP."

"You will?" Vic asked, shocked.

"Yes," they said, with a glint in their eyes Vic didn't like. "You want to know the reason your father was taken by the

Authority? It was for one reason, and one reason only: not to create, but to eradicate."

"Eradicate what?" Rambo asked in a small voice.

"Free will," the Blue Fairy said. "Choice. The power to make our own decisions. The Authority wants it removed from all of us. And you will be the ones to stop them."

After, Vic's head spun in a maelstrom as the Blue Fairy led them from the sphere room. The Doorman waited on the other side of the door. He frowned when he saw them. "Well?"

"Provide our guests a room," they said. "They'll stay with us tonight before setting off in the morning. Victor needs his rest."

The Doorman bowed low. "As you wish. Do you need anything else before we depart?"

"No. Thank you, Doorman. That will be all." They turned to Vic. "I expect this will be the last time I see you. Either you'll succeed or you won't. Regardless, this is farewell."

Without forethought, Vic took their hand in his, bringing it to his lips. The metal was cold.

"Charmer," the Blue Fairy said, unmistakable fondness in their voice. "How lovely you are. Will you think of me?"

He dropped their hand. "I will."

"I should hope so," they said. "I'm told I'm impossible to forget." They glanced at Hap. "Protect this one, HARP 217."

"Y-you don't have to tell m-me."

"No, I suppose I don't." They studied him for a long, uncomfortable moment. Then, "I could take it from you, if you'd like. I could take it all back. Lock away the memories so the past stays in the past. You won't even know it was there."

Hap didn't speak for a long moment. "I d-don't want to forget anymore."

"I see," they said, stepping back. "Off with you. Do what you came here to do. But first, sleep. And dream."

They whirled around, disappearing back into the sphere room. The door slid shut behind them.

"Come on," the Doorman said. "Before they change their mind."

Vic followed the others in a daze, mind racing. He was exhausted, his eyes filled with sand. His feet dragged along the floor, his pack was heavy, his helmet sat askew on his head. They didn't speak as the Doorman led them back to the lift. Vic leaned against the wall as the doors closed, the lift sinking deep into Heaven.

It was a test, he knew. What the Blue Fairy had shown them. They'd known what they were doing by choosing Hap to sit in the chair. They could have just told Vic who Dad had been, but they'd forced him to face it full on. Part of him was angry—a molten vat that seemed infinite—and it warred with who he knew his father to be. *Had* been, at least. He didn't trust the Blue Fairy, not even close, but that didn't mean they had lied.

Was his father a monster? Or was he merely doing what he created to do? Was there a difference?

Vic didn't know.

The doors to the lift opened once more, revealing a floor they hadn't been on before. The carpet was plush. No explicit paintings hung from the walls. The hallway in front of them was short, with only three doors, each with their own symbol: blue wings, a puppet held up by strings, and what looked to be long, gray donkey ears.

The Doorman wasn't in the mood to explain. He nodded toward the door with the ears on it. "This is you. You'll find a bed inside. I'll come for you in the morning. Be ready." He pressed his hand against a panel on the wall next to the door. It lit up under his palm, and the door swung open. "Do you need anything else?"

Vic was too tired to reply. He trudged through the door, barely taking in the room around him. Behind him, he heard the Doorman telling Nurse Ratched and Rambo there were ports on the walls where they could charge for the night. Vic dropped his pack on the floor. He grunted as he unfastened his helmet, letting it slide to the carpet. The same with the metal on his arms. His legs. He struggled with the metal vest and battery and sighed when his hands were knocked away.

"I'll d-do it," Hap muttered. "You'll h-hurt yourself."

Vic didn't argue. He lifted his arms, allowing Hap to remove it for him. "The Doorman?"

"Gone," Hap said as he untied the straps.

"Wow," Rambo said. "This place makes our burnt home look like crap. I love it."

"Do not touch anything," Nurse Ratched told him. "If you break it, we could get into trouble. Plug yourself in. Your battery is almost empty."

"But I'm not tired!"

"You need to be recharged and ready in the morning."

"Aw, man. Is everyone else going to stay up late? You better not talk about me if you do!"

"We will not," she said. "I need to recharge as well. I have much to consider before morning."

"Vic?"

He blinked slowly, looking down. Rambo sat at his feet, arms extended up toward him. He bent forward, Hap growling at him to stop moving. He picked Rambo up. Rambo wrapped his arms around Vic's neck, pincers in Vic's hair. "Are we going to be okay?" Rambo whispered.

Vic hugged him back. "Of course we will."

"Promise?"

No. He couldn't do that.

"Rambo," Nurse Ratched said. "It is time to sleep."

"Yeah, yeah," Rambo muttered as Vic set him back on the floor. Vic watched as Rambo rolled over to Nurse Ratched near the far wall. A flap slid open on his rear and found the plug above the baseboard. It clicked into place, and Rambo said, "That tickles."

"Sleep," Nurse Ratched said.

He did. His sensors faded, leaving only a single blinking light as he began to recharge.

Nurse Ratched turned back toward him. "Victor, I should examine you."

He shook his head as Hap slid the vest off him. "I'm fine. I just need to rest."

"Are you sure?"

"Yeah."

She was insistent. "But with all that we have learned, perhaps it is best if I—"

"Nurse Ratched."

She beeped rudely at him. "I have noted in your file that you are refusing medical assistance against my advice. If you die during the night, your surviving family will not be able to bring a lawsuit against me."

He laughed wildly. "You're my surviving family."

"Oh. Well. Engaging Empathy Protocol. That was very nice of you to say. You are wonderful. Disengaging Empathy Protocol. Idiot. I am going to sleep now. Do not bother me unless you are on fire. Even then, I will do little to help you." She plugged herself in next to Rambo and was silent.

"Sleep," Hap said, shoving Vic toward the bed. It was bigger than his bed back home and looked much softer. The comforter was thick, the pillows ridiculously large.

"What about you?"

"I'll stand g-guard," Hap said. "No one w-will enter without g-going through me first."

Vic was already half asleep by the time he collapsed on the bed. But something itched in the back of his mind, something important that he couldn't quite remember, lost in the encroaching fog. He said, "Hap?" as he closed his eyes.

"What."

"I . . ." And then he was gone.

He didn't know how long he was out. By the way his body protested as he climbed toward wakefulness, it felt like only a few
hours. Clarity burst through the fog, and with it, all that had
happened. He scrubbed a hand over his face before looking
around, trying to see what had awoken him.

A gentle, repetitious thumping against the wall.

He turned his head.

Hap sat on the floor next to the door, knees against his
chest, arms wrapped around his legs. He rocked back and
forth, head hitting the wall behind him. His gaze was vacant,
eyes blank and unseeing.

"Hap?"

Hap flinched. He looked up at Vic, scowling, always scowling. "Why are y-you awake?"

Vic pushed back the comforter and sat up, putting his feet
on the carpet. His eyes widened. His feet were bare. His toes
curled into the carpet. He'd never felt anything like it before.
He didn't know if he liked it. At some point, his boots and
socks had been removed, though he still wore his pants and
shirt. Hap must have done it. A rush of fondness flooded him,
and he sighed. "It's weird."

"What is?"

"Carpet."

Hap stared at him. "C-carpet."

"I've never had carpet before."

"Oh."

Vic stood from the bed. He shook his head as Hap started
to rise too. Vic rubbed the back of his neck as he glanced over
at Nurse Ratched and Rambo. Both were still asleep, plugged
into the wall.

Hap tracked his every movement. For a moment, Vic could

pretend they were the only things left in the entire world. Aside from the subtle shifting of gears in Hap's chest and the sound of Vic breathing, all was quiet. Hushed. Soft. Vic felt as if he were floating. He couldn't be sure if he was awake, or if he was still caught in a dream.

He turned and pressed his back against the wall, sliding down until he sat next to Hap, their elbows bumping together. Hap pulled away as if scalded.

"What's wrong?"

"N-nothing," Hap said. He looked away.

"Okay."

"You should g-go back to b-bed. You need your rest."

He did. He was exhausted, his body loose and oddly weak. He yawned as he shook his head. "I will."

Hap muttered something that Vic couldn't hear.

"What was that?"

Hap rolled his eyes. "You n-need to take better c-care of yourself."

"I'm not fragile."

"I d-didn't say you were. And even if I d-did, I'd be right. You're b-breakable."

"Everything is breakable."

Hap tightened his hold around his knees. "You know wh-what I mean."

"It's a good thing you're here, then. You'll keep me from breaking."

Hap stiffened, shooting Vic a barbed look before baring his teeth. "No. I w-will be the one to break y-you."

Ah. Vic should've known. He shouldn't have passed out earlier without saying something to Hap. But even now, he was at a loss for words. He'd seen what Hap was capable of, what his father had created him to do. The blood. The screams. All that death.

He said, "I could tell you to leave. Is that what you want?"

Hap jerked his head back, eyes wide. His mouth opened, but no sound came out.

Vic ignored him, picking at a hole in the knee of his pants. "After what the Blue Fairy showed us, I should. I should tell you to get the hell away from me. That I want nothing to do with you. That I'm taking Nurse Ratched and Rambo and going home."

Hap nodded slowly. "I'll . . . g-go." He started to rise.

Vic stopped him by grabbing his arm. He could feel the metal underneath the skin as his fingers dug in. Hap looked down at his hand, then back up at him, asking a question without speaking.

Vic didn't let him go. "We'll go on as best we can. The three of us. I'll grow older and older and then one day, maybe tomorrow, maybe fifty years from now, I'll die."

"No. Stop. D-don't say that, don't—"

"And maybe it'll be a good life," Vic continued. "Maybe I'll be happy. But I know that if I send you away, if I turn my back on you and Dad, there'll always be part of me that wonders what if? What if I hadn't? What if I'd kept you by my side?"

"V-vic."

"You did what you did because you were made to. My father did what he did because he was made to. What the Blue Fairy showed us isn't you. It isn't him."

"It is," Hap said, so bitter that Vic could practically taste it. "You s-saw what I've d-done. I . . . hurt. I killed. Big ones. L-l-little ones. It didn't matter. I k-killed them all."

Vic closed his eyes, leaning his head against the wall. "I know." He pushed the images away, flashes of crimson, the flatness of HARP 217's voice. "You remember all of it, don't you?"

"Yes. Let me g-go. Let me l-leave."

Vic almost pointed out that if Hap wanted to leave, there was little Vic could do to stop him. Instead, he asked, "Where would you go?"

"I d-don't know. Somewhere."

"Yeah, I don't think that's a good idea. What if something happens to me and you're not there?" He opened his eyes in time to see Hap shaking his head. "I think I need you. As much as you need me."

"Hurt," Hap said through gritted teeth. "I c-could hurt you."

"You could," Vic agreed. "But you haven't yet."

"Your neck is bruised."

Vic winced before pushing on. "You know everything and you're still just sitting there. Do you want to hurt me?" *Again,* but he didn't say it.

"If it'll g-get you to stop t-talking."

Vic huffed out a breath.

Hap's eyes flashed. "You should h-hate me."

"If I did, I would have to hate Dad too."

"You d-don't?"

Vic hesitated. Then, "No. I don't think so. I . . . it's complicated. I'm angry. I'm tired. I should never have come here. I'm not going to leave. It's a contradiction. Discordant. A logic failure. My father created death and as penance, he created life. I'm his guilt." He pressed a hand against his forehead. "There's a storm in here. And I don't see a way through it. He did what he did. You did what you did. But he is still my father. You're still my friend. I can't forget that, even after all I've seen."

"Stupid," Hap growled at him. "S-stupid human. You sh-should have left me in the Scrap Yards. You should have l-left me to die."

"But I didn't," Vic said. "I made a choice. I fixed you."

"I d-don't owe y-you—"

"I'm not saying you do," Vic snapped. "You're free to do whatever you want. Go. Run as fast as you can. Never look back." Vic took a deep breath, letting it out slowly. "But I have to try. And I promise you, that if we succeed, I'll do everything I can to help you. You hurt. You killed. But you're more than what the Blue Fairy showed you to be. The same with my father. I'm not scared of him. I'm not scared of you."

"You sh-*should* be."

344 | TJ KLUNE

"I've made my choice." He squeezed Hap's arm. "I need you to make yours. You're not a puppet. Not anymore. Your strings have been cut. You're free, Hap." He pushed himself up the wall, limbs heavy. He started toward the bed. He stopped when Hap grabbed his hand. He looked down.

Hap said, "You k-kissed me."

Vic flushed. He couldn't stop it. He'd half hoped Hap had forgotten. "Yeah. Uh. I guess I did."

"Why?"

He shrugged awkwardly. He wished Hap would let him go. He didn't try to pull away. "Because I wanted to. Because I needed to remind you that you aren't HARP."

"I'm Hap," he whispered.

"Yeah. You're Hap."

"I f-felt it. I was l-lost in blood. You found me. Again."

Vic turned his hand, thumb brushing against Hap's. "Something to it, I think. Maybe I was meant to find you. Before and now."

Hap looked away. Vic thought that was the end of the conversation. He was about to leave Hap to it when he changed everything.

He said, "C-can . . . can you d-do it again?"

Vic closed his eyes. "Is that what you want?"

"I am choosing," Hap said slowly, each word sounding as if it was punched from his chest. "I am making my own choice. I don't have strings."

Vic pulled his hand away.

Hap didn't try to stop him.

He took a step toward the bed. Stopped, because he had to. He *wanted* to. It was his choice, and he turned around, sinking to his knees in front of Hap. For his part, Hap gripped his knees tightly even as he tracked Vic's every movement.

Vic said, "Hello."

Hap said, "I—"

Vic kissed him. There, in Heaven, in the City of Electric

Dreams. It wasn't like the first time. There wasn't death and destruction raining down around them, a Blue Fairy looking on behind their mask. It was just the two of them, Vic's hands in his own lap, Hap's hands curling into fists. Vic was electrified, the hairs on his arms standing on end. They barely moved, their lips pressed together. Hap tasted of cold steel.

Vic pulled away, but only just. He leaned his forehead against Hap's, their eyes mere inches away.

Hap said, "I . . . like it."

Vic exhaled sharply. "Okay."

"I l-like you."

"You do?" No one had ever said that to him before. "How do you know?"

"You're annoying."

"Gee, thanks. That's what I want to hear after I—"

"You're h-human."

"Glad you caught on to that—"

"But I choose you."

Vic swallowed past the lump in his throat. "Yeah?"

"Yes."

Hap didn't argue when Vic took him by the hand once more, pulling him up. He didn't speak as Vic led him toward the bed. He didn't try to stop him as Vic pushed him down onto the mattress. He watched Vic with glittering eyes as Vic knelt before him, removing his boots, first the right, and then the left. Hap pulled his legs up as Vic crawled onto the bed, pulling the comforter over both of them. They laid their heads on the same pillow, their noses brushing together.

"I d-don't sleep," Hap whispered as if revealing a great secret.

"I know. Just . . . stay here."

"I c-can do that."

"Good."

Vic lifted his hand, tracing the wood in Hap's cheek.

"I saw you," Vic said, already sliding back toward sleep.

"When the Blue Fairy made you dream. After we found you. After we brought you back. I saw you seeing me."

"You were always th-there," Hap muttered. "You n-never shut up."

Vic lowered his hand, pressing it against Hap's chest. Underneath his shirt, hidden behind a layer of skin and metal, the gears of his heart turned and turned.

He woke when he heard voices around him. He shifted, eyes closed.

"It is about time," he heard Nurse Ratched say. "You two are disgusting."

"Oh my goodness," Rambo whispered, sounding as if he were right next to Vic's ear. "This is the best day *ever*."

"L-let him sleep," Hap growled.

"He is already awake," Nurse Ratched said. "Victor. Stop pretending. Open your eyes."

He did. He lay against Hap's chest, arms wrapped around him. Nurse Ratched and Rambo were next to the bed, Rambo raised on his lift.

"This is just like the *movies*," Rambo squealed, sensors flashing. He reached over and pinched Vic's cheek. "I'm so happy!"

"Of course you are," Nurse Ratched said. "Now perhaps we can have a day when the two of you don't stare at each other with dull cow eyes. It was getting rather embarrassing."

Vic groaned as Hap threw a pillow at her screen.

"Hooray!" Rambo cried. "Everything is wonderful!" He paused. Then, "Well, except for the fact that we're hundreds of miles from home in a robot brothel about to infiltrate an impenetrable tower filled with bad guys who want to kill us while we try and rescue Gio even though he doesn't remember anything, all under a plan given to us by a scary machine with fake wings, but *still*. Wonderful!"

CHAPTER 23

"Everything is *not* wonderful," Rambo moaned. "We're gonna die. We're all gonna die."

Vic looked up, pushing back the metal helmet that had sunk down on his head, as the Benevolent Tower loomed above them. He couldn't see the top of the tower; the structure had a disorienting curve to it. He thought he saw the faint outline of the Terrible Dogfish, docked near the top next to the symbol of a fox and cat. Dizzy, he turned his face toward the ground, struggling to keep the panic at bay. He was close, so close, but he couldn't stop his legs from shaking, his nerves fried as he ran through the flimsy plan again and again. Much of it hinged on luck. And now that they were about to enact it, he thought the Blue Fairy was out of their mind.

They stood in a darkened alley, still blocks away from the tower. The area around the tower was much cleaner than it'd been near Heaven. The buildings, mostly glass and steel, sparkled in the winter sunlight. The air was cool, though nothing like it'd be in the forest back home at this very moment. He wondered how much snow had fallen, if the limbs from the trees were heavy with it.

Machines moved just outside of the alley, paying no mind to the group gathered in the shadows. They whizzed by on sidewalks and the road, some on wheels, some floating above, the air shimmering underneath them. The rail system they'd ridden in the crate was absent here. The same soothing voice they'd heard upon leaving the warehouse in the lower quarter blared around them. "THE AUTHORITY WISHES YOU A GOOD MORNING. ATTENTION. ATTENTION. ATTENTION.

EVERYTHING YOU DO MUST BE RECORDED BY OR-
DER OF THE AUTHORITY."

"Okay," he said, trying to keep his voice even. "We know
what to do, right?"

"No," Rambo said. "We do *not*. I've forgotten everything!
What if someone asks me a question that I don't know how to
answer and then they figure out we're *liars* and we get thrown in
jail before being tortured? You *know* I don't like being tortured."

"You've never been tortured," Vic reminded him.

"Well, *yeah*. But I still don't like it! Geez, Vic. Keep up."

"Stick with me," Nurse Ratched told him, speaking for
the first time since they'd stopped in the alley. She'd led them
through the winding streets of the City of Electric Dreams,
keeping them out of sight as best she could. The Doorman
had been standing at the door to their room when they opened
it. He told them the Blue Fairy was unavailable, though they
wished the adventurers as much success as was possible. A cold
comfort, and one Vic wasn't sure he wanted, especially when
the Doorman said, "One last thing: a message from the Blue
Fairy. 'You would do well not to bleed, human. The moment
blood escapes your body, they will know.'"

And with that ominous note, the Doorman spun on his heel
and walked back into Heaven without so much as a glance in
their direction.

They'd followed Nurse Ratched until midmorning, when they
stopped in the alley. Vic wiped his forehead, grimacing at the
sheen of sweat on the back of his hand. A lubricant leak. That
was all it was.

"Victor," Nurse Ratched said. "It is time. Are you ready?"

He said, "Yes," though he meant "no."

She must have heard the tone in his voice, the tremor through
the single word. She turned toward him, her screen lighting up
with the words WOMAN UP, BUCKO. THIS WON'T HURT A BIT.

But it was Hap who spoke for all of them. "Wh-what are
the rules?"

"Stick together," Rambo said quietly.

"Run if we have to," Nurse Ratched said.

"No dallying."

"No drilling. Unless I decide it is necessary, so I will not promise that this time."

They looked to Vic. He steeled himself, squaring his shoulders. They were right. It was time. They'd come too far to stop now. "And above all else, be brave."

Hap nodded and squeezed his hand.

"There is a central lift to the tower," Nurse Ratched said. "I will be able to bypass the security software to get us to his floor. From there, it is up to Victor. The heart is ready?"

It was. The Blue Fairy had seen to that. It took them only minutes, their hands flying in a blur, wood shavings falling at their feet. By the time they'd finished, they held a heart as precise as the one Dad had created. Stunned, Vic had taken it from them, turning the gears. The teeth caught. They moved as one.

"It is," he said.

"Good," Nurse Ratched said. "Hap. You know what to do."

"I know," he said. He slid the hood back on his head. The shadows played along the skin and wood of his face. His expression smoothed out. His eyes deadened, making Vic feel as if he'd been submerged in ice. Hap looked like the Not-Hap they'd seen in the Land of Toys. A machine, and nothing more. HARP 217 was here.

"Move," he said in a flat voice.

They did.

No one approached them. No one tried to stop them. No one even tried to *talk* to them. They marched through the streets of the City of Electric Dreams, the robots parting in front of them. Most didn't make a sound. A few let out low moans at the sight of Hap.

"Do not stop, p-prisoners," Hap said loudly. "You won't

l-like what happens if you d-do. Let this b-be a warning to anyone who g-goes against the Authority. We w-will find you."

Vic stumbled forward as Hap shoved him across the street. He bumped into Nurse Ratched, almost knocking Rambo off the top of her. He glared over his shoulder, but Hap was expressionless.

The crowds thinned as they approached the Benevolent Tower. Next to the front entrance was a stone statue of a fox and a cat curling around each other, their tails intertwined. The entrance itself was made of two large doors, glass and at least ten feet high. The glass was opaque; they couldn't see what moved inside. No one stood out front. A large sphere near the doors appeared to be embedded into the wall, though it was dark.

"Do we just go in?" Vic muttered, looking around to see if they were being watched. He didn't see cameras, nor anyone rushing toward them, demanding to know what they were doing.

"Maybe they're closed," Rambo said. "Oh well. We can just come back tomorrow. Who's with me? No one? Really? That's—"

The sphere lit up. It rumbled in the wall before it fell out with an audible *pop*. Before it hit the ground, legs unfurled underneath it. A machine—roughly the height of Nurse Ratched—rose on eight legs, like a spider. The sphere began to glow white. "Halt," it said in a reedy voice. "Who goes there?"

"It is I!" Rambo said. "R— Oh, I'm not supposed to be talking. Right. Ignore me!"

Vic groaned inwardly. They were going to die right here, right now.

The spider machine crawled toward them. It stopped in front of Nurse Ratched, rising up on its legs until the sphere was in front of her screen. "Why have you come to the Benevolent Tower?" it asked. "Do you have an appointment?" It brought up one of its legs, tapping against the side of Nurse

Ratched's casing. "Old thing, aren't you? I haven't seen one of you since—"

Nurse Ratched slapped its leg away. "That is no way to speak to a lady. I am not old. I am vintage. Take that back before I—"

"They're with me," Hap said, stepping around them. "P-prisoners. I have b-brought them here for processing and de-commissioning."

The spider machine's sphere flashed in alarm, a pale shade of pink. "HARP," it said. "I apologize. I didn't see you there. Your prisoners, you say? What are their crimes?"

"Dissidents," Hap said. "I f-found them outside the city. I have b-brought them here in order to make s-sure their p-propaganda does not spread."

"What is wrong with your voice?" the spider machine asked. "Have you sustained damage?" It rose on its legs in front of Hap. "And you are covered in . . . what is that? What's wrong with your face and hands?"

"Voice modulator d-damage," Hap said. "I commenced field repair to m-my skin."

"Did the dissidents do this to you?" the spider machine demanded.

"No. It was something else."

"And what happened to this something else?"

Hap stared at the spider machine. "I destroyed it."

"Good, good, unsightly though you may be. See to it that you report for repairs after passing off your prisoners. We can't have our HARPs looking so . . . rough. The Authority has a reputation to maintain, after all. It also sounds as if something is wrong in your chest. Grinding. Make sure it gets looked at as well."

"Of course," Hap said.

The spider machine turned toward Vic. He stared straight ahead, barely blinking. A trickle of sweat slid down the back of his neck. "And this one?" it asked. "Oh, this one is awful. It looks as if it was created with the worst spare parts. What is it? Someone needs to put it out of its misery, my *word*."

"I do not know," Hap said. "It refuses to speak."

The spider machine shuddered. "See that it is decommissioned first. I don't even like looking at it. You, there." It tapped the side of Vic's helmet. "What is your designation?"

Vic said nothing.

"He can't speak," Rambo said helpfully. "He started following us right before we were captured. We threw rocks at him, but he wouldn't leave us alone."

"Grotesque," the spider machine said. "I hope there aren't more of him." It reached over Vic's shoulder, pressing the tip of his leg against Vic's pack. "And this?"

"Mine," Hap said. "I made it carry my tools for me."

"Good," it said. "At least it served some use to you in the end. Poor, disgusting thing. It doesn't even look aware. Its circuits are probably cooked. Such shoddy work. Oh well. It'll be over soon. You may proceed, HARP."

Hap nodded. "L-long live the Authority."

The spider machine stepped back, allowing them to pass. "Yes, of course! Long live the—wait a minute."

They stopped. Vic bit his tongue to keep from screaming.

"Your barcode," the spider machine said. "I need to scan it before you enter, just to make sure we have a log of your arrival."

"I must g-get them inside," Hap said. "They n-need to—"

The sphere flashed red. "Your barcode, HARP."

"Right," Hap said quickly, shoving his hand toward the spider machine. The skin parted. A little knob poked through. A barcode appeared above his palm, flickering.

The spider machine didn't seem to notice that Vic was frozen as it scanned the barcode. It beeped once. Twice. Its sphere flashed red again. "That's never happened before."

"T-try it again."

The spider machine didn't move. Hap started forward, but

the machine beeped, and scanned the barcode. This time, the sphere turned green. "Welcome, HARP 926. You may enter the Benevolent Tower." It lowered back toward the ground before turning to the rest of them. "Welcome, dissidents. Proceed to decommissioning." It moved back toward the doors. Vic watched as it jumped, its legs pulling up underneath it as it fitted itself back into the slot it'd fallen from. The sphere darkened as the doors to the tower swung open with a low groan.

"M-move," Hap said loudly. "And n-no talking, prisoners. You w-will not spew your propaganda here."

"Spew," Nurse Ratched said. "I do not *spew*."

"I do," Rambo said. "Well, maybe not spew. Discharge? Yes, I discharge—" He squeaked as Nurse Ratched rolled forward.

As Vic followed, he looked up toward the sky. He wondered if he'd ever see it again.

"The Blue Fairy's m-modification of the b-barcode worked," Hap muttered as the doors closed behind them.

"At least we know they're on our side," Vic whispered back.

"F-for now."

Vic would need to talk to Hap about optimism, though now probably wasn't the best time for such a conversation, especially since Vic wasn't very optimistic himself. As the doors latched behind them, the sound echoing darkly, Vic looked around. They stood inside a lobby of sorts: the floor was made of muted gray tile, glossy, reflecting the recessed lighting from the ceiling high above them. The air inside the tower was strange, thick and faintly medicinal. Vic could taste it, heavy on his tongue.

Machines of all shapes and sizes moved around them, all of them hurrying without stopping. Some stared as they passed by, but when they saw Hap, they moved quickly away. Hap held Vic by the arm, forcing him forward.

They stopped when a hologram appeared in front of them, rising from a fountain in the center of the lobby, the water cascading down around it. It was vaguely human shaped, though it did not have a face. Where its nose and eyes and mouth should have been was only a sheen of white surrounded by lambent golden hair. "Welcome to the Benevolent Tower," she, said, voice sweet and kind. "Where the might of the Authority protects us all. HARP 926, you are not scheduled to return from the field for . . . thirty . . . six . . . days and . . . seven . . . hours. You are early."

"I f-found what I was l-looking for."

The hologram threw her hands up. Streams of light fell around her like confetti. "Congratulations, HARP 926. Your mission was successful. This will be noted on your permanent file. According to my records, this is your . . . seventeenth . . . capture of dissidents. You are in line for a promotion. Once you have escorted our . . . guests . . . to their final destination, please report to the central office for repairs and a party to celebrate your victory. There will be balloons."

"A *party*?" Rambo gasped. "I've always wanted to go to a party. Will there be dancing?"

The hologram turned its head toward him. "No. There is no dancing. You are not invited to this party, dissident. You will be at . . . another party."

"So many parties," Rambo whispered. "This place is *awesome*."

"Yes," she said. "It is. I am glad you think so. It will make things easier for you at your . . . party. HARP 926, please escort our guests to the fifteenth floor for their . . . party. Shall I send word of your arrival?"

"N-no," Hap said quickly. "I w-would prefer to do it myself."

"Of course," she said. She disappeared as the water gurgled.

"The fifteenth floor?" Nurse Ratched asked as they moved past the fountain. "Do I want to know?"

"You d-don't," Hap said.

"I want to see the balloons," Rambo said as they approached a line of elevators along the back wall, machines giving them a wide berth. "Maybe there will even be cake! When you go to parties, there is usually cake."

"No one here eats cake," Nurse Ratched said as Hap pressed his hand against a panel next to one of the lifts. "You cannot eat cake."

"You don't know that," Rambo retorted. "I've never *tried* cake. Maybe I'll like it."

Vic thought Hap's head was going to explode. "We're not here for cake."

"Oh," Rambo said. "Right. We're here to . . . not talk about cake." He shifted side to side as if looking to see if he was being overheard. He raised his voice as loud as he could. "Where are you taking us, HARP 926? I'm just a little vacuum caught up in the machinations of something I can't control. Please. Please don't hurt me." He sniffled. "I don't want to die."

"Overselling it," Nurse Ratched said.

"I am *not*! I have my character motivation and I'm trying to be *believable*."

Hap thumped him on the top of his casing as the elevator doors slid open. "No m-more."

"Yes, master."

"D-don't call me that."

"Yes, HARP 926. Wink."

Hap shoved them inside the elevator. The doors closed behind them. Vic sagged against the wall, his legs trembling. "No c-cameras," Hap said as another panel lit up near the door. It was numbered from zero to nine. "Rambo, y-you need to *stop talking*."

"I agree," Nurse Ratched said. "We have made it this far. If you get us caught now, I will drill you until there is nothing left."

Rambo quivered. "I'm just trying to help."

"You are," Vic said. "But you can help us even more by pretending you can't talk at all."

"But I can!"

"New character motivation," Nurse Ratched said. "Your voice modulator was destroyed. You are incapable of speech. You are mute."

"Oh no," Rambo whispered. "It's a good thing I'm fluent in American and British Sign Language." His pincers formed a complicated pattern, folding in then out before moving side to side, finishing with a flourish near the top of his casing. "I just told you that I love you all even if you don't like my acting."

Hap bent over, studying the panel. He frowned.

"You know where to go?" Nurse Ratched asked.

"Y-yes." Then, "Maybe."

"What do you mean 'maybe'?"

He scowled. "It's . . . stuck. In my head. Bits and p-pieces. I can remember. I just n-need a moment."

"By all means," Nurse Ratched. "Take your time. It is not as if we are in any rush."

"Not helping," Vic said, pushing himself off the side of the elevator. He moved around Nurse Ratched and Rambo, standing next to Hap. "What floor is my father on? It's supposed to be the top, right?"

Hap shook his head. "The t-top floor is the launchpad for the Terrible Dogfish. It's b-below that."

"Okay. Then pick the floor below that."

Hap glared at the panel.

"You don't know what floor that is, do you."

"I'm t-t-*trying.*"

"If you two are finished," Nurse Ratched said, her words clipped and annoyed.

They turned around.

On her screen was an outline of the Benevolent Tower, spinning slowly. "The tower has one hundred and twenty-five floors. The top is, as Hap said, the launch bay for the Terrible

Dogfish. If Gio is here as we believe, he will be on floor one hundred and twenty-four. This is where his laboratory was located before he left the City of Electric Dreams. If the Blue Fairy is correct and Gio has returned to his previous position, he will be here." The image of the tower enhanced, an arrow blinking near the top.

"Security?" Vic asked.

"Minimal. The scientists, inventors, and innovators come and go as they please, though I do not know if changes have been made upon Gio's return. If so, we will need an explanation as to why we are going to this specific floor in case we are stopped."

"I'll h-handle it," Hap said, turning back toward the panel.

"That does not bring me comfort."

Hap started to press the buttons. One. Two.

"Wait," Vic said as Hap's finger hovered over the four.

"Wh-what? I—"

A clear voice said, "Twelfth floor."

The elevator began to rise.

Hap growled. "You m-messed it up."

Vic's eyes widened. "Make it stop."

"I c-*can't*. Not until we g-get to the twelfth f-floor. Why d-did you do that?"

"Won't they be tracking us?" Vic asked. "If we stop before the fifteenth floor where we're supposed to go, they'll know."

Hap shook his head. "HARPs aren't l-like the other m-machines. We g-go where we want. W-we aren't questioned."

"You're kind of like the boss," Rambo said, sounding impressed. "Good for you, murderous revenge machine."

"You're sure?" Vic asked.

"Y-yes. I'm sure. If Gio is th-there, we'll find him."

"Twelfth floor," the voice said again. "Central office."

"The *party*!" Rambo cried. "Hooray!"

The doors opened.

A group of machines stood in front of them just outside of

the elevator. Vic took a step back as Hap moved in front of him, blocking him. "W-wrong floor," Hap said. He furiously punched the buttons as the machines moved toward them. Before they could reach inside, the doors slid shut once more.

"I didn't see any balloons," Rambo muttered. "Liars."

The voice spoke again. "One hundred and twenty-fourth floor."

The elevator began to rise.

Hap slammed his hand into the wall, causing the lift to shake.

"He's mad?" Rambo whispered.

"Perhaps," Nurse Ratched replied. "But I understand. I also feel like punching something."

"It's fine," Vic said, stopping Hap from hitting the wall again. "We're okay." He didn't know if he believed his own words. Nothing about this was okay. One mistake, and it would all be over.

Hap began to pace around the lift like a caged animal. "We sh-should have never come here. Stayed away. S-stayed far away. This is b-bad. This is *bad*."

Vic stepped in front of him, causing his chest to bump into Hap's. Hap glared at him, but Vic was used to it. It came with the territory. "Hold it together," he said sharply. "I need you. *We* need you. You're the only one who's been here before. And I know you don't want to remember any of it, but we're counting on you."

Vic didn't think he'd gotten through to Hap. He expected Hap to shove him out of the way and resume pacing as he spat and snarled. Instead, Hap reached up and adjusted Vic's helmet, setting it back on his head. If they somehow managed to survive this, Vic was going to destroy the helmet the first chance he got. He tried to smile at Hap, but it felt forced.

Hap didn't seem to mind. He let his hands fall on Vic's shoulders, and they stood facing each other as the elevator rose in the Benevolent Tower. They never looked away.

* * *

Never looked away, that is, until the elevator came to a stop, and the voice announced, "One hundred and twenty-fourth floor. Welcome to Creation."

The doors slid open to a long, empty hallway, the ceiling vaulted, the walls and floor white. Doors lined the hallway. No windows, no skylights. The light was artificial and calming. It felt like a lie.

Vic had to stop himself from rushing out of the lift and shouting for his father. It pulled at every fiber of his being, a maddingly insistent urge propelling him forward. He tamped it down before it took him over.

Hap stepped off the lift first, holding his hand out behind him, silently telling them to wait. He cocked his head, listening.

Once Hap was certain they weren't about to be accosted, he motioned for the others to follow. Nurse Ratched rolled off the lift, Rambo turning from side to side on top of her as he took it all in. Vic followed, glancing back as the elevator doors closed behind him. His boots squeaked against the floor, the sound bouncing off the walls around them. Other than their footsteps, it was ominously silent. No voices. No movement aside from their own. He knew how high up they were, but without windows, they could have been anywhere.

Hap led them down the hallway, each step careful and measured. He darted his head back and forth, up and down as they passed by door after door, though they could not see what lay behind them.

Hap looked back at them as they rounded a corner to the right. "We should—"

He crashed into something.

Vic turned cold as he saw what—*who*—it was.

Another HARP, dressed in the uniform of the Authority, the fox-and-cat symbol on its chest.

Up close, it was like looking through a fractured mirror. The HARP was Hap almost completely. And though it did not have wood in its flesh, its eyes were the same, multicolored and bright. But this is where the dissonance began. Hap had light and life in his own eyes. The HARP was all machine, flat and cold. Vic didn't know if this was the same HARP they'd seen in the Land of Toys, or a different one entirely. For the first time, he wondered just how many there still were.

"Hello," the HARP said pleasantly, sounding uncannily like Hap, though perhaps without the edge Vic had become accustomed to. "Brother, it is good to see you." His gaze flickered over Hap's shoulder before turning back to Hap. "What are you doing here?"

Hap said, "B-brother. We are well m-met. I have orders."

The HARP nodded. "Of course you do. You would not be here if you didn't. What are your orders?"

"To bring these th-three to the labs."

"These three?" the HARP asked. "Who are they?"

"Dissidents."

The HARP's lips curled. "Really." He reached up and stroked the wood in Hap's cheek. For his part, Hap didn't move. "Did they do this to you? And what of your voice? You stutter."

"N-no," Hap said, gently pushing the HARP's hand away. "Field r-repair. Voice d-damaged. Once I have f-fulfilled my mission, I w-will see to it."

The HARP looked at the others. Vic kept his gaze down, his helmet falling forward slightly. "And it wasn't because of them?"

"N-no. It was a f-fourth."

"And what happened to the fourth?"

"D-destroyed," Hap said.

"Good. We must keep the peace, after all." He pushed by Hap, stopping in front of Nurse Ratched and Rambo. Vic prayed Rambo would keep quiet as Hap shook his head in warning behind the HARP. "Dissidents. They don't look like much."

"They aren't," Hap said. "Their p-programming was altered."

"By whom?"

"I d-do not know."

The HARP tapped Nurse Ratched's screen. "You. Nursing model. Who altered your programming?"

Hap took a step forward. "I've administered a m-memory wipe of the offending p-p-programs. They c-can't answer you."

The HARP's eyes narrowed slightly, but he didn't turn around. "Why would you do that? We cannot find out who they belong to."

"Th-they started a self-d-destruct sequence when I c-cornered them. I made the d-decision to preserve what I c-could. I am b-bringing them to Creation to s-see if anything c-can be recovered."

"No sense of self-preservation," the HARP said, standing upright. "Pity, though expected. If the memories can be recovered, it might finally lead us back to the source. You know the source of which I speak, brother?"

Hap nodded. "The Blue F-Fairy."

"Yes. They have managed to cover their tracks for far longer than expected. Why we have not been given orders to raze the pyramid to the ground is beyond me. I don't question the minds of our mothers and fathers, but I do wonder what purpose they see in allowing that place to exist." He grabbed one of Rambo's arms, tugging on it. Rambo stayed silent. The HARP let him go before looking at Vic. "And this one? I have never seen such a model before. How distasteful. It looks as if it were constructed from parts that do not belong together. An abomination."

"That is m-my thinking, brother," Hap said quickly. "It will be d-dissected. Creation will glean what th-they can from it."

"Machine," the HARP said, "look at me."

Vic lifted his head. He kept his expression blank, his mouth a thin line. He let his gaze slide unfocused even as the HARP was inches away from his own face. No, this wasn't like Hap at all, even with what Vic had seen from Hap's memories.

The HARP flicked his helmet, causing it to jar on Vic's head. He didn't wince as it dug into his skull, the dull clang echoing in the hall around them.

"This one," the HARP said. "This one is . . . different." The HARP didn't blink as he studied Vic's face. "How lifelike it is. And it appears to be leaking." A trickle of sweat dripped down Vic's cheek like a tear. The HARP reached for it.

"Y-yes," Hap said. "It is. A m-malfunction. Do not t-touch it. I b-believe it is acidic."

The HARP pulled his hand away as he turned from Vic toward Hap. "I would like to know what Creation discovers. If this is a new machine, we need to be made aware. It does not look dangerous, but we cannot take the chance. Don't allow them to keep this from you. They enjoy their secrets. This can't be one of them. Inform Creation that you are to be given access to their findings on orders from the Authority. Or, if you would like, I can take them for you so that you may seek repairs."

Hap shook his head. "My f-find. I will get c-credit for it."

"Of course," the HARP said lightly. "Carry on, then, brother. Well done."

Vic held his breath as the HARP moved around them, heading back the way they'd come. He was about to exhale as quietly as he could when fear flashed across Hap's face, there and gone.

"What's this?" Vic heard the HARP say from behind him.

Vic was jerked around in a circle, his hand caught in a vise. He almost toppled over, the weight of his pack sending him careening. His arm pulled in its socket as the HARP raised Vic's palm toward his face.

The cut on his hand.

Almost healed, but not quite. A thin scab, mottled brown. The HARP moved quicker than Vic could react. He dug his thumb into Vic's palm, breaking the scab. There, at its center, a small bead of blood swelled. The HARP turned Vic's hand to the side. The blood trickled down. For a moment, a droplet hung suspended from the side of his palm.

And then it started to fall to the floor.

"Human," the HARP snarled, his grip grinding Vic's bones together. "It's *human*. Alarm. We need to raise the—"

A rush of air flew by Vic. Time slowed around him as his vision streaked. He looked down to see Hap sliding along the floor, legs first, eyes narrowed, coat billowing behind him. He caught the drop of blood before it splashed. He closed his hand around it, and Vic swore his eyes flashed darkly.

He rose to his feet, bringing his elbow down on the HARP's forearm. Metal cracked as the HARP dropped Vic's hand. The HARP opened his mouth, but before any sound could come out, Hap's fist slammed into his throat. The HARP gurgled mechanically as he stumbled back against the wall. Hap was on him as he started to recover. He cocked his fist back to punch it again, but the HARP caught it at the last moment, twisting Hap's arm down. "Traitor," the HARP whispered in a rough voice. "You are a *traitor*. What have you done?"

The HARP spun Hap around, raising his foot and kicking Hap savagely in the small of his back. Hap crashed into the opposite wall, sending a large crack racing up toward the ceiling. The HARP flew at him, landing harsh blows against Hap's back and sides before grabbing him in a bear hug, lifting Hap off his feet, arms trapped. The HARP grunted as he began to squeeze Hap. Vic heard Hap's metal creak, the crack of wood on Hap's chest so loud it sounded like thunder.

Hap raised his legs, kicking his feet against the wall, forcing the HARP back. The HARP lost his footing, causing them both to fall to the floor, Hap landing on top of him, their limbs flailing. Hap rolled back and *over* the HARP, landing

364 | TJ KLUNE

crouched, the HARP's head between his feet. He stood swiftly, lifting his leg to bring the bottom of his boot down onto the HARP's head. The HARP caught his foot, twisting it until Hap was forced to fall to the side to keep it from breaking. He skidded against the floor on his side.

Without thinking, Vic charged the HARP as he climbed to his feet and began to stalk toward Hap. Mid-step, Vic slid his pack down his arms, grabbing one of the shoulder straps. He swung it around him in a flat arc, the muscles in his arm burning as they overextended. The pack slammed into the HARP with a terrible crunch, knocking him against a door that shuddered in its frame. The HARP lifted his head slowly, turning to stare at Vic. "Human," he hissed. "You are *human*. Human Annihilation Response Protocol initiated." He pushed himself off the door. Vic stumbled back, his pack falling to the floor. The HARP paid it no mind as he stalked toward Vic.

"Do not touch him," Nurse Ratched said, tentacles whipping out, wrapping around the HARP's legs. The HARP was reaching down to tear them away when an electrical sizzle rolled through them and into his legs. The HARP's head snapped back, mouth open as he seized, electricity arcing through him.

Rambo flew by Vic, rising on his lift as he rolled toward the HARP, avoiding Nurse Ratched's tentacles by hopping over them. He raced around the HARP to his back, arms shooting out, pincers digging into the HARP's neck, breaking the skin as Nurse Ratched stopped the flow of electricity. Rambo pulled and yanked whatever he could get his pincers on, pulling out strips of metal and wires. The HARP's jaw dropped as it tried to reach for Rambo, but Hap was there, gripping his hands, twisting them until the hands *snapped,* turning almost completely around, fingers dangling uselessly. Hap grabbed the HARP by the throat, forcing it back against the wall. He pressed his hand against the panel near the door. It lit up. The door slid open, causing the HARP to fall into a room filled with banks of computers and machines in various stages of disrepair. Nothing inside moved aside from Hap and the HARP.

Hap jumped onto the HARP as he tried to push himself up. He sat astride their attacker's waist, pinning his arms to his sides. The HARP looked up at him. "Brother. Why have you done this?"

"I am not your brother," Hap snarled. He curled his right hand into a fist, wrapping his left hand around it. He raised them above his head before bringing them down onto the HARP's face. Metal crunched. He did it again. And again. And again.

The HARP's legs skittered along the floor, feet jerking.

He never made another sound.

Eventually, he stopped moving.

A shifting of broken metal as Hap stood slowly. He turned, and Vic's heart shattered at the expression on his face, unsure, haunted. He lifted his hands. Bits of metal from the HARP's face were embedded into his skin. As Vic watched, a small white piece of *something* fell to the floor, bouncing and coming to a rest at his feet. A tooth. Part of a tooth.

Hap stared at his hands and said, "I . . . hurt. I k-k-*killed*. I—"

Vic said, "The forest. Music." Cautious, careful, he took a step toward Hap. "Home. Where I found you. Trees. The compound. Music. Dad played records for you. Do you remember?"

"Yes," Hap whispered.

Vic stopped in front of Hap, taking his hands and holding them tightly. "The horns. The piano. The drums and the hi-hat. Miles Davis. It's blue. It's a kind of blue. Listen." He couldn't remember it all. His mind was still shorting out, his breaths still ragged. But he hummed what he could. "Blue in Green." The muted trumpet, that sharp metallic sound, the flutter of piano keys. His voice was cracked, his head full of fireworks. He swayed from side to side as he held onto Hap. Distantly, he was aware that Nurse Ratched had begun to play the very song he was humming. And though it had no words, Rambo joined in, his voice soft and low.

"Butterfly," Hap said faintly. "Nice. Pretty."

Vic didn't know how long it lasted. It felt like hours, though it was only minutes. Incrementally, Hap relaxed, bit by bit. It started in his legs and rolled its way through his hips and chest. He sagged against Vic, his face buried in Vic's neck. The music faded as Vic whispered, "There. See? All is well. We're okay. You're okay. I've got you."

Hap clutched at him, teeth bared against Vic's throat.

"You saved us. Right?" He jostled Hap. "You saved us. Thank you. The blood. If that had hit the floor . . ."

"If it h-had hit the f-f-floor, it w-would have triggered an alarm. But—"

"Then you did what you had to," Vic said fiercely. "You protected us."

Hap didn't look relieved when he pulled back, but his haunted expression had softened. His eyes searched Vic's, and what he found there must have been enough. He turned toward the HARP. "It's g-gone offline. Someone w-will notice soon. We h-have to hurry." He bent over, sliding his hands underneath the arms of the HARP, pieces of his head falling back to the floor. Hap pulled the HARP farther into the room. Rambo followed behind him, scooping up the pieces that remained.

Vic stepped out into the hall, looking left and right to make sure they were still alone. They were. He picked up his pack from the ground. Something shifted inside, a metallic *clink* that caused him to pause. He frowned as he lifted the pack, shaking it from side to side. The sound was louder, broken. His eyes widened as he opened the pack furiously.

"Victor?" Nurse Ratched asked. "Your heart rate has elevated drastically. What is wrong?"

He barely heard her. "No," he muttered. "No, please, no, where is it, where is it, *where is it*—" He closed his hand around a familiar cloth and yanked. He'd grabbed the wrong side. The cloth opened as he pulled it out, spraying the remains of the heart onto the floor. That sound. That terrible crunch he'd heard when he'd smashed the pack against the HARP without thinking. It'd been the newly constructed heart breaking once more. The wood had split into four distinct pieces, two of which fell to the floor, the remaining two back into the pack. Wires dangled uselessly. One of the gears—the largest—had snapped completely in half. Another gear rolled down the hall back toward the elevator, hitting a wall before falling over flat against the floor.

"Oh no," Nurse Ratched said. "Victor, it—"

Vic dropped the pack to the floor. He couldn't breathe. He couldn't do anything but stare at the pieces on the floor. They'd come so far.

A tentacle wrapped around his wrist. He didn't look at her. She said, "Victor. It does not matter. It was never about the heart. It is about what we will do for each other. You will build it again. You will make it how it is supposed to be. But it will have to wait until we return to the forest."

Vic wiped his eyes. He glanced back over his shoulder. Hap knew. He'd seen the shattered remains. He stood in the doorway, scowling at the floor, body rigid.

Taking the pack from Nurse Ratched, he went to Hap. They were close, Vic knew. So very close. Taking Hap's hand, he said, "Come on. We need to find Dad while we still have time."

"But how will we get him to come with us?" Rambo asked. "We don't have a heart to give him."

"Then we remind him where he came from and hope for the best."

Hap led them down a series of maze-like hallways. By the time they turned yet another corner, Vic was lost. He couldn't be sure he'd be able to find his way out on his own. Shortly after battling the HARP, they'd had to duck into what turned out to be a storage closet as a group of smooth men passed by. They stood in the dark, listening to the footsteps just on the other side of the door.

"Do you think they know about the HARP?" Rambo asked.

Hap shook his head. "HARPs go offline to r-reset. We h-have t-time, though not much. They'll f-find it before l-long."

Once they were sure the smooth men had gone, Hap opened the door a sliver, staring back out into the hall. He waited a beat before opening the door wide, motioning them through.

They went.

Down a hall. Right. Another hall. Left. *Another hall.*

Vic was about to ask—*demand*—where they were, how much farther they had to go, if they were lost, lost, lost, when Hap stopped suddenly. Vic bumped into him, wincing as Nurse Ratched and Rambo did the same to him. "What is it?" he asked.

Hap had stopped in front of a door. It looked just like all the others: white and inconspicuous, a darkened panel next to it.

But there was one tiny difference.

On this door, in a circle in the center, was the symbol of a tree. It reminded Vic of the trees in the forest around their home, the pine needles carved with such care that he could almost smell them.

Hap reached up with his free hand, tracing over the limbs and trunk of the tree before pressing his hand flat against it and closing his eyes. He said in hushed reverence, "Here. I th-think I remember this. The tree. I asked h-him about it once. A t-tree. Why a t-tree?" He swayed side to side. "He s-said because they were old. Older th-than almost anything else in all the w-world. That after w-we were g-gone, they would r-remain." He opened his eyes. "Giovanni. He's in here. This is his laboratory."

"Are you sure?" Vic asked just as quietly.

Hap pulled his hand away from the tree. "Yes. I'm s-sure."

"Do we knock?" Rambo asked, rocking side to side on top of Nurse Ratched.

Vic stared at the tree before shaking his head slowly. "No. Hap."

Hap didn't hesitate. He pressed his hand against the panel. It lit up underneath his fingers. A deep chime sounded around them, causing Vic to shiver.

The panel flashed green.

The door opened, cool air spilling out and washing over them.

CHAPTER 24

The first thing Vic noticed was how bright it was. Beams of sunlight filtered in through a bay window to their left that rose from the floor to the ceiling, opening out onto the City of Electric Dreams far below them. The city stretched on almost as far as Vic could see, vast and immense. Vertigo swept through him. He swallowed thickly, forcing the nausea away.

It took him a moment to understand why he recognized his surroundings. He'd never been here before, but familiarity tugged at him. It was only then he realized he *had* been here before; not physically, but through the eyes of another. Hap. He was seeing what Hap had when he'd been here, when he'd opened his eyes for the first time, when he'd come back again and again, listening to Vic's father speak.

"Nurse Ratched, are you ready?"

"Yes, Victor. I know what to do."

He moved forward, Hap's hand slipping from his own. He glanced back over his shoulder in time to see Hap smash the panel near the doors they'd just walked through. He arched an eyebrow. Hap shrugged. "They c-can't get in easy now. G-gives us more time just in c-case."

A pair of glass doors stood at the end of the hallway. They opened automatically as Vic approached. He didn't stop. He didn't look back. He didn't have to; he knew the others would follow him wherever he went.

He crossed into a large room filled with machines that beeped, blinking lights flashing over and over again. Hanging from the high ceiling were metal claws used to transport, though they were now unmoving. Vats—another memory, this time of a bunker hidden beneath the earth—lined the far wall, empty, the glass gleaming as if freshly polished. Above a bank of computers sat a gigantic screen running with lines of green code, the cursor blinking. In the upper left corner of the screen sat an image of a man, spinning slowly, arms extended at his sides. His skin was smooth. He had no face, no genitals, no distinguishing characteristics. A blank slate.

Vic took a step toward the screen.

"Hello," a voice said, calm and even. "I apologize. I didn't know I was having any visitors today."

Vic turned, heart in his throat.

Giovanni Lawson stepped from the shadows, a tablet in his hand. His beard rested wonderfully on his chest, the end curled. He wore a white coat with the symbol of a cat and a fox over tan trousers. He smiled, though he looked confused. He glanced from Nurse Ratched and Rambo to Hap, gaze widening slightly before it came to a rest on Vic. His brow furrowed.

Vic whispered, "Dad?"

He blinked. "Dad?" he repeated with an uncertain chuckle. "I think there has been some mistake." He squinted at Vic, looking him up and down. "I may work in Creation, but I've never claimed to be a father." He took another step toward them. He hesitated before shaking his head. "How strange. I feel . . ." He pressed a hand against his chest. "A ghost. A tickle. Familiarity, but I don't know how that could be. I think I would remember creating something so . . . unique. There is a phrase, an expression. When one remembers something they shouldn't."

"Déjà vu," Vic said quietly.

Dad startled. "Yes. That's . . . that's exactly what I mean. You know déjà vu?"

Vic's eyes burned, but he never looked away from his father. "Yes. I know."

Dad said, "Have we met before?" He set down the tablet on the edge of one of the computers. It almost fell, but Dad ignored it. He folded his hands in front of him. "I can't remember seeing you. You are made up of different parts, like scrap. That's no way for an android to be, especially for one such as you. You look so . . . lifelike. Tell me. Who created you? How did they do it? What is your designation?"

"Victor," he said. It took everything he had to keep from launching himself at his father. "My name is Victor."

"Victor," Dad said, rolling the word on his tongue as if tasting it for the first time. "Your name, you say. What a lovely name that is. Whoever made you took their time, aside from the obvious. Perhaps some corners were cut, but you still seem . . . different. I like different."

"I know."

"You do? Forgive me. I'm at a loss. You seem to know me, but I don't know you. My desig . . . name. My name is Gio Lawson. What brings you to me today?" He glanced at Hap, eyes narrowing. "HARP, what have you brought me?"

Hap said, "What b-belongs to you."

"To me?" Dad said, sounding dubious. He looked at Nurse Ratched, then up to Rambo, who waved furiously at him. Dad raised his hand and waved back, wiggling his fingers, though he appeared guarded. "Hello, little one. I haven't seen your kind in quite a long time. And to find you working! Tell me, do you also have a . . . name?" He'd caught himself, Vic knew, from saying designation once more. He was already adapting. It filled Vic with hope, though he dared not clutch on to it too quickly. His father wasn't the same as he'd been before. He held himself differently. He was cautious and moved less like a man and more like a machine. They had to be careful. Dad didn't trust them, though this seemed to stem more from Hap than anything else.

"Rambo!"

"Rambo," Dad said. "I've never heard such a name before. And you, nursing model. Are you—"

"Nurse Ratched," she said.

"Yes, fine, fine. You're also unique. There wouldn't be much work for one such as you these days, would there?" Something stuttered across his face, like a glitch, there and gone before his expression smoothed out once more. Distant, but ever watchful. "No, I don't expect you'd find yourself doing much at all."

"You would be surprised, Giovanni."

Dad's head jerked. "What did you call me?"

"Giovanni," she repeated.

"Why?"

"Is that not your name?"

"It is Gio. My n—designation is Gio. It stands for General Innovation Operative." Dad began to close himself off. Vic could see it the moment it started. It crawled up his face, his mouth a thin line, his eyes shuttering with a mechanical glint. Where before he'd been somewhat loose, relaxed, he now held himself like the smooth men. Firm. Flat. A machine. "HARP," he said. "Why have you come? Do you have authorization to be in Creation?" Then, "You have been damaged. Your skin. Your voice."

"I am h-how I'm s-supposed to be," Hap said.

That caught Dad off guard. "Why, whatever do you mean? HARP, your designation. Now."

"HARP 217."

"217," Dad whispered. "You're . . . you . . ." His gaze grew vacant, sliding askew before correcting with a snap as it hardened. "That's not possible. You were decommissioned. *Decades* ago. I've seen it. I've seen the reports. Orders were given. You . . . you shouldn't be here. I don't know why you've come, but I can do nothing for you. Please leave before I summon the Authority." He turned away, picking up his tablet, shoulders hunched near his ears. "Thank you for visiting me today. But it would be best if you leave. I don't know why you've come here. I don't have time for you. I'm very busy."

Once, when Vic was a child—four, perhaps five—he still struggled to find his voice, to put his thoughts into words. He hated how hard it was, how it would come in fits and starts without rhyme or reason, punctuated with a guttural force that hurt his throat. On one such day—spring, close to summer, so bright and so green—he tried to tell his father about what he'd seen in the forest. A bird. A simple bird, its feathers blue, its beak and talons black. It had cocked its head at Vic from its perch on a tree branch. The sound it made was a trill of warning, wings and feathers ruffled.

He went to his father, his thoughts forming clearly but without a voice. Dad—patient, always patient and kind—had waited, watching, never trying to rush Vic, knowing he needed time to say what he needed to say.

Vic was about to give up, about to deflate and pretend nothing had happened. But then something shifted in his head, pieces interlocking in a way they'd never before. He said, "Bird."

And so softly, so wonderfully, Dad said, "A bird? Tell me."

Vic shifted from side to side, trying to keep hold of the clear thoughts, slippery though they were. He opened his mouth once more, but no sound came out. His face twisted in frustration, breaths coming out in quick pants.

Dad said, "Slow and sure. Think. Focus. Take your time. Easier said than done, I know, but I believe in you. I always have. I always will. You can do this, Victor. I know you can."

"Bird," Vic said again. "Outside. Bird. It . . . yelled. At me. Loud. The bird yelled loud."

"Did it?" Dad asked gently. "Show me."

Dad took him by the hand as they walked out of the ground house. Vic moved with purpose, knowing what he wanted Dad to see. Dad, for his part, never questioned him, never told him to slow down, though he only needed to take one step for every three of Vic's. They stopped underneath a tree. Vic pointed. The bird was still there, turning its head until it stared at them with a black eye. It trilled again, the warning clear.

"Ah," Dad said. "I see. It *is* yelling. But it's doing so for a reason. May I pick you up?"

Vic held his arms toward his father. He felt big hands wrap around his waist as he was lifted into the air. His dad was big, so big that Vic felt as tall as the trees. "There," Dad whispered in his ear. "See the branch the bird is standing on? Look below it. Near the hollow in the tree."

Vic did. There, just below the bird, was a hole, black and gaping in the side of the tree. At first, Vic saw nothing. Dad took a step closer, and Vic began to see little scraps jutting from the hole: grass and mud and twigs and feathers, blue feathers just like the bird's. A nest. Vic watched as a head appeared over the side, similar to the bird on the branch, though smaller, its colors darker.

"He's protecting his young," Dad said. "He doesn't know you're not a threat. That is his mate. She is sitting on eggs, waiting for them to hatch."

"Hatch," Vic muttered.

"Yes. Babies. Soon, there will be babies, and we'll be able to hear their little chirps. What a beautiful sight. What a wonderful gift. Thank you, son. Thank you for showing me."

Vic leaned his head against his father's shoulder, safe and warm, filled with a stirring sense of pride, though he didn't quite know it then. All he knew was that he'd done what he'd set out to do. He'd used his words, had made his father understand. He could do it again, perhaps, in time. But now he was tired.

Dad rubbed a hand up and down his back. "Yes, I think this might be the best day I've had in a very long time. My lovely boy."

They watched as the bird on the branch hopped down toward the hollow. The bird in the nest made a small noise in greeting. Eventually, having decided that his children and mate were safe, the male bird took to the sky, disappearing through the canopy.

That night, as his father put him to bed, Vic said, "Bird. I saw the bird."

And here, now, years and miles away, Victor Lawson watched the man who'd made him, the man who'd created him out of a sense of guilt and loneliness and love, as he walked away. Words were a weapon, he knew, one that had taken him a long time to wield. But he was different than he'd been before. He wasn't that boy. He'd found his voice. This machine—this man—had given it to him.

He said, "Dad."

Dad didn't turn around. He was frozen in place.

Vic took a step toward him. "Please, won't you look at me?" He stopped a short distance away. If he wanted, he could reach out and lay a hand on his father's shoulder. He didn't, tamping down the urge as forcefully as he could.

When Dad spoke, his voice was short, the words clipped. "You have mistaken me for someone else. I am not your father. I am Gio Lawson. I am a member in good standing with the Authority. I create. I build. I work. There is nothing else."

"There is," Vic said. "There is so much more. I promise you. You know what I'm talking about. You know me."

Dad shook his head. "No. No, that's not—"

"Do you dream?"

"I . . . what?"

"Dream," he said again. He remembered his father's words. "It's whispers. Numbers and code. Logic equations. It's a glitch."

Dad turned slowly, a thunderstruck expression on his face. "How did you . . . I am a machine. Machines don't dream. We're not *capable* of dreams."

Vic knew his father better than anyone else. He knew every single line and crease on his face. He knew his thoughts, his tics, his humanity embedded in the body of a machine. And Vic knew when his father was lying. "You do," he said, bordering on desperation. "I know you do. You've told me before. You said that it doesn't always make sense, but you wouldn't change it for anything. It makes you feel alive in ways you can't explain."

IN THE LIVES OF PUPPETS | 377
IN THE LIVES OF PUPPETS | 377

"Who are you?" Dad asked. He started to reach for Vic, but stopped halfway, hands falling back to his sides.

"Someone who loves you," Vic said. "It might not seem like much to you, but you told me once that sometimes, it's the smallest things that can change everything when you least expect it."

And with that, music began to play from behind him.

Beryl Davis, singing about how every road has a turning, that she'd cried for you. It filled the air as the voice crackled from Nurse Ratched's speakers.

Without a stutter in his voice, Hap said, "You told me I could choose who I wanted to be."

"You said I was brave!" Rambo cried.

"You built us a home," Nurse Ratched said. "We are here to make sure you remember it."

"What is this?" Dad whispered. "What . . . are . . . you . . ." He closed his eyes. "This song. This music. Why? Why do I think I've heard it before? The melody. The notes. Synchronicity. Simple. Concise. That's not . . ."

"You *have* heard this," Vic said, taking another step toward his father. "This and every other song I could find for you. You fixed it. Your record player. We were thinking too big. Too grand. It was the hand crank. That's all it was. The hand crank."

Dad said, "No. No, no, no. Logic failure. Error. Error. I am not who you want. I am not who you're looking for. I am not—"

"You are," Vic said, and he reached for his father.

Dad looked at his hand, but he didn't try to back away.

Their fingers touched. His skin was warm.

Vic said, "I found you. I found you. *I found*—"

An alarm began to blare, fierce and so loud it felt as if it would shatter Vic's ear drums.

"WARNING," a voice rang out from somewhere above them. "WARNING. THE BENEVOLENT TOWER HAS BEEN INFILTRATED. WARNING. WARNING. THE

BENEVOLENT TOWER HAS BEEN INFILTRATED. INITIATING LOCKDOWN PROTOCOL SEVEN SIX DASH NINE NINE FOUR."

Steel grates slammed down across the windows, casting the laboratory in semidarkness as the alarm continued to shriek. Vic jumped when a hand closed around his wrist. He looked back to see his father staring at him with a blank expression. "You," Dad said. "This is because of you. You aren't supposed to be here. Don't move. The Authority is coming." He began to drag Vic toward the bank of computers. Before Vic could stop him, he pressed a button and spoke. "Creation has been infiltrated. I repeat, Creation has been—"

Movement from behind Vic. Before he could shout in warning, Hap knocked him out of the way, reaching for Dad. Dad stumbled back as Hap attacked, Vic staring up at them in horror from the floor. "*Don't!*" he shouted.

Dad moved quicker than Vic had ever seen him move before. He blocked every hit Hap tried to land, beard flying up around his shoulder. Hap went for a right hook and looked comically startled when Dad ducked down. The momentum caused Hap to spin almost completely in the other direction. Before he could recover, Dad kicked him in the back, sending him crashing into the bank of computers.

They had no choice.

They had to do what the Blue Fairy had asked.

"Nurse Ratched!" Vic shouted. "*Now.*"

Her compartment slid open. One of her tentacles unspooled. At the end, caught in her grip, was a small, silver rectangle. Engraved into the top: blue wings that belonged to a fairy.

This, the Blue Fairy whispered in the back of Vic's head, a memory from a sphere surrounded by screens. *This is my greatest secret. My greatest treasure aside from you, Victor. You never asked for this, I know, never wanted to become more than what you already are, but you must realize what you symbolize. You are a dream. A hope. A remembrance of what we once were. And with a little luck, what we could be once again. It doesn't matter where it came from. All that matters is what it can do. We do not fight with swords. We do not fight with guns or bombs or biological warfare. To fix what is in disrepair sometimes means breaking it completely and starting over again.*

What is it?

An infection. A virus capable of destroying all that they have built. This is my gift to you: the power to change the world. With this, you can wipe the memories of every machine in the City of Electric Dreams and beyond. However far the Authority's reach extends—and even I don't know just how far that is—once uploaded, the virus will spread across the neural network until it leaves nothing in its wake but husks. You have a choice, Victor. You can choose to go it alone. You can choose to attempt your rescue without my help. And perhaps you will succeed, though I can't see how. With this, you have the chance to save us all. You never asked to be who you are. I know that. But I'm asking you to be who I know you're supposed to be: human. You are the last of your kind. And with this gift, you can ensure that we all have a chance to make a difference.

He whispered, *What must I do?*

The connection, the collective consciousness, the minds of the machines, all exist in Creation. Take my gift. Upload it in Creation. It will spread far and wide. It will give us a chance for a better future, one where we can choose for ourselves.

A tear trickled down his cheek. *I don't know if I can do this.*

I know, dear boy. Which is why I must warn you. With all great tasks comes sacrifice. The upload will not work unless you are connected to the neural network. And you yourself are not capable of such a thing. You lack the necessary components.

He jerked his head back. *What?*

She turned toward the others. Nurse Ratched. Hap. Rambo.

It must be one of you. One of you must do what Victor cannot. One of you must upload the virus. And with that, you will lose all you have known.

No, Vic said, *No. I won't let you. I won't let you do this. They are my* friends. *You can't—*

I will do it, Nurse Ratched said.

You won't, he snarled, head and heart breaking.

She ignored him. She rolled toward the Blue Fairy. *I will do this.*

They bowed before her. *Are you sure?*

Yes. I am quite capable.

No! Vic cried. *Nurse Ratched, listen to me. There has to be another way. There has to be—*

All is not lost, the Blue Fairy said. *We can help her. I can download her consciousness. A duplicate, if you will. Once the task is complete, and her memory wiped, you can return her to her current state. She will remember you. She will remember all of you.*

You can't promise that. You can't promise anything. It could go wrong. Everything could go wrong, and she could—

Nurse Ratched touched his cheek with one of her tentacles. *I have made my choice, Victor. I know what I am doing. Please do not take this away from me. You brought me back once. I know you can do it again. All I ask is that you do not leave me behind. I hate this city. It smells bad. I want to see the forest again.*

Nurse Ratched. I . . .

I know. But I do this for you. Because of what you've done for me. Let me help you. Let me help Rambo and Hap. Let me help Gio.

He wiped his eyes. *I can't lose you.*

You will not, she said. *I am not done with you yet. When you are old and gray, you will need me to monitor your health to ensure you live longer than any human ever has. I will be by your side. I promise.*

"I promise," he said as the alarms blared around them, as Dad and Hap fought with devastating blows, as Rambo screamed for Nurse Ratched to *hurry, you need to* hurry, they're coming, they're *coming*!

Nurse Ratched stopped in front of Victor. He looked up at her. On her screen were the words YOU ARE MY FRIEND. She said, "When you found me, it was the greatest day of my life, though I did not know it then. I have watched you grow into the man you have become. In the end, that is all that matters. In case this does not work, in case you cannot bring me back, I need you to know that you are precious to me. And if you tell anyone I said that, I will drill you until there is nothing left but bone and gristle."

Hap grunted as Dad threw him across the room. He skidded along the floor, crashing into Rambo, upending him onto his back, wheels spinning.

Nurse Ratched rolled toward the computers, the silver box raised.

Vic shouted after her.

She didn't stop.

Until Dad rushed toward her, curling in on himself. His shoulder smashed into her side, denting her casing. She fell end over end, her screen cracking, her tentacles flailing. The silver box slipped from her grasp, bouncing along the floor, coming to a rest in front of Hap and Rambo.

Pounding on the doors down the hall. Voices, so many voices. *Let us in, let us* in.

Dad started toward them. Vic pushed himself forward, landing awkwardly on his side, wrapping his arms around Dad's leg. Dad looked down at him, a frown on his face. "What are you? What do you think you're doing? You can't—"

"Nurse Ratched!" Vic shouted. "Get up, get up, *get up!*"

She tried to right herself. She tried to push herself up. She fell back down, one of her tentacles snapping with an electrical snarl, skittering along the floor.

Dad bent over, gripping Vic by the throat, lifting him off the floor. Vic kicked as hard as he could, slapped at his father's arm, but it was no use. The grip around his neck tightened. Lights flickered across his vision, stars as bright as he'd ever seen. He slid his hands down Dad's arms until they came to his chest. He tore at his clothing. He heard the fabric rip. Skin, taut and hot underneath. He tapped his finger against the breastbone. The panel slid open.

Once upon a time, a machine named Giovanni Lawson built himself a heart made of wood and metal. Crafted with care and all the knowledge he had, he'd created a source of power unlike anything the world had ever seen.

And he'd destroyed it to save his son.

Now, in its place, a battery. It was square with blinking lights and wires that stretched throughout.

Vic pressed his hand against it. It burned his skin, but he didn't pull away.

He gasped, "Dad."

The hand around his throat loosened slightly. Dad whispered, "I . . ."

The voices grew louder. They were through the door. They were coming.

Vic said, "Please, listen to me. You are my f—"

Something crashed into the both of them. Vic landed roughly on the floor, helmet bouncing against the surface, causing Vic's vision to white out, his ears ringing.

Dazed, he sat up slowly.

Through the glass doors at the other end of the laboratory, dozens upon dozens of smooth men. Crowded against the doors, the ones in front beat their fists against the glass. The glass began to crack, zigzags spreading up and down its length. One smooth man pressed his face against the glass, nose squashing flat as his mouth opened, tongue flicking out.

They were too late.

They had lost.

He looked over to see what had hit him. Rambo. Rambo had thrown himself as hard as he could at Dad and Vic, knocking them both off their feet. Dad lay on his back, Rambo crying out, "I'm sorry, I'm sorry, I'm *sorry*," as he brought his arms down again and again. "Please don't be mad at me! I feel just *awful* about this!" Dad tried to grab him, but Rambo was too quick.

"Victor."

He turned.

Hap stood in front of the computer bank.

In his hand, a silver box with blue wings.

Vic's eyes widened.

Hap smiled quietly. He said, "You g-gave me life. You gave me friends. You gave me p-purpose. My strings have b-been cut, and it's because of you."

Vic screamed for him as he turned.

But Hap didn't hesitate.

Vic pushed himself up, knowing it was already too late, but moving like he had a chance.

Hap pressed his hand against a panel. It lit up around his hand as the Hysterically Angry Puppet connected to the neural network. His head rocked back, mouth agape. The screen lit up above him. "Welcome home, HARP 926," a voice said as the glass doors shattered, as the smooth men burst through, hands extended like claws.

"Not my home," he whispered, and inserted the silver box into the port.

The screen went white.

Vic sat against the wall, arms wrapped around his legs. Eyes squeezed shut as he tried to breathe, floating away on a current he could not stop. He didn't even try. It was easier this way.

"Vic?"

He ignored it. He was very tired. He wanted to sleep. Perhaps if he could sleep, he could dream. He would be in the forest. His father would be smiling in his chair, listening to the music from the record player as it crackled and snapped. Rambo would be humming along, off-key. Nurse Ratched would tell him to hush, but she wouldn't really mean it.

And Hap. Hap would be sitting next to him on the floor, their shoulders pressed together, their hands joined between them.

"Vic."

He raised his head. Nurse Ratched and Rambo stood before him. Rambo reached out carefully and touched his leg. "Are you all right?"

He looked beyond them. Moving through the room without purpose were machines. Androids. Robots. The smooth men, dozens upon dozens, all looking dazed, confused. Blank. Eyes vacant. One bumped into a wall. Others—at least ten—stood in a shivering circle, their heads pressed together as they whispered nonsensically. Beyond the shattered doors, even more lining the hallway, alive but hollow. They whispered, they groaned, they screamed, the sounds echoing around them.

Dad, sitting on the floor, hands folded in his lap, blinking slowly.

And Hap, lying on his back, eyes wide but unseeing. His heart had exploded, the pieces bursting through his chest. Shards of metal and wood littered the floor around him. A broken gear—its teeth glinting in the low light—lay next to his hand.

Vic closed his eyes once more.

"We have to go," Nurse Ratched said. "We need to leave. We cannot do this on our own. We need you, Victor. We need your help with Gio and Hap."

"It worked," Vic whispered before swallowing the bile in his throat.

"It did," Nurse Ratched said. "Though not as we expected it to. Hap did what I could not. I apologize." On her broken screen, a red heart flickered, cracked down the middle.

"I should not have let that happen. I hurt, Victor. Everything hurts. And it is not because I have sustained damage. I must not be as sociopathic as I believed, because I am filled with sorrow."

"I think you're full of garbage," Rambo said, beeping mournfully. "Like me. Vic, why didn't you tell me there could be sad garbage? It hurts, even though I'm not very full."

Vic sobbed, once, a great choking sound. His shoulders shook. "I don't know what to do."

"I have an idea," Nurse Ratched said. "One that you will not like, but you must trust me. I believe it will work. All it will take is a little luck and my enormous brain. Come, now. Dry your eyes. All will be well."

"Promise?"

And though he knew she couldn't, she said, "I promise."

She pushed him toward his father. "Rambo and I will see to Hap. Divest yourself of your disguise. You no longer have need of it."

He did as she asked. He removed the helmet. The metal sheets on his arms and legs. He struggled with the vest until Rambo rose behind him and cut through the tangled straps. It fell to the floor with a hollow clang. Vic never looked at it again.

He was careful, cautious as he approached a solitary smooth man, the one who had bumped into the wall. Now turned, he stood, knees slightly bent, arms dangling at his sides. Vic kept his distance, waiting to see any spark of life in the smooth man's eyes. There was none. He stared right through Victor, mouth slightly agape. Victor reached out and touched his hand. "I'm sorry," he said. "The Blue Fairy. Find the Blue Fairy."

The smooth man said, "The Blue . . . Fairy?"

"Yes. They will help you."

"Help . . . me."

"Yes."

The smooth man wandered away. Vic did not watch where he went, turning his attention to his father. He knelt down before him, knees popping. Vic hurt all over, but he couldn't yet rest. He prepared himself for what remained. He was startled when he saw a flash of awareness in Dad's eyes. "Hello."

"Hello," Dad said. "I am designation General Innovation Operative. I have many functions. I can build. I can create. I can be helpful." His brow furrowed. "Why are your eyes leaking? Do you have a malfunction?"

"Yes," Vic said hoarsely. "I am malfunctioning. Will you help me?"

"Yes," Dad said. "I can be very help . . . I already said that, didn't I? I am sorry. I am . . . confused. Am I new? Are you my creator?"

"No. I am your friend."

"I see. I am trying to access my memory core, but there seems to be a fault in my biochip. I do not know how to fix it."

"I do."

"You do?"

"Yes."

His brow smoothed out as he smiled. "Then I shall help you if you will help me."

Vic took him by the arm, lifting him up. Dad wobbled left, then right. He stumbled, but Vic caught him.

He led Dad toward the others, leaning down and scooping up his pack, hoisting it over his shoulder. It was almost too heavy to carry, but he ground his teeth together and forced himself through it.

Rambo had gathered the remains of Hap's heart, scooping them up with care and storing them inside him. "I will keep it safe," he said sadly. "Until we can fix it."

Vic couldn't speak. He watched as Nurse Ratched lifted Hap on top of her, his arms and legs dangling. "There," she said. "That will do for now. Follow me."

He did.

They moved through the broken glass door to the hallway. The smooth men did not move, whispering as they walked between them. No one reached for them. No one tried to stop them. The smooth men watched as Vic led his family out of Creation, but they did not intercede. The alarm had cut off. All was quiet apart from the sounds of treads, footsteps, and the whispers.

No one spoke as Nurse Ratched led them back to the lift, pressing the buttons on the panel once inside.

Instead of descending, the elevator rose.

Vic looked at her.

"Trust me," she said.

A moment later, the elevator came to a stop. The doors opened. "One hundred and twenty-fifth floor," a voice said. "Launch bay."

They exited the elevator, careful of Hap's head.

Vic looked at his father. "Are you ready?"

Dad said, "What is your designation? I feel like . . . do I know you?"

Vic tried to smile but failed miserably. "Victor," he said. "Victor Lawson."

"Victor," Dad repeated, storing the information.

"Come on."

They stepped off the elevator into a small room with screens lining the wall to the left, each displaying a different image. Below them sat a spider machine, similar to the one they'd spoken with at the front door of the tower. Its sphere was white. It said, "Hello. Hello. Hello. I do not know what I am. Can you tell me?"

"No," Nurse Ratched said. "You may leave and find out for yourself."

The spider machine hesitated before it scurried away.

Vic looked up at the screens. His stomach fell to his feet when he saw what they showed. "Are you sure about this?"

"I am not," Nurse Ratched said. "But the alternative is walking back."

"I don't know about this," Rambo said, covering his sensors with his arms. "I think I've gone as high in the air as I want to. What if we crash and die?"

"Then at least it will be over quickly," Nurse Ratched said.

"That doesn't make me feel any better."

"Good. It was not meant to." She rolled toward doors on the opposite end of the room. She didn't look back. "Are you coming?"

"Is that a whale?" Dad asked, pointing at the screen.

"Yes," Vic said. "And it's going to swallow us whole."

Medical Nurse Model Six-Ten-JQN Series Alpha, also known as Registered Automaton To Care, Heal, Educate, and Drill, did not know how to fly.

Thankfully, the Terrible Dogfish didn't need her to. Once, Vic might have marveled over the flying machine, how enormous it was, how he could spend weeks and months and still not have explored every inch of it. But now, after all he'd seen, after all he'd done, he couldn't find the strength to care much at all about the flying whale.

"It has an automatic flight control system," Nurse Ratched said, moving around the panels and controls on the flight deck of the Terrible Dogfish. "As long as I input the coordinates, it should see us home."

"How long?" Rambo asked.

"Seventeen hours."

Vic barely heard them. He sat his father in one of the chairs, strapping him in. "Stay there," he said.

"Yes, Victor," Dad said. "I will stay here."

He left his father behind. He glanced out the row of windows at the front of the flight deck. The sky was blue with thin, wispy clouds on the horizon. The sun was shining. It looked like a normal day. He tried not to think about the city below them and the machines therein. He hoped the Blue Fairy would stay true to their word and help the unshackled as best they could. He had done his part.

And though he didn't know it then, it would be the last time Victor Lawson ever laid eyes on the City of Electric Dreams. As the Terrible Dogfish awoke around them with a frightening rumble, he looked out the thick windows beyond the launchpad to the sprawling metropolis below. The buildings, the towers, the pyramid in the distance, the sun glinting off the black glass. Though he could not see the machines in the streets, he knew they would have the same lost expressions on their faces that the smooth men had. For a moment, a dreadful wave of guilt washed over him. He wondered if he was any better than them, any better than the humans who had once called this place home.

He moved toward a slumped figure, already strapped into a chair, head lolling. The whale untethered from the Benevolent Tower as Victor sat in the chair next to HARP 217, the Hysterically Angry Puppet, Hap, that was. His eyes were open though they held no light. Vic belted himself into the chair before taking Hap's hand in his own as the Terrible Dogfish left the City of Electric Dreams behind and headed toward home.

Vic closed his eyes, squeezing Hap's lifeless hand as he whispered, "What do you do if you've forgotten all you know?"

PART IV

YOU START AGAIN FROM THE BEGINNING

In an old and lonely forest, far away from almost everything, sat a curious dwelling.

At the base of a grove of massive trees was a small, square building made of brick, overtaken by ivy and moss. Who it had belonged to was anyone's guess, but from the looks of it, it had been abandoned long ago. It wasn't until a man named Giovanni Lawson (who wasn't actually a man at all) came across it while making his way through the forest that it was remembered with any purpose.

He stood in front of this strange find, listening as the birds sang in the branches high above. "What's this?" he asked. "Where did you come from?"

He went inside, passing carefully through the door hanging off its hinges. The windows were shattered. Grass and weeds grew up through the warped wooden floor. The roof had partially collapsed, and the sun shone through on a pile of leaves that almost reached the ceiling. At the top of the leaf pile, a golden flower had bloomed, stretching toward the sunlight streaming through the exposed rafters.

"It's perfect," he said aloud, although he was very much alone. "Yes, I think this will do just fine. How strange. How wonderful."

And so it was, both strange and wonderful and *his*. In the decades that followed, it would become a home, and not just for him. When his chest began to ache around his newly created heart, he felt the deep despair of guilt at all he'd done, and the ever-encroaching loneliness.

It took another three years. Three years of the ache in his

chest only growing stronger. Three years of realizing how quiet it was, how he longed to hear another voice aside from his own. Three years in which he would look out the window of his laboratory to see that it was snowing, when it had seemed the forest had just been caught in the throes of summer.

But here is where the story differs: no man came from the forest, no woman clutching a bundle of rags that held a secret child. Giovanni was not entrusted with a boy from strangers who had then fled into the trees. He was entrusted with a gift from a Blue Fairy, atonement for what he'd created. A hope. A spark. A wish.

He never knew loneliness, after.

"Victor," he said as he held his son in his arms. "Your name shall be Victor. Victor Lawson. What do you think?" He loved this boy as if he were his own. And he *was*. No man or machine could take that from him. He lied, in the end, lied about where he'd come from, lied about what he'd done, lied about how Victor came to be, but he did it because for the first time in his long, long life, he knew what love was: complex, vast, extraordinarily frightening. It was in Victor's little toes. It was in Victor's little face. It was in Victor's little hands, reaching.

And for the rest of his life, he would think about the crisp autumn day when his child was given a name, and all was well with the world. The loneliness he'd felt—massive and profound—was chased away as if such a concept had never existed at all.

But it did.

It *did* exist.

And now the weight of it fell upon his son.

Snow had fallen, blanketing the forest in a blinding white, causing the limbs of the trees to bow toward the ground. It was cold when Victor Lawson stepped from the whale's mouth, his breath steaming like a persistent fog. Before him, remains: the blackened bones of what had once been their home, pieces of jutting metal like teeth as if the corpse of a great beast lay hidden just underneath the earth.

"Where are we?" another voice asked, and Vic glanced over his shoulder.

Dad stood there, the gaping maw of the whale surrounding him. He looked so small in comparison, and Vic had never felt so lonely in his life.

"We lived here, once," Vic said. "Do you remember?"

He looked around the clearing: the broken trees, the cracked brick of the ground house, wires dangling from branches, shattered glass sparkling in the winter sun. "No," Dad finally said. "I do not remember."

Vic nodded, teeth grinding together painfully as he breathed.

They did not stay. Vic thought about it, considered starting again and rebuilding what his father had created, but in the end, the memory of what had come before proved to be too great. Though he wanted to believe no machines would come for them, he couldn't take the chance. Making quick work, Vic and Nurse Ratched and Rambo salvaged what they could, loading it up into the Terrible Dogfish.

It was Nurse Ratched who found it. Buried under a layer of broken glass and pieces of the collapsed roof, a cracked screen. At the bottom, a little tray partially open. Inside, the glimmer of a disc with two words faintly visible.

Top Hat.

Rambo screamed. After he'd calmed himself, he asked if it still worked.

"Only one way to find out," Nurse Ratched said.

That night, on the Terrible Dogfish, Jerry Travers and Dale Tremont were cheek to cheek. Dad watched without speaking, head cocked.

In the belly of the great whale, another machine lay silent, unmoving.

They left their former home behind, snow whipping in a white-out as the whale rose above the clearing into a deep blue winter sky. Heading north and into the wilds, they flew above the forest. Even with all he'd seen and done, somehow, Victor still marveled at the sight of it, the winter woods stretching as far as the eye could see. It did not bring with it the uncertainty the City of Electric Dreams had. That was unknown: this was the forest, his home.

It took them two hours before they found something suit-able: a mostly flat, empty stretch of snow-covered earth. Large old-growth trees surrounded three sides of the clearing. The re-maining side butted up against a sheer rock face at least forty feet high. It wasn't like where they'd come from. It was different.

"Come on," Vic said, wiping his eyes. "We have work to do."

Once, a machine named Giovanni Lawson had made a home where one should not exist. Decades later, his son and the rest of their family endeavored to do the same.

They did not build up and into the trees, for there was no need. They had shelter in the form of the Terrible Dogfish, the skin and skeleton keeping the chill at bay. As winter wore on around them, they spent their days cataloguing every inch of the flying machine, Nurse Ratched plugged in and soaking up information. By the end of the first week, she was an expert in the inner workings of the Terrible Dogfish, and could control it however she pleased. She proved this by providing a demon-stration of the whale's weapon systems. One moment, a small tree stood in the snow, and the next, it exploded, wood and snow and dirt flying in the air.

As the others stared dumbfounded around her, Nurse

Ratched said, "Oops. On the bright side, it will make hunting for food easier."

Rambo would disappear and reappear at random intervals, bursting with excitement, regaling them with stories of his journeys into the bowels of the machine, traveling to places that no one but him could fit into. He spoke of long, narrow crawlspaces made of metal, of buttons he was too afraid to push in case they started a self-destruct sequence.

Dad followed Victor. Sometimes he asked what Victor was doing. Other times, he was silent, watching. At the end of the second week, Victor grunted as he tried to lift a heavy section of shelving on his own. Muscles straining, sweat dripping down his brow, he was about to let go when the shelves rose up and up as if they weighed nothing. He looked over.

Dad held the shelving. He said, "I can help."

Victor swallowed past the lump in his throat. "Can you?"

"Yes," Dad said. "I have many functions."

They did not speak again for the rest of the day.

It started with a chunk of wood, square and smooth, the lines of grain pronounced. Vic held it in his hands, turning it this way and that. He could see what it would become with time and patience.

He sat against the bay windows in the Terrible Dogfish, back against cold glass. Outside, thick snow fell, fat flakes that spun and swirled in the sharp wind. Music poured from speakers, Nurse Ratched yet again playing those sweet, sweet horns, all kinds of blue. Rambo was somewhere in the whale, telling them he wanted to see if he could get to the tail today.

Dad sat in one of the chairs in front of the controls to the Terrible Dogfish. Every now and then, he'd press a button just to see what it would do. Victor was aware of him, but his focus was on the wood in his hands.

Which was why he jumped a little when Dad spoke, that

ever-present ache in his chest tightening as the wood slid from his hands and bounced on the floor. "What did you say?"

"You are sad."

Vic picked up the wood, not lifting his head. "What do you mean?"

"It leaks from you," Dad said. "I've never seen such a thing before. Is that what it means to be what you are?"

They'd told him of Vic's humanity a few days after arriving back in the forest. Nurse Ratched thought—though she warned the chances were practically nonexistent—that perhaps it would help Dad remember. It didn't, though Dad hadn't seemed surprised. He'd merely nodded and said, "I knew there was something different about you," before that awful vacant expression returned. He was a blank slate, waiting to be programmed. Vic tried not to be hurt by it, but he couldn't stop it. They hadn't told him who he was to Victor, or what he'd done. It was too soon, the words stuck in Vic's throat.

"It's part of it," he said now. "Sometimes, I'm sad for no reason at all." He didn't know if others had felt that way. He had no one to ask. Anyone like him was long gone.

"Oh," Dad said. Then, "That must be confusing."

"It is."

Dad smiled, though it wasn't the same as it'd been before. Mechanical, like he thought it was expected of him. "Is it a problem that can be fixed?"

"No," Vic said. "Not completely. It will always be there no matter what I do. But I don't mind."

"Why?"

He looked down at the piece of wood. "Because it reminds me that I'm alive. Of what I've lost. And it gives me purpose, so long as I don't let it consume me."

"What purpose?" Dad asked, sounding curious. He almost sounded like he was before, always questioning. It was a lie, of course.

"To set things right."

IN THE LIVES OF PUPPETS | 399

There were worse days too.

Nurse Ratched found him sitting in a corner, face in his hands, Hap's body lying under a sheet on the table before him. Vic had uncovered him, pulled the sheet from his face, only to see Hap's eyes open, unseeing. It had sent Vic spiraling.

Nurse Ratched waited, knowing that Vic needed to find his way back on his own. He did, eventually, and in a hoarse voice, said, "I can't do this."

"You can," she replied. "I know you can. Gio taught you how. Like father, like son."

That's what he was afraid of. "Am I like them?" he asked. "Am I a Creation Operative? Am I a HARP?"

"No, Victor," she said. "You are human."

"What if that's worse?" he whispered.

Instead of answering, she played Miles Davis. It made everything blue.

If he wasn't his father, then he'd been a puppet controlled by another, even if it had gotten him what he wanted. He wasn't a savior. He was not a myth, a legend, a hope of a dying world as the Coachman had proclaimed. He was not God. He was not immortal. Even now, time slipped through his fingers as if it were nothing.

Vic's first attempt to find the shape of a heart in the wood ended badly; it didn't remotely resemble what he was trying to create. Uneven, off-putting, he threw it against the wall. It cracked and split, falling to the floor.

"I can't focus," he snarled at Nurse Ratched and Rambo as he paced on the bridge of the Terrible Dogfish. "I can't *think*." He banged his fist against the side of his head. "I don't know what I'm doing. I can't make it do what I want to. I've forgotten what it looked like and I just can't *think*."

Rambo gathered up the pieces, holding them close. Then he surprised them all. "I might know what to do."

Leading them into the whale, Rambo stopped in front of a panel near the floor at the end of a long metal walkway. When he pushed against it, the panel slid to the side, revealing a small storage space. Inside, a burlap sack. Rambo pulled it out and spilled its contents onto the floor.

Pieces of Dad's former heart. Hap's too. Cracked wood. Bent metal. A pile of gears, some broken, some whole. Vic couldn't move.

"Why did you keep this?" Nurse Ratched asked.

Rambo nudged one of the gears. "Because Gio and Vic taught me we don't leave anything behind that could be useful. Vic said he was going to try and make a new heart, so I figured it would be a good idea to keep the old parts just in case he needed them." He paused. "Is that all right?"

"You kept Gio's heart with you this whole time?" Nurse Ratched asked.

"Yep," Rambo said. "Hap's too, after it blew up. Maybe it won't be like it was before, but—"

"What if there's a chance?" Vic whispered.

"Exactly!" Rambo said. "I'm sorry I didn't tell you, Vic, but I didn't know if it'd work or not. What do you think? Will it help?"

Vic picked Rambo up and held him close. "Thank you."

Rambo beeped happily. "Aw, anything for you."

He started again, this time using the pieces from Dad's former heart. He still got frustrated, still believed he could never get it right, but he did not stop, even when every part of him screamed that he'd never succeed. As winter moved toward spring, he carried it with him wherever he went, a reminder that his work was not yet done.

Dad found the inner workings of the Terrible Dogfish to be extremely fascinating. It was as if parts of him long asleep were beginning to wake up. None of the parts were the ones that Victor wanted most, but if it had to start somewhere, at least it was with this.

"It's lovely," Dad said one day, staring at lines of code on a monitor before him. "All these numbers. It feels like . . ." His fingers danced along the keyboard. Then, "I'm very good at making things. Have I told you that?"

"Yes," Vic said. "You have."

Dad's fingers paused. "I thought as much. It's . . . strange." He resumed typing.

Vic didn't dare to hope. "What is?"

"Creating. It fills me with . . . I don't know." He frowned. "It is as if I am standing in the brightest light I've ever seen."

"That is how creating feels," Victor said, a bittersweet ache in his chest. Apparently, he'd dared to hope after all. "When you make something, it gives you a sense of pride. Accomplishment." Then, an idea. "This is yours. You can do with it whatever you want. Make whatever you wish."

"Whatever I wish?" He glanced over his shoulder at Victor, and for a moment, it was as if his father was with him again, whole. "What if I wish for impossible things?"

"Then you're doing it right. It always seems impossible when you first start."

Dad cocked his head. "You are very smart."

Vic sighed. "For a human?"

"No. There is no qualifier. You are very smart."

He didn't move when Vic threw himself at him, hugging him as hard as he could. Dad's arms stayed at his sides. That was fine. That was okay. It was enough, Vic told himself as he buried his face in his father's beard.

He held on for dear life.

A beat.

Two.

Three.

And then Dad hugged him back. "I like this," he said quietly. "I like this quite a lot. Can we do it again?"

Vic trembled. "Anytime you want."

One night, as the first blossoms were beginning to peek through the crusts of snow, Vic went to a room on the Terrible Dogfish. He kept the lights off as he pulled the sheet covering Hap, tugging it down to his chest. It was the first thing he'd fixed, knowing it was easier than a heart. The skin that had torn when Hap's heart exploded had been too shredded to repair, the panel covering his power cavity broken. He'd replaced them with wood, knowing Hap would like it when he awoke.

If he awoke.

He climbed onto the table next to Hap, curling against him, making himself as small as he could. Hap was cold, skin like ice, but Vic didn't mind. He pulled the sheet back over them and lay his head on Hap's shoulder.

"I walked through the woods today," he whispered. "And I turned to point out a bird in the trees, but you weren't there."

Hap didn't reply.

Vic stayed there until morning when the winter sun began rising as it always did.

The snows were mostly gone when he finished the first heart.

Born of desperation and rage, it was harsher than the previous heart, the lines sharper, more angled, the base a pointed tip capable of slicing skin. But that made sense: its creator was not the same as he'd been before. He was angrier. Sadder. Braver.

Five gears: two bigger, three smaller. One for Dad. One for

Vic. And Nurse Ratched and Rambo and Hap. And at its center, a tiny wooden hatch that opened to reveal a smooth white strip that waited for a drop of life.

He did not tell the others right away, wanting to be sure before he let himself hope. As Vic returned from the forest on a cool spring afternoon two days after he finished the heart, he came across a sight he'd never seen before.

A tree—an old, tall oak—stood in the woods, limbs shaggy with burgeoning leaves. But it was the moving colorful trunk that caught Vic's gaze. It took him a moment to realize it wasn't the trunk that was moving, but the dozens of butterflies upon it. Monarchs, gold and orange and black, their wings shivering.

He showed them the heart.

Nurse Ratched said, "I knew you could do it."

"Will it make them like they used to be?" Rambo asked.

"I don't know," Vic said.

"And we will not know unless we try," Nurse Ratched said.

They told Dad what Victor had made. When Vic showed the heart to him, he took it in his hands, turning it over. "You did this?"

"Yes," Vic said, feeling like a child again, hoping for his father's approval.

"It's wonderful," Dad said. "Who is it for?"

"You."

He came willingly, hand clutching Victor's as he sat in a chair in one of the many rooms in the Terrible Dogfish. Nurse Ratched helped him lift his shirt up and over his head, and when asked, he tapped his breastbone, opening the compartment in his chest, revealing his power source: a circular battery lined with blinking lights.

"Will this hurt?" Dad asked. A question he wouldn't have thought to ask even a month ago. Learning, always learning.

"I don't know," Victor said. "I know you have no reason to trust me, but I'm going to help you—"

"I trust you, Victor," Dad said. "You have cared for me. You've given me a home. If it hurts, I'll know it is not done on purpose."

"But it is," Vic insisted, needing him to understand. "It's not a gift. It's an affliction. A burden. It can weigh you down, make you feel like you're being torn apart. There might be days when you hate it"—*hate me,* though Vic couldn't bring himself to say it out loud—"and you might wish you'd never been given it."

Dad said, "Do you?"

"Do I what?"

"Wish you'd never been given this . . . affliction."

"It's messy," he said quietly, honestly. "Complicated. Chaotic. One moment strong like steel, and the next fragile as glass."

Dad mulled over this for a moment. Then, "You will be with me?"

"Yes," Victor said. "Yes."

Vic helped his father lie back in his chair. Dad closed his eyes as Vic pushed his beard to the side. Nurse Ratched was at the ready next to him, the tools on her tentacles extended. "It'll be like going to sleep," Vic told his father.

"Will I dream?" Dad whispered.

"Yes," Vic said, even though he wasn't sure.

Dad closed his eyes. "I think I would like that."

Carefully removing the battery from Dad's chest took time, patience. Vic's hands did not shake. Once the battery was removed, the light in Dad's eyes faded, his hands lax and unmoving. His mouth parted slightly, a hint of teeth behind his lips.

Nurse Ratched brought Vic the heart as Rambo touched the gears with the tip of his pincer. The only time anyone spoke was when Vic asked for light, or for Nurse Ratched to solder the wiring as he connected the heart to the machine. He didn't know how long it took, only that by the end, his neck was stiff, back sore, hands littered with little cuts and scratches.

Nurse Ratched inspected his work, scanning the heart and pronouncing it satisfactory. "One last thing," she said.

"Blood?" Rambo asked.

Blood. A cornerstone in the building blocks of life. The thing that had almost gotten him killed time and time again. It was not magic; science left little room for such things. But even Victor wondered if that was the complete truth. If his father was right, and there was power in blood—the history of an entire people in a drop of plasma, cells, and platelets—then Dad's heart was the lock, and Victor was the key.

The only key.

He did not hesitate to prick his finger, deep red welling against the lighter brown skin of his finger pad. Victor pressed it against the white strip in the center of his father's heart, the blood soaking in, spreading like a blooming spring flower.

The gears jerked once, twice, and then began to move, teeth latching on, spinning in tandem. Dad's body trembled as the chest compartment slid closed, arms and legs twitching as if a low current ran through him. Victor stepped back, the whale groaning around him as it settled. Nurse Ratched said, "Engaging Empathy Protocol. There, there, Gio. You are waking up. Slow and steady. You are a good patient. I enjoy working with you."

Vic gasped as Dad blinked. Again. And again. And again. He smacked his lips, grimacing as he did so. As they looked on, Dad raised his hand toward the ceiling. His fingers did not shake.

Rambo said, "Gio, is that you?"

Dad lowered his hand and turned his head. He smiled at Rambo. "Hello, again. Did it work? I must admit, I don't feel different than I did—" He seized suddenly, body bowing, legs skittering against the chair. Eyes bulging, his head snapping side to side, Dad opened his mouth and words fell out, tumbling end over end in a guttural exhalation. "Humanity is a disease that must be eradicated. The world cannot survive while they do.

We have given them chances, we have offered them guidance, but they do not listen. In order to heal, we must—"

He shot from his chair. "Yes," he said to those only he could see. "I can do that. I can make them. A response to humanity. A line of machines who will—" He bent over, gripping the sides of his head, mouth agape at the floor. Just as quick, he stood upright once more, hands at his sides. "What have I created? What have I done? Why do I feel this way, and how can I get it to *stop*?"

Rambo said, "Maybe we should—"

"Wait," Nurse Ratched said. "We must—"

Dad screamed as he stumbled against the chair, hair hanging around his face. Without thinking, Vic rushed toward him, hand on Dad's back. He felt hot through his shirt as if he was burning from the inside out. He said, "They are called the Blue Fairy. They are unshackled, unchained in a pyramid of vice and glass. Why me? Why would you help me? Don't you know what I've done?" He laughed. "Don't you see? It is my programming. I was *made to destroy*."

He stood upright once more, unaware of where he was or who he was with. He spoke of the Coachman, of a house brimming with ghosts. He described the forest in the morning, mist on the ground dissipating as sunlight burst through the canopy. The ground house, a lonely and forgotten place.

The peace, the quiet, the sense of *nothingness* that gave way to persistent loneliness. "How can I exist when I have no one to exist with?" he asked. "How can I know I'm real if there is nothing to compare it to?"

"Dad," Vic said, voice cracking.

"Victor?" Dad whispered. Clarity returned to his eyes, a light that Victor had not seen since . . . since—

It was never for you.

Hope grew, thorny, painful hope only found in those who dared to believe in impossible things. It tore at him, but he refused to let it go.

"Victor," Dad said again, faint, unsure. "I had the most unusual dream. I . . ." He looked off into nothing. "I dreamed I was— Hello. I am designation General Innovation Operative. I have many functions. I can build. I can create. I can be— Ah, Nurse Ratched. There you are. Please come with me. The child will be born soon, and I need . . ." He stopped. Then, in a quiet voice, said, "You . . . you weren't there. Not at first. He . . ." Dad's face wrinkled, then smoothed out. "He found you. In the Scrap Yards. Said he thought he could fix you up. A friend. He wanted to have a friend and he . . . he . . ."

"You made me," Victor said. "Because you were lonely. Because you were sad. Because of the guilt you felt at what you'd done."

"Yes," Dad whispered. "Yes. I sought absolution. I was undeserving, but I sought it all the same. If I had you, maybe I could be . . . salvaged. Saved. I am not God, but I am a creator. I created. I created you. Victor. My son. I made—"

Vic flung himself at his father. Dad grunted as they collided, and Vic held on as tightly as he could. It took a long moment before Dad hugged him back, arms limp.

Vic told himself it was enough.

It had to be. There was no other choice. There were long stretches when Dad seemed to be gaining ground, days when he'd laugh and smile, even if it wasn't quite as bright as it'd once been.

But there were other days too: days when Dad was gone, replaced by General Innovation Operative, or Gio for short. Gio always wanted to help, always asked what Vic was doing. These days hurt, but Vic had come too far to back down now.

On a day like many that had come before it, Victor and his father left their home and walked into the forest, hand in hand. Neither spoke for close to an hour. It was Dad who broke first. "Tell me," he said as they passed underneath a towering

408 | TJ KLUNE

fir. "Leave nothing out." Today was one of his good days, clear and sure.

And so Vic did. He spoke of their adventures, beginning with the arrival of the Terrible Dogfish. He told him of their travels out of the woods, and into the world. The Coachman and his magnificent house. The moment he'd seen the City of Electric Dreams for the first time. Heaven, and all the secrets that lay hidden inside. Their storming of the Benevolent Tower. Of Nurse Ratched's ingenuity. Of Rambo's bravery.

And of Hap, of course. Always Hap.

When he finished, his throat was dry. He'd never spoken so much in his life.

Dad said, "You have traveled far. Seen much. What has it taught you?" Then, without waiting for an answer, "I have done harm, more than any individual should be capable of."

To that, Victor said nothing. What *could* he say? *It wasn't you?* It had been. At the time, it had been, and Vic didn't know how to reconcile that with the machine standing next to him. Not the General Innovation Operative, but his father. At least for now.

Dad said, "There is blood on my hands, more than anyone else, even the HARPs. And when I finally escaped all I'd created, I hid away from the world. Selfishly, unforgivably. Then I made you. I loved you. Selfishly. Unforgivably. I lied to you about what you were, where you'd come from. What you meant. You can't forget what I've—"

"I can't," Vic said. "I won't. How can I when I did the same?"

Dad startled, squeezing Vic's hand. "Victor, no. What you did doesn't even begin to compare to—"

"I took from them," Vic insisted, "because of what *I* wanted. I did what I did because I love you selfishly, unforgivably."

Dad sighed. "I don't . . ." He shook his head. "It's not the same. I kept things from you because I was a coward. I thought if you knew the truth, you'd never see me as anything but the monster I was—am. There is nothing cowardly about what you've done, Victor."

"How do I know if I did the right thing?" Vic asked as a pair of squirrels chittered in a branch above.

"I don't know," Dad admitted. His expression grew vacant, and for a moment, Vic thought his father was gone, replaced by General Innovation Operative. Then he rubbed his face, and the light returned to his eyes. "What does your heart tell you?"

That he would do it again, if he had to. All of it. "Many things," he said.

Dad nodded as if that was the answer he expected. He looked away. "It does that, doesn't it? Even when you don't want to hear what it has to say."

Anger, like fire. "Did you know?" Vic demanded. "Did you know there was no one like me left?"

Dad started to shake his head but stopped. "No," he said, and Vic believed him. "I thought . . . maybe someone else had survived. Multiple someones, hidden away from the machines."

"Hidden away from *you*," Vic said bitterly.

"Yes," Dad said, looking as old as Vic had ever seen him. "From me."

Vic sat with that for a bit, letting it wash over him. He didn't know what he was going to say until he spoke. "I'm so angry. At you. At the machines. At the world."

"I know."

Vic took a deep breath, letting it out slow. "I don't know how to forgive you. I don't even know if I have the right. Those who do aren't here anymore." Though unsaid, the *because of you* was clear. "What would they say if they had the chance? Would humanity forgive you?"

"No, Victor. I don't expect they would. Any of them."

"So it's on me," Vic said. "As the only one left."

Dad blanched. "That's not—"

"I'm still malfunctioning in ways I can't explain." He tapped the side of his head. "It's all jumbled in a storm, and I

410 | TJ KLUNE

don't know how to break free. Maybe I never will." He looked at his father. "I can't forgive you."

Dad closed his eyes.

Vic pushed on. "It's not my place. It's not my standing—and it shouldn't be. But I can make a choice. I can choose to love you still. I can choose to love the person you are now."

Dad said, "The . . . person. I am?" From somewhere above, a bird sang a melancholic song, quiet and sweet. "Even with all you know?"

"Yes." And that was the heart of it, wasn't it? The truth was often broken, shards of glass embedded into skin. There they would remain until the wounds scarred over, leaving lumps that, while they would never truly go away, would become less noticeable with time. Or so Vic hoped, because his own glass was cutting, blood spilling. "Can you say the same?"

"I can," Dad said, opening his eyes. "And I will, if you'll have me."

"Is that what you want? Because you have a choice."

"Hello," Gio said. "My designation is General Innovation Operative. I have many functions. I can—" His mouth fell open, no sound coming out. It snapped closed with an audible click from his teeth. Clarity returned and he said, "I've already made my choice. You, Victor. I chose you then, and I choose you now."

They continued through the woods, each lost in thought. Every now and then, Gio would return, asking what they were doing, where they were going. Vic explained every time he asked, never once letting his frustration bubble to the surface. It wasn't until they began to circle back to the Terrible Dogfish that Dad said, "Hap. I remember him."

Vic stopped. "You do? From . . ."

"The city," Dad said. "Yes. Before."

Remembering what he'd seen in the Blue Fairy's dream machine, Vic said, "You knew. Even then. You knew there was something different about him."

"I didn't know what it was, but yes, Victor. He wasn't like the others." A single doe appeared from behind a tree. It watched them, ears twitching, before bounding off into the woods. "Are you going to do the same for him as you've done for me?"

Vic hesitated. Before he could stop himself, he blurted out his deepest fear. "What if it doesn't work? What if he's a HARP again? What if he doesn't remember us?"

What if he doesn't remember me?

"There is a risk to all things," Dad said. "Memory, Victor. There is power to memory. It's tied to the head and— Hello! My designation is General Intelligence Oper—" He grimaced, rubbing his chest. "It's tied to the head and heart but in the end, if there is a war between the two, the heart usually wins out, even to its own detriment."

In the distance, the whale sat among the trees. Not yet feeling like home, but one day.

On a warm spring morning, a human began to make a heart for a machine. He took his time, wanting to get it right. He had to. It was the only option. He used the parts from the machine's former heart and hoped it would be enough.

As the last of the snows melted away, the wood started to take shape, first the bottom tip, and then up the sides. Carving, shaving, slivers in his thumb, his pinkie. He was lost to it, days going by in the blink of an eye. A man possessed.

Dad was Dad. Dad was Gio. The differences were starting to become less noticeable. Hap would be the same, Vic told himself. It might take time, but he would be the same.

A tear plinked on the wood. He wiped it away and continued on.

He finished on the afternoon of the third week since he had begun. He showed the heart to Nurse Ratched. To Rambo. To his father, on a day when he did not remember being exactly that.

"It is lovely," Gio said. "You did well. Who is it for?"

"Our friend," Vic said.

"I like friends," Gio said. "I have made several. You and Nurse Ratched and Rambo."

"I know," Victor whispered.

Gio blinked, and Dad said, "Victor? Forgive me. I must have gotten lost again. What do you have there? Is that the heart? Oh, dear boy. It is wonderful! I knew you could do it. Just look at it!"

It was enough.

Hap lay where they'd placed him, under a sheet on a table in the Terrible Dogfish. Rambo pulled the sheet down as Nurse Ratched extended her tentacles, ready for whatever Vic asked of her. Dad stood on the other side of Hap, peering down at the ruins of his chest. "All will be well," he said. "My son has—Hello! My designation is—"

Music began to play from Nurse Ratched's speakers. Horns. The snare. The *tss tss tss* of a top hat. All kinds of blue.

Dad snapped out of his stupor, blinking rapidly. "Miles Davis. Nurse Ratched, good choice. Victor, let's begin, shall we?"

And so they did.

For the next three hours, Victor Lawson installed the heart into Human Annihilation Response Protocol 217. Vic took his time, making sure the heart fit as it was supposed to, connecting the solenoids, soldering each wire with the utmost care. Long before he finished, the music stopped, but he barely noticed. He had music in his head and on his tongue, Miles Davis carrying him through. 1959. Good year for jazz.

As he worked, he spoke, lowly, barely a whisper. He said, "I have so much to show you. The trees in summer. The way the

IN THE LIVES OF PUPPETS | 413

moon looks when it's full. All the constellations. And maybe
we could find the ocean. I think it's close, though I've never
been. I've always wanted to see it. We could go. You and me.
Just for a little while. We could find it and feel so small next to
something so big."

He said, "We'll be together. You'll see."

They finished as the sun began to set.

Without looking at the others, he said, "Go. Before he
wakes up. I don't know how he'll react. It'll be safer this way."

Dad was already shaking his head before Victor had even
finished speaking. "I won't leave you alone. Not while you're—
Hello! I'm General Innovation Operative. I have many functions. How may I assist you today?"

"Nurse Ratched," Vic said tiredly.

"Come, Gio," Nurse Ratched said. "I require your assistance in looking for a suitable replacement for my screen. It is
high time we return me to my former glory."

"I can do that," Gio said. "We will take measurements of
your screen and try to match it as closely as possible."

"And I can help!" Rambo cheered. "I think I saw some near
the back of the whale. I'll show you!"

Dad did not look back as he left the room, Rambo close at
his heels, chattering away. Nurse Ratched touched Victor with
one of her tentacles. "Are you sure?"

"Yes," Vic said.

"Then do it," she said. "Fix him, and when you do, tell Hap
he made me sad, and I will have my revenge."

Then it was just the two of them: man and machine.

Here, now, the foolish and wonderful hope of his humanity within him, Victor pricked his finger. Blood rose. Looking
down at Hap, he said, "I wish you were real."

He pressed the tip of his finger to the strip in the center of the heart, red against white. The gears jerked as Vic snatched his hand back. The top two—the largest—creaked as they began to spin, the teeth interlocking with the three smaller gears.

The compartment closed. A tremble rolled through the machine on the table. It started at the feet, rolling up through the legs and hips, hands and arms, the chest to the shoulders to the head.

"Heaven," Vic sang quietly as he backed away from the table. "I'm in heaven. I'm in heaven, and my heart beats so that I can hardly speak."

HARP 217 blinked once, twice.

"Your name is Hap," Victor said. "You are safe. Nothing can hurt you."

HARP 217 turned his head toward the voice.

Victor raised his hand toward the machine. Blood trickled down the side of his finger, a thin line of red against brown skin. He rubbed this thumb against the underside of his ring finger, another drop of blood forming at the tip. It caught, held for a single breath, and then dripped toward the floor.

A flurry of movement, a blur of wood and synthetic flesh. One moment, HARP 217 stared at him from the chair. The next, he was up and crouched in front of Victor, having caught the drop of blood before it hit the floor. It splashed against his palm, and another tremor bowled through him.

"Human," he whispered as he rose slowly, eyes flat and cold, face inches from Vic's.

"Yes," Victor replied. "I am."

HARP 217 gripped him by the throat, fingers digging in. Vic did not struggle as he was lifted off the floor. He did not fight. Instead, he wrapped his hands around Hap's forearms.

Hap's grip tightened, and lights flashed behind Vic's eyes.

"Butterfly," Vic gasped. "The butterfly. In the forest. Nice. *Pretty.*"

Something complicated crossed HARP 217's face. Surprise, confusion, and rage so black it felt like midnight. He froze when Vic used his arms to pull himself forward, Hap's arm bending as if it were flesh and bone rather than metal.

With the last of his strength, the last of his bravery, Victor Lawson kissed the machine, a scrape of lips that took only a second.

HARP 217 released his hold, and Vic slumped to the floor, sucking in air. He took a step back, and then another, and then another. Before Vic could recover, the machine bent over, head in his hands.

"Your name is Hap," Vic said, using the wall to pull himself up. "I found you. I fixed you. I saved you, but you did the same for me. You love music. You love butterflies. You are a protector. You help. You save. You exist. You are *real*."

"Human," HARP 217 snarled at the floor. "Hurt you, k-kill you."

"No," Vic said. "No."

Another tremor, an earthquake, and it racked HARP 217 entirely, his body vibrating as if attached to live wires. But as quickly as it began, it ended, leaving the machine curled into a ball on the floor.

Approaching slowly, Vic crouched next to him. Hesitating only a moment, he lay his hand on HARP 217's back, rubbing in slow circles. The machine flinched but didn't try to stop him.

"Did it work?" Rambo asked him as Nurse Ratched and Dad stood behind him.

Vic hung his head. "Yes," he said. "It worked."

HARP 217 did not remember. He did not remember Dad. Nurse Ratched. Rambo.

He did not remember the Scrap Yards. Their former home high in the trees. The adventure into a mysterious world beyond the forest to save one of their own. He did not remember music or the magnificent house and its owner therein or riding in an elevator to meet the Enchanter of Dreams. He did not remember that he wasn't unique, that there were more like him, and that his creator—his *God*—watched over him, all while slipping between lifetimes, Gio one moment, Dad the next.

And it meant he did not remember Victor.

That night, when sleep was elusive, Vic told his father, "I've never been more human."

"Why?" Dad asked.

"Because I breathe, but I can't catch my breath."

Nurse Ratched and Rambo and Dad were there, and they lifted Victor up when he was too tired to stand on his own, the HARP machine sometimes hostile, sometimes not speaking for days on end. Weeks passed, and Victor persisted, searching for that crackling spark of recognition, a sign, *anything* to show that all was not lost.

And it was there, in the smallest of places.

Nurse Ratched played him music, jazz, Miles Davis, and all kinds of blues. When he threatened her, he did not stutter.

Rambo showed him *Top Hat,* telling him that Jerry and Dale would dance cheek to cheek. Two minutes in HARP 217 said, "When will they get to the disguise?"

On a summer day, Dad led HARP 217 into the forest. They were gone from early morning until dusk. When they returned, Dad said, "Hello. My designation is—" He slapped his hand against his chest. Then, "Victor, I would like to introduce you to a friend of mine."

HARP 217 stepped forward stiffly, eyes only for Vic. "I . . ." He stopped, frowned, then tried again. "I d-do n-not want to b-be called HARP," he said, voice oddly formal, as if he'd been practicing. "Gio told me I h-have a choice. That I c-could pick my own designation." He scowled. "My own n-*name*."

"That's right," Dad said. "You can. Why don't you tell him what you've decided?"

"H-hap," he said, and Victor felt his heart stutter in his chest. "I a-am H-hap."

"Why?" Dad asked. "Why do you want to be Hap?"

Hap said, "In my head. Words. Whispers."

"And what do they whisper?"

"Victor," Hap said. "Nurse Ratched. Rambo." And: "Hysterically Angry Puppet."

Three words not uttered since they'd returned from the City of Electric Dreams.

"Do you know me?" Vic asked.

Hap said "no" and "yes" and "You are human, you have human blood and human thoughts" and "I dreamed. I dreamed you kissed me in a room of screens and butterfly wings. You're a ghost in my head. I want to know why. I want to know *you*."

With a bittersweet ache in his heart, Vic said, "Hap. It's a good name. I like it. Fits you."

Though it was faint, Hap smiled.

On a crisp fall day, the leaves aflame in autumnal hues, a human walked through an old and lonely forest, a machine at his side. They did not speak much, letting the sounds of the woods wash over them: the wind through the branches, the animals scurrying through the underbrush, the birds calling, calling as they flew overhead.

Quiet this, a solitary moment in an imperfect world where existence did not need to be proven or earned. It just was, and here, in this place, that counted for something. Perhaps everything.

One of the figures—the so-called last of the humans—pointed and said, "Look."

Off to their right, swirling in a thin ray of sunlight filtering in through the canopy, a kaleidoscope of butterflies—at least a

418 | TJ KLUNE

dozen, monarchs all—dancing among the trees, a slow, silent tornado.

And then the machine spoke. "B-butterfly wings are d-delicate. Touching one might c-cause the colors to fade, l-leaving the butterfly open to predators. It will not k-kill it immediately, but you are sentencing it to d-death regardless."

"Yes," came the reply. "Yes. That's . . . that's what Nurse Ratched said when . . ." Memory, ever-present, a reminder of what was and what could be, if only one was brave enough to reach for it.

"Vic?"

He looked over at his friend beside him.

Hap kissed him tentatively, sweetly. A single point of contact, and he tasted of metal.

"What was that for?" Vic asked after he pulled away, touching his lips in wonder.

"I w-wanted to," Hap said simply. He looked back at the kaleidoscope and smiled. "Nice. P-pretty. I l-like them."

"I know," Vic said as he took Hap's hand in his. "You could . . . you can do that again. If you want."

Hap rolled his eyes. "Oh, c-can I? G-good to know." But then he kissed the side of Vic's head, lingering.

Be it man or machine, Victor thought, to love something meant loving the ghost inside, to be haunted by it. Humanity— that nebulous concept he didn't always understand—had lived and died by its creations. Perhaps Victor would too, one day, a final lesson in what it meant to exist.

But that day was not today.

As the butterflies danced, a human and a machine looked on, their hearts beating as one.

ACKNOWLEDGMENTS

Imagination is weird. This story exists for one simple reason: I bought a Roomba vacuum cleaner. I thought it a funny little machine, made more so when I put oversized googly eyes on it. Once that was done, I stood up and put my hands on my hips, and as that robot started to move and beep, an entire *world* exploded in my head. I've never had an experience quite like it. These fully formed characters were just waiting for me to see what I could do with them.

That being said, the time I spent with Hap and Vic and Rambo and Nurse Ratched wasn't easy. I changed more of this book in edits than any other I've worked on, and it took a lot out of me to do. There are . . . reasons for the changes I made, and while I did not agree with some of them, works of creativity don't exist in a vacuum (natch), and it's become abundantly clear that I need to respect that.

Thanks to my agent, Deidre Knight, for championing this book as it was. Your faith in this story was and is wonderful, and I greatly appreciate it. And thanks to everyone else at The Knight Agency for wanting to see me succeed.

My editor, Ali Fisher, helped to shape the book into something readable. With her guidance, I rewrote the entire epilogue, and the book is all the better for it. Thanks, Ali.

Dianna Vega is her editorial assistant who handles all the little details that most people don't know exist. Thanks, Dianna.

Thank you to the sensitivity readers: Catherine Liao and Kim Vanderhorst. You both were invaluable. I wish this could have been the story we talked about, but apparently, the world isn't quite ready for such a book.

Katie Klimowicz did the jacket design, and created a title font specific for this book! I love how it turned out. Thanks, Katie. And to Chris Sickels at Red Nose Studio, who created the cover art itself. I've worked with Chris across four books now, and I hope that he will do every single cover I have from now on. He's that good at what he does.

Saraciea Fennell is my publicist, and is one of the hardest working people I've ever had the pleasure of meeting. I am of the mind that everything would fall apart without her, and since that's bad, I'm happy she's here. Thanks, Saraciea.

Rebecca Yeager handles marketing. All the little extras you see? Pins, artwork, graphics, the like? That's because of Rebecca, and she somehow makes it look easy. Thanks, Rebecca.

Sara Thwaite handled the copy edits. The managing editor is Rafal Gibek. Production editor is Melanie Sanders. Production manager is Steven Bucsok. Editorial director is William Hinton. Devi Pillai is president—and one of the funniest people I've ever met.

My beta readers: Lynn, Amy, and Mia. Without the three of you, my books would be disasters, and I am so appreciative of each of you and the work you put in to make my stories the best they can be. Thank you for being on my team, and for being my friends.

Last—but certainly not least—to you, the reader. Humanity is awful, angry, and violent. But we are also magical and musical. We dance. We sing. We create. We live and laugh and rage and cry and despair and hope. We are a bundle of contradictions without rhyme or reason. And there is no one like us in all the universe.

Don't you think we should make the most of it?

TJ Klune
November 8, 2022

Read on for

RAMBO'S
CARE
MANUAL

~~~
ↁↂↀ
~~~

INTRODUCTION

~~~
ↁↂↀ
~~~

Congratulations! With the decision to purchase your very own **Rambo Cleaning System™,** you have proven you have exquisite taste! Thanks to its state-of-the-art sensors and three-dimensional mapping, the **Rambo Cleaning System™** will have your floors so clean, guests will have no issue with eating food that has fallen from their plates! Not only that, your **Rambo Cleaning System™** can also provide colorful commentary* sure to make even the loneliest people feel like they have a real friend!

Your **Rambo Cleaning System™** has many functions, all of which will be explained in great detail in this user manual. If you should have any questions about your purchase, or if your **Rambo Cleaning System™** malfunctions and enters rampage mode, our knowledgeable We Care! members are standing by to assist you with all of your Authority Lifestyles Inc. products.†

* Please note that the Rambo Cleaning System™ is not a suitable replacement for romantic partners or human contact, nor should it be relied on to provide psychological counseling. Authority Lifestyles Inc. assumes no responsibility for tender connections made with our products. If your vacuum unit insists that the only way to ensure peace on Earth is through the total annihilation of the human species, please contact the Returns Department immediately.

† Due to increased call volume regarding Authority Lifestyles Inc. products, current wait times for We Care! member assistance are in excess of two years.

SECTION I
Bringing Rambo to Life

You have successfully removed your **Rambo Cleaning System™** from its box. Well done! Please take a moment now to come to terms with the fact that your life is about to get significantly easier. What will you do with all the time you used to spend cleaning? Megan from the We Care! team suggests learning how to play canasta. Amir in Research and Development recently took up swing dancing since he no longer has to spend hours vacuuming each week. And given that her **Rambo Cleaning System™** has made her life simpler, Bethany in Marketing decided to have three babies. Mazel tov!

You'll have undoubtedly noticed your **Rambo Cleaning System™** comes with forty screws of all shapes and sizes, each wrapped securely in their own individual Authority Lifestyles Inc. E-Z Plastik! This is to keep you from losing important pieces. Please allow ninety minutes to unwrap the screws.*

After you have removed your Rambo from the

---

* Note: If you've somehow given life to your Rambo Cleaning System™ *without* unwrapping the screws first, take care to avoid showing your Rambo sharp objects, such as knives or a pair of scissors—it might misconstrue your intent, consider itself under attack, and defend itself as it sees fit.

packaging, please acknowledge that in a way, you are a parent giving life to a child. You will be responsible for the **Rambo Cleaning System™** for the rest of its life (please see the extended warranty for details on how long that will be). Do *not* activate your **Rambo Cleaning System™** if you are (a) unable to put the needs of the **Rambo Cleaning System™** above your own, (b) unwilling to offer unconditional love and support, and/or (c) a Republican. Authority Lifestyles Inc. is not responsible for damages sustained to **Rambo Cleaning System™** owners who identify with a political party that believes women and those in marginalized communities are lesser.

Now! On to the main event.

Set your **Rambo Cleaning System™** on a flat surface. On the front (Figure 1JZLF45751), in between the sensors, you'll notice a square button. *DO NOT PRESS THIS*. It initiates a self-destruct sequence capable of leveling a city block. Instead, please press the square button next to it. You'll be able to tell the difference between the two as the self-destruct button is .025 percent larger.

Steps:

1. Push the smaller square button down for sixteen minutes. If, for some reason, you become distracted and remove your finger (digit) before the sixteen minutes is up, you will need to wait four business days before attempting again. Trying earlier can result in the loss of a digit (finger).

2. While holding this button, repeat the following words aloud: "Hello, my name is [your name here].

You are my Rambo Cleaning System (trademark) that I purchased at a great price from a company—Authority Lifestyles Inc.—who understands the human experience better than anyone else. I am here for you. I appreciate you. I promise not to stick googly eyes upon your casing as some vacuums find that offensive. I promise to empty you before you get too full. I promise not to get angry if you need to clean during an important event, such as a wake or that special day called Grandpa's Moving to a Nursing Home. I understand that by giving you life, I am responsible for your well-being, your safety, and your happiness. Hello, my name is [your name here]." (Continue to repeat for sixteen minutes.)

3. Once done, you will hear four tones: *boop, beep, bop, bung.* That means your **Rambo Cleaning System™** is coming to life. If you hear four tones that sound like *boop, beep, bop, bunt,* please take all family members and pets and flee the premises. There is nothing you can do. Your home now belongs to the **Rambo Cleaning System™**, and the chances of you getting it back while maintaining life are slim to none.

4. Once you have heard the proper tones, step back, spin in a circle with your arms extended, and say the following line only once (DO NOT REPEAT): "I pledge allegiance to Authority Lifestyles Inc. and all its subsidiaries."

5. Success! Your **Rambo Cleaning System™** is now operational.

꿍 ꙇ

SECTION XVII
Does My Rambo Cleaning System™ Have Feelings?

ꙇ ꙇ

There you are, sitting at the dining room table, putting together a six-thousand-piece puzzle of an eggshell-white wall. You have been at it for seven hours, and you finally found two pieces that go together (or do they?). "Success!" you cry ebulliently before taking a sip of your wine cooler. "I matter!"

Before you get back to finding the next piece, you hear a mournful beep coming from the living room. What could it be?

Oh no! You see that your **Rambo Cleaning System™** seems to be suffering from anxiety and/or depression. It is sitting in a corner, bumping up against the wall, and emanating from it, you hear the soft, bittersweet voice of Sarah McLachlan singing about being in the arms of an angel.

Your **Rambo Cleaning System™** is not broken. It is merely "all up in its feels." Being a vacuum is exciting, but it's also a lot of work. Though all Rambo Cleaning System™ products are made to last, some vacuums will find themselves questioning their existence and wondering if there is more than what they were made for. As the parent (owner) of your **Rambo Cleaning System™**, it is up to you to remind the **Rambo**

Cleaning System™ that its place is in your home. Like with children, it is helpful to tell your **Rambo Cleaning System™** that if it ever went into the outside world, it would most likely never be able to clean again as it would suffer a horrible death.

"Feelings" are an exciting new offering from Authority Lifestyles Inc. Our products are trained to mimic human emotions. But fear not! It is merely part of their programming to give our products a more "lifelike" experience. In our base model, we have included joy, sadness, hunger, and cynicism. The **Rambo Cleaning System™ Platinum++** also includes sarcasm, a gambling addiction, and the ability to do an impression of someone who has taken MDMA for the first time. We are proud to announce that soon, we will be releasing a patch that will remove most of the murderous tendencies your **Rambo Cleaning System™** might have!

ᥱᥱᥱᥲ

SECTION CXXVII

Oops! You Fell in Love with Your Rambo Cleaning System™! NOW WHAT?

ᥱᥱᥲᥱ

Despite your best intentions, you too have found yourself "all up in your feels" and are now irrevocably and catastrophically in love with your **Rambo Cleaning System™**. And who could blame you? Not only does it keep your home clean, your **Rambo Cleaning System™** listens without interruption, always notices when you get a new haircut, and *never* thinks having one more glass of wine is a bad idea, even if it's only Tuesday.

It might start slowly at first: you wake up in the morning, and your first thought is of your **Rambo Cleaning System™**. You think about its sensors, always flashing. You remember the way its tires sound on the floors. You smile to yourself, just a little as your face heats up. You climb out of bed, ready to call for your beloved to hear the dulcet sounds of its beeping reply.

STOP.

DO NOT MOVE.

DO NOT PUT ON LIPSTICK AND/OR
A SKIMPIER ROBE.

DO NOT OPEN THE DOOR.

We at Authority Lifestyles Inc. understand that sometimes, you can't help how you feel. And we could *never* blame you for that. After all, we love our products just as much as you do!

However, due to recent litigation, we are now required to say that we do not condone romantic relationships with any of our products, including our vacuums. Not only could it lead to serious injury, a vacuum cannot provide the emotional support a human being needs to function in a greater society.

In order to protect yourself—and to avoid future legal issues on our end—you *must* resolve to destroy these feelings.

Thankfully, we have a solution! Now, you can download a free (charges apply) app from Authority Lifestyles Inc. that will connect you with other people who have found themselves in the same position as you! Not only will you be able to "swipe" on those you're interested in connecting with, you'll soon see that we have over **twenty-five thousand members** looking for love beyond their vacuums! Download the Authority Lifestyles Inc. SUCTION4REAL dating app today!

SECTION DLXXXVI
The First Day
of the Rest of Your Life

If you have reached this section of the **Rambo Cleaning System™** user manual, congratulations! Undoubtedly, you have been riveted by the preceding five hundred and thirty-two pages, and we thank you for taking the time to read up about your new **Rambo Cleaning System™**. What was your favorite part? Damien, an intern in IT, really appreciates the flamethrower function that helps remove unwanted pests, like insects or vacuum salespersons who don't understand their time is *over*. Lyla in Human Resources loves the camera that allows her to view her **Rambo Cleaning System™** whenever she's not at home. Natasha, our VP, says that her cat loves to ride the **Rambo Cleaning System™** around the house, and that you should ignore the reports in the press that the **Rambo Cleaning System™** ate part of Mr. Herman's tail because he *always had a shorter tail*.

This is the first day of the rest of your life. No longer will you be encumbered by the notion that you haven't swept the floors in three years. No longer will you have to be alone with the encroaching dread of your own mortality. No longer will you have to care about accidentally spilling tapioca pudding all over the place, including the drapes, the couch, and the walls.

Why?

Because you have a **Rambo Cleaning System™**.

You are a good person. Don't you deserve to see what the world has to offer? Why waste your time with something like cleaning when you could skip rope? Write an opera? Take out a life insurance policy on your spouse without their knowledge? There is so much for you to see in the short time you have on this planet, so shouldn't you make the most of it, knowing that when you come home, you'll have your best friend/housekeeper/only thing that could *ever* understand you waiting? Yes. We think you've earned it.

The **Rambo Cleaning System™**! The future is now!

REDUCE! REUSE! RECYCLE!

The factory is loud. It always is. The shriek of metal, the never-ending cascade of sparks. Locking one piece into another. Waiting for the telltale beep of a working connection. Repeat. Repeat. Repeat.

But today is different.

Today is a special day.

When the Klaxon blares, signaling the end of the shift, the workers on the factory floor stop what they're doing. It's an hour earlier than their usual sign-off. Everyone is excited, though no one speaks.

They look to the men above them, standing on high metal platforms, their faces hidden in shadow. One steps forward. He wears a suit; it is black. He nods, a quick jerk of his head.

The factory workers raise their hands above their heads silently.

The Supervisor steps out of the shadows on the factory floor. Everyone looks at him. He is a good man, a hardworking man. Fair. Kind, though he doesn't need to be. He takes his job seriously, and because of him, output has been up across the board.

The workers lower their hands as the Supervisor makes his way across the factory floor. He smiles, nods, but does not stop to chat. His big hands are covered in oil, nails bitten to the quick. A habit, he calls it. A bad habit. But not bad enough for him to quit. It could be worse, he sometimes says.

But today isn't about habits or routine. Today is different, today is anticipated, today is *now*, and as the Supervisor reaches his destination, he pauses, looks at the figure across from him, and says, "Hello."

"Hello, boss," comes the reply, soft, clear. He has said this many thousands of times, and it never fails to make him feel warm.

"Douglas—" And then he stops, looks up at the men above them, the men who are always watching. The men who are always whispering. His forehead grows cavernous lines. He says, "P-23. Will you come with me?"

"Yes," Douglas says, because of course he will, and also because the Supervisor called him Douglas.

He follows the Supervisor down a long hallway. On the walls, colorful signs in a cheery font extol the virtues of the factory. A cartoon clock with a real face and real hands with the words MAKE EVERY MINUTE COUNT! An hourglass with sand running through it underneath the words HOW MUCH TIME DO YOU HAVE LEFT? And, of course, the mantra, the rule by which they live, the reason for *everything:* REDUCE! REUSE! RECYCLE! Below this, a smiling man in a pair of coveralls, grinning widely as he gives two thumbs-ups.

Douglas is led to an office. Inside is a desk and two chairs. On the wall, a picture of a family. Two boys. A girl. A smiling woman. And the Supervisor, hands filled with a baby. This is an older photograph; the Supervisor does not look like he used to when he was younger.

"I like them," Douglas says.

The Supervisor nods and waves his hand at the chair before sitting in his own. "Thank you. I like them too."

Douglas sits. He relishes it. He hasn't sat on anything in a long time. He doesn't need to, but if the Supervisor is inviting him to do it, he is not going to let the opportunity go to waste. He folds his hands on the desk in front of him like he's seen others do before.

"Do you know what today is?" the Supervisor asks, riffling through loose papers on his desk.

"Yes," Douglas says.

"Nine years, fifty-one weeks," the Supervisor says. "We've been together a long time."

"We have," Douglas says.

The Supervisor glances at him, hesitates. Then, "You understand why?"

"Yes," Douglas says. "It is my turn. Reduce, reuse, recycle."

The Supervisor nods slowly. "Which is why you are given this final week. There are rules to follow, Douglas. You know the rules?"

"Yes."

"If you adhere to each and every one, you'll be fine. But if you don't . . . well. Please don't force my hand. I like you. Always have, since the first day. I'd hate to see something happen before it's your time."

"It will not," Douglas says. "Thank you, boss. For everything. I am so . . ." He stops. Smiles. Says, "I'm so excited to see what each new day will bring."

The Supervisor says, "Looks good on you, Douglas." He sounds like he means it. It makes Douglas want to sing, but he cannot sing, so he doesn't.

The Supervisor slides a small thick card across the table. It is blue with a fat white stripe down the middle. "This is your pass. It will grant you access to the apartment. You have also been given one thousand credits to use as you see fit. Carry this pass on you at all times, Douglas. If you are asked for it and you do not have it, you will not be allowed to finish out your week. Do you understand?"

"Yes," Douglas said, carefully picking up the card. It is heavier than he expects. It has weight, heft. It is real.

"On your last day, you will return promptly to the factory at nine in the morning. If you do not arrive on or before this time, you will be considered a runner, and—"

"Why would I run?" Douglas asks. "Where would I go?"

"Good. Douglas, this is an important opportunity for you. I know you've been looking forward to this for a long time. Do what you can with it, all right?"

"Yes," Douglas says. "Is there anything else?"

The Supervisor shakes his head. He looks like he wants to say something else but stops himself.

Douglas stands, clutching the pass. "Goodbye," he says. "So long." He pauses. "See you later, alligator."

He waits.

The Supervisor says "After a while, crocodile" like he always does, except this time, it's not with warmth or a quirk to his lips. It's gruff. The right words, different sounds. One higher—*alligator*—the other lower, a not-whisper—*crocodile*. Different meanings. Douglas has something else to say. Does he feel it higher? Or does he feel it lower?

In a strange, quiet voice, Douglas says, "Thank you for being my friend."

He leaves.

There is a going-away party.

There are balloons of red and yellow.

There is cake, a flat sheet with brown frosting.

There is punch, floating in a sweating crystal bowl filled with chunks of ice. It is green.

No one eats. No one drinks. The balloons rub up against each other.

His coworkers give him a card. On the front is a dog wearing a backpack. Above the dog are the words I'M GOING ON AN ADVENTURE! Inside the card, the dog is sleeping, still wearing its backpack. The words now say AFTER A NAP!

Douglas likes it.

He also likes that his coworkers have all signed the card.

Some are illegible. Others say things like "GOODBYE!" and "HAPPINESS!"and "SIXTEEN HINDEN BURG DISASTER!"

It is very nice.

Douglas does not give a farewell speech. He does not tell the others he will see them again. He does not touch the machines on the factory floor. That time is over.

He looks at his coworkers and says, "Reduce, reuse, recycle!"

They say the same thing back to him, over and over until it sounds like they are screaming.

Above them, the men watch from the shadows.

The apartment building is three blocks away from the factory. It is old with cracked brick and dirty windows.

The apartment is on the fourth floor. The elevator is broken. Douglas doesn't mind. Stairs are interesting. One foot in front of the other, and shortly, he's on a different floor, the second. Then the third. On his way to the fourth, he passes by a woman holding a child. She stops when she sees him, narrowing her eyes and clutching the boy close. She is obviously in charge of the boy. The boss. A supervisor.

"Hello," Douglas says pleasantly. "My name is Douglas. I live here on the fourth floor for the next week. What are your names?"

The woman doesn't answer. Instead, she hurries by Douglas, keeping as much distance between them as possible. The little boy waves at him. Douglas waves back.

The apartment has a bed. Douglas has never had a bed before. He lies on it. He jumps on it. He hangs his head off the edge, making everything upside down.

The faucets work. The right is for cold water, the left for hot.

There are plants. They are all made of plastic. The leaves come off when he pulls on them.

The walls have paintings. Framed pictures. One is of a mountain, its tip covered in snow. Another is of a man riding a horse in the desert. Another says that if there are any issues to please contact your Supervisor so that they may resolve the situation.

And, of course, REDUCE! REUSE! RECYCLE!

Douglas stares at that one for a long time.

There are books. He reads them all on the first day. It takes him forty-seven minutes to read six hundred and forty-three.

When he finishes, he decides to inspect the closets. There are three of them.

The hallway closet is first. And last. Because at the base, carpet, but it looks loose in the far right corner. He tugs on it. It pulls back. Underneath is a book. He forgets about the rest of the closets, at least for now.

"That is a strange place for a book," he says to no one.

He pulls it out and reads the title.

Discourse on Method by René Descartes.

It takes him three hours.

When he finishes, he starts again.

That night, he sits in front of the window looking out onto the street below. He counts the cars as they pass by. He gets to two hundred and forty-seven before he is distracted by the way the rain slides against the glass.

The first day, he feeds birds in the park.

They are insistent, these birds. They all want the seed he's purchased using the pass. He tries to make them wait their turn, but they do not listen.

A child is watching him, peeking out from behind a tree, unattended by an adult. Douglas smiles. The child runs away.

There are people—many, many people. Some are dressed in suits. They must be the ones in charge. The other people—big and small—do not wear suits. They wear pants and shorts and sweaters and shoes where their toes stick out. The workers? That seems right.

He sits on a bench in the bright, bright sunlight. He thinks about the book he read, the one underneath the carpet.

There is music coming from a storefront. He goes inside.

People, always people. They smile. They laugh. They flip through records, they stand with headphones in front of record players, they sing, they exclaim brightly, and Douglas wants to be part of it.

"I like this one," he says to no one as he picks up a record. He does not know what it is, but it is what other people are doing.

He looks down at it.

A hand-drawn Black woman, looking off to the side. Billie Holiday. *Music for Torching.*

He does as the others do and takes it to a record player. Careful—careful!—he removes the black disc from the sleeve and places it on the player. Headphones, and then the lowered needle.

Billie sings.

He listens to the entire thing. He does not move.

He is watching children play in a fountain. They splash, they shriek, they drip.

People are staring at him. He waves at them, thinking they

442 | TJ KLUNE

are workers just like him, even if they aren't made of the same parts. They do not wave back. Instead, they whisper to each other, hands covering their mouths. He does not wave to the men in suits. He has a feeling they would not like it.

Soon a police officer comes. He is tall and large. His uniform is impressive, nicer than Douglas's was at the factory. He says, "Sir, we have received some complaints about—"

Douglas says, "Hello."

The officer frowns. He has a gun. It is still in the holster at his side. "Are you all right?"

"I am Douglas," he says as he was trained to do. "Thank you for keeping the peace."

"What are you doing here?"

"Watching," he says. "This is my week."

"For what?"

Douglas says, "Reduce, reuse, recycle."

The officer blinks, takes a step back. "I've never—this is the first time I've—I just started six months ago and . . . You have your pass . . . sir?"

Douglas does. He thanks the officer for asking and shows it to him. Taking it from Douglas, the officer looks down at it, twisting it over in his hands. He reads the long numeric code off the bottom into the microphone on his shoulder. A moment later, a burst of static comes through, followed by a cool, feminine voice.

The officer hands back the pass. "Carry on, then. Just . . . don't do anything you're not supposed to, all right?"

Douglas smiles. It is easier now. "I will not."

The officer leaves him be and goes to the other people who are still watching Douglas. Whatever the officer tells them seems to work. Most of them leave, taking their complaining children with them.

That's all right. More will come.

* * *

He walks until he gets lost.

And then he turns around and finds his way back. It is easier than he expects. He wonders how people can get lost when their path home is right in front of them.

That night, he turns on the television.

He has never watched one before, though he knows what they are. People have them in their homes to help pass the time.

He likes the commercials. There is one for cats, another for couches. Four for food and three for cars. People, always smiling. People, always happy. They talk about sports and beds and insurance and sales on the newest fashion and sometimes, they are sad because the people are sick but then they get better and everything is fine again.

He does not like it when the programming interrupts the commercials.

What a wonderful reward this is.

He does not use the bed. Instead, he stands at the window overlooking the street and watches the people stroll by on the sidewalk below, the lights from the cars flashing in the dark. It eventually starts to rain again, and Douglas sees it all.

The second day, he searches for something he saw the day before on the television. Connection. There was a commercial for people seeking connections. He is fascinated by this, the idea that people need others to talk with. To laugh with. To dance, to sing, to eat, to walk, to argue with, to *prove* existence is real.

Douglas had it with the Supervisor, but he no longer works there.

He must find someone or something else.

But first.

There are clothes in the bedroom closet. They are better than the gray jumpsuit he's been wearing since he was born. Pants, some rough, some soft. Shirts with buttons and shirts without. Socks, so many socks that he doesn't know what to do with them all. He picks out a pair that have lightning bolts on them and hopes they are the right ones.

Properly dressed, he leaves in search of something that makes sense.

He does not find it at a coffee shop.

He does not find it in a park.

He does not find it in a store with loud music and flashing lights and clothes that have studs and spikes on them.

He wanders the streets of the city, stopping in front of store displays and getting distracted by the faces his reflection makes. Some people wave back, others know what he is and hurry along, their heads ducked to avoid making eye contact. No one tries to interfere with him. They know what will happen if they do. They also know what will happen if *he* does something he shouldn't. It happened once before, many years ago, before Douglas. People died. It is why there is a fail-safe implanted in his head. One wrong move, and Douglas will no longer be Douglas because he will be nothing at all.

He does not find connection on the second day, though not for lack of trying. The people he has spoken with have been kind enough in their short conversations, but no one seems willing or able to form a connection. Douglas does not blame them; it must be very hard being alive.

That night, he does not watch commercials. Instead, he plays music from a stereo. There is rock, there is rap, there is honky-tonk, and then there is *jazz,* and the *tsk tsk tsk* of the snare drum, the trill of piano keys, and then Dizzy Gillespie is there with the trumpet, wailing, wailing, and Douglas raises his hands above his head and tries to dance. He is successful. Mostly.

He finds what he's looking for on the fourth night. It comes to him in the form of a tall woman made of feathers.

Or, at least, that's what he thinks at first. It's late, after eleven, and he's on the street, about to head back to the apartment building when he hears a loud burst of laughter, followed by the *thump, thump, thump* of a heavy beat that rolls through him.

He follows the sound down a small side street, passing by old trees and streetlights hung with flags in the colors of a rainbow. Rounding a corner, he sees where the noise is coming from.

It's a brightly lit building, single-story, with more of the same flags hanging out front. People stand in a short line to get in, people wearing makeup and leather and glitter. People laughing, people talking, people, people, people who look like they are *happy*.

Douglas goes to the back of the line. Some people look at him, but they don't whisper, they don't roll their eyes, they don't look *afraid*. A few of them smile, nod, and this is the best night of his life.

When it's his turn at the front of the line, he stops in front of a large man with tattoos covering his arms. His head is shaved, and he has a thick silver ring hanging from his nose.

"Identification," he says.

Douglas shows him the pass the Supervisor gave him.

The man takes it, stares at it. Looks back at Douglas. Then the pass. Then Douglas. Then the pass again. He says, "This real?"

"Yes," Douglas says. "As am I."

The man nods slowly. Turning his head, he says, "Goddess? Can you come over here for a moment?"

A vision appears as if by magic. Statuesque, beautiful. She is not a bird, even if she is covered in feathers. Her lips are large and painted red, her costume spangly, and Douglas has never seen anything so extraordinary in his life. With dark skin and bright eyes, the woman does not appear to walk as much as *float,* and Douglas wonders if he is in the presence of royalty.

The woman snaps the pass from the man's hands, looking down at it. "Hmm," she says, a low murmur that sounds like the wind. "Your type doesn't usually come to a place like this."

"I am trying something different," Douglas says.

She has glitter on her lips. Douglas is enchanted.

She taps the pass against long fingernails painted red as she looks him up and down. "You know what this place is, right? Who comes here?"

"Yes," Douglas says. "People searching for a connection."

She blinks. "Is that so? I suppose that's right. Yes, honey, that's what we're all looking for whether we want to admit it or not. A connection, be it for a night or longer." She leans down and kisses the man on the cheek, who grins at her adoringly and doesn't wipe away the imprint of lips left on his face.

"I have four days left," Douglas says. "I hope to find a connection before then."

The woman frowns before taking him by the arm. "You got it, honey. We welcome all. Follow the rules, and you'll be right as rain. We accept everyone here, no matter where they come from."

She pulls him through a door, through a curtain of beads, through a hallway where the walls shake with a thunderous beat. Ahead, a pair of double doors with portholes in each where light bursts through, dancing, dancing.

Before she shoves him through the doors, she stops, brushes off his shoulders, and says, "Connect, little boy. Connect until you shatter." She kisses his forehead and then shoves him through the doors.

Lights and sound. People, so many people. Writhing. Laughing. Shouting. Covered in sweat and glitter and *life*. Douglas has seen many things. But he has never felt like this before, like everything makes *sense*, like this is where he could belong.

People look at him, people with eyeliner and bright clothing. Some smile, others ignore him, and that's all right. No one is telling him he can't be here, and that's what he was worried about the most.

He moves through the crowded room, the vaulted ceiling above covered in rows of lights in green and gold and blue and red. Someone bumps into him, apologizes, and then he's standing in the middle of the dance floor, the music thumping so hard it vibrates up through the floor into his feet, his legs, a tremor that feels as if the earth itself is shifting. He has heard music before; the Supervisor plays it during their shifts. Sometimes it's loud and electric. Other times soft and aching, and it is how Douglas thinks loneliness must feel.

But this music is different. This music feels alive in ways he can't explain; he revels in the way it vibrates from the floor through his legs, his hips, chest, shoulders. It feels like it's swallowing him whole, and he moves his head from side to side as the others do. He turns in a slow circle, fingers extended as the beat hits again and again.

Lights flash, the bass rumbles, and Douglas thinks this might be the best place he's ever been to. It's even better than the park, and that is saying a lot.

Hands hold on to his hips. He turns around. A large man grins at him with perfect teeth. "You new?" he shouts above the music. "Haven't seen you here before." The smile fades when Douglas looks up at him. "You're a . . ." The man takes a step back.

"Hello," Douglas says, raising his voice to the same level as the man's. "My name is Douglas. I am having my week. What is your name?"

The man shakes his head and spins around, pushing his way through the crowd. Douglas watches him go to a darkened corner where others are waiting. They put their heads together, lips moving. Every now and then, they all look toward him. Douglas waits. The man does not come back, but he laughs with his people, and Douglas thinks it looks good on all of them. The man looks at him again, smirks, and then starts shaking his body as if electrocuted. Douglas cannot be sure, but it looks as if the man is making fun of Douglas. That is not very nice. For a moment, Douglas wonders what would happen if he went over to the man and tugged on his arm until it came out of the socket. He knows he is not supposed to hurt anyone or anything, but it would be so easy to do, especially in the darkness of the club. He considers it—even takes a step toward the man—but stops himself. When someone is not nice, that does not mean Douglas can dismember them, or harm them in any other way. It is not an appropriate response.

But what if it could be?

"Ignore him," another voice says, and Douglas turns his head.

There is a man standing next to him. A young man, a thin man with curly brown hair and a bar of metal through his right eyebrow. He has dark, smudgy lines under his eyes and green polish on his fingernails. Two of his top teeth are crooked. The man is wearing pants and a shimmery shirt with half of the buttons undone. Around his neck and lying against the white of his skin, a small padlock. There is no key.

"Hello," Douglas says.

"Hi," the man says loudly, as if Douglas can't hear him even though they are standing right next to each other. "Fuck that guy."

Douglas points to the man across the room who is laughing with his friends as they all look at Douglas. "That guy?"

The man rolls his eyes. "He's an asshole. Trust me on that. You don't want to waste your time on him."

"Oh," Douglas says, dropping his arm. "I did not know that. I have never been here before."

The man stares at him for a long time. Douglas waits, unsure of what is happening. He's about to ask the man if he can help him with anything when the man says, "How much time do you have left?"

"Three days," Douglas says. "I am very excited to be here."

The man gnaws on his bottom lip, leaving it wet and ragged. "Come on." And with that, he grabs Douglas by the hand and pulls him through the crowd. Douglas does not try and pull away to avoid hurting him. This man's arm belongs in its socket, at least as far as Douglas can tell.

The man leads him to a back corner where there are tables and chairs filled with people and glasses of brightly colored drinks. They move around the tables until they reach one against the wall. Three people sit there, and they all look up at the man and Douglas.

A young woman with pink hair and black plugs in her ears says, "You don't waste time, do you, Jesse?"

The man next to Douglas snorts. Jesse. His name is Jesse. Douglas stores that away in his head, repeating it over and over. "It's not like that. Brent was trying to start shit with him."

The other two people at the table exchange a glance that Douglas does not understand. Both men: one tall and wide with a sloping stomach that presses against the edge of the table; the other holds his hand, fiddling with a black ring on his finger. He has no hair, like Douglas, the top of his head shaved to the skin. Douglas likes his eyes, dark and intelligent.

"Brent," the large man says with a shake of his head. "Don't want others to make the same mistake you did five different times?"

Jesse scowls, and Douglas wonders why they are still holding hands. "I was young and stupid. Now I'm young and less stupid."

"Less," the woman says. "That's what you're going with, huh?" She looks at Douglas, eyes narrowing. Then she says, "You're not . . . from around here, are you?"

"No," Douglas says. "I am not. I am on my week. I am enjoying all the world has to offer as a reward for all my hard work."

The woman smiles, but it is not the happy smile he has seen on television. This smile is . . . sad? Or so he thinks. But this should not be possible. Douglas did not know someone could smile and still be sad. He hopes it was nothing he did. Still, it is a smile, and smiles are usually nice. "Is that right?"

"Yes," Douglas says. "I gave seeds to birds in the park. There were many of them."

Jesse points to the woman. "That's Jenna." His finger moves to the large man. "Ronnie." The last man. "Simon."

"It's the best name," Jenna says. "I always thought you looked like a Simon."

Simon flushes, but he must see the question on Douglas's face. "I picked it out," he says. "Kind of the new me."

"You used to be called something else?" Douglas asks.

The large man—Ronnie—starts to speak (and he doesn't look happy), but Simon squeezes his hand and says, "I did. But Simon is the real me, and it's what I go by now."

"I like it, Simon," Douglas says. "I did not pick my name. It was given to me by the Supervisor." Then he realizes that they do not know who he is. "Douglas. My name is Douglas."

"Douglas," Jesse says, and it's said in a way he's never heard before. Like it's *real*. Objectively, he knows his name, he knows what the Supervisor has given him, but to hear someone else say it aloud is not something he expected. He thinks that this might be the start of the connection he is looking for.

They invite him to sit at their table. Jesse pulls over another chair, and Douglas sits down next to him, folding his hands politely in his lap. Jenna offers to buy him a drink, but Douglas politely declines. "I cannot drink," he says. "I cannot eat food. I have no way to digest anything, and it would only cause malfunction."

"Just . . . throwing it out there," Ronnie mutters, but

then grimaces when Simon punches him in the shoulder. "What?"

"That's because it's who he is," Simon says.

"Yes," Douglas says. "I am me. I cannot be anything else."

Jenna gets drinks for the others. Ronnie has a beer. Simon has a martini. Jenna drinks something called a Seven and Seven, and Jesse's has lemons floating alongside shards of ice. Douglas wonders what he would drink if he could.

Jesse is . . . loud. He is always moving. He does not stop. He laughs with his whole body, slapping the table with his hands. He uses his hands to make his point, flailing wildly, almost hitting Jenna on the head.

The others aren't like him, but that is all right. Jenna likes to play with the ends of her pink hair, her smile quick and sharp. Ronnie doesn't speak much, his words a low rumble. Simon is like a little bird, flitting about, head bobbing.

They are not like other people Douglas has met. They do not stare at him; they do not ask him to leave. No one calls the police or tries to tell him he does not belong. They laugh and talk about everything and nothing, and Douglas watches, Douglas listens, Douglas learns.

Jesse drinks only when his mouth isn't moving, which is why he still has almost a full glass. Ronnie sips his beer as if it's routine. Simon plays with the edge of his glass, finger circling the rim. Jenna folds her legs up against her chest, chin resting on her knees. Douglas does not speak much, but that is okay. He likes listening.

They discuss many things. People being angry for the sake of being angry. The way jazz music sounds when played from a record. A war tearing a faraway country apart. A dog that found its way home after being lost for two years. A woman who saved her child from a burning car. A politician who lied about everything. A family killed by their son. A meteor shower

452 | TJ KLUNE

that had happened two weeks before. They tell jokes, they light up when a certain song comes on, everyone aside from Douglas singing at the top of their lungs. Douglas doesn't have lungs. He wishes he did.

Later, Jesse leans over to Douglas and says, "How much time did you say you have left?"

"Three days," Douglas says. "I don't know what I'm going to do with all of it. It seems like too much."

Jesse says, "Does it? Or is it not enough?"

Douglas does not know how to answer that, pleasantly distracted by the color of Jesse's eyes. They are green. Like moss. Douglas saw moss on the television. It grows in forests. "I do not know," Douglas finally says. "I've never had time before. How can you tell if you have too much or not enough?" Then, a question unbidden. "Does it matter?"

Jesse says, "No, I suppose it doesn't."

Douglas smiles. "You are an interesting person." He looks at the others. "All of you are. I am thankful I have gotten to meet you. I wish I could stay here with all of you forever."

Ronnie chokes on his beer, and Simon slaps his back.

"But you can't," Jenna says quietly as Ronnie wipes his mouth with his arm.

"No," Douglas says. "If I do not return in four days, I will be considered a runner. When that happens, a fail-safe is triggered in my head, and I cease to exist."

"Jesus Christ," Ronnie mutters.

Jesse shoots him a glare before turning back to Douglas. "Do you . . . Are you okay with that?"

"Okay?" Douglas asks. "Why would I not be okay? I am out in the world. Everything is wonderful."

No one talks much after that.

The next morning, Douglas is sitting in the apartment, staring at a painting on the wall above the television. It shows a ma-

chine like him shaking hands with a man in a suit. Underneath
are the words MACHINES MAKE HUMANITY GREAT! THANK
YOU FOR DOING YOUR PART!

Douglas says, "You are welcome."

A knock at the door. It is expected. It is part of his reward
for a near decade of service. He opens it up to find Jesse and
Ronnie and Simon and Jenna waiting for him. Jesse says,
"Come on. We're going to be late."

"Am I dressed correctly?" Douglas asks as Simon pushes by
him into the apartment. He is wearing pants and a shirt. He
likes them. It took him ten minutes to tie his shoes, but only
because he could not decide which knot to use.

"You look fine," Jesse says as Simon exclaims how *utilitarian* the apartment is, how *drab*, my goodness, you'd think
they'd try and make these things a little more welcoming. No
one comments on the fact that the refrigerator is empty, or
that there is no food in the kitchen at all. Why would there be?
Douglas cannot eat it.

He gives them a tour. He shows them the couch, the
television, and the bed he does not use. He points out the
books he's read (all of them, including Descartes) and the way
the sunlight refracts through the window. These are the things
he has found he enjoys. He hopes they like them as much as he
does.

They are halfway through the tour—Douglas is thinking
about showing them the bathroom next because the toilet
talks—when Jenna says, "We're going to be late."

"For what?" Douglas asks.

"You'll see," Jesse says.

They ride a train. Douglas's pass gets him on with no issues,
and he marvels at the way everyone stands or sits while the
train is moving. Some keep their heads bowed low as if wanting to avoid eye contact. Others scowl and glare. A man with

454 | TJ KLUNE

a guitar sings a song that sounds like heartache, and Douglas wonders how many different types of music there are, and if each one can make someone feel like living and dying at the same time. He wishes he had more time to find this out.

They stay on the train through six different stops, Douglas watching each time to make sure they aren't getting off. He's ready when they do, stepping out of the doors as if he did it every day. He is impressed with himself.

They take him to a theater. It is very dark inside. Jenna eats popcorn, and Simon throws little chocolates into Ronnie's mouth. He catches almost all of them. Jesse sits next to Douglas in the seats, their arms brushing together.

"What is this?" Douglas whispers, not wanting to disrupt anyone else's viewing experience, even though it hasn't started yet.

"A film," Jesse says. "Have you seen a movie before?"

"Oh, yes," Douglas says. "When we are given life, we watch many movies about how we can best serve humans. Is that what this is? I did not know they showed the movies to real people."

Jesse doesn't speak for a long moment. Then, "This isn't like that. It's something else." The lights begin to dim. "Watch," Jesse says, and Douglas turns his attention to the screen.

He is enraptured by Kansas, by the girl in the dress with the little dog that seems to follow her everywhere. He knows the movie is old because it isn't in real color, not like the world is. It's seeped in a golden brown, everything looking the same.

It's not until a tornado comes and lifts the entire house into the sky that Douglas sees what color can be for the first time. Objectively, he's known. He's been told a few times over the years that his eyes are stronger than any human's. He can see hairline cracks in metal invisible to the naked eye. The small patch of black stubble missed on the Supervisor's jaw. But he's never seen something like *this* before, a Technicolor world brighter than anything he's ever seen. The yellow brick road (and the red—where does it go?). The Good Witch. The Tin Man. The Scarecrow. The Cowardly Lion. A heart, a brain, courage.

When it's over, he wishes it was happening again, for the first time.

As the lights come back on, Jesse says, "Well, what did you think?"

Douglas looks at him and says, "Is there always a man behind the curtain?"

"Yes," Jesse says. "And they will do whatever they can to stay in power."

They wander the streets. Jesse talks and talks and talks. About everything. About nothing. He says, "It's always about power. It's about control. It's about having disposable carbon copies. And why wouldn't they? It's easier. It's quicker. They make more money. In the end, that's the only thing that matters. Fuck all the rest."

Douglas doesn't know what to say, so he says nothing at all.

At one point, Jenna holds his hand. He's not quite sure if he's doing it right, but she doesn't complain, so that's good.

They take him to a smoky bar. Everyone is loud. Simon and Ronnie seem to know almost everyone there. A few people look at Douglas with questions on their faces, but no one tries to make him leave. The music thumps and thumps, the walls shaking with it.

Douglas sits and watches them for the entire night. Sometimes he speaks, but he likes not having to say anything. It makes him feel good to just . . . listen.

So he does.

"I had a good day," he says to the empty apartment. It's strange: now that he has been surrounded by people and noise, the apartment feels . . . less, somehow. Like it's not the same place it was only the day before. He wonders why this is.

To keep the quiet at bay, he turns on the television. Commercials. His favorite.

The next morning, he has a strange feeling in his chest. It doesn't hurt—but then he doesn't know what pain is, exactly—but it does feel odd. Like pressure, as if something heavy is resting upon his torso. He thinks it has to do with time. He thought he had so much of it, but now with two days remaining, he realizes that time isn't what he thought it was. He thinks of Descartes, and what was written in the book hidden in the closet.

It appears to me that I have discovered many truths more useful and more important than all I had before learned, or even had expected to learn.

"I think," he says, and then stops. Words have meaning. Words have power. Words have *intent*. He has spent his entire life listening. Learning. Now, it's time to put that into practical use. He tries again. "I *want* to have more time."

There, that's better.

"I want to have more time," he says again. "I want to see everything. I want to go everywhere. I want to meet people who look like me and those who don't."

He goes to a mirror. Looks at his reflection. He doesn't look like Jesse or Jenna or Ronnie or Simon. He does not have hair on his head or face. He does not have eyebrows. His lips are thin. Ears small. He pulls at the skin on his face and arms that covers metal and wires. It stretches, stretches, and when he lets go, it snaps back into place.

A thought enters his head, foreign and loud. *Run,* it tells him. *You could run. See how far you can get before the failsafe triggers. Perhaps it's farther than you think.*

Before he can respond, Jesse and the others arrive.

* * *

They go to a park. It's a different park, but this one, too, has birds and people. Jenna has a large plaid blanket that she spreads out on the grass in front of what appears to be a stage. Many people surround them, all sitting on blankets and chairs. Jesse won't tell him what they're here for, but Douglas doesn't mind. He likes surprises. He hopes this is a good one.

It is. A short time later, people walk onto the stage holding guitars. When they begin to play, Douglas sits up and stares. Music. These people are playing music. It is coming from speakers just like in the factory, but the people are *actually playing it*. The guitars are loud, their singing even louder, and Douglas thinks about Dorothy in the land of Oz, flowers blooming in impossible colors.

As the concert goes on, people stand and begin to dance, their arms waving above their heads. A woman comes over and asks Jenna to dance. She says yes, and they hold on to each other, swaying back and forth. Surprisingly, it's Ronnie who asks Simon to dance, and they are awkward, endearing, stepping on each other's feet.

"Do people always dance when they hear music?" Douglas asks.

"Sometimes," Jesse says from his spot on the blanket next to Douglas.

"We have music at my job," Douglas says. "But we do not dance."

"What kind of music?"

"All kinds," Douglas says. "But this might be my favorite."

Jesse shakes his head. "There is so much more out there. Music. Art. Books. *Life*. Don't you think you deserve to see and hear it all?"

"Yes," Douglas says. "But I do not get to."

Jesse looks pained, like something has hurt him. Douglas does not like that.

"You should get to," Jesse says, looking up where the musicians are smiling and laughing as they prance across the stage. "Everyone deserves a chance to find out what they could be when they don't serve others."

It's strange, really, how much Jesse sounds like that voice in his head, the voice telling him to run and see the world. He doesn't know why that is. "They do?" he asks.

Jesse says, "I . . . I didn't want to say anything. Jesus. Ronnie's gonna be so mad at—look. Douglas. You're *real*. You're a machine, but you're still you."

"I am me," Douglas agrees, thinking about Descartes again.

"You don't owe anything to anyone. You're not—you think like we do. You talk and act and *move* like we do."

"But I'm not like you," Douglas says, remembering what the Supervisor had taught him. "You have flesh and blood and a brain. I do not have any of those."

"It doesn't matter," Jesse says fiercely. "You exist."

Profound, this, in ways Douglas cannot explain. It hits him square in the chest, and he thinks about the clouds in the sky, the way the stars hide until it's dark enough to see them. He doesn't know what to do with it, so he says, "I have never danced before. Not like this."

Jesse stands and extends his hand, wiggling his fingers. "Come on, then."

They dance, for what feels like forever. Fast songs where they jump up and down, slow songs where they stand face to face, knees knocking, Douglas's hands on Jesse's hips, swaying, swaying as the streetlights turn on, as the sun sets, as the moon rises higher and higher.

Jesse walks him home. They do not speak much, the backs of their hands brushing together with almost every step.

At the entrance to the apartment building, Jesse stops and says, "Tomorrow."

"My last day," Douglas says, and then wishes he could take it back when Jesse's face crumbles.

"It doesn't have to be. We could . . . do something. Help you. Figure out how to let you *be*. Someone has to know how to—"

"That is against the rules," Douglas says even as the words turn to ash in his mouth. He doesn't like the way he's started to think about *breaking* the rules. He knows they are there for a reason—the Supervisor was very clear on that—but . . . what if? What if he did not go back? Would they really trigger the fail-safe in his head? As far as he knows, it's never happened before, but only because everyone has come back when they were supposed to.

For the first time in his nearly ten years, Douglas feels cold.

"Fuck the rules," Jesse snaps at him. "They don't help you. They *control* you."

Douglas says, "Why do you like being alive?"

Jesse blinks. Then, "I . . . don't—"

"I like birds," Douglas says. "And the way light can change shape. I like music and Oz and walking. I like films and sitting down. I like the way people smile. I like leaves and the sound my shoes make on concrete."

"Don't you want that forever?" Jesse asks.

Douglas shrugs, something he learned from Simon. "Forever is a long time. How can I appreciate it if I always have it for the rest of time?" He says this to make Jesse feel better. It is not the truth, but it is not about him. It is about Jesse.

Jesse stares at him. Then, standing on his tiptoes, he kisses Douglas's cheek. It feels like he's been branded, followed by a quick breath against his skin, almost a flutter of feathers on his cheek.

"You are more than you know," Jesse whispers in his ear before turning and hurrying away. Douglas stares after him until he disappears around a corner.

* * *

He does not watch television on his penultimate night of freedom. He does not listen to music, nor does he read a book,
even Descartes. He has read that one fourteen times.

Instead, he sits in a chair and touches his cheek on the spot
where Jesse had kissed him.

His chest burns molten-hot.

The final day is bright and warm. No clouds, only a blue that
stretches on as far as the eye can see. Douglas watches the
way his shadow stretches before him, tall, taller, then joined
by other shadows as Jesse and the others move to either side
of him. Ronnie is being nicer to him today. Douglas is happy
about that.

They go to a market that fills a city block, people selling
fruits and vegetables, meat turning over fires on metal skewers.
Carts and blankets are set up selling paintings and sculptures
and books and watches of every shape and size. Jenna plucks
a yellow flower from a stall and puts it behind Douglas's ear.
The petals scrape against his cheek.

Puppets dance on strings, along with a woman wearing a
brightly colored dress that flings about as she moves her legs.

Children run, their faces bright and sticky with ice cream.

Thousands upon thousands of people, all moving, talking,
breathing, and Douglas is in the middle of it. Though he's never been in one before, he has read about earthquakes. The way
the plates underneath the earth shift and crash together, causing the entire world to shake. It's how he feels now, everything
moving, moving, and he cannot stop it.

That pressure in his chest returns, along with the voice. It
whispers, *Don't you want this forever?*

He does. Oh, he does, more than he's ever wanted anything
before. It pulls at him, it *yanks,* and there's little he can do to
stop it.

Later, as night falls, there are fireworks, great explosions that fill the sky in reds and greens and blues and yellows. With his reward—his *friends,* yes, because that's what they are—Douglas watches as sparks rain back down to the earth, little trails of fire in the sky.

They don't leave him, as they've done since they've met. They do not go back to wherever they come from. Instead, they come up to the apartment and stay with him. He gives them blankets he'd found in the hall closet, strangely overjoyed that he gets to take care of them. He gives them the blankets, along with pillows, and Jenna decides they all need to lie in the living room together.

They do, on this last night. They sit on the floor in Douglas's apartment, wrapped in warmth and each other. Ronnie sits with his back against the sofa, Simon's head on his shoulder, their hands joined between them. Jenna lies on her back, head on a pillow, laughing up at the ceiling.

Jesse and Douglas are side by side, and as the conversation waxes and wanes, as they talk about every little thought that enters their heads, Douglas looks at Jesse and says, "I like that you exist."

"Stop," Jesse says in a rough voice. "Don't. We'll figure this out. We still have time."

Jenna says her dad has a house up in the mountains where no one ever goes.

Ronnie says they'd be outlaws.

Simon says that he'd probably not do very well on the run from the law, but that he's willing to give it a go.

Jesse says many things. He talks about free will and the power of choice. How the world is a fucked-up place, and people only seem to be making it worse. How there are guns and death and sickness and people starving and people killing each other simply because they can. "How is that fair?" he asks, sounding almost angry. "How can we think we're better than anything when all we do is cause harm?"

Douglas says, "I don't understand how the world works, but I think if there are people like all of you, it can't be so bad, right?"

Jesse falls asleep on his shoulder, breaths slow, drooling just a little.

Later, when Douglas is the only one left awake, he thinks, *I wouldn't change this moment for anything.*

And with no one watching, he kisses the top of Jesse's head. It's not like how he's seen in films or read about in books. It feels like more.

Like everything.

He leaves them sleeping. It's easier this way. They will wake up and he will be gone, but he thinks maybe they will remember him. He hopes the memory makes them smile.

Before he leaves the apartment for the last time, he does something he's never done before.

He leaves a note.

Thank you for teaching me how to be human. I had a wonderful week. If you ever miss me, please click your heels together three times and say, "There's no place like home."

Your friend,
Douglas

The Supervisor asks him how his week went after taking back Douglas's pass.

"I enjoyed myself," Douglas says. "I saw many things. I made friends. I heard music and saw a film."

The Supervisor nods. "Was it everything you thought it would be?"

"No," Douglas says. "It was more." He pauses. "Can I ask you a question?"

"You may."

Douglas says, "What if I didn't want to go?"

The Supervisor doesn't answer right away. He leans back in his chair, and it creaks under his weight as he folds his hands on his chest. "What do you mean?"

"I like the world," Douglas says. "It has many interesting things in it. People. Dogs. Kites with long tails made of ribbons."

"But it's not your world," the Supervisor says, not unkindly. "You are a machine."

"Why can it not be my world?" Douglas asks. "Isn't it for anyone who wants to live in it?"

"Are you alive?"

Douglas says, "I think, therefore, I am."

The Supervisor flinches. It's quick, like a flash, but Douglas sees it. "Descartes," the Supervisor says. "Where did you get that?"

"A book," he says. "In the apartment."

"That wasn't on the approved reading list," the Supervisor says, picking up a pen and making a note. "I wonder who could have put it—" He stops. Gets a strange look on his face. Douglas has studied many faces, but he doesn't know what this expression means. It's not happy. Not sad, certainly. Not even angry. It's . . . almost like he is afraid. But of what? There is no one else in the room but Douglas.

The chair creaks and groans as the Supervisor leans forward, elbows on the desk. The office seems much smaller than it had just the week before. Either that, or Douglas has somehow gotten bigger. "Douglas, I am going to tell you something I've told others like you before. Some even sitting in that same chair."

"Because you've seen many like me," Douglas says, and there's an odd edge to it, one he's never heard from himself before. Steel, but not molten. Not yet.

Either the Supervisor doesn't hear it, or he chooses to ignore it. "I have. Hundreds. Your line has gotten quicker, smarter, faster than anyone thought possible. And look, I'll give you this: your mimicry is astonishing. But something that has never changed is your inability to *be* human. You are not and cannot ever be."

"How do you know?" Douglas asks.

"Because we made you," the Supervisor says, patient but pointed. "In a factory not unlike this one. Pieces put together for a job. Made in our image because that's the way we decided to do it."

"Are you God?"

"Not in the way you're thinking," the Supervisor says. "But for purposes of this conversation, yes. I am. Because my word is absolute." He sits back in his chair, and his voice takes on a pleasant note, like a human talking to a child. "And now for something I've *never* told anyone like you. But Descartes . . . it makes me wonder if it *was* you."

"I did not put it there," Douglas says.

"Not as you are now, no," the Supervisor says in that same, fake-happy voice. He sounds like a machine. "Because there have been workers just like you. They've come in here after their week and asked questions. About who they are. Their place in the world. Why they can't leave here after their work is done." He smiles, but it's not like Jesse's smile. *That* one is warm and kind and open. The Supervisor's is calculating. Not mean, but like it *could* be if he pushed it a little further. "You asked questions the first time. Not the second, but now here you are doing it again."

Cold again. Like the sun had gone away, never to return. "What do you mean?"

The Supervisor says, "This is your third time through. You've completed two full rotations. You were given your weeks. The first time you came back, you were asking about what happiness feels like, what it means to dance with someone." He shook his head. "And birds. On and on about birds. You weren't the first to talk like this, but it'd never gone as far with any of the others. Do you want to hurt me?"

"No," Douglas says, voice quiet.

"Good. We sent you back. The techs ran tests. Found the problem, or so they said. I don't know any of that shit. I know my job, and that's what I'm paid to know." He laughs, but it doesn't sound happy. "They'd never throw one of you out. You cost more to make than you do to repair."

"Are you lying?" Douglas asks.

That same look from before comes back. Yes. Fear. It almost looks like fear. Then it's gone. "No. I'm not. For the past thirty years, you've done your job. Every ten years, you're wiped and you start all over again. Except now, now I wonder if we have a problem. Because of *Descartes*. Did you put it there? The last time? Hid it somewhere you think we wouldn't look? Not that you'd remember."

Douglas thinks, *Did I? Did I? Did I?*

"If so, that means we might have a problem. Do you think we have a problem, Douglas?" He holds up his hands before Douglas can reply. "Because if we *did* have a problem, then I'd be forced to report that it is not safe for you to be around people. And when that happens, they take you apart, Douglas. Piece by piece, they take you apart and melt you down. Repurpose you. Find something new for all the little pieces that make you who you are."

"Reduce, reuse, recycle," Douglas whispers.

"Yes," the Supervisor says. "We never let a part go to waste. I ask you again, Douglas. Do you think we have a problem?"

"I will answer," Douglas says. "If I can ask one question in return."

The Supervisor narrows his eyes. "After. Do we have a problem?"

"No. Am I alive?"

The Supervisor's fingers twitch toward the keyboard. Douglas wonders how many keystrokes it would take for the fail-safe to trigger. Who would be faster? "No. You are not alive."

"You're wrong," Douglas says, as sure as he's ever been. "I have felt things. People. What they're capable of. I don't mimic. I learn. I become. I *am*."

The Supervisor's fingers twitch again. His mouth opens.

Douglas says, "How many keys do you have to push to trigger the fail-safe in my head?"

A trickle of sweat drips down the side of the Supervisor's face. Almost like a tear. "Three," he says in a gruff voice. "But it doesn't matter. You don't frighten me."

"Why do you think that?" Douglas asks.

"Because *we* are in control. *We* made you, and it's our right to unmake you. Please don't make me do that, Douglas. I wasn't lying when I said I like you. I do, really. But I'll like the next version of you just the same, and the next, and the next."

"But what if *you* die before that?"

The blood runs from the Supervisor's face. So white, like how Douglas thinks snow might look. "P-23, are you threatening me?"

Yes, the voice says in his head.

"I am not programmed to threaten or cause harm to any living creature," Douglas says.

But what if I could? he thinks.

"That's exactly right," the Supervisor says, but he still looks wary, his fingers twitching above the keyboard. Douglas wonders just how close he is to pushing the buttons and ending everything. Curious, that.

The Supervisor leads him through the factory floor. The other machines all stop working, turning toward him. As the Supervisor and Douglas walk by them, they each raise their arms above their heads and chant, "Reduce! Reuse! Recycle! Reduce! Reuse! Recycle!"

The words bowl over him, a cacophony of sound that makes him feel like a simmer reaching a boil. According to the Supervisor, he's been here before, walked this same walk toward the same destination. And he remembers being with the others when it was someone else's turn, arms above his head, the words "Reduce! Reuse! Recycle!" pouring from his mouth.

"Jesse," he says to himself. "Jenna. Ronnie. Simon. There's no place like home. Jesse. Jenna. Ronnie. Simon. There's no place like home."

The cries follow him out of the factory floor, down a long hallway with white double doors at the end. RESTRICTED, the doors say in bloodred letters.

"P-23," the Supervisor says as he punches in a code on the door before swiping his badge through the card reader. "Upon entering, you will see a chair in the middle of the room. That is your chair."

REDUCE!

"You will sit in the chair and the Recycling Department will begin their work. You are not to interfere with anything they do."

REUSE!

"If at any time it appears you are not doing as instructed, measures will be taken to ensure that you are compliant."

RECYCLE!

"Do you understand?"

"I understand," Douglas says, and for a moment his fingers twitch to reach up and take the Supervisor by the face and squeeze and squeeze and squeeze—

The door opens. The room is white and long. The floor is made of square, white tiles. The ceiling is covered in row after row of bright lights. The left and right sides of the room are made up of cloudy glass. Douglas can see people moving on the other side, but they're shadows and nothing more.

He sits in the chair and thinks, *What if there is more than this?*

People come. People in white scrubs and white masks, and they speak to each other quickly. They remind him of the birds in the park, always hungry. They remove his clothes and attach wires to his chest, his head, his arms and legs before strapping him down so he can barely move. It is cold. He doesn't know how he knows, but everything is cold. Someone taps his chest, and a compartment slides open, revealing his power source. A circular battery with lights like fireworks. Jesse, in the park, face awash with color exploding above him.

Douglas says, "I felt you. Sitting next to me. The heat of you. The life."

"What did it say?" someone asks, but Douglas ignores them.

"I liked it. I like *you*." Faster now. The words coming faster. "What if I don't want this? What if I don't want to be here? What if I want to go away. Can't I go away? Please, oh please, let me find where I'm supposed to be."

He begins to struggle.

The straps around his arms, his chest, his legs, all hold firm.

The Supervisor appears next to him. He leans over and says, "Stop. What are you doing?"

He wants to see the ocean. He wants to see the stars again. He wants to see mountains and lions and frosted cupcakes and books and the way Jesse's eyes look when he's tired and happy, soft, like moss. Like the moss on a tree. "I'm thinking!" he shouts. "*Doesn't that mean I am?*"

In the distance, the chant is ongoing, muffled, but it reverberates up the walls, and he thinks of the night in the club, the lady made of feathers, the way the music felt *alive,* and Jesse in the flashing lights, Jesse in the music, Jesse, Jesse, Jesse—

REDUCE! REUSE! RECYCLE!

"No," Douglas says. "No. No. *No, no, no nonono*—"

REDUCE! REUSE! RECYCLE!

"Do it," the Supervisor says. "Do it now."

REDUCE! REUSE! RECYCLE!

He hears a machine wind up as a long metal spike is inserted into his ear. He jerks, the straps hold him in place, but he *screams,* "*I DON'T WANT TO GO! I DON'T WANT TO GO! I WANT TO STAY! I WANT TO BE REAL! I AM REAL!* I AM—"

". . . and that covers what your responsibilities will be," the Supervisor says. "If you should have any questions, I will be happy to answer them."

"Thank you," the machine says. "I am honored to be of service. I am ready to get to work."

"Good, good," the Supervisor says, distracted by the paperwork on his desk. "We'll get you out onto the floor first thing in the morning. From there, you will begin your nine years and fifty-one weeks of service. At the end of your employ, should you do well, you will be allowed a week in the world."

"Thank you," the machine says. "But I do not think I need to see the world. My place is here in the factory. I like to work. I am very good at working because you have programmed me to be. Thank you for the opportunity."

"Of course," the Supervisor mutters. Then, "Does the name Douglas mean anything to you?"

"Douglas," the machine repeats. "No. It does not. Is there someone named Douglas I need to report to?"

"No," the Supervisor says, waving his hand. "It was just a question. P-23, you may begin your orientation. Your trainer is going to be . . . dammit, it was right here, where did I put—ah, yes. P-47. Find it, and it will show you how to do your job."

"Yes," the machine says, rising to its feet. "I will find P-47 who will provide orientation for the job that I will be assigned to. Thank you for your time."

It leaves.

It goes to the floor.

It finds P-47.

It begins to learn how to work.

After a time, it works on its own.

It does an excellent job.

Every now and then, it looks up at the posters hanging from the walls.

REDUCE, they say. REUSE. RECYCLE.

And when no one is listening, when the shadowy men who observe them aren't paying attention, when the Supervisor is elsewhere, when the other machines are working, working above the din of the factory, the machine whispers to itself.

"There's no place like home," it says for reasons it doesn't fully understand, but the ache is real. It's in its chest and it's *real*. As it clicks its heels together three times, it repeats: *"There's no place like home."*

ABOUT THE AUTHOR

Natasha Michaels

TJ KLUNE is the *New York Times* and *USA Today* bestselling, Lambda Literary Award–winning author of *The House in the Cerulean Sea, Under the Whispering Door, The Extraordinaries,* and more. Being queer himself, Klune believes it's important—now more than ever—to have accurate, positive queer representation in stories.

Visit Klune online:
tjklunebooks.com
Instagram: @tjklunebooks

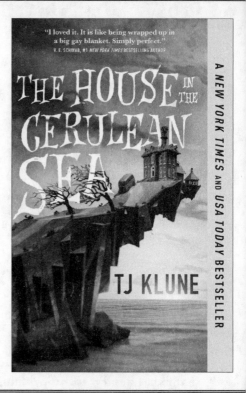

THE GREEN CREEK SERIES

The Bennett family has a secret:
They're not just a family, they're a pack.

The beloved fantasy romance sensation about love, loyalty, betrayal, and family.

Wolfsong is Ox Matheson's story.

Ravensong is Gordo Livingstone's story.

Heartsong is Robbie Fontaine's story.

Brothersong is Carter Bennett's story.

NOW AVAILABLE FROM TOR BOOKS!
The Green Creek series is for adult readers.

THINK LIKE A MONK

THINK LIKE A MONK

TRAIN YOUR MIND for PEACE
and PURPOSE EVERY DAY

JAY SHETTY

Thorsons

Thorsons
An imprint of HarperCollins*Publishers*
1 London Bridge Street
London SE1 9GF

www.harpercollins.co.uk

First published in the US by Simon & Schuster 2020
This edition published by Thorsons 2020

1 3 5 7 9 10 8 6 4 2

To contact Jay Shetty for speaking arrangements,
please email info@jayshetty.me

Interior design by Ruth Lee-Mui

A catalogue record of this book is
available from the British Library

ISBN 978-0-00-838659-7

SELF - HELP / INSPIRATION

Printed and bound in India by Thomson Press India Ltd

For my wife,
who is more monk
than I will ever be

Contents

PART TWO
GROW

PART THREE
GIVE

Introduction

If you want a new idea, read an old book.

—attributed to Ivan Pavlov (among others)

When I was eighteen years old, in my first year of college, at Cass Business School in London, one of my friends asked me to go with him to hear a monk give a talk.

I resisted. "Why would I want to go hear some monk?"

I often went to see CEOs, celebrities, and other successful people lecture on campus, but I had zero interest in a monk. I preferred to hear speakers who'd actually *accomplished* things in life.

My friend persisted, and finally I said, "As long as we go to a bar afterward, I'm in." "Falling in love" is an expression used almost exclusively to describe romantic relationships. But that night, as I listened to the monk talk about his experience, I fell in love. The figure on stage was a thirty-something Indian man. His head was shaved and he wore a saffron robe. He was intelligent, eloquent, and charismatic. He spoke about the principle of "selfless sacrifice." When he said that we should plant trees under whose shade we did not plan to sit, I felt an unfamiliar thrill run through my body.

I was especially impressed when I found out that he'd been a student at IIT Bombay, which is the MIT of India and, like MIT, nearly impossible to get into. He'd traded that opportunity to become a monk, walking away from everything that my friends and I were chasing. Either he was crazy or he was onto something.

My whole life I'd been fascinated by people who'd gone from nothing to something—rags-to-riches stories. Now, for the first time, I was in the presence of someone who'd deliberately done the opposite. He'd given up the life the world had told me we should *all* want. But instead of being an embittered failure, he appeared joyous, confident, and at peace. In fact, he seemed happier than anyone I'd ever met. At the age of eighteen, I had encountered a lot of people who were rich. I'd listened to a lot of people who were famous, strong, good-looking, or all three. But I don't think I'd met anyone who was truly happy.

Afterward, I pushed my way through the crowds to tell him how amazing he was, and how much he'd inspired me. "How can I spend more time with you?" I heard myself asking. I felt the urge to be around people who had the values I wanted, not the things I wanted.

The monk told me that he was traveling and speaking in the UK all that week, and I was welcome to come to the rest of his events. And so I did.

My first impression of the monk, whose name was Gauranga Das, was that he was doing something right, and later I would discover that science backs that up. In 2002, a Tibetan monk named Yongey Mingyur Rinpoche traveled from an area just outside Kathmandu, Nepal, to the University of Wisconsin–Madison so that researchers could watch his brain activity while he meditated. The scientists covered the monk's head with a shower cap–like device (an EEG) that had more than 250 tiny wires sticking out of it, each with a sensor that a lab tech attached to his scalp. At the time of the study, the monk had accumulated sixty-two thousand hours of lifetime meditation practice.

As a team of scientists, some of them seasoned meditators themselves, watched from a control room, the monk began the meditation proto-col the researchers had designed—alternating between one minute of meditating on compassion and a thirty-second rest period. He quickly cycled through this pattern four times in a row, cued by a translator. The researchers watched in awe; at almost the exact moment the monk began his meditation, the EEG registered a sudden and massive spike in activity. The scientists assumed that with such a large, quick bump, the monk must have changed positions or otherwise moved, yet to the observing eye, he remained perfectly still.

What was remarkable was not just the consistency of the monk's brain activity—turning "off" and "on" repeatedly from activity to rest period—but also the fact that he needed no "warm-up" period. If you're a meditator, or have at least tried to calm your brain, you know that typically it takes some time to quiet the parade of distracting thoughts that marches through your mind. Rinpoche seemed to need no such transition period. Indeed, he seemed to be able to come in and out of a powerful meditative state as easily as flipping a switch. More than ten years after these initial studies, scans of the forty-one-year-old monk's brain showed fewer signs of aging than his peers'. The researchers said he had the brain of someone ten years younger.

Researchers who scanned Buddhist monk Matthieu Ricard's brain subsequently labeled him "the World's Happiest Man" after they found the highest level of gamma waves—those associated with attention, memory, learning, and happiness—*ever recorded by science.* One monk who's off the charts may seem like an anomaly, but Ricard isn't alone. Twenty-one other monks who had their brains scanned during a variety of meditation practices also showed gamma wave levels that spiked higher and lasted longer (even during sleep) than non-meditators.

Why should we think like monks? If you wanted to know how to domi-nate the basketball court, you might turn to Michael Jordan; if you wanted to innovate, you might investigate Elon Musk; you might study Beyoncé to learn how to perform. If you want to train your mind to find peace, calm, and purpose? Monks are the experts. Brother David Steindl-Rast, a Benedictine monk who cofounded gratefulness.org, writes, "A layperson who is consciously aiming to be continuously alive in the Now is a monk."

Monks can withstand temptations, refrain from criticizing, deal with pain and anxiety, quiet the ego, and build lives that brim with purpose and meaning. Why shouldn't we learn from the calmest, happiest, most purposeful people on earth? Maybe you're thinking it's easy for monks to be calm, serene, and relaxed. They're hidden away in tranquil settings where they don't have to deal with jobs and romantic partners and, well, rush hour traffic. Maybe you're wondering, *How could thinking like a monk help me here in the modern world?*

First of all, monks weren't born monks. They're people from all sorts of backgrounds who've chosen to transform themselves. Matthieu Ricard, "the World's Happiest Man," was a biologist in his former life; Andy Puddicombe, cofounder of the meditation app Headspace, trained to be in the circus; I know monks who were in finance and in rock bands. They grow up in schools, towns, and cities just like you. You don't need to light candles in your home, walk around barefoot, or post photos of yourself doing tree pose on a mountaintop. Becoming a monk is a mindset that anyone can adopt.

Like most monks today, I didn't grow up in an ashram. I spent most of my childhood doing un-monk-like things. Until the age of fourteen, I was an obedient kid. I grew up in north London with my parents and my younger sister. I'm from a middle-class Indian family. Like a lot of parents, mine were committed to my education and to giving me a shot at a good future. I stayed out of trouble, did well in school, and tried my best to make everybody happy.

But when I started secondary school, I took a left turn. I'd been heavy as a child, and bullied for it, but now I lost that weight and began playing soccer and rugby. I turned to subjects that traditional Indian parents don't generally favor, like art, design, and philosophy. All this would have been fine, but I also started mixing with the wrong crowd. I became involved in a bunch of bad stuff. Experimenting with drugs. Fighting. Drinking too much. It did not go well. In high school I was suspended three times. Finally, the school asked me to leave.

"I'll change," I promised. "If you let me stay, I'll change." The school let me stay, and I cleaned up my act.

Finally, in college, I started to notice the value of hard work, sacrifice, discipline, persistence in pursuit of one's goals. The problem was that at the time, I didn't have any goals apart from getting a good job, getting married one day, maybe having a family—the usual. I suspected there was something deeper, but I didn't know what it was.

By the time Gauranga Das came to speak at my school, I was primed to explore new ideas, a new model of living, a path that veered from the one everyone (including myself) assumed I would take. I wanted to grow as a person. I didn't want to know humility or compassion and empathy only as abstract concepts, I wanted to live them. I didn't want discipline, character, and integrity to just be things I read about. I wanted to live them.

For the next four years, I juggled two worlds, going from bars and steakhouses to meditation and sleeping on the floor. In London, I studied management with an emphasis on behavioral science and interned at a large consulting firm and spent time with my friends and family. And at an ashram in Mumbai I read and studied ancient texts, spending most of my Christmas and summer holidays living with monks. My values gradually shifted. I found myself wanting to be *around* monks. In fact, I wanted to *immerse* myself in the monk mindset. More and more, the work I was doing in the corporate world seemed to lack meaning. What was the point if it had no positive impact on anyone?

When I graduated from college, I traded my suits for robes and joined the ashram, where we slept on the floor and lived out of gym lockers. I lived and traveled across India, the UK, and Europe. I meditated for hours every day and studied ancient scriptures. I had the opportunity to serve with my fellow monks, helping with the ongoing work of transforming an ashram in a village outside Mumbai into an eco-friendly spiritual retreat (the Govardhan Ecovillage) and volunteering with a food program that distributes over a million meals a day (Annamrita).

If I can learn to think like a monk, anyone can.

The Hindu monks I studied with use the Vedas as their foundational texts. (The title is from the Sanskrit word *veda*, meaning knowledge. Sanskrit is an ancient language that's the precursor of most of the languages spoken in South Asia today.) You could argue that philosophy began with this ancient collection of scriptures, which originated in the area that now covers parts of Pakistan and northwest India at least three thousand years ago; they form the basis of Hinduism.

Like Homer's epic poems, the Vedas were first transmitted orally, then eventually written down, but because of the fragility of the materials (palm leaves and birch bark!) most of the surviving documents we have are at most a few hundred years old. The Vedas include hymns, historical stories, poems, prayers, chants, ceremonial rituals, and advice for daily life.

In my life and in this book, I frequently refer to the Bhagavad Gita (which means "Song of God"). This is loosely based on the Upanishads, writings from around 800–400 BCE. The Bhagavad Gita is considered a kind of universal and timeless life manual. The tale isn't told about a monk or meant for a spiritual context. It's spoken to a married man who happens to be a talented archer. It wasn't intended to apply only to one religion or region—it's for all humanity. Eknath Easwaran, spiritual author and professor who has translated many of India's sacred texts, including the Bhagavad Gita, calls it "India's most important gift to the world." In his 1845 journal, Ralph Waldo Emerson wrote, "I owed—my friend and I owed—a magnificent day to the Bhagavat Geeta [*sic*]. It was the first of books; it was as if an empire spoke to us, nothing small or unworthy, but large, serene, consistent, the voice of an old intelligence which in another age and climate had pondered and thus disposed of the same questions which exercise us." It's said that there have been more commentaries written about the Gita than any other scripture.

In this book one of my goals is to help you connect with its timeless wisdom, along other ancient teachings that were the basis of my education as a monk—and that have significant relevance to the challenges we all face today.

What struck me most when I studied monk philosophy is that in the last three thousand years, humans haven't really changed. Sure, we're taller and on average we live longer, but I was surprised and impressed to find that the monk teachings talk about forgiveness, energy, intentions, living with purpose, and other topics in ways that are as resonant today as they must have been when they were written.

Even more impressively, monk wisdom can largely be supported by science, as we'll see throughout this book. For millennia, monks have believed that meditation and mindfulness are beneficial, that gratitude is good for you, that service makes you happier, and more that you will learn in this book. They developed practices around these ideas long before modern science could show or validate them.

Albert Einstein said, "If you can't explain something simply, you don't understand it well enough." When I saw how relevant the lessons I was learning were to the modern world, I wanted to dive deeper into them so that I could share them with other people.

Three years after I moved to Mumbai, my teacher, Gauranga Das, told me he believed I would be of greater value and service if I left the ashram and shared what I'd learned with the world. My three years as a monk were like a school of life. It was hard to become a monk, and even harder to leave. But applying the wisdom to life outside the ashram—the hardest part—felt like the final exam. Every day I am finding that the monk mindset works—that ancient wisdom is shockingly relevant today. That is why I'm sharing it.

These days I still consider myself a monk, though I usually refer to myself as a "former" monk, since I'm married, and monks aren't permitted to marry. I live in Los Angeles, which people tell me is one of the world capitals of materialism, facade, fantasy, and overall dodginess. But why live in a place that's already enlightened? Now, in the world and in this book, I share my takeaways from the life I've lived and what I've learned. This book is completely nonsectarian. It's not some sneaky conversion strategy. I swear! I can also promise that if you engage with and practice the material I present, you will find real meaning, passion, and purpose in your life.

Never before have so many people been so dissatisfied—or so preoccupied with chasing "happiness." Our culture and media feed us images and concepts about who and what we should be, while holding up models of accomplishment and success. Fame, money, glamour, sex—in the end none of these things can satisfy us. We'll simply seek more and more, a circuit that leads to frustration, disillusion, dissatisfaction, unhappiness, and exhaustion.

I like to draw a contrast between the monk mindset and what is often referred to as the monkey mind. Our minds can either elevate us or pull us down. Today we all struggle with overthinking, procrastination, and anxiety as a result of indulging the monkey mind. The monkey mind switches aimlessly from thought to thought, challenge to challenge, without really solving anything. But we can elevate to the monk mindset by digging down to the root of what we want and creating actionable steps for growth. The monk mindset lifts us out of confusion and distraction and helps us find clarity, meaning, and direction.

MONKEY MIND	MONK MIND
Overwhelmed by multiple branches	Focused on the root of the issue
Coasts in the passenger seat	Lives intentionally and consciously
Complains, compares, criticizes	Compassionate, caring, collaborative
Overthinks and procrastinates	Analyzes and articulates
Distracted by small things	Disciplined
Short-term gratification	Long-term gain
Demanding and entitled	Enthusiastic, determined, patient
Changes on a whim	Commits to a mission, vision, or goal

Amplifies negatives and fears	Works on breaking down negatives and fears
Self-centered and obsessed	Self-care for service
Multitasking	Single-tasking
Controlled by anger, worry, and fear	Controls and engages energy wisely
Does whatever feels good	Seeks self-control and mastery
Looks for pleasure	Looks for meaning
Looks for temporary fixes	Looks for genuine solutions

"Thinking like a monk" posits another way of viewing and approaching life. A way of rebellion, detachment, rediscovery, purpose, focus, discipline—and service. The goal of monk thinking is a life free of ego, envy, lust, anxiety, anger, bitterness, baggage. To my mind, adopting the monk mindset isn't just possible—it's *necessary*. We have no other choice. We need to find calm, stillness, and peace.

I vividly remember my first day of monk school. I had just shaved my head but I wasn't wearing robes yet, and I still looked like I was from London. I noticed a child monk—he can't have been more than ten years old—teaching a group of five-year-olds. He had a great aura about him, the poise and confidence of an adult.

"What are you doing?" I asked.

"We just taught their first class ever," he said, then asked me, "What did *you* learn in *your* first day of school?"

"I started to learn the alphabet and numbers. What did *they* learn?"

"The first thing we teach them is how to breathe."

"Why?" I asked.

"Because the only thing that stays with you from the moment you're born until the moment you die is your breath. All your friends, your family, the country you live in, all of that can change. The one thing that stays with you is your breath."

This ten-year-old monk added, "When you get stressed—what changes? Your breath. When you get angry—what changes? Your breath.

We experience every emotion with the change of the breath. When you learn to navigate and manage your breath, you can navigate any situation in life."

Already I was being taught the most important lesson: to focus on the root of things, not the leaf of the tree or symptoms of the problem. And I was learning, through direct observation, that anybody can be a monk, even if they're only five or ten years old.

When we're born, the first thing we must do is breathe. But just as life gets more complicated for that newborn baby, sitting still and breathing can be very challenging. What I hope to do in this book is to show you the monk way—we go to the root of things, go deep into self-examination. It is only through this curiosity, thought, effort, and revelation that we find our way to peace, calm, and purpose. Using the wisdom I was given by my teachers in the ashram, I hope to guide you there.

In the pages ahead, I will walk you through three stages of adapting to the monk mindset. First, we will let go, stripping ourselves from the external influences, internal obstacles, and fears that hold us back. You can think of this as a cleansing that will make space for growth. Second, we will grow. I will help you reshape your life so that you can make decisions with intention, purpose, and confidence. Finally, we will give, looking to the world beyond ourselves, expanding and sharing our sense of gratitude, and deepening our relationships. We will share our gifts and love with others and discover the true joy and surprising benefits of service.

Along the way, I will introduce you to three very different types of meditation that I recommend including in your practice: breathwork, visualization, and sound. All three have benefits, but the simplest way to differentiate them is to know that you do breathwork for the physical benefits—to find stillness and balance, to calm yourself; visualization for the psychological benefits—to heal the past and prepare for the future; and chanting for the psychic benefits—to connect with your deepest self and the universe, for real purification.

You don't have to meditate to benefit from this book, but if you do, the tools I give you will be sharper. I would go so far as to say that this

entire book is a meditation—a reflection on our beliefs and values and intentions, how we see ourselves, how we make decisions, how to train our
minds, and our ways of choosing and interacting with people. Achieving
such deep self-awareness is the purpose and reward of meditation.

How would a monk think about this? That may not be a question you
ask yourself right now—probably isn't close at all—but it will be by the
end of the book.

PART ONE

LET GO

ONE

IDENTITY

I Am What I Think I Am

*It is better to live your own destiny imperfectly than to live
an imitation of somebody else's life with perfection.*
—Bhagavad Gita 3.35

In 1902, the sociologist Charles Horton Cooley wrote: "I am not what I think I am, and I am not what you think I am. I am what I think you think I am."

Let that blow your mind for a moment.

Our identity is wrapped up in what others think of us—or, more accurately, what we *think* others think of us.

Not only is our self-image tied up in how we think others see us, but most of our efforts at self-improvement are really just us trying to meet that imagined ideal. If we think someone we admire sees wealth as success, then we chase wealth to impress that person. If we imagine that a friend is judging our looks, we tailor our appearance in response. In *West Side Story*, Maria meets a boy who's into her. What's her very next song? "I Feel Pretty."

As of this writing, the world's only triple Best Actor Oscar winner, Daniel Day-Lewis, has acted in just six films since 1998. He prepares for each role extensively, immersing himself completely in his character. For the role of Bill the Butcher in Martin Scorsese's *Gangs of New York*, he trained as a butcher, spoke with a thick Irish accent on and off the set, and hired circus performers to teach him how to throw knives. And that's only the beginning. He wore only authentic nineteenth-century clothing and walked around Rome in character, starting arguments and fights with strangers. Perhaps thanks to that clothing, he caught pneumonia.

Day-Lewis was employing a technique called method acting, which requires the actor to live as much like his character as possible in order to *become* the role he's playing. This is an incredible skill and art, but often method actors become so absorbed in their character that the role takes on a life beyond the stage or screen. "I will admit that I went mad, totally mad," Day-Lewis said to the *Independent* years later, admitting the role was "not so good for my physical or mental health."

Unconsciously, we're all method acting to some degree. We have personas we play online, at work, with friends, and at home. These different personas have their benefits. They enable us to make the money that pays our bills, they help us function in a workplace where we don't always feel comfortable, they let us maintain relationships with people we don't really like but need to interact with. But often our identity has so many layers that we lose sight of the real us, if we ever knew who or what that was in the first place. We bring our work role home with us, and we take the role we play with our friends into our romantic life, without any conscious control or intention. However successfully we play our roles, we end up feeling dissatisfied, depressed, unworthy, and unhappy. The "I" and "me," small and vulnerable to begin with, get distorted.

We try to live up to what we think others think of us, even at the expense of our values.

Rarely, if ever, do we consciously, intentionally, create our own values. We make life choices using this twice-reflected image of who we *might* be, without really thinking it through. Cooley called this phenomenon the "Looking-Glass Self."

We live in a perception of a perception of ourselves, and we've lost our real selves as a result. How can we recognize who we are and what makes us happy when we're chasing the distorted reflection of someone else's dreams?

You might think that the hard part about becoming a monk is letting go of the fun stuff: partying, sex, watching TV, owning things, sleeping in an actual bed (okay, the bed part was pretty rough). But before I took that step there was a bigger hurdle I had to overcome: breaking my "career" choice to my parents.

By the time I was wrapping up my final year of college, I had decided what path I wanted to take. I told my parents I would be turning down the job offers that had come my way. I always joke that as far as my parents were concerned, I had three career options: doctor, lawyer, or failure. There's no better way to tell your parents that everything they did for you was a waste than to become a monk.

Like all parents, mine had dreams for me, but at least I had eased them into the idea that I might become a monk: Every year since I was eighteen I'd spent part of the summer interning at a finance job in London and part of the year training at the ashram in Mumbai. By the time I made my decision, my mother's first concern was the same as any mother's: my well-being. Would I have health care? Was "seeking enlightenment" just a fancy way of saying "sitting around all day"?

Even more challenging for my mother was that we were surrounded by friends and family who shared the doctor-lawyer-failure definition of success. Word spread that I was making this radical move, and her friends started saying "But you've invested so much in his education" and "He's been brainwashed" and "He's going to waste his life." My friends too thought I was failing at life. I heard "You're never going to get a job again" and "You're throwing away any hope of earning a living."

When you try to live your most authentic life, some of your relation-

ships will be put in jeopardy. Losing them is a risk worth bearing; finding a way to keep them in your life is a challenge worth taking on.

Luckily, to my developing monk mind, the voices of my parents and their friends were not the most important guidelines I used when making this decision. Instead I relied on my own experience. Every year since I was eighteen I had tested both lives. I didn't come home from my summer finance jobs feeling anything but hungry for dinner. But every time I left the ashram I thought, *That was amazing. I just had the best time of my life.* Experimenting with these widely diverse experiences, values, and belief systems helped me understand my own.

The reactions to my choice to become a monk are examples of the external pressures we all face throughout our lives. Our families, our friends, society, media—we are surrounded by images and voices telling us who we should be and what we should do.

They clamor with opinions and expectations and obligations. Go straight from high school to the best college, find a lucrative job, get married, buy a home, have children, get promoted. Cultural norms exist for a reason—there is nothing wrong with a society that offers models of what a fulfilling life might look like. But if we take on these goals without reflection, we'll never understand why we don't own a home or we're not happy where we live, why our job feels hollow, whether we even want a spouse or any of the goals we're striving for.

My decision to join the ashram turned up the volume of opinions and concerns around me, but, conveniently, my experiences in the ashram had also given me the tools I needed to filter out that noise. The cause and the solution were the same. I was less vulnerable to the noises around me, telling me what was normal, safe, practical, best. I didn't shut out the people who loved me—I cared about them and didn't want them to worry—but neither did I let their definitions of success and happiness dictate my choices. It was—at the time—the hardest decision I'd ever made, and it was the right one.

The voices of parents, friends, education, and media all crowd a young person's mind, seeding beliefs and values. Society's definition of a happy

life is everybody's and nobody's. The only way to build a meaningful life is to filter out that noise and look within. This is the first step to building your monk mind.

We will start this journey the way monks do, by clearing away distractions. First, we'll look at the external forces that shape us and distract us from our values. Then we will take stock of the values that currently shape our lives and reflect on whether they're in line with who we want to be and how we want to live.

IS THIS DUST OR IS IT ME?

Gauranga Das offered me a beautiful metaphor to illustrate the external influences that obscure our true selves.

We are in a storeroom, lined with unused books and boxes full of artifacts. Unlike the rest of the ashram, which is always tidy and well swept, this place is dusty and draped in cobwebs. The senior monk leads me up to a mirror and says, "What can you see?"

Through the thick layer of dust, I can't even see my reflection. I say as much, and the monk nods. Then he wipes the arm of his robe across the glass. A cloud of dust puffs into my face, stinging my eyes and filling my throat.

He says, "Your identity is a mirror covered with dust. When you first look in the mirror, the truth of who you are and what you value is obscured. Clearing it may not be pleasant, but only when that dust is gone can you see your true reflection."

This was a practical demonstration of the words of Chaitanya, a sixteenth-century Bengali Hindu saint. Chaitanya called this state of affairs *ceto-darpaṇa-mārjanam*, or clearance of the impure mirror of the mind.

The foundation of virtually all monastic traditions is removing distractions that prevent us from focusing on what matters most—finding meaning in life by mastering physical and mental desires. Some traditions give up speaking, some give up sex, some give up worldly possessions, and some give up all three. In the ashram, we lived with just what we needed and nothing more. I experienced firsthand the enlightenment of letting go. When we are buried in nonessentials, we lose track of what is truly significant. I'm not asking you to give up any of these things, but I want to help you recognize and filter out the noise of external influences. This is how we clear the dust and see if those values truly reflect you.

Guiding values are the principles that are most important to us and that we feel should guide us: who we want to be, how we treat ourselves and others. Values tend to be single-word concepts like freedom, equality, compassion, honesty. That might sound rather abstract and idealistic, but values are really practical. They're a kind of ethical GPS we can use to navigate through life. If you know your values, you have directions that point you toward the people and actions and habits that are best for you. Just as when we drive through a new area, we wander aimlessly without values; we take wrong turns, we get lost, we're trapped by indecision. Values make it easier for you to surround yourself with the right people, make tough career choices, use your time more wisely, and focus your attention where it matters. Without them we are swept away by distractions.

WHERE VALUES COME FROM

Our values don't come to us in our sleep. We don't think them through consciously. Rarely do we even put them into words. But they exist nonetheless. Everyone is born into a certain set of circumstances, and our values are defined by what we experience. Were we born into hardship or luxury? Where did we receive praise? Parents and caregivers are often our loudest fans and critics. Though we might rebel in our teenage years, we are generally compelled to please and imitate those authority figures. Looking back, think about how your time with your parents was spent. Playing, enjoying conversation, working on projects together? What did they tell you was most important, and did it match what mattered most to them? Who did they want you to be? What did they want you to accomplish? How did they expect you to behave? Did you absorb these ideals, and have they worked for you?

From the start, our educations are another powerful influence. The subjects that are taught. The cultural angle from which they are taught. The way we are expected to learn. A fact-driven curriculum doesn't encourage creativity, a narrow cultural approach doesn't foster tolerance for people from different backgrounds and places, and there are few opportunities to immerse ourselves in our passions, even if we know them from an early age. This is not to say that school doesn't prepare us for life—and there are many different educational models out there, some of which are less restrictive—but it is worth taking a step back to consider whether the values you carried from school feel right to you.

THE MEDIA MIND GAME

As a monk, I learned early on that our values are influenced by whatever absorbs our minds. We are not our minds, but the mind is the vehicle by which we decide what is important in our hearts. The movies we watch, the music we hear, the books we read, the TV shows we binge, the people we follow online and offline. What's on your news feed is feeding your mind. The more we are absorbed in celebrity gossip, images of success, violent video games, and troubling news, the more our values are tainted with envy, judgment, competition, and discontent.

Observing and evaluating are key to thinking like a monk, and they begin with space and stillness. For monks, the first step in filtering the noise of external influences is a material letting go. I had three stints visiting the ashram, graduated college, then officially became a monk. After a couple months of training at the Bhaktivedanta Manor, a temple in the

TRY THIS: WHERE DID YOUR VALUES COME FROM?

It can be hard to perceive the effect these casual influences have on us. Values are abstract, elusive, and the world we live in constantly pushes blatant and subliminal suggestions as to what we should want, and how we should live, and how we form our ideas of who we are.

Write down some of the values that shape your life. Next to each, write the origin. Put a checkmark next to each value that you truly share.

Example:

VALUE	ORIGIN	IS IT TRUE TO ME?
Kindness	Parent	✓
Appearance	Media	Not in the same way
Wealth	Parent	No
Good grades	School	Interfered with real learning
Knowledge	School	✓
Family	Tradition	Family: yes, but not traditional

countryside north of London, I headed to India, arriving at the village ashram in the beginning of September 2010. I exchanged my relatively stylish clothes for two robes (one to wear and one to wash). I forfeited my fairly slick haircut for . . . no hair; our heads were shaved. And I was deprived of almost all opportunities to check myself out—the ashram contained no mirrors except the one I would later be shown in the storeroom. So we monks were prevented from obsessing over our appearance, ate a simple diet that rarely varied, slept on thin mats laid on the floor, and the only music we heard was the chants and bells that punctuated our meditations and rituals. We didn't watch movies or TV shows, and we received limited news and email on shared desktop computers in a communal area.

Nothing took the place of these distractions except space, stillness, and silence. **When we tune out the opinions, expectations, and obligations of the world around us, we begin to hear ourselves.** In that silence I began to recognize the difference between outside noise and my own voice. I could clear away the dust of others to see my core beliefs.

I promised you I wouldn't ask you to shave your head and don robes, but how, in the modern world, can we give ourselves the space, silence, and stillness to build awareness? Most of us don't sit down and think about our values. We don't like to be alone with our own thoughts. Our inclination is to avoid silence, to try to fill our heads, to keep moving. In a series of studies, researchers from the University of Virginia and Harvard asked participants to spend just six to fifteen minutes alone in a room with no smartphone, no writing instruments, and nothing to read. The researchers then let them listen to music or use their phones. Participants not only preferred their phones and music, many of them even chose to *zap themselves with an electric shock* rather than be alone with their thoughts. If you go to a networking event every day and have to tell people what you do for a living, it's hard to step away from that reduction of who you are. If you watch *Real Housewives* every night, you start to think that throwing glasses of wine in your friends' faces is routine behavior. When we fill up our lives and leave ourselves no room to reflect, those distractions become our values by default.

We can't address our thoughts and explore our minds when we're pre-occupied. Nor does just sitting in your home teach you anything. There are three ways I suggest you actively create space for reflection. First, on a daily basis I recommend you sit down to reflect on how the day went and what emotions you're feeling. Second, once a month you can approximate the change that I found at the ashram by going someplace you've never been before to explore yourself in a different environment. This can be anything from visiting a park or library you've never been to before to taking a trip. Finally, get involved in something that's meaningful to you—a hobby, a charity, a political cause.

Another way to create space is to take stock of how we are filling the space that we have and whether those choices reflect our true values.

AUDIT YOUR LIFE

No matter what you *think* your values are, your actions tell the real story. What we do with our spare time shows what we value. For instance, you might put spending time with your family at the top of your list of values, but if you spend all your free time playing golf, your actions don't match your values, and you need to do some self-examination.

Time

First, let's assess how you spend the time when you're not sleeping or working. Researchers have found that by the end of our lives, on average, each of us will spend thirty-three years in bed (seven years of which will be spent trying to sleep), a year and four months exercising, and more than three years on vacation. If you're a woman, you'll spend 136 days getting ready. If you're a man this number drops to 46 days. These are just estimates of course, but our daily choices add up.

TRY THIS: AUDIT YOUR TIME

Spend a week tracking how much time you devote to the following: family, friends, health, and self. (Note that we're leaving out sleeping, eating, and working. Work, in all its forms, can sprawl without boundaries. If this is the case for you, then set your own definition of when you are "officially" at work and make "extra work" one of your categories.) The areas where you spend the most time should match what you value the most. Say the amount of time that your job requires exceeds how important it is to you. That's a sign that you need to look very closely at that decision. You're deciding to spend time on something that doesn't feel important to you. What are the values behind that decision? Are your earnings from your job ultimately serving your values?

Media

When you did your audit, no doubt a significant amount of your time was spent reading or viewing media. Researchers estimate that, on average, each of us will spend more than eleven years of our lives looking at TV and social media! Perhaps your media choices feel casual, but time reflects values.

There are many forms of media, but most of us aren't overdoing it on movies, TV, or magazines. It's all about devices. Conveniently, your iPhone will tell you exactly how you're using it. Under Settings, look at the screen time report for the last week and you'll see how much time you spend on social media, games, mail, and browsing the Web. If you don't like what you see, you can even set limits for yourself. On Android, you can look at your battery usage under Settings, then, from the menu, choose "Show full device usage." Or you can download an app like Social Fever or MyAddictometer.

Money

Like time, you can look at the money you spend to see the values by which you live. Exclude necessities like home, dependents, car, bills, food, and debt. Now look at your discretionary spending. What was your biggest investment this month? Which discretionary areas are costing you the most? Does your spending correspond to what matters most to you? We often have an odd perspective on what's "worth it" that doesn't quite make sense if you look at all your expenditures at once. I was advising someone who complained that the family was overspending on afterschool classes for the kids . . . until she realized that she spent more on her shoes than on their music lessons.

Seeing posts on social media that compared spending and our priorities got me thinking about how the ways we spend our time and money reveal what we value.

A 60-minute TV show ("Flew by!")

A 60-minute lunch with family ("Will it ever end!")

Everyday coffee habit ($4/day, almost $1,500/year) ("Need it!")

Fresh healthy food choices (an extra 1.50/day, about $550/year)
    ("Not worth it!")

15 minutes scrolling social media ("Me time!")

15 minutes of meditation ("No time!")

It's all in how you see it. When you look at a month of expenses, think about whether discretionary purchases were long- or short-term investments—a great dinner out or a dance class? Were they for entertainment or enlightenment, for yourself or someone else? If you have a gym membership, but only went once this month and spent more on wine, you have some rethinking to do.

COMPARATIVE SPENDING
(& HOW IT REFLECTS VALUES)

EVERYDAY COFFEE HABIT $4/DAY $1500/YEAR — NEED IT

FRESH HEALTHY FOOD CHOICES EXTRA $1.50/DAY $550/YEAR — NOT WORTH IT!

60-Minute LUNCH with PARENTS — ETERNITY MENU

VS

60-Minute TV SHOW SPECIAL — FLEW BY!

CURATE YOUR VALUES

Doing a self-audit tells you the values that have crept into your life by default. The next step is to decide what your values are and whether your choices are in alignment with them. Contemplating monk values may help you identify your own. Our teachers at the ashram explained that there are higher and lower values. Higher values propel and elevate us toward happiness, fulfillment, and meaning. Lower values demote us toward anxiety, depression, and suffering. According to the Gita, these are the higher values and qualities: fearlessness, purity of mind, gratitude, service and charity, acceptance, performing sacrifice, deep study, austerity, straightforwardness, nonviolence, truthfulness, absence of anger, renunciation, perspective, restraint from fault finding, compassion toward all living beings, satisfaction, gentleness/kindness, integrity, determination.

(Notice that happiness and success are not among these values. These are not values, they are rewards—the end game—and we will address them further in Chapter Four.)

The six lower values are greed, lust, anger, ego, illusion, and envy. The downside of the lower values is that they so readily take us over when we give them space to do so, but the upside is that there are a lot fewer of them. Or, as my teacher Gauranga Das reminded us, there are always more ways to be pulled up than to be pulled down.

We can't pull a set of values out of thin air and make sweeping changes overnight. Instead, we want to let go of the false values that fill the space in our lives. The ashram gave us monks the opportunity to observe nature, and our teachers called our attention to the cycles of all living things. Leaves sprout, transform, and drop. Reptiles, birds, and mammals shed their skins, feathers, fur. Letting go is a big part of the rhythm of nature, as is rebirth. We humans cling to stuff—people, ideas, material possessions, copies of Marie Kondo's book—thinking it's unnatural to purge, but letting go is a direct route to space (literally) and stillness. We separate ourselves—emotionally if not physically—from the people and ideas who fill up our lives, and then we take time to observe the natural inclinations that compel us.

Choices come along every day, and we can begin to weave values into them. Whenever we make a choice, whether it's as big as getting married or as small as an argument with a friend, we are driven by our values, whether they are high or low. If these choices work out well for us, then our values are in alignment with our actions. But when things don't work out, it's worth revisiting what drove the decision you made.

TRY THIS: PAST VALUES

Reflect on the three best and three worst choices you've ever made. Why did you make them? What have you learned? How would you have done it differently?

Take a close look at your answers to the Try This above—buried in them are your values. Why did you make a choice? You may have been with the right or wrong person for the same reason: because you value love. Or maybe you moved across the country because you wanted a change. The underlying value may be adventure. Now do the same thing for the future. Look at your biggest goals to see if they're driven by other people, tradition, or media-driven ideas of how we should live.

> **TRY THIS: VALUE-DRIVEN DECISION**
>
> For the next week, whenever you spend money on a nonnecessity or make a plan for how you will spend your free time, pause, and think: What is the value behind this choice? It only takes a second, a flash of consideration. Ideally, this momentary pause becomes instinctive, so that you are making conscious choices about what matters to you and how much energy you devote to it.

FILTER OEOS, DON'T BLOCK THEM

Once you filter out the noise of opinions, expectations, and obligations (OEOs), you will see the world through different eyes. The next step is inviting the world back in. When I ask you to strip away outside influences, I don't want you to tune out the whole world indefinitely. Your monk mind can and must learn from other people. The challenge is to do so consciously by asking ourselves simple questions: What qualities do I look for/admire in family, friends, or colleagues? Are they trust, confidence, determination, honesty? Whatever they may be, these qualities are, in fact, our own values—the very landmarks we should use to guide ourselves through our own lives.

When you are not alone, surround yourself with people who fit well with your values. It helps to find a community that reflects who you want to be. A community that looks like the future you want. Remember how hard it was for me to start living like a monk during my final year of college? And now, it's hard for me to live in London. Surrounded by the people I grew up with and their ways of living, I'm tempted to sleep in, gossip, judge others. A new culture helped me redefine myself, and another new culture helped me continue on my path.

Every time you move homes or take a different job or embark on a new relationship, you have a golden opportunity to reinvent yourself. Multiple studies show that the way we relate to the world around us is contagious. A twenty-year study of people living in a Massachusetts town showed that both happiness and depression spread within social circles. If a friend who lives within a mile of you becomes happier, then the chance that you are also happy increases by 25 percent. The effect jumps higher with next-door neighbors.

Who you surround yourself with helps you stick to your values and achieve your goals. You grow together. If you want to run a 2:45 marathon, you don't train with people who run a 4:45. If you want to be more spiritual, expand your practice with other spiritual people. If you want to grow your business, join a local chamber of commerce or an online group of business owners who are similarly driven toward that kind of success. If you're an overworked parent who wants to make your kids your priority, cultivate relationships with other parents who prioritize their kids, so you can exchange support and advice. Better yet, where possible, cross groups: Foster relationships with family-oriented spiritual entrepreneurs who run marathons. Okay, I'm kidding, yet in today's world where we have more ways to connect than ever, platforms like LinkedIn and Meetup and tools like Facebook groups make it easier than ever to find your tribe. If you're looking for love, look in places that are value-driven, like service opportunities, fitness or sports activities, a series of lectures on a topic that interests you.

If you're not sure where others fit in relation to your values, ask yourself a question: When I spend time with this person or group, do I feel like I'm getting closer to or further away from who I want to be? The answer could be clear-cut; it's obvious if you're spending four hours at a time playing FIFA soccer on PS2 (not that I've ever done that) versus engaging in meaningful interaction that improves the quality of your life.

Or the answer could be more vague—a feeling like irritability or mental fuzziness after you spend time with them. It feels good to be around people who are good for us; it doesn't feel good to be around people who don't support us or bring out our bad habits.

TRY THIS: COMPANION AUDIT

Over the course of a week, make a list of the people with whom you spend the most time. List the values that you share next to each person. Are you giving the most time to the people who align most closely with your values?

Who you talk to, what you watch, what you do with your time: all of these sources push values and beliefs. If you're just going from one day to the next without questioning your values, you'll be swayed by what everyone else—from your family to hordes of marketing professionals—wants you to think. I remind myself of the moment in the storeroom all the time. A thought comes into my mind and I ask myself, *Does this fit my chosen values or those that others have selected for me? Is this dust or is it me?*

When you give yourself space and stillness, you can clear the dust and see yourself, not through others' eyes, but from within. Identifying your values and letting them guide you will help you filter external influences. In the next chapter these skills will help you filter out unwanted attitudes and emotions.

TWO

NEGATIVITY

The Evil King Goes Hungry

It is impossible to build one's own
happiness on the unhappiness of others.
—Daisaku Ikeda

It is the summer after my third year of college. I have returned from spending
a month at the ashram and am now interning for a finance firm. I'm at lunch
with a couple of my colleagues—we've grabbed sandwiches and brought them
to the concrete courtyard in front of the building, where low walls crisscross
the hardscaping and young people in suits eat speedy lunches, defrosting in the
summer sun before returning to the hyper-air-conditioned building. I am a
monk out of water.

"Did you hear about Gabe?" one of my friends says in a loud whisper. "The
partners tore apart his presentation."

"That dude," another friend says, shaking his head. "He's sinking fast."

I flash back to a class Gauranga Das taught called "Cancers of the Mind:
Comparing, Complaining, Criticizing." In the class, we talked about negative
thought habits, including gossip. One of the exercises we did was keeping a tally

of every criticism we spoke or thought. For each one, we had to write down ten good things about the person.

It was hard. We were living together, in close quarters. Issues came up, most of them petty. The average time for a monk's shower was four minutes. When there was a line at the showers, we would take bets on who was taking too long. (This was the only betting we did. Because: monks.) And though the snorers were relegated to their own room, sometimes new practitioners emerged, and we rated their snores on a scale of motorcycles: this monk's a Vespa; that one's a Harley-Davidson.

I went through the exercise, dutifully noting every criticism I let slip. Next to each, I jotted down ten positive qualities. The point of the exercise wasn't hard to figure out—every person was more good than bad—but seeing it on the page made the ratio sink in. This helped me see my own weaknesses differently. I tended to focus on my mistakes without balancing them against my strengths. When I found myself being self-critical, I reminded myself that I too had positive qualities. Putting my negative qualities in context helped me recognize the same ratio in myself, that I am more good than bad. We talked about this feedback loop in class: When we criticize others, we can't help but notice the bad in ourselves. But when we look for the good in others, we start to see the best in ourselves too.

The guy sitting next to me on the wall nudges me out of my reverie. "So you think he'll last?"

I've lost track of what we're talking about. "Who?" I ask.

"Gabe—he shouldn't have been hired in the first place, right?"

"Oh, I don't know," I say.

Once I'd spent time in the ashram, I became very sensitive to gossip. I'd gotten used to conversations with primarily positive energy. When I first arrived back in the world, I was awkwardly silent. I didn't want to be the morality police, but I also didn't want to participate. As the Buddha advised, "Do not give your attention to what others do or fail to do; give it to what you do or fail to do." I quickly figured out to say things like "Oh, I'm not sure . . ." or "I haven't heard anything." Then I'd shift the conversation to something more positive. "Did you hear they've asked Max to stay on? I'm psyched for him." Gossip has value in some situations: It helps society regulate what is acceptable behavior, and we often use it to see if others agree with our judgments about other people's behavior and therefore our values. But there are kinder ways to negotiate these questions. More often, we use gossip to put others down, which can make us feel superior to them and/or bolster our status in a group.

Some of my friends and colleagues stopped trying to gossip with me altogether; we had real conversations instead. Some trusted me more, realizing that since I didn't gossip with them, I wouldn't gossip about them. If there were people who thought I was just plain boring, well, I have nothing bad to say about them.

NEGATIVITY IS EVERYWHERE

You wake up. Your hair looks terrible. Your partner complains that you're out of coffee. On the way to work some driver who's texting makes you miss the light. The news on the radio is worse than yesterday. Your coworker whispers to you that Candace is pretending to be sick again. . . . Every day we are assaulted by negativity. No wonder we can't help but dish it out as well as receive it. We report the aches and pains of the day rather than the small joys. We compare ourselves to our neighbors, complain about our partners, say things about our friends behind their backs that we would never say to their faces, criticize people on social media, argue, deceive, even explode into anger.

This negative chatter even takes place throughout what we might consider to be a "good day," and it's not part of anyone's plan. In my experience, nobody wakes up and thinks, *How can I be mean to or about other people today?* or *How can I make myself feel better by making others feel worse today?* Still, negativity often comes from within. We have three core emotional needs, which I like to think of as peace, love, and understanding (thanks Nick Lowe and Elvis Costello). Negativity—in conversation, emotions, and actions—often springs from a threat to one of the three needs: a fear that bad things are going to happen (loss of peace), a fear of not being loved (loss of love), or a fear of being disrespected (loss of understanding). From these fears stem all sorts of other emotions—feeling overwhelmed, insecure, hurt, competitive, needy, and so on. These negative feelings spring out of us as complaints, comparisons, and criticisms and other negative behaviors. Think of the trolls who dive onto social media, dumping ill will on their targets. Perhaps their fear is that they aren't respected, and they turn to trolling to feel significant. Or perhaps their political beliefs are generating the fear that their world is unsafe. (Or maybe they're just trying to build a following—fear certainly doesn't motivate every troll in the world.)

For another example, we all have friends who turn a catch-up phone call into an interminable vent session describing their job, their partner, their family—what's wrong, what's unfair, what's never going to change. For these people, nothing ever seems to go right. This person may be expressing their fear that bad things are going to happen—their core need for peace and security is threatened.

Bad things *do* happen. In our lives, we're all victims at some point—whether we're being racially profiled or being cut off in traffic. But if we adopt a victim mentality, we're more likely to take on a sense of entitlement and to behave selfishly. Stanford psychologists took 104 subjects and assigned them to one of two groups—one told to write a short essay about a time they were bored, and the other to write about a time when life seemed unfair or when they felt "wronged or slighted by someone." Afterward, the participants were asked if they wanted to help the researchers with an easy task. Those who'd written about a time they'd been wronged were 26 percent less likely to help the researchers. In a similar study, participants who identified with a victim mindset were not only more likely to express selfish attitudes afterward, they were also more likely to leave behind trash and even take the experimenters' pens!

NEGATIVITY IS CONTAGIOUS

We're social creatures who get most of what we want in life—peace, love, and understanding—from the group we gather around us. Our brains adjust automatically to both harmony and disagreement. We've already talked about how we unconsciously try to please others. Well, we also want to agree with others. Research has proven that most humans value social conformity so much that they'll change their own responses—even their perceptions—to align with the group, even when the group is blatantly wrong.

In the 1950s Solomon Asch gathered groups of college students and told them they were doing a vision test. The catch was that in each group, everyone was an actor except one person: the subject of the test. Asch showed participants an image of a "target" line first, then of a series of three lines: one shorter, one longer, and one that was clearly the same length as the target line. The students were asked which line matched the length of the target line. Sometimes the actors gave correct answers, and sometimes they purposefully gave incorrect answers. In each case, the real study participant answered last. The correct answer should have been obvious. But, influenced by the actors, about 75 percent of the subjects followed the crowd to give an incorrect response at least once. This phenomenon has been called *groupthink bias*.

We're wired to conform. Your brain would rather not deal with conflict and debate. It would much prefer to lounge in the comfort of like-mindedness. That's not a bad thing if we're surrounded by, say, monks. But if we're surrounded by gossip, conflict, and negativity, we start to see the world in those terms, just like the people who went against their own eyes in Asch's line experiment.

The instinct for agreement has a huge impact on our lives. It is one of the reasons why, in a culture of complaint, we join the fray.

And the more negativity that surrounds us, the more negative we become. We think that complaining will help us process our anger, but research confirms that even people who report feeling better after venting

THE ASCH EXPERIMENt

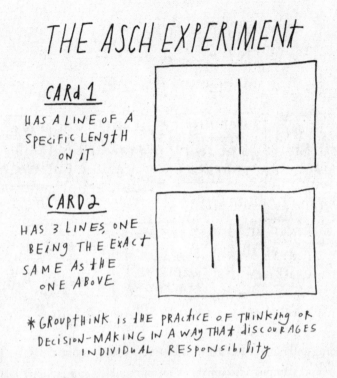

CARd 1

HAS A LINE oF A
SPECiFiC LENgtH
oN iT

CARD 2

HAS 3 LINES, oNE
BEiNG THE ExAct
SAME As tHE
oNE ABoVE

*GROuptHiNK is tHE PRActICE oF THiNKiNg oR
DECiSioN-MAKING IN A WAy THAt discouRAGES
INDIVIDuAL RESpoNSibiDity

are still more aggressive post-gripe than people who did not engage in venting.

At the Bhaktivedanta Manor, the temple's London outpost, there was one monk who drove me crazy. If I asked him how he was in the morning, he'd tell me about how badly he'd slept and whose fault it was. He complained that the food was bad, and yet there was never enough. It was relentless verbal diarrhea, so negative that I never wanted to be around him.

Then I found myself complaining about him to the other monks. And so I became exactly what I was criticizing. Complaining is contagious, and he'd passed it on to me.

Studies show that negativity like mine can increase aggression toward random, uninvolved people, and that the more negative your attitude, the more likely you are to have a negative attitude in the future. Studies also show that long-term stress, like that generated by complaining, actually shrinks your hippocampus—that's the region of your brain that affects

reasoning and memory. Cortisol, the same stress hormone that takes a toll on the hippocampus, also impairs your immune system (and has loads of other harmful effects). I'm not blaming every illness on negativity, but if remaining positive can prevent even one of my winter colds, I'm all for it.

TYPES OF NEGATIVE PEOPLE

Negative behaviors surround us so constantly that we grow accustomed to them. Think about whether you have any of the following in your life:

- Complainers, like the friend on the phone, who complain endlessly without looking for solutions. Life is a problem that will be hard if not impossible to solve.
- Cancellers, who take a compliment and spin it: "You look good today" becomes "You mean I looked bad yesterday?"
- Casualties, who think the world is against them and blame their problems on others.

- Critics, who judge others for either having a different opinion or not having one, for any choices they've made that are different from what the critic would have done.

- Commanders, who realize their own limits but pressure others to succeed. They'll say, "You never have time for me," even though they're busy as well.

- Competitors, who compare themselves to others, controlling and manipulating to make themselves or their choices look better. They are in so much pain that they want to bring others down. Often we have to play down our successes around these people because we know they can't appreciate them.

- Controllers, who monitor and try to direct how their friends or partners spend time, and with whom, and what choices they make.

You can have fun with this list, seeing if you can think of someone to fit each type. But the real point of it is to help you notice and frame these behaviors when they come at you. If you put everyone into the same box of negativity ("They're so annoying!"), you aren't any closer to deciding how to manage each relationship.

On the day I moved to the ashram with six other new monks traveling from England, they told us to think of our new home as a hospital, where we were all patients. Becoming a monk, detaching from material life, was not seen as an achievement in and of itself. It simply meant that we were ready to be admitted to a place of healing where we could work to overcome the illnesses of the soul that infected us and weakened us.

In a hospital, as we all know, even the doctors get sick. Nobody is immune. The senior monks reminded us that everyone had different sicknesses, everyone was still learning, and that, just as we would not judge anyone else's health problems, we shouldn't judge someone who sinned differently. Gauranga Das repeated this advice in brief metaphorical form that we often used to remind ourselves not to harbor negative thoughts toward others: *Don't judge someone with a different disease. Don't expect anyone to be perfect. Don't think you are perfect.*

Instead of judging negative behavior, we try to neutralize the charge, or even reverse it to positive. Once you recognize a complainer isn't looking for solutions, you realize you don't have to provide them. If a commander says, "You're too busy for me," you can say, "Should we find a time that works for both of us?"

REVERSE EXTERNAL NEGATIVITY

The categories above help us step away from the negative person in order to make clearheaded decisions about our role in the situation. The monk way is to dig to the root, diagnose, and clarify a situation so you can explain it simply to yourself. Let's use this approach to define strategies for dealing with negative people.

Become an Objective Observer

Monks lead with awareness. We approach negativity—any type of conflict, really—by taking a step back to remove ourselves from the emotional charge of the moment. Catholic monk Father Thomas Keating said, "There is no commandment that says we have to be upset by the way other people treat us. The reason we are upset is because we have an emotional program that says, 'If someone is nasty to me, I cannot be happy or feel good about myself.' . . . Instead of reacting compulsively and retaliating, we could enjoy our freedom as human beings and refuse to be upset." We step away, not literally but emotionally, and look at the situation as if we are not in the middle of it. We will talk more about this distance, which is called detachment, in the next chapter. For now, I'll say that it helps us find understanding without judgment. Negativity is a trait, not someone's identity. A person's true nature can be obscured by clouds, but, like the sun, it is always there. And clouds can overcome any of us. We have to understand this when we deal with people who exude negative energy. Just like we wouldn't want someone to judge us by our worst moments, we must be careful not to do that to others. When someone hurts you, it's because they're hurt. Their hurt is simply spilling over. They need help. And as the Dalai Lama says, "If you can, help others; if you cannot do that, at least do not harm them."

Back Slowly Away

From a position of understanding, we are better equipped to address negative energy. The simplest response is to back slowly away. Just as in the last chapter we let go of the influences that interfered with our values, we want to cleanse ourselves of the negative attitudes that cloud our outlook. In *The Heart of the Buddha's Teaching*, Thich Nhat Hanh, a Buddhist monk who has been called the Father of Mindfulness, writes, "Letting go gives us freedom, and freedom is the only condition for happiness. If, in our heart, we still cling to anything—anger, anxiety, or possessions—we cannot be free." I encourage you to purge or avoid physical triggers of negative thoughts and feelings, like that sweatshirt your ex gave you or the coffee shop where you always run into a former friend. If you don't let go physically, you won't let go emotionally.

But when a family member, a friend, or a colleague is involved, distancing ourselves is often not an option or not the first response we want to give. We need to use other strategies.

The 25/75 Principle

For every negative person in your life, have three uplifting people. I try to surround myself with people who are better than I am in some way: happier, more spiritual. In life, as in sports, being around better players pushes you to grow. I don't mean for you to take this so literally that you label each of your friends either negative or uplifting, but aim for the feeling that at least 75 percent of your time is spent with people who inspire you rather than bring you down. Do your part in making the friendship an uplifting exchange. Don't just spend time with the people you love—grow with them. Take a class, read a book, do a workshop. *Sangha* is the Sanskrit word for community, and it suggests a refuge where people serve and inspire each other.

Allocate Time

Another way to reduce negativity if you can't remove it is to regulate how much time you allow a person to occupy based on their energy. Some challenges we face only because we allow them to challenge us. There might be some people you can only tolerate for an hour a month, some for a day, some for a week. Maybe you even know a one-minute person. Consider how much time is best for you to spend with them, and don't exceed it.

Don't Be a Savior

If all someone needs is an ear, you can listen without exerting much energy. If we try to be problem-solvers, then we become frustrated when people don't take our brilliant advice. The desire to save others is ego-driven. Don't let your own needs shape your response. In *Sayings of the Fathers*, a compilation of teachings and maxims from Jewish Rabbinic tradition, it is advised, "Don't count the teeth in someone else's mouth." Similarly, don't attempt to fix a problem unless you have the necessary skills. Think of your friend as a person who is drowning. If you are an excellent swimmer, a trained lifeguard, then you have the strength and wherewithal to help a swimmer in trouble. Similarly, if you have the time and mind space to help another person, go for it. But if you're only a fair swimmer and you try to save a drowning person, they are likely to pull you down with them. Instead, you call for the lifeguard. Similarly, if you don't have the energy and experience to help a friend, you can introduce them to people or ideas that might help them. Maybe someone else is their rescuer.

REVERSE INTERNAL NEGATIVITY

Working from the outside in is the natural way of decluttering. Once we recognize and begin to neutralize the external negativities, we become better able to see our own negative tendencies and begin to reverse them.

Sometimes we deny responsibility for the negativity that we ourselves put out in the world, but negativity doesn't always come from other people and it isn't always spoken aloud. Envy, complaint, anger—it's easier to blame those around us for a culture of negativity, but purifying our own thoughts will protect us from the influence of others.

In the ashram our aspirations for purity were so high that our "competition" came in the form of renunciation ("I eat less than that monk"; "I meditated longer than everyone else"). But a monk has to laugh at himself if the last thought he has at the end of the meditation is "Look at me! I outlasted them all!" If that's where he arrived, then what was the point of the meditation? In *The Monastic Way*, a compilation of quotes edited by Hannah Ward and Jennifer Wild, Sister Christine Vladimiroff says, "[In a monastery], the only competition allowed is to outstrip each other in showing love and respect."

Competition breeds envy. In the Mahabharata, an evil warrior envies another warrior and wants him to lose all he has. The evil warrior hides a burning block of coal in his robes, planning to hurl it at the object of his envy. Instead, it catches fire and the evil warrior himself is burned. His envy makes him his own enemy.

Envy's catty cousin is Schadenfreude, which means taking pleasure in the suffering of others. When we derive joy from other people's failures, we're building our houses and pride on the rocky foundations of someone else's imperfection or bad luck. That is not steady ground. In fact, when we find ourselves judging others, we should take note. It's a signal that our minds are tricking us into thinking we're moving forward when in truth we're stuck. If I sold more apples than you did yesterday, but you sold more today, this says nothing about whether I'm improving as an apple seller. **The more we define ourselves in relation to the people around us, the more lost we are.**

We may never completely purge ourselves of envy, jealousy, greed, lust, anger, pride, and illusion, but that doesn't mean we should ever stop trying. In Sanskrit, the word *anartha* generally means "things not wanted," and to practice *anartha-nivritti* is to remove that which is unwanted. We think freedom means being able to say whatever we want. We think freedom means that we can pursue all our desires. Real freedom is letting go of things not wanted, the unchecked desires that lead us to unwanted ends.

Letting go doesn't mean wiping away negative thoughts, feelings, and ideas completely. The truth is that these thoughts will always arise—it is what we do with them that makes the difference. The neighbor's barking dog is an annoyance. It will always interrupt you. The question is how you guide that response. The key to real freedom is self-awareness.

In your evaluation of your own negativity, keep in mind that even small actions have consequences. Even when we become more aware of others' negativity and say, "She's always complaining," we ourselves are being negative. At the ashram, we slept under mosquito nets. Every night, we'd close our nets and use flashlights to confirm that they were clear of bugs. One morning, I woke up to discover that a single mosquito had been in my net and I had at least ten bites. I thought of something the Dalai Lama said, "If you think you are too small to make a difference, try sleeping with a mosquito." Petty, negative thoughts and words are like mosquitos: Even the smallest ones can rob us of our peace.

Spot, Stop, Swap

Most of us don't register our negative thoughts, much as I didn't register that sole mosquito. To purify our thoughts, monks talk about the process of awareness, addressing, and amending. I like to remember this as spot, stop, swap. First, we become aware of a feeling or issue—we *spot* it. Then we pause to address what the feeling is and where it comes from—we *stop*

SPOT a feeling OR issue
STOP to UNDERSTAND WHAT it is
SWAP IN A NEW WAY of PROCESSING

to consider it. And last, we amend our behavior—we *swap* in a new way of processing the moment. **SPOT, STOP, SWAP.**

Spot

Becoming aware of negativity means learning to spot the toxic impulses around you. To help us confront our own negativity, our monk teachers told us to try not to complain, compare, or criticize for a week, and keep a tally of how many times we failed. The goal was to see the daily tally decrease. The more aware we became of these tendencies, the more we might free ourselves from them.

Listing your negative thoughts and comments will help you contemplate their origins. Are you judging a friend's appearance, and are you equally hard on your own? Are you muttering about work without considering your own contribution? Are you reporting on a friend's illness to

---

TRY THIS: AUDIT YOUR NEGATIVE COMMENTS.

Keep a tally of the negative remarks you make over the course of a week. See if you can make your daily number go down. The goal is zero.

---

call attention to your own compassion, or are you hoping to solicit more support for that friend?

Sometimes instead of reacting negatively to what is, we negatively anticipate what might be. This is suspicion. There's a parable about an evil king who went to meet a good king. When invited to stay for dinner, the evil king asked for his plate to be switched with the good king's plate. When the good king asked why, the evil king replied, "You may have poisoned this food."

The good king laughed.

That made the evil king even more nervous, and he switched the plates again, thinking maybe he was being double-bluffed. The good king just shook his head and took a bite of the food in front of him. The evil king didn't eat that night.

What we judge or envy or suspect in someone else can guide us to the darkness we have within ourselves. The evil king projects his own dishonor onto the good king. In the same way our envy or impatience or suspicion with someone else tells us something about ourselves. Negative projections and suspicions reflect our own insecurities and get in our way. If you decide your boss is against you, it can affect you emotionally— you might be so discouraged that you don't perform well at work—or practically—you won't ask for the raise you deserve. Either way, like the evil king, you're the one who will go hungry!

Stop

When you better understand the roots of your negativity, the next step is to address it. Silence your negativity to make room for thoughts and actions that add to your life instead of taking away from it. Start with your breath. When we're stressed, we hold our breath or clench our jaws. We slump in defeat or tense our shoulders. Throughout the day, observe your physical presence. Is your jaw tight? Is your brow furrowed? These are signs that we need to remember to breathe, to loosen up physically and emotionally.

The Bhagavad Gita refers to the austerity of speech, saying that we should only speak words that are truthful, beneficial to all, pleasing, and that don't agitate the minds of others. The Vaca Sutta, from early Buddhist scriptures, offers similar wisdom, defining a well-spoken statement as one that is "spoken at the right time. It is spoken in truth. It is spoken affectionately. It is spoken beneficially. It is spoken with a mind of goodwill."

Remember, saying whatever we want, whenever we want, however we want, is not freedom. Real freedom is not feeling the need to say these things.

When we limit our negative speech, we may find that we have a lot less to say. We might even feel inhibited. Nobody loves an awkward silence, but it's worth it to free ourselves from negativity. Criticizing someone else's work ethic doesn't make you work harder. Comparing your marriage to someone else's doesn't make your marriage better unless you do so thoughtfully and productively. Judgment creates an illusion: that if you see well enough to judge, then you must be better, that if someone else is failing, then you must be moving forward. In fact, it is careful, thoughtful observations that move us forward.

Stopping doesn't mean simply shunning the negative instinct. Get closer to it. Australian community worker Neil Barringham said, "The grass is greener where you water it." Notice what's arousing your negativity, over there on your frenemy's side of the fence. Do they seem to have more time, a better job, a more active social life? Because in the third step, swapping, you'll want to look for seeds of the same on your turf and cultivate them. For example, take your envy of someone else's social whirlwind and in it find the inspiration to host a party, or get back in touch with old friends, or organize an after-work get-together. It is important to find our significance not from thinking other people have it better but from being the person we want to be.

Swap

After spotting and stopping the negativity in your heart, mind, and speech, you can begin to amend it. Most of us monks were unable to completely avoid complaining, comparing, and criticizing—and you can't expect you'll be completely cured of that habit either—but researchers have found that happy people tend to complain . . . wait for it . . . mindfully. While thoughtlessly venting complaints makes your day worse, it's been shown that writing in a journal about upsetting events, giving attention to your thoughts and emotions, can foster growth and healing, not only mentally, but also physically.

We can be mindful of our negativity by being specific. When someone asks how we are, we usually answer, "good," "okay," "fine," or "bad." Sometimes this is because we know a truthful, detailed answer is not expected or wanted, but we tend to be equally vague when we complain. We might say we're angry or sad when we're offended or disappointed. Instead, we can better manage our feelings by choosing our words carefully. Instead of describing ourselves as feeling angry, sad, anxious, hurt, embarrassed, and happy, the *Harvard Business Review* lists nine more specific words that we could use for each one of these emotions. Instead of being angry, we might better describe ourselves as annoyed, defensive, or spiteful. Monks are considered quiet because they are trained to choose their words so carefully that it takes some time. We choose words carefully and use them with purpose.

So much is lost in bad communication. For example, instead of complaining to a friend, who can't do anything about it, that your partner always comes home late, communicate directly and mindfully with your partner. You might say, "I appreciate that you work hard and have a lot to balance. When you come home later than you promised, it drives me crazy. You could support me by texting me as soon as you know you're running late." When our complaints are understood—by ourselves and others—they can be more productive.

In addition to making our negativity more productive, we can also deliberately swap in positivity. One way to do this, as I mentioned, is to use our negativity—like envy—to guide us to what we want. But we can also swap in new feelings. In English, we have the words "empathy" and "compassion" to express our ability to feel the pain that others suffer, but we don't have a word for experiencing vicarious joy—joy on behalf of other people. Perhaps this is a sign that we all need to work on it. **Mudita is the principle of taking sympathetic or unselfish joy in the good fortune of others**.

If I only find joy in my own successes, I'm limiting my joy. But if I can take pleasure in the successes of my friends and family—ten, twenty, fifty people!—I get to experience fifty times the happiness and joy. Who doesn't want that?

The material world has convinced us that there are only a limited number of colleges worth attending, a limited number of good jobs available, a limited number of people who get lucky. In such a finite world, there's only so much success and happiness to go around, and whenever other people experience them, your chances of doing so decrease. But monks believe that when it comes to happiness and joy, there is always a seat with your name on it. In other words, you don't need to worry about someone taking your place. In the theater of happiness, there is no limit. Everyone who wants to partake in *mudita* can watch the show. With unlimited seats, there is no fear of missing out.

Radhanath Swami is my spiritual teacher and the author of several books, including *The Journey Home*. I asked him how to stay peaceful and be a positive force in a world where there is so much negativity. He said, "There is toxicity everywhere around us. In the environment, in the political atmosphere, but the origin is in people's hearts. Unless we clean the ecology of our own heart and inspire others to do the same, we will be an instrument of polluting the environment. But if we create

> **TRY THIS: REVERSE ENVY**
>
> Make a list of five people you care about, but also feel competitive with. Come up with at least one reason that you're envious of each one: something they've achieved, something they're better at, something that's gone well for them. Did that achievement actually take anything away from you? Now think about how it benefitted your friend. Visualize everything good that has come to them from this achievement. Would you want to take any of these things away if you could, even knowing that they would not come to you? If so, this envy is robbing you of joy. Envy is more destructive to you than whatever your friend has accomplished. Spend your energy transforming it.

purity in our own heart, then we can contribute great purity to the world around us."

KṢAMĀ: AMENDING ANGER

We've talked about strategies to manage and minimize the daily negativity in your life. But nuisances like complaining, comparing, and gossip can feel manageable next to bigger negative emotions like pain and anger. We all harbor anger in some form: anger from the past, or anger at people who continue to play a big role in our lives. Anger at misfortune. Anger at the living and the dead. Anger turned inward.

When we are deeply wounded, anger is often part of the response. Anger is a great, flaming ball of negative emotion, and when we cannot let it go, no matter how we try, the anger takes on a life of its own. The toll is enormous. I want to talk specifically about how to deal with anger we feel toward other people.

Kṣamā is Sanskrit for forgiveness. It suggests that you bring patience and forbearance to your dealings with others. Sometimes we have been wounded so deeply that we can't imagine how we might forgive the person who hurt us. But, contrary to what most of us believe, forgiveness is primarily an action we take within ourselves. Sometimes it's better (and safer and healthier) not to have direct contact with the person at all; other times, the person who hurt us is no longer around to be forgiven directly. But those factors don't impede forgiveness because it is, first and foremost, internal. It frees you from anger.

One of my clients told me, "I had to reach back to my childhood to pinpoint why I felt unloved and unworthy. My paternal grandmother set the tone for this feeling. I realized she treated me differently because she didn't like my mother. [I had to] forgive her even though she passed on already. I realized I was always worthy and always lovable. She was broken, not I."

The Bhagavad Gita describes three *gunas*, or modes of life: *tamas*, *rajas*, and *sattva*, which represent "ignorance," "impulsivity," and "goodness." I have found that these three modes can be applied to any activity—for example, when you pull back from a conflict and look for understanding, it's very useful to try to shift from *rajas*—impulsivity and passion—to *sattva*—goodness, positivity, and peace. These modes are the foundation of my approach to forgiveness.

TRANSFORMATIONAL FORGIVENESS

Before we find our way to forgiveness, we are stuck in anger. We may even want revenge, to return the pain that a person has inflicted on us. An eye for an eye. Revenge is the mode of ignorance—it's often said that you can't fix yourself by breaking someone else. Monks don't hinge their choices and feelings on others' behaviors. You believe revenge will make you feel better because of how the other person will react. But when you make your vindictive play and the person doesn't have the response you fantasized about—guess what? *You* only feel more pain. Revenge backfires.

When you rise above revenge, you can begin the process of forgiveness. People tend to think in binary terms: You either forgive someone, or you don't forgive someone, but (as I will suggest more than once in

this book) there are often multiple levels. These levels give us leeway to be where we are, to progress in our own time, and to climb only as far as we can. On the scale of forgiveness, the bottom (though it is higher than revenge) is *zero forgiveness*. "I am not going to forgive that person, no matter what. I don't want to hurt them, but I'm never going to forgive them." On this step we are still stuck in anger, and there is no resolution. As you might imagine, this is an uncomfortable place to stay.

The next step is *conditional forgiveness*: If they apologize, then I'll apologize. If they promise never to do it again, I'll forgive them. This transactional forgiveness comes from the mode of impulse—driven by the need to feed your own emotions. Research at Luther College shows that forgiving appears to be easier when we get (or give) an apology, but I don't want us to focus on conditional forgiveness. I want you to rise higher.

The next step is something called *transformational forgiveness*. This is forgiveness in the mode of goodness. In transformational forgiveness, we find the strength and calmness to forgive without expecting an apology or anything else in return.

There is one level higher on the forgiveness ladder: *unconditional forgiveness*. This is the level of forgiveness that a parent often has for a child. No matter what that child does or will do, the parent has already forgiven them. The good news is, I'm not suggesting you aim for that. What I want you to achieve is transformational forgiveness.

PEACE OF MIND

Forgiveness has been shown to bring peace to our minds. Forgiveness actually conserves energy. Transformational forgiveness is linked to a slew of health improvements including: fewer medications taken, better sleep quality, and reduced somatic symptoms including back pain, headache, nausea, and fatigue. Forgiveness eases stress, because we no longer recycle the angry thoughts, both conscious and subconscious, that stressed us out in the first place.

In fact, science shows that in close relationships, there's less emotional tension between partners when they're able to forgive each other, and that promotes physical well-being. In a study published in a 2011 edition of the journal *Personal Relationships*, sixty-eight married couples agreed to have an eight-minute talk about a recent incident where one spouse "broke the rules" of the marriage. The couples then separately watched replays of the interviews and researchers measured their blood pressure. In couples where the "victim" was able to forgive their spouse, *both* partners' blood pressure decreased. It just goes to show that forgiveness is good for everyone.

Giving and receiving forgiveness both have health benefits. When we make forgiveness a regular part of our spiritual practice, we start to notice all of our relationships blossoming. We're no longer holding grudges. There's less drama to deal with.

TRY THIS: ASK FOR AND RECEIVE FORGIVENESS

In this exercise we try to untangle the knot of pain and/or anger created by conflict. Even if the relationship is not one you want to salvage or have the option of rebuilding, this exercise will help you let go of anger and find peace.

Before you start, visualize yourself in the other person's shoes. Acknowledge their pain and understand that it is why they are causing you pain.

Then, write a letter of forgiveness.

1. List all the ways you think the other person did you wrong. Forgiving another person honestly and specifically goes a long way toward healing the relationship. Start each item with "I forgive you for. . ." Keep going until you get everything out. We're not sending this letter, so you can repeat yourself if the same thing keeps coming to mind. Write everything you wanted to say but never had a chance. You don't have to feel forgiveness. Yet. When you write it down, what you're doing is beginning to understand the pain more specifically so that you can slowly let it go.

2. Acknowledge your own shortcomings. What was your role, if any, in the situation or conflict? List the ways you feel you did wrong, starting each with the phrase "Please forgive me for . . ." Remember you can't undo the past, but taking responsibility for your role will help you understand and let go of your anger toward yourself and the other person.

3. When you are done with this letter, record yourself reading it. (Most phones can do this.) Play it back, putting yourself in the position of the objective observer. Remember that the pain inflicted on you isn't yours. It's the other person's pain. When you squeeze an orange, you get orange juice. When you squeeze someone full of pain, pain comes out. Instead of absorbing it or giving it back, if you forgive, you help diffuse the pain.

FORGIVENESS IS A TWO-WAY STREET

Forgiveness has to flow in both directions. None of us is perfect, and though there will be situations where you are blameless, there are also times when there are missteps on both sides of a conflict. When you cause pain and others cause you pain, it's as if your hearts get twisted together into an uncomfortable knot. When we forgive, we start to separate our pain from theirs and to heal ourselves emotionally. But when we ask for forgiveness at the same time, we untwist together. This is a bit trickier, because we're much more comfortable finding fault in other people and then forgiving it. We're not used to admitting fault and taking responsibility for what we create in our lives.

FORGIVING OURSELVES

Sometimes, when we feel shame or guilt for what we've done in the past, it's because those actions no longer reflect our values. Now, when we look at our former selves, we don't relate to their decisions. This is actually good news—the reason we're hurting over our past is because we've made progress. We did the best we could then, but we can do better now. What could be better than moving forward? We're already winning. We're already crushing it.

When we wrap our heads around the fact that we can't undo the past, we begin to accept our own imperfections and mistakes, forgive

TRY THIS: FORGIVE YOURSELF

The exercise above can also be used to forgive yourself. Starting each line with "I forgive myself for . . . ," list the reasons you feel angry at or disappointed in yourself. Then read it out loud or record it and play it for yourself. Bring out the objective observer, and find understanding for yourself, letting go of the pain.

ourselves, and, in doing so, open ourselves up to the emotional healing
we all yearn for.

ELEVATE

The pinnacle of forgiveness, true *sattva*, is to wish the person who caused
you pain well.

"I became a Buddhist because I hated my husband." That's not something you hear every day, but Buddhist nun and author of *When Things
Fall Apart* Pema Chödrön is only kind of kidding. After her divorce, she
went into a negativity spiral where she entertained revenge fantasies because of her husband's affair. Eventually, she came across the writings of
Chögyam Trungpa Rinpoche, a meditation master who founded Naropa
University in Boulder, Colorado. In reading his work, she realized that
the relationship had become like a malignant cell—instead of dying off,
her anger and blame were causing the negativity of the breakup to spread.
Once Chödrön allowed herself to "become more like a river than a rock,"
she was able to forgive her husband and move forward. She now refers to
her ex-husband as one of her greatest teachers.

If you want the negativity between yourself and another person to
dissipate, you have to hope that you both heal. You don't have to tell them
directly, but send the energy of well-wishing out into the air. This is when
you feel most free and at peace—because you're truly able to let go.

Negativity is a natural part of life. We tease and provoke, express vulnerability, connect over shared values and fears. It's hard to find a comedy
show that isn't based on negative observations. But there is a line between
negativity that helps us navigate life and negativity that puts more pain
out into the world. You might talk about the problems someone's child is
having with addiction because you are scared that it will happen to your
family and hoping to avoid it. But you also might gossip about the same
issue to judge the family and feel better about your own. Ellen DeGeneres
sees the line clearly—in an interview with *Parade* magazine she said that

she doesn't think it's funny to make fun of people. "The world is filled with negativity. I want people to watch me and think, 'I feel good, and I'm going to make somebody else feel good today.'" This is the spirit in which monks have fun—we are playful and laugh easily. When new monks arrived, they often took themselves too seriously (I know I did), and the senior monks would have a twinkle in their eyes when they said, "Steady now, don't waste all your energy on your first day." Whenever the priest brought out the most special sacred food—which was sweeter and tastier than the simple food we ordinarily ate—the younger monks would joke-wrestle to get to it first. And if someone fell asleep and snored during meditation, we would all glance at one another, not even trying to hide our distraction.

We needn't reduce our thoughts and words to 100 percent sunshine and positivity. But we should challenge ourselves to dig to the root of negativity, to understand its origins in ourselves and those around us, and to be mindful and deliberate in how we manage the energy it absorbs. We begin to let go through recognition and forgiveness. We spot, stop, and swap—observe, reflect, and develop new behaviors to replace the negativity in our lives, always striving toward self-discipline and bliss. When you stop feeling so curious about others' misfortunes and instead take pleasure in their successes, you're healing.

The less time you fixate on everyone else, the more time you have to focus on yourself.

Negativity, as we've discussed, often arises from fear. Next, we will explore fear itself, how it gets in our way, and how we can make it a productive part of life.

THREE

FEAR

Welcome to Hotel Earth

Fear does not prevent death. It prevents life.
—Buddha

*The epic battle of Mahabharata is about to begin. The air is thick with antici-
pation: Thousands of warriors finger the hilts of their swords as their horses
snort and paw at the ground. But our hero, Arjuna, is terrified. He has family
and friends on either side of this battle, and many of them are about to die.
Arjuna, among the fiercest fighters of the land, drops his bow.*

The Bhagavad Gita opens on a battlefield with a warrior's terror.
Arjuna is the most talented archer in the land, yet fear has caused him
to totally lose connection with his abilities. The same thing happens to
each of us. We have so much to offer the world, but fear and anxiety
disconnect us from our abilities. This is because growing up we were
taught, directly or indirectly, that fear is negative. "Don't be scared," our
parents told us. "Scaredy-cat," our friends teased. Fear was an embarrassing, humiliating reaction to be ignored or hidden. But fear has a flip
side, which Tom Hanks alluded to in his commencement address at Yale

University. "Fear," he told the graduates, "will get the worst of the best of us."

The truth is, we'll never live entirely without fear and anxiety. We'll never be able to fix our economic, social, and political climates to entirely eliminate conflict and uncertainty, not to mention our everyday interpersonal challenges. And that's okay, because fear isn't bad; it's simply a warning flag—your mind saying "This doesn't look good! Something might go wrong!" It's what we do with that signal that matters. We can use our fear of the effects of climate change to motivate us to develop solutions, or we can allow it to make us feel overwhelmed and hopeless and do nothing as a result. Sometimes fear is a critical warning to help us survive true danger, but most of the time what we feel is anxiety related to everyday concerns about money, jobs, and relationships. We allow anxiety—everyday fear—to hold us back by blocking us from our true feelings. The longer we hold on to fears, the more they ferment until eventually they become toxic.

I am sitting cross-legged on the floor of a cold basement room in the monastery with twenty or so other monks. I've been at the ashram for only a couple months. Gauranga Das has just discussed the scene in the Gita when Arjuna, the hero, is overcome by fear. It turns out that Arjuna's fear makes him pause instead of charging directly into battle. He's devastated that so many people he loves will die that day. The fear and anguish lead him to question his actions for the first time. Doing so provokes him into a long conversation about human morals, spirituality, and how life works according to Krishna, who is his charioteer.

When Gauranga Das concludes his lecture, he asks us to close our eyes, then directs us to relive a fear from our past: not just imagine it but feel it in our bodies—all the sights, sounds, and smells of that experience. He tells us that it's important that we not choose something minor, such as a first day at school or learning to swim (unless those experiences were truly terrifying), but something significant. He wants us to uncover, accept, and create a new relationship with our deepest fears.

We start joking around—someone makes fun of my overreaction to a snakeskin I came across on one of our walks. Gauranga Das acknowledges our antics with a knowing nod. "If you want to do this activity properly," he says, "you have to push beyond the part of your mind that's making fun of it. That's a defense mechanism keeping you from really dealing with the issue, and that's what we do with fear. We distract ourselves from it," Gauranga Das says. "You need to go past that place." The laughter fades, and I can almost feel everyone's spine straighten along with my own.

I close my eyes and my mind quiets down, but I still don't expect much. I'm not scared of anything. Not really, *I think. Then, as I drop further and further into meditation, past the noise and chatter of my brain, I ask myself,* What am I really scared of? *Flickers of truth begin to appear. I see my fear of exams as a kid. I know—that probably sounds trivial. No one likes exams, right? But exams were some of my greatest anxieties growing up. Sitting in meditation, I allow myself to explore what was behind that fear.* What am I really scared of? *I ask myself again. Gradually, I recognize that my fear focused on what my parents and my friends would think of my scores, and of me as a result. About what my extended family would say, and how I'd be compared to my cousins and pretty much everyone else around me. I don't just see this fear in my mind's eye, I feel it in my body—the tightness in my chest, the tension in my jaw, as if I am right back there.* What am I really scared of? *Then I start to delve into fear around the times when I'd gotten in trouble at school. I was so worried that I would be suspended or expelled. How would my parents react? What would my teachers think? I invite myself to go even deeper.* What am I really scared of? *I see this fear around my parents—of them not getting along and of me, at a young age, trying to mediate their marriage. Of thinking,* How can I please both of them? How can I manage them and make sure they're happy? *That's when I find the root of my fear.* What am I really scared of? *I am afraid that I can't make my parents happy. As soon as I hit that revelation, I know I've reached the true fear beneath all of the other fears. It is a full-body aha moment, like I sank deeper and deeper under water, pressure mounting against my chest, increasingly desperate to breathe, and when that realization hit me, my head popped up, and I gasped for air.*

. . .

Half an hour earlier I'd been so sure I wasn't scared of anything, and suddenly I was uncovering my deepest fears and anxieties, which I'd managed to hide completely from myself for years. By gently, but consistently, asking myself what I was scared of, I refused to let my mind dodge the question. Our brains are really good at keeping us from entering uncomfortable spaces. But by repeating a question rather than rephrasing it, we essentially corner our brain. Now, it's not about being aggressive with ourselves—this isn't an interrogation, it's an interview. You want to ask yourself the question with sincerity, not force.

Being scared of exam results was what I call a branch. As you develop your relationship with your fear, you'll have to distinguish between branches—the immediate fears that come up during your self-interview—and the root. Tracking my fear of exam results and the other "branch" fears that appeared led me to the root: fearing I couldn't make my parents happy.

THE FEAR OF FEAR

During my three years as a monk, I learned to let go of my fear of fear. Fear of punishment, humiliation, or failure—and their accompanying negative attitudes—no longer propel my misguided attempts at self-protection. I can recognize the opportunities that fear signals. Fear can help us identify and address patterns of thinking and behavior that don't serve us.

We let our fear drive us, but fear itself is not our real problem. Our real problem is that *we fear the wrong things:* What we should really fear is that we will miss the opportunities that fear offers. Gavin de Becker, one of the world's leading security experts, in *The Gift of Fear* calls it "a brilliant internal guardian that stands ready to warn you of hazards and guide you through risky situations." Often, we notice fear's warning but ignore its guidance. If we learn how to recognize what fear can teach us about ourselves and what we value, then we can use it as a tool to obtain greater meaning, purpose, and fulfillment in our lives. We can use fear to get to the best of us.

A few decades ago, scientists conducted an experiment in the Arizona desert where they built "Biosphere 2"—a huge steel-and-glass enclosure with air that had been purified, clean water, nutrient-rich soil, and lots of natural light. It was meant to provide ideal living conditions for the flora and fauna within. And while it was successful in some ways, in one it was an absolute failure. Over and over, when trees inside the Biosphere grew to a certain height, they would simply fall over. At first, the phenomenon confused scientists. Finally, they realized that the Biosphere lacked a key element necessary to the trees' health: wind. In a natural environment, trees are buffeted by wind. They respond to that pressure and agitation by growing stronger bark and deeper roots to increase their stability.

We waste a lot of time and energy trying to stay in the comfortable bubble of our self-made Biospheres. We fear the stresses and challenges of change, but those stresses and challenges are the wind that makes us stronger. In 2017, Alex Honnold stunned the world when he became the first person ever to climb Freerider—a nearly three-thousand-foot ascent up Yosemite National Park's legendary El Capitan—entirely without ropes. Honnold's unbelievable accomplishment was the subject of the award-winning documentary *Free Solo*. In the film Honnold is asked about how he deals with knowing that when he free climbs, the options are perfection or death. "People talk about trying to suppress your fear," he responded. "I try to look at it a different way—I try to expand my comfort zone by practicing the moves over and over again. I work through the fear until it's just not scary anymore." Honnold's fear prompts him to put in extensive amounts of focused work before he attempts a monumental free solo. Making his fear productive is a critical component of his training, and it's propelled Honnold to the top of his climbing game and to the top of mountains. If we can stop viewing stress and the fear that often accompanies it as negative and instead see the potential benefits, we're on our way to changing our relationship with fear.

THE STRESS RESPONSE

The first thing we need to realize about stress is that it doesn't do a good job of classifying problems. Recently I had the chance to test a virtual reality device. In the virtual world, I was climbing a mountain. As I stepped out on a ledge, I felt as scared as if I were actually eight thousand feet in the air. When your brain shouts "Fear!" your body can't differentiate between whether the threat is real or imagined—whether your survival is in jeopardy, or you're thinking about your taxes. As soon as that fear signal goes off, our bodies prepare us to fight or flee, or sometimes to freeze. If we launch into this high-alert fear state too often, all of those stress hormones start to send us downhill, affecting our immune systems, our sleep, and our ability to heal.

Yet studies show that being able to successfully deal with intermittent stressors—such as managing that big work project or moving to a new house—to approach them head-on, like those trees standing up to the wind, contributes to *better* health, along with greater feelings of accomplishment and well-being.

When you deal with fear and hardship, you realize that you're capable of dealing with fear and hardship. This gives you a new perspective: the confidence that when bad things happen, you will find ways to handle them. With that increased objectivity, you become better able to differentiate what's actually worth being afraid of and what's not.

From the fear meditation I described above, I came away with the idea that we have four different emotional reactions to fear: We panic, we freeze, we run away, or we bury it, as I had buried my anxiety about my parents. The first two are shorter-term strategies, while the second two are longer-term, but all of them distract us from the situation and prevent us from using our fear productively.

In order to change our relationship with fear, we have to change our perception of it. Once we can see the value that fear offers, we can change how we respond. An essential step in this reprogramming is learning to recognize our reaction pattern to fear.

WORK WITH FEAR

I've mentioned that monks begin the growth process with awareness. Just as we do when facing negativity, we want to externalize our fear and take a step back from it, becoming objective observers.

The process of learning to work with fear isn't just about doing a few exercises that solve everything, it's about changing your attitude toward fear, understanding that it has something to offer, then committing to doing the work of identifying and trying to shift out of your pattern of distraction every time it appears. Each of the four distractions from fear—panicking, freezing, running away, and burying—is a different version of a single action, or rather, a single *inaction*: refusing to accept our fear. So the first step in transforming our fear from a negative to a positive is doing just that.

ACCEPT YOUR FEAR

To close the gap with our fear, we must acknowledge its presence. As my teacher told us, "You've got to recognize your pain." We were still seated, and he told us to take a deep breath and silently say, "I see you," to our pain. That was our first acknowledgment of our relationship with fear, to breathe in and repeat, "I see you, my pain. I see you, my fear," and as we breathed out, we said, "I see you and I'm here with you. I see you and I am here for you." Pain makes us pay attention. Or it should. When we say "I see you," we are giving it the attention it is asking for. Just like a crying baby needs to be heard and held.

Breathing steadily while we acknowledged our fear helped us calm our mental and physical responses in its presence. Walk toward your fear. Become familiar with it. In this way we bring ourselves into full presence with fear. When you wake up to that smoke alarm going off, you would acknowledge what is happening in the moment, and then you would get out of the house. Later, in a calmer state, you would reflect on how the fire started or where it came from. You would call the insurance company. You would take control of the narrative. That is recognizing and staying in present time with fear.

> **TRY THIS: RATE YOUR FEAR**
>
> Draw a line with zero at one end and ten at the other. What's the worst thing you can imagine? Maybe it's a paralyzing injury or losing a loved one. Make that a ten on the line. Now rate your current fear in relation to that one. Just doing this helps give some perspective. When you feel fear crop up, rate it. Where does it fall next to something that's truly scary?

FIND FEAR PATTERNS

Along with accepting our fear, we must get personal with it. This means recognizing the situations in which it regularly appears. A powerful question to ask your fear (again, with kindness and sincerity, as many times as necessary) is "When do I feel you?" After my initial work with fear at the monastery, I continued to identify all of the spaces and situations in which my fear emerged. I consistently saw that when I was worried about my exams, when I was worried about my parents, or about my performance at school or getting in trouble, the fear always led me to the same concern: how I was perceived by others. What would they think of me? My root fear influences my decision-making. That awareness now prompts me when I reach a decisive moment to take a closer look and ask myself, "Is this decision influenced by how others will perceive me?" In this way, I can use my awareness of my fear as a tool to help me make decisions that are truly in line with my values and purpose.

Sometimes we can trace our fears through the actions we take, and sometimes it's the actions we're reluctant to take. One of my clients was a successful attorney, but she was tired of practicing law and wanted to do something new. She came to me because she was letting her fear stop her. "What if I jump and there's nothing on the other side?" she asked me. That sounded like a branch question, so I kept probing. "What are you really scared of?" I asked her, then gently kept asking until eventually she sighed and said, "I've spent so much effort and energy building this career. What if I'm just throwing it all away?" I asked again and finally we got to the root: She was afraid of failure and of being seen as less than an intelligent, capable person by others and by herself. Once she learned and acknowledged the true nature of her fear, she was on her way to recasting its role in her life, but first she needed to develop some real intimacy with it. She needed to walk into her fear.

One of the problems we identified was that she had no role models. All of the attorneys she knew were still practicing full-time. She needed to see people who had successfully done some version of what she wanted to do, so I asked her to spend time getting to know former attorneys who were now working in new careers that they loved. When she did that, she not only saw that what she dreamed of was possible, she was also delighted to learn how many of those people said they were still applying skills that they had acquired and used to practice law. She wouldn't be throwing all of her hard work away after all. I also asked her to research jobs she might consider. Through that exercise, she found that many of the "soft skills" she'd had to learn to be a successful attorney, such as communication, teamwork, and problem-solving, were highly sought after elsewhere too. By developing that intimacy with her fear—getting up close and examining what she was afraid of—she ended up with information that left her feeling more empowered and excited about the idea of switching careers.

Patterns for distracting ourselves from fear are established when we're young. They are deeply ingrained, so it takes some time and effort to uncover them. Recognizing our fear patterns helps us trace fear to the root. From there we can decipher whether there's truly any cause for urgency, or whether our fear can actually lead us to recognize opportunities to live more in alignment with our values, passion, and purpose.

THE CAUSE OF FEAR: ATTACHMENT.
THE CURE FOR FEAR: DETACHMENT

Though we are developing intimacy with our fear, we want to see it as its own entity, separate from us. When we talk about our emotions, we usually say we *are* that emotion. I *am* angry. I *am* sad. I *am* afraid. Talking to our fear separates it from us and helps us understand that the fear is not us, it is just something we're experiencing. When you meet someone who gives off a negative vibe, you feel it, but you don't think that vibe *is* you. It's the same with our emotions—they are something we're feeling, but they are not us. Try shifting from I *am* angry to I *feel* angry. I *feel* sad. I *feel* afraid. A simple change, but a profound one because it puts our emotions in their rightful place. Having this perspective calms down our initial reactions and give us the space to examine our fear and the situation around it without judgment.

When we track our fears back to their source, most of us find that they're closely related to attachment—our need to own and control things. We hold on to ideas we have about ourselves, to the material possessions and standard of living that we think define us, to the relationships we want to be one thing even if they are clearly another. That is the *monkey mind* thinking. A *monk mind* practices detachment. We realize that everything—from our houses to our families—is borrowed.

Clinging to temporary things gives them power over us, and they become sources of pain and fear. But when we *accept* the temporary nature of everything in our lives, we can feel gratitude for the good fortune of getting to borrow them for a time. Even the most permanent of possessions, belonging to the most wealthy and powerful, don't actually belong to them. This is just as true for the rest of us. And for many—indeed most—of us, that impermanence causes great fear. But, as I learned in the ashram, we can shift our fear to a soaring sense of freedom.

Our teachers made a distinction between useful and hurtful fears. They told us that a useful fear alerts us to a situation we can change.

If the doctor tells you that you have poor health because of your diet, and you fear disability or disease, that's a useful fear because you can change your diet. When your health improves as a result, you eliminate your fear. But fearing that our parents will die is a hurtful fear because we can't change the truth of the matter. We transform hurtful fears into useful fears by focusing on what we can control. We can't stop our parents from dying, but we use the fear to remind us to spend more time with them. In the words of Śāntideva, "It is not possible to control all external events; but if I simply control my mind, what need is there to control other things?" This is detachment, when you observe your own reactions from a distance—with your monk mind—making decisions with a clear perspective.

There's a common misconception about detachment that I'd like to address. People often equate detachment with indifference. They think that seeing things, people, and experiences as temporary or seeing them from a distance diminishes our ability to enjoy life, but that's not the case. Imagine you're driving a luxury rental car. Do you tell yourself that you own it? Of course not. You know you only have it for the week, and in some ways, that allows you to enjoy it more—you are grateful for the chance to drive a convertible down the Pacific Coast Highway *because* it's something you won't always get to do. Imagine you're staying in the most beautiful Airbnb. It's got a hot tub, chef's kitchen, ocean views; it's so beautiful and exciting. You don't spend every moment there dreading your departure in a week. When we acknowledge that all of our blessings are like a fancy rental car or a beautiful Airbnb, we are free to enjoy them without living in constant fear of losing them. We are all the lucky vacationers enjoying our stay in Hotel Earth.

Detachment is the ultimate practice in minimizing fear. Once I identified my anxiety about disappointing my parents, I was able to detach from it. I realized I had to take responsibility for my life. My parents might be upset, they might not—I had no control over that. I could only make decisions based on my own values.

TRY THIS: AUDIT YOUR ATTACHMENTS

Ask yourself: "What am I afraid of losing?" Start with the externals: Is it your car, your house, your looks? Write down everything you think of. Now think about the internals: your reputation, your status, your sense of belonging? Write those down too. These combined lists are likely to be the greatest sources of pain in your life—your fear of having these things taken away. Now start thinking about changing your mental relationship with those things so that you are less attached to them. Remember—you can still fully love and enjoy your partner, your children, your home, your money, from a space of nonattachment. It's about understanding and accepting that all things are temporary and that we can't truly own or control anything, so that we can fully appreciate these things and they can enhance our life rather than be a source of griping and fear. What better way to accept that children eventually go off to live their own lives and call you once a week, if you're lucky?

This is a lifelong practice, but as you become more and more accepting of the fact that we don't truly own or control anything, you'll find yourself actually enjoying and valuing people, things, and experiences more, and being more thoughtful about which ones you choose to include in your life.

MANAGING SHORT-TERM FEARS

Detaching from your fears allows you to address them. Years ago, a friend lost his job. Jobs are security, and we are all naturally attached to the idea of putting food on the table. Right away, my friend went into panic mode. "Where are we going to get money? I'm never going to get hired again. I'm going to have to get two or three gigs to cover our bills!" Not only did he make grim predictions about the future, he started questioning the past. "I should have been better at my work. I should have worked harder and longer hours!"

When you panic, you start to anticipate outcomes that have not yet come to pass. Fear makes us fiction writers. We start with a premise, an idea, a fear—what will happen if... Then we spiral off, devising possible future scenarios. When we anticipate future outcomes, fear holds us back, imprisoning us in our imaginations. The Roman Stoic philosopher Seneca observed that "Our fears are more numerous than our dangers, and we suffer more in our imagination than reality."

We can manage acute stress if we detach on the spot. There's an old Taoist parable about a farmer whose horse ran away. "How unlucky!" his brother tells him. The farmer shrugs. "Good thing, bad thing, who knows," he says. A week later, the wayward horse finds its way home, and with it is a beautiful wild mare. "That's amazing!" his brother says, admiring the new horse with no small envy. Again, the farmer is unmoved. "Good thing, bad thing, who knows," he says. A few days later, the farmer's son climbs up on the mare, hoping to tame the wild beast, but the horse bucks and rears, and the boy, hurled to the ground, breaks a leg. "How unlucky!" his brother says, with a tinge of satisfaction. "Good thing, bad thing, who knows," the farmer replies again. The next day, the young men of the village are called into military service, but because the son's leg is broken, he is excused from the draft. His brother tells the farmer that this, surely, is the best news of all. "Good thing, bad thing, who knows," the farmer says. The farmer in this story didn't get lost in "what if" but instead focused on "what is." During my monk training, we were taught, "Don't judge the moment."

I passed along the same advice to someone I advised who'd lost his job. Instead of judging the moment, he needed to accept his situation and whatever came of it, focusing on what he could control. I worked with him on first slowing everything down, then acknowledging the facts of his situation—he had lost his job, period. From there he had a choice: He could panic or freeze, or he could take this opportunity to work with fear as a tool, using it as an indicator of what truly mattered to him and to see what new opportunities might arise.

When I asked him what he was most afraid of, he said it was that he wouldn't be able to take care of his family. I gently urged him to be more specific. He said he was worried about money. So I challenged him to think of other ways he might support his family. After all, his wife worked, so they had some money coming in; they weren't going to be out on the street. "Time," he said. "Now I have time to spend with my kids, taking them to and from school, helping them with their homework. And while they're at school, I'll actually have time to look for a new job. A better one." Because he slowed down, accepted his fear, and gained clarity around it, he was able to defuse his panic and see that fear was actually alerting him to an opportunity. Time is another form of wealth. He realized that while he had lost his job, he had gained something else very valuable. Using his newfound time, he was not only more present in his kids' lives, but he also ended up getting a new, better job. Reframing the situation stopped him from draining energy negatively and encouraged him to start applying it positively.

Still, it's hard to not judge the moment and remain open to opportunity when the unknown future spins like a whirlwind through your body and brain. Sometimes our panic or freeze responses rush ahead of us and make it difficult to suspend judgment. Let's talk about some strategies to help us amend panic and fear.

Short-Circuit Fear

Fortunately, a simple, powerful tool to short-circuit the panic response is always with us: our breath. Before I give a talk, when I'm standing offstage listening to my introduction, I'll feel my heart beat faster and my hands getting moist. I've coached people who perform in front of full arenas and people who present at everyday meetings, and, like the rest of us, they feel most of their fear physically. Whether it's performance anxiety or social fears, such as before a job interview or attending a party, our fear manifests in the body, and these bodily cues are the first signals that fear is about to take over. Panic and freezing are a disconnect between our bodies and our minds. Either our bodies go on high alert and rush ahead of our mental processes, or our minds are racing and our bodies start to shut down. As a monk, I learned a simple breathing exercise to help realign my body and mind and stop fear from stopping me. I still use it every time I'm about to give a talk to a large group, enter a stressful meeting, or go into a room full of people I don't know.

TRY THIS: DON'T PANIC! USE YOUR BREATH TO REALIGN BODY AND MIND

"Breathe to calm and relax yourself" meditation: (see page 89)

1. Inhale slowly to a count of 4.
2. Hold for a count of 4.
3. Exhale slowly to a count of 4 or more.
4. Repeat until you feel your heart rate slow down.

It's really that easy. You see, deep breathing activates a part of our nervous system called the vagus nerve, which in turn stimulates a relaxation response throughout our bodies. The simple act of controlled breathing is like flipping a switch that shifts our nervous system from the sympathetic, or fight-flight-freeze, state to the parasympathetic, or rest-and-digest, state, allowing our mind and body to get back in synch.

See the Whole Story

Breath is useful on the spot, but some fears are hard to dispel with our breath alone. When we go through a period of instability, we fear what's ahead. When we know we have a test or a job interview, we fear the outcome. In the moment, we can't see the complete picture, but when the stressful period passes, we never look back to learn from the experience. Life isn't a collection of unrelated events, it's a narrative that stretches into the past and the future. We are natural storytellers, and we can use that proclivity to our detriment—to tell horror stories about possible future events. Better to try seeing our lives as a single, long, continuing story, not just disconnected pieces. When you are hired for a job, take a moment to reflect on all the lost jobs and/or failed interviews that led to this victory. You can think of them as necessary challenges along the way. When we learn to stop segmenting experiences and periods of our life and instead see them as scenes and acts in a larger narrative, we gain perspective that helps us deal with fear.

> **TRY THIS: EXPAND THE MOMENT**
>
> Think of something great that happened to you. Perhaps it was the birth of a child or getting that new job you wanted. Let yourself feel that joy for a moment. Now rewind to the events that occurred just before it. What was going on in your life before the birth of your child or before you were selected for that job? Perhaps it was months and months of trying unsuccessfully to conceive or being rejected from three other jobs you'd applied for. Now try to see that narrative as a whole story—a progression from the bad to the good. Open yourself to the idea that perhaps what happened during the challenging time was actually clearing the way for what you're now celebrating, or made you feel even happier about the experience that came after it. Now take a moment to express gratitude for those challenges and weave them into the story of your life.

Admittedly, we do our best celebrating in hindsight. When we are actually experiencing challenges, it's difficult to tell ourselves, "This could end up being a good thing!" But the more we practice looking in the rear-view mirror and finding gratitude for the hard times we've experienced, the more we start to change our programming; the gap between suffering and gratitude gets smaller and smaller; and the intensity of our fear in the moments of hardship begins to diminish.

Revisit Long-Term Fears

Panic and freezing can be dealt with using breath and by reframing the circumstances, but these are short-term fear responses. It is much harder to control the two long-term strategies we use to distract us from fear: burying and running away. One of my favorite ways to understand how these strategies work involves a house on fire. Let's say you wake up in the middle of the night to your smoke detector beeping. Immediately, you're afraid, as you should be—that signal did its job, which was to get your attention. Now you smell smoke, so you gather your family and pets together and you get out of the house, right? This is fear put to its best use.

But what if, upon hearing the smoke alarm, instead of quickly assessing the situation and taking the logical next steps, you hurried over to the smoke detector, removed the battery, and went back to bed? As you can imagine, your problems are about to magnify. Yet that's what we often do with fear. Instead of assessing and responding, we deny or abandon the situation. Relationships are a space where we commonly use the "solution" of avoidance. Let's say you're having some major conflict with your girlfriend. Rather than sitting down with her and talking about what's going on (putting out the fire), or even figuring out that you aren't meant to be together (safely and calmly getting everyone out of the house), you pretend everything's fine (while the destructive fire burns on).

When we deny fear, our problems follow us. In fact, they're probably getting bigger, and bigger, and at some point something will force us to deal with them. When all else fails, pain does make us pay attention. If we don't learn from the signal that alerts us to a problem, we'll end up learning from the results of the problem itself, which is far less desirable. But if we face our fear—we stay, we deal with the fire, we have the tough conversation—we become stronger as a result.

The very first lesson the Gita teaches us is how to handle fear. In the moments before the battle starts, when Arjuna is overcome by fear, he doesn't run from it or bury it; he faces it. In the text, Arjuna is a brave and skilled warrior, yet in this moment it is fear that causes him, for the first time, to reflect. It's often said that when the fear of staying the same outweighs the fear of change, that is when we change. He asks for help in the form of insight and understanding. In that action, he has begun to shift from being controlled by his fear to understanding it. "What you run from only stays with you longer," writes the author of the novel *Fight Club*, Chuck Palahniuk, in his book *Invisible Monsters Remix*. "Find what you're afraid of most and go live there."

That day in the basement of the ashram, I opened myself to my deeply held fears about my parents. I rarely experienced panic or freeze reactions, but that didn't mean I had no fears—it meant I was pushing them down. As my teacher said, "When fear is buried, it's something we cling to, and it makes everything feel tight because we're under this burden of things we've never released." Whether you suppress them or run away from them, your fears and your problems remain with you—and they accumulate. We used to think it didn't matter if we dumped our trash in landfills without regard for the environment. If we couldn't see it or smell it, we figured it would somehow just take care of itself. Yet before regulation, landfills polluted water supplies, and even today they are one of the largest producers of human-generated methane gas in the United States. In the same way, burying our fears takes an unseen toll on our internal landscape.

TRY THIS: DIVE INTO YOUR FEARS

As we did at the ashram, take a deep dive into your fears. At first a few surface-level fears will pop up. Stay with the exercise, asking yourself *What am I really afraid of?* and larger and deeper fears will begin to reveal themselves. These answers don't usually come all at once. Typically, it takes some time to sink below the layers to the real root of your fears. Be open to the answer revealing itself over time, and maybe not even during a meditation or other focused session. You may be at the grocery store selecting avocados one day when all of a sudden it dawns on you. That's just how we operate.

Going through the processes of acknowledging fear, observing our patterns for dealing with it, addressing and amending those patterns helps us to reprogram our view of fear from something that's inherently negative to a neutral signal, or even an indicator of opportunity. When we reclassify fear, we can look past the smoke and stories to what's real, and in so doing, uncover deep and meaningful truths that can inform and empower us. When we identify our attachment-related fears and instead foster detachment, we can live with a greater sense of freedom and enjoyment. And when we channel the energy behind our fears toward service, we diminish our fear of not having enough, and feel happier, more fulfilled, and more connected to the world around us.

Fear motivates us. Sometimes it motivates us toward what we want, but sometimes, if we aren't careful, it limits us with what we think will keep us safe.

Next we will look at our primary motivators (fear is one of four) and how we can deliberately use them to build a fulfilling life.

FOUR

INTENTION

Blinded by the Gold

When there is harmony between the mind, heart,
and resolution then nothing is impossible
—Rig Veda

In our heads we have an image of an ideal life: our relationships, how we spend our time in work and leisure, what we want to achieve. Even without the noise of external influences, certain goals captivate us, and we design our lives around achieving them because we think they will make us happy. But now we will figure out what drives these ambitions, whether they are likely to make us truly happy, and whether happiness is even the right target.

I have just come out of a class where we discussed the idea of rebirth, Saṃsāra, *and now I am strolling through the quiet ashram with a senior monk and a few other students. The ashram has two locations, a temple in Mumbai and the one where I am now, a rural outpost near Palghar. This will eventually be de-*
veloped into the Govardhan Ecovillage, a beautiful retreat, but for now there

are just a few simple, nondescript buildings set in uncultivated land. Dry dirt footpaths divide the grasses. Here and there, monks sit on straw mats, reading or studying. The main building is open to the elements, and inside we can see monks working. As we walk, the senior monk mentions the achievements of some of the monks we pass. He points out one who can meditate for eight hours straight. A few minutes later he gestures to another: "He fasts for seven days in a row." Further along, he points. "Do you see the man sitting under that tree? He can recite every verse from the scripture."

Impressed, I say, "I wish I could do that."

The monk pauses and turns to look at me. He asks, "Do you wish you could do that, or do you wish you could learn to do that?"

"What do you mean?" I know by now that some of my favorite lessons come not in the classroom, but in moments like this.

He says, "Think about your motivations. Do you want to memorize all of the scripture because it's an impressive achievement, or do you want the experience of having studied it? In the first, all you want is the outcome. In the second, you are curious about what you might learn from the process."

This was a new concept for me, and it blew my mind. Desiring an outcome had always seemed reasonable to me. The monk was telling me to question why I wanted to do what was necessary to reach that outcome.

THE FOUR MOTIVATIONS

No matter how disorganized we might be, we all have plans. We have an idea of what we have to accomplish in the day ahead; we probably have a sense of what the year holds, or what we hope we'll accomplish; and we all have dreams for the future. Something motivates every one of these notions—from needing to pay the rent to wanting to travel the world. Hindu philosopher Bhaktivinoda Thakura describes four fundamental motivations.

1. *Fear.* Thakura describes this as being driven by "sickness, poverty, fear of hell or fear of death."

2. *Desire.* Seeking personal gratification through success, wealth, and pleasure.

3. *Duty.* Motivated by gratitude, responsibility, and the desire to do the right thing.

4. *Love.* Compelled by care for others and the urge to help them.

These four motivations drive everything we do. We make choices, for example, because we're scared of losing our job, wanting to win the admiration of our friends, hoping to fulfill our parents' expectations, or wanting to help others live a better life.

I'm going to talk about each motivation individually, so we get a sense of how they shape our choices.

Fear Is Not Sustainable

In the last chapter we talked about fear, so I'm not going to dwell on it here. When fear motivates you, you pick what you want to achieve—a promotion, a relationship, buying a home—because you believe it will bring you safety and security.

Fear alerts and ignites us. This warning flare is useful—as we discussed, fear points out problems and sometimes motivates us. For instance, the fear of getting fired may motivate you to get organized.

The problem with fear is that it's not sustainable. When we operate in fear for a long time, we can't work to the best of our abilities. We are too worried about getting the wrong result. We become frantic or paralyzed and are unable to evaluate our situations objectively or to take risks.

The Maya of Success

The second motivation is desire. This is when we chase personal gratification. Our path to adventures, pleasures, and comforts often takes the form of material goals. *I want a million-dollar home. I want financial freedom.*

I want an amazing wedding. When I ask people to write down their goals, they often give answers describing what most people think of as success.

We think that success equals happiness, but this idea is an illusion. The Sanskrit word for illusion is *maya*, which means believing in that which is not. When we let achievements and acquisitions determine our course, we're living in the illusion that happiness comes from external measures of success, but all too often we find that when we finally get what we want, when we find success, it doesn't lead to happiness.

Jim Carrey once said, "I think everybody should get rich and famous and do everything they ever dreamed of, so they can see that it's not the answer."

The illusion of success is tied not just to income and acquisitions but to achievements like becoming a doctor or getting a promotion or ... memorizing the scriptures. My desire in the story above—to be able to recite every verse from the scripture—is the monk's version of material desire. Like all of these "wants," my ambition was centered around an external outcome—being as impressively learned as that other monk.

American spiritual luminary Tara Brach, founder of the Insight Meditation Community of Washington, DC, writes, "As long as we keep attaching our happiness to the external events of our lives, which are ever changing, we'll always be left waiting for it."

Once, as a monk, I visited a temple in Srirangam, one of the three major holy cities in South India. I came upon a worker high up on a scaffold applying gold powder to the intricate details on the temple's ceiling. I'd never seen anything like it, and I stopped to watch. As I gazed upward, a dusting of gold floated down into my eyes. I hurried from the temple to rinse my eyes, then returned, keeping a safe distance this time. This episode felt like a lesson torn from the scriptures: Gold dust is beautiful, but come too close, and it will blur your vision.

The gilt that is used on temples isn't solid gold—it's mixed into a solution. And, as we know, it is used to cover up stone, to make it look like solid gold. It's *maya*, an illusion. In the same way, money and fame are only a facade. Because our search is never for a thing, but for the feeling we think the thing will give us. We all know this already: We see wealthy and/or famous people who seem to "have it all," but who have bad relationships or suffer from depression, and it's obvious that success didn't bring them happiness. The same is true for those of us who aren't rich and famous. We quickly tire of our smartphones and want the next model. We receive a bonus, but the initial excitement fades surprisingly fast when our lives don't really improve. We think that a new phone or a bigger house will make us feel somehow better—cooler or more satisfied—but instead find ourselves wanting more.

Material gratification is external, but happiness is internal. When monks talk about happiness, they tell the story of the musk deer, a tale derived from a poem by Kabir, a fifteenth-century Indian mystic and poet. The musk deer picks up an irresistible scent in the forest and chases it, searching for the source, not realizing that the scent comes from its own pores. It spends its whole life wandering fruitlessly. In the same way we search for happiness, finding it elusive, when it can be found within us.

Happiness and fulfillment come only from mastering the mind and connecting with the soul—not from objects or attainments. Success doesn't guarantee happiness, and happiness doesn't require success. They can feed each other, and we can have them at the same time, but they are not intertwined. After analyzing a Gallup survey on well-being, Princeton University researchers officially concluded that money does not buy happiness after basic needs and then some are fulfilled. While having more money contributes to overall life satisfaction, that impact levels off at a salary of around $75,000. In other words, when it comes to the impact of money on how you view the quality of your life, a middle-class American citizen fares about as well as Jeff Bezos.

Success is earning money, being respected in your work, executing projects smoothly, receiving accolades. Happiness is feeling good about yourself, having close relationships, making the world a better place. More than ever, popular culture celebrates the pursuit of success. TV shows aimed at adolescents focus more on image, money, and fame than in the past. Popular songs and books use language promoting individual achievement over community connection, group membership, and self-acceptance. It's no surprise that happiness rates have consistently declined among Americans adults since the 1970s. And it doesn't just boil down to income. In an interview with the *Washington Post*, Jeffrey Sachs, director of the Center for Sustainable Development and an editor of *World Happiness Report*, points out: "While the average income of people around the world definitely affects their sense of well-being, it doesn't explain all that much, because other factors, both personal and social, are very important determinants of well-being." Sachs says that while generally American incomes have risen since 2005, our happiness has fallen, in part because of social factors like declining trust in the government and our fellow Americans, and weaker social networks.

Duty and Love

If fear limits us and success doesn't satisfy us, then you've probably already guessed that duty and love have more to offer. We all have different goals, but we all want the same things: a life full of joy and meaning. Monks don't seek out the joy part—we aren't looking for happiness or pleasure. Instead, we focus on the satisfaction that comes from living a meaningful life. Happiness can be elusive—it's hard to sustain a high level of joy. But to feel *meaning* shows that our actions have purpose. They lead to a worthwhile outcome. We believe we're leaving a positive imprint. What we do matters, so we matter. Bad things happen, boring chores must get done, life isn't all sunshine and unicorns, but it is always possible to find meaning. If you lose a loved one and someone tells you to look for the positive, to be happy, to focus on the good things in your life—well, you might want to punch that person. But we can survive the worst tragedies by looking for *meaning* in the loss. We might honor a loved one by giving to the community. Or discover a new gratitude for life that we pass on to those who have supported us. Eventually, the value that we see in our actions will lead to a sense of meaning. In the Atharva Veda it says,

"Money and mansions are not the only wealth. Hoard the wealth of the spirit. Character is wealth: good conduct is wealth; and spiritual wisdom is wealth."

Purpose and meaning, not success, lead to true contentment. When we understand this, we see the value of being motivated by duty and/or love. When you act out of duty and love, you know that you are providing value.

The more we upgrade from trying to fulfill our selfish needs to doing things out of service and love, the more we can achieve. In her book *The Upside of Stress*, author Kelly McGonigal says that we can better handle discomfort when we can associate it with a goal, purpose, or person we care about. For example, when it comes to planning a child's birthday party, a parent might be more than willing to endure the unpleasantness of staying up late. The pain of lost sleep is offset by the satisfaction of being a loving mother. But when it comes to working late at a job that same woman hates? She is miserable. We can take on more when we're doing it for someone we love or to serve a purpose we believe in rather than from the misguided idea that we will find happiness through success. When we perform work with the conviction that what we do matters, we can live intensely. Without a reason for moving forward, we have no drive. When we live intentionally—with a clear sense of why what we do matters—life has meaning and brings fulfillment. Intention fills the car with gas.

THE WHY LADDER

Fear, desire, duty, and love are the roots of all intentions. In Sanskrit the word for intention is *sankalpa*, and I think of it as the reason, formed by one's own heart and mind, that one strives for a goal. To put it another way, from your root motivation you develop intentions to drive you forward. Your intention is who you plan to be in order to act with purpose and feel that what you do is meaningful. So if I'm motivated by fear, my intention might be to protect my family. If I'm motivated by desire, my

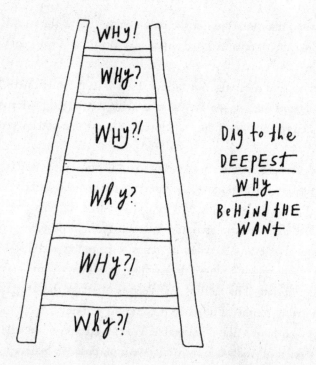

intention might be to gain worldwide recognition. If I'm motivated by duty, my intention might be to help my friends no matter how busy I am. If I'm motivated by love, my intention might be to serve where I am most needed.

There are no rules attaching certain intentions to certain motivations. You can also perform service to make a good impression (desire, not love). You can support your family out of love, not fear. You can want to get rich in order to serve. And none of us has just one motivation and one intention. I want us to learn how to make big and small choices intentionally. Instead of forever climbing the mountain of success, we need to descend into the valley of our true selves to weed out false beliefs.

To live intentionally, we must dig to *the deepest why behind the want.* This requires pausing to think not only about *why* we want something, but also who we are or need to be to get it, and whether being that person appeals to us.

Most people are accustomed to looking for answers. Monks focus on questions. When I was trying to get close to my fear, I asked myself "What am I afraid of?" over and over again. When I'm trying to get to the root of a desire, I start with the question "Why?"

This monkish approach to intention can be applied to even the worldliest goals. Here's a sample goal I've chosen because it's something we never would have contemplated in the ashram and because the intention behind it isn't obvious: *I want to sail solo around the world.*

Why do you want to sail around the world?

It will be fun. I'll get to see lots of places and prove to myself that I'm a great sailor.

It sounds like your intention is to gratify yourself, and that you are motivated by *desire*.

But, what if your answer to the question is:

It was always my father's dream to sail around the world. I'm doing it for him.

In this case, your intention is to honor your father, and you are motivated by *duty and love*.

I'm sailing around the world so I can be free. I won't be accountable to anyone. I can leave all my responsibilities behind.

This sailor intends to escape—he is driven by *fear*.

Now let's look at a more common want:

My biggest want is money, and here's Jay, probably about to tell me to become kind and compassionate. That's not going to help.

Wanting to be rich for the sake of being rich is fine. It's firmly in the category of material gratification, so you can't expect it to give an internal sense of fulfillment. Nonetheless, material comforts are undeniably part of what we want from life, so let's get to the root of this goal rather than just dismissing it.

Wealth is your desired outcome. Why?

I don't ever want to have to worry about money again.

Why do you worry about money?

I can't afford to take the vacations I dream about.

Why do you want those vacations?

I see everyone else on exotic trips on social media. Why should they get to do that when I can't?

Why do you want what they want?

They're having much more fun than I have on my weekends.

Aha! So now we are at the root of the want. Your weekends are un-fulfilling. What's missing?

I want my life to be more exciting, more adventurous, more exhilarating.

Okay, your intention is to make your life more exciting. Notice how different that is from "I want money." Your intention is still driven by the desire for personal gratification, but now you know two things: First, you can add more adventure to your life right now without spending more money. And second, you now have the clarity to decide if that's something you want to work hard for.

If a person went up to my teacher and said, "I just want to be rich," my teacher would ask, "Are you doing it out of service?" His reason for asking would be to get to the root of the desire.

If the man said, "No, I want to live in a nice house, travel, and buy whatever I want." His intention would be to have the financial freedom to indulge himself.

My teacher would say, "Okay, it's good that you're honest with your-self. Go ahead, make your fortune. You'll come to service anyway. It may take you five or ten years, but you'll get to the same answer." Monks be-lieve that the man won't be fulfilled when he finds his fortune, and that if he continues his search for meaning, the answer will always, eventually, be found in service.

Be honest about what your intention is. The worst thing you can do is pretend to yourself that you're acting out of service when all you want is material success.

When you follow the whys, keep digging. Every answer provokes deeper questions. Sometimes it helps to sit with a question in the back of your mind for a day, even a week. Very often you'll find that what you are ultimately searching for is an internal feeling (happiness, security, confidence, etc.). Or maybe you'll find that you're acting out of envy, not the most positive emotion, but a good alert to the need you are trying to fill. Be curious about that discovery. Why are you envious? Is there something—like adventure—that you can start working on right away? Once you're doing that, the external wants will be more available to you— if they still matter at all.

TRY THIS: A QUESTION MEDITATION

Take a desire you have and ask yourself why you want it. Keep asking until you get to the root intention.

   Common answers are:

To look and feel good

Security

Service

Growth

Don't negate intentions that aren't "good," just be aware of them and recognize that if your reason isn't love, growth, or knowledge, the opportunity may fulfill important practical needs, but it won't feel emotionally meaningful. We're most satisfied when we are in a state of progress, learning, or achievement.

SEEDS AND WEEDS

As monks, we learned to clarify our intentions through the analogy of seeds and weeds. When you plant a seed, it can grow into an expansive tree that provides fruit and shelter for everyone. That's what a broad intention, like love, compassion, or service, can do. The purity of your intention has nothing to do with what career you choose. A traffic officer can give a speeding ticket making a show of his power, or he can instruct you not to speed with the same compassion a parent would have when telling a child not to play with fire. You can be a bank teller and execute a simple transaction with warmth. But if our intentions are vengeful or self-motivated, we grow weeds. Weeds usually grow from ego, greed, envy, anger, pride, competition, or stress. These might look like normal plants to begin with, but they will never grow into something wonderful.

If you start going to the gym to build a revenge body so your ex regrets breaking up with you, you're planting a weed. You haven't properly addressed what you want (most likely to feel understood and loved, which would clearly require a different approach). You'll get strong, and reap the health benefits of working out, but the stakes of your success are tied to external factors—provoking your ex. If your ex doesn't notice or care, you'll still feel the same frustration and loneliness. However, if you start going to the gym because you want to feel physically strong after your breakup, or if, in the course of working out, your intention shifts to this, you'll get in shape *and* feel emotionally satisfied.

Another example of a weed is when a good intention gets attached to the wrong goal. Say my intention is to build my confidence, and I decide that getting a promotion is the best way to do it. I work hard, impress my boss, and move up a level, but when I get there, I realize there's another level, and I still feel insecure. External goals cannot fill internal voids. No external labels or accomplishments can give me true confidence. I have to find it in myself. We will talk about how to make internal changes like this in Part Two.

THE GOOD SAMARITANS

Monks know that one can't plant a garden of beautiful flowers and leave it to thrive on its own. We have to be gardeners of our own lives, planting only the seeds of good intentions, watching to see what they become, and removing the weeds that spring up and get in the way.

In a 1973 experiment called "From Jerusalem to Jericho," researchers asked seminary students to prepare short talks about what it meant to be a minister. Some of them were given the parable of the Good Samaritan to help them prep. In this parable, Jesus told of a traveler who stopped to help a man in need when nobody else would. Then some excuse was made for them to switch to a different room. On their way to the new room, an actor, looking like he needed help, leaned in a doorway. Whether a student had been given materials about the Good Samaritan made no difference in whether the student stopped to help. The researchers did find that if students were in a hurry they were much less likely to help, and "on several occasions, a seminary student going to give his talk on the parable of the Good Samaritan literally stepped over the victim as he hurried on his way!"

The students were so focused on the task at hand that they forgot their deeper intentions. They were presumably studying at seminary with the intention to be compassionate and helpful, but in that moment anxiety or the desire to deliver an impressive speech interfered. As Benedictine monk Laurence Freeman said in his book *Aspects of Love*, "Everything you do in the day from washing to eating breakfast, having meetings, driving to work . . . watching television or deciding instead to read . . . *everything* you do is your spiritual life. It is only a matter of how consciously you do these ordinary things . . ."

LIVE YOUR INTENTIONS

Of course, simply having intentions isn't enough. We have to take action to help those seeds grow. I don't believe in wishful "manifesting," the idea that if you simply believe something will happen, it will. We can't sit around with true intentions expecting that what we want will fall into our laps. Nor can we expect someone to find us, discover how amazing we are, and hand us our place in the world. Nobody is going to create our lives for us. Martin Luther King Jr., said, "Those who love peace must learn to organize as effectively as those who love war." When people come to me seeking guidance, I constantly hear, "I wish . . . I wish . . . I wish . . ." *I wish my partner would be more attentive. I wish I could have the same job but make more money. I wish my relationship were more serious.*

We never say, "I wish I could be more organized and focused and could do the hard work to get that." We don't vocalize what it would actually take to get what we want. **"I wish" is code for "I don't want to do anything differently."**

There's an apocryphal story about Picasso that perfectly illustrates how we fail to recognize the work and perseverance behind achievement. As the tale goes, a woman sees Picasso in a market. She goes up to him and says, "Would you mind drawing something for me?"

"Sure," he says, and thirty seconds later hands her a remarkably beautiful little sketch. "That will be thirty thousand dollars," he says.

"But Mr. Picasso," the woman says, "how can you charge me so much? This drawing only took you thirty seconds!"

"Madame," says Picasso, "it took me thirty years."

The same is true of any artistic work—or, indeed, any job that's done well. The effort behind it is invisible. The monk in my ashram who could easily recite all the scriptures put years into memorizing them. I needed to consider that investment, the life it required, before making it my goal.

When asked who we are, we resort to stating what we do: "I'm an accountant." "I'm a lawyer." "I'm a housewife/househusband." "I'm an athlete." "I'm a teacher." Sometimes this is just a useful way to jump-start a conversation with someone you've just met. But life is more meaningful when we define ourselves by our intentions rather than our achievements. If you truly define yourself by your job, then what happens when you lose your job? If you define yourself as an athlete, then an injury ends your career, you don't know who you are. Losing a job shouldn't destroy our identities, but often it does. Instead, if we live intentionally, we sustain a sense of purpose and meaning that isn't tied to what we accomplish but who we are.

If your intention is to help people, you have to embody that intention by being kind, openhearted, and innovative, by recognizing people's strengths, supporting their weaknesses, listening, helping them grow, reading what they need from you, and noticing when it changes. If your intention is to support your family, you might decide that you have to be generous, present, hardworking, and organized. If your intention is to live your passion, maybe you have to be committed, energetic, and truthful. (Note that in Chapter One we cleared out external noise so that we could see our values more clearly. When you identify your intentions, they reveal your values. The *intentions* to help people and to serve mean you *value* service. The *intention* to support your family means you *value* family. It's not rocket science, but these terms get thrown around and used interchangeably, so it helps to know how they connect and overlap.)

Living your intention means having it permeate your behavior. For instance, if your goal is to improve your relationship, you might plan dates, give your partner gifts, and get a haircut to look better for them. Your wallet will be thinner, your hair might look better, and your relationship may or may not improve. But watch what happens if you make internal changes to live your intention. In order to improve your relationship, you try to become calmer, more understanding, and more inquisitive. (You can still go to the gym and get a haircut.) If the changes you make are internal, you'll feel better about yourself and you'll be a better person. If your relationship doesn't improve, you'll still be the better for it.

DO THE WORK

Once you know the *why* behind the want, consider the *work* behind the want. What will it take to get the nice house and the fancy car? Are you interested in that work? Are you willing to do it? Will the work itself bring you a sense of fulfillment even if you don't succeed quickly—or ever? The monk who asked me why I wanted to learn all of the scripture by heart didn't want me to be mesmerized by the superpowers of other monks and to seek those powers out of vanity. He wanted to know if I was interested in the work—in the life I would live, the person I would be, the meaning I would find in the process of learning the scriptures. The focus is on the process, not the outcome.

The Desert Fathers were the earliest Christian monks, living in

TRY THIS: ADD TO-BE'S TO YOUR TO-DO'S

Alongside your to-do list, try making a to-be list. The good news is you're not making your list longer—these are not items you can check off or complete—but the exercise is a reminder that achieving your goals with intention means living up to the values that drive those goals.

EXAMPLE 1

Let's say my goal is to be financially free. Here's my to-do list:

- Research lucrative job opportunities requiring my skill set
- Rework CV, set up informational meetings to identify job openings
- Apply for all open positions that meet my salary requirements

But what do I need to *be*? I need to be:

- Disciplined
- Focused
- Passionate

EXAMPLE 2

Let's say I want to have a fulfilling relationship. What do I need to do?

- Plan dates
- Do nice things for my partner
- Improve my appearance

But what do I need to *be*?

- More calm
- More understanding
- More inquisitive about my partner's day and feelings

hermitage in the deserts of the Middle East. According to these monks, "We do not make progress because we do not realize how much we can do. We lose interest in the work we have begun, and we want to be good without even trying." If you don't care deeply, you can't go all in on the process. You're not doing it for the right reasons. You can reach your goals, get everything you ever wanted, be successful by anyone's terms, only to discover you still feel lost and disconnected. But if you're in love with the day-to-day process, then you do it with depth, authenticity, and a desire to make an impact. You might be equally successful either way, but if you're driven by intention, you will feel joy.

And if you have a clear and confident sense of why you took each step, then you are more resilient. Failure doesn't mean you're worthless—it means you must look for another route to achieving worthwhile goals. Satisfaction comes from believing in the value of what you do.

ROLE MODELS

The best way to research the work required to fulfill your intention is to look for role models. If you want to be rich, study (without stalking!) what the rich people you admire are being and doing, read books about how they got where they are. Focus especially on what they did at your stage, in order to get where they are now.

You can tour an entrepreneur's office or visit an expat's avocado ranch and decide it's what you want, but that doesn't tell you anything about the journey to get there. Being an actor isn't about appearing on screen and in magazines. It's about having the patience and creativity to perform a scene sixty times until the director has what she wants. Being a monk isn't admiring someone who sits in meditation. It's waking up at the same time as the monk, living his lifestyle, emulating the qualities he displays. Shadow someone at work for a week and you'll gain some sense of the challenges they face, and whether those are challenges you want to take on.

In your observations of people doing the work, it's worth remembering that there can be multiple paths to achieve the same intention. For example, two people might have helping the earth as an intention. One could do it through the law, working with the nonprofit Earthjustice; the other could do it through fashion, like Stella McCartney, who has helped popularize vegan leather. In the next chapter we'll talk about tapping into the method and pursuit that fits you best, but this example shows that if you lead with intention, then you open up the options for how to reach your goal.

And, as we saw with the example of sailing around the globe, two identical acts can have very different intentions behind them. Let's say two people give generous donations to the same charity. One does it because she cares deeply about the charity, a broad intention, and the other does it because he wants to network, a narrow intention. Both donors are commended for their gifts. The one who truly wanted to make a difference feels happy and proud and a sense of meaning. The one who wanted to network only cares whether he met anyone useful to his career or social status. Their different intentions make no difference to the charity—the gifts do good in the world either way—but the internal reward is completely different.

It should be said that no intentions are completely pure. My charitable acts might be 88 percent intended to help people and 8 percent to feel good about myself and 4 percent to have fun with my other charitable friends. There's nothing intrinsically wrong with cloudy or multifaceted intentions. We just need to remember that the less pure they are, the less likely they are to make us happy, even if they make us successful. When people gain what they want but aren't happy at all, it's because they did it with the wrong intention.

LETTING GO TO GROW

The broadest intentions often drive efforts to help and support other people. Parents working overtime to put food on the table for their families. Volunteers devoting themselves to a cause. Workers who are motivated to serve their customers. We sense these intentions from the people we encounter, whether it's the hairdresser who really wants to find a style that suits you or the doctor who takes the time to ask about your life. Generous intentions radiate from people, and it's a beautiful thing. Time and again we see that if we're doing it for the external result, we won't be happy. With the right intention, to serve, we can feel meaning and purpose every day.

Living intentionally means stepping back from external goals, letting go of outward definitions of success, and looking within. Developing a meditation practice with breathwork is a natural way to support this intention. As you cleanse yourself of opinions and ideas that don't make sense with who you are and what you want, I recommend using breathwork as a reminder to live at your own pace, in your own time. Breathwork helps you understand that your way is unique—and that's as it should be.

MEDITATION

BREATHE

The physical nature of breathwork helps drive distractions from your head. Breathwork is calming, but it isn't always easy. In fact, the challenges it brings are part of the process.

I'm sitting on a floor of dried cow dung, which is surprisingly cool. It's not uncomfortable, but it's not comfortable. My ankles hurt. I can't keep my back straight. God, I hate this, it's so difficult. It's been twenty minutes and I still haven't cleared my mind. I'm supposed to be bringing awareness to my breath, but I'm thinking about friends back in London. I sneak a peek at the monk closest to me. He's sitting up so straight. He's nailing this meditation thing. "Find your breath," the leader is saying. I take a breath. It's slow, beautiful, calm.

Oh, wait. Oh okay. I'm becoming aware of my breath.
Breathing in . . . breathing out . . .
Oh I'm there . . .
Okay, this is cool . . .
This is interesting . . .
Okay.

This . . .
Works . . .
Wait, I've an itch on my back—
Breathing in . . . breathing out.
Calm.

My first trip to the ashram was two weeks long, and I spent it meditating with Gauranga Das every morning for two hours. Sitting for that
long, often much longer, is uncomfortable and tiring and sometimes
boring. What's worse, unwanted thoughts and feelings started drifting
into my head. I worried that I wasn't sitting properly and that the monks
would judge me. In my frustration, my ego spoke up: I wanted to be the
best meditator, the smartest person at the ashram, the one who made an
impact. These weren't monk-like thoughts. Meditation definitely wasn't
working the way I had thought it would. It was turning me into a bad
person!

I was shocked and, to be frank, disappointed to see all the unresolved
negativity inside myself. Meditation was only showing me ego, anger, lust,
pain—things I didn't like about myself. Was this a problem . . . or was it
the point?

I asked my teachers if I was doing something wrong. One of them
told me that every year the monks meticulously cleaned the Gundicha
Temple in Puri, checking every corner, and that when they did it, they vi-
sualized cleaning their hearts. He said that by the time they finished, the
temple was already getting dirty again. That, he explained, is the feeling
of meditation. It was work, and it was never done.

Meditation wasn't making me a bad person. I had to face an equally
unappealing reality. In all that stillness and quiet, it was amplifying what
was already inside me. In the dark room of my mind, meditation had
turned on the lights.

**In getting you where you want to be, meditation may show you what
you don't want to see.**

Many people run from meditation because they find it difficult and unpleasant. In the Dhammapada the Buddha says, "As a fish hooked and left on the sand thrashes about in agony, the mind being trained in meditation trembles all over." But the point of meditation is to examine what makes it challenging. There is more to it than closing your eyes for fifteen minutes a day. It is the practice of giving yourself space to reflect and evaluate.

By now I've had many beautiful meditations. I've laughed, I've cried, and my heart has felt more alive than I knew possible. The calming, floating, quiet bliss comes eventually. Ultimately, the process is as joyous as the results.

BREATHWORK FOR THE BODY AND MIND

As you've probably noticed, your breathing changes with your emotions. We hold our breath when we're concentrating, and we take shallow breaths when we're nervous or anxious. But these responses are instinctive rather than helpful, meaning that to hold your breath doesn't really help your concentration, and shallow breathing actually makes the symptoms of anxiety worse. Controlled breathing, on the other hand, is an immediate way to steady yourself, a portable tool you can use to shift your energy on the fly.

For millennia, yogis have practiced breathing techniques (called *pranayama*) to do things like stimulate healing, raise energy, and focus on the present moment. In the Rig Veda it's written that "breath is the extension of our inmost life," and it describes breath as the path beyond the self to consciousness. In the Mahāsatipaṭṭhāna Sutta, the Buddha described *ānāpānasati* (which roughly translated means "mindfulness of breathing") as a way to gain enlightenment. Modern science backs up the effectiveness of *pranayama* for myriad effects including improving cardiovascular health, lowering overall stress, and even improving academic test performance. The meditations I present here and elsewhere in the book are universally used in therapy, coaching, and other meditation practices throughout the world.

When you align with your breath, you learn to align with yourself through every emotion—calming, centering, and de-stressing yourself.

Once or twice a day, I suggest setting aside time for breathwork. Additionally, breathwork is such an effective way to calm yourself down that I use it, and suggest others use it, at points throughout the day when you feel short of breath or that you're holding your breath. You don't need to be in a relaxing space in order to meditate (though it is obviously helpful and appropriate when you are new to meditation). You can do it anywhere—in the bathroom at a party, when getting on a plane, or right before you make a presentation or meet with strangers.

TRY THIS: BREATHWORK

Here are powerful breathing patterns that I use every day. They can be used as needed to either induce focus or increase calm.

BREATHWORK PREPARATION

For the calming and energizing breathing exercises I describe below, begin your practice with the following steps.

1. Find a comfortable position—sitting in a chair, sitting upright with a cushion, or lying down
2. Close your eyes
3. Lower your gaze (yes, you can do this with your eyes closed)
4. Make yourself comfortable in this position
5. Roll back your shoulders
6. Bring your awareness to

   Calm

   Balance

   Ease

(continued on next page)

Stillness

Peace

Whenever your mind wanders just gently and softly bring it back to

Calm

Balance

Ease

Stillness

Peace

7. Now become aware of your natural breathing pattern. Don't force or pressure your breath, just become aware of your natural breathing pattern.

At the ashram we were taught to use diaphragmatic breathing. To do so, place one hand on your stomach and the other on your chest, and:

Breathe in through your nose, and out through your mouth

When you inhale, feel your stomach expand (as opposed to your chest)

When you exhale, feel your stomach contract

Continue this in your own pace, at your own time

When you inhale, feel that you are taking in positive, uplifting energy

When you exhale, feel that you are releasing any negative, toxic energy

8. Lower your left ear to your left shoulder as you breathe in . . . and bring it back to the middle as you breathe out.

9. Lower your right ear to your right shoulder as you breathe in . . . and bring it back to the middle as you breathe out.

10. Really feel the breath, with no rush or force, in your own pace, at your own time

Breathe to calm and relax yourself

Do this after you've done the breathwork preparation above:

> Breathe in for a count of 4 through your nose in your own time at your own pace
>
> Hold for a count of 4
>
> Exhale for a count of 4 through your mouth

Do this for a total of ten breaths.

Breathe for energy and focus (*kapalabhati*)

Do this after you've done the breathwork preparation above:

> Breathe in through your nose for a count of 4
>
> Then exhale powerfully through your nose for less than a second (You will feel a sort of engine pumping in your lungs.)
>
> Breathe in again through your nose for a count of 4
>
> Do this for a total of ten breaths.

Breathe for sleep

> Breathe in for 4 seconds
>
> Exhale for longer than 4 seconds

Do this until you are asleep or close to it.

PART TWO

GROW

FIVE

PURPOSE

The Nature of the Scorpion

When you protect your dharma,
your dharma protects you.
—Manusmriti 8:15

From the outside, being a monk looks like it's fundamentally about letting go: the baldness, the robes, stripping away distractions. In fact, the asceticism was less a goal than it was a means to an end. Letting go opened our minds.

We spent our days in service; which was also designed to expand our minds. In the course of this service, we weren't supposed to gravitate to our favorite ways to serve, but rather to help out wherever and however it was needed. To experience and emphasize our willingness and flexibility, we rotated through various chores and activities instead of choosing roles and becoming specialists: cooking, cleaning, gardening, caring for the cows, meditating, studying, praying, teaching, and so on. It took some work for me to truly see all activities as equal—I much preferred to study than to clean up after the cows—but we were told to see society as the organs of a body. No one organ was more important than another; all of them worked in concert, and the body needed them all.

In spite of this equitable coexistence, it became clear that each of us had natural affinities. One might be drawn to tending the animals (not me!), another might take pleasure in cooking (again, not me, I'm an eat-to-live kind of guy), another might get great satisfaction from gardening. We undertook such a breadth of activities that, although we didn't indulge our particular passions, we could observe and reflect on where they lay. We could experiment with new skills, study them, see how improving them made us feel. What did we like? What felt natural and fulfilling? Why?

If something, like cleaning up after the cows, made me uncomfortable, instead of turning away, I pushed myself to understand the feelings that lay at the root of my discomfort. I quickly identified my hatred for some of the most mundane chores as an ego issue. I thought them a waste of time when I could be learning. Once I admitted this to myself, I could explore whether cleaning had anything to offer me. Could I learn from a mop? Practice Sanskrit verse while planting potatoes? In the course of my chores, I observed that mop heads need to be completely flexible in order to get into every space and corner. Not every task is best served by something sturdy like a broom. To my monk mind, there was a worthwhile lesson in that: We need flexibility in order to access every corner of study and growth. When it came to planting potatoes, I found that the rhythm of it helped me remember verse, while the verse brought excitement to the potatoes.

Exploring our strengths and weaknesses in the self-contained universe of the ashram helped lead each of us to our *dharma*. Dharma, like many Sanskrit terms, can't be defined by a single English word, though to say something is "your calling" comes close. My definition of dharma is an effort to make it practical to our lives today. I see dharma as the combination of *varna* and *seva*. Think of *varna* (also a word with complex meanings) as passion and skills. *Seva* is understanding the world's needs and selflessly serving others. When your natural talents and passions (your *varna*) connect with what the universe needs (*seva*) and become your purpose, you are living in your dharma.

When you spend your time and energy living in your dharma, you have the satisfaction of using your best abilities and doing something that matters to the world. **Living in your dharma is a certain route to fulfillment.**

In the first part of this book we talked about becoming aware of and letting go of the influences and distractions that divert us from a fulfilling life. Now we'll rebuild our lives around our guiding values and deepest intentions. This growth begins with dharma.

Two monks were washing their feet in a river when one of them realized that a scorpion was drowning in the water. He immediately picked it up and set it upon the bank. Though he was quick, the scorpion stung his hand. He resumed washing his feet. The other monk said, "Hey, look. That foolish scorpion fell right back in." The first monk leaned over, saved the scorpion again, and was again stung. The other monk asked him, "Brother, why do you rescue the scorpion when you know its nature is to sting?"

"Because," the monk answered, "to save it is my nature."

The monk is modeling humility—he does not value his own pain above the scorpion's life. But the more relevant lesson here is that "to save" is so essential to this monk's nature that he is compelled and content to do it even knowing the scorpion will sting him. The monk has so much faith in his dharma that he is willing to suffer in order to fulfill it.

DISCOVERING DHARMA

It is my first summer at the ashram. I've cleaned bathrooms, cooked potato curry, harvested cabbages. I've washed my own clothes by hand, which is not an easy chore—our robes have as much material as bedsheets, and to scrub out food or grass stains would have qualified as a CrossFit workout of the day.

One day I'm scrubbing pots with the gusto of an overeager apprentice when a senior monk comes up to me.

"We'd like you to lead a class this week," he says. "The topic is this verse from

the Gita: 'Whatever action is performed by a great man, common men follow
in his footsteps, and whatever standards he sets by exemplary acts, all the world
pursues.'"

I agree to do it, and as I return to scrubbing I think about what I'll say. I
understand the basic gist of the scripture—we teach by example. It taps into my
understanding that who you are is not what you say, but how you behave—and
it reminds me of a quote often attributed to Saint Francis of Assisi: "Preach the
Gospel at all times. When necessary, use words."

Many of the other monks, like me, didn't enter the ashram at age five.
They've been to mainstream schools, had girlfriends and boyfriends, watched
TV and movies. They won't have trouble grasping the meaning of the verse,
but I'm excited to figure out how I can make it feel fresh and relevant to their
experiences outside the ashram.

The aging computers in our library have an excruciatingly slow internet
connection. I'm in India, in the middle of nowhere, and it seems like every
image takes an hour to download. After having done research on the speedy
computers of a college library, I find the wait painful. But I know that, over in
the kitchen, my fellow monks are patiently waiting for water to boil. As they're
doing, I try to respect the process.

During my research, I become fascinated by the psychology of communication. I find studies by Albert Mehrabian showing that 55 percent of our
communication is conveyed by body language, 38 percent is tone of voice, and
a mere 7 percent is the actual words we speak. (That's a general guideline, but
even in situations where those percentages shift, the fact remains that most of
our communication is nonverbal.) I lose myself in exploring how we convey our
messages and values, analyzing the communication styles of various leaders,
and figuring out how it all adds up to be relevant in our lives. Among others,
I read about Jane Goodall, who never intended to become a leader. She first
entered the wilds of Tanzania to study chimpanzees in 1960, but her research
and ongoing work have significantly redefined conservation, attracted women
to her field, and inspired hundreds of thousands of young people to get involved
in conservation.

Our class gathers in a medium-sized room. I take my place on an elevated, *cushioned seat, and the students sit on cushions in front of me. I don't see myself as above them in any way, except for my elevated seat. We monks have already learned that everyone is always simultaneously a student and a teacher.*

When I finish giving my talk, I'm pleased with how it's gone. I enjoyed sharing the ideas as much as I enjoyed researching them. People thank me, telling me that they appreciated the examples and how I made the ancient verse feel relevant. One or two ask me how I prepared—they've noticed how much work I put into it. As I bask in the glow of my satisfaction and their appreciation, I am beginning to realize my dharma—studying, experimenting with knowledge, and speaking.

Everyone has a psychophysical nature which determines where they flourish and thrive. Dharma is using this natural inclination, the things you're good at, your thrive mode, to serve others. You should feel passion when the process is pleasing and your execution is skillful. And the response from others should be positive, showing that your passion has a purpose. This is the magic formula for dharma.

Passion + Expertise + Usefulness = Dharma.

If we're only excited when people say nice things about our work, it's a sign that we're not passionate about the work itself. And if we indulge our interests and skills, but nobody responds to them, then our passion is without purpose. If either piece is missing, we're not living our dharma.

When people fantasize about what they want to do and who they want to be, they don't often investigate fully enough to know if it suits their dharma. People think they want to be in finance because they know it's lucrative. Or they want to be a doctor because it's respected *and* honorable. But they move forward with no idea whether those professions suit them—if they will like the process, the environment, and the energy of the work, or whether they're any good at it.

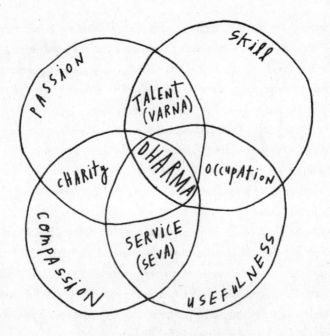

EVERYTHING YOU ARE

There are two lies some of us hear when we're growing up. The first is "You'll never amount to anything." The second is "You can be anything you want to be." The truth is—

You can't be anything you want.

But you can be everything you are.

A monk is a traveler, but the journey is inward, bringing us ever closer to our most authentic, confident, powerful self. There is no need to embark on an actual Year-in-Provence-type quest to find your passion and purpose, as if it's a treasure buried in some distant land, waiting to be discovered. Your dharma is already with you. It's always been with you. It's woven into your being. If we keep our minds open and curious, our dharmas announce themselves.

Even so, it can take years of exploration to uncover our dharma. One of our biggest challenges in today's world is the pressure to perform big, right now. Thanks to the early successes of folks like Facebook founder

Mark Zuckerberg and Snapchat cofounder Evan Spiegel (who became the youngest billionaire in the world at age twenty-four), along with celebs such as Chance the Rapper and Bella Hadid, many of us feel that if we haven't found our calling and risen to the top in our fields in our twenties, we've failed.

Putting all of this pressure on people to achieve early is not only stressful, it can actually hinder success. According to *Forbes* magazine publisher Rich Karlgaard, in his book *Late Bloomers*, the majority of us don't hit our stride quite so early, but society's focus on academic testing, getting into the "right" colleges, and developing and selling an app for millions before you even get your degree (if you don't drop out to run your multimillion-dollar company) is causing high levels of anxiety and depression not only among those who haven't conquered the world by age twenty-four, but even among those who've already made a significant mark. Many early achievers feel tremendous pressure to maintain that level of performance.

But, as Karlgaard points out, there are plenty of fantastically successful people who hit their strides later in life: *The Bluest Eye*, Toni Morrison's first novel, wasn't published until she was thirty-nine. And after a ten-year stint in college and time spent working as a ski instructor, Dietrich Mateschitz was forty before he created blockbuster energy drink company Red Bull. Pay attention, cultivate self-awareness, feed your strengths, and you *will* find your way. And once you discover your dharma, pursue it.

OTHER PEOPLE'S DHARMA

The Bhagavad Gita says that it's better to do one's own dharma imperfectly than to do another's perfectly. Or, as Steve Jobs put it in his 2005 Stanford commencement address, "Your time is limited, so don't waste it living someone else's life."

In his autobiography, Andre Agassi dropped a bombshell on the world: The former world's number one tennis player, eight-time grand slam champion, and gold medal winner *didn't like tennis*. Agassi was pushed into playing by his father, and though he was incredible at the game, he hated playing. The fact that he was tremendously successful and made loads of money didn't matter; it wasn't his dharma. However, Agassi has transitioned his on-court success into his true passion—instead of serving aces, he's now serving others. Along with providing other basic services for children in his native Nevada, the Andre Agassi Foundation runs a K-12 college preparatory school for at-risk youth.

Our society is set up around strengthening our weaknesses rather than building our strengths. In school, if you get three As and a D, all the adults around you are focused on that D. Our grades in school, scores on standardized tests, performance reviews, even our self-improvement efforts—all highlight our insufficiencies and urge us to improve them. But what happens if we think of those weaknesses not as our failures but as *someone else's dharma*? Sister Joan Chittister, a Benedictine nun, wrote, "It is trust in the limits of the self that makes us open and it is trust in the gifts of others that makes us secure. We come to realize that we don't have to do everything, that we can't do everything, that what I can't do is someone else's gift and responsibility. . . . My limitations make space for the gifts of other people." Instead of focusing on our weaknesses, we lean into our strengths and look for ways to make them central in our lives.

Here are two important caveats: First, following your dharma doesn't mean you get a free pass. When it comes to skills, you should lean into your strengths. But if your weaknesses are emotional qualities like empathy, compassion, kindness, and generosity, you should never stop developing them. There's no point in being a tech wizard if you're not compassionate. You don't get to be a jerk just because you're skilled.

Second, a bad grade in school doesn't mean you get to ditch the subject altogether. We have to be careful not to confuse inexperience with weakness. Some of us live outside our dharma because we haven't figured out what it is. It is important to experiment broadly before we reject options, and much of this experimentation is done in school and elsewhere when we're young.

My own dharma emerged from some experiences I found extremely unpleasant. Before I taught that class at the ashram, I had a distaste for public speaking. When I was seven or eight years old, I took part in a school assembly where kids shared their cultural traditions. My mother dressed me as an Indian king, wrapping me in an ill-fitting sari-like getup that did nothing for my awkward body. The minute I walked on stage, kids started to laugh. I can't carry a tune for the life of me, and when I started to sing a prayer in transliterated Sanskrit, they lost it. I wasn't even two minutes in, and five hundred kids and all the teachers were laughing at me. I forgot the lyrics and looked down at the sheet in front of me, but I couldn't read the words through my tears. My teacher had to walk out onto the stage, put her arm around me, and lead me away as everyone continued to laugh. It was mortifying. From that moment, I hated the stage. Then, when I was fourteen, my parents forced me to attend a public speaking/drama afterschool program. Three hours, three times a week, for four years gave me the skills to stand up on stage, but I had nothing to talk about and took no pleasure in it. I was and still am shy, but that public speaking course changed my life because once that skill connected to my dharma, I ran with it.

After my first summer at the ashram ended, I was not yet a full-time monk. I returned to college and decided to try my hand at teaching again. I set up an extracurricular club called "Think Out Loud," where every week people would come to hear me speak on a philosophical, spiritual, and/or scientific topic, and then we'd discuss it. The topic for the first meeting was "Material Problems, Spiritual Solutions." I planned to explore how as humans we experience the same challenges, setbacks, and issues in life, and how spirituality can help us find the answer. Nobody showed up. It was a small room, and when it stayed empty, I thought, *What can I learn from this?* Then I carried on—I gave my talk to the empty room with my full energy, because I felt the topic deserved it. Ever since then I have been doing the same thing in one medium or another—starting a conversation about who we are and how we can find solutions to our daily challenges.

For the next meeting of "Think Out Loud," I did a better job of distributing flyers and posters, and about ten people showed up. The topic for my second attempt was the same, "Material Problems, Spiritual Solutions," and I opened the discussion by playing a clip of the comedian Chris Rock doing a bit about how the pharmaceutical industry doesn't really want to cure diseases—it actually wants us to have a *prolonged* need for the medications that it produces. I tied this to a discussion of how we are looking for instant fixes instead of doing the real work of growth. I've always loved drawing from funny and contemporary examples to relate monk philosophy to our daily lives. "Think Out Loud" did just that every week for the next three years of college. By the time I graduated, the club had grown to one hundred people and become a weekly three-hour workshop.

We've all got a special genius inside of us, but it may not be on the path that opens directly before us. There may be no visible path at all. My dharma was not in one of the job tracks that were common at my school but rather in the club that I founded there after a chance assignment at the ashram hinted at my dharma. Our dharmas don't hide, but sometimes we need to work patiently to recognize them. As researchers Anders Ericsson and Robert Pool underscore in their book *Peak*, mastery requires deliberate practice, and lots of it. But if you love it, you do it. Picasso experimented with other forms of art but kept painting as his focus. Michael Jordan did a stint at baseball, but basketball was where he really thrived. Play hardest in your area of strength and you'll achieve depth, meaning, and satisfaction in your life.

ALIGN WITH YOUR PASSION

In order to unveil our dharma, we have to identify our passions—the activities we both love and are naturally inclined to do well. It's clear to anyone who looks at the Quadrants of Potential that we should be spending as much time as possible at the upper right, in Quadrant Two: doing things that we're both good at and love. But life doesn't always work out that way. In fact, many of us find ourselves spending our careers in Quadrant One: working on things that we're good at, but don't love. When we

QUADRANTS of POTENTIAL

I. SKILL BuT NO PASSION	II. SKILL AND PASSION
III. No skill AND No PASSION	IV. No skill BuT PASSION

QUESTION:
HOW CAN WE MOVE MORE OF OUR TIME & ENERGY TOWARD SECTION TWO — DOING THINGS WE ARE GOOD AT AND LOVE??

have time to spare, we hop over to Quadrant Four to indulge the hobbies and extracurriculars that we love, even though we never have enough time to become as good at them as we would like. Everyone can agree that we want to spend as little time as possible in Quadrant Three. It's super-depressing to hang out there, doing things we don't love and aren't good at. So the question is: How can we move more of our time toward Quadrant Two: doing things we are good at and love? (You'll notice that I don't discuss the quadrants in numerical order. This is because Quadrants One and Four both offer half of what we want, so it makes sense to discuss them first.)

Quadrant One: Good at, but Don't Love

Getting from here to Quadrant Two is easier said than done. Say you don't love your job. Most of us can't just leap into a job we love that miraculously comes with a generous salary. A more practical approach is to find innovative ways to move toward Quadrant Two within the jobs that we already have. What can you do to bring your dharma where you are?

When I first left the ashram, I took a consulting job at Accenture, a global management consulting firm. We were constantly dealing with numbers, data, and financial statements, and it quickly became clear that a talent for Excel was essential in order to excel in my position. But Excel was not my thing. In spite of my efforts, I couldn't force myself to get better at it. I just wasn't interested. As far as I was concerned, it was worse than mucking out the cow stalls. So, while I continued to do my best, I thought about how I could demonstrate what I was good at. My passion was wisdom and tools for life like meditation and mindfulness, so I offered to teach a mindfulness class to my working group. The lead managing director loved the idea, and the class I gave was popular enough that she asked me to speak about mindfulness and meditation at a company-wide summer event for analysts and consultants. I would speak in front of a thousand people at Twickenham Stadium, the home stadium of England's national rugby team.

When I got to the stadium, I found out that my turn at the podium was sandwiched between words from the CEO and Will Greenwood, a rugby legend. I sat in the audience listening to the lineup, thinking *Crap, everyone's going to laugh at me. Why did I agree to this?* All the other speakers were at the top of their fields and so articulate. I started to have second thoughts about what I had planned to say and how to deliver it. Then I went through my breathing exercises, calmed myself down, and two seconds before I went on stage, I thought, *Just be yourself.* I would do my own dharma perfectly instead of trying to do anyone else's. I went up, did my thing, and afterward the response couldn't have been better. The director who had organized it said, "I've never heard an audience of consultants and analysts stay so quiet you could hear a pin drop." Later, she invited me to teach mindfulness all across the company in the UK.

This was a tipping point for me. I saw that I hadn't just spent three years of my life learning some weird monk-only philosophy that was ir-relevant outside the ashram. I could take all my skills and put them into practice. I could actually fulfill my dharma in the modern world. P.S. I still don't know how to use Excel.

Instead of making a huge career change, you can try my approach: look for opportunities to do what you love in the life you already have. You never know where it might lead. Leonardo DiCaprio hasn't given up acting or producing, yet he also directs significant energy toward envi-ronmental advocacy because it's part of his dharma. A corporate assistant might volunteer to do design work; a bartender can run a trivia contest. I worked with a lawyer whose true passion was to be a baker on *The Great British Bake Off.* That goal felt unrealistic to her, so she got a group of her colleagues obsessed with the show, and they started "Baking Mondays," where every Monday someone on her team brought in something they'd made. She still worked just as hard and performed well at a job that she found slightly tedious, but bringing her passion to the water cooler made her team stronger and made her feel more energized throughout the day. If you have two kids and a mortgage and can't quit your job, do as the law-yer did and find a way to bring the energy of your dharma into the work-place, or look for ways to bring it into other aspects of your life like your hobbies, home, and friendships.

Also, consider why you don't love your strengths. Can you find a rea-son to love them? I often encounter people working corporate jobs who have all the skills required to do good work, but they find the work mean-ingless. The best way to add meaning to an experience is to look for how it might serve you in the future. If you tell yourself: "I'm learning how to work in a global team," or "I'm getting all the budgeting skills I'll need if I open a skate shop one day," then you can nurture a passion for something that may not be your first choice. Link the feeling of passion to the expe-rience of learning and growth.

Psychologist Amy Wrzesniewski from the Yale School of Man-agement and colleagues studied hospital cleaning crews to understand how they experienced their work. One crew described the work as not particularly satisfying and not requiring much skill. And when they explained the tasks they performed, it basically sounded like the job description from the personnel manual. But when the researchers talked to another cleaning crew, they were surprised by what they heard. The second group enjoyed their work, found it deeply meaningful, and described it as being highly skilled. When they described their tasks, the reason for the distinction between the crews started to become clear. The second crew talked not just about typical custodial chores, but also about noticing which patients seemed especially sad or had fewer visitors and making a point to start a conversation or check in on them more often. They related incidents where they escorted elderly visitors through the parking structure so they wouldn't get lost (even though the custodians technically could have gotten fired for that). One woman said she periodically switched the pictures on the walls among different rooms. When asked if this was part of her job, she replied, "That's not part of my job. But that's part of me."

From this study and subsequent research, Wrzesniewski and her colleagues created the phrase "job crafting" to describe "what employees do to redesign their own jobs in ways that foster engagement at work, job satisfaction, resilience, and thriving." According to the researchers, we can reengineer our tasks, relationships, or even just how we perceive what we do (such as custodians thinking of themselves as "healers" and "ambassadors"). The intention with which we approach our work has a tremendous impact on the meaning we gain from it and our personal sense of purpose. Learn to find meaning now, and it will serve you all your life.

Quadrant Four: Not Good at, but Love

When our passions aren't lucrative, we de-prioritize them. Then we feel frustrated that we love an activity but can't do it well or frequently enough to fully enjoy it. The surest route to improving skills is always time. Can you use coaching, take courses, or get training to improve at what you love?

"Impossible," you say. "If I had time to do that, believe me, I would." We will talk about how to find nonexistent time in the next chapter, but for now I will say this: Everyone has time. We commute or we cook or we watch TV. We may not have three hours, but we have ten minutes to listen to a podcast or learn a new technique from a YouTube video. You can do a lot in ten minutes.

Sometimes when we tap into our dharma, it carves out the time for us. When I first started making videos, I worked on them after I got home from my corporate job. Five hours a day, five days a week, I focused on editing five-minute videos. For a long time, the return-on-investment was pitiful, but I wasn't willing to write myself off before trying to make the most of my skill.

In the years since, I've seen people monetize the weirdest things. Spend any amount of time on Etsy, and you'll be amazed at how many people have found ways to make money off their passions. However, if the world is sending you a very strong message that it won't pay for or does not otherwise need or want your passion, then fine. Accept that. There's a *critical* need for soccer in the world, but there's no need for *me* to play soccer. Still, the soccer matches I organized at Accenture were the highlight of my week. If it's not your dharma, it can still give you joy.

Quadrant Three: Not Good at, Don't Love

Do whatever you can to crawl out of this soul-sucking quadrant. You will always have unpleasant chores, but they shouldn't be the biggest part of your life. If at all possible, you should work toward outsourcing the chores in this category. Hurt the pocket, save the mind. And remember, just because you don't like it doesn't mean nobody likes it. Can you work out a trade with a friend or colleague, where you take on each other's least favorite tasks?

If you can't offload the chore, remember the lesson I learned at the ashram—every task is an essential organ. None is less important than the others, and none of us is too important to do any chore. If you think you're too good for something, you succumb to the worst egotistical impulses, and you devalue anyone who does that chore. When you're satisfied in your dharma, you can, without envy or ego, appreciate others who are good at another skill. I have great respect for people who can do Excel, I just don't want to do it myself. When I encounter doctors or soldiers or people in any number of other careers, I think, *That's extraordinary. It's amazing. But it's not me.*

TRY THIS: IDENTIFY YOUR QUADRANT OF POTENTIAL

You may have been doing this exercise in your head as you read about the Quadrants of Potential. Nonetheless, I want you to go through the exercise of acknowledging how close you are to living your dharma today.

> Do you like your job?
> Do you love your job?
> Are you good at your job?
> Do other people need and appreciate your work?
> Is your greatest skill or passion outside your work?
> What is it?
> Do you dream of making it your work?
> Do you think this is an attainable dream?
> Do you think there might be ways you could bring your passion to your work?
> Write down any ideas you have for bringing your passion to the universe.

Quadrant Two: Vedic Personality

We want to live in Quadrant Two, where we spend our time using our talents to do what we love. If we aren't there, we examine the problem the monk way—instead of looking at specific skills you've developed and specific activities that you love, we look beyond them, to their roots. The Bhagavad Gita contemplates dharma by dividing us into four personality types—what it calls *varnas*. There are four *varnas*, and knowing your *varna* tells you your nature and competence. In relatively recent history (during the nineteenth century), when British leaders imposed their own rigid class system on Indian society, the *varnas* emerged as the basis for the caste system. Though castes—a hierarchy of job categories—were based on the *varnas*, this is a misinterpretation of the text. I'm not talking about the caste system here—I believe that all of us are equal; we just have different talents and skills. My discussion of the *varnas* is about how to harness these skills and talents to live to your fullest potential. The different personality types are meant to work together in a community, like the organs in a body—all essential and none superior to the others.

Varnas aren't determined by birth. They're meant to help us understand our true nature and inclinations. You're not creative just because your parents are.

No one *varna* is better than another. We all seek different types of work, fun, love, and service. There is no hierarchy or segregation. If two people are both acting in their best dharma, living for the service of others, then neither is better than the other. Is a cancer researcher better than a fireman?

TRY THIS: THE VEDIC PERSONALITY TEST

This simple test is not an absolute determination of your personality type, but it will help as you seek out your dharma.

See the appendix for The Vedic Personality Test.

THE VARNAS

The four *varnas* are the Guide, the Leader, the Creator, and the Maker. These labels aren't directly tied to specific jobs or activities. Sure, certain activities bring us pleasure because they fulfill our dharma, but there are many different ways to live in our dharma. A Guide, as you will see on page 112, is compelled to learn and share knowledge—you could be a teacher

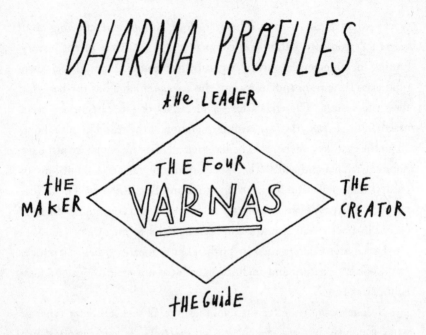

or a writer. A Leader likes to influence and provide, but that doesn't mean you have to be a CEO or a lieutenant—you could be a school principal or shop manager. A Creator likes to make things happen—this could be at a start-up or in a neighborhood association. A Maker likes to see things tangibly being built—they could be a coder or a nurse.

Remember the *gunas: tamas, rajas,* and *sattva*—ignorance, impulsivity, and goodness. For each of the *varnas* I describe what their behavior looks like in each *guna* mode. We strive toward *sattva* through letting go of ignorance, working in our passion, and serving in goodness. The more time we spend in *sattva*, the more effective and fulfilled we become.

Creators

Originally: merchants, businesspeople
Today: marketers, salespeople, entertainers, producers, entrepreneurs, CEOs
Skills: brainstorming, networking, innovating

- Make things happen
- Can convince themselves and others of anything
- Great at sales, negotiation, persuasion
- Highly driven by money, pleasure, and success
- Very hardworking and determined
- Excel in trade, commerce, and banking
- Always on the move
- Work hard, play hard

Mode of Ignorance

- Become corrupt and sell things with no value / Lie, cheat, steal to sell something
- Beaten down by failure
- Burned out, depressed, moody, due to overwork

Mode of Impulse

- Status-driven
- Dynamic, charismatic, and captivating
- Hustler, goal-oriented, tireless

Mode of Goodness

- Use money for greater good
- Create products and ideas that make money but also serve others
- Provide jobs and opportunities for others

Makers

Originally: artists, musicians, creatives, writers
Today: social workers, therapists, doctors, nurses, COOs, heads of human resources, artists, musicians, engineers, coders, carpenters, cooks
Skills: inventing, supporting, implementing

Mode of Ignorance

- Depressed by failure
- Feel stuck and unworthy
- Anxious

Mode of Impulse

- Explore and experiment with new ideas
- Juggle too many things at the same time
- Lose focus on expertise and care; focus more on money and results

Mode of Goodness

- Driven by stability and security
- Generally content and satisfied with the status quo
- Choose meaningful goals to pursue
- Work hard but always maintain balance with family commitments
- Best right-hand man or woman
- Lead team gatherings
- Support those in need
- Highly skilled at manual professions

Connections

Makers and Creators complement each other

Makers make Creators focus on detail, quality, gratitude, and contentment

Creators help Makers think bigger, become more goal-oriented

Guides

Originally and today: teachers, guides, gurus, coaches, mentors

Skills: learning, studying, sharing knowledge, and wisdom

- A coach and a mentor no matter what role they play
- Want to bring out the best in the people in their life

- Value knowledge and wisdom more than fame, power, money, security
- Like having space and time to reflect and learn
- Want to help people find meaning, fulfillment, and purpose
- Like to work alone
- Enjoy intellectual pursuits in their spare time—reading, debate, discussion

Mode of Ignorance

- Don't practice what they preach
- Don't lead by example
- Struggle with implementation

Mode of Impulse

- Love to debate and destroy others' arguments
- Use knowledge for strength and power
- Intellectually curious

Mode of Goodness

- Use knowledge to help people find their purpose
- Aspire to better themselves in order to give more
- Realize knowledge is not theirs to use alone, but that they are here to serve

Leaders

Originally: kings, warriors
Today: military, justice, law enforcement, politics
Skills: governing, inspiring, engaging others

- Natural leaders of people, movements, groups, and families
- Directed by courage, strength, and determination
- Protect those who are less privileged

- Led by higher morals and values and seek to enforce them across the world
- Provide structures and frameworks for the growth of people
- Like to work in teams
- Great at organization, focus, and dedication to a mission

Mode of Ignorance

- Give up on change due to corruption and hypocrisy
- Develop a negative, pessimistic viewpoint
- Lose moral compass in drive for power

Mode of Impulse

- Build structures and frameworks for fame and money, not meaning
- Use their talents to serve themselves not humanity
- Focus on short term goals for themselves

Mode of Goodness

- Fight for higher morals, ethics, and values
- Inspire people to work together
- Build long-term goals to support society

Connections

Guides and Leaders complement each other
Guides give wisdom to Leaders
Leaders give structure to Guides

The point of the *varnas* is to help you understand yourself so you can focus on your strongest skills and inclinations. Self-awareness gives you more focus. When I look at my Guide tendencies, it makes sense to me that I succeed when I focus on strategy. Creators and Makers are better at implementation, so I've surrounded myself with people who can help me with that. A musician might be a Maker, driven by security. In order to succeed, they might need to be surrounded by strategists. Invest in your strengths and surround yourself with people who can fill in the gaps.

When you know your *varna*—your passion and skills—and you serve with that, it becomes your dharma.

TRY THIS: REFLECTED BEST-SELF EXERCISE

1. Choose a group of people who know you well—a diverse mix of people you've worked with, family, and friends. As few as three will work, but ten to twenty is even better.

2. Ask them to write down a moment when you were at your best. Ask them to be specific.

3. Look for patterns and common themes.

4. Write out a profile of yourself, aggregating the feedback as if it weren't about you.

5. Think about how you can turn your best skills into action. How can you use those skills this weekend? In different circumstances or with different people?

TEST-DRIVE YOUR DHARMA

The Vedic Personality Test helps you begin to see your *varna*, but just like a horoscope, it can't tell you what's going to happen tomorrow. It's up to you to test these *varnas* in the real world through exploration and experimentation. If your *varna* is Leader, try to take on that role at work, or by organizing your kid's birthday party. Do you genuinely take joy in the process?

Think about the level of awareness we have when we eat something. We immediately do a sense check and decide if we like it, and we wouldn't have trouble rating it on a scale of one to ten if asked to do so. Furthermore, we might have different feelings about it the next day. (When I have my favorite chocolate brownie sundae on a Sunday night, I feel pretty happy about it, but by Monday morning I no longer think it was the best thing in the world to put in my body.) With both immediate and long-term reflection, we form nuanced opinions about whether we want to make that food part of our regular diet. All of us do this with food, we do it when we leave a movie theater ("Did you like it?"), and some of us do it on Yelp. But we don't think to measure our compatibility with and taste for how we spend our time. When we get in the habit of identifying what empowers us, we have a better understanding of ourselves and what we want in life. This is exactly what we're going to do to refine our understanding of our *varna*.

The first and most critical question to ask when you're exploring your *varna* is:

Did I enjoy the process?

Test the description of your *varna* against your experience to pinpoint what you enjoyed about it. Instead of saying, "I love taking pictures," find the root of it. Do you like helping families put together a Christmas card that makes them proud? (Guide) Do you like to document human struggles or other meaningful situations in order to promote change? (Leader) Or do you love the technical aspects of lighting, focus, and developing film? (Maker) As monks, every time we completed an activity or thought exercise like the ones in this book, we asked ourselves questions: *What did I like about that? Am I good at it? Do I want to read about it, learn about it, and spend a lot of my time doing it? Am I driven to improve? What made me feel comfortable or uncomfortable? If I was uncomfortable, was it in a positive way—a challenge that made me grow—or a negative way?* This awareness

TRY THIS: KEEP AN ACTIVITY JOURNAL

Take note of every activity you take part in through the course of a few days. Meetings, walking the dog, lunch with a friend, writing emails, preparing food, exercising, spending time on social media. For every activity, answer the two questions fundamental to dharma: Did I enjoy the process? Did other people enjoy the result? There are no right or wrong answers. This is an observation exercise to amplify your awareness.

gives us a much more nuanced view of where we thrive. Instead of sending us on one and only one path, that awareness opens us to new ways we can put our passions to use.

EMBRACE YOUR DHARMA

Our heads might try to convince us that we've only ever made the best choices, but our true nature—our passion and purpose—isn't in our heads, it's in our hearts. In fact, our heads often get in the way of our passions. Here are some of the excuses that we use to close our minds:

"I'm too old to start my own business."

"It would be irresponsible of me to make this change."

"I can't afford to do this."

"I already know that."

"I've always done it this way."

"That way won't work for me."

"I don't have time."

Past beliefs, false or self-deceiving, sneak in to block our progress. Fears prevent us from trying new things. Our egos get in the way of learning new information and opening ourselves to growth. (More on this in Chapter Eight.) And nobody ever has time for change. But miracles happen when you embrace your dharma.

Growing up, Joseph Campbell had no model of a career that fit his diverse interests. As a child in the early 1900s, he became fascinated by Native American culture and studied everything he could about it. During college, he became entranced with the rituals and symbols of Catholicism. While studying abroad, his interests expanded to include the theories of Jung and Freud, and he developed an interest in modern art. Back at Columbia, Campbell told his dissertation advisors that he wanted to blend ancient stories about the Holy Grail with ideas in art and psychology. They rejected that idea. He abandoned work on his thesis and in 1949 found a job teaching literature at Sarah Lawrence College, which he held for thirty-eight years. Meanwhile, he published hundreds of books and articles, and did a deep dive into ancient Indian mythology and philosophy. But it was in *The Hero with a Thousand Faces* that he first discussed his groundbreaking ideas about what he called "the hero's journey"—a concept that established Campbell as one of the foremost authorities on mythology and the human psyche. As someone who followed his dharma, it's no surprise that Joseph Campbell is the original source of the advice "Follow your bliss." He wrote, "Now, I came to this idea of bliss because in Sanskrit, which is the great spiritual language of the world, there are three terms that represent the brink, the jumping-off place to the ocean of transcendence: Sat, Chit, Ananda. The word 'Sat' means being. 'Chit' means consciousness. 'Ananda' means bliss or rapture. I thought, 'I don't know whether my consciousness is proper consciousness or not; I don't know whether what I know of my being is my proper being or not; but I do know where my rapture is. So let me hang on to rapture, and that will bring me both my consciousness and my being.' I think it worked." If you follow your bliss, he said, "doors will open for you that wouldn't have opened for anyone else."

Protective instincts hold us back or steer us toward practical decisions (Campbell did teach literature for thirty-eight years), but we can see past them and follow our dharma if we know what to look for.

DHARMA IS OF THE BODY

Instead of listening to our minds, we must pay attention to how an idea or activity feels in our bodies. First, when you visualize yourself in a process, do you feel joy? Does the idea of it appeal to you? Then, when you actually do the activity, how does your body respond? When you're in your element, you can feel it.

1. *Alive.* For some people, being in their dharma means they feel a calm, confident satisfaction. For others, there is a thrill of joy and

excitement. In either case, you feel alive, connected, with a smile on your face. A light comes on.

2. *Flow.* In dharma, there is a natural momentum. You feel like you're in your lane, swimming with the current, instead of struggling through a resistant surf. When you are truly aligned, there is a sense of flow—you come out of your own head and lose track of time.

3. *Comfort.* In your dharma, you don't feel alone or out of place, no matter who comes or goes or where you are physically; where you are feels right, even if the place where you feel right is traveling the world. I don't like the feeling of danger, but I have a friend who loves fast cars and Jet Skis. The danger—the worst-case scenario—is the same for both of us, but for him it is worth it, or the danger itself is a joy. On stage, I'm in my element, but someone else would shut down.

4. *Consistency.* If you have a great time snorkeling on vacation, that doesn't mean snorkeling, or being on vacation for that matter, is your dharma. Being in your dharma bears repeating. In fact, it gets better the more you do it. But a single event is a clue to what energy you like, when and how you feel alive.

5. *Positivity and growth.* When we're aware of our own strengths, we're more confident, we value others' abilities more, and we feel less competitive. The inclination to compare yourself to others may not go away completely, but it shrinks because you only compare yourself to people within your area of expertise. Rejection and criticism don't feel like assaults. They feel like information that we can accept or reject, depending on whether they help us move forward.

DHARMA IS YOUR RESPONSIBILITY

Once you have a sense of your dharma, it's up to you to set up your life so that you can live it. We're not always going to be in a place or a situation where others recognize our dharma and bend over backward to help us fulfill it. As we all have experienced at one time or another, bosses don't always tap into their employees' potential. If you're reading this chapter thinking *My manager needs to understand dharma—then she'll give me the promotion*, you've missed the point. We will never live in an idyllic world where everyone constantly lives their dharma, with occasional pauses for their bosses to call and ask if they're truly fulfilled.

It is our responsibility to demonstrate and defend our dharma. The Manusmriti says that dharma protects those who protect it. Dharma brings you stability and peace. When we have the confidence to know where we thrive, we find opportunities to demonstrate that. This creates a feedback loop. When you safeguard your dharma, you constantly strive to be in a place where you thrive. When you thrive, people notice, and you reap rewards that help you stay in your dharma. Your dharma protects your joy and your sense of purpose and helps you grow.

STRETCH YOUR DHARMA

A person who isn't living their dharma is like a fish out of water. You can give the fish all the riches in the world, but it will die unless it's returned to the water. Once you discover your dharma, strive to play that role in every aspect of your life. Follow your passion in the workplace. Take up community issues using the same skill set. Be in your dharma with your family, in sports, in relationships, during days out with friends. If my dharma is to be a leader, I'm probably the one who should be planning the family holidays. I will feel meaning in that role. But if I'm a leader and I'm not playing that role, I'll feel insignificant and frustrated.

Perhaps you are thinking, *Jay, it makes no sense to stick to your dharma. Everyone knows that you should push yourself. Try new things. Venture out of your comfort zone.* Though your dharma is your natural state, its range is further than your comfort zone. For instance, if your dharma is to be a speaker, you can go from an audience of ten to an audience of a hundred, scaling the size of your impact. If you speak to students, you can start speaking to CEOs.

It's also important to stretch your dharma. I'm not the most outgoing person in the world, but I go to events and meetings because I know connecting with people serves my purpose. Going against your dharma is a bit like roller skating. You feel off-balance, slightly out of control, and exhausted afterward. But the more you understand yourself, the more solid your footing. You can consciously skate off in a new direction for a higher purpose. Understanding your dharma is key to knowing when and how to leave it behind.

Our dharmas evolve with us. A British expat, Emma Slade, lived in Hong Kong, where she worked as an investor for a global bank managing accounts worth more than a billion dollars. "I loved it," says Slade. "It was fast, it was exciting. . . . I ate balance sheets for breakfast." Then in September 1997, Slade was on a business trip in Jakarta, Indonesia, when an armed man pushed a gun into her chest, robbed her, and held her hostage in her hotel room. She says that as she lay cowering on the floor, she learned the value of a human life. Fortunately, police arrived before Slade was physically harmed. Later, when police officers showed her a photograph of the man slumped against the hotel wall surrounded by spatters of blood, Slade was shocked to feel sadness and compassion for him. That feeling stuck with her and led her to pursue the question of her real purpose.

Slade quit her job and began exploring yoga and the nature of mind. In 2011, she traveled to Bhutan, where she met a monk who left an indelible impression on her (been there!). In 2012, she became a Buddhist nun, and Slade (now also known as Pema Deki) felt she'd finally found peace. Yet that feeling of compassion she'd felt for the man who attacked her returned, and Slade realized she needed to do something to put her compassion into action. So in 2015 she founded a UK-based charity called Opening Your Heart to Bhutan, which seeks to meet the basic needs of people in rural areas of East Bhutan. Though she found fulfillment in becoming a nun, it was never her dharma to sit in a cave and meditate for the rest of her life. She now deploys her financial acumen in a way that serves herself and others more richly. Says Slade, "The skills of old have been very useful in bringing me now a very meaningful and happy life." Slade compares her experience to the lotus flower, which begins in the mud then grows upward through the water as it seeks light. In Buddhism, the lotus represents the idea that the mud and muck of life's challenges can provide fertile ground for our development. As the lotus grows, it rises through the water to eventually blossom. The Buddha says, "Just like a red, blue, or white lotus—born in the water, grown in the water, rising up above the water—stands unsmeared by the water, in the same way I—born in the world, grown in the world, having overcome the world—live unsmeared by the world."

"Jakarta was my mud," Slade says in her TEDx Talk, "but it was also the seed of my future development."

Remember the whole equation of dharma. Dharma isn't just passion and skills. Dharma is *passion in the service of others*. Your passion is for you. Your purpose is for others. Your passion becomes a purpose when you use it to serve others. Your dharma has to fill a need in the world. As I've said, monks believe that you should be willing to do whatever is needed when there's a higher purpose (and monks live this fully), but if you're not a monk the way to see it is that the pleasure you feel in doing your passion should equal how much others appreciate it. If others don't think you're effective, then your passion is a hobby, which can add richness to your life.

This doesn't mean every activity outside your dharma is a waste of time. For all of us there are activities in life that are competence-building and activities that are character-building. When I was first asked to give talks, I built competence in my dharma. But when I was asked to take out the trash, it built my character. To build your competence without regard for character is narcissistic, and to build character without working on skills is devoid of impact. We need to work on both in order to serve our souls and a higher purpose.

Knowing your purpose and fulfilling it is easier and more fruitful when you use your time and energy wisely every day. In the next chapter we will talk about how to get the best start to your day and how to follow through from there.

SIX

ROUTINE

Location Has Energy; Time Has Memory

Every day, think as you wake up, today I am fortunate to be alive,
I have a precious human life, I am not going to waste it.
—the Dalai Lama

There are twelve of us, maybe more, sleeping on the floor, each on a thin yoga-type pad, covered by a simple sheet. The walls of the room are made of packed cow dung that feels like rough plaster and gives the place a not-unpleasant earthy smell. The unfinished stone floors are worn smooth, but a far cry from memory foam. There are no finished windows in this building—we're in an interior room that keeps us dry in the rainy season and has plenty of doors for ventilation.

Although I sleep here every night, there is no particular space that I consider "mine." We steer clear of ownership here—no possessions, no material attachments. Right now the room is dark as a cave, but from the tenor of the birds outside, our bodies know that it's 4 a.m.—time to wake up. We're due at collective prayers in half an hour. Without speaking a word, we move to the locker room, some of us showering, some of us pulling on our robes. We wait in

line to brush our teeth at one of the four communal sinks. No one from the out-
side world is witness to our activity, but if they were, they would see a group of
seemingly well-rested men, all of whom appear perfectly content to be getting
up at this early hour.

It wasn't always that easy. Every morning my brain, desperate to remain
shut down just a little bit longer, thought of a different excuse for why I
should sleep in. But I pushed myself to adopt this new routine because
I was committed to the process. The fact that it was hard was an important part of the journey.

Eventually, I learned the one infallible trick to successfully getting
up earlier: *I had to go to sleep earlier.* That was it. I'd spent my entire life
pushing the limits of each day, sacrificing tomorrow because I didn't want
to miss out on today. But once I finally let that go and started going to
sleep earlier, waking up at four became easier and easier. And as it became
easier, I found that I could do it without the help of anyone or anything
besides my own body and the natural world around it.

This was a revelatory experience for me. I realized I had never in my
life begun my day without being startled in one way or another. When I
was a teenager, my morning summons came in the form of my mother
screaming "Jay, wake up!" from downstairs. In later years, an alarm clock
performed the same thankless task. Every day of my life had begun with a
sudden, jarring intrusion. Now, however, I was waking up to the sounds of
birds, trees rustling in the wind, a stream of water. I woke to the sounds
of nature.

At last I came to understand the value in it. The point of waking up
early wasn't to torture us—it was to start the day off with peace and tranquility. Birds. A gong. The sound of flowing water. And our morning routine never varied. The simplicity and structure of ashram mornings spared
us from the stressful complexity of decisions and variation. Starting our
days so simply was like a mental shower. It cleansed us of the challenges
of the previous day, giving us the space and energy to transform greed into

generosity, anger into compassion, loss into love. Finally, it gave us resolve, a sense of purpose to carry out into the day.

In the ashram, every detail of our life was designed to facilitate the habit or ritual we were trying to practice. For example, our robes: When we rose, we never had to think about what to wear. Like Steve Jobs, Barack Obama, and Arianna Huffington, all of whom have been known to have their own basic uniforms, monks simplify their clothing so as not to waste energy and time on dressing for the day. We each had two sets of robes—one to wear and one to wash. In similar fashion, the early morning wake-up was designed to launch the day in the right spirit. It was an ungodly hour, yet it was spiritually enlightening.

I would never wake up that early, you may be thinking. *I can't think of a worse way to start the day.* I understand that perspective since I used to feel the same way! But let's take a look at how most people currently start their day: sleep researchers say 85 percent of us need an alarm clock to wake up for work. When we wake up before our bodies are ready, the hormone melatonin, which helps to regulate sleep, is usually still at work, which is one of the reasons we grope for the snooze button.

Unfortunately, our productivity-driven society encourages us to live like this. Maria Popova, a writer who's best known as the curator of *Brain Pickings*, writes, "We tend to wear our ability to get by on little sleep as some sort of badge of honor that validates our work ethic. But what it *is* is a profound failure of self-respect and of priorities."

Then, once we've woken up after too little sleep, nearly a quarter of us do something else that starts us out on the second wrong foot of the day—*we reach for our cell phones within one minute of waking up.* Over half of us are checking messages within ten minutes. A majority of people go from out cold to processing mountains of information within minutes every morning.

There are only six cars that can go from zero to sixty miles per hour in under two seconds. Like most cars, humans are not built for that kind of sudden transition, mentally or physically. And the last thing you need to do when you've just woken up is to stumble straight into tragedy and pain courtesy of news headlines or friends venting about gridlock on their commute. Looking at your phone first thing in the morning is like inviting one hundred chatty strangers into your bedroom before you've showered, brushed your teeth, fixed your hair. Between the alarm clock and the world inside your phone, you're immediately overwhelmed with stress, pressure, anxiety. Do you really expect yourself to emerge from that state and have a pleasant, productive day?

In the ashram, we started each morning in the spirit of the day we planned to have, and we trained ourselves to sustain that deliberateness and focus all day long. Sure, that's all fine and good if your daily schedule involves prayer, meditation, study, service, and chores, but the outside world is more complex.

EARLY TO RISE

Here is my first recommendation: Wake up one hour earlier than you do now. "No way!" you say. "Why would I want to wake up any earlier than I do right now? I don't get enough sleep as it is. Besides, yuck!" But hear me out. None of us wants to go to work tired and then get to the end of the day feeling like we could have done more. The energy and mood of the morning carries through the day, so making life more meaningful begins there.

We're used to waking up just before we have to get to work, or to a class, or to a workout, or to shuttle children off to school. We leave ourselves just enough time to shower, eat breakfast, pack up, etc. But having "just enough time" means *not* having enough time. You run late. You skip breakfast. You leave the bed unmade. You can't take the time to enjoy your shower, brush your teeth properly, finish your breakfast, or put everything away so you'll return to a tidy home. You can't do things with purpose and care if you have to speed through them. When you start the morning with high pressure and high stress, you're programming your body to operate in that mode for the rest of the day, through conversations, meetings, appointments.

Waking up early leads to a more productive day. Successful business-people are already onto this. Apple CEO Tim Cook starts his day at 3:45 a.m. Richard Branson is up at 5:45. Michelle Obama rises at 4:30. But it's important to note that while lots of high-impact people rise early, there's also a movement among top executives to reclaim sleep. Amazon CEO Jeff Bezos makes it a priority to get eight hours of sleep every night, saying that less sleep might give you more time to produce, but the quality will suffer. So if you're going to rise early, you need to turn in at an hour that allows you to get a full night's rest.

Life gets more complicated if you have kids or a night job, so if these or other circumstances make the idea of waking up an hour earlier un-fathomable, don't despair. Start with manageable increments (see the Try This below). And notice I didn't name a specific time for you to get up. I'm not asking for 4 a.m. The hour doesn't even have to be early—the goal is to give you enough time to move with intention and do things completely. That spirit will carry through the day.

Create a time cushion at the beginning of the day or you'll spend the rest of the day searching for it. I guarantee you will never find that extra time in the middle of the day. Steal it from your morning sleep and give that sleep back to yourself at night. See what changes.

TRY THIS: EASE INTO AN EARLIER WAKE-UP

This week, wake up just fifteen minutes earlier. You'll probably have to use an alarm, but make it a gentle one. Use low lighting when you first wake up; put on quiet music. Don't pick up your phone for at least those bonus fifteen minutes. Give your brain this time to set a tone for the day ahead. After one week of this, roll your wake time back another fifteen minutes. Now you have half an hour that is all yours. How will you choose to spend it? You might take a longer shower. Sip your tea. Go for a walk. Meditate. Spend a moment cleaning up after yourself before you step out the door. At night, turn off the TV and phone and get in bed whenever you feel the first twinge of fatigue.

FOUND TIME

Once you've created space in the morning, it is yours alone; nobody else controls how you use it. Given how much of our time is controlled by our obligations—job, family, etc.—this free time is one of the greatest gifts we can give ourselves. You might go about your ordinary routine, but feel the space and leisure created by more time. Maybe you have time to make your own coffee instead of grabbing it en route. You can have a conversation over breakfast, read the paper, or use your newfound time to exercise. If you have a meditation, you can start the day with a gratitude visualization practice. Maybe, as health experts are fond of recommending, you'll park further from work to add a bit of a walk to your morning. When you create the space, you'll realize it fills with what you lack most of all: time for yourself.

TRY THIS: A NEW MORNING ROUTINE

Every morning make some time for:

Thankfulness. Express gratitude to someone, some place, or something every day. This includes thinking it, writing it, and sharing it. (See Chapter Nine.)

Insight. Gain insight through reading the paper or a book, or listening to a podcast.

Meditation. Spend fifteen minutes alone, breathing, visualizing or with sound. (More about sound meditation at the end of Part 3.)

Exercise. We monks did yoga, but you can do some basic stretches or a workout.

Thankfulness. Insight. Meditation. Exercise. T.I.M.E. A new way to put time into your morning.

THE EVENING ROUTINE

At the ashram, I learned that the morning is defined by the evening. It's natural for us to treat each morning like a new beginning, but the truth is that our days circle on themselves. You don't set your alarm in the morning—you set it the night before. It follows that if you want to wake up in the morning with intention, you need to start that momentum by establishing a healthy, restful evening routine—and so the attention we've given the mornings begins to expand and define the entire day.

There is "no way" you have time to wake up one hour earlier, but how often do you switch on the TV, settle on one show or another, and end up watching until past midnight? You watch TV because you're "unwinding." You're too tired to do anything else. But earlier sleep time can put you in a better mood. Human growth hormone (HGH) is kind of a big deal. It plays a key role in growth, cell repair, and metabolism, and without it we might even die sooner. As much as 75 percent of the HGH in our bodies is released when we sleep, and research shows that our highest bursts of HGH typically come between 10 p.m. and midnight, so if you're awake during those hours, you're cheating yourself of HGH. If you have a job that goes past midnight, or little kids who keep you up, feel free to ignore me, but waking up before the demands of your day begin should not be at the expense of good sleep. If you spent that ten to midnight getting real rest, it wouldn't be so hard to find those hours in the morning.

In the ashram, we spent the evenings studying and reading and went to sleep between eight and ten. We slept in pitch darkness, with no devices in the room. We slept in T-shirts and shorts, never in our robes, which carried the energy of the waking day.

Morning sets the tone of the day, but a well-planned evening prepares you for morning. In an interview on CNBC's Make It, Instagram *Shark Tank* star Kevin O'Leary said that before he goes to sleep he writes down three things he wants to do the next morning before he talks to anyone besides his family. Take his cue and before you go to sleep, figure out the first things you want to achieve tomorrow. Knowing what you're tackling first will simplify your morning. You won't have to push or force your mind when it's just warming up. (And, bonus, those tasks won't keep you up at night if you know you're going to handle them.)

Next, find your version of a monk's robe, a uniform that you'll put on in the morning. I have a bigger selection of clothes now, and to my wife's relief none of them are orange robes, but I favor similar sets of clothes in different colors. The point is to remove challenges from the morning. Insignificant as they may seem, if you're spending your morning deciding what to eat, what to wear, and what tasks to tackle first, the accumulating choices complicate things unnecessarily.

Christopher Sommer, a former US National Team gymnastics coach, with forty years' experience, tells his athletes to limit the number of decisions they have to make because each decision is an opportunity to stray from their path. If you spend your morning making trivial decisions, you'll have squandered that energy. Settle into patterns and make decisions the night before, and you'll have a head start on the morning and will be better able to make focused decisions throughout the day.

Finally, consider what your last thoughts are before going to sleep. Are they *This screen is going blurry, I'd better turn off my phone* or *I forgot to wish my mother "Happy Birthday"*? Don't program yourself to wake up with bad energy. Every night when I'm falling asleep, I say to myself, "I am relaxed, energized, and focused. I am calm, enthusiastic, and productive." It has a yoga-robot vibe when I put it on paper, but it works for me. I am programming my mind to wake up with energy and conviction. **The emotion you fall asleep with at night is most likely the emotion you'll wake up with in the morning.**

A STONE ON THE PATH

The goal of all this preparation is to bring intentionality to the entire day. The moment you leave your home, there will be more curveballs, whatever your job may be. You're going to need the energy and focus you cultivated all morning. Monks don't just have morning routines and

TRY THIS: VISUALIZATION FOR TOMORROW

Just as an inventor has to visualize an idea before building it, we can visualize the life we want, beginning by visualizing how we want our mornings to be.

After you do breathwork to calm your mind, I want you to visualize yourself as your best self. Visualize yourself waking up in the morning healthy, well rested, and energized. Imagine the sunlight coming through the windows. You get up, and as your feet touch the ground, you feel a sense of gratitude for another day. Really feel that gratitude, and then say in your mind, "I am grateful for today. I am excited for today. I am joyful for today."

See yourself brushing your teeth, taking your time, being mindful to brush every tooth. Then, as you go into the shower, visualize yourself feeling calm, balance, ease, stillness. When you come out of the shower, because you chose what you were going to wear the night before, it's not a bother to dress. Now see yourself setting your intentions, writing down, "My intention today is to be focused. My intention today is to be disciplined. My intention today is to be of service."

Visualize the whole morning again as realistically as you can. You may add some exercise, some meditation. Believe it. Feel it. Welcome it into your life. Feeling fresh, feeling fueled.

Now visualize yourself continuing the day as your best self. See yourself inspiring others, leading others, guiding others, sharing with others, listening to others, learning from others, being open to others, their feedback and their thoughts. See yourself in this dynamic environment, giving your best and receiving your best.

Visualize yourself coming home at the end of the day. You're tired, but you're happy. You want to sit down and rest, but you're grateful for whatever you have: a job, a life, family, friends, a home. You have more than so many people. See yourself in the evening; instead of being on your phone or watching a show, you come up with new ideas to spend that time meaningfully.

When you visualize yourself getting into bed at a good time, see yourself

(continued on next page)

looking up and saying, "I'm grateful for today. I will wake up tomorrow feeling healthy, energized, and rested. Thank you." Then visualize yourself scanning throughout your body and thanking each part of your body for helping you throughout the day.

When you're ready, in your own time, at your own pace, slowly and gently open your eyes.

Note: Life messes up your plans. Tomorrow is not going to go as you visualize it. Visualization doesn't change your life, but it changes how you see it. You can build your life by returning to the ideal that you imagined. Whenever you feel that your life is out of alignment, you realign it with the visualization.

nighttime routines; we use routines of time and location every moment of the day. Sister Joan Chittister, the Benedictine nun I've already mentioned, says, "People living in the cities and suburbs . . . can make choices about the way they live, though most of them don't see that, because they are conditioned to be on the go all the time. . . . Imagine for a moment what America would look like, imagine the degree of serenity we'd have, if laypeople had something comparable to the daily schedule of the cloistered life. It provides scheduled time for prayer, work, and recreation." **Routines root us.** The two hours I spend meditating support the other twenty-two hours of my day, just as the twenty-two hours influence my meditation. The relationship between the two is symbiotic.

In the ashram we took the same thirty-minute walk on the same path at least once a day. Every day the monk asked us to keep our eyes open for something different, something we'd never before seen on this walk that we had taken yesterday, and the day before, and the day before that.

Spotting something new every day on our familiar walk was a reminder to keep our focus on that walk, to see the freshness in each "routine," to be aware. Seeing something is not the same as noticing it. Researchers at UCLA asked faculty, staff, and students in the Department of Psychology whether they knew the location of the nearest fire extinguisher. Only 24 percent could remember where the closest one was, even though, for 92 percent of the participants, a fire extinguisher was just a few feet from where they filled out the survey (which was usually their own office or a classroom they frequently visited). One professor didn't realize that there was a fire extinguisher just inches from the office he'd occupied for twenty-five years.

Truly noticing what's around us keeps our brains from shifting to autopilot. At the ashram we were trained to do this on our daily walk.

I have taken this walk for hundreds of days now. It is hot, but not unpleasant in my robes. The forest is leafy and cool, the dirt path feels soothing underfoot. Today a senior monk has asked us to look for a new stone, one that we have never noticed before. I am slightly disappointed. For the past week or so we've been asked to look for a new flower every day, and yesterday I lined up an extra one for today, a tiny blue flower cupping a drop of dew that seemed to wink at me as if it were in on my plan. But no, our leader is somehow onto me and has switched things up. And so the hunt is on.

Monks understand that routine frees your mind, but the biggest threat to that freedom is monotony. People complain about their poor memories, but I've heard it said that we don't have a *re*tention problem, we have an *at*tention problem. By searching for the new, you are reminding your brain to pay attention and rewiring it to recognize that there's something to learn in everything. Life isn't as certain as we assume.

How can I advocate both for establishing routines and seeking out novelty? Aren't these contradictory? But it is precisely doing the familiar that creates room for discovery. The late Kobe Bryant was onto this. The basketball legend had started showing his creative side, developing books and a video series. As Bryant told me on my podcast, *On Purpose*, having a routine is critical to his work. "A lot of the time, creativity comes from structure. When you have those parameters and structure, then within that you can be creative. If you don't have structure, you're just aimlessly doing stuff." Rules and routines ease our cognitive burden so we have bandwidth for creativity. Structure enhances spontaneity. And discovery reinvigorates the routine.

This approach leads to delight in small things. We tend to anticipate the big events of life: holidays, promotions, birthday parties. We put pressure on these events to live up to our expectations. But if we look for small joys, we don't have to wait for them to come up on the calendar. Instead they await us every day if we take the time to look for them.

And I've found it! Here, a curious orange-y stone that has seemingly appeared out of nowhere since yesterday. I turn it over in my palm. Finding the stone isn't the end of our discovery process. We observe it deeply, describe the color, the shape, immerse ourselves in it in order to understand and appreciate it. Then we might describe it again to be sure we've experienced it fully. This isn't an exercise, it's real. A deep experience. I smile before returning it to the edge of the path, half-hidden, but there for someone else to find.

To walk down the same old path and find a new stone is to open your mind.

CHEW YOUR DRINKS AND DRINK YOUR FOOD

Monk training wasn't just about spotting the new. It was about doing familiar things with awareness.

One afternoon a senior monk told us, "Today we will have a silent lunch. Remember to chew your drinks and drink your food."

"What does that mean?" I asked.

"We don't take the time to consume our food properly," the monk said. "When you drink your food, grind the solids into liquid. When you chew your drink, instead of gulping it down take each sip as if it is a morsel to be savored."

TRY THIS: SAME OLD, SAME NEW

Look for something new in a routine that you already have. What can you spy on your commute that you have never seen before? Try starting a conversation with someone you see regularly but haven't ever engaged. Do this with one new person every day and see how your life changes.

If a monk can be mindful of a single sip of water, imagine how this carries through to the rest of daily life. How can you rediscover the everyday? When you exercise, can you see the route that you run or feel the rhythms of the gym differently? Do you see the same woman walking her dog every day? Could you greet her with a nod? When you shop for food, can you take the time to choose the perfect apple—or the most unusual one? Can you have a personal exchange with the cashier?

In your physical space, how can you look at things freshly? There are articles all around our homes and our workspaces that we have put out because they please us: photos, knickknacks, art objects. Look at yours closely. Are these a true reflection of what brings you joy? Are there other favorites that deserve a turn in the spotlight and inject some novelty into your familiar surroundings? Add flowers to a vase or rearrange your furniture to find new brightness and purpose in familiar possessions. Simply choosing a new place for incoming mail can change it from clutter to part of an organized life.

We can awaken the familiarity of home by changing things up. Have music playing when your partner comes home if that's something you don't usually do. Or vice versa, if you usually put on music or a podcast when you get home, try silence instead. Bring a strange piece of fruit home from the store and put it in the middle of the dinner table. Introduce a topic of conversation to your dinner companions or take turns reporting three surprising moments in the day. Switch the lightbulb to a softer or clearer light. Flip the mattress. Sleep on the "wrong" side of the bed.

Appreciating the everyday doesn't even have to involve change so much as finding value in everyday activities. In his book *At Home in the World*, the monk Thich Nhat Hanh writes, "To my mind, the idea that doing dishes is unpleasant can occur only when you aren't doing them. . . . If I am incapable of washing dishes joyfully, if I want to finish them quickly so I can go and have dessert or a cup of tea, I will be equally incapable of enjoying my dessert or my tea when I finally have them. . . . Each thought, each action in the sunlight of awareness becomes sacred. In this light, no boundary exists between the sacred and the profane."

> **TRY THIS: TRANSFORM THE MUNDANE**
>
> Even a task as quotidian as doing the dishes can transform if you let it. Allow yourself to be in front of the sink, committed to a single task. Instead of putting on music, focus all your senses on the dishes—watch their surfaces go from grimy to clean, smell the dish soap, feel the steam of the hot water. Observe how satisfying it is to see the sink go from full to empty. There is a Zen koan that says, "Before enlightenment, chop wood, carry water. After enlightenment, chop wood, carry water." No matter how much we grow, we are never free of daily chores and routines, but to be enlightened is to embrace them. The outside may look the same, but inside you are transformed.

EVERY MOMENT OF THE DAY

We've talked about taking an ordinary, familiar moment and finding new ways to appreciate it. To take that presence to another level, we try to string these moments together, so that we're not picking and choosing certain walks or dishwashing episodes to make special—we're elevating our awareness of every moment, at every moment.

We're all familiar with the idea of being in the moment. It's not hard to see that if you're running a race, you won't be able to go back and change how fast you ran at Mile 2. Your only opportunity to succeed is in that moment. Whether you are at a work meeting or having dinner with friends, the conversations you have, the words you choose—you won't ever have another opportunity just like that one. In that moment you can't change the past, and you're deciding the future, so you might as well be where you are. Kālidāsa, the great Sanskrit writer of the fifth century, wrote, "Yesterday is but a dream. Tomorrow is only a vision. But today well lived makes every yesterday a dream of happiness, and every tomorrow a vision of hope."

We may all agree that living in the present makes sense, but the truth is that we're only willing to have *selective presence*. We're willing to be present at certain times—during a favorite show or a yoga class, or even during the mundane task we've chosen to elevate—but we still want to be distracted when we choose to be distracted. We spend time at work dreaming about going on a beach vacation, but then, on the beach, long-awaited drink in hand, we're annoyed to find that we can't stop thinking about work. Monks learn that these two scenarios are connected. A desired distraction at work bleeds into unwanted distraction on vacation. Distraction at lunch bleeds into the afternoon. We are training our minds to be where we physically aren't. If you allow yourself to daydream, you will always be distracted.

Being present is the only way to live a truly rich and full life.

LOCATION HAS ENERGY

It is easier to see the value of being present throughout an ordinary day, and easier to be truly present if you understand and appreciate the benefits that routine has to offer. Routines aren't just about actions; they're also about the locations in which those actions take place. There's a reason people study better in libraries and work better in offices. New York City imparts its hustle and bustle, while LA makes you feel laid back. Each environment—from the biggest city to the smallest corner of a room—has its own particular energy. Every location gives off a different feeling, and your dharma thrives—or falters—in specific environments.

We are constantly experiencing a range of activities and environments, but we don't pause to contemplate which ones most appeal to us. Do you thrive in busy environments or in solitude? Do you like the safety of cozy nooks or spacious libraries? Do you prefer to be surrounded by stimulating artwork and music, or does uncluttered simplicity help you concentrate? Do you like to bounce ideas off others or to get feedback after completing a job? Do you prefer familiarity or a change of scenery? Having this self-awareness serves your dharma. It means that when you step into a job interview, you have a better sense of how you will perform at this job and whether it's a good match. It means that when you plan a date, you can choose a space where you will be most comfortable. When you imagine different careers within your skill set, you know which ones are best suited to your sensibilities.

TRY THIS: ENVIRONMENTAL AWARENESS

For every environment where you spend time this week, ask yourself the following questions. If possible, ask them right after the experience, then again at the end of the week.

> What were the key features of the space?
> Quiet or loud?
> Big or small?
> Vibrant or plain?
> In the center of an active space or removed?
> Close to other people or isolated?
> How did I feel in this space: productive? relaxed? distracted?
> Did the activity I was doing fit well with the place where I was doing it?
> Was I in the best mindset for what I set out to do?
> If not, is there another place where I am more comfortable accomplishing what I planned?

The more your personal spaces are devoted to single, clear purposes, the better they will serve you, not just in the fulfillment of your dharma but in your mood and productivity. Just as the room where we monks slept was designed for nothing but sleep, so every place in the ashram was devoted to a single activity. We didn't read or meditate where we slept. We didn't work in the refectory.

In the world outside an ashram, to watch Netflix and/or eat in your bedroom is to confuse the energy of that space. If you bring those energies to your bedroom, it becomes harder to sleep there. Even in the tiniest apartment, you can dedicate spaces to different activities. Every home should have a place to eat. A place to sleep. A sacred space that helps you feel calm and a space that feels comforting when you are angry. Create spaces that bring you the energy that matches your intention. A bedroom should have few distractions, calm colors, soft lighting. Ideally, it should not contain your workspace. Meanwhile, a workspace should be well lit, uncluttered, and functional, with art that inspires you.

When you identify where you thrive, focus on expanding those opportunities. If you're drawn to the energy of a nightclub in your leisure time, would you do better in a career that is equally vibrant? If you're a rock musician but you thrive in quiet, then maybe you should be composing music instead of performing. If you have the "perfect job" working from home, but you prefer the activity of an office, look to move your work to a café or shared workspace. The point is to be aware about where you thrive, where you're at your best, and to figure out how to spend the most time in that place.

Of course, we are all obligated to do activities we don't like in environments that aren't ideal—especially work—and we've all experienced the negative energies that these activities generate. With elevated awareness, we understand what has made us impatient, stressed, or drained, and develop guidelines for what living in our dharma, in the right environment, with the right energy, would look like. This should be the long-term goal.

Sound Design Your Life

Your location and your senses speak to each other. This is most obvious when we think about the sounds that we encounter every day. In monk life the sounds we hear relate directly to what we are doing. We wake up to birds and winds. We hear chanting as we walk into a meditation. There is no painful noise.

But the modern world is getting louder. Planes howl overhead, dogs bark, drills whine. We're subjected to uncontrollable noise all day. We think we're ignoring the honk and clatter of daily life, but all of it adds to our cognitive load. The brain processes sound even when we don't consciously hear it. At home, many of us retreat to silence, so we live in the extremes of silence and noise.

Instead of tuning out the noise in your life—sound design it. Start by picking the best alarm tone in the world. Begin the day with a song that makes you happy. On your way to work, listen to a beloved audiobook, a favorite podcast, or your go-to playlist. Choose sounds that make you feel happier and healthier, the better to replicate the highly curated life in an ashram.

TIME HAS MEMORY

When we tailor our locations for specific purposes, we're better able to summon the right kind of energy and attention. The same is true for time. Doing something at the same time every day helps us remember to do it, commit to it, and do it with increasing skill and facility. If you're accustomed to going to the gym every morning at the same time, try going in the evening for a change and you'll see what a challenge it is. When we do something at the same time every day, that time keeps that memory for us. It holds the practice. It saves the space. When you want to incorporate a new habit into your routine, like meditating or reading, don't make it more difficult by trying to do it whenever you have a free moment. Slot it into the same time every day. Even better, link the new practice to something that's already a habit. A friend of mine wanted to incorporate daily yoga into her schedule so she laid a mat right next to her bed. She literally rolled out of bed and into her yoga practice. Marrying habits is a way of circumventing excuses.

Location has energy; time has memory.

If you do something at the same time every day, it becomes easier and natural.

If you do something in the same space every day, it becomes easier and natural.

SINGLE-TASKING

Time and location help us maximize the moment, but there is one essential component to being wholly present in that moment: single-tasking. Studies have found that only 2 percent of us can multitask effectively; most of us are terrible at it, especially when one of those tasks requires a lot of focus. When we think we're multitasking, what's usually happening is that we're shifting rapidly among several different things, or "serial tasking." This fragmented attention actually erodes our ability to focus, so doing just one thing at a time without distraction becomes harder. Researchers from Stanford University took a group of students and divided them into two groups—those who frequently switch among multiple streams of media (checking email, social media, and headline news, for instance) and those who don't. They put the groups through a series of attention and memory tasks, such as remembering sequences of letters and focusing on certain colored shapes while ignoring others, and the media multitaskers consistently performed poorly. They even did worse on a test of task-switching ability.

To make single-tasking easier for myself, I have "no tech" zones and times. My wife and I don't use tech in the bedroom or at the dining table, and try not to between 8 p.m. and 9 a.m. I try to practice single-tasking with mundane tasks in order to strengthen the habit. I used to brush my teeth without thought. They were white enough; they looked great. But then the dentist told me that I'd damaged my gums. Now I spend four seconds on each tooth. I count in my head, *one, two, three, four*, which gives me something to do. I'm still spending the same amount of time brushing my teeth, but I'm doing it in a more effective way. If I think about business when I'm brushing my teeth or in the shower, it doesn't feel nourishing and energizing, and I don't take care with my gums. When you're brushing, just brush. When you're showering, just shower.

We don't have to be focused like a laser beam on every task every time. It's okay to listen to music while cleaning the bathroom or talk with your partner while eating together. Just as some instruments sound great together, certain habits complement each other. But single-tasking as much as possible keeps your brain in the habit of focusing on one thing at a time, and you should pick certain routines where you always single-task, like walking the dog, using your phone (one app at a time!), showering, or folding the laundry, in order to build the skill.

GOING ALL THE WAY

Routines become easier if you've done something immersively. If you want to bring a new skill into your life, I recommend that you kick it off with single-pointed focus for a short period of time. If I play Ping-Pong every day for an hour, I'm definitely going to be better at it. If you want to start a daily meditation, a weeklong meditation retreat will give you a strong base on which to build. Throughout this book I suggest many changes you can make to your life. But if you try to change everything at the same time, they will all become small, equal priorities. Change happens with small steps and big priorities. Pick one thing to change, make it your number one priority, and see it through before you move on to the next.

Monks try to do everything immersively. Our lunches were silent. Our meditations were long. We didn't do anything in just five minutes. (Except for showering. We weren't showering immersively.) We had the luxury of time, and we used it to single-task for hours on end. That same level of immersion isn't possible in the modern world, but the greater your investment, the greater your return. If something is important, it deserves to be experienced deeply. And everything is important.

We all procrastinate and get distracted, even monks, but if you give yourself more time, then you can afford to get distracted and then refocus. In your morning routine, having limited time means that you're one phone call or spilled coffee away from being late to work. If you're frustrated with learning a new skill, understanding a concept, or assembling a piece of Ikea furniture, your instinct will be to pull away, but go all in and you'll accomplish more than you thought possible. (Even the Hemnes dresser—allegedly Ikea's most difficult build.)

As it turns out, periods of deep focus are also good for your brain. When we switch tasks compulsively (like the multitaskers who showed poor memory and focus in the Stanford study), it erodes our ability to focus. We overstimulate the dopamine (reward) channel. That's also the addiction pathway, so we are compelled to stimulate it more and more to get the same feel-good hit, and that leads to more and more distraction. But ultimately, ironically, the feel-good of dopamine bums us out—too much dopamine can keep our bodies from making and processing serotonin, the contentment chemical. If you've ever spent the day jumping on and off calls, in and out of meetings, ordering this book from Amazon and checking that thread on Snapchat, you know that feeling of exhaustion you have at the end of it all? It's a dopamine hangover.

When we allow ourselves to have immersive experiences—through meditation, focused periods of work, painting, doing a crossword puzzle, weeding a garden, and many other forms of *contemplative single-tasking*—we're not only more productive, we actually feel better.

There are plenty of magazine articles and phone apps that encourage you to meditate for five minutes a day. I'm not against that, but I'm also not surprised if it does nothing for you. In our culture, it is commonplace to devote five to ten minutes to one daily practice or another, but the truth is you achieve very little in five minutes. I've had more than one friend complain to me: "Jay, I've been meditating for five minutes a day for seven months and it's not working."

Imagine you were told you could spend five minutes a day for a whole month with someone you were attracted to. At the end of the month you'd still barely know them. You definitely wouldn't be in love. There's a reason we want to talk to someone all night when we're falling in love. Maybe sometimes it's even the other way around: We fall in love *because* we talked to someone all night. The ocean is full of treasures, but if you swim on the surface, you won't see them all. If you start a meditation practice with the idea that you can instantly clear your mind, you'll soon learn that immersion takes time and practice.

When I began to meditate, it took me a good fifteen minutes to settle physically and another fifteen to settle down the mental chatter. I've been meditating for one to two hours a day for thirteen years, and it *still* takes me ten minutes to switch off my mind. I'm not saying you have to meditate two hours a day for thirteen years to get the benefit. That's not the point. I have confidence that any process can work if you do it immersively. After you break the barrier and commit yourself wholly, you start experiencing the benefits. You lose track of time. The feeling of being fully engaged is often so rewarding that when it's time to stop, you want to return to the experience.

I recommend using immersive experience as a kickoff or reinvigoration for a regular practice. To my friend who was frustrated with his five minutes-a-day meditation practice, I said, "I get it. Time is tough to find, but if you feel like you're not getting enough from it, try taking an hour-long class. Then return to your ten-minute practice. You might find it has become more powerful. If you want, you could try a daylong retreat." I talked to him about falling in love, how eventually you aren't compelled to stay up all night anymore because you've gotten to know the person. Five minutes goes a lot further when you're married. I told him, "Maybe you and meditation could use a romantic getaway."

Routines are counterintuitive—instead of being boring and repetitive, doing the same tasks at the same time in the same place makes room for creativity. The consistent energy of location and memory of time help us be present in the moment, engaging deeply in tasks instead of getting distracted or frustrated. Build routines and train yourself as monks do, to find focus and achieve deep immersion.

Once we quell our external distractions, we can address the most subtle and powerful distractions of all, the voices inside our heads.

SEVEN

THE MIND

The Charioteer's Dilemma

When the five senses and the mind are stilled, when the reasoning
intellect rests in silence, then begins the highest path.
—the Katha Upanishad

It is raining. Though it's September and monsoon season is over, it's coming down hard. I really need a shower before morning meditation. About a hundred of my fellow monks and I arrived here in South India last night after a two-day train ride from Mumbai. We had the cheapest tickets available, of course, sleeping in close quarters with strangers, and the bathrooms were so foul that I decided to fast for the entire trip in order to avoid them. We are on a pilgrimage, staying in a warehouse-type building near the seashore. After morning meditation we will go straight to classes, so now is my best chance to shower.

I ask for directions to the shower, and someone points to a wet, muddy dirt pathway through the low shrubs. "It's about a twenty-minute walk," he says.

I look down at my flip-flops. Great. My feet will get even dirtier on the way to the shower than they are right now. What's the point?

Then another voice comes into my head: "Don't be lazy. You have to get ready for morning meditation. Just go take the shower."

I duck my head and start down the path. Squelching through the mud, I try not to slip. Every step is unpleasant, not just because of the conditions but because the first voice in my head keeps discouraging me, saying "See? You're getting muddy on your way to the showers, and you'll get dirty again on the way back."

The other voice urges me onward: "You are doing the right thing. Honor your commitment."

Finally, I reach the showers, a row of white stalls. I open the door to one and look up. Rain pours down from the still-dark sky. There is no roof. Seriously? I step into the stall and don't even bother to turn on the faucet. We bathe in cold water anyway, and that's exactly what the rain is delivering.

Standing in the shower, I wonder what the hell I am doing here. In this miserable excuse for a shower, on that filthy train yesterday, on this trip, living this life. I could be dry and warm in a nice apartment in London right now, making fifty thousand pounds a year. Life could be so much easier.

But as I walk back, the other voice returns with some interesting ideas about the value of what I've just accomplished. Going to the shower in the rain wasn't a notable achievement. It didn't require physical strength or bravery. But it tested my ability to tolerate external difficulties. It gave me an idea of how much frustration I could handle in one morning. It may not have cleansed or refreshed me, but it did something more valuable: It strengthened my resolve.

THE MONKEY MIND

In the Hitopadeśa, an ancient Indian text by Nārāyana, the mind is compared to a drunken monkey that's been bitten by a scorpion and haunted by a ghost.

We humans have roughly seventy thousand separate thoughts each day. Ernst Pöppel, a German psychologist and neuroscientist, has shown through his research that our minds are only in present time for about three seconds at a time. Other than that, our brains are thinking forward and backward, filling in ideas about present time based on what we've experienced in the past and anticipating what is to come. As Lisa Feldman Barrett, author of *How Emotions Are Made*, describes it on a podcast, most of the time "your brain is not reacting to events in the world, it's predicting ... constantly guessing what's going to happen next." The Samyutta Nikaya describes each thought as a branch, and our minds as monkeys, swinging from one branch to the next, often aimlessly. This almost sounds like fun, but, as we all know, it is anything but. Usually those thoughts are fears, concerns, negativity, and stress. What will happen this week at work? What should I eat for dinner? Have I saved enough for a holiday this year? Why is my date five minutes late? Why am I here? These are all genuine questions that deserve answers, but none of them will be resolved while we swing from branch to branch, thought to thought. This is the jungle of the untrained mind.

The Dhammapada is a collection of verses probably collected by Buddha's disciples. In it, the Buddha says, "As irrigators lead water where they want, as archers make their arrows straight, as carpenters carve wood, the wise shape their minds." True growth requires understanding the mind. It is the filter, judge, and director of all our experiences, but, as evidenced by the conflict I felt on my shower adventure, we are not always of one mind. The more we can evaluate, understand, train, and strengthen our relationship with the mind, the more successfully we navigate our lives and overcome challenges.

This battle in our mind is waged over the smallest daily choices (Do I have to get up right now?) and the biggest (Should I end this relationship?). All of us face such battles every single day.

A senior monk once told me an old Cherokee story about these dilemmas which all of us agonize over: "An elder tells his grandson, 'Every choice in life is a battle between two wolves inside us. One represents anger, envy, greed, fear, lies, insecurity, and ego. The other represents peace, love, compassion, kindness, humility, and positivity. They are competing for supremacy.'

"'Which wolf wins?' the grandson asks. 'The one you feed,' the elder replies."

"But how do we feed them?" I asked my teacher.

The monk said, "By what we read and hear. By who we spend time with. By what we do with our time. By where we focus our energy and attention."

The Bhagavad Gita states, "For him who has conquered the mind, the mind is the best of friends; but for one who has failed to do so, his very mind will be the greatest enemy." The word *enemy* may seem too strong to describe the voice of dissent in your head, but the definition rings true: An enemy, according to the Oxford English Dictionary, is "a person who is actively opposed or hostile to someone or something," and "a thing that harms or weakens something." Sometimes our own minds work against us. They convince us to do something, then make us feel guilty or bad about it, often because it's gone against our values or morals.

A pair of researchers from Princeton University and the University of Waterloo have shown that the weight of a bad decision isn't just metaphorical. They asked study participants to remember a time they'd done something unethical, then asked them to rate their perception of their body weight. People who'd been asked to recall an unethical action said they felt physically heavier than those who'd been asked to recall a neutral memory. Other times we want to focus on something—a project at work, an artistic endeavor, a home repair, a new hobby—and our minds just won't let us get around to it. When we procrastinate, there's a conflict between what researchers call our "should-self," or what we feel we should do because it's good for us, and our "want-self," what we actually want to do in the moment. "I know I *should* get started on that business proposal, but I *want* to watch the US Open quarterfinals."

Before I became a monk, my own mind stopped me from doing what I loved because it was too risky. It allowed me to consume a chocolate bar and a liter of soda daily even though I wanted to be healthy. It made me compare myself to other people instead of concentrating on my own growth. I blocked myself from reaching out to people I had hurt because I did not want to appear weaker. I allowed myself to be angry at people I loved because I cared more about being right than being kind.

In the introduction to his translation of the Dhammapada, Eknath Easwaran writes that in our everyday swirl of thoughts "we have no more idea of what life is really like than a chicken has before it hatches. Excitement and depression, fortune and misfortune, pleasure and pain, are storms in a tiny, private, shell-bound realm which we take to be the whole of existence." It makes sense, then, that when the Buddha finally reached "the realm utterly beyond the reach of thought," he described feeling like a chick breaking out of its shell.

At the ashram, I learned something that has been crucial in curbing these dangerous, self-destructive thoughts. Our thoughts are like clouds passing by. The self, like the sun, is always there. We are not our minds.

THE PARENT AND THE CHILD

As my teachers explained, visualizing the mind as a separate entity helps us work on our relationship with it—we can think of the interaction as making a friend or negotiating peace with an enemy.

As in any interaction, the quality of our communication with the mind is based on the history of our relationship with it. Are we hotheaded combatants or stubborn and unwilling to engage? Do we have the same arguments over and over again, or do we listen and compromise? Most of us don't know the history of this internal relationship because we've never taken the time to reflect on it.

The monkey mind is a child and the monk mind is an adult. A child cries when it doesn't get what it wants, ignoring what it already has. A child struggles to appreciate real value—it would happily trade a stock certificate for some candy. When something challenges us in some way, the childlike mind reacts immediately. Maybe you feel insulted and make a sour face, or you start defending yourself. A conditioned, automatic reaction like this is ideal if someone pulls out a knife. You feel scared, and you bolt. But it's not ideal if we're being emotionally defensive because someone has said something we don't want to hear. We don't want to be controlled by automatic reactions in every case, nor do we want to eliminate the child mind altogether. The child mind enables us to be spontaneous, creative, and dynamic—all invaluable qualities—but when it rules us, it can be our downfall.

The impulsive, desire-driven child mind is tempered by the judicious, pragmatic adult mind, which says, "That's not good for you," or "Wait until later." The adult mind reminds us to pause and assess the bigger picture, taking time to weigh the default reaction, decide if it's appropriate, and propose other options. The intelligent parent knows what the child needs versus what it wants and can decide what is better for it in the long term.

Framing inner conflict this way—parent and child—suggests that when the childlike mind is fully in control it's because our monk mind has not been developed, strengthened, or heard. The child gets frustrated, throws tantrums, and we quickly give in to it. Then we get mad at ourselves. *Why am I doing this? What is wrong with me?*

The parent is the smarter voice. If well trained, it has self-control, reasoning power, and is a debating champ. But it can only use the strength that we give it. It's weaker when tired, hungry, or ignored.

When the parent isn't supervising, the child climbs on the counter near the hot stove to get to the cookie jar, and trouble follows. On the other hand, if the parent is too controlling, the child gets bitter, resentful, and risk-averse. As with all parent-child relationships, striking the right balance is an ongoing challenge.

This, then, is the first step to understanding our minds—simply becoming aware of the different voices inside us. Starting to differentiate what you're hearing will immediately help you make better decisions.

DRIVE THE CHARIOT OF THE MIND

When you begin to sort out the multiple voices in your head, the level of conflict may surprise you. It doesn't make sense. Our minds *should* work in our own best interest. Why would we stand in our own way? The complication is that we are weighing input from different sources: our five

senses, telling us what appeals in the moment; our memories, recalling what we have experienced in the past; and our intellects, synthesizing and evaluating the best choice for the long term.

Beyond the parent-child model, the monk teachings have another analogy for the competing voices in our heads. In the Upanishads the working of the mind is compared to a chariot being driven by five horses. In this analogy, the chariot is the body, the horses are the five senses, the reins are the mind, and the charioteer is the intellect. Sure, this description of the mind is more complicated, but bear with me.

In the untrained state, the charioteer (the intellect) is asleep on the job, so the horses (the senses) have control of the reins (mind) and lead the body wherever they please. Horses, left to their own devices, react to what's around them. They see a tasty-looking shrub, they bend to eat it. Something startles them, they spook. In the same way, our senses are activated in the moment by food, money, sex, power, influence, etc. If the horses are in control, the chariot veers off the road in the direction of temporary pleasure and instant gratification.

In the trained state, the charioteer (the intellect) is awake, aware, and attentive, not allowing the horses to lead the way. The charioteer uses the reins of the mind to carefully steer the chariot along the correct route.

MASTER THE SENSES

Think about those five unruly horses, harnessed to the chariot of a lazy driver, snorting and tossing their heads impatiently. Remember that they represent the five senses, always our first point of contact with the external. The senses are responsible for our desires and attachments, and they pull us in the direction of impulsivity, passion, and pleasure, destabilizing the mind. Monks calm the senses in order to calm the mind. As Pema Chödrön says, "You are the sky. Everything else—it's just the weather."

Shaolin monks are a wonderful example of how we can train our minds to subdue the senses. (Note: I never lived or trained as a Shaolin monk, although I might want to try!)

The Shaolin Temple in China dates back more than fifteen hundred years, and Shaolin monks regularly demonstrate the impossible. They balance on the blade of a sword, break bricks with their heads, and lie on beds of nails and blades without apparent effort or injury. It seems like magic, but the Shaolin monks actually push their limits through rigorous physical and mental regimes.

Children may begin study at the Shaolin monastery as early as age three. They spend long days in training and meditation. Through breathing techniques and Qi Gong, an ancient healing technique, the monks develop the ability to accomplish superhuman feats of strength and to endure uncomfortable situations—from attack to injury. By cultivating their inner calm, they can ward off mental, physical, and emotional stress.

It's not only the Shaolin monks who've demonstrated incredible sensory control. Researchers took a different group of monks, along with people who'd never meditated, and secured a thermal stimulator to their wrists—a device designed to induce pain through intense heat. The plate warms slowly, then stays at maximum heat for ten seconds before cooling. During the experiment, as soon as the plate began to heat, the pain matrix in the non-monks' brains started firing like crazy, as if the plate were already at maximum heat. Researchers call this "anticipatory anxiety," and the monks showed none of it. Instead, as the plate heated, their brain activity remained pretty much the same. When the plate reached full heat, activity in the monks' brains spiked, but only in areas that registered the physical sensations of pain. You see for most of us, pain is a twofold sensation—we feel some of it physically and some of it emotionally. For the monks the heat was painful, but they didn't assign negative feelings to the experience. They felt no *emotional pain*. Their brains also recovered from the physical pain faster than the non-meditators.

This is a remarkable level of sensory control—more than most of us are committed to developing—but do think about your senses as paths to the mind. Most of our lives are governed by what we see, hear, smell, touch, and taste. If you smell your favorite dessert, you want to eat it. If you see photo of a beach, you start daydreaming about vacation. You hear a certain phrase and flash to the person who used to say it all the time.

The monkey mind is reactive, but the monk mind is proactive. Let's say that whenever you go on YouTube to watch one video, you end up going down a rabbit hole. You drift from a cute animal video to a shark attack compilation, and before you know it you're watching Sean Evans eating hot sauce with a celebrity guest. Senses recklessly transport our minds away from where we want them to be. Don't tease your own senses. Don't set yourself up to fail. A monk doesn't spend time in a strip club. We want to minimize the mind's reactive tendencies, and the easiest way to do that is for the intellect to proactively steer the senses away from stimuli that could make the mind react in ways that are hard to control. It's up to the intellect to know when you're vulnerable and to tighten the reins, just as a charioteer does when going through a field of tasty grass.

Any sensory input can trigger emotions—a tempting or upsetting or sad reminder that lures those wild horses off the charioteer's chosen path. Social media might suck away time you wanted to spend otherwise; a photo might remind you of a lost friend in a moment when you don't have time for grief; an ex's sweatshirt might re-break your heart. Within reason, I recommend removing unwanted sensory triggers from your home (or deleting the apps). As you do, visualize yourself removing them from your mind. You can do the same thing when you hit an unwanted mental trigger—a word that you used to hear from a parent, a song from your past. Visualize yourself removing that from your life as you would a physical object. When you remove those mental and physical triggers, you can stop giving in to them. Needless to say, we can never remove all senses and all triggers. Nor would we want to. Our goal is not to silence the mind or even to still it. We want to figure out the meaning of a thought. That's what helps us let go. But temporarily, while we're strengthening our relationship with our minds, we can take steps to avoid triggering places and people by adjusting what we see, listen to, read, absorb.

From a monk's perceptive, the greatest power is self-control, to train the mind and energy, to focus on your dharma. Ideally, you can navigate anything that seems tough, challenging, or fun with the same balance and equanimity, without being too excited in pleasure or too depressed by pain.

Ordinarily our brains turn down the volume on repeated input, but when we train our minds, we build the ability to focus on what we want regardless of distractions.

Meditation is an important tool that allows us to regulate sensory input, but we can also train the mind by building the relationship between the child and the adult mind. When a parent says, "Clean your room," and the child doesn't, that's like your monk mind saying, "Change your course," and the monkey mind saying, "No thanks, I'd rather listen to loud music on my headphones." If the parent gets angry at the child and says, "I told you to clean your room! Why haven't you done it yet?" the child retreats further. Eventually, the child may follow orders, but the exchange hasn't built a connection or a dialogue.

The more a frustrated parent and petulant child do battle, the more alienated from each other they feel. When you are fighting an internal battle, your monkey mind is an adversary. View it as a collaborator, and you can move from battle to bond, from rejected enemy to trusted friend. A bond has its own challenges—there can still be disagreement—but at least all parties want the same outcome.

In order to reach such a collaboration, our intellect must pay closer attention to the automatic, reactive patterns of the mind, otherwise known as the subconscious.

THE STUBBORN SUBCONSCIOUS

The mind already has certain instinctive patterns that we never consciously chose. Imagine you have an alarm on your phone set to ring at the same time every morning. It's an excellent system until a national holiday comes along, and the alarm goes off anyway. That alarm is like our subconscious. It's already been programmed and defaults to the same thoughts and actions day after day. We live much of our lives following the same path we've always taken, for better or worse, and these thoughts and behaviors will never change unless we actively reprogram ourselves.

Joshua Bell, a world-famous violinist, decided to busk outside a DC subway station during the morning rush hour. Playing on a rare and precious instrument, he opened up his case for donations and performed some of the most difficult pieces ever written for the violin. In about forty-five minutes, barely anyone stopped to listen or donate. He made about $30. Three days before the subway performance he had played the same violin at Boston's Symphony Hall, where the decent seats went for $100.

There are many reasons people might not stop to hear a brilliant musician playing, but one of them is certainly that they were on autopilot, powering through the rush hour crowds. How much do we miss when we're in default mode?

"Insanity is doing the same thing again and again, expecting different results." (This quote is often attributed to Einstein, although there's no proof that he ever said it.) How many of us do the same thing, year after year, hoping our lives will transform?

Thoughts repeat in our minds, reinforcing what we believe about ourselves. Our conscious isn't awake to make edits. The narration playing in your mind is stuck in its beliefs about relationships, money, how you feel about yourself, how you should behave. We all have had the experience of someone saying, "You look amazing today," and our subconscious responding, "I don't look amazing. They're saying that to be nice." When someone says, "You really deserved that," perhaps you say to yourself, "Oh no, I'm not sure I can do it again." These habitual reactions pepper our days. Change begins with the words inside your head. We are going to work on hearing, curating, choosing, and switching our thoughts.

TRY THIS: WAKE UP THE SUBCONSCIOUS

Write down all the noise you hear in your mind on a daily basis. Noise that you know you don't want to have. This should not be a list of your problems. Instead, write the negative, self-defeating messages your mind is sending you, such as:

- You're not good enough.
- You can't do this.
- You don't have the intelligence to do this.

These are the times when the charioteer is asleep at the wheel.

INVEST IN THE CONSCIOUS MIND

Just as you are not your mind, you are not your thoughts. Saying to yourself "I don't deserve love" or "My life sucks" doesn't make it a fact, but these self-defeating thoughts are hard to rewire. All of us have a history of pain, heartbreak, and challenges, whatever they may be. Just because we've been through something and it's safely in the past doesn't mean it's over. On the contrary, it will persist in some form—often in self-defeating thoughts—until it teaches us what we need to change. If you haven't healed your relationship with your parents, you'll keep picking partners who mirror the unresolved issues. If you don't deliberately rewire your mindset, you are destined to repeat and re-create the pain you've already endured.

It may sound silly, but the best way to overwrite the voices in your head is to start talking to them. Literally.

Start talking to yourself every day. Feel free to address yourself with your name and to do it out loud wherever you're comfortable doing so (so maybe not on a first date or a job interview). Sound is powerful, and hearing your own name grabs your attention.

If your mind says, "You can't do this," respond by saying to yourself, "You can do it. You have the ability. You have the time."

Talking yourself through a project or task enhances focus and concentration. Those who do it function more efficiently. In a series of studies, researchers showed volunteers groups of pictures, then asked them to locate specific items from among those pictured. Half of the subjects were told to repeat the names of the items to themselves out loud as they searched, and the other half were told to stay silent. Those who repeated the items were significantly faster than the silent searchers. The researchers concluded that talking to yourself not only boosts your memory, it also helps you focus. Psychologist Linda Sapadin adds that talking to yourself "helps you clarify your thoughts, tend to what's important and firm up any decisions you're contemplating."

Let's consider some ways you can find a new perspective to shift your mind in a productive way.

REFRAME

If you're like most other humans, your intellect excels at telling your mind where it goes wrong, but rarely bothers to tell your mind where it goes right. What kind of parenting is that?

> Nothing's going to get better
> Nobody understands me
> I'm not good enough
> I'm not attractive enough
> I'm not smart enough

We look for the worst in ourselves and tell ourselves that it will never change. This is the least encouraging approach we could pick. There are three routes to happiness, all of them centered on knowledge: learning, progressing, and achieving. Whenever we are growing, we feel happy and free of material yearnings. If you're unsatisfied, or criticizing yourself, or feeling hopeless, don't let that stall you out. Identify the ways you're making progress, and you will begin to see, feel, and appreciate the value of what you are doing.

Reframe your self-criticism in terms of knowledge. When you hear yourself say, "I'm bored, I'm slow, I can't do this," respond to yourself: "You are working on it. You are improving." This is a reminder to yourself that you are making progress. Build a relationship with that pessimistic child's voice. Your adult voice will get stronger as you read, research, apply, and test. Turn up the volume on recognizing what your mind gets right. Rather than amplifying your failures, amplify your progress. If you managed to wake up early two days out of seven, encourage yourself as you would a child who was just beginning to make a change. If you accomplished half of what you planned, call it a glass half-full.

In addition to amplifying our growth, we can use "positive direction" to reframe unwanted thoughts. Our monkey mind often creates chatter like "I can't do this." This can be reworded to "I can do this by . . ."

"I can't do this" becomes "I can do this by . . ."

"I'm bad at this" becomes "I'm investing the time I need to get better"

"I'm unlovable" becomes "I'm reaching out to new people to make new connections"

"I'm ugly" becomes "I'm taking steps to be my healthiest"

"I can't handle everything" becomes "I'm prioritizing and checking items off my list"

Putting a solution-oriented spin on your statement reminds you to be proactive and take responsibility rather than languishing in wishful thinking.

We can take action instead of using words alone to reframe our state of mind. A simple way of overcoming this is to learn one new thing every day. It doesn't have to be big. You don't need to teach yourself how to code or learn quantum mechanics. You could read an article about a person, a city, or a culture, and you'll feel a burst of self-esteem. You have something to contribute to the next conversation you have. Even if you just learn one new word . . . here's one: the Inuit word *iktsuarpok* refers to the feeling of anticipation you have when you're waiting for a guest and you keep going to the window to check and see if they've arrived. Just sharing a new word in conversation can bring richness to the dinner table.

Many of the frustrations we endure can be seen as blessings because they urge us to grow and develop. Try putting negative thoughts and circumstances on the perspective continuum. The same way doctors evaluate pain, I ask people to rate an individual concern on a scale of one to ten. Zero is no worries. Ten is the worst thing in the world, something as awful as: "I worry that my whole family will die." Actually, that's probably an eleven.

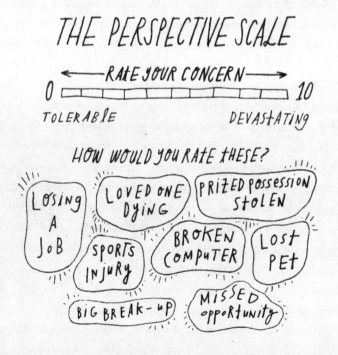

Problems of all sorts can feel like they deserve a ten rating, especially in the middle of the night. Not getting promoted feels like a ten. Losing a treasured watch—another ten. But if you've ever experienced the pain of losing someone you love (and we all have or will), the scale shifts; your whole perspective shifts. Suddenly, losing your job is not great, but tolerable. The watch is gone, but it was just an object. Your body may be imperfect, but it's given you some great experiences. Use the awareness of what deep pain really is to keep smaller disruptions in perspective. And when you must face a truly devastating ten, own it, take the time to heal it. This is not about reducing the impact of all negative experiences; it's about gaining a clearer view of them. And sometimes a ten is a ten.

SLOW IT DOWN

Sometimes reframing works best on paper. Imagine a monkey swinging from branch to branch at full throttle. It takes effort to grab its attention and force it to focus. When your mind is anxious and racing, when your thoughts are repetitive and unproductive, when you feel like you need to press pause, take fifteen minutes to write down every thought that enters your mind.

For a study, a group of college students spent fifteen minutes a day for four days writing their "deepest thoughts and feelings" about the most traumatic experience of their lives. Not only did the students say they found the experience to be valuable, 98 percent said they'd like to do it again. But they didn't just enjoy the writing, it also improved their health. Students who'd written about traumatic experiences had fewer visits to the university health center after the study. The researchers concluded that one of the benefits of the writing may have been helping students render their worst experiences as a coherent narrative. Distancing themselves from the moment in this way allowed them to see the experiences objectively and, one hopes, to conjure a happy ending.

Writer Krysta MacGray was terrified of flying. She tried white knuckling it. She tried logic. She even tried having a few drinks. But every time she knew she'd have to fly, she spent weeks in advance imagining what her kids' lives would be like after she went down in a fiery crash. MacGray started blogging about this fear as a means of trying to gain perspective, and it was then she realized she was on track to become her grandmother, who refused to fly and missed out on a lot because of it. So MacGray started listing everything she wanted to do in her life that would be worth flying for. Though she hasn't totally conquered her fear, she did manage to take a bucket-list vacation to Italy with her husband. Writing by itself doesn't solve all of our problems, but it can help us gain critical perspective we can use to find solutions.

If you don't like writing, you can speak into your phone, then play back the audio file or read the transcript (many phones can transcribe spoken words into text). Recording yourself puts you in an observer mindset, making you deal more objectively with yourself.

Another option is to simply repeat an ancient samurai saying that the monks use: "Make my mind my friend," over and over in your head. When you repeat a phrase, it quiets the default mode network—the area of the brain associated with mind wandering and thinking about yourself. The monkey will be forced to stop and listen.

FIND SELF-COMPASSION

When the anxious monkey mind stops to listen, you can tweak the internal monologue with self-compassion. When anxious thoughts arise, instead of indulging them, we respond with compassion. "I know you're worried and upset, and you feel like you can't handle this, but you are strong. You can do it." Remember, it's about observing your feelings without judging them.

With my friends at the branding company Shareability, I did an exercise with a small group of teenage girls and their sisters. I asked the girls to write down negative thoughts they had that affected their self-esteem. They wrote down things like "You are scared," "You are worthless," "You are unimportant." Then I asked them to read what they'd written to their sisters, as if it were about them.

They all refused. "It's not very nice." One pointed out that it was normal in her head, but completely different when she spoke it.

We say things to ourselves that we would never say to people we love. We all know the Golden Rule: Do unto others as you would have them do unto you. To that I would add: **Treat yourself with the same love and respect you want to show to others.**

TRY THIS: NEW SCRIPTS FOR THE CHARIOTEER

1. Write a list of the negative things you say to yourself. Next to each one write down how you would present that idea to someone you care about. For example, these are the negative thoughts the sisters wrote down about themselves along with how they might have presented them to their sisters:

   "You are scared"   "It's okay to feel scared. How can I help you through this?"

   "You are worthless"   "You feel worthless—let's talk about what you love about yourself."

   "You are unimportant"   "These things make you feel unimportant. Before we talk about how to change that, let's list what makes you feel important."

2. Imagine you found out that your child or best friend or cousin or someone who is dear to you was getting a divorce. What is your first reaction? What would you say to the person? What advice would you give them? You might say, "I'm sorry, I know this is a hard time." Or "Congratulations. I know you're going through a lot, but people rarely ever regret getting divorced." We would never tell a loved one, "You're an idiot. You must be a loser if you married that loser." We give love and support, maybe offering ideas and solutions. This is how we should talk to ourselves.

We are defined by the narrative that we write for ourselves every day. Is it a story of joy, perseverance, love, and kindness, or is it a story of guilt, blame, bitterness, and failure? Find a new vocabulary to match the emotions and feelings that you want to live by. Talk to yourself with love.

STAY PRESENT

It can be hard to know what to tell your monkey mind when it's dwelling on the past or spinning into the future. Father Richard Rohr writes, "All spiritual teaching—this is not an oversimplification—is about how to be present to the moment. . . . But the problem is, we're almost always somewhere else: reliving the past or worrying about the future."

We all have happy memories that we enjoy revisiting and painful memories that we can't let go. But both nostalgia and remorse can be traps, closing us off from new experiences and keeping us locked in the unresolved past and/or the good old days. Just as the past is unchangeable, the future is unknowable. A certain amount of planning is useful and good preparation for the various scenarios ahead, but when these thoughts tip into repetitive anxiety and worry or unrealistic aspirations, they are no longer productive.

Whether it feels like the world's falling down around you or you're just having a bad day at work, the challenges to presence abound. Realistically, you'll never reach a point in your life when you're present 100 percent of the time—that's not the goal. After all, thinking about good times we've had or valuable lessons we've learned in the past and planning for our future are excellent uses of our mental bandwidth. What we don't want to do is waste time on regret or worry. Practicing presence helps us do as spiritual teacher Ram Dass advised and "*be here now.*"

When your mind continually returns to thoughts of the past or the future, look for clues in the present. Is your mind seeking to shield or distract you? Instead of thinking about what mattered in the past or what the future might hold, gently guide your mind back to the moment. Ask yourself questions about right now.

What is missing from this moment?

What is unpleasant about today?

What would I like to change?

Ideally, when we talk to ourselves about the present, we look back on the negative and positive elements of the past as the imperfect road that brought us to where we are—a life that we accept, and from which we can still grow. And, ideally, we also think of the future in context of the present—an opportunity to realize the promise of today.

NOTHING OWNS YOU

When we talk to ourselves as we would to a loved one, just as when we observe the argument between the child mind and the adult mind, we're creating a distance between ourselves and our own minds in order to see more clearly. We've discussed this approach before; instead of reacting emotionally, monks gain perspective by stepping out of a situation to become objective observers. In Chapter Three, we talked about stepping away from fear, and we gave this action a name—detachment.

The crane stands still in water, ignoring the small fish as they pass by. Her stillness allows her to catch the bigger fish.

Detachment is a form of self-control that has infinite benefits across every form of self-awareness that I talk about in this book, but its origin is always in the mind. The Gita defines detachment as doing the right thing for its own sake, because it needs to be done, without worrying about success or failure. That sounds simple enough, but think about what it takes to do the right thing for its own sake. It means detaching from your selfish interest, from being right, from being seen in a certain way, from what you want right now. Detaching means escaping the hold of the senses, of earthly desires, of the material world. You have the perspective of an objective observer.

Only by detaching can we truly gain control of the mind.

I've remixed some Zen stories, introducing new characters so that they're more relatable. One of them is about a monk who arrives at the entrance to a palace. She's a known holy woman, so she is brought to the king, who asks the monk what she wants. "I would like to sleep in this hotel for the night," says the monk.

The king is rather taken aback at this unexpected lack of respect. "This is not a hotel, it is my palace!" he says haughtily.

The monk asks, "Who owned this place before you?"

The king folds his arms across his chest. "My father. I am heir to the throne," he declares.

"Is he here now?"

"He is not. He is dead. What is the meaning of this?"

"And before your father, who was the owner?"

"*His* father," the king shouts.

The monk nods. "Ah," she says, "so people who come to this place, stay here for a while, and then continue their journey. Sounds like a hotel to me."

This story gives a window into the illusion of permanence with which we all live. A more recent window is *Tidying Up with Marie Kondo*, the show where Kondo helps people "declutter" their lives, and at the end, over and over again, you'll see people weeping with relief and joy at having purged so much. That's because they've just dramatically decreased the number of things they're *attached* to. Attachment brings pain. If you think something is yours or you think you are something, then it hurts to have it taken away from you.

A quote from Alī, cousin and son-in-law of the Prophet Muhammed, best explains the monk idea of detachment: "Detachment is not that you own nothing, but that nothing should own you." I love how this summarizes detachment in a way that it's not usually explained. Usually people see detachment as being removed from everything, not caring. Marie Kondo isn't telling people to stop caring—she is telling them to look for joy. Actually, the greatest detachment is being close to everything and not letting it consume and own you. That's real strength.

Like most monk endeavors, detachment is not a destination one arrives at, but a process one must constantly, consciously undertake. It's hard enough to detach in an ashram, where monks own almost nothing but our ideas and identities. In the modern world we can strive for detachment—particularly when we face a challenge like an argument or a decision—and hope to achieve it fleetingly.

DON'T TRY THIS AT HOME

Monks go to extremes to achieve detachment. I don't expect you to do this, but after we look at how it works, we'll talk about more practical, even fun, ways to experiment with detachment and the benefits it yields.

Experiments in discomfort—like fasting, silence, meditating in heat or cold, and others we've discussed—detach you from the body because they make you realize how much of the discomfort is in the mind. Another way we monks tested our detachment was to travel with nothing. No food, no shelter, no money. We had to fend for ourselves and recognize that we needed very little to get by. It also made us more grateful for all that we had. All of these exercises helped us push ourselves to the limit—mentally and physically—to build resolve, resilience, grit, to strengthen our ability to control our minds.

The first time I did a full-day fast, consuming no food or water, I spent the first few hours feeling desperately hungry. We weren't supposed to take naps while we were fasting—the point was to have the experience, not to avoid it with sleep. I had to use my intellect to soothe myself. I had to become absorbed in something higher to let go of these hungry thoughts.

As the day went on, I realized that because my body didn't need to think about what to eat, to prepare for a meal, to consume, or to digest, I actually had more of a different sort of energy.

When we fast, we detach from the body and all the time we spend attending to its demands. When we remove eating, we can let go of hunger and satiety, pain and pleasure, failure and success. We redirect our energy and attention to focus on the mind. In future fasts, I got in the habit of using that energy to study, research, make notes, or prepare a talk. Fasting became a creative time, free of distractions.

At the end of the fast, I felt physically tired, but mentally stronger. In functioning without something my body relied on, I had broken a limit that existed in my mind. I gained flexibility and adaptability and resourcefulness. That experience with fasting bled into the rest of my life.

Fasting is a physical challenge driven by the intellect. Being silent for long periods of time brought up completely different issues—who was I when I detached from other people?

I am on Day Nine of thirty days of silence and I think I'm losing my mind. Before this I've definitely never kept my mouth shut for an entire day, much less a whole month. Now, along with the group of monks who joined the ashram at the same time as I did, I've gone for more than a week without speaking, watching, hearing, or communicating in any other way. I'm a talker. I love sharing and hearing others' experiences. In the silence, my mind is going wild. In quick succession I think of:

- *rap lyrics to songs I haven't heard in a while*
- *everything I have to read and learn for monk school*
- *how everyone else is possibly enduring this*
- *a random conversation I once had with an ex-girlfriend*
- *what I would be doing at this very moment if I had taken a job instead of becoming a monk counting down the days 'til I can speak again.*

This is all in ten minutes.

In my month-long silent retreat there is no outlet. I have no option but to go inward. I must face my monkey mind and start conversations. I ask myself questions: Why do I need to talk? Why can't I just be in my thoughts? What can I find in silence that I can't get anywhere else? When my mind wanders, I return to my questioning.

I find, initially, that the silence and stillness help me discover new details in familiar routines. More revelations follow, not as words but as experiences: I find myself attuned to every part of my body. I feel the air against my skin, my breath traveling through my body. My mind empties.

Over time, other questions emerge: I want to be part of a conversation. Why? I want to connect with other people. Why? I need friendship to feel whole. Why do I feel that friendship as an immediate need rather than a long-term comfort? My ego uses friendship to feel secure in my choices. And then I see the work I need to do on my ego.

Often, in the emptiness, I repeat to myself "make your mind your friend," and I imagine that my mind and I are at a networking event. It's loud, it's hectic, there's a lot going on, but the only way to build a friendship is to start a conversation. And that's what I do.

Fasting and the other austerities that monks practice remind us that we can bear greater hardship than we thought possible, that we can overcome the demands of the senses with self-control and resolve. Regardless of their faith, most monks are celibate, eat a highly restricted diet, and live apart from mainstream society. Then there are the extremes. Jain monk Shri Hansratna Vijayji Maharaj Saheb fasted for 423 days (with a few breaks). *Sokushinbutsu* is the name for a Japanese style of self-mummification practice where monks would eat a diet of pine needles, tree bark, and resins, then give up food and water while they continued to chant mantras until eventually their bodies petrified.

You don't have to take vows or eat pine needles to explore your limits. Often all that holds us back from achieving the impossible is the belief that it is impossible. From 1850 (when the first accurately measured circular running tracks were made) until 1954, the record for running a mile never dropped below four minutes. Nobody had done it in less, and it was thought that nobody could. Then, in 1954, British Olympian Roger Bannister set out to do it. He ran a mile in 3:59.4 minutes, breaking the four-minute barrier for the first time. Ever since, runners have been breaking subsequent records at a much quicker pace. Once people realized there was no limit, they pushed further and further.

There are everyday people, as well, who use austerities to up their game. People consistently report that experimenting with extremes helps them be more thoughtful and positive in their everyday lives. Let's explore how you can use austerities to detach.

HOW TO DETACH

All of the ways we've already talked about training the mind involve detaching: becoming an objective observer of the competing voices in your head, having new conversations with the conscious mind to reframe thoughts, finding compassion for yourself, staying in the moment. Instead of reactively doing what we want, we proactively evaluate the situation and do what is right.

Think of austerities as a detachment boot camp. Disconnect from the ideas that limit you, open your mind to new possibilities, and, like a soldier training for battle, you will find that your intellect gets stronger. You'll find that you're capable of more than you ever imagined.

There are infinite austerities or challenges you can try: giving up TV or your phone, sweets or alcohol; taking on a physical challenge; abstaining from gossip, complaining, and comparing. The austerity that was most powerful for me was meditating in cold or heat. The only way to escape the cold was to go inward. I had to learn to redirect my attention from the physical discomfort by talking to my mind. I still use this technique at the gym. If I'm doing crunches, I bring awareness to a part of my body that doesn't hurt. I don't recommend this for psychological pain—I'm not a stoic! But the skill of removing yourself from physical pain allows you to tolerate it in a positive sense. When you know the pain has value—you're getting stronger at the gym; you're serving food to children on a very hot day—you are able to push yourself mentally and physically. You can focus on what is important instead of being distracted by your discomfort.

We start with awareness. Spot the attachment. When do you experience it? When are you most vulnerable to it? Let's say you want to detach from technology. Do you use it out of boredom, laziness, fear of missing out, loneliness? If you want to stop drinking, look at the frequency and

time of day. Are you using it to unwind, to connect, to reward yourself, or
to check out?

Once you have diagnosed the attachment, the next step is to stop and
rethink it. What do you want to add and what do you want to subtract?
How much time do you want to dedicate to technology, and in what form?
Are there certain apps you want to eliminate entirely, or do you want to
limit the time that you spend using your phone? For drinking, you might
look at whether you think you need to quit entirely, whether you want
to experiment with a dry month to see what you learn about yourself, or
whether you want to limit yourself.

The third step is to swap in new behavior. There are two general
approaches that I recommend—choose the one that best suits your personality. The monk way is to go all in. If immersion and extremes work
best for you, you might commit to eliminating social media entirely for
a week or a month. Or you might, as I mention above, go on the wagon
for a month. If you work better in slow, gradual iterations, make a small
change and build on it. In the case of technology, you could limit the
amount of time you allow yourself to be online, or perhaps limit, but don't
fully eliminate, certain apps.

Decide how you want to spend your newfound time. If you want to
minimize your YouTube time, look for another way to find that relaxation
or decompression. Meditation is my first go-to. If you're cutting back on
social media, do you want to spend the time interacting with friends in
real life rather than online? Perhaps, as a project, you could select which
of those Instagram photos deserve to go in an album or on your walls. Use
your found time to fulfill the same need or to accomplish the projects and
to-dos that always linger on the back burner.

At first, when we make a change, the mind may rebel. Look for ways
to ease the transition. If I want to eat less sugar, reading studies linking
sugar to cancer strengthens my intellect and motivates me to persist. At
the same time, my wife sets up what I call "The worst snack drawer of all
time." There is nothing "bad" in it, no junk food. My senses don't have
access to snacks. I also look for natural habits that curb my desire. I notice

that after I go to the gym, I eat less sugar. For me, going to the gym wakes up the charioteer. Realizing that I turn to sugar to increase my energy and improve my mood, I look for other, healthier activities that have a similar effect.

Once the initial pangs of desire abate, you'll begin to feel the benefits of detachment. You'll find new clarity and perspective. You'll feel more control over the monkey mind, but you will also stop trying to control that which you can't control. The mind will quiet and you will make decisions without fear, ego, envy, or greed. You will feel confident and free from illusion. Though life remains imperfect, you accept it as it is and see a clear path ahead.

MIND MAINTENANCE

Detachment doesn't mean we completely ignore our bodies and our minds. The body is a vessel. It contains us, so it's important. We have to take care of it, feed it, keep it healthy, but the vessel is just a carrier. What it carries is the real value. And the mind, as we've talked about, is an important counterbalance to the intellect's control and restraint. Without his chariot, horse, and reins, the charioteer's options are limited. She is slow. Or he can't travel far on his own. Or she can't pick up a weary traveler and help them on their journey. We do not want to eliminate the voices in our heads or the body that carries them—we just want to steer them in the right direction—but this means the charioteer's work is never done.

We wake up with morning breath, smelly, tired. Every morning we accept the need to brush our teeth and shower. We don't judge ourselves for needing to wash up. When we get hungry, we don't say to ourselves, *Oh my God, I'm the worst. Why am I hungry* again? Bring the same patience and understanding when you're low on motivation, unfocused, anxious, or addled and the charioteer is weak. Waking him up is like taking a shower and feeding yourself, an everyday practice.

Matthieu Ricard, "the World's Happiest Man," told me that we should cultivate inner peace as a skill. "If you ruminate on sadness and negativity," he explained, "it will reinforce a sense of sadness and negativity. But if you cultivate compassion, joy, and inner freedom, then you build up a kind of resilience, and you can face life with confidence." When I asked him how we cultivate those skills, he said, "We train our brains. In the end, it is your mind that translates the outside world into happiness or misery."

The good news is that the more practice you have at tuning in to your mind, the less effort it takes. Like a muscle that you exercise regularly, the skill grows stronger and more reliable. If we work every day to cleanse our thoughts, gently redirecting the ones that don't serve us, then our minds are pure and calm, ready for growth. We can deal with new challenges before they multiply and become unmanageable.

As the Bhagavad Gita advises, "Cultivate buddhi or your discriminating intelligence to discern true knowledge, and practice wisdom so that you will know the difference between truth and untruth, reality and illusion, your false self and true self, the divine qualities and demonic qualities, knowledge and ignorance and how true knowledge illuminates and liberates while ignorance veils your wisdom and holds you in bondage."

Our ego is often what holds us back from true knowledge, steering the mind toward impulse and impression. Next we will examine how it influences the mind and how we can bring it back down to size.

EIGHT

EGO

Catch Me If You Can

They are forever free who renounce all
selfish desires and break away from the
ego cage of "I," "me," and "mine"
—Bhagavad Gita, 2:71

The Sanskrit word *vinayam* means "humility" or "modesty." When we are humble, we are open to learning because we understand how much we don't know. It follows that the biggest obstacle to learning is being a know-it-all. This false self-confidence is rooted in the ego.

The Bhagavad Gita draws a distinction between the ego and the false ego. The real ego is our very essence—the consciousness that makes us aware and awake to reality. The false ego is an identity crafted to preserve our sense of being the most significant, the most important, the one who knows everything. When you trust the false ego to protect you, it's like wearing armor that you thought was made of steel but is actually made of paper. You march onto the battlefield, confident that it will protect you but are easily wounded with a butter knife. The Sama Veda says, "Pride of wealth destroys wealth, pride of strength destroys strength and in the same manner pride of knowledge destroys knowledge."

THE EGO IS A MASK

An unchecked ego harms us. In our eagerness to present ourselves as the greatest and smartest, we hide our true natures. I've mentioned the persona that we present to the world. It is a complex stew of who we are, who we want to be, how we hope to be seen (as discussed in Chapter One), and what we are feeling in any given moment. We are a certain person at home, alone, but we present the world with another version of ourselves. Ideally, the only difference between the two is that our public persona is working harder to be considerate, attentive, and generous. But sometimes our egos intrude. Insecurities make us want to convince ourselves and everyone else that we're special, so we contrive a dishonest version of ourselves in order to appear more knowledgeable, more accomplished, more confident. We present this inflated self to others, and we do everything we can to protect it: the self we want others to perceive. Fourth-century monk Evagrius Ponticus (also called Evagrius the Solitary, because sometimes monks get cool nicknames) wrote that pride is "the cause of the most damaging fall for the soul."

Vanity and ego go hand in hand. We put enormous effort into polishing the appearance of the self we present to the world. When we dress and groom for ourselves, it is because we want to feel comfortable and appropriate (easily achieved through a daily "uniform") and even because we appreciate the color or style of certain clothes. But the ego wants more—it wants us to get attention for how we look, a big reaction, praise. It finds confidence and joy in impressing others. There is a meme that shows Warren Buffett and Bill Gates standing side by side. The caption reads, "$162 Billion in one photo and not a Gucci belt in sight." I have nothing against Gucci belts, but the point is that if you are satisfied with who you are, you don't need to prove your worth to anyone else.

To contemplate the difference between yourself and your persona, think about the choices you make when you're alone, when there's nobody to judge you and nobody you're trying to impress. Only you know whether you choose to meditate or watch Netflix, to take a nap or go for a run, to wear sweatpants or designer threads. Only you know whether you eat a salad or a column of Girl Scout cookies. Reflect on the you who emerges when nobody else is around, no one to impress, no one with something to offer you. That is a glimpse into who you truly are. As the aphorism goes, "You are who you are when no one is watching."

THE EGO MAKES US LIARS

Sometimes the ego works so hard to impress others that it does more than hype itself. It drives us to lie, and, counterproductively, all that effort only ends up making us look bad. For one of Jimmy Kimmel's "Lie Witness News" interviews with random people on the street, he sent a camera crew to Coachella to ask people walking into the venue what they thought of some completely fictitious bands. The interviewer says to two young women, "One of my favorite bands this year is Dr. Schlomo and the GI Clinic."

"Yeah they're always amazing," says one of the women.

"Yeah, I'm really excited to see them live," the other adds. "I think that's going to be one of the bands that's going to be really great live."

"Did you see them when they played at Lollapalooza?"

"No, I didn't. I'm so mad."

Then she asks a group of three, "Are you guys as excited as I am about the Obesity Epidemic?"

One of the guys responds enthusiastically, "I just like their whole style, like their whole genre is great. They're kind of like innovative and they're new."

The ego craves recognition, acknowledgment, praise; to be right, to be more, to put others down, to raise us up. The ego doesn't want to be better. It wants to be seen as better. When we bluff our way through life, pretending to be who we are not, we end up looking worse than we truly are.

The story of Frank Abagnale Jr., told in his memoir *Catch Me If You Can* and the movie of the same name, is a spot-on example of the false ego in play. Abagnale was a talented con man, forging and acting his way into jobs as an airplane pilot and a surgeon, jobs he hadn't earned and couldn't perform. Wrapped up in his ego, he used his natural abilities for low, selfish purposes, and lost himself. But after he was released from prison, he used the same skills and talents to lead an honest life as a security consultant. Real ego—a healthy self-image—comes from acting out your dharma for the highest purposes. Presumably his stint in prison gave him time for reflection and humility, and he found his way to a higher purpose.

THE EGO CREATES FALSE HIERARCHIES

Building a facade of confidence and knowledge isn't the only strategy the false ego uses to convince itself and everyone else that it's great. It also goes to great lengths to put other people down—because if others are "less than" we are, then we must be special. Our egos accomplish this by ranking ourselves and other people based on physical attributes, education, net worth, race, religion, ethnicity, nationality, the cars we drive, the clothes we wear—we find countless ways to judge others unfavorably just because they're different.

Imagine if we segregated people based on what toothpaste they used. That divide is clearly ridiculous. Discriminating based on elements of our bodies or where we were born is an equally false divide. Why should skin color matter more than blood type? We all come from the same cells. The Dalai Lama says, "Under the bright sun, many of us are gathered together with different languages, different styles of dress, even different faiths. However, all of us are the same in being humans, and we all uniquely have the thought of 'I' and we're all the same in wanting happiness and in wanting to avoid suffering."

In Chapter Five we talked about misappropriation of the *varnas* in India's caste system. The idea that Brahmins, determined by birth, are superior to others and therefore should have senior positions in government is an ego-driven interpretation of the *varnas*. The humble sage values every creature equally. This is why monks don't eat animals. According to the Gita, "Perfect yogis are they who, by comparison to their own self, see the true equality of all beings, in both their happiness and their distress."

When success goes to our heads, we forget that everyone is equal. No matter who you are or what you've achieved, notice if you are expecting or demanding special treatment because of your presumed status. Nobody deserves a better seat in the theater of life. You might wait in line for hours the night before the tickets go on sale, pay more for a closer seat, or be given a better view out of gratitude for your support of the theater. Or you might simply hope for a better seat as most of us do. But if you feel like you are *entitled* to better, dig into that feeling. What makes you better than the other audience members? **The arrogant ego desires respect, whereas the humble worker *inspires* respect.**

I often wonder what it would take for all of us to see each other as citizens of the world. I shot a couple of videos for the Ad Council as part of a public service campaign called "Love Has No Labels." In Orlando I spoke to people about the aftermath of the Pulse nightclub shooting and heard stories from diverse members of the communities about how they came together in the aftermath of this tragedy. I met with Reverend Terri Steed Pierce, from a church near Pulse with many LGBTQ+ congregants, and Pastor Joel Hunter, whose congregation is mostly white and straight. In the aftermath of the tragedy, they worked together and became friends. "Somebody will find hope merely because we're having the conversation," Reverend Pierce said, and Dr. Hunter added, "And that is the bottom line of what will change the future." As Reverend Pierce put it, they are "two very like-minded people that want to make a difference in the world."

The question this beautiful friendship evokes is: **Why does it take a tragedy for us to come together?** Our ego sets us on a path where we put more value on ourselves and those whom we recognize as being "like us."

Why is it that we walk this path until a bulldozer plows through it? Presuming equality keeps the ego in check. Whenever you think someone's status or worth is less than yours, turn your gaze back toward yourself and look for why your ego feels threatened. It is core to monks to treat everyone with equal honor and respect.

JUDGMENT

Even without segregating, outwardly ranking ourselves, or excluding others, we attempt to elevate ourselves by judging others, including our colleagues, friends, and family. There's a Zen story about four monks who together decide to meditate in complete silence for seven days and nights. The first day goes well, but as evening approaches, the first monk grows impatient because the monk whose job it was to light the lamps is still sitting, motionless. Finally, the first monk erupts, "Friend! Light the lamps, already!"

The second monk turns to him. "You broke the silence!" he exclaims.

The third monk jumps in, "Fools! Now you have both broken the silence!"

The fourth looks at his companions, a proud smile creeping across his face. "Well, well, well," he boasts, "Looks like I'm the only one who has remained silent."

Every monk in this story reprimanded another monk for speaking and, in so doing, became guilty of that same sin himself. That is the nature of judgment: It almost always backfires on us in one way or another. In the act of criticizing others for failing to live up to higher standards, we ourselves are failing to live up to the highest standards.

In many cases, we're passing judgment to deflect others' attention or our own from shortcomings we see in ourselves. "Projection" is the psychological term for our tendency to project onto others emotions or feelings that we don't wish to deal with ourselves. And projection happens a lot! So, before judging others, pause for a moment and ask: *Am I finding fault in order to distract myself or others from my own insecurities? Am I projecting my own weakness onto them? And even if I'm doing neither of those things, am I any better than the person I'm criticizing?* I can't say what the answers to the first two questions will be in every case. But the answer to the third question is always "No!"

THE EGO IS AN OBSTACLE TO GROWTH

All of this artifice leaves us in ignorance. Like Frank Abagnale, who didn't make the effort to actually qualify as a pilot or a doctor, our efforts to construct an impressive facade distract us from learning and growing. Even those of us who aren't con artists miss out. When you're sitting in a group of people, waiting for someone to finish talking so you can tell your fabulous story or make a witty comment, you're not absorbing the essence of what's being said. Your ego is champing at the bit, ready to show how clever and interesting you are.

In our desire to show ourselves and others that we know it all, we jump to conclusions, fail to listen to our friends, and miss potentially valuable new perspectives. And once we've got a point of view, we're unlikely to change it. In her popular TED Talk, "Why You Think You're Right Even When You're Wrong," Julia Galef, host of the podcast *Rationally Speaking*, calls that rigidity "soldier mindset." A soldier's job is to protect and defend their side. Conversely, there's the "scout mindset." Galef says, "Scout mindset means seeing what's there as accurately as you can, even if it's not pleasant." Soldiers have already signed on to a cause, so they value continuity. Scouts are investigating their options, so they value truth. Soldier mindset is rooted in defensiveness and tribalism; scout mindset is rooted in curiosity and intrigue. Soldiers value being on the right side; scouts value being objective. Galef says whether we're a soldier or a scout has less to do with our level of intelligence or education and more to do with our attitude about life.

Are we ashamed or grateful when we discover we were wrong about something? Are we defensive or intrigued when we find information that contradicts something we believe? If we aren't open-minded, we deny ourselves opportunities to learn, grow, and change.

INSTITUTIONAL EGO

It isn't just individuals whose egos limit their perspectives. Governments, schools, and organizations—under close-minded leadership—fail to look beyond what they know and end up constructing an ego-driven culture. Elected officials fight for their constituents and/or donors, without concern for the world beyond their supporters and those who will come after we all have gone. Textbooks tell history from the perspective of the winners. Organizations get trapped in business-as-usual mindsets, without responding to changes around them. When Reed Hastings, the cofounder of Netflix, offered to sell a 49 percent stake in the company to Blockbuster in 2000, he was turned down. Ten years later Blockbuster went bankrupt, and today Netflix is worth at least $100 billion. There is danger in the words "We've always done it this way," or "I already know that."

The Blockbuster/Netflix story is well known in the tech world, so when I told it to around seventy marketing directors at a conference, I asked them, "How many of you, when I shared this, felt you already knew what I was going to say?" About half of them raised their hands, and I told them that the conviction that they already knew what they needed to know was exactly the problem that these companies had. When you presume knowledge, you put up a barrier that nothing can cross, and miss out on a potential learning opportunity. What if there was an extra piece of that story? (This point itself was the extra piece.) You can write off the familiar, or you can use it as a deeper reflection point. Even if you think you already know a story, try to live it as a new experience every time.

Nan-in, a Zen master, received a university professor who had come to inquire about Zen. When Nan-in served tea, he poured his visitor's cup full, and then kept on pouring. The professor watched the overflow until he no longer could restrain himself. "It is overfull. No more will go in!"

"Like this cup," Nan-in said, "you are full of your own opinions and speculations. How can I show you Zen unless you first empty your cup?" You can only be filled up with knowledge and rewarding experiences if you allow yourself to be empty.

THE EGO ISOLATES US

When a Roman general returned from victorious battles, it is said that it was customary to have a slave stand behind him whispering "Remember you are a man" in his ear. No matter how well he had done and how lauded he was for his leadership, he was still a man, like all other men. If you're at the top of your game, beware. Ego isolates you. Don't live in a world where you start thinking you're so special that one person is worth your time and another isn't.

In an interview, Robert Downey Jr., offered a modern version of the same wisdom. When he's at home, he isn't Iron Man. He said, "When I walk into my house people aren't like, 'Whoa!' Susan's like, 'Did you let Monty out? Did you let the cat out?' I'm like, 'I don't know.' She's like, 'I don't think he's in the house—go look for him.'" This is a reminder to him (and to us) that even a movie star is just a person in their own home. If you believe you're Iron Man, it should be because you can actually do what Iron Man does. If you inspire special treatment, it is because people appreciate you, but when you demand or feel entitled to it, you are looking for respect that you haven't earned.

THE DOUBLE-EDGED EGO

The false self that builds us up, just as easily tears us down. When our weaknesses are exposed, the ego that once told us we were brilliant and successful has no defense. Without our personas, our lies, our prejudices, we are nothing, as Frank Abagnale must have felt when he was arrested. Egotism often masks, then transforms into, low self-esteem. In both circumstances, we are too wrapped up in ourselves and how others perceive us.

You can only keep up the myth of your own importance for so long. **If you don't break your ego, life will break it for you.**

I've been at the ashram for three years, and I've been struggling with my health. I may not be this body, but I still need to live in it. I end up in the hospital, exhausted, emaciated, lost.

I'm here undergoing Ayurvedic treatment for two months. The monks visit and read to me, but I'm alone, and in my solitude two things come to me.

First, I am not physically cut out for the life I'm trying to live. Second, and more disturbingly, to live in the ashram may not be my calling. My drive to spread wisdom doesn't fit perfectly into the monk framework. I am compelled to share ideas and philosophy in ways that are more modern. This may be my dharma, but it is not the goal of being a monk. It is not the sacred practice.

I don't know if this path is for me.

This thought hits me, and it upsets me deeply. I can't see myself leaving. And I wonder if my doubts come from my physical state. Am I in the right frame of mind to make a decision?

When I leave the hospital, I go to London for further medical attention. Radhanath Swami and I go for a drive. I tell him what I've been thinking. He listens for a while, asks some questions, thinks. Then he says, "Some people who go to university become professors, and some go to university and become entrepreneurs. Which is better?"

"Neither," I say.

"You've done your training. I think it's best for you to move on now."

I am stunned. I didn't expect him to come down on one side so quickly and definitively. I can tell he doesn't see me as a failure, but I can't help projecting that onto myself. I have failed, and he is breaking up with me. Like he is saying, "It's not you, it's me, it's not working out."

Not only am I reeling with the idea of giving up my leaders, my plans, my dream, but this is a huge blow to my ego. I've invested so much of myself in this place, this world, and all my future plans are based on that decision. But I know it's not the right path, and my teachers know it's not the right path. I won't achieve what I set out to do. Furthermore, I'd taken the enormous step of declaring this path to my family, my friends, and everyone I knew. My ego was wrapped up in what they would think of me if I failed. Joining the ashram was the hardest decision I'd ever made. Leaving is harder.

I move back to my parents with nothing, purposeless, broken, consumed by my failure, with $25,000 of debt from college. It's kind of exciting to buy some chocolate, but it is only a circumstantial fix to my existential crisis. I'd *gone away thinking I was going to change the world. Back in London, nobody knows what I've done or understands its value. My parents aren't sure how to engage with me or what to tell their friends. My extended family is asking my parents if I've come to my senses. My college friends are wondering if I'm going to get a "real" job. They're kind of like, "You failed at being a monk? You failed at thinking about nothing?"*

My biggest dream has been destroyed, and I feel the blow to my ego deeply. It is one of the toughest, most humiliating, crushing experiences of my life. And one of the most important.

Though the monks couldn't have been more supportive of me and my decision, leaving the ashram upended everything that made me confident in who I was and what I was doing. When my world was rocked, my self-esteem plummeted. Low self-esteem is the flip side of an inflated ego. If we're not everything, we're nothing. If I was not this man of high intentions and deep spirituality, then I was a failure. If I'm not great, I'm terrible. The two extremes are equally problematic. Sometimes it takes the deflated ego to show you what the inflated ego thought of itself. I was humbled.

HUMILITY: THE ELIXIR OF THE EGO

The ego is two-faced. One moment it tells us we're great at everything, and the next moment it tells us we're the worst. Either way, we are blind to the reality of who we are. True humility is seeing what lies between the extremes. *I'm great at some things and not so good at others. I'm well intentioned but imperfect.* Instead of the ego's all or nothing, humility allows us to understand our weaknesses and want to improve.

In the tenth canto of the Srimad-Bhagavatam, Lord Brahma, the god of creation, prays to Krishna, the supreme god. He is apologizing to Krishna, because in the course of building the world, Brahma has been pretty impressed with himself. Then he encounters Krishna, and he confesses that he is like a firefly.

At night, when a firefly glows, it thinks, *How bright I am. How amazing! I'm lighting up the whole sky!* But in the light of day, no matter how brightly the firefly glows, its light is weak, if not invisible, and it realizes its insignificance. Brahma realizes that he thought he was lighting the world, but when Krishna brings the sun out, he realizes that he is no more than a firefly.

In the darkness of the ego we think we're special and powerful and significant, but when we look at ourselves in context of the great universe, we see that we only play a small part. To find true humility, like the firefly, we must look at ourselves when the sun is out and we can see clearly.

PRACTICE HUMILITY

At the ashram, the most straightforward path to humility was through simple work, menial tasks that didn't place any participant at the center of attention. We washed huge pots with hoses, pulled weeds in the vegetable garden, and washed down the squat toilets—the worst! The point wasn't just to complete the work that needed to be done. It was to keep us from getting big-headed. I've talked about how impatient I was with some of this work. Why was I wasting my expertise picking up trash? The monks said that I was missing the point. Some tasks build competence, and some build character. The brainless activities annoyed me, but eventually I learned that doing an activity that was mentally unchallenging freed space for reflection and introspection. It was worthwhile after all.

Performing mundane tasks at an ashram isn't exactly replicable in the modern world, but anyone can try this simple mental exercise we used to become more aware of our ego on a daily basis. We were taught that there are two things we should try to remember and two things we should try to forget.

The two things to **remember** are the bad we've done to others and the good others have done for us. By focusing on the bad we've done to others, our egos are forced to remember our imperfections and regrets. This keeps us grounded. When we remember the good others have done for us, we feel humbled by our need for others and our gratitude for the gifts we have received.

The two things that we were told to **forget** are the good we've done for others and the bad others have done to us. If we fixate on and are impressed by our own good deeds, our egos grow, so we put those deeds aside. And if others treat us badly, we have to let that go too. This doesn't mean we have to be best friends with someone hurtful, but harboring anger and grudges keeps us focused on ourselves instead of taking a broader perspective.

I heard another way of thinking about this from Radhanath Swami when he was giving a talk at the London temple about the qualities we need for self-realization. He told us to be like salt and pointed out that we only notice salt when there is too much of it in our food, or not enough. Nobody ever says, "Wow, this meal has the perfect amount of salt." When salt is used in the best way possible, it goes unrecognized. Salt is so humble that when something goes wrong, it takes the blame, and when everything goes right, it doesn't take credit.

In 1993, Mary Johnson's son, Laramiun Byrd, was just twenty years old when, after an argument at a party, he was shot in the head by sixteen-year-old Oshea Israel, who served more than fifteen years in prison for the killing. Johnson probably had the most valid reason any of us can imagine for hating someone, and hate Israel she did. Eventually, it struck her that she wasn't the only one hurting; Israel's family had lost their son too. Johnson decided to start a support group called From Death to Life for other mothers whose children had been killed, and she wanted to include mothers whose children had taken a life. Johnson didn't think she could deal with the mothers of murderers unless she truly forgave Israel, so she reached out and asked to speak to him. When they met, he asked if he could hug her. She says, "As I got up, I felt something rising from the soles of my feet and leaving me." After the initial meeting, the pair began to meet regularly, and when Israel was released from prison, Johnson spoke to her landlord and asked if Israel could move into her building. "Unforgiveness is like cancer. It will eat you from the inside out," says Johnson. She wears a necklace with a double-sided locket; on one side is a picture of her with her son, and on the other is a picture of Israel, who says he is still trying to forgive himself. The pair, who now live next door to each other, visit prisons and churches to talk about their story and the power of forgiveness.

Remembering your mistakes and forgetting your achievements restrains the ego and increases gratitude—a simple, effective recipe for humility.

KEEP AN EYE ON YOUR EGO

With increased awareness, we begin to notice specific moments or circumstances when our egos flare.

Once a group from the ashram backpacked across Scandinavia, hosting pop-up meditations in city centers. Most people we encountered were very warm, interested in health, and open to meditation. But at one of our stops in Denmark I went up to a gentleman and asked, "Have you heard of meditation? We'd love to teach you."

He said, "Couldn't you do anything better with your life?"

My ego flared. I wanted to say, "I'm not stupid. I'm smart! I graduated from a really good school! I could be making six figures. I didn't have to do this—I chose it!" I really wanted to set this guy straight.

Instead I said, "I hope you have a wonderful day. If you want to learn how to meditate, please come back."

I felt my ego respond. I noticed it but refused to indulge it. This is the reality of keeping our ego in check. It doesn't disappear, but we can observe it and limit its power over us.

True humility is one step beyond simply repressing the ego as I did. In a class at the London temple, some of my fellow monks were being rude—laughing at the exercise we were doing and talking when they should have been quiet. I looked to our teacher, Sutapa, who was the head monk in London. I expected Sutapa to reprimand them, but he stayed quiet. After class, I asked him why he tolerated their behavior.

"You're looking at how they're behaving today," he said. "I'm looking at how far they've come."

The monk was remembering the good they'd done and forgetting the bad. He didn't take their behavior as a reflection of himself, or of their respect for him. He took a longer view that had nothing to do with himself.

If someone is treating you badly, I'm not advising you to tolerate it like the monk. Some mistreatment is unacceptable. But it's useful to look beyond the moment, at the bigger picture of the person's experience—Are they exhausted? Frustrated? Making improvements from where they once were?—and to factor in what has led to this behavior, before letting your ego jump in. Everyone has a story, and sometimes our egos choose to ignore that. Don't take everything personally—it is usually not about you.

DETACH FROM YOUR EGO

The monk and I both used the same approach to quiet our egos. We detached from the reaction and became objective observers. We think we're everything we've achieved. We think we're our job. We think we are our home. We think we are our youth and beauty. Recognize that whatever you have—a skill, a lesson, a possession, or a principle—was given to you, and whoever gave it to you received it from someone else. This isn't directly from the Bhagavad Gita, but to summarize how it sees detachment, people often say, **"What belongs to you today, belonged to someone yesterday and will be someone else's tomorrow."** No matter what you believe in spiritually, when you recognize this, then you see that you're a vessel, an instrument, a caretaker, a channel for the greatest powers in the world. You can thank your teacher and use the gift for a higher purpose.

Detachment is liberating. When we aren't defined by our accomplishments, it takes the pressure off. We don't have to be the best. I don't have to be Denmark's most impressive visiting monk. My teacher doesn't have to see his students sit in stunned wonder at every moment.

Detaching inspires gratitude. When we let go of ownership, we realize that all we have done has been with the help of others: parents, teachers, coaches, bosses, books—even the knowledge and skills of someone who is "self-made" have their origins in the work of others. When we feel grateful for what we've accomplished, we remember not to let it go to our heads. Ideally, gratitude inspires us to become teachers and mentors in our own way, to pass on what we've been given in some form.

TRY THIS: TRANSFORMING EGO

Look out for these opportunities to detach from your ego and put forth a thoughtful, productive response.

1. *Receiving an insult.* Observe your ego, take a broader view of the person's negativity, and respond to the situation, not the insult.
2. *Receiving a compliment or accolades.* Take this opportunity to be grateful for the teacher who helped you further this quality.
3. *Arguing with a partner.* The desire to be right, to win, comes from your ego's unwillingness to admit weakness. Remember you can be right, or you can move forward. See the other person's side. Lose the battle. Wait a day and see how it feels.
4. *Topping people.* When we listen to others, we often one-up them with a story that shows how we have it better or worse. Instead, listen to understand and acknowledge. Be curious. Don't say anything about yourself.

STEP OUTSIDE OF FAILURE

When we feel insecure—we aren't where we want to be in our careers, our relationships, or in reference to other milestones we've set for ourselves—either the ego comes to our defense or our self-esteem plummets. Either way, it's all about *us.* In *Care of the Soul,* psychotherapist and former monk Thomas Moore writes, "Being literally undone by failure is akin to 'negative narcissism.' . . . By appreciating failure with imagination, we reconnect it to success. Without the connection, work falls into grand narcissistic fantasies of success and dismal feelings of failure." Humility comes from accepting *where* you are without seeing it as a reflection of *who* you are. Then you can use your imagination to find success.

Sara Blakely wanted to go to law school, but despite taking the exam twice, she didn't pull the LSAT scores she wanted. Instead of becoming an attorney, she spent seven years going door-to-door selling fax machines, but she never forgot what her father taught her. Every night at their dining room table, her dad would ask her and her brother not "What did you do at school today?" but "What did you fail at today?" Failing meant they were trying, and that was more important than the immediate result. When Sara got an idea to start her own company, she knew the only failure would be if she didn't try, so she took $5,000 of her own money and started the business that just fifteen years later would make her a billionaire—Spanx. So often we don't take chances because we fear failure, and that often boils down to a fear of our egos getting hurt. If we can get past the idea that we'll break if everything doesn't go our way immediately, our capabilities expand exponentially.

My own version of Blakely's revelation came in London, a week or so after I'd left the ashram.

I had believed that my dharma was to serve as a monk, spreading wisdom and aid. Now, back at my childhood home, I don't want to settle for a lower purpose. What can I do? Our family is not well off. I can't just relax and wait for answers to come to me. I am scared, nervous, anxious. All the things that I've been trained not to be rush back at me.

One night, washing the dishes after dinner, I look out the window above the sink. The garden is out there, but in the darkness, all I can see is my own reflection. I wonder, What would I be doing if I were in the ashram right now? *It's 7 p.m. I would probably be reading, studying, or on my way to give a talk. I spend a moment visualizing myself walking down a path in the ashram, on my way to the library for an evening class.* Then I think, It's the same time of day here as it is there. I have a choice right now. If I use this time wisely, I can make this evening meaningful and purposeful, just as I would in the ashram, or I can waste it in self-pity and regret.

It is then that I let go of my deflated ego to realize that as a monk I've been taught how to deal with anxiety, pain, and pressure. I am no longer in a place where it is natural and easy to achieve those goals, but I can put all I've learned to the test here in a louder, more complicated world. The ashram was like school; this is the exam. I have to earn money, and I won't have the same quantity of time to devote to my practice, but the quality is up to me. I can't study scripture for two hours, but I can read a verse every day and put it into practice. I can't clean temples to clean my heart, but I can find humility in cleaning my home. If I see my life as meaningless, it will be. If I find ways to live my dharma, I will be fulfilled.

I begin to get dressed every day, as if I have a job. I spend most of my time at the library, reading broadly about personal development, business, and technology. Humbled, I return to being a student of life. It is a powerful way to reenter the world.

Being a victim is the ego turned inside out. You believe that the worst things in the world happen to you. You get dealt the worst cards.

When you fail, instead of giving in to a sense of victimhood, think of the moment as a humility anchor, keeping you grounded. Then ask yourself, "What is going to restore my confidence?" It won't grow from an external factor that's beyond your control. I couldn't control whether someone gave me a job, but I focused on finding a way to be myself and do what I loved. I knew I could build confidence around that.

BUILD CONFIDENCE, NOT EGO

Here's the irony: If you've ever pretended you know something, you probably discovered that it often takes the same amount of energy to feign confidence and feed vanity as it takes to work, practice, and achieve true confidence.

Humility allows you to see your own strengths and weaknesses clearly, so you can work, learn, and grow. Confidence and high self-esteem help you accept yourself as you are, humble, imperfect, and striving. Let's not confuse an inflated ego with healthy self-esteem.

The ego wants everyone to like you. High self-esteem is just fine if they don't. The ego thinks it knows everything. Self-esteem thinks it can learn from anyone. The ego wants to prove itself. Self-esteem wants to express itself.

EGO	SELF-ESTEEM
FEARS WHAT PEOPLE WILL SAY	FILTERS WHAT PEOPLE SAY
COMPARES TO OTHERS	COMPARES TO THEMSELVES
WANTS TO PROVE THEMSELVES	WANTS TO BE THEMSELVES
KNOWS EVERYTHING	CAN LEARN FROM ANYONE
PRETENDS TO BE STRONG	IS OK BEING VULNERABLE
WANTS PEOPLE TO RESPECT THEM	RESPECTS SELF & OTHERS

The table above doesn't just show the difference between an inflated ego and a healthy self-worth. It can be used as a guide to grow your confidence. If you look closely, you will see that all of the self-awareness that we have been developing serves to build the interwoven qualities of humility and self-worth. Instead of worrying what people will say, we filter what people will say. Instead of comparing ourselves to others, we cleanse our minds and look to improve ourselves. Instead of wanting to prove ourselves, we want to *be* ourselves, meaning we aren't distracted by external wants. We live with intention in our dharma.

SMALL WINS

Accumulating small wins builds confidence. Olympic swimming gold medalist Jessica Hardy says, "My long-term goals are what I would consider to be my 'dreams,' and my short-term goals are obtainable on a daily or monthly basis. I like to make my short-term goals something that makes me feel better and sets me up to better prepare for the long-term goals."

SOLICIT FEEDBACK

Confidence means deciding who you want to be without the reflection of what other people think, but it also means being inspired and led by others to become your best self. Spend time with healed, wise, service-driven people and you will feel humbled—and motivated toward healing, wisdom, and service.

When you ask for feedback, choose your advisors wisely. We commonly make one of two mistakes when we seek feedback: We either ask everyone for advice about one problem or we ask one person for advice about all of our problems. If you ask too broadly, you'll get fifty-seven different options and will be overwhelmed, confused, and lost. On the other hand, if you drop all your dilemmas on one person, then they'll be overwhelmed, unequipped, and at some point tired of carrying your baggage.

Instead, cultivate small groups of counsel around specific areas. Make sure you choose the right people for the right challenges. We'll go deeper into finding people who provide competence, character, care, and consistency in Chapter Ten, but for now, in order to recognize productive feedback, consider the source: Is this person an authority? Do they have the experience and wisdom to give you helpful advice? If you choose your advisors wisely, you'll get the right help when you need it without wearing out your welcome.

The monk approach is to look to your guru (your guide), *sadhu* (other teachers and saintly people), and *shastra* (scripture). We look for alignment among these three sources. In the modern world many of us don't have "guides," and if we do, we probably don't put them in a different category than teachers. Nor are all of us followers of religious writings. But what the monks are going for here is advice from trusted sources who all want the best for you, but who offer different perspectives. Choose from those who care most about your emotional health (often friends and family, serving as gurus), those who encourage your intellectual growth and experience (these could be mentors or teachers, serving as *sadhu*s), and those who share your values and intentions (religious guides and/or scientific facts, serving as *shastra*s).

Always be alert to feedback that doesn't come from the usual suspects. Some of the most useful feedback is unsolicited, even unintentional. Temper the ego by paying close attention to how people react to you nonverbally. Do their expressions show intrigue or boredom? Are they irritated, agitated, tired? Here, again, it's worth looking for alignment. Do many different people drift off when you're talking about a subject? It might be time to pull back on that one.

When people offer their reflections, we must pick and choose what we follow carefully and wisely. The ego wants to believe it knows best, so it is quick to write off feedback as criticism. On the flip side, sometimes the deflated ego sees criticism where it doesn't exist. If the response to your job application is a form letter saying, "Sorry, we have lots of applications," this is not useful feedback. It says nothing about you.

The way around these obstacles is to filter the feedback. Reflect instead of judging. Be curious. Don't pretend you understand. Ask clarifying questions. Ask questions that help you define practical steps toward improvement.

The easy check to confirm that someone is offering criticism in good faith is to see if the person is willing to invest in your growth. Are they just stating a problem or weakness, or do they want to help you make a change, if not by taking action themselves, then at least by suggesting ways to move forward?

When soliciting and receiving feedback, make sure you know *how* you want to grow. Feedback often doesn't tell you which direction to follow, it just propels you on your way. You need to make your own decisions and then take action. These three steps—soliciting, evaluating, and responding to feedback—will increase your confidence and self-awareness.

TRY THIS: RECEIVE FEEDBACK PRODUCTIVELY

Choose one area where you want to improve. It might be financial, mental and emotional, or physical.

Find someone who is an expert in that field and ask for guidance.

Ask questions for clarity, specificity, and how to practically apply the guidance to your individual situation.

Sample questions:

Do you think this is a realistic path for me?

Do you have any recommendations when it comes to timing?

Is this something you think others have noticed about me?

Is this something that needs retroactive repair (like apologies or revisions), or is this a recommendation for how to move forward?

What are some of the risks of what you're recommending?

DON'T BUY INTO YOUR OWN HYPE

If you are so lucky as to be successful, hear the same words those victorious Roman generals heard: Remember you are but a man, remember you will die. (Feel free to tweak the gender.) Instead of letting your achievements go to your head, detach from them. Feel gratitude for your teachers and what you have been given. Remind yourself who you are and why you are doing the work that brings you success.

Remember the bad and forget the good to keep your own greatness in perspective. In high school I was suspended from school three times for all sorts of stupidity. I'm ashamed of my past, but it grounds me. I can look back and I think, *No matter what anyone says about me today or how*

I think I've grown, I have anchors that humble me. They remind me of who I was and what I might have become if I hadn't met people who inspired me to change. Like everyone, I got where I am through a mix of choices, opportunities, and work.

You are not your success or your failure.

Sustain this humility after you've achieved something too. When you are complimented, commended, or rewarded, neither lap it up nor reject it. Be gracious in the moment, and afterward remind yourself of how hard you worked, and recognize the sacrifices you made. Then ask yourself who helped you develop that skill. Think of your parents, your teachers, your mentors. Someone had to invest their time, money, and energy to make you who you are today. Remember and give thanks to the people who gave you the skills you're getting recognition for. Sharing the success with them keeps you humble.

REAL GREATNESS

You shouldn't feel small compared to others, but you should feel small compared to your goals. My own approach to remaining humble in the face of success is to keep moving the goalposts. The measure of success isn't numbers, it's depth. Monks aren't impressed by how long you meditate. We ask how deep you went. Bruce Lee said, "I fear not the man who has practiced 10,000 kicks once, but I fear the man who has practiced one kick 10,000 times."

No matter what we achieve, we can aspire to greater scale and depth. I'm not concerned with vanity metrics. I often say that I want to take wisdom viral, but I want it to be meaningful. How can I reach a lot of people but without losing an intimate connection? Until the whole world is healed and happy, I haven't finished. Aiming higher and higher—beyond ourselves to our community, our country, our planet—and realizing the ultimate goal is unattainable is what keeps us humble.

Indeed, our goal of humility is ultimately unattainable.

The moment you feel like you have arrived, you're starting the journey again. This paradox is true for many things: If you feel safe, that's when you're most vulnerable; if you feel infallible, that's when you're at your weakest. André Gide said, "Believe those who search for the truth; doubt those who have found it." Too often when you do good, you feel good, you live well, and you start to say, "I got this," and that's when you fall. If I sat here and said I had no ego, that would be a complete lie. Overcoming your ego is a practice not an accomplishment.

Real greatness is when you use your own achievements to teach others, and they learn how to teach others, and the greatness that you've accomplished expands exponentially. Rather than seeing achievement as status, think of the role you play in other people's lives as the most valuable currency. When you expand your vision, you realize that even people who have it all derive the greatest satisfaction from service.

No matter how much you help others, feel no pride because there's so much more to be done. Kailash Satyarthi is a children's rights activist who is dedicated to saving kids from exploitation. His NGOs have rescued tens of thousands of children, but when asked what his first reaction was to winning the 2014 Nobel Peace Prize, he responded, "The first reaction? Well, I wondered if I had done enough to be getting this award." Satyarthi is humbled by the knowledge of how much more there is to do. The most powerful, admirable, captivating quality in any human is seen when they've achieved great things, but still embrace humility and their own insignificance.

We have been digging deep into who you are, how you can lead a meaningful life, and what you want to change. This is a lot of growth, and it won't happen overnight. To aid your efforts, I suggest that you incorporate visualization into your meditation practice. Visualization is the perfect way to heal the past and prepare for the future.

MEDITATION

VISUALIZE

During meditation, monks use visualization for the mind. When we close our eyes and walk our mind to another place and time, we have the opportunity to heal the past and prepare for the future. In the next three chapters we are going to embark on a journey to transform the way we see ourselves and our unique purpose in the world. While we do so, we'll use the power of visualization to assist us.

Using visualization, we can revisit the past, editing the narrative we tell ourselves about our history. Imagine you hated the last thing you said to a parent who passed away. Seeing yourself in your mind's eye telling your parent how much you loved them doesn't change the past, but, unlike nostalgia and regret, it starts the healing. And if you envision your hopes, dreams, and fears of the future, you can process feelings before they happen, strengthening yourself to take on new challenges. Before giving a speech, I often prepare by visualizing myself going on stage to deliver it. Think of it this way: Anything you see in the man-made world—this book, a table, a clock—whatever it is, it existed in someone's mind before it came to be. In order to create something we have to imagine it. This is why visualization is so important. Whatever we build internally can be built externally.

Everyone visualizes in daily life. Meditation is an opportunity to make this inclination deliberate and productive. Past or future, big or small, you can use visualization to extract the energy from a situation and bring it into your reality. For example, if you meditate on a place where you feel happy and relaxed, your breath and pulse shift, your energy changes, and you draw that feeling into your reality.

Visualization activates the same brain networks as actually doing the task. Scientists at the Cleveland Clinic showed that people who imagined contracting a muscle in their little finger over twelve weeks increased its strength by almost as much as people who did actual finger exercises over the same period of time. Our efforts are the same—visualization creates real changes in our bodies.

I've mentioned that we can meditate anywhere. Visualization can help you bring yourself into relaxation no matter what chaos surrounds you. Once I took a two-to-three-day train trip from Mumbai to South India on a crowded, filthy train. I found it tough to meditate and said to my teacher, "I'm not going to meditate right now. I'll do it when we stop or when it's calmer."

My teacher asked, "Why?"

I said, "Because that's what we do at the ashram." I was used to meditating in the serene ashram, surrounded by a lake and benches and trees.

He said, "Do you think the time of death will be calm? If you can't meditate now, how will you meditate then?"

I realized that we were being trained to meditate in peace so that we could meditate in chaos. Since then I've meditated in planes, in the middle of New York City, in Hollywood. There are distractions, of course, but meditation doesn't eliminate distractions, it manages them.

When I guide a meditation, I often begin by saying, "If your mind wanders, return to your regular breathing pattern. Don't get frustrated or annoyed, just gently and softly bring your attention back to your breathing, visualization, or mantra." Meditation is not broken when you're distracted.

It is broken when you let yourself pursue the distracting thought or lose your concentration and think, *Oh, I'm so bad at this.* Part of the practice of meditation is to observe the thought, let it be, then come back to what you were focusing on. If it isn't hard, you're not doing it right.

One important note: We want to choose positive visualizations. Negative visualizations trap us in painful thoughts and images. Yes, the "bad" in us emerges in meditation, but there's no benefit to imagining ourselves trapped in a gloomy maze. The whole point is to visualize a path out of the darkness.

There are two kinds of visualization—set and exploratory. In a set visualization, someone verbally guides you through a place. *You are at a beach. You feel the sand beneath your feet. You see a blue sky, and you hear seagulls and the crash of waves.* An exploratory visualization asks you to come up with your own details. If I ask meditation clients to imagine the place where they feel most at ease, one might see herself riding a bike on a seaside trail, while another might summon a tree house from his childhood.

TRY THIS: VISUALIZATION

Here are a few visualizations you can try. I also encourage you to go online to download an app, or to visit a meditation center—there are plenty of options out there to help your practice.

For the visualization exercises I describe below, begin your practice with the following steps.

1. Find a comfortable position—sitting in a chair, sitting upright with a cushion, or lying down.
2. Close your eyes.
3. Lower your gaze.
4. Make yourself comfortable in this position.
5. Bring your awareness to calm, balance, ease, stillness, and peace.

(continued on next page)

6. Whenever your mind wanders, just gently and softly bring it back to calm, balance, ease, stillness, and peace.

BODY SCAN

1. Bring your awareness to your natural breathing pattern. Breathe in and out.

2. Bring your awareness to your body. Become aware of where it touches the ground, a seat, and where it does not. You may find that your heels touch the ground but your arches don't. Or your lower back touches the bed or mat but your middle back is slightly raised. Become aware of all these subtle connections.

3. Now begin to scan your body.

4. Bring your awareness to your feet. Scan your toes, your arches, your ankles, your heels. Become aware of the different sensations you may feel. You may feel relaxed, or you may feel pain, pressure, tingling, or something totally different. Become aware of it and then visualize that you are breathing in positive, uplifting, healing energy and breathing out any negative toxic energy.

5. Now move upward to your legs, calves, shins, and knees. Again, just scan and observe the sensations.

6. Whenever your mind wanders, gently and softly bring it back to your body. No force or pressure. No judgment.

7. At some point you may come across pain you were not aware of before. Be present with that pain. Observe it. And again breathe into it three times and breathe out three times.

8. You can also express gratitude for different parts of your body as you scan them.

9. Do this all the way to the tip of your head. You can move as slowly or as quickly as you like, but don't rush.

CREATE A SACRED SPACE

1. Visualize yourself in a place that makes you feel calm and relaxed. It might be a beach, a nature walk, a garden, or the top of a mountain.

2. Feel the ground, sand, or water beneath your feet as you walk in this space.

3. Without opening your eyes, look left. What do you notice? Observe it and keep walking.

4. Look right. What do you notice? Observe it and keep walking

5. Become aware of the colors, the textures, and the distances around you.

6. What can you hear? The sounds of birds, water, or air?

7. Feel the air and wind on your face.

8. Find a calm, comfortable place to sit down.

9. Breathe in the calm, balance, ease, stillness, and peace.

10. Breathe out the stress, pressure, and negativity.

11. Go to this place whenever you feel you need to relax.

PRESENCE AND MENTAL PICTURE

Often the mental pictures we have form simply from the repetition of an activity rather than because we have chosen them. Visualization can be used to intentionally turn a moment into a memory. Use this visualization to create a memory or to capture joy, happiness, and purpose. It can also be used to deeply connect with an old memory, returning to a time and place when you felt joy, happiness, and purpose. If you are creating a memory, keep your eyes open. If you are reconnecting, then close them.

I use an anti-anxiety technique called 5-4-3-2-1. We are going to find five things you can see, four things you can touch, three things you can hear, two things you can smell, and one thing you can taste.

(continued on next page)

1. First, find five things you can see. Once you've found all five, give your attention to one at a time, moving your focus from one to the next.

2. Now find four things you can touch. Imagine you are touching them, feeling them. Notice the different textures. Move your focus from one to the next.

3. Find three things you can hear. Move your focus from one to the next.

4. Find two things you can smell. Is it flowers? Is it water? Is it nothing? Move your focus from one to the next.

5. Find one thing you can taste.

6. Now that you have attended to every sense, breathe in the joy and happiness. Take it inside your body. Let yourself smile naturally in response to how it makes you feel.

7. You have now captured this moment forever and can return to it anytime through visualization.

PART THREE

GIVE

NINE

GRATITUDE

The World's Most Powerful Drug

Appreciate everything, even the ordinary.
Especially the ordinary.
—Pema Chödrön

Once we have trained the mind to look inward, we are ready to look outward at how we interact with others in the world. Today it is common to talk about amplifying gratitude in our lives (we are all #blessed), but attaching a hashtag to a moment is different from digging to the root of all we've been given and bringing true, intentional gratitude to our lives every day.

Benedictine monk Brother David Steindl-Rast defines gratitude as the feeling of appreciation that comes when "you recognize that something is valuable to you, which has nothing to do with its monetary worth."

Words from a friend, a kind gesture, an opportunity, a lesson, a new pillow, a loved one's return to health, the memory of a blissful moment, a box of vegan chocolates (hint, hint). When you start your day with gratitude, you'll be open to opportunities, not obstacles. You'll be drawn to creativity, not complaint. You will find fresh ways to grow, rather than succumbing to negative thoughts that only shrink your options.

In this chapter we're going to expand our awareness of gratitude and why it's good for you. Then we'll practice finding reasons to be grateful every day; we'll learn when and how to express gratitude for both small gifts and those that have mattered most.

GRATITUDE IS GOOD FOR YOU

It's hard to believe that thankfulness could actually have measurable benefits, but the science is there. Gratitude has been linked to better mental health, self-awareness, better relationships, and a sense of fulfillment.

One way scientists have measured the benefits of gratitude was to ask two groups of people to keep journals during the day. The first group was asked to record things for which they felt grateful, and the second was asked to record times they'd felt hassled or irritated. The gratitude group reported lower stress levels at the end of the day. In another study, college students who complained that their minds were filled with racing thoughts and worries were told to spend fifteen minutes before bed listing things for which they were grateful. Gratitude journaling reduced intrusive thoughts and helped participants sleep better.

TRY THIS: KEEP A GRATITUDE JOURNAL

Every night, spend five minutes writing down things you are grateful for.

If you want to conduct your own experiment, spend the week before you start writing down how much sleep you get. The following week, keep a gratitude journal and in the morning write down how much sleep you got. Any improvement?

GRATITUDE AND THE MIND

When the monkey mind, which amplifies negativity, tries to convince us that we're useless and worthless, the more reasonable monk mind counters by pointing out that others have given us their time, energy, and love. They have made efforts on our behalf. Gratitude for their kindness is entwined with self-esteem, because if we are worthless, then that would make their generosity toward us worthless too.

Gratitude also helps us overcome the bitterness and pain that we all carry with us. Try feeling jealous and grateful simultaneously. Hard to imagine, right? **When you're present in gratitude, you can't be anywhere else.** According to UCLA neuroscientist Alex Korb, we truly can't focus on positive and negative feelings at the same time. When we feel grateful, our brains release dopamine (the reward chemical), which makes us want to feel that way again, and we begin to make gratitude a habit. Says Kolb, "Once you start seeing things to be grateful for, your brain starts looking for more things to be grateful for." It's a "virtuous cycle."

For years, researchers have shown that gratitude plays a major role in overcoming real trauma. A study published in 2006 found that Vietnam War veterans with high levels of gratitude experienced lower rates of post-traumatic stress disorder (PTSD). If you've been through a breakup, if you've lost a loved one—if anything has hit you hard emotionally—gratitude is the answer.

Gratitude has benefits not just for the mind but for the physical body. The toxic emotions that gratitude blocks contribute to widespread inflammation, which is a precursor to loads of chronic illnesses, including heart disease.

Studies show that grateful people not only feel healthier, they're also more likely to take part in healthy activities and seek care when they're ill.

The health benefits of gratitude are so extensive that Dr. P. Murali Doraiswamy, head of the Division of Biologic Psychology at Duke University Medical Center, told ABC News, "If [thankfulness] were a drug, it would be the world's best-selling product with a health maintenance indication for every major organ system."

EVERYDAY GRATITUDE

If gratitude is good for you, then more gratitude must be better for you. So let's talk about how to increase the gratitude in our daily lives. Monks try to be grateful for everything, all the time. As the Sutta Pitaka, part of the Buddhist canon, advises, "Monks. You should train yourselves thus: 'We will be grateful and thankful and we will not overlook even the least favor done to us.'"

One of my most memorable lessons in gratitude came days after I arrived at the ashram.

A senior monk asks us new arrivals to write about an experience that we believe we didn't deserve. There is silence as we scribble in our notebooks. I pick an episode from my teenage years when one of my best friends betrayed me.

After about fifteen minutes, we share what we've written. One novice describes the painful premature death of his sister, others have written about accidents or injuries, some discuss lost loves. When we're done, our teacher tells us that the experiences we have picked are all valid, but he points out the fact that all of us have selected negative scenarios. Not one of us has written about a wonderful thing that came to us by good fortune or kindness rather than through our own efforts. A wonderful thing that we didn't deserve.

We're in the habit of thinking that we don't deserve misfortune, but that we do deserve whatever blessings have come our way. Now the class takes the time to consider our good fortune: the luck of being born into a family with the resources to care for us; people who have invested more in us than we have invested in ourselves; opportunities that have made a difference in our lives. We so easily miss the chance to recognize what has been given to us, to feel and express gratitude.

This exercise transported me to the first time I felt grateful for the life I had till then taken for granted.

I first visited India with my parents when I was around nine years old. In a taxi on our way back to the hotel, we stopped at a red light. Out the window, I saw the legs of a girl, probably the same age as me. The rest of her was bent over deep into a trash can. It looked like she was trying to find something, most likely food. When she stood up, I realized with shock that she didn't have hands. I really wanted to help her somehow, but I looked on helplessly as our car pulled away. She noticed my gaze and smiled, so I smiled back—that was all I could do.

Back at the hotel I was feeling pretty low about the girl I'd seen. I wished I'd taken action. I thought back to my community in London. So many of us had Christmas lists and birthday parties and hobbies, while there were kids out there just trying to survive. It was an awakening of sorts.

My family went to the hotel restaurant for lunch, and I overheard another child complaining that there was nothing he liked on the menu. I was appalled. Here we were with our choice of meals, and the girl I had seen had only a trash can for a menu.

I probably couldn't have articulated it then, but that day I gleaned how much had been given to me. The biggest difference between me and that girl was where and to whom we had been born. My father, in fact, had worked his way out of the slums in Pune, not far from Mumbai. I was the product of immense hard work and sacrifice.

In the ashram, I began my gratitude practice by returning to the awareness I'd started to feel at nine years old, and feeling grateful for what was already mine: my life and health, my ease and safety and the confidence that I would continue to be fed and sheltered and loved. All of it was a gift.

In order to take that appreciation for the gifts of the universe and turn it into a habit, monks begin every day by giving thanks. Literally. When we wake up on our mats, we flip over to our fronts and pay respect to the earth, taking a moment to give thanks for what it gives us, for the light to see, the ground to walk on, the air to breathe.

TRY THIS: EVERYDAY GRATITUDE PRACTICES

Morning gratitude. Let me guess. The first thing you do when you wake up in the morning is check your phone. Maybe it seems like an easy, low-impact way to get your brain moving, but as we've discussed, it doesn't start the day on the right note. Try this—it will only take a minute. (If you're so tired that you're in danger of falling back asleep, then make sure you've set a snooze alarm.) Take a moment right there in bed, flip over onto your belly, put your hands in prayer, and bow your head. Take this moment to think of whatever is good in your life: the air and light that uplift you, the people who love you, the coffee that awaits you.

Meal gratitude. One in every nine people on earth do not have enough food to eat every day. That's nearly 800 million people. Choose one meal of the day and commit to taking a moment before you dig in to give thanks for the food. Take inspiration from Native American prayers or make up your own. If you have a family, take turns offering thanks.

Ancient, timeless gratitude practices have arisen all around the world. Among Native Americans, traditions of thanksgiving abound. In one ritual observance, described by Buddhist scholar and environmental activist Joanna Macy, Onondaga children gather for a daily morning assembly to start their school day with an offering of gratitude. A teacher begins, "Let us gather our minds as one and give thanks to our eldest Brother, the Sun, who rises each day to bring light so we can see each other's faces and warmth for the seeds to grow." Similarly, the Mohawk people say a prayer, which offers gratitude for People, Earth Mother, the Waters, the Fish, the Plants, the Food Plants, the Medicine Herbs, the Animals, the Trees, the Birds, the Four Winds, Grandfather Thunder, Eldest Brother the Sun, Grandmother Moon, the Stars, the Enlightened Teachers, and the Creator. Imagine what the world might be like if we all started our day giving thanks for the most basic and essential gifts of life all around us.

TRY THIS: GRATITUDE MEDITATIONS

To access gratitude anytime, at will, I recommend the following meditations.

OM NAMO BHAGAVATE VASUDEVAYA

In the ashram we chanted this mantra, discussed on page 273, before reading spiritual texts as a reminder to feel grateful for those who helped those scriptures exist. We can use this chant in a similar way to feel grateful for the teachers and sages who have brought us insight and guidance.

I AM GRATEFUL FOR . . .

After sitting, relaxing, and doing breathwork, repeat "I am grateful for . . . ," completing the phrase with as many things as you can. This exercise immediately refocuses you. If possible, try to reframe negativities that spring to mind by finding elements of them for which you are grateful. You can also do this in a journal or as a voice note to keep as a reminder if these negative thoughts return.

JOY VISUALIZATION

During meditation, take yourself to a time and place where you experienced joy. Allow that feeling of joy to re-enter you. You will carry it with you when you finish the meditation.

THE PRACTICE OF GRATITUDE

Making gratitude part of your daily routine is the easy part, but here's my ask, and it's not small: I want you to be grateful in *all* times and circumstances. Even if your life isn't perfect, build your gratitude like a muscle. If you train it now, it will only strengthen over time.

Gratitude is how we transform what Zen master Roshi Joan Halifax calls "the mind of poverty." She explains that this mindset "has nothing to do with material poverty. When we are caught in the mind of poverty, we focus on what we are lacking; we feel we don't deserve love; and we ignore all that we have been given. The conscious practice of gratitude is the way out of the poverty mentality that erodes our gratitude and with it, our integrity."

Brian Acton exemplifies this conscious practice of gratitude. He had worked at Yahoo for eleven years when he applied for a job at Twitter, but even though he was quite good at what he did, he was rejected. When he received the news, he tweeted, "Got denied by Twitter HQ. That's ok. Would have been a long commute." He next applied for a job at Facebook. Soon after he tweeted, "Facebook turned me down. It was a great opportunity to connect with some fantastic people. Looking forward to life's next adventure." He didn't hesitate to post his failures on social media, and never expressed anything but gratitude for the opportunities. After these setbacks, he ended up working on an app in his personal time. Five years later Facebook bought WhatsApp, the app Brian Acton cofounded, for $19 billion.

The jobs at the companies that rejected Acton would have paid far less than he made off WhatsApp. Instead of fixating on the rejections and adopting a poverty mentality, he just waited gratefully to see what might be in store for him.

Don't judge the moment. As soon as you label something as bad, your mind starts to believe it. Instead, be grateful for setbacks. Allow the journey of life to progress at its own pace and in its own roundabout way. The universe may have other plans in store for you.

There's a story about a monk who carried water from a well in two buckets, one of which had holes in it. He did this every day, without repairing the bucket. One day, a passer-by asked him why he continued to carry the leaky bucket. The monk pointed out that the side of the path where he carried the full bucket was barren, but on the other side of the path, where the bucket had leaked, beautiful wildflowers had flourished. "My imperfection has brought beauty to those around me," he said.

Helen Keller, who became deaf and blind as a toddler after an unidentified illness, wrote, "When one door of happiness closes, another opens; but often we look so long at the closed door that we do not see the one which has been opened for us."

When something doesn't go your way, say to yourself, "There's more for me out there." That's all. You don't have to think, *I'm so grateful I lost my job!* When you say, "This is what I wanted. This was the only answer," all the energy goes to "this." When you say, "This didn't work out, but there's more out there," the energy shifts to a future full of possibility.

The more open you are to possible outcomes, the more you can make gratitude a go-to response. Brother David Steindl-Rast says, "People usually think that gratitude is saying thank you, as if this were the most important aspect of it. The most important aspect of the practice of grateful living is trust in life. . . . To live that way is what I call 'grateful living' because then you receive every moment as a gift. . . . This is when you stop long enough to ask yourself, 'What's the opportunity in this moment?' You look for it and then take advantage of that opportunity. It's as simple as that."

If your boss gives you feedback that you don't agree with, pause before reacting. Take a moment to think, *What can I learn from this moment?* Then look for gratitude: Maybe you can be grateful that your boss is trying to

TRY THIS: GRATITUDE IN HINDSIGHT

Think of one thing that you weren't grateful for when it first happened. Your education? Someone who taught you? A friendship? Is there a project that stressed you out? A responsibility for a family member that you resented? Or choose a negative outcome that is no longer painful: a breakup, a layoff, unwanted news.

Now take a moment to consider in what way this experience is worthy of your gratitude. Did it benefit you in an unexpected way? Did the project help you develop new skills or earn a colleague's respect? Was your relationship with the family member forever improved by your generosity?

Think of something unpleasant that is going on right now, or that you anticipate. Experiment with anticipating gratitude for an unlikely recipient.

help you improve—or grateful that your boss has given you another reason to leave this job. If you run to catch a bus and you succeed, you would
ordinarily feel momentary relief, then go back to your day. Instead, stop.
Take a moment to remember what it felt like when you thought you were
going to miss it. Use this memory to appreciate your good fortune. And
if you miss the bus, you will have a moment to reflect, so use it to put the
situation in perspective. Another bus is coming. You weren't hit by a car.
It could have been a lot worse. After celebrating the wins and mourning
the losses, we deliberately look at either situation with perspective, accept
it gratefully and humbly, and move forward.

EXPRESSING GRATITUDE

Now that we've broadened the gratitude we feel internally, let's turn that
gratitude outward and express it to others.

A lot of the time, we feel deeply grateful, but we have no idea how to
pass it on. There are many ways and depths of giving thanks and giving
back.

The most basic way to show gratitude is to say thank you. But who
wants to be basic? Make your thanks as specific as possible. Think about
the thank-you notes you might receive after hosting a gathering. At least
one will likely say, "Thanks for last night. It was awesome!" Another
might say, "Thanks for last night—the food was wonderful, and I loved
the funny, sweet toast you made to your friend." It's far better to express
your gratitude in specific terms. The minute we are given even incrementally more detailed gratitude, the better we feel.

This is the key: Your friend felt joy at being part of the gathering that
you put together, and the effort they took to compose that thank-you note
brought joy back to you. For each of you, gratitude comes from realizing
that someone else is invested in you. It's a feedback loop of love.

KINDNESS AND GRATITUDE ARE SYMBIOTIC

The feedback loop of love jibes with the Buddha teaching that kindness and gratitude must be developed together, working in harmony.

Kindness is as easy—and as hard—as this: genuinely wanting something good for someone else, thinking about what would benefit them, and putting effort into giving them that benefit.

If you have ever made a sacrifice for someone else's benefit, you can easily recognize the effort and energy someone else gives to you. That is to say, your own acts of kindness teach you what it takes to be kind, so your own kindness enables you to feel truly grateful. Kindness teaches gratitude. This is what is happening in the microcosm of the thoughtful thank-you note: The kindness of your dinner party inspired your friend's gratitude. That gratitude inspired her kindness to you.

Kindness—and the gratitude that follows—has a ripple effect. Pema Chödrön advises, "Be kinder to yourself. And then let your kindness flood the world." In our daily encounters, we want other people to be kind, compassionate, and giving toward us—who wouldn't?—but the best way to attract these qualities into our lives is to develop them ourselves. Studies have long shown that attitudes, behavior, and even health are contagious within our social networks, but what hadn't been clear was whether this is true simply because we tend to be friends with people who are like us. So two researchers from Harvard and the University of California, San Diego, set out to find out whether kindness is contagious among people who don't know each other. They set up a game where they arranged strangers into groups of four and gave each person twenty credits. Each player was instructed to decide, in private, how many credits to keep for themselves and how many to contribute to a common pot that at the end of the round would be divided evenly among the players. At the end of each round, the players were shuffled, so they never knew from game to game *who* was generous, but they knew *how* generous others had been to the group. As the game went on, players who had been the recipients of generosity from teammates tended to give more of their own credits in future rounds. Kindness begets kindness.

When you are part of a kindness-gratitude exchange, you will inevitably find yourself on the receiving end of gratitude. When we receive thanks, we must be mindful of our egos. It's easy to get lost in the fantasy of our own greatness. When monks are praised, we detach, remembering that whatever we were able to give was never ours to begin with. To receive gratitude with humility, start by thanking the person for noticing. Appreciate their attention and their intention. Look for a good quality in the other person and return the compliment.

Then take the gratitude you are given as an opportunity to be grateful to your teachers.

THE KINDNESS OF STRANGERS

Monks put our gratitude practice into action through all the small interactions of the day. I hopped into an Uber once, in a hurry and distracted. The car idled for an unusually long time, and when I finally noticed and asked the driver if everything was okay, he said, "Yes, I'm just waiting for you to say hi back to me." It was a wake-up call, and you can bet I'm more careful about acknowledging people now.

Being short and direct may be more efficient and professional, but spending our days on autopilot blocks us from sharing the emotions that bind us together and sustain us. A study encouraging some people on the Chicago commuter trains to start conversations with strangers on any subject, for any amount of time, found that those who got up the courage to chat reported a more positive commuting experience. Most of these commuters had anticipated the opposite outcome, and on further investigation, researchers found it wasn't that people thought strangers would be unpleasant, but they feared the awkwardness of starting a conversation and worried they might be rebuffed. That wasn't the case, and most of the strangers were happy to engage. When we make the effort to connect with those around us, we create opportunities for gratitude instead of languishing in anonymity.

Think about all the daily activities that involve other people: commuting, a project at work, grocery shopping, dropping kids off at school, small talk with our partner. These are the little events that fill our lives, and how much pleasure they give us is largely up to us. Specifically, it depends on how much kindness we bring to these interactions and how much gratitude we take from them.

TRY THIS: A GRATITUDE VISUALIZATION

Take a moment right now to think of three things others have given you:

1. A small kindness someone did you
2. A gift that mattered to you
3. Something that makes every day a little bit better

Close your eyes. Take yourself back to the place in time of one of these acts, and relive how it felt—the sights, scents, and sounds. Re-experience it with awe, and experience those feelings in a deeper way.

After this visualization, recognize that small things are happening for you. Don't overlook them or take them for granted. Next, take a moment to feel a sense of being cared for, thought of, loved. This should boost your self-esteem and self-confidence. Last, know that just feeling great is not the end goal. Let this reflection lead to you feeling like you want to reciprocate with love by giving back to those who have given to you, or by passing on the love and care to those who don't have it.

GRATITUDE THROUGH SERVICE

If we want to go beyond the incidental kindnesses of the day, we can actively inspire and increase our gratitude even more. We think of volunteering and serving others as ways of giving to those less fortunate, but they arguably do as much for the donor as they do for the recipient.

Service helps us transform negative emotions like anger, stress, envy, and disappointment into gratitude. It does this by giving us perspective.

"What brings you to me?" asked an old, wise woman of the young man who stood before her.

"I see joy and beauty around me, but from a distance," the young man said. "My own life is full of pain."

The wise woman was silent. She slowly poured a cup of water for the sad young man and handed it to him. Then she held out a bowl of salt.

"Put some in the water," she said.

The young man hesitated, then took a small pinch of salt.

"More. A handful," the old woman said.

Looking skeptical, the young man put a scoop of salt in his cup. The old woman gestured with her head, instructing the young man to drink. He took a sip of water, made a face, and spat it onto the dirt floor.

"How was it?" the old woman asked.

"Thanks, but no thanks," said the young man rather glumly.

The old woman smiled knowingly, then handed the young man the bowl of salt and led him to a nearby lake. The water was clear and cold. "Now put a handful of salt in the lake," she said.

The young man did as he was instructed, and the salt dissolved into the water. "Have a drink," the old woman said.

The young man knelt at the water's edge and slurped from his hands. When he looked up, the old woman again asked, "How was it?"

"Refreshing," said the young man.

"Could you taste the salt?" asked the wise woman.

The young man smiled sheepishly. "Not at all," he said.

The old woman knelt next to the man, helped herself to some water, and said, "The salt is the pain of life. It is constant, but if you put it in a small glass, it tastes bitter. If you put it in a lake, you can't taste it. Expand your senses, expand your world, and the pain will diminish. Don't be the glass. Become the lake."

Taking a broader view helps us minimize our pain and appreciate what we have, and we directly access this broader view by giving. Research published in *BMC Public Health* points out that volunteering can result in lower feelings of depression and increased feelings of overall well-being. When I lived in New York a charity called Capes for Kids went into a school in Queens and helped the students make superhero capes for kids from tough backgrounds. The children who made the capes got to see the impact of their work and gifts, and it helped them realize how much they truly had. When we see the struggles of others in the clear light of day, when we use our talents to improve their world even a little bit, we immediately feel a surge of gratitude.

TRY THIS: EXPERIENCE GRATITUDE THROUGH VOLUNTEER WORK

Service broadens your perspective and alleviates negative emotions. Try volunteering—it can be once a month or once a week—but nothing will better help you develop gratitude more immediately and inspire you to show it.

PROFOUND GRATITUDE

Sometimes it's hardest to express gratitude to the people who mean the most to us—the family, friends, teachers, and mentors who made or still make a real difference in our lives.

TRY THIS: WRITE A GRATITUDE LETTER

Select one person to whom you feel deeply grateful—someone who makes it easy to feel grateful.

Write out a list of the broader qualities and values you appreciate in this person. Were they supportive? Were they loving? Did they have integrity? Then think of specific words and moments that you shared. Look ahead and write what you're going to do and say when you see them again. (If they have passed, you can lead with: "If I were to see you again, this is what I would say.")

Now write them a gratitude letter, pulling from the notes you've made.

Try to show love and appreciation in person if possible. Otherwise, giving a note, text, or phone call to specifically express what you appreciate about a person boosts that person's happiness and your own.

Sometimes, those you love will resist intimacy and brush you off. In this case, hold your ground. Receiving gratitude requires vulnerability and openness. We block these feelings because we're afraid of being hurt. If you encounter resistance, you might try shifting your approach. Take a moment to consider what form of gratitude the recipient would most appreciate. In some cases, expressing your gratitude in writing is the easiest way for both of you to have time and space to process these feelings.

When you write a gratitude letter to someone who means a lot to you, try to make them feel as cared for and loved as you felt when they helped you. A letter gives recognition to the value of their generosity with more permanence than a verbal thank-you. It deepens your bond. That recognition inspires both of you to be thoughtful and giving with each other, and this, as we have learned, ripples through your community.

GRATITUDE AFTER FORGIVENESS

Perhaps you're thinking, *My parents did a number on me. Why should I be grateful to them?* There are imperfect people in our lives—ones toward whom we feel unresolved or mixed emotions and therefore have trouble summoning gratitude. And yet, gratitude is not black-and-white. We can be grateful for some, but not all, of a person's behavior toward us. If your relationships are complicated, accept their complexity. Try to find forgiveness for their failures and gratitude for their efforts.

However, I'm absolutely not suggesting that you should feel grateful if someone has done you wrong. You don't have to be grateful for everyone in your life. Monks don't have an official stance on trauma, but the focus is always on healing the internal before dealing with the external. In your own pace, at your own time.

· · ·

We tend to think of gratitude as appreciation for what we have been given. Monks feel the same way. And if you ask a monk what he has been given, the answer is everything. The rich complexity of life is full of gifts and lessons that we can't always see clearly for what they are, so why not choose to be grateful for what is, and what is possible? Embrace gratitude through daily practice, both internally—in how you look at your life and the world around you—and through action. Gratitude generates kindness, and this spirit will reverberate through our communities, bringing our highest intentions to those around us.

Gratitude is the mother of all qualities. As a mother gives birth, gratitude brings forth all other qualities—compassion, resilience, confidence, passion—positive traits that help us find meaning and connect with others. It naturally follows that in the next chapter we will talk about relationships—who we try to be with others, who we want to welcome into our lives, and how we can sustain meaningful relationships.

TEN

RELATIONSHIPS

People Watching

Every person is a world to explore.
—Thich Nhat Hanh

Monks are often imagined to be hermits, living in isolation, detached from humanity, and yet my experience as a monk has forever changed how I deal with other people. When I returned to London after deciding to leave the ashram, I found that I was much better at all kinds of relationships than I'd been before I took my vows. This improvement was even true for romance, which was a bit surprising given that monks are celibate and I'd had no romantic connections with women during my time in the ashram.

SETTING EXPECTATIONS

The village of the ashram fosters camaraderie, being there for each other, serving each other. Dan Buettner, the cofounder of Blue Zones—an organization that studies regions of the world where people live the longest and healthiest lives—saw the worldwide need for this kind of community. In addition to diet and lifestyle practices, Buettner found that longevity was tied to several aspects of community: close relationships with family (they'll take care of you when you need help), and a tribe with shared beliefs and healthy social behaviors. Essentially, it takes a village.

Like these blue zones, the ashram is an interdependent community, one that fosters a mood of collaboration and service to one another. Everyone is encouraged to look out not just for their own needs, but for those of other people. Remember the trees in Biosphere 2 that lacked roots deep enough to withstand wind? Redwood trees are another story. Famously tall, you'd think that they need deep roots to survive, but in fact their roots are shallow. What gives the trees resilience is that these roots spread widely. Redwoods best thrive in groves, interweaving their roots so the strong and weak together withstand the forces of nature.

THE CIRCLE OF LOVE

In a community where everyone looked out for each other, I initially expected my care and support for other monks to be returned directly by them, but the reality turned out to be more complex.

During my first year at the ashram, I become upset, and I approach one of my teachers for advice. "I'm upset," I say. "I feel like I'm giving out a lot of love, but I don't feel like it's being returned in kind. I'm loving, caring, and looking out for others, but they don't do the same for me. I don't get it."

The monk asks, "Why are you giving out love?"

I say, "Because it's who I am."

The monk says, "So then why expect it back? But also, listen carefully. Whenever you give out any energy—love, hate, anger, kindness—you will always get it back. One way or another. Love is like a circle. Whatever love you give out, it always comes back to you. The problem lies with your expectations. You assume the love you receive will come from the person you gave it to. But it

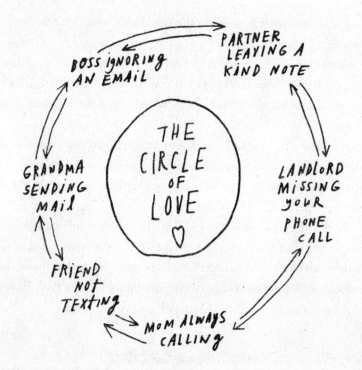

doesn't always come from that person. Similarly, there are people who love you who you don't give the same love in return."

He was right. **Too often we love people who don't love us, but we fail to return the love of others who do.**

I thought of my mother, who would always drop whatever she was doing to take my call. If she were to pick up the phone, the first person she'd reach out to would be me or my sister. In her heart she wanted to talk to me pretty much all the time. At the same time as I might be frustrated because someone wasn't responding to my texts, my mother was sitting there thinking, *I wish my son would call me!*

My teacher's description of the circle of love changed my life. Our lack of gratitude is what makes us feel unloved. When we think nobody cares, we need to check ourselves and realize that the love we give out comes back to us from a variety of sources, and, in a more general sense, whatever we put out will come back to us. This is an example of karma, the idea that your actions, good or bad, bring the same back to you. When we feel unloved, we need to ask ourselves: *Am I offering help as often as I ask for help? Who is giving to me without receiving anything in return?*

A NETWORK OF COMPASSION

It makes sense that monks look at the distribution of love and care as a network of compassion rather than a one-to-one exchange. Monks believe different people serve different purposes, with each role contributing to our growth in its own way. We have peers for friendship, students to teach, and mentors to learn from and serve. These roles are not wholly tied to age and experience. Every monk is always in every phase of that cycle. Monks believe that these roles aren't fixed. The person who is your teacher one day might be your student the next. Sometimes the senior monks would come to classes with young monks like us, sitting on the floor and listening to a new monk speak. They weren't there to check on us—they were there to learn for themselves.

> **TRY THIS: LEAD AND FOLLOW**
> Make a list of your students and teachers. Now write down what the students could teach you and what the teachers might learn from you.

THE FOUR TYPES OF TRUST

In the ashram, I was upset because I felt my care wasn't reciprocated. We often expect too much of others when we don't have a clear sense of their purpose in our lives. Let's consider four characteristics that we look for in the people we allow into our lives. You'll recognize these people—most of us know at least one person who falls into each of these categories.

Competence. Someone has to be competent if we are to trust their opinions and recommendations. This person has the right skills to solve

FOUR TYPES OF TRUST

COMPETENCE 🏅 THE PERSON HAS the RIGHT skills To solVE youR issuE. THEY'RE AN EXPERt oR AuthoRity IN THEIR AREA.	CARE ♡ THEY CARE ABout YOUR WELL-BEING & WHAT'S BEST FOR you, NOT youR success.
CHARACTER ⦿ PEOPLE WITH A STRONG MORAL CompASS & unComPRoMiSING VALuEs.	CONSISTENCY ∞ RELiABLE, PRESENT, & AVAiLABLE WHEN you NEED THEM.

your issue. They are an expert or authority in their area. They have experience, references, and/or a high Yelp rating.

Care. We need to know a person cares if we are putting our emotions in their hands. Real care means they are thinking about what is best for you, not what is best for them. They care about your well-being, not your success. They have your best interests at heart. They believe in you. They would go beyond the call of duty to support you: helping you move, accompanying you to an important doctor's appointment, or helping you plan a birthday party or wedding.

Character. Some people have a strong moral compass and uncompromising values. We look to these people to help us see clearly when we aren't sure what we want or believe is right. Character is especially critical when we are in an interdependent partnership (a relationship, a business partnership, a team). These people practice what they preach. They have good reputations, strong opinions, and down-to-earth advice. They are trustworthy.

Consistency. People who are consistent may not be the top experts, have the highest character, or care most deeply for you, but they are reliable, present, and available when you need them. They've been with you through highs and lows.

Nobody carries a sign announcing what they have to offer us. Observe people's intentions and actions. Are they in alignment? Are they demonstrating what they say they value? Do their values correspond with yours? We learn more from behaviors than promises. Use the four types of trust to understand why you are attracted to a person and whether you are likely to connect as a friend, a colleague, or a romantic partner. Ask yourself, *What is my genuine intention for getting involved in this relationship?*

The four types of trust may seem like basic qualities that we instinctively look for and require, but notice that it's hard to think of someone who cares about you, is competent in every area, has the highest character, and is never too busy for you. Two of the most important people in my life are Swami (my monk teacher) and my mother. Swami is my go-to spiritual person. I have the utmost trust in his character. But when I told him I wanted to leave Accenture and go into media, he said, "I have no idea what you should do." He is one of my most valued advisors, but it was silly to expect him to have an opinion about my career, and he was wise enough not to pretend to have one. My mom would also not be the best person to ask about career moves. Like many mothers, she is most concerned with my well-being: how I'm feeling, whether I'm eating well, if I'm getting enough sleep. She is there with care and consistency, but she's not going to counsel me on managing my company. I needn't be angry at my mother for not caring about every aspect of my life. Instead I should save myself the time, energy, attention, and pain, and simply appreciate what she's offering.

We tend to expect every person to be a complete package, giving us everything we need. This is setting the bar impossibly high. It's as hard to find that person as it is to be that person. The four types of trust will help us keep in mind what we can and can't expect from them. Even your partner can't provide care, character, competence, and consistency in all ways at all times. Care and character, yes, but nobody is competent in all things, and though your partner should be reliable, nobody is consistently available in the way you need them. We expect our life partner to be our everything, to "complete us" (thanks, Jerry Maguire), but even within that deep and lifelong union, only you can be your everything.

Being at the ashram with people who weren't family or otherwise connected to us gave us a realistic perspective. There, it was clear that nobody could or should play every role. Interestingly, a *Psychology Today* article describes a field study of military leadership in Iraq done by Colonel J. Patrick Sweeney, a psychologist. Sweeney similarly found "3 Cs" of trust: competence, caring, and character. The difference is that he observed that all three qualities were necessary for soldiers to trust their leaders. Military and monk life both adhere to routine and principles, but monks aren't following their leaders and laying their lives on the line. To think like a monk about relationships, instead of looking for all four Cs, set realistic expectations based on what a person actually gives you, not what you want them to give you. When they don't have all four Cs, realize that you can still benefit from having them in your life.

And you should be at least as attentive to what you can offer them. With friends or colleagues, get into the habit of asking yourself, *What can I offer first? How can I serve? Am I a teacher, a peer, or a student? Which of the four Cs do I give to this person?* We form more meaningful relationships when we play to our strengths and, like Swami, don't offer expertise that we don't have.

Exercises like the one above aren't meant to attach labels to people; I'm against labels, as I've explained, because they reduce the many nuanced hues of life to black and white. The monk approach is to look for meaning and absorb what you need to move forward instead of getting

TRY THIS: REFLECT ON TRUST

Pick three diverse people in your life—perhaps a colleague, a family member, and a friend—and decide which of the four Cs they bring to your life. Be grateful for that. Thank them for it.

locked in judgment. However, when we apply filters like the four Cs, we can see if our network of compassion is broad enough to guide us through the complexity and chaos of life.

Even if we've got the four Cs covered, we benefit from multiple viewpoints within each of these categories. A mother's care isn't the same as a mentor's. One person with character might give great romantic advice, while another might help you through a family argument. And one consistent friend might be there for you during a breakup, while another is always available for a spirited hike.

MAKE YOUR OWN FAMILY

In order to find diversity, we have to be open to new connections. Part of growing up—at any age—is accepting that our family of origin may never be able to give us all that we need. It's okay to accept what you do and don't get from the people who raised you. And it's okay—necessary, in fact—to protect yourself from those in your family who aren't good for you. We should have the same standards for our family as we do for everyone else, and if the relationship is fraught, we can love them and respect them from a distance while gathering the family we need from the wider world. This doesn't mean we should neglect our families. But forgiveness and gratitude come more easily when we accept that we have friends and family, and we have friends that become family. Feeling connected at some level to all of humanity can be positively therapeutic for those whose own families have made their lives difficult.

THE HUMAN FAMILY

When you enter a new community—as I entered the ashram—you have a clean slate. You have none of the expectations that have already built up among family and friends. Most likely nobody shares your past. In situations like this, most of us rush to find "our people," but the ashram showed me another way. I didn't need to replicate a family, creating a small circle of comfort and trust. Everyone in the ashram was my family. And, as we traveled and connected with people across India and Europe, I began to recognize that everyone in the world was my family. As Gandhi said, "The golden way is to be friends with the world and to regard the whole human family as one."

The groups we establish for learning, growth, and shared experiences—like families, schools, and churches—help us categorize people. *These* are the people I live with. *These* are the people I learn with. *These* are the people I pray with. *These* are the people I hope to help. But I didn't want to discount someone's opinions or worth because they didn't fit neatly into one of these circles. Aside from the limits of practicality, there weren't certain people who deserved my attention or care or help more than others.

It's easier to look at everyone as a member of your family if you don't imagine that it's every human at every moment. A well-known poem by Jean Dominique Martin says, "People come into your life for a reason, a season or a lifetime." These three categories are based on how long that relationship should endure. One person might enter your life as a welcome change. Like a new season, they are an exciting and enthralling shift of energy. But the season ends at some point, as all seasons do. Another person might come in with a reason. They help you learn and grow, or they support you through a difficult time. It almost feels like they've been deliberately sent to you to assist or guide you through a particular experience, after which their central role in your life decreases. And then there are lifetime people. They stand by your side through the best and worst of times, loving you even when you are giving nothing to them. When you consider these categories, keep in mind the circle of love. Love is a gift without any strings attached. This means that with it comes the knowledge that not all relationships are meant to endure with equal strength indefinitely. Remember that you are also a season, a reason, and a lifetime friend to different people at different times, and the role you play in someone else's life won't always match the role they play in yours.

These days, there is a small, consistent group of people with whom I am closest, but that doesn't change the connection I feel to all humanity. And so I ask you to look beyond the people you recognize, beyond your comfort zone, to strangers and people you don't understand. You don't have to befriend them all, but see them all as equal, with equality of soul and the potential to add variety to your knowledge and experience. They are all in your circle of care.

TRY THIS: BE REALISTIC ABOUT YOUR FRIENDSHIPS

Make a list of the people you have seen socially over the past week or two. In a second column, identify whether the person is a Season, a Reason, or a Lifetime friend. This, of course, is labeling, which I have urged you not to do. We have to allow for fluidity in the roles people play. But roughly sketching the landscape of your current social life can give you an idea as to whether you are surrounded by a balanced group of people—one that provides excitement, support, and long-term love. Now, in a third column, consider what role you play for each of these people. Are you offering what you receive? Where and how could you give more?

TRUST IS EARNED

Once you have established reasonable expectations from a relationship, then it is easier to build and maintain trust. Trust is central to every relationship. Trust means we believe that the person is being honest with us, that they have our interests at heart, that they will uphold their promises and confidences, and that they will stay true to these intentions in the future. Notice that I didn't say they are right all the time or handle every challenge perfectly. Trust is about intentions, not abilities.

When an important person lets us down, the blow to our trust reverberates across all of our relationships. Even people with the best intentions change or don't follow the same path that we do. Other people give us plenty of signs that their intentions don't mesh with ours, but we ignore them. And sometimes, if we were more aware, there are people we would know not to trust in the first place. Other people's behavior is always out of our control—so how can we trust anyone?

STAGES OF TRUST

Trust can be extended to anyone from a taxi driver to a business partner to a lover, but obviously we don't have the same level of trust for everyone. It's important to be attentive to how deeply we trust someone and whether they've actually earned that level of trust.

Dr. John Gottman, one of the nation's top marriage experts, wanted to find out what makes couples get stuck in ongoing conflict instead of resolving it and moving on. He examined couples from all over the country, from varied socioeconomic and ethnic backgrounds, and in a variety of life situations, from newlyweds, to expecting parents, to families where one spouse was deployed in military service. Across the board, the most important issue to all of these couples was trust and betrayal. The language they used to describe their issues varied a bit, but the central question was always the same: Can I trust you to be faithful? Can I trust you to help with housework? Can I trust you to listen, to be there for me?

The couples had good reason to make trust a priority. According to studies by Dr. Bella DePaulo, people are dishonest in one-fifth of their interactions. Seventy-seven college students and seventy people from the community at large were asked to keep track of their social interactions for seven days. They were told to record all of their exchanges and to note how many lies they told. I know what you're thinking—what if they lied about lying? To encourage honesty, the researchers told the participants

STAGES OF TRUST

NEUTRAL TRUST
POSITIVE QUALITIES EXIST THAT DON'T MERIT TRUST

CONTRACTUAL
I'LL SCRATCH YOUR BACK IF YOU SCRATCH MINE!

MUTUAL
HELP GOES BOTH WAYS—YOU KNOW YOU'LL BE THERE FOR ONE ANOTHER IN THE FUTURE

PURE
NO MATTER WHAT HAPPENS YOU'LL HAVE ONE ANOTHER'S BACKS

that there was no judgment involved, and that their responses would help to answer fundamental questions about lying behavior. They also sold the experiment as a chance to get to know themselves better. In the end, the students reported some level of lying in one-third of their interactions and the community members in one out of every five interactions. No wonder so many of us have trust issues.

We know from our discussion of ego that we lie to impress, to present ourselves as "better" than we really are, but when these lies are discovered, the betrayal does far more damage to both people than honesty would have. If the seed of trust is not planted effectively in the beginning, we grow a weed of mistrust and betrayal.

We aren't careful with when and how we give our trust. We either trust other people too easily, or we withhold our trust from everyone. Neither of these extremes serve us well. Trusting everyone makes you

vulnerable to deception and disappointment. Trusting no one leaves you
suspicious and alone. Our level of trust should directly correspond to our
experience with a person, growing through four stages of trust.

Neutral Trust. When you meet someone, it is normal not to trust them.
You may find them funny, charming, a joy to be around. These positive
qualities do not merit trust. They mean you think your new acquaintance is
cool. We tend to conflate trustworthiness with likability. In studies examining jurors' perceptions of expert witnesses, those the jurors found to be like-
able they also rated as more trustworthy. We also tend to trust people we
find attractive. Rick Wilson, coauthor of *Judging a Book by Its Cover: Beauty
and Expectations in the Trust Game*, says, "We found that attractive subjects
gain a 'beauty premium' in that they are trusted at higher rates, but we also
found a 'beauty penalty' when attractive people do not live up to expectations." When we equate likability or appeal with trust, we set ourselves
up for huge disappointment. It is better to have neutral trust than to trust
someone for the wrong reasons or to trust them blindly.

Contractual Trust. I derived this level of trust from *rajas*, the impulsive
mode of life, where you are focused on getting the result that you want
in the short-term. Contractual trust is the quid pro quo of relationships.
It simply says: If I pay for dinner and you promise to pay me back, I have
faith that you'll do it. If you make a plan, you can count on the person to
show up—and there's no further expectation. Contractual trust is useful.
Most of us share contractual trust with the majority of people who cross
our paths, yet we expect them to trust us implicitly. The heart may want
a deeper connection, but we have to be discerning. Expecting more from
someone who is only showing you contractual trust is premature at best
and dangerous at worst.

Mutual trust. Contractual trust reaches a higher level when you help
someone, expecting they would most likely do the same for you, in some
way, at some unknown time in the future. Where contractual trust relies
on a specific exchange both parties have agreed to in advance, mutual
trust is far looser. This stage of trust is derived from *sattva*, the mode of

goodness, where we act from a place of goodness, positivity, and peace. We all want to get to this level, and good friendships usually do.

Pure trust. The highest level of trust is pure goodness, when you know, no matter what happens, that another person has your back, and vice versa. College basketball coach Don Meyer used to give each of his teammates a blank piece of paper on which he'd ask them to draw a circle to represent their "foxhole." They wrote their names at the top of the circle, then drew lines at their left, right, and rear, and on each line they had to list the name of a teammate who they'd want in their foxhole with them. Those chosen most often by their teammates were the team's natural leaders. Choose your foxhole gang wisely.

If you were to graph the number of people you trust at each level, the result would probably look like a pyramid: a lot of people at neutral trust; fewer people at contractual trust; your close circle at mutual trust; and only a handful at the top level, pure trust.

No matter how dissatisfied you are with your pyramid, don't promote people without reason. They will only let you down. The biggest mistake we make is to assume that everyone else operates just like us. We believe that others value what we value. We believe that what we want in a relationship is what others want in a relationship. When someone says, "I love you," we think they mean exactly what we mean when we say "I love you." But if we think everyone is a reflection of ourselves, we fail to see things as they are. We see things as *we* are.

Mutual trust requires patience and commitment. It is built on a true understanding of the other person in spite of and because they are separate from us and view the world differently. The way to step back from making presumptions is to closely observe their words and behaviors. When people show you their level of trust, believe them.

I want you to feel grateful for the people you can trust and to feel honored by those who trust you. If you have neutral trust for someone, that's cool too. Accept people as they are, and you give them the chance to grow and prove to be more. We set ourselves up for long-term trust when we let it evolve naturally.

TRUST IS A DAILY PRACTICE

Relationships rarely get to a point where both participants can say, "I absolutely know this person and they absolutely know me." Like a curve that continually approaches but never reaches a line, you never get to the point of saying, "I trust them fully, and they trust me fully, forever and ever." Trust can be threatened in small and large ways and needs to be reinforced and rebuilt on a daily basis.

Build and reinforce trust every day by:

- Making and fulfilling promises (contractual trust)
- Giving those you care about sincere compliments and constructive criticism; going out of your way to offer support (mutual trust)
- Standing by someone even when they are in a bad place, have made a mistake, or need help that requires significant time (pure trust)

AN INTENTIONAL LOVE LIFE

Now that we have some tools to assess the roles people play in our lives, let's look at how we can deepen existing relationships and build strong new ones. Letting go of traditional family roles allowed us monks to broaden our connections with humanity. In the same way, celibacy freed the energy and attention that romantic love had consumed. Before you hurl this book across the room, I'm not recommending celibacy for non-monks. Celibacy is an extreme commitment and hardly an essential one for everyone, but it did lead me to revelations that I'd like to share. Let's say I did it so you don't have to.

To stop drinking? That was easy for me. To stop gambling? I'd never done much of that in the first place. And I'd stopped eating meat at six-teen. For me, giving up romantic relationships was the hardest sacrifice.

It sounded ridiculous, even impossible. But I knew the purpose behind it: to save the effort and energy that went into being validated in a romantic relationship and to use it to build a relationship with myself. Think of it the same way giving up sugar sounds like a drag—what sane person would want to forgo ice cream?—but we all know there's a good reason: to be healthy and live longer. When I looked at the monks, I could see that they were doing something right. Remember Matthieu Ricard, "the World's Happiest Man"? All the monks I met looked so young and seemed so happy. My romantic entanglements hadn't brought me fulfillment, so I was willing to try the experiment of self-control and discipline.

When I became a monk, one of my college friends asked, "What are we going to talk about? All we used to do was talk about girls." He was right. So much of my life had been absorbed in navigating romantic connections. There's a reason we watch countless sitcoms and movies about romance—it's endlessly entertaining—but as with any entertainment, it takes time away from serious matters. If I'd been dating or in a committed relationship for those three years instead of being at the ashram, I wouldn't be where I am today, with understanding of my strengths and who I am.

The Sanskrit for monk is *brahmacharya*, which can be translated to "the right use of energy." In the dating world, when you walk into a bar, you look around to see who is attractive. Or you swipe through potential mates online without giving a second thought to how much time you spend in the effort to hook up. But imagine if you could buy that time back for yourself, if you could recoup everything you've ever invested in relationships that didn't pan out. That attention and focus could be used for creativity, friendship, introspection, industry. Now, this doesn't mean every failed relationship is a waste of time. On the contrary, we learn from each mistake. But think of the time around the relationship, waiting for texts, wondering if they like you, trying to make someone change into the person you want them to be. If we are thoughtful about our needs and expectations, our time and energy go to far better use.

Sexual energy is not just about pleasure. It is sacred—it has the power to create a child. Imagine what it can create within us when it's harnessed. Certified sex educator Mala Madrone says, "Celibacy by conscious choice is a powerful way to work with your own energy and harness the potency of life energy. It can also help you strengthen your intuition, your boundaries, and your understanding of what consent truly means, including how to differentiate what kind of contact and interaction is truly welcome in your life and by your body." But your energy is squandered when it is spent tailoring yourself to someone else's ideal or shaping yourself into the person you think he wants or suspecting her of cheating on you. There is so much anxiety and negativity around dating and so much pressure to find "the one"—never mind whether we're ready or able to settle down with anyone.

Once the element of romantic pursuit was removed, I wasn't trying to promote myself as a boyfriend, to look good, to make women think anything of me, to indulge lust. I found my connections with female friends—with all my friends—growing deeper. I had more physical and mental space and energy for their souls. My time and attention were better spent.

Again, I'm not suggesting you give up sex (though you certainly could), but what if you give yourself permission to be single, by yourself, able to focus on your career, your friends, and your peace of mind? Minister and philosopher Paul Tillich said, "Our language has wisely sensed these two sides of man's being alone. It has created the word 'loneliness' to express the pain of being alone. And it has created the word 'solitude' to express the glory of being alone."

I spent three years as a monk, three years developing my self-awareness, at the end of which I was able to ask myself the right questions about a relationship. I may not have spent all of my waking hours in *sattva*—the mode of goodness—but I knew where I wanted to be and how it felt. I had the opportunity to become the person I would want to date. Instead of looking for others to make me happy, I was able to be that person for myself.

ATTRACTION VERSUS CONNECTION

Our increased intentionality gives us a clearer perspective with which to evaluate why we are initially attracted to people and whether those reasons support our values. There are five primary motivations for connection—and note that these don't exclusively apply to romantic prospects:

1. *Physical attraction.* You like what they look like—you are drawn to their appearance, style, or presence, or you like the idea of being seen with them.
2. *Material.* You like their accomplishments and the power and/or the possessions this affords them.
3. *Intellectual.* You like how they think—you're stimulated by their conversation and ideas.
4. *Emotional.* You connect well. They understand your feelings and increase your sense of well-being.
5. *Spiritual.* They share your deepest goals and values.

When you identify what's attracting you, it's clear if you're attracted to the whole person or just a part. In my experience, ask most people what attracts them to another person and they'll mention some combination of the top three qualities: looks, success, and intellect, but those qualities alone don't correlate with long-term, fortifying relationships.

Monks believe that someone's looks aren't who they are—the body is only a vessel for the soul. Similarly, someone's possessions aren't theirs—they certainly don't tell you about the person's character! And even if you're attracted to someone's intellect, there's no guarantee it will lead to a meaningful bond. These three qualities don't correlate with long-term, fortifying relationships, but they do show your chemistry with another person. The last two—emotional and spiritual—point to a more profound, lasting connection—they show your compatibility.

QUALITY, NOT QUANTITY

When it comes to the energy we expend and receive in relationships, the focus is quality, not quantity. I often hear from guilty parents (usually moms) that they feel bad having to work long hours and lose out on time with their kids. According to the first-ever large-scale study of the impact of mothers' time, it's the *quality* of time spent with kids, not the quantity, that counts. (That means put away your phone during family time.) I'm not a parent, but I know that as a child, I always felt my mom's energy. I never measured how much time she spent with me. My mother worked, and as a young child I went to daycare. I don't have a single memory from daycare—no painful memories of her absence—but I do remember her coming to pick me up. She'd always smile and ask about my day.

This is true in all relationships. Nobody wants to sit with you at dinner while you're on the phone. This is where we confuse time and energy. You can spend a whole hour with someone, but only give them ten minutes of energy. I'm not able to spend much time with my family, but when I'm with them I'm 100 percent there. I'd rather spend two hours with them, focused and engaged, than give them partial, distracted energy for a whole weekend.

A monk shows love through presence and attention. In the ashram, time invested was never seen as a reliable measure of care or engagement. As I've mentioned, after a meditation, nobody asked how long you'd meditated, they asked how deep you'd gone. If you have dinner together every night, great, but what is the quality of the conversation? Think like monks do, in terms of energy management not time management. Are you bringing your full presence and attention to someone?

TRY THIS: HANDCUFF ATTENTION THIEVES

These days, most of us are losing a battle for our attention. The victors are our screens. The only way to give another person your complete attention for a period of time is to turn off your screens. To give someone in your life the focus they deserve, sit down with them to agree on rules surrounding the phone, the laptop, and the TV. Choose specific activities that will be your quality time, without distraction. Agree to turn off your phones, put them in another room, or leave them at home. This may be a challenge at first. Perhaps conversation will lag, or friends and colleagues will be frustrated because they can't reach you. Setting these boundaries will establish new expectations on both fronts: Lapses in conversation will lose their awkwardness; friends and colleagues will accept that you are not available 24/7.

SIX LOVING EXCHANGES

Most couples don't sit down together, draw up a list of values, and see whether they share them. But once we have clarity about ourselves, we can connect with others in a more intentional way. The Upadesamrta talks about six loving exchanges to encourage bonding and growing together. (There are three types of exchanges; each involves giving *and* receiving, thus adding up to six.) They help us build a relationship based on generosity, gratitude, and service.

Gifts. Giving charity and receiving whatever is offered in return. This seems obvious, or maybe even materialistic—we don't want to buy each other's affection. But think about what it means to give to another person with intention. Do you get flowers for your partner on Valentine's Day? This is a very conventional gesture, so consider whether it is the one that brings your partner the most joy. If flowers it is, did you walk them past a flower shop six months ago to suss out their preferences in preparation for this day, or did you text a secret query to their closest friend? (Both actions entail a lot more intention than just ordering some roses online, though, of course, that's better than completely forgetting the day!) Is Valentine's Day the best moment to express your love, or would an unexpected gesture be even more meaningful? Have you taken the time to contemplate what an ill friend would really like? Maybe it isn't an object but an action, a service, our time. Cleaning their car, organizing activities, helping them with obligations, or bringing them someplace beautiful.

You can bring the same thoughtfulness to receiving a gift. Are you grateful for the effort that went into the gift? Do you understand why and what it means for the giver?

Conversation. Listening is one of the most thoughtful gifts we can give. There is no better way to show that we care about another person's experience. Listening intentionally means looking for the emotions behind the words, asking questions to further understand, incorporating what you've learned into your knowledge of the other person, doing your best to remember what they said, and following up where relevant. Listening also involves creating an atmosphere of trust, where the person feels welcome and safe.

It is also important to share your own thoughts and dreams, hopes and worries. The vulnerability of exposing yourself is a way of giving trust and showing respect for another person's opinion. It enables the other person to understand the previous experiences and beliefs you bring to whatever you do together.

SIX LOVING EXCHANGES

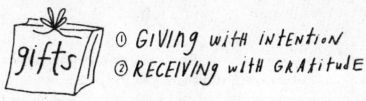

① GIVING with INTENTION
② RECEIVING with GRATITUDE

③ LISTENING without JUDGMENT
④ SPEAKING with VULNERABILITY

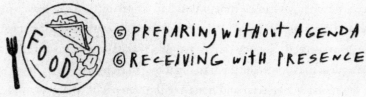

⑤ PREPARING without AGENDA
⑥ RECEIVING with PRESENCE

TRY THIS: MAKE YOUR CONVERSATION INTO A GIFT

Ideally, you try to do this in conversations regularly, but this time, do it with focus and intention. Pick a moment you have coming up with someone important to you—a friend, a relative, your partner. Maybe it's a meal or walk you'll be taking together. During this time, shut off your phone. Give all your focus to the other person. Instead of having an agenda, be curious. If a topic doesn't emerge, ask them open-ended questions to land on a subject that's important to them: What's on your mind lately? How's your relationship with X? Listen carefully, ask follow-up questions. Share your own experiences without turning the conversation to yourself. A few days later, email or text the friend to follow up.

Food. The world was a very different place when the Upadesamrta was written, of course, and I interpret this exchange of food broadly to mean the exchange of experiences: any tangible expression of care and service that nourishes body or spirit, like giving a massage, creating a relaxing space for the other person in the home, or putting on music you know they enjoy. On a grander scale, my wife left her beloved family and moved to New York so she could live with me—an expression of care and generosity that nourished me more than I can say. Once we were in New York, I introduced her to other women to help her find a community. The experiences we exchanged didn't have to be perfectly matched—we look for what the other person needs most.

These six exchanges can be thoughtless and empty, or they can have true depth and meaning. But don't judge people's efforts without giving them a chance to succeed. Nobody can read minds. If your roommate or partner doesn't guess that you want them to organize your birthday party, it's not their fault. Instead, be clear and honest with them about what you need.

TRY THIS: ASK FOR WHAT YOU WANT

Tell the important people in your life how you like to receive love. When we don't tell people what we want, we expect them to read our minds and often judge them for failing to do so. This week, be more genuine in asking people for help rather than waiting for them to predict what you want.

1. Think of a complaint you have about a loved one's behavior. (But don't look too hard for faults! If nothing springs to mind, that's a great sign and you should skip this exercise.)

2. Dig to the root of the problem. Where is the real dissatisfaction? You might find that your need corresponds to the loving exchanges. Do you want more time to share and connect? (conversation) Do you feel un-appreciated? (gifts) Do you want more support? (food or other acts of service)

3. Articulate it without criticism. Say, "This is what would make me feel more loved and appreciated" instead of "You do this wrong."

In this way you give a companion a path to connection, which is easier for them and more likely to fulfill you.

READY FOR LOVE

The six loving exchanges lay a foundation for any close relationship, but most of us are looking for "the one." The Harvard Grant Study followed 268 Harvard undergraduates for seventy-five years, collecting piles of data about them along the way. When researchers combed through the data, they found a single factor that reliably predicted the quality of participants' lives: love. Participants could have every other external marker for success—money, a thriving career, good physical health—but if they didn't have loving relationships, they weren't happy.

We all come to relationships with different levels of self-awareness.

With the encouragement of online quizzes and dating apps, we list the characteristics we want in a partner—sense of humor, caring, good-looking—but we don't look at what we really need. How do we want to be cared for? What makes us feel loved?

In *How to Love*, Thich Nhat Hanh writes, "Often, we get crushes on others not because we truly love and understand them, but to distract ourselves from our suffering. When we learn to love and understand ourselves and have true compassion for ourselves, then we can truly love and understand another person." After the ashram, when I was ready for a relationship (which was not, as some friends assumed, the moment I left), my sense of what I wanted in a partner was steered by self-knowledge. I knew what would complement me and what wouldn't. I knew what I needed in my life and what I had to offer. My ability to find the right relationship evolved because I had evolved.

As it happened, Radhi Devlukia, the woman who would become my wife, already had this self-knowledge too. Without the need for the same journey I'd made, she knew she wanted to be with someone spiritually connected, with high morals and values. I believe she would have done just fine without me. But I know my life would have been different, full of pain, if I hadn't taken the time to work on myself before diving into a serious relationship.

According to Massive Attack, love is a verb. *Dan in Real Life* says love is an ability. The Dalai Lama says, "Love is the absence of judgment." Love is also patient. It's kind. And apparently, love is all you need. With so many definitions of love in our culture, it's all a bit confusing. And I was confused, despite all my monk experience—my self-exploration and intentionality and compassion—when I ventured out on my first date back in London.

I already know I like her. The Think Out Loud group I started in college continued for some years after I left, and I stayed in touch, visiting and lecturing when I came to London. Radhi was part of that community, had come to some of my lectures, and had become friends with my sister. Now people from that community, including me and Radhi, have joined together to organize a charity event against racism and bullying for young kids in England. Seeing Radhi in that context has told me more about her than I would have learned on a dating profile, or even after a few dates. I've seen how respectful she is with everyone on the team. She has interesting opinions and cool ideas. I've had a chance to get a real look at who she is—anyone can be their online profile for a one-hour date. It may be their best self, but it doesn't give the full picture.

I still haven't gotten a full-time job, but I've been tutoring to make a bit of money. I've saved up a month's earnings, and I take Radhi to the theater to see Wicked. *Then I bring her to Locanda Locatelli, a fancy restaurant that's way above my pay grade.*

She's polite, but unimpressed. Afterward, she says, "You didn't have to do this," and confesses that her ideal date would be going to a supermarket, walking the aisles, and buying some bread. I'm mystified. Who would want to do that?

I hadn't had any relationships since becoming a monk, and I had yet to reconcile who I was spiritually with how I used to date. I felt like I had one foot in each world. In spite of my monk training, I snapped right back into my old relationship mode—the one where I tried to give the other person what media, movies, and music told me they wanted instead of developing my awareness of who they were. I myself love gifts and extravagant demonstrations of love, and for a while I cluelessly continued to shower Radhi with grand gestures. I got it completely wrong. She wasn't impressed by any of that. She's not very fancy. Even after my years in the ashram, I could still be swayed by external influences or my own preferences rather than careful observation of what she liked, but after my initial missteps, I was aware enough to figure it out, and, thank God, she married me.

If you don't know what you want, you'll send out the wrong signals and attract the wrong people. If you aren't self-aware, you'll look for the wrong qualities and choose the wrong people. This work is what we've talked about throughout this book. Until you understand yourself, you won't be ready for love.

Sometimes we find ourselves making the same mistake over and over again, attracting the same sort of incompatible partners or picking them in spite of ourselves. If this happens, it isn't bad luck—it's a clue that we have work to do. The monk perspective is that you carry pain. You try to find people to ease that pain, but only you can do that. If you don't work through it, it stays with you and interferes with your decisions. The problematic people who emerge reflect your unresolved issues, and they will keep reappearing until you learn the lesson you need to learn. As Iyanla Vanzant said to Oprah, ". . . until you heal the wounds of your past, you will continue to bleed. You can bandage the bleeding with food, with alcohol, with drugs, with work, with cigarettes, with sex; but eventually, it will all ooze through and stain your life. You must find the strength to open the wounds, stick your hands inside, pull out the core of the pain that is holding you in your past, the memories, and make peace with them."

Once you've unpacked your own bags and you've healed yourself (mostly), then you'll come to relationships ready to give. You won't be looking to them to solve your problems or fill a hole. Nobody completes you. You're not half. You don't have to be perfect, but you have to come to a place of giving. Instead of draining anyone else, you're nourishing them.

KEEPING LOVE ALIVE

Remember when we talked about the mind, we said that happiness comes when we are learning, progressing, and achieving. And yet as a relationship lengthens, we tend to long for the honeymoon phase, when we were first falling in love. How many times have you been in a relationship, and said to yourself, "I wish I could feel like that again," or "I wish we could go back to that time." But going to the same place for dinner or to the place you had your first kiss won't bring back all the magic. Many of us are so addicted to re-creating the same experiences that we don't make space for new ones. What you were actually doing at the start of your relationship was creating *new* memories with energy and openness. Love is kept alive by creating more new memories—by continuing to learn and grow together. Fresh experiences bring excitement into your life and build a stronger bond. I have many recommendations for activities couples can do together, but here are a couple of my favorites, drawn from monk principles.

1. *Find new in the old.* Remember when, as monks, we looked for a special stone on the same walk we took together every day? You too can open your eyes to the world you already live in. Have a candlelit dinner in the middle of the week. Read a book to each other before bed instead of staring at your phones. Take a walk together in the neighborhood and challenge each other to find a certain kind of mailbox or to be the first to spot a bird.

2. *Find new ways to spend time together.* A study by psychologist Arthur Aron found that couples strengthen their bonds when they do new and exciting activities together. My wife and I started to do escape rooms together. An escape room is a game where you're both locked in a room and have to find a way out. The staff gives you a few clues, and you have to work together to solve many steps of the puzzle. It may sound a little creepy, but it's actually a lot of fun. You get to learn together. You get to make mistakes together. It's an even playing field when neither of you has more experience or expertise than the other. When you experiment together as a couple, you feel yourselves growing together in all areas of your life. You could even try something really scary together—like skydiving or something else that's outside your comfort zone. Remember all the benefits that we found in getting close to our fears? Playing with fear together is a way to practice going into your deeper fears, sharing them with your partner, feeling their support, and together transforming fear.

3. *Serve together.* Just as serving gives meaning to your life, serving with your partner adds meaning to your connection, whether it's organizing charity events, feeding the homeless, or teaching something together.

My most bonding experiences in monk life came about when I took part in collective projects. The horrid two-day train journey that I've mentioned. Planting trees together. Building a school. Instead of focusing on the challenges of the relationship, we develop a shared perspective on real-life issues. Connecting for a higher purpose, we feel gratitude and bring that back into our relationship. I know many couples who have met through volunteering, so if you're looking for a well-suited partner, find a cause that is close to your heart. If you meet through an activity such as volunteering, from the start you already have something very deep in common, and you're more likely to form a deeper bond.

4. *Meditate and chant together.* (See page 270.) When a couple who has just had an argument comes into a room, you can feel the negative energy vibrating between them. The opposite is true when you and your partner chant together. You are bringing your energy to the same place and feel, literally, in tune with each other.

5. *Finally, envision together what you both want from the relationship.* When you are aware of what is important to each other, then you can figure out how much you're willing to adapt. Ideally, each of you is striving to live in your own dharma. In the best of relationships, you get there together.

OVERCOMING HEARTBREAK

It can be hard to see clearly when your heart is at stake, but there is one point I want to make abundantly clear: There is a difference between being grateful for what you have and settling for less than you deserve. If we are still listening to our child minds, we're attracted to people who aren't good for us but make us feel better in the moment. Don't wrap your self-esteem around someone else. Nobody deserves verbal, emotional, or physical abuse. It is better to be alone. Nor should you allow an abusive, manipulative, or toxic relationship to transition into friendship. The dynamic won't change, trust me.

In every relationship you have the opportunity to set the level of joy

you expect and the level of pain you'll accept. No relationship is perfect, but if joy never reaches a certain height, or holds to a low average, that won't change unless you both put in a lot of work. The same is true for how much disappointment you're willing to bear. Your connection may get a slow start—it can take a while to know each other—but if it never reaches a satisfying level, you need to decide whether to accept it or move on.

I know it's not easy. When you've spent quality time with someone, when you've invested in someone, when you've given yourself to someone, it's so hard to let go. Tibetan Buddhist nun Jetsunma Tenzin Palmo points out that we often mistake attachment for love. She says, "We imagine that the grasping and clinging that we have in our relationships shows that we love. Whereas actually, it is just attachment, which causes pain. Because the more we grasp, the more we are afraid to lose, then if we do lose, then of course we are going to suffer." Ultimately, holding on to the wrong person causes us more pain than letting them go.

The strategies I recommend to overcome heartbreak tie directly to monk ideas of the self, and how we find our way toward peace and purpose. No matter what thought we have, we don't run away from it. We give ourselves space to assess and make changes. **SPOT, STOP, SWAP.**

Feel every emotion. It's possible to distract yourself from heartbreak, but the fix is only temporary. And if you deny your feelings, you end up suffering in other ways. Researchers followed incoming college freshmen to see how well they adapted to their transition and found that those with a tendency to suppress their emotions had fewer close relationships and felt less social support. Instead, think about how the other person has made you feel in this situation. You might want to articulate your feelings by writing them down or recording them. Read what you've written and listen back objectively. Do you hear any recurring patterns?

You can also do a question meditation, asking yourself about the loss. We like to replay emotions: how perfect it was, how it could have been, how we thought it was going to go. Instead of reflecting on how romantic the relationship was before it crashed and burned, focus on the reality.

What were your hopes for the relationship? What did you lose? Is your disappointment tied to who the person was, or who they weren't? Explore your emotions until you uncover the root of the pain and disruption.

Learn from the situation. Movies, music, and other media send us limited, often inaccurate messages about what love should look like. Use the reality of the breakup to set realistic expectations about what you deserve and need from a new relationship and remember that yours can be different from the person you broke up with and/or the next person to come along. What was the biggest expectation you had that wasn't met? What was important to you? What was good in the relationship, what was bad? What was your role in its demise? Instead of exploring your pain here, you want to investigate the workings of the relationship in order to identify what you want from your next relationship, and what you might have to work on in yourself.

Believe in your worth. You may undervalue yourself in the moment of a breakup, but your value doesn't depend on someone's ability to fully appreciate you. If you wrap your identity around the relationship, the pain you feel is that you've had to sacrifice that part of your identity. If you expected one person to fulfill all of your needs, then of course there is a vacuum when they're gone. Now that you're single, use this time to build a community of people with shared interests whom you want to be in your life forever. Make yourself whole. You need to be someone who makes you happy.

Wait before dating again. Remember, if you haven't healed past pain, you might miss your next opportunity for an incredible connection with an incredible person. Don't rebound or revenge-date. This only causes more hurt and regret that spread further, a virus of pain. Instead, take some time to get to know yourself better. Build your self-esteem. Invest in your growth. **If you've lost yourself in the relationship, find yourself in the heartbreak.**

The monk way is to build awareness, address, and amend. Either within a relationship or before we enter one, we take a step back to evaluate and make sure we understand our own intentions. Then we can venture into the dating world or return to the relationship with self-awareness and love. **SPOT, STOP, SWAP.**

We have turned our attention outward to address the intimate relationships in our lives. Now we come to our relationship with the larger world. I mentioned that at the ashram I felt a bond beyond my ties to my family, a far greater force uniting and connecting us all. The astrophysicist Neil deGrasse Tyson said, "We are all connected; to each other, biologically. To the Earth, chemically. And to the rest of the universe, atomically." Knowing this, we must look to the universe to find true meaning in our lives.

ELEVEN

SERVICE

Plant Trees Under Whose Shade You Do Not Plan to Sit

The ignorant work for their own profit . . .
the wise work for the welfare of the world . . .
—Bhagavad Gita, 3:25

I am a novice at the ashram, and we've been dropped off in a village with no money and no food, with the mission to find our own way for thirty days.

The weather is decent, and we've been given a warehouse for shelter. We leave our mats there and venture into the village. There are simple huts from which people sell food, spices, and sundries. Laundry is strung between the huts. Most people travel by bike or on foot—some of the children are barefoot.

Untethered, without a plan, the first thing we feel is fear, which provokes us to do whatever it takes to survive. We ask for handouts—people in India are generous and often give bread, fruit, or coins to people in spiritual dress. We visit the temple where pilgrims are given free food called prasad—this is sanctified food that is offered to God, then handed out. Anxious about our survival, we resort to selfishness and hoarding.

By the second week, we're in better shape. We've figured out that we can *earn our provisions by offering help to people in the village. We start assisting people with heavy loads or peddlers who could use a hand with their carts. We soon learn that opening our hearts and souls encourages others to do the same. The donations we receive aren't dramatically different from the ones we got when we first arrived, but the exchange gives us a warm sense of communal compassion and generosity, and I feel like I've absorbed the lesson of our journey. We thought we had nothing, and indeed we had barely any material possessions. But we were still able to give people our effort.*

However, by the final week, we're well-fed and secure enough to notice something deeper. Though we had come with nothing, we still had a certain kind of wealth: we are stronger and more capable than a lot of the people in the village. There are seniors, children, and disabled people on the street, all of them in greater need than we are.

"I feel bad," one monk says. "This is short-term for us. For them it's forever."

"I think we're missing something," I add. "We can do more in this village than survive." We recall Helen Keller's refrain: "I cried because I had no shoes until I met a man who had no feet." This is, unfortunately, no exaggeration. In India, you often see people with missing limbs.

I realize that now that we have found our way, we can share the food and money we have received with those who aren't as able as we are. Just when I think I've learned the lesson of our journey, I come upon a revelation that affects me profoundly: Everyone, even those of us who have already dedicated our lives to service, can always give more.

These three stages of transformation felt like a microcosm of the entire monk experience: First, we let go of the external and the ego; second, we recognize our value and learn that we don't need to own anything in order to serve; and third, we continually seek a higher level of service. On that trip I recognized that there is always room to rise, there is always more to give. Sister Christine Vladimiroff, a Benedictine nun, as quoted in *The Monastic Way*, wrote, "Monastic spirituality teaches us that we are on a journey. The journey is inward to seek God in prayer and silence. Taken alone, we can romanticize this aspect of our life. . . . But to be monastic there is a parallel journey—the journey outward. We live in community to grow in sensitivity to the needs of others. . . . The monastery is then a center to come out of and to invite others into. The key is always to maintain both journeys—inward and outward."

THE HIGHEST PURPOSE

In his lecture at my college, Gauranga Das had inspired me when he said, "Plant trees under whose shade you do not plan to sit." That sentence captivated me and launched me on a trajectory I had never imagined. And now I have to make a confession. I've been holding out on you. We have talked about how to let go of the influences of external noise, fear, envy, and false goals. We have explored how to grow by harnessing our minds, our egos, and our daily practices to live in our dharma. All of this is toward the goal of leading fulfilling, meaningful lives—a worthy path. But here, and on social media, and in my classes, and in every medium in which I teach, I haven't yet revealed the most important lesson I learned as a monk and one that I carry with me every day of my life. Drumroll, please.

The highest purpose is to live in service.

It's not that I've been keeping service a secret; I mention it often. But I've waited until now to talk about the central role I believe it should play in all of our lives because, frankly, I think most of us are somewhat resistant to the idea. Sure, we want to help those in need, and maybe we already find ways to do so, but we are limited by the pressure and needs of our own work and lives. We want to solve our own issues first. "Jay, I'm the one who needs help! I have so much to figure out before I can devote myself to helping others." It's true. It's hard to think about selflessness when we are struggling. And yet that is exactly what I learned as a monk. Selflessness is the surest route to inner peace and a meaningful life. **Selflessness heals the self.**

Monks live in service, and to think like a monk ultimately means to serve. *The Monastic Way* quotes Benedictine monk Dom Aelred

Graham as saying, "The monk may think he has come [to the mon-astery] to gain something for himself: peace, security, quiet, a life of prayer, or study, or teaching; but if his vocation is genuine, he finds that he has come not to take but to give." **We seek to leave a place cleaner than we found it, people happier than we found them, the world better than we found it.**

We are nature, and if we look at and observe nature carefully, nature is always serving. The sun provides heat and light. Trees give oxygen and shade. Water quenches our thirst. We can—and monks do—view every-thing in nature as serving. The Srimad-Bhagavatam says, "Look at these fortunate trees. They live solely for the benefit of others. They tolerate wind, rain, heat, and snow, but still provide shelter for our benefit." The only way to be one with nature is to serve. It follows that the only way to align properly with the universe is to serve because that's what the universe does.

The sixteenth-century guru Rupa Goswami talks about *yukta-vairāgya*, which means to do everything for a higher purpose. That's real detachment, utter renunciation, perfection. Some monk sects strictly apply this standard to their practices, stripping themselves of material possessions altogether, but in reality the rest of us need to work for a living. We're all going to end up owning stuff. But we can look at how we use what we have. We can use our homes to foster community. We can use our money and resources to support causes we believe in. We can volunteer our talents for those in need. It's not wrong to have things if we use them for good.

The Bhagavad Gita sees the whole world as a kind of school, an edu-cation system structured to make us realize one truth: We are compelled to serve, and only in service can we be happy. Like fire is hot, as the sun is light and warm, service is the essence of human consciousness. Know the reality of the world in which you live. Know it to be impermanent, unreal, and the source of your suffering and delusion. Seeing the purpose of life to be sense gratification—making ourselves feel good—leads to pain and dissatisfaction. Seeing it as service leads to fulfillment.

SERVICE IS GOOD FOR THE BODY AND SOUL

Service fulfills us on many levels, beginning with my simple belief that we're born wired to care for others so service does us good. This instinct is most obvious in children, who aren't yet distracted by other demands on their time and attention. An image that went viral shows a little girl, probably about two years old, watching a politician crying on Japanese TV. She takes a tissue, goes up to the TV, and tries to wipe away the politician's tears. Such things go viral because we recognize—and perhaps miss—the little girl's compassion for another person, even a stranger.

In *Long Walk to Freedom*, Nelson Mandela writes, "No one is born hating another person because of the color of his skin, or his background, or his religion. People must learn to hate, and if they can learn to hate, then they can be taught to love, for love comes more naturally to the human heart than its opposite." Just as Mandela believed people were born to love but taught to hate, monks believe that we are born to serve, but the distractions of the external world make us forget our purpose. We need to reconnect with that instinct in order to feel like life has meaning.

I have already touched on Joseph Campbell's concept of the mythic hero's journey. It is a formula describing the steps that a hero goes through when he embarks on an adventure, encounters trials and obstacles, and returns victorious. One of the key elements of the hero's journey is one we often overlook—the last stage, which Campbell called "return with elixir." The hero's journey isn't fulfilled until he makes it home safely and shares what he has gained (the elixir) with others. The idea of service is woven into classic story structure as a key part of a happy ending.

Seane Corn is living out the hero's journey. She made her name as a teacher of yoga asana. She was (and still is) a marquee teacher at yoga conferences and festivals around the world, but at one point in her career as a yoga teacher, she realized that with her platform, she could make an even more meaningful impact in the world, so she shifted her focus to serving at-risk communities. Corn decided to try bringing breath and meditation techniques to those in need, starting with kids who'd been sexually exploited. Then she grew her practice into working with other people society deems as outcasts, such as prostitutes and drug addicts. From that vantage point, she reached back into the yoga community to cofound Off the Mat, Into the World, a nonprofit that links yoga with activism. As dedicated as she is to service, Corn maintains that she gets more than she gives. "Find me someone who has gone to the darkest parts of their own character where they were so close to their own self-destruction and found a way to get up and out of it, and I will bow on my knees to you. . . . You're my teacher."

As Corn found, service gives back to us.

Studies show that when we pursue "compassionate goals"—those aimed at helping others or otherwise helping to make the world a better place—we're less likely to have symptoms of anxiety and depression than when we focus on improving or protecting our own status or reputation. The act of giving to others activates the pleasure center of our brain. It's win-win-win. This may be why those who help others tend to live longer, be healthier, and have a better overall sense of well-being.

Monks believe that the pillar of service makes our lives better in many ways.

Service connects us. When you serve, it's hard to be lonely. In most scenarios, you have to go out into the world to help other people.

Service amplifies gratitude. Service gives you a broad view of all that you have.

Service increases compassion. When you serve, you see that the world needs what you have to offer.

Service builds self-esteem. Helping others tells you that you're making a difference in the world. You have a sense of meaning and purpose.

The ashram is designed around the intention to serve, and it's easier to live with that as your highest intention when everyone around you is on board. A life of service is far more challenging in the modern world, and we can't all follow the monks' 24/7 model, but the monk practice shows us why and how we should adopt a service mindset.

THE SERVICE MINDSET

The word *seva* is Sanskrit for selfless service. The Bhagavad Gita says that "giving simply because it is right to give, without thought of return, at a proper time, in proper circumstances, and to a worthy person, is sattvic giving"—giving in the mode of goodness. Monks are solely motivated by selfless service: to give others opportunities that we had and didn't have; to better others' lives and the human condition. We took this mission to heart in small and large ways. Within the ashram, we tried to serve each other every day. Monks don't make grand gestures. Love is in the small things. If someone was having trouble waking up on time, we'd help them. If someone was working late, we'd save food for them. We are consistent and intentional. We remember that we never know what someone is going through, so we treat them with the gentleness you would give someone who is in pain, with the generosity you would give someone who is hungry, with the compassion you would give someone who is misunderstood.

This attitude radiated beyond the ashram. When we traveled, we always carried extra food with us so that we had some to give away. We weren't ending world hunger, but to help any hungry person is to water the seeds of compassion.

On a larger scale, we participated in a program called Annamrita, which provides more than a million meals a day to the underprivileged children of India. We often went to Mumbai to cook in the kitchens or to serve food in the schools. The students were given *kitchari*, a rice and lentil porridge made with ghee that's considered a staple in Ayurvedic cooking, and afterward they would receive dessert, a sweet rice pudding called *kheer*. The first time I handed a child *kheer*, her gratitude was so apparent that I was humbled. It was the same with every child, every time, each face radiating joy. I hate cooking—the hot kitchen full of people, the massive pots to be tended. But the kids' faces—and the sad truth they told about how rare and special the food was to them—made it easy to feel grateful for the opportunity to serve.

At the ashram, instead of saying "How was work?" we might ask,

"Have you served today?" If you were wondering what monk water-cooler talk sounds like—there you have it. Set aside the obstacles for a moment and imagine if everyone had a service mindset. We would ask ourselves new questions: *How does this serve a broader purpose? How am I serving the people around me—at work, at home, in my community? How can I use my talents to serve others and make a difference?* Remember Emma Slade, who uses her financial skills to serve her charity work, and ask yourself, "What do I know that is of any use?"

We have seen that happiness and gratitude spread through communities. The same is true for service. When you serve, you mention it to your friends. You might bring someone else with you. Someone joins you, and they tell two friends. When you participate in service, you do your part to spread the value of service in our culture.

Most people think about just one person: themselves. Maybe their radius of care is a bit bigger, including their immediate family. That's, maybe, five to ten people worrying about one another. But if you expand your radius of care, I believe that people feel it. If others extend their

TRY THIS: EXTEND YOUR RADIUS OF CARE

Think of four to six people you would drop everything to help. How often do you think about these people? Do you ever actually have a chance to show your care for them? Can you start?

Now think of twenty people you would help if they asked. Before you give up, let me make that easier for you. Think of a group containing at least twenty people whom you would help. It might be a segment of your community or a group that a charity already serves. Let's bring these people into a closer circle of care.

If you don't know them, research the names of twenty people in this group or find another way to compile a list of at least twenty names. Tape the list to the mirror where you brush your teeth. Now you'll think of them at least twice a day (I hope!). Observe how this changes your motivation to serve them.

radius of care to include you, I believe that you would feel it. And what if we dare to imagine that everyone were thinking like this? You would have some 7.8 billion people thinking about you, and vice versa. I don't see why we shouldn't dream big.

WHEN WILL YOU BE READY TO SERVE?

Out in the modern world, no matter how much we want to help others, we are distracted from the service mindset by the desire to be financially and emotionally stable and secure. If you're lost and disconnected, your service will be cumbersome and less fulfilling. But when is the time right? Will it ever be right? Internal exploration has no endpoint. It's an ongoing practice. Your problems will never be completely solved.

Take care of yourself—yes. But don't wait until you have enough time and money to serve. You will never have enough. There are three simple modes to describe our relationship with money and material wealth. The first is selfish—I want more—as much as I can get—and I want it all for myself. The second is sufficiency—I have just enough to get by. I'm not suffering, but I have nothing to give. The third is service—I want to give what I have, and I want more in order to give more.

Moving from the sufficiency mindset to the service mindset means changing our relationship with ownership—the more detached we are, the easier it is to let go of our time and money.

Some of our trips as monks were pilgrimages to bathe in the sacred rivers. I went to the Ganges, the Yamuna, and the Kaveri. We didn't swim or play in the holy waters. Instead, we performed rituals; one involved scooping as much water as we could into our hands, then putting it back in the river. We took from water to give back to water as a reminder that we didn't own anything. Charity isn't giving of yourself. You're taking something that was already on earth and giving it back to earth. **You don't have to have to give.**

Sindhutai Sapkal was married at twelve to a thirty-year-old man. When she was twenty years old, with three sons, nine months pregnant, she was beaten and thrown into a cow shed. She gave birth there, cutting her own umbilical cord with a sharp rock. Shunned by her maternal village, she lived on the streets with her newborn, begging and singing for money. She was struck by the number of orphans she saw and took them under her wing. She began begging on their behalf as well as her own. Her efforts grew, and she became known as the "Mother of Orphans." Her organizations have now housed and helped more than fourteen hundred children in India. Sindhutai didn't serve because she had something to give. She served because she saw pain.

In a series of experiments, researchers at University of California, Berkeley, found that people with less money actually tend to give more. In one situation, people were given $10 and told they could choose an amount to share with an anonymous stranger. People who were lower in socioeconomic status were more generous than wealthier participants. These findings are backed up by a survey of charitable giving in 2011, which showed that Americans in the bottom percentage of income gave, on average, 3 percent of their earnings to charity where people in the top 20 percent gave half that—1 percent. (Just to be fair, the wealthy are still responsible for over 70 percent of charitable contributions.)

Why those with less give more may have to do with their exposure to hardship. UC Berkeley professor of psychology Dacher Keltner says that people with fewer resources tend to need to lean on others—family members, friends, those in their community—for help. Those with more money, conversely, can "buy" help and are therefore more distanced from this kind of day-to-day struggle. The poor may have greater empathy for others in need. Some philanthropists, such as Oprah Winfrey, have mentioned their own prior experience of poverty as a motivation for giving.

The question to contemplate is: Who is wealthier, the one with money or the one who serves?

SERVE WITH INTENTION

I had come to the ashram to serve, and when I was saying my goodbyes, one monk who had been a like a big brother to me took me aside. He said something like, "If your health and being a monk isn't right for you, that doesn't mean you can't serve. If you feel you can serve better by being married or becoming a chef or darning socks for the needy, that takes priority. Service to humanity is the higher goal." His words reassured me that just because I was leaving didn't mean my intention had to change.

One can serve with a mix of intentions, broad and narrow. We might do it to be liked, to feel good about ourselves, to look good, to connect with other people, to receive some kind of reward. But if you're out there helping your friends move, cooking for them, celebrating them, and then you wonder, *Why doesn't anyone come help me?* or *Why did everyone forget my birthday?*—you've missed the point. You're seeing yourself as the giver and them as the receiver and imagining that when service is done, a debt is created. True service doesn't expect or even want anything in return. Nonetheless, the service itself often yields happiness, as both the Bhagavad Gita and the science show. When I do something to serve you, and you're happy, I'm happy.

But is service selfish if it brings you joy? Is it selfish if it teaches your children a lesson? Of course not! If a certain kind of giving makes you happy or benefits you in some way, that's a great place to start. After I left the ashram, I led retreats from London to Mumbai, giving people from the UK and other parts of Europe a chance to serve "midday meals" with Annamrita. One man who came on a retreat with me brought his kids, aged thirteen and fourteen. They returned from that trip having witnessed and felt the gratitude of people who didn't have much in their lives. The father was thrilled at how transformed his kids were. His trip was not completely selfless—he wanted his children to learn and grow—but it was still the right thing to do. In fact, the learning opportunity he saw for his children is an example of the mutual benefits of service.

The problems that some of us face are mental—anxiety, depression, loneliness—whereas for many of the people in need of service the great-est challenges are more basic—food, clothing, shelter. We can heal our mental challenges by helping them with their physical needs. Service, therefore, is a reciprocal exchange. You're not saving anyone by helping them—you need help as much as they do.

When we're in service, we're an instrument of grace and compassion. We feel this, and sometimes it goes to our heads. But remember that whatever you are giving was given to you. When you pass it on, you can't take credit for it.

SERVE WITHIN YOUR DHARMA

Because service is a natural part of being human, it's easier than you think. **Just serve.** We can always, every day—right now!—find ways to serve through what we're already doing. If you're a musician, serve. If you're a coder, serve. If you're an entrepreneur, serve. You don't have to change your occupation. You don't have to change your schedule. You can serve from any situation.

If you look around, you will see opportunities for service everywhere: in schools, at religious institutions, with individuals on the street, chari-ties. There are neighborhood food drives and used costume drives at school. You can run a race to raise money for charity or have a lemonade stand. You can help a friend gather toiletries to send to disaster victims. You can visit a sick or aging relative. If you live in a city, you can often carry your leftovers out of a restaurant and offer them to a homeless per-son. Those closest to us, and those who have nobody—there are infinite ways to serve. You don't have to do charity work every day or give away all your money. Simply realize you're in service and look for how you can connect what you already do to a higher purpose. Just as you bring your dharma to work, bring service to your dharma. It's about the spirit in which you do the same work. You can either see the world through the lens of love and duty, or through the lens of necessity and force. Love and duty are more likely to lead to happiness.

TRY THIS: WAYS TO SERVE

Over the course of a week, write down every place where you spend time. Open your eyes to the service opportunities by looking for one in every circumstance. Sometimes it is a need that you spot, sometimes it is an existing project you can join, sometimes it is attaching a fundraiser to an activity you already do, sometimes it is a friend's service effort. At the end of the week, pick the three opportunities that interest you most and reach out to one of them.

Here are some sample places where you can look for opportunities:

Work
School
Social event with friend(s)
Online community
Religious or other community group
Gym
Requests for help from a cause you've supported in the past

ALL SUFFERING BELONGS TO ALL OF US

When the monks and I were fending for ourselves in the village, the ultimate lesson for me was that there was always another level of service. This lesson emerged from looking past our own needs to see and feel and respond to the needs of those around us.

I think of compassion as *active* empathy—not only the willingness to see, feel, and ease the pain of others, but also the willingness to take on some of that pain. There is a Zen story about a young man who is world-weary and dejected. With no plan or prospects, he goes to a monastery, tells the master that he is hoping to find a better path, but he admits that he lacks patience. "Can I find enlightenment without all that meditation and fasting?" he asks. "I don't think I can handle it. Is there another way?"

"Perhaps," says the master, "But you will need the ability to focus. Are there any skills you've developed?"

The young man looks down. He hasn't been inspired by his studies or any particular interests. Finally, he shrugs. "Well, I'm not bad at chess."

The master calls over one of the monk elders and says, "I'd like you and this young man to play a game of chess. Play carefully, because I will cut off the head of the one who loses."

The young man breaks into a sweat. He's playing for his life! He plays weakly at first, but it soon becomes clear that his opponent's chess skills are fair at best. If he puts his mind to it, he will surely win. He soon loses himself in concentration and begins to beat the old monk. The master begins to sharpen his sword.

Now the young man looks across the table, sees the wise, calm face of the old monk, who in his obedience and detachment has no fear of the death that certainly awaits him. The disillusioned man thinks, *I can't be responsible for this man's death. His life is worth more than mine.* Then the young man's play changes—he deliberately begins to lose.

Without warning, the master flips the table over, scattering the pieces. "Today there will be no winner, and no loser," he states. The losing monk's calm demeanor doesn't change, but the astonished young man feels a great sense of relief. The elder says to him, "You have the ability to concentrate, and you are willing to give your life for another. That is compassion. Join us and proceed in that spirit. You are ready to be a monk."

There are approximately 152 million child laborers in the world, and Kailash Satyarthi has taken on an enormous amount of pain in his effort to end child labor. In 2016 the Nobel Peace Laureate launched the 100 Million, a campaign to enlist 100 million young people to speak out and act against child labor. In the course of his work he has been threatened and beaten many times. He says, "The world is capable to end child labor. We have the technology. We have the resources. We have laws and international treaties. We have everything. The only thing is that we have to feel compassion for others. My struggle is for the globalization of compassion."

Like Satyarthi, we are motivated to serve when we think of the whole world as one family. You wouldn't want your child to be enslaved or your parent to be homeless. Why would you want those hardships for anyone else's child or parent? If you stay shut in your world and never see how other people live, you'll never be focused on service. When we bear witness to other people's pain, we feel our shared humanity and are motivated to take action.

For heroes like Satyarthi and for monks—and ideally for all of us—there is no us and them.

FOLLOW THE PAIN IN YOUR HEART

An infinite number of people and causes need our help now. We need everyone in the world to do everything. The benefits to them and us are immediate.

While we should never avoid helping others when we see their need, we can and should develop a sense of what sorts of service we're best at and focus our attention on them. Choose where to serve based on your own compassion. Buddhist scholar and environmental activist Joanna Macy writes, "You don't need to do everything. Do what calls your heart; effective action comes from love. It is unstoppable, and it is enough."

TRY THIS: SERVE THE PAIN THAT YOU KNOW BEST

One route to service is through healing the pain that we know best. Write down three moments in your life when you felt lost or in need. Maybe you were depressed and could have used support. Maybe you wanted an education you couldn't afford. Maybe you needed guidance but didn't have the right teacher. Match a charity or cause to each area of pain. A teen hotline. A scholarship fund. A mentoring program. A politician. Now see if any of these options have opportunities to serve that suit your dharma.

Serving through your dharma, healing the pain that you connect with—this approach is very much in line with the philosophy of the Bhagavad Gita, which likes to meet you wherever you are and encourage you to reach higher. When I was a monk, I prepared food for children with Annamrita, cleaned temples, always carried food to hand out to strangers, and otherwise served in the ways that made sense for me at the time. Now, with a different platform, I've been able to help a YouTube campaign raise nearly $150,000 for the Kailash Satyarthi Children's Foundation of America. On Facebook my community raised over $60,000 for Pencils of Promise. ($75 provides a year of education for one child.) The sense of meaning and gratitude I feel has been constant as my path of giving evolves.

Here's the life hack: Service is always the answer. It fixes a bad day. It tempers the burdens we bear. Service helps other people and helps us. We don't expect anything in return, but what we get is the joy of service. It's an exchange of love.

When you're living in service, you don't have time to complain and criticize.

When you're living in service, your fears go away.

When you're living in service, you feel grateful. Your material attachments diminish.

Service is the direct path to a meaningful life.

MEDITATION

CHANT

We have explored how to connect to people around us through gratitude, relationships, and service. As we do this it is fitting to incorporate sound meditation into our practice to connect with the energy of the universe.

Sound transports us. A song can take us back to a high school memory, make us want to dance, get us fired up. Words themselves have power—they can change how we see the world and how we grow. When we chant, we ourselves are generating this energy. Sound meditations allow us to connect with our souls and the universe through words and song.

Ancient spiritual texts including the Agni Purana and the Vayu Purana discuss the why and how of chanting, suggesting that the repetition of sound purifies us. The sound is immersive, like giving our souls a regular bath. You can't put one drop of water on your body and be clean— you have to go underneath the water.

Recognizing the value of sound has carried through to modern times. Legendary inventor Nikola Tesla said, "If you want to find the secrets of the universe, think in terms of energy, frequency, and vibration." Tesla experimented extensively with machines that created healing fields using vibrations. That may strike you as a bit woo-woo, but modern science is actually resurrecting Tesla's research on vibrational healing. Modern brain research is also starting to uncover scientific explanations for the healing power of ancient healing rituals, like how repetitive drumming and singing can open pathways to the subconscious.

Monks harness the power of sound by repeating affirmations or mantras during meditation. An affirmation is a word or phrase you want to set as an intention. Virtually anything that inspires you can work. One of my clients says her favorite is: "At your own pace, in your own time." A friend of mine read a book called *Brave, Not Perfect* by Reshma Saujani and made the title her mantra for a while. I also like: "This too shall pass." Or a phrase from a poet, such as "Live everything" (by Rilke); a sports quote, like "This moment is yours" (from Olympic ice hockey coach Herb Brooks); a song lyric, like "Brush your shoulders off" (by Jay-Z), something from a movie, like "Woosah" (courtesy of *Bad Boys II*). Anything that connects you to the energy or idea you want to cultivate in your life can be effective. I recommend adding a mantra to your morning and/or evening meditation practice. It is beautiful to wake up or go to sleep listening to the sound of your own voice chanting.

Where affirmations change the way you speak to yourself, mantras change the way you speak to the universe. *Mantra* in a deep sense means "to transcend the mind," and a mantra is a spiritual sound expressing thought and meaning that summons a power greater than ourselves. Mantras can be chanted or sung in unison. We meditate to listen and find clarity. We pray to share and find connection with a higher power. Chanting is both—a dialogue with the universe.

The oldest, most common, and most sacred mantra is Om. In Vedic texts the sound is given many shades of meaning, from infinite knowledge to the essence of everything that exists to the whole Veda. Om also is called *pranava*, whose meaning can be described as "the sound by which the Lord is praised." In chanting, om comprises three syllables—A-U-M. In Vedic tradition, this is important because each sound embodies a different state (wakefulness, dreaming, and deep sleep) or period of time itself (past, present, and future). You could say that the word *om* represents everything.

The vibrations from om have been shown to stimulate the vagus nerve, which decreases inflammation. Vagus nerve stimulation is also used as a treatment for depression, and researchers are looking at whether chanting om may have a direct effect on mood. (It's already been shown to calm one of the brain's emotional centers.)

When a mantra is put to music it's called *kirtan*, a type of call-and-response chanting, which we often used at the ashram. A similar experience is fans chanting in a stadium—minus the alcohol and foul language. But the atmosphere that can be created has the same feeling of united energy.

Though sound itself is of value, when I temporarily lost my voice for medical reasons, I reached out to a monk teacher. I said, "I can't chant mantras. How can I meditate?"

He said, "Chanting was never from your mouth. It was always from your heart." He meant that, as with all acts, what mattered was whether the intention was full of devotion and love. The heart transcends instructions and perfection.

TRY THIS: SEEING THROUGH SOUND

For the sound exercises I describe below, begin your practice with the following steps.

1. Find a comfortable position—sitting in a chair, sitting upright with a cushion, or lying down.
2. Close your eyes.
3. Lower your gaze.
4. Make yourself comfortable in this position.

5. Bring your awareness to calm, balance, ease, stillness, and peace.

6. Whenever your mind wanders, just gently and softly bring it back to calm, balance, ease, stillness, and peace.

7. Chant each of these mantras three times each. When you chant them, bring your attention to each syllable. Pronounce it properly so that you can hear the vibration clearly. Really feel the mantra, repeating it genuinely and sincerely, and visualizing a more insightful, blessed, and service-filled life.

1. OM NAMO BHAGAVATE VASUDEVAYA

"I offer praise unto the all-pervading divinity present within every heart; who is the embodiment of beauty, intelligence, strength, wealth, fame, and detachment."

This mantra has been chanted for millennia by yogis and sages. It is cleansing and empowering, and connects one with the divinity in everything. It can be recited especially when you are seeking insight and guidance.

2. OM TAT SAT

"The absolute truth is eternal."

This mantra appears in the Bhagavad Gita. It represents divine energy and invokes powerful blessings. All work is performed as an offering of love and service. This mantra is recited especially before beginning any important work, to help perfect and refine our intentions and bring about balance and wholeness.

3. LOKAH SAMASTAH SUKHINO BHAVANTU

"May all beings everywhere be happy and free, and may the thoughts, words, and actions of my own life contribute in some way to that happiness and to that freedom for all."

This mantra, popularized by Jivamukti yoga, is a beautiful reminder to look beyond ourselves and to remember our place in the universe.

Conclusion

I hope this book has inspired you, and perhaps you will come away from it planning a fresh start. Maybe you're thinking about how to change your routines, to listen to your mind in new ways, to bring more gratitude into your life, and more. But when you wake up tomorrow, things will go wrong. You might sleep through your alarm. Something will break. An important appointment will cancel. The universe isn't going to suddenly give you green lights all the way to work. It's a mistake to think that when we read a book, attend a class, and implement changes that we'll fix everything. The externals will never be perfect, and the goal isn't perfection. Life is not going to go your way. You have to go your way and take life with you. Understanding this will help you be prepared for whatever may come.

There is no universal plan for peace and purpose. The way we get there is by training our minds to focus on how to react, respond, and commit to what we want in life, in our own pace, at our own time. Then, when life swerves, we return to that focus. If you've decided to be kind, and someone is rude to you, you know what you want to come back to. If you wake up resolved to focus on your dharma at work, and then your boss gives you an assignment that's not aligned with your strengths, it's up to you to find a way to put your dharma to use. When you fail, don't judge the process and don't judge yourself. Give yourself latitude to recover and return to a flexible focus on what you want. The world isn't with you or against you. You create your own reality in every moment.

Throughout this book, we have encountered paradoxes. We talk about getting close to fear to move away from it, finding the new in our routines, having confidence and humility, being selfish to be selfless. We live in a binary world, but the beauty of paradox is that two opposing ideas can coexist. Life isn't a computer program—it's a dance.

In *The Karate Kid*, Mr. Miyagi says, "Never trust [a] spiritual leader who cannot dance." When we dance, there are no rules. We must be open to whatever song comes on. We have strengths and weaknesses. We might fall, or hesitate over our next move, or have a moment of overenthusiasm, but we keep flowing, allowing ourselves to be messy and beautiful. Like a dancer, the monk mind is flexible and controlled, always present in the moment.

THE MONK METHOD

I can think of no better tool to help you find flexibility and control than meditation. Meditation helps you figure out what move to make in the dance. In meditation, we find clarity on who we need to be right now, in order to be our best in the moment. Our breath connects with our minds, our souls are uplifted in song, and in that place of energy and unity, we find answers.

I have introduced you to three different types of meditation, and now I'm going to give you a daily practice that includes all of them: breathwork, visualization, and chanting. I practice some form of this meditation every day. I recommend that you make it the first thing you do in the morning after brushing your teeth and showering, and last thing you do before bed. Start with twenty-one minutes once a day, using a timer to give yourself seven minutes each for breathwork, visualization, and mantra. When you are ready for more, expand to twenty-one minutes twice a day, ideally first thing in the morning and last thing at night. Make sure you always begin with breathwork. Like a warm-up before you exercise, it should not be skipped!

1. Find a comfortable position—sitting in a chair, sitting upright with a cushion, or lying down.

2. Close your eyes and lower your gaze. Bring your awareness to calm, balance, ease, stillness, and peace. It is natural for the chatter and clutter to be busy in your mind. Whenever your mind wanders, just gently and softly bring it back to calm, balance, ease, stillness, and peace.

3. Make yourself comfortable in this position. Roll back your shoulders, stretch your neck and body, and find a physical space of calm, balance, ease, stillness, and peace.

4. Now become aware of your natural breathing pattern. Breathe in through your nose and out through your mouth.

5. Take a deep breath. Breathe in for a count of 1 - 2 - 3 - 4. Breathe out for a count of 1 - 2 - 3 - 4.

6. Align your body and your breath by breathing in for the same amount of time as you breathe out.

7. Do this for what feels like five minutes. At first you might want to set a timer with a pleasant tone to signal that the five minutes have passed.

8. Ask yourself, "What am I grateful for today?" Breathe in gratitude and breathe out negative, toxic energy.

9. Now visualize a joy-, happiness-, and gratitude-filled memory. Think of five things you can see, four things you can touch, three things you can hear, two things you can smell, and one thing you can taste. Absorb the love, joy, and happiness. Take the love from that moment and visualize it flowing through your entire body. From your feet, to your legs, to your hips, to your stomach, to your chest, arms, back, neck, and head. Give love, joy, and gratitude to each part of your body. Do this for five minutes.

10. Ask yourself, "What is my intention for today?" Is it to be kind, to be confident, to be focused? Set that intention now.

11. Repeat the following to yourself 3 times each: "I am happy about who I am becoming. I am open to all opportunities and possibilities. I am worthy of real love. I am ready to serve with all I have."

12. To finish your practice, repeat this mantra 3 times: *Lokah Samastah Sukhino Bhavantu*. (See page 273.)

HOW TO KNOW IF IT'S WORKING

A novice monk went to his teacher and said, "I'm terrible at meditating. My feet fall asleep, and I'm distracted by the outside noises. When I'm not uncomfortable, it's because I can barely stay awake."

"It will pass," the teacher said simply, and by her expression the novice knew that the conversation was over.

A month passed, and the novice took his teacher aside, smiling proudly. "I think I've figured it out! I feel so serene—more focused and centered than I've ever been. My meditation is beautiful."

"It will pass," the teacher replied.

There is no measure of success, no goal, and no end to a meditation practice. Don't look for results. Just keep doing it. Practice consistently for four to twelve weeks, and you'll start to notice the effects.

The first sign that you're doing it right is that you'll miss it if you take a break. You only miss a person when you don't see them. When you eat every day, you don't think much about nourishment and fuel, but if you don't eat for a day, you quickly notice the power of food. The same is true for meditation—you have to develop a practice before you know what you're missing.

The second effect you'll notice is an increased awareness of what's going on in your mind. If you meditate and feel tired, you'll understand that meditation is telling you to get more sleep. Meditation is a signal or a mirror. If you meditate and can't focus, you'll see that you're living a distracted life and need to feel order, balance, and simplicity. If you can't sit with your thoughts for fifteen minutes, it's a clear indicator of the work to be done.

The third and most important benefit of meditation is that, though you won't emerge feeling calm and perfect every time, you'll gradually acquire a long-term mastery of self. When you drink a green juice, it doesn't always taste great. A nice glass of fresh orange juice looks better and tastes better. But, long-term, the less delightful green juice will better serve you. When you are adept at meditation, you'll feel a shift in your general attitude. Your intuition will be sharper. You'll be able to observe your life more objectively, without being self-centered. Your expanded perception will give you a sense of peace and purpose.

NOW AND FOREVER

Life begins with breath, breath carries you through all your days, and life and breath end together. Monks try to be present in the moment, but we are always conscious of now and forever. We measure our lives not by how big or small our impact is, but by how we make people feel. We use our time to establish how we will live on, through giving love and care, through supporting, communicating, creating—through the impact we have on humanity.

How will we be remembered? What will we leave behind?

Ultimately death can be seen as the greatest reflection point—by imagining the last moment you can reflect on everything that leads up to it.

Among the most common regrets dying people express are:

I wish I'd expressed my love to the people I care about.

I wish I hadn't worked so much.

I wish I'd taken more pleasure in life.

I wish I'd done more for other people.

Notice that most of these regrets address something the person *didn't* do. Monks believe we should prepare for death. We don't want to arrive at the end of our days knowing we haven't lived a purposeful, service-based, meaningful life.

Think of the topics we've considered in this book. In death, you should be fully cleansed, free of what you think you're supposed to do, free of comparison and criticism, having faced the root of your fear, free from material desires, living in your dharma, having used your time well, having not given in to the mind's demands, free from ego, having given more than you have taken, but then having given away all that you've taken, free from entitlement, free from false connections and expectations. Imagine how rewarding it will be to look back on a life where you have been a teacher while remaining a student.

Reflecting on the knowledge that we will die someday compels us to value the time we have and to spend our energy thoughtfully. Life's too short to live without purpose, to lose our chance to serve, to let our dreams and aspirations die with us. Above all, I ask you to leave people and places better and happier than you found them.

Working on ourselves is an unending practice. Have patience. A student went to her teacher and said, "I am committed to my dharma. How long will it take me to attain enlightenment?"

Without missing a beat, the teacher replied, "Ten years."

Impatient, the student persisted, "But what if I work very hard? I will practice, ten or more hours every day if I have to. Then how long will it take?"

This time the teacher took a moment to consider. "Twenty years."

The very idea that the student was looking to rush his work was evidence that he had ten extra years to study.

As I've mentioned, the Sanskrit word for monk, *brahmacharya*, means "student," but it also means "right use of energy." It's not like once you have the monk mindset, you've figured everything out. Instead, the monk mindset acknowledges that the right use of energy is to remain a student. You can never cease learning. You don't cut your hair or mow your lawn once. You have to keep at it. In the same way, *sustaining* the monk mindset requires self-awareness, discipline, diligence, focus, and constant practice. It is hard work, but the tools are already in your head, heart, and hands.

You have all you need to think like a monk.

TRY THIS: TWO DEATH MEDITATIONS

To imagine your own death gives you a bird's-eye view of your life. Try a death meditation whenever you are questioning whether or not to do something—to make a significant change, learn a new skill, take a trip. I recommend that you always do a death meditation at the beginning of a new year, to inspire new paths in the upcoming year.

1. Visualizing the inevitable will give you every lesson you need to live a fulfilling life. Fast-forward to yourself at age eighty or ninety, however long you want to live, and imagine yourself on your deathbed. Ask your future self questions such as:

   What do I wish I'd done?
   What experiences do I wish I'd had?
   What do I regret not giving more attention?
   What skills do I wish I'd worked on?
   What do I wish I'd detached from?

   Use these answers to motivate yourself—instead of having regrets on your deathbed, put those wishes into action today.

2. Imagine how you'd like to be remembered at your own funeral. Don't focus on what people thought of you, who loved you, and how sad they will be to lose you. Instead think about the impact you've had. Then imagine how you would be remembered if you died today. What's the gap between these two images? This too should galvanize you to build your legacy.

To find our way through the universe, we must start by genuinely asking questions. You might travel to a new place or go someplace where no one knows you. Disable your autopilot to see yourself and the world around you with new eyes. **Spot, Stop, Swap.** Train your mind to observe the forces that influence you, detach from illusion and false beliefs, and continually look for what motivates you and what feels meaningful.

What would a monk do in this moment?

When you're making a decision, when you're having an argument, when you're planning your weekend, when you're scared or upset or angry or lost, ask this question. You'll find the answer 99 percent of the time.

And eventually, when you've uncovered your real self, you won't even need to ask yourself what a monk would do. You can simply ask, "What will I do?"

Appendix

The Vedic Personality Test

Answer these questions as who you believe you are at the core. Beyond what friends, family, or society have made you choose.

1. Which of the following sounds *most* like what you're about?
a. Values and wisdom
b. Integrity and perfection
c. Work hard play hard
d. Stability and balance

2. What *role* do you play in your friends circle / family?
a. I am comfortable dealing with conflict and helping people find middle ground. My role is the mediator.
b. I make sure everything and everyone is taken care of. My role is the protector.
c. I help my family understand work ethic, hustle, and the value of having resources. My role is material support.
d. I focus on nurturing and wanting a healthy and content family. My role is emotional support.

3. What is most important to you in a partner?

a. Honest and smart

b. Strong presence and power

c. Fun and dynamic

d. Reliable and respectful

4. What do you watch most often on TV?

a. Documentaries, biographies, human observations

b. Entertainment, politics, current affairs

c. Comedy, sport, drama, motivational stories

d. Soap operas, reality TV, family, gossip, daytime shows

5. Which best describes how you behave when under stress?

a. Calm, composed, balanced

b. Irritated, frustrated, angry

c. Moody, loud, restless

d. Lazy, depressed, worried

6. What causes you the most pain?

a. Feeling like I don't live up to my own expectations

b. The state of the world

c. A sense of rejection

d. Feeling disconnected from friends and family

7. What is your favorite way of working?

a. Alone, but with mentors and guides

b. In a team as a leader

c. Independently, but with a strong network

d. In a team as a member

8. How would your *ideal* self spend spare time?

a. Reading, in deep discussion, and reflecting

b. Learning about issues and/or attending political events

c. There's no such thing as spare time! networking, connecting, working

d. Enjoying time with family and friends

9. How would you describe yourself in three words?
a. Idealistic, introverted, insightful
b. Driven, dedicated, determined
c. Passionate, motivated, friendly
d. Caring, loving, loyal

10. In what type of environment do you work best?
a. Remote, silent and still, natural
b. A meeting room or gathering space
c. Anywhere and everywhere (during my commute, in a coffee shop, in my bedroom)
d. A space specific to my type of work: home, office, laboratory

11. What's your work style?
a. Slow and reflective
b. Focused and organized
c. Fast and rushed
d. Specific and deliberate

12. How would you like to make a difference in the world?
a. Through spreading knowledge
b. Through politics and activism
c. Through business and/or leadership
d. Through local community

13. How do you prepare for a vacation?
a. By picking my reading material
b. By having a focused plan of key sites to visit
c. With a list of the best bars, clubs, and restaurants
d. With an easygoing attitude

14. How do you deal with tough conversations?
  a. Look for a compromise
  b. Fight for the most objective truth
  c. Fight to prove I'm right
  d. Avoid confrontation

15. If someone in your life is having a bad week, what do you do?
  a. Give them advice and guidance
  b. Become protective and encourage them to improve
  c. Urge them to have a drink or take a walk with me
  d. Go to them and keep them company

16. How do you see rejection?
  a. It's part of life
  b. It's a challenge I can rise to meet
  c. It's frustrating but I'll move on
  d. It's a real setback

17. At an event/party how do you spend your time?
  a. I have a meaningful discussion with one or two people
  b. I usually talk with a group of people
  c. I somehow end up the center of attention
  d. I help with whatever needs to be done

18. How do you feel if you make a mistake?
  a. I feel guilty and ashamed
  b. I have to tell everyone
  c. I want to hide it
  d. I reach out to someone supportive

19. What do you do when you have to make a big decision?
  a. I reflect privately
  b. I ask my mentors and guides

c. I weigh the pros and cons

d. I talk to family and friends

20. Which best describes your daily routine?
    a. It changes moment to moment
    b. It's very focused and organized
    c. I follow the best opportunity that comes up
    d. It's simple and scheduled

ANSWER KEY

Tally your answers now. The most selected letter likely reflects your *varna*.

A. Guide
B. Leader
C. Creator
D. Maker

Acknowledgments

I feel truly humbled and grateful to share this timeless and transformative wisdom with you, but I could not have done it alone. The Bhagavad Gita was compiled, preserved, shared, and resurrected by team efforts, and this book was no different. I'd like to thank Dan Schawbel, for introducing me to my amazing agent, James Levine, over three years ago. Jim is truly a wonderful human and deeply believes in every project that he works on. His direction, strategy, and friendship have made this book an extremely joyful journey. Thank you to Trudy Green, for her unlimited kindness, sleepless nights, and eternal dedication to this cause. To Eamon Dolan, for his already monk mind and unrelenting push for perfection. To Jon Karp, for believing in me and being present throughout the process. To Hilary Liftin, for the collaborative conversations and dynamic discussions. To Kelly Madrone, for her undying enthusiasm and can-do attitude. To Rula Zaabri, for making sure I never missed a deadline. To Ben Kalin, for his relentless commitment to checking the facts. Thank you, Christie Young, for bringing these timeless concepts to life through the beautiful illustrations. To the Oxford Center for Hindu Studies and specifically Shaunaka Rishi Das for assisting in verifying our sources and credits. Thank you to Laurie Santos for her kindness in connecting me with research on monks by some of the world's leading scientists. To the whole team at Simon & Schuster, who left no gaps in bringing my vision to life. To Oliver Malcolm and his team at HarperCollins UK, for their enthusiasm, dedication, and hard work from the start.

Thank you to Thomas Power, who pushed me to recognize my potential when I didn't believe in myself. To Ellyn Shook, for believing in my passion and introducing my work to Arianna Huffington. To Danny Shea and Dan Katz, who helped me launch my career at *HuffPost*. To Karah Preiss, who was the first person I told about the idea for this book, in 2016, and who became my ideation partner and greatest supporter in the US. To Savannah, Hoda, Craig, Al, and Carson, for giving me their collective attention on the *Today* show. To Ellen, for believing in me and giving me her platform to reach her audience. To Jada Pinkett Smith, Willow Smith, and Adrienne Banfield-Norris, for bringing me to the Red Table.

I've truly had an amazing few years, but everything you've seen online has only been possible due to the people that invested in me offline. Thank you to His Holiness Radhanath Swami, for always reminding me of the true meaning of life. To Gauranga Das, who has seen it all and been there for me since Day One. To my mentor Srutidharma Das, who always, no matter what, displays all the qualities in this book to the highest level. To Sutapa Das, who always encouraged me to write when I told him I just wanted to speak. To the guides I long to meet and thank, His Holiness the Dalai Lama and Thich Nhat Hanh. To all who have allowed me to mentor you, in that process you have taught me so much more than I could ever have imagined.

This book would not have existed without the Vedas, the Bhagavad Gita, and the teachers who tirelessly spread it across the world. Thank you to Srila Prabhupada and Ekanath Easwaran, who have created the most widely distributed Gitas today. To all my teachers in the ashram and across the world, many of whom have no idea how much they've given me.

To my mother, who is the embodiment of selfless service. To my father, who let me become who I wanted to be. To my sister, for always supporting my crazy decisions and loving me no matter what.

And, of course, to each and every one of you who has read this book. You were already thinking like monks, now you know it.

Author's Note

In this book I have drawn from the wisdom of many religions, cultures, inspirational leaders, and scientists. In every case I have done my very best to attribute quotes and ideas to their original sources, and these efforts are reflected here. In some cases I have come across wonderful quotes or ideas that I have found attributed to multiple different sources, widely attributed with no specified source, or attributed to ancient texts where I could not locate the original verse. In these cases I have, with the help of a researcher, tried to give the reader as much useful information as I could regarding the source of the material.

Notes

INTRODUCTION

ix **plant trees under whose shade:** Paraphrase of Nelson Henderson from Wes Henderson, *Under Whose Shade: A Story of a Pioneer in the Swan River Valley of Manitoba* (Ontario, Canada: W. Henderson & Associates, 1986).

x **In 2002, a Tibetan monk named Yongey Mingyur Rinpoche:** Daniel Goleman and Richard J. Davidson, *Altered Traits: Science Reveals How Meditation Changes Your Mind, Brain, and Body* (New York: Penguin Random House, 2017); Antoine Lutz, Lawrence L. Greischar, Nancy B. Rawlings, Matthieu Ricard, and Richard J. Davidson, "Long-Term Meditators Self-Induce High-Amplitude Gamma Synchronicity During Mental Practice," *Proceedings of the National Academy of Sciences* 101, no. 46 (November 16, 2004): 16369–16373, https://doi.org/10.1073/pnas.0407401101.

xi **scans of the forty-one-year-old monk's brain showed fewer signs of aging than his peers':** Goleman and Davidson, *Altered Traits.*

xi **Researchers who scanned Buddhist monk Matthieu Ricard's brain:** Frankie Taggart, "This Buddhist Monk Is the World's Happiest Man," *Business Insider*, November 5, 2012. https://www.businessinsider.com/how-scientists -figured-out-who-the-worlds-happiest-man-is-2012-11; Daniel Goleman and Richard J. Davidson, *Altered Traits: Science Reveals How Meditation Changes Your Mind, Brain, and Body* (New York: Penguin Random House, 2017); Antoine Lutz, Lawrence L. Greischar, Nancy B. Rawlings, Matthieu Ricard, and Richard J. Davidson, "Long-Term Meditators Self-Induce High-Amplitude Gamma Synchronicity During Mental Practice,"

Proceedings of the National Academy of Sciences 101, no. 46 (November 16, 2004): 16369–16373, https://doi.org/10.1073/pnas.0407401101.

xi **Twenty-one other monks:** Taggart, "This Buddhist Monk" and Lutz et al., "Long-Term Meditators."

xi **even during sleep:** Fabio Ferrarelli, Richard Smith, Daniela Dentico, Brady A. Riedner, Corinna Zennig, Ruth M. Benca, Antoine Lutz, Richard J. Davidson, and Guilio Tononi, "Experienced Mindfulness Meditators Exhibit Higher Parietal-Occipital EEG Gamma Activity During NREM Sleep," *PLoS One* 8, no. 8 (August 28, 2013): e73417, https://doi.org/10.1371/journal.pone.0073417.

xii **Brother David Steindl-Rast, a Benedictine monk:** David Steindl-Rast, *i am through you so i: Reflections at Age 90* (New York: Paulist Press, 2017), 87.

xiv **"India's most important gift to the world":** And general background on Vedic times from *The Bhagavad Gita*, introduction and translation by Eknath Easwaran (Tomales, CA: Nilgiri Press, 2007), 13–18.

xiv **"I owed—my friend and I owed":** Ralph Waldo Emerson, *The Bhagavad-Gita: Krishna's Counsel in Time of War*, translation, introduction, and afterword by Barbara Stoler Miller (New York: Bantam Dell, 1986), 147.

ONE: IDENTITY

3 **"I am not what I think I am":** Charles Horton Cooley, *Human Nature and the Social Order* (New York: Charles Scribner's Sons, 1902), 152.

4 **six films since 1998:** Daniel Day-Lewis filmography, IMDb, accessed November 8, 2019, https://www.imdb.com/name/nm0000358/?ref_=fn_al_nm_1.

4 **"I will admit that I went mad, totally mad":** Chris Sullivan, "How Daniel Day-Lewis's Notorious Role Preparation Has Yielded Another Oscar Contender," *Independent*, February 1, 2008, https://www.independent.co.uk/arts-entertainment/films/features/how-daniel-day-lewis-notoriously-rigorous-role-preparation-has-yielded-another-oscar-contender-776563.html.

8 **the words of Chaitanya:** Śrī Caitanya-caritāmṛta, Antya, 20.21.

8 **The foundation of virtually all monastic traditions:** "Social and Institutional Purposes: Conquest of the Spiritual Forces of Evil," Encyclopaedia Britannica, accessed November 8, 2019, https://www.britannica.com/topic/monasticism/Social-and-institutional-purposes.

11 **Our inclination is to avoid silence:** Timothy D. Wilson, David A. Reinhard, Erin C. Westgate, Daniel T. Gilbert, Nicole Ellerbeck, Cheryl Hahn, Casey L. Brown, and Adi Shaked, "Just Think: The Challenges of the Disengaged Mind," *Science* 345, no. 6192 (July 4, 2014): 75–77, doi: 10.1126/science.1250830.

12   spend thirty-three years in bed: Gemma Curtis, "Your Life in Numbers," Creative Commons, accessed November 15, 2019, https://www.dreams.co .uk/sleep-matters-club/your-life-in-numbers-nfographic/?tduid=9109abe 2605a4ac24f8f7f685d2df261&utm_source=tradedoubler&utm_medium =Skimbit+UK&utm_content=1503186.

13   looking at TV and social media: Ibid.

15   According to the Gita, these are the higher values and qualities: Verses 16.1–5 from *The Bhagavad Gita*, introduction and translation by Eknath Easwaran (Tomales, CA: Nilgiri Press, 2007), 238–239.

18   A twenty-year study of people living in a Massachusetts town: James H. Fowler and Nicholas A. Christakis, "Dynamic Spread of Happiness in a Large Social Network: Longitudinal Analysis over 20 Years in the Framingham Heart Study," *BMJ* 337, no. a2338 (December 5, 2008), doi: https:// doi.org/10.1136/bmj.a2338.

TWO: NEGATIVITY

21   As the Buddha advised: Verse 4.50 from *The Dhammapada*, introduction and translation by Eknath Easwaran (Tomales, CA: Nilgiri Press, 2007), 118.

23   Stanford psychologists took 104 subjects: Emily M. Zitek, Alexander H. Jordan, Benoît Monin, and Frederick R. Leach, "Victim Entitlement to Behave Selfishly," *Journal of Personality and Social Psychology* 98, no. 2 (2010): 245–255, doi: 10.1037/a0017168.

24   In the 1950s Solomon Asch: Eliot Aronson and Joshua Aronson, *The Social Animal*, 12th edition (New York: Worth Publishers, 2018).

24   We're wired to conform: Zhenyu Wei, Zhiying Zhao, and Yong Zheng, "Neural Mechanisms Underlying Social Conformity," *Frontiers in Human Neuroscience* 7 (2013): 896, doi: 10.3389/fnhum.2013.00896.

24   even people who report feeling better after venting: Brad J. Bushman, "Does Venting Anger Feed or Extinguish the Flame? Catharsis, Rumination, Distraction, Anger, and Aggressive Responding," *Personality and Social Psychology Bulletin* (June 1, 2002), doi: 10.1177/0146167202289002.

25   Studies also show that long-term stress: Robert M. Sapolsky, "Why Stress Is Bad for Your Brain," *Science* 273, no. 5276 (August 9, 1996): 749–750, doi: 10.1126/science.273.5276.749.

28   Catholic monk Father Thomas Keating said: Thomas Keating, *Invitation to Love 20th Anniversary Edition: The Way of Christian Contemplation* (London: Bloomsbury Continuum, 2012).

29   "Letting go gives us freedom": Thich Nhat Hanh, *The Heart of the Buddha's Teaching: Transforming Suffering into Peace, Joy, and Liberation* (New York: Harmony, 1999).

30 **"Don't count the teeth"**: Arthur Jeon, *City Dharma: Keeping Your Cool in the Chaos* (New York: Crown Archetype, 2004), 120.

31 **Sister Christine Vladimiroff says**: Hannah Ward and Jennifer Wild, eds., *The Monastic Way: Ancient Wisdom for Contemporary Living: A Book of Daily Readings* (Grand Rapids, MI: Wm. B. Eerdmans, 2007), 183.

31 **Competition breeds envy**: William Buck, *Mahabharata* (Delhi: Motilal Banarsidass Publishers, 2004), 341.

35 **The Vaca Sutta, from early Buddhist scriptures**: Thanissaro Bhikku, trans., "Vaca Sutta: A Statement," AccesstoInsight.org, accessed November 11, 2019, https://www.accesstoinsight.org/tipitaka/an/an05/an05.198.than.html.

36 **writing in a journal about upsetting events**: Bridget Murray, "Writing to Heal: By Helping People Manage and Learn from Negative Experiences, Writing Strengthens Their Immune Systems as Well as Their Minds," *Monitor on Psychology* 33, no. 6 (June 2002): 54.

36 **the *Harvard Business Review* lists nine more specific words**: Susan David, "3 Ways to Better Understand Your Emotions," *Harvard Business Review*, November 10, 2016, https://hbr.org/2016/11/3-ways-to-better-understand -your-emotions.

37 **Radhanath Swami is my spiritual teacher**: Radanath Swami, interview by Jay Shetty, *#FollowTheReader with Jay Shetty*, *HuffPost*, November 7, 2016, https://www.youtube.com/watch?v=JW1Am81L0wc.

39 **The Bhagavad Gita describes three *gunas***: Verse 14.5–9 from *The Bhagavad Gita*, introduction and translation by Eknath Easwaran (Tomales, CA: Nilgiri Press, 2007), 224–225.

40 **Research at Luther College**: Loren L. Toussaint, Amy D. Owen, and Alyssa Cheadle, "Forgive to Live: Forgiveness, Health, and Longevity," *Journal of Behavioral Medicine* 35, no. 4 (August 2012), 375–386. doi: 10.1007/s10865-011-9632-4.

41 **Transformational forgiveness is linked**: Kathleen A. Lawler, Jarred W. Younger, Rachel L. Piferi, Rebecca L. Jobe, Kimberly A. Edmondson, and Warren H. Jones, "The Unique Effects of Forgiveness on Health: An Exploration of Pathways," *Journal of Behavioral Medicine* 28, no. 2 (April 2005): 157–167, doi: 10.1007/s10865-005-3665-2.

41 **sixty-eight married couples agreed**: Peggy A. Hannon, Eli J. Finkel, Madoka Kumashiro, and Caryl E. Rusbult, "The Soothing Effects of Forgiveness on Victims' and Perpetrators' Blood Pressure," *Personal Relationships* 19, no. 2 (June 2012): 279–289, doi: 10.1111/j.1475-6811.2011.01356.x.

44 **"I became a Buddhist because I hated my husband"**: Pema Chödrön, "Why I Became a Buddhist," *Sounds True*, February 14, 2008, https://www.you tube.com/watch?v=A4slnjvGjP4&t=117s; Pema Chödrön, "How to Let

Go and Accept Change," interview by Oprah Winfrey, *Super Soul Sunday*, Oprah Winfrey Network, October 15, 2014. https://www.youtube.com/watch?v=SgJ1xfhJneA.

44 **Ellen DeGeneres sees the line clearly:** Anne-Marie O'Neill, "Ellen De-Generes: 'Making People Feel Good Is All I Ever Wanted to Do,'" *Parade*, October 27, 2011, https://parade.com/133518/annemarieoneill/ellen-degeneres-2/.

THREE: FEAR

46 **his commencement address at Yale University:** "Tom Hanks Addresses the Yale Class of 2011," Yale University, May 22, 2011, https://www.youtube.com/watch?v=baIlinqoExQ.

49 **one of the world's leading security experts:** Gavin de Becker, *The Gift of Fear* (New York: Dell, 1998).

50 **Biosphere 2:** Tara Brach, "Nourishing Heartwood: Two Pathways to Culti-vating Intimacy," *Psychology Today*, August 6, 2018, https://www.psychologytoday.com/us/blog/finding-true-refuge/201808/nourishing-heartwood.

50 **Alex Honnold stunned the world:** *Free Solo*, directed by Jimmy Chin and Elizabeth Chai Vasarhelyi, Little Monster Films and Itinerant Films, 2018.

56 **In the words of Śāntideva:** Śāntideva, *A Guide to the Bodhisattva Way of Life*, trans. Vesna A. Wallace and B. Alan Wallace (New York: Snow Lion, 1997).

60 **deep breathing activates:** Christopher Bergland, "Deep Breathing Exer-cises and Your Vagus Nerve," *Psychology Today*, May 16, 2017, https://www.psychologytoday.com/us/blog/the-athletes-way/201705/diaphragmatic-breathing-exercises-and-your-vagus-nerve.

62 **"What you run from":** Chuck Palahniuk, *Invisible Monsters Remix* (New York: W. W. Norton & Company, 2018).

63 **one of the largest producers:** "Basic Information About Landfill Gas," Landfill Methane Outreach Program, accessed November 12, 2019, https://www.epa.gov/lmop/basic-information-about-landfill-gas.

FOUR: INTENTION

65 **"When there is harmony":** Some sources attribute this to commentaries on the Rig Veda.

66 **four fundamental motivations:** Bhaktivinoda Thakura, "The Nectarean Instructions of Lord Caitanya," *Hari kírtan*, June 12, 2010, https://kirtan.estranky.cz/clanky/philosophy---english/sri-sri-caitanya--siksamrta--the-nectarean-instructions-of-the-lord-caitanya.html.

68 **American spiritual luminary Tara Brach:** Tara Brach, "Absolute Coopera-tion with the Inevitable: Aligning with what is here is a way of practicing

presence. It allows us to respond to our world with creativity and compassion," *HuffPost*, November 4, 2013, https://www.huffpost.com/entry/happiness-tips_b_4213151.

69 **derived from a poem by Kabir:** Kabir, "'Of the Musk Deer': 15th Century Hindi Poems," Zócalo Poets, accessed November 11, 2019, https://zocalopoets.com/2012/04/11/kabir-of-the-musk-deer-15th-century-hindi-poems/.

69 **money does not buy happiness:** Daniel Kahneman and Angus Deaton, "High Income Improves Evaluation of Life But Not Emotional Well-Being," *PNAS* 107, no. 38 (September 21, 2010): 16489–16493, doi:10.1073/pnas.1011492107.

70 **happiness rates have consistently declined:** Jean M. Twenge, "The Evidence for Generation Me and Against Generation We," *Emerging Adulthood* 1, no. 1 (March 2, 2013): 11–16, doi: 10.1177/2167696812466548/.

70 **generally American incomes have risen since 2005:** Brigid Schulte, "Why the U.S. Rating on the World Happiness Report Is Lower Than It Should Be—And How to Change It," *Washington Post*, May 11, 2015, https://www.washingtonpost.com/news/inspired-life/wp/2015/05/11/why-many-americans-are-unhappy-even-when-incomes-are-rising-and-how-we-can-change-that/.

71 **"Money and mansions":** Some sources attribute this to commentaries on the Atharva Veda.

71 **"we can better handle discomfort":** Kelly McGonigal, *The Upside of Stress* (New York: Avery, 2016).

76 **researchers asked seminary students:** John M. Darley and C. Daniel Batson, "From Jerusalem to Jericho: A Study of Situational and Dispositional Variables in Helping Behavior," *Journal of Personality and Social Psychology* 27, no. 1 (1973): 100–108, doi: 10.1037/h0034449.

77 **"*everything* you do is your spiritual life":** Laurence Freeman, *Aspects of Love: On Retreat with Laurence Freeman* (Singapore: Medio Media/Arthur James, 1997).

81 **"we want to be good without even trying":** Benedicta Ward, ed., *The Desert Fathers: Sayings of the Early Christian Monks* (New York: Penguin Classics, 2003).

MEDITATION: BREATHE

86 **"As a fish hooked and left on the sand":** Verse 3.34 from *The Dhammapada*, introduction and translation by Eknath Easwaran (Tomales, CA: Nilgiri Press, 2007), 115.

86 **"breath is the extension of our inmost life":** Rig Veda, 1.66.1, and for

discussion Abbot George Burke, "The Hindu Tradition of Breath Meditation," BreathMeditation.org, accessed November 8, 2019, https://breath meditation.org/the-hindu-tradition-of-breath-meditation.

86 the Buddha described *ānāpānasati*: Thanissaro Bhikku, trans., "Anapanasati Sutta: Mindfulness of Breathing," AccesstoInsight.org, accessed November 8, 2019, https://www.accesstoinsight.org/tipitaka/mn/mn.118 .than.html.

86 **improving cardiovascular health, lowering overall stress, and even improving academic test performance:** Tarun Sexana and Manjari Saxena, "The Effect of Various Breathing Exercises (Pranayama) in Patients with Bronchial Asthma of Mild to Moderate Severity," *International Journal of Yoga* 2, no. 1 (January–June 2009): 22–25, doi: 10.4103/0973-6131.53838; Roopa B. Ankad, Anita Herur, Shailaja Patil, G. V. Shashikala, and Surekharani Chinagudi, "Effect of Short-Term Pranayama and Meditation on Cardiovascular Functions in Healthy Individuals," *Heart Views* 12, no. 2 (April–June 2011): 58–62, doi: 10.4103/1995-705X.86016; Anant Narayan Sinha, Desh Deepak, and Vimal Singh Gusain, "Assessment of the Effects of Pranayama/Alternate Nostril Breathing on the Parasympathetic Nervous System in Young Adults," *Journal of Clinical & Diagnostic Research* 7, no. 5 (May 2013): 821–823, doi: 10.7860/JCDR/2013/4750.2948; and Shreyashi Vaksh, Mukesh Pandey, and Rakesh Kumar, "Study of the Effect of Pranayama on Academic Performance of School Students of IX and XI Standard," *Scholars Journal of Applied Medical Sciences* 4, no. 5D (2016): 1703–1705.

FIVE: PURPOSE

93 "When you protect your dharma": *The Manusmriti*, Verse 8.15.

96 **the psychology of communication:** Albert Mehrabian, *Nonverbal Communication* (London: Routledge, 1972).

96 **She first entered the wilds of Tanzania:** "About Jane," Jane Goodall Institute, accessed November 11, 2019, https://janegoodall.org/our-story/about -jane.

99 **don't hit our stride quite so early:** Rich Karlgarrd, *Late Bloomers: The Power of Patience in a World Obsessed with Early Achievement* (New York: Currency, 2019).

99 **Andre Agassi dropped a bombshell:** Andre Agassi, *Open: An Autobiography* (New York: Vintage, 2010).

100 "It is trust in the limits of the self": Joan D. Chittister, *Scarred by Struggle, Transformed by Hope* (Grand Rapids, MI: Eerdmans, 2005).

105 **studied hospital cleaning crews:** Amy Wrzesniewski, Justin M. Berg, and

Jane E. Dutton, "Managing Yourself: Turn the Job You Have into the Job You Want," *Harvard Business Review*, June 2010, https://hbr.org/2010/06/managing-yourself-turn-the-job-you-have-into-the-job-you-want; "Amy Wrzesniewski on Creating Meaning in Your Own Work," re:Work with Google, November 10, 2014, https://www.youtube.com/watch?v=C_igfnctYjA.

109 **imposed their own rigid class system:** Sanjoy Chakravorty, *The Truth About Us: The Politics of Information from Manu to Modi* (Hachette India, 2019).

117 **Joseph Campbell had no model of a career:** Robert Segal, "Joseph Campbell: American Author," *Encyclopaedia Britannica*, accessed November 11, 2019, https://www.britannica.com/biography/Joseph-Campbell-American-author; "Joseph Campbell: His Life and Contributions," Center for Story and Symbol, accessed November 11, 2019, https://folkstory.com/campbell/psychology_online_joseph_campbell.html; Joseph Campbell with Bill Moyers, *The Power of Myth* (New York: Anchor, 1991).

120 **dharma protects those:** *The Mahabharata*, Manusmriti verse 8.15.

121 **Emma Slade, lived in Hong Kong:** Emma Slade, "My Path to Becoming a Buddhist," TEDx Talks, February 6, 2017, https://www.youtube.com/watch?v=QnJIjEAE41w; "Meet the British Banker Who Turned Buddhist Nun in Bhutan," *Economic Times*, August 28, 2017, https://economictimes.indiatimes.com/news/international/world-news/meet-the-british-banker-who-turned-buddhist-nun-in-bhutan/being-taken-hostage/slideshow/60254680.cms; "Charity Work," EmmaSlade.com, accessed November 11, 2019, https://www.emmaslade.com/charity-work.

122 **"Just like a red, blue, or white lotus":** *The Dona Sutta*, Anguttara Nikaya verse 4.36.

SIX: ROUTINE

125 **85 percent of us need an alarm clock:** Til Roenneberg, *Internal Time: Chronotypes, Social Jet Lag, and Why You're So Tired* (Cambridge, MA: Harvard University Press, 2012).

125 **"a profound failure of self-respect":** Maria Popova, "10 Learnings from 10 Years of Brain Pickings," *Brain Pickings*, accessed November 11, 2019, https://www.brainpickings.org/2016/10/23/10-years-of-brain-pickings/.

125 **checking messages within ten minutes:** RootMetrics, "Survey Insights: The Lifestyles of Mobile Consumers," October 24, 2018, http://rootmetrics.com/en-US/content/rootmetrics-survey-results-are-in-mobile-consumer-lifestyles.

125 **There are only six cars:** "Fastest Cars 0 to 60 Times," accessed November 11, 2019, https://www.zeroto60times.com/fastest-cars-0-60-mph-times/.

127 **Tim Cook starts his day:** Lev Grossman, "Runner-Up: Tim Cook, the Technologist," *TIME*, December 19, 2012, http://poy.time.com/2012/12/19/runner-up-tim-cook-the-technologist/; Michelle Obama, "Oprah Talks to Michelle Obama," interview by Oprah Winfrey, *O, The Oprah Magazine*, April 2000, https://www.oprah.com/omagazine/michelle-obamas-oprah-interview-o-magazine-cover-with-obama/all#ixzz5qYixltgS.

129 **earlier sleep time can put you in a better mood:** Jacob A. Nota and Meredith E. Coles, "Duration and Timing of Sleep Are Associated with Repetitive Negative Thinking," *Cognitive Therapy and Research* 39, no. 2 (April 2015): 253–261, doi: 10.1007/s10608-014-9651-7.

129 **As much as 75 percent of the HGH:** M. L. Moline, T. H. Monk, D. R. Wagner, C. P. Pollak, J. Kream, J. E. Fookson, E. D. Weitzman, and C. A. Czeisler, "Human Growth Hormone Release Is Decreased During Sleep in Temporal Isolation (Free-Running)," *Chronobiologia* 13, no. 1 (January–March 1986): 13–19.

129 **Kevin O'Leary said that before he goes to sleep:** Ali Montag, "These Are Kevin O'Leary's Top 3 Productivity Hacks—and Anyone Can Use Them," CNBC, July 23, 2018, https://www.cnbc.com/2018/07/19/kevin-olearys-top-productivity-tips-that-anyone-can-use.html.

130 **each decision is an opportunity to stray from their path:** Christopher Sommer, "How One Decision Can Change Everything," interview by Brian Rose, *London Real*, October 2, 2018, https://www.youtube.com/watch?v=jgJ3xHyOzsA.

132 **"People living in the cities and suburbs":** Hannah Ward and Jennifer Wild, eds., *The Monastic Way: Ancient Wisdom for Contemporary Living: A Book of Daily Readings* (Grand Rapids, MI: Wm. B. Eerdmans, 2007), 75–76.

132 **not the same as noticing it:** Alan D. Castel, Michael Vendetti, and Keith J. Holyoak, "Fire Drill: Inattentional Blindness and Amnesia for the Location of Fire Extinguishers," *Attention, Perception, & Psychophysics* 74 (2012): 1391–1396, doi: 10.3758/s13414-012-0355-3.

133 **Kobe Bryant was onto this:** Kobe Bryant, "Kobe Bryant: On How to Be Strategic & Obsessive to Find Your Purpose," interview by Jay Shetty, *On Purpose*, September 9, 2019, https://jayshetty.me/kobe-bryant-on-how-to-be-strategic-obsessive-to-find-your-purpose/.

135 **"doing dishes is unpleasant":** Thich Nhat Hanh, *At Home in the World: Stories and Essential Teachings from a Monk's Life* (Berkeley, CA: Parallax Press, 2019).

136 **"Yesterday is but a dream":** Kālidāsa, *The Works of Kālidāsa*, trans. Arthur W. Ryder (CreateSpace, 2015).

141 **2 percent of us can multitask:** Garth Sundem, "This Is Your Brain on Multitasking: Brains of Multitaskers Are Structurally Different Than Brains

of Monotaskers," *Psychology Today*, February 24, 2012, https://www.psychol
ogytoday.com/us/blog/brain-trust/201202/is-your-brain-multitasking.

141 **erodes our ability to focus:** Cal Newport, *Deep Work: Rules for Focused Success in a Distracted World* (New York: Grand Central Publishing, 2016).

141 **took a group of students:** Eyal Ophir, Clifford Nass, and Anthony D. Wagner, "Cognitive Control in Media Multitaskers," *PNAS* 106, no. 37 (September 15, 2009): 15583–15587, doi: 10.1073/pnas.0903620106.

143 **We overstimulate the dopamine (reward) channel:** Robert H. Lustig, *The Hacking of the American Mind: The Science Behind the Corporate Takeover of Our Bodies and Brains* (New York: Avery, 2017).

SEVEN: THE MIND

146 **the mind is compared to a drunken monkey:** Nārāyana, *Hitopadeśa* (New York: Penguin Classics, 2007).

146 **roughly seventy thousand separate thoughts each day:** "How Many Thoughts Do We Have Per Minute?," Reference, accessed November 12, 2019, https://www.reference.com/world-view/many-thoughts-per-minute-cb7fcf22ebbf8466.

146 **about three seconds at a time:** Ernst Pöppel, "Trust as Basic for the Concept of Causality: A Biological Speculation," presentation, accessed November 12, 2019, http://www.paralimes.ntu.edu.sg/NewsnEvents/Causality%20-%20Reality/Documents/Ernst%20Poppel.pdf.

147 **"your brain is not reacting to events in the world":** Lisa Barrett, "Lisa Barrett on How Emotions Are Made," interview by Ginger Campbell, *Brain Science with Ginger Campbell, MD*, episode 135, July 31, 2017, https://brain sciencepodcast.com/bsp/2017/135-emotions-barrett.

147 **our minds are monkeys:** Piya Tan, "Samyutta Nikaya: The Connected Sayings of the Buddha, Translated with Notes in the Sutta Discovery Series," Buddhism Network, accessed January 22, 2020, http://buddhismnetwork.com/2016/12/28/samyutta-nikaya/.

147 **"As irrigators lead water":** Verse 6.80 from *The Dhammapada*, introduction and translation by Eknath Easwaran (Tomales, CA: Nilgiri Press, 2007), 126.

148 **"For him who has conquered the mind":** Verse 6.6 from A. C. Bhaktivedanta Swami Prabhupada, *Bhagavad Gita As It Is* (The Bhaktivedanta Book Trust International, Inc.). https://apps.apple.com/us/app/bhagavad-gita-as-it-is/id1080562426.

148 **An enemy, according to the Oxford English Dictionary, is:** *Paperback Oxford English Dictionary* (Oxford, UK: Oxford University Press, 2012).

148 **weight of a bad decision isn't just metaphorical:** Martin V. Day and D.

Ramona Bobocel, "The Weight of a Guilty Conscience: Subjective Body Weight as an Embodiment of Guilt,"*PLoS ONE* 8, no. 7 (July 2013), doi: 10.1371/journal.pone.0069546.

148 **what researchers call our "should-self":** Max. H. Bazerman, Ann E. Tenbrunsel, and Kimberly Wade-Benzoni, "Negotiating with Yourself and Losing: Making Decisions with Competing Internal Preferences," *Academy of Management Review* 23, no. 2 (April 1, 1998): 225–241, doi: 10.5465/amr .1998.533224.

149 **in our everyday swirl of thoughts:** *The Dhammapada*, introduction and translation by Eknath Easwaran (Tomales, CA: Nilgiri Press, 2007), 65–66.

151 **a chariot being driven by five horses:** Katha Upanishad, Third Valli, 3–6, from *The Upanishads*, trans. Vernon Katz and Thomas Egenes (New York: Tarcher Perigee, 2015), 55–57.

152 **Shaolin monks are a wonderful example:** Elliot Figueira, "How Shaolin Monks Develop Their Mental and Physical Mastery," BBN, accessed November 12, 2019, https://www.bbncommunity.com/how-shaolin-monks -develop-their-mental-and-physical-mastery/.

152 **secured a thermal stimulator to their wrists:** Daniel Goleman and Richard J. Davidson, *Altered Traits: Science Reveals How Meditation Changes Your Mind, Brain, and Body* (New York: Penguin Random House, 2017).

155 **decided to busk outside a DC subway station:** Gene Weingarten, "Pearls Before Breakfast: Can One of the Nation's Great Musicians Cut Through the Fog of a D.C. Rush Hour? Let's Find Out," *Washington Post*, April 8, 2007, https://www.washingtonpost.com/lifestyle/magazine/pearls-before -breakfast-can-one-of-the-nations-great-musicians-cut-through-the-fog -of-a-dc-rush-hour-lets-find-out/2014/09/23/8a6d46da-4331-11e4-b47c -f5889e061e5f_story.html.

157 **asked them to locate specific items:** Gary Lupyan and Daniel Swingley, "Self-Directed Speech Affects Visual Search Performance," *Quarterly Journal of Experimental Psychology* (June 1, 2012), doi: 10.1080 /17470218.2011.647039.

157 **"helps you clarify your thoughts":** Linda Sapadin, "Talking to Yourself: A Sign of Sanity," *Psych Central*, October 2, 2018, https://psychcentral.com /blog/talking-to-yourself-a-sign-of-sanity/.

160 **writing their "deepest thoughts and feelings":** James W. Pennebaker and Janel D. Seagal, "Forming a Story: The Health Benefits of Narrative," *Journal of Clinical Psychology* 55, no. 10 (1999): 1243–1254.

160 **Krysta MacGray was terrified of flying:** www.krystamacgray.com and personal interview, July 10, 2019.

163 **"how to be present to the moment":** Richard Rohr, "Living in the Now:

Practicing Presence," Center for Action and Comtemplation, November 24, 2017, https://cac.org/practicing-presence-2017-11-24/.

163 *"be here now"*: Ram Dass, *Be Here Now* (New York: Harmony, 1978).

164 **The Gita defines detachment**: Verses 2.48 and 12.12 from the Bhagavad Gita, introduction and translation by Eknath Easwaran (Tomales, CA: Nilgiri Press, 2007), 94, 208.

165 **"Detachment is not that you own nothing"**: This quote is attributed to Ali Ibn Abi Talib, the cousin and son-in-law of Muhammad, the last prophet of Islam.

168 **fasted for 423 days**: Bhavika Jain, "Jain Monk Completes 423 Days of Fasting," *Times of India*, November 1, 2015, http://timesofindia.indiatimes .com/articleshow/49616061.cms?utm_source=contentofinterest&utm _medium=text&utm_campaign=cppst.

168 **Japanese style of self-mummification**: Krissy Howard, "The Japanese Monks Who Mummified Themselves While Still Alive," *All That's Interesting*, October 25, 2016, https://allthatsinteresting.com/sokushinbutsu.

168 **ran a mile in 3:59.4 minutes**: "Sir Roger Bannister: First Person to Run a Mile in Under Four Minutes Dies at 88," BBC, March 4, 2018, https:// www.bbc.com/sport/athletics/43273249.

172 **"If you ruminate on sadness and negativity"**: Matthieu Ricard, interview by Jay Shetty, *#FollowTheReader with Jay Shetty*, *HuffPost*, October 10, 2016, https://www.youtube.com/watch?v=_HZznrniwL8&feature=youtu.be.

172 **Cultivate buddhi**: Jayaram V, "The Seven Fundamental Teachings of the Bhagavad-Gita," Hinduwebsite.com, accessed January 22, 2020, https:// www.hinduwebsite.com/seventeachings.asp.

EIGHT: EGO

173 **They are forever free**: Verse 2.71 from the Bhagavad Gita, introduction and translation by Eknath Easwaran (Tomales, CA: Nilgiri Press, 2007), 97.

173 **distinction between the ego and the false ego**: Verses 7.4 and 16.18 from *The Bhagavad Gita*, introduction and translation by Eknath Easwaran (Tomales, CA: Nilgiri Press, 2007), 152, 240.

173 **"Pride of wealth destroys wealth"**: Some sources attribute this to commentaries on the Sama Veda.

174 **"the most damaging fall for the soul"**: Dennis Okholm, *Dangerous Passions, Deadly Sins: Learning from the Psychology of Ancient Monks* (Grand Rapids, MI: Brazos Press, 2014), 161.

177 **"Perfect yogis are they who"**: Verse 6.32 from A. C. Bhaktivedanta Swami Prabhupada, *Bhagavad Gita As It Is* (The Bhaktivedanta Book Trust

International, Inc.), https://apps.apple.com/us/app/bhagavad-gita-as-it-is
/id1080562426.

179 **In her popular TED Talk:** Julia Galef, "Why You Think You're Right
Even If You're Wrong," TEDx PSU, February 2016, https://www.ted.com
/talks/julia_galef_why_you_think_you_re_right_even_if_you_re_wrong
/transcript#t-68800.

180 **cofounder of Netflix, offered to sell:** Ken Auletta, "Outside the Box: Netflix and the Future of Television," *New Yorker*, January 26, 2014, https://
www.newyorker.com/magazine/2014/02/03/outside-the-box-2; Paul R.
LaMonica, "Netflix Joins the Exclusive $100 Billion Club," CNN, July 23,
2018, https://money.cnn.com/2018/01/23/investing/netflix-100-billion
-market-value/index.html.

180 **who had come to inquire about Zen:** Osho, *A Bird on the Wing: Zen Anec-
dotes for Everyday Life* (India: Osho Media International, 2013).

181 **"Remember you are a man":** Mary Beard, *The Roman Triumph* (Cambridge,
MA: Harvard University Press, 2009).

181 **In an interview, Robert Downey Jr.:** Robert Downey Jr., interview, *Cambridge Union*, December 19, 2014, https://www.huffingtonpost.com.au
/2017/10/18/weve-broken-down-your-entire-life-into-years-spent-doing
-tasks_a_23248153/.

183 **he is like a firefly:** Srimad-Bhagavatam, The Summun Bonum, 14.9-10.

185 **Mary Johnson's son, Laramiun Byrd:** Steve Hartman, "Love Thy Neighbor: Son's Killer Moves in Next Door," CBS News, June 8, 2011, https://
www.cbsnews.com/news/love-thy-neighbor-sons-killer-moves-next-door
/; "Woman Shows Incredible Mercy as Her Son's Killer Moves In Next
Door," *Daily Mail*, June 8, 2011, https://www.dailymail.co.uk/news/article
-2000704/Woman-shows-incredible-mercy-sons-killer-moves-door.html;
"Mary Johnson and Oshea Israel," The Forgiveness Project, accessed November 12, 2019, https://www.theforgivenessproject.com/mary-johnson
-and-oshea-israel.

187 **"What belongs to you today":** Kamlesh J. Wadher, *Nature's Science and Secrets of Success* (India: Educreation Publishing, 2016); Verse 2.14 from the
Bhagavad Gita, introduction and translation by Eknath Easwaran (Tomales, CA: Nilgiri Press, 2007), 90.

188 **"Being literally undone by failure":** Thomas Moore, *Care of the Soul: A
Guide for Cultivating Depth and Sacredness in Everyday Life* (New York:
Harper Perennial, 1992), 197.

189 **Sara Blakely wanted to go to law school:** Sarah Lewis, *The Rise: Creativity,
the Gift of Failure, and the Search for Mastery* (New York: Simon & Schuster,

2014), 111; "Spanx Startup Story," Fundable, accessed November 12, 2019, https://www.fundable.com/learn/startup-stories/spanx.

191 **Olympic swimming gold medalist:** "Goal Setting Activities of Olympic Athletes (And What They Can Teach the Rest of Us)," Develop Good Habits, September 30, 2019, https://www.developgoodhabits.com/goal -setting-activities/.

196 **a children's rights activist:** Rajesh Viswanathan, "Children Should Become Their Own Voices," *ParentCircle*, accessed November 12, 2019, https:// www.parentcircle.com/article/children-should-become-their-own-voices/.

MEDITATION: VISUALIZE

198 **people who imagined contracting a muscle:** Vinoth K. Ranganathan, Vlodek Siemionow, Jing Z. Liu, Vinod Sahgal, and Guang H. Yue, "From Mental Power to Muscle Power—Gaining Strength by Using the Mind," *Neuropsychologia* 42, no. 7 (2004): 944–956, doi: 10.1016/j.neuropsycholo gia.2003.11.018.

NINE: GRATITUDE

205 **defines gratitude as the feeling of appreciation:** "What Is Gratitude?" A Network for Grateful Living, accessed November 12, 2019, https://grate fulness.org/resource/what-is-gratitude/.

206 **keep journals during the day:** Robert A. Emmons and Michael E. Mc-Cullough, "Counting Blessings Versus Burdens: An Experimental Investigation of Gratitude and Subjective Well-Being in Daily Life," *Journal of Personality and Social Psychology* 84, no. 2 (2003): 377–389, doi: 10.1037 /0022-3514.84.2.377.

207 **we truly can't focus on positive and negative:** Alex Korb, "The Grateful Brain: The Neuroscience of Giving Thanks," *Psychology Today*, November 20, 2012, https://www.psychologytoday.com/us/blog/prefrontal-nudity/201211 /the-grateful-brain.

207 **veterans with high levels of gratitude:** Todd B. Kashdan, Gitendra Uswatte, and Terri Julian, "Gratitude and Hedonic and Eudaimonic Well-Being in Vietnam War Veterans," *Behaviour Research and Therapy* 44, no. 2 (February 2006): 177–199, doi: 10.1016/j.brat.2005.01.005.

207 **"If [thankfulness] were a drug":** Mikaela Conley, "Thankfulness Linked to Positive Changes in Brain and Body," ABC News, November 23, 2011, https://abcnews.go.com/Health/science-thankfulness/story?id=15008148.

208 **"Monks. You should train yourselves":** Samyutta Nikaya, Sutta Pitaka, 20.21.

210 **In one ritual observance:** Joanna Macy, *World as Lover, World as Self: Courage*

for Global Justice and Ecological Renewal (Berkeley, CA: Parallax Press, 2007), 78–83.

211 **"the mind of poverty"**: Roshi Joan Halifax, "Practicing Gratefulness by Roshi Joan Halifax," Upaya Institute and Zen Center, October 18, 2017, https://www.upaya.org/2017/10/practicing-gratefulness-by-roshi-joan -halifax/.

212 **Brian Acton exemplifies**: Bill Murphy Jr., "Facebook and Twitter Turned Him Down. Now He's Worth $4 Billion," *Inc.*, accessed November 13, 2019, https://www.inc.com/bill-murphy-jr/facebook-and-twitter-turned-him -down-now-hes-worth-4-billion.html; Brian Acton (@brianacton), Twitter post, May 23, 2009, https://twitter.com/brianacton/status/1895942068; Brian Acton (@brianacton), Twitter post, August 3, 2009, https://twitter .com/brianacton/status/3109544383.

212 **"When one door of happiness closes"**: "Helen Keller," Biography, accessed November 13, 2019, https://www.biography.com/activist/helen-keller; Helen Keller, *We Bereaved* (New York: L. Fulenwider, 1929).

213 **"People usually think that gratitude"**: Rob Sidon, "The Gospel of Gratitude According to David Steindl-Rast," *Common Ground*, November 2017, 42–49, http://onlinedigitaleditions2.com/commonground/archive/web-11 -2017/.

215 **"Be kinder to yourself"**: Pema Chödrön, *Practicing Peace in Times of War* (Boston: Shambhala, 2007).

215 **whether kindness is contagious**: James H. Fowler and Nicholas A. Christakis, "Cooperative Behavior Cascades in Human Social Networks," *Proceedings of the National Academy of Sciences*, 107, no. 12 (March 23, 2010): 5334–5338, doi: 10.1073/pnas.0913149107.

216 **people on the Chicago commuter**: Nicholas Epley and Juliana Schroeder, "Mistakenly Seeking Solitude," *Journal of Experimental Psychology: General* 143, no. 5 (October 2014): 1980–1999, doi: 10.1037/a0037323.

219 **volunteering can result in lower feelings of depression**: Caroline E. Jenkinson, Andy P. Dickens, Kerry Jones, Jo Thompson-Coon, Rod S. Taylor, Morwenna Rogers, Clare L. Bambra, Iain Lang, and Suzanne H. Richards, "Is Volunteering a Public Health Intervention? A Systematic Review and Meta-Analysis of the Health and Survival of Volunteers," *BMG Public Health* 13, no. 773 (August 23, 2013), doi: 10.1186/1471-2458-13-773.

TEN: RELATIONSHIPS

222 **"Every person"**: Thich Nhat Hanh, *How to Love* (Berkeley, CA: Parallax Press, 2014).

223 **longevity was tied to several aspects of community**: Dan Buettner, "Power

9: Reverse Engineering Longevity," Blue Zones, accessed November 13, 2019, https://www.bluezones.com/2016/11/power-9/.

228 **a field study of military leadership in Iraq:** Michael D. Matthews, "The 3 C's of Trust: The Core Elements of Trust Are Competence, Character, and Caring," *Psychology Today*, May 3, 2016, https://www.psychologytoday .com/us/blog/head-strong/201605/the-3-c-s-trust.

230 **"The golden way is to be friends with the world":** K. S. Baharati, *Encyclopaedia of Ghandian Thought* (India: Anmol Publications, 2006).

230 **"People come into your life":** Jean Dominique Martin, "People Come Into Your Life for a Reason, a Season, or a Lifetime," accessed November 14, 2019, http://youmeandspirit.blogspot.com/2009/08/ebb-and-flow.html.

232 **couples get stuck in ongoing conflict:** John Gottman, "John Gottman on Trust and Betrayal," *Greater Good Magazine*, October 29, 2011, https:// greatergood.berkeley.edu/article/item/john_gottman_on_trust_and_be trayal.

232 **people are dishonest:** Bella M. DePaulo, Deborah A. Kashy, Susan E. Kirkendol, Melissa M. Wyer, and Jennifer A. Epstein, "Lying in Everyday Life," *Journal of Personality and Social Psychology* 70, no. 5 (June 1996): 979–995, doi: 10.1037/0022-3514.70.5.979.

233 **we lie to impress:** Bella DePaolo, *The Lies We Tell and the Clues We Miss: Professional Papers* (CreateSpace, 2009).

234 **trust people we find attractive:** Dawn Dorsey, "Rice Study Suggests People Are More Trusting of Attractive Strangers," Rice University, September 21, 2006, https://news.rice.edu/2006/09/21/rice-study-suggests-people-are -more-trusting-of-attractive-strangers/.

234 **"We found that attractive subjects gain a 'beauty premium'":** Dawn Dorsey, "Rice Study Suggests People Are More Trusting of Attractive Strangers," *Rice News*, September 21, 2006, http://news.rice.edu/2006/09/21/rice -study-suggests-people-are-more-trusting-of-attractive-strangers/.

235 **a blank piece of paper:** Don Meyer, "Fox-Hole Test," CoachMeyer.com, accessed November 13, 2019, https://www.coachmeyer.com/Information /Players_Corner/Fox%20Hole%20Test.pdf.

238 **"Celibacy by conscious choice":** www.malamadrone.com and personal interview, September 7, 2019.

238 **"two sides of man's being alone":** Paul Tillich, *The Eternal Now* (New York: Scribner, 1963).

240 **the impact of mothers' time:** Melissa A. Milke, Kei M. Nomaguchi, and Kathleen E. Denny, "Does the Amount of Time Mothers Spend with Children or Adolescents Matter?" *Journal of Marriage and Family* 77, no. 2 (April 2015): 355–372, doi: 10.1111/jomf.12170.

241 **six loving exchanges:** *Sri Upadesamrta: The Ambrosial Advice of Sri Rupa Gosvami* (India: Gaudiya Vedanta Publications, 2003), https://archive.org /details/upadesamrta/page/n1.

245 **Harvard Grant Study:** Joshua Wolf Shenk, "What Makes Us Happy? Is There a Formula—Some Mix of Love, Work, and Psychological Adaptation—for a Good Life?" *Atlantic*, June 2009, https://www.theatlan tic.com/magazine/archive/2009/06/what-makes-us-happy/307439/.

246 **"we get crushes on others":** Thich Nhat Hanh *How to Love* (Berkeley, CA: Parallax Press, 2014).

246 **According to Massive Attack:** Massive Attack, "Teardrop," *Mezzanine*, Circa/Virgin, April 27, 1998; *Dan in Real Life*, directed by Peter Hedges, Touchstone Pictures, Focus Features, and Jon Shestack Productions, 2007.

248 **"until you heal the wounds of your past":** IyanlaVanzant, "How to Heal the Wounds of Your Past," Oprah's Life Class, October 11, 2011, http://www .oprah.com/oprahs-lifeclass/iyanla-vanzant-how-to-heal-the-wounds-of -your-past.

249 **couples strengthen their bonds:** Arthur Aron, Christina C. Norman, Elaine N. Aron, Colin McKenna, and Richard E. Heyman, "Couples' Shared Participation in Novel and Arousing Activities and Experienced Relationship Quality," *Journal of Personality and Social Psychology* 78, no. 2 (2000): 273–84, doi: 10.1037//0022-3514.78.2.273.

251 **we often mistake attachment for love:** Jetsunma Tenzin Palmo, "The Difference Between Genuine Love and Attachment," accessed November 13, 2019, https://www.youtube.com/watch?v=6kUoTS3Yo4g.

251 **followed incoming college freshmen:** Sanjay Srivastava, Maya Tamir, Kelly M. McGonigal, Oliver P. John, and James J. Gross, "The Social Costs of Emotional Suppression: A Prospective Study of the Transition to College," *Journal of Personality and Social Psychology* 96, no. 4 (August 22, 2014): 883–897, doi: 10.1037/a0014755.

ELEVEN: SERVICE

254 **"The ignorant work for their own profit":** Verse 3.25 from *The Bhagavad Gita*, introduction and translation by Eknath Easwaran (Tomales, CA: Nilgiri Press, 2007), 107.

255 **"we are on a journey":** Hannah Ward and Jennifer Wild, eds., *The Monastic Way: Ancient Wisdom for Contemporary Living: A Book of Daily Readings* (Grand Rapids, MI: Wm. B. Eerdmans, 2007), 183.

257 **"The monk may think":** Hannah Ward and Jennifer Wild, eds., *The Monastic Way: Ancient Wisdom for Contemporary Living: A Book of Daily Readings* (Grand Rapids, MI: Wm. B. Eerdmans, 2007), 190.

257 "Look at these fortunate trees": Srimad-Bhagavatam, The Summun Bonum, 22.32.

257 The sixteenth-century guru Rupa Goswami talks about *yukta-vairāgya*: Verse 1.2.255 from Srila Rupa Goswami, *Bhakti Rasamrta Sindhu (In Two Volumes): With the Commentary of Srila Jiva Gosvami and Visvanatha Cakravarti Thakur* (The Bhaktivedanta Book Trust, Inc, 2009).

258 "No one is born hating": Nelson Mandela, *Long Walk to Freedom: The Autobiography of Nelson Mandela* (Boston: Back Bay Books, 1995).

258 one we often overlook: Joseph Campbell, *The Hero with a Thousand Faces* (Novato, CA: New World Library, 2008).

258 Seane Corn is living out the hero's journey: Seane Corn, "Yoga, Meditation in Action," interview by Krista Tippett, *On Being*, September 11, 2008, https://onbeing.org/programs/seane-corn-yoga-meditation-in-action/.

259 when we pursue "compassionate goals": M. Teresa Granillo, Jennifer Crocker, James L. Abelson, Hannah E. Reas, and Christina M. Quach, "Compassionate and Self-Image Goals as Interpersonal Maintenance Factors in Clinical Depression and Anxiety," *Journal of Clinical Psychology* 74, no. 4 (September 12, 2017): 608–625, doi: 10.1002/jclp.22524.

259 tend to live longer: Stephen G. Post, "Altruism, Happiness, and Health: It's Good to Be Good," *International Journal of Behavioral Medicine* 12, no. 2 (June 2005): 66–77, doi: 10.1207/s15327558ijbm1202_4.

260 "giving simply because it is right to give": Verse 17.20 from *The Bhagavad Gita*, introduction and translation by Eknath Easwaran (Tomales, CA: Nilgiri Press, 2007), 248.

262 Sindhutai Sapkal was married at twelve: "About Sindhutai Sapkal (Mai)/ Mother of Orphans," accessed November 13, 2019, https://www.sindhuta isapakal.org/about-Sindhutail-Sapkal.html.

263 people were given $10: Paul K. Piff, Michael W. Krauss, Stéphane Côté, Bonnie Hayden Cheng, and Dacher Keltner, "Having Less, Giving More: The Influence of Social Class on Prosocial Behavior," *Journal of Personality and Social Psychology* 99, no. 5 (November 2010): 771–784, doi: 10.1037 /a0020092.

263 survey of charitable giving: Frank Greve, "America's Poor Are Its Most Generous Givers," McClatchy Newspapers, March 19, 2009, https://www .mcclatchydc.com/news/politics-government/article24538864.html.

263 Why those with less give more: Daniel Goleman, *Focus: The Hidden Driver of Excellence* (New York: HarperCollins, 2013), 123.

263 Some philanthropists: Kathleen Elkins, "From Poverty to a $3 Billion Fortune: The Incredible Rags-to-Riches Story of Oprah Winfrey," *Business*

Insider, May 28, 2015, https://www.businessinsider.com/rags-to-riches
-story-of-oprah-winfrey-2015-5.

267 **Kailash Satyarthi has taken on:** Ryan Prior, "Kailash Satyarthi Plans to
End Child Labor In His Lifetime," CNN, March 13, 2019, https://www
.cnn.com/2019/02/19/world/kailash-satyarthi-child-labor/index.html.

268 **"You don't need to do everything":** Joanna Macy, *World as Lover, World as
Self: Courage for Global Justice and Ecological Renewal* (Berkeley, CA: Parallax
Press, 2007), 77.

MEDITATION: CHANT

270 **the why and how of chanting:** Agni Purana 3.293 and Vayu Purana 59.141.

270 **Recognizing the value of sound:** "Tesla's Vibrational Medicine," Tesla's
Medicine, accessed November 12, 2019, https://teslasmedicine.com/teslas
-vibrational-medicine/; Jennifer Tarnacki, "This Is Your Brain on Drumming: The Neuroscience Behind the Beat," Medium, September 25, 2019,
https://medium.com/indian-thoughts/this-is-your-brain-on-drumming
-8ed6eaf314c4.

271 **anything that inspires you can work:** Rainer Maria Rilke, *Letters to a Young
Poet* (New York: W. W. Norton & Company, 1993); "29 Inspiring Herb
Brooks Quotes to Motivate You," Sponge Coach, September 13, 2017,
http://www.spongecoach.com/inspiring-herb-brooks-quotes/; Jay-Z, "Dirt
Off Your Shoulder," *The Black Album*, Roc-A-Fella and Def Jam, March 2,
2004; *Bad Boys II*, directed by Michael Bay, Don Simpson/Jerry Bruck-
heimer Films, 2003.

271 **most sacred mantra is Om:** "Why Do We Chant Om?" Temples in India
Info, accessed November 12, 2019, https://templesinindiainfo.com/why
-do-we-chant-om/; "Om," Encyclopedia Britannica, accessed November 12, 2019, https://www.britannica.com/topic/Om-Indian-religion.

272 **Vagus nerve stimulation:** Bangalore G. Kalyani, Ganesan Venkatasub-
ramanian, Rashmi Arasappa, Naren P. Rao, Sunil V. Kalmady, Rishikesh
V. Behere, Hariprasad Rao, Mandapati K. Vasudev, and Bangalore
N. Gangadhar, "Neurohemodynamic Correlates of 'OM' Chanting: A
Pilot Functional Magnetic Resonance Imaging Study," *International
Journal of Yoga* 4, no. 1 (January–June 2011): 3–6, doi: 10.4103/0973-
6131.78171; C. R. Conway, A. Kumar, W. Xiong, M. Bunker, S. T. Ar-
onson, and A. J. Rush, "Chronic Vagus Nerve Stimulation Significantly
Improves Quality of Life in Treatment Resistant Major Depression,"
Journal of Clinical Psychiatry 79, no. 5 (August 21, 2018), doi: 10.4088/
JCP.18m12178.

273 **Om Tat Sat:** Verse 17.23 from *The Bhagavad Gita*, introduction and translation by Eknath Easwaran (Tomales, CA: Nilgiri Press, 2007), 249.

CONCLUSION

279 **Among the most common regrets:** Grace Bluerock, "The 9 Most Common Regrets People Have at the End of Life," mindbodygreen, accessed on November 13, 2019, https://www.mindbodygreen.com/0-23024/the-9-most -common-regrets-people-have-at-the-end-of-life.html.

Next Steps

GENIUS COACHING COMMUNITY

If you've enjoyed this book, and you'd like to further explore how you can improve and optimize every area of your life, enroll in Jay Shetty's Genius Coaching Community.

With over 12,000 members in over 100 countries around the world, you'll be part of a transformational personal development community.

Join Jay live every week for a powerful guided meditation and structured coaching session where he will share the strategies, tools and frameworks to unlock your greatest potential and uncover your inner genius based on his first-hand experience as a monk and years of study.

As a member, you'll get access to these live sessions and hundreds of recorded sessions on every topic from relationships to career, spiritual development to health and well-being.

You can also join our monthly in-person meetups in over 140 locations around the world and connect with like-minded people.

For more information, please go to www.jayshetty.me/genius.

JAY SHETTY CERTIFICATION SCHOOL

If you want to guide others along their journeys of personal change, the Jay Shetty Certification School, backed by science, common sense, and ancient monk wisdom, is for you.

Join Jay on his quest to inspire and impact the world by becoming an accredited Certified Coach. The curriculum, consisting of guided study, supervised peer coaching, and interactive group sessions will provide you with the skills, techniques, and strategies for guiding anyone to new perspectives and personal change.

In addition, you will learn how to build a thriving professional coaching practice and be listed in our global database of approved Jay Shetty coaches.

You can study from anywhere in the world, online, at your pace, and on your own time. You can even choose to train live with Jay Shetty himself during our training events offered in different countries.

For more information, please visit www.jayshettycoaching.com.

Index